GOTREK & FELIX

THE THIRD OMNIBUS

GIANTSLAYER • ORCSLAYER • MANSLAYER

Dwarf Trollslayer Gotrek Gurnisson and his human companion Felix Jaeger continue their epic journeys. They head to Albion to combat the evil that terrorises the citizens there before it can grow to threaten the whole world. And if that wasn't enough, on their return to the southern coast of the Old World they discover that orcs are running rampant... With the Empire's armies desperately fighting off a major Chaos invasion, the world is laid bare. Can our intrepid heroes defeat the villains in time to save the day?

Collecting the seventh, eighth and ninth action-packed novels in the Gotrek & Felix series, *Gotrek & Felix: The Third Omnibus* is crammed with classic fantasy adventure.

• THE GOTREK & FELIX SERIES •

GOTREK & FELIX: THE FIRST OMNIBUS
by William King
(Contains books 1-3: *Trollslayer, Skavenslayer & Daemonslayer*)

GOTREK & FELIX: THE SECOND OMNIBUS
by William King
(Contains books 4-6: *Dragonslayer, Beastslayer & Vampireslayer*)

GOTREK & FELIX: THE THIRD OMNIBUS
by William King and Nathan Long
(Contains books 7-9: *Giantslayer, Orcslayer & Manslayer*)

Book 10 – ELFSLAYER
by Nathan Long

Featuring characters from Gotrek & Felix

• THANQUOL & BONERIPPER •

GREY SEER
by C. L. Werner

A WARHAMMER OMNIBUS

GOTREK & FELIX

THE THIRD OMNIBUS

William King & Nathan Long

A Black Library Publication

Giantslayer copyright © 2003 Games Workshop Ltd.
Orcslayer copyright © 2006 Games Workshop Ltd.
Manslayer copyright © 2007 Games Workshop Ltd.

This omnibus edition published in Great Britain in 2009 by
BL Publishing,
Games Workshop Ltd.,
Willow Road, Nottingham,
NG7 2WS, UK.

10 9 8 7 6 5 4 3 2

Cover illustration by Geoff Taylor.
Map by Nuala Kinrade.

A CIP record for this book is available from the British Library.

ISBN 13: 978 1 84416 733 3

See the Black Library on the Internet at
www.blacklibrary.com

Find out more about Games Workshop
and the world of Warhammer at
www.games-workshop.com

Printed and bound in the US.

THIS IS A DARK age, a bloody age, an age of daemons and of sorcery. It is an age of battle and death, and of the world's ending. Amidst all of the fire, flame and fury it is a time, too, of mighty heroes, of bold deeds and great courage.

AT THE HEART of the Old World sprawls the Empire, the largest and most powerful of the human realms. Known for its engineers, sorcerers, traders and soldiers, it is a land of great mountains, mighty rivers, dark forests and vast cities. And from his throne in Altdorf reigns the Emperor Karl Franz, sacred descendant of the founder of these lands, Sigmar, and wielder of his magical warhammer.

BUT THESE ARE far from civilised times. Across the length and breadth of the Old World, from the knightly palaces of Bretonnia to ice-bound Kislev in the far north, come rumblings of war. In the towering Worlds Edge Mountains, the orc tribes are gathering for another assault. Bandits and renegades harry the wild southern lands of the Border Princes. There are rumours of rat-things, the skaven, emerging from the sewers and swamps across the land. And from the northern wildernesses there is the ever-present threat of Chaos, of daemons and beastmen corrupted by the foul powers of the Dark Gods. As the time of battle draws ever near, the Empire needs heroes like never before.

Claws

North of Here Lie The
Dreaded Chaos Wastes.

Erengrad.

Here Be Trolls...

Praag.

Middle Mountains.

Kislev

Kislev.

nheim.

Wolfenburg.

Talabheim.

The Empire

ltdorf.

Nuln.

The
Moot.

Sylvania.
Dracken
-hof.

Karak Kad

Zhufbar.

Averheim.

Black
Water.

Black fire Pass.

arak
Norn.

CONTENTS

INTRODUCTION 11

GIANTSLAYER 15

REDHAND'S DAUGHTER 263

ORCSLAYER 321

MANSLAYER 571

Introduction

I FEEL KIND of funny writing this introduction. After all, I only wrote two thirds of the omnibus, and Gotrek and Felix are not my characters, but, well, they asked, so here goes…

As I've said before in numerous places, taking over the Slayer series from William King was both an honour and a terrifying responsibility. Gotrek and Felix are amongst the most popular characters in the Warhammer universe, and I was, at the time, an almost untested newcomer with only a few moderately successful novels under my belt. In fact, one of the most common questions asked after they announced that Nathan Long was going to write the series was, 'Who?'

I was terrified that legions of die-hard Gotrek fans were going to show up at my door with torches and rune axes and call for my head, and there was, to be sure, a fair amount of grumbling. But, much to my relief, there were many who liked the books, and praised what I had done. In the end I decided that it was impossible to please all of the people all of the time, and the only thing I could do was try my best to stay as true to the spirit of the series and the characters of Gotrek and Felix as I could. This omnibus – with books from both William King and I side by side – is your opportunity to judge how well I succeeded.

Gulp!

One of the things that I came to realise as I continued to work on the series was how much fun Gotrek and Felix were to write, and just how superb a literary pairing they truly are. Bill's genius in this can be proven by the fact that, while they work perfectly together, they would fail entirely if separated.

Imagine Gotrek without Felix – a morose, taciturn, unkillable killing machine who does nothing but stomp from fight to fight and cares for nothing but his doom. That would get old in a story or two. There would be no twists, no drama, no conflict between Gotrek's desire to die and his higher, more heroic nature – no ego to ride herd on his id.

Imagine Felix without Gotrek – a rich young dilettante poet, prone to melancholic introspection, who would never leave Altdorf, and who would eventually settle down to work in his father's business when that writing career didn't work out. There is no story at all in that life. There would be no action, no adventure, no conflict between Felix's desire for literary renown and his wilder, more restless nature – no id to goose his ego.

In putting them together, however, Bill created the perfect recipe for sword and sorcery stories. Gotrek's id drags Felix into danger. Felix's ego reminds Gotrek of his duty to protect the weak. Gotrek charges headlong at certain death. Felix hesitates at the edge of the pit, torn between loyalty and fear. Gotrek spits out pithy certainties. Felix ponders murky subtleties. Gotrek is led by rage and honour. Felix is led by romance and compassion. Their characters are so strong and well laid out that they tell me what they would do in any situation. Their actions write themselves. In that way at least, writing them is the easiest job in the world.

In other ways, of course, it is the most difficult job in the world. How do I keep the stories fresh, yet at the same time recognisably Gotrek and Felix stories? How do I bring the duo back to the Empire without repeating the adventures that have come before? How do I reintroduce the old characters that everybody knows and loves without making it feel cheap and cheesy? How do I keep the audience guessing? What does Gotrek slay next? How do I top the last book?

Answering all these questions is always hard, but at the same time it's one of the things that makes writing the series fun. In some ways, it's like putting together a giant puzzle, taking this bit of lore, this monster or race, this location, and this character who we haven't seen in a while, and coming up with a plot that will hold them all. Sometimes it takes a lot of twisting and turning to get all the pieces to lock together and fit into the hundred thousand word box I have to put them in, and sometimes I have to take them all out and start all over again, but it is extremely satisfying once I've got them all neatly tied together and I can start on the actual writing.

It's at that point that Gotrek and Felix take over and the job gets much easier. As the above has shown, I am a very meticulous – obsessive? – plotter, and so one might think that I know everything that will happen in a book before I write it, but that's not the case. I know what *has* to happen, but very often, I don't know exactly *how* it will happen – and that's where Gotrek and Felix come in. As I run them through the plot and introduce them to the people they meet along the way, they know better than I how they're going to react, and I just have to watch and listen. When they meet some pompous fool I can see Gotrek's brow lowering and his hand inching toward his axe, while Felix sweats bullets and tries to keep the slayer from killing him. When they meet some beautiful woman, I can see Gotrek ignoring her, while Felix trips all over his tongue as he tries to talk to her. When they finally encounter some nameless horror from the pit, I know Gotrek is going slay first and ask questions later, and Felix is going to fight by his side, even as his guts are churning with terror. It's what they do.

Occasionally, however, they surprise me, and those are the parts I love best. I did not expect Gotrek's reaction at the end of *Orcslayer*, and yet it felt right to me once I wrote it. I did not expect Felix's relationship with his brother to go the way it did in Manslayer, and yet once it was down on paper, it seemed it could have gone no other way. This is what always makes me eager to write another Slayer book – the chance to follow Gotrek and Felix and learn new things about them as I find out what they're going to do next. Who could pass up an adventure like that?

Not me, that's for certain.

So, thank you, Black Library, for giving me such a wonderful opportunity, and thank you, Mister King, for creating characters that are such a joy to write about. I owe you both a great and lasting debt.

Nathan Long
Hollywood
2008

GIANTSLAYER

'Sylvania had proven to be a haunt of horror. The dire events at Drakenhof Castle left us filled us with sadness and fear. We had prevented the rising of a great terror but paid an awful price. And there was to be no respite from battle and dread. No sooner had we overcome our undead foe than we found ourselves thrown headlong into another even more desperate adventure, one that was to involve the titanic legacy of a long dead race and an encounter with the greatest living sorcerer of this age of the world, as well as battles with foes more horrible and deadly than almost anything we had faced before. During the course of these adventures I was to learn far more about the secret history of our world than I ever wanted to learn, and found my life and soul in the greatest of peril. Even now, looking back on these terrible events I am amazed that I survived. Many of my companions were not to prove so lucky...'

– From *My Travels With Gotrek*, Vol IV,
by Herr Felix Jaeger (Altdorf Press, 2505)

PROLOGUE

THE EARTH SHOOK. All around him people screamed. Huge buildings shuddered. The statues of the gods toppled from their alcoves in the shrines of ancient temples, shattering into a thousand pieces as the earth writhed like a dying serpent. He ran through the streets of the ancient city, seeing the looks of horror on the faces of his people. He passed decaying mansions where the desiccated ghosts of previous owners gibbered thinly in their fear. Ahead of him the mighty column of the Seafarer teetered and then collapsed. The Phoenix King flew from his high perch, his outstretched hand seeming to wave in terror as he tumbled earthward.

As he crested the high hills overlooking the mighty harbour, a glance at the peaks rimming the city told him the worst. The mountains blazed with light as wild magic ran out of control. He could sense its unbridled power even at this distance, and knew without having to cast any divinations that something was deeply, deeply amiss with the old spells that protected his land and his people.

Somehow, he was not sure how, he was atop the mighty wall that had guarded the harbour for a dozen ages. Looking out to sea, he saw the thing he had feared most of all. A towering wave, twice as high as the wall, driven by a force that would shatter the city, raced ever closer. Within it mighty leviathans, raised up from the deeps that surrounded the island continent, roared and bellowed and sought to break free. Strength that could shatter the largest ship in seconds was useless in the grip of that terrible tsunami.

Knowing that it was futile, that there was no way he could endure this, he prepared himself to resist, drawing on all his power, readying his mightiest warding magics, but somehow, as he had known it must be, nothing came. Power trickled into him where once it would have flooded.

A hundred times the height of the tallest man, the wave towered over his head, cresting, ready to break. For an instant he gazed into the eyes of a trapped sea monster, feeling a certain kinship with it; then its huge pink maw gaped, teeth the size of swords glinted in the shadows, and the mighty wave tumbled forward to break against the wall with awesome irresistible power.

It swept over him, crushing him, drowning him, smashing him down into the depths, and it rushed forward to sweep the last and greatest city of the elves from the face of the planet.

Suddenly he was elsewhere, in a place that was not a place, in a time that was outside time. There were presences there, not dead, not living, mighty mages all. Their faces were etched with aeons of pain, scarred from fighting a battle that no mortal should have been asked to fight. Even he, who was accounted mighty among the wizards of the world, was daunted by the power of the spells around him. More than that, he was frightened by where he knew himself to be, and when.

The shadowy presences danced around him, constantly performing a ritual that they must never stop, lest they bring disaster upon the world. They were wraith-like, and their movements were slow and pained, like the clockwork figures of the dwarfs whose mechanisms were slowly winding down. Once, he knew, they had been elves, the greatest wizards of their age, and they had sacrificed themselves to save their land and their people.

'Greetings, blood of Aenarion,' said an ancient voice, dry, dusty, but with the faint lilting accent of the mountains of Caledor still.

'Greetings, Lord of Dragons,' he replied, knowing who he faced, wondering if this was a dream, knowing it was not.

'We are remembered still among the living then?' said the voice.

'Remembered and honoured.'

'That is good. That is some repayment for our sacrifice.' There was more than a hint of self-pity in the voice. Understandable, he supposed. He would probably have felt sorry for himself if he had been trapped at the centre of the great vortex for five millennia, struggling to hold together the web of spells that kept the island continent afloat.

The scene shimmered, like a reflection on the surface of disturbed water. The ghastly, ghostly figures seemed to recede, and he was glad. He ought to let them go, but he knew he had been brought here for a purpose.

'Why am I here?' he shouted, and his words seemed to echo through infinite caverns, and resound into distant ages.

'The old barriers are falling. The Paths of the Old Ones are opened. We cannot hold the Weave against it.'

'What am I to do?'

'Seek the source of disorder. Find the Oracle of the Truthsayers. She will tell you what you need to know. Close the ancient pathways. Go swiftly and go alone. You will find the allies you need along the way and in the most unexpected forms. Go. There is little time left. Even this sending is weakening us and we must conserve the little strength we have left.'

Even as the words echoed up from the bottom of infinity, the voice was fading. A great fear came over him.

The Archmage Teclis sat bolt upright, pulling the silken sheets from the naked forms of his companions. Cold sweat covered him; he could smell it even through the musky scents worn by the two courtesans.

'What is it, my lord?' asked Shienara. Concern showed in her beautiful narrow face. 'What ails you?'

'Nothing,' he lied, rising from the bed and limping across the room. He reached for a goblet and a crystal decanter of wine cut in the shape of a dragon.

'Is it the dreams again, the nightmares?'

He shot her a cold glance. 'What do you know of nightmares?' he asked.

'You talk in your sleep, my lord, and lash out, and I guessed.'

He looked at her, long and hard. These were words his many enemies would pay much to hear.

'There were no nightmares,' he said, reaching out for the power. Unlike in the dream, it flowed strongly into him. 'There were no dreams. You should forget these things.'

A slight blankness came over her beautiful face as the spell took her. She looked at him and smiled quizzically. 'Sleep,' he told her, 'and when you wake remember nothing.'

Instantly she slumped next to the form of her twin. He shrugged, wishing that he could sleep so soundly, knowing that he never would again without the aid of magic, and that was something he could no longer afford. Momentary guilt afflicted him that he should treat a fellow elf so, but these were strange and evil times, and the need for security was paramount. Ancient enemies stirred. Old gods were awakening. Every oracle and soothsayer between here and far Cathay predicted doom. His own star charts spoke of as much. He took a sip of the bitter wine. It flowed down easily.

He gestured and his robe fluttered across the room, wrapping itself around his naked form. He pulled on a pair of slippers made from the finest Cathayan silk. He reached out and his staff leapt to his hand. He limped from the chamber, and down the cold echoing hallways of his ancestral home. He made his way to the workroom, knowing that he would do as he always did, and seek comfort in knowledge. The few aged servants still awake scurried away, knowing from his frown that it would be best not to interrupt his reverie.

Dark times were coming, he knew. The dreams were impossible to ignore now, and he had long ago learned the unwisdom of doing that anyway.

In the deepest cellars beneath the mansion, his workroom provided him with a haven. As he entered, he spoke the words of command. Immediately wards sprang into place. The air shimmered with their bridled power. Not even the mightiest daemon could penetrate them.

A trapped homunculus stirred slowly in a jar of preservative fluid. It gestured at him obscenely as he limped past. The creature was not best pleased with its home. Tiny gills pulsed in its neck. Its thin leathery wings stirred the liquid, turning it cloudy. He gave it a cold smile, and it froze in mid-gesticulation. Few things in this world or beyond had the courage to cross him when an evil mood was upon him.

He moved through the chamber, past the ordered alcoves containing mystical paraphernalia and the elaborately indexed series of volumes in a hundred languages, living and dead. Eventually he found what he sought, the strange apparatus he had unearthed in the ruins of the ancient Cathayan city nearly two centuries ago. A massive sphere of verdigrised bronze, engraved with strange runes that reminded him of the work of the decadent denizens of Lustria.

Teclis sat cross-legged before the Sphere of Destiny and contemplated his dream. It was the third time in less than a month it had come to him, each time more clear and vivid than the last. This was the first time the ancients had spoken to him, though. Had he really talked with ghosts of the ancestral wizards who protected his land? Had they reached out through the barriers that bound them and communicated with him? He smiled sourly. He knew that dreams could be sent to warn or to harm, but he knew equally that sometimes dreams were only his own deeper mind talking to him, giving shape to his fears and intuitions. Either some friendly power or his own deepest instincts were trying to warn him of something – it was irrelevant which. He needed to act.

You did not have to be a high wizard to know that something was amiss in the world. Reports from Eagle captains brought tales of disaster from the furthest lands. In Cathay, the warlords had risen in rebellion against the Mandate of Heaven. In Araby a fanatic who called himself the Prophet of Law was stirring up the natives to cleanse their land of evil... and his definition of evil included anyone who was not human. In the cities of their under-empire, the skaven stirred. The forces of the Witch King once more strode the soil of Ulthuan. Elven armies mustered to head northwards and oppose them, and elven fleets patrolled the northern seas constantly. But a month ago, he had been summoned here to Lothern and the court of the Phoenix King to discuss these matters, and having done so was told to prepare for war.

He passed his hands over the sphere. The casing of metal bands contracted in on themselves, revealing a milky white gem that pulsed with its own internal light. He spoke the words of the invocation he had found in a scroll from the reign of Bel Korhadris, near three thousand years old, and the lights danced over its surface. He snapped his fingers and the candles of hallucinogenic incense, concentrated from the leaves of the black lotus, sprang to life and began to burn. He breathed deeply of them, and opened his mage senses to the fullest, feeling his point of view being sucked into the depths of the crystal. For long moments, nothing happened. He saw only blackness, heard only the muted drumbeat of his heart. He continued the invocation, working effortlessly on a spell that it would have taken a lesser mage a lifetime to master.

Now his vision seemed to hover over Ulthuan. He could see perfectly even in the darkness, and he could view those things that would be visible only to a mage. He saw the flows of magic pinioned by the watchstones that kept the island continent above the waves. Raised by elder world magic millennia ago, it needed the same magic now to prevent it sinking beneath the surface of the sea. In his dreams he had spoken to those who maintained those spells. He knew that was significant. He saw the tiny glints that were his fellow wizards working magic, the intricate structures of spells as they were woven by masters of the most magical of all the world's peoples.

Sensing a disruption in the flows of power, he sent his consciousness racing in the direction from which it came. Far to the north he sensed the abomination that waited at the farthest pole. It pulsed with energy, no longer quiescent, promising the end of the world. Still, it had not fully woken, but yet...

Within heartbeats his spirit eyes soared over the Chaos Wastes, as close to the influence of the polar abomination as he dared go, taking in the vast hordes of black armoured warriors camped on the cold plains, and the hideous legions of horned beastmen who followed them. He saw the huge flows of Chaotic energy that the winds of magic blew over them, but he saw nothing there to cause any disturbance to his island home. All the same, it was disturbing, the size of that huge invasion force. It was larger than anything the diminished power of the elves could muster and he knew it was only a small fraction of what the dark powers were amassing.

He sent the sphere arcing through the sky towards the ancient city of Praag and saw that it was still in ruins, although its people were making valiant efforts to rebuild it. Interestingly, dwarfs were present. It seemed the ancient enemies of his own people had come to help the humans in this hour of need.

He let his eyes dwell on the massive citadel, wrapped as it was by spells that not even he could penetrate, and wondered what it was that was kept in the depths beneath that fortified pinnacle. What ancient secret brought the armies of Chaos back to this spot again and again? What ancient oaths bound the humans to rebuild their haunted city in the face of the unbreaking cycle of destruction? The speculation was interesting but it was getting him nowhere. It merely confirmed what he had heard: that the greatest invasion in centuries was taking place in the Old World, and he feared it would take more than the might of man and dwarf to repel it.

He raised his point of view higher until the curve of the sleeping world lay beneath him, the lines of power flowing through the night like an enormous web were visible to him even through the white turbulent spirals of the clouds. He inspected them closely, looking for clues, and found them. From the northern island of Albion the lines of power that would normally have flowed to Ulthuan did so weakly. Sometimes they flickered and faded. Sometimes they blazed brightly and massive pulses of energy raced out over the sea in the direction of the island continent. Out of the Chaos Wastes pulses of power rushed towards Albion and then diminished. From Albion, the flows raced onwards, rippling towards the Empire, Bretonnia, Ulthuan.

What was going on here? What magic was this? Those webs of energy dated back to the most ancient days – what could be using them for its own ends? Nothing good, he was certain. He sent the point of view of the sphere rushing towards Albion. It hurtled towards the magical barriers that surrounded the island, into the mists, and there it was stopped utterly and completely.

Not good, he thought. Albion had always been surrounded by spells of great potency intended to ward it from the eye of outsiders. Those spells obviously still held. No, he thought, that was not quite true. They felt different now. There was a subtle taint to them, of evil and something else.

Briefly he considered what he had seen, and a horrible suspicion began to grow in his mind. Fragments of certain ancient forbidden texts, written by mad elven wizards in the dawn ages of the world came back to him. Legends of the world's most ancient gods, that talked of things best forgotten. But apparently someone *had* remembered them. Someone had disturbed the things that were best left untouched. Fear clutched at his heart as he considered this. He needed to consult certain ancient sources, and he needed to do so now. If what he suspected was true, there was indeed not a moment to waste.

DAWN FOUND TECLIS on the balcony outside the library, a book spread on his lap, his face resting in his hands. The old mansion built on the side of the highest hills overlooking the city of Lothern gave him a fine view of the harbour. It was flat and serene as a pond; not the slightest hint of the enormous tidal wave of his nightmares menaced it.

Briefly, he wished he was back in the tower of Hoeth, with the greatest library in the world close at hand, and his fellow mages to consult with, but that was a foolish wish. Politics had brought him here. He did not like this place, the ownership of which he shared with his brother. He had not liked it when they were children, and he did not like it now. Too many old memories, he supposed, too many recollections of long evenings of illness and infirmity. It reminded him too much of a hospice or one of those temples of euthanasia where the old and the weary of life went to end their lives in peace and comfort.

He dismissed these thoughts. Even as he did so, the earth quivered. It was very mild. The wine in his goblet merely rippled. The walls of the old palace barely quivered. It might have been a natural earthquake, but he doubted it. All the signs were clear. Something was interfering with the ancient spells that bound the island continent of Ulthuan together, that stopped it from disappearing once more beneath the waves. And if something was not done, his nightmares would come true.

Aldreth, one of his oldest servants entered. Teclis knew it was important. The old elf had orders not to disturb him for anything less than a summons from the Phoenix King himself. 'Your brother wishes to speak with you,' he said.

Teclis smiled sourly. There was no way of denying he was at home. This place was as much Tyrion's as his own, and the servants were as loyal to his twin as they were to him. More loyal, he thought acidly. Of course, his brother would depart if he indicated a wish for privacy. His manners were as perfect as everything else about him. Teclis turned his gaze back to the sea. You are in a vile mood today, he told himself.

'Show my brother in,' he said. 'And prepare food if he wishes it.'

'It is a little early to be drinking that vintage,' said Tyrion as he strode out onto the balcony. There was a hint of reproof in his voice that was equivalent to a thunderous chorus of disapproval from anyone else. Teclis looked up at his brother. So tall, so straight. The limbs so clean and so unbent, the face so honest and open. The voice as beautiful as a temple bell being rung to greet the dawn. Astonishing, he thought, that this golden creature should be my twin. It seemed that the gods had lavished all their gifts on him, and left me an ill-made thing.

'I take it that means you won't be joining me, brother?'

He knew he was being unfair. The gods had given him a gift for magic unequalled in this age of the world, and the will necessary to use that power as it should be used. Still, there were times when he would have gladly swapped all of that for Tyrion's effortless popularity, his ease and courtesy, his ability to be happy even in the unhappiest of times, and his blazing good health.

'On the contrary, it is my brotherly duty to keep you from drinking alone. The gods alone know what that might lead to.' And there it was, the famous charm, the ability to change the mood of the situation with a smile and a seemingly thoughtless joke. Tyrion reached out for the decanter and poured himself a full goblet. There was no formality there, none of the endless empty ritual that Teclis so despised in elvish social gatherings. It was the casual gesture of the warrior more at home in camp than the Phoenix King's court, and yet it was exactly the thing his brother knew would put him most at ease. Teclis could understand why there were those at court who compared his brother to Malekith in ancient times, before the Witch King revealed his true colours. He had known his brother all their lives, and even he was not sure how much art went into that carefully contrived artlessness.

Tyrion waved, and Teclis looked up. On the balcony above them, Shienara and her sister, Malyria, waved back. They looked at Tyrion with the mixture of open desire and admiration he had always commanded from women. Useless, of course, as his brother had eyes only for his consort, the Everqueen. He had not, unlike most elf males, ever been unfaithful.

'What is this early morning toast in honour of?' Tyrion asked.

'The end of the world,' said Teclis.

'That bad?' said Tyrion.

'The end of our world, at least.'

'I do not think the Dark One will overcome us this time,' said Tyrion. It was exactly what Teclis would have expected him to say, but there was a watchfulness about him now, a wariness. Suddenly he looked exactly like what he was, the deadliest elf warrior in twenty generations.

'It is not our dear kinsman and his lackeys I am worried about, it is Ulthuan itself. Someone, or something, is tampering with the watchstones or the power that underlies them.'

'These earthquakes and eruptions are not coincidence then? I had suspected as much.'

'No, they are not.'

'You will be leaving soon then.' It was not a question. Teclis smiled as he nodded. His brother had always understood him better than any other living being.

'Do you want some company on your journey? I am supposed to be leading the fleet northwards, to face the spawn of Naggaroth, but if what you say is true, I am sure the Phoenix King could spare my services.'

Teclis shook his head. 'The fleet needs you. Our armies need you. Where I am going, spells will be more useful than swords.'

Teclis slammed his drink down on the fine ivory table. It almost spilled over the parchments that sat there. He had spent most of the night writing them. 'Please see that these are copied and delivered to his majesty and the masters at Hoeth,' he told Aldreth. 'Now I must go. I have a long way to travel and a short time to do it in.'

CHAPTER ONE

With a heavy heart, Felix Jaeger watched the last of the remaining Kislevite warriors place the corpse of Ivan Petrovich on the pyre. The old warrior looked somehow smaller, shrunken in death. His face showed none of the peace that was supposed to belong to those who had entered the realm of Morr, God of Death, but then, Felix supposed, Ivan's last few moments had been anything but pleasant. He had witnessed his only child, Ulrika, transformed into a vampire, a soulless blood-sucking thing, and he himself had met his death at the hand of her undead master's minions. Felix shivered and drew his faded red Sudenland wool cloak about him. Once he had thought himself in love with Ivan's daughter. What was he supposed to feel now?

The answer was that he did not know. Even when she had still walked among the living he had been unsure. Now, he realised, he would never really have the chance to find out. Somewhere deep within him a slow, sullen, smouldering resentment against the gods was fanned to flame. He was starting to understand how Gotrek felt.

He looked over at the Slayer. The dwarf's brutal features were uncharacteristically thoughtful. His squat massive form, far broader than any human's, looked out of place among the Kislevite horse soldiers. He knuckled the patch covering his ruined eye with one massive hand, then scratched his shaved and tattooed head reflectively. His great crest of red dyed hair drooped in the cold and snow. He looked up and caught Felix's glance and shook his head. Felix guessed that in his own strange way Gotrek had liked the old march boyar. More than that, Ivan Petrovich had in some way been a link to the Slayer's mysterious past. He had known the dwarf since the time of his first expedition to the Chaos Wastes many years before.

The thought made Felix realise just how far from home Ivan had fallen. It must be three hundred leagues at least from here in the dark forests of Sylvania to the cold lands on the edge of Kislev that he had once ruled. Of course, the old boyar's realm was gone now, swept away by the vast Chaos invasion that had driven as far south as Praag.

'Snorri thinks Ivan died a good death,' said Snorri Nosebiter. He looked glum. Despite the cold, the second Slayer was no better dressed than Gotrek. Perhaps dwarfs simply did not feel discomfort like humans. More likely they were simply too stubborn to admit it. Snorri's normally stupidly cheerful features were masked by sadness. Perhaps he was not quite so insensitive as he seemed.

'There are no good deaths,' Felix muttered under his breath. When he realised what he had done, he offered up a silent prayer that neither of the dwarfs had heard him. He had, after all, sworn a vow to follow Gotrek and record the Slayer's doom in an epic poem what seemed like a lifetime ago. The dwarfs lived only to atone for some supposed sin or crime by meeting their doom at the hands of a mighty monster, or in the face of overwhelming odds.

The surviving Kislevites filed past and offered up their last respects to their former lord. Many of them made the sign of the wolf god Ulric with the fingers of their left hand, then cast a glance over their shoulder and made it again. Felix could understand that. They were still almost within the shadow of Drakenhof Castle, that mighty citadel of evil the vampire lord Adolphus Krieger had sought to make his own. He had possessed an ancient amulet and a plan to bring all the aristocracy of the night under his command. Instead he had succeeded only in bringing his own doom.

But at what cost? So many had lost their lives. There was another mass pyre nearby that the surviving Kislevites had hastily constructed for their own fallen. A second one contained the remains of the vampire's followers. Here in the cursed land of Sylvania these men were not about to leave any corpses unburned to face a possible dark resurrection at the hands of a necromancer.

Max Schreiber strode forward, leaning on his staff, looking every inch the imposing wizard in his golden robes. Not even the bloodstains and sword rips in the clothes detracted from the man's dignity, but there was something dead in his eyes and a bleakness to his features that matched Gotrek's. Max had loved Ulrika, probably more than Felix ever had, and now he too had lost her forever. Felix hoped that in his grief the wizard would not do something stupid.

Max waited until the last of the Kislevites had filed past the boyar's body, then he looked at Wulfgar, the ranking leader. The horse soldier nodded. Max spoke a word and banged the butt of his staff on the ground three times. With each strike, one of the pyres burst into flames. The sorcery was strong and obvious. Golden flames flickered into being around the damp wood and then settled on them. The nails driven into Snorri's skull reflected the light, making it look like he had a small blaze atop his shaven head.

Slowly smoke rose, the wood blackened and then burst into more natural flame. Felix was glad of the wizard's magic. There was no way under these conditions that even the dwarfs would have been able to light a fire.

Swiftly the fires spread and soon the sickly sweet smell of roasting flesh filled the air. Felix was not prepared to stay and watch Ivan be consumed. The man was a friend. He turned and strode out from the ruined hall into the cold air. The horses were waiting, and the wagons of the wounded. Snow covered the land. Somewhere out there was Ulrika and her new mentor, the Countess Gabriella, but they were out of his reach now.

War waited in the north. Chaos was coming, and it was there the Slayers expected to find their destiny.

THE OLD WOMAN looked weary. The children marching along beside her looked starved. They wore the usual rags common to Sylvanian peasantry. Their eyes were studies in hopeless misery. Beside them a few men in blood-spattered tunics grasped pitchforks in frozen fingers. Felix saw tiredness war with fear in their faces and slowly win out. They were scared of the riders and the dwarfs but they were too tired and too hungry to run.

'What happened to you?' asked Gotrek in a manner that was anything but reassuring. The massive axe he held in one fist made him even more threatening. 'Why do you wander these roads in winter?'

It was a good question. Any sensible peasant would be huddling in his hovel right now. Felix already knew the answer. These were refugees.

'Beasts came,' said the old woman eventually. 'Out of the woods. They burned our houses, burned the inn, burned everything, killed most and carried others off.'

'Most likely wanted breakfast,' said Gotrek. The expressions on the faces of the refugees told Felix that they had not needed to know that.

'Beastmen?' Snorri had perked up, as he always did at the prospect of a fight.

'Aye, scores of them,' said the old woman. 'Came out of nowhere in the middle of winter. Who would have thought it? Maybe the zealots are right. Maybe the end of the world is coming. They say the pale lords have returned and that Drakenhof Castle is inhabited once more.'

'That's something you don't need to worry about any more,' said Felix, then wished he hadn't. The hag was looking at him as if he were an idiot, which he supposed he was for saying such a thing. Of course, any Sylvanian peasant would worry about Drakenhof Castle and its inhabitants, no matter what some ragged stranger said.

'You say they burned down the inn?' said Max.

'Aye. Killed the innkeeper and most of the guests.'

'Snorri was looking forward to a bucket of vodka,' said Snorri. 'Snorri thinks those beastmen need to be taught a lesson.'

Gotrek nodded agreement. Felix had been afraid of that. The fact that there were less than a dozen unwounded Kislevite horse archers, the two Slayers, and Felix and Max to face what sounded like a mass of beastmen did not daunt either dwarf in the least. The Kislevites, hardened warriors from the march lands where human territories bordered Chaos, had sense enough to be worried, Felix could tell from their expressions.

'Don't go,' said the old woman. 'Ye'll just get yourselves killed. Best come with us. Stephansdorp is just a couple of days' walk south of here. It's less than a day without the snow.'

'If it has not been burned to the ground too,' said Gotrek, somewhat unhelpfully. A couple of the children whimpered. One or two of the men looked as if they were fighting back tears themselves. Felix could not blame them. Doubtless only the thought of sanctuary among their kin in the nearby village had kept them going. Even as Felix watched, one man collapsed onto his knees, letting his pitchfork fall from numbed fingers. He made the sign of Shallya on his breast and bowed his head. Two of the children went over to him and began to tug his sleeves, whispering, 'Da-da.'

'Best get going if we're going to overtake these beastmen,' said Gotrek. Snorri nodded agreement. Wulfgar shook his head. 'We will guard these folk en route to their kin,' he said. 'We must find a place for our wounded.'

He looked almost shamefaced as he said it. Felix did not blame him, though. The Kislevites had been sorely demoralised by the death of Ivan, and the events at Drakenhof had been enough to dent the courage of even the bravest. Gotrek stared at Wulfgar for a moment. Felix feared the Slayer was about to give the horse soldier the benefit of a few well-chosen words concerning the courage and hardiness of Kislevite humanity, but he just shrugged and shook his head.

'What about you, Max?' Felix asked. The wizard considered for a moment before saying, 'I will come with you. These beastmen should be cleansed from our land.'

The tone of the wizard's voice worried Felix. He seemed well nigh as bitter and full of rage as Gotrek. Felix hoped that he was not becoming unhinged by grief over what had happened with Ulrika. On the other hand, he was glad Max was coming with them. The wizard was worth a company of horse archers when it came to a fight.

Briefly, Felix considered sloping off with the horse archers himself, but decided against it. Not only would it have gone against the oath he had sworn to follow the Slayer, but Felix felt far safer in the company of Gotrek, Snorri and Max than he would in the company of the Kislevites, even if they were going hunting for beastmen.

'Best be getting on then,' he was surprised to hear himself saying, 'if we want to get there by nightfall.'

'THIS PLACE HAS certainly changed since we were last here,' said Felix, looking at the still smouldering ruins of what had once been a walled village. Nobody paid him the slightest attention. They were all too busy looking at the wreckage for themselves.

There was not much left. Most of the hovels had been made of wattle and daub with thatched roofs. Their walls had been kicked in, their roofs burned. Only the inn had been a more substantial structure, of timber and stone. It had taken a fair time to collapse, he guessed. The flames must have been fierce indeed to consume the structure. A pity it was gone, he thought, for the weather was already starting to worsen.

Even as he watched, shadowy figures moved within it. They were too big and too misshapen to be human. There was only one thing that looked like that. Beastmen! Snorri almost howled with joy when he realised what they were seeing and brandished his axe and his hammer in the air. Gotrek raised his axe, ran his thumb along the blade until it drew blood and then spat a curse.

If this intimidated the beastmen, they gave no sign. A group of them emerged from the ruins of the inn. Some of them possessed bovine heads, while others had the heads of goats or wolves or other beasts. All of them were massive and muscular. All of them were armed with crude spears, massive spiked clubs or hammers. They were an incongruous sight. The last time Felix had passed through this place, the Green Man had been occupied by humans and he had passed an evening in bizarre conversation with the vampiric countess. Now the whole small village surrounding the inn had been swept away. In his lifetime Felix had seen a great deal of slaughter and a number of villages razed, but he knew he would never get used to it. The senseless carnage fuelled his anger and his resentment.

The dozen beastmen swept forward. They obviously felt no fear at facing such a small group of opponents. Answering calls came from elsewhere, from the snow-girt woods around the sacked hamlet. Felix hoped he and the others had not bitten off more than they could chew.

As the beastmen loped forward, Gotrek and Snorri raced to meet them. Raced was probably the wrong word under the circumstances, Felix decided. The dwarfs' short legs carried them at what would have been a comfortable jog for Felix. In any case, the distance between them closed swiftly. Felix looked at Max to see if the wizard was going to cast a spell. Max scanned their surroundings looking for other attackers. He seemed confident that the Slayers could handle the beasts.

Gotrek hit the pack slightly ahead of Snorri. His axe hurtled through a tremendous arc, lopping off the arm of the nearest beastman, opening the stomach of another to send a wave of blood and bile spraying to the ground, and smashing through the raised club with which a third attempted to parry. A moment later Snorri took down the disarmed beastman with a stroke of the hammer he held in one hand, and buried his axe in the skull of another. There was a sickening crunch like rotten wood splintering as he drove it home.

Within a few heartbeats five of the beastmen were down. Gotrek and Snorri barely slowed. Gotrek leapt forward and chopped a wolf-headed creature clean in two, sending its upper body one way and its lower body another. Snorri whirled like an Arabyan dervish and brought both his weapons smashing into another Chaos spawn. The hammer tenderised flesh even as the axe smashed ribs and bit deep into the creature's lungs. It stood for a moment, blowing bubbles of bloody froth from its chest before it collapsed.

The surviving beastmen had not even had time to realise the scale of the casualties they had taken. They swept forward, trying to overwhelm their foes. They obviously had confidence in the sheer brutal power of their blows, but they had reckoned without the strength of

Gotrek and Snorri's stark ferocity. Gotrek whirled his axe in a massive double arc, driving them back. Snorri dived forward to land on his side and hit the snow rolling. He barrelled into the legs of one beastman, tripping it, while his axe took another behind the knee sending it stumbling to the ground. Without breaking stride, Gotrek brought his axe down twice with all the force of a thunderbolt. Felix knew that neither of the fallen beastmen would rise again, given the sickening power of those blows. A heartbeat later, the axe had risen again to behead another beastman.

Now the Chaos creatures were dismayed. They turned and fled. Gotrek's axe took another in the back. Snorri pulled himself to his feet and lobbed his hammer, catching another on the back of the skull, sending it tumbling forward into the snow. A few moments later, Snorri had reclaimed his hammer and turned the beastman's skull to jelly with it.

Felix glanced around. More groups of beastmen had emerged from the wood, just in time to witness the rout of their fellows. Felix could see that there were not nearly as many as he had feared. There were three groups with, at most, five members. It looked like the largest part of their force had emerged from the inn. Nonetheless they looked like they were considering a charge when Max raised his arms and began incanting a spell. In seconds a sphere of light brighter than the sun appeared in each of his clenched fists. When he opened his fingers bolts of pure blazing golden power lashed forward. They ravened among the brutes, charring flesh and melting bone. It was all too much for the Chaos creatures. They turned tail and fled into the woods.

Felix was amazed. Events had moved so swiftly, he had not even managed to bloody his sword. He felt almost embarrassed when he considered it. Seeing his expression, Gotrek spoke up.

'Don't worry, manling. You will get your chance to kill Chaos spawn when we follow these beasts to their lair!'

'I was afraid you were going to say that,' Felix said. He moved into the ruins of the inn. Butchered bodies were everywhere. Human bones lay in the snow, cracked for marrow and gnawed by powerful jaws. He felt like being sick but he controlled himself.

'Looks like they stopped here for a snack,' said Gotrek.

Two hours later, massive trees loomed all around them. The snow was falling so heavily that Felix could barely see ten feet ahead of him. They had long ago lost all sight of the beastmen's tracks. Now it was only a matter of trudging forward through the storm, making sure to keep his eyes fixed firmly on Gotrek's broad back. The wind whined in his ears. The snowflakes melted in his hair. His breath emerged in frosty clouds. His fingers felt too numb to hold a sword. He was not sure that if he was attacked now, he would even be capable of fighting. He sincerely hoped the Slayers were in a better way. Right now he desperately wished he had gone off with the Kislevites. Now was not the time to be caught in the Sylvanian woods by a sudden blizzard.

They needed to find shelter soon, or they were doomed.

CHAPTER TWO

'I WANT TO KILL Gotrek Gurnisson myself,' said Grume of Night Fang. He loomed out of the shadows like a small mountain of metal and armour. The intricate net of potent enchantments on his armour was almost dazzling to Kelmain's mage sight. The warlord had been like a man demented ever since the defeated scouts had returned out of the blizzard, bearing word of the dwarf's presence. Kelmain wished he had never mentioned it now, but he had been at Praag and knew from the descriptions of their adversaries that only Gotrek Gurnisson and his associates matched the scouts' descriptions.

'Why?' asked the Chaos wizard, just to be contrary. Kelmain looked around the stone walls of the ancient antechamber, trying to gather his patience. The runes fascinated him and so did those bizarre carvings, but the smell was so distracting. He covered his mouth and his nose with one clawed hand. Grume stank of sweat and the old blood and congealed brains that covered his armour. Normally Kelmain did not consider himself fastidious, it was not something anyone in his line of work could afford to be, but this was the limit.

'Because his axe killed Arek Daemonclaw and I want it for my own. Such a weapon would be worthy of me. All considered Arek's armour unbreachable,' Grume's deep voice bellowed.

Outside, the wind and snow whirled past, deflected by the spells Kelmain had woven around them.

Kelmain gazed into the hovering crystal and saw his identical twin, Lhoigor, reflected within. He might as well have been standing in the room, not a thousand leagues away within that dreary temple on the island of Albion. Tall, thin, vulpine of features, pale of skin. The difference was that Lhoigor was clad in gold instead of black, and had a runestaff of gold as opposed to his own staff of ebony and silver. Lhoigor flapped a hand beneath his nose and then raised a hand to his mouth. Kelmain knew what he meant. Why, of all the Chaos warlords gathered, did it have to be Grume who accompanied him on this reconnaissance, he wondered? Why could it not be Kestranor the Castrator? At least the musky scent of the Slaanesh worshipper was pleasant. Even Tchulaz Khan, the festering follower of Nurgle, was almost preferable to this. It was a pity he had drawn the short straw and been forced to accompany this scouting mission. He would even have preferred the miserable wet weather of that pestilential island to this. Still, he told himself, someone had to do it. Their acolytes were all busy shepherding forces through the paths, and if truth be told, the idea of using the ancient web of extra-dimensional roadways had excited him.

'That is a very dangerous weapon,' said Kelmain, and immediately wished he had not opened his mouth. The stench almost made him gag. Perhaps there was something sorcerous to it. He was not normally so squeamish. Or perhaps it had something to do with that hideous weapon the Khorne worshipper carried. Just looking at it with his mage sight made the wizard squirm. That was not something he wanted to be killed with. Death would be the least of his worries then.

'All weapons are dangerous, but I am a follower of Khorne,' said Grume with a grin of contempt. He was every inch the great warlord, talking down to his wizardly minions.

Idiot! Kelmain thought. Why did they always have to work with these muscle-headed buffoons? He sometimes suspected that the Great Powers of Chaos chose their warrior champions for their stupidity – particularly the Blood God.

Indeed he is, murmured Lhoigor's voice within his head, and Kelmain knew his twin was thinking exactly the same as he was.

'I do not like working with you followers of the Changer of Ways, any more than you like working with me,' said Grume, 'but the Great Ones have spoken and daemons have brought me their words. The time has come for us to unite and overthrow the weak kingdoms of men.'

Indeed it has, thought Kelmain. And I wonder if you realise how much the place in which we stand has to do with this. He glanced around at the remains of the ancient arch that dominated the chamber. Here was spellwork of great cunning, god-like in its complexity, so intricate that even when dormant it threatened to overwhelm his mind. The Paths of the Old Ones, Kelmain marvelled. We have opened them, or rather our masters have, and we may use them as we will. Soon, he thought, they will put this entire ancient and corrupt world within our grasp, and we will reshape it to fit our dreams. But to do this we must work with idiots who want to use us only for their own stupid purposes.

Grume opened his visor to reveal his bloated and ugly features. A glint of feral cunning showed in the warlord's small pig-like eyes. Kelmain could almost read his thoughts. The Axe of Gotrek had become a legend among the followers of Chaos. At the Siege of Praag, it had breached the supposedly invincible armour of the great Chaos Warlord Arek Daemonclaw. The death of that mighty champion had led to the breaking of his army and the siege of the City of Heroes. Rumour whispered that the dwarf had even destroyed the physical form of one of the Great Daemons of Khorne in the lost city of Karag Dum.

Kelmain was one of the few in a position to know exactly how true those rumours were. Grume already had several powerful weapons forged with the imprisoned souls of mighty daemons and champions. It was obvious that he wanted to add the dwarf's axe to his collection. It was equally obvious that when the time came, after the forces of Chaos were triumphant, he fully intended to use the weapon against those who opposed him.

It was a plan admirably suited to one of his utter stupidity, but who prided himself on his cunning. It would hardly do, thought Kelmain, to explain to him the full perils of trying to use that axe. There, indeed, was a weapon that would take enormous power to pervert to the ways of Chaos, and a tremendous understanding of magic. Grume had absolutely no knowledge of such things. Kelmain did, although he was loath to risk using his powers in so dangerous a pursuit at so critical a time. They were needed to oversee the use of the Old Ones' devices and ensure that they served Chaos well. Still, perhaps Grume's ambition could be put to another use? He glanced into the crystal once more to see if his brother was following his thoughts. Lhoigor's answering smile showed that he was.

'Do you know what happened to the last wizard who mocked me?' Grume asked, his voice full of menace. He had the confidence of one who knows he has a small army of beastmen close at hand. The casualties the Slayer and his comrades had inflicted had reduced their numbers only by a fifth or so. Kelmain stifled a yawn.

'I believe his soul went to feed the daemon that resides in your bludgeon,' he said. 'Or did you not offer him up as a snack to your patron daemon prince? I forget. One meets so many mighty champions of Chaos these days, one simply cannot remember all the dreadful punishments they meted out to those who mocked them.'

'You play a dangerous game, wizard,' said Grume. Wrath twisted his bestial features. He loomed over the mage, nearly twice his height. His hand rested on the hilt of the odd magical mace that normally dangled from his wrist. 'By Khorne, you will pay the ultimate price.'

'You are showing the lack of intellect for which the followers of Khorne are so justly renowned,' said Kelmain in a tone of apology and abject grovelling that clearly confused the Chaos warrior. 'If you were to kill me or feed my soul to your mighty weapon, there would be no one to open the Paths of the Old Ones for you... or locate the Slayer on your behalf.'

'Then you will do what I command,' said Grume, self-satisfaction evident in his voice. He had chosen to listen to the tone, and not the words, as Kelmain had known he would. Here was a brute used to bullying his way forward over the objections of others.

'Why not? If you succeed, we will have one enemy less. I have no love for Gotrek Gurnisson and would be glad to see him dead.'

'I will give you enchantments to let you locate the Slayer and his axe,' said Kelmain. 'When you find him... kill him.'

'If you can,' he added, so quietly that Grume did not hear.

KELMAIN WATCHED GRUME's force assemble within the antechamber. The carved heads of obscene toad-like gods seemed to watch them mockingly. Looking into the viewing crystal, he met the gaze of his brother. Lhoigor looked a little weak. Using the spell of speaking over so vast a distance was draining even to a mage of his power.

'You have found Gotrek Gurnisson,' said Lhoigor. It was not a question.

'Yes. My divinations show our fleeing beastmen were right. He is near where we are, at the Sylvanian nexus. One would almost think it was fate,' said Kelmain.

'Perhaps it is. Destiny seems to have marked that one. Or the powers that oppose us.'

'It will most likely prove unfortunate for that giant idiot,' he added, gesturing at Grume with his staff. The huge Chaos warrior ignored him and concentrated on bullying a score of his troops into position. 'I should close this portal and leave him to get cold feet treading through the winter snows of the Empire.'

'Call him back, brother, and you could always send him to Lustria, if you are worried about his health in the winter.' Lhoigor's smile was cold but there was an evil humour in it.

'Or to the gateway in sunken Melay – that would clean his armour for him,' said Kelmain.

'I don't think our last scouting team returned from testing the path we thought led into the heart of Firemount. Some lava might heat our large friend up nicely.'

'Or to Ulthuan, to teach the elves what happens to those who defy the champions of the Blood God,' said Lhoigor in an almost perfect copy of the Chaos champion's booming manner. Kelmain laughed, and so eerie was the sound of his mirth that the beastmen looked up and shuddered.

'Get on with it,' bellowed Grume. Kelmain shrugged and gestured expansively.

'I see you have another plan, brother,' said Lhoigor, a look of wicked mirth upon his face.

'As ever, you understand me perfectly. There is more than one way to doom a dwarf.' He picked up the orb of seeing he had taken from the ruins of ancient Lahmia. It felt cold as rock in his hands. The gem in the centre of the perfect sphere glittered with magical energy. He muttered the spell, and it rose into the air and swooped down to circle the Chaos warrior. Kelmain shut his eyes and concentrated on the link. His point of view shifted to that of the gem. It was his eye and he could see through it now.

'This will lead you to that accursed dwarf,' said Kelmain, and the spell allowed his voice to emerge from the Eye. 'And allow us to witness your great victory! Go kill Gotrek Gurnisson,' said Kelmain.

A little tired from the strain of the ritual, Kelmain yawned. His brother did likewise. A small significant feeling of triumph filled Kelmain as he prepared to shift his consciousness into the Eye. One way or another, Gotrek Gurnisson was as good as dead. And so was anybody with him.

Grume and his warriors were already heading out of the antechamber into snow.

'You do not think that Grume can overcome Gotrek Gurnisson?'

'He is tough and his force is very numerous, but even if he does not, it will serve our purposes. If they fail to overcome the Slayer, they will lure him here – there are things within the Paths of the Old Ones which can kill even him.'

CHAPTER THREE

THE SERVANTS LOOKED at him with awe as he entered the stable. Teclis was garbed for battle, wearing the war crown of Saphery and bearing the staff of Lileath. Ignoring their stares, he inspected the griffon. It was a magnificent beast, a winged eagle-headed lion, large enough for an elf to ride. It opened its mouth and let out an ear-piercing scream that caused the courtesans to shriek nervously and then giggle. It was a warcry that down through the ages had terrified the enemies of the elves. Now that the great dragons lay mostly dormant, these mighty magical creatures were the favoured aerial steeds of the elves. Of course, they were rare. This one, a champion racer, would have cost the ransom of a human king. The great breeder Ranagor had reared it with her own hand from an egg she had taken from the highest slopes of Mount Brood.

There were times Teclis wished he had learned to properly master a griffon, but he never had. It was a skill that only the strongest of elves could learn, and it was an art that had to be learned young. In his youth he had been too sickly. He would never be able to ride one of these magnificent creatures into battle without first paralysing its fierce will with magic, which would defeat the whole point. He would need to use a spell of stupefaction to make the thing docile enough to ride.

A spasm of dizziness passed through him. They were getting worse. He counted slowly to twenty and there was no surprise when the earth shook and the building quaked. His uncanny sensitivity to fluctuations in the level of magical energy around him, a side-effect of the spells he used to give himself normal health and energy, had forewarned him of the quake. He knew that he needed to get busy, that time was running out for his land and his people and, if the binding spells failed, for himself too, most likely.

He took a deep breath of the stable air. It held the overpowering stink of animal flesh and dung, and of feathers. His aged servants hooked the great saddle to the creature's back, all the while trying to be careful of its mighty claws and great scimitar-like beak. They checked the girth and the bridle and then looked at him. He shrugged and exerted his will, muttering the words of the charm. He felt the flow of energy round about him, warming him as it always did, and he sent tendrils of it out to touch the great beast, to calm its fierce heart and sooth its burning brain. The creature's eyelids drooped and its posture slumped as the spell took hold. It some-how looked smaller now, far less regal.

Teclis muttered an apology and limped forward, dragging himself wearily into the saddle and buckling himself in. Not for him the bravado of some young elves who rode bareback and unharnessed, and performed tricks on the backs of their steeds. He made sure all the buckles were in place, feeling slightly embarrassed as he did so. This was the way a child would ride, but he was taking no chances of falling from the saddle. Certainly, he knew spells of levitation, but were he to be stunned for a moment or distracted, or should the winds of magic simply not blow strong enough, a fall might prove fatal nonetheless.

His brother strode forward to look at him, ignoring the grif-fon's enormous beak and huge claws with a calm that Teclis envied. Even the bravest usually showed signs of nervousness around the beasts, but not Tyrion. He seemed as comfortable and at ease as he had done over the dinner table, and it was no false bravado either.

'Are you sure you do not wish me to accompany you?' he said.

'Your duties lie here, brother, with our fleet, and this is a task best accomplished by sorcery alone.'

'I bow to your superior knowledge, then, but it's been my experi-ence that a well-honed blade can prove useful at the most unexpected of moments.'

Teclis tapped the blade that hung at his side with his left hand. 'I have a well-honed blade, and I was taught to use it by a master,' he said.

Tyrion grinned and shrugged. 'I hope you learned my lessons well, little brother.'

The affection and condescension in his tone irritated Teclis no end, but he hid them behind a sour smile. 'May you live a thousand years, brother.'

'And thee, Teclis of the White Tower.' With his usual impeccable timing, Tyrion stepped back out of the griffon's way and executed a perfect courtly bow.

He waved to the women and to his servants, drew back on the reins and waited. The griffon's haunches bunched beneath him as its muscles tensed for the spring. He felt a momentary dizzy lurch in his stomach as the creature bounded forward and launched itself into space through the opening in the balcony. For a brief giddy moment he saw the entire city spread out beneath him, from the palace-temple of the Phoenix King to the great statue of Aenarion that greeted the returning sailors in the harbour, all illuminated by the golden sunlight of Ulthuan.

His stomach lurched further as the griffon dropped earthward. He felt a momentary panic. The restraining harness that had seemed like such a good idea a few moments ago now felt like a death-trap. In the moments it would take to release it and cast a spell of levitation, he and his mount would be spattered on the hard marble below. He fought down the urge to close his eyes, and watched as the purple-tiled rooftops of the villas of the lesser nobles came closer.

Then, the griffon spread its enormous pinions with a crack. They beat the air with the force of thunderbolts. For a moment, the heart-stopping descent was arrested and the creature seemed to float on the very air, caught for a heartbeat between the power of gravity and the force of its own upward motion. For a second Teclis felt weightless, caught between horror and exhilaration, then the griffon increased the force of its wingbeats, and its gigantic, magical strength triumphed over the earth's pull.

Beneath him, Teclis could feel its chest expand and contract as it breathed in time with its wing movements. He could feel the metronome of its heart, driving blood to muscles, powering sinews like some mighty engine. The griffon let out an ear-piercing shriek of pure triumph and Teclis knew exactly how it felt. Looking down at the city stretched beneath him like the model town in some elvish infant's playroom, he was exultant. Perhaps this was how the gods felt, he thought, when they looked down from the heavens to see how their mortal pawns were behaving.

He saw the people in the street – the Tiranoci in their chariots, proud dragonlords on their horses, scholar-slaves from far Cathay, merchants from a dozen lands of men – all look up at him. Did they recognise him, the premier wizard of this land, going about his business? It did not really matter. They looked up in awe and wonder at the sight of an elven lord passing overhead and they shouted and waved in greeting. He waved back, letting the steed skim over the rooftops out towards the harbour, to the thousands of towering masts that marked the position of the ships.

He passed over the decaying mansions, and the empty houses, noticed the half-empty streets built to accommodate ten times the current number of inhabitants and some of the feeling of triumph drained out of him. The realisation struck him with the force of a hammer blow, as it always did, that his people were a dying race. No amount of pomp and circumstance could conceal that. The endless parades and ceremonies could not hide it. The towering genius that had lined every avenue with mighty statues and soaring columns was fading from this world. Slaves and outsiders inhabited many of the buildings round the harbour, filling them with buzzing life that counterfeited the ancient glories of Lothern. But it was not elvish life. It was the life of outsiders, of people who had come to this island continent but recently, and who had never set foot outside the foreigners' quarter of this one city.

As it often did, a vision took form in his mind, of the inevitable death of all he held dear. One day, he knew, these streets, this city, this whole continent would be empty of elves. His people would be gone, leaving not even ghosts, and only the footsteps of those strangers would echo through the ruins of what had once been their homes.

He tried to dismiss the image but he could not. Like all elves he was prone to melancholy, but unlike his kindred, he did not revel in it. He despised it as a weakness, but now, leaving this ancient glorious city for what might prove to be the last time, he could not resist giving in to the impulse. Already, he could see that the number of human ships in the harbour near outnumbered the elvish ones.

True, there were many mighty Eagles, Falcons and Bloodhawks, their long lean lines designed to penetrate the waves like a spear. Driven by magical winds they were the fastest, most manoeuvrable craft on the sea, but even here in their home city, in the greatest of all elf ports they were hemmed in by the craft of others. Here were mighty galleons from Bretonnia and Marienburg. Below him he could see dhows from Araby, their sails like the fins of sharks, and junks from Far Cathay, with towering stern-castles and lateen rigs designed to catch the winds of distant seas. They had all come here to trade, to purchase the magical wares, and powerful drugs and medicines for which the elves were famous, and in return they had brought silk, exotic woods, perfumes, spices, and trained pleasure slaves; all the things required to make comfortable the twilight years of his people.

The salt tang of the sea caught his nostrils. He caught sight of a human gazing up at him with a spyglass from the crow's nest of one of the ships. He fought down the catlike malign urge to send his griffon flying close to the man's head to terrify him and pulled on the reins turning his mount upwards and northwards, towards the clouds and the distant mountains wreathed in the powerful aura of ancient and mighty spells. He realised for a moment he had been tempted by the old cruelty of his people, who saw the lives of other lesser races as nothing more than playthings, and he felt a surge of the sickness and self-hatred that made him so unlike the rest of his people.

There were times when he felt that the elves, in their arrogance, deserved to be replaced, to be superceded by the younger races. At least they still strove to build things, to learn, to make things anew, and in many ways they were succeeding. Instead his people lived in the past, in dreams of long-gone glories. To them all knowledge worth possessing was already known, all sorceries perfected to their highest level by elvish adepts. Teclis had studied the mysteries of magic long and hard, and he knew how deeply his people deceived themselves. In his youth, he had dreamed of uncovering new spells and recovering lost arts, and he had done so; but in recent years even that had lost its savour, and there were things he sometimes wished he had not learned.

He thought of the letter he had left with his brother to give to the Phoenix King explaining what was happening. He thought of the messages already dispatched by sorcerous means to the adepts of the White Tower. He had done what he could to forewarn those he was sworn to protect, and now he had to do his duty or die in the attempt. Considering the magnitude of the task that faced him, the latter eventuality seemed not unlikely.

He tugged the reins of the docile griffon and sent it arcing towards the distant mountains.

BENEATH HIM HE could see the carved peaks of Carillion. Ancient magic had reformed them into gigantic statues, a testimony to the power of the elves. Teclis shuddered to think how much magical energy, how many years of wizardly labour, had gone into carving those stones into the shapes of great beasts. Here two mighty pegasi flanked the valley, each a hundred times the height of an elf. Clouds gathered beneath their wings. Each was poised to take flight or strike with a massive hoof. It seemed like at any moment they might come to life and crush him like a small and pathetic insect.

They were not simply for show either. His mage sight showed him that they were wrapped around with spells of fantastic complexity, lattices of pure mystical energy that pulsed and crackled with power. They were part of the huge web of spells that covered the continent of Ulthuan and kept it stable. Without it to bleed off power and shape it to other uses, the entire land would become unstable and sink once more beneath the waves or be torn apart in immense volcanic convulsions. These huge statues were far from the mightiest works of his people. In the northlands entire mountains had been carved into the semblance of ever more fantastic and grotesque beasts.

There is a mad strain in us, he thought, it burns stronger in the hearts of our dark kindred of Naggaroth but it lurks in the heart of every elf. Pride, madness and a warped genius for art showed in those statues, just as it showed in every elf city. Perhaps the dwarfs are right about us, he thought. Perhaps we are indeed cursed. He dismissed the thoughts and concentrated on the task at hand.

He circled the griffon over the valley, seeking the thing he knew he would find in the shadow of those mighty wings. It blazed in his mage sight now, even more brightly than the flows of magic through the waypaths. This was new. It had not been so before, when last he had passed this way. Something was interfering with the work of the ancients here.

He dropped the griffon closer. An enormous standing stone stood there, and it was this which the pegasi had been set to guard. It was monolithic, eroded by millennia of strange weather, and yet it still stood.

In the side of the hill, in the shadow of the stone, was an entranceway. It led down into an antechamber that had been sealed for millennia, and with good reason. Behind it lay the work of those capable of challenging all the power and wisdom of the elves, artefacts of a people who had left these lands while his ancestors were still barbarians. This was the accursed place Tasirion had mentioned in his book, one of several to be found in ancient Ulthuan.

He dragged on the top rein giving the griffon the signal to land. He could see nothing threatening, but he was cautious. Many strange monsters were to be found in these lands, and sometimes, war parties of dark elves made it even this close to Lothern. It would not do to take every precaution against sorcery and find himself chopped down by some poisoned arrow.

Even as the beast descended, a wave of weakness passed through him again, and the earth shook. The stone danced. The mighty winged horses shivered as if afraid. In the distance, burning mountains spouted strange multi-coloured clouds into the sky. Teclis cursed. Whatever it was, it was getting stronger, either that or he was nearer the epicentre.

The griffon's claws touched earth. He felt the beast's muscles contract beneath him as it absorbed the force of impact. It paused there, uncertain as to what to do as the earth quivered beneath it. A moment later things had settled once more. Teclis descended from the saddle, struggling with the illusion that the earth would begin to shake once more or that he would somehow sink into it as if it were water. An earthquake was something that unsettled the senses in many ways, and made the brain doubt many things. He was almost surprised when the ground did not give way.

He strode closer to the entrance now, studying it. There was a stone arch and stone gates blocking the way forward. On the gate was inscribed the ancient edict forbidding any elf to proceed further. Teclis knew he was breaking laws made in the time of making itself by opening them. It was a crime punishable by death. This was one reason he had not wanted his brother with him.

Not that such things would have mattered to most elves. The spells to unlock these forbidden vaults were known to very few: the Everqueen, a few of the masters of the White Tower, and himself. Tasirion had read them and used them to his eternal regret centuries ago. His fate had been a warning to others who might disturb what lay here. Teclis considered this for a moment, and then spoke the spell. The wards laid by his forebears opened and the huge door slid silently inwards, leading down into a massive darkened antechamber. On the far side of the chamber was an archway, and through it he could see a road that led down into darkness.

The great arch was many times his height. It was carved in ancient-looking runes and the toad-like heads of an ancient race were carved in it. He could see the flow of powerful magic within it. It emanated a sense of evil that was almost palpable. Teclis shuddered and muttered a charm against Chaos even as he strode out of the balmy sunlight and into the cool shadows. The doorway slid shut behind him. He proceeded downwards under several more archways. The walls were huge blocks of dressed stone carved with odd linear runes. He sensed evil within them too.

No, he told himself, it was not the stones themselves that were evil; it was the stuff that seeped through them. Here was pure dark magic, the raw stuff of Chaos, a radiation that could twist mind and body in many ways. The spells built into the arch had been designed to contain it, but he could see now that they were ancient, flawed and unravelling, and that it was their weakness that allowed the sinister energy to flow through.

This was why ward spells were placed around this site, and his people were forbidden to enter. The whole area would eventually become tainted and corrupt, a cancer at the heart of Ulthuan, a stain of darkness that would slowly spread across the land. For now, though, he had other worries. If he did not solve the mystery of what was causing the quakes, there would be no need to worry about the corruption of anything but a few deep sea fishes, for his homeland would vanish beneath the cleansing waves. He must seek out the Oracle of the Truthsayers and find out what must be done.

He reached out and touched the surface of one of the stones. It was not smooth – strange angular runes had been carved on it, pictographic glyphs similar to those that elven explorers had brought back from the lost continent of Lustria and the steaming, jungle-girt cities of the lizard folk. Beneath them he could feel the magic flow, strong currents, powerful and deep. From his readings he knew this was not supposed to be the case. The ways were supposed to be dormant, sealed. This amount of power should not be passing through them.

He knew his suspicions were correct now. This place, and the others like it, were the source of the imbalance that threatened Ulthuan. Their activation was draining power from the watchstones, unsettling the precarious balance of the spells that protected the land. They were drawing massive amounts of magical energy out of the system and if they were not stopped, it would only be a matter of time before they caused a catastrophe.

Who could have done this thing, he wondered? It was always possible that it was all a colossal cosmic accident, or that the ancient wards had simply worn away. With a system so complex and ancient and fragile you could not rule such a thing out. Still, his instincts told him that such was not the case. He mistrusted anything to do with the dark power of Chaos. Too many other things were happening in the world for him to be happy with the thought that all of this was coincidence.

In the Old World, the armies of darkness swept across the land like a crimson tide, leaving red ruin in their wake. The seas had become dangerous, as monsters rose from the depths and the black ships of Chaos ravaged all they encountered. In the north, the ancient enemy stirred. War was coming to Ulthuan, just as it had already come to the rest of the world. At times like these, it was foolish to believe in coincidence.

He strode around the last and deepest arch buried deep below the earth, studying the runes, and the underlying pattern of magic that they channelled. He spoke a spell of divination that laid the entire intricate pattern bare. A work of breathtaking genius indeed, he thought, as he looked on the lines of magic. It was as if a million spiders had spent a thousand years spinning a web of near-inconceivable complexity. For all his centuries of study, this was a work that dazzled him.

He did not need to understand how the thing was created, any more than the drinker of a virility potion need understand the alchemical process by which it was made. He needed only to understand what the thing was used for, and that seemed clear enough.

Some of the spells were wards, designed to block passage through them. They were mostly frayed and gone now, no longer potent enough to fulfil their maker's purpose. It was what they guarded that interested him now. The wards guarded a doorway, an opening into somewhere else. Elf sorcerers had long known that these things existed but the ancients had closed them for their own incomprehensible reasons and the old elves had thought it best to leave them undisturbed. In these later ages they could only be opened at certain times, when the stars were right, when the flaws in the old spells were temporarily revealed. Until now, Teclis reminded himself. Now someone or something had clearly found a way to open them again.

He sat down cross-legged in the centre of the chamber. He considered the ancient network of spells his ancestors had built to keep the island continent stable. It was commonly assumed that they had been the creation of elves, a unique product of elvish genius. Was it possible those ancient mages had simply built on top of the work of the ancients, tapping its power for their own purposes? Now that someone had reactivated these artefacts of the Old Ones, they would draw power out of Ulthuan's magical wards. Yes, he thought, it was entirely possible that such was the case. It was a road to catastrophe.

There was only one thing to do now, he must find the source of all this and reverse it. He must find a way of passing through the gate, and shutting it down again. Teclis closed his eyes and began to meditate. He knew time was getting short.

CHAPTER FOUR

'I WISH THIS weather would ease up,' said Felix Jaeger, drawing his faded red Sudenland wool cloak tighter about himself, and leaning closer to the small sputtering fire. It just about lit the whole cave. Felix was glad of it. Another few minutes in the snowstorm would have done for him.

'It's winter, and it's Sylvania, manling, what do you expect? It's supposed to be as cold as an elvish heart.'

Felix looked over at the Slayer. If the massive dwarf felt any discomfort at the biting chill, he showed no sign of it. Snow clustered in his massive crest of bright orange hair, and covered the tattoos of his shaven skull, but he was still dressed as always only in his thick leather waistcoat, britches, and boots. His massive rune-covered axe lay close at hand. He drew a little further from the fire as if to emphasise his toughness. There were times when Felix hated travelling with dwarfs. He looked over at Max to see how the wizard was taking this display of rugged outdoor toughness, but he was lost in thought, staring into the fire as if he could discern some mystical pattern there.

He had been like this ever since they had discovered Ulrika's fate back at the keep. He had responded only to Felix's request to use his magic to light their fire when even the dwarfs' attempts with flint and tinder had failed. The wizard looked like a man caught in a particularly evil waking dream. Felix could understand that. Just the thought of Ulrika and what had happened to her drove a knife blade of conflicting emotions into his own heart. Whatever had once lay between them, it was over now, her transformation into one of the undead had seen to that. He tried to push the thought away. These were things he did not want to consider here in these dark woods in this ancient haunted land.

'Snorri was hoping there was a bear in this cave,' observed Snorri. He did look disappointed as well. An almost comic look of dismay passed over his broad, stupid face. He reached up with one massive paw and stroked the painted nails that had been driven into his skull. Like Gotrek, Snorri was almost as broad as he was tall and he was solid muscle, although in Snorri's case that included the space between his ears, thought Felix.

'Why?' Felix asked. 'Did you want to skin it and wear it for a cloak?'

'What would Snorri need a cloak for, young Felix? This is like a summer picnic compared to winter in the Worlds Edge Mountains.'

If I hear that line about summer picnics once more I will hammer some more nails into your head, thought Felix sourly. He had listened to the dwarfs' cheery comments on the worsening weather with increasing hostility for some days now.

'You think this is cold, manling?' said Gotrek. 'You should have been in the High Passes in the Grim Winter. Now that was cold!'

'I am sure you are going to tell me about it,' said Felix.

'Snorri remembers that,' said Snorri. 'Snorri was with Gurni Grimmson's warband chasing orcs. It was so cold that one night Forgast Gaptooth's fingers all turned black and dropped into the soup he was stirring. Good soup it was too.' He laughed as if at a fond memory. 'So cold that his beard froze solid and broke off in chunks like icicles.'

'You're making this up,' said Felix.

'No, Snorri isn't.'

Probably true, thought Felix. Snorri didn't have the imagination to make anything up.

'Very proud he was of that beard too; when he came home his wife didn't recognise him. He was so ashamed he shaved his head. A troll ate him at the end. Course, he choked it on the way down.'

'Now there was a Slayer,' said Snorri approvingly. Gotrek nodded. Felix was not surprised. The Slayers lived only to die in combat with the nastiest and largest monsters, to redeem themselves for crimes or sins they had committed. Felix was not sure that he would count choking a troll to death as it ate you a heroic death, but he was not about to mention that now.

'Wish there had been a bear in this cave,' said Snorri wistfully. 'A big one. Maybe two. Good eating in bears.'

'You would know,' said Felix.

'Better than squirrels, or rabbits, or hares,' said Snorri. 'Wish there was a bear in this cave.'

'Some say the caves about here are haunted,' said Max. It was his first contribution to the conversation in a long time, but it seemed to suit his gloomy mood.

'What do you mean?' Felix asked.

'In *Legends of Sylvania*, Neumann mentions that the caves around Drakenhof were meant to be haunted. The locals avoided them. Some claim that their roots went all the way down into Hell.'

'Perhaps you should have mentioned this before Snorri and Gotrek led us into these caves,' said Felix.

'It's only a story, Felix. And considering the alternative was freezing to death, would you really have let it put you off?'

Felix supposed not, but he still felt peeved. 'You think there is anything to these stories, Max?'

'Some stories contain hints of truth, Felix.'

'Is there anything else you forgot to tell us?'

'They say folk who went deep into the caves went missing, never to be seen again.'

'Maybe there was bears in them,' said Snorri. 'Bears could have eaten them.' He was glancing at the back of the cave hopefully, as if expecting to see it run deeper. Felix was glad he had already checked it earlier. The cave ran just a few more strides back under the hill.

'And there were lots of altered ones who sometimes used them for shelter.'

'The bears?' said Snorri, confused.

'The caves,' said Max.

Felix noticed that Gotrek had stopped listening, and was glancing over his shoulder out into the night. His fingers had tightened on his axe. Max was sitting up and glancing out into the darkness too.

'What is it?' Felix asked, already fearing the worst.

'Something is out there,' said Gotrek. 'I smell beasts. There is the taint of Chaos on the wind.'

Snorri cheered up at once. 'Let's go get them.'

'Yes,' said Felix sarcastically. 'Let's not worry about little things like how many of them there are, or whether they might be ready for us.'

'Course not,' said Snorri. 'Why would Snorri do that?'

'There is magic out there,' said Max, and his voice sounded sepul-chral. 'Dark magic. The winds of Chaos blow strong this night.'

Felix groaned. Why was it, that just when he thought a situation could not get any worse, it always did? Sitting in a frozen cave by a sputtering fire with two death-seeking dwarfs and a gloomy wizard while a blizzard raged outside had been bad enough. Now, it seemed like the forces of Chaos and dark magic were about to take a hand. Why do the gods hate me so, Felix wondered?

'And there's something more,' said Max. His gaunt face looked strained and there was a feverish light in his eyes.

'I am no longer capable of being surprised,' sneered Felix. 'But do tell, anyway.'

'I don't know what it is. There is a power here the like of which I have not encountered before. There is a strange magic at work. I sensed it an hour ago.'

'Nice of you to mention that too,' said Felix. The two dwarfs stared at them impatiently.

'There was no sense in disturbing you while you rested, until I had a clearer idea of what it was. It might have had nothing to do with us.'

'Apparently it does.'

'Yes. Why else would the beastmen be coming this way? How could they have found us on a night like tonight?'

'You are saying they are coming for us?' said Felix, drawing his sword.

'They are already here, manling,' said Gotrek. Felix looked past the Slayer into the blizzard. He could see massive forms that bore only the vaguest resemblance to humans, and mighty black armoured warriors the likeness of which he knew only too well.

'Did they follow us all the way from Praag?' Felix asked, curling his lip.

'If so, then they've come a long way to die, manling.'

'Snorri thinks Snorri should go first,' said Snorri, suiting actions to words and charging out, brandishing his axe in one hand, and his hammer in the other. Within heartbeats he was amid the beastmen, cleaving through them like a thunderbolt, raising a tempest of snow around his booted feet. The look of glee on his simple, brutal face reminded Felix of children snowball fighting.

Gotrek moved in his wake, moving through the snow as if it was not there, no more slowed by the deep drifts than the beastmen or the Chaos warriors. Behind him, Felix heard Max begin to chant a spell. He knew better than to look around. A lapse of concentration in combat was often fatal, and he did not take his eyes from his opponents.

There were at least a score of beastmen. As always, they were shambling parodies of humanity, with the heads of goats or wolves or oxen. They clutched a variety of crudely made weapons in their mutated hands and talons. Their shields bore the symbol of Chaos, eight arrows radiating out from a huge cat-like eye. A monstrous Chaos warrior led them, quite the biggest Felix had ever seen. He was as huge as an ogre – perhaps he had once been one. He was more than half again as tall as Felix, and Felix was a tall man. Felix guessed the Chaos warrior outweighed him by a factor of four, and that was not counting the rune-encrusted armour that covered his massive form.

There was nothing else for it. He had put off entering the fray quite long enough. It was either fight or be cut down. And though a few minutes ago he might have thought that a mercy compared to the tedium of dwarfish conversation, he found that now his life was at risk, even Snorri's banalities were not without charm.

Howling like a madman, he charged at the nearest beastman, swinging his dragon-hilted blade as hard as he could. The beastman raised his spear to parry. The sharp blade bit chunks from the shaft. Felix brought his boot up, catching the beastman between the legs. The thing howled in agony, and bent over. Felix's next strike separated its head from its shoulders.

He did not wait for another beastman to come to him, but lunged forward, hampered by the snow and the slickness of footing beneath it. He had learned his fighting in the arms houses of Altdorf's sword masters, on floors of hard wood and stone. I wonder why my fencing masters never bothered to tell me that most fights would not take place under those ideal circumstances, he thought bitterly.

Briefly, he wished he had a pistol, but then realised that in the damp and wet he would have been lucky to get one to work. He crossed blades with a massive beastman, a head shorter than he was but twice as wide. One of the creature's hands ended in a mass of slimy suckered tentacles. When it lashed out at his face, he could see a leech-like mouth in the middle of the palm. Once, the horror of the sight might have frozen him, but he had become used to such things over the past few years. In his time travelling with the Slayer, he had seen far worse things.

The tentacles slapped his face, and he felt something sting. The slime was corrosive, he thought, or worse – poisoned. Loathing and fear made him lash out all the harder. His blade took the creature in the wrist, shearing away its mutated paw. His next blow split the thing from breastbone to groin.

Something bright hissed and sputtered overhead. He knew enough to cover his eyes. There was a brilliant explosion of golden light. A blast of steaming snow scalded his face. He looked up to see that a crater had been cleared from the snow by Max's fireball, and many of the beastmen stood shaking their heads and blinking stupidly as they tried to clear their vision. A couple of roasted bodies lay in a pool of steaming meltwater at the centre of the crater.

Now was not the time for fighting honourably, Felix realised, particularly not since by the light of a few sputtering bushes he could see scores more beastmen approaching. He raced forward, lashing out with his blade, killing as many of the blinded beastmen as he could. Snorri and Gotrek moved among them doing the same as they headed towards the oncoming mass. Only the mighty black armoured giant held his ground. Overhead something strange moved, orbiting it. A magical gem of some sort, Felix guessed.

More fireballs arced overhead, bursting among the oncoming mass of beastmen, turning one or two into blazing torches of melting flesh, knocking others to the ground with the force of impact. Knowing it was madness but unable to think of anything else, Felix shouted, 'Follow me, Snorri. Let's get them!'

There was method in his madness. Snorri followed him with a will, ignoring the huge Chaos warrior, unable to allow a mere human to get ahead of him in the race to kill the beastmen. So far, so good, Felix thought. At least my back is covered. He knew that if anybody could take care of the huge Chaos warrior, it was Gotrek. The dwarf had yet to lose a fight, and Felix doubted that he intended to start now.

Felix aimed at the wounded and the fallen as he ploughed into the beastmen, picking off the easy targets, lashing out at any that were blinded. Snorri showed no such discrimination. He attacked whatever was closest, whether it was wounded, unwounded, sighted, blind or running away. He laughed as he killed, happy as a child with a new toy.

Max sent more fireballs arcing overhead. Their explosions turned night briefly to day, and snow to steam. Felix saw one beastman fall, his face a mass of blisters, skin falling away from flesh and flesh falling from bone like an overcooked ham-hock. He took a second to orientate himself and then threw himself forward, following Snorri into the deepest mass. Behind him, an enormous clanging sound told him that Gotrek's axe had met the blade of the huge Chaos warrior.

'Now, Slayer of Arek, prepare to die,' boomed a voice deeper than any human's by at least an octave. 'Your axe will be mine.'

'Do tell,' said Gotrek, his grating voice audible even over the roar of battle. Felix ducked the swipe of another beastman, and lunged forward, getting his blade beneath the creature's guard and through the wall of its stomach. He turned it upward, beneath the ribs, sending point to heart, and then withdrew it. Blood gouted and the creature fell forward, blood pouring from a wolf-like mouth, huge teeth snapping so close to Felix's throat that he could smell its foul breath. He lashed out again, clearing a circle around him, and found that the wild swirl of battle had brought him around facing Gotrek and his opponent.

The Chaos warrior was really huge, Felix realised grimly. Felix had not seen anything so big in human shape since he had fought Grey Seer Thanquol's mutated bodyguard back at the Lonely Tower. And in terms of combat prowess there was no comparison. This thing wore the glowing rune-encrusted armour of a Chaos warrior, the black metal surface etched with strange sigils and inlaid daemon heads. In its right hand was a monstrous shield, moulded to resemble the leering features of a bloodthirster, one of the greatest of daemons. In his left hand was a mace of some odd metal, its head shaped like the skull of some other enormous daemon. Perhaps it was one, burnished in black and gold. It radiated a strange power. The empty eyesockets glowed with an infernal light that made it seem as if the daemon was alive. As the Chaos warrior raised it, the mace emitted an eardrum-shattering shriek so loud it threatened to wake the dead.

'I am Grume of Night Fang and I will not grant you a swift death,' bellowed the Chaos warrior. 'I will break your knees and beat your joints to jelly and then I will throw your maimed body to my followers for their sport.'

'Did you come here to boast or to fight?' sneered Gotrek.

'Your death shall be long and terrible and your kin will wail and gnash their teeth when they hear of it.'

'I have no kin,' said Gotrek, and just uttering the words made his beard bristle with fury. He lashed forward with his axe. The blade clanged against the shield. The daemon's face seemed to twist and grimace in surprise as the axe bit home. Molten metal flowed forth like blood or tears. Strange sorcery was at work here, Felix thought, then ducked as another beastman tried to take his head off.

He whirled and brought the pommel of his sword down on the beastman's snout. There was a crunch as bone and cartilage gave way. He punched the creature on the newly sensitive spot with his free fist and was rewarded by a howl of anguish. As the beastman reeled backward, he sheared away half its face with his sword, leaving teeth and white bone momentarily visible before he put the thing out of its agony by severing its head.

More fireballs exploded around him, clearing the area. Felix stood blinking. Either Max had acquired pinpoint accuracy with his magic or he simply did not care whether he hit Felix or not. It was not a thought calculated to reassure.

Felix glanced around. The main force of beastmen were sweeping around the melee and avoiding the killing ground now, trying to get to Max before he could unleash more magic. For a moment, Felix and Snorri stood gazing at each other. The Slayer had killed everything within reach. He blinked and glared stupidly at Felix, unable to understand where all of his foes had suddenly gone. Felix saw Grume bring his howling mace smashing down at Gotrek. The move was incredibly swift and should have reduced the dwarf to a pulp, except that the Slayer was no longer there. With a shift of his footing, he had moved away from the point of impact.

Felix could tell from the look on Gotrek's face that he was having to concentrate ferociously on the fight. That was hardly surprising since the unearthly shrieking of the daemonic mace was distracting enough from fifty strides away. The gods alone knew what it must be like closer to the source. Only someone who had seen the dwarf fight as often as Felix had would have spotted that he seemed slower than usual and that he did not move with quite his customary blinding speed.

The monstrous Chaos warrior chuckled horribly, as if he understood the effect his weapon was having and had seen it often before. When he spoke his voice was full of confidence. 'The Skull Mace of Malarak is not to be opposed. It freezes the limbs and chills the hearts of those who face it. Prepare to greet your ancestors.'

Felix measured the distance between himself and the Chaos warrior, taking aim at what looked like a weak point in the backplate of his armour. Even as he did so, he knew that he was too far away to get there in time. Had the hour of the Slayer's doom finally arrived?

CHAPTER FIVE

As FELIX RUSHED forward he noticed a strange stink, like of rotting flesh and congealed blood. It came from the Chaos warrior, he was sure, and it was as nauseating as it was appropriate. Closing the distance revealed to him how huge Grume was – a veritable mountain of armoured flesh. The shrieking of his mace made Felix's head ache and his teeth grind. He felt like his ears were starting to bleed. How the Slayer withstood this, he could not guess.

Through the stinking fog he could see Gotrek still stood frozen as the mace descended. True to his word, Grume was not aiming for the Slayer's head but for his axe arm. He obviously did intend to capture and torture the Slayer. This did not bode well for the rest of them. Behind him, Felix could barely hear the sounds of carnage as Snorri fought with the beastmen.

Grume's insane booming laughter was barely audible over the daemonic shriek of his weapon. Gotrek's face looked pale and flinty. The mace descended like the hammer of some mad war god. At the last second, Gotrek's axe lashed out. The rune-covered blade bit into the daemonic skull. Lines of fire flashed along the star-metal. The daemon's head shattered into a thousand pieces. The shrieking ceased instantly and the stinking cloud began to disperse.

'You will break my bones, will you?' said Gotrek, almost conversationally. The axe lashed out, catching the giant just behind the

58

knee. The ornate armour buckled as if it were made from tin. Blood
gouted. Grume began to topple backwards like a massive tree. Felix
had to jump to one side to avoid being crushed.

'You will throw my battered form to your followers for their
sport, will you?' The axe descended again on the giant's other leg,
cutting through armour and tendons, paralysing it. Grume began
to push himself upwards with both hands. The axe flickered out,
taking off the left hand at the wrist. Another blow lopped off the
right arm at the elbow. Gotrek spat on his recumbent form and
turned to face the beastmen. There was an awful casual cruelty
about the Slayer's actions that chilled Felix. The virtually limbless
form of the Chaos warrior thrashed in the snow, bleeding to
death.

Gotrek strode purposefully towards the beastmen, axe held ready.
It was too much for them. They turned and fled in a mad rush. As
they did so, Felix noticed the strange eye-like object still hovered
there, almost invisible in the gloom. It swivelled backwards and forwards, like an eye tracking them.

What new evil was this, he wondered?

KELMAIN TURNED TO consult his brother's floating image. 'So much
for the mighty Grume,' he said. The image of the dying Chaos warrior was still imprinted on his mind.

'It was predictable. The likes of Gotrek Gurnisson are not to be
overcome by the Grumes of this world. That axe carries a mighty
freight of destiny.'

'Best we should remove it from the gameboard of the world then,'
said Kelmain smiling.

'Proceed with your plan,' said Lhoigor. 'Spring the trap.'

'NO!' SHOUTED FELIX as Gotrek and Snorri disappeared into the
gloom. 'Wait, we must have a plan!'

It was already too late, he knew. He turned and saw Max Schreiber
walking closer. A glow surrounded him. The snow seemed to sizzle
away at his feet, turning to steam. It was an eerie sight and made the
magician seem somehow less than human.

'Too late, Felix,' he said. 'We'd best go after them.'

'Did you see that strange floating eye?' Felix asked.

Max nodded. 'A magical construct of considerable power – the
focus of some sort of observation spell would be my guess.'

'You mean we are being watched by a wizard?'

'Aye – and a very powerful one too. Most likely the one who
planned this attack, and led the Chaos worshippers to us.'

'A Chaos wizard as well as that monster, great,' said Felix sourly. 'Is there anything you can do about it?'

'We shall see when we find the others,' said Max Schreiber. 'Best get going, or we'll never catch up with them.'

'Don't worry,' said Felix. 'Dwarfs have short legs. There's no way they are going to outrun us.'

EVERY FEW HUNDRED strides, they found evidence of where the beastmen had turned at bay and sought to rend the dwarfs. Their lack of success was evident by the number of mutated corpses that lay in the snow. Now bigger, thicker flakes were starting to fall and fill the tracks and cover the corpses. Soon, he knew, there would only be odd-looking humps where once living, breathing beings had been. It was all rather depressing, he supposed.

Beside him, Max strode along, seemingly impervious to the cold. Felix was glad the mage was near. The aura surrounding him gave off enough heat to ward the worst of the chill. Perhaps Max was directing it that way, to help him. Felix did not feel like asking. It also provided enough light to see by.

'They went that way,' said Felix, pointing in the direction of Gotrek's tracks. The Slayer had a very recognisable print. His feet were larger and broader than a man's, and his stride was shorter.

'That does not surprise me,' said Max.

'I have the feeling you're about to tell me something I won't like,' said Felix, studying the gloom beyond the circle of light, looking for the reflected glint of beastmen's eyes. Without the Slayers, he and Max might be overcome. All it would take would be one lucky spear cast to incapacitate the wizard, and then he would be alone against the monsters.

A frown of concentration passed across Max's face. 'There is a massive source of magical energy in that direction. It blazes like a beacon. I can sense it even from here. It's powerful beyond belief and tainted by the power of Chaos.'

'Why did you not tell us this earlier? Didn't want to worry us, I suppose.'

'No, Felix, I did not tell you earlier because it was not there earlier.'

What new horror waits now, Felix wondered?

FROM UP AHEAD came the sound of fighting. Felix thought he recognised Gotrek's bellowing and Snorri's warcry. He raced up the slope through the snow and emerged into a clearing in the woods. Ahead of them lay what a great barrow or a small hill, incredibly

weathered and ancient-looking. In its side was an arch, comprised
of two massive uprights and a stone crossbar. All of the barrow
except the arch was encrusted with newly fallen snow. It glowed
oddly, and when the snow touched it, the flakes melted
immediately. He guessed the stench of burning vegetation in the air
came from incinerated moss.

'What the hell is going on here?' he asked.

'Magic,' said Max. 'Of a very powerful kind.'

Felix could see a battle was taking place at the entrance to the
barrow. Snorri and Gotrek hacked and slew their way through a
mass of beastmen. The retreating monsters fought a desperate
rearguard action as they fled within. Felix and Max followed to the
entrance. The way down was peculiar, unlike anything Felix had
ever seen before. The walls were massive blocks of undressed stone
covered in strange angular runes. Several more arches supported the
ceiling, as the corridor descended down at an angle into the gloom.
Somewhere off in the darkness was another intensely glowing arch.

The mass of the beastmen raced through the glowing arch and
simply disappeared. It was uncanny. One moment they were there,
the next they were gone, leaving only a pattern of ripples in the
glowing air. Looking closely, Felix could see that the glowing eye
hovered over the scene, shifting its location with blurring speed as
it moved to position itself for a better view of the combat.

Felix decided that he had better go do his part. He raced forward,
feeling a strange shiver run down his spine as he passed underneath
one of the stone arches. He did not need to be a powerful magician
like Max to know there was something supernatural going on here.

Snorri slashed and whirled his way through the beastmen
corpses, hacking limbs and crushing heads with merry abandon. As
he got within range of the glowing arch something odd occurred. A
massive tentacle, thick as the hawser cable on a moored ship,
emerged from the glow and wrapped itself around him. Before Felix
could shout a warning, the tentacle contracted, and Snorri was
dragged through into the glow. In a heartbeat he had vanished.

Gotrek roared a curse, and redoubled his efforts, chopping down
the last few beastmen. Felix strode up to his side. 'What was that
thing that took Snorri?' he asked.

'A daemon, most likely, and soon to be a dead one, or my doom
will be upon me,' replied the Slayer. Without a backward glance, he
leapt forward into the glow. In a second he too was gone.

'Wait!' shouted Max. 'You have no idea where that portal leads.'

Felix stood before the glowing arch and wondered what to do.
There was no trace of the Slayers, the beastmen or the tentacled

monster. He could hear no sounds. Even as he watched, the shimmering began to vanish. Suddenly something blurred overhead. There was a sickening crunch. Looking back, he could see that Snorri had been cast out through the portal with the speed of a stone shot from a sling. Either by accident or design he had been thrown directly into Max. The two of them lay sprawled unconscious on the ground.

Instinct told Felix that he had mere moments to come to a decision. He knew that if he stood here until the light vanished, whatever portal the Slayer had passed through would be closed, and with it any chance of following him. Even as he stood there undecided, something small and round and hard smashed into his back, and propelled him forward into the light. Of course, he thought. I forgot all about the floating eye.

A wave of cold passed through him, and for a moment a dizzying sense of vertigo threatened to overwhelm his senses. He felt like he was falling down a huge mineshaft, accelerating at enormous velocity. He braced himself for an impact and was surprised to find himself stumbling along on solid ground. A moment later he wished he wasn't as a terrifying sight greeted his gaze.

Up ahead was a vast tentacled thing, a cross between a squid and a serpent, some hideous mutant daemon of Chaos. Its tentacles lashed out attempting to grasp Gotrek but the Slayer stood his ground and slashed away at them with his axe, severing the tips of some, drawing great gouts of gore from others. All around lay the shattered bodies of dozens of beastmen. A few more still fought, grasped in its giant tentacles. Obviously whatever this enormous brute was, it did not discriminate between its fellow Chaos worshippers and anybody else when it came to seeking its prey.

Something whizzed over Felix's head, and he saw the glittering eye hurtle past. For a second he could have sworn he heard chilling infernal laughter and then the thing flashed out of view. In the distance behind the daemonic thing, Felix thought he saw a black robed figure reach up and catch the gem, then race off into the gloom.

Felix felt a blaze of heat behind him, and the shimmering glow of light dimmed. He turned to look back the way he came, and was surprised to see nothing but a huge archway that seemed to look out onto infinite space. Blazing lights passed to and fro in the gloom. Not stars, he thought, but will-o'-the-wisps of sorcerous light.

Briefly he felt his sanity totter. Somehow, he had been transported to an entirely different location beyond his normal ken. There was no sign of the snow-covered forest, or the great barrow, or Max Schreiber or Snorri either. There was only an arch reminiscent in shape of the one he had passed through, but somehow newer-looking and carved with the gargoyle faces of some strange toad-like beings. This was indeed strong magic, he thought, wishing that he had paid more heed to what Max had said.

A howling war cry behind him reminded him that battle still raged and he was part of it. Even as he watched, the last of the beastmen were raised high in the tentacles of the daemon and dropped into its huge gaping beak-like maw. There was a hideous crunching sound as bones were broken, and blood splattered the daemon's mouth. At the same time, more of the monstrous tentacles snaked past Gotrek and came looping towards him. He threw himself to one side, avoiding its suckered grasp, and lashed out with his sword. The blade bit deep into rubbery flesh. Black blood oozed slowly forth. He dodged and weaved forward, hacking at tentacles that came near him as he battled his way towards Gotrek's side. At times like this, it seemed like the safest place to be.

A rush of displaced air warned him, and he threw himself forward as a massive tentacle swept through where his head had been. He hit the ground rolling and noticed that the floor looked odd. It was made of old stone that looked as if it has been eaten away by something like acid. Set in each of the blocks were odd runes, straight lines and serpent-like squiggles. They were unlike anything he had ever seen before.

He let his momentum carry him to his feet, and found himself within a hairsbreadth of being decapitated. Gotrek's axe stopped mere fingerbreadths from his face. Felix felt a surge of relief that the Slayer had such control, otherwise he would surely be dead.

'I've seen better-looking creatures,' Felix said, gazing up at the thing. It was huge, the tentacled maw arched nearly four times his height overhead. He could see that it dripped slime. The eyes that looked down on him, though, were filled with a baleful and awfully human intelligence.

'It's probably thinking the same thing about you, manling,' said Gotrek, ducking the sweep of a massive tentacle, retreating step by step before the oncoming bulk of the thing. Felix realised that this was a hopeless battle. Even the Slayer's mighty axe was all but useless against a monster of such size and power. Gotrek's mighty hacks were like a small boy hitting a bull with a table-knife. They were causing the beast discomfort, but it was doubtful they would kill it.

Felix felt a surge of despair. How had it come to this? A few minutes ago they had been seated around a cheery fire in a comfortable cave, and now they were, well, the gods alone knew where, fighting some hideous daemonic thing.

Unless he did something desperate he could see no chance of surviving. Snarling, he drew back his sword and cast it like a spear directly into the one huge eye of the beast. It flew straight and true and embedded itself in the foul jelly of the great unwinking orb. The sword buried itself deep and Felix hoped it had lodged in the creature's brain.

A second later he regretted his actions. The monster let out an evil high-pitched shriek and began to lash the air blindly with its tentacles. Felix saw Gotrek sent tumbling head over heels to land on the floor by a convulsion of the thing's tentacles. Felix threw himself flat to keep himself from being swatted like a bug.

The huge monster began to retreat away from them, still lashing the air. A few seconds later a foul cloud of black inky gas billowed from orifices near its beak. Felix had just enough time to hold his breath before the cloud overwhelmed them, cutting off sight.

Felix noticed that his skin was stinging and tears billowed from his eyes. A foul stench filled his nostrils worse even than that of the giant Chaos warrior. That the gas was as poisonous as that from some vile skaven weapon, he did not doubt. Desperately he launched himself backwards, hoping to get out of it before his lungs gave out and the fumes overcame him.

Even as he did so, he saw the blurred outline of something huge and snake-like emerge from the mist. He had only a second to recognise it as one of the daemon's tentacles before it made contact with his skull. The force of the impact of the great rope of muscle smashed him flat. Involuntarily he opened his mouth, and took a lungful of the foul polluted air.

Damn, he thought, as his chest felt like it was catching fire, and a wave of blackness sent him tumbling down into the darkness.

CHAPTER SIX

TECLIS THOUGHT HE had found the key to opening the ways now. He paused for a moment to check that all his defensive wards were in place, that all the manifold protective charms and amulets he wore were active. He murmured the spell of opening, then drew power to himself and sent tendrils of it out to touch the spells of the ancients. Ever so gently, like a master thief inserting a pick into a lock, he brought his magic into contact with theirs. For a moment, nothing happened. He stifled a curse, then faintly at first, and with ever-increasing force, he felt a tremor within the mystical structure of the spells. Light danced from stone to stone illuminating the archway. They swirled in a manner reminiscent of the auroras he had once seen in the uttermost north.

The way was open. He was free to enter the Paths of the Old Ones. Far off, he felt the faintest of tremors, as magical energy surged within the system. He could see nothing amiss. He had activated no traps – none that he could perceive anyway, although it was certain that those who had built this place would be capable of creating spells of the utmost subtlety. He wondered whether to proceed. This was useless. He could remain here until doomsday wondering about such things. Acting on instinct, he decided to follow it and strode through the archway.

William King

The transition was instantaneous. One moment, he was standing in the vault in Ulthuan, the next he was somewhere else. It resembled nothing so much as a huge corridor carved from stone, every block of which bore runes of that ancient inhuman pattern. Closer examination revealed that the stonework was corroded in places, vilely tainted and mutated, and he knew at once that Chaos was loose within the paths. Overhead, strange gems set in the ceiling gave dim greenish illumination.

He looked back over his shoulder. Behind him, the way was still open. He stepped back through to the vault just to make sure he could. He considered returning to the surface for the griffon but he knew that attempting to compel it to follow him into this vast labyrinth would drive the creature to the brink of madness and perhaps beyond. He released it from the spell and set upon it a compulsion to return to Lothern.

What now, he wondered? Leaving this entrance open was not a good idea. Some innocent might wander in, or more importantly something might emerge into the land of Ulthuan. He shrugged, stepped through the portal once more and uttered the charm that would close the way. As swift as the dropping of a headsman's axe the gate closed. The vault vanished to be replaced by a view of a long stone corridor. He was committed now.

All around him he felt the surge of magical energies pulsing through the ancient network. They permeated the stonework and the runes. He thought of the few extant descriptions of this place, written by Tasirion and other sorcerers who had dared study it. Most claimed that it was dead; others that it was dormant, with the merest trickle of power. Such was not the case now. The place was alive with it.

Were these the forebears of the rune workings of the dwarfs, he wondered, or did they represent some parallel development? Perhaps they were not connected at all. He had no way of telling. The sorcerer in him was fascinated and he wished he had time to study these things and make sketches to show his fellow mages, but there were more urgent matters to consider, and he needed to push on into this vast magical maze.

He was in a halfway house, he realised, a place somewhere beyond the world he knew and close to the realm of Chaos though not yet part of it. He felt like he was standing on the edge of a great shaft that proceeded downwards to near infinite depths. Somewhere up ahead was another larger and more powerful portal.

Even as that thought came to him, he realised that he was not alone. He could sense other presences: vast, powerful and most likely daemonic. They had not yet sensed him, he realised, but it was only a matter of time. Wrapping himself in his most potent charms of concealment, he pushed on.

The corridor was strange. It seemed to become higher and wider as he strode through it, as if time and space were being distorted. He realised that this might actually be the case, for it was the only thing he could think of that would allow what should have been journeys of several months to be completed in several days. Or perhaps this was merely a trick being played on his mind by his senses? Such things were possible when a lot of magical energy was involved.

There had been hints in Tasirion's book that somehow these ancient roads ran through the daemonic realms of Chaos itself, although they constrained it in some way to make it manageable. That would be necessary, for the raw stuff of Chaos was a baneful thing, capable of warping the body and spirit of those who encountered it. Some claimed it was the very essence of magic, mutable, potent and destructive. It was not a thought calculated to reassure one whose chosen vocation was sorcery.

Of course, elves were more resistant to the baleful power of Chaos than most other forms of life. It was said that they had been created that way. Even so, resistant did not mean immune. Teclis had often suspected that the power of the Dark Gods had had more effect on the elves than they were prepared to admit. He sometimes suspected that the dark elves had been a product of Chaos's influence acting on the elvish spirit over a period of millennia. It was one of those things that could never be proven, but to him seemed all too likely.

He noticed as he walked that the walls were becoming higher and thinner. In places they seemed to have worn away, and bizarre patterns of light shone through. It appeared the further he walked this road, the more corrupt it was becoming. He was grateful now that he was wearing his most potent protective amulets. If anything, he only wished that they were more powerful. He sensed he was close now to the portal he sought.

He wondered whether the ancients had walked these paths this way. Certain texts had hinted otherwise. They claimed the Old Ones had ridden in fiery chariots traversing these paths at greater speeds, that they could pass between continents in hours rather than days. That must have been something. He considered other theories that he had read.

Some claimed that the skaven had dug great tunnel systems under the continents. He had seen some of their works in his time and knew the terrifying magnitude of the ratmen's delvings but tunnels that covered thousands of leagues seemed unlikely. Was it possible that the skaven had somehow gained entrance to this ancient network and used it for their own foul ends? All too possible, he decided, particularly since his nostrils had started to detect the faint but unmistakeable taint of warpstone in the air. There was nothing those vile creatures would not do to possess that evil substance, and no doubt if it was to be found here they would sniff it out.

Warpstone was not the only thing down here, he decided. The sense of presence he had felt earlier returned, redoubled. He cast a glance over his shoulder. He was not nervous, not yet anyway. He knew his own capabilities and there were few things in this world or the next that daunted him. Even so, he felt some need to be cautious. He reviewed all the deadly spells he knew, and prepared himself to unleash them instantly.

Whatever it was, it was coming closer. In the distance, by the light of the glowing runes, he could see things moving. He spoke a spell of perception and his point of view rocketed towards them. To his astonishment, he saw that they were beastmen, led by a black armoured Chaos warrior. There were at least a hundred of them moving through the Paths of the Old Ones, moving towards the gate that emerged in Ulthuan.

Immediately he realised the full horrific implications of what he was witnessing. One hundred beastmen were no threat to the realm of the elves, but these might simply be the first of many. Whole armies could move along these paths, and invade the kingdom long before any force could be marshalled to meet them. Elvish domination of the seas around Ulthuan would mean nothing under these circumstances, would in fact be merely a liability. All the warriors crewing ships would not be available to meet an invasion force on land. And if these beastmen were to share their secret with the Dark Ones of Naggaroth...

He told himself he was leaping to conclusions. He had no idea whether these Chaos worshippers were the vanguard of an advancing army or merely hapless fools who had somehow stumbled into this strange realm. Even if they did hold the key to entering the Paths of the Old Ones at will, perhaps no gates emerged in the land of the Witch King.

Teclis was not reassured. Tasirion's book had hinted at a vast network of gateways, and surely the Old Ones had been capable of building a system of such tunnels that would span the entire world.

The intensity of the threat posed to his homeland had doubled. Not only were these ancient ways threatening the stability of the continent by their very existence, they were an invasion route for the deadliest enemies of all sane people, the followers of Chaos. More than ever, he realised that he needed to track this threat to its source, and deal with it.

Briefly he considered turning back to warn his people of what was coming, but he realised that there was no time. Any moment wasted might prove critical if the gates were not returned to dormancy. A heartbeat later any decision was taken from his hands. The Chaos warrior looked up, as if sensing something, and gestured for his beastmen to move forward.

Too late, Teclis realised that this was no mere Chaos warrior but one gifted with sorcerous powers by the Changer of Ways. His spell had been sensed and now ruthless opponents sought him. The elf wizard considered standing and fighting, but realised that he could not afford to do so needlessly. He needed to conserve his power for greater challenges, not fritter it away in random conflicts with chance-met encounters in this vast extra-dimensional warren.

He wove a spell of levitation, feeling resistance to his spell as he did so. The corrupting influence of Chaos was interfering with his pure elven sorcery here. Even as he cast it he could see the beastmen come closer. He was not afraid… yet. He had overcome greater odds in the past. The spell took effect and he strode upward. The ceiling here was perhaps ten times the height of a man above him, and each step took him closer to it. If the beastmen chose to lob missiles at him there might be some problems, but he knew spells that would ward him against that. He was not too worried about any spells the Chaos warrior might possess. He had complete confidence in his own ability to deal with such things. He had long ago learned that there were few magicians in this world that he need fear.

Having achieved a position of safety he considered his offensive options. There were many spells capable of dealing with even such a huge crowd of beastmen. He could spray them with molten plasma or blast them with fireballs. He could send a rain of magical missiles showering down on them. He could surround them with mists and illusions that would set them at each other's throats. If worst came to worst he could simply reduce them to their component atoms, although that would require more power than he cared to expend.

So engrossed did he become in these calculations that it took him a few moments to realise that the beastmen were not charging towards him, but fleeing away from something. Wonderful, he thought. That puts an entirely different complexion on things. As the sour moment passed, he smiled. There is a lesson here, he thought. The entire world does not rotate around you.

He strode higher and cloaked himself in refractory spells, bending light about him to conceal himself. Within ten heartbeats he was glad he had. The thing that pursued the beastmen was horrific, a titanic creature that looked like a cross between a slug and a dragon. Its huge armoured form slithered softly along the roadway leaving a trail of bubbling corrosive slime behind it. The thing was as large as a ship, and its long serpentine neck raised its huge head nearly as high as Teclis's present position.

There was something about it, an aura of menace and power that made even the elf wizard's stout spirit quail. He did not blame the beastmen and their leader for fleeing before it. Even as he watched, the creature opened its mouth. Teclis had seen the great dragons of Ulthuan, and he thought he knew what was coming. Once again he was surprised. Instead of a gout of flame, a foul festering mass of mucus vomited forth to splatter the beastmen. Where it touched them it hardened swiftly, immobilising them, holding them in place. It seemed to have some of the properties of a spider's web, and a butterfly's cocoon, and one thing more. When it touched the beastmen, they screamed like souls in torment.

The alchemist in Teclis was fascinated. Poison or corrosive, he wondered? Whatever it was, it seemed to cause a great deal of agony. Teclis felt no sympathy for the beastmen. They were vile creatures living only for killing, torture and rape. Whatever they got now, they doubtless deserved.

Even as he watched, the great head swooped down, and the monster began to feed. Tearing his gaze away, Teclis proceeded along the Paths of the Old Ones. He needed to follow this path to the source of the disturbance. Up ahead, the corridor ended in a ledge. It was through this that both beastmen and monster must have come. There was nothing else there save another glowing arch; beyond it, he sensed, the real danger began.

CHAPTER SEVEN

'WELL, MANLING, YOU are alive,' said Gotrek. He sounded neither pleased nor displeased. The expression on his face could have been carved from stone.

Felix pulled himself to his feet. He felt a little dizzy and the inside of his lungs felt rough. He coughed and noticed that his phlegm was stained black when he spat. That was probably not a good sign, he thought.

'What happened?'

'You blinded the beast, and it belched that noxious cloud and then retreated.' Felix's hand felt for his empty scabbard. The only weapon he had now was his knife. Realising what he was thinking, Gotrek jabbed his thumb towards the floor. Felix saw that his blade lay there glittering.

'Must have fallen out when the thing shook its head,' Felix said, moving over to pick it up. Traces of a jelly-like substance marred the blade. He wiped them off with a strip cut from his cloak and then returned the blade to his scabbard. He gave his attention to his surroundings once more.

'Where are we?' he asked. The Slayer shook his head.

'I have no idea, manling. These tunnels are not dwarf work and they stink of sorcery.'

'Tunnels?' said Felix. He was thinking aloud. Of course, they were tunnels, they just did not feel like any tunnels he had ever been in before. It was more like being caught within some vast alien structure, a labyrinth or a maze. And mazes in legends were always full of monsters.

'Aye, tunnels, manling, although unlike any ever delved by dwarf. Still they have the feeling of runework to them. There is sorcery being channelled here, and no mistake.'

'You don't say,' said Felix ironically. 'I would never have suspected that from the way we passed through that arch and disappeared.'

Gotrek gave him a flat unreadable glance. Felix felt that perhaps he was amused. There was something about sarcasm that appealed to the dwarfish sense of humour, and Felix occasionally suspected that the Slayer possessed one. 'More to the point, how do we get back?'

'I don't think we can, manling. I think the way behind us is closed.'

Felix had an awful feeling he knew what Gotrek was going to say next, and sure enough, he was not disappointed. 'The only thing we can do is press on and hope to find a way out, or our doom.'

Wearily, Felix trudged after the dwarf, coughing unpleasant black stuff up with every second step.

'WHAT DO YOU think those monsters eat when they can't get beastmen?' Felix asked. The question was much on his mind. He was starting to feel very hungry. It had been a long time since he had eaten, and his rations were all in the packs they had left back in the cave. Come to think of it, so was his water flask. As soon as the thought hit him, his mouth felt dry.

'Curious humans,' grunted Gotrek. Felix wondered if he was making a joke.

'Perhaps they wander in through the stone arches.'

'Perhaps. I don't know, manling, I am not a wizard.'

'Speaking of wizards, where do you think our black-robed friend went?'

'As far away from me as possible, if he has any sense. Or maybe the monster ate him.'

'Somehow I doubt we should be that lucky.'

KELMAIN EMERGED FROM the Paths of the Old Ones and into the chamber of the temple. He was grateful to have avoided the Slayer's axe. He was even more thankful to be out, for no matter how great the protective power of the amulets his masters had showed him how to make, he always felt there was an element of terrible danger within the place. You could never be sure when some ancient protective device would spring to life or some rogue daemon of the Twisted Paths, unheedful of the warning runes on the talisman, would seek to gulp down your soul.

He was pleased to see that his acolyte's face showed the apprehension he kept so well concealed. Young Tzeshi was paler even than usual, despite the fact that he had at least a hundred beastmen and Chaos warriors at his back. He bowed on seeing Kelmain and sketched a gesture of deepest respect on the air. Kelmain nodded to him and indicated that he should continue. As he departed he could hear the youthful mage begin the chant that would extend the protective spells enfolding him to enclose all of his followers.

There was no reason why he should not. Their experiments so far had been successful and their scouting parties had covered half the globe. Soon, if all went according to plan, the armies of Chaos would be able to move swiftly from the Chaos Wastes to any nation on the surface of the planet, bypassing borders and fortifications, emerging deep within the territory of their foes.

Filled with a vision of glory, he strode through the ancient haunted hallways to speak with his brother.

FELIX SHUDDERED. THEY had walked for hours now, and the road had become stranger. The stones had a melted, fused look that he had come to associate with the warping influence of Chaos. Sometimes it looked like faces leered out of the walls or that bodies were trapped frozen within the stone. Sometimes he felt like they were moving very slowly whenever he took his eyes off them. The strange jewels in the ceiling overhead sometimes vanished, taking with them their illumination. When that happened, he had to move forward trusting in the dwarf's keen tunnel-bred senses, following the glow of the runes on the axe. They were lighted all the time now, and that was never a good sign. In the past it had always predicted the presence of evil magic or vile monsters.

Moving through the gloom was not reassuring. It felt like anything could be there, waiting. Sometimes he could imagine the presence of strange formless things in the dark, just behind him. He could picture huge jaws opening to snap at him. Even though he knew it was useless, he often turned and glared behind him. He had to fight down the urge to take out his sword and sweep the air all around. He told himself that had anything been there the Slayer would know, and would do something about it. The thought provided cold comfort.

'These tunnels do not run below the earth,' said Gotrek. He sounded almost thoughtful.

'What do you mean?'

'A dwarf can sense depth. Only a cripple would not know how deep below the mountains he was. All my life I have had this knowledge and never once had to think about it. Now, it is gone. It is like the loss of sight, almost.'

Felix could not quite picture it being that bad, but he realised that he was in no position to know. How would he feel if he suddenly lost all sense of up and down, he wondered, and then realised that he simply could not get his head around the idea.

'I really do wonder where that magician went to.' Felix said. It was not that he was keen to catch up with the Chaos sorcerer. He simply wondered how he had gotten away. Presumably there must be some way in or out of this strange place, and he must know it. If they could only find him, perhaps they could convince him to get them out of here. He doubted that even the wickedest of wizards could withstand the Slayer's powers of persuasion under the circumstances. Come to think of it, he would help Gotrek himself, if the need arose.

'Doubtless he is running as fast as his legs will carry him, manling. I never yet met a wizard who would stand and face cold steel, given any choice.'

Felix wondered about this. He could recall facing several magicians who had not run away from them. Still, this did not seem like the time to point this out to the Slayer. 'He might be our only way out of here.'

'We need place no reliance in the followers of Chaos.'

'We may have to. Otherwise your heroic doom will take the form of starving.'

Gotrek grunted. He did not sound impressed. 'If that be so, that be so.'

For the first time Felix was really forced to consider the fact that they might die here. There was no food and nothing to drink. Not unless they went back and ate the beastman corpses and drank their blood, and that was not a thing he could imagine the Slayer doing. They were probably poisonous anyway, and that was assuming they had not already been eaten by some other foul denizens of these supernatural ways.

Get a grip on yourself, he told himself. A dozen heartbeats after the thought occurs to you, and you are already considering eating beastmen and the gods alone know what other horrors. Things have not come to that pass yet, and you've been through worse. You've been through battles and sieges and treks through frozen mountains. You've fought dragons and daemons and monsters of all descriptions. You're not dead yet. In spite of himself, though, Felix could not help but feel they had never been so isolated or so far from home.

TECLIS FOLLOWED THE oddly glowing runes up to the ledge. Ahead of him the path ended at another archway within which flowed the strange polychromatic swirls of energy he had seen earlier. The sense of immense controlled energies contained within was awesome. He paused for a moment, knowing what he must do, but not quite prepared to do it.

This was the path Tasirion had written about. All he had to do was pass within it. All of these strange interdimensional corridors he had passed through so far had merely been a preparation for this. They were simply the approaches to the true Paths of the Old Ones. He had a feel for their structure now. They were like tunnels dug down through the surface of reality. What loomed before him was more like the entrance to an underground river.

The trail was clear. Why was he hesitating? He already knew the answer. Things had decayed since the time of the Old Ones. That much was obvious. Their works were potent but they had been infiltrated and corrupted by the powers of Chaos. Who could tell whether they would work the way they were supposed to, or even the way they had when Tasirion passed this way all those scores of years ago?

As it was he had two choices. He could turn and go back the way he came, and try to find another way to avert the doom of Ulthuan. If such were possible in the limited time he had available. Or he could press on, trusting to his knowledge and his spells as he had always done. He allowed himself a smile. Many had called him arrogant, and he supposed it was too late now to prove them wrong.

He stepped forward and touched the surface of the glowing substance. It felt cool and liquid and it flowed around his fingers, engulfing them. He took a deep breath and pushed through. In a heartbeat he was swept into the raging currents beyond. He had a brief glimpse of a huge corridor along which tumbled thousands upon thousands of glittering many-coloured spheres, hurtling along like asteroids through space. He sensed dark malign presences and prepared himself to meet them.

* * *

'AT LEAST THE lights are back on,' said Felix, realising that he was whining. They could see again. The path curved upward, or perhaps it was downward at a strange angle; he could no longer tell. All he knew was that even though it felt like they were walking on the flat, he could see the curve of the path. It was an effect that was most disorientating. Perhaps, after all, he could understand what Gotrek had been talking about earlier when he mentioned how confusing it was to no longer be able to sense depth. The cues that his eyes were giving him no longer matched the cues his body felt. It created an immense sense of dislocation.

'There is another source of light,' Gotrek said. Felix realised that he was right. The pathway ahead split into two, one going upwards, the other going downwards. Both ended after about fifty strides in glowing archways. No, he realised, it was not just the archways that glowed, it was what was within them. They appeared to be filled with some substance like mercury, except that it glowed and pulsed with all colours. Shimmering patches drifted over the surface like oil on water, pulsing as they went. The effect was eerie and definitely supernatural.

Even as the thought occurred to him, Felix heard an immense slithering sound behind him. Something huge was dragging itself from the dark tunnels through which they had passed. His forebodings had proven themselves to be true after all.

Out of the darkness a massive creature dragged its bloated body. Its head was draconic, but where its mouth should have been was a mass of squid-like tentacles. As they writhed, Felix saw a huge leech-like mouth the size of a manhole cover in its midst. If anything, it was worse than the first beast they had encountered.

It stank awfully and its skin seemed putrid. When he looked closely, enormous maggots writhed beneath it, sometimes biting their way through and inching away. It took Felix a moment to realise what they were: young. The thing was being eaten alive by its own progeny, although that did not appear to do anything to damp its own appetite. There was something about the look and the stench that was familiar, that reminded him of the followers of the Plague God Nurgle he had seen at the Siege of Praag. Was it possible that this thing was some sort of pestilential daemonic creature of the lord of pestilence? He did not suppose it would matter all that much if the creature ate him. Even as he watched he realised that something worse might happen. The maggots bursting forth from within it were crawling towards him.

Worse still, hideous high-pitched laughter emerged from somewhere high atop the beast's skull. When he looked he could see that one of the excrescences looked suspiciously like a human head. As the realisation struck he heard the creature speak. 'Once I was like you – soon you will be like me – ha ha! Lord Nurgle's gift will be yours, and you will be his – ha ha!'

Felix had once seen a caterpillar being eaten alive by the larvae of a wasp that had been implanted within it. He wondered if this was what would happen to him if those bloated, squelching sacs of foulness bit him. He braced himself for combat even as their foul parent loomed over him. Its shadow fell across him, bringing with it an awful stench. Then it leaned forward like an avalanche of flesh and pus.

I have fought some awful things, Felix thought, but surely this must be the worst.

THE CURRENTS OF magic swept Teclis down the endless corridor of many-coloured lights. He touched things, smashed through gossamer webs of energy and emerged on the other side. Before he could orientate himself, he tumbled headlong. Strange hallucinations overtook him. He passed through scenes he well remembered. His childhood, his first book of spells, the battles that had wracked Ulthuan when the Dark Kindred had invaded while he was still a youth. The mighty confrontation at Finuval Plain where he had fought with the Witch King and eventually triumphed. They flickered past. Between them were intervals where he hurtled down the long extra-dimensional corridor.

Sometimes the scenes were subtly different. In some, he looked into the book and saw there spells of convoluted evil that turned him to the darkness. In some of the battles he fought not against the Witch King but with him, clad in dark armour that was a reflection of Malekith's own. In others he saw himself standing over the body of his dying twin and laughing. Even as he felt horror he realised that these things reflected something within himself, some possibility. Were these his secret dreams and nightmares, or were they something else?

He touched the protective amulet on his breast and concentrated his mind, clearing the images from his thoughts. As sanity returned, a phrase came to him, an expression from Tasirion's book: *The Paths of the Old Ones have been corrupted by Chaos, you must be wary of the Twisted Paths.*

He saw now what the mad mage had meant. Tasirion had claimed that the Twisted Paths were where the work of the Old Ones intersected with bubbles of pure Chaos. The stuff was malleable. It responded to the thoughts and dreams and sometimes the simple presence of sentient minds. He realised he had been falling through them and as he did so he had altered them.

In a way they were windows into other worlds, temporary things, bubbles rising through the seething extra-dimensional sea of Chaos, places that would exist for one heartbeat, or ten, or perhaps a lifetime or a millennium. He knew that he could, if he wished, guide himself towards them and enter them.

What would it be like, he wondered, to be caught in such a bubble, a miniature universe sculpted from his own innermost wishes, reflecting his own secret history? Could he make a paradise? Could he create a place where his illness had not struck him, where he was as strong and perfect as Tyrion, where the darkness within him would never have to come to light, where he would never need to feel jealousy or envy or bitter pain?

Was this the secret of the Old Ones' disappearance? Had they departed from our world to this place and created their own bubble universes, nestled within the sea of Chaos? Was such a thing even possible? It was a concept to boggle the mind. Even as it struck him, he accelerated faster through the corridors of this strange space. As he did so he saw that the bubbles of the Chaos stuff were travelling along like droplets of mercury dropped down the funnel of an alembic. Sometimes two would impact and merge, sometimes they would split and go their separate ways. It was like watching some primordial life forms. He moved to avoid any that came too close, fearing that they might be semi-sentient or drawn to him in some way and that they might consume him. The hallucinations stopped, as he had thought they would.

He studied his surroundings closely, noticing that the tumbling spheres were agitated by great pulses of energy, flowing first one way and then the other like seaweed being dragged about by the tides. He realised almost at once that the energy flows were linked to the disturbances in Ulthuan and elsewhere. By tracking them to their source, he could most likely find the cause of the disturbance.

There were other presences here too, none of them mortal. Some were alien and uninterested in him. Others were malign and followed in his wake like sharks following a ship. They were daemons who had somehow found their way into this colossal labyrinth. He knew that only his protective amulets kept them at bay, and that at the first touch of weakness they would take him.

Suddenly a strange intuition touched him, a feeling of dry ghostly presences such as there had been in his dreams. Was it a product of his imagination, he wondered, or had those trapped sorcerers really reached out for him? Or was it some subtle form of attack projected by the creatures following him? He willed himself to slow and as he did so, noticed an archway that glowed in a strangely familiar way. Moreover, he noticed a trace of an awesomely powerful magical resonance created by a thing that was not in itself Chaotic. It was in fact the resonance of a weapon or device that was powerfully resistant to Chaos, an artefact of near-godlike power. Was this some treasure lost long ago in the paths? Was this something he was supposed to seek?

Such a thing might prove very useful to him on his quest. By an effort of will, he pushed himself towards the archway. Within what seemed like heartbeats he hurtled through it and emerged to face horror.

FELIX DIVED TO one side as tendrils descended towards him. He lashed out, hacking the tips of a few and hit the ground rolling, just in time to see a mass of bloated white maggots moving towards him. He noticed that on each side of their leech-like mouths were small clusters of eyes that reminded him of a spider's, only these contained a strange intelligence and a glittering malice that was uncanny. Large as they were, though, he could not see what harm they could do him as long as they did not get close enough to bite. And he had no intention of allowing that to happen.

Gotrek was already amid the mass of maggot-things, hacking at them with the axe. Their jelly-like quivering flesh gave no resistance. The things burst under the impact, sending milky fluid that stank like rotten curdled milk everywhere. Overhead, the high-pitched laughter of the daemonic thing sounded anew. Felix wondered what it knew that he did not.

He threw himself forward, keeping behind the Slayer, guarding his back against anything that threatened to get past. Not that there was much danger of that with all the carnage the dwarf was wreaking. The huge monster leaned forward, tentacles stretching once more. Long rubbery limbs, suckered like a squid's, threatened to wrap around him. He cut at them, and his blade bit deep, causing more of the hideous milky fluid to surge forth. He noticed that the floor beneath his feet was becoming sticky, and his movements slower. The sheer nauseating stench was threatening to overwhelm him.

Gotrek showed no sign of slowing. Whenever a tentacle looped near him, he chopped it in two. The thing did not die, though. It hit the ground and began to writhe away like a snake, showing a life, if not an intelligence, independent of its original owner. Even as Felix watched, the severed tentacle began to heal and regrow, like the limbs of the fabled troll, or the heads of some daemonic hydra.

The huge bloated body of the monster had started to expand like a balloon as it sucked in air. Felix had the feeling that this was the prelude to nothing good, but he could not for the life of him predict what was going to happen. The thing was too alien, their circumstances beyond the ambit of all his previous experience. He was starting to wonder if they had somehow been cast into hell. At this moment, it seemed all too likely.

The monster exhaled, a gust of stinking, buzzing breath unlike anything Felix had ever quite experienced. It was a black gale that thundered around his ears, then he realised that the buzzing had nothing to do with the breath; it was the foul wingbeat of millions upon millions of flies. These were not any normal flies, either. They were huge things with fat glistening jewelled bodies, and eyes just as intelligent and malicious as that of the monster or the maggots. Perhaps they were all part of the same thing; perhaps they all shared the same intelligence.

That was the last conscious thought he had for a few moments as horror swept over him. Millions of fat buzzing bodies crept over him, their wings stroking his flesh softly and obscenely, the creatures battering against his eyes, and threatening to fill his mouth and his nostrils. He lashed out frantically, but it was like fighting with mist. He crushed hundreds, perhaps thousands as he rolled over but more and more of them came. He could imagine himself under a huge crawling mound of the creatures, covering every inch of his body. He felt them try to force their way through his lips, climbing into his ears. The smell intensified and the buzzing of the wings seemed to have a voice all of its own. He thought he heard the words *Nurgle* and *Praise* and *Pestilence* carried in that strange droning but could not tell if it was real or the product of his own terrified imagination.

Just when he thought things could not get any worse, he felt a massive rope of muscle encircle him. Suckers bit into his body. Something lifted him upwards as though he were weightless and he did not doubt that he was being carried towards the maw of the monstrous creature that was the lord of all these flies.

CHAPTER EIGHT

TECLIS EMERGED THROUGH the archway and found himself looking down upon a scene of battle. Two humanoid figures were engulfed within a carpet of flies, amid a vile white mist that smelled worse than an orcish midden. One of the figures was quite plainly a dwarf. His outline was more visible through the flies that carpeted him, and he held in one hand an axe that could only be a dwarfish rune weapon, and one of great power at that. No flies covered it. Where they touched the blade they vanished and the runes blazed a little brighter.

This was the thing he had sensed. This was the thing he had deludedly thought might help him. It could only be the axe. There was another magical weapon present, one of cruder make and lesser power. Its wielder was gripped by the tentacle of the monster.

Teclis had studied all the grimoires of his ancestors who had lived in age when daemons had walked the earth. Moreover, he had personally as much experience of daemons as anyone not a follower of Chaos was likely to have, and he could not recognise the thing. It bore some resemblance to a beast of Nurgle, one of the lesser entities that followed the Lord of Disease, but grown almost as huge as a dragon, and mutated almost out of recognition. Moreover, it seemed to be spawning lesser beings at an appalling rate, and in his blinded state, Teclis realised that it was only a matter of time before one of them reached the dwarf. What would happen then would be interesting, for he guessed the maggots were infectors of some type, who would pass the taint of Chaos on through their venom, if they were not already doing so with their gore. Could even that appallingly powerful weapon protect the dwarf, if that happened, or would it use its power against him as it would another Chaos-tainted thing?

Tempted though he was to conduct the experiment, Teclis resisted. Two magical weapons, Teclis thought, borne by two heroes. Here were two allies who might prove invaluable in the quest to come, if they could be persuaded to see reason. Perhaps this was why they had been drawn to his attention. First of all, though, he had better deal with the daemon and its spawn.

Teclis drew on the powers stored within his staff, preferring to rely on it rather than the tainted but potent energies flowing through the Paths of the Old Ones. He chanted a spell of exorcism and banishment. The casting was sure and steady and bands of high magic danced from his outstretched hands, separating the weaves of power that bound the flies, reducing them at once to mindless insects, and he added a small incendiary component to the spell that caused the flies to combust. He shaped another spell to purify the foul air tainted by daemon effluvia, and then concentrated his efforts on the great beast itself, sending multiple lines of energy arcing and spinning towards its head. The magical fire passed through its body like so many red-hot wires through rancid lard. The creature screamed and its tittering stopped.

With his sight clear of the buzzing insects, the dwarf did not need any more encouragement to strike. He raced forward and the massive axe crashed through the slimy skin of the beast. The creature's wails intensified as the glowing rune-encrusted blade bit home. The massive tentacles uncoiled as the creature writhed in agony. The man in its grip was sent flying across the corridor as if flung from a catapult.

Teclis summoned a small pseudo-sylph to catch him and cushion his fall. It was a tiny air creature formed from magical energy to do his will, an extension of himself rather than a true elemental, but this was the shape in which he found it easiest to manifest his powers.

Such was the velocity with which the man was flung that Teclis was too slow. By the time he had commanded the sylph to act, he had already passed through the archway and vanished into the Paths of the Old Ones.

The dwarf seemed barely to have noticed. A quick glance was all he took. His one good eye narrowed when he saw Teclis, though, and then he returned to carving the massive Chaos creature. Now the daemon was in full retreat, slithering away into the darkness, its maggot children inching along after it. Teclis knew he must end this farce soon if he was to take advantage of the opportunity with which he had been presented. He sent another wave of magical power after the creature, incinerating the maggots and charring its flesh. The creature screamed as it died.

The dwarf spat on its smouldering remains and then turned to face the wizard.

'Now, elf, I will deal with you.'

FELIX FELT A sudden surge of heat around him, and then the buzzing stopped. He opened his eyes and saw a charred halo of dust falling away from him. The grip of the tentacle tightened painfully around his ribs, cutting off his breath. He felt as if his bones were about to break. Desperately he gripped his sword and tried to bring it to bear on the monstrous limb, but the angle was wrong.

He heard Gotrek's war cry ring out and axe bite home. A golden glow filled the air, and a swirling breeze dissipated the cloying stink of the beast. What was going on here, he wondered, as the glow intensified and lines of fire pierced the body of the daemon? Magic was at work – that was quite obvious. Had Max followed them?

Before he had time to consider things further, the creature's tentacles uncurled and he found himself hurtling through the air. Involuntarily, he closed his eyes. He knew that if he hit the ground or a wall from this height at this speed, at very best bones would be broken, at worst he would die a pulped gelatinous mass like the maggots. He braced himself for the impact that he knew could only be seconds in coming.

Instead, he felt himself engulfed in coolness. He opened his eyes, and saw that he was on the other side of the glowing barrier, caught amid swirling colours. He had but a few seconds to take this in, and then he felt himself gripped by acceleration. It was as if his velocity, already great, had increased by several orders of magnitude.

Desperately he looked around but what he saw was meaningless. He seemed to be hurtling though a breathable atmosphere along an infinite corridor whose walls changed colour every heartbeat. Strange glittering spheres moved through it as well, pulsing and changing, flowing into each other like droplets of quicksilver. Inside each seemed to be a shimmering vision. He had no idea where he was or where he was going. The sense of disorientation he had felt in the darkness of the corridors returned, increased tenfold.

Worse yet, he was alone and caught in some vast sorcerous trap from which he knew he would never escape.

TECLIS LOOKED AT the dwarf and considered the possibility of his own death. The more he looked at that axe the more his respect for its power increased. That it was an ancient rune weapon of the highest order, he had no doubt. The aura of antiquity surrounding it was clear. The runes were dazzling bright, more potent than any he had ever seen, and in his time, he had seen many.

Its wielder was no less frightening. He appeared to be a normal dwarf, albeit one of great size and physical power, but his aura told Teclis's keen and sensitive mage sight a different story. The dwarf had been changed in many ways. Magic permeated his being. Magic that flowed from the axe and changed him utterly. It was changing him still. He was far tougher and stronger than any dwarf had a right to be, and far more immune to the effects of magic as well. Fascination warred with fear. Here was a being in the process of transformation into something else, under the influence of a magic older than elven civilisation. Teclis would have given a king's ransom to be able to study this weapon, but at the moment he had other worries.

'I have no quarrel with you, dwarf,' he said.

'I can change that,' said the dwarf. He moved closer, the menacing axe held high.

Teclis considered his options. He had used much of the power stored in the staff, and the magical energies he could draw on here within the paths would all be tainted by Chaos, and thus most likely resisted by the axe. He would not have bet gold that under these circumstances he could overcome the protective runes on that blade. In Ulthuan things might have been different, but this was not Ulthuan.

Nor did drawing his sword and facing the dwarf seem like an acceptable option. He was a fair swordsman, but one look at this dwarf told him that even a magical blade in the hands of a competent fighter would not be nearly enough for victory.

'I saved your life and that of your companion,' he said, backing towards the archway. Under the circumstances, discretion seemed the better part of valour. Still, he was loath to simply run. He had the pride of all the line of Aenarion, and more, he felt that this dwarf was important to him somehow, that this meeting was not simply chance.

'I do not take kindly to that suggestion,' said the dwarf in a voice like stone grating on stone.

Of course not, thought Teclis, looking at the strange hairstyle and the tattoos, and the dwarf's generally morose demeanour – you are a Slayer, sworn to seek death in battle. I have done you no favours then. He kept backing away as the Slayer advanced, kept considering his options, looking for the key that would give him an advantage here. There was only one thing that sprang immediately to mind.

'If you wish to save your companion, you must work with me now,' said Teclis.

FELIX BEGAN TO see things as he tumbled headlong into the spheres. At first they seemed almost formless, but then he began to recognise pictures, fleeting glimpses of himself and others. Some of them were quite obviously memories. Others he did not recall. They might have been the dreams of another, save that he recognised those within them.

He saw himself as a youth in his father's house, quarrelling with the old man. He saw himself as a young radical student at the University of Altdorf, drinking and posturing and writing verses of no great worth in taverns of no great respectability. He saw the duel he fought with Wolfgang Krassner and the corpse at his feet, bloody foam still oozing from its lips. He saw the wild night when he had met Gotrek in the Axe and Hammer, and swore an oath to accompany him and record his doom. He saw their fatal encounter with the Emperor's cavalry during the window tax riots.

More images filled his eyes as his senses became somehow more real and more dream-like. What was going on here? What was this medium through which he moved? It seemed to respond to thought and memory with magical speed. He could not comprehend it. He was not a sorcerer and had no wish to be. He had read in some books of natural philosophy that the pure stuff of Chaos was supposed to be like this. He had heard of similar strange things happening during the first Siege of Praag before Magnus the Pious had intervened and saved the city. Stone had flowed like water, hideous monsters had been made flesh, nightmares had walked the street.

More scenes flickered around him. He saw an ancient castle in Sylvania where he and Gotrek confronted a vampire and rescued a girl. He recognised the vampire from a picture he had once seen in Drakenhof Castle. It was Mannfred von Carstein.

He saw a great battle in which the armies of the Empire confronted a horde of orcs, and Snorri Nosebiter fell in battle to be mourned by a regiment of Slayers. He saw a huge burning mountain on top of which Gotrek fought with a bat-winged daemon that looked like a combination of man and elf, only much larger. These things had never happened, he knew. Perhaps they were delusions given form by his feverish brain, prophesies of the future, glimpses of worlds that might have been if he had walked a different path?

He did not know, and he did not care. Already he felt his senses were about to be overwhelmed, that if this kept up his mind would collapse under the sheer rush of information, and he would be reduced to a mad gibbering thing. Then he saw that some of the other objects were coming closer and taking new forms. He sensed the presences around him, closing in, coming closer through the aether like sharks surrounding a thrashing swimmer. A tendril of thought, silky and malevolent and evil, reached out and infiltrated his brain.

We will feed soon, it said. *Your soul is ours.*

THE DWARF STOPPED his advance.

'Is this some elvish treachery?' he said. Teclis shook his head.

'Your friend has gone through the Portal of the Old Ones. He has no protective charms or amulets of spells. He has no idea of how to shield himself. He has no runes such as are to be found on your formidable axe. If he is not found soon, he will die or be devoured by those who dwell beyond.'

The dwarf raised his axe once more, and advanced, a look of pure determination on his face. Teclis feared that he was going to have to fight. Instead the dwarf strode towards the gateway. 'I will find him. I do not need your help, elf.'

'It is not so simple. You are no sorcerer. You could not find him within the ways. Nor could you find your own way out without the correct key. You will be lost in there forever or until you meet something that not even your axe can slay.'

'But you will help me?' said the dwarf. There was harsh irony in his voice. 'Why do I feel there is a catch?'

'Because in return, you will help me to discharge my quest. A simple bargain. Something a dwarf should understand.'

The dwarf glared at him. 'Do not worry. I will require nothing that would compromise your dwarfish pride or your peculiar notions of honour.'

'What would an elf know of honour?'

Teclis smiled. 'Then after we have saved your friend I will leave it to you to decide whether what I ask of you is honourable.'

The dwarf cocked his head. He suspected a trap. So might I look, thought the wizard, if I were bargaining with a daemon. He smiled again, having just been given some insight into what was going on in the dwarf's head.

'Very well,' said the dwarf. 'But if this is a trick or you betray me, then you will most assuredly die, if I have to climb out of the pit of hell to kill you.'

The smile vanished from Teclis's lips. The dwarf sounded like he would do exactly what he said. He had the look of someone who could do it, too.

'If we are to travel together we should know each other's names. I am Teclis, of the line of Aenarion,' he said, giving a courtly bow as to one of uncertain status.

'I am Gotrek, son of Gurni,' said the dwarf. He did not bow.

'And if my rememberer is dead,' he said, 'you will soon join him.'

We'll see, thought Teclis, knowing that once they were within the Paths of the Old Ones, the balance of power would tip back into his favour.

FELIX WONDERED IF he were dead and passed within Morr's iron-gated halls. That seemed the one likely possibility, although if this was the afterlife it was a peculiarly hellish one.

Perhaps that was what had happened. Perhaps he had been condemned to one of the purgatories where evildoers were punished for their sins. He had not considered himself a particularly evil man in life, but perhaps the gods judged mortals by different standards.

He stood now in a strange dark place. Fire pits were everywhere. Suffering mortals were chained to walls and daemonic entities tortured them. The weight of his own chains was enormous, and their heat was uncomfortable against his limbs.

Worse yet, something large, horned and bat-winged was coming closer. It reminded him of daemons he had seen before. It had the same malicious eyes, and the same air of inhuman cruelty. It paused before him and looked up at where he hung.

'You are ours now,' it said. 'We will feast on your flesh and upon your soul. For us it will be a moment of mild diversion. For you, an eternity of pain.'

'WAIT,' SAID TECLIS. 'I must cast the spells of warding and tracking before we pass through this archway.'

The dwarf spat on the ground, and ran his thumb over the edge of the axe. A bead of bright blood appeared there. It was a disconcerting sight. Teclis reactivated the charms of protection woven into his amulets and extended their influence to an area about three strides from his body. The axe would most likely protect its wielder from the worst influences of Chaos within the paths, but he was taking no chances.

He next considered locating the man. Such divination was not easy at the best of times and he had barely caught a glimpse of the human. Still, the sword had a very distinctive magical pattern, and Teclis had the recall of an elvish sorcerer. In his youth he had performed thousands of exercises designed to increase the capacity of his memory. The application of such skills was invaluable to a sorcerer in countless ways, as he was just about to prove.

He visualised the man, freezing the instant in which he had been flung clear of the daemon-thing. He saw again the straw-blond hair, the scared blue eyes, the lined and tanned face with its horrified expression. He pictured the tall form wrapped in the ragged red cloak. He pictured the man's aura and the aura of the blade. The image of a great dragon sprang to his mind, and he realised as he contemplated the memory that a dragon's head had been the pattern on the hilt of the blade. Once he was certain he had the image as perfect as he was going to get it, he cast the spell of divination and location, sending tendrils of force through the gateway, relying on the principle of sympathetic magic to guide them to their source. For a moment, he feared he would find nothing, that the link was too tenuous, that even his skills were not equal to the task, then he felt something far off and receding.

As soon as he made contact, he wished he had not. The man was in great fear, and the shadow of another presence had fallen on his mind. Teclis suspected it was the shadow of a daemon.

'We must go now. Your friend is in grave danger,' said Teclis.

'Lead on,' said the dwarf as Teclis stepped through the glowing arch and into the nightmare reality of the Twisted Paths.

CHAPTER NINE

THE OTHER WORLD was different this time, Teclis realised. He was not
seeing the same things at all. Maybe it was because he had increased
the diameter of the weave of his protective spells, but he suspected
it was the presence of that axe. The more time he spent in its presence, the more he realised how powerful it was. More than that,
now that Gotrek Gurnisson was in the ambit of his spells, he could
sense the strong magical links between the dwarf and the weapon.

He had heard of such phenomena before, but this was the first
time he had seen it acted out so powerfully. Over time psychic links
could be formed between any magical device and the person who
wielded it. Such was an inevitable by-product of magical forces but
this was something more. Power flowed down those links into the
dwarf, power subtle enough to change even a creature so resistant
to magic as a dwarf, and powerful enough to hold at bay the currents of Chaos here. He would have given a lot to know the history
and provenance of that weapon, he thought. He doubted that the
dwarf was going to share it with him though.

If the Slayer was daunted by the bizarre nature of their surroundings he gave no sign. Teclis wondered if they were seeing the same
things. At the moment, they floated within a bubble of clear air
defined by the boundaries of his spell. Outside, the magical currents
of the Paths of the Old Ones flowed. Teclis sensed the inhabitants

out there. Some were neutral spirits, elementals and other creatures who could feed on the direct flow of magic. Most were actively inimical, creatures of Chaos who had entered the pathways and been trapped there. Or perhaps they simply chose to live there. There were resonances of older things, spirits that had been hostile to Chaos, who had perhaps been set there as guardians by the Old Ones themselves, but who had been swamped and submerged and perhaps corrupted long ago.

Once again, he felt the fascination of the scholar. There was so much to learn and so little time to learn it in, even with the lifespan of an elf prince. There was material for a hundred studies contained within this place, if only he survived to write it. He fought to bring his thoughts back to the task at hand. First he needed to find the human, and then he needed to return to his quest. Had he not felt such a strong intuition about the dwarf and his axe he doubted that he would have even offered to help. Yet some instinct had told him that this was the right thing to do. You did not just encounter the wielder of such a weapon by chance. Their destinies had touched and intertwined at this point, of this he was sure. One thing had not changed, though; the great tidal swirl of energy still moved to and fro through the Twisted Paths, pushing the bubbles of reality hither and yon.

He reached out with the divination spell again, and sensed the human's pain and fear. If they did not reach him soon, it would be too late to do anything. He urged the sphere onwards through the aether, hoping that by sheer force of will, he could make it get there in time.

FELIX WATCHED AS another of the daemons came closer. He threw himself forward against the chains, knowing already that it was useless. They were strong enough to resist even Gotrek's massive strength. His sword lay just out of reach, positioned there to add to his torment and his hopelessness.

The daemon leaned closer. He could see that its eyes were not like a human's. At first they appeared like pits of pure flame, but if you looked into them, you could see that a malign intelligence dwelt there. Instead of pupils, small flames danced in the ember pits that filled its sockets – sentient flames, flames of pure evil.

The daemon laughed, and the sound was chilling even in the heat. It was the laugh of a creature to whom the most unspeakable cruelty was the most natural of things, that found pleasure in the pain and fear of others, that somehow fed on them as an epicure might feast on pickled lark's tongues. Its mouth opened wider and he could see yellow teeth and a long snaky bifurcated tongue. It leaned forward, and he could feel the heat radiating from it. The thing emanated it like a furnace. The tongue snaked forward and licked his face.

This is not real, Felix thought. This is merely a horrible dream. But he knew it was not. The daemon knew it too.

'You are mine,' it said. 'By Tzeentch, you should not have come here.'

'It was not my idea,' he said. The creature backhanded him with its open palm. He could see that it had long talon-like nails.

'I do not like your human humour,' it said. 'I like your fear, and your pain.'

'Not many openings for a jester around here, then,' said Felix because he could think of nothing better. It was a weak joke, but it annoyed the daemon, and that was about all he could manage at the moment. The thing moved eye-blurringly swiftly again. His head smacked against the warm rocks. Small stars danced before his eyes. Pain blurred his vision. Felix lashed out with his foot, but the heavy chains slowed him, and the thing danced aside easily.

'I like it when my food struggles,' it said, in the sort of voice a cat might have used to a mouse, if it were capable of speech.

'I'll see what I can do to oblige,' said Felix, throwing himself forward against the chains once more, hoping to catch it with one of the links. It danced away and returned slashing with its claws.

TECLIS SAW THE glowing oval ahead, and the shapes that surged around it. He knew then that this was not going to be easy. The man had been sucked into one of the reality bubbles floating through the paths. Perhaps even one constructed by his own thoughts and fears. He was trapped within it, and there were daemons all around it. A few had entered already to feed. Teclis had no idea what was awaiting them within it, but he knew that in order to rescue the human, they were going to have to go in.

'There are daemons ahead,' he said to the dwarf.

'Bring them on,' said Gotrek Gurnisson. 'My axe has a thirst.'

FELIX BIT BACK a scream as the daemon's needle-like talons pierced his bicep. Blood stained his shirt. Blood filled his mouth. It was all his, too, despite his best efforts to hit the daemon.

'Giving up so soon,' it said, malicious humour filling its voice. 'I have barely started and my kindred have yet to have their turn. It's been an age since we had such sport, or so it feels to us. It's not

often you humans are foolish enough to enter the Paths of the Old
Ones unprotected.'

'Go to hell,' said Felix.

'We're already there, or hadn't you guessed?'

As SOON AS they contacted the bubble reality, Teclis knew it was
going to be bad. Humans always had vivid imaginations and quaint
superstitions about hell, and he guessed that he was now inside one
of them. Still, he thought, it could be worse, we could be caught in
a dark elf's dreams.

'I can smell daemons,' said the dwarf. 'Where are we?'

'You would know what a daemon smells like, would you?'
sneered Teclis before he could stop himself. Clever, he thought, very
diplomatic.

'Actually, elf, I would. And I can smell them now. Along with
brimstone and sulphur.'

'I'll take your word for it,' said Teclis. 'We're in a bubble reality created from the stuff of Chaos. I am guessing it is one of the human
hells.'

'A bubble what?' said the dwarf, stomping forward across the reddish stone between the fire pits. 'Never mind. I think we have found
what we came for.'

A smiling daemonic figure looked up, and said, 'Oh good, more
food.'

Teclis smiled back at it. The daemon's face froze and he looked
closer at what he was seeing, and then the smile vanished from his
face completely. Swiftly Teclis wove a low-level spell of interference
which would prevent any of the creature's kindred from coming to
its aid, at least for a time. He cast spells of inhibition over the area
to restrict the creature's powers. He did not want to try anything
more ambitious because he wanted to conserve his power against
more pressing need. He did not want to have to draw on the tainted
magical energies within the Paths of the Old Ones unless he was in
the direst straits.

The daemon realised what he was doing and turned from the
human. He threw himself at Teclis, his form changing in mid-air
even as he did so. He became a creature much larger, far more ugly
with scaly reptilian skin and huge jaws full of needle-like teeth. Teclis
had his sword out instantly but before he could do anything the
massive axe flashed forward. The daemon's wings opened with a
snap, hurling it backward out of the way at the last instant. Still,
despite its eye-blurring speed, the dwarf had managed to connect.
Where the axe had hit, the daemon's flesh was scorched as if by

flame. Its eyes widened with malice and hate. Anger and fear flickered over its expression. It opened its mouth and let out a long wailing howl, like a wolf summoning its pack to fight. From far off in the distance came the sound of response, and Teclis felt daemons press forward against the wards he had set. The spells were not intended to stop them, only slow them and cause them pain. He was gratified to realise that they were performing their work well, even here in this strange realm.

The daemon was less pleased. 'Soon, we shall feast upon your souls,' it said, but it sounded less than confident.

'I grow tired of endless bombast,' said the dwarf. 'Now you die.'

Teclis noted that their surroundings had changed. The crumbling cavernous walls now resembled well-dressed stone. There was even a hint of delicate elvish sculpting. He guessed that his presence and that of the dwarf was altering this bubble of reality subtly. It was only to be expected in a place so malleable.

The daemon looked at the dwarf and then at his axe. He was measuring himself against his opponent and quite obviously found himself wanting. He turned swiftly and lunged for the human, intent on killing him rather than letting him be rescued. Teclis could not allow that. He sent a bolt of energy surging towards the daemon. It was not enough to destroy it, but it was enough to cause it considerable pain. Using the lightning as a whip, he drove the creature away from its prey. It disappeared howling into the stone corridors.

'It will be back,' Teclis said. 'And it will bring friends.'

'I care not,' said the dwarf, moving over to the human. The axe flashed. The chains snapped, and the man slumped forward but recovered himself so that he did not fall. A moment later he reached down and picked up his sword. As soon as it was in his fist, he stood taller and straighter, and seemed ready for action.

'I am grateful for the rescue,' he said. 'Have you found an ally or is this another daemon of this foul place?'

'Worse than that, manling,' said Gotrek Gurnisson. 'It's an elf.'

Teclis ignored the jibe; he had other things to do. The daemons were coming closer, pushing into this bubble reality, in search of their prey. They were in sufficient number that he doubted that even he and the dwarf could stand against them all, at least in this place, and the daemons were trying a new strategy. Rather than trying to painfully push through his wards, they were collapsing the bubble reality, pricking its edges and allowing the magical energies to flow in and sweep away his delicate spell weave like the tide overwhelming a child's sandcastles on the beach.

'Elf or daemon, you have my gratitude, sir,' said the human. They exchanged names and introductions.

'You are very welcome, but now we must go,' said Teclis. The dwarf glared at him. Teclis felt that given the Slayer's avocation it would not be the cleverest of things to inform him that an overwhelming horde of opponents was about to descend upon them. He decided on telling the lesser, but still worrying enough, truth.

'This bubble reality is about to collapse, and a tide of wild magical energy flow in. I doubt this is the sort of doom you seek, Slayer. It would be a rather pointless death.'

The dwarf nodded. Teclis gathered his magical energies around him once more, cloaking himself and the dwarf and the human. Heartbeats later the bubble did indeed give way. He could feel the tide of magical energy smashing through his delicate weaves. A moment later, the walls glowed and vanished and they were back in the seething sea of magical energy. This was not a good place to attempt to fight the daemons. It was their natural home and their senses were far more attuned to such a place than any mortal being's, even his. He thought that perhaps he could impose his will on a bubble reality and create a place more suited to himself and his companions, but that would be a futile strategy in the end. He would have to maintain it against the combined efforts of the daemonic horde to tear it down, and en masse they would prove stronger than he, at least in this space and time. What they needed more than anything else at this moment was to get out of here, and there was only one way to do that.

He let the protective sphere of enchantments rush free into the currents. It hurtled forward like an inflated wine bladder thrown into a stream. He wove his most powerful and painful protective enchantments around its edges, and bound them as tight as he could. He applied the force of his will to sending them hurtling ever faster down the energy stream in the direction he wanted to go. For a moment they tumbled onwards faster and faster, and he thought they might outdistance the horde that pursued them, but then like sharks scenting blood the daemons set off in pursuit.

Teclis sensed them drawing closer. The runes on the dwarf's axe grew brighter. The human's face seemed strained, which given the circumstances they had just rescued him from was hardly surprising. They might all find themselves in similar circumstances soon, if he did not find a way out of here. Or they might find their flesh rent asunder and their souls the food of daemons.

* * *

FELIX LOOKED OUT beyond the confines of the strange shimmering spell-sphere in which they floated and wondered if what he was seeing was real. His experience with the daemon had left him doubting the evidence of his senses. Had Gotrek and this elf really shown up and rescued him, or was this all some sort of subtle torment dreamed up by the hell spawn? At any moment, was he likely to find himself back in that evil-smelling dungeon, in the clutches of that nightmarish creature? His heart beat faster and his palms grew sweatier at the mere thought of it. For a moment, he felt as if his sanity might be overthrown by the hideous prospect. He felt himself teeter on the edge of a vast abyss. What if he really was dead, and this really was some sort of hell?

Slowly, one step at a time, he stepped back from the edge. If this was a hell, it was a peculiar one indeed, and he doubted that even a daemon's imagination would extend so far as having Gotrek appear in the company of an elf. That was stretching probability entirely too far. To distract himself from his uncertain thoughts, he concentrated on his companions.

The Slayer looked deeply, deeply unhappy. He glared daggers at the elf and then at Felix and muttered to himself in dwarfish. Felix wondered what he had done to deserve such looks, but slowly it dawned on him that the elf was a wizard, and Gotrek must have made some sort of pact with him in order to win Felix's freedom. He could easily imagine that such a debt of honour was not the sort of obligation the dwarf cared to be under.

But who was this stranger and where had he come from? It seemed unlikely he had just been wandering about through these strange extra-dimensional passages. Felix studied the elf. He had never really had the opportunity to study one at such close range before although he had seen a few in the streets of Altdorf in his youth.

Teclis was taller than a man and much thinner. Indeed, he was quite feeble-looking, more so than any elf Felix could ever recall seeing before. He was extremely thin, and his flesh seemed almost translucent. His hands had long, extremely thin and fine fingers. His face was narrow and whatever physical weakness he might suffer from was not reflected there. It was a face that should have belonged to a fallen god, sculpted by centuries of pain. The almond-shaped eyes were clear and cold and cruel. The thin lips were curved in a malicious smile. Felix could understand why the dwarfs were so prejudiced against elves if they all looked like that. He seemed to be looking out on the world with a constant sneer, judging everything by the high standards of his race and finding it all unworthy.

Be careful, Felix told himself, you do not know this. You may simply be judging him in the light of Gotrek's attitude. He has done you no harm, indeed he helped rescue you, and at this moment seems to be doing his best to get us all out of this terrible place. As he thought this, Felix recognised another source of his prejudices.

Teclis was a mage and obviously a very powerful one. With a man like Max Schreiber he could accept this. He knew that he possessed a common humanity, a shared set of values with the wizard, but looking at this elf he was not at all sure he could say the same thing. There was something almost as alien about those coldly beautiful features as there was about an orc, or a vampire. Teclis might superficially look like a human, more so in some ways even than Gotrek, but Felix could not help but think that his point of view was even more remote from mankind's than the Slayer's.

He tried to recall all his tutors had told him of elves. He knew they were an ancient race, civilised when men had still been barbarians. They were mighty sailors and explorers and wizards without equal. They were said to be cruel and degenerate and given over entirely to pleasure. Elvish slavers often raided the coast of the Old World, and mortal man never saw those they took again. Some scholars claimed that there were two types of elves, some sworn to light, some sworn to darkness, and that it was the latter that enslaved mankind. Others claimed this was simply a convenient fiction that allowed elf traders to disclaim responsibility for their cruel corsair kindred. How was Felix to know what or who to believe? His own experience of such things was extremely limited.

Some said they were immortal, others only that they were extremely long-lived. This elvish wizard might well be the same Teclis who had fought against the last great Chaos incursion during the time of Magnus the Pious over two centuries ago. Was that possible? More likely he was simply named for that mighty wizard.

Felix shook his head. Looking at that ancient, smooth and ageless face, he could believe that this was the same mage. Perhaps if they got out of this, he would ask him. Then the implications of that thought struck him – was it possible that he had been rescued from daemons by a hero of ancient times, a being whose name he had read in books? Did legends still walk the earth by the light of day?

Suddenly he heard the wizard say: 'Beware! Danger is near!'

CHAPTER TEN

FELIX SAW THAT the shifting currents of the alien space around them were changing again. Hideous faces were pressing against the outside of the sphere. Some of them resembled people he had once known – Ulrika, Max, Snorri, Albrecht and many others – but their faces were hideously changed, fanged and malevolent. Some of them were like his father and brothers and others were completely unrecognisable, although all shared the same eerie and evil appearance.

Some had the faces of dwarfish women and children as well as males; some even bore a distinct family resemblance to the Slayer. Others were elven, beautiful and deadly-looking. There were handsome elf males and beautiful females, and a towering figure in black rune-encrusted armour. He heard his companions gasp as if they recognised some of the visages. Gotrek spat a curse and aimed his axe at the edge of the sphere.

It passed through and bit into one of the laughing faces. An eerie scream sounded as the sphere shuddered and appeared about to collapse. The elf let out a pained gasp and said, 'Do not do that! If you break the sphere then we will all drown in this vile stuff. It is the only thing that protects us at this moment.'

'I need no protection,' said Gotrek angrily.

'Do not be so sure, dwarf,' said the elf, and there was an edge to that musical voice that had not been there before. 'Even that axe can only protect you for so long in these mystical currents. Soon you would become like them – lost souls, daemons, a dishonour to your clan.'

The elf added the last as if it was an afterthought, but Felix thought he saw the subtle barb there. Gotrek grimaced. 'I am already a dishonour to my clan.'

'Then you will have no chance of redemption, only a chance to deepen their dishonour.' Elf though he might be, the wizard obviously knew something of dwarfs. Gotrek fell silent, save for the occasional muttered curse.

Before Felix had a chance to say anything, an eerie high-pitched sound penetrated the sphere. It was a sound such as souls in rapture might make – calm, peaceful and wonderful. It promised everything your heart might desire. Peace if you were weary of struggle, happiness if you were tired of melancholy, outright joy even seemed possible now and forever.

At first, it seemed ludicrous that those faces should sing such a song, and he realised that this was just some subtle spell, used by the daemons to try and ensnare him. It was a pathetic trick, an obvious lure, and it was as easy to ignore as to see through. Then he looked closer and he could see that the faces had altered. They were friendlier now, and smiled at him as one might at a long-departed loved one who had just returned.

'They cannot yet break through my shield, unless your companion aids them with his axe,' said Teclis. 'But it is only a matter of time. Pray to your human gods that we can escape before they do so. In this place none of us will have the strength to resist them for long.'

What did the wizard mean, Felix thought? It was becoming increasingly obvious that the beings out there meant them no harm. They were friendly, welcoming – all of what had happened earlier had merely been a misunderstanding. They were willing to share with them the secret of eternal happiness. All you had to do was to be willing to listen.

Part of Felix knew this was simply not true. These were the false promises of daemons, but the part of him that was frightened and tired wanted desperately to believe that what they said was true, to put an end to this suffering and anxiety forever. He offered up a prayer to Sigmar. These were the ways the subtlest of daemons worked on men, tempting them when they were at their lowest ebb, promising them a surcease from their travails. He knew he should not want to believe them, but still he did. Worse yet, he knew that as his desire increased, so the spells protecting him weakened. His own connection to the daemons was weakening the wards.

He saw another face he recognised. It was that of the creature that had tormented him. It no longer looked so wicked. It looked ashamed, apologetic. It beckoned to him to come closer, so that it might apologise. In spite of himself, Felix felt the urge to respond.

Outside the sphere, the Paths of the Old Ones flickered past. All around the daemons crowded in, preparing for the moment when the protective spells would give way.

TECLIS KNEW IT was only a matter of time now before his wards eroded. The dwarf's axe had severed the weave. Given the chance, he might have resealed them, but at the moment it was all he could do to hold them closed. Worse yet, Felix Jaeger was faltering. He already had a connection with the daemons out there, having once fallen into their clutches. If they got out of this alive, Teclis knew he might eventually have to perform some rituals of exorcism to remove the taint from the man's soul and sever any residual link to the creatures of hell. If they survived... Right now, he needed to find a way to ensure that they did.

A glance at the dwarf showed no weakness there. If anything, the dwarfish kind were even more resistant to the lures of Chaos than elves – a certain stubbornness had been bred into them early in creation. And even if that were not the case, the weapon Gotrek Gurnisson bore would have protected him from any of their wiles. Doubtless the first few of the creatures to break through his defences would die the final death, but after that Teclis did not see how even the mighty dwarf could survive in this place.

Frustratingly, he could sense that they were getting close to the source of the disturbances he had been tracking. With every heartbeat, they were nearer to the great pulses of power that threatened to destroy this ancient network. If only they had the time, he felt certain he could locate the source of the disturbance and neutralise it. In terms of the distances within the paths, they did not have much further to go. Unfortunately, it was only a matter of heartbeats before his defences were overwhelmed and they were thrown into the current to deal with the daemons as best they could.

Even as this thought passed through his mind, he noticed a swirling vortex of force nearby. It was an exit path, of that he was sure. Given a few seconds they could reach it, and return to the world of men and elves and dwarfs. The siren song grew louder, and a taloned hand reached through the protective sphere. He sensed the presence of the daemons all around them. There was no other choice – if they were going to escape they were going to have to do it now, and face the consequences of his decision later.

'Prepare to do battle,' he said and sent them tumbling headlong towards the portal.

FELIX HEARD THE elf speak and braced himself. He had no idea what was about to happen, but he guessed that it was not going to be good. He was almost sorry that the elf had interrupted his reverie, for he felt he had come closer to understanding the inhabitants of this strange and wonderful place than any man ever had before. He knew that if only he could communicate with those strange intelligences, he might achieve wonderful things, far beyond the dreams of normal mortals.

All such thoughts were swept aside as he felt a sudden tremendous burst of acceleration. They tore free from the pursuing beings and headed towards a swirling whirlpool of light. Moments later they were flung through what felt like a normal atmosphere, and landed on hard stone. Felix felt all the air being blasted from his lungs by the force of the impact. He hit the ground rolling, doing his best to kill his velocity. He knew he had acquired a few more scrapes as he did so.

Quickly he pulled himself to his feet. They were once more in a long stone corridor like the one he and Gotrek had been in before he had been cast into the maelstrom of alien energy. Behind them was a glowing archway, the like of which he had seen before although this one was marked with different runes. Gotrek was already on his feet, quick as a cat, and had turned to face the archway. The elf somehow remained floating in the air at about shoulder height, surrounded by a strange mystical glow. Chained lightning circled his staff, the gems set in his armlets and towering headpiece gave forth an eerie light. The look on his face was as grim as Gotrek's. Both of them seemed prepared to fight.

Felix took in a lungful of air, grateful for the substantial feel of it even though it was damp and smelled musty. Whatever he had been breathing in the paths had been much rarer stuff. He felt slightly dizzy now but held himself upright and waited for whatever it was his companions expected.

Nor did he have to wait long. Within moments daemonic shapes, humanoid, but winged and fanged and taloned, had taken shape in the glowing light of the archway, emerging from it like swimmers from water. The sight of them in no way reassured Felix. Some of them were feminine but with shaven heads and massive crab-like claws. They gave forth a strange musk. Along with them were hounds with long, prehensile tongues and soft doe-like eyes that held the glitter of evil humour. Felix had seen their like before, during the Siege of Praag. The thought that he could recognise such things was a profoundly disturbing one.

Their leader was the batwinged humanoid that reminded him of the creature who had tortured him, but who here seemed at once more beautiful and more horrible. Behind him he could see more of the creatures trying to push through. The runes on the gateway glowed, and ruddy lightning bolts flickered over the surface of the light. The daemons and their hounds screamed but kept coming. It was obvious they had triggered some ancient device set to defend against their kind, but whatever it was, it was too enfeebled now to hold them for long.

Gotrek laughed and threw himself forward. The great axe cleaved through the daemons, rending them asunder. They disintegrated into a shower of sparks and a sickly sweet odour. They left no corpses. As Felix watched, some of the sparks tried to return through the archway, but they were met by the red lightning and over- whelmed.

Despite seeing the fate of their comrades, more of the daemons and their long snouted beasts pushed forward. By sheer weight of numbers they drove the Slayer away from the portal. Gotrek con- tinued to hack and cleave, destroying them as they came at him. A few decided to seek easier prey and swept around the edges, flank- ing the Slayer and coming towards Felix and the elf.

Felix met the first of the daemon women head on. She aimed a claw at his head. The huge lobster-like pincer looked as if it would snap his neck like a twig. He ducked beneath it, aiming a blow upward and taking her through the throat. She disappeared into a cloud of sparks leaving only that peculiar musky perfume behind.

Felix had fought these creatures before, and they had seemed much tougher then. He doubted that he himself had become any stronger, so he could only conclude that something about the sor- cery in this place was weakening them and leaving them vulnerable. It seemed that if he and his companions had been at a disadvantage within the sorcerous web of the paths, then the shoe was quite defi- nitely on the other foot here.

The winged creature that had tortured him was hurtling over the Slayer's head towards Teclis. It hit the glow surrounding him and bounced away screaming. Filled with rage and a lust for revenge, Felix leapt upward, jabbing his blade through the crea- ture's crotch and twisting. It too vanished, its essence trying futilely to return to the place beyond the portal.

Felix smiled grimly and moved to aid Gotrek, although the Slayer did not appear to need his help. He had already carved his way through the daemons opposing him. The onslaught from beyond slackened, and at that point the elf began to chant a spell. Instantly the remaining creatures were sucked backwards towards the void, coming apart as if sliced by fine invisible wires when they hit the red light web of the ancients. In seconds the corridor was clear although the howling mass of the mob was visible beyond. Even as Felix watched, the ruddy light seemed to thicken and congeal forming first a translucent film and then a hard opaque layer over the portal. He shook his head, not quite understanding what was going on.

'It seems that this incursion has activated some ancient ward,' said the elf. 'Unfortunately, it will prevent us from using this portal again ourselves for quite some time, although I doubt that using it would be quite such a good idea. Doubtless the daemons are waiting beyond, hoping we are foolish enough to stumble back through and allow them to take their revenge.'

Gotrek sucked his teeth loudly but said nothing. The elf's presence was something of a strain for him. He looked as if he would like nothing more than to take his axe and start hewing. Felix was glad that he restrained himself. It was obvious that they owed a debt of honour to the wizard.

'Where are we? What is this place? How do we get out?' he asked.

'We are within an artefact of the Old Ones, and this is not the time or place to discuss it. As to how we get out – follow me. If you please, sir dwarf,' the elf added with exaggerated politeness. Gotrek's fingers tightened around the haft of his axe. Felix could see his knuckles whitening. A sensible man would have fled at that point, but the elf seemed oblivious. Felix was wondering whether his own nerves could stand the strain of this for much longer.

He fell into step behind the elf, and considered his words. The Old Ones were a legend, a race of god-like beings that had vanished from the world long ago. Some scholars claimed that they were the fathers of the present gods banished by their rebellious children. Others wrote that they had brought some cosmic doom upon themselves and fled. Most tomes said nothing about them at all. Only the vaguest of hints could be found in even the most ancient texts.

In spite of this, the elf seemed certain of what he had said, and he, of all people, ought to know. Felix paid more attention to his surroundings now, looking for clues about the beings that had made these things. The stonework was rough-hewn but marked by glyphs of some oddly reptilian design. Felix was not quite sure how he got that impression, but get it he did. Perhaps they were mere decoration, perhaps they were protective wards. How could he tell? Max Schreiber would doubtless have had a theory about this, he thought. Why was he never around when you needed him?

Suddenly, a thought struck him. These corridors were obviously a link between the real world and the odd world beyond the portal. 'An antechamber,' he said aloud.

'A good guess, Felix Jaeger,' said the elf. 'Yes. Doubtless this place is a bridge between our world and the place through which those paths run. It is neither here nor there, caught between the two worlds.

'And that would mean at the far end of this corridor, we will find a way back into our world,' said Felix.

'I most certainly hope so,' said Teclis. 'Otherwise we may well prove to be stuck here forever.'

'Entombed forever with an elf,' muttered Gotrek. 'Truly this is the gateway to hell.'

CHAPTER ELEVEN

ALTHOUGH HE DID his best to hide it, Teclis was desperate. The way back into the Paths of the Old Ones was effectively sealed from this point. Even if he could break through the ancients' protective spells, doubtless the daemons would still wait beyond. They were immortal and malicious and could take as much time as they liked. He could not risk waiting for them to depart.

Inwardly he cursed his decision to rescue the human and the dwarf. They had cost him valuable time and energy on his quest, and what had he got for his trouble? An ungrateful surly wretch of a Slayer, and a human who appeared on the verge of madness, or giving way to Chaos. He knew he would have to check later for the possibility of daemonic possession. Certainly once they were out of the paths an exorcism would have to be performed.

He matched his breathing to his stride and performed the calming mental exercises he had learned as an apprentice. What was done was done. There was no sense in regretting it. And he could not believe it was simple chance that brought the dwarf and that axe into his path. The gods were taking a hand here, he felt. The question was – which gods? Not the powers of Chaos as far as he could tell, not with that weapon. Perhaps the Ancestor Gods of the dwarfs, perhaps those of his own people. A meeting between the bearer of that axe and the mightiest elven wizard of the age, bearer of the staff of Lileath and the war crown of Saphery, had to hold a deeper significance.

Calmness returned. He took in his surroundings. The stones here appeared to be less worn and less corrupted by Chaos than the ones in Ulthuan. He asked a question that had been nagging at the back of his mind for some time. 'How did you come to be within the Paths of the Old Ones?'

'It was an accident,' said Felix Jaeger. 'We were pursuing a Chaos sorcerer and his minions when a large daemon appeared and...'

Teclis laughed softly. The man's manner was quite matter of fact, even though he was discussing things that would have terrified many an ancient elf.

'Something funny, elf?' asked the dwarf. Teclis shook his head.

'I find your composure in the face of such things... refreshing.'

'I was not very composed at the time,' said the man. 'But things happened so suddenly once we entered the chamber...'

Doubtless it was a chamber just like the one in Ulthuan. The Chaos sorcerer must have been the one to open it. That meant the beastmen he had seen had not simply wandered into the paths by accident. It seemed that followers of darkness had indeed gained access to the Paths of the Old Ones. They must be using them to move swiftly between various places. The question was, were they aware or unaware of the other consequences of what they were doing? Did it matter? The followers of the Four Powers of Destruction were insane enough to keep using the paths anyway, regardless if it meant the destruction of Ulthuan, perhaps particularly if it meant the sinking of the island continent.

'The strange thing is that I believe I have seen the wizard before,' said Felix Jaeger.

'Yes?'

'At Praag, during the siege. He was one of those who summoned daemons, but was also doing other worse things.'

'Worse things?'

'Max Schreiber claimed the Chaos wizards were drawing the powers of dark magic down from the North.'

'Max Schreiber? Who is he?'

'A wizard of our acquaintance.'

'He knows what he is talking about. If daemons were summoned at Praag, something would have to increase the level of ambient magical energy for them to be able to manifest.'

'Max said something similar. He knows more about such things than I.'

'You already know as much as many wizards, Felix Jaeger.'

'And much good it has done me.'

Teclis considered this. These men had been at Praag, and so had the wizard they pursued. He considered Praag and its ancient hidden secret, and the way the forces of Chaos attacked the place so constantly and the rulers of Kislev constantly rebuilt it again. Oblivious to his dark thoughts, the man continued to speak, recounting their adventures within the great extra-dimensional labyrinth. Teclis nodded and encouraged him as they neared what he sensed was the exit.

He paused before the stone archway and studied the runes, then uttered the spell of opening. They emerged into what appeared to be another stone corridor running upwards and moved onwards in silence towards the light. Up ahead was another sealed doorway. He opened it with a spell. A moment later he was hit in the face with a gust of cold wet air and a flurry of driving rain. He stepped through into a puddle and looked around, pursing his lips in distaste.

The wind drove a lock of his hair into his eyes, and he pushed it back into place. In the distance he could smell marsh. The skies overhead were leaden, and full of clouds. All around were dark gloomy trees. Somewhere in the distance, thunder rumbled and the brief intense flash of lightning flickered across the sky. There was something odd about the way the winds of magic blew here. Their energies flowed turbulently through the sky. He would need to be careful with his spell casting. Still, it helped him evaluate where they were.

'As I suspected,' he said. 'We are in Albion.'

FELIX GROANED AT the elf's words. 'That's not possible,' he said.

'You have just come through the Paths of the Old Ones, fought with daemons and witnessed the creation of a bubble reality, and you are telling me that this is impossible?' said Teclis sardonically.

'But Albion is a thousand leagues to the north of the Old World, a place of mists and giants and fog...' Felix looked around him. The place was certainly cold and wet enough to be Albion.

'Albion is perhaps a hundred leagues at most north of your land, Felix Jaeger,' said Teclis. 'Elf ships pass its coast all the time.'

'Elf ships!' The words burst explosively from Gotrek's mouth. They had all the ring of an obscenity. Given how the Slayer felt about elves and ships, Felix supposed that was understandable. He was still surprised that the Slayer had not buried his axe in the wizard's skull.

'But Albion...' he said. Suddenly he realised how far he was from home. Even if what the elf said was correct, they had been in

Sylvania – scores, if not hundreds of leagues from the coast. In what seemed like a matter of a day at most, they had crossed a huge chunk of the continent and passed over the sea. This was magic to stun the mind. He looked around again, searching the forests for monsters. Nothing seemed inclined to emerge, but that might change at any moment.

Felix shook his head, and pulled up the hood of his cloak against the rain. Guiltily he realised that he had no idea what had happened to Snorri or Max, or if they were even still alive. Now there would be no way of finding out for months, if they could even find a way back home. Felix was not at all keen on the idea of re-entering the Paths of the Old Ones. Once had been quite enough for this lifetime.

'How are we going to get home?' he asked. The portal was already closed. Briefly, very briefly, he considered asking the elf to open the way and stepping back through it, then dismissed the thought out of hand. He would rather swim home than return the way they had come.

'We have other things to do first,' said the elf.

'*We?*' said Felix. He felt indebted to the elf but he was not sure he liked the assumption that he would automatically do his bidding. He liked even less the thought of the wizard implying such a thing to Gotrek. Dwarfs were a proud race, and touchy as impoverished noblemen with a string of debts. To his surprise, the Slayer said nothing. He merely shrugged and said; 'What would you have us do? I am in a hurry to pay off my debt.'

'It will take some time to explain,' said the elf. 'And first we should get away from this place. Who knows what might stumble through those portals.'

'I do not care,' said Gotrek.

'Alas, I do. It is difficult to explain such things as the Paths of the Old Ones while you are trying to beat off the onslaught of dae-mons. I do not think it likely they will find a way through, but I am loath to take the chance.'

'I see your point,' said Felix, who was, if anything, even less keen than the elf to confront any monsters that might materialise. 'Let's see if we can find some place to shelter. You can explain things to us as we walk.'

They strode downhill away from the stone ring. The rain fell harder. The lightning flashed closer. The thunder rumbled louder.

To HIS SURPRISE, Teclis found that his two companions grasped his explanation of events on Ulthuan quickly. Whatever else they might be, Felix Jaeger and Gotrek Gurnisson were not stupid. They listened and they absorbed what he said.

'You are telling me that if we do nothing Ulthuan will fall beneath the waves,' said the dwarf. 'I don't see the problem.'

'I might expect a dwarf to say something like that,' said Teclis, unexpectedly touchy. The dwarf's surliness was getting on his nerves, and he was not used to having to be cautious around anyone.

'All of elvenkind would be destroyed,' said Felix Jaeger.

'Not all, but most,' said Teclis.

'I still don't see the problem.'

'Then perhaps I can explain,' said Teclis trying to keep the sneer from his voice, and not entirely succeeding. 'What do you know of the Old Ones?'

'They are a legend,' said Gotrek Gurnisson. 'A race of gods older than the gods. Some claim they created this world. Others that they never existed at all.'

'They existed.'

'If you say so, elf.'

'I have consulted the Book of Isha within the Library of the Phoenix Kings. It was written in the time before Aenarion. A record of the golden age when elves and dwarfs were at peace, and the Old Ones still watched over the world. I have read the *Book of Valaya*…'

'You have what?' sputtered the dwarf.

'I have read the *Book of Valaya*.'

'An elf has read one of the sacred books…'

'There is a copy of the book in the Library at Hoeth.'

'The world has changed. Now only the Priestesses of Valaya consult those iron-bound tomes.' Another thought seemed to occur to the Slayer.

'You have read a book written in the High Tongue of the dwarfs?'

'Elves and dwarfs were not always enemies, Gotrek Gurnisson. In times gone past there were grammars and dictionaries written. Old Dwarfish is not a language much studied now among the elves, but I have an interest in such things…'

The dwarf glared at Teclis but did not speak further. He seemed on the verge of exploding.

'Both books claim the same thing. The Old Ones possessed powers greater even than our gods in many ways. They not only altered our world's climate, they did so by moving its position in space. They altered the seasons and the shape of the continents themselves. They raised Ulthuan up out of the sea, and made it a home for the elves.'

'Spare me the lessons in elvish mythology,' sneered the dwarf.

'These are not myths, they are truths. They used magic that almost beggars imagination to fix the continents in place and to keep Ulthuan above the waves. They span a web of magic from pole to pole, a lattice of forces that encircles the planet. The Paths of the Old Ones are part of that.'

'Why?' asked the man. He seemed to have no trouble believing this, but he possessed a very human curiosity.

'I do not know. Who can guess the motives of such beings? Not I!' Teclis wondered if he should avoid telling them his suspicions. All of the events of the past few hours tended to confirm his theories. He decided that he needed these two on his side. They were his only allies here, and they were potentially very powerful ones. 'It may be that the whole project, the shifting of the planet, the raising of continents, the lifting of both our peoples out of the mire of barbarism, was nothing more than a tiny part of some great cosmic scheme, the purpose of which I do not know.

'I do know that when the Old Ones left our world, Chaos came. The two things are connected, I am sure. The Old Ones built this whole system so that it connected with a mighty portal at the Northern Pole, a gateway on a size and scale that makes the portals we have passed through seem like a child's plaything. I suspect the Old Ones may have used it to pass to another world unimaginably remote. Perhaps they were like sailors shipwrecked here and what they built was a beacon or a lifeboat.

'Whatever its purpose, as they departed they worked some mighty ritual and it failed at least in part. Something went wrong with the portal. It opened a way to somewhere else. The dark powers of Chaos used it to enter our world and almost overran it. To this day, it remains there in the north, mostly quiescent but sometimes erupting like a volcano.'

'The god Grimnir passed into the North in search of it, and to find a way to close it. So much is written in the *Book of Stone and Pain*, in the time when the skies rained fire and the world was changed forever,' said Gotrek. It sounded like the words were torn out of him unwillingly.

'Then our myths agree on something, Gotrek Gurnisson, for so it is written in the *Book of Isha* as well.'

'I still do not see what this has to do with the Paths of the Old Ones.'

'All of these things are interlinked. Before I can tell you more I must have your word that you will tell no one of this.'

Felix nodded. Gotrek considered, as if wondering if the words contained some sort of snare, and then said, 'You have it.'

'Ages ago, evil mages attempted to destroy Ulthuan. They did so by unravelling the network of energies used to keep it above the sea. The attempt failed thanks to the effort of many heroic elven mages who gave their lives to prevent it. They stabilised the system and rewove the great net as best they could but they discovered that the work of the Old Ones was more damaged than they had imagined. Chaos was using the Paths of the Old Ones as a way to invade our world, and as a source of corruption. The places where they touched the earth became tainted places. My ancestors needed the power within the paths to stabilise Ulthuan. I suspect they got it by draining energy from the paths.'

'And now someone has opened the paths again,' said the man.

'The magical energy needed to maintain my homeland is being bled off and if something is not done soon, it will be destroyed.'

Gotrek Gurnisson cursed. He turned to a tree, lifted his axe. There was an awful crack as with one blow he sheared through it. Splinters flew everywhere. The tree began to topple. Teclis gasped; it was the most awesome feat of strength he had ever seen. The oak had been almost as thick through as his body, and solid. The tree's branches made a terrible noise as they impacted on those of other trees as it fell. The sound was like a mastodon stampeding through the forest.

'I hate trees almost as much as I hate elves,' said Gotrek Gurnisson.

'What has got into you, dwarf?' said Teclis.

'You have just given me the means to avenge the Beard,' said the Slayer.

'The what?' said Felix.

'It is an old tale,' said Teclis, 'and one best not dwelt on. An elven king insulted a dwarf ambassador in a shameful way. Suffice to say that because of it, the elves and dwarfs fought the bloodiest war in history. It's an insult the dwarfs still wish to avenge to this day.'

'You mean to say you would let a continent full of people be slain to avenge a beard?' Felix Jaeger asked the dwarf. He sounded incredulous.

'A land full of elves,' said the dwarf, in a grating voice. 'And not merely to avenge the clipping of the beard, but to right the many wrongs that are set to the elven account in the *Great Book of Grudges.'*

'Well, that's different, then,' said Felix Jaeger sarcastically. Teclis was pleased to see that the man was on his side, for it occurred to him that the simplest way for Gotrek Gurnisson to ensure the doom of Ulthuan was for him to use the axe and take Teclis's head. After that there would be no one capable of stopping the impending catastrophe in time. Perhaps, thought Teclis, now would be the time to use his most destructive spells. Best to slay the dwarf before the dwarf slew him. Still, he had one last throw of the dice.

'You swore to aid me,' he said.

'If it was not dishonourable,' said Gotrek Gurnisson. 'And you left that decision up to me.'

Teclis cursed inwardly. 'It is said dwarfs would haggle over a contract while the world burned.'

'It is said the words of an elf are as slippery as machine oil.'

'This is foolish,' said the man. 'You two stand and argue while the lives of a nation are at stake.'

'More than a nation,' said Teclis. 'If that will make any difference.'

'What do you mean by that?'

'The old ley lines do not just underpin Ulthuan. They run through other places – the Worlds Edge Mountains, for instance.'

'I do not believe you,' said the dwarf.

'Was there not a time when the mountains shook and many dwarfish cities suffered? Did not the skaven emerge to take one of your holds?'

'Karag Eight Peaks,' said the man.

'The skaven once experimented with machines that tapped the power of the ley lines. I do not know if they did this deliberately or unknowing. I would guess the latter, knowing the ratmen. In any case, the devices proved too deadly even for them...'

'Unless they are the ones behind our present troubles,' said the man.

'How would you know what the skaven do? Unless you consort with rats, which is not a thing I would put past elves.'

'We intervened when we sensed their sorceries, and sent a force of mages and warriors to destroy them. A few returned to tell us of the battle.'

'It must be a famous one, to be so well renowned,' sneered Gotrek Gurnisson.

'Not all who fight seek glory,' said Teclis, feeling his patience coming to an end. 'Nor do their names live forever afterwards. Some give their lives willingly so others might live on, and ask no reward.'

'And you would be one of those, would you, elf?'

Teclis smiled nastily. 'I have no intention of dying at all if I can help it,' he said.

'Sensible man,' he heard the human mutter under his breath.

'Are you with me? Or do you wish to go back on your word? Surely not even a dwarf can see something dishonourable in staving off a disaster that might engulf the mountain halls themselves.'

'Aye, if what you say is true.'

'If I am lying to you, kill me,' said Teclis.

'That goes without saying,' said the dwarf.

'What do you want us to do?' asked the human. He was visibly reluctant, caution and a desire for self-preservation obviously warring with the urge to help.

'Whatever I am doing, two such mighty warriors could be of help,' said Teclis. 'I fear I shall need swords and axes before this all ends.'

'I thought as much,' said the man. 'What I meant was – what do you want us to do now?'

'We need to find the source of the trouble and eliminate it. I must locate the Oracle of the Truthsayers, whoever she is. If we cannot now... well, we are on Albion, and perhaps close to our goal, for the records say that this is where the greatest temples of the Old Ones were in the ancient times. The main nexus of the ley lines is here, the grand confluence of all their magical energies. We must find it, and from there we must find a way to close the paths.'

'You are the wizard,' said Felix Jaeger. 'You know more of these things than us. Lead us to the temple and we will help you get in. After that, it's up to you.'

The man looked at the dwarf as if expecting disagreement, and was obviously surprised to find none.

'Very well,' said Teclis. 'But first we must rest and there are rituals that need to be performed.'

'Rituals?' said the man.

'First we must make sure the daemons cannot take you once more.'

'That sounds like a good idea to me. How will you ensure that?'

'There are spells I can perform that will secure your soul and your body, and break any links that might remain.'

'Links? You're telling me that those things in that weird other world might be able to find me again?'

'Unless I do something, it's almost certain. They will come to you in your dreams... at first.'

The man fell silent. He looked thoughtful and scared. The dwarf just looked angry, but that seemed to be the natural state of things.

'Best cast your spells then,' said the man.

'This will hurt somewhat,' said the elf.

'I suspected as much,' said the man. 'Let's get it over with.'

TECLIS LED THE way along the forest path, hoping that the two would follow him. He was impressed by the human's courage. He had endured the spells of exorcism with very little complaint and Teclis knew how painful they could be. The process had left its mark, though. The man's fingers constantly sought out the amulet Teclis had given him. Teclis considered the wisdom of that decision. It was worth parting with some of his own protections in order to ensure that his companion was not possessed. He was fairly certain that his spells had been successful, but with the strange flow of magic in Albion, it was best to take no chances. And there were other reasons for giving the human the talisman. If the dwarf turned against him, it would be as well to have an ally, willing or unwilling.

Even now he could sense the dwarf bubbling with rage, and the man's anxiety about their future peril. Felix Jaeger was right to be anxious, he thought. Whoever or whatever could open the Paths of the Old Ones would be a mighty foe indeed.

He let out a long sigh. He would face that peril when he came to it. Right now, his greatest worry was an axe in the back from a demented dwarf. His brother could have handled this situation so much better, he thought.

CHAPTER TWELVE

FELIX PULLED HIS sodden cloak tighter about him, and watched the air mist as he breathed. It was winter here, he thought, but winter was different from back in the Empire. In the Empire, snow lay thickly on the ground. Here it merely rained, although the rain was so cold it was like a thousand icy knives biting into your flesh. The ground squelched below his feet. The sky was the colour of lead. Stones erupted through the turf. He would almost have preferred the snow, he thought. Here it seemed like the skies wept along with the land.

For all that, the scenery was not without beauty. Occasionally when they came to gaps in the trees, he caught glimpses of rolling rugged hills, down whose sides streams scampered and played. Now and again, he thought he managed a glimpse of a stag or some roe deer moving through the forest. At the moment, in the distance he caught sight of a thin column of smoke rising into the sky. At first he was not certain, for it blended into the sky in such a way as to be almost invisible, but after a few more leagues of weary trudging, he knew that they were approaching habitation, and that it was towards this the elf had been guiding them all this time. His eyes are much, much keener than mine, Felix realised.

He wondered at the confidence of the elf. He could not have maintained the elf's air of supreme self-possession with Gotrek

114

muttering at his back. The elf, however, gave no impression of caring. He moved calmly and fastidiously down the slope, never missing a stride no matter how slippery the turf. For all his enfeebled appearance, he seemed tireless. Studying him, Felix noticed other things. His own boots were sodden with mud, and some of it spattered his cloak and britches. Gotrek's boots were filthy and streaks of red clay marked his bare arms. Yet Teclis was as clean as when they had started. His boots gleamed. His blue robes shimmered. Not even the tip of his staff was stained where it hit the ground.

How was this possible, Felix wondered? Were his clothes enchanted in such a way as to repel dirt, or was there some spell at work here? From listening to Max Schreiber, Felix knew that it cost a wizard some of his personal strength and endurance each time he used magic, that it tired them out the way running a race might tire any normal man. Surely not even a wizard as powerful as the elf appeared to be would waste his strength merely on keeping clean? Or perhaps he would, Felix thought; there was a cat-like fastidiousness about Teclis that Felix guessed was typical of elves. Not only that, at any time he got downwind of the elf, he caught the scent of a faint musky perfume such as a woman might wear. Nobles of the Empire carried pomanders to ward of the stinks of the street, but he had heard of few of them wearing perfumes. Another area in which elves differed from men, he thought.

Even in the elaborate headgear and jewellery, and the fine silk robes, there was nothing effeminate about the elf. He was dressed to a different standard than a man, that was all. Human nobles dressed like peacocks for show, to display their wealth. Perhaps it was the same for elves. There was something very aristocratic about the elf, an air of hauteur and languor that Felix would have found infuriating in a nobleman, but which somehow he did not mind in the elf. He did not feel as if the elf were behaving like this to put him in his place, as the son of an uppity merchant mingling with the upper classes, but that it was just the natural air of the Elder Race.

A thought occurred to Felix – was it possible that much of the pose of the human aristocracy was modelled on the behaviour of the older and more cultured race? He would never be in a position to know anyway. Nor did it matter all that much in their present situation.

He looked at the rising column of smoke again and felt a shiver of vague apprehension. They were strangers here, and he had heard rumours that all the folk of Albion were cannibals. Perhaps they were merely seamen's stories. There were other tales of human sacrifice and strange monsters in the swamps. The whole land was cloaked in impenetrable mists and ringed round by sharp savage rocks so that sailors rarely made landfall there save by shipwreck, and fewer still returned to tell of the treacherous voyage. And who knew if the tales could be trusted anyway? Sailors were not known for their honesty when speaking of their travels in taverns.

Looking back, the nightmarish trip through the Paths of the Old Ones was already starting to take on the quality of a dream. He doubted that the human mind could really absorb what he had seen there. It all seemed so unreal, particularly now that he was soaking in the all too real rain of Albion. He pushed his dark thoughts aside.

Albion! Were they really in Albion? Teclis seemed certain and he was in the best position of all to know. And what of his other claims, that the daemons could sense Felix and might even come looking for him? That part of his experience was all too easy to accept. He had encountered such creatures before in Praag, and in Karag Dum. He had no doubt of their malice or the fact that they might take his escape from their clutches personally. He offered up a prayer to Sigmar, for the safety of his soul, but given how effective his prayers had been in the past, he did not expect any help from the hammer wielder now. His hand strayed once more to the protective amulet the elf had given him, along with a warning never to remove it, even when he slept. It was a beautiful thing of elven workmanship. The chain was of some silvery alloy and the amulet itself was a disc of ivory inlaid with the curved elf runes, all of silver. Felix hoped that it was as powerful as it was beautiful. The thought of having his soul devoured by daemons was not a pleasant one.

He gave his attention back to Gotrek. The Slayer was being even more than usually surly. His one good eye was fixed on the elf's back as if he were contemplating using it for axe practice. Remembering the way Gotrek had casually chopped through that tree, Felix was more impressed than ever by the elf's composure. Still, he did not expect Gotrek to go for the elf, not without any warning anyway. Hacking an unarmed opponent down from behind was not the Slayer's way.

He fell into step beside the Slayer, but Gotrek merely glared at him, and looked away. Felix shrugged and strode forward to talk with the elf. Anything to distract himself from this freezing, constant rain.

'Are you related to the Teclis who fought alongside Magnus the Pious?'

'I am he.'

It was all Felix could do to keep his jaw from dropping. It was one thing to speculate about such a thing, but another entirely to have it confirmed. The elf gave him a look of malicious amusement.

'Long are the lives of elves,' he said.

'Short are the tempers of dwarfs,' Gotrek muttered, just loud enough to be heard.

Felix did not quite know what to say next. What did you say when you met a character you had once read about in your history books as a child, one who had mingled with the contemporaries of your great-great-great-great-grandfather? He supposed there were many questions his old professors would have killed to have him ask, but right now his mind was blank. 'So what was it like?' he said.

'Desperate, dirty, bloody and vile,' said the wizard. 'Like most battles. I saw friends die before they should have. There are few elves now, and every one lost is a tragedy.'

'That's a matter of opinion,' grumbled the Slayer. The elf ignored him with admirable composure. Felix knew that he could not have.

'Did you really fight the Witch King of Naggaroth?'

'I am surprised that you have heard of such matters,' said Teclis.

'My father is a merchant. He often does business in Marienburg. There is a colony of elves there even to this day. Word gets out. Stories get told.'

'I can imagine. Merchants are forever gossiping. I suppose it must be part of their trade.' Felix realised something else about the elf. His speech had the same sort of accent he had once heard his grandfather use back when he was a very small child. There was an archaic lilt to the tone of his words that suggested a being of great age, a fact that was singularly at odds with the elf's youthful appearance. He was suddenly reminded of the Countess, the ancient vampire he had encountered back in Sylvania, and he shivered. This time it was not from the cold.

'Is there something wrong?' asked the elf politely. 'Did my words upset you?'

'No. You just remind me of someone I once met.'

'From your expression, it was not a pleasant memory.' Felix was surprised that the elf was so perceptive about humans; then again, he supposed that after several centuries of meeting them you might have insights that few others would have. Once again, his thoughts drifted back to vampires, and from there to Ulrika, and that was not pleasant either.

'It was a vampire,' Felix blurted out.

Gotrek gave a short bark of laughter. Felix guessed that he found the comparison all too apt.

'You have encountered one of the arisen?' Teclis asked. Felix saw that he was interested.

'Several, actually.'

'You seem to have had an interesting career, Felix Jaeger. I am constantly surprised at how much you humans manage to cram into your short lives.' Felix could tell that Teclis did not mean to be offensive, but he was starting to understand what it was that dwarfs disliked about elves. He was starting to revise his earlier opinion about the elf's manner. The tone was faintly patronising without intending to be, and that just made it worse.

'I can see that I have offended you somehow,' said the elf. His tone made it clear that he did not care in the slightest. Perhaps the feelings and opinions of lesser beings were of no relevance if you were a powerful wizard, centuries old. Felix forced himself to smile blandly. Two could play this game, he thought.

'Not at all. It was I who offended you, perhaps, by inadvertently comparing you to one of the undead. If I gave offence, I apologise.'

'No apology is necessary, Felix Jaeger. I have taken no offence.'

Which was probably just as well, thought Felix. The last thing he wanted was to have this powerful mage angry with him. The current situation was potentially explosive enough without him adding to it.

'What did you think of the arisen?' The elf's tone was genuinely curious. 'Why do I remind you of one of them?'

'It's not exactly that you remind me of them,' said Felix, choosing his words carefully. 'It's merely that I was thinking that being so long-lived you might have similar attitudes and insights into the human mind.'

'No. The arisen regard your kind as their prey,' said Teclis. 'There are several fascinating monographs from the period of your Vampire Counts which expound their point of view quite cogently. Manheim's *Reflections on Mortality, Immortality and Immorality*, for example.'

'Never heard of it,' said Felix. He was quite surprised. He considered himself quite the scholar, and yet he had never heard of either the author or the book.

'The author was one of the arisen, a lackey of one of the von Carsteins. He fancied himself as something of a philosopher. His books were privately printed and distributed among his kind. Some of them fell into the hands of Finreir after the wars of the Vampire Counts. He brought them back to Ulthuan with him.'

'Any others that were found were most likely burned by the witch hunters,' said Felix.

'I know,' said the elf. 'Now there was a heinous crime.'

'A heinous crime? I do not think so. What could be so heinous about destroying a work by one of those evil creatures?'

'Destroying knowledge is never good,' said Teclis. 'And who is to say what is good and evil? Manheim regarded himself as no more evil than a human farmer. Indeed he regarded himself as less evil, for he did not kill his cattle but rather did his best to look out for their welfare.'

'That is something only an elf would say,' said Gotrek.

'Manheim said it, not me. He was not an elf.'

'Comparing people to cattle implies ownership,' said Felix. 'Is it right to own people?'

'Elves have done so in the past. Humans still do.'

'Dwarfs never have,' said Gotrek.

'Yes, yes,' said Teclis. 'Shall we take it as given that your race enjoys moral superiority over all others? That way we will be in agreement with the dwarfs themselves.'

'Elves still own people. Humans, dwarfs, elves,' said Gotrek. 'Slavers still attack the coasts.'

'This is true,' said Felix.

'Dark elves,' said Teclis.

'Are there any other kind?' asked Gotrek.

Teclis halted for a moment and turned to look at the Slayer. He seemed on the verge of losing his temper. Gotrek grinned in anticipation.

'There are dwarfs who worship Chaos. Does that mean all dwarfs are Chaos worshippers?'

Gotrek's knuckles whitened as he gripped his axe tight. He reached up and ran his thumb along the edge of the blade. A drop of bright blood showed. Felix knew he had to do something before violence inevitably erupted.

'Surely only the followers of Chaos will benefit if we fall out among ourselves now. We have a quest to fulfil that is more important than petty bickering.'

'There is nothing petty about such accusations, manling,' said Gotrek. There was a very hard edge to his voice.

'I was merely pointing out the flaw in your logic, not making an accusation,' said Teclis.

'And once again is proven the old saying: an elf will twist the meaning of his words to suit any purpose.'

'That is a dwarf saying, I imagine. I could reply with an elvish saying...'

What was it about these two, Felix wondered? Gotrek was rarely particularly rational but he was not stupid. Surely he could see the need for cooperation here? Teclis seemed like a very intelligent being but there was obviously something about the dwarf that goaded him to cold fury. It was like watching a cat and a dog eying each other. To tell the truth, he felt his own temper starting to fray.

'Cats and dogs, elves and dwarfs, men and Bretonnians,' he said.

'What?' said Teclis. Gotrek merely glared.

'It's an old joke,' said Felix. 'In the Empire, where I come from. I thought while we were all exhibiting our prejudices I might as well exhibit mine.'

'Has your trip through that hell damaged your mind, manling?' asked Gotrek.

'A fine example of your human humour, I am sure,' said Teclis. His tone of voice was a good deal chillier than the wind. Wonderful, thought Felix. I managed to distract them from each other by getting them angry with me. He could see it was an effective strategy, but he was not sure he could survive it for many days.

Felix shrugged. The sopping wet cloak shifted uncomfortably on his shoulders. He felt like comparing their behaviour to that of children but he was fairly certain it would not be good for his health. Instead he said, 'Perhaps we should concentrate on the matter at hand. I thought you wanted to save your people, Teclis of Ulthuan. And I believed that you had made a pledge to aid him, Gotrek.'

The dwarf bristled for a moment, and Felix feared for his life, but then like an attack dog deciding not to go for the throat, Gotrek settled back and lowered his axe. 'It has come to something when a dwarf needs to be reminded of his word by a human,' he said.

He actually sounded slightly ashamed. Felix was glad that Teclis had the good grace not to gloat. Indeed the elf looked a little abashed himself. Perhaps I might survive this after all, Felix thought. He considered the volatile nature of his companions and the situation – then again, perhaps not.

THEY STOOD ON a rise looking down on a most unusual village. Even in the gathering misty twilight, its strangeness was evident. It was built in the middle of a lake, amid a mass of reeds, and the houses appeared to either be on stilts or situated atop small artificial islands. Actually, houses was the wrong word for them. They looked far more primitive even than Sylvanian peasant dwellings. Causeways of mud and logs linked them. Fires glowed within. A few people were still abroad. Some sat on the causeways fishing. Others drifted on the lake in coracles. A few appeared to be walking on the surface of the fen, and Felix suspected magic until a closer look revealed that they were wearing stilts.

Felix looked at Teclis. 'What now?' he asked.

'We may as well seek shelter here for the night. There will be food and warmth and perhaps sanctuary where I can perform the needed rituals.'

'And what rituals would those be?' asked a voice from near at hand. Both the elf and the dwarf reacted instantly. Gotrek raised his axe and whirled. Teclis raised his staff and a nimbus of light played around it. Felix was impressed. He had never known anybody to take the Slayer off guard before. Nor did the elf look like one who could easily be ambushed.

He moved his hand to the hilt of his sword but did not draw it. 'Peace,' said the voice. It had a soft lilting accent but there was nothing weak in it. 'There is no need for violence between us. I merely asked a civil question.'

'Where I come from,' said Felix, 'it is customary for a man to introduce himself before questioning others.'

'And where would that be, my young friend?' Felix peered into the darkness to see who this suicidal maniac might be. He had given the man an excuse to make a civil introduction to two of the most dangerous beings Felix had ever met, and he seemed hell-bent on not taking it.

He could just see the figure of an old man, gnarled as an oak branch and just as tough-looking. He was wearing trews and a pleated cloak of a tartan pattern that blended into the undergrowth. A long sword was slung across his back. He leaned on a long spear as if it were a staff. His nose was small and snub, his smile wide, his teeth yellow and feral-looking. There was a malicious glint in his bright blue eyes as he returned Felix's inspection. Strange angular tattoos blotched his cheek and brow. 'The Empire,' said Felix. The old man laughed.

'No one from the Empire has made it through the mists in a long time, not since my grandfather's time, when those hell-spawned greenskins arrived.'

'You mean orcs – they are not from the Empire,' said Felix.

'They occupy the same clanlands,' said the old man.

'And men from the Empire arrived at the same time?' asked Teclis. The old man gave him a look of studied contempt.

'Only your folk come and go as they please, spawn of Naggaroth,' said the old man. 'And by the time this night is out, there will be one less of those unless you surrender your weapons.'

Gotrek simply gave him an incredulous look. The stranger raised his hand and gave a piercing whistle.

From out of the long grass a score of archers appeared. Most astonishingly of all for Felix, from out of the mere more spearmen appeared, their long harpoons like spears drawn back to cast.

'There's no need for violence,' said Teclis.

'I'm afraid there is,' said the old man. 'Unless you surrender your weapons now.'

'You will take this axe from my cold dead hand,' said Gotrek. 'Though it pains me to have to defend an elf.'

Felix flinched, expecting at any moment to feel an arrow bury itself in his back or his eye. Things were certainly not looking good, he thought. Just then the rain started again.

CHAPTER THIRTEEN

THE OLD MAN gestured again, and suddenly arrows flashed through the air. Felix threw himself flat, aiming for the oldster, but with surprising agility for a man his age, he had already rolled behind the rock, out of sight. Felix cursed and glanced back to see if Gotrek or the elf had been hit. He was astounded by what he saw.

The arrows bounced away from the area around them, repelled by a glowing sphere centred on the elf mage. Teclis gestured again and the men of Albion all stood frozen. A few gave gasps of fear, but they stood still as stone. Felix looked at the ones who had seemingly emerged from the water like mermen. He could see that each of them held a cut reed in his mouth, most likely as a tube to breathe through. It was a trick he had heard of, but it spoke of enormous patience, not to mention courage, to actually be able to use it.

Felix looked behind the rock and saw that the old man stood there. Frozen. Beads of sweat ran down his forehead, as he tried to resist the spell. Felix considered very briefly running him through with his sword, but resisted the impulse. He was tired and scared but there was no need for killing just on that account. Yet.

'Your magic is strong, servant of Malekith, but the Light will overcome.'

Felix glanced at the elf, expecting him to look angry. Instead he looked amused. 'It seems that we have another who shares your opinion of elves, Gotrek Gurnisson.'

'A sensible man,' said Gotrek. 'It would pain me to have to slay him. And there's no honour in taking an axe to men who stand like sheep for the slaughter.'

'Your familiar speaks truth,' said the old man. 'Free us and let us settle this like warriors.'

Wrath clouded Gotrek's face. He looked as if he was going to take his axe to the old man there and then. 'I have never been familiar with an elf,' he said.

Felix shook his head. Diplomacy was obviously not the strong suit of anybody around here. He looked closer at the old man. His face was tattooed in odd geometric patterns that reminded Felix of something. Of course, he thought, the runes on the standing stones. 'Are you really so tired of living, old man?' he said. 'Not content with ordering an attack on a powerful wizard, you must insult a dwarf Slayer. There is a fine line between courage and stupidity, and you have crossed it.'

'And you are obviously enthralled by elvish magic. I have seen it often. Good men often return as slaves in the service of the Dark Ones.'

'That makes all three of us now,' said Felix. He looked at the elf for a lead. Max Schreiber had told him how draining magic could be, but the elf showed no sign of any strain at holding a score of warriors immobile. What were they to do, Felix wondered? We can't just slit these men's throats, can we?

'I am not what you think I am,' said Teclis. 'I am no servant of the Witch King. Indeed I have been his enemy for many years.'

'So you say,' said the old man. 'But I have only your word for that.'

'Tell me, does it mean nothing to you that I hold you in my power, and yet have spared your lives, despite your insults to myself and my companions?'

'This could just be some elvish trick. You may wish to enthral us or bring doom on us in some dark and terrible way...'

Fire entered the wizard's eyes and when he spoke his words were full of menace. He became a figure of immense power, suddenly cloaked in a strange majesty. His face looked carved from stone.

'I am Teclis, of the line of Aenarion, of the firstborn of Ulthuan. If I wished to destroy you or enthral you or bring doom down upon your pitiful barbarian village, it would already be done and there is nothing that you or your followers or your childish magic could do to stop me, old man.'

Felix believed him. At that moment, he was as menacing as anything Felix had ever seen, and he had looked upon powerful daemons in his time. At that moment there was something almost daemonic about the elf himself. Then Teclis shrugged and the spell was broken. Suddenly the old man and his followers were free to move. They slumped to the ground, weapons slipping from nerveless fingers.

'Fortunately for you, I do not,' said Teclis. 'We require food and shelter and a place to sleep for the night. You will give it to us, and in the morning we will be on our way. You will be recompensed for your trouble.'

Almost as if the words were torn from his throat unwillingly, the old man said, 'Aye, as you wish. For this night and this night only you will be guests in Crannog Mere.'

Felix had heard heartier welcomes. He wondered if the elf knew what he was doing. Maybe they would wake up in the night to find knives buried in their throats. He looked at the elf and then at Gotrek and decided no, that was not going to happen. Whatever doom might lie in wait for this pair, it would not be a knife in the dark from some barbarian tribesman.

THEY FOLLOWED THE barbarians down to the edge of the water. Felix never took his eyes off them, for he feared that at any moment, despite their leader's words, they might turn and attack. If that happened, he knew there would be carnage.

At the water's edge the men walked straight in. Felix gasped, for they seemed to be walking on water. Their feet barely sank below the surface even though the water had been deep enough to conceal spearmen. Was this some new form of magic, he wondered?

Teclis followed them and so did Gotrek with barely a shrug and a sniff. Knowing that the others were waiting for him, Felix put his feet in the water and the answer to the mystery became clear. Just below the surface was a narrow causeway, cunningly concealed so that it could only be seen from close at hand. The men of Crannog Mere obviously knew the way by heart for they did not need to look down. Nor did Gotrek, who always seemed sure-footed in these situations. Close inspection revealed that the elf really was floating just slightly above the surface of the water, effortlessly and doubtless by the use of magic. Felix had to keep his eyes down as he moved for the causeway wound about like a snake, to confuse attackers. It was a simple and effective system, as simple as using this fen as a moat.

As they approached the gate, women armed with bows and spears hailed them. They were mounted on the low wooden parapet that surrounded the main island, certainly the central fortification for the community. It was obvious they had been hiding while their menfolk waited. It was equally obvious that at least some of the women here were prepared to fight alongside their men.

'They are guests, Klara,' said the old man. 'They are not enemies for this night at least.'

'But one of them is a Dark One...'

Gotrek cackled.

'And the other appears to be some form of squat daemon.' The dwarf's laughter stopped abruptly and he stroked his axe-blade meaningfully.

'I am a dwarf of the Worlds Edge Mountains,' he said.

'Och, and what might they be?' the woman enquired. Gotrek did not deign to reply, although he looked like he was considering taking an axe to the gate. Felix wondered at the isolation of this place. He had grown up in a city where elves and dwarfs could oft times be seen walking the streets. He supposed that a tiny village in the middle of a bog was slightly less cosmopolitan.

'Nonetheless they are our guests,' said the old man. 'They had us in their power and they did not kill us. They say they are not our foes and until they prove differently we will take them at their word.'

'I wondered why ye were standing there like big glaked nambies,' said the woman. 'Magicians, are they?'

'One of them is, and very powerful too. More so even than the Wise One, unless I miss my guess.'

'She'll no thank ye tae be saying that,' said the woman.

'Are we going to stand here all night discussing this, woman, or shall you open the gate?' The old man asked.

'I suppose we shall be opening the gate then.' It creaked open and they strode within, to be greeted by the smell of peatsmoke and middens and fish, and the barking of dogs and the crying of children. Teclis raised his hands to his nose and coughed delicately.

'I've smelled worse,' said Gotrek.

'I doubt you ever bathe,' said the elf. It took some time for Felix to realise that he was making a joke. He suspected that Gotrek ever would. He glanced around as they walked through the street. One small boy, cheeks stained with soot, looked at him and burst into tears. Other children were hustled away by their mothers. They moved to the huge turf-roofed hall that dominated the central mound. The eyes that watched them were hostile. If Felix had had to guess he would have said most of the hostility and fear were aimed at Gotrek and Teclis, but still the villagers managed to reserve a small portion for him too. It looked like it was going to be an uncomfortable night.

THE HALL WAS long and low and dimly lit by torches soaked in pitch and lamps that contained some sort of scented oil. The place was obviously some sort of communal feasting and living chamber. A massive fireplace dominated one wall. Another was covered in what appeared to be small kegs of spirit. The men tossed off their cloaks and threw themselves down where they could, to sit cross-legged or squat as they saw fit. Their weapons never left them, though, and Felix noticed that there were still sentries at the gate.

'I am Murdo Mac Baldoch, welcome to this hall,' said the old man.

'I am Teclis of Ulthuan, I thank you for your welcome.'

'Gotrek, son of Gurni.'

'Felix Jaeger of Altdorf. I thank you for your welcome.'

Murdo went round the room and introduced each of the men in turn. From outside he could see the women peering in. They looked curious and frightened in equal measure. Felix guessed that they did not see too many strangers in these parts, and those that they did were most likely enemies. The fortifications gave that much away about this place. Men did not build such things without good need for them.

The old man picked up a goblet from the stands and tapped one of the kegs. The smell of strong alcohol became obvious as some form of golden spirit emerged. He took the goblet, sampled it himself, and then handed it to Teclis. The elf looked at it, sniffed it, and said; 'The fabled whisky of Albion. I thank you.'

He drank a sip and held the goblet. Murdo repeated the process with Gotrek who gave the elf a contemptuous glance and then tossed it back in one. The feat drew gasps of what Felix took to be admiration from the tribesmen.

'Och, you are a drinking man, Gotrek Gurnisson,' said Murdo.

'I am a dwarf,' said Gotrek. 'The whisky is good – for a human brew.'

'You'll be having another then?'

'Aye.'

Murdo refilled Gotrek's goblet and brought one to Felix. He sniffed it. The smell of the alcohol was very powerful. He took a sip and almost spluttered. It burned his tongue and sent powerful fumes racing up the back of his throat and into his nostrils. The taste was slightly smoky but not unpleasant if you were used to it. It was certainly no worse than Kislevite potato vodka.

'Very good,' he said, noting that Gotrek had drained the second goblet and looked no worse for wear. This time there was general applause from the tribesmen. Whatever else they might think of strangers, the men of Albion obviously appreciated a good drinker. As if this were a signal, each of the men took up a goblet and tapped a cask. It seemed like each had his own separate one, or perhaps it was that each family had one. He noticed that groups of men all drank from the same cask, but that was the only pattern he could put to it.

All of them took up places by the walls, sitting with their backs to it, looking inwards into the circle. Someone produced a set of small windpipes and what appeared to be a fiddle, and music began to play. The scent of cooking food began to overcome the midden murk.

'And what brings you to Albion, wizard of Ulthuan?' Murdo asked. His face was bland but keen interest showed in his eyes. Felix noticed that he only sipped at his whisky while others attempted to repeat Gotrek's feat. Felix could tell the Slayer was listening even though he appeared to be doing nothing more than staring into the fire.

'I am on a quest,' said Teclis. 'As are my companions.'

'A quest is it? The work of wizards and wise ones, no doubt. I shall not pry.'

'You are not prying, friend Murdo. Perhaps you can be of assistance. I seek the Oracle of the Truthsayers, or failing that, an ancient temple perhaps recently occupied by the forces of darkness.'

Felix could have sworn that the glint in the old man's eyes grew brighter. He nodded. 'And what would you do if you found her?'

'I would ask her help. I have great need of it.'

'It is not often one of your kind would admit that.'

'These are dark times.'

'Aye, the world over, it seems. You spoke of a temple – what do you know of this?'

'It is said to be the work of the Old Ones. Do you know ought of them?'

This time the old man definitely flinched. Felix could see his fingers toy with an amulet on his breast. For the first time, Felix noticed there were runes on the stone tip of the old man's spear. He was undoubtedly a wizard of some sort.

'I know of them, although these are not the sort of things a wise man speaks of in public. There are sacred mysteries involved.'

'It is a matter for the Truthsayers then?' The old man looked a little shocked now.

'You are very learned.'

The elf smiled with what Felix took to be mock self-depreciation.

'What would you do if you found a temple like the one you seek and it was occupied by dark powers?'

'I would cast them out, or failing that make sure they could not use the power that lies within the temple for their own evil purposes.'

'You and your two companions are going to do this? You have set yourself no easy task.'

'You know of the things of which I speak then?'

'I know of such things.'

'Will you tell me of them? I cannot reveal all of my reasons but I believe that my quest will also help your people.'

'In what way?'

'Has the earth recently shook? Has the weather gotten worse?'

'The weather is always bad in Albion but recently it has seemed particularly so. Great storms lash the lands. Rivers flood. Villages are swept away. A great curse has settled on our land, Teclis of Ulthuan. First the greenskins descended from the mountains in their hordes and then all of the things you have described have happened. Some say the Gods of Light have turned their faces from Albion and that the Seven watch over us no longer.'

'All of these things are linked, I am sure,' said the elf. 'Old magics have been woken by evil men. These spells are centred on Albion. If there is a curse, it has a source, and that source can be cleansed.'

'So the Oracle claims and I believe her. She says the old paths have been opened and daemons are creeping through them. Some claim she is senile and that the sight has left her, but I myself am not so sure.'

'Your people are divided in this matter?'

'The Truthsayers are.'

'Again you speak of the order of wizards of Albion…'

'Aye, how came you to be familiar with such things?'

'There are texts in my library in… but you are the first I have met.'

'First and least, Teclis of Ulthuan. I am not a great wizard, so do not judge the power of my brotherhood by my own.'

'You are not the least of mortal wizards I have faced, Murdo, and there is no shame in being bested by me. In my time I have faced down the Witch King himself.'

'That is a boast that few would ever dare make lest it bring the anger of the Dark One down on them.'

'It is nothing short of the truth.' Such was the elf's manner that Felix could see the old man was swayed.

'They say the elves have silver tongues,' he said.

'It was yellow livers I always heard,' muttered Gotrek. A massive tattooed man was staring at him. Gotrek looked up and downed another goblet of whisky.

'What are you looking at?' the man asked.

'I don't know,' said Gotrek, 'but it's looking back.'

Felix studied the warrior. He was as broad as Gotrek and near as brutal-looking. His nose had been mashed several times by the look of things, and his ears were as cauliflowered as those of a prize fighter. His head was bald and he had a long ginger beard. He was muscled like a blacksmith. He was soon to be a dead man if he provoked the dwarf, Felix thought.

If a fight broke out here in this enclosed space there would be carnage, thought Felix. If the wizard joined in, the village would most likely be levelled and these people so far had done them no harm. They seemed more scared by their own troubles than anything else, and Felix could understand their mistrust of outsiders. It had to be said that after the rigours of the past few days, he was not keen on fighting himself at the moment.

'You think you're strong, wee man,' said the stranger, grinning. He interlinked his fingers and cracked his knuckles.

'I am a dwarf, but can see you are too thick-skulled to remember that.'

The whole place had fallen silent. 'Now, Culum,' said Murdo. 'These folk are our guests and we be wanting no trouble.'

'I was thinking more of some sport,' said the bruiser.

'And what sort of sport would that be?' said Gotrek.

'Can ye arm-wrestle?'

Gotrek laughed. 'Can you ask stupid questions?' he retorted. Felix was pleased to see that the whisky had apparently mellowed the Slayer enough so that he did not reach for the axe. He stood and flexed his fingers. Both of them leaned forward over the table and grasped hands. The tribesmen had begun to chant Culum's name. 'He has never lost a bout,' said Murdo proudly. Felix could see that there was some family resemblance between the two.

Huge muscles flexed. Felix studied the pair. Culum was even more massive than Gotrek and his shoulders were huge but his arms were not as thick, and there was something about dwarfs, Felix knew, that made them stronger than humans of comparable mass. He had never worked out quite what it was. And Gotrek was strong, even for a dwarf.

Watching them Felix was aware that enormous power was at war here. Culum looked capable of uprooting treestumps with his bare hands. His muscles bulged, sweat beaded his brow. Slowly but surely, the Slayer's arm was forced backward. The tribesmen cheered louder. The smile on the human's face widened. Gotrek took a slug of whisky with his free hand, and grinned, showing his rotten teeth. The movement of his arm towards the table slowed and stopped. Felix was amazed that he could hold it at that angle. Culum grinned back and pushed harder. Great cables of sinew writhed in his arm and neck.

And yet, Gotrek's arm did not move. Culum's grin became sicklier as he pushed harder and harder. Veins bulged in his forehead and he looked as pop-eyed as a fish. Gotrek began to exert his strength. The human's arm quivered and then was pushed back. The tribesmen's cheering stopped. A hairsbreadth at a time, his arm was pushed back to the upright position, then slowly, inexorably, the human's arm was forced back to the tabletop. It hit the wood with a slamming sound, and there was for a moment total silence. Then the tribesmen began to cheer and applaud. Gotrek glared at them, but it did not stop them from beating their goblets on the table or praising his strength.

'That's a feat of which the harpers will sing for many a moon,' said Murdo. 'I would not have believed it if I had not seen it myself.'

After the initial shock even Culum seemed to be taking it well. He grinned ruefully and offered Gotrek his hand. The Slayer grasped it briefly and then returned to his drinking.

Food was brought, soup and coarse bread and cheese and cooked ham. The folk seemed friendlier now, but that might just have been the whisky. Felix noticed that the elf sipped his, and his goblet did not seem to empty by much after each sip. Felix decided that he had better emulate the elf. While the people were friendly enough now, he did not want to wake with his throat cut.

As these dark thoughts raced through his mind, he noticed that the elf and the old man had been talking and seemed to have reached some sort of agreement. He glanced over at the Slayer, who helped himself to the food with melancholy relish. He noticed that Gotrek's axe was within easy reach. Drunk or not, the dwarf was taking no chances. Felix wondered what was going on in the minds of their putative hosts.

CHAPTER FOURTEEN

FELIX WOKE THE next day to the sound of water washing against the walls of the village and the patter of rain on the roof. He felt quite warm and threw off his cloak, noticing that his sword lay within easy reach where he had left it. He glanced around the hall, and noticed that most of the men were still asleep, snoring loudly. Teclis sat on a wooden chair, his eyes open and fixed on the middle distance. He appeared to be in a trance. The Slayer was nowhere to be seen.

Felix got up and rubbed his back. There was an ache there that lying on a straw pallet had done nothing to improve. He shrugged and reached down and fastened his sword belt to his waist. Somewhere in the distance he could smell fish cooking. He stepped outside into the mist and the rain. The chill bit him immediately and began to clear his head. He stretched and shrugged and did his best to loosen up.

Strange dreams had troubled him the night before – dreams of daemons and the things he had seen within the Paths of the Old Ones. He touched the elvish amulet for reassurance and wondered what would happen if he slept without it. Was it really possible that he might become a victim of daemonic possession, or had the elf only said that to frighten him? It was one of those things that he was in no position to judge. Teclis was a wizard and he was not.

More than that, he was an elf, and Felix had no way of guessing his motives. He had no idea what went on behind those cold slanted eyes. The thoughts might be as alien as those of a spider or a skaven for all he knew.

'Good morning, bonnie lad,' said a clear voice behind him.

'Good morning, Klara,' said Felix, turning to look at the wench who had greeted them at the gates yester eve.

'You remembered my name,' she said. 'That be good.'

'I am Felix Jaeger,' he said, bowing and feeling stupid when she laughed.

'An unusual name.'

'Not where I come from,' he said.

'Och, and that would be the Empire.'

'It seems word spreads fast around here.'

'Fast as a dugout in a stream,' she said. 'This is a small village, and we are a small clan and to tell the truth, the men were bellowing so loudly about all manner of things that the womenfolk find them out whether they will it or no.'

Felix laughed, amused more by her expression than her words. She seemed good-humoured and she was pretty. Her complexion was fair and freckled, her hair a deep reddish brown. Her lips were wide and her eyes clear blue. 'And you'll be going to see the Oracle,' she said. 'And she'll decide what's to be done with your elvish friend and his wee familiar.'

'I would not let Gotrek hear you say that if I were you.'

'Why not?'

'He's not a familiar, he's a dwarf, and they have no liking to be associated with elves in any way, shape or form.'

'And yet you are all travelling together…'

'Circumstances are unusual,' he said.

'Must be. Must be. It's been a strange year and your appearance no the least strange thing.'

Felix felt his curiosity being piqued. 'Is that so?' he said, letting the words hang in the air.

'Aye,' she said. 'That is so. There have been great storms and strange portents. Lightning dancing on the hilltops and horned men walking the marshes and the greenskins everywhere – a pox upon them all.'

'Orcs, you mean?'

'Yrki, orcs, greenskins, whatever word you wish to use. They be as bad as the Dark Ones – only 'tis said they herd folk for eating instead of for slaves.'

'I have heard that is so, though I have never seen it.'

'And how would you know, pretty boy? You look more like a candidate for the Bardic college and you have not a scar upon ye, save for that wee scratch on your face.'

Felix was not offended. He realised that he did not look or sound like most people's idea of a warrior and he did not think of himself as one. 'Nonetheless I have killed my share of greenskins,' he said. 'And maybe a few more.'

'Och, away wi' ye.'

'It's true, though if truth be told, Gotrek did most of the killing.'

'The familiar? He has the look of a fell-handed one right enough, and that axe looks like it could dae some damage.'

'It has,' said Felix, and resisted the temptation to tell her a few stories. He realised that he was being pumped for information in exactly the same way as he was hoping to obtain knowledge from her. 'But you were telling me of the strangeness of the year.'

'Aye. 'T'as been a bad one. The fishing has no been good, and the barley barely sprouted in the hills. They say the clans in the mountains be starving and the swamp beasts be on the prowl once more.'

'Swamp beasts?'

'Big bad things all covered in moss-like stuff and strong enough tae uproot trees if they have the mind.'

'Like treemen?' Felix asked, trying to relate them to something within his knowledge. Although, if truth be told, all he knew of treemen was what he had read in books. They were supposed to be allies of the elves, living beings half man, half tree and stronger than trolls, capable of crushing boulders within their gnarly fists.

'I hae never seen a treeman, so I couldnae tell ye.'

Felix shrugged and told her what he knew. 'And you'll be telling me you have fought these as well, I suppose,' she said.

'No. Not yet anyway, although the way my life has been going it's only a matter of time.'

'What do ye mean by that?'

'It sometimes seems like I have fought just about half the monsters out of the old tales,' he said.

'Och, you're just saying that tae impress me.'

Felix laughed. 'No, it's true. Although to be honest, Gotrek did most of the fighting. I was really just there to watch.'

'What do you mean?'

'I swore an oath to follow him and record his doom. He swore an oath to seek death in battle against the mightiest and most monstrous of foes.'

'He disnae seem to have kept his oath very well then.'

'It's not for lack of trying.'

'Aye, he has that driven look. I've seen it before on the faces of those who think they've heard their death spirits a-wailin' although he has a face that would frighten even one of the Deaths.'

'That he does.'

'Perhaps he'll be wanting to seek out one of the swamp beasts then, to try his luck against them.'

'Don't say that too loud, he might hear you.'

'I take it you're no too keen on seeing his doom then.'

'I've always thought that anything tough enough to bring Gotrek's doom about would bring mine about very soon afterwards.'

'You're saying you're a-feared o' death then.'

'Isn't any sensible person?'

'You will not hear too many o' the menfolk around here admit such a thing. And I would not say it too loudly if I were you, lest they think you less than a man.'

'Is that so?'

'A man here is proud of courage and of his deeds. He tells them at every opportunity. A boastful bunch they are, but they have much to boast about.'

Felix was suddenly reminded of Teclis. Perhaps the elf would fit in here better than they. She misread his smile.

'Don't misjudge them,' she said. 'They are a fell-handed bunch of men.'

'I better hope they don't misjudge me then.'

'I would not worry if I were you, Felix Jaeger. There are few around here who would make that mistake.'

'I worry that there will be a misunderstanding. We did not come here looking for trouble. We came here on a quest of our own.'

'This is Albion, bonnie laddie, trouble always finds you soon enough. And speaking of which, here is my husband…'

Felix looked up to see Culum striding towards them. There was a scowl on his face when he looked at them. Felix suddenly regretted his easy manner. It had never occurred to him that anybody as free-spoken and flirtatious as Klara would be anything other than unmarried. The look on Culum's face told him that it might be a fatal mistake if he made it again. Felix strode off quickly. Gotrek was the one who was seeking his doom here, not him.

THE SLAYER LOOKED out from the wooden ramparts into the gathering mists. He seemed unbothered by the rain and untroubled by the cold. Felix wished him a good morning.

'What's good about it, manling?'

'We're still alive,' Felix was about to say, and then realised it was the wrong thing. 'What's so bad about it?' he countered.

'I have sworn an oath to aid a pox-ridden elf,' he said.

'And why would you do that?' Felix asked. Gotrek merely glared at him. Of course, Felix thought, he did it to help me. Gotrek's no sorcerer. There was no chance he could have found me without the elf's help, was there? Felix was actually quite astonished and more than a little grateful. 'I am sure it will not reflect to your discredit,' he said eventually.

'I am aiding one of the beard-clippers,' he said.

'What do you mean by that?'

'The locks of a dwarf were once shorn like those of a sheep by those elves.'

'Is that such a bad thing?'

'There is no greater insult to a dwarf.' Felix considered this. He knew nothing of the religious taboos of the dwarfs, but he was quite prepared to believe that there were many connected with facial hair.

'Even so, is that really reason enough for the long feud between the Elder Races?'

'Aye, manling, it is. Not least because the beard belonged to the brother of a dwarfish king. No dwarf may rest until such an insult is avenged. And if the grudge is not settled in his lifetime, it passes to his descendants.'

'Remind me never to get on a dwarf's bad side,' said Felix. Gotrek ignored him, lost in his own gloomy thoughts.

'But it's not the only reason. Ever the elves have betrayed us, slaughtered our people in sneak attacks, used their foul sorceries to ambush us. They betrayed our trusts and our ancient treaties. They took slaves and sacrifices to their dark gods.'

'Teclis does not seem to want to sacrifice anybody to the Dark Gods.'

'Who can tell what an elf thinks? Who can tell if they lie or are simply bending the truth the way a blacksmith works hot metal?'

Felix studied his companion. 'You are troubled because he may be telling the truth?'

'Aye manling, I am. I care not whether the island of the elves sinks or floats. The world would best be rid of the primping, perfumed, pointed-eared…'

'But?'

'But what if he is telling the truth about what may befall the Worlds Edge Mountains and the lands of men? My people swore an ancient oath of allegiance to yours and we do not forget our oaths…'

Gotrek sounded almost embarrassed. Felix guessed it was because of the oath he had sworn to the elf, and which he had threatened to go back on.

'Gotrek – if there is even a chance he is correct, we must help him. It is a risk we cannot take.'

'Aye, manling, that is the conclusion that I have come to. Although when that matter is settled, there may yet be a reckoning.'

'Great,' murmured Felix so low that he hoped not even the Slayer could hear. 'That will give us something to look forward to.'

'Aye,' said Gotrek. 'It will.'

Felix drew his cloak tighter about him, and studied the mist. It seemed to him that huge menacing shapes moved in it, but he hoped they were merely the outlines of the trees.

When they had returned to the hall, Teclis greeted them. 'I have talked with Murdo. He has agreed to take us to see the Wise One.'

Felix stared at the old wizard. 'You have changed your tune,' he said. 'Yesterday we were the spawn of the Dark Ones. Today you are prepared to help us.'

'Let's just say that there is nothing like drinking with a man – or an elf or a dwarf for that matter – to give you a better idea of their character.'

Felix wondered about that. He was not sure he trusted the old man. On the other hand, it did not look like he had much choice.

'I HATE BOATS almost as much as I hate elves,' said Gotrek as they clambered aboard the barge.

'I am glad you shared that with us,' said Felix looking around to see how Teclis and the boat owners of Crannog Mere were taking the statement. He was pleased that they appeared to be diplomatically ignoring it. 'I suppose you would prefer to walk to where we have to go?'

'Aye, given a choice, manling.'

'The water would be above your head if you tried,' said Murdo, then seeing the Slayer's black look added, 'Mine too.'

He was surprised to see Murdo and twenty warriors clamber aboard behind them. It looked like the men of Crannog Mere were giving them an honour guard. He was less pleased to see that Culum was one of them. He glared at Felix suspiciously as he passed. Surely the man could not be that jealous, he thought, but common sense told him otherwise.

He studied the boat. The construction was strange. It was flat-bottomed with a very shallow draft, not at all like the ships that sailed the Reik, more like a barge in fact. Felix supposed that it was because the waters here were comparatively shallow. They were in a huge marsh after all, not the open sea or a mighty river. Some of the men had taken up long poles and begun to push the ship out into the water away from the island. On the walls, the women watched quietly, a few children waved goodbye. Somewhere in the distance a piper played what sounded like a lament. It was not a cheery farewell.

'Why does everybody look so happy?' Gotrek asked sarcastically.

'No trip through the great swamp is ever taken lightly, Gotrek Gurnisson,' said Murdo. 'There are many strange perils – the swamp fiends, the marsh daemons, the walking dead, all manner of curses lie on this land. Who knows when or if we will see our homes again?'

Felix did not like the look of interest that appeared on the Slayer's face. 'If any of your swamp fiends show up, leave them to me,' he said. 'They will taste my axe.'

'Well spoken,' said Murdo.

Some of the men had taken up bows and spears and stood watchful. They seemed to be more interested in what they could hear than what they could see. Felix supposed it was because the mist limited their vision.

Old Murdo stood on a platform at the front of the ship, guiding them, making the choice whenever they came to a fork in the channel. As they rode along, Felix realised that in addition to everything else, the swamp was a huge labyrinth of murky water and unstable land. He doubted that he would ever be able to find his way back to Crannog Mere even if he wanted to. Perhaps that was part of the plan.

'What is the matter, Felix Jaeger?' Teclis asked. 'You look pensive.'

An open boat where everybody could hear was no place to go voicing his suspicions, Felix knew. Matters were delicate enough between them and the men of Albion. Right now they were dependent on them to get where they wanted to go.

'I was thinking about how we are going to get home after this,' he said. The elf laughed.

'It is good that you look on the bright side of things, Felix Jaeger.'

'What do you mean?'

'Who says we will be going home afterwards?'

'It's always good to have a plan.'

'Let us cross that bridge when we come to it,' said the elf and gave his attention back to the waterways. He looked as if he intended to memorise them. Perhaps he could, Felix thought, and cursed the mist and rain.

'Is it always like this?' he asked Murdo.

'It's no usually so nice,' said Dugal, one of the Crannogmen, with a cheery grin. Felix laughed until he realised that the fellow was not joking.

AT FIRST AS they travelled, Felix only noticed the sound of the water lapping against the side of the boat, and the swishing of the poles through the water. Occasionally a man would grumble something and then fall silent as if realising what he had just done. After a time, he began to notice other noises – the calls of birds, the growls of animals, distant furtive splashings as something big entered the water. The air was dank and damp and smelled of rot. There was something about the swamp that reminded him of an old half-ruined house by the river he and his brother had once gone into as a dare when they were children. There was the same air of abandonment and chill gloom, and a sense that things were stirring just out of sight. Looking back on that long ago adventure, Felix was certain that the worst things in the place had been merely the phantoms produced by their own imagination. He was not so sure here.

Albion was a haunted land. You did not have to be a magician like Teclis or Max Schreiber to know this. You could sense it. Old powers stirred here, strong magic was in the very air you breathed. He thought of Teclis's tale of how the island was integral to the magical fabric of the world, and he could now believe it.

All around he could see the twisted trees rising out of the murky water. They looked trollish and menacing, more like twisted evil giants than plants. Things scuttled along their branches. Once something dropped onto the deck of the boat in front of him, and began to slither across the floor. At first Felix thought it was a snake, but then he realised that it was segmented and insect-like. Culum brought a heavy sandaled foot down on it, and glared at Felix as if he wished the thing were his throat.

Murdo came back to study it. Felix examined the remains with him. It resembled a giant millipede but its jaws were enormous and ant-like. 'Treescuttle,' said the old man. 'Lucky it did not bite you.'

'Poisonous?' Felix asked.

'Aye – saw a man bit once. Before he could be treated his arm had swelled and turned black and bloated with the venom. We had to amputate. Still he died, raving about daemons and fiends. Some of the other shamans and wizards collect the venom, and use it in small quantities to bring on visions. That way lies madness, I think.'

Teclis strode over and looked down on the scuttler's corpse. His eyes were bright with curiosity. 'Interesting,' he said, tipping the thing onto its back with his dagger. 'I have never seen one this big before.'

Felix wondered how he could be so cold about the thing. Just the sight of the creature made him shudder. Its legs were moving despite the fact that its body was crushed in the middle. Teclis produced a small sack from within his robes and carefully sliced open the head, revealing the venom sacs. He took them out on the knife-point and placed them in the sack. A gesture and a word and the sack was sealed.

'You never know, I may have the chance to sample this at some later date.'

'Decadent beard-clipper,' came a voice from the back of the ship. Felix felt sure that it belonged to Gotrek.

FELIX SAT AT the back of the ship and listened to the sounds of the twilight. They had taken on a different quality. The bird songs were lower and less musical. Something large and winged sometimes flapped overhead hooting. Glowing bugs emerged from out of the water and swirled around them like lost souls. The shadows lengthened. There was a strange and rather frightening beauty about the whole thing.

'How much further?' he asked Murdo. The old man stood rock-still, showing no fatigue although he had been there most of the day.

'Such impatience, laddie. It will take more than a day's poling to get us to the Wise One, but our journey is almost done for the day. We will tie up near the Haunted Citadel.'

'That sounds inviting,' said Felix sarcastically.

'There's nae need to be afeared – the place has been deserted for a dozen lifetimes.'

'Let's hope so,' said Felix, as a gigantic ominous stone shape rose out of the mists.

CHAPTER FIFTEEN

THE MEN OF Crannog Mere brought the barge coasting to a halt just out of bowshot of the island. They did it by the simple expedient of driving the poles down into the water and tying the ship to them with long hempen ropes. One man apiece stood watch at prow and stern. The others broke out meat and bread and cheese from the knapsacks and began to sip whisky from their flasks, mixing it with what smelled like beer from huge leather skins. Murdo offered Felix some.

'Best take it, the water here is oft undrinkable and haunted by the foul spirits of plague.'

Felix helped himself. It was small beer, malty and watered. He had heard some claim that the process of brewing purified water. He was quite glad to have it anyway. Teclis stood at the prow examining the ruins. The mist had parted slightly and the moons were wanly visible overhead. Just looking at the stonework, Felix could tell that the structure had not been built by men. There was something about the construction he could not quite put his finger on.

'The gates are too low and square,' said Gotrek, as if reading his thoughts. 'The stonework is carved with runes. You can see them near-buried beneath the moss.'

'If you can see in this gloom like a dwarf,' said Felix, although he did not doubt the Slayer was correct.

'This place was not built by my people or yours,' said Gotrek. 'Nor by the elves. I have never seen anything like it.'

'I have,' said Teclis. 'On the coasts of Lustria. One of the abandoned cities of the slann, overgrown by the steaming jungle.'

'I thought the slann naught but a legend,' said Felix.

'You will find that there are truths behind many legends, Felix Jaeger.'

'I was taught they became extinct long ago. Scourged from the earth by the gods, wiped out by fire and flood and plague for their sins.'

'I believe they still live,' said the elf carefully, as if considering his words. 'I believe that in the heart of Lustria there are still cities where they practise their ancient rituals.'

'Why would there be a slann fortress here? We are a long way from Lustria.'

'I do not know. The slann prefer places that are warm. They are a cold-blooded race and chill makes them sluggish. This place is very old – perhaps when it was built the climate was different. Or perhaps there are other reasons.' The elf looked as if he might have some idea of what those reasons were, but did not want to discuss them. 'I would never have guessed we would have found such a thing here in the heart of Albion.'

'You did not find it,' said Murdo. 'We have known about it for centuries.'

'I wish to take a closer look at this,' said the elf.

'In the morning,' said Murdo. 'There will be more light and it will be safer.'

'I do not need light,' said Teclis. 'And I do not fear anything we might find here. And tomorrow we need to start moving again.'

'You propose going ashore then?'

'I do.'

'Then I will accompany you and so will Culum and Dugal. I have sworn to help you, and it would shame me if any harm came tae ye.'

Felix looked at Gotrek knowing what the Slayer was going to say already. 'Anywhere the elf can go, a dwarf can go too.'

Felix shrugged. There was something about this place he did not like, an eeriness that had nothing to do with it being deserted but rather suggested some strange inhuman presence brooding over the ruins. It's just your imagination, he told himself, affected by the hour, the mist and the talk of the pre-human slann.

Part of him knew it was more than that.

* * *

THE MEN OF Crannog Mere poled the barge close to the shore, to where a great tree root ran through a broken wall and disappeared beneath the water like the finger of some giant clutching the island's edge. Teclis bounded up from the boat and onto it effortlessly, running along the bark until he had vanished through the walls.

Gotrek went next. His axe bit into the wood easily and he pulled himself up its haft. As cat-footed as the elf, he too vanished silently through the gap in the walls. The luminescent insects swirled around them.

'Some say they are the souls of the dead drowned in the swamp,' said Dugal. 'The fireflies, I mean.'

No one seemed inclined to disagree with him. He sprang up, scrambled onto the branch and away. Murdo and Culum followed. Some more of the tribesmen passed them torches. Felix threw himself upwards and was surprised by how wet, slick and slimy the surface was. He felt his fingers begin to slip, and frantically and ungracefully pulled himself up. The surface of the branch seemed slick and slippery as well. How did Teclis and Gotrek make this look so easy, he wondered, as he reached down for the torch offered to him? Arms wide, torch in one hand, sword in the other, he moved cautiously along the branch and into the ruins of a structure built by an Elder Race.

'WOULD YE LOOK at that?' said Dugal, swearing softly.

'No wonder men avoid this place,' said Teclis. Felix could see what he meant looking down onto the ruins. There were many smaller buildings within the walls. What might have been streets between them were now canals, or at the very least sluggish channels of brackish water. Huge webs hung between some of the buildings. In some of them dangled bodies the size of large animals or men.

'I would not want to meet the spider that spun those,' said Felix.

'I would,' said Gotrek, running his finger along the blade of his axe meaningfully.

'Seen enough?' Felix asked the elf. He was half hoping that the mage would be discouraged and retreat. He might have guessed he could no more expect common sense from Teclis than he could from Gotrek.

'There is something about this place,' said Teclis. 'I sense power here, like the power at the stone ring. Perhaps we have found another entrance to the Paths of the Old Ones.'

'Excellent,' said Felix sardonically. 'Is that why you wanted to explore this place – you had already sensed something?'

'In part, yes. But I am genuinely interested in this place.'

'I'll bet you are.'

Somewhere in the distance, Felix could have sworn he saw something large moving. He pointed it out to the others. 'It's a spider,'
said Teclis. 'A big one. I am starting to understand something about
this swamp. These twisted trees and luminous mutated insects are
all of a piece. They are being warped by the power buried within
these ruins. Its evil influence must contaminate everything for
leagues around.'

'That would be why it is unhealthy to drink the waters in these
parts then,' said Murdo, as if what the elf said jibed with something
he already knew.

'Certainly. Drink nothing and eat nothing found anywhere near
here.'

'Thanks for mentioning that,' said Gotrek. 'I was planning a feast.'

'You can never tell with dwarfs,' said Teclis. 'I have heard you feast
on blind fish and fungus found in the darkest depths beneath the
mountains.'

'And your point is?'

'There's no telling what a dwarf will eat.'

'That's good coming from someone who eats larks' tongues pickled in sheep vomit.'

'In aspic,' said Teclis.

'Same thing, isn't it?'

'Are we going to stand here all night discussing culinary matters
or shall we proceed?' asked Felix. The elf and dwarf glared at him.
Felix was starting to suspect that in some sick way the two of them
enjoyed baiting each other.

They moved along the wall. Ancient slippery stairs carried them
down to the water's edge. Murdo tested the depth with a spear, and
they found out it came only waist high. The glittering bugs swirled
around them.

Felix looked at them. 'You can't seriously intend to walk through
this, can you? Who knows what lurks beneath this muck?'

'Only one way to find out, manling,' said Gotrek, splashing down
into the water. It came up to about half the height of the dwarf's
chest. He carefully held the axe above the water as he proceeded.
Teclis followed, but his feet did not descend below the surface.
Instead he seemed to walk smoothly along the top of it. His fine
footwear did not even appear to be slightly wet.

The others followed Gotrek, holding the torches high so that they
would not be extinguished. Briefly Felix considered offering to wait
here until they returned. There was something about this stinking,

stagnant water that he did not like. He felt that at any second something might emerge from beneath its surface and seize him. He
halted for half a heartbeat and then gritted his teeth as he entered
the water. Wetness sloshed around him. It was warmer than he
expected. The smell of rottenness increased.

Slowed by the water's clammy grip he pushed onwards in the
wake of the others. Wonderful, he thought. Surrounded by barbarians and giant mutated insects, up to my waist in slime, in a misty
haunted swamp in a land hundreds of leagues from home – how
could it get worse?

At that moment he noticed an insect had bitten him and the bite
was beginning to swell. I suppose the gods had to give me that
answer, he thought. He looked at Teclis with something like hate. It
was very annoying that the elf could look so calm and clean and in
control while all of the rest of them suffered. He felt an irrational
urge to splash him with muck or tug his cloak until he too was
pulled down into the slime. And he knew at least one person here
would support him if he did it too.

Get a grip, he told himself. You are just tired and scared and
focusing all your aggression on the nearest easy target. If events run
true to form there will soon be other things to worry about. And he
knew that was what really scared him.

Ahead of them, the others had come to something. A fallen tree
branch had been run between two buildings over the stagnant
water. It looked for all the world like a crude bridge. Was there some
sort of intelligence at work here, he wondered? That is all we need
– smart giant spiders. Although why a spider would need a bridge
eluded him.

'This looks like the work of men,' he heard Teclis say.

'I have heard tales of mutants and other degenerates dwelling
deep in the swamp. Perhaps they had sought this shunned place as
a refuge.'

'Why did we come here again?' Felix asked, but no one paid any
attention to him. They were too busy climbing up onto the log and
striding into the opening in the nearby building. Felix decided to
follow.

Inside, the structure was massive, hewn from great cyclopean
blocks of stone. The stone was unmortared but fitted into place so
cunningly that it seemed immovable, an illusion that the creepers
and branches and roots running through the gaps did little to dispel. They seemed almost like organic parts of the place, part of a
great design, rather than a random intrusion of nature. Felix told
himself he was imagining things.

He noticed Gotrek running his massive stubby fingers over the stonework. A closer look showed him the Slayer was tracing more of those odd runic patterns. Once again they were all right angles, and they reminded him of the tattoos of the men of Crannog Mere. What is the significance of those things, he wondered?

Water dripped from the ceiling above them, forming puddles on the floor. Things with glittering eyes retreated before their torches, and Felix was glad that he only got the slightest glimpse of them. He was not fond of things so big that scuttled. They entered a chamber, and saw bones scattered all over the floor. They had been cracked open for the marrow. The Slayer inspected these too. 'Human,' he said. 'Or my mother was a troll.'

Murdo and Dugal nodded agreement. 'And they ate them raw,' said Teclis shuddering slightly. As if that made a great deal of difference, Felix thought. He doubted that the inhabitants of this place found it easy to light fires. A moment later he asked himself: what has become of me? I am speculating on the difficulties of lighting a fire to cook people over. Once there was a time when the mere thought would have had me run screaming from this place. Now noticing my own reaction just leaves me amused and a little scared. He knew then that he had come a long way from home in more ways than one.

'Looks like there's nobody home now,' said Gotrek.

'Maybe they went shopping,' said Felix. The elf lifted his hand and a glow surrounded it, brightening until it was almost the intensity of the sun. The whole chamber was thrown into relief. At first Felix flinched, expecting to see some huge monster about to attack them, but then he noticed the elf's attention had been drawn to a massive stone table set in the middle of the floor. Teclis laid his hand on it, and fire spread, burning the moss and lichen causing it to shrivel and vanish in wisps of strange-smelling smoke. As it did so, Felix noticed that it revealed a pattern on the table top, one that was oddly familiar although for the life of him he could not quite work out why.

'What is it?' he asked. The elf continued to stare at the table-top.

'Unless I am much mistaken, and I doubt I am, this is a map.'

The lines graved on the stone certainly looked that way. 'What of?' Felix asked.

'The world.'

Felix laughed, realising what had looked familiar. Parts of the pattern resembled the maps his father possessed of the Old World. Only parts, though.

'It can't be. There is no land so close to the coast of Estalia,' he said. 'If there was our mariners would have found it.'

Teclis traced part of the pattern with his finger. It was a ring of islands surrounding a central sea. 'This looks like Ulthuan,' he said, 'but it is not. Quite.'

He moved his hand again. 'This is the coastline of Northern Lustria, but it's in the wrong place. And this is the cold hell of Naggaroth but its relationship to the area that should be Ulthuan is wrong.'

'Maybe the mapmaker did not have eyes quite like ours,' suggested Gotrek. Felix was not entirely sure he was being sarcastic.

'Possibly,' said Teclis. 'Or maybe it was a map of the world in a different time. When the continents were different. It is said the Old Ones shifted the lands and pinned them in new places as part of their great design.'

'Or maybe,' suggested Felix, 'it's a map of the world as it was intended to be.'

'That, Felix Jaeger, is a terrifying thought,' said Teclis.

'Why?'

'Because perhaps someone still intends to make it so?'

Felix looked at the elf, not quite knowing how to respond. Teclis seemed lost in thought.

'Perhaps the Old Ones' plans were never completed. Perhaps they were interrupted. Perhaps the opening of the paths is a sign that other things have reactivated.'

'That is insane,' said Felix, unable to contain his thoughts.

'Is it, Felix Jaeger? We are dealing with the work of beings as far beyond you and I as we are above an insect. How would we qualify to judge what is sane or not for them? We might as well judge the sanity of gods.'

'The Chaos Gods are insane,' said Gotrek.

'Perhaps not from their point of view, Gotrek Gurnisson.'

'Only an elf could say something like that.'

'Perhaps because we are not as rigid in our thinking as dwarfs.'

'Or your morals.'

'Only an elf and a dwarf would argue about such things while they discussed the end of the world,' said Felix. Both of them looked at him dangerously. 'If the continents are intended to shift like carpets, our people and our cities will be so much dust.'

'If,' said Gotrek. 'So far all we have heard are some long-winded speculations from a pointy-eared, tree-loving, spellsinging...'

'If there is even the possibility he is correct, something must be done,' said Felix quickly before the argument could erupt in its full glory. 'The earth would shake, the mountains would rain fire, foul warpstone dust would fall from the skies...'

Even as he said the words, Felix realised that he was describing events from the legendary age before Sigmar and the rise of the Empire. He could see that the thought had struck the elf too. 'Perhaps all of this has happened before,' said Teclis. 'During the Dawn Ages, before even the War of the Beard, when elf and dwarf were allies against a common foe.'

'It was not the dwarfs who betrayed their sworn oaths,' said Gotrek testily.

'Quite,' said the elf. 'But putting that predictable interruption to one side for a moment, I believe Felix Jaeger is right. If there is even the remotest possibility of something like this happening, then our ancient animosities must be put aside... until a better time, for I know how unlikely it is that a dwarf will ever lay down a grudge.'

'It seems to me that you are engaging in a mighty load of speculation on the basis of one old map. Who says this has anything to do with the Old Ones and their works?' asked Murdo. There was something odd in the old man's manner, Felix thought. He wondered if the others had noticed this.

'All of Albion is connected with them,' said Teclis. 'It is the nexus of their work. It formed some mighty part in their great scheme of things, no less so than Ulthuan. This fortress is part of some greater design, I am sure of it.'

Murdo looked troubled, as if the elf was touching on matters that he felt were best left unspoken.

How much does Murdo really know about such things, Felix wondered? He is more familiar with these ancient secrets than he lets on.

'Perhaps we should be getting back now,' said Felix.

'Not yet,' said the mage. 'We are close to the mouth of another portal. I can sense it. We must investigate it before we leave. We must get closer to the heart of this structure.'

'I was afraid you were going to say something like that,' said Felix. The elf laughed as if he were joking.

The mists closed in as they left the hall. Somehow they were coming through the walls. Luminescent insects drifted among them. Their buzzing whines keened in Felix's ears. Their bites blotched his skin. He noticed that not one of them ever seemed to close with the elf, even though the others were all troubled by them. Infuriating, Felix thought. The elf led them deeper into the ancient structure, through a labyrinth of stonework that made Felix's head spin. Sometimes they came to dead ends and were forced to retrace their steps. At others, the passageways would take ninety-degree turns for no foreseeable reason. The elf did not seem discouraged. He merely nodded his head, as if this confirmed something.

He strode over to Gotrek, who was far more at home in such places than he could ever be.

'Can you find your way out of here?' he asked in a whisper.

'Aye, manling, no dwarf ever got lost in such a simple maze as this. I could find my way out blindfolded if need be.'

'I don't think that will be necessary. Impressive as it would be.'

'There is something odd about this place.'

'What?'

'This maze is laid out seemingly without rhyme or reason. Look to your left and you will see a dead end. To the right if we went that way, I have no doubt that once that corridor turns it too would reach a dead end.'

'Why are you so certain?'

'There is a pattern here. It's obvious.'

'Not to me,' said Felix.

'You are not a dwarf brought up in the endless corridors of Karaz-a-Karak.'

'True. What is this pattern you see?'

'Unless I miss my guess, it is the same as one of the ones we have seen on the stones in the Paths of the Old Ones, and inscribed on the rock walls of the barrow in Sylvania, and on the walls of this place. Similar even to the ones tattooed on the faces of our friends.'

'You can remember all of these?' said Felix, amazed.

'Dwarfs have a good memory for more things than grudges.' Felix thought about this and decided that it was most likely true. He had never known the Slayer to lie. But if it were, then somehow this was all part of a vast puzzle, one that Felix did not quite understand. And if the elf was right, he most likely never would. His mind was not equipped to grasp what creatures that were close to gods might have been about when creating such a thing.

The maze continued until they found themselves standing in a huge chamber, gazing down into a vast pit. The ceiling had collapsed above and tons of rock had fallen downward, crushing whatever was below. Massive webs formed a new roof overhead and blocked out part of the moonlight. Rain dripped through and the wet droplets made Felix shiver.

'We are in the centre of this place. The entrance to the paths is directly below us,' said Teclis.

Gotrek's bitter mad laughter rang out. 'Then you will go no further. Give me a hundred dwarfish miners and a month and we might get through those rocks. Might. Unless you can use magic there is no way through.'

'The stones here are still partially protected by runework,' said Teclis. 'With ten mages and ten days we might clear this, but now is not the time.'

'So what now?' Felix asked.

'We go back and seek another way to our goal,' said Teclis, looking at Gotrek as if daring him to say something.

The dwarf stiffened and glanced around, head cocked as if listening. His stance bespoke the utmost wariness and preparation to do violence.

'Something is approaching,' said Gotrek, raising his axe. 'And I doubt it's friendly.'

CHAPTER SIXTEEN

'WHAT IS IT?' Felix asked.

'Nothing natural,' said the Slayer. The humans had already readied their weapons. Dugal and Murdo stood with spears raised. Culum had produced a huge hammer with a stone head. Teclis had his hand on his sword. Quicksilver runes flowed along the blade.

The things emerging from the other entrances were not entirely spider-like. They pranced along the edge of the great pit on only six long spidery legs for one thing – it was funny how you could notice such details at a time like this, Felix thought – and they had faces that looked sinisterly human mounted high on their abdomens. Their eyes burned with an intelligence that no spider had ever possessed. Luminous fungus blotched their sides. A wild ululating wail emerged from their mouths. There were perhaps a dozen of them. Felix noticed that they had two smaller manipulative arms at the front of their bodies. Perhaps they were the ones who had crunched the bones after all. Several of them scuttled up and along the walls, magically attached. Behind the spiders came a host of human mutants. Twisted beings marked by the stigmata of Chaos who looked on the spiders with a mixture of fear and reverence emerged from every entrance to the huge hall. They were armed with spears and slings and clubs.

'Perhaps we should leave here,' said Felix. Gotrek charged along the pit edge towards the leading spider thing. Teclis raised his arms and sent a wave of golden fire lancing towards the humans. A few cast spears which ignited as they arced towards him, shrivelling to black ash in flight. Screams echoed around the ancient walls as flesh melted and ran like wax. Through it all, the spiders kept coming. When the magical flames touched them the blotched patterns on their sides blazed brighter and they seemed to move faster. Are they immune to spells, Felix wondered?

Teclis strode into the air, taking up a position above the centre of the great pit, and gestured. Lightning lashed from his hands, whipping the stone. Sparks arced up from the puddles of water. Felix saw a reptile-faced mutant flung into the air on a pillar of lightning. The spiders ignored it and kept on coming.

'They are ancient guardian daemons,' shouted Murdo. 'Save your spells.'

Gotrek meanwhile had met the leading spider. His axe thunked into its armoured side. Instead of cleaving straight through as it normally would, it bit deep into the chitin and stuck. Felix shuddered to think at how resistant the creatures must be to withstand the appalling force of the Slayer's blows. Was it possible that their end was in sight, here in this god-forsaken pesthole in the backwaters of Albion?

He had no more time for such thoughts. A flicker of movement caught from the corner of his eye caused him to duck. A slingstone shattered against the rock walls behind him. He cursed and kept moving, looking for cover, wondering if he dared ditch the torch that made him such an obvious target. There was enough light here to see by but he had to get back through the stone corridors. If any of the others were present there would be no problem but if they were separated...

Above him he saw a huge daemon spider moving along the walls. A spray of webbing spurted from its bulbous rear and hit the ground near Felix. He leapt back to avoid the sticky stuff and saw another spider closing the ground between them with appalling speed. It sprang down from the wall and landed amid the men of Albion, scattering them. With unerring instinct it came straight at Felix.

'Do not let them take you alive!' shouted Murdo. 'They will implant their eggs within you, make you into one of them.'

Now that is a disgusting idea, thought Felix, whirling the torch so that it flared brighter. As the creature neared him, he struck it in the face with his torch, hoping to blind it. Moments later his blade bit into the tough chitin of its leg. He aimed for the weakest point, shearing through the joint. The thing squealed with pain as its leg separated. Black stuff oozed from the wound, sealing it. Another leg flicked forward. It hit Felix with the force of a hammer blow, knocking him onto his back. The torch left his numbed fingers. He only just managed to keep his grip on his sword.

He rolled aside as the thing moved its bulk above him, and brought its foreleg down again. He could see there were hooks on it that could slash skin to the bone. He barely managed to evade it, but it snagged his cloak pinning him to the ground. Using his left hand, Felix desperately attempted to free the clasp of the cloak, while stabbing upward with his sword. The blade pierced the thing's underbelly, and dark stuff dropped from the wounds. It burned where it touched his skin. Perhaps that was not such a good idea, he thought, noticing the legs of the approaching mutants as they came ever closer.

The stench was near overpowering, of rot and mould and something old and fusty, mingled with a smell like rotten eggs and curdled milk. It made him want to gag. Instead he gritted his teeth and grabbed the hilt with both hands, twisted the sword, and proceeded to saw into the wound. The burning blood boiled over his hands. The spider-thing screamed louder. Felix felt like joining in, but did not.

Lightning flashed and flames danced. Whirlwinds of golden fire swept across the room. Felix found himself being dragged along beneath the spider as it headed up the wall once more. He tucked his head into his chest to avoid having it bumping on the stone. The strain made his neck ache and the muscles bulge until they felt like taut wire beneath his skin. Slowly his blade was dragged from the wound. He glanced down and saw that most of the mutants were in retreat, unable to cope with the blazing energies that the elf wizard sent ravening across the chamber. Felix pulled his blade clear and dropped to the floor. Overhead the thing he had wounded seemed to be deflating like a punctured sac of bile as it limped and scurried upwards towards the shadows.

Elsewhere things were not going well for his party. Gotrek had overcome his beast by the simple expedient of chopping it to pieces. No matter how tough the spiders were, they were not tough enough to withstand that terrible axe for long. However, even as Felix watched, three more of the creatures began to surround the Slayer, spurting sticky web stuff from their abdomens that was slowing the dwarf down. Two more pressed on the men of Crannog Mere. If there were any more to be dealt with, they were hidden from view.

Felix raced over towards Gotrek. A flying leap took him onto the back of the spider. His fingers caught on the fine mesh of hair that covered its back and he pulled himself up. The thing roared as it realised what he was about. It tried to reach back with its small fore-arms to get him but they were not long enough, and its other legs were not positioned to enable it to dislodge him. He gritted his teeth and brought his sword down onto the back of the thing's humanoid face. His fingers were numb now from the poison that had spilled on them earlier, and he was desperate to do damage before they froze completely.

As the blade bit home, the face screamed, a sound oddly like a human child. The daemon spider began to buck and shake itself from side to side, hoping to throw its burden clear. Felix held grimly on and kept stabbing away, and the thing's struggles eventually grew weaker and weaker. As the spider jigged backwards and forwards he caught glimpses of the others.

Culum had partially pulped one of the spiders with his massive hammer and Murdo was jabbing his spear into its vulnerable eyes. Dugal, though, shrieked as he was lifted up by a set of fiendish mandibles. The spider carrying him backed away towards the exit. Felix wanted to help but there was nothing he could do.

A wave of fire descended from the elf wizard and engulfed Gotrek. What treachery was this, Felix wondered? Was Teclis mad to strike down their mightiest warrior in the midst of this desperate affray? Or had he been in league with these foul daemons all along? Had his mind been poisoned by some evil magic? Felix felt a wave of despair pass through his numbed and pain-wracked frame. If the elf was against them all hope was gone.

Heartbeats later, though, the method behind the wizard's mad-ness became clear. The flames flickered around Gotrek shrivelling away the sticky webs that threatened to immobilise him. A second later, a mighty blow from the axe chopped through the thorax of one of the creatures. Both halves kept moving for a moment before collapsing to the floor. The struggles of the thing beneath Felix were subsiding, which was just as well since his numbed fingers were finding it increasingly difficult to maintain their grip. He stabbed one last time for good measure and then let go, rolling to absorb the impact as he hit the floor.

Swiftly he pulled himself to his feet and went to aid Dugal. Think-ing he spied a weakness in the things, he aimed at the place where the leg merged with body and the armour seemed less substantial. It was a difficult strike to place and his first blow went awry. His sec-ond bit home and he was rewarded. The blade found a weak spot in the armour and slid home easily. Once more he twisted it. The thing bucked and writhed in agony, dropping Dugal. A moment later, Culum and Murdo were on it hammering and stabbing with a vengeance. It swiftly retreated backwards into the gloom, leaving them alone to watch Gotrek dismember his foe.

Felix inspected Dugal. The screaming had stopped. He lay still and cold as a corpse. Felix could see there were punctures in his tunic. He took out his knife and cut it away. The flesh beneath was bruised and bled slowly where the mandibles had penetrated flesh. He could tell by the look of horror in the man's eyes that he was still conscious and aware of what was happening to him.

Murdo dropped to his haunches beside Dugal. His ran his hands over the wound and muttered an incantation. A light passed from his tattooed fingers to the wound. Dugal's eyes closed and his breathing became even shallower. The old man shook his head.

Teclis drifted down to earth like a falling leaf and knelt beside Murdo. 'A fine casting. There's not much more I can do at the moment – without the right herbs or access to an alchemical laboratory. All I can do is slow the spread of the poison.'

'It might be enough,' said Murdo. 'If we can get him to the Oracle in time. There is no one quite as skilled at healing as she.'

A slightly sullen expression passed over the elf's face. Surely he was not so vain, Felix thought. He held up his own hands and looked at them, wondering if there was any chance that the bile of the spider thing could have poisoned him too. They were dyed bluish and hurt very badly.

The elf looked at them, and spoke a word. A spark passed from his hand to Felix's. The blue colouring hardened, cracked and flaked away, taking what looked like the top layer of skin with it. Felix's hands now looked pinkish and raw, and felt even more painful, like a graze swabbed with alcohol. Liquid fire coursed through the veins on the back of his hands. The tendons jumped and spasmed and were still.

'If there was any poison, it is cleansed now, Felix Jaeger,' said the elf.

'Thanks, I think,' said Felix. His hands still stung and it was painful for him to hold a sword. Still if the alternative was death, this was preferable.

'There is nothing here for us now,' said Teclis, glancing backwards into the pit. 'We'd best be going. Quickly.'

Gotrek looked wistfully after the spiders, and Felix could tell he was considering hunting them down. At this point, it was not something he felt like doing. Eventually, though, the dwarf shook his head and turned to follow them. Culum carried Dugal as easily as a baby. His expression managed to tell Felix that somehow this was all his fault.

THEY EMERGED INTO the moonlight. It gleamed in the dark oily waters covering the semi-sunken structures. The remaining tribesmen greeted them worriedly.

'We wondered if the daemons had taken you,' said a short squat man even more tattooed than the others. 'I was going to come looking for you.'

'No need, Logi,' said Murdo gently. 'We're back.'

'Dugal disnae look well,' said Logi.

'Bitten by one of the lurkers within.'

'That isnae good.'

'No.'

Felix saw that the tribesmen were all staring hard at him, as if they too blamed him for what had happened to their kinsman. It took him a few fraught seconds to realise that they were actually looking past him at the elf. The wizard gave no sign of either noticing or caring, although he could not have been unaware of the hostile crowd. Felix envied him his self-possession, or perhaps it was simply arrogance.

Without saying a word, the elf moved over to Dugal, who now lay on the soaking wooden boards at the foot of the barge. He cocked his head to one side as if considering something, and then began to slowly chant what sounded like a dirge. At first nothing happened, then Felix noticed that the beams of the greater moon all appeared to be drawn to his staff. Slowly it grew brighter with a gentle radiance. He noticed that over and over again the elf invoked the name of Lileath, doubtless some god or goddess of his pantheon. The others watched, hands on weapons, not quite sure what was happening. Despite the stinging in his hands, Felix did the same. He noticed that his skin was starting to tingle, and felt the hair stand on the nape of his neck. He sensed strange presences, hovering just outside the line of his vision, but whenever he turned his head, he could see nothing, and merely got the maddening feeling that whatever it was, it was still there, just out of sight.

Eventually a web of light spun itself out from the elvish staff. Long silver threads, seemingly woven from moonbeams, unravelled away from it, as from a spindle. They leapt from the staff to Dugal's twitching, moaning form, and entwined it, until he shimmered like the moon reflected on water, then slowly they began to fade, leaving him seemingly unchanged. Felix wondered if he was the only one who had noticed that the man's chest had ceased to rise or fall. He did not have long to wait.

'You've killed him,' said Culum, lifting his hammer menacingly.

The elf shook his head. The big man reached down and touched Dugal's chest. 'There is no heartbeat,' he said.

'Wait,' said Teclis. An expression of baffled concentration clouded Culum's features. The silence deepened as the long moment dragged on.

'I felt a heartbeat,' said Culum. 'But now it is gone.'

'Keep waiting.' Felix counted thirty more of his own quickening heartbeats before Culum nodded again.

'It's a spell of stasis,' Teclis said. 'I have slowed down his life functions – breathing, heartbeat, everything. For him time passes at a fraction of the speed as the rest of us. The spread of the poison has been slowed, and the time before death increased.'

'His pain has been somewhat decreased as well,' the elf added, almost as an afterthought.

'But he will still die,' said Murdo softly.

'Unless this Oracle of yours can do something for him, yes,' said Teclis.

'Then we had best make speed.'

'You wish to go now?'

'In this light and fog? I do not see how.'

'If you need light, I can give it to you,' said Teclis.

Murdo nodded. A huge flash lit the night. For a moment, Felix wondered if Mannsleib had come to earth and settled on the end of the elf's staff, then he saw it was only the chilly glow of another spell. He flexed his fingers, noticing that the pain was already starting to fade, and the healing had begun at what seemed an unnatural rate.

The tribesmen settled down at their poles and pushed the boat on through the misty channels. From the ancient, haunted city behind them came the sound of drumming. Felix wondered what it meant, and feared that it boded no good whatsoever.

'Perhaps we will be pursued,' he said.

'If it's by those altered things, we have nothing to fear,' grated Gotrek.

'I suspect there are worse things waiting in this swamp,' said Felix. The Slayer looked unusually thoughtful. He sniffed the sour air and then ran his thick fingers through the massive crest of dyed hair.

'Aye, manling, I think you might be right,' he said almost cheerfully. For Felix, that was the worst portent of all.

CHAPTER SEVENTEEN

Dawn came slowly. The wan sunlight had a hazy quality as it shone through the thinning mist. Felix sat slumped in the back of the boat, listening to the slosh of water against bow and pole and the chirruping of the early morning birds. Behind them the drums were fading, but were still evident. To Felix they sounded like the heart-beat of the great monster that was the swamp.

He ran his fingers through his stubble and rubbed his reddened eyes. He had slept fitfully at best on the hard wet boards of the boat, all too aware that nearby Dugal lay dying. Even though the man's silence was eerie, he still cast a pall over the entire crew. They all knew how close he was to death too, and it was affecting them. Probably more than it does me, Felix thought. After all, he is virtually a stranger to me, they grew up with him.

He shook his head and offered up a prayer to Shallya. Even though he no longer believed in her mercy, it seemed old habits died hard. How often have I done this now, Felix wondered. How often have I sat and watched a not-quite-stranger die? It felt like a hundred times. He felt like he was a thousand years old. He felt like he was being worn thin by the constant friction of events. He asked himself, if he had known it would be like this on that drunken night, would he have still sworn to follow Gotrek? Sadly, he knew the answer was yes.

Dugal might be dying, but Felix was still very much among the living, and keenly aware of it. Even this sour, reeking air tasted sweeter and he could see hints of the strange beauty amid the swamplands. Monstrous flowers blossomed on long creepers hanging from the branches overhead. Huge lilies floated on massive pads in the channels. Even the weeds that clogged the waterway and impeded their passage gave forth an odd narcotic perfume.

Ahead on the prow, Teclis stood, immobile as the figurehead of a sailing ship. His strange chiselled features held no human expression, and he showed no more sign of weariness than a wooden carving. As the dawn light filtered through the canopy, he had let his spell dim, and now simply watched as Murdo guided the ship with soft commands, telling the men with the poles to go left or right as their route dictated.

There was nothing about the elf's physical appearance to suggest his great age. He looked as fit and fair as a youth of eighteen summers. And yet there was something there that spoke of his years; Felix could not quite tell what. Perhaps it was the controlled expression of his face. Perhaps the aura of wisdom he projected or perhaps, Felix thought, it is simply his imagination.

Gotrek slumped with his back to the wood of the hull, as immobile as the elf, and as watchful. Whatever he had sensed the night before had not shown up, but that had not reduced his wariness. Rather, it seemed to have increased it. His coarse rough-hewn features might have belonged to some primordial statue. He looked aged and powerful as some warrior god from the morning of the world. The axe looked older still. What stories might it not be able to tell if it had a voice, Felix wondered?

He rose slowly and walked the length of the ship, carefully avoiding the men sprawled in sleep. The men of Crannog Mere had taken watches and rested in shifts. They seemed determined to keep the barge moving until they reached their final destination, and perhaps succoured their comrade. Felix could almost feel Culum's eyes boring into his back. It was starting to get on his nerves. He felt like saying, 'All I did was talk to her', but he knew that it would not help. He had met Culum's type before. The big man had made up his mind to dislike him, and nothing Felix could say would change his mind.

Well, he thought, if there's going to be violence between us, then there will be violence. There was nothing he could do about it at the moment. Still, in that instant, he could not help envying the elf his magical powers.

* * *

TECLIS STOOD IN the prow and drank in everything he saw. He knew he might never pass this way again, and he wanted to fix it in his memory. It was rare these days for him to experience a completely novel situation, and he wanted to milk it for everything it was worth.

He looked at the slippery branches dripping with creepers and large evil-looking blooms. His eyes were keen enough to pick out the lurking millipedes and the noxious spiders as well as the glittering jewel-eyed dragonflies resting on the leaves. He could see the shadow and silver shapes of the fish moving in the murky mere. He could smell at least seven different kinds of narcotic bloom, and vowed that if he got the chance he would come back here, and sample and catalogue them. If he lived, there would be plenty of time.

He could feel the resentful gaze of the humans on him, and it amused him. He felt like an adult surrounded by a pack of angry children. They might bristle and look surly but there was nothing they could do to hurt him. He fought to keep a smile off his face. He knew he was starting to behave like all the elves he so despised, in the way they looked down on all the younger races. How easily it crept up on you, he thought.

Perhaps it was merely a response to the events of the night before. He had been shocked to encounter creatures so resistant to his magic. They had obviously been intended to be so. Doubtless guardians left by the Old Ones to deal with any intruders in their temple-fortress. It had been a long time since Teclis had encountered anything against which his magic could not protect him, and it had left him feeling more unbalanced than he would have believed.

Still, in a way, he welcomed it. There had been a thrill to that combat he had not experienced in some time, a sense of having laid his life on the line that had become rare in his life. It almost made him feel young again. Almost.

He considered the nature of last night's foe. His theory was not quite pure speculation on his part. Certain hidden books had hinted that the Old Ones had left guardians, but those things had been tainted by Chaos. Was it possible that millennia of exposure to the energies seeping through the portal beneath the tower could have changed them? Yes, he supposed it was. No matter how resistant the Old Ones had made their creations, they were no less likely than the paths to be tainted. Chaos warped living things far more easily than it warped unliving matter. He supposed the same thing might happen to elves, given time. After all, Ulthuan had a heavier density of magical portals, gates and ways than almost any other place on the planet, as well as a higher concentration of magical energy.

Perhaps, he thought, the change has already happened. Perhaps the split between the dark elves and his own people was rooted in a simple physical cause. Or perhaps, his own people had been changed as well. Perhaps over the millennia they had altered too. Certainly in some ways this was the case. Fewer elves were born now. Were there other changes? Only Malekith and his dreadful mother would be in a position to know for certain, and somehow he doubted he would ever get the truth from them, even if they met somewhere other than on a battlefield.

Not for the first time, he felt the temptation of the darker side of his nature tug him. Perhaps he could arrange such a visit sometime. Perhaps knowledge might be exchanged. He almost laughed at his own folly. The only knowledge he would ever be able to extract from a visit to Naggaroth would be the intimate knowledge of pain inflicted on him by the dark elf torturers. No, that was a path that was closed for all time.

He could feel the dwarf's eyes boring into his back. He considered Gotrek Gurnisson. There was an enigma there that would need solving some day. The axe he bore was a weapon of awesome power, and it had changed the dwarf in many ways. The signs written all over his aura had become far clearer last night during the battle when dwarf and weapon had seemed to become almost as one. Power had flowed both ways during that conflict, he was certain, although the manner in which it had done so had baffled even him. The knowledge of those ancient dwarven runesmiths had been enormous. The Old Ones had revealed mysteries to them they had kept even from the elves. Oh, for a year to study that weapon. He smiled. That was an eventuality as likely as him gaining knowledge from the Witch King of the dark elves, and only marginally less dangerous.

Still, the dwarf would make a mighty ally in whatever trials lay ahead. The encounter with the spider daemons had shown Teclis that there were areas where an axe might come in handy. Nor was the human, Felix Jaeger, to be discounted. The man was brave and resourceful. Perhaps the gods had sent them to aid him.

He considered the dying man, for so Teclis thought of him. Unless this Oracle was skilled beyond all reason, Dugal's fate was already sealed. All Teclis had done was delay it, and that had been as much a matter of political expediency as charity. He had needed to be seen to help the man, otherwise the blame for his fate could quite easily have fallen on Teclis and he still needed the men of

Crannog Mere as allies, at least for the present. And it would not do any harm for the tribesmen to think that the fate of their companion was linked to the wizard's under the present strained circumstances.

Of course, should Dugal die, that would change. It was a hurdle he would leap when he came to it. He did not wish Dugal or the tribesmen any harm, but if it came to a choice between survival for himself and Ulthuan, or their lives, then there was no choice at all. Teclis knew he would sacrifice all of those present, including himself, and ten thousand times more if need be to preserve the kingdom of the elves.

He could almost feel the dwarf's cold stern eye judging him. Nonsense, he told himself, you are merely projecting your own doubts outwards. Under the circumstances Gotrek Gurnisson would make the same choices as you. Not that it mattered what the dwarf thought anyway. At the present moment, he was simply another tool to be used to achieve Teclis's ends.

The thought amused him. Perhaps the dwarfs are right to judge us as they do. He considered this for a moment and saw that in this he was the dwarf's superior. No dwarf would ever admit that an elf might be right about such a thing. They were stern, inflexible, judgemental and unforgiving, always had been and always would be.

Still, even that had its uses.

FELIX LOOKED UP at the open sky. At last the swamp was behind them, and the rains had ceased. Even the midge and mosquito bites seemed momentarily less troubling. Ahead of them now lay a range of low barren foothills, rising to huge snow-capped peaks. Down the mountain's flanks ran hundreds of small rivers and streams, transporting the near-constant rains and depositing them in the swamp. Some spears of sunlight had managed to break through the leaden clouds and pierce the gloom. This land had a cruel beauty, he thought, but a beauty nonetheless.

The men of Crannog Mere had fallen silent. They seemed to be nervous now, as if leaving the swamp had the opposite effect on Felix as it had on them. They looked around shiftily like city dwellers suddenly deposited in the middle of a wood. Felix realised that they were leaving the lands they knew for parts more or less unknown, and it was affecting them. Felix had made such transitions so many times now himself that often he barely noticed them. Had it only been days ago he had walked the snow-covered forests of Sylvania? Somehow it seemed much longer. It was amazing how swiftly the mind could accept changes in circumstance when it had to.

He studied his companions. The Slayer looked grim and stolid as ever. Teclis looked quite genuinely pleased to see the sun. He stretched his arms almost in greeting. Murdo looked less nervous than the others, like a man making a journey he had done many times before. Culum simply glared at Felix as if quietly hating him just for being there. Suddenly the day seemed less bright, and the wind a fraction more chill.

They poled the barge across the open lake towards the shore. Felix could see the grey rocks of the bottom. Some were sharp as sword blades and would gut the boat if they hit them. Murdo guided them warily with short terse commands. Ahead of them the mountains loomed. Overhead a single huge eagle stretched its wings to catch the breeze, lazily scanning the land below for prey.

What other things might there be out there, Felix wondered, doing the same? Old powerful magic and Chaos had tainted this land. Surely they had not seen the last of monsters.

THEY BEACHED THE boat, dragged it ashore and into the long grass and rushes where it might be at least partially concealed. Half the men were detailed to watch it. The others would accompany them to the Oracle's cave. Felix was not thrilled to note that Culum would be one of their escorts. Still, at least he seemed to have his hands full carrying the unconscious Dugal.

'We follow the stream to its source,' Murdo said. 'If you get separated from us, find it and follow it. Downhill, it will bring you back to the lake and the boat. Uphill, it will lead eventually to the Oracle's home. Doubtless she will find you, if she wants to.'

The others laughed nervously, making Felix wonder about the role that this Oracle played in the society of Albion. The men's attitude seemed equal parts reverence and fear. He supposed it was hardly surprising if she was a witch. An image of the old hags in the fairy tales of his youth sprang to mind, of bubbling cauldrons and feasts on unhallowed flesh. Try as he might, he could not force it from his mind.

'Keep your eyes peeled for orcs,' said Murdo.

'Orcs?' Felix asked.

'Aye, many have been the sightings of greenskins in these hills in the past few months. Something has stirred them up. And stirred them up badly.'

As ever he looked as if he knew more than he was saying. What secrets are you hiding, Murdo, Felix wondered?

CHAPTER EIGHTEEN

FELIX BREATHED HARD as he walked, and cursed the constant rain. The land sloped upwards steeply. The path was slippery with scree. They followed the curve of the river, and all they saw for many long hours were wild long-horned sheep and some goats. The men of Crannog Mere marched stolidly along, wary now as only men out of their element could be. Gotrek seemed almost happy to be back amid barren hills and distant mountains. The chill breeze did not daunt him, and not even the return of the constant rain dampened his spirits. Teclis seemed preoccupied, concentrating on something far removed from their surroundings. As Felix approached him, he shivered as he noticed that the rain did not touch the elf's garments. Instead, repelled by some invisible shield, it halted a finger's breadth away. Close up it lent the elf a shimmering aura that added to his unearthly appearance.

'What is it?' Felix asked him, wondering if it was wise to interrupt the sorcerer while he concentrated.

'There are currents of magic passing through these hills, deep and old and tainted. Chaos has touched this land deeply, not just on the surface.'

'I have seen much worse,' said Felix, thinking of the lands through which he and Gotrek had once ventured in their search for the lost city of Karag Dum. The elf looked at him and cocked an eyebrow disbelievingly. 'The northern Chaos Wastes,' he added.

'You've been there? And you returned untainted. That is an impressive feat, Felix Jaeger.'

'Not one I would care to repeat,' Felix said. He was sure the dwarf would not thank him for sharing the tale of the voyage of the airship *Spirit of Grungni* with an elf, so he resisted the urge to tell it. Instead he said, 'You say these lands are tainted – in what way? What can we expect to encounter?'

'I think the contamination here runs deep. For some reason Albion has attracted a great deal of dark magical energy. I have heard tales that the Ogham Rings, the great stone circles, attract it and somehow render it harmless. Perhaps that was once true, but I suspect that now they are malfunctioning. All spells eventually wear out, all devices eventually reach the end of their usefulness. Perhaps they still attract the dark magic, but their capacity to store it or purify it has been reduced or lost. Perhaps it has something to do with the opening of the Paths of the Old Ones. Perhaps it is all part of the same great pattern. I do not know. I do know that there is a stone ring nearby and it is bending the flow of magic here, and altering the weather. Perhaps that accounts for the rains. The rains certainly account for why so much of these hills are barren.'

'How so? Everybody knows that rain is needed to make crops grow.'

Teclis shrugged. 'In most cases that is true. But flooding does not help corn grow.'

'It's difficult to flood a hill,' said Felix. 'At least in the way you mean. The water runs downslope. It does not lie.'

'Aye, and if it's heavy enough, it carries the topsoil with it, leaving only exposed rock on which only moss and lichen can grow.'

Looking around them, Felix could see that what the elf had said was true. Near the fast-flowing river there was only stone and rock, nothing grew save for a few hardy plants rooted in patches of soil trapped between boulders. Only away from the river did the green return. Felix considered this.

Some of his natural history professors maintained that the world was shaped by elemental forces – wind and rain and volcanoes and ice – that the lands were as they were because of the way they interacted. Others, and the priests, claimed the world was as it was because the gods had made it that way. What Teclis had said about the Old Ones sculpting continents tended to support that theory. What he said about the topsoil supported the first. Was it possible both were true? Or perhaps the elements were merely the tools the gods had used.

No, that could not be right. It would take centuries, if not millennia, for a river to wear away the bones of mountains. But perhaps the Old Ones' perception of time was different from ours, perhaps for them centuries were but an eyeblink.

'You look confused, Felix Jaeger. What are you thinking about?'

Felix told the elf.

'Perhaps the Old Ones used the elements as you think, but our legends tell us otherwise. They had no need to wait for millennia for erosion and geological forces to do their work. They could cut through tectonic plates with blades of cosmic fire, and level mountains with their spells. And this they did. They sculpted continents the way I might sculpt a statue.'

Felix was not quite willing to give up on his idea yet. 'You speak as if they were artists seeking to create a finished work of art. What if they were more like gardeners? Perhaps they pruned a branch here, irrigated an area there. Planted seeds that would not reach their final form for ages. Perhaps they did not shape the continents exactly to their design. Perhaps they merely put certain forces in motion, knowing that they would eventually one day lead to a certain end.'

Felix expected mockery, but instead the elf looked thoughtful. 'That is an original thought, Felix Jaeger, and one I had not considered. Nor has any elf that I know of. What you say may be correct or not, but you have given me something to think about.'

'I am glad to have been of some service to one of the Elder Race,' said Felix sardonically. 'Let me know when you have finished your deliberations.'

'You may not be alive then, Felix Jaeger. I may not reach any conclusions for a hundred years, if then.'

Felix was a little shocked by the sudden yawning gulf that had opened in the conversation and the glimpse it gave him of his own mortality. In the Empire few men reached the age of sixty. A man of fifty was considered old. Felix might be long in his grave while this youthful-seeming creature still thought upon his words. It sparked a certain resentment in him.

'If you are still alive then. We might all be dead within days.'

THE SLOPE STEEPENED. The going got tougher. They were on a mountain trail now and the rain-slicked gradient was becoming dangerous. Felix breathed in gasps and sweat started to mingle with the rain soaking his clothing.

He looked around. The peaks loomed larger now, and the clouds seemed thicker. Behind them the swamp was a low grim mass of trees and water. He thought he could see the huge stone structure of the Haunted Citadel emerging from the gloom, but it might just have been his imagination.

The land around them now looked gloomier, the rain had leeched even its drab colours. The waters of the river rushed by louder now, boiling white in places where they clashed against rocks and passed through narrow channels. In these last few dying hours of daylight, they had passed a succession of rushing falls whose spray had wet their faces, noticeable even in the rain. Here and there massive rocks far higher than a man flanked the path like sentinels. Sometimes Felix thought they bore some resemblance to ancient statues, their outlines blurred by time, and he was reluctant to put this down entirely to his imaginings.

The men of Crannog Mere all huffed and puffed worse than he. They were not mountain men, and this constant uphill walking was tiring them. Felix knew what a strain it could be to the calves and thighs when you were not used to it. He had walked in the Worlds Edge Mountains often enough to be familiar with it.

It was getting colder and wetter by the minute, and Felix felt like the chill that had settled in his bones was so deep that no fire would ever entirely remove it. It was like the cold of the grave. Only the dwarf and the elf showed no signs of strain. Gotrek strode along tirelessly like a man out for a summer stroll through an Altdorf park. Teclis was even more annoying – for all his feeble appearance, and his limping walk, he showed not the slightest signs of fatigue. Felix supposed that it must help that the wizard's spells protected him from the wet and cold, but that did not make it any easier to watch him. At least he might throw his shield over the rest of us, Felix thought; the selfish, elvish bastard.

His fingers found the amulet the elf had given him, the one Teclis claimed would shield him from daemons. He was not that selfish, at least not if what he had told Felix was true. Felix had not been troubled by the evil ones, but it had only been a few days so he had no basis for deciding about that. On the other hand, there was no doubt Teclis had rescued them from the Paths of the Old Ones. Even Gotrek had to admit that, albeit through gritted teeth. It was not a subject Felix ever expected to bring up again with the dwarf, at least if he could help it. The dwarf was touchy enough at the best of times.

Footsteps crunched on the scree beside him. He looked up, and was surprised to see Murdo had fallen into step beside him. 'I have been watching you,' said the old man.

'And what have you seen?'

'You do not seem to be under any enchantment that I can tell of, and you fought bravely enough against the spider daemons. I think you are what you say you are, and your companions are what they claim too.'

'Thank you, I think.'

'The problem is that if I accept that I have to accept much o' what else they claim, and that is frightening, laddie.'

'Yes, I suppose it is. We live in frightening times.'

'Aye, the weather has worsened, and the orcs and beastmen have come out of their fastnesses and war stirs across the land. There are rumours of other things, of evil mages abroad in the land.'

'They are abroad in every land,' said Felix sourly. 'Why should yours be different?'

'For in our land, every man and woman who shows a trace of the talent is inducted into a brotherhood, sworn to preserve our ancient ways, watched over by their fellows. I have the talent myself, enough tae ken that yon Teclis there is more powerful than any mage now living in Albion, maybe than any who ever lived here. And he is scared, although he hides it well. That scares me.'

'I think you are wise.'

Murdo nodded his head.

'Why are you telling me this?'

'Because I think maybe we got off on the wrong foot, and that we are all in the same boat and it has a hole in it. And I want you to know that whatever comes, you may rely on the men of Crannog Mere.'

'That is always good to know, but why tell me? Why not tell Teclis or Gotrek?'

'Because you are a man, and it is easier to say to you. And those two are not exactly the sort you can open your heart to.'

Or maybe you are planning treachery, Felix thought, and you think it easier to hoodwink me than them. But somehow he could not quite bring himself to believe that. The old tribesman seemed painfully sincere, and genuinely intimidated by the pair, which was something Felix could understand only too well. He had known Gotrek for years, and he still found him unapproachable, and the elf carried himself with a bearing that might intimidate the Emperor Karl Franz.

Having said his piece, Murdo moved back among his men, as if waiting to see what Felix would do. Felix shrugged. He would mention it to the others when and if the need arose.

Something had been nagging at the back of his mind for a while and it chose this moment to come forth. He had always

intended to set down the tale of Gotrek someday, when it came
to its inevitable end, but perhaps he should begin setting it down
soon, in case something happened to him before it was over. He
had seen things worth recounting in these journeys, and met people who would surely leave their names in the histories and
legends. Perhaps, if ever he got back to the Empire, he should
make a record of his travels with Gotrek and leave it somewhere
safe. With his brother, perhaps, or Max Schreiber, assuming the
wizard was even still alive. He squared his shoulders and came to
a decision. He would do it, and do it soon if the opportunity presented itself.

Another worrying thought occurred to him. Often in the past he
had been confronted with the reality of death, his own and other
people's. There had been times when he had thought he was going
to die, but now, for some reason, in this far distant place, he was
confronted by the certainty of it. Perhaps it was his time in the daemon's dungeon, or perhaps it was meeting the ageless elf and
talking about time, but something had brought the reality of his
mortality home to him.

Even if he avoided all the sword blades, and evil spells and the
teeth of monsters, if he did not fall foul to plague, pestilence or accident, some day he would not be here. Death was as certain as
tomorrow, just a little further away perhaps, and he now felt as he
never had before the urge to do something to be remembered himself, to write his name alongside those of Gotrek and Teclis and the
others he had met.

At that moment, he felt he understood just a little of what the
Slayer must have felt when Felix had sworn to record his doom. I
will record it, he thought – yours and mine and all the others I have
seen. There are some things that should be remembered. Assuming,
he thought, I am still here to write them down once this is all over.
It will not be an epic poem though, he thought. I cannot imagine
contriving one of those now. It will be a book or a series of them,
setting it all down as it had happened to the best of his recollection.
My Travels with Gotrek, or *The Trollslayer's Doom*. Something like that,
he thought.

He considered this, and all the books he had read as a youth, and
as a scholar at the university, and began to think of what he would
need to know. Certainly, he would need to record something about
Albion, for little was known of it back in the Empire. Here was a
chance to add to the sum of that knowledge, and share it – assuming that any survived the coming Chaos invasion or what might
happen if what Teclis claimed was true.

He shrugged. He had to assume that someone would. It was a commitment made to the future when times might be better and Chaos might be vanquished. However remote that possibility might seem now, he would proceed on the assumption that it might happen. It was a small, perhaps futile, gesture of faith in the face of events of cosmic malignity. And it was his gesture. Somehow just the thought made him feel a little better, although he was not entirely sure why. He strode back to join the old Truthsayer.

'Tell me about your land,' he said to Murdo.

'What do you want to know?'

As THEY WALKED, the thunder of rushing water grew louder ahead of them. It echoed through the rocks like the booming voice of an angry giant. Felix was worried. Such a sound could cover the hubbub of an approaching army, and visibility was already low because of the clouds, mist and the wilderness of tortured rocks through which they proceeded.

The river was narrower now and moved faster, and several times they had passed gigantic waterfalls tumbling down from above, separated from them as the path wound away and rejoined them later, higher upslope. It was getting dark now, and they were well up the mountainside. Felix tried not to think that mountains were the haunt of orcs, and concentrated on what old Murdo was telling him.

Under normal circumstances, Felix would have been fascinated, for the tattooed man was an interesting speaker, with a fund of knowledge and tales about his land. Felix learned that the men of Albion were divided into many tribes of the highlands and the low. The tribes were interrelated and once, not so long ago, there had been a golden age of peace, but that was before the orcs came, and the other raiders from over the seas. It seemed that the dark elves had found some way to penetrate the eternal mists that surrounded the enchanted island, and so had others. Felix immediately thought of the way he and Gotrek and Teclis had arrived but kept his peace about it. The outsiders had brought war with them. Felix struggled to get his head around the situation.

The orcs had arrived centuries back, few in number at first, as they must have been shipwrecked on the islands. They had bred quickly, swarming everywhere, and only the unification of the tribes under the hero Konark had let men triumph eventually and drive the orcs back into the mountains. The orcs had taken refuge amid ancient ruins in the remote valleys.

Occasional wars had been needed to pen them there. Now it seemed the orcs had multiplied again and something had driven them from the mountains onto the plains. They had even penetrated the great swamp that had kept the folk of Crannog Mere safe for ages. The orcs were bad, but the thought of something wicked and powerful enough to drive them from the mountains was worse. Now the tribes of men needed a leader to unite them once more, or they would be swept away. It was said that in these very mountains a hero by the name of Kron, who claimed to be a descendant of Konark, had done that for a few tribes. Felix gathered that Murdo was helping them because he thought Teclis was capable of discovering the mystery behind the orcs' sudden onslaught, and perhaps even stopping it. Felix certainly hoped so.

He considered what he knew. It seemed no part of the world was immune from its troubles. The great continent of the Old World was being ravaged by Chaos. Ulthuan shook with earthquakes. Albion was plagued by orcs and terrible storms. He would not have been surprised to learn that even in far Cathay, cataclysm had struck. Perhaps all the seers prophesying the end of the world had the truth of it.

He gave his attention back to Murdo. A picture of Albion emerged. It was less advanced than the Old World. The secret of making gunpowder was unknown and armour heavier than leather rare, manufactured by the tribes of the coast who seemed to be the main builders of large towns and cities. Great stone rings, focuses of magical force and energy, and other legacies of the ancients were everywhere. Ruined cities, haunted towers, odd labyrinths open to the sky, whose walls were scribed with mystical runes. Some of these were guarded by monstrous mutated giants, others by strange creatures such as hippogryphs and manticores and other daemonic mutants. Most of the gods of the Old World were known here, but seemed to be regarded more as great spirits than the deities with which he was familiar. Ulric was a wolf spirit of war and winter. Taal, the nature god, was regarded as supreme. In the Empire, there were some primitives who still worshipped the Old Faith, and what Murdo said reminded Felix of what he had read of them. Sigmar was unheard of here, which did not surprise Felix.

Dwarfs were things of legends and old tales. If ever there had been dwarfish cities here, they existed no more. Felix was hardly surprised – Albion was an island and dwarfs were not fond of ships. From what he had gathered from Gotrek, their steamboats were relatively recent developments in a history that stretched back millennia. Elves were known as Dark Ones here and had a reputation for deceit and treachery. Chaos was feared and the four powers of darkness were known but never to be named, whispered Murdo, lest you draw their attention to you. The old man had no idea of the geography of the world beyond

his island, had never heard of Araby or Cathay. Bretonnia was a legend
of which tales had been brought by shipwrecked sailors. Kislev was an
icy island at the north of the world. The Empire was another island,
larger and ruled by three emperors who fought constantly. Felix smiled
at this distorted notion of history until he realised that his own ideas
about Albion would have seemed just as strange to Murdo before he
came here. And, he was forced to remind himself, perhaps what the old
man was telling him was no more than stories. Certainly he believed
them to be true, but he was an uneducated tribesman from a tiny isolated village in a huge swamp in the back end of beyond. It was
possible, conceded Felix, that his tale held errors.

Still, on the details of what lay near his home, he seemed sound
enough. Felix resolved to keep an open mind until he saw something that contradicted what Murdo said. He pulled his cloak
tighter and studied his surroundings. They had emerged onto a
wide flat ledge mostly filled with a lake of bubbling water, fed by a
huge waterfall that leapt down from overhead to boil and bubble
on the rocks below. Massive boulders covered in damp green moss
ringed the lake, save where the water poured out over the stone edge
to continue to journey to lands below. Spray was everywhere. The
roaring was like that of a great wounded beast.

It took him a few moments to realise that there were dead bodies
ringing the edge of the lake. It took him a few more seconds to
realise that they belonged to women. He rushed over to the nearest
one. She had been young and lithe and she had died from a spear in
the back. Judging from the bloody foam on her lips, it looked like
she had drowned in her own blood. A spear lay near her cold, clutching fingers. Felix noticed the green hand protruding from the water,
and the swirl of greenish blood that told him an orc lay dead there.

'Taal's breath,' murmured Murdo. 'That is Laera, who was a chieftain of the Oracle's maiden-guard. There are others nearby – it looks
like they were wiped out by orcs.'

Felix looked around. He saw now that some of what he had
thought were moss-covered boulders were in fact orcish corpses.
The mist and spray and fading light had tricked his eyes.

'Where are the orcs now?' Felix asked.

Stone crunched as Gotrek strode up to the lakeside. He spat on
the submerged orcish body casually. 'If they are here, we will find
them,' he said.

'Wonderful,' said Felix. 'Can't wait.'

All around the men of Crannog Mere made ready for battle.

CHAPTER NINETEEN

THE MEN OF Crannog Mere stood with weapons ready. Culum had gently placed Dugal on the ground and unslung his stone-headed hammer. Teclis scanned their surroundings warily, as if expecting a horde of ravening greenskins to race down from the surrounding slopes at any minute. Gotrek cackled gleefully and swung his axe a few times, like a woodsman limbering up before chopping down a tree.

'Perhaps they drove the orcs off,' said Felix.

'Nae, laddie. If they had we would be challenged by the maiden-guard. It is the way.'

'Maybe the orcs have left.'

'These corpses are barely stiff, manling,' said Gotrek. 'This fight happened within the hour.'

'Why does this always happen to us?' Felix wondered aloud, and then wished he hadn't. The glances of the tribesmen showed that they were more than willing to suspect that the three companions were somehow responsible for all this. No matter what Murdo said, it appeared that the majority of the men did not trust them. Or perhaps it was just Teclis, he thought, noticing that most of the murderous looks were aimed at the elf.

'Why indeed?' Teclis asked. 'It cannot be purely chance that the orcs struck here mere hours ahead of us, can it?' He gave the impression of one who talked to himself and did not expect any answers from others.

'What now?' Felix asked.

'The Oracle is below, unless the orcs have her. Perhaps her maiden-guard are with her waiting for succour even now,' said Murdo.

'If there's greenskins to be killed, let's get to it,' said Gotrek with more enthusiasm than Felix liked.

'Below?' said Felix pointedly. 'Where exactly is that? I can see no caves.'

In answer, Murdo walked to the edge of the lake, to the cliffs where the waterfall dropped. He seemed to vanish into the water itself, and one by one the men of Albion trooped after him, leaving Dugal in the shelter of the rocks.

Impelled by curiosity, Felix moved forward to where the men had vanished. He could see that there was a clear space wide enough for two people abreast behind where the waterfall fell. A ledge of rock ran there, but there were no men to be seen. Gotrek strode past onto the ledge, ignoring the tons of furious water passing so close, and he too seemed to vanish into the wall. Felix followed and within ten strides found a cave mouth opening to the left. The men were within, along with the Slayer, looking at more dead bodies of women and orcs. Felix found the sight very disturbing. He was not used to looking at so many dead girls. Most of them had been beautiful, too, he noted in passing.

Teclis came behind him and studied the scene. He pushed past Felix and the man felt the spray hit him, repelled by the mage's spells. It seemed a little impolite but Felix was not about to say anything, particularly not since he was already soaked. Teclis gestured and light filled the cave. Felix could see that it vanished deeper into the darkness beneath the mountains.

'Tunnels full of orcs,' he said. 'How can it get any worse?'

'How can it get any better?' said Gotrek. In the strange witch-light cast by the elf, his shadow danced menacingly along the walls.

Murdo fumbled amid the nooks and crannies of the walls until he found torches. Teclis lit them with a word. At first, Felix wondered why they were bothering, since the elf was capable of illuminating their passage, then the thought occurred to him that something might happen to him. It was not a reassuring one.

Gotrek moved to the fore, Murdo looming over him with a lit torch in one hand, spear in the other. It seemed logical in this dark underground space that the dwarf should lead; he was far more at home here than any human or elf could ever be. Felix stood beside Teclis, weapon bared. The tribesmen followed behind them.

Gotrek strode confidently into the gloom. Felix took a deep breath.

'Here we go,' he said.

THERE WERE SIGNS of combat everywhere. Armed warrior women had fought a desperate rearguard action into the depths of the cavern complex. They lay where they had been hacked down, surrounded by the bodies of orcs and goblins. Once, not so long ago, Felix had found something pathetic in the sight of the child-sized corpses of goblins. Not any more. Whatever sympathy he might have had was long gone. Now they just looked like any other small malevolent monster, with their bulging eyes and rows of razor-edged serrated teeth. In some ways they were just as terrifying as their larger orcish kin. They usually attacked in packs. The massive orcs did not need to.

So far the torches and the magelight had proved unnecessary. There were oil lanterns set in niches in the walls, providing a faint flickering illumination. In places they had been tumbled and smashed but the damp floor of the tunnels must have extinguished any blaze. A faint perfume filled the air, from the lantern oil and from some incense that had been added.

He felt the weight of the mountain begin to press in on him, became acutely aware of the mass of stone and rock hanging just above him, ready to crush him. Barely conscious of what he was doing, he listened for the creak of the earth as the mountain settled. He heard nothing but that did not keep him from imagining things. He felt, for instance, that it was getting warmer with every step.

A glance at the elf told him that Teclis was faring little better than he. The elf looked deeply uneasy for the first time that Felix could ever remember. His shoulders were hunched and he stooped, though there was plenty of room even for someone of his height in the tunnel. His gaze flickered everywhere as if seeking threats. Felix knew without being told that the elf was feeling the strain of being underground even more than he was.

Only the Slayer seemed unconcerned. He stood taller and strode with even more confidence than usual. Felix could have sworn that he was even whistling some almost jaunty tune. Nonetheless, Gotrek held his axe ready. Even as Felix watched he paused, sniffed the air and said, 'There are orcs nearby. Lots of orcs.'

* * *

THE TUNNELS DEEPENED. The floor became less damp. At first Felix
had wondered why anyone would choose to dwell in such a chill,
wet place, but now it was warm, and the perfume in the air was
almost musky. He could see that all year around, even in the cold of
winter, this could be comfortable.

'How does this Oracle live?' he asked Murdo. He was not surprised that his voice came out in a whisper and that the old man
replied in kind. He was only talking to cover his nervousness. He
knew it was foolish to make a noise when there might be orcs near,
but he could not help himself. 'Where do they find food?'

'The tribes bring offerings, and the maiden-guard keep goats and
sheep on the higher ground. Perhaps the orcs found those and followed them here, I am thinking.'

'That would seem logical,' said Felix. 'But why would they dwell
here anyway? Why not in some more accessible location?'

'This place is sacred, Felix Jaeger. The light has blessed it. The first
Oracle communed with the Great Spirits here after wandering lost
through the mountains. The gods led her to shelter in these caves in
a snowstorm while wolves hunted her. She found the altar of light
in their depths and it granted her magical powers.'

For a moment, Teclis looked less queasy and showed a glimmer
of professional interest. Felix supposed that any wizard would when
matters magical came up. 'It was an ancient artefact?' he asked.

'I do not know, Teclis of the elves. I am not an initiate of these
mysteries. I know that in return for taking the sight of her eyes, it
granted another sort of sight. And I know that from that first day to
this, there has been an Oracle in this place. They come when they
are summoned from whatever corner of Albion where they be living.'

'Summoned?' Felix asked. Murdo shrugged.

'They know when it is their time to come here, just as the old Oracle knows when the hour of her dying will come on her. The light
grants them this knowledge.'

Felix wondered how much of this was mere superstition and how
much truth. He had seen so many strange things in his time that
anything seemed possible. It might prove interesting meeting this
Oracle, he thought. Under any other circumstances but these.

THE TUNNEL WIDENED out into an area of caves. Felix could see that
these had once been occupied chambers. Sleeping pallets lay strewn
about the ground. Rent and torn clothing lay everywhere, golden
torcs and glittering jewellery caught the light. There were more bodies and from up ahead came the sound of combat. A horde of

greenskins packed the entrance of a cave mouth. They seemed to be trying to force their way in against stiff resistance. A dark cloaked figure armed with a stone-tipped spear urged them on.

Gotrek needed no more encouragement, and with a bellowing roar, he raced ahead as fast as his short legs would carry him. The men of Albion followed, overtaking him easily with their long strides. Felix decided to stick close to the Slayer, and the elf had obviously decided to do the same. He barely seemed to lengthen his limping stride and he was beside Gotrek. As he walked, he spread his arms and chanted. A wall of flame erupted ahead of them, and the screams and bellows of dying orcs and goblins filled the air.

The men of Albion stopped, unable to push their way through the roaring flames. Felix could feel their heat from where he stood. It was like being next to an open furnace. Nothing, it seemed, could live within that incandescent fury.

He was wrong. With a bestial roar, a massive orc burst out of the flames. His clothing smouldered. His greenish skin was seared a sooty black in places, but he came on undaunted. Moments later, another and then another burst through. All of them were huge, bigger than a man and far more muscular. Their yellowish tusks glistened with froth. Massive scimitars gleamed in their huge fists. Their eyes were filled with mad hatred and insensate fury. There were only half a dozen of them, but the sight of them, and the way they had burst through the flames, seemed to fill the folk of Crannog Mere with dismay. Felix understood their feelings only too well. The orcish leader, even more massive than the rest and wearing a helmet of bronze inlaid with bullhorns, grunted something to his fellows in their brutal tongue, and they laughed madly as they advanced.

Felix did not doubt that at that moment the men of Albion would have run had not Gotrek stood his ground. He was sorely tempted to do so himself. Instead, he moved to a position slightly to the left and slightly behind the Slayer, judging this the best place to ward his back. Teclis moved over to the right, a gleaming runeblade clutched in his left hand, the staff blazing with power in his right.

'Steady, lads,' said Murdo. 'These greenskin devils owe us blood for what they did here.'

That was all it took. The men formed up into a fighting line on either side of the three companions. Culum lifted his hammer menacingly. Felix watched the green giants move closer. He was aware of the dryness in his mouth and the beating of his heart. He felt suddenly weak, and everything seemed to be happening much slower than usual. He ignored the sensations, having experienced them in battle many times before, and braced himself for the impact. It was not long in coming.

He saw one orc leap forward and impale itself on the barrier of spears. Undaunted, it drove itself forward, reaching out to snap one man's neck and chop another down with its blade. More spears slammed home into its body. But it fought on, cackling madly, seemingly unkillable by normal weapons, such was its unnatural vitality. Another went for Culum. Sparks flashed as blade met hammer and the big man was driven back by a strength even more prodigious than his own.

Two of the orcs came for Gotrek. He did not wait for them to reach him, instead he strode forward, ducking the sweep of a scimitar and catching the back of an orc's knee with his return blow. The beast fell forward headlong, unable to walk on the amputated stump of its leg. The Slayer's second blow was met by a scimitar and partially deflected. Gotrek snorted with contempt, and aimed another blow that sent the orc leaping backwards, desperately avoiding a stroke that would have caved in its ribs had it connected.

It was Teclis that surprised Felix. Showing no more restraint than Gotrek, he hurled himself forward to confront the orcish leader. The creature was even taller than the elf, and far more massive. Enormous cable-like sinews rippled under its glistening green skin. It snarled something in orcish and laughed when the elf's reply was delivered in the same tongue. The guttural syllables sounded strange in the elf's far higher voice.

'Wait,' shouted Felix, knowing that their situation might yet become desperate if the elf were killed. 'Leave this one for me.'

He moved forward to meet the orc but by then it was far too late. The greenskin chieftain struck with the speed and fury of a summer storm. His blow fell like a thunderbolt, but the elf was simply not there. Moving with a swiftness that blurred sight, he moved around the orc's strike, and his own blade bit home into the orc's upper arm. The creature bellowed with fury and aimed a stroke that would have decapitated the slim elf had it connected. Teclis ducked to one side, executing what seemed almost a courtly bow, and the blade passed above his head. His return stroke was driven upwards with all the force of an uncoiling spring. It bit into the orc's ribs, drawing greenish blood. Only the orc chief's own lightning swiftness had kept the blade from burying itself in his bowels. Strokes passed between the two almost too fast for Felix's eye to follow. The elf gave ground gracefully, moving backward like water flowing over stone. The orc pursued, grunting mightily, until he was almost past Felix. In his fury, his concentration was entirely on the mocking elf who danced away taunting him in his own language and who was slowly inflicting a dozen small cuts on him with his ripostes.

Seeing the opportunity, Felix lunged forward. His blade took the orc in the side, finding its way beneath the ribs and passing right through the stomach. Felix withdrew it, and threw himself back as the orc, striking like a dying scorpion, lashed out at him reflexively. In that fatal moment of distraction, the elf's blade took him through the eye and he slumped to the earth, dead before he hit the ground.

'That was not very sporting, Felix Jaeger,' said Teclis.

'This is not a game,' said Felix angrily, annoyed by the elf's insouciance. 'You can die here the same as anybody else.'

'Is that not part of the thrill of the thing?' said Teclis dangerously. Felix wondered if his ennui could really be that great.

'And who will save Ulthuan if you fall here?' said Felix, turning to enter the battle once more. Even as he did so, he saw the dark cloaked figure had raised his hand. A wave of magical power flowed towards Felix. For a brief moment, he thought he saw the folk around him transformed into daemons. All around he heard the men of Crannog Mere gasp in terror. The irrational urge to turn and flee filled him and he could see the others waver. Looks of horror were on their faces as if they had just seen their worst nightmares materialise in front of them.

The amulet on Felix's chest glowed and a warmth spread through him, dispelling the fear. He heard a cold chill laugh and realised that it had come from the elf. The sound of that dry mirth was more chilling in its way than even the vision of his manifold fear.

'Try your simple sorceries on me would you, man of Albion? I return them to you, redoubled and redoubled again.' The elf spoke a spell and the dark-cloaked figure emitted a high-pitched shriek of pure fear before clutching his chest and collapsing to the ground. The men of Albion steadied and fought on.

Gotrek had chased his orc until it was backed against the wall. His axe flashed once and the creature's chest caved in, entrails exploding everywhere from the force of the impact. Felix looked around to see how the men of Albion were doing. Culum finally saw an opening and aimed his hammer squarely at the beast's head. The force of the impact took the head clean from the shoulders, caving in one side and sending it flying through the air to hit the ground rolling like a ball. It landed at Felix's feet, almost as if the big man had intended it that way, and looked up at him with fierce hatred in the dying light of its eyes.

The other tribesmen had managed to surround the last two orcs and harried them like hounds pulling down a stag. Spears flickered forward, fast as the tongues of snakes, and pierced green flesh. Bleeding and gored from a dozen wounds, the orcs finally went down. They had taken their share of men to hell with them, though, thought Felix. Only half a dozen of the men of Crannog Mere were left.

Gotrek headed towards the opening from which the sounds of fighting had come. Felix followed him into the final caves.

THERE WERE GOBLINS in here, and dead orcs and more dead women. A few of the amazons still stood, battling a scuttling horde of bow-legged goblins. Beyond them was a white-shrouded figure that the women seemed willing to give their lives to protect. Felix raced forward, overtaking the Slayer, and leapt the last few strides that separated him from the goblins.

Wielding his blade with both hands, he hewed about him, taking many of the little monsters before they even knew he was upon them. Their death screams panicked their comrades and they turned frantically to face the new threat, giving the women time to hustle their charge back out of range of the combat.

Excellent, thought Felix, alone against a horde of greenskins. This is where chivalry gets you. He continued to fight though, back-pedalling desperately, knowing that the Slayer could not be too far away. Nor was he disappointed. Within heartbeats, a massive axe flashed past his shoulder and chopped a howling goblin clean in two. Then Gotrek was moving through them like a whirlwind of destruction. Nothing lived that fell within the arc of his blade. His blows smashed through shields, made parries futile for the small creatures. They could no more withstand the Slayer than Felix could have withstood the charge of a bull.

Moments later the men of Albion arrived and the slaughter was complete. That's that, thought Felix, glancing back at the scene of the carnage. He turned around to find himself facing a row of spears, all aimed at his chest.

CHAPTER TWENTY

THE WOMEN WERE armed with spears and small leather shields. They did not look friendly. Felix wondered why they pointed their spears at him so menacingly. Had he not helped save them? Had he not killed orcs? He kept very still anyway. Mistakes get made. Misunderstandings can easily be fatal when there are weapons involved.

'This is sacred ground,' said one of the women. She was almost as tall as Felix and her hair was tied into many locks. Tattoos covered her face and arms and gave her a wild barbaric look.

'I'm sorry – next time I will respect your taboos, and let the orcs slaughter you on your sacred ground.' He could not quite keep the bitterness from his voice. The woman looked as if she was going to attack him. Felix prepared himself to spring clear.

'Be at peace, Siobhain,' said a quavering voice. 'He is a stranger here and he helped save all of our lives. He is entitled to be here.'

'But he is not of our blood,' said Siobhain. 'Any fool can see that…'

Her mouth sprang shut like a steel trap as if she had just realised what she had said. A flush, visible even in the dim light, passed beneath her facial tattoos. A moment later Felix understood why. The old woman to whom she had been talking had eyes of milky white. She was quite obviously blind. The girl gave Felix a glare as if it was all somehow his fault. Felix shrugged.

'You are Felix Jaeger,' said the old woman. Felix kept his own mouth closed with effort. How could she have known his name? Carrier pigeon, a messenger slipped away from Crannog Mere in the dead of night, lots of different ways, the rational part of his mind whispered, but he knew it was wrong. There was magic involved. This old woman was quite plainly a witch of some sort. 'Well met,' said the old woman, her fingers moving through an intricate gesture that might have been part of a spell or a benediction. Felix flinched but nothing happened.

'Well met,' he said back, bowing with as much grace as he could muster. It seemed somehow the right thing to do. He sensed the old woman's attention sliding away from him and took the opportunity to study her. She was a tall woman, sharp faced, but still beautiful. Her robes were of thick grey wool. Her braids were even more complex than Siobhain's. There were tattoos on her face too, but they had faded to near invisibility, like markings on parchment that has been left too long in the sun. How could that have happened, Felix wondered?

'You are welcome here too, Teclis of Ulthuan. You are the first of your kind to set foot in this place for millennia.'

The elf's voice was sardonic. 'As far as I know I am the first of my kind ever to set foot in this place, Oracle.'

'Then you do not know everything,' said the old woman. Her voice had a sharp, brittle quality now. Felix guessed she was used to being treated with more respect. Certainly the tribesmen seemed in awe of her. The expressions on their faces said as much.

'I have been aware of that for more centuries than you have lived,' said Teclis. His own tone was just as sharp. The gods preserve us from the vanity of wizards, thought Felix. A strange smile passed across the old woman's face, almost as if she knew what he was thinking. Gotrek grunted at the elf's words and strode forward.

'I am Gotrek, son of Gurni,' he said, not giving the old woman time to name him. 'Who are you?'

The maiden-guard and the tribesmen bristled at his tone. Hands stiffened on weapons. Gotrek looked supremely unconcerned by the prospect of imminent violence. Felix wished he could share the dwarf's attitude.

'You too are welcome, Slayer.' If Gotrek wondered how she knew what he was, no sign of it appeared on his face. 'I gave up my name when I took the title Oracle.'

The Slayer shrugged. He even managed to make that action somehow menacing. Felix wondered if they had really come all this way just to get into a fight with the people who should have been their allies. Something needed to be done and quickly.

'How did those orcs get here?' he asked. 'This is not the sort of place you just stumble on.'

'They were led here,' said the Oracle.

'Led!' said Murdo. He sounded shocked.

'Aye, Murdo Mac Baldoch, led.'

'What man of the tribes would have led them here? Surely no one could so turn their face from the light?'

'It was more than a man of the tribes, Murdo. It was one of the Council. Siobhain, make yourself useful! You and Mariadh bring the body of the dark-cloaked stranger to us.'

There was silence until the two warrior-maidens returned bearing the body of the sorcerer. The Oracle moved over to it and pulled back the cowl to reveal a lean, pale, tattooed face. The man's features were distorted by terror even in death. Spittle was still on his lips. It looked like he had died of pure fright.

Murdo's face went white. 'Baldurach!' he said. There was both fear and disbelief in his tone. The old man's shoulders slumped and he studied the floor at his feet. 'We are betrayed then, and by one of our own,' he said very softly.

'Some there are who listen to the whispers of the Dark Spirit,' said the Oracle.

'This is not the place to talk of this,' Murdo said, glancing significantly at the three companions. His glance even seemed to take in his own kin, although Felix thought this might have been his own imagination.

'If not here, where?' said the Oracle. 'These three must hear what is said here. Send the others away.' She gestured to her guardians and they began to herd the men out. The Oracle turned and walked deeper into the caves. She did so easily and gracefully, with no hint of the fact that she was blind. Felix felt the hairs stir on the nape of his neck. *There are other senses than sight,* he told himself. *Or perhaps she has simply walked these halls so long she has all the obstructions memorised.* Once again something told him that this was not the case.

Gotrek and Teclis fell into step behind her. The elf's magelight dimmed somewhat but still gave enough illumination to see by. Murdo looked at him with what might have been fear, respect or awe and gestured for Felix to proceed. Felix followed them down into the gloom. The old man's heavy tread told him Murdo was right behind him.

THIS CHAMBER WAS smaller. The walls were carved with more abstract patterns that seemed to map some cosmic maze. In the centre was a massive, perfect stone egg, on which was inscribed similar patterns. Just looking at them made Felix feel slightly dizzy. On the top of the stone egg was a dimple in which something lay.

'Are you sure you want these strangers here?' asked Murdo.

'They are part of this,' said the Oracle. She sat cross-legged in the shadow of the egg and gestured for them to sit likewise. Felix and Teclis joined her. Gotrek lounged against the wall, his axe held nonchalantly in both hands. Murdo glared at him and then he, too, sat.

'What?'

'Dark shadows gather, Murdo. Things long imprisoned will be free. Some of our brothers and sisters have turned from the truth and the light and now serve that which we sought to contain. The ancient brotherhood is broken. A time of schism and chaos is come.'

'Impossible!'

'No, Murdo, not at all. We are mere mortals and it is undying. We are fallible and corruptible. Some have fallen. As was predicted.'

'That it should happen in our time. That the ancient trust should be betrayed.'

'Yet betrayed it is. And orcs found their way into the heart of this sacred place. We should be grateful it was only orcs Baldurach led and not something worse.'

Felix wondered if the elf and dwarf were as confused by this as he. They gave no sign. Teclis appeared to be concentrating hard on everything said. Gotrek merely stared into space as if bored.

'You say they are part of this.'

'Yes. Outsiders have taken over the Temple of the Old Ones. They have opened the ancients' paths. In doing so, they have left an opening through which the ancient enemy can escape.'

'Who is this enemy of which you speak?' Felix asked.

'An ancient spirit of darkness, imprisoned long ago, bound by mighty spells at the dawn of history. It seeks power and the domination of all.'

'It was imprisoned using the power of the paths and the leylines,' said Teclis. He sounded like a physician discussing a case of fever. The Oracle nodded.

'It was the only way. No mortal would have had the power otherwise.'

'And now the flows of power have been disturbed, its shackles have loosened.'

'Yes. Though that is not your problem. Your concerns are more pressing. You seek to prevent the sinking of your homeland, do you not?'

'Yes. How do you know this?'

'Thoughts and visions can pass through the Paths of the Old Ones as well as living beings. I have talked with the same undying ones who talked with you. They told me of your coming. Our fortunes are linked. For you must clear the Temple of the Old Ones and close the paths once more, or your land is doomed.'

'We must do it?' said Felix. 'Why us?'

'For no one else in Albion has the power or the knowledge to do what needs to be done. The temple is in the hands of the fell powers of Chaos. They have driven forth the orcs and bound the god the greenskins worshipped.'

'They have bound a god?' said Felix. 'With all due respect, I think beings who can do that are a little beyond our ability to deal with.'

He did not look around for fear that either the elf or the dwarf might disagree with him. They remained silent.

'It is no true god, Felix Jaeger. It is one of the creations of the Old Ones, a guardian set to watch over their temple and their creations.'

Felix thought about the spider things they had fought back in the swamp. The memory did nothing to increase his liking for the task that was being proposed. 'What sort of monsters are these?'

'One of the giants of Albion, Felix Jaeger.' Felix suppressed a groan. He did not need to be able to see the Slayer to know how interested he was. 'The giants were made long ago, by the Old Ones, to guard their treasures and their secrets. They are near immortal but over the years, it is said, they have become altered, a degenerate parody of the noble creatures they once were. They fell to the worship of Chaos, and other vile practices. They became wicked, predatory creatures, that preyed on all things weaker than they, but still they kept to their duties in an odd way, bound by the geas the Old Ones placed on them. They haunted the old places and made them their lairs, filled them with their ill-gotten treasures.'

This was getting worse and worse – treasures as well as monsters! He was surprised Gotrek was not foaming at the mouth by now. 'And you say one of them has been bound by the forces of Chaos.'

'Aye, Magrig One Eye, mightiest of the giants of old, a slayer of dragons and behemoths in his day, before his brain became clouded and he acquired the lust for manflesh.'

'Oh good, not just an ordinary gigantic monster then,' said Felix.

'No. He is large as a hillock and can smash castle walls with a blow of his club.'

'And now he has been bound to the service of Chaos?' said Teclis.

'Aye, by Kelmain and Lhoigor, two of the foulest and most powerful of all the Changer's servants.'

The old woman gestured and a vision appeared in the glowing mist that sprang up between her hands. It showed two miniature sorcerers, albino twins, one garbed in black, one in gold. Their heads were bald or shaven, their fingers were like claws.

'I know them,' said Felix, unable to keep the surprise from his voice. 'We followed one of them into the Paths of the Old Ones. And they were at Praag with the Chaos horde,' he added hastily, before his words could be misinterpreted.

'Aye,' said Gotrek. 'They were. They advised Arek Daemonclaw and his warlords. They summoned those great living siege engines and the daemons who stormed the walls.'

'They are old enemies of yours?' said Murdo.

'They won't get much older if they come within reach of my axe,' said Gotrek.

'That is good,' said the Oracle, 'for they are evil men and much in need of killing.'

Felix toted up the foes. 'One giant, two sorcerers of great power, what else? Three dragons?'

'The mages have their bodyguards, and every day they bring more and more Chaos warriors through the paths. They plan to use the ancient ways to invade many lands. They either do not know or do not care about the consequences of what they have done.'

'A Chaos army as well then. Good – that seems simple enough. Shall we just walk in and challenge them all to single combat?'

'I do not think you are taking this entirely seriously, Felix Jaeger,' said the Oracle.

'You spotted that, did you? I can see why they call you the Oracle.' Felix seemed unable to keep his mouth shut.

Murdo's hand reached for his knife. 'You will show some respect…'

'Or what? You'll kill me. It seems your Oracle is going to do quite well on that score anyway.'

Felix knew he was sounded hysterical and bitter, but he could not help it. That was the way he felt. It seemed like it was out of the troll's cookpot and into the flames. How could three of them achieve anything under these conditions? It was impossible. There was an army of monsters. There was a giant. There were two of the most powerful and evil magicians on the face of the planet. It did not matter how mighty a warrior Gotrek was or how powerful a sorcerer was Teclis, the odds were very much stacked against them. He shook his head, fighting for self-control. So what else was new? He had faced overwhelming odds before and survived. He and the Slayer had fought their way out of many dark places. This was just going to be one more. He looked at the Oracle.

'I apologise,' he said softly. 'I am just tired and scared.'

'Those are understandable things to be under the circumstances, Felix Jaeger. It does you credit that you know it.'

'For a moment there I just didn't see how we could do it.'

'And you do now?' said Teclis smiling.

'It's simple,' he said. 'All we need is an army to keep the Chaos warriors occupied. Gotrek and I will kill the giant, and you can deal with the wizards. Nothing could be simpler.'

'A good plan, manling,' said Gotrek. Felix thought he detected a hint of sarcasm in the Slayer's voice, but he was not entirely sure. 'And if the elf can't deal with those spellcroakers, I will.'

'I wished I shared your confidence, Gotrek Gurnisson,' said the elf. His manner did not entirely reassure Felix.

'I think parts of what you require can be arranged,' said the Oracle. 'It is only a matter of looking in the right place.'

Excellent, thought Felix, I am going to take advice on how to look for something from a blind woman. He kept his thoughts to himself though. The blind woman smiled as if reading them anyway.

'Now, Teclis of the elves,' she said. 'You must take this, and I will instruct you in its use, and then I will see to Dugal.'

She lifted the amulet from atop the intricate rune-worked egg. Felix could see that it was made of stone, and covered in the now familiar runes. Since it was clear that she intended only the elf to remain, he got up, bowed, and left.

'I hope she is teaching him some powerful magic,' he said, as the sound of murmuring voices faded behind him. 'We are going to need it.'

CHAPTER TWENTY-ONE

FELIX DREW HIS cloak tight about him. The wind blew chill and cold here in the mountains. As they walked over the crest, he could see how deceptive the landscape really was. What looked like a range of high peaks were in fact many intersecting ranges of mountains, and between them lay many valleys and lakes.

Up here, snow lay on the ground still and vegetation was scant. The only wildlife were some high-flying birds, and some wild sheep that bounded warily away when they saw humans. Below them were more pinewoods that rolled almost down to the shores of the lakes in some places. To the north, he could see what looked like a barren valley. What makes one valley fertile and another not he wondered, then shrugged. It was just one more of those questions to which he would most likely never find an answer.

Behind him the tribesmen of Crannog Mere straggled out in a line. At the head of the column were the maiden-guard the Oracle had sent to guide them. The elf mage and the dwarf stood on the brow of the hill, staring around them. It was not the wild beauty of the landscape that held their attention, Felix could tell, but the cluster of circular stone towers that clung to the next ridge top. They were massive brutal structures designed to resist siege. Their only ornamentss were the omnipresent runes that echoed the tattoo patterns on the faces of the warriors. These had been painted in blazing lurid colours on the stonework. Doubtless they held some mystical significance. Perhaps he would ask the elf, he thought.

From the tower a group of warriors had emerged and raced along the ridgeback towards them. There were several score at a rough count, and all of them armed. Felix moved closer to Gotrek and Teclis. He did not doubt that there would be a warm welcome for the Oracle's followers, but he was not so sure how well things would go for strangers. Under the circumstances, he decided, it was better to be on the safe side.

THE FOLK OF Carn Mallog were more bearish than wolvish, Felix decided. They were big men, burly and hard-faced. Their hair was long and shaggy, beards of almost dwarfish length sprouted from their faces, braided and twisted into all manner of fantastic patterns. Tattoos marked their cheeks and sword arms. Huge two-handed swords hung strapped to their backs. Long spears were clutched in their hands. Their clothes consisted of leather jerkins and woollen kilts. Long plaid cloaks covered the shoulders of most. Some had bearskins or wolfskins instead. They seemed to be the men of most importance. They eyed Teclis and Gotrek warily. Their looks made it clear that their reservations applied to Felix as well.

'These men have swords,' Felix said to Gotrek. 'The men of Crannog Mere do not. Why do you think that is?'

'It's hard to work metal in a swamp, manling,' said the dwarf.

'Murdo has a sword,' said Felix, just to be contrary.

'I would guess he traded for it with the mountain men. Mountains and hills are where you find mines and metals, mostly.'

'Why is that?'

The dwarf shrugged. 'Ask the gods,' he said. 'They put the metal there. Dwarfs just dig it out.'

Felix could see he was not going to get any better answer. Teclis returned the men's stares blandly, ignoring their open hostility. Murdo led a huge bear of a man over towards them and swiftly made the introductions. It turned out the man's name was Bran MacKerog, chieftain of the men of Carn Mallog. There was no warmth in the greetings he gave them, only suspicion and perhaps a wary respect.

'I give you thanks for aiding the Oracle,' he said. 'The light watch over her.'

'No thanks are necessary,' said Felix, seeing that his companions were not going to respond. 'We merely did what any men would have under the circumstances.'

As soon as he said it, Felix knew it was not the right thing. He doubted whether Gotrek or Teclis would thank him for comparing them to men. He could see that the thought that neither was human had already passed through Bran's head. For all his brutal features there was a quick intelligence written in those cold blue eyes and that hard-hewn face. Felix doubted that a man got to be chieftain in the mountain tribes by birth alone.

'You will take whisky with us,' he said. Felix was not sure whether it was a request, a command or an invitation.

'We will,' he said quickly in case the others took it the wrong way. They moved towards the towers as night began to gather around the peaks like a cloak.

Teclis limped along with Murdo on one side and Siobhain on the other. They had returned from their talks with the men of Carn Mallog. In the days it had taken them to get this far, both seemed to have accepted him. He supposed it made it easier for them that the Oracle had. Both talked freely and softly in his presence, at least as long as they were out of earshot of the others. Teclis listened with half his attention while his mind pondered the mysteries the Oracle had revealed to him. They had come to him as a profound shock.

'It is bad,' said Murdo. 'The orcs are gathering in the mountains once more. Rumour has it that their shamans have whipped them up to try and retake their valley. Some sort of prophet has arisen among them. It seems they have dwelled there so long they regard it as their own.'

'Is that so?' said Teclis. It seemed his suspicions had been correct. The temple was the key to all of this. It lay at the centre of the vast web of the Paths of the Old Ones, and only from there could those arcane ways be closed once more, although it seemed the price to be paid might be very high. He wondered once more at the other things the old woman had told him. Was it really possible that the Truthsayers had been made privy to certain secrets of the Old Ones that not even the elves had been taught?

'Indeed, Teclis of Ulthuan, it is so,' said the woman. She smiled at him rather oddly, he thought, and touched his arm when she spoke. That raised interesting possibilities if his suspicions were correct.

He smiled and returned his thoughts to their earlier track. Such a thing would certainly be a blow to the vanity of his people if it were true and became common knowledge. According to the Oracle it seemed the formation of the order of Truthsayers dated back to the legendary times when the Old Ones had walked the earth. Why had the elves not been told this? The Old Ones must have had their reasons. Perhaps there were factions among the Old Ones just as with every other race. Perhaps they did not want only one race to possess all magical knowledge. After all, they had given the skill of rune-crafting only to the dwarfs.

'It seems we may face an army of greenskins as well as army of Chaos worshippers,' said Murdo. He looked off at the distant peaks as if he suspected they might be hiding enemies.

'That would not be good,' said Teclis, shifting his attention back to the man. 'We must reach the Chamber of Secrets in the Temple of the Old Ones if I am to do what must be done.'

'I will help you all I can,' said Murdo. 'In any way I can.'

'As will I,' said Siobhain. There was definitely a glint in her eye, Teclis thought. Well, many human women had found him attractive down the ages, but at the moment he needed to keep his mind on other things.

It appeared that the Old Ones had foreseen something of the coming catastrophe, and taught these human wizards to prepare for it. The great stone rings were a means of trapping and controlling the energy of Chaos. If what the Oracle had said was true, then it had not been the elven wizards who turned the tide in the ancient war against Chaos, but the Truthsayers and their stone rings. By draining off the magical power of Chaos at the crucial time, they had blunted its sorcerously driven assault on the world, although at the cost of polluting their own land as the stones' power worked too well.

Perhaps here was the real reason the Paths of the Old Ones had become contaminated. Perhaps it was from magical energy drained from Albion into them. Teclis dismissed the theory. He did not know enough. He reviewed what the Oracle had told him about the temple, and the amulet that now hung from his chest.

It seemed that there were no Truthsayers left with the power to use it as it should be used, so it had fallen to him. He only hoped that he would be up to the task. He touched it with his long fingers. Of course he would. He was Teclis, greatest wizard of this age of the world. If he could not close the paths, nobody could. And that was the most worrying thought of all. If he could not do it…

Ahead of them loomed the first of the great stone towers. It looked like they would arrive just in time for nightfall. Soon he would talk with Bran and the others about the Oracle's plan. And after that… He smiled at the woman. She smiled back at him. We shall see what we shall see, Teclis thought.

* * *

'How LARGE AN army has your Empire then, Felix Jaeger?' asked
Bran. Instantly all the large burly men surrounding him paid more
attention.

'I do not know the exact numbers, but many regiments,' said Felix.
On the walk to the tower, the mountain chieftain had shown great
interest in the Empire and its weapons. War was his business, Felix
supposed, and he was merely showing a professional interest.
Either that or he was pumping him for information with a view to
a future invasion. In any case, the questions and the talk always
seemed to circle back to the question of military strength.

Felix was not intimidated by the thought. From what he had seen
of the men of Albion, the Empire had little to fear. As far as he could
tell, they had no knowledge of gunpowder; they had no organised
colleges of battle magic and no access to war machines such as
steam tanks or organ guns. Their metalworking skills appeared
quite primitive compared to Empire men or dwarfs. Still there was
something about the mountain chieftain, a naked ambition in his
eye that made Felix cautious whenever he spoke.

'Your people are merchants, you say? Not warriors?' The warriors
of his bodyguard nudged each other and laughed as if the chieftain
had made a joke. Felix was getting a bit tired of this.

'My father is a merchant.'

'That is not what I meant. You say the wealth of your nation is in
trade. Is it a very wealthy nation?'

Felix smiled coldly. Bran looked at him the way a robber might
size up a rich merchant, or an extortionist a shopkeeper. There was
a naked greed in his eye now that was quite obvious.

'Very wealthy,' said Felix. If this backcountry warlord wanted to
harbour fantasies of pillaging the Empire, who was he to disabuse
him? 'But the dwarfs have even more gold than we...' he added
maliciously.

'Aye, but if their warriors are all like Gotrek Gurnisson, 't'would
be hard fighting to take it from them.' Felix saw his meaning at once.
He was taking Gotrek as representative of all dwarfs and Felix as representative of the men of the Empire. Felix did not take any offence.
The simple truth of the matter was that Gotrek was a lot tougher
than he was, although there was something rankling about the
assumption.

'You might find Felix Jaeger's people harder than you think,' said
Murdo, as he fell into step beside them. 'He is.'

Felix was surprised to see him. Murdo had become thick as
thieves with Teclis. A glance behind him showed the elf was walking close to Siobhain. Surely what Felix was thinking was

happening there could not be happening. Maybe it was. Maybe Murdo was being discreet.

'We will talk further about such things when we get within the brocht,' said Bran. He did not seem to want to continue the conversation with the Truthsayer present. 'Now I must speak with my chieftains. It has been a pleasure, Felix Jaeger. And to see you too, Murdo MacBaldoch.'

As he watched the huge mountain men swagger away, Murdo laughed. 'A good man, Bran is, but greedy and famous as a raider too.'

'So I had gathered,' said Felix.

'A word to the wise,' said the Truthsayer. 'Do not talk to him too much about the riches of your homeland, or he is likely to forget all about the matter at hand and try and talk you into an expedition against your Empire.'

'Are all of your chieftains like him?'

'Unfortunately, most of them are. They would rather raid than rear their own cattle. It's what makes our people so difficult to unite except in the face of a massive threat.'

'Well, you face one now, don't you?'

'That we do, Felix Jaeger. That we do.'

ONCE THE TOWER door was barred, Felix felt like a prisoner. The walls were massive and thick and the place was dim and smelled of unwashed human flesh and animals and wood smoke. Bodies pressed all around in the gloom. It would be all too easy to stick a dagger into someone's back in such circumstances, he realised. Unless they could see in the darkness, like an elf or a dwarf.

There was nothing to be frightened about, he told himself. They had come with the Oracle's blessing and no one would attack them. To do so would be an unforgivable insult to her and to their gods. He smiled sourly to himself. You have only their word for that, he told himself. And had not the ancient seeress herself hinted that there were those who worked against her, and her kind? What exactly were her kind, he wondered?

He felt like he was once again trapped in a huge maze. He did not know his way around here. He could take nothing for granted. The dwarf stomped into view. Well, almost nothing. He could rely on the Slayer to be his usual obstreperous self. He was not sure that was an advantage when you were cooped up in a sealed fortress with a horde of armed men. Against so many, he doubted even Gotrek could prevail.

He studied the place, looking for a way out. There was none that he could see. The place was barbarically simple. There was only one huge room with a massive wooden fire in the centre. The smoke ascended through a series of holes in the wooden floors above to escape through the tower top. The whole place was one enormous chimney, he realised. From what he gathered, each of these massive towers belonged to one family, and all of the families were part of one extended clan. Such was the social organisation of this part of Albion.

From the shadows in which he stood, he could hear voices speaking. One was the booming voice of Bran. 'We have sent messengers to the other clans with word of your coming. They will meet with us at the Ring of Ogh. The greenskins went too far when they attacked the sacred caves.'

'Aye,' Murdo agreed. 'They did.'

'Time enough for a drink,' said Bran. All of the guests were brought to the long table and whisky was produced. All of them were within easy shouting distance of the chieftain. Bran clapped his hands, and fiddlers and pipers began to play as platters of food were brought out. Soon Teclis and Murdo were at work on either ear of the chieftain explaining the situation, answering his probing questions. He seemed to take in the situation very quickly even as he swilled down whisky and chomped on a sheep shank. Felix found his attention drifting – he had heard enough about the paths and disasters to last him a lifetime, and the whisky was leaving a pleasant fire in his belly. Perhaps, he thought, when the others leave this place, I shall stay here. It's come to something, he thought, when that is what qualifies as a pleasant fantasy.

He felt a soft presence wriggle into place beside him. It was Morag, one of the maiden-guard. She was pretty with a freckled face and snub nose and short cropped reddish brown hair. She smiled up at him. He smiled back.

'So tell me about the elf,' she said. 'How long have you been travelling with him?' Felix groaned and began to talk.

The slamming of a goblet on the table brought his attention back to Teclis and Bran.

'No. It is madness,' said Bran. 'I will not lead my people into such a trap.'

There was a distinct vehemence in his voice. 'If you do not show us the high road into the valley the Oracle spoke of, then no one will. The curse will continue on the land. And in part it will be your fault.' The elf's voice was persuasive but Bran did not seem to have much trouble resisting his logic.

'The orcs know of the road. It will be watched. Wait until the clans assemble, then we will force a passage.'

'We do not have time,' said Teclis. 'It will take weeks to assemble an army and we don't have weeks any more. We have days at most.'

Felix suddenly gave the conversation his full attention. This was a new development. He had thought they were going into the valley with an army, but now it looked like the plan had changed. It was nice to be entrusted with such details, Felix thought.

'I tell you the passes will be watched.'

'The greenskins are concentrating their forces on the temple. They will leave only a small force at best.'

'A small force is all it will take to hold us in the passes. Even if I take all my warriors it would be impossible to force passage against determined resistance.'

'I am a wizard of great power. It would be difficult but not impossible, I am sure.'

'I don't care if you wield the power of the gods, I am not going with you,' said Bran. 'Even if you entered the valley, it will be full of orcs.'

'If we can get into the valley, I believe I can conceal us from prying eyes, at least for as long as it takes to reach the temple.'

'And if you cannot? I will join the High King at the Stones of Ogh and we will deal with the greenskins in force.'

'The land may not live that long,' said Murdo. 'If the power within the temple is fully unleashed...'

'No, Murdo,' said Teclis. 'I can see noble Bran's mind is made up. Do not press him. We shall go forward on our own. After all, when we reach the Chamber of Secrets, it will be all the fewer to share in its treasures...'

'Treasures?' said Bran, an entirely new note entering his voice. 'Tell me about these treasures!'

'No. Your mind is made up. Why do you wish to hear about treasure?'

'Why does any man wish to hear about treasure; speak on, elf!' Gotrek gave him a look of disgust but Felix could see that he paid attention too.

The night wore on. Morag drifted away. Felix got drunker and drunker until he could barely keep his eyes open. He found a shadowy spot under a huge wooden support and wrapped himself in his cloak. Despite the sound of drinking, he plunged into an exhausted sleep almost immediately.

CHAPTER TWENTY-TWO

IN THE WAN morning sunlight of the mountain valleys, the events of the previous night seemed like a dream. Felix did his best to ignore his aching head and churning stomach. No more whisky for me, he thought. Still, at least the elf's tales of treasure had done the trick. Felix vaguely remembered roaring drunken toasts being made to the treasures of the Old Ones. He wondered if they really existed or were merely bait for Bran's greed. Did anybody here really think they were going to get their hands on ancient treasures? The odds were a thousand to one against.

He glanced over at the Slayer. Despite the enormous amounts of alcohol he had consumed, Gotrek looked none the worse for the night's drinking. Felix wished fervently that he felt the same way. He glanced back along the path. There were many of the mountain men there, and the swamp dwellers of Crannog Mere, as well as the Oracle's maiden-guard. The elf strode along conversing casually with Siobhain, seemingly completely unaware of the admiring glances of the women, and the jealous glances of many of the men. Felix began to understand why elves were so disliked. The resentment of the men was almost palpable.

At this point they moved along the side of a sheer drop, and he was not taking the risk of anyone accidentally pushing him over the edge. They had taken a very narrow path up the mountainside. It was very cold now and there were clouds visible below them. Felix squinted sidelong at the Slayer. He appeared surprisingly jaunty.

Well, why not, Felix thought? We are back in the bloody mountains, and the prospect of a suicidal quest into enemy lands is before us. Soon his doom will be upon him most likely. Felix shrugged. With this hangover, he did not really care. He continued to trudge wearily up the mountainside, feeling about a thousand years old.

'WHAT ARE YOU thinking?' asked the woman, Siobhain. She seemed concerned.

'Many things. None of which I can talk about now,' he said. She held her peace, although Teclis could tell she was desperate to know more. Teclis wondered if he was doing the right thing. This was all going too slowly for his liking. He could feel the mad raging power ahead of them now. It seemed so palpable that he was surprised the others could not, even without his sensitivity to magic.

What he was attempting now was madness. These mountains were full of orcs. The temple was full of Chaos worshippers and all he had was this small band of barbarians, a dwarf and a reluctant Imperial swordsman. The odds against success were immense. Still, what could he do?

What were his options? He could leave this small army and make his own way to the temple. By wrapping himself in spells of warding and concealment, he could conceivably make his way through undetected into the heart of the temple complex, but what then?

Kelmain and Lhoigor were both powerful mages, and would be fighting on a battlefield of their choosing, most likely woven round with their own protective spells. Perhaps they might even have subverted the defences of the Old Ones to their will.

Confident as he was in his own powers, the odds were not in his favour. Unless he could overcome the Chaos mages quickly, their guardians would be able to overcome him physically. All it would take would be one sword blow, and his long life would be over. And it would not just be swords, he knew. There would be all manner of Chaos-worshipping monsters, and this giant of whom the Oracle had spoken. He needed to have physical protection if he were to close the Paths of the Old Ones and battle hostile magic, and that meant more than magic. He needed an army and he needed Gotrek Gurnisson's axe, for the moment anyway.

He considered the pair. The longer he stayed in their company, the longer he saw the hand of destiny at work. Some power watched over them – for good or ill, the elf was not sure, but he was certain that old and powerful forces were at work there, which he could only half glimpse.

He smiled. He was becoming as superstitious as one of the elves of Athel Loren. Fate or chance or the hand of gods, it did not matter. He knew he would most likely need their help before the end. Up ahead, the unleashed energy of the ancients sent billows of power, visible only to a magician, into the sky. He knew just from looking at it that such power could not be contained for long. He only hoped that they would be in time.

He would have given a lot to know more about what his enemies were up to right at this moment.

KELMAIN LOOKED DOWN at Magrig from the stone platform in the side of the ziggurat. The giant glared back up at him with its one good eye. You are not a handsome creature, are you, thought Kelmain, studying the mutated face and huge stinking body. Well, I suppose I would not be either if I had fought as many battles as you. The last one with your late and unlamented brother must have been quite a combat, judging by the fact that you lost your eye, and he lost his life.

'The little greenskins came! Magrig kill many but more will come,' said Magrig in a voice like the rumble of thunder overhead. 'There are many of them and they have powerful magic. Maybe too many even for Magrig to smash.'

'I am sure you will do your best,' said Kelmain. He studied the distant hills with their covering of odd mutated foliage. The swamp smell of the surrounding forest assaulted his nostrils almost as much as the giant's stink. He wondered why the giant seemed so intimidating today. To be sure, he radiated the immense physical power of a being the size of a siege tower, but that was not it – after all, the giant's tiny mind was still firmly under control of the binding spell. He had been ever since they had surprised him in his sleep when they first emerged from the portals into this ancient complex. No, it was not that they were losing control of him.

It took a moment for illumination to strike. Of course: with his squatly massive form, his red matted hair and his one empty socket the giant reminded him of a monstrously huge parody of Gotrek Gurnisson. Was that somehow significant, Kelmain wondered? Was there an omen here? Perhaps he should sacrifice one of the captives the beastmen had brought back and search the entrails for signs. Was it possible the dwarf had somehow escaped from the paths? No. Powerful as he was, the dwarf was no magician. He would be trapped there until the end of the world.

On the other hand, time was getting short. Lhoigor reported that the paths were becoming increasingly hard to control. Some of them vented constant eruptions of Chaotic energy now, and the madness was starting to spread from the Twisted Paths into the unchanged ones. More than one of their acolytes and his warband had failed to return and there were fewer Chaos warriors here than he would have liked with the greenskin tribes massing in the hills. It seemed their awe and fear of Magrig was starting to wear off. Perhaps this had not been such a good plan after all.

Why did our masters put us up to it then, he wondered? Why are we keeping that altar below slick with the heartsblood of human sacrifices? Why do we keep our acolytes and ourselves working around the clock against whatever odd force it is that is trying to shut down the paths? Was that the work of the accursed elves, he wondered? Or was it something else, some nasty surprise the ancients had left to prevent interlopers using their toys? If so, they would fail. Chaos rules this world, he thought. Nothing will be denied to us. Nothing.

Kelmain could sense their awful greenskin magic being worked up in those hills. Perhaps their shamans have some inkling of what we do here, and are trying to stop us, he thought. Much good it would do them.

'Stay within the temple and smash anything that comes this way!' he told Magrig. 'But come if I call you.'

'I hear and obey, ancient one,' said Magrig.

It pleased Kelmain to be addressed by the title the giant must have used to talk to his creators long ago. Once more he sensed the green flash of orcish magic. What can they be up to, he wondered, as he turned and walked back down the steps and into the heart of the ziggurat.

ZARKHUL WOKE FROM his trance. He was uneasy even though he could sense the comforting mass of thousands of orcs all around and draw power from their presence. They had come from all over the island to be here. Battled their way to join his clans, summoned by the ancient mass instincts of the orcish kind. Something bad was going on. He sensed it. The weather had worsened. Magrig, the sleeping god they had made offerings to for so long, had turned against his people and now his visions spoke of a time and death and hunger for the tribes.

Over and over again the twin gods had shown him visions of the land breaking apart and eating the orcs, of the foul beastmen of Chaos emerging from the temple city like maggots from a corpse, of skies the colour of blood that rained fire and foul warpstone dust. Somehow he knew in his very bones that if they did not reclaim the city and cast the outsiders from its sacred stones then disaster would overtake all of his people. The gods had spoken to him. They had granted him conviction and the mantle of authority that made the chieftains listen to him, even though many of them were his sworn enemies, and had often fought him for control of one ziggurat or another.

Now, like a herd of bison all swinging to face a common threat, the tribes were acting as one. Such things happened to the people when the gods spoke to them. Now they would lay aside their differences and follow him into the great waaargh. They would need to. For in his latest vision he had seen that time was running out and they would need to act soon to avert disaster.

He sensed a tugging at his thoughts and opened his spirit eyes. The spirit of the shaman Gurag hovered before him, invisible to all eyes save his. He spoke with a voice inaudible to all but Zarkhul. 'The men of the mountain are coming along the secret paths. They have allied with elves.'

'Take your force and grind them to a pulp! Gorge on their marrow!' said Zarkhul, speaking in a voice that was not a voice.

'Aye, we will eat manflesh this night, and elf flesh too.' The spirit shimmered and vanished as Gurag returned to his body. Strange, thought Zarkhul, that one so obese in the flesh should see himself as such a proud and muscular warrior in spirit form.

Dismissing the thought, the orc war leader gave his attention to the ziggurats of the temple city below. A lifetime of warfare among their streets against his former rivals had gifted him with knowledge of the best lines of attack, as well as the secret ways beneath the city. With luck the newcomers would not know about those. He would build a mountain of their skulls high as one of the ziggurats as an offering to the Twin Gods. At its peak would be the skull of Magrig and his two strange human familiars. Only when he had made this offering would the gods be appeased. Only then would disaster be averted.

All he needed now was a sign from the shamans to let him know when to begin the attack. He hoped it would not be long in coming.

In the distance lightning flashed and thunder rumbled. Zarkhul wondered if that was the sign. Probably not, he thought. Such weather was too common around here to constitute an omen.

* * *

FELIX STRODE ALONG the mountain paths, not at all reassured by his conversation with the elf. The air was colder now, the weather changing swiftly as it always did in the mountains. Clouds were visible in the valley below them, and slowly they crept up along the flanks of the mountain until they became a mist that reduced even nearby men to blurred shapes. Felix wondered whether this was some doing of the elf's or the work of their enemy, then he realised he did not care.

A squat massive figure appeared out of the gloom before him. He was reassured to hear the dwarf's gruff voice ahead, muttering something in dwarfish. Suddenly thunder rumbled, and in the distance lightning flashed. The flare was diffused by the mist into a brief intense glow and then vanished. Felix wondered whether it was dangerous and lightning might strike him. He felt very vulnerable, as an insect crawling across a window pane where at any time a great hand might swat him.

'Curse this weather,' he said.

'It is strange,' said Gotrek. 'In all my years in mountains, I have never seen clouds come in so fast and thunder so strong.'

'The weather here in Albion is a curse,' said Felix.

'You could be right, manling. Something twists it here, that's for sure.'

Murdo emerged from the mist, silent as a wraith. 'The Stones of Ogham.'

'I take it that has some significance,' said Felix.

'Sometimes. In the areas of the stone rings the weather is often warped. In recent years it has become much worse.'

'These stones hold great magical power then?'

'Aye, they are the work of the ancients.' He looked as if he could say more if he wanted to, but had no intention of doing so. Maybe he did. It was always hard to tell with any sort of wizards. Sometimes they were deep and mysterious because they knew something. Sometimes because they were hiding their ignorance. As a layman Felix was in no position to judge.

'Why have the orcs come here at the same time as us? It cannot be coincidence?'

'Who can tell with the greenskins? Sometimes a mass madness seems to come over them and for no discernable reason they do things in a mass. It's like lemmings throwing themselves off a cliff or the migration of birds. Maybe their gods speak to them. Perhaps the stones are holy to the orcs as well. In places of power it is often easier to attract the attention of the gods and great spirits. '

'Well, tonight would be a night for that,' said Felix. 'This weather is certainly not natural.'

'No,' said Murdo. 'It is not. Perhaps when you have succeeded in your task the world will return to normal, if what the elf says is true.'

'Perhaps,' said Felix.

There was another brilliant flare of light diffused through the mist, then a thunderclap, this time much closer, and the whole mountain seemed to shake. It was all Felix could do to keep from flinching, so sudden and violent was the outburst. He wondered how great the chances of avalanches were here, then decided he did not want to know. The way things were going he knew the kind of answer he would get. A few moments later a drizzle of rain hit his face. It was chill as mountain ice.

'Perfect,' he said. 'Just what I needed to make this day complete.'

The words were no sooner out of his mouth when a scream echoed through the gloom.

'As ever, I spoke too soon,' he said, turning towards its source.

CHAPTER TWENTY-THREE

FELIX RACED THROUGH mist and confusion. Some of the highland warriors had drawn their huge swords, others brandished their spears as they looked around for the new menace. Howling war cries emerged from the gloom all around, great bellowing roars that told of the presence of massive bull orcs and the yips and gibbers that spoke of goblins.

Suddenly the clang of weapon on weapon rang through the gloom, followed by the crunch of bone and the screams of wounded men. Felix ran into something big and bounced. It took him a second to realise that he had run smack into the back of an orc. It took him another heartbeat to plunge his sword into its spine. Now was not the time for chivalry, he thought.

The fight was a nightmare. He had only heartbeats to decide whether the shadow emerging from the clouds was a man or a monster. If it was an orc, he struck, if it was a man he tried to hold his blows. He was not entirely sure that he succeeded every time. His flesh crawled. At any moment he expected a blow from some unexpected direction to smash into his flesh and send his soul screaming to Morr's dark kingdom. He knew from the sounds all around him that it was happening often enough.

He needed to move cautiously, for he knew that the edge of the path hung over a vertiginous drop. It would be pointless to avoid the strike of a foe only to plunge to his death in the abyss below. The image almost paralysed him. He stood frozen on the spot for a moment, petrified by the thought of dropping into the gloom below. Somewhere off to his left there was a flash of light, a golden glow that was not lightning, but the casting of an elvish spell. He knew that Teclis was fighting for his life out there in the dark.

Closer yet came Gotrek's fierce bellow. It was followed by the butcher-shop sounds of an axe hitting flesh. From force of habit, Felix made his way towards the noise, knowing that in a wild melee like this, the Slayer's side would be the safest place to be.

TECLIS CURSED THE mist and the strange flows of magic through the mountains of Albion. His ward spells had given him only a heart-beat's warning of the attack. In that instant he had thrown a shield spell around himself.

'Stay with me,' he told Siobhain and drew his sword. It was not pure chivalry on his part. He needed someone to guard his back and he was sure the woman would not plunge a spear into it.

'I am with you,' answered Siobhain.

The flows of magic were sluggish here. Unless he missed his guess, they were currently all being drawn off to the Stone of Ogham, which was most likely the source of this foul weather. He considered trying to channel the winds towards him but decided against it. There was too much chance of some strange feedback effect. The stones distorted magic mightily. This being the case he would need to draw on his personal power and that of the staff of Lileath. Hopefully that would be sufficient.

Swiftly, he wove a web of divination, sending feelers of magic out in a network all around him. They would trip at the presence of orcs and greenskins and warn him of any within about thirty strides. Next he channelled a normal wind towards him, cleaving through the mist. Momentarily it parted the clouds giving him a clear view of the path. Half a dozen orcs raced towards him. He snarled and sent a blast of destructive energy towards them. They bellowed in rage and pain as it ripped through them, boiling flesh from bone like overcooked meat on a joint. One of them, on the very fringe of the spell, was only mildly singed. He leapt forward with eye-blurring speed, his huge scimitar raised in both hands, ready to smite the sorcerer.

Teclis stepped to one side and swung the staff downward, tripping the orc. As it sprawled on its face, he inserted his blade below the flange of its helmet, severing the vertebrae in the neck and cutting the spinal cord like a surgeon. The creature spasmed interestingly as it lost control of its motor functions and began to die. Teclis saw no reason to put it out of its misery and turned to look for a new target. Siobhain put her spear into its back.

A horde of small greenskins scuttled forward. A wave of short spears blurred towards him. There was no time for anything subtle. He spoke a word of command and a wave of flame consumed most of the missiles. He sprang to one side away from the area targeted just in time to hear them clatter onto the stones.

Annoyed by being taken off guard by such crude creatures, he strode into their midst. His blade flickered out, piercing an eyeball here, a windpipe there. The goblins responded with their own weapons, but they were partially deflected by the energy field he had already woven around himself. It was a subtle spell of his own devising which used the force of an enemy's blow against itself. The harder they hit, the more violently their blades were repelled. The danger was that they might strike with enough force to overload the spell. That was why it was best to keep moving and dodge and duck and weave.

Teclis smiled now. In every elf, he suspected, there was a core of bloodlust and what some would call cruelty. In battle this was drawn to the surface. He had seen the mask of culture fall from the faces of too many of his warrior kin not to recognise its presence in himself. It did not disgust him, as it might a human, it was merely another interesting emotion to be catalogued and, if he was honest, enjoyed. Perhaps it was the tainted blood of Aenarion, he thought?

He laughed, and was surprised to see that his laughter elicited looks of horror from Siobhain and the humans around him. Of course, perhaps they did not feel the battle joy flowing through their veins. They were not elves, after all. Nor could they understand what this meant to him personally. He ducked another blow and brought the tip of the staff crunching down on a booted goblin foot. The little creature screeched in pain and clutched its toes, hopping almost comically for the few seconds before he impaled it on his blade.

No, he thought, they could not understand. In his youth, he had been Teclis the weakling, Teclis the cripple, Teclis the pitied. That had been before he had learned to strengthen himself with spells and potions. Now his breath came as easily as any other elf's, and the only sign of his former weakness was a slight limp in his left leg that left him barely less swift and graceful than any other elf. Once these creatures could have overwhelmed him. Once his brother had been needed to protect him from them. No more, he thought, pulling his blade out in a burst of green blood, and then lunging at

full extension to skewer another. Now I can look after myself, and
enjoy combat as it was meant to be.

His laughter became louder, and the humans looked away. Only
Siobhain fought beside him, and even her face showed fear.
Thoughts flickered like lightning flashes through his mind. He
seemed to be moving so swiftly that he had time to contemplate
eternity between blows. It was strange, the only elf he had ever met
who seemed to take no pleasure out of this wild battle joy was his
brother, quite possibly the deadliest elf who ever lived. Why should
that be, Teclis wondered?

'Why should that be?' he asked the goblin that spewed its last
meal over itself as the blade took it in the belly. It did not understand elvish, of course, and looked at him as if he were mad. There
was something so irresistibly comic in the thought that he simply
laughed all the more. He was still laughing as a huge bolt of magical power tore out of the night, and drowned him in a sea of pain.

FELIX HEARD THE cruel hideous laughter ringing out through the
mist. What could it be, some orc laughing at the death agonies of
its foe, a daemon summoned by one of their shamans? No. There
was something familiar about it.

'It's the elf, manling,' said Gotrek from beside him. The dwarf
chopped back-handed at a charging orc and cut it in two. Felix
threw up his arm to avoid being blinded by the spray of blood and
found himself engaged with another huge orc. The force of the creature's strokes numbed his arm. He backed away, parrying as he
went, cursing the dim light that made it twice as difficult to concentrate on his foe's flashing blade. He felt something squelch
under his heel. He had trodden on a corpse. He fought to keep his
balance and had to match the orc blow for blow to avoid being driven back and tripping on the uncertain footing. He heard the
dwarf's battle cries recede into the gloom.

It was a mistake. Felix was a strong man but the orc was stronger.
Its blows almost sent the blade flying from his hand. He knew that
he could not long hold his own in this sort of combat. He needed
to take a chance and end this quickly. He ducked, letting the orc's
blade pass over his head and then thrust forward with his sword,
piercing the orc's belly. The thing roared deafeningly and swiped at
him with its massive fist. The force of the impact made stars dance
before Felix's eyes. The pain was sickening. He reeled away in one
direction, and the orc reeled away in the other to be swallowed by
the mist. From all around came the sounds of battle and that
hideous piercing laughter.

Concentrate, Felix told himself, fighting to hold down his food, and not simply collapse on the blood-slick ground. It took a massive effort of will to hold himself upright. From all around he heard the sound of scuttling. Small greenish shapes garbed in hooded leather jerkins surrounded him. They cackled and capered as they closed.

This was not looking good, he thought. There was a flash of greenish light and the hideous elvish laughter stopped.

TECLIS FOUGHT TO remain conscious. He knew he was lucky. His magical defences had absorbed most of the impact but still pain surged along every nerve end as he fought to contain and dispel the deadly energy pulsing through him.

Fool, he told himself, his thoughts cold and clear. This is what you get for giving way to the murder lust. You were taken by surprise by a wielder of the power. A crafty one, too. He had shielded himself and husbanded his power until close enough to deliver what should have been a killing stroke. And he had almost succeeded too. Still, almost was not quite good enough.

Now that he had uncloaked himself, the orc shaman was as visible as a beacon burning on a hilltop on a clear night to Teclis's mage sight. He smiled, seeing the greenish-yellow glow of greenskin energy surrounding his foe. It was the familiar magical signature of the shaman. They tapped their energies in some unusual way. The aura brightened as the shaman unleashed another blast. This time Teclis was prepared and his own counter-spell unwove the mesh of alien energy before it had covered half the distance between them. Teclis countered with a bolt of power but the orc's counter-spell was swift and strong. He had the advantage of being fresh and his senses were clear. Teclis still had to deal with the consequences of the shaman's first blast. He hoped that would not prove fatal.

Worse still, his divination web told him that more greenskins were closing on either side; three of them at least and more coming. Where was the girl, he wondered? Lost somewhere in this damned mist, unfortunately. With his attention focused on the shaman he was vulnerable. He could try and defend himself physically and most likely be struck down by the shaman. He could deal with the shaman and take a sword blow for his pains. He could split his attention and fight at less than full effectiveness on two fronts. None of the choices were particularly attractive. Still, he needed to make one and soon. Death stalked ever closer.

* * *

Felix forced himself upright, determined to die on his feet at least. Seeing that their prey was about to put up a fight, the goblins slowed.

'Not too brave, eh?' he said, brandishing his sword menacingly. The goblins in front of him retreated, but others took advantage of his distraction to rush in from left and right. Only the scrape of booted feet on rocks warned him. He swung his blade left and right, driving them back, whirled in case any were coming from behind and then whirled again to face his original attackers who had regained their courage and were closing again.

This was getting him nowhere, he thought. If he stayed here he would die. Acting instantly he threw himself forward slashing with his blade, crashing into the packed mass of greenskins, bowling them over with superior weight and ferocity. He struck left and right furiously, and was rewarded by the jarring of blade on bone, and the agonised squeals of his foes. A moment later and he was clear, back in the main swirl of the battle. He found himself face to face with Murdo and Culum and the men of Crannog Mere.

'I am glad to see you,' he said, joining their ranks as they prepared to face another rush of orcs and goblins.

Teclis hurled himself upwards, invoking the spell of levitation. He strode into the sky at the end of his leap, hoping that it would confuse his foes and get him clear of their blades. There were grunts of dismay from below as the greenskins realised that their prey had eluded them. As he had intended, the mist had covered his movements.

He had not eluded the shaman, though. The nightmarish green glow erupted upwards, a volcanic rush of power that took him all his skill to parry. The deadly sting of the previous blast had gone now and he was free to concentrate on the task at hand. He contained his opponent's spell in an orb of energy and then sent an arc of power crashing down on him. Briefly the shaman's counterspells held out, then one by one they collapsed. Talismans burst in coruscating showers of sparks as they overloaded. The shaman's figure became a statue of molten bronze light in the shape of a monstrously obese orc, then the flesh was stripped from his body, the skeleton vanished and he was gone from the world forever.

Teclis rose above the battle and for a moment stood above the clouds of mist. It was a god-like sensation. He could hear the sounds of battle below, but for the moment he was not part of it. He was free to consider his options.

Not wanting to be taken off guard again, Teclis sent divinatory probes outwards, tendrils of magic designed to alert him to the presence of any enemy mage or spell. It was not flawless, he doubted that such a wide-scale scan could detect the presence of someone under a spell of concealment, but he hoped that he might sense something amiss. It was difficult here in Albion with the flows of magic so disturbed by the presence of the stone rings.

Nothing. That was good. Now he would unleash some power and see what he could do about this attack. Just at that moment something hurtled out of the gloom towards him. He moved to one side and it rocketed by him. The wind of its passage rippled his robes. For a moment, he caught a brief unbelievable glance of what looked like a goblin wearing a pointed helm, and flapping massive leather wings. He shook his head almost unable to believe his eyes. The thing must have been fired from a catapult, that was the only explanation. He could hear its mad giggles as it disappeared out of sight into the clouds and then into the abyss below.

Teclis scanned all around him. From a clump of rocks above he saw more of the goblins and some strange engines that they used to launch themselves into the air. Was it possible, he wondered, that these suicidal creatures had been raining down on the fight all this time, and he had been unaware of it? It certainly looked that way. Even as he watched, several more of them hurtled into the air and vanished into the clouds of mist. Moments later came the sound of screaming.

Now what looked like some kind of leader was directing them to look at him. He could see some of the engines were being realigned in his direction. He lashed out with a storm of light, clearing the ridgetops with blast after blast of pure magical energy. Engines and flyers alike caught light. Once he was sure he had taken care of the visible foes, he asked himself what he was going to do next.

CHAPTER TWENTY-FOUR

FELIX STOOD SHOULDER to shoulder with Murdo and Culum and they began to fight their way through the mass of orcs and goblins. The rock underfoot was slick with condensation and gore. The way it sloped was no help to balance either. The uncertain edge of the path was a cause for constant concern, and in the mist, there was no way to know who was winning.

Felix's arms ached from hacking at orcs. His breath came in gasps. He wondered what had become of the Slayer and the elf. If anything had happened to either of them, his position here was very precarious indeed. He was a stranger in a land of which he knew very little.

The battle became merely a matter of parry, hack or stab whenever a foe came near him. He watched his comrades' backs and they watched his. In the maelstrom of battle, personality and animosities were forgotten. More than once he parried a blow aimed at Culum's back. On several occasions the big hammer-man erupted from the mist to smash the head of an orc attacking Felix to pulp.

Strangest of all were the bat-winged goblins that seemed to descend from the sky, spearing men on their pointed helmets, carrying them off over the edge of the cliffs. The greenskins appeared to have no notion of self-preservation. Froth billowed from their mouths and their wide eyes spoke of some sort of drug abuse.

Felix had seen their sort before, in the mountains of the World's Edge back on the boundary of the Empire. It seemed strange to encounter something even vaguely and repulsively familiar so far from home.

Somewhere in the mist, thunder rumbled and golden light flickered. Felix felt vaguely reassured, confident that the elf wizard was still in the fray. More than once he thought he heard Gotrek's bellowed war-cry.

Eventually, after what seemed liked an eternity in hell, the clamour of battle dimmed. The bellows of the orcs grew less and took on a fearful note as they receded into the mist. The shrieks and giggles and wild yips of the goblins faded into the distance. Gradually the voices of men became dominant, and war-cries were replaced by shouts of concern and queries as to the health of brothers and comrades and kin.

Felix found himself looking over at Murdo and wondering if he looked half as bad as the old man. Blood dripped from the Truthsayer's face and arms, the red of men and the green of orc. He had taken a few wounds. A patch of skin on his forehead had been shaved away to reveal pink and bleeding meat beneath. Murdo reached up and muttered an incantation and the wound closed, leaving only a fresh pink scar. Felix noticed that he himself carried a few cuts on his arms and chest but his mail shirt appeared to have preserved him from worse harm.

As if an evil spell had lifted, the mist parted to reveal a scene of awesome carnage. The pathway was covered in the corpses of men and orcs and goblins and even some huge and shapeless monsters of a type that Felix could not name. The men of Carn Mallog had fought bravely but over half of them were down. Only about five of the original war-party from Crannog Mere was left. In the air above them, circled with an aura of power, the elf hovered. Felix could smell burning and saw the flames where strange wooden war engines blazed on the cliffs above.

Gotrek stomped through the shambles like a gore spattered daemon of war. He looked grimly pleased with himself and he booted the severed head of an orc chieftain ahead of him like a child playing kickball.

'I see you still live,' said Felix.

'Aye, manling, I do. These were weak creatures and it would have been an unworthy doom to fall to them.'

Felix looked at the piles of dead men and wondered if they would agree with the Slayer's assessment of their foes. Somehow it seemed unlikely. 'Maybe we'll find something more deadly on our quest,' he said sourly.

Gotrek shrugged and glared up at the elf as if annoyed to see that he still lived. Either that or he was considering whether the wizard would make a worthy enough opponent to put him out of his misery. Felix sincerely hoped not. Then he noticed that the elf was gesturing at something.

'I suppose we'd better see what he has found,' Felix said.

BELOW THEM, THEY could see a vast valley, ringed around with mountains. In the middle of the valley, surrounded by boiling black clouds, illuminated by lightning bolts, they could see an enormous structure.

'The Temple of the Old Ones,' said Felix.

'Indeed,' said Teclis. 'The Temple of the Old Ones.'

Felix studied the buildings. To be visible from this height, they must be huge. Each was built as a ziggurat, a stepped pyramid with seven huge levels. Each level was marked with runes, and was reached by a ramp from the level below. Strange ramps and tunnels linked the ziggurats running through the trees that seemed to have swallowed the rest of the city. Glowing lights inside indicated that the place was either occupied, haunted or home to some unspeakable sorcery, perhaps all three.

Gotrek was shaking his head in a puzzled manner.

'What is it?' Felix asked.

'I am reminded of something, that is all.'

'What?'

'The ziggurats of the chaos dwarfs.'

'You think there might be some connection?' asked Teclis.

'I do not know, elf. Nor do I wish to speculate further.'

'As you wish,' said the elf. 'I will tell the others to get some rest. They will need all their strength for the morrow.'

THE PATH WOUND down the far side of the mountains, into the hidden valleys. They all moved cautiously, not quite believing that the elf's spells shielded them as he claimed. They had not seen any orcs this morning, but you never knew.

'Are you sure your magic is working?' Felix asked. 'I can see no difference.'

The elf gave him a strained smile. 'You are within the ambit of the spell.'

'How does it work?'

'It misdirects prying eyes and divinatory magic. Only if someone comes within a dozen strides of us will they notice us. Now if you please, until we are under cover of the trees, I must concentrate on maintaining it.'

As they moved, Felix noticed a change in their surroundings. The air was warmer and there was a foul putrid scent to it, worse than any decay he had smelled back in the swamp. As they descended, it became wetter and there was more vegetation. At first only a few gnarled black trees clung to the mountainside with their roots inter-mingled with the stone and soil. These proved only to be the first sentries of a vast army of vegetation, a horde of mighty trees and bushes. None of them looked remotely normal. Fungus blighted their branches. Creepers strangled them like serpents. Strange ani-mals scampered along their huge boles. Enormous glistening spiderwebs caught the dim sunlight. Felix felt no urge to see the creatures that had spun them.

Gotrek looked upon them and spat. 'I hate trees almost as much as I hate elves.'

Teclis laughed. 'What have trees ever done to you, Gotrek Gur-nisson?' he asked. Felix wondered if the elf liked living dangerously. The Slayer was not someone you provoked lightly.

Gotrek glared back. The men of Carn Mallog moved silently now. A few had shucked their furs as the heat increased. Bran moved alongside Murdo and Siobhain. A faint sheen of perspiration glis-tened on his face. He looked nervous and slightly shifty. Whatever he might once have thought, it was obvious that he did not like the idea of going any further into this corrupt place. Felix could not say he blamed him, for he had finally recognised the faint tingling brimstone taste in the air.

'Warpstone,' he murmured. 'This is not good.'

'You are correct, Felix Jaeger,' said Teclis. 'It is indeed the bane of the ancients.'

Felix looked at the elf. For once, he knew he was in the presence of someone who could answer his questions, and unlike the Slayer, who seemed to enjoy lecturing. 'What is warpstone?' he asked, aware that he was not the only one listening. His question seemed to have gotten everyone's attention.

'The raw stuff of Chaos,' said Teclis. 'Solidified, congealed, dis-tilled, some combination of all three. It is the pure product of dark magic.'

'I saw a skaven once consume the stuff,' said Felix.

'Then it was a most unusual skaven, for warpstone is very poiso-nous even to mutants such as the ratmen. I have read that some of the Grey Seers can absorb quantities of a refined form and draw energy from it. If so, I cannot imagine that they would remain sane or healthy for very long, although their sorcerous power would be immense.'

Felix thought of the ratman sorcerer he and Gotrek had so often encountered. The elf's description would easily fit such a creature.

'Warpstone comes from Morrsleib, the Chaos moon,' said Murdo. 'Chunks of it break off and fall to earth in great meteor showers. Such showers regularly land on Albion. Something seems to draw them. Perhaps the stone rings. Perhaps that is their purpose.'

'I do not think so,' said Teclis, but seeing the look of vexation on the old man's face, he corrected himself. 'Let me rephrase that. I believe that Morrsleib may well be made of warpstone, and certainly such meteor showers as you describe have been corroborated by many elvish chroniclers, but I do not believe Morrsleib is the sole source of warpstone. It is merely a huge, strange astronomical phenomenon. And I do not believe the stone rings were made to attract the meteors, although they may well do so. I believe they have another function.'

'You could well be right,' said Murdo, obviously not wanting to argue with the elf.

'This is all very interesting,' said Felix, 'but I am rather more concerned with the effects that the stuff may have on us.'

'There are only minute traces in the air,' said Teclis. 'And one way or another, I doubt we are going to be here long enough for it to have much effect on us.'

'That's very reassuring,' said Felix. He resisted the urge to point out that while the elf was most likely protected by his magic, the rest of them were not.

The path wound lower down the mountainside. The foliage surrounding them thickened. From the undergrowth came many strange grunts and snuffles and the sounds of huge beasts moving among the branches. Bran's warriors became visibly more nervous. The tension increased. Gotrek's head swung from side to side as he scanned the undergrowth for threats.

'I can see why the giant became corrupt,' said Teclis, 'if this was his dwelling place. A thousand years here would warp anybody's mind.'

'If their mind was not already warped to start with,' said Gotrek pointedly.

'His physical form may well have mutated as well,' said the elf, ignoring the Slayer.

'In what way?' Felix asked, his mouth suddenly dry.

'He will most likely be larger and bear many stigmata of Chaos. He may possess many mutations that will make him harder to kill.'

Felix thought about the troll he and Gotrek had once fought beneath the ruins of Karag Eight Peaks. Someone had chained a bit of warpstone around its neck, and all of the things the elf had described had happened to it. Felix wondered at the depth of the wizard's knowledge. He seemed to know a lot about many things. I suppose it's one of the advantages of living for centuries and being a powerful sorcerer, he thought. It would be something worth noting when he came to write his chronicle of the Slayer's adventures, though. Some scholars would be willing to pay for that sort of information alone, although Felix was not sure he wanted his work to interest those sorts of people. It made the book of interest to witch hunters and the Imperial censors too. Perhaps he would just leave it out then, he thought.

The thin layer of earth covering the rocky path thickened as they descended into the valley, and as it did so it transmuted into a horrible blackish-brown mud that clung to Felix's boots and made sucking sounds as he raised his feet to walk. Something wet and slimy touched his face. He shuddered, thinking of the fingers of drowned men or the tentacles of some particularly obnoxious monster. Instead he saw it was only a creeper dangling from the branches above. The branches arched overhead now, forming a passageway through the dense forest that surrounded them. Felix marvelled at the change in environment. Only a few hours ago they had been shivering on the misty heights. Now they were in a warm near-jungle that reminded him of tales about the Dark Continent he had read as a youth. The silence deepened. He could hear his own breathing. He felt certain that something terrible was about to happen.

The long moments drew themselves out, slow as slugs sliding their way down a wall. He let out a long breath, filled with his own sense of relief. He walked forward and found himself on the edge of a huge puddle filled with brown and muddy water. The edges of the earth came up like those of a cup to hold it, and there was something obscurely familiar about the shape.

He shook his head wondering why a massive outline seen here in the wild back country of Albion should seem familiar to a city boy from Altdorf. Slowly the realisation filtered into his brain, slowly the enormity of what he was seeing descended onto his mind. He told himself that it could not be so. It was merely random chance that had caused the pattern to look as it did.

'It is a footprint,' said Teclis.

'Aye,' said Gotrek with a certain grim satisfaction. 'That it is.'

'It can't be,' said Felix quietly. He paced the side of the mighty tread. It was exactly two of his strides long. If he lay down beside it, it would be almost as long as he was. 'The creature who made it would have to be at least six times as tall as me.'

'And what's your point, manling?' Felix considered what he had just said, realising that he did not want to believe that anything so huge could walk the earth clothed in the shape of a man. On the other hand, just because he feared an encounter with such a creature did not mean it could not exist. In the past he had encountered many huge monsters, why not a giant?

He tried to remember whether any of the noises they had heard earlier might have been the tread of such a monster. How could he tell? What was the point of speculating? Instead he considered the thought of encountering such a creature, trying to scale the thing in his mind. At best he would come up to its calf. Striking it with his sword would be like a child attacking him with a pin. It could lift him one-handed, take off his head with one bite. Hastily dismissing the image from his mind, he turned to Teclis and said; 'I hope you know some spells for controlling giants?'

'The giants of Albion are wilful creatures, and very resistant to magic, so it is said.'

'And yet these Chaos mages control one.'

'Perhaps those reports are incorrect. Perhaps the creature is pacted to Chaos. Perhaps they have access to spells I do not, Felix Jaeger. I am one of the greatest of wizards, it's true, but I do not know everything.'

'This is a historic moment,' sneered Gotrek. 'Perhaps the first time in recorded history an elf has ever admitted that. Be sure to make a record of that, manling.'

'Be sure to make a record of everything,' said Teclis. 'If you survive.'

Somewhere in the distance, something huge bellowed. The cry was answered by the sound of horns and drums.

'Not just giants, it seems,' said Teclis. 'It sounds like orcs and goblins as well.'

'That's reassuring,' said Felix, as they pushed along the path.

CHAPTER TWENTY-FIVE

THE PATH RAN on and on through the stinking forest. The mud grew thicker, but no more massive tracks were visible, a thing for which Felix was profoundly grateful. Instead the forest became more blighted, the trees more twisted, the animals more mutated. A deer with two heads came into view. Spiders big as a man's fist and shimmering like jewels scuttled overhead. They forded a stream of blackish water in which faint glowing particles were visible. Felix guessed that the water here was contaminated with warpstone. His fear was confirmed when Teclis said, 'Pass the word: do not drink of the water or eat anything found here, no matter how edible it might look.'

'I don't think anybody needed to be told that,' said Gotrek.

'You can never be too careful,' said the elf. For once the dwarf did not disagree. The air became thicker and more oppressive with the sort of feel to it that often presages a storm. Suddenly Felix felt nostalgia for the clean air and cold rain of the mountains. He leapt from rock to rock across the ford, not wanting that tainted water to touch even his boots. What are you scared of, he asked himself? Mutated boots? The thought did not seem very funny. He had heard of stranger things in the haunted city of Praag. He cursed to all the gods. It seemed to be his destiny to visit all the worst places in the world. Just once he wished Gotrek's quest would take them to the harem of the Sheik of Araby or the Palace of the Emperor. The way our luck runs, he thought, we would find them overrun with mutants or inhabited by evil mages.

Rain began to fall. It was warmer than mountain rain, and Felix did not like the way it touched his skin. Many of the drops had been filtered through the leaves and branches of those noxious gnarled trees. The gods alone knew what poisons they might contain.

He glanced again. Overhead he thought he caught the glitter of saucer-like eyes. He concentrated. Among the blotched green, he caught sight of a hideous snaggle-toothed face. Before he could say a word, a spear flashed out and smashed into it and a goblin corpse splashed down into the sucking mud.

'I wonder how many more like that there are around here?' he said. Siobhain retrieved her spear from the corpse. The warriors of Albion moved on. Felix had visions of wild-eyed goblin tribesmen peering from the murky undergrowth. It did nothing to improve his mood.

He forced himself to consider what was going on here. It seemed that they were not the only ones with an interest in the Temple of the Old Ones. Did the orcs intend to seize it for their own use, or was there something more sinister afoot?

Teclis shook his head. 'I can see I will have to swathe us in the cloak of unseeing once more,' he said.

'Don't strain yourself, elf,' said Gotrek.

THE LAST BATTERED survivors of Gurag's orcs limped into Zarkhul's camp. He looked at their crestfallen leader. Kur was his name.

'What happened?'

'Gurag was killed by the elf. They made it past us. They are in the valley. They march on the temple.'

Was this the sign he had been waiting for, Zarkhul wondered? Perhaps. All of the tribes were gathered now, they had returned from capturing the stone rings and the shamans had harvested their power. Now seemed as good a time as any for the attack.

'Get your swords out! You can prove your courage to us all. We are going into the city!'

A great roar arose from the gathered horde as his words spread like magic through their ranks. He was certain that even the most distant clans cried with one voice as they responded to his order. At such times as this the orcs would act as one body, could be wielded as one sword, and he was their leader.

* * *

AHEAD OF THEM lay the brow of the hill. Felix, Gotrek, Teclis and Murdo made their way up to the crest. They kept to the shadow of the trees and moved quietly although how anything might hear them over the constant lashing of the rain eluded him. At the brow of the hill, they could see that below them, the land cleared. It was wild, open and rocky all the way down to where the temple stood.

The nearest ziggurat was as large as a hill, Felix realised. The temple complex covered an area as large as many human cities. Perhaps only the massive sprawl of Altdorf was larger among all the places he had visited. Over it hung an aura of immense antiquity and strangeness. He could easily believe that no human being had built this place, nor any being remotely man-like such as an elf or a dwarf. Huge glyphs were embedded in the sides; they were rectangular, right-angled mazes which somehow seemed to draw the eye into them. He had to fight to break his gaze away, to keep it from following the patterns. He felt that if he did so, all the way to the end, he might be gifted with strange cosmic insights, but they were not things he wanted. To understand those runes, he felt, might be to leave humanity and sanity behind.

A thought struck him. 'Maps,' he said.

'What, manling?' said Gotrek.

'The runes are maps, of the paths, or of the structure of the paths, or something to do with the…' he let his sentence drag to an end lamely. He realised he must sound like a madman to the others.

'Perhaps you are right,' said the elf. 'It's an interesting theory. Or perhaps they are wards. Symbols can bear within themselves representations of spells. They are patterns of mystical force. Dwarfish rune magic works in this way, I believe.'

'Believe what you like,' said Gotrek. 'But this is getting us no closer to our goal.'

As if in answer to his words, the ziggurats shook. 'And we are running out of time,' said Teclis. 'The power within is starting to run out of control.'

'We go in?' said Felix.

'We go in,' the others agreed. As they spoke, drums thundered around the valley. The orcs too appeared to have come to a decision. Murdo returned and spoke to his men, Bran to his. The maiden-guard hefted their spears and made ready.

Before they knew it, all were engaged in a wild rush downhill, running as fast as they could, using the rocks for cover. Felix was not sure why they did so. Some instinct made them want to cover that open ground as swiftly as possible. The walls of the ancient temple

held no promise of shelter or safety and yet somehow they seemed
preferable to being caught exposed in the open.

Just the sight of one man running was enough to get the whole
nervous crew moving. As they approached the great stone structures
he felt as if he was somehow being watched by some vast implacable presence within the temple of the Old Ones, and he wanted
more than anything to get himself out from under its gaze as
quickly as possible.

He felt almost relieved when he set foot on the first ramp leading up the side of the pyramid. He felt less than relieved when he
looked behind him. The whole forest on the hills surrounding the
pyramid was suddenly alive with orcs. They emerged from the vile
woods in their thousands, whooping and chanting. What have we
disturbed here, Felix wondered, knowing that there was no turning
back? Against so many there was no chance of returning. Even as
they watched, the orcish horde began to rumble downhill, moving
with the irresistible force of an avalanche. Perhaps it was the gaze
of the orcs we felt, he thought, but knew he was wrong.

'There's a doom for you,' he said to Gotrek, gesturing back
towards the mighty horde.

'My doom lies within this pyramid,' said Gotrek, his eyes fixed on
the elf's back. Felix was not exactly sure what he meant by that, but
it reassured him even less than the sight of all those orcs.

'What now?' he asked Teclis.

'Inside,' he said. 'We are close to the locus of all this power, I can
sense it. Our quest is almost over.'

The battle-cries of the greenskins rose behind them. 'One way or
another, I think you are right,' Felix said.

FELIX GAUGED THE size of the archway under which they passed. It
was ten times the height of a man, large enough to let the giants of
his imagination pass through. Wonderful, he thought. As if there
was not enough to worry about already.

The place was lit by odd green lights set in the ceiling. They
reminded Felix of the ones he had seen in the Paths of the Old
Ones. The stonework too was reminiscent of that at the entrance to
the paths, although on a far more heroic scale. Why had the mysterious Old Ones felt the need to built roadways so big here? What
was it they had taken through from Albion that was so large? Or was
his imagination simply too prosaic for the subject? Perhaps the
arches were so huge for a completely different purpose. Perhaps
there was some mystical significance to their size, shape and form
that he simply could not grasp. Perhaps they were part of some sort

of rune that could only be read by a god. Not that it mattered much at this hour, Felix thought. If those orcs get their claws on us, all such speculation will be ended. Filled with trepidation, he passed under the arch and into the vast gloomy corridors beyond.

As they did so, the walls shook once more. 'We must hurry now. To the Chamber of Secrets!'

The walls around them shook once more and the lights in the ceiling died. A few of the men let out howls of fear. The dark chamber was suddenly filled with menace. Teclis strode ahead of them, filled with confidence. From the tip of his staff came light to illuminate their way and send things scuttling back away from its circle. Felix caught sight of vast bat-shapes rising into the darkness below the ceilings. Once more he was aware of the huge weight of stones pressing down all around them. He was within the depths of an artificial mountain and something about it oppressed his very soul.

With every step into the ancient darkness he became more certain that the place was haunted. He was not sure what by – perhaps the ghosts of the Old Ones, perhaps the spirits of other long-dead things – but he felt certain that something was there. Very often it seemed to him that just as they entered a chamber, some vast shadow departed, hovering just beyond their sight, waiting and watching with malign intelligence for them to make some misstep or perhaps just to lose their way in the eternal gloom.

Worse yet, the taint of warpstone on the air was getting stronger. There was a pressure in his ears, on the top of his head, within his cheeks, that intensified until it was almost painful. Even his teeth ached. He did not doubt that the elf was right. They were nearing the heart of the most powerful magic Felix had ever encountered. He sensed long-dormant forces coming awake all around them.

Even Gotrek seemed to sense it. His movements were cautious and his head scanned from side to side watchfully. Felix noticed that the runes on the dwarf's axe had begun to glow with their own internal light. That had never been a good sign, in Felix's experience.

Behind them they could hear the echoing shouts of the orcs. The sound seemed to rumble through the old chambers like thunder. The bestial roaring was amplified a dozen-fold until it became the voice of an angry god. In his mind's eye, Felix could picture that vast army of greenskins filing out through the corridors, slowly, inexorably, an irresistible green tide filling up the whole structure.

It seemed unlikely to Felix that they should have got this far without running into some sort of resistance. In his experience, the forces of Chaos never gave up anything they had taken without some sort of fight. Unless of course, it was all a trap. The sudden certainty of it shook him. Were they being lured further into the pyramid to their dooms? Would they be sacrificed in some unspeakable way as part of some dreadful ritual? Had they already been swallowed alive by the vast dark god that was the pyramid itself?

He tried to push the thought from his mind and noticed something else. The amulet the elf had given him was warm enough that he could feel it on his chest. He touched it with his fingers and was surprised by how hot it was, and he saw that the runes on it, written in flowing graceful elvish script, were alight. Something had activated its protective power.

Now in the distance, he heard other sounds, the bellowing of warcries, the clash of weapon on weapon. Somewhere men or things close to men chanted the names of dark gods. Orcs responded with guttural shouts in their bestial language. So far, on the path they had taken they had encountered nothing. It felt even more like a trap, like walking down the throat of a mighty beast that at any moment might gulp them down into its huge stomach. He gripped tight on his sword as if by holding it tighter he could somehow hold onto his fears as well.

Another thought insinuated itself into Felix's mind. They were not in the body of some great beast, they were trapped in the toils of some great infernal machine, like the engines the dwarfs used to process ore and work metal, only this one processed souls and produced... what? He could not begin to guess. Suddenly he found himself longing for action. His nerves were stretched, his brow covered in cold sweat. Waiting for whatever dreadful doom that was about to ensnare them seemed intolerable. He had to fight down an urge to run towards that distant melee, to throw himself into the mindless carnage, to drown out his consciousness in waves of berserker bloodlust.

The charm grew warmer on his breast. The runes on Gotrek's axe glowed brightly. The auras blazing on Teclis's amulets almost dazzled him. In the strange glow he could see the faces of the other humans. They all looked strange and bestial, their shadows were the shadows of slouching apes, their features chiselled into expressions of elemental hatred and violence. Culum glared at him malignly. Siobhain's face seemed twisted with insane hatred. Bran looked furtively about as if he feared one of his kin would plunge a spear into his back and claim his crown for their own. They all seemed caught up in some mad dream.

The elf glanced at him and concern passed across his hateful, alien features. 'It's this place,' he said. 'It twists your mind. Chaos and the magic of the Old Ones have intertwined to produce something that mortals were not meant to endure the like of. Be calm. Resist it. Soon we shall be where we need to be.'

As if to mock his soothing words the sounds of violence intensified and the whole pyramid shook as if struck with a giant hammer. The lights flickered to life once more, and a strange keening whining noise filled the air. Felix did not want to consider what could cause such a vast stone structure to quake like a shivering beast. He sensed that forces were being unleashed that might crack the whole world like an egg. He wished he were anywhere but here.

AHEAD OF THEM lay a massive square, open to the sky. That the place had once possessed a roof was evidenced by the fact that huge shattered stones lay everywhere. Mighty stone pillars jutted upwards to support a ceiling that was no longer there. They too showed signs of erosion. Moss had grown on their intricate carved stonework. Tufts of ochre outlined some of the lines and submerged others.

Overhead dark clouds boiled in the sky, glittering redly as if tainted with warpstone dust. Huge thunderbolts lashed down. They must be striking fairly close now. The sight of the open sky increased Felix's claustrophobia rather than the reverse. It reminded him that in another few moments they would plunge back into the stygian gloom. The air here was not fresh. It carried hints of some new corruption. Teclis uttered what might have been an oath in Elvish and moved towards the base of one pillar.

It had been corroded utterly and a white hand stuck out from the rock. Felix moved closer and looking over the elf's shoulder, saw that it was not a human hand. It had only three fingerbones and those were broader and thicker than the fingers of any man. The elf tapped the stonework with the tip of his staff, and rock crumbled to reveal a skeleton that was only remotely human.

It tumbled forward and clattered onto the floor. The elf must have exerted some arcane energy for it did not shatter into a thousand pieces as Felix would have expected. Instead it flipped over as if animated. For a second Felix feared the thing was being returned to some sort of unlife, like the skeletons and zombies he had fought in the ruins of Drakenhof. Others shrank away as well. Only Gotrek and the elf held their ground.

Seeing no immediate danger he moved cautiously forward. The skeleton belonged to a being almost as tall as a man and broader – something about the shape of the head and the disposition of the limbs suggested the batrachian. If a toad and an ape had been crossed, it might have a skeleton like that, Felix thought.

'Slann,' said Teclis. 'One of the Eldest Race, the Old Ones' chosen servants. It was immured here amid these pillars. You would find a similar skeleton at the base of each of these columns. They were entombed alive.'

'But why?' Felix asked.

'As part of some ritual designed to consecrate this place. Their souls were intended as guardians. Maybe they were offerings to whatever it was the Old Ones worshipped. Or maybe the purpose was so alien we could not begin to understand it. Who can tell? Someday when we have more time, I would like to come back and examine this place. Who knows what secrets it contains?'

'This is getting us nowhere,' said Gotrek, raising his axe meaningfully. 'Lead on, elf. Bring us to the heart of this thing.'

Teclis shook himself from his reverie, but paused for a last wondering glance at the skeleton. Felix thought he understood. How long had it been since that creature had lived and breathed and walked in sunlight? Millennia at least. Before the birth of the Empire. Before the first human civilisations arose in ancient Nehekhara. What kind of world had it looked on? What strange marvels had it witnessed? For a brief moment, Felix understood part of the attraction of necromancy. To be able to make such a creature speak and give up its secrets. He shivered and pulled his gaze away, wondering where those dark thoughts had come from. This place really was affecting him, he thought.

As one they passed out of the great courtyard, and back into the bowels of the temple.

FELIX STUDIED THE corridor around him as they marched. At this point it was as wide as a road and the only protective barriers were where support arches jutted out of the walls every fifty strides or so. If there were any chambers leading out of the corridors they had been sealed so cunningly as to be undetectable. Ever since the discovery of the skeleton in the base of the pillar, Felix had suspected that concealed chambers and corpses and secrets were everywhere around them. He found it only too easy to imagine sealed chambers in which legions of batrachian bodies had laid down their lives for their perverse gods, in which sinister engines pulsed with the energies of ancient sorceries.

Overhead the greenish lights glowed eerily. They provided a dim and ghastly luminescence that hid almost as much as it illuminated. Shadows danced grotesquely as the light flickered then surged. They spoke of secret energies ebbing and flowing all around as much as the shaking earth. Once more the image of some huge, complex and ultimately incomprehensible machine struck Felix. But he was prepared to believe that powers that could slowly and inexorably shift continents were being marshalled here.

As the thought struck him, he heard the sounds of battle echo once more through the huge structure.

THE NOISE OF furious conflict came ever closer. Felix squinted into the distant gloom. Orcs and beastmen fought savagely at the next crossroads. Two mighty inexorable tides of monsters had met and neither was willing to give ground. Felix could not tell who was winning, nor did he care. He wanted merely to be out of this place, and away from the eternal gloom surrounding them.

Teclis raised his hand and gestured for them to stop. All around, men and women readied their weapons, levelling their spears, limbering up their swords. Felix was not sure what use such mighty claymores might have even in these wide corridors. He doubted that there was room for more than two or three men armed in such a way to fight abreast. In a confined space they would prove almost as much a threat to their friends as their enemies.

'No,' said the elf. 'We do not fight. Not yet. We must find another way.'

They waited tensely to see if the battle flowed towards them, but it did not. Instead it receded away from them, flowing into the distance. The small army of humans began its advance once more.

THEY CAME TO another ramp, this one leading down into the depths. From it emerged a foul smell, of stagnant warpstone-polluted water, and old decay. Mould clung to the walls here, a peculiar black stuff that seemed somehow poisonous. It had eaten away at the ancient carvings and formed new and grotesque shapes that hinted at gargoyles and monsters without quite being them.

Without stopping Teclis led them downward into the eternal gloom. Felix looked at the dwarf but he seemed absorbed with his own dark thoughts, his mind appeared to have turned inwards on itself as it often did before moments of extreme and explosive violence.

Even the downward-leading ramp was huge. It descended steeply into a gloom that became ever deeper as the green ceiling lights became ever more intermittent. Felix strode along at the head of the column beside the elf and the dwarf. He found their presence reassuring even here. Then his eyes caught sight of something that left him stunned.

The way ahead was barred by what looked like a huge broken wall of spikes. He strode closer and saw that they were not spikes but bones, part of another, much larger skeleton. A monstrous ribcage loomed above him. He walked along a shattered spine towards a fairly human-looking skull that had been smashed by some titanic blow.

It was the skeleton of a giant. It blocked the entire corridor. Its size was entirely consistent with the creature he had imagined when he saw the huge print in the forest mud.

'I don't think he was entombed here as part of some ancient ritual,' said Felix.

He inspected it for the stigmata of mutation and could see none. The bones were huge, much thicker than those of an ordinary man in proportion to their size, and Felix guessed that the giant had been much broader in life in proportion to his size than a man. Still, there were no horns or claws. A few of the bones from legs and arms were missing but he saw their cracked and broken remains lay close by. It reminded him of the way orcs and beastmen broke bones to suck out the marrow. He suppressed a shudder.

'What could have killed and eaten a giant?' he asked, not really expecting an answer.

'Another giant,' said Gotrek grimly. He strode forward under the huge ribcage and paused to contemplate it for a second as if measuring himself against it. Felix wondered what was passing through his mind. Compared to this huge creature, even Gotrek's mighty axe was less than a child's toy. It was not a reassuring thought. The print they had seen outside was recent and the image of a cannibal giant strong enough to kill even its mighty kin sprang into his mind.

He could tell by the expressions of all the men around him that the same thought had occurred to them. It was with visible reluctance that they continued their trek down into the depths of the pyramid.

CHAPTER TWENTY-SIX

TECLIS STUDIED THE threads of power he sensed all around him. He was close now. Close to the black heart of the mystery he had crossed continents to solve. Close to the source of the dreadful eruptions of power that spelled doom for his homeland unless they were resolved. He felt the flow of vast energies around him, greater even than those pinned down by the watchstones of Ulthuan. Compared to them, this was like measuring a mountain stream against the flow of the mighty river Reik.

There was something wrong here. The flows of energy were not steady. They stuttered. They erupted mightily one instant and faded away to nothing the next, as if someone had invoked their mighty energies but could not quite control them, was in fact battling to contain them. The thought sent fear shuddering through even his perfect self-control. That someone had awoken this sleeping daemon without knowing its true name, had aroused all this power without having the means to completely control it, was almost more frightening than the idea that evildoers had bound it to the service of Chaos.

For if the power that underpinned continents and could shift worlds in their orbit was allowed to raven unchecked then the end of the whole world was perhaps nigh. Certainly the end of this temple and perhaps this island, and as an inevitable consequence,

Ulthuan. Worse than that, even the partial control that was going on here was the mark of mighty sorcerers, perhaps more than his equals. He did not relish the prospect of facing them.

His options were scant indeed. They needed to go on, to get to the very core of this, and soon. He led the way downwards into the heart of the pyramid. All around him power surged. All around him battle raged.

THE ROAD ENDED at a mighty arch. Beyond it lay a huge chamber, with many entrances and exits. Felix looked at it. There seemed no rhyme or reason to the place. It was a huge maze laid out according to principles he could not understand. Above them were many galleries and walkways. Ahead of them was open space, and when he went to the edge and looked down, he could see more galleries dropping away beneath them. It was like looking into a huge well.

He was reminded once more of the strange city he and Gotrek and Snorri had gotten lost in during their trek across the Chaos Wastes. Was there some connection between this place and that? Certainly there were similarities between the architecture, but this temple was built on an even more epic scale. In his mind's eye, he suddenly pictured dozens of such places scattered about the world, linked by a web of strange powers, laid out in a pattern just as incomprehensible to a mortal mind as their interiors.

He was distracted from his reverie by the appearance of a horde of orcs on the gallery above and opposite them. Their leader was some sort of shaman, carrying a skull-tipped staff. He shrieked and pointed at them. So much for spells of concealment, Felix thought. Noticing the men below, the orcs raised their bows and sent a wave of arrows hurtling towards them. The distance was great but one could not count on all the force of the missiles being spent. Felix ducked down below the level of the stone banister. Arrows clattered down all around him. A second wave came in and Teclis incinerated them with a spell. Seeing this, the greenskins held their fire and shouted taunts and abuse in their vile tongue. Gotrek answered with a few of his own, and was joined by the human warriors. The elf seemed more concerned with getting them moving again.

The orcs began to surge along the gallery seeking some way to get to their opponents. As Felix watched, beastmen and black armoured Chaos warriors emerged from another entrance and met the greenskins head on. A monstrous melee ensued.

Felix wondered at their luck. Why had they encountered no resistance? Why were the Chaos warriors concentrating on the greenskins? An answer immediately struck him. They were the greater threat. They were, after all, a huge army compared to this small band. Perhaps the Chaos warlords had failed to notice the humans in their midst. If that was the case, Felix thought, it would only be a matter of time before they rectified this oversight.

His premonition proved true, not a hundred strides from where he had it. The elf led them off the massive balcony along which they marched and into a huge chamber containing more strange pillars. These ones glowed with an eerie green light. Felix could almost sense the power flowing through them. The massive runes glowed along their length. From an entrance at the other end of the chamber, a horde of beastmen suddenly emerged. At their head was a black armoured Chaos warrior on whose chest blazed a glowing Eye of Chaos symbol.

At the sight of the interlopers, the beastmen howled challenges and prayers to their dark gods and threw themselves forward. The warriors of Albion leapt to meet them breast to breast. Within moments a mad melee swirled among the pillars.

'Stay close,' said Teclis. 'We cannot afford to get pinned down here. Time is getting very short.'

'So is my patience,' said Gotrek. Even as he spoke, he hacked down a wolf-headed creature armed with a massive spear, and then split open a goat-head from gizzard to groin. Felix parried the blow of another goat-headed giant and then stabbed over its spear with the tip of his sword. The creature shrieked as it leapt away to avoid being spitted. Its back came into contact with one of the glowing pillars. Immediately, its shrieks intensified and a terrible smell of burning flesh filled the air. As it toppled forward, Felix could see its shoulders and spine were blackened, charred meat. He almost felt like he was putting the thing out of its agony when he cut it down.

Gotrek and Teclis pushed forward, dwarfish axe and elvish blade flickered in unison. Felix could see that Teclis was more than a match for even a master human swordsman, but his prowess fell far short of the dwarf's. For every one beastman the elf cut down, the Slayer hewed down four. Still, Felix thought, for an effete wizard, the elf was not doing at all badly. Every now and again, he stopped and spoke a word of power and gestured. A bolt of energy lashed from his staff to disintegrate his foes.

The three of them formed a spearhead behind which the warriors of Albion chopped their way through their inhuman foes. The dwarf and the elf were unstoppable at least by any power that currently opposed them. The folk of Albion were not quite so lucky. Even as Felix watched he saw the ranks around Bran thinning, clawed down by desperate beastmen. Murdo and Culum went to his aid, hewing their way through the monstrous ranks, bolstering up the hill-king's guard and enabling them to fight their way free of the ruck. Gotrek and the Chaos warrior came into contact. For a few brief moments, starmetal axe clashed with hell-forged black steel, then the Chaos champion was down and his forces begun to retire in disarray.

'Push on, push on,' yelled Teclis. 'We must get to the heart of the pyramid before it is too late.'

Such was the urgency of his tone that not even Gotrek gainsaid him. Once more the pyramid shivered. The glow surrounding the rune-carved pillars grew so bright as to be almost dazzling and then swiftly faded. Where it touched, corpses or living, it burned. Felix hurried on, sensing the elf's desperation and not liking the thought of finding its cause one little bit.

THE DEEPER THEY penetrated into the pyramid, the more difficulty Teclis had in keeping them concealed from spells of prying and warding. Once already his concentration had faltered and they had been seen by the orc shaman. The flows of magical energy were becoming chaotic, partially from the invocation of the powers centred on the temple and partially from the vast surges being unleashed by greenskin shamans and Chaos warlocks. The latter were tiny changes compared to the former, but under such conditions, they introduced uncertainties into the matrix.

Each casting was like a tiny grain of sand shifting in a desert. Of itself it was nothing, but the tiniest piece of extra weight and pressure it created could cause a whole dune to tremble and fall into a new pattern. So it was here. Perhaps one day, if he lived, he would set his theories about this to paper. At the moment, he had other concerns.

In order to avoid contributing to the maelstrom, he was drawing on the power contained in the staff, and his own personal energies and these were tiring in the extreme. He possessed certain powdered roots and herbs that would aid him, but preferred not to use them unless he absolutely must. The price to be paid for renewed energy was a loss of concentration and intellectual sharpness, and at the moment, he needed all his wits about him.

His force was too small to risk it being caught up in another melee. Time was growing short. He needed to find the safest path to the heart of this labyrinth and confront the sorcerers at work there, and he needed the blades of the men and dwarf to shield him. He knew he was going to have to risk a spell of his own, and trust to the fact that any other mage present was most likely too caught up in the intricacies of battle magic to notice something as subtle as he was going to attempt.

He gestured for the others to wait, closed his eyes and murmured the spell of All Seeing. At first, as always, there was no change, then slowly the frontiers of his perception began to expand outwards like a slowly inflating bubble. Suddenly he was able to stand outside himself and look down, seeing in three hundred and sixty degrees. He felt dizzy as his mind struggled to adjust to perceptions it had never been intended to deal with, to see things from a perspective no mortal normally viewed from. Had it not been for decades of practice and the discipline of centuries he doubted he could have done so. As far as he knew no human had ever achieved the mental flexibility needed to perform this ritual without the use of potent hallucinogenic drugs. Even then, he doubted the spell was very useful to them. Only elves it seemed could perform this, and the Old Ones who had taught them it, of course. Perhaps the slann could as well, but who could tell what that strange batrachian race were capable of?

He realised that he was becoming distracted, as his mind sought to escape the pressure to which he was subjecting it. He breathed deeply, stilled his racing heart with a thought and let his consciousness continue to balloon.

He became aware of all the corridors radiating away from his current position. He saw most were empty, but that in some beastmen raced and orcs moved stealthily. It seemed that nearby the battle for the pyramid had reached a new phase, of stealthy stalking, as each side sought to take the other by surprise. Outwards his perceptions raced like the ripples from a dropped stone racing towards the edge of a dark still pool.

He saw pockets of savage conflict where orc and beastman battled. He saw shamans cast spells with wands of bone and warlocks respond with spells of subtle Tzeentchian intricacy. He felt the tearing of the fabric of reality these caused like a pain inside his skull.

Onwards and outwards his vision ranged until he saw the whole pyramid as a vast seething ant-heap of violence and conflict filled with hordes of monsters bent on doing each other harm. He saw huge trolls and monstrous dragon-ogres. He saw bizarre limbless pit-bred monsters, all mouth and eyes, bouncing into battle with shrieking goblins on their backs. He saw harpies flap among the galleries and descend on bellowing black orcs to claw at their eyes with razor-sharp talons.

There was much he could not see. Certain areas were shielded by strange runes. Others were blocked from his sight by dazzling swirls and flows of cosmic energy which blinded him when he attempted to concentrate on them. He forced his mind to drink in what it could and memorise what it must, and then he focused his attention on what he sought, the strange vast vortex of power that lurked deep in the heart of this mad structure.

This part was easy. His attention was drawn to it like a moth to a flame or a drowning swimmer to the centre of a whirlpool. He saw the spells of warding set up to protect it. They were potent and strong but they lacked the subtlety and power of the slann wards. With luck and skill and concentration he could avoid them. He sent his consciousness flowing along the intricate patterns, avoiding the mystical tripwires and pitfalls, trying not to set off any of the alarms. It felt like agonisingly slow, painful work, but he knew that in reality he was still caught in the moment between one heartbeat and another. In passing he saw the warriors who waited at the centre and the huge thing that stalked the heart of the pyramid, he sensed its primordial rage and hunger. Then at last his mind found what it sought: the central chamber, the heart of the madness, the place where the power flowed out of the world beyond and into the mortal realm.

He saw a massive structure that somehow suggested a sacrificial altar slicked with blood and the controls of some intricate machine. He saw the piles of corpses that had been offered up to the gods alone knew what. He saw giant pillars at either end of the hall through which all the condensed and collected magical energy was focused, and he saw the vast and intricate web of forces that radiated out from this place and into hundreds of others. Here was one of the great nexi of the Paths of the Old Ones, perhaps the greatest, save for that vast abyss that gaped at the northern pole.

He could see now where all the Chaos warriors and beastmen were coming from. They were entering through the Paths of the Old Ones and emerging here. Even as he watched, a burst of energy told him of the arrival of another warband. He watched them immediately take orders from the wizards who controlled this place, and race outwards to do battle.

Here then, at last, were the beings who had worked to open this place – near identical albino twins of vulpine aspect. One was clad in spun gold and the other in deepest black. He could sense at once that they were mages of vast dark power. Something linked them, a tie of blood and magic that reminded him of the one that linked himself and his twin, only greater. He sensed their malice and glee as they worked and realised that they were in no sense sane. They did not care if they destroyed this island or this world. Perhaps they would be glad. There was no way he could persuade them to stop, so that slim chance was gone. Two such as these were going to have to be overcome by force. He only hoped he possessed enough to do the work.

Even as he watched he could see that one of them was working spells similar to his own to guide the forces of Chaos against the orcs. The other supervised the engine at the chamber's heart, seemingly unaware or unconcerned that he had woken forces beyond his power to control.

Teclis cancelled his spell and his consciousness immediately flowed back into the vessel that was his body. He shook his head and checked the spells of concealment he had laid over the party. Now more than ever they were needed. If one of those mages sensed them before they reached the innermost sanctum, he could throw enough of the Chaos warriors and beastmen forward to overwhelm them. He believed that his weaves were tight and effective. At the moment his greatest fear was that they would be reported to the wizards by one of their lackeys. Against that, haste was the only defence.

CHAPTER TWENTY-SEVEN

ZARKHUL PUSHED ON into the heart of the pyramid. He led his body-guard out into this, the heart of the largest ziggurat. He was close to his goal. Soon he and his warriors would slay the interlopers who defiled the temple. They would cleanse this place in blood. He summoned the spirit power of his people and his gods and brought his blessing down on his warriors. Now, he thought, there would be a reckoning.

KELMAIN SENSED A disturbance in the wards. He thought he had sensed one before but he had not been sure. The tides of power here were so turbulent that it had been hard to tell. This was different. This bore the imprint of greenskin magic and it was close, very close and immensely powerful. Somehow it seemed the orcs had found their way into the heart of the city. There were too many of them to be resisted, at least until reinforcements could be summoned. They needed time to calm the seething energies of the paths and bring them back under control, then once more they could summon aid. He needed all his remaining forces here to guard the Chamber of Secrets until that could happen. He cast the spell of summoning that would draw Magrig to him.

* * *

FELIX GASPED FOR breath. The elf had led them at a fast trot through the labyrinth. Felix was not sure how he found his path and kept to it, but it seemed to be working. As they descended into the depths, they managed to avoid any more marauding bands of beastmen or orcs. Their way was clear. From the pressure in his head, he could tell they were getting closer and closer to their goal. Powerful evil magic was at work.

From up ahead now, he could see a strange pulsing glow. It blazed brighter then receded almost to invisibility. More than ever he felt like a bug crawling through the chambers of some huge creature's house. The scale of the corridors was oppressive. Large enough for even the dead giant to have moved through. What had been brought here, he wondered? Why did these ways need to be so large? Had the Old Ones brought ships down here? Or were they giants themselves? So many questions and so few answers.

Suddenly from close by, he heard the sound of insane enraged bellowing so loud that it was almost earsplitting, and so terrifying he almost froze on the spot. Only a creature far larger than a man could have made that much noise. Only a giant. Moreover, even as he listened the screaming came closer, bringing with it the sounds of battle.

Felix exchanged looks with Gotrek and Teclis. They knew what was coming too. The elf looked calm. Gotrek looked angry. His beard bristled and he ran his thumb along the blade of his axe until a bead of blood showed. The men of Albion looked poised for flight. This horror looked like it might prove the final one for their shattered nerves. They looked ready to break and run in a moment.

What happened next happened almost too quickly for the mind to comprehend. A huge shadow appeared far down the passageway, blocking out the ceiling lights with its bulk. From all around it came a whirlwind of screams and war-cries. These seemed like the reedy piping of swamp birds compared to the bellowing of the huge monster.

Carried by its huge stride the giant was on them almost before they could react. Felix got a quick glance of the thing. It had once looked like a man, but that time had been long ago. Now it was warped hideously. Its proportions were almost dwarf-like. Its shoulders were immensely huge. Its legs like the boles of massive trees. The comparison was an easy one to make, for in one hand it held a club that was little more than the branch-stripped remains of a tree. But it was the face that Felix would remember in his nightmares.

Once perhaps, it had borne the features of a nobly proportioned man, albeit one with a monumentally huge jaw. Now those features had run like melted wax, so that flabby jowls hung down almost to the creature's chest. Idiot fury and pain filled its one good eye. Drool dribbled from between teeth the size of tombstones. The smell was appalling. It reeked like a legion of beggars who had spent all day trawling through a sewer for the vilest refuse. Felix started to gag.

All around the creature were orcs and Chaos warriors, fighting with it and each other. The giant did not care. It lashed out with its club, reducing them to jelly-like smears. The force of its blows was irresistible. One would have been enough to smash a warship to flinders. As it moved, it stamped on the small creatures surrounding it, like a man might crush vermin underfoot.

It took them in with one glance, casually smashed a dozen of the men of Albion to paste and passed on into the depths of the pyramid, leaving them trapped in the furious melee.

'Quickly,' said Teclis. 'We must follow it.'

'You're joking,' said Felix, blocking the blow of a massive orc, a second before Gotrek's axe chopped it in two.

The elf shook its head. 'It is heading into the depths to the axis of power. It is being drawn there or summoned.'

'Summoned?' said Felix. 'What could summon that?'

'I do not know,' said Teclis. 'But I am sure we will find out.'

Even as the elf spoke, the dwarf surged past him, hewing frantically, desperate it seemed to get on the trail of a monster worthy of guaranteeing his doom.

Felix followed. There was nothing else to do.

AND SO THEY came to the heart of the temple, to the secret chambers where the ancient engines of the Old Ones had been reactivated by the dark sorcery of Chaos. They emerged into a huge chamber where a dozen portals had opened. Through two of them emerged the warriors of Chaos, beastmen, minotaurs, harpies, iron-collared daemonic hounds, all the nightmare creatures Felix had hoped never to meet again. All around them were piles of dead bodies, both greenskin and beastman.

Standing atop a huge altar were Kelmain and Lhoigor. One of them manipulated the energies by passing his hands over the controls of the ancient machines. The other appeared to be frozen. The giant loomed before him, listening to the seductive voice of evil. Immediately Felix saw why the creature had been summoned. Hordes of greenskins flowed through several other entrances to the huge chamber, enough to overcome even those temporarily guarding it. How they had got there Felix had no idea, but according to the men of Albion the greenskins had been at home here for centuries before being driven out, so perhaps they knew some secret way. Not that it mattered. It looked like he and his companions were going to be caught between the hammer of Chaos and the anvil of orcdom. There were thousands of foes in this chamber, and two of the deadliest sorcerers he had ever seen along with their enthralled gigantic servitor. He offered up a last prayer to Sigmar. He knew he was not going to survive this.

Even as the thought passed through his mind, the walls shook. The runes along the walls glittered. The face of Lhoigor twisted as he tried to control the mystical backlash. Even to Felix's untrained eye, it was obvious that he was not able to do it.

Suddenly he understood what was going on and why there were so few Chaos warriors. The mages had unleashed forces they could not control. Through the open portals, Felix could see a seething sea of energy. It was slowly advancing through the portals, as inexorable and irresistible as lava. There would be no more reinforcements from the Chaos Wastes, Felix realised. They had most likely been swallowed by raw stuff of Chaos that flowed within the paths. He could not find any sympathy in himself for such creatures.

Another thought passed through his mind. The orcs could win here and their victory would be as bad as that of Chaos. For unless the ancient engines were shut down, the forces unleashed would tear apart Ulthuan and Albion and eventually perhaps the world.

'What are we going to do?' Felix said.

'Guard me,' said Teclis. 'I must reach that altar.'

'Typical of an elf,' said Gotrek, his tone almost humorous. 'The world is ending and all he is concerned about is his own safety.'

Still, when the elf moved, the Slayer followed, and Felix went with him.

THEY BATTLED THEIR way across the chamber, the human warriors forming a tight knot around the elf. They had no idea what he was going to do but they seemed determined to defend him in any case. All around them orc fought with beastman and Chaos warrior.

Felix could see that this worked to their advantage. Only rarely did their foes make anything like a concerted rush towards them. At those times the fighting became hot and deadly and men and women died. Felix ducked the sweep of a Chaos warrior's blade, lashed out a counter-blow against the cold black metal armour. His sword almost dropped from fingers numbed by the force of impact. The ancient magical blade cut through the enchanted vambrace and bit into the Chaos warrior's arm. Another stroke took him through the gorget and buried the blade deep in his throat.

Up ahead Gotrek and Teclis fought like daemons, chopping down anything that got in their path. Man or monster, beast or orc, nothing withstood them. The destruction they wrought was immense. They were almost halfway to their goal when it all went horribly wrong.

Teclis knew it was only a matter of time before the Chaos sorcerers spotted him. His spells had prevented them from being detected by wards as they had moved through the pyramid, but they would be visible to magesight now. One of the twins was busy, trying to control the immense flow of power through the master altar. The other appeared to be feeding him strength while at the same time guiding the forces of Chaos. Teclis could sense the summons going out to every part of the pyramid. He did not need to understand the language to know that it was urging them to return to this chamber by the swiftest route possible.

Once the spell was complete the black-clad albino opened his eyes and gazed around. Their eyes met. Teclis felt the spark of recognition pass between them. Each knew the other for what they were immediately – a master sorcerer. The Chaos mage smiled evilly and bellowed something in an ancient half-recognisable tongue. Teclis ducked the sweep of an orcish blade, frantically trying to make out what his foe had shouted through the din of battle. He felt certain it was not a spell. The next thing he chanted was though – a moment later an enormous arc of power smashed outwards towards him and the Slayer. Desperately Teclis prepared a counter-spell. Even as he did so a monstrous shadow passed over the elf.

FELIX LOOKED UP. His gaze travelled up enormous columnar legs, along a mighty misshapen body and came to rest once more on that hideous gigantic face. Everyone around him stood as if paralysed. He did not blame them. The sheer ferocity of the giant's howl was enough to unman most people. For a moment, all was silent. All around them, nothing seemed to move.

Felix was not sure whether this was really the case or if it was an illusion. Often in the past, in moments of crisis, things had seemed to freeze or move with extreme slowness. Perhaps this was one of them.

A moment later he was certain of it. The huge monster raised its club and brought it down in a sweeping arc, designed to reduce the elf to bloody sludge. Felix's thoughts raced as he tried to work out what to do. Nothing came. He could not block the blow. He began to move forward, thinking perhaps that he could push the elf to one side, then he noticed that with painful slowness the Slayer appeared to be doing exactly that.

One of Gotrek's ham-sized hands thrust the elf out of harm's way, then the Slayer bounded aside himself. Such was the force of the Slayer's blow that the elf was hurled from his feet and sent rolling away. Felix suspected that the dwarf had most likely enjoyed doing that. A heartbeat later there was a thunder-crack as the club connected with stone. The impact hurled chips of gravel everywhere. One caught Felix on the face, gashing a bloody weal across his cheek.

Undaunted by the enormous size of his foe, Gotrek bounded forward. His axe smashed into the giant's ankle. Blood flowed from an enormous cut. The dwarf's mad laughter rang out as he hacked once more. The runes on his axe glowed ever brighter as it bit into the giant's Chaos-tainted flesh. Was it possible that he might succeed in bringing down even this titanic beast, Felix wondered?

Behind the giant, he noticed the Chaos mage launch another spell. Felix knew it boded nothing good. He glanced at Teclis to see if the elf mage was doing anything but he was still flipping himself to his feet. A second later a sphere of glowing red left the mage's hand and, rotating as it came, flickered towards the Slayer, leaving a glowing blood-red contrail in its wake.

Gotrek did not hesitate. His axe flashed upwards to intercept it, and this proved to be his undoing. The moment the sphere touched the axe, it disintegrated in an enormous flash of light. A second later the Slayer reeled backwards, moving awkwardly, obviously blinded. The Chaos mage bellowed something again, in some obscure language.

The giant gave an idiot giggle, bent down and grabbed Gotrek in one enormous hand. Felix momentarily expected to see the fist close and reduce the dwarf to a bloody mess and now he was too far away to do anything to help the Slayer.

TECLIS PULLED HIMSELF to his feet. His ribs were sore from the blow the Slayer had landed when pushing him out of the giant's way. He did not know whether to be grateful or enraged. It felt as if some of his ribs were broken. Not only that, his pride was hurt. He would not have believed it possible for anyone to landed a blow on him unawares, and yet the Slayer had. It said much for the dwarf's prowess. The thoughts flickered through his mind as he pulled himself clear of the struggle between dwarf and giant. He felt fairly sure that this time even Gotrek Gurnisson had bitten off more than he could chew. Regrettably, Teclis was in no position to help him. He had another, even larger problem – how to overcome the Chaos sorcerers and close the Paths of the Old

Ones before the tide of Chaos overran this temple, and undermined the whole geo-mystical pattern of the Old Ones' work,
sinking Ulthuan and ravaging the lands of men.

At the moment, the roaring giant cut them off from his sight. He
bounded off to the right, chopping down a beastman who came too
close, parrying a blow from a goblin spear as it rose to impale him.
Murdo was at his back, his spear flashing. The elf had no time to be
grateful.

'You must stop them!' the old man bellowed. Teclis did not
reply to this redundant statement. He was too busy concentrating on how to do it. Seeing himself ignored, the old man
muttered a prayer. Runes burned along the length of his spear
and he cast it directly at the black-robed mage. It flew with
incredible speed, like a thunderbolt, so swift that even Teclis's
sight could barely follow it. He was surprised when it was only
partially deflected by the mage's protective spells, slashing his
side like a sword-blow. Even more impressively, the spear
swerved in flight and began to return to the old man's hand. It
seemed that the magic of men was still capable of surprising
him.

The Chaos sorcerer was not best pleased. He gestured, and a polychromatic sphere of light flickered around his hand. He gestured
again and a geyser of the raw stuff of Chaos appeared – hurtling
towards Murdo. The Truthsayer sprang to one side. The stuff hit two
of the men behind him and they fell apart as if hosed down with
acid.

A bellow of pain somewhere to the left and behind them told
Teclis that against all odds Gotrek Gurnisson appeared to be alive
and keeping the giant occupied. Knowing that the dwarf could not
last much longer Teclis decided he'd better make his move while the
monster was still distracted.

Gathering all his strength, he prepared to act.

SOMEHOW, SINEWS BULGING, Gotrek resisted that enormous force. His
axe arm was outside the giant's grip and still flailed away, drawing
blood with every swipe. The giant raised him to the level of its
mouth. Felix watched, horrified, knowing what was coming next.
The creature's mouth was so huge it could take the Slayer in one
bite.

At the last second, just before his struggling form was stuffed into
the thing's mouth, Gotrek shook his head and appeared to regain
his sight. His situation was awful. Even if he freed himself, he could
do nothing except fall to his death on the hard stone below. As if

realising this, the dwarf bellowed defiance and chopped down with his axe, slicing through the giant's fingers. The giant's grip came free and Gotrek leapt forward, pushing himself off the giant's palm with his feet, burying his blade right into the middle of the giant's enormous forehead. Magrig let out a bellow of pain that almost burst Felix's eardrums.

Hanging from his axe like a climber using a pick to hold onto the face of a mountain, Gotrek reached over and stuck his hand into the giant's plate-sized eye. Felix winced as he reached under the lid and tugged the remaining eyeball free of the socket. The giant spasmed and tried to swat at the dwarf. Gotrek tugged his axe free and let himself drop, still clutching at the ball of jelly that had once been an eye. Felix thought he would drop to his doom, but was surprised to see a cable of veinous substance come loose behind the eye. It occurred to him that the Slayer was swinging from what remained of the giant's optic nerve. The giant's blow slapped into its own head with enormous force. It had dropped its club now as it howled and raged in its agony. It stopped and shook its head as if that would somehow get rid of the pain. Of course, it only increased it.

Gotrek swung backwards and forwards like the pendulum on a clock, dropping ever lower as the giant bent double. Blood and brain fluid were starting to leak through the enormous wound on the giant's forehead. At the lowest point of his orbit, Gotrek reached up and slashed the nerve with his axe, falling the last dozen feet to the ground and rebounding to his feet. He was an awful sight, covered in gore, blood leaking from the corners of his own mouth, but still he refused to slow down. He lashed out with his axe once again, catching the giant behind the ankle, cutting a tendon the size of a ship's cable. The giant teetered on its feet, unable to see or control one of its legs. Slowly, like a huge tree falling in the forest, it began to topple. Felix was already moving, throwing himself clear of the monster as it collapsed. Many of the orcs and goblins were not so lucky. They fell crushed beneath its huge weight, never to rise again.

Still, the giant was not finished. With an awful vitality it rolled and flailed at anything around it. Perhaps it could still hear movements, perhaps it was merely lashing out at random. Felix did not wait around to conclude his investigation at close range. He backed away swiftly. Gotrek did not. Moving with startling speed considering his wounds, he raced in closer, under the arm of the flailing giant.

Felix paused in his flight to watch what happened next. The Slayer struck twice. One blow opened the giant's windpipe, the other its jugular vein. A torrent of red flowed forth, billowing upwards like a geyser. At the same time a hideous gurgling rasping sounded, as the giant tried to fill its lungs, while air wheezed out through the incision the Slayer had left. Had that been deliberate, Felix wondered, an act of malicious cruelty, or had the Slayer merely missed his first stroke? He doubted he would ever find out.

Even as the Slayer jogged clear, the giant lashed out frantically, desperate to avenge itself on its tormentor. One of its massive arms caught the Slayer a glancing blow and sent him hurtling across the room as if launched by a giant catapult. The last Felix saw of his semiconscious form was as it descended into a horde of screaming goblins who let up a horrible shriek of triumph, and turned to tear their prey to pieces.

CHAPTER TWENTY-EIGHT

TECLIS INVOKED THE spell of levitation and marched upwards into the air, determined to put himself above the melee. At the same time he invoked multiple overlapping shields, reinforcing those created by his charms and amulets. A brilliant golden sphere surrounded him. The din of battle decreased as the warding spells blocked it out. Even so, the giant's screech of pain was almost deafening, as was the thunderous crash at it fell to the ground. What was going on, he wondered, unwilling to take his eyes off the Chaos mages? Surely the Slayer could not have killed the giant? It was a feat that beggared belief.

Naturally a golden glowing figure hovering over the battle chamber attracted the attention of other foes. In a sense he had made himself a very attractive target. Spears and rocks rose to greet him and angled away, repelled by the power of his wards.

A smile twisted the face of the black-robed Chaos mage. Teclis noted that the wound along his flank was already sealing itself, as powerful regenerative magic went to work. He had expected something similar. This pair would have all manner of devious protections. Now was the time to start testing them.

Teclis gestured and invoked the name of Lileath. Power sang in his veins as he forged a spell of awesome power. Spheres of destructive energy danced on his fingertips and left comet contrails in the air as he directed them towards his foe. The Chaos mage raised his staff in a barring gesture and a barrier of pure power shimmered into being in the air between them. The golden spheres hit it and exploded, sending shock waves rippling outwards from the point of impact. The force of the blast sent men, mutants and orcs to their knees. It caused the outer layer of his wards to flare into incandescent brightness as it neutralised them.

His opponent was both swift and skilled, that much was clear, but his speed was no match for an elf's. Even as his foe began to shape an offensive spell, Teclis unleashed another attack. Wave after wave of destructive energy rippled out from him, a torrent of power that could have reduced a castle wall to so much slag.

A black aura sprang into being around the Chaos mage as his own talismans and wards sought to protect him. They blazed ever brighter as he strove to neutralise the ever-increasing amount of energy the elf mage brought to bear. More than that, they had bought Kelmain time enough to abort his offensive spell and begin to invoke protections of his own. Teclis gritted his teeth and threw ever greater amounts of power at him, confident that eventually he would be victorious.

At that point, he sensed a bolt of colossal energy scything towards him from the direction of the altar. It was too late for him to do anything but pray that his wards would hold. It seemed that the other Chaos mage had decided to abandon trying to control the portals and entered the fray.

INSIDE THE CENTRAL chamber Felix saw all was chaos and carnage. Towering, grotesque shadows danced everywhere as the mages fought like angry gods overhead. The gore spattered giant, blinded, throat cut, hamstrung, raised its hands and tried to staunch the flow of gore from its neck. All around goblins, orcs and beastmen filled with bloodlust pranced and shouted and stabbed, like daemons tormenting a fallen deity in some nether hell. Unable to endure the torments, the giant lashed out with its fists, crushing a few of its tormentors, sending the rest shrieking away. It ended up sprawling in a spreading pool of its own blood. A few of the beastmen, too berserk to retreat, were crushed as it thrashed about.

Briefly, Felix lost sight of the Slayer as he sought to avoid joining them. Out of the gloom emerged a few of the men of Albion and the last of the maiden-guard, led by Siobhain. Murdo was with them too, a strange glow surrounding his spear, and black corrupt-looking mist evaporating from its point as if he had stabbed some evil thing with acidic blood.

'By the light, it does my heart good to see you yet live, Felix Jaeger,' said the old man. 'We shall make a last stand here worthy of the heroes of old. We must slay those foul wizards or die in the attempt.'

The others brandished their weapons and formed up around them. Felix was less interested in heroic last stands than he was in finding Gotrek. He knew that with the Slayer down, his chances of escape from this hellhole were exactly nil. And he was not at all sure that a last-ditch attempt to kill the wizards would do any good. With the sorcerers defeated, the forces they had unleashed here could raven out of control. Still, that was what Teclis was here for, he supposed.

'We must find the Slayer,' he bellowed. Seeing the looks of the men of Albion, he added, 'his axe can slay those spellcasters.'

At that moment, out of the corner of his eye, he caught sight of the goblins. They seemed to be swarming over something. Not waiting to see if the others followed, Felix charged towards them. A dozen strides and he bowled over the first of the little greenskins and skewered another on his sword. Two swift strokes beheaded another pair. Noticing their new attacker, they turned to face him. Momentum carried Felix forward over another goblin. He lashed out with his boot and sent a greenskin flying like a kicked cat and stabbed another through the chest. Taking his sword in both hands he hewed like a woodcutter at those in front of him and found himself face to face with Gotrek.

The Slayer looked done in. He bled from a dozen small wounds, he leaned on the shaft of his axe for support, and the corpse of a goblin dangled from his fist, hanging there like a rabbit with a broken neck. Others lay trampled underfoot.

Gotrek gave him a dazed uncomprehending glance, which was hardly surprising considering the amount of punishment he had taken.

'You,' he said. 'You have come to record my doom, then.'

'Some doom,' said Felix, hoping to snap the Slayer from his trance. 'Overwhelmed by a horde of snotlings.'

'These are not snotlings, manling. They are too big.'

Murdo arrived beside him.

'You have healing magic – do something!' Felix snapped.

Murdo nodded and gestured to the others. They formed a circle around him and the Slayer. The old man began to chant. Felix hoped the spell would work, for the way things were going, they desperately needed the Slayer's axe.

Overhead, the golden figure of Teclis blazed with light; attacked on both sides by the two Chaos wizards it looked like his defences were starting to fail. The brimstone stench of warpstone filled the air as the raw stuff of Chaos started to emerge from one of the gates. The temple shook as if hit by a giant hammer. The earth bucked and shook beneath their feet. Felix did not need to be a wizard to know that the end was very close.

TECLIS CURSED HIS overconfidence as agony wracked his body. He had gone from attack to desperate defence in a heartbeat. Secure in the knowledge that he could overwhelm Blackstaff, and certain that the Chaos mage's twin would be kept busy trying to control the energies he had unleashed, he had not reckoned on him abandoning the task to come to his brother's aid. In doing so he had made the situation doubly desperate, for unless something was done about the swiftly unravelling nexus of forces around them, disaster would overwhelm them all. Unfortunately at the moment, all Teclis could do was try to shore up his defences and endure, hoping against hope that some miracle would happen to give him the advantage over his foes before death took him.

He forced his lips into a smile that had as much agony in it as mirth. Whatever happened, he would go down fighting. If worst came to the worst he would unleash all the energies in his helm and staff in one final cataclysmic strike. In his own death he would take this pair down with him. But who then will save Ulthuan? The thought nagged away at the back of his mind, but he had no answer to it.

'ENOUGH, OLD MAN, enough,' said a familiar gruff voice. 'Any more of your spells and my head will explode.'

Felix glanced around to see that the Slayer looked better. Not exactly well, but capable of thought and movement. His blood-caked form was a grim sight but his grip on the axe was firm, and his stride was sure. All around came the sounds of battle as the last of the folk of Albion held their ground against the oncoming hordes. Felix's arm was tired from swinging it at orcs and beastmen.

'There's sorcerers to be killed,' said Felix.

'Is one of them an elf?' said Gotrek.

'No.'

'Too bad – but I suppose those Chaos-worshipping swine will have to do.' The Slayer barged forward through the line of men, and like a swimmer casting himself from a high crag into deep water, dove into the battle once more. Felix was right behind him.

* * *

LHOIGOR LAUGHED AS he summoned more and more energy to throw at the elvish wizard. He was surprised that the mage still endured. He and his twin had thrown enough power at him to have killed a daemon, or levelled a small mountain. Amazingly, their foe still lived, although now Lhoigor could sense him weakening. In a few more heartbeats he would be done. Just as well really, considering how close the nexus point was to erupting. And if that went, this temple, the whole island, and a fair chunk of the continent would go with it.

Lhoigor smiled. Would that be such a bad thing, he asked himself? Granted, they would no longer be able to move the armies of Chaos through the paths. On the other hand, the lands of men and elves would suffer such devastation as they had not endured in millennia. The cities of men would be overthrown. The survivors would be thrown back into barbarism and be easy prey. The hordes of Chaos would sweep over them. The survivors would grovel before the idols of their new gods, before offering up their weeping souls on the blackened altars.

Of course, there was the little matter of the fact that he and Kelmain might die as well, but even that might be avoided. There were still means of escape along a few of the Old Ones' open routes. They could kill the elf and withdraw, leaving their followers and their attackers to their fate. The more he thought of it, the more this appealed to Lhoigor.

At that moment, he saw a familiar dwarfish figure coming towards him through the press of battle. Even more astounding than the fact that the elf lived was the fact that Gotrek Gurnisson was still alive. That decided him – there was no way he was remaining to face that axe if he could help it. So be it, he thought. Let these fools fight to the death. They could kill the elf and make good their escape.

FELIX DODGED A massive chunk of fallen masonry that had crashed down from the ceiling. As he advanced through the melee, he reeled like a drunk man on the deck of a storm-tossed ship. The tremors were getting worse, he knew, the smell of brimstone more intense. Of them all, only Gotrek moved easily, keeping his footing with the sureness of a cat.

Panic spread through the battle. Even the ferocity of the orcs and the rage of the beastmen could not maintain itself in the face of the collapsing temple. The dying giant in the middle of the battle had cleared a space for itself. Already many of the combatants were starting to flee, hoping to escape the imminent destruction of the temple. Where they thought they were going to hide eluded Felix.

If the structure collapsed, as seemed all too likely, there was nowhere safe to go.

A few of them, in their fear, were throwing themselves into the open portals. Some were swallowed up by the oncoming waves of Chaotic matter. Others vanished into the shadows. After his own encounters within that alien extra-dimensional labyrinth Felix did not envy them. The panic created a different problem. Now they had to fight their way forward through a press of bodies determined to escape at any cost. Goblins scrambled over the shoulders of orcs, beastman and greenskin ran shoulder to shoulder, their animosity overwhelmed by the magnitude of the impending catastrophe.

Felix followed in the wake of the Slayer as he hewed a path through the press of bodies. Everyone present seemed to have been caught up in the wild panic. All of them shared the same sense of impending doom. Felix stabbed out at anyone who looked like they would get around the Slayer, and so at last, they came to the great plinth atop which stood the altar.

Enormous whips of dreadful energy leapt from it to lash the floating form of the elven mage. The shields of light protecting him seemed to dim by the second. Felix knew that if they did not save him soon, they would be too late.

Gotrek vaulted onto the plinth and raced at the golden-robed Chaos sorcerer. The vulture-like man sensed his presence and raised his staff, the smell of ozone and brimstone filling the air as a gigantic bolt of energy arced towards the Slayer. Gotrek raised his axe. The runes blazed so brightly their after-image was engraved on Felix's field of vision. He half expected the Slayer to be incinerated but no, Gotrek stood although his hair and beard were singed. If anything this seemed to goad him to a berserk madness. Dwarfs took harm to their facial hair very seriously.

The Slayer charged forward and as he did so, Murdo's spear hurtled over his shoulder to embed itself in the sorcerer's flesh. A look of panic crossed his face. Felix knew he would never forget that expression. He looked more stunned than in pain, as if he could not quite believe what was happening to him, then Gotrek was upon him.

The sorcerer raised his staff to parry the axe. Gotrek laughed dementedly as he brought the axe down in a glittering arc. It impacted on the staff and broke it asunder. Brilliant energy burst forth explosively but the axe continued inexorably and clove the mage in two. Not content with this, Gotrek chopped his corpse into smaller parts. Small lightning bolts earthed themselves from the body as if many spells were being discharged into the altar.

The second Chaos mage screamed as his twin died. He turned to look at the body and for a second terrible pain, all the agony his brother seemed to have avoided, was written on his face. His concentration lapsed and at that moment a river of molten elvish power descended on him. For a moment, he stood silhouetted in its blaze. Felix saw small lines of darkness unravel within the glow, and then the Chaos mage was gone. The river of power lashed over the corpse of his brother cleansing the earth of its foulness.

Felix found himself standing with the survivors of the men of Albion atop the great plinth in the central chamber of the Temple of the Old Ones. Teclis descended from above to join them. They stood in what appeared to be an island of sanity as Chaos erupted all around.

'What now?' Felix said.

'I must unravel the work of these madmen,' said the elf. 'You must go before this place is destroyed.'

'An idea I am all in favour of,' said Felix, 'but how do you propose we do it?' He gestured to the crowds of fleeing enemies and the walls that seemed ready to collapse all around them.

'There is only one way,' said the elf. He pointed to the still open portals that led down into the Paths of the Old Ones. Several of them appeared clear of the Chaos contamination. Felix shook his head. 'Oh no,' he said. 'I am not going in there again.'

'There is no other way,' said the elf.

'We don't know how to find our way through the paths. There are daemons in there.'

'Not all the paths are twisted. I know the way,' said Murdo. 'I know the rituals. I can get us out.'

'Very good,' said the elf. 'Now get going. I have work to do here.'

'Are you sure you can do it?' asked Murdo.

'If I cannot, no one can,' said the elf. 'Go.'

'Is there anything I can do?' said Murdo.

'Pray,' said the elf. 'Now go!'

Murdo led the pitiful band of survivors to the opening in the wall. He glanced at the runes on the archway and gestured for them to pass through it. Gotrek watched the elf as he turned towards the altar. He paused for a long moment, as if about to say something, and then turned on his heel to follow Murdo. He seemed to realise that this was work for wizards and there was nothing he could do here.

Felix touched the elf on the shoulder. 'Good luck,' he said.

'And to you, Felix Jaeger,' replied the elf. 'Be careful. In the paths those things might still come for you.'

Felix reached the arch.

'I hope he succeeds,' he said to Gotrek.

'If he fails there's one good thing about it,' said the Slayer.

'What?'

'One less elf in the world.'

They moved down into the ancient darkness that led to the Paths of the Old Ones. Behind them, the elf began to sing a spell.

CHAPTER TWENTY-NINE

TECLIS STOOD ATOP the ancient altar in the Chamber of Secrets. All around him were signs of imminent catastrophe. The walls shook and huge chunks of rock descended from the ceiling, crushing greenskin and beastman alike. The giant still moved and thrashed, albeit slower now, and its howling was audible even over the shattering of fallen masonry and the panicked screams. The sulphur stench of warpstone and Chaos filled the air. To his mage sight vast interlocking patterns of energy shimmered and danced.

He touched the amulet the Oracle had given him. Now was the time to use it. Briefly he considered following the others, and seeking refuge within the paths. The scale of the task daunted him. He had minutes at most to shut down the vast network of magic the Old Ones had created. There was no option. There was no place for him to run if he failed anyway, and he would not let down his people. He must do what the Oracle had sent him to do. He must awaken the guardians of the Old Ones.

He offered up a prayer to Asuryan and took a deep breath, seeking to clear his mind, then he turned to confront the altar. It was a vast square block covered in familiar-looking angular runes. Most of them glowed. All of them represented something. At first they were bafflingly alien, but he realised that somehow his former foes had managed to activate them, and this meant they were not beyond his ability either. Particularly not when he held this ancient talisman. He held it up to the light and recited the spell he had been taught. Instantly power was drained from him into the amulet. Cords of energy seemed to flow out of it to the altar, binding him to it. The runes glowed ever brighter. The earth shook like a frightened beast.

It was pointless trying to understand the runes themselves. They were merely symbols anyway. What he needed was to comprehend the forces they represented. He opened his mind, bringing all of his mystical acuteness to bear on the problem. One rune was as good as any other for his purposes, so he chose one he recognised as having been present on every portal he had seen, and focused his mage sight on it.

As his point of view zoomed in, he saw that it was a work of breathtaking delicacy. The rune itself was connected to all the other runes by a vast web of interlocking forces. It was virtually a universe of them in itself. As above, so below, he thought, wondering if by manipulating the rune he could manipulate the forces themselves. Now was not the time to experiment though. Swiftly, working between one heartbeat and another, he allowed his consciousness to flow through the talisman and expand outwards to encompass the whole vast mystical lattice as earlier he had struggled to understand the layout of the pyramid.

Everything he saw tended to confirm his suspicions. The altar was the fulcrum of a vast system; its pattern held a deeper meaning and there was something about it that was oddly and hauntingly familiar, although at the moment he could not quite put his finger on what.

The pattern shimmered and started to fade. He saw that the whole thing was on the verge of disintegration and his heart hammered against his ribs. The plinth shook beneath his feet. More stones were dislodged. The giant's death howls set his teeth on edge. For a moment, he realised that the whole vast intricate web was about to explode and there was nothing he could do about it. The whole unstable system was about to unleash all its energy in a final destructive torrent. He waited for the end to come, knowing that he was at the very epicentre of the coming destruction.

A moment passed and then another. Nothing happened. He breathed again, and considered what he had witnessed. He knew now what the pattern reminded him of. Seen from certain angles it was almost identical to the map inscribed in the Haunted Citadel. Swirls of Chaotic energy were moving through the whole structure. The complex of energy represented by the runes was nothing less than a map of the Paths of the Old Ones and the whole complex system of tectonic forces they were interlinked with. He saw how the whole system had its roots in the realm of Chaos, that other space of infinite dangerous energies. He saw how it lay halfway between this world and the realm of daemons. He saw in one sudden blinding flash of insight all the nodal points through which power pulsed.

He saw too that the system was corrupted now, infected by Chaos, the ancient safeguards destroyed, perhaps by some colossal cosmic accident, perhaps by malevolent design. No matter, he thought. Unless he did something soon it would be too late. But, great though his understanding of sorcery was, whatever was controlling this whole vast world-spanning net of magic was beyond him. There was no way he could hope to understand it in the very limited time he had available. That would be the work of a lifetime, and even then he was not sure mortal minds could comprehend the thing in its entirety. So far he had found no sign of the guardians. He had expected them to come in response to his summons, but there was nothing. Perhaps they had passed into death.

Frustration and fear gnawed at him. He had come so far and done so much and it looked like he was a lifetime too late. He and all his people were the butt of some vast cosmic joke. He had been brought all this way merely to witness the final doom of his people. He stifled a curse. There must be something he could do. There must be some way to save the situation. If only he could find it.

FELIX FOLLOWED MURDO down into the bowels of the earth. His mouth felt dry and his hand returned constantly to the amulet the elf had given him. He did not want to go any further. He realised that he had never feared anything as much in his life as he feared returning to the Paths of the Old Ones. His feet felt like they were encased in boots of lead. It was a massive effort to take one step further. I would rather die than pass into that eldritch other world one more time, he thought.

And that's exactly what will happen if you don't. If you stay you will be buried alive at best, or swallowed by the oncoming tide of Chaos at worst. But if you pass through the portal you may lose even your soul. There had to be another way. Perhaps he could find a way back through the tunnels. Even as the thought occurred to him, he knew it was madness. There was no way he could cover that whole vast distance before the temple collapsed. And even if the gods smiled on him, and he did manage it, he would be in a huge haunted forest surrounded by the survivors of the Chaos army and the greenskins and hundreds of leagues from home. There was no chance of escape that way. He felt like a rat cornered by a cat. He wanted to lash out and hit something, but he knew it would do no good.

Ahead of him Murdo had stopped at a familiar-looking ramp. Beyond it lay a shimmering portal filled with many shifting colours. Felix thought he could see daemonic forms taking shape in there but told himself it was just his imagination. The old Truthsayer had begun a chant and a change took place in the glistening surface. It began to dim and solidify and Felix thought he saw himself and the others reflected as in some vast dull mirror. What was going on? At least it seemed like the old man had not been lying when he claimed to know something of the secrets of the paths.

The walls shook once more. The odour of warpstone increased. Felix felt that if he stayed here he would be suffocated by it. It seemed that the elf had failed in his task. The quakes came more swiftly now.

Murdo spoke to his people. One by one they stepped through the gate and vanished. Felix looked at the Slayer. Gotrek strode forward, axe held ready as if to smite some foe. Felix moved to join him. He felt a hand on his shoulder.

'I have opened the way, lad. It is safe – have no fear. I must return now and help the elf.'

Felix paused, half grateful for the interruption, half desperate to get the ordeal over with. 'Are you sure? He wanted to do it alone.'

'There are some things that cannot be done alone, and this is one. I go now. May the light watch over you.'

'And you,' said Felix, watching the old man limp back up the corridor. 'Good luck.'

Then he strode forward into the vortex. Cold slithered over him. Panic filled him. There was a sudden sensation of tremendous acceleration.

TECLIS DESPERATELY SCANNED the great rune map, looking for something, anything that would aid him. He knew his task was all but hopeless, but he refused to give up. In heartbeats he scanned the outer limits of the paths, and found nothing useful, so he returned his attention closer to home, to the pyramid itself. It was the centre of all this. Surely there must be something here. The ghosts of the Isle of the Dead would not have sent him here otherwise.

Another memory flickered through his mind: the pillars containing the skeletons of long-dead slann. He did not know why that thought came to him at the moment, except perhaps the idea of ghosts was in his mind. Perhaps the trapped sorcerers had sent the idea to him. It did not matter. He sought the glyph that simulated the mystical structure of the great ziggurat and let his attention flow to the hall of the pillars. Yes, he thought, there was something there. Something faint, but still present. He reached out with a faint tendril of magical essence and activated the pillars.

At once, he sensed another presence reaching out to touch him, through the intricate network of energy. At first he was wary, wondering if this was some sort of trap, whether a daemon was making its presence felt through the disintegrating Chaos-contaminated system. He shielded his mind but the presence was persistent and it did not have the feel of Chaos. There was something slow and alien and cold about it. A sense of power and baffled intelligence, of some great cold-blooded creature awakening from a long sleep.

Who are you? The thought was not in Elvish and he could not quite grasp its full range of meaning, but the gist was clear. *Why have you wakened us?*

'I am Teclis of the elves, and I seek your aid in averting disaster.' He pictured what was going on in his mind and projected it outwards.

Ah, you are one of the young races, the ones we helped teach back in the days of life. Your race has changed a great deal in a very short time.

Teclis smiled ironically. That was not what the elves thought. They thought themselves conservative and unchanging with a civilisation that had lasted ages.

An eyeblink in the time of the Old Ones, the Great Ones.

'Who are you?' asked Teclis.

We are the wardens charged by the Old Ones to oversee the great design. We gave our lives so that our spirits might remain and watch over the work but something went wrong and we had to close the paths to avoid catastrophe. We have slept and our power has been leeched away and now catastrophe looms. Others have interfered with the pattern, moulding it to their own designs, and they have caused great harm.

Images flickered into the elf's mind. He saw his own people building their watchstones and siphoning off power. He saw the ancestors of the men of Albion, tall and proud and far more advanced than the men of today, build their great stone circles. He saw how, well-intentioned though they might have been, they had distorted things. More images flickered though his mind and he saw further back in time, to the opening of the great warp gate and the havoc that wrought on the pattern magic of the Old Ones.

Ah, there is the cause. Alas, even had we our full strength, undoing that would be beyond us. Undoing that would be beyond the power of gods.

'Then there is nothing to be done?' queried Teclis. 'The work of the Old Ones will be unravelled and my homeland will be destroyed.'

No, young one, if you are willing, there is a way. You have great power and with it we can perhaps close the paths and seal them, at least temporarily.

'Any respite would be good, but how long?'

Heartbeats of the Great Watcher. Ten cycles of the world around the eye of heaven. Perhaps twenty.

Teclis considered this. 'Not long.'

Not long, and there is a price.

'Name it,' stated Teclis.

One of the pillars was shattered. One of our souls was lost. We need a replacement to make our pattern complete once more.

'You are talking about death, a living sacrifice. Myself.'

Yes.

Teclis took no time to reach his decision. 'I accept. What must I do?'

That will not be necessary, elf, said another voice. Teclis recognised it as belonging to Murdo. He knew the old man was standing at the altar now, hand on his shoulder, linked to him by contact, at once there and in this netherspace.

I know more of this than you do, continued Murdo. *My people have studied the mysteries of the patterns. My ancestors were taught by these cold-blooded ones. I have a better chance. Also I am old and must pass from this world soon. You have centuries yet.*

'Only if we succeed,' replied Teclis.

We must *succeed.*

'Very well. Let us proceed.'

FELIX FELT AS if his head was going to explode. Something had gone very wrong. Thousands of images coruscated through his mind. He saw visions of many things, of places and worlds and bubbles within the paths. The moment seemed to stretch forever. He sensed hungry things coming for him and knew the daemons were once more on his trail. He felt like he was tumbling endlessly down the corridors of infinity at fantastic speed. Somewhere far off he sensed power pulsing through the Paths of the Old Ones, as if something long dormant had woken. The hungry things came ever closer, and there was a terrifying sense that it was him and him alone they were after, that somehow they sensed his presence, and wanted to feast on his soul.

Suddenly up ahead was another vortex. He wondered whether he could possibly reach it in time.

* * *

GUIDED BY THE spirits of the ancient guardians, Teclis went to work. Knowledge flowed into him. He began to understand the huge complex of energies that flowed through the paths. He saw how every part was designed like a finely constructed machine. Now the machine was broken, and the fact that it still partially functioned was leading it to disaster, like a chariot still being dragged along an open road even though its axle was broken. What he needed was to close the portals so that they would not draw on those ravening runaway energies.

He opened his eyes and looked around the main chamber. Murdo lay now atop the altar. Teclis considered what he was going to do and was repelled by it. His whole life had been spent thinking that the sacrifice of sentient beings was a barbarous act. That they performed such things was what separated the dark elves from his own people.

He told himself that Murdo had volunteered for this, that he was giving up his life willingly and for the greater good, just as the ancient slann masters had done millennia ago. Doubts assailed him. Murdo was not a slann, perhaps the ritual would not even work, how could he hope to join with those ancient ghosts of an alien species? Teclis knew he could perform the sacrifice and it might all still be in vain. There was a very good chance of it. And even if they succeeded the solution would only be temporary. Decades at the most. The old open wound at the northern gate would still be there. The paths would be forced open once more. To an elf like himself, a decade was not a huge amount of time. What was the point?

He tried to shrug off his despair. The point was that they would buy more time. In a decade he could learn more, muster greater forces, return here with greater knowledge and more power. It was worth taking the chance, worth buying the time. If they succeeded.

'Ready?' he asked Murdo. The old man nodded. He clearly wanted to speak but could not. Despite his bravado, there was fear in his eyes. Teclis considered his own doubts and found them small compared to those that must assail the Truthsayer. He lay spreadeagled on the altar in the position they had been directed to by the slann, with his head and feet aligned with the ancient mystical poles of power.

Teclis spoke the words that he had been taught, his throat twisting as he struggled to spit out the alien syllables. Only centuries of practice in the arcane tongues allowed him to do it. As he spoke the words, he found his inner vision twisting, comprehension and power flowed through him. He had no sacred knife, as the old mage priests had, but his sword would do in its place. As he reached the climax of the ritual with the temple shuddering around him like a frightened beast, and the smell of warpstone and decay in his nostrils, he plunged the blade home, ripping open Murdo's chest and pulling out his heart, spraying the altar with blood. He winced at the pain in the old man's eyes. Yet part of him, hidden and dark, half felt only by himself, felt a secret satisfaction. The gap between even the highest of high elves and the darkest of dark was not so great after all, he thought, with a thrill at the sickness of his satisfaction. Blood flowed outwards, emptying itself over the altar, flowing through the ancient runic channels.

Teclis waited for a sign. Nothing happened. After all that, nothing. Murdo had given up his life in vain, and Teclis had violated the laws of his people for nothing. He stifled a curse, and controlled the urge to unleash a powerful bolt of energy at the altar. He studied it with his eyes and his mage sight and still saw no difference. Blood continued to gush, the light passed from the old man's eyes. Still nothing.

Wait. From the corner of his eye, he thought he saw the runes begin to glow in a new configuration. He felt a tug of power, through the spell that linked him with the altar, and fed it more. The blood-drenched runes began to glow. He saw Murdo's spirit drawn from his body, and dragged downward into the altar. While his lips chanted, and his own heart still beat, he freed his own spirit to pursue it. Once more his vision was drawn into the infinite maze of energy. He saw the old man's spirit, young-looking now and bathed in light, draw towards twelve others. They looked like great upright toads, but there was a suggestion of intelligence about them, and nobility and power that impressed even Teclis. He joined with them, filling a gap in their ranks, and at once began to work their great spell. Teclis joined in, feeding them his own power, performing the role that in ancient times living mage priests would have performed, providing a link between the world of the living and them.

There will be pain, the voice in his head told him. It did not lie. As he became one with them, he realised that they were one with the great pattern of the paths, and they could feel the corruption within them as purest agony. The polar warpgate was indeed a wound to them and one that gave them great pain. Worse, it was one they could do nothing about. Teclis could understand now why they had closed the paths and retreated into dormancy. Enduring ages of such pain would surely have driven them mad.

Instead they concentrated on the rune markers of the paths, the things that drew power from the realm of Chaos. Closing the way was not going to be easy here. The raw primal power of the dae-monic realm was forcing its way through the gaps the runes provided, like lava erupting through the crust of the earth.

He felt agony increase as they exerted themselves to shut the paths down. It was a pressure well nigh unbearable. He forced him-self to concentrate, draw on the deepest reserves of his being and focus on the spell. Somewhere very far off, his body still chanted. He wanted to retreat into it, make the pain stop, just for an instant, but he knew that would be fatal – if he left the circle now before the spell was complete, all would fail.

Teclis kept chanting as one by one the runes were sealed. The pain mounted. He wondered if it would ever stop or if he would die of his agony and his spirit would be trapped here forever.

A small still part of his mind prayed that the others had gotten clear. It would not be a good thing to be trapped within the Paths of the Old Ones when the way was finally sealed. Pain mounted in his mind, searing at him. Blackness hovered at the edge of his mind. Desperately he tried to hold onto consciousness, as they made one final effort.

FELIX FELT AN enormous wave of pressure pass over him. He was not sure what was happening, but his speed seemed to be falling. At the same time, the sense of evil presence increased, as if the things stalk-ing him were closing the distance. He willed himself to move faster but nothing happened. In the back of his mind, he thought he heard daemonic howls of triumph. He knew he was doomed if he fell into their clutches. Teclis could not save him now, and Gotrek was nowhere to be seen.

Feeling claws reaching for him, he stretched out, reaching for the vortex. It was close now, but perhaps not close enough, he thought he felt phantom fingers on his cloak. He reached further, stretched himself to the utmost. Almost there. He was certain something touched him now. Gossamer fingers that grew stronger and scalier. The howls of triumph were loud in his mind. An eternity of torture loomed.

Then something changed. Some power shifted within the strange extra-dimensional labyrinth. The vortex up ahead seemed to swirl slower, its energy draining away. The howls of triumph turned to shrieks of fear. Something had scared his pursuers. He sensed them retreat, moving off into the distance as if desperate to reach sanctu-ary before some dreadful event occurred. Perhaps the elf had succeeded. Perhaps he had closed the Paths of the Old Ones to Chaos.

Another thought struck Felix. Perhaps he had closed the paths to everyone else too. If that was the case he would be trapped in here. Along with the daemons, if they did not make good their escape. Desperately he twisted, throwing himself towards the vortex. It was smaller now, weaker, closing rapidly. He aimed himself like a diver and prayed to Sigmar to preserve him. For a long moment, nothing happened, then somehow he was through, falling back once more into the world he knew.

He landed sprawling on his face on hard stone. He lay there gasping. When he looked up, the Slayer was standing over him. Over the dwarf's shoulder he could see the human survivors and a slice of blue sky. The air smelled of salt and sea water.

'What kept you, manling?' Gotrek asked.

'You don't want to know.'

'Where's Murdo?'

'He won't be joining us, and neither will Teclis is my guess.'

'No great loss there.'

'Do you think they succeeded?'

'Well, so far there's no sign of the world ending, but maybe we had better wait a few days to be sure.'

Felix rose to his feet and limped towards the light. They had emerged halfway up a chalk cliff, looking out to a misty sea. Gulls called, and watery sunlight filtered down through the thick cloud. Siobhain and Culum glared at him but he would not let their hostility get to him, at least not right now. He felt like a man granted a new lease of life, and he intended to enjoy it.

Even as the thought occurred to him, it began to rain.

TECLIS FELT AS if he had been beaten very thoroughly with a large wooden club. His bones ached, his muscles ached, his head throbbed as if a goblin were using it for a drum. The air was foetid and smelled of warpstone and death. Near the altar the dead giant's corpse stunk worse than a cesspit. He was thousands of leagues from home with no means of transportation in the tumbled-down remains of an ancient haunted temple, most likely surrounded by orcs and beastmen.

He let none of this bother him. He was still alive and the Paths of the Old Ones were closed. The threat of continent-shattering doom was temporarily withdrawn. They had succeeded. He looked down at the corpse of Murdo and gently closed the wide-staring eyes. He wondered where the old man's spirit was now. Trapped in the stones along with the slann? Without his own pillar it would inevitably decay, and with it, the spell they had woven.

Teclis knew that he would need to return here and see what he could do about that, probably with an army and a host of mages, but right now, he was tired and a long way from home, and he needed a place to sleep. Leave tomorrow's problems for tomorrow, he told himself as he limped off in search of a safe spot to recover his powers and begin the long journey home to Ulthuan.

REDHAND'S
DAUGHTER

ONE
The Storm

THE DWARF STEAMSHIP *Storm Hammer* crashed through the waves, trailing clouds of smoke and seagulls behind it. Its paddles thrashed the ocean, driving it into the wind with a speed that would have been inconceivable for a sailing ship in these rough seas. In the distance, great thunderheads threatened.

Felix Jaeger leaned against the rail and watched the sea break against the prow. Riding the bow wave a pod of dolphins easily paced the ship, leaping from the water, turning on their backs in mid air to show their bellies before splashing back into the water. Such was their speed that they gave the impression more of flying under water than swimming. Just looking at them made Felix happy, for no reason he could put his finger on. Perhaps it was their faces – something about the shape of their mouths made them seem to smile. It went well with the exuberance of their motion and contrasted directly with the sour expressions of the dwarfs around him.

Felix had never seen a more miserable-looking group, and he had plenty of experience of a race that specialised in gloom. Most of these dwarfs had a slightly greenish tinge. Many had just returned from throwing up over the side. From where Felix stood he could see a line of them hanging over the guardrail, heaving the contents of their stomachs into the sea. Was this why the gulls followed the ship, Felix wondered, doing his best to ignore the retching sounds? To find food?

He understood the dwarfs' misery. During the first few hours out of harbour, when the *Storm Hammer* had hit the rolling swells of the Gulf of Araby, he had felt something of their discomfort himself. He had spent several hours sitting on the cannon turret trying to keep the contents of his stomach firmly in place. The sickness had been as bad as the hangover after a three-day drinking session. Then, as suddenly as it had come, it passed. He did not exactly feel fine, but he had adjusted. The dwarfs were taking longer about it. It seemed that as a race, they were peculiarly prone to seasickness.

Felix recalled reading somewhere that dwarfs, being bound to the elemental affinity of the earth, were unwelcome to the sea gods. That was one theory; another was that the same sensitivity of the inner ear that allowed dwarfs to tell depth and distance so unerringly while underground, made them vulnerable to the rocking motion of ships. Whatever the reason, he was in a position to confirm it was true.

He looked around for Gotrek but the Slayer was nowhere in sight. Doubtless he was down below inspecting the massive engines, or perhaps he had broached a cask of ale and was working his way through it. According to dwarfs, ale was a cure for all ills, particularly seasickness.

Certainly most of the crew capable of going about their business stank of it. Up on the bridge, Captain Ahabsson glugged back a stein with one hand while his hook rested on the wheel. Even as Felix watched, he leaned forward and said something into the speaking tubes. A few seconds later, as if in response, a steam-whistle sounded, its long lonely scream racing outwards over the water, startling the gulls into higher flight. Moments later, a shortbeard – a young dwarf – clambered up the ladder onto the bridge with another jack of ale foaming in his hand. The captain eyed it appreciatively before taking a slug.

Ahabsson pushed a lever beside the wheel, in response the ship picked up speed, smashing through the next wave in a cloud of spray. Wetness splashed Felix's face. He wiped salt water away with the hem of his old red cloak and returned to studying the dolphins.

Oncoming storm or no, he felt glad to be here, glad that the haunted desert lands of Araby, with their fanatical warriors, hollow-eyed prophets and liche-haunted tombs were falling below the horizon behind them. He had had enough of the mazy cities and teeming bazaars to last him a lifetime. If he never saw them again, it would be too soon. Enough of doomed princesses, treacherous dancing girls and hidden treasures, he thought, and then smiled cynically.

He doubted he and Gotrek would ever stop looking for treasure. Though such quests had never brought them any luck and always ended in a confrontation with huge monsters or wicked magicians, dwarfen goldlust combined with the Slayer's doomed quest for death would ensure they followed up every rumour.

He glanced at the black sky ahead, and the huge wave of cloud rushing toward them. Ahabsson sighted his spyglass on the horizon and studied the storm clouds. He raised a huge speaking trumpet to his mouth and bellowed orders.

'Avast ye! Batten down the hatches! Ready the pumps! It looks like a mighty blow be coming!'

Well spotted, thought Felix sourly. The seasick dwarfs heaved themselves upright, wiped their mouths and stomped about their business, grabbing steins and filling them from the open barrels as they went. They still looked sick and drunk, but they moved with the purposefulness that Felix had come to associate with dwarfs, but their appearance was as strange as any he had seen. Some wore headscarves, and their clothes were a motley assortment of rags and finery. Some went barefoot while wearing what might have been the cast-off jacket of a Bretonnian admiral over ragged britches. Others were stripped to the waist, showing tanned arms and shoulders and huge white patches of belly when the rising wind blew their beards aside. Many had hooks or peg-legs or eyepatches and all bore an assortment of villainous-looking scars. Most had their beards and hair plaited, the knots sealed with tar.

No, these were hardly typical dwarfs he thought. But he supposed that was only to be expected. According to Gotrek, few dwarfs went to sea, and those that did were all considered mad. Felix considered this judgement a little rich given the lunacy of the Slayer's own vocation.

Caught on a steamship, with half the crew drunk and the other half sea-sick, heading into a storm, he thought – what more could possibly go wrong? He looked around again and saw that the dolphins had disappeared, vanished as though they had never been. The reason became clear. A huge head had broached the surface: a leviathan of the deep! A long sinuous neck and massive body followed. The beast was almost as large as the ship, with a mouth that could swallow a man whole. It looked at the ship with evil beady eyes as if it wanted to challenge this intruder in its domain. It blew a huge spout of water and then vanished below the surface. The last Felix saw of it was the flukes of its vast tail before it too slid beneath the surface. It seemed even the sea monsters had enough sense to avoid the coming storm. He was glad it had vanished before someone had summoned Gotrek to challenge it.

More than ever, Felix felt useless. All of the dwarfs had something to do. They rushed around turning windlasses and closing pressure spigots, slugging back ale, and slamming down hatches. Some sealed the ale barrels and rolled them below. A few banged rivets into place with hammers. Water spouted through tubes on the ship's sides as the pumps were tested. Felix felt like the only one on board with nothing to do. He was a useless, purposeless outsider here.

Still, he thought, he should not complain. The steamship was a blessing. Lone armed merchantmen out of Barak Varr were rare in this part of the world. When it had steamed into the harbour at Quadira, they had been only too glad to take passage on it. Gotrek had even managed to put aside his prejudice against ships in order to escape the astonishing summer heat. It had cost them the last of the gold they had taken from Sulmander's tomb, and the promise to aid in any fighting if the ship was attacked, but it had been a way out of the hot empty lands and back to civilisation, or at least somewhere near it.

It was not so hot now. The gusting winds had picked up speed and carried with it the first drops of rain. The sea was suddenly a lot rougher too. He could hear the engines strain to drive the paddles.

On impulse, Felix strode over to the bottom of the conning tower, and looked up at the captain. 'Permission to come up, sir,' he asked. He had learned early that no one set foot on that tower without either being invited or ordered there. Surprisingly, it was something even the usually rebellious Slayer seemed to accept.

'Aye, Felix Jaeger, climb up and have some brew.' The captain seemed remarkably less taciturn, now that he had ten or so beers in him, Felix thought.

He pulled himself up the metal ladder that was riveted to the wall and surveyed the command deck.

'Aye, manling, I bet you've never looked on the likes of this before!' bellowed Ahabsson.

'Actually, I have,' said Felix. Ahabsson sputtered out some of his ale.

'Where?' he shouted. 'Speak up, lubber!'

Felix found himself shouting back: 'It looks remarkably similar to the command deck of the airship *Spirit of Grungni!*'

A look of astonishment passed over the captain's face. 'I knew a dwarf once who was always talking about building an airship. They said he was mad, you know!'

'Malakai Makaisson,' said Felix. 'I know him.'

'You know Makaisson? The greatest dwarf shipwright who ever lived? Although I understand his *Unsinkable* had a few teething troubles.'

'I understand it sank,' said Felix. He eyed the oncoming storm clouds warily. They filled most of the sky ahead now, and the waves looked the size of mountains. The *Storm Hammer* was already beginning to climb up the side of one long swell.

'Aye, but she was a beautiful ship,' said Ahabsson. 'Beautiful. I watched her pull out of port the day of her shakedown cruise. She never came back of course. He shaved his head afterwards, or so the wharf rats say.'

'He became a Slayer,' said Felix.

'A rare pity. Malakai Makaisson's compressor engines are still the best ever designed.'

'He built his airship. I travelled on it. To the Chaos Wastes.'

Spray whipped into Felix's face. The wind had turned very cold and rain pattered off the decks, forming puddles in the indented metal. All of the dwarfs were below now, save the watchman in the crow's-nest and the captain on the tower. All of the hatches were sealed. Felix suddenly felt very lonely and exposed.

'If you were not travelling in the company of Gotrek Gurnisson, human, I would be inclined to doubt ye.'

Felix looked at the controls. 'That would be the throttle, for controlling the power to the engines,' he said, pointing to the lever next to the captain's hand. 'Those gauges monitor steam pressure. The compass there points to true north, when it's not been distorted by the influence of Chaos, and you can navigate by it, and by the stars.'

'In truth, I thought these were secrets known only to dwarf mariners and engineers,' said the captain. 'How did you come by them?'

'Malakai Makaisson taught me how to fly the *Spirit of Grungni.*'

'Then he overstepped himself, laddie, but then he was a dwarf that never cared too much for the proprieties. Ye reckon ye can handle a ship then?'

'I could probably steer her if need be,' said Felix.

'Aye, as long as we are out in the deeps, maybe ye could. But I'll bet you have no knowledge of tides or currents or...'

'No need if you're flying,' said Felix.

'No, I suppose not,' said Ahabsson. The howling of the wind made his bellow almost inaudible. Huge waves had begun to break over the ship's prow. Sheets of white water ran down the decks as the ship rose into the crest. Felix felt a hint of his sea-sickness return.

'Best get below, laddie,' said Ahabsson. 'This is going to be a rough one.'

Felix dropped down the ladder as he had seen the dwarfs do, keeping his feet on the outside, sliding rather than climbing. His palms were hot from friction as he hit the deck. Suddenly he wished he were back above again.

The air was close and foetid. It reeked of ale, vomit and the acrid stink of metal. There was a sulphurous stench that came from the boiler rooms, along with the clangour of pistons rising and falling and paddlewheels turning. It was like being trapped inside a huge drum while a giant beat time. He had to crouch, for the ship had been built for people shorter and wider than himself. He was suddenly abruptly aware of being on a moving tube of metal surrounded on all sides by water. The pounding of the waves on the deck above reminded him that sometimes he was well under water. A look out of a porthole showed him only blackness and rising bubbles.

He pushed forward into the mess room, and saw Gotrek Gurnisson at the bench next to the metal table. The benches had been riveted to the floor. The table itself was a sheet of iron, mounted on top of a steel pillar that rose directly from the deck. Other queasy looking dwarfs surrounded Gotrek. They drank ale dourly. The Slayer looked utterly different from the sailors. He was much broader and heavier and half a head taller than all of the other dwarfs, even without the huge crest of orange dyed hair that rose above his tattooed scalp. A patch covered his ruined eye. In one massive fist he clutched a tankard. In the other was an axe, the like of which a strong man would have struggled to wield with two hands.

'It was on a night such as this that the *Karak Varn* went down,' shouted Ugly Urli. The marine sergeant wore an expression of sour pleasure on his shrapnel pocked face. 'Aye a terrible storm that was.'

'She was washed up on the beach at Kregaerak, a huge hole in the hull. Some say she hit a rock, others that it was one of the terrors of the deep, the giant dragon shark,' said Mobi. He was short, even for a dwarf, and very, very wide.

'No,' said Tobi, one of the shortbeards. 'It was a kraken.'

Gotrek showed some interest now, despite his queasy appearance. Talk of huge monsters always got his attention. It was hardly surprising. After all, he had sworn an oath to seek his death in combat with such creatures. To tell the truth, Felix could have done without hearing these tales. It seemed that no matter what the situation, dwarfs could always find a way to make it worse by recalling great disasters from their history.

Felix hunched across the chamber, almost on all fours, and was suddenly glad of it when the ship shuddered and rocked hugely. A surge of nausea filled him, and he was convinced that something massive had struck the ship. The image of the *Storm Hammer* hurtling to the bottom like a huge water-filled metal coffin jumped into his mind.

The ship shook again, and all of the dwarfs grabbed the table, the benches or the door handles, whatever came to hand. Felix found himself tossed right across the room. He felt briefly weightless and wondered what was going on. Had the ship been lifted from the sea by some huge monster, or simply tossed by one of the mountainous waves?

The dwarfs returned to swilling their drinks as if nothing had happened. 'And a ship crewed by dead men rose from the among sea-weed,' said Narli, a wizened ancient with a face like a diseased prune and a long, shaggy beard that came almost to his feet.

Felix could feel the hull creaking and flexing below him, and wondered how much strain the ship could take before being broken in two. He wished he was an engineer, and knew about such things, but one look at Gotrek's face convinced him that perhaps it was better not to know. The Slayer rose to his feet and padded across the deck, heading for the ladder.

'Where are you going?' Felix asked.

'To get some fresh air,' the Slayer replied. Gotrek reached the stairs at the end of the cabin and was greeted by a rush of water when he thrust open the door. It was almost as if someone had thrown a filled bucket in the dwarf's face. Undaunted, Gotrek strode out onto the soaking deck. Just before the other dwarfs shut the door, Felix could see him raise both arms above his head and bellow defiance at the lightning-scored sky. He seemed to be daring the gods of the sea to take him.

The door closed. The last Felix saw of the Slayer was him reeling across the deck, bellowing madly at the uncaring sky. Then the ship surged forward into another huge wave. Felix turned and looked at the drunken dwarfs. They avoided his gaze, their faces filled with superstitious dread, as they muttered to themselves in Dwarfish.

TWO
Wild Orcish Reavers

FELIX PULLED HIMSELF wearily onto the deck. The sky was blue and clear. The gulls had returned overhead. A huge albatross rode the air above their stern, ignoring the pot shots the dwarfs took at it with the gymbal-mounted stern cannon. The sea was calm and flat as a mirror.

Gotrek stood at the prow, looking ahead, still and stolid as a statue. A glance showed Felix that Captain Ahabsson was asleep in a metal chair on the conning tower while one of the other dwarfs had taken the wheel. The ship looked the way Felix felt. Many plates on the deck were bent out of shape. He could tell just by the sound of the wheels and engines that there was some damage. The amount of water the side pumps were spewing spoke of a hull that had sprung leaks. The sound of hammering from below told him that the dwarfs were busy about their repairs.

He touched his bruises. They were still tender. He had been tossed around all night by the motion of the ship as it crashed through the storm. He had dozed fitfully, plagued by nightmares and he had woken often to the sound of screaming metal and tortured engines as the *Storm Hammer* clove a path through the mountainous seas. Sometimes he had been sick. At other times he was so certain that he was going to die by being swallowed by

the waves that he had considered throwing himself overboard
just to get it over with.

In the bright calm light of the quiet morning such thoughts
seemed like mad fantasies, but he knew they had passed through
his mind the previous night. He strode over to Gotrek.

'Where are we?'

'Damned if I know, manling,' the Slayer replied. 'Are those
islands?'

Felix shaded his eyes with one hand. It certainly looked as if
there were peaks on the horizon, and perhaps something else,
something moving. 'Looks like another ship,' he said.

'I'll take your word for it. Your eyes are better than mine.'

Felix clambered up to the crow's-nest on the mainmast. It had
been abandoned sometime during the storm. He hoped the
watcher had made it below and had not been carried off by the
sea. He unlimbered the huge spyglass from its protective case
and trained it on the distant spot, turning the eyepiece and tracking wheels to bring it into focus as he had been taught. The
telescope was a powerful one, and it seemed like his vision had
been sent flashing towards the horizon. When it reached its target, he wished it had not. Another ship was indeed out there, and
it was like no vessel Felix had ever seen before.

It looked like a cross between a raft and a Bretonnian galleon,
propelled by a combination of oars, paddle-wheels and sails. It
had a makeshift look combined with a brutal functionality that
told Felix who its builders were even before he caught sight of his
first green skin. He banged the alarm bell and shouted: 'Beware!
Orcs!'

If he had claimed that the ship was sinking he could not have
received a swifter response. Suddenly the decks seethed with
dwarfs, all straining to see in the direction of the oncoming ship.
Ahabsson had risen from his chair and trained his spyglass on
the horizon. Felix returned to gazing into his.

He guessed that the orc ship was twice the size of the *Storm
Hammer*, and it had perhaps four or five times the crew. A number of massive orcs filled the vessel's huge stern and forecastles.
Goblin sailors swarmed over the sails and rigging. Strange crude
rune signs had been painted on the sails. The skull of some large
beast and its thighbones crossed beneath it had been nailed to
the largest mast. A large catapult was mounted on some sort of
rotating platform at the fore. Another smaller one dominated the
stern.

The dwarfs' response was not what he had expected. Ahabsson leaned forward and pulled a lever before returning to the wheel. The speed of the *Storm Hammer* picked up as it swerved towards the orc craft. What were these maniacs up to, Felix wondered? He had expected flight before a craft so obviously superior. After all, Gotrek was the only Slayer on board, and they were carrying a cargo of precious spices. Felix shouted into the speaking tube: 'Captain. We are heading towards the orcs!'

Even distorted by the speaking tube, Ahabsson's cackle was recognisable. 'Don't fret laddie. We'll have her soon enough for ye. Keep your eyes peeled and let me know of any surprises.'

'You intend to sink her?' Felix asked incredulously.

'No! Board her, and take her treasure. Thon's an orc freebooter. She's bound to have loot in her hold.'

'I didn't know you were a pirate captain,' said Felix, instantly regretting the words.

'Privateer, laddie, and don't you forget it. We've letters of marque from the Shipwrights' Council at Barak Varr.'

'Well, that's a relief,' muttered Felix. Steam hissed below, as the ironclad's turret began to bring itself to bear on the orc hulk. There was a strange grinding sound as it moved, and one of the shortbeards moved to lubricate the base with oil. Felix wondered how much damage the ship had really sustained during the storm.

Most of the dwarfs had gone back below to their battle stations. The marines prepared their crossbows or stood by the large gymbal-mounted handcannons. Gotrek watched from the prow. Even from this height, Felix could see the tension in him.

He gave his attention back to the freebooter. As they closed more details became clear, and the more he saw, the less he liked their situation. Even though the *Storm Hammer* was built of metal, and their foe of wood, they seemed grossly outmatched to him. The orc craft was much larger and the crew far more numerous. Worse still, there seemed to be some sort of shaman on the forecastle of the ship, dancing around the catapult and shouting spells.

Teams of goblins, naked save for loincloths, glistened with sweat as they turned the winches that drew the catapult's arm into the firing position, or provided the motive power to rotate its mounting platform. Lordly orcs stood by, bellowing instructions. Obviously it was too much for the warriors to sully their claws with manual work. The orcs were huge creatures, twice as tall and many times the weight of the lean stringy goblins. Most were wearing britches and headscarves tied around their bald pates. Many were armed with cutlasses, a few carried bows. All were festooned lavishly with jewellery.

Felix shifted his point of view to the sterncastle, where the orc captain stood surrounded by his cronies. He was a massive creature, his head adorned with a Bretonnian admiral's tricorn hat. His tusks gleamed gold in the sunlight and he bore a cutlass in each hand.

Felix shouted the description into the speaking tube.

'Better and better,' replied Ahabsson. 'Uragh Goldtusk is the most feared pirate on the Gulf. The sultans have posted a reward of its own weight in gems for his head.'

The name made Felix shiver. In the bazaars and hostelries of Quadira, the boldest sailors muttered Goldtusk's name with fear. The tales of his ferocity and cruelty were dark legends within themselves! When the orc captain moved, Felix's eyes came to rest on a figure his bulk had previously hidden.

She was a human woman, tall, lithe and well formed, and very beautiful despite being garbed in what looked like the garments of a Bretonnian sailor. Her hair, which fell to her shoulders, was raven black and curly. Her hands were bound in chains, but she held her head high and showed no fear. Felix was too dumbstruck to inform the captain of what he saw.

The sea around the *Storm Hammer* churned white as she picked up speed. Clouds of sparks and black smoke emerged from her funnels. The gulls squawked and shrieked. The ship heeled and turned to take a better line towards its foe.

Felix saw the distant catapult arm swing forward. A blazing fireball rose from it and arced towards the *Storm Hammer*. The huge sphere left a fiery comet trail behind it that glowed unnaturally, with just the faintest hint of green. It flew further and faster than any natural stone could have and landed in the water just in front of the *Storm Hammer's* prow, sending up an enormous column of steam and boiling water, before sinking into the depths. When he looked down, Felix could see it still glowing as it plunged towards the sea bottom.

The islands were closer now, a smudge of black peaks smeared on the horizon, one much larger and more prominent than the others. Felix knew that they were much too far away to swim to it, even if sharks didn't get them. Ahabsson had set them on a course that could easily lead to their deaths, for Felix doubted the orcs would let them escape in the ship's boats. The best they could hope for would be capture, in which case they would be enslaved or eaten. His glance rested for a moment on Gotrek. The Slayer brandished his axe and bellowed challenges at the enemy. There was one who would suffer neither. Only death or victory lay ahead for him.

The goblins worked the winches again, and once more the catapult arm bent back into position. The shaman continued his relentless dance, and Felix could see a faint nimbus of greenish light playing around his head. It was still too far for a crossbow shot. He was sure that the greenskin sorcerer would work more deviltry before this day was through.

The *Storm Hammer* continued to cleave through the waves, moving inexorably closer to the orc ship. The barrel of the cannon in the turret had elevated now. There was an enormous boom, and a cloud of sparks and smoke billowed out, momentarily obscuring his view of the enemy ship. Felix heard the whistle of the cannonball, and seconds later saw it impact on the side of the orc hulk, smashing through the timber and leaving a gaping hole.

Ahabsson barked more instructions to the gunners in dwarfish, and the turret continued to swivel as the *Storm Hammer* maintained its course. Felix began to see method in the captain's madness. The orc ship was tacking towards them, but on their present course the *Storm Hammer* would emerge upwind and behind the freebooter. Hopefully they could smash its paddles and destroy its catapult and pick off the crew at will.

Felix heard the grinding of gears around the left wheel, and hoped that whatever damage the dwarf ship had taken in the storm would not fatally weaken her now.

The catapult opened fire once more. The shaman danced and capered, and as he did so, the huge fireball altered its course in mid-flight, veering towards the *Storm Hammer*. Felix watched gape-mouthed. He had seen a great deal of sorcery in his life but this was something new. If Ahabsson was surprised, he gave no sign. He merely swivelled his head to track the fireball as it came towards them. Felix felt his mouth go dry as the blazing sphere seemed almost to creep closer. It occurred to him that the fireball could actually hit him, and that he may die here. Indeed, it would not need to hit him. It could simply strike the steel mast to which the crow's-nest was attached and send him crashing into the sea. He had never felt more acutely vulnerable in his entire life. Looking at the blazing sphere, he could see that it had a core of molten stone surrounded by a nimbus of magical fire.

As the fireball came near the end of its downward arc, Ahabsson swung the wheel and pulled violently on one of the levers beside him. There was a grinding of gears as one of the great paddle wheels went into reverse. The *Storm Hammer* yawed wildly, and took a new course. The fireball struck the ship only a glancing blow, but it was enough. There was a blinding flash and a searing wave of heat swept over the steamship. She shuddered with the impact. Felix heard a hail of shrapnel patter on the metal hull. A few of the dwarfs shouted or screeched in pain. Felix ducked as small blazing stones pinged off the metal cupola around him. A moment later he heard a couple of secondary bangs.

When he looked up he could see part of the *Storm Hammer*'s hull was scorched black, some metal plates appeared to have buckled and two of the rail-mounted handcannons had exploded in the heat of the impact. Several dwarfs lay in crumpled heaps on the deck. The ship's chirurgeon and his assistants raced towards them. Another fear smote Felix. There was no sorcerer present to magically heal his wounds. Looking at the hacksaw the surgeon carried, it became obvious why so many of the dwarfs had peg-legs and hooks instead of hands. Shattered limbs were hacked off. Stumps were plunged into hot tar. It was a testimony to the ruggedness of the dwarf sailors that none of them screamed, although even from here, Felix could see their faces were masks of sweating agony.

That might happen to him, he thought. He might lose a limb or an eye. The realisation made his stomach churn. Looking down, he could see that the marines had broken out the casks of ale again, and something stronger. Urli and Mobi were distributing tots of some foul black liquid from a leather flask, and the dwarfen marines consumed it with relish before washing it down with more ale.

Only Gotrek stood apart, his whole attention focused on the orcish ship, like a hound straining at the leash. He radiated frustration, and looked as if he was considering throwing himself over the side and swimming towards the freebooter. Felix thought he understood. This was a battle where the Slayer had no control over his destiny. He could not close with his foe until Ahabsson decided to. And who could tell when that would be?

The cannon spoke again, and either by luck or design, struck the forecastle of the oncoming hulk. The ensuing explosion smashed the catapult to splinters. When the smoke cleared, fire raged and the shaman was nowhere to be seen. Relief filled Felix.

With the sorcerer out of action there was a chance they would survive this.

A cheer went up from the marines and they bellowed catcalls and challenges at their foe. Goblins scurried across the ship, encouraged by cuffs and kicks from the orcs, hastily throwing bucket after bucket of water onto the blazing weapon. One catapult down, one to go, Felix thought.

Ahabsson held his line, and the *Storm Hammer* sped past the stern of the hulk so close that Felix could see the faces of the orcs without needing to use the spyglass. The dwarf ship began to come round in a great figure of eight turn that would position them directly to the rear of the orcs, with the turret in direct line to fire. As they did so, Felix could see that the second, smaller, catapult on the sterncastle was being wheeled to bear on them. At least, he told himself, there was no shaman present now to guide its stones with spells, only the bellowing Goldtusk and his lieutenants and their prisoner.

Felix considered telling Ahabsson about the girl, but realised that by now the captain could see her for himself. It was unlikely he was going to change his plan simply because there was one human woman present either. His duty was to his own ship and people, and his goldlust was focused on his prize.

The *Storm Hammer* had almost completed her turn now and was in a position right behind Goldtusk's vessel. So swiftly had they executed the manoeuvre that their own white wake was visible before them, crossing that left by the orc craft. Goldtusk raised one huge arm then lowered it: the second catapult spoke. A huge boulder spun through the air and impacted on the turret of the steamer. The whole ship shuddered. The turret rang like a bell. At first Felix thought there was no damage, save for a massive dent in the armoured plate, but then he noticed that the turret had stopped tracking and smoke was emerging from below. It seemed that the mechanism had been damaged, and perhaps the gun crew stunned. The shortbeard who had been oiling the machine lay in a pool of blood half covered by a boulder as big as a man's body. Nothing the chirurgeon could do there, Felix thought.

Ahabsson bellowed something into another of the speaking tubes. He appeared to be demanding to know why the gunners were asleep on the job. His shouts got no response. The dwarfen crossbows opened up now, a hail of somewhat inaccurate fire raking the orcish sterncastle. Felix saw Goldtusk push the woman away behind him. A couple of orcs and goblins went down, but the captain himself was unharmed.

As Felix watched, more and more greenskins flooded onto the sterncastle, bellowing and grunting, seemingly oblivious of the black smoke rising up behind them. They appeared more concerned with getting into the fight than with the fact that their own craft might soon become a floating funeral pyre.

What was Ahabsson going to do, Felix wondered? Now that the *Storm Hammer's* main offensive weapon was out of action, his plan had been negated. The best Felix could think of was that they should pull back out of range and wait for the fire to spread through the enemy vessel. Of course that would mean foregoing the treasure and leaving the woman to her doom, but it would certainly spare their own lives. Even if the orcs succeeded in getting the blaze under control, it would take some of their lives, and damage their ship still further.

The captain seemed to have come to the same conclusion, for the great paddlewheels ground into reverse, allowing them to hold their position. Evidently Ahabsson was still hoping that his gun crew could eventually fire their weapon, for he held the prow in line with the hulk. Even if the turret could not track, they could still shoot at the enemy.

Arrows began to descend on the decks of the dwarfen ship, but the crew merely ducked behind the turret and the guardrails and the shafts merely fell onto the deck. Felix was glad none of the greenskins had thought to take a shot at him, but realised it was only a matter of time. He debated whether to risk climbing down or waiting for the smoke from the fire to cover him. The decision was taken from his hands when disaster struck.

A grinding crunching sound came from below, and the wheels ceased their spinning. A smell of burning rose from beneath him. It seemed that the storm damage had been worse than Felix thought, or perhaps it had been the impact of the sorcerous fireball, or some combination of them both, but now the *Storm Hammer* was slowing. Soon she would be wallowing dead in the water.

Worse still, the orcs had reefed their sails and begun to slow themselves. They had reversed their own paddle wheels. Even as Felix watched, the hulk slowed to a stop and then backed up towards the dwarfen ship. The orc's paddles were not nearly so swift and efficient as the *Storm Hammer's*, but they were doing the job.

From below Felix could hear the sound of hammering as dwarfen engineers worked to get the ship moving again, but even he could see that there was no chance of it happening before they were attacked. Arrows sleeted down on the deck now, pinning down the marines. Even Gotrek had taken cover, standing ready behind the huge moulded figurehead at the prow. They had gone from predator to prey in the space of a heartbeat.

The hulk came ever closer, and as it did so, it loomed ever larger. To Felix's fevered imagination it took on the massiveness of a mountain, looming over the steamer like one of the icebergs of the frozen northern seas. The top of the sterncastle was almost level with Felix's crow's-nest. He ducked down so that only his eyes were above the level of the cupola.

The orcs bellowed in triumph, crowding the railings. They were close enough for Felix to see that the guardrails had been salvaged or stolen from a Bretonnian ship. Goblins and orcs filled the rigging, clinging to the lines, obviously preparing themselves to swing down onto the *Storm Hammer*.

As they did so, Felix noticed that the barrel of the turret had started to elevate and that Ahabsson was bellowing something about grapeshot. If the orcs noticed, most of them gave no indication of caring. Only Goldtusk shouted something to his closest followers and herded them back from the rails.

A moment later smoke billowed from the turret once more and there was a sound like thunder. Grapeshot ripped across the front of the sterncastle and into sails, tearing canvas, peppering the wood with holes, ripping through the flesh of orc and goblin alike. Their shouts of triumph momentarily turned to screams. Goblins lost their foothold in the rigging and dropped into the sea. Sleek black-finned shapes told Felix that the sharks were waiting to feast.

As the orcish arrow fire slackened off, the dwarf marines emerged from cover. Muskets, crossbows and handcannons raked the enemy decks. More greenskins fell. For a moment, it looked like panic would spread among the orcs, but Goldtusk re-emerged. He had been saved by stepping back out of the line of the upward-angled cannon shot. Now he shrieked instructions at his followers, cuffed and booted them into some semblance of order.

At that moment the *Storm Hammer's* hull rang like a bell as the two ships careered into each other. The first wave of orcs and goblins swung down from the rigging on their lines. Orcs hastily tossed boarding nets over the side, and tried to snag the *Storm Hammer* with grapnels.

Doubtless, had not the grapeshot depleted their numbers, Goldtusk's crew would have overwhelmed the dwarfen mariners in the initial assault. As it was, a few of the dwarfs let off a ragged volley of musketry and crossbow fire, before snatching up their sea-axes, hammers and cutlasses to make ready to repel boarders.

THREE
The Prisoner

ORC AND DWARF clashed. Hammer splintered bone. Cutlass clove through dwarfen flesh. Blood, green and red mingled on the metal decks. Felix felt useless, high above the fight. He snatched out his sword and considered his options. He could try to abseil down the mast using the line, but that would be difficult with a weapon in one hand. He could climb down slowly on the handholds but that would leave him vulnerable to arrow fire. Or he could stay where he was and do nothing.

More and more orcs and goblins swarmed down the boarding nets. While they were engaged in a melee there was little the dwarfs could do to prevent them. Ahabsson had produced a set of pistols and blasted away at the greenskins, picking up another with his good hand as soon as he had discharged the first.

'Get off my ship!' he bellowed. Then Gotrek emerged from the shadow of the prow. He raced among the orcs chopping left and right with the axe. Nothing could stop him. He reaped lives like a peasant scything corn, clove through the greenskin ranks like a runaway chariot, scattered his foes like a whirlwind scatters leaves. It was as if some ancient dwarfen god of war had emerged onto the blood-slick decks and strove to avenge his people on their ancient enemies. Goblins threw themselves over the guardrails into the shark-infested waters to escape him. Orcs held their ground and died. The dwarfen marines, moments before in disarray, suddenly took heart. Their line stiffened, they threw themselves forward in Gotrek's wake, and tore into the ever-increasing number of orcs that still dropped onto their decks from the boarding nets.

Felix was suddenly distracted as some freak of wind or wave rolled the ship. The mast tipped downwards towards the sterncastle of the orc vessel. Through the clouds of smoke, Felix caught a glimpse of the woman struggling in the grasp of her brutal green-skinned captors and, acting on instinct, grabbed a line and flung himself out into space.

Seconds later his boots clattered down on the deck of the orc sterncastle. He raced through the smoke across the wooden deck towards where he had last seen the woman. She stood at bay, her back to a guard rail, trying to drive back an orc with bunched chains wrapped around her wrists.

Felix rammed his sword into the orc's back. It passed right through its stomach and out of the other side. When he withdrew it the orc tumbled forward, only to have its skull crushed by the woman's flailing chains. Felix stood face to face with her. Even blood-spattered and smoke-smudged she was lovely. She smiled briefly, then gave him a haughty look, and said, 'What are you waiting for? Free me!'

Her voice was low and husky, the accent Tilean. Felix did not like her tone, but now was not the time or place to tell her this.

'Where are the keys?'

'Goldtusk has them!'

Felix put his foot on the loop of chain, inserted the blade of his sword into the links and twisted. As he did so, he noticed that there were strange runes on the cuffs, and at first the metal seemed to tingle when he touched it. The tip of his sword bored into the deck and the blade flexed. A normal sword would have broken under the strain, but Felix was confident that the magical blade he had found under Karag Eight Peaks would endure. The link widened and Felix stooped until the connecting loop fell out. 'What's your name?' Felix asked as he inspected the chain on her arms. Yes, definitely some sort of rune work there. Perhaps the orcs had a system for designating whose property their captive was.

'Katja Murillo. And yours?'

'Felix Jaeger.'

'Well, Felix Jaeger, pleased as I am to make your acquaintance, I would appreciate it if you could hurry up and remove these chains from my arms.'

'I'm working on it.' He saw the woman's eyes widen as she glanced over his shoulder, and he turned to see what the fuss was about.

The smoke clouds had parted momentarily and Captain Goldtusk stood revealed. He looked surprised to see a human on his command deck. Felix seized the opportunity and aimed a two handed stroke at his head. The orc responded with cat-like quickness. One of the cutlasses rose to block Felix's blow, while the other lashed out to strike.

Felix leapt backwards, bringing his blade up into the guard position. Sparks flashed as the weapons clashed. The brutal strength of the orc's blow almost knocked the sword from Felix's hand. He was aware that the orc was a head taller than he was, and much heavier. Huge muscles rippled smoothly beneath the taut green skin as Goldtusk advanced, driving Felix backwards.

For long moments it was all he could do to defend himself. He had never faced a swordsman quite as deadly as the pirate captain. He seemed equally adept at using his blade with either hand, and his speed and power were devastating. Felix considered himself a better than able swordsman, and a stronger than average man, but it was instantly obvious to him that he was grossly outmatched.

He glanced around, looking for a way out, but saw none. The woman had vanished into the smoke, and all that was visible was the looming figure of the orcish captain. Their blades crossed again, and a slash from the orc's left hand blade left a bloody weal across the front of Felix's tunic. If he had been a heartbeat slower Felix knew the blow would have smashed through his ribs and cut through vital organs.

The crackling heat of the blaze was like an inferno. Sweat soaked his shirt now, and the acrid reek of smoke and gunpowder filled his nostrils. The screams of the dying rose from the deck of the *Storm Hammer* behind him. He could hear Gotrek's bellowed war-cry and the shouts of the dwarf privateers mingled with the grunts and shrieks of the orcs. Under the circumstances there was no way of telling how the battle was going, but it was obvious he could expect no help from that direction. It looked like Gotrek would have to find someone else to write his death saga. Felix was going to be too dead to do it.

At that moment, he heard the hiss of chains whipping through the air, and the heavy links connected with the orc's head, knocking him off balance. Katja Murillo was there, using the severed lengths of chain as a weapon. Goldtusk twisted to see the source of the new threat, and Felix lashed out with his weapon. Even half stunned, the orc's astonishing quickness saved him. He half-sprang, half-reeled to one side, taking only a long cut across the forehead. He glared hatred at Felix for an instant before vanishing into the smoke.

'We'd best get off this ship,' said Katja. 'It's going to go down. There's no way that fire is going to be brought under control now.'

'Wonderful,' said Felix. 'How do you suggest we do that?'

The woman had already gone, vanishing off in the direction of the screams. Felix followed and found himself looking down from the sterncastle of the hulk onto a scene of utter carnage. Orc and goblin bodies were piled high on the decks of the *Storm Hammer*. Gotrek stood atop the heap, bellowing challenges and ranting insanely in dwarfish. Orcs still responded to his shouts, clambering over the corpses of their dead comrades to get to the Slayer while goblins clambered back up the boarding nets. Felix readied his sword to meet them. At the stern of the *Storm Hammer* the few surviving marines had rallied around Ahabsson and were more than holding their own.

Suddenly the dwarf ship's wheels started to churn the sea, and the *Storm Hammer* began to shudder. Perhaps some of the engineers had carried on making repairs below while the battle raged. Perhaps the obstruction had cleared itself. Felix could only guess. What he was absolutely certain of was that if he did not get back onto the steamship now, he would be swimming back to her through shark-infested waters. He looked around to see if he could find Katja and noticed that the woman had already abseiled halfway down the side of the hulk. She had found a rope and looped it around her waist and was using it to help her. Felix did not have time for that. Instead he threw himself over the barrier, and scampered down the net, lashing out with his boots at any goblins that got in his way. As if by silent agreement, they allowed him unobstructed passage, and he dropped the last span to the steel deck. Katja was already there.

It was obvious that the *Storm Hammer's* paddles were not working perfectly, that one was churning the water quicker than the other, for the steamer had begun a slow rotation as she backed away from the hulk. A glance told him that the wooden wheels at the back of the orc ship had been broken by the impact.

The orcs seemed to realise at last what was happening. Some of them threw themselves over the side into the sea to return to their blazing ship. Others made the mistake of taking their eyes off the Slayer for a fatal instant, and never looked upon anything again in this life. The dwarfs made a final heroic effort and drove the last of the boarders into the sea. Within a few seconds not a single greenskin was left alive on the decks of the *Storm Hammer*.

Bellowing instructions, Ahabsson made his way back to his command deck and began to tug levers and batter gauges with his fist. The crippled steamship and the blazing hulk drifted apart. Felix could see the fire had spread from stem to sterncastle across the huge ship, the sails were alight, and the rigging ablaze. Frantic efforts by the orcs and goblins to stem the blaze went to no avail.

As the morning wore on, the two ships continued to drift apart. Eventually the surviving greenskins took to the boats, and rowed off towards the islands. Shortly thereafter, the blazing hulk slid beneath the surface and was seen no more.

Mobi strode up to Felix's side. 'There goes Goldtusk's treasure,' he said regretfully. 'There goes our chance to be rich.'

'You're wrong,' said Katja from behind him. Felix suspected that it would have been better for his health and his peace of mind if she had kept her mouth shut.

'What do you mean?' asked Mobi. 'And who are you anyway?'

'I'd better tell that to your captain,' said Katja.

'Aye,' said Mobi. 'No doubt he'll be wanting a word anyway!'

'First find a hammer and strike these chains from my hands,' said the woman haughtily.

'I take orders from Captain Ahabsson, not from you, woman,' said Mobi, and led her away.

FOUR
The Island of Fear

'WHO ARE YOU and what are you doing on my ship?' asked Ahabsson. He nursed an ale in his now bandaged hand. Felix and Gotrek watched interestedly as the woman prepared to reply. Faint splashes told Felix of orcish bodies being unceremoniously tossed over the side. Felix noticed that some of the goblins had hugely distended earlobes from which copper chains dangled. Others had copper pins struck through their noses. Most all of them were covered in barbaric scar tattoos.

'I am Captain Katja Murillo, out of Tobaro in Tilea.'

'Captain of what?'

'The *Golden Gull.*'

'Women captains? What will the manlings think of next?' grumbled Ahabsson. 'How came you to be Goldtusk's prisoner?'

'I was cruising these waters in search of Redhand's treasure when Goldtusk took my ship. He fired some of my crew from the catapults and ate the rest.'

There was a near imperceptible change in the atmosphere, the dwarfs suddenly glanced around furtively and seemed to radiate attentiveness. They always did when treasure was mentioned. Urli licked his lips.

'Why here?'

'The treasure is to be found on those islands,' she said.

'And how do you know this? Redhand vanished a decade ago, and neither man nor dwarf knows where he went or what happened to his loot.'

'He was my father,' she said. Ahabsson shrugged.

'That would make a difference, I suppose.'

'He left a map. It was etched onto the lid of a jewellery box he gave my mama before his last voyage. The pattern was concealed within a standard Arabian design. It was only when I got my master's ticket that I realised what it was myself.'

'And where is this box now?'

'At the bottom of the sea. It most likely went down with Gold-tusk's ship.'

'Then the treasure is gone, isn't it?'

'No. I memorised the pattern. I can find it.'

'Can you now, girl? You sure?'

'Aye.'

'And I suppose you will split it with us if we take you to the islands and bring it back.'

'Aye. Three shares to one. If you'll give me your word on the deal.'

'That would be three shares in my favour would it?' said Ahab-sson.

'No. In mine.'

'I have a ship to fuel and a crew that needs paying.'

'Three quarters of nothing is nothing. And you'll have to harbour in the islands anyway for repairs judging by the looks of your ship here.'

'We could just set you down on the island and leave you there.'

'You would not do that to another mariner, captain.'

'Would I not?'

The woman just looked at him. Ahabsson shrugged and said, 'I suppose you're right. One for one and my word on it.'

'A deal.'

They both spat on their hands and shook. Felix looked at Gotrek. The Slayer was bandaged in half a dozen places. He looked a terrible sight but Felix knew he would heal with near supernatural speed. He always did. Gotrek's face was stone hard and enigmatic. For once he did not look all that excited by the prospect of gold. The chirurgeon had already slathered healing salve over Felix's own wounds. It had burned at first but now the pain was all but gone.

'Is that treasure the reason why the orc spared you when he killed your crew?'

'Aye,' she said. 'I told him about it. It was that or be eaten like my men.'

'That's two ships that have gone down looking for this treasure then,' said Gotrek. 'Let's hope we're not the third.'

'Aye,' said Ahabsson. 'Now we best begin repairing the ship.'

THE ENGINEERS HAD got the wheels working properly once more, albeit very slowly. Felix watched the island come closer. He could see a mighty peak in the centre, and as they approached, huge cliffs of most unusual aspect. At their highest they towered to perhaps a hundred times the height of a man. The stone was predominantly reddish brown and layered in many different shades. Here and there streamers of rock ran down through the layers, as if the stone had run like wax and then solidified. Gulls hurled themselves outwards from the cliffs but Felix could see no way to climb up from where they were. Indeed, the base of the cliffs appeared to have been eroded inwards by the foaming breakers surging against its side. It would be an impossible climb, Felix realised.

'Lava made those cliffs,' said Gotrek. 'That mountain is a volcano.'

Felix did not ask how he knew. Dwarfs were incredibly knowledgeable in the ways of stone and earth.

'Let's hope it does not erupt while we are here,' said Felix, eying the peak warily.

'Aye, let us hope so.'

'What is twisting your face? You do not seem as happy as a dwarf with a prospect of treasure before him should be.'

'There is something about this place I do not like, manling. I do not like it at all.'

Felix considered this and shivered despite the late afternoon heat. Anything that made Gotrek Gurnisson uneasy was something that should give any sane man nightmares.

Ahabsson and Katja stood on the conning tower. The engineers had struck off her chains, and found her a cutlass. She looked almost as piratical as Goldtusk. Looking at her, it was easy to believe she was Redhand's daughter.

The captain relayed her instructions into his speaking tube. The *Storm Hammer* limped along at a fraction of her normal speed. Ahead of them a natural harbour loomed, a ribbon of black sand beach fringed by palm trees. Cliffs flanked the bay on either side, and jungle rose on the hills behind it. There was no sign of human habitation Felix could see.

The *Storm Hammer* shuddered to a halt. In the hours it had taken to find the harbour, Felix got some idea of the casualties they had suffered. Every one of the crew had been wounded. Some had been scratches, others had resulted in amputations. Some had been scalded badly by steam gushing from broken pipes. Half of them had died. Normally they would have been sewn into their shrouds and tossed overboard but given the presence of land so close, Ahabsson had decided to bury them there. Given the choice any dwarf would prefer to be buried on earth or stone, and the captain was willing to grant that if he could.

The ship herself had fared about as well as her crew. She was still capable of movement, but slowly and painfully. She had suffered a great deal of damage, and according to Malgrim, the chief engineer, it would take a lot of work to make her seaworthy again. There was no way she could survive another storm like the one the night before, let alone a sea-battle if it came to it. For all that the crew seemed happy enough to go about their business, even the wounded helping as much as they could. It was amazing how the prospect of finding hidden gold perked up a dwarf.

'I will not be sorry to feel land under my feet again, manling,' said Gotrek. Felix agreed, although there was something about the riotous life of the jungle that made him uneasy as well. He felt as if anything could be lurking in there, watching them with malignant eyes.

'What do you know about these islands?' Felix asked.

'Nothing, manling, I am not a sailor.'

'They might be part of the Megalean Chain,' piped up Mobi. 'It could extend this far south. Or it might be some place no mariner has heard of. We were driven pretty far off course by the storm.'

'One woman at least had heard of them,' said Felix, nodding significantly in the direction of Katja. 'And one man: her father.'

'It's possible,' said Old Narli, scratching his wizened face with an equally wizened hand. 'Redhand was the terror of these seas for twenty years, long afore Goldtusk and his orc freebooters appeared. At one time, Redhand had a fleet. They sailed everywhere they pleased. Even stormed the walls of Magritta. Although that was the end of them. The King of Estalia took exception, or so they say, and sent out all of his admirals. The pirate fleet was smashed at Bounty Bay. They say Redhand escaped with his treasure, and was never heard of again. Many a strange tale is told of Redhand. They say he was married to a sea-witch, who ruled him with a hand of iron, and wove wind and wave to her bidding. An evil pair they were. Drank blood and offered up the souls of their captives to her dark gods. I would not be surprised if this treasure was cursed. Still gold's gold for all that.'

'I wonder what happened to him,' said Felix.

'I think you might find out, manling.'

'What do you mean?'

'If you were a pirate with a cache of buried gold, would you not come back to collect it?'

'I suppose so. And if he did not simply desert his family and take up refuge somewhere else, then he might still be here.'

'Or his corpse. Assuming he's not in Far Cathay, laughing at us and all the other fools trying to find his treasure. And that's assuming the chit of a girl's story is really true.'

'Oh, it's true,' said Katja. Felix had not heard her approach, but he had to assume that Gotrek had. The Slayer's ears were far keener than his own. Either he did not care whether he offended the girl, or he wanted her to hear for reasons of his own. 'And truthfully I do not know whether I hope to find it or not. If my father took it and is living somewhere right now, then may the gods watch over him. If he died here, I hope to find that out. And if the treasure is here, I hope to claim my legacy.'

She smiled at Gotrek and then at Felix. 'A party is going ashore to bury the dead and look for water. Would you care to accompany us? We can take a look around and see if we can find the trail.'

'I will,' said Felix quickly.

'I would like to feel the earth beneath my feet once more,' said Gotrek. Felix was glad that the Slayer would accompany them. The more he saw of the jungle, the more his unease grew.

'I wonder if Goldtusk made it to land yet?' he said. No one answered.

It felt strange to be back on solid ground. Even with sand crunching beneath his feet, Felix still swayed slightly, as if compensating for the subtle movements of a deck beneath him. It made him feel off-balance and he realised how used he had become to the ship's rocking movement, even in the few days they had been aboard.

The dwarfs were already returning to the ship to bring ashore more of the dead for burial. A few small shrouded corpses already lay in the sand. It was strange to think that they would lay for eternity so many hundreds of leagues from home. A deep feeling of melancholy settled on Felix as he realised that the same fate would probably befall him one day.

Gotrek seemed to read his thoughts. 'At least they will be within sight of a mountain, albeit one with fire in its heart.'

Almost as if the earth had heard him, the ground shivered. The shrouds flapped in response to more than the wind. Felix could feel the vibration through the soles of his boots. The sand shook like a frightened beast.

'What was that?' he muttered.

'An earthquake,' said Gotrek. 'A mild one. The spirit of this mountain grows restless in its sleep, it seems.'

'Let's hope it does not wake up while we are here,' said Felix.

'This island is a place where the earth was restless, and the mountains belch fire and smoke,' said Katja. Noticing Felix stare she said, 'I can remember my father speaking of it from when I was a little girl.'

'Did he speak of anything else?' asked the Slayer.

'Aye, he spoke of ruins and a fallen city of some ancient people. I think we will see them on our trek inland.'

'Oh good,' said Felix, thinking of all the other tumbled-down and monster-haunted places he had barely escaped with his life from during his long association with the Slayer. His thoughts went from Karag Eight Peaks in the Worlds Edge Mountains to the Temple of the Old Ones in Albion. None of them were places he would care to revisit. 'More ruins.'

They found a stream. The water appeared pure and fresh. Light dappled the grass beneath them as if filtered through the leaves. Brightly coloured parrots squawked in the branches above them. There were the tracks of deer of some sort, and large predators. The air was warm and balmy and only slightly humid. Despite himself Felix was starting to relax a little. There were food and water here so they were not about to die of hunger or thirst.

They trekked uphill, following the path of the stream. After days on a ship, Felix found it hard going. Katja went up the path like a gazelle, seemingly glad to have the free use of her limbs once more. Of course, to Gotrek, a dwarf, the steepest of slopes were no more of an impediment than a flat plain. He was not even slightly out of breath by the time they reached the top and found the first ruin. It looked like a small watchtower, built on a lookout point. Stone had been piled on stone crudely, but strongly. It looked like nothing Felix had seen before in his travels.

'Human work,' said Gotrek, after considering it for a moment. 'Very shoddy. Destroyed by orcs, judging by those bones.'

'But long ago?' said Felix, wanting reassurance, although the facts were plain to see. Birds nested amid the tumbled stonework, white guano splattering the rocks. There was no sign of greenskin presence here. Briefly Felix considered helping himself to some of the eggs but decided against it. Perhaps the time would come for that later, before they left. He was not even sure how edible gull eggs were, although he was ready to try anything in a pinch. 'There are no orcs here now.'

'Many orc tribes are nomadic. They might have moved inland in search of better hunting, or because their gods sent them some sign, or because their chief felt like feeding on the flesh of his kin on the other side of the island. You can never tell with orcs.'

Felix had known the Slayer long enough to begin to follow the track of his thoughts. 'You think Goldtusk and his merry crew might have come from around here?'

'Maybe. Perhaps he recruits from among these islands. Or has a stronghold here.'

'Goldtusk recruits from this island, I am sure of it. These waters were familiar to him. My father said there were orcs on the island. They often attacked his men.'

'You picked a fine time to tell us about this, Katja,' said Felix.

'No dwarf would have let that affect their decision,' said the woman.

Gotrek grunted agreement but Felix was aggrieved. 'Perhaps not but it would not do any harm for them to know what dangers they might face.'

The girl grinned. She had cleaned up well and she clearly knew the charm her snub-nosed beauty gave her. 'Volcanoes. Orcs. Goblins. Earthquakes. Savage animals. They already knew, or could have guessed.'

'Anything else? Your father didn't mention any evil sorcerers, curses on the treasure, fearsome dragons, huge monsters, did he? And when was the last time you saw him anyway?'

'I told you. Ten years ago more or less, before he left on his final voyage. I begged to go with him, but he said I was too small.'

'Very touching,' said Felix, unsure quite why he was so annoyed. There was something about the woman that made him suspicious. 'Do you expect us to believe that the local folk just let a pirate live among them?'

'In Tilea things are very hard, Felix Jaeger. There is little difference between a pirate and a fisherman, sometimes. My father returned to his village often, and his relatives were always pleased to see them. He lived like a prince and he was generous.'

'And what of your mother. Was she not some sort of daemon-worshipping sorceress?'

'Lies. My mother was a simple Tilean farmer's daughter.' There was a slightly hysterical tone to her voice. Felix had obviously touched a raw nerve. He felt an obscure urge to apologise, but he did not. He was still nettled by the fact that the girl had not mentioned the orcs. It felt a little like a betrayal, although he was not quite sure why it should. He had known her for less than a day. He simply stared at her.

'There was something else,' she said, glancing at the dwarf.

'Yes,' said Felix.

'My father mentioned that there was something that lived in the ruins, a monster that guarded a magical gem as big as your fist. It was too powerful to be overcome by his men. He swore he would return with a greater force and overcome it. That was the last time I saw him. '

Gotrek looked interested now. Talk of mysterious monsters was a sure way of getting his attention. Felix wondered how much the girl knew of the Slayer cult and whether she was deliberately pitching this story at Gotrek. She was clever enough, he was sure. There was clearly more to this woman than met the eye.

'No need for us to worry about that,' said Felix. 'We'll be happy with Redhand's treasure.'

'I don't know about that, manling,' said Gotrek, just as Felix had feared he would.

'You'll get a chance at both. My father left his treasure in the city.'

'How convenient,' said Felix. He definitely had the feeling that they were being manipulated. Still, he could understand why. Katja Murillo had neither ship nor crew, and words were her only way to get them to do what she wanted.

From somewhere down below came the sound of a single musket shot. Felix was startled, but it was not repeated. Perhaps it had been a signal for them to return.

'We'd best be getting back,' he said. 'The others might need our help.'

FIVE
Into the Jungle

WHEN THEY RETURNED to the beach they discovered Urli had shot a deer. The dwarfs were excited, for this would be the first fresh meat they had seen in days. Already someone had started to build a fire on the beach from driftwood and fallen branches. Urli was at work gutting and skinning the creature. A boat had been sent back to invite more of the dwarfs to the feast. It looked like only a skeleton crew would be left aboard for the night. Felix didn't like this situation at all.

It was not just dwarfs the ship's boats had brought, there was ale as well. Soon the fire was blazing merrily; the deer was being roasted along with yams and tubers the shortbeards had collected.

Despite feeling the tug of the bottle, Felix did not drink anything stronger than water. He lacked the dwarfs' ability to see in the dark and their keen senses of hearing and smell, so he wanted his head clear. At night, the sense of danger had increased, although there was nothing physically menacing to be seen. The white breakers rolled cheerfully to the shore. The larger moon, Mannslieb, viewed its face in the mirror of the waters. Morrslieb had yet to appear.

Gotrek too seemed subdued. He held a tankard in one hand, but did not drink with his usual gloomy relish. Often he would leave the fire and the tales and songs of the sailors to go stand at the jungle's edge and peer into the dark. He seemed to be considering actually going into the jungle to hunt. Felix was glad that he did not.

He was equally glad when the dwarfs decided to return to their ship about midnight when the meat was gone and the fire was low. Most of them, save a few who were already too inebriated to move, rowed drunkenly back to the ship. Felix was not too thrilled when Gotrek decided to remain on land, but he hunkered down on the beach with his back to the jungle and stared out at the distant running lights of the steamship.

He was surprised when a few minutes later, Katja dropped down beside him. She offered him a tankard of ale, but he shook his head.

'I wanted to thank you for saving me from Goldtusk,' she said. 'I didn't do it very well at the time. You can understand why, I hope. Things were crazed. Emotions were running high...'

'Think nothing of it,' said Felix, unwinding a little. Perhaps she was not so bad after all, he thought. But still there was something about her that unsettled him. She seemed determined to put him at his ease.

'It's lovely here, don't you think?' she said, gesturing towards the sea. Felix understood what she meant, but he could not quite bring himself to agree.

'It is, but there is something about this place I don't like.'

The girl sighed. 'Aye, you are right. It looks beautiful by day or by night, but there is a presence here that sometimes makes my blood run cold.'

'Do you really think your father's treasure is here?'

'Aye. I am certain of it.'

'Why did he pick this place? There must be a dozen more welcoming islands in this chain.'

'Perhaps that is why he picked this place. He knew it would be shunned.'

'That makes a certain amount of sense, but if it had been me, I would have left this island undisturbed and gone somewhere else.'

She shrugged. 'Something brought him back here to his doom. I am sure of it. He wanted that gem more than he ever wanted anything.'

'Why?'

'I'm guessing he thought it held the secret of great power and eternal life.' Felix almost laughed, but there was something in her voice that compelled belief and undercurrents of the same lust she claimed had driven her father.

'That sounds more like something your mother would want.'

'My mother was a normal mortal woman.'

'Narli seems convinced otherwise…'

'Many dark tales followed Redhand and his crew. The same tales have dogged many other pirates.'

'They have not always been lies.'

'Perhaps not. Why are you travelling aboard a ship full of dwarfs?' Felix laughed at the transparently obvious attempt to change the subject.

'A long story. In a moment of drunken madness years ago, I swore an oath to follow Gotrek and record his doom in an epic poem.'

'He does not seem to have found it yet.'

'You have no idea how strong Gotrek is. I have lost count of how many monsters he has killed.'

'He certainly killed a lot of orcs today.'

'He hates orcs.'

'I have heard it said dwarfs hate anything that is not a dwarf.'

'They don't hate humans. They are allied with us.'

'They are allied with your Empire. That's something different.'

'I suppose it is. What's Tilea like?'

'Beautiful. Rugged. Poor. Wealthy nobles, ancient city-states. Corrupt. There are many prejudices, many superstitions. There are many wars. Our men become mercenaries and bandits and seafarers…'

'Your women too, it seems.'

'I am a seafarer, yes.'

'And you came looking for pirate gold.'

'Why not? The people who it belonged to once have no use for it now.'

Felix felt like reminding her that it was her father who killed them, but he did not. Maybe she was no more responsible for who her father was than he was. Gustav Jaeger was a wealthy merchant after all, and no man became as rich as his father without having a few crimes on his conscience, Felix was sure.

He lay back and gazed up at the stars. They looked different here than in the cold skies of the Empire. He wondered why that was, and filed it among the many questions he could not answer. He noticed that Katja had stood up and was looking back over her shoulder.

'The little dwarf is taking an awful long time to come back,' said Katja.

Felix realised she was right. He rose to his feet and strode over to where Gotrek sat slumped by the fire. 'Mobi is taking a long time about making water.'

'What do you want me to do about it manling, go and give him instructions on how it's done?'

'Maybe something happened to him.'

'Mobi!' Gotrek bellowed, startling some drunkards awake, and not a few animals under the tree line as well by the sounds of it. 'Mobi!'

There was no response. Gotrek got up and stomped over to where the shortbeard had last been seen. There were tracks in the sand leading in one direction, but none coming back. Felix's unease returned. He did not like this at all.

They moved along the edge of the woods but found no sign of the youngster at all. 'Maybe he wandered off into the woods and got lost,' said Felix unconvincingly.

'Maybe. There's no sense in looking for tracks now. It will have to wait until morning.'

But when morning came they found no tracks either, and no sign of where or how the shortbeard had vanished. The search parties found no trace.

Katja led the dwarfs deeper into the forest. There were ten of them, the toughest of the marines, led by Urli. Ahabsson had elected to stay with the ship and supervise the repairs. Felix supposed it showed that the captain trusted them. On the other hand, they were not about to go anywhere without the ship, so he could afford to.

Now they were on solid ground again, the dwarfs had broken out far more traditional war gear. They wore chainmail and carried shields on their backs. They had helmets too, but in the sweltering heat most let them dangle from their straps around their necks. All of the dwarfs carried muskets or crossbows, except Urli who carried a wicked-looking blunderbuss. Even Felix had borrowed a couple of pistols from the captain and stuck them in his belt. He had donned his old chainmail shirt. Even though it turned clambering uphill in the enervating heat into a nightmare, he was glad of its protection. Only Gotrek and Katja wore no armour.

There were mosquitoes in the jungle, and leeches and large ants with a fiery bite that Felix discovered for himself when he tried to brush them from his armour with his bare hands. The dwarfs looked as out of place among the lush tropical vegetation as orcs at an elvish wedding. Felix did not feel any more at home himself. He had grown up in Altdorf, the capital of the Empire and would much have preferred to be back there now.

Only Katja gave no signs of unease as they followed the stream along deeper into the woods, and Felix suspected that was merely because she masked her feelings well. She sat on the bole of a toppled palm tree and took a swig from her flask. The dwarfs stood around peering off into the gloom, swigging ale from leather bladders.

'What now?' Felix asked. 'What are we looking for?'

'An old road of some sort, or a path. There was a line on the map that could only have been that.'

'You're placing an awful lot of faith in a design on a jewellery box, aren't you?'

'My father was a cunning man, Felix Jaeger, and a meticulous one. Also I can recall him speaking of some ancient highway that ran across the island through the jungle.'

Felix realised exactly what a wild goose chase they were on. They were relying on this girl's memories of a pattern on a box, and her scant recollection of her father's old stories to guide them across an island as large as an Imperial county in search of a treasure that might or might not actually be there. And that was assuming Katja was telling the truth, a thing of which he was not entirely sure.

Only dwarfs would leap at such a long shot, he thought, and then realised that he was deluding himself. Many adventurers had done far stranger things on the strength of even vaguer rumours. He and Gotrek had done such things themselves. And, he supposed, they had nothing better to do while the ship was being repaired.

When he considered things, Felix realised that Ahabsson was risking nothing save the lives of the marines. All of the essential crew, the engineers, gunners and sailors were still aboard ship. The captain had insisted on keeping them there, despite their clamour to accompany the treasure hunters. If the search party never returned from the jungle, he could simply finish repairs, up anchor and sail away. Felix wondered how much credence the captain really put in the girl's story, and realised that it did not need to be much. He was gambling the lives of his passengers and some of his warriors against the possibility that there might be loot to be had. That was all. Felix felt his respect for the captain's business acumen rise in proportion with his resentment of it.

'Once we find the highway, what then?' Felix asked. He realised that every dwarf present had fallen silent as they waited for the girl's answer.

'I will let you know when we get there,' she said. Now they were in the forest, Felix realised her manner had changed. It was far more regal. She had assumed the bearing of someone who was used to being obeyed without question.

'What if something should happen to you?'

'You'd best make sure it doesn't,' she said, laughing, but it was obvious there was some real mistrust there.

'We'll do our best,' he said, as she got up and made ready to go again.

They found the road at noon. In many places it was overgrown. Long grass had sprouted through cracks in the stone giving the impression of great age. It was made of dressed stone, and there were weather-eroded patterns on it that reminded him of things he had seen a long way away on the other side of a continent.

'This looks a little like the stonework we saw on the Paths of the Old Ones, and the temples in Albion,' he said to Gotrek.

'Aye, manling. I wondered when you would notice. They are not exactly the same though. More like human copies of those ancient runes.' Katja shot them a sidelong glance.

'You have been to Albion?' she asked. Felix nodded.

'You are extraordinarily well travelled.'

'Some people would say so,' said Felix, pushing ahead of the dwarfs and following the path deeper into the jungle. He had very dark memories of the Paths of the Old Ones and no wish to relive them. Leaves from overhanging branches stroked his face. The screech of parrots mocked him.

'Come back, Felix,' he heard the girl shout. 'You are going the wrong way.'

'You think the Old Ones have been here?' Felix asked Gotrek as they strode along. The Slayer tipped his head to one side as he considered his answer.

'Perhaps. This is not orc work.'

Felix noticed that the girl was staring at them. 'What do you know of the Old Ones?' she asked. 'I thought only scholars and sorcerers possessed that lore.'

'Very little. We encountered some of their handiwork once. A long way from here. You give the impression of knowing more about them than I.'

'My father was a learned man in his own way. He claimed some pre-human race had made the temples and the city, but that the orcs had taken them over for their own. It's more likely that men lived here after the Old Ones and before the orcs. The Old Ones are long gone. I have talked with many scholars about them myself.'

'Ask five scholars about the Old Ones and you will get fifteen opinions,' said Felix. 'There is little known for sure about them.'

'I am more interested in the treasure, anyway,' said Katja, but there was something in the look of her that made Felix disbelieve that.

'The Old Ones left many guardians for their temples,' said Felix, remembering some of the vile monsters they had encountered in Albion. 'And much of their work was corrupted by the coming of Chaos.'

'Is that one of fifteen opinions, Felix Jaeger?'

'No, that comes from bitter experience.' Felix's thoughts turned to the monsters of Albion, ancient guardians corrupted by the power of Chaos. Could the same kind of creatures be present on this island? Felix feared it was all too likely.

Night found them still toiling along the ancient road. It had led them up jungle-covered hills and down into tree-filled valleys. It had passed near stinking swamps and festering bogs, but over time Felix knew that they were climbing slowly upwards towards the great volcanic peak at the mountain's heart.

'Could your father not have picked an easier place to bury his treasure?' Felix asked, surveying the seemingly endless jungle that lay before them. He felt every extra pound of the chainmail now, but was more reluctant than ever to take it off. He slapped a mosquito that had settled on his cheek. His hand came away splotched with blood, most likely his own.

'I think the idea was to make it difficult to find,' the girl replied with maddening equanimity.

'I would have thought burying it on an island not found on civilised maps would have gone a long way towards ensuring that.'

'Aye, but these islands are not unknown to pirates, merchant voyagers, and the dhows of Araby. Elvish ships pass this way occasionally as well.'

Her words caused a stir of grumbling among the dwarfs, which did not in the least surprise Felix. The animosity between elves and dwarfs was age old and bone deep. Just the faint possibility of elves finding this treasure would keep the crew searching from now until doomsday. Felix wondered if Katja knew that, and then wondered why he was so suspicious. Maybe it was this island, he thought. There was something about it that bred an atmosphere of fear and mistrust. He hoped that was just his imagination.

Ahead of them another small ruined tower emerged from the jungle. Urli returned from inspecting it. 'There's orc marks all over the place. Recent, but not fresh. Looks like there are green-skins on the island, for sure.'

'Good,' said Gotrek. 'My axe thirsts.'

Felix wished the dwarf had not spoken quite so loudly. He could not quite rid himself of the thought that there was something out there listening.

They decided to camp for the night in the ruins. It was warm, so there really was no need for a fire, but Felix was glad when they built one anyway. Dwarfs might be able to see in the darkness but he could not, and it would help to keep wild beasts at bay. Hopefully, the thick jungle all around would keep them from being spotted by watchful eyes.

Felix lay down in a corner of the tower, and watched the dwarfs draw lots to see who would stand sentry. He and the girl were excluded from the process, which left him feeling at once glad and vaguely insulted. He was sure it reflected some dwarfish prejudice against human hardihood, and he mentioned it to Katja.

'Perhaps they simply want sentries who can see in the dark,' she said. 'And I don't blame them. Now it's time to sleep.'

Felix found that sleep did not come easily. At night the jungle was just as loud as during the day. Things crashed through the trees. Raucous birdcalls erupted at odd moments. Out there he knew things were killing and being killed, and eaten. In here the mosquitoes whined annoyingly close to his face. The roof of the tower was long gone, and he could see stars through the clear patches in the canopy of leaves overhead. He felt infinitely far from home, and almost as far from safety. Even though the *Storm Hammer* was only just over a day's march away, she might as well be on the far side of a moon for all the difference it made. The expedition was completely isolated.

He wondered whether the ruins would contain an opening into the ancient extra-dimensional warren of the Paths of the Old Ones, and if so, was the corrupting influence of Chaos seeping through there? He shivered when he thought of the daemonic creatures he had encountered, and his hand stole towards the amulet that the elvish mage Teclis had given to him. To his surprise, he found that it was cool, which was usually a good sign. It grew warm in the presence of inimical sorcery. If the amulet was responding to some threat, it did not appear to be imminent.

Gotrek rose to his feet and moved towards the entrance. His cocked his head, listening for something, and then returned to his place, where he sat with his back to the wall and his good eye focused on the entrance. There was one who was not going to be caught off guard, Felix thought, stifling a yawn. Sleep snuck up on him before he was even aware of it.

Just before consciousness left him, he thought he saw a dark silent shadow pass between himself and the stars.

The rain woke him. It was dark and droplets sizzled down in the vanishing remnants of the fire. The dwarfs paid it not the slightest heed. Felix scratched at an insect bite and rose to his feet. He grabbed a handful of waybread and dried meat from his backpack and stuffed it into his mouth. The dwarfs and Katja were ready to move.

The rain was warm but it seeped through his tunic and britches and made him uncomfortable. He did not complain though, knowing that it would simply expose him to the mockery of the dwarfs.

'Where's Snelli?' Urli asked. 'If he wandered off and found a place to kip instead of taking his watch, he'll feel my boot on his backside. Snelli!'

The shout echoed through the wood, startling the birds and smaller animals, but there was no response. Once again, they found themselves searching for a missing dwarf. They found tracks leading off to the edge of the wood, where the dwarf had gone to relieve himself, but after that, just as with Mobi, they vanished.

'Sorcery!' Urli muttered. Gotrek shook his head. He looked upwards into the trees. Felix followed his thoughts. Maybe something had grabbed the dwarf from above and carried him off along the branches. His thoughts returned to the shadow he had seen the previous evening. It might just have been a figment of his imagination, but he thought he had better mention it.

'If you saw something why did you not wake us?' asked Urli.

'I was asleep by then, and it might just have been something I dreamed.'

'And it might not.' The dwarfs were grumbling amongst themselves again. They were a hard crew, but they were out of their element, and two of their number had disappeared without any explanation whatsoever. Felix could understand why they were upset. There was something out there that could sneak up on a wary dwarf in the dark without detection, and carry him off in silence. This alarmed them all.

Only Gotrek looked undismayed as they set out along the old road, but Felix noticed that even he kept a careful eye on the branches overhead. At noon they paused to eat. Ignoring all entreaties Gotrek moved off into the woods alone. He had drunk a lot of ale and reeled visibly. Felix thought this unusual, for normally the Slayer could consume barrels of the stuff without seeming the worse for wear. He decided he had better follow him, and strode off in the direction he had headed. He entered a grove of trees where the branches were thick overhead. Gotrek sat with his back to one of the trees, his head lolling drunkenly.

Suddenly a noose of rope dropped from above. This time the overconfident attacker had picked the wrong target. Before the loop of rope could close over his neck, Gotrek's eyes snapped open and he grabbed it. A sharp tug brought two tattooed goblins tumbling down out of the tree. The axe flashed and before either body hit the ground, it was relieved of its head.

'There'll be fewer disappearances now,' said the Slayer. Seeing Felix's quizzical look he added, 'They have been following us overhead all day.'

'You think there will be more?'

'Almost certainly, manling. The signs are getting more numerous the further inland we go.'

'That's reassuring,' said Felix, following the Slayer back to where the expedition rested. He showed no signs of drunkenness now.

SIX
Treasure, Traps and Guardians

LATE AFTERNOON FOUND them high up the volcano's side. The
road had ended. They looked down into a valley full of ruins.
Once there had been a large city here, Felix was sure. Several of
the ruins were stepped pyramids that reminded him of things he
had seen in Albion. Others were massive halls, perhaps palaces.
The jungle had swallowed the place. Trees filled what had once
been streets. Creepers obscured the walls of many buildings. It
had been an age since this place was occupied.

'Quiet as an elvish wake,' muttered Narli.

'This the place?' Gotrek asked. Katja nodded.

'I hope we don't have to search it all,' said Urli.

'No. We find the central hall. That's where my father left his
treasure.'

'And this magical jewel?' said Gotrek.

'That's there too.'

'Let's get on with it then.'

They pressed on through the heavy undergrowth and down
into the ruins of the dead city.

'Quiet here, isn't it?' said Felix.

'It was until you started talking, manling,' said Gotrek. The
Slayer seemed pre-occupied, straining to hear something, his
head tracking from side to side warily.

'It is though,' Felix insisted. The quiet was unnerving after the cacophony of the jungle. It seemed like even the beasts were scared into silence here, and Felix did not blame them.

Katja led them onwards through the streets. They were laid out in a rectangular grid pattern between the pyramids and the palaces. They would have been easy to navigate before the jungle came.

'Makes you think, doesn't it?' he said to Katja, just to break the unnerving quiet.

'About what?' she asked. Like the Slayer, she seemed preoccupied, but in her case it was doubtless because she was so near to finding her father's legacy. Felix could see the tension and excitement in her very stance. Her face was pale. Felix doubted it was because of fear.

'About how this happened. Maybe one day Altdorf will be like this, swallowed by the endless forests.'

'We can only hope, manling,' muttered Gotrek. He glanced at the nearest tree as if considering taking his axe to it. 'I hate trees,' he muttered apropos of nothing.

'You've come to the wrong place then,' said Felix.

Urli returned from scouting along a sidestreet. 'There are orcs here,' he said. 'In this city. Tracks are everywhere. Climbed up onto the roof. I thought I saw our friend Goldtusk and a horde of goblins.'

Felix looked at the dwarf. 'What is he doing here?'

'He knows the treasure is here somewhere,' said Katja. 'I told him.'

'It's more than you told us,' said Felix. 'When did you get so friendly with him?'

Felix noticed that Katja's expression was angry. Her fingers were flexing in complicated patterns that reminded him of the way Max Schreiber's used to when he was about to cast a spell. Did the girl know sorcery, Felix wondered? Abruptly she seemed to realise what she was doing and her expression changed.

'When he threatened to torture me,' she said. 'I had to tell him something.'

'If we hang about here,' said Urli. 'He'll come and torture us all. He has quite an army of those little savages.'

'Excellent,' muttered Gotrek. 'Lead me to them.'

'At least let us get the treasure first before you start a fight,' said the marine. 'Not all of us have shaved our heads.'

Gotrek considered this. Like any dwarf he was subject to gold-lust.

'Good idea,' he said. 'First the gold, then the killing.'

The place had once been a palace, and a big one, perhaps the home of the city's ruler. Katja led them through one massive entranceway and down a long hall. Felix was in no way surprised to see that this was lit by glowing green gems, set in the ceiling. Such gems had lit the Temple of the Old Ones on Albion.

A strange glow coming from one of the chambers attracted Felix's attention. Cautiously he moved through the doorway to check it out.

As he did so, hot air washed over his face. His eyes felt suddenly dry, and his skin taut. He moved cautiously forward, with the Slayer at his side. Ahead of them was a pit from which emerged an orange-red glow. He made his way to the very edge and saw a long way below what looked like molten rock.

'Lava,' said Gotrek. He looked baffled. 'Why would anyone build a palace with vents leading down into a lava flow?'

'Perhaps they wanted to heat the place,' said Felix, not entirely facetiously. The Slayer shook his head as if he took the suggestion seriously.

'On a tropical island? No. They must have had some other purpose.'

'Sorcery?' Felix asked. He could not imagine how this could be but it was one possible explanation.

'Maybe,' said Gotrek. 'Perhaps it was a place of sacrifice?'

Felix shivered. The Slayer's words made a terrible sort of sense. 'You mean they propitiated the mountain with human sacrifices?'

'They would not have to be human, manling. But yes. It would not be the first time this sort of thing has occurred in history.'

'The Old Ones were too civilised for that,' said Felix.

'No one, least of all you, knows what the Old Ones were like. Perhaps they were some sort of degenerate remnant of the Old Ones who fell into barbarism. Or perhaps this place was not built by the Old Ones, but one of their slave races, or someone else entirely.'

Felix could see something about this place had caught the Slayer's imagination. That had been just about the longest speech he had ever heard Gotrek make that did not concern the sad decline of human civilisation or how much better things were in the old days. He sensed eyes on them and turned to see Katja and the dwarfs standing in the doorway staring at them. The dwarfs looked impatient. The girl looked thoughtful. He wondered how much of what they had said had been overheard.

'We'd best be getting on,' said Urli. 'There's greenskins about, remember?'

Gotrek looked contemplatively into the firepit for a moment, then spat into it. Felix felt no inclination to do the same. He was too busy wondering what it would be like being thrown into that pit. He did not want to consider what thoughts might run through his mind during that last long fall. He stood looking into it for a while, until he realised that the others had left without him, then he raced to catch up. Instinct told him that this was no place to wander alone.

They made their way down a central aisle until they came to a large square, open to the sky, with an altar in it. The altar was covered in carvings of some sort of lizard-like beings.

'This is the place,' she said.

'I don't see any treasure,' said Urli.

'My father discovered this by accident,' she said, moving over and beginning to twist the carvings on the altar. Gotrek nodded as if he understood what she was doing. He strode straight over to one gargoyle and tugged at it. Instead of breaking, it moved, and a moment later there was a grinding sound as the altar slowly slid into a new position, revealing a flight of stairs leading down into the darkness below.

'Amazing that he managed to inscribe all this on the lid of a jewellery box,' said Felix sardonically. Katja shrugged.

'There was a tale he told me when I was a child, about a princess and a dragon and a hidden treasure. As soon as I saw this altar I recognised it, and knew what to do.'

'Whatever you say.'

'Why do you doubt me, Felix Jaeger?'

'I don't doubt you. I just think there are things you are not telling us.'

'Of course there are. When this is over and we have time I will gladly tell you the story of my entire life if you so desire, but at the moment we must hurry.' She strode down into the stairwell and vanished. Events were moving too fast now. There were orcs about, and Felix felt sure that Katja was deceiving them in some way.

'I wonder if this goes all the way down into the lava pits?' said Gotrek nastily. Felix wished he hadn't.

They emerged into a vault. There were more patterns woven into the floor and Felix did not need to be a magician to know that they were of some sorcerous significance. He wished that

Max Schreiber, or even Teclis, were here to tell him what they were. Well, perhaps not the elf, not with all these dwarfs present.

It was sweltering hot down here. All of their faces glistened with sweat. Felix felt like he had been stuck inside an oven. He looked over at Katja. There was a peculiar look of triumph on her face. She must be very pleased at getting so close to her father's treasure, he thought. Or perhaps it was something else.

'Be careful,' she said. 'Try not to step on any of those lines.'

'Why not?' Gotrek demanded. 'Scared it will bring us bad luck?'

'No. They form some sort of protective spell here.'

'Now, how would you know that?' Felix asked, but she ignored him. She was already edging closer to the door on the far side of the chamber, carefully moving along the channels formed between the lines. It was like walking a labyrinth, but she eventually got to her goal without incident. The dwarfs followed her. Gotrek shrugged and then did the same. Felix watched them carefully. There was something very wrong here, but he could not quite put his finger on it. Then he noticed that the runes along Gotrek's axe were glowing. He touched his own elvish amulet. It was very warm, more so even than the heat down here would suggest. Perhaps Katja was right. Perhaps there were sorcerous defences here.

He doubted that it would make much difference if he told anyone. The dwarfs' faces were transformed by goldlust and Katja's by a strange exultation. Even as he watched, Gotrek touched a series of runes, obviously depressing some sort of pressure plate. The massive vault door slid open silently to reveal another chamber beyond.

The dwarfs gave a cry of pure pleasure and leapt through it, oblivious of Felix's shout telling them to wait. Felix could see the glitter of gold in that room, and of something else. Hastily he pushed forward, walking through the mazy pattern on the floor.

The chamber inside was smaller than the outer one, and it held gold indeed. There were piles of it on the floor. Some of it was in the shape of strange square coins with holes in the middle, some of it in the shape of odd draconic masks. There were also chests full of silver and gold that looked more modern and of human design.

For a moment, Felix felt himself being carried away by greed, just like the dwarfs were. They were, beyond a shadow of a doubt, rich beyond their wildest dreams of avarice. There was a king's ransom here. But it was what lay beyond that got Felix's attention.

At the far end of the chamber was another large lava pool. A pathway ran out into the centre and from the middle of the bubbling lake rose a stone spike carved with strange runes. Atop the spike was a huge gem. It glowed blood-red with its own internal fire. It was very beautiful and even to Felix's untrained eye, it was obvious that this was the greatest treasure present.

Certainly Katja thought so, for she ignored the heaps of gold amid which the dwarfs played and strode straight towards it. Only Felix and Gotrek watched her. The rest of the expedition were too busy whooping with joy. Despite his present avarice, Felix was watchful. He had been in many other treasure chambers and he had never found things so easy. Surely there must be some guardian present.

He was not disappointed. Even as Katja set foot on the walkway, lava gusted up from below. The heat in the chamber, already intense, became more so. Lava had begun to slop up over the edges of the pit.

In defiance of gravity, the lava continued to flow upwards and it flowed into a massive humanoid figure, at least half again as tall as a man. Its skin was molten stone. Veins of darker fire flowed across its surface. When it spoke, its words came out like the bubbling of a pool of magma.

'I am the guardian of this place, mortals. Begone, lest you bring doom upon yourselves and this island. The fire mountain's heart is not for you. Be warned the Ancients bound me here to protect their handiwork and see their spells did not fail. I will not fail in that trust!'

Katja stood for a moment and then looked over at Gotrek. 'Here is a foe worthy of your axe.'

'Indeed,' said Gotrek.

The lava creature bellowed, and stepped over the side of the pit. The floor bubbled where it set foot. There was a stench of brimstone in the air. The dwarfs hastily stuffed their knapsacks and pockets with loot, torn between greed and fear. Fear triumphed as the lava man advanced. A wave of heat came from it that was like the open door of a blast furnace. Gotrek licked his lips and moved towards it.

'What is that thing?' yelled Felix, kneeling to stuff a gold necklace into his own tunic and snatch up a fistful of the strange ancient coins.

'A fire elemental trapped in a body of molten stone,' Katja replied. 'Do not fear. Its long imprisonment has weakened it.'

'I recognise you now, sorceress,' bellowed the elemental as it reached for the woman, 'You failed the last time you came here. You will fail now. I am still strong enough to kill you all.'

'That remains to be seen,' said Gotrek, charging. Felix considered the monster's words. He could not help but feel they were making a terrible mistake here. What did the elemental mean about the last time Katja had been here? Surely she could not have come here before. And why had it called her a sorceress? A terrible suspicion filtered into Felix's mind.

The elemental gave its attention to the Slayer. Flames danced over its body. Molten stone extruded from its left forearm to form a shield. A sword of stone and fire appeared in its right fist. It met the swing of Gotrek's axe with the shield and riposted with the blazing blade.

Sparks flew on impact, showering over the Slayer. Even from where he stood Felix could smell burning hair and flesh. If he felt any pain, Gotrek gave no sign. He returned the creature's blow with one of his own which cracked the creature's shield and bit into its forearm. The elemental emitted a bubbling howl and struck once more. The weight of its blow drove the Slayer back. The creature strode forward again, and Felix could see that it left a blazing footprint in the stone behind it.

Taking advantage of the guardian's distraction, Katja had stepped onto the narrow platform, and advanced cautiously towards the glittering gem. Felix was astonished at her greed. Now was not the time to be thinking of grabbing loot, now was the time to follow in the footsteps of the crew, and beat a hasty retreat.

Briefly he considered doing so himself, but knew he could not. He was obligated to at least witness the Slayer's doom before making a run for it. No, more than that, he thought, he was obliged to make an attempt to fight the beast. The gods alone knew how often Gotrek had saved his life. Even if he sought his own death, Felix was honour bound to help him. Steeling himself, he advanced into the chamber.

With every stride the heat became more intense. It radiated from the blazing figure ahead. He was not at all sure how the Slayer withstood it. He forced himself to put one foot in front of the other, even though his skin felt like it was about to crack and his eyes felt dry as the desert sands. Even the dreadful heat of the deserts in which he and the Slayer had almost died of thirst was nothing compared to this.

Gotrek and the monster continued to exchange blows. The creature was much stronger than the Slayer, but Gotrek was quicker. He ducked the burning sword and sidestepped attempts to knock him from his feet with the stone shield. His counterblows bit into the creature's flesh, sending lava splashing like lost blood onto the floor. But the very success of the Slayer hampered him. Lava splashed onto his flesh, burning him. Nor did his blows appear to be effective. Each time the creature was hit, its molten flesh flowed together again, and it came on, apparently unharmed.

Felix wracked his brain for a plan. They had faced many monsters in the past, but this one appeared all but invincible, a product of pure sorcery, and it looked like only pure sorcery could stop it. Unable to think of anything better to do, he lashed out at the monster with his sword.

It was like striking rock. The shock passed up his arm along with a wave of heat. He noticed that even the tip of the magical blade glowed cherry red, and it was a weapon that had withstood dragon fire in its time. The elemental responded by lashing out with its shield arm. A wave of crackling heat preceded the blow and Felix threw himself backward to avoid it. He landed on his back and rolled to one side as the monster followed through. Its fist impacted on the floor and sent up a spray of molten stone that set his cloak smouldering. Felix was suddenly very glad to be wearing his armour.

A swift glance around showed him two things. Katja had picked up the gem, and Gotrek had aimed an enormous swipe at the distracted creature's back. Such was the force of his blow that the elemental broke in two. Its substance seemed to lose all shape and it became a pool of molten stone on the floor.

'At last, I have it,' said Katja. 'The Heart of Fire is mine.'

Her face looked almost daemonic in its triumph and, not for the first time in their career, Felix suspected that he and the Slayer might indeed have made a terrible mistake. She reached out and picked up the glowing gem. As she lifted it on high, the earth shook. From deep below, in the lava pit came a sound like the roar of a dragon.

'Foolish mortal, what have you done?' bubbled the elemental as it rose once more, taking on its human shape. 'You have doomed yourselves. That stone was all that kept the mountain quiescent. It was all that preserved the city until the master's return. Now...'

The elemental's words were cut off when Katja gestured and uttered a spell. A wave of cold swept over the monster. Its skin turned greyer as it cooled. Gotrek took advantage of the moment to strike it again, smashing it into a thousand pieces. Then he glared up at the woman.

'What is going on here?'

'I thank you for your aid, Slayer. You made a better ally than Goldtusk ever was, even before he turned traitor. Now I suggest you depart this place. Terrible things are going to happen here.'

'One of them will happen to you, girl, if you do not tell me what is going on.'

'This stone is an object of great magical power. Long have I coveted it... since before I was wed to Redhand. He was not strong enough to overcome the guardian. You were. Now I bid you farewell.'

Even as she spoke, her outline shimmered, and before either Felix or the Slayer could move. It faded and the woman with it.

'Wizards!' said Gotrek. Felix looked at the space from which the woman had vanished. He was still confused as to what had happened but he needed no great insight to tell him it was time to go. The whole structure shook and lava was beggining to bubble over the mouth of the pit. The Slayer seemed to agree, for he too turned to leave.

As he raced up the stairway, Felix considered what the elemental had said. In Albion, the elf wizard Teclis had told him that ancient leylines underpinned the continents, keeping some of them stable. It seemed that the same thing had happened here and that the power had been focused through that ancient gem. Now the gem had been removed, it seemed like terrible volcanic forces had been unleashed.

As they entered the old palace, he heard the howls of orcs and goblins coming from all around. The greenskins had followed them and were now trapped. From all around a terrible orange glow told him that lava was going to swallow the city. Briefly he wandered what had happened to the other dwarfs, then dismissed the thought. Now was a time to think about saving their own skins.

A yell from up ahead told him that he and the Slayer had been spotted. The corridors seethed with orc and goblins. Behind them lava bubbled upwards. The temperature had risen. Given a choice between being boiled alive and facing the greenskins, there was only one decision to be made. Ignoring the fact they were outnumbered a hundred to one, they charged directly at the astonished goblins.

Gotrek's axe lashed out, killing everything in its path. It clove right through spears and shields and bodies, leaving red ruin in its wake. Felix booted a goblin out of the way and took another through the throat with his blade. He strode along in the Slayer's wake, protecting his back, from any of the greenskins that sought to flank him. In two minutes of hard fighting, they had battled their way into another huge chamber. All around them the earth shook. Pillars had started to topple. Behind them orange light spoke of the onward rush of the lava. Felix knew that they had to get out soon or the palace would fall on top of them, and bring the Slayer's inglorious career to end with no one left alive to write its epitaph.

The sounds of carnage had obviously attracted more and more greenskins; confused and scared by the eruption, they seemed to be drawn towards the fight. In the centre of the chamber was a plinth, where once some statue had stood. Felix looked at the greenskin horde and realised that the end had come one way or another. He exchanged a glance with the Slayer, and saw only mad battlelust in Gotrek's one good eye.

'Let's go,' he said and launched himself forward into the fray once more.

They battled forward through the horde, hacking and slaying as they went. All around them was a vast press of greenskin bodies. Felix did not bother with subtle swordplay. He merely lashed, killing as he went. In these circumstances, attack was the best and only form of defence. Slowly, they pushed forward through the throng.

All around, Felix could see leering, gibbering faces. Drool dribbled from their lips and glistened on yellow teeth. Plate-sized goblin eyes glared up at him, lantern bright in the reflected light of the lava. Small figures thrust spears at him. Some he parried with his blade. Others were turned aside by his mail. Some scored his flesh, leaving bloody weals. He knew it was only a matter of time before one of them hit something vital. Nonetheless he fought on.

Ahead of him, Gotrek hewed and cleaved as if possessed. Blood flowed from dozens of small cuts, but nothing slowed him down. The terror he inspired in the greenskins worked to his advantage. Sometimes foes froze for a crucial instant before the axe connected. Sometimes they turned to run, and hurled themselves into the press of their companions, tangling themselves with others and leaving them easy prey for the Slayer. Gotrek moved among them like a tiger among small dogs, smashing skulls, pulping limbs and breaking bodies with every blow. Each time the axe swung forward there came a terrible slaughterhouse noise, like a cleaver smashing through flesh and bone, and more foes fell.

It seemed impossible that anything could stand in his way, but driven on by weight of numbers and the inexorable push of the crowd, the goblins kept at it. Ahead of them, Felix could see the plinth. A bound took him onto it, and a heartbeat later the Slayer followed. Together they looked out over a sea of green faces. The goblins screeched and yammered at them, brandishing spears and shields. Felix could make out details of individual faces now with their long noses and huge eyes and sharp, sharp teeth. Some wore collars festooned with spikes. Others frothed at the mouth as if rabid. At the back of the chamber, he could see Goldtusk with his bodyguard of orcs. The orc pirate recognised him and bellowed with hatred. He and his followers started to push their way through the throng. Felix thought it would be a good idea to avoid them.

The noise of falling stone and toppling pillars was deafening. The heat was intense. Searing yellow-orange light illuminated everything. In one brilliant instant the whole scene was seared into his mind, then the goblins pushed forward again, swarming over the base of the plinth and into combat once more.

Felix lashed out with his blade, severing hands that reached for his ankles. He stamped down, crushing the fingers of those who sought to clamber onto the altar. He smashed his sword into faces, slicing flesh and exposing bone. Goldtusk and his lackeys had pushed their way almost within striking distance now. He roared a challenge at the Slayer, brandishing both cutlasses high above his head.

Bellowing in defiance, Gotrek threw himself forward into the oncoming mass, like a swimmer diving into a sea of green. For a moment, it closed over him and then he surfaced, clearing a space around himself with his terrible axe, killing anything that came within his reach. Felix followed swiftly.

In a heartbeat, they were engaged with the orcs. Several of them swarmed towards Gotrek. Felix found himself once more engaged with Goldtusk. The orc's blows did not seem to possess their former savagery. 'Where is she? Where is that treacherous witch? Where treasure she promised? Tell me and you die quick. Else you die slow and painful.'

'That's an attractive choice,' said Felix, lashing out with his blade, determined to seize any advantage he could. Goldtusk wanted him alive; Felix had no such desire to preserve the orc's life. Sparks flew as their blades met. Once more Felix caught a glimpse of how appallingly strong the orc was. Even pulling his blows, he had almost managed to drive the blade from Felix's hands.

A spear point blurred in from the right. One of the goblins had obviously decided to take advantage of his distraction. Felix batted it aside and realised that he had left himself wide open. It was fortunate indeed that the orc captain wanted him alive, he thought, otherwise he would now be a headless corpse. As it was he barely managed to duck in time as Goldtusk smashed the hilt of his sword down on Felix's head. Even the glancing blow sent stars dancing before Felix's eyes. He felt strength drain from him like spilled wine. Desperately, he gathered the last of his strength and put it all into one savage blow at the orc. Goldtusk laughed as he parried it easily with one cutlass. He laid the point of the other against Felix's heart. 'Tell me or you die!' he said.

'Over there,' said Felix, pointing behind the orc. Goldtusk half turned his head. He did not see Katja, instead he saw Gotrek who had just finished butchering his lieutenants. The Slayer grinned evilly at the huge orc and attacked.

The duel was brief and intense. Axe and cutlasses flickered almost too fast for the eye to follow. Goldtusk sprang forward, aiming a sweeping blow down at the Slayer. Gotrek parried it with the blade of the axe. The second cutlass swept round and for a moment Felix feared that it would connect, but the Slayer brought up the haft of the axe, and the blade rebounded from the ancient rune-encrusted shaft. Gotrek jabbed the butt of the shaft into Goldtusk's belly. Air was expelled from the orc's lungs as from a blacksmith's bellows. He bent double, presenting his neck as an easy target. The blade flashed downward and Goldtusk's severed head rolled on the floor. Gotrek had only a moment of stunned silence in which to enjoy his triumph before the goblins let out a horrified roar and charged forward once more.

It was obvious that even the Slayer was tiring. He bled from dozens of small cuts. His skin had been burned in many places. Almost imperceptibly he was slowing. Felix knew that it would not be long before he was overwhelmed by sheer weight of numbers. There was no chance of survival.

Then from the back of the goblin horde came the sound of screams. Felix's first thought was that the dwarfs had returned in a vain attempt to save them, but a few seconds of inspection told him this was not the case. The smell of scorched flesh filled the air as the heat intensified once more. Looking back Felix could see that the rear of the packed goblin mass was being drowned beneath the oncoming lava. As their cries reached their comrades' ears panic was beginning to spread.

Felix did not blame them. He felt no great urge to be roasted alive himself. He bellowed, 'We have to get out of here now!'

'I am not running away from a fight with mere goblins, manling!' A savage sweep of the axe clove clean through one goblin and buried itself in the chest of another. There was a horrid sucking sound as Gotrek withdrew his weapon, and the goblin's still-beating heart was revealed.

Felix ducked the stab of a goblin spear and took the greenskin through the heart with his riposte. 'It's not the goblins I'm worried about, it's the lava.'

The goblins all around had begun to back away, the ones nearest cautiously, those out of axe reach less so. Gotrek and Felix crashed into them once more, driving the greenskins ahead of them like cattle. The fight had become a rout, although Felix knew it was less thanks to their efforts than the lava. Whatever the reason, he was grateful. Now all they had to do was get out of the city without being overwhelmed themselves.

Once more, the earth shook. Behind them, the pillars supporting the roof toppled, and the ceiling caved in. Hundreds of tons of rock crashed down, burying alive many of the goblins in the chamber. Any that survived would soon be covered in bubbling magma.

It was indeed time to get out of this place.

They stood on top of the valley, watching the streets below fill up with orange lava. Felix nursed his bruises and was grateful for the fact that the goblins, in their panic, had scattered to the four winds. Overhead, black clouds billowed from the mouth of the volcano as lava boiled up over the top of the crater. Soon it would reach the jungle and fire and terror would begin. Felix bent double and panted for breath. He was tired, but he could not stop the thoughts racing through his head. He felt he understood most of what had happened now. Katja had been the sorceress who had wed Redhand. She had accompanied the pirate on his last fatal adventure when they had found the jewel. No doubt Redhand had died in a futile effort to get it for her. She had made her escape and returned to civilisation and must have spent years preparing for her return to the island. Perhaps she had been captured by Goldtusk, more likely she had made a deal with him and had been betrayed. The runes on her chains had most likely been meant to contain her magic. Gotrek had proven to be an opportune means of overcoming the guardian elemental. That, or something like that, must have been the way it went.

'There goes Redhand's treasure,' said Gotrek mournfully, watching as the central palace was swallowed.

'Not all of it,' said Felix, producing the necklace and coins he had saved.

'There was enough to ransom a dwarf king down there, manling. That would not ransom an elf's doxie.'

'Some people are never happy,' said Felix. 'Let's see if we can find the others and get back to the ship?'

'I would almost rather stay on this accursed island than go out to sea again.'

'You may well have to if we don't get a move on.'

'At least there will be some goblins to kill.'

As they set off on the long trek back to the ship, Felix wondered if they would ever see more of Redhand's so-called daughter. He had a feeling somehow, that they had not heard the last of her.

ORCSLAYER

'At long last we were sailing home. After nearly two decades following the Slayer as he chased his doom east and south and east again, through Araby, Ind and Cathay, I was returning with him to the Old World and the lands of our birth. Years had I longed for this day, but when it came, it was not to bring either of us the joy or peace we hoped it would. Instead, we found terror and strife waiting for us the moment our feet touched land. My companion met an old friend, and was asked to honour an old oath; little knowing what horror and bloodshed would come of these things.

Before the nightmare came to its bitter, bloody end, I saw the Slayer happier than I had ever known him to be, but also more miserable. It was a strange time, and it is with great reluctance that I stir those sad memories in order to record them here.'

— From *My Travels With Gotrek*, Vol VII,
by Herr Felix Jaeger (Altdorf Press, 2527)

CHAPTER ONE

'ORCS?' GOTREK SHRUGGED. 'I've fought enough orcs.'

Felix peered at the Slayer in the gloom of the merchant ship's cramped forward cabin. The thick-muscled dwarf sat on a bench, his flame-bearded chin sunk to his chest, an immense stein of ale in one massive fist, and a broached half-keg at his side. The only illumination came from a small porthole – a rippling, sea-sick-green reflection from the waves outside.

'But they've blockaded Barak Varr,' said Felix. 'We won't be able to dock. You want to get to Barak Varr, don't you? You want to walk on dry land again?' Felix wanted to dock, that was for certain. Two months in this seagoing coffin where even the dwarf had to duck his head below decks had driven him stir-crazy.

'I don't know what I want,' rumbled Gotrek, 'except another drink.'

He took another drink.

Felix scowled. 'Fair enough. If I live, I will write in the grand epic poem of your death that you drowned heroically below decks, drunk as a halfling on harvest day, while your comrades fought and died above you.'

Gotrek slowly raised his head and fixed Felix with his single glittering eye. After a long moment where Felix thought the Slayer might leap across the cabin and rip his throat out with his bare hands, Gotrek grunted. 'You've a way with words, manling.'

He put down his stein and picked up his axe.

BARAK VARR WAS a dwarf port built inside a towering cliff at the easternmost end of the Black Gulf, a curving talon of water that cut deeply into the lawless badlands south of the Black Mountains and the Empire. Both the harbour and the city were tucked into a cave so high that the tallest warship could sail under its roof and dock at its teeming wharves. The entrance was flanked by fifty-foot statues of dwarf warriors standing in massive stone ship prows. A squat, sturdy lighthouse sat at the end of a stone spit to their right, the flame of which, it was said, could be seen for twenty leagues.

Felix could see almost none of this architectural wonder, however, for a boat-borne horde of orcs floated between him and Barak Varr's wide, shadowed entrance, and a thicket of patched sails, masts, crude banners and strung-up corpses blocked his view. The line looked impenetrable, a floating barricade of captured and lashed-together warships, merchantmen, rafts, barges and galleys that stretched for nearly a mile in a curving arc before the port. Smoke from cooking fires rose from many of the decks, and the water around them bobbed with bloated corpses and floating garbage.

'You see?' said Captain Doucette, an extravagantly moustachioed Bretonnian trader from whom Gotrek and Felix had caught a ride in Tilea. 'Look like they build from every prize and warship that try to pass; and I must land. I have to sell a hold full of Ind spices here, and pick up dwarf steel for Bretonnia. If no, the trip will make a loss.'

'Is there some place you can break through?' asked Felix, his long blond hair and his red Sudenland cloak whipping about in the blustery summer wind. 'Will the ship take it?'

'Oh, oui,' said Doucette. 'She is strong, the *Reine Celeste*. We fight off many pirates, smash little boats in our way. Trading is not easy life, no? But… orcs?'

'Don't worry about the orcs,' said Gotrek.

Doucette turned and looked Gotrek from bristling crimson crest, to leather eyepatch, to sturdy boots and back again. 'Forgive me, my friend. I do not doubt you are very formidable. The arms like trunks of the trees, yes? The chest like the bull, but you are only one man – er, dwarf.'

'One *Slayer*,' growled Gotrek. 'Now fill your sails and get on. I've a keg to finish.'

Doucette cast a pleading look at Felix.

Felix shrugged. 'I've followed him through worse.'

'Captain!' a lookout called from the crow's-nest. 'More ships behind us!'

Doucette, Gotrek and Felix turned and looked over the stern rail. Two small cutters and a Tilean warship were angling out of a small cove and racing towards them, sails fat with wind. All the fancy woodwork had been stripped from them, replaced with rams, catapults and trebuchets. The head of the beautiful, bare-breasted figurehead on the warship's prow had been replaced with a troll's skull, and rotting corpses dangled by their necks from its bowsprit. Orcs stood along the rail, bellowing guttural war cries. Goblins capered and screeched all around them.

Doucette hissed through his teeth. 'They make the trap, no? Pinch like the crayfish. Now we have no choice.' He turned and scanned the floating barrier, and then pointed, shouting to his pilot. 'Two points starboard, Luque. At the rafts! Feruzzi! Clap on all sail!'

Felix followed Doucette's gaze as the steersman turned the wheel and the mate sent the waisters up the shrouds to unfurl more canvas. Four ramshackle rafts, piled with looted barrels and crates, were lashed loosely together between a battered Empire man-o'-war and a half-charred Estalian galley. Both of the ships were alive with orcs and goblins, hooting and waving their weapons at Doucette's trader.

The merchantman's sails cracked like pistols as they filled with wind, and it picked up speed.

'Battle stations!' called Doucette. 'Prepare to receive boarders! 'Ware the grapnels!'

Greenskins large and small were pouring over the sides of the man-o'-war and the galley, and running across the rafts towards the point where the merchantman meant to break through. True to the captain's warning, half of them swung hooks and grapnels above their heads.

Felix looked back. The cutters and the warship were gaining. If the merchantman made it through the blockade it might outrun the pursuers, but if it were caught...

'By the Lady, no!' gasped Doucette suddenly.

Felix turned. All along the raft-bound man-o'-war, black cannon muzzles were pushing out of square-cut ports.

'We will be blown to pieces,' said Doucette.

'But... but they're orcs,' said Felix. 'Orcs can't aim to save their lives.'

Doucette shrugged. 'At such a range, do they need to aim?'

Felix looked around, desperate. 'Well, can you blow them up? Shoot them before they shoot us?'

'You joke, mon ami,' laughed Doucette. He pointed to the few catapults that were the merchantman's only artillery. 'These will do little against Empire oak.'

They were rapidly approaching the blockade. It was too late to attempt to turn aside. Felix could smell the greenskins, a filthy animal smell, mixed with the stink of garbage, offal and death. He could see the earrings glinting in their tattered ears and make out the crude insignia painted on their shields and ragged armour.

'Throw me at it,' said Gotrek.

Felix and Doucette looked at him. The dwarf had a mad gleam in his eye.

'What?' asked Doucette. 'Throw you?'

'Put me in one of your rock lobbers and cut the cord. I'll deal with these floating filth.'

'You... you want me to catapult you?' asked Doucette, incredulous. 'Like the bomb?'

'The grobi do it. Anything a goblin can do, a dwarf can do, better.'

'But, Gotrek, you might...' said Felix.

Gotrek raised an eyebrow. 'What?'

'Er, nothing, never mind.' Felix had been about to say that Gotrek might get himself killed, but that was, after all, the point, wasn't it?

Gotrek crossed to one of the catapults and climbed onto the bucket. He looked like a particularly ugly bulldog sitting on a serving ladle. 'Just make sure you put me over the rail, not into the side.'

'We will try, master dwarf,' said the chief of the catapult's crew. 'Er, you will not kill us if you die?'

'I'll kill you if you don't start shooting!' growled Gotrek. 'Fire!'

'Oui, oui.'

The crew angled the gun around, huffing at Gotrek's extra weight, until it faced the man-o'-war, and then cranked the firing arm a little tighter.

'Hold onto your axe, master dwarf,' said the crew chief.

'Perhaps a helmet,' said Felix. 'Or a... '

The crew chief dropped his hand. 'Fire!'

A crewman pulled a lever and the catapult's arm shot up and out. Gotrek flew through the air in a long high arc, straight for the man-o'-war, bellowing a bull-throated battle cry.

Felix stared blankly as Gotrek flattened against the patched canvas of the man-o'-war's mainsail and slid down to the deck into a seething swarm of orcs. 'The real question,' he said to no one in particular, 'is how I'm going to make it all rhyme.'

He and the catapult's crew craned their necks, trying to find Gotrek in the chaos, but all they could see was a swirl of hulking green bodies and the rise and fall of enormous black-iron cleavers. At least they're not stopping, Felix thought. If they were still fighting, then Gotrek was still alive.

Then the orcs stopped fighting, and instead began running to and fro.

'Is he...?' asked Doucette.

'I don't know,' said Felix, biting his lip. After all the dragons, daemons and trolls Gotrek had fought, would he really die facing mere orcs?

The lookout's voice boomed down from above. 'Impact coming!'

With a jarring crunch, the merchantman crashed into the line of rafts, smashing timber, snapping cord, and sending barrels and crates and over-enthusiastic orcs flying into the cold, choppy water. The side of the man-o'-war rose like a castle wall directly to their right, her cannon ports level with Doucette's deck.

Grapnels whistled through the air to the left and right, and Felix ducked just in time to miss getting hooked through the shoulder. They bit into the rail and the deck and the sails, their ropes thrumming tight as the ship continued forwards. The *Reine Celeste*'s crew chopped at them with hatchets and cutlasses, but two more caught for each one they cut.

A thunderous boom went off in Felix's right ear, and one of the man-o'-war's cannon, not fifteen feet away, was obscured in white smoke. A cannonball whooshed by at head level and parted a ratline.

Felix swallowed. It looked like Gotrek had failed.

'Boarders!' came Doucette's voice.

The merchant ship had broken through the orc line and was inside the blockade, but was slowing sharply, towing the grapnel-hooked rafts and the rest of the ships with it. The man-o'-war was turning as it was pulled, and its guns remained trained on Doucette's ship as waves of roaring green monsters climbed up the lines and the sides and clambered over the rail. Felix drew his dragon-hilted sword and joined the others as they raced to hold them off – men of every colour and land stabbing, hacking and shooting at the age-old enemy of humanity – Tileans in stocking caps and baggy trousers, Bretonnians in striped pantaloons, men of Araby, Ind and further places, all fighting with the crazed desperation of fear.

There was no retreat, and surrender meant an orc stew-pot. Felix sidestepped a cleaver-blow that would have halved him had it connected, and ran his towering opponent through the neck. Two goblins attacked his flanks. He killed one and kicked the other back. Another orc surged up in front of him.

Felix was no longer the willowy young poet he had been when, during a night of drunken camaraderie, he had pledged to record Gotrek's doom in an epic poem. Decades of fighting at the Slayer's side had hardened him and filled him out, and made a seasoned swordsman of him. Even so, he was no match – physically at least – for the seven-foot monster he faced. The beast was more than twice his weight, with arms thicker than Felix's legs, and an under-slung jaw from which jutted up cracked tusks. It stank like the back end of a pig.

Its mad red eyes blazed with fury as it roared and swung a black iron cleaver. Felix ducked and slashed back, but the orc was quick, and knocked his sword aside. There was another boom and a cannonball punched through the rail ten feet to Felix's left, cutting a swath through the melee that killed both merchants and orcs alike. Red blood and black mixed on the slippery deck. Felix deflected a swipe from the orc that shivered his arm to the shoulder. The catapult's crew chief fell back in two pieces beside him.

Another series of booms rocked the ship, and Felix thought the orcs had somehow got off a disciplined salvo. He glanced past his orc to the man-o'-war. Smoke poured from the cannon ports but, strangely, no cannonballs. The orc slashed at him. Felix hopped back and tripped over the crew chief's torso. He landed flat on his back in a puddle of blood.

The orc guffawed and raised his cleaver over his head.

With a massive *ka-rump* the man-o'-war exploded into a billowing ball of flame, bits of timber and rope and orc parts spinning past. The fighters on the deck of the merchantman were blown off their feet by a hammer of air. Felix felt as if his eardrums had been stabbed with spikes. The orc above him staggered and looked down at his chest, surprised. A cannon's cleaning rod was sticking out from between his ribs, the bristly head dripping with gore. It toppled forwards.

Felix rolled out of the way and sprang to his feet, looking towards the flame-enveloped man-o'-war. So Gotrek had done it after all. But at what cost? Surely there was no way the dwarf could have survived?

Out of the boiling fireball toppled the man-o'-war's mainmast, crashing towards the merchantman's deck like a felled tree – and racing out across it, half climbing, half running, was a broad, compact figure, face and skin as black as iron, red crest and beard smouldering and singed. The top of the mast smashed down through the merchantman's rail and pulverised a knot of goblins that was just climbing over. With a wild roar, Gotrek leapt from this

makeshift bridge into the merchantman's waist, right in the middle
of the crowd of orcs that was pushing Doucette's crew back towards
the sterncastle with heavy losses.

The Slayer spun as he landed, axe outstretched, and a dozen orcs and
goblins went down at once, spines and legs and necks severed. Their
companions turned to face him, and seven more went down. Heartened, the merchant crew pressed forwards, attacking the confused orcs.
Unfortunately, more were running across the rafts, and the merchantman was still caught in a net of grapnels, and pinned in place by the
fallen mast.

Felix leapt the forecastle rail, yelling to Doucette as he plunged into
the circle of orcs and goblins towards Gotrek. 'Cut the lines and clear
the mast! Forget the orcs!'

Doucette hesitated, then nodded. He screamed at his crew in four
languages and they fell back, chopping at the remaining ropes and
heaving together to push the man-o'-war's mast off their starboard
rail, while the greenskins pressed in to take down the crazed Slayer.

Felix took up his accustomed position, behind, and slightly to the
left of Gotrek, just far enough away to be clear of the sweep of his axe,
but close enough to protect his back and flanks.

The orcs were frightened, and showed it by trying desperately to kill
the object of their fear. But the harder they tried, the faster they died,
getting in each other's way in their eagerness, forgetting Felix until he
had run them through the kidneys, fighting each other for the chance
to kill Gotrek. The deck under the dwarf's feet was slick with black
blood, and orc and goblin bodies were piled higher than his chest.

Gotrek caught Felix's eye as he bifurcated an orc, topknot to groin.
'Not a bad little scrap, eh, manling?'

'Thought you'd died at last,' said Felix, ducking a cutlass.

Gotrek snorted as he gutted another orc. 'Not likely. Stupid orcs
had all the powder up on the gun deck. I cut some ugly greenskin's
head off and stuck it in a cook fire until it caught.' He barked a sharp
laugh as he decapitated two goblins. 'Then bowled it down the gun-
line like I was playing ninepins. That did it!'

With a screeching and snapping of rending timbers, the merchant-
man's crew finally pushed the man-o'-war's mainmast clear of the rail.
Grapnel lines parted with twangs like a loosed bow's as the *Reine
Celeste* surged forwards, straightening out before the wind.

The crew cheered and turned to fight the last few orcs. It was over
in seconds. Felix and the others wiped their blades and looked back
just in time to see the three orc pursuit ships smash together as they
all tried to shoot the gap through the blockade at once. Roars of fury
rose from them, and the three crews began to hack at each other

while their boats became inextricably fouled in the mess of rafts, ropes and floating debris.

Next to the three-ship squabble, the remains of the burning man-o'-war sank slowly into the gulf under a towering plume of black smoke. Orcs from further along the line were hastily cutting it free so it didn't pull anything else down with it.

Captain Doucette stepped up to Gotrek and bowed low before him. He had a deep gash on his forearm. 'Master dwarf, we owe you our lives. You have saved us and our cargo from certain destruction.'

Gotrek shrugged. 'Only orcs.'

'Nonetheless, we are extremely grateful. If there is anything we may do to repay you, you have only to name it.'

'Hrmm,' said Gotrek, stroking his still smouldering beard. 'You can get me another keg of beer. I've nearly finished the one I left below.'

IT WAS A tense twenty minutes, sailing into the harbour from the blockade, the crew warily watching the rafts and rowboats of orcs that chased after them from the floating barricade until they at last gave up and fell behind. As the *Reine Celeste* got closer to Barak Varr's cavernous opening, they had to pick their way through a litter of wrecked orc ships half-sunk around the sea wall. Signals flew from the lighthouse, which Captain Doucette answered speedily. Grim-faced dwarf cannon crews watched them from fortified emplacements below it. Dwarf masons were at work on the lighthouse itself, repairing a great hole blasted in its side.

Felix gazed in wonder as the *Reine Celeste* sailed between the two statues and into the shadow of the harbour cavern, staggered by the beauty and immense proportions of the place. The cave was so wide and so deep that he could not see the walls.

Hundreds of thick chains hung down from the darkness of the roof. At the end of each was an octagonal lantern the size of a nobleman's carriage, which provided an even yellow light that allowed ships to find their way to the docks.

The harbour filled the front half of the cave, a wide, curving frontage from which the branching stone fingers of quays and wharves extended. They were laid out with typical dwarfish precision, evenly spaced and perfectly positioned, to make manoeuvring in and out of the slips as easy as possible for the ships that docked there. There were thirty ships berthed there now, and room for at least fifty more.

A city of stone rose beyond the harbour. It was strange for Felix, who had visited more dwarf holds than most humans, to see such human structures as houses and mercantile buildings arranged along broad avenues under the shadow-hidden roof of the cave, but the dwarfs had made these surface-world forms their own. Never had Felix seen squatter, more massively built houses, all steel grey granite and decorated to the roof peaks with intricate geometric dwarf ornamentation. Even the smallest looked as if it could withstand a cannon-blast.

As they approached the embankment, a tiny dwarf steam ship, little more than a dinghy with a furnace, puffed out to them, and then guided them to an empty slip. A cheer erupted from the dock as the crew threw out their lines and extended the gangplank. There was a crowd of nearly a hundred on hand to welcome Captain Doucette and his crew as they stepped off the ship. Most were dwarfs, but there were a fair number of men as well.

The harbourmaster, a fat dwarf in slashed doublet and breeches, stumped forwards amid the general hubbub of congratulation and greeting. 'Welcome, captain, and twice welcome. You are the first ship to dock here in three weeks, since the accursed orcs set their barricade. A great deed, sir.'

Doucette turned to Gotrek. 'This one do the deed, sir. He blow up the man-o'-war with the single hand, hien?'

'Then we are indebted to you, Slayer,' said the harbourmaster, bowing low. Then, without further ado, he took out his ledger and got to business. 'Now, sir, what do you carry?' He licked his lips eagerly.

'I bring cinnamon and other spices from Ind,' said Doucette grandly, 'and oil of palm, patterned rugs of Araby, and little lace caps for the ladies. Very pretty, yes?'

The harbourmaster's smile crumpled, and many in the crowd fell silent. 'Spices? All you have is spices?'

'And rugs and caps.'

'Spices,' grunted the harbourmaster. 'What good are spices when we have no meat? You can't make a meal of pepper and salt.'

'Monsieur, I...'

'The orcs have been blocking the harbour for three weeks?' interrupted Gotrek. 'What ails you? Why haven't you blasted them out of the water?'

A dwarf sailor with his beard and hair in tarred braids spoke up before the harbourmaster could reply. 'Grungni-cursed greenskins got lucky and sank one of our ironclads, and the other is transporting dwarfs to the war in the north.'

'It's true,' said the harbourmaster. 'With so many gone to aid the Empire, we've barely enough dwarfs and ships to keep the orcs from

entering the harbour, let alone chase them away. They infest the
landside entrance as well. We're besieged land and sea.'

Gotrek and Felix glanced at each other.

'War?' asked Gotrek. 'What war?'

'You don't know of the war?' asked the harbourmaster. 'Where
have you been?'

'Ind and Araby,' spat Gotrek, 'chasing our tails.'

'You say this war is in the Empire?' asked Felix.

'Aye,' said the sailor. 'The Chaos hordes coming south again: usual
madness. Some "chosen one" and his lads making a try for the
world. A lot of holds sent dwarfs north to help turn them back. Our
ships carried many of them.'

'Chaos,' said Gotrek, his one eye shining. 'Now there's a challenge.'

'It were better if we left men's troubles to men,' said the harbourmaster bitterly. 'The orcs have taken advantage of the clans being
away and are rising all over the Badlands. Many small holds and
human towns have been put to fire and sword. Even Karak Hirn is
lost. The other holds have buttoned themselves up tight until
they're at full strength again.'

'But how goes the war?' asked Felix. 'Does the Empire still stand?
Have they reached... Nuln?'

'The harbourmaster shrugged. 'Who can say? The overland cara-
vans stopped coming more than a month ago, and every ship that
docked before the orcs strung their rafts across our mouth had a different story. One said Middenheim had fallen, another that Altdorf
was in flames. The next said the hordes had been pushed back to the
Wastes and never got further than Praag. It might already be over for
all we know. Grimnir make it so. These orcs must be put down or
we shall starve.'

Gotrek and Felix turned back to Captain Doucette.

'Take us out of here,' said Gotrek. 'We must get north.'

'Yes,' said Felix. 'I must get to Nuln. I must see if it still exists.'

Doucette blinked. 'But... but, my friends, it is impossible. We
must make the repairs, no? And I must take on water and supplies,
and cargo. It will take a week at least.' He gestured to the entrance
of the harbour, glowing orange in the late afternoon sun. 'And what
of the green ones? Will we make the escape the way we make the
entrance? It may not be so easy, eh?'

'Damn your excuses,' said Gotrek. 'I've a doom waiting for me.
Let's go.'

Doucette shrugged. 'My friend, I cannot. Not for a week. It is
impossible.'

Gotrek glared at him, and Felix was afraid he was going to grab the captain by the scruff of the neck and drag him back on board, but at last the Slayer cursed and turned away.

'Where's Makaisson when you need him?' he growled.

'Forgive me, harbourmaster,' said Felix, bowing, 'but can you tell me where we can find lodgings for a week?'

The harbourmaster barked a laugh. 'Good luck. The city is filled to bursting with refugees from every hold and human town in the Badlands. There isn't a bed to let at any price, and not much food either, but you've cinnamon to dine on, so you'll make out all right.'

Gotrek balled his fists as the crowd laughed. For once Felix was in a like mood. He wanted to punch everyone within reach in the nose. This was maddening. He had to get north. He had to learn what had become of his family – his father, his brother Otto. He didn't want to stay in some out of the way port while his home, his country, was ravaged by bloodthirsty barbarians. He had seen what the hordes had done to the lands of Kislev. That the same thing might be happening in the Empire – in the Reikland and Averland – while he was far away and powerless to stop it, was almost more than he could bear.

'Come, manling,' said Gotrek at last, turning towards the city and hefting his axe. 'Let's go make some empty beds.'

CHAPTER TWO

THE HARBOURMASTER'S prediction proved true. Gotrek and Felix visited thirteen taverns and not one had a bed to spare. Most had rented out their stables and haylofts to desperate refugees as well. Others had been taken over by the city as barracks and hospitals for the dwarfs and men who defended the city against the orcs in the harbour and on the walls of the dwarf fort that protected the port's landside entrance. Even the bawdy houses in the human quarter were taking in boarders, and making their girls ply their trade in downstairs parlours and alcoves.

Barak Varr's lantern-lit underground streets were crowded with dwarfs and men of every description, traders, sailors, merchants, gaunt farmers with their families in tow and their belongings on their backs, angry men-at-arms talking of retaking their castles or exacting vengeance on the orcs, lost children crying for their mothers, the sick and the maimed and the dying moaning and ignored in alleys and dark corners.

The long-time residents of Barak Varr – both dwarf and human – who had three weeks ago welcomed the refugees with open arms, were now glaring at them behind their backs, their patience stretched to breaking point. Supplies of food and ale were dwindling rapidly, and with the orc blockade in place, there was little possibility of more supplies coming soon. Felix heard voices raised in complaint and argument on every street they turned down.

By the fourteenth tavern, the Sea Chest, Gotrek gave up and ordered an ale.

'Enough drinks, it won't matter where I sleep,' he said with a shrug.

Felix was not so easy about accommodations, but he needed a drink too. It had been a long day. They shoved in at a circular table with a crowd of dwarfs and men in the uniform of the city guard and stared for a long moment at the foaming mugs of ale the barmaid set down before them. Beads of condensation ran down the sides, and a heady scent of hops wafted from them like a memory of summer.

Gotrek licked his lips, but didn't reach for the mug. 'Real dwarf ale,' he said.

Felix nodded. He too was mesmerised at the vision of liquid gold before him. 'Not that damned palm wine we had in Ind.'

'Or the Bretonnian slop Doucette served on the *Celeste*,' said Gotrek. He snorted dismissively. 'Human beer.'

'Or the sugar water they served in Araby,' said Felix with feeling.

Gotrek spat a fat gob of phlegm on the floor, disgusted. 'That rot was poison.'

At last they could stand it no longer. They snatched up the steins and downed them in long, greedy pulls. Gotrek finished first, banging down his mug and leaning back, his eyes glazed, licking foam from his moustache. Felix finished a moment later and sat back as well. He closed his eyes.

'It's good to be back,' he said at last.

Gotrek nodded, and signalled the barmaid for another round. 'Aye,' he said.

After they had drunk their second and third in silence, Gotrek's brow began to cloud, and his one eye stared off into nothingness. Felix knew the signs and was therefore not surprised when a few moments later Gotrek grunted and spoke.

'How many years were we gone?'

Felix shrugged. 'I can't remember. Too long, at any rate.'

'And still alive.' Gotrek wiped the foam from his moustache and traced distracted circles on the patinated planks of the table. 'My best dooms are behind me, manling. I've slain trolls, vampires, giants, dragons, daemons, and each was to be my death. If they couldn't kill me, what will? Am I to spend the next three hundred years killing skaven and grobi? A Slayer must die to be complete.' He raised his axe high into the air, holding the haft by the very end so that the razor sharp edge glinted in the light. 'The axe must fall.'

'Gotrek…' said Felix uneasily.

Gotrek blinked blankly at the gleaming blade, then let it drop.

'Gotrek!' Felix squawked.

Gotrek stopped the blade a hairsbreadth from his nose as he caught it again, and then lowered it to his side as if he had done nothing untoward. 'Imagine a Slayer who died of old age. Pathetic.' He sighed, then took another long draught.

Felix's heart was pounding with reaction. He wanted to scream at the dwarf for being a fool, but after years in his company, he knew that any protestations would only make Gotrek dig his heels in and do something even more stupid.

'We must go north,' Gotrek continued after a moment. 'That daemon was the beast that came closest to killing me. I want another go at–'

'Pardon, Slayer,' said a voice behind them. 'You are Gotrek, son of Gurni?'

Gotrek and Felix turned, hands moving to their weapons. Two young dwarfs in travel-stained doublets and worn boots stood at a respectful distance.

Gotrek eyed them levelly. 'Who wants to know?'

The nearer of the two, whose sandy hair was pulled up in a clubbed topknot, ducked his head. 'I am Thorgig Helmgard, son of Thane Kirhaz Helmgard, of the Diamondsmith clan of Karak Hirn, at your service and your clan's. This is my friend and clan brother Kagrin Deepmountain.' The second dwarf, a round-faced youth with a brown beard even shorter than Thorgig's, ducked his head, but said nothing. His eyes remained fixed on the floor.

'We… We recognised your axe when you raised it,' continued Thorgig, 'though we have only heard it described.'

Gotrek frowned at the name of the hold. 'And that's excuse enough to interrupt a dwarf in his drinking, shortbeard?'

Felix glanced at Gotrek. That was unusually brusque, even for him.

Thorgig coloured a little, but kept himself in check. 'Forgive me, master Slayer. I only wanted to ask if you had come to Barak Varr to help your old friend, my liege, Prince Hamnir Ranulfsson, recover Karak Hirn, which was lost to the grobi not three weeks ago. He is organising an army among the refugees.'

'Old friend, is it?' said Gotrek. 'I wouldn't help Hamnir Ranulfsson finish a keg. If he's lost his father's hold it's no more than I'd expect.' He turned back to his mug. 'Off with you.'

Thorgig's fists clenched. 'You border close to insult, Slayer.'

'Only close?' said Gotrek. 'Then I've missed my mark. Hamnir Ranulfsson is an oathbreaking dog, not fit to shape tin or dig middens.'

Felix edged back.

'Stand, Slayer,' said Thorgig, his voice trembling. 'I would not hit a sitting dwarf.'

'Then I'll stay sitting. I don't want your death on my hands.'

Thorgig's face was as red and mottled as Felix's cloak. 'You won't stand? Are you a coward as well as a liar?'

Gotrek's hands froze on his mug and the muscles in his massive arms flexed, but then he relaxed. 'Go back to Hamnir, lad. I've no grudge against you.'

'But I've one against you.' The young dwarf's posture was rigid with a mixture of fear and fury.

'Fair enough,' said Gotrek, looking into his mug. 'Come back when your beard reaches your belt and I'll take your measure, but at the moment, I'm drinking.'

'More cowardice,' said Thorgig. 'You are a Slayer. You will be long dead by then.'

Gotrek sighed morosely. 'I'm beginning to doubt it.'

Thorgig and his companion continued to stare at Gotrek while the Slayer downed his ale, lost in moody reflection, and Felix eyed the scene anxiously, every muscle ready to jump away at the first sign of a fight. He had watched Gotrek's back in battles with daemons, dragons and trolls, but only a madman got in the middle of brawling dwarfs.

After a long moment, the awkwardness of his position at last became too much for the young dwarf and he turned to his companion. 'Come, Kagrin, we are fools to expect a Slayer to defend his honour. Do they not take the crest because they lost it long ago?'

Gotrek tensed again as the two dwarfs pushed through the crowd to the door, but he successfully stopped himself from going after them.

'What was all that about?' asked Felix when they were gone.

'Not your concern, manling.' Gotrek drained his mug and stood. 'Let's find another place.'

Felix sighed and rose. 'Another place will be better?'

'It won't be this place,' came the reply.

LODGINGS SUDDENLY BECAME available at the next tavern, a filthy dive called the Blind Alley, when two Tilean traders who had been staying there got in a fight with three Estalian sailors over the favours of a tavern girl, and all five of them were thrown out. There was a fierce bidding war for the room among the tavern's customers, but Gotrek showed the landlord a diamond the size of his thumbnail and the auction came to an abrupt end. He ordered a half keg of the tavern's best brew sent up and retired immediately.

Felix shook his head when he looked around the cramped, grimy room. There were mould stains on the walls, and the sheets on the two narrow cots tucked under the eaves were blotched and grey. 'That diamond was the gift of the Caliph of Ras Karim,' he said. 'It might have bought a townhouse in Altdorf, and you used it to pay for this?'

'I want some peace,' rumbled Gotrek, 'and if you go on about it, you can sleep in the hall.'

'Not I,' said Felix, pulling back his cot's patched blanket dubiously. 'I'll be too busy wrestling bed-bugs to speak.'

'Just be quiet about it.'

There was a deferential tap on the door, and two of the landlord's barmen waddled in with a half-keg. The mark of a Barak Varr dwarf brewery was branded on the side. They set it on the floor between the cots, then tapped it, left two mugs, and withdrew.

Gotrek turned the tap and let a few inches of ale slide down the side of the mug. He took a sip, then nodded, satisfied. 'Not Bugman's, but not bad. Ten or twelve of these and I could sleep in a pig sty.' He filled the mug to the brim and sat in the room's only chair.

'A pig sty might have been cleaner,' said Felix. He filled his mug too, and took a swallow. The rich amber liquid flowed, cool and pleasingly sharp, down to his stomach, and sent a warm tingle through his limbs. At once, a mellow glow spread over the whole room, a golden patina that blinded one to the dirt and disrepair. 'On the other hand, a pig sty wouldn't have this,' he said, lifting the mug. He took a longer drink and sat down on his cot. A slat creaked ominously, and he slid toward the centre. He sighed. 'So, is this what you mean to do while we wait out the week for the _Celeste_? Sit in this room and drink?'

'You have a better plan?'

Felix shrugged. 'It just seems a waste of time.'

'That's the trouble with men,' said Gotrek, 'no patience.' He took a drink. Felix tried to think of a better plan, but couldn't, so he had another drink too.

Four or five mugs later another knock came on the door. Felix thought it was the landlord again, bringing up another half keg, and levered himself out of the swaybacked bed, but when he opened the door, a prosperous-looking dwarf stood in it, four more behind him in the shadows of the hall. Felix recognised young Thorgig and his silent friend Kagrin among them.

The dwarf in the door looked of an age with Gotrek – though it was hard to tell with dwarfs – but considerably less weathered. His chestnut brown beard flowed down his green and gold doublet, bulged over a comfortable paunch, and was tucked neatly under his belt. A pair of gold spectacles dangled from a gold chain clipped to his collar. He had square, broad features and clear brown eyes, currently flashing with suppressed anger. 'Where is he?' he asked.

Gotrek looked up at the voice and glared balefully at the speaker from across the room. 'Found me, did you?'

'There aren't many one-eyed Slayers in town.'

Gotrek burped. 'Well, now you can go again. I already told your boot-boy I wouldn't help.'

The dwarf – Felix assumed it must be the aforementioned Hamnir Ranulfsson – stepped forwards, ignoring Felix entirely. 'Gotrek–'

'You set foot in this room,' said Gotrek, interrupting him. 'I'll kill you. After what has passed between us, you've no reason to expect anything from me except a cleft skull.'

Hamnir hesitated for a second, and then stepped deliberately into the room. It was an act of courage for, compared to Gotrek, he looked small and soft and fat. 'Then kill me. I've swallowed a lot of pride coming here. I'll speak my piece.'

Gotrek looked him over coldly from his chair. He shook his head. 'You've become a shopkeep.'

'And you've become a tavern bully by all accounts,' said Hamnir.

'I told your boy my grudge was with you. I didn't fight him.'

'I know our grudge, Gurnisson,' said Hamnir, 'which is why I don't come asking for myself, but for Karak Hirn, and all its clans, and for all the dwarfs and men of the Badlands as well. With Karak Hirn fallen there is no bastion to stop the grobi from raiding the countryside. It burns. Trade twixt dwarf and man has ceased. No grain for ale. No human gold for dwarf swords. The holds are slowly starving.'

'And how did this tragedy come about?' asked Gotrek, sneering. 'No fault of yours, surely.'

Hamnir looked down, colouring. 'The fault is mine more than anyone else's, I suppose. My father and older brother went north to join the forces fighting the Chaos invasion and left me with the running of Karak Hirn. As second son, I have dealt primarily with trade, as you know, and it has been my custom to come to Barak Varr to negotiate with the Tilean grain merchants, as they are known for their sharp practices and slippery ways.'

'No sharper or slipperier than yours, I'm sure,' muttered Gotrek.

Hamnir ignored him. 'So I left the hold in the hands of Durin Torvaltsson, one of my father's advisors, too old to go to war, and–'

'The orcs took the hold while you were away arguing over wheat?' Gotrek's disgust was palpable.

Hamnir clenched his jaw. 'We had no reason to expect an attack. The orcs were running wild in the Badlands, but they hadn't attacked the holds. Why would they when there were so many easier targets among the human settlements? But... but they did attack. We had been here three days when Thorgig and Kagrin slipped through the siege by night and found me. They said the orcs had come up from our mines, in overwhelming force. We were taken entirely unawares. Our alarms, our traps, all failed. Durin is dead, as are many others: Ferga, my betrothed, Thorgig's sister, may be one of them. I–'

'So you *are* to blame,' said Gotrek.

'And if I am,' said Hamnir, hotly, 'does it change what has been lost and what more will be lost because of it? Can a true dwarf turn away?'

'I am a true *Slayer*, Ranulfsson,' growled Gotrek, 'sworn to seek a great death, and I won't find that fighting grobi in Karak Hirn. I'm going north. There are daemons in the north.'

Hamnir spat. 'That for Slayers: vain and selfish. They seek great deaths, not great deeds.'

Gotrek stood, taking up his axe. 'Get out.'

The dwarfs in the hall put their hands on their axes and hammers, and stepped forwards, but Hamnir waved them back.

He glared at Gotrek. 'I hoped it wouldn't come to this. I hoped you would do the right thing and come to the aid of Karak Hirn out of loyalty to your race, but I see that you are still the same old Gotrek Gurnisson, still more concerned with your own glory than the common good. Very well.' He raised his chin, pushing his beard out like an auburn waterfall. 'Before the oath was made that birthed the grudge between us, there was another, spoken when we first became friends.'

'You dirty–' said Gotrek.

'We vowed,' continued Hamnir, talking over him, 'with blood passed between us, that come what may on life's bitter road, if called upon, we would aid and defend each other as long as there was still blood in our veins and life in our limbs to do so. I call on that vow now.'

Gotrek's single eye blazed and he advanced on Hamnir, axe raised. Hamnir paled, but stood firm. Gotrek stopped before him, trembling, and then whipped the axe down, so close to Hamnir's side that it shaved some stray threads from his sleeve, then bit into the floorboards.

Hamnir let out a relieved breath.

Gotrek punched him in the nose so hard that he landed on his neck at the feet of his dwarfs. They stepped forwards to cover him, but Gotrek stayed where he was.

'You've some gall calling on an oath, after what you've done,' Gotrek said as Hamnir tried to raise his bleeding head, 'but, unlike some, I have never broken a vow. I'll join your army, but this foolishness better be finished before the war is over in the north.' He turned his back on the dwarfs in the door and picked up his mug. 'Now, get out. I'm drinking.'

CHAPTER THREE

A WIDE BOULEVARD, the Rising Road, ran straight through Barak Varr from the docks to the back wall of the enormous cavern where the holds of the port's founding clans were built into the solid rock in the more traditional dwarf manner, each with a fortified front door topped with the clan sigil. The boulevard pierced the back wall and continued on, rising, straight and broad and gradual, through the earth to the surface, where it opened within a sturdy dwarf fortress, built to defend the landside entrance.

On this road, three days later, Hamnir Ranulfsson, Prince of Karak Hirn, mustered his army of refugee dwarfs – five hundred doughty warriors from a score of clans, along with dwarf smiths and surgeons, and bustling dwarf wives, overseeing wagons full of food, camp gear and supplies, all headed for Rodenheim Castle, a human keep near Karak Hirn where, according to Thorgig, the survivors of the orc invasion had taken refuge. The castle too had been ravaged by orcs, Baron Rodenheim slaughtered with all his vassals, but the green horde had soon abandoned it for fresh pillage, and the dwarfs had moved in.

Banners waved proudly at the head of Hamnir's column. The force was well kitted out with armour, shields, axes, crossbows, handguns and cannon – as well as provisions and fodder – for Barak Varr had helped outfit the army. Felix didn't doubt that this was because the dwarfs of the port wished Hamnir every success in regaining Karak Hirn and assuring the security of the dwarf race, but no doubt the fact that, with his force gone, they would have six hundred less mouths to feed probably had something to do with it as well.

Felix was the only man in the long column. This was not yet an army of general liberation. The dwarfs were going to take back Karak Hirn, and men were not invited freely into a dwarf hold, no matter how desperate the situation. Only Felix's status as 'Dwarf Friend' and Gotrek's 'rememberer' allowed him to join the dwarfs' solemn ranks. He stood with Gotrek near the front of the force while they waited for all the clans to form up.

There was a fair amount of argument about the order of march, with each clan claiming some ancient honour or precedent that would put them closer to the front, and Felix could see Hamnir standing in the centre of a crowd of clan leaders doing his best to keep his temper while he arbitrated amongst them.

Gleaming gromril armour covered Hamnir head-to-toe – if a little snug about the waist – and over this was belted a dark green surcoat stitched with Karak Hirn's sigil of a horn over a stone gate. A shield over his back had the same design, and he wore on his head an elaborate winged helm, the cheek and nose guards of which did not quite hide his lumpy broken nose and his two purple-tinged black eyes.

Gotrek swayed beside Felix, moaning, and propping himself up with his axe. True to his original intention, he had spent the last three days in their filthy room, blind drunk for the few hours he was awake each day. Yet it had been him – with a dwarf's uncanny ability to know the time under or above ground, in light or dark – that had woken Felix two hours ago and told him to get ready. Now, however, with nothing to do but wait and, eventually, march, the effects of the previous night's binge had caught up with him.

'Would you mind very much not breathing so loudly?' he growled.

'I could stop breathing entirely, if you like,' Felix said, snappily, for he too had been less than sparing with the ale the night before.

Gotrek pinched his temples. 'Yes, do. And don't shout.'

At last, after another hour of argument and re-forming, an order of march was settled upon, and the dwarf army got underway. They were accompanied by Odgin Stormwall, commander of the landside fortress, a stout, white-bearded old veteran, and a company of Barak Varr's city guard – fifty dwarfs in ringmail and blue and grey surcoats accompanied them. Odgin explained the situation above as they marched.

'The grobi filth besiege the fort,' Odgin explained as they marched, 'though they're not trying very hard to take it. Mostly, they're eating and drinking every bit of forage to be had within fifty leagues, and slaughtering every caravan that comes to trade with us. When they get restless, they make a run at the walls and we turn them back. Usually they just lob rocks and gobbos at us.'

'Why don't you just march out and destroy them?' asked Thorgig, who walked at Hamnir's side with his silent friend Kagrin.

Odgin exchanged an amused smile with Hamnir, and then nodded at Thorgig. 'Oh, we'd like to, lad, but there's more than a few of them. Why should we put ourselves at risk when we're nice and safe behind our walls?'

'But you're starving in here,' said Thorgig.

'Aye, and they'll starve out there sooner,' said Odgin. 'When they've killed all the livestock and looted all the towns within a day's march, their hunger will win out over their patience and they'll move on. They always do.'

'What if you starve before they do?'

Odgin chuckled. 'Your orc isn't much on rationing. Our lads may complain about tightening their belts and running out of beer, but we can feed the hold for another two months or so on biscuit and spring water.' He turned to Hamnir. 'Now, Prince Hamnir, here's how we'll get you away. If you were to march out of the main gate, you'd have every orc in the camp after you, but there's a hidden sally port round the back. It goes underground for a bit and comes up in one of our old barns.' He grinned. 'Orcs smashed it up a bit, and burnt the roof off it, but they never found the door.'

'And the greenskins won't see us when we march out?' asked Gotrek. 'There are six hundred of us.'

'That's what these lads are for,' said Odgin, jerking a thumb over his shoulder at the company of Barak Varr city guard. 'It's them who'll march out the front gate, and when the greenskins come running to get stuck in, you will slip out of the sally port and away.'

Hamnir blinked and looked back at the dwarf guards. 'They mean to sacrifice themselves for us? That is more than we wished. I–'

'Oh, it won't be any sacrifice. They're like that shortbeard there,' he said, nodding at Thorgig. 'They've been wanting to come to grips with the greenskins since this business started. We'll pull them out of the fire once you're away. They'll go no further than the gate.'

'Nonetheless,' said Hamnir, 'they put themselves in danger in order to help us, and I thank them for it.'

'There isn't a dwarf in Barak Varr that doesn't want to see Karak Hirn restored, Prince Hamnir,' said Odgin. 'The Hirn holds the

Black Mountains together. It protects the Badlands. We'd not survive long without it.'

WHEN HAMNIR'S COLUMN reached the top of the Rising Road, great granite doors swung out and they marched into the wide central courtyard of Kazad Varr, a massively built dwarf fortress with thick walls and square towers at each corner. Felix looked behind him, momentarily disoriented. He had expected the doors to the long tunnel to be built into a cliff-face or mountainside, as was usual with the entrances of dwarf holds, but here there was no mountain. The doors were built into a squat, arrow-slotted stone structure that occupied the space where, in a castle, the central keep would have stood.

Within the fort all was calm. Dwarf quarrellers in blue and grey surcoats patrolled the walls, and cannon crews watched from the towers. They hardly raised their heads when, after a distant thud, an oddly shaped missile arced high over the wall and slammed, screaming, into the flagstones, not thirty feet to Hamnir's left.

Felix looked at it. It was a scrawny goblin with a spiked helmet and poorly made leather wings tied to its arms. Its neck was broken and its body burst. Blood spread out from it in black rivulets.

'Idiots,' said Gotrek.

Felix blinked at him. 'But you... on the ship, you did the same...'

'I made it.'

As the dwarfs of the Barak Varr city guard continued on towards the main gate, Odgin led Hamnir and his army towards the back of the fort to a stone stables, built out from the back wall. At the rear of the stables, Odgin unlocked and opened a pair of big ironbound doors. Behind them, a broad ramp descended into a tunnel that passed under the fortress wall.

'Hold here until the guard is fully engaged and the signal is given,' said Odgin. 'When you leave the barn, march straight ahead. The west gate of the old pasture wall is only a hundred yards beyond, and once through it, your force will be shielded from the eyes of the orcs.'

Gotrek spat, a disgusted sneer twisting his face. Felix smirked. Even when it made tactical sense, Gotrek didn't care to hide from an enemy.

There was a short wait. Then, from across the fortress came the clatter of chains and gears, and Felix could see the huge doors of the main gate swinging out and the portcullis rising. With a fierce shout, the Barak Varr guard marched forwards into the mouth of the gate, helms and axe blades flashing in the morning sun.

A rising roar from beyond the wall echoed their shout. It grew louder and more savage with each second.

'They've seen the bait,' said Thorgig, chewing his lip. It looked to Felix as if the young dwarf would rather be at the main gate than here.

Soon after came the unmistakable sound of two armies slamming together shield to shield and axe to axe. Thorgig's eyes glowed, and the other dwarfs shifted restlessly, gripping their weapons and muttering to themselves.

Gotrek groaned and massaged his temples. 'Don't suppose they could fight quietly?' he grumbled.

The sound of battle intensified. Felix could see violent movement in the open arch of the main gate – flashes of steel, falling bodies, surging lines of green and grey.

Finally, a flutter of red came from the wall above the gate – a banner waving back and forth.

'That's it,' said Odgin. 'The whole horde's coming now. Off you go.'

Hamnir saluted Odgin, fist over his heart. 'You have my thanks, Odgin Stormwall. Karak Hirn will not forget this.'

Odgin returned the salute, grinning. 'Remember it next time we come to trade sea pearls for sword steel, prince.'

Hamnir motioned his troops forward and marched down the ramp into the tunnel. It was a cramped space compared to the Rising Road, with only room enough for four dwarfs to march abreast. After less than two hundred paces it ended in another ramp, rising, it seemed, to a blank ceiling.

Hamnir called a halt as Thorgig stepped to a lever in the left wall.

'Companies ready!' called Hamnir.

The dwarfs drew their axes and hammers. Quarrellers set bolts on strings. Gotrek took a drink from his canteen. Felix hefted his sword, nervous.

'Open!' called Hamnir.

Thorgig pulled the lever. With a rumble of hidden gears, the ceiling rose and split, and bright morning sunlight poured into the darkness.

Hamnir raised his axe. 'Forward, sons of Grungni! March!'

The column started up the ramp, Hamnir in the lead, Gotrek and Felix in the first rank with Thorgig and Kagrin. They came up in a ruined barn. The building was roofless – the walls mere heaps of rubble. Skeletons of sheep and cattle were littered everywhere, bits of rotting meat still stuck to them.

As the dwarfs stepped from the barn and began marching towards the pasture gate directly ahead of them, Felix looked around at the orc camp to their right – an endless clutter of ragged skin tents, gutted and toppled outbuildings, make-shift boar pens and refuse, that spread out in all directions from the front gate of the dwarf fortress. Crude, leering faces were painted on the tents in blood and dung. Flies buzzed over heaps of rotting garbage on which human bodies and bones had been tossed. Primitive totems hung above the bigger tents, proclaiming the dominance of this or that chieftain.

From all over this shambles, orcs ran towards the main gate. The entire camp seethed with movement. Warbosses and their lieutenants chivvied their fractious troops towards the open gate with curses, kicks and slaps. Hulking green warriors snatched up their weapons and beat their chests. Tiny goblins unleashed fang-toothed, four-legged beasts that looked like deformed pigs. Blood-daubed war banners, decorated with severed human and dwarf heads, waved above swarms of enraged orcs, all roaring challenges.

There was a mob mustering directly behind a stand of tents just to the right of the dwarf column – so close that Felix could have seen the yellows of their eyes if they had been facing towards them.

The bulk of the fort was between Hamnir's force and the main gate, so it was impossible to see how well the Barak Varr guards were faring, but the sound of steel on steel still rang in Felix's ears, so he knew they weren't dead yet.

Thorgig ground his teeth. 'Not fair,' he said, under his breath.

Felix shook his head. Imagine wanting to be in the way of that savage green avalanche. He, for one, was happy to be slipping out of the back door. He looked around. They were almost halfway to the pasture wall gate, but the tail of the column had not yet emerged from the tunnel in the barn.

Suddenly, from the right, came a belligerent shriek, very close. The entire dwarf column looked right. A goblin that had been trying to corral one of its unruly pets had seen them. It turned tail and ran, bug-eyed. The dwarf quarrellers fired, and a score of crossbow bolts flashed after it. They were too late. The little greenskin dodged around a tent and ran towards the mustering orcs, screaming at the top of his lungs.

'That's done it,' said a dwarf behind Felix.

'Good,' said Thorgig.

Orcs were turning and pointing and calling to their mates. Warbosses were screaming orders.

Hamnir cursed. 'Double time!' he shouted. 'Double time! Hurry it up!'

'You running, shopkeep?' asked Gotrek as the dwarf column picked up its pace. 'Can't stomach a good set-to any more?'

'If I lose half my troops here for the sake of "a good set-to"', snarled Hamnir, his face tight, 'what am I to do at Karak Hirn, when the battle means something?'

Gotrek glared at Hamnir's logic, but continued trotting along with the others, much to Felix's relief.

The orcs were coming. A mob of massive green-skinned warriors poured around the shattered houses, roaring for dwarf blood, bone and skin totems bobbing like grisly marionettes overhead. Goblins scampered in their wake, long knifes glinting.

Hamnir's head swivelled from them to the gate and back. 'We're not going to make it,' he muttered. 'We're not going to make it.'

'Then turn and fight, Grimnir curse you!' said Gotrek.

Thorgig looked uneasily at Hamnir. 'Your orders, prince?'

'Orders,' said Hamnir, as if he didn't know what the word meant. 'Yes, of course. I...' He looked around again, eyes showing white. The orcs were fifty feet away and closing fast. 'Grungni take it. Quarrellers, right! Fire! Fire! Column, dress right!' His voice was thin with tension.

The quarrellers fired, and twenty greenskins went down. There was no time for a second volley. The orcs were on them, slamming into the right side of the column in a piecemeal charge as the dwarfs belatedly turned out to face them.

Axe and cleaver met blade-to-blade and haft-to-haft in an impact that Felix could feel through his feet. Notched black iron smashed through shining dwarf mail and sturdy dwarf shields, biting deep into dwarf flesh. Gleaming dwarf axes chopped through leather and scrap armour, cleaving green orc-flesh and shattering white orc-bone.

Gotrek pushed to the front line and laid about him like a thresher, separating orcs from their sinewy limbs and their ugly, thick-skulled heads. Felix drew his dragon sword, Karaghul, and joined him, keeping just out of the sweep of the Slayer's great axe. He stabbed a goblin in the mouth and ducked a club like a tree stump, swung by an orc with brass hoops piercing his up-jutting tusks.

Dwarfs fell right and left under the orc onslaught, but the line never wavered. They took the orcs' savage blows on their shields with stoic determination, and fought back with grim, glowering calm. There were no wild attacks, no desperate lunges, only a steady, relentless butchery that dropped orcs one after another. Even Hamnir was calming, as if the physical work of swinging his axe was steadying him.

A mob of orcs broke and ran, pin-cushioned with bolts and driven back by the dwarfs' implacable attack. The gang beside them caught their panic and retreated as well, bellowing savage curses.

'We're turning them,' said Hamnir, dodging back from a cleaver swipe and cutting its owner's wrist to the bone. 'We just might–'

A thunderous roar came from the cluster of tents. Felix kicked a goblin in the face and looked up. An enormous orc warboss was stomping towards the battle with a crowd of black orc lieutenants surrounding him. He bellowed at the fleeing orcs and pointed an angry finger at the dwarf column.

The orcs cringed from his displeasure and reluctantly turned back towards the dwarfs.

'Luck of the dwarfs,' growled Hamnir, bashing an orc in the knee with his shield.

'The big one's put the fear of Gork in them,' said Gotrek. He seemed almost pleased.

The warboss smashed into the centre of the dwarf column, his black orcs and the backsliders beside him. His huge cleaver cut a bloody trench through a company of Ironbreakers. It seemed to glow with a greenish light. Dead dwarfs flew back, severed limbs spinning away as the boss chopped and hewed. His black orc lieutenants ploughed in after him. Bolstered by his presence, the orcs attacked with renewed fury all along the dwarf line.

Hamnir cursed under his breath. 'You wanted a good set-to, Gurnisson,' he snapped over his shoulder. 'On your way, then.'

Gotrek was already out of earshot, charging down the column towards the rampaging orc chieftain. Felix hurried after him, as did Thorgig and Kagrin.

'Want to see the crested coward in action,' Thorgig grunted. 'Maybe he'll punch the orc in the nose when he isn't ready.'

Kagrin smirked, but said nothing.

The warboss was huge – twice the height of a dwarf, and nearly as wide as it was tall. Its armour was a patchwork of scrap metal and looted plate. Dwarf breastplates served it for shoulder pieces. A necklace of staring human heads hung around its tree-trunk neck, woven together by their hair. As Gotrek and Felix got closer, Felix heard an angry, high-pitched screaming, and realised it was the boss's green-glowing cleaver, keening for blood. The runes on Gotrek's axe glowed red as it neared the fell weapon.

All around the brute was chaos – dwarf warriors pushing forwards to get into the fight, quarrellers angling to get a clear shot, the warboss's hulking lieutenants hacking and chopping right and left, trying to win favour with feats of mad savagery.

The warboss cut a dwarf in two, the cleaver slicing through the warrior's heavy ringmail as if it were butter. The metal literally melted and flowed at its touch.

Gotrek leapt up on a pile of dwarf bodies and swung his axe, its runes trailing red. The orc threw up his cleaver and the weapons came together in a shivering clash. Sparks flew. The cleaver shrieked like a wounded daemon. The warboss roared and lashed out, furious at being thwarted. Gotrek blocked and bashed back, and the axe and cleaver began weaving a whirling cage of steel and iron as he and the orc hacked and countered.

The boss's black orc lieutenants surged forwards, howling for blood. Felix, Thorgig and Kagrin closed with them to protect Gotrek's flanks. Felix dodged a serrated axe swung by a one-eyed orc, then stepped in and stabbed the monster in its remaining eye. It bellowed in rage and pain, striking out blindly in all directions. A wild swing gutted one of its comrades. Two more killed it and thrust it behind them.

Felix jumped back as the orcs slashed at him. There was no sense parrying. The massive axes would only shatter his blade and numb his arm. On Gotrek's left, Thorgig bashed an orc's club aside with his shield and chopped through its knee. It toppled like a tree. A cleaver caught the wings of Thorgig's helmet and knocked it flying. He blocked another attack with his axe. The force of the blow nearly flattened him. Kagrin, who had been hanging back, darted in and gashed the orc in the side with a beautifully made hand axe. Thorgig finished it off.

Gotrek parried another swing of the warboss's cleaver, then turned his axe so it screeched down the cleaver's haft and severed the orc's fingers. They dropped away like fat green grubs, and the glowing cleaver fell. The warboss roared and fumbled uselessly for it with its bloody stumps. Gotrek jumped up onto its knee and split its bony skull down to its sternum.

The black orcs stared as Gotrek rode the huge orc's collapsing body to the ground, and two died from dwarf axes before they recovered themselves. Three leapt at Gotrek, all trying to reach him first. He fanned them back with his axe and snatched up the warboss's cleaver. It crackled with angry green energy where it touched his skin. Gotrek didn't flinch.

'Who's the next boss?' he called. 'Who wants it?'

As the three black orcs advanced again, Gotrek tossed the humming cleaver behind them. They lifted their eyes, following its arc, then turned and dived, elbowing and punching each other to get at it. The other lieutenants looked back at the commotion and saw the first three fighting for the cleaver. They roared and joined the scuffle, their dwarf opponents forgotten.

The dwarfs pressed forwards, swinging for the orcs' backs, but Gotrek threw out a hand.

'Don't engage!' he shouted. 'Let them fight.'

The dwarfs stepped back. The orc brawl was turning deadly. One of the lieutenants buried his axe in the chest of another. Others were bellowing for their followers to come to their aid. Orcs began peeling away from their fights all along the dwarf column to rally to their leaders. Felix saw the glowing cleaver cut an orc's head off, but its wielder was stabbed in the back and another took it up.

Gotrek wiped his axe on the trampled grass. 'That's done it,' he said, satisfied, and started to the front of the column again. Felix joined him.

Thorgig glared at Gotrek's back as he retrieved his dented helmet and followed with Kagrin. He seemed disappointed that the Slayer had prevailed.

More and more orcs were deserting the dwarf line to join the scrum over the cleaver. Others were fighting amongst themselves. By the time Gotrek and Felix rejoined Hamnir, the dwarfs' line of march was clear.

Hamnir grunted, reluctantly impressed. 'Thought you'd take the Slayer's way, and try to fight them all while we died behind you.'

'I swore to protect you,' Gotrek said, coldly. 'I don't break my oaths.'

The column started forwards as the orcs fought on.

CHAPTER FOUR

THE DWARFS' MOOD, already grim because of the casualties the orcs had inflicted upon them during their exit from Barak Varr, grew grimmer still the deeper they travelled into the Badlands. Though they saw few orcs, signs of their rampage were everywhere.

The land had been plagued by the orc hordes for as long as dwarfs and men had settled there. Their invasions were as common as spring floods, and almost as predictable, and the hardy folk of the plains protected themselves from them as if from a storm. The few settlements huddled tightly around strong keeps, into which the farmers and their livestock could retreat when the greenskins came. There they would wait out the ravaging of their farms until the savage tide receded, then return to their land and rebuild.

This time, because so many men and dwarfs had gone north to fight, it had been much worse. There had been no one to stop them, and the orcs had followed their lust for slaughter wherever it took them. The devastation was entirely random. Hamnir's army came upon villages burned to the ground, everyone slain, and then, not five miles on, others absolutely untouched, the farmers harvesting their fields with nervous eyes straying to the horizon and look-outs posted on every hill.

They passed castles with banners waving, and others that were nothing but charred ruins. The farms and houses around these were razed to the ground, the picked bones of the peasants and their families strewn about the blackened circles of cooking fires. Nothing edible was left where the orcs had been. Livestock had been eaten, fruit trees and grain bins stripped, hogsheads of ale and wine drained and smashed.

The only men who hadn't been thrown into the stew pot were those who had been used for sport. Rotting corpses in ruined armour had been nailed, spread-eagled, to trees, crude targets painted on their chests. Dozens of black arrows stuck out of them. Most had missed the bulls-eye. Other corpses hung from the battlements of castles as warnings, savagely mutilated.

It was a grim march, and Gotrek was grim company, even more taciturn and dour than usual. He kept as far from Hamnir as he could, walking at the back near the baggage train, while Hamnir marched at the head. Only when the scouts reported orcs or other dangers in the vicinity did Gotrek return to the front and take up a guard position near his old companion.

The Slayer spoke to Felix hardly more than to Hamnir. He seemed entirely withdrawn, staring at the ground ahead of him as he marched, and muttering under his breath, ignoring Felix entirely. The other dwarfs ignored him too, eyeing him warily if they looked at him at all. Felix couldn't remember any other time in his travels with Gotrek when he felt more of an outsider, more alone. On all their other adventures, there had been at least a few other humans with them – Max, Ulrika – though she wasn't human any more, was she? Here, he seemed the only member of his species for a hundred leagues. It was a strange, lonely feeling.

At every stop, while the other dwarfs smoked pipes or cooked up sausages and mushrooms, or took their ease, and Felix penned the day's events in his journal, Thorgig's silent friend Kagrin took out a gold-trimmed dagger and a set of tiny files, chisels and gouges, and worked impossibly intricate designs into the pommel and crosspiece. He did these entirely freehand, and yet the work was perfectly symmetrical and precise, the epitome of the angular geometric style the dwarfs favoured. Even the other dwarfs were impressed, stopping in the middle of setting up their tents to watch him work and give him praise or advice. He took both without a word, only nodding curtly and bending even more intently over his work.

Felix watched him too, as much for his oddity as his workmanship. He had never seen a quieter dwarf. The race as a whole seemed born to bluster and brag, but Kagrin hardly ever raised his eyes, let alone his voice. On one or two occasions, however, Felix caught Kagrin frowning at him, only to look away as soon as Felix met his eyes. Other dwarfs in the camp stared at Felix as well, belligerent, challenging glares as if they were offended by his mere presence and asking him to defend the existence of his whole race. Kagrin's gaze was different – more curious than angry.

Then, on the evening of the fourth day, after they had made camp and eaten dinner, Kagrin sat down near Felix and began to work on the dagger as usual. It took him an hour of filing and tooling before, at last, he looked up at Felix and cleared his throat.

'Aye, goldsmith?' said Felix, when Kagrin failed to speak.

Kagrin looked around, as if fearful of being overheard. 'Er, I... I wished to ask, as you are human...' He trailed off. Felix was about to prompt him again when he finally found his voice, rumbling almost inaudibly. 'Are... are dwarfs well thought of in the lands of men?'

Felix paused. He didn't know what question he had been expecting, but that wasn't it. He scratched his head. 'Er, well, yes, generally. Their craftsmanship is highly praised, as is their honour and steadfastness. There are some among the less learned who look upon dwarfs with suspicion and jealousy, but most treat them with great respect.'

Kagrin seemed heartened by this answer. 'And... and there are places where dwarfs live peacefully beside men?'

Felix looked at him surprised. 'There have been dwarf enclaves in the cities of the Empire for a thousand years. You haven't heard of them?'

Kagrin's shoulders tightened and he looked around again. 'Shhh! Aye, I have, but I've heard... I've heard it said that dwarfs must lock themselves in at night, for fear of men out to murder and rob them. They say dwarfs have been burnt at the stake as enemies of man.'

'Who says this?' asked Felix, frowning.

'Dwarfs of my clan.'

'Ah.' Felix nodded. 'Forgive me if I impugn the motives of your clan brothers, but perhaps they are reluctant to lose a goldsmith of your calibre, and tell you tall tales of the barbarity of man to dissuade you from leaving.'

'I haven't spoken of leaving!' hissed Kagrin angrily. His fists clenched.

'Of course not, of course not,' said Felix holding up his palms. 'I can see that you are only curious. So, er, to satisfy that curiosity: I have never heard of dwarfs being burnt at the stake or called enemies of men. It is true that there have been accounts of mobs – instigated usually by jealous and desperate smiths – attacking dwarf houses, but it is rare. I haven't heard of it happening in this century at all. Dwarfs are long established in the Empire. Most of these passions cooled long ago. A dwarf who did contemplate setting up shop in the Empire would have little fear of trouble, and great prospects for success, particularly if he was as skilled a goldsmith as... well, as some I could name.'

Kagrin nodded brusquely, and then shot a guilty look towards Thorgig, who sat with a handful of other dwarfs, playing a game with stone pawns and dice.

He turned back to Felix and bowed his head. 'Thank you, human. You... you have, er, satisfied my curiosity.'

Felix nodded. 'My pleasure.'

He watched after Kagrin as he gathered up his tools and retired to his tent. It was strange to think of someone who no doubt had thirty years on him, as a 'poor lad', but Felix couldn't help it. It was clear that Kagrin felt torn between the lure of the wide world and the bonds of friendship and family. He had a hard road ahead of him, whatever road he chose. Felix wished him well.

AFTER SIX DAYS marching at the slow but steady dwarf pace, the Black Mountains, which had been a low saw-toothed line on the horizon when the dwarfs had left Barak Varr, filled the northern sky, an endless line of giants that stood shoulder to shoulder for as far as the eye could see to the east and west. Dark green skirts of thick pine forest swept up to the towering black granite crags that gave the range its name. Their snowy peaks shone blood red in a blazing sunset.

'Home,' said Thorgig, inhaling happily as he gazed up at the splendid peaks.

For mountain goats, thought Felix, groaning at the thought of all the climbing to which he would soon be subjected. A cold wind blew down off the slopes. He pulled his old red cloak tighter around him and shivered.

And perhaps he shivered for reasons other than the cold, for, although the dwarfs thought fondly of the place as home, it stirred in Felix less pleasant feelings. It had been not far from here that Gotrek and Felix had helped the ill-fated Baron von Diehl try to found a settlement, only to have it razed to the ground by wolf-riding greenskins. At Fort von Diehl Gotrek had lost his eye, and Felix had lost his first love. He shook his head, trying to keep her ghost at bay. Kirsten. He wished he hadn't been able to remember her name.

'There is Rodenheim Castle,' said Hamnir, a little further on, pointing to a stern, squat-towered castle perched on one of the forest-covered foothills that splayed out from the mountains like claws. 'It is a great shame that Baron Rodenheim won't be among those who muster here to help us. He was a true Dwarf Friend. May his gods receive him.'

The army started up the weedy cart track that wound up the hill to the castle, and soon began to see signs of its demise. The little village that clung to the slopes below it was shattered and burned, the stone houses roofless and toppled, the shrines desecrated. Cracked bones were heaped in corners like snowdrifts. A horrible stench came from the town well. Flies hovered above it. The red twilight painted the scene with a bloody brush. Felix had seen a lot of slaughter and ruin in his years with Gotrek, so it no longer turned his stomach, but it never failed to depress him.

The castle too was the worse for wear. Though its walls still stood, they were scorched and black in places, and great chunks had been knocked off the battlements. Flags with the insignia of Karak Hirn flew over the roofs of burned towers.

As the dwarf army approached, a horn echoed from the walls, and Felix could see stout figures carrying long-guns marching to their positions behind the crenellations. Torches flared to life above them, revealing dwarf crews readying catapults and trebuchets and kettles of boiling lead. The horn was answered by another, followed by cries and commands from within.

A white-bearded thunderer in well worn chainmail climbed onto the battlements above the gate, his finger on the trigger of his gun. 'No closer, by Grimnir!' he bellowed, when the head of Hamnir's column had come in range. 'Not until you announce yourself and your purpose!'

'Hail, Lodrim!' called Hamnir. 'It is Prince Hamnir Ranulfson, and I've brought six hundred brave dwarf volunteers. Have we leave to enter?'

The thunderer leaned forwards, blinking myopically. 'Prince Hamnir? Is it you? Valaya be praised!' He turned and shouted over his shoulder. 'Open the gates! Open the gates! It's Prince Hamnir, come with reinforcements!'

With a creaking of winches, the portcullis went up and the drawbridge came down. Both showed signs of recent battle, but also fresh repair.

Even before the bridge had thudded to rest, a dwarf was running across it, arms outstretched. 'Hamnir!' he cried. 'Prince!'

He was tall for a dwarf – almost four and a half feet, and powerfully built. His receding brown hair was pulled back in a club, and bright white teeth flashed through a thick beard that spilled down his barrel chest to his belt.

'Gorril! Well met!' said Hamnir, as the two dwarfs embraced and slapped each other's backs.

'I am relieved to see you alive,' said Gorril.

'And I, you,' replied Hamnir.

Gorril stepped back and bowed, grinning. 'Come, prince, enter your hold, meagre human surface hut though it may be.' He turned to the cluster of dwarf warriors who stood in the castle door. 'Away with you! Prepare Prince Hamnir's quarters! And see if you can find beds for six hundred more!'

Hamnir turned and signalled the column forwards, then strode with Gorril through the gates and into the castle's courtyard, as Gotrek and Felix, Thorgig and the rest marched in after. The yard was crowded with cheering dwarfs, and more were pouring from every door, all hailing Hamnir and the new troops.

'You made it unscathed?' asked Gorril as they pushed through the crowd of wellwishers.

'Some trouble with orcs as we left Barak Varr,' said Hamnir. 'Nothing since.' He looked at Gorril hopefully. 'Any word of Ferga?'

'Or my father?' asked Thorgig, urgently.

Gorril's brow clouded. 'None. I'm sorry.' He gave Thorgig a sympathetic look. 'You and Kagrin are the only dwarfs of the Diamondsmith clan to have escaped. Many died in the defence, and your father is believed to have locked the others in his hold. They may still live, though food will be growing short.'

Thorgig clenched his fists. 'I should be with them. If they are hurt...'

'You can't blame yourself,' said Gorril. 'You held your position as ordered, and then there was no going back.'

'Then I should have died.'

Hamnir laid a hand on the young dwarf's shoulder. 'Easy now. If the worst has happened, at least we will have opportunity to avenge them.' He looked around at the cheering crowd and nodded approvingly at Gorril. 'Thorgig told me you were sending for aid. It seems you were successful.'

Gorril made a face. 'Not so many as we could have wished. The other holds hadn't many dwarfs to spare. Too many gone north.' He shrugged. 'But let's leave that for tomorrow, aye? Tonight's for feasting!'

He turned to the crowd. 'Set the board, you layabouts. Your prince has come home!'

There was a great cheer and axes and fists were thrust in the air. But as Gorril led Hamnir toward the keep, two dwarfs pushed forward.

'Prince Hamnir,' said the first, a hammerer with a braided red beard. 'As leader of this throng, we ask you to dismiss the dwarfs of the Goldhammer Clan, who have dishonoured the good name of the Deephold Clan by denying my great-great-great-grandfather the rightful command of his Ironbeards in the battle of Bloodwater Grotto, fifteen hundred years ago!'

'Don't listen to him, prince,' said the other dwarf, a broadshouldered miner with jutting blond eyebrows. 'We are guilty of nothing but common sense. A troll had his great-great-great-grandfather's arm off at the shoulder before that battle. What was my great-great-great-grandfather to do? A general must think of what is best for the battle. We-'

Two other dwarfs pushed in front of the first two. 'Prince, you must hear us first!' cried one, a burly, black-bearded ironbreaker. 'Their paltry dispute is nothing compared to the feud that exists between we of the-'

'Enough!' roared Gorril, waving them all away. 'Will you badger the prince before he has his helmet off? Hamnir will hold council tomorrow and hear grievances then. Surely grudges that have stood for a thousand years can wait one more day.'

The dwarfs grumbled their displeasure, but stepped aside.

Gorril rolled his eyes at Hamnir. 'It has been like this since the others began to arrive. All want to help. None want to work with anyone else.'

'It never changes,' said Hamnir.

Gotrek grunted, disgusted.

'TELL ME WHAT happened,' said Hamnir. 'Thorgig and Kagrin told us what they knew when they came to Barak Varr, but their stories were a bit... confused.'

The feast was over, and Hamnir, Gorril, Gotrek and Felix, and a handful of the survivors from Karak Hirn were gathered in Baron Rodenheim's private apartments, which had been set aside for Hamnir, to discuss the coming action.

Despite Gorril's words, it hadn't been much of a feast, as supplies were low, but the dwarfs had done their best, and none at the head table had wanted for food or ale. Felix had had an uncomfortable time of it, for the dwarfs, being handy with their tools, and unwilling to suffer the indignity of trying to use human-scale furniture, had sawn down the legs of all the tables and chairs in the keep's great hall so that they better fit their short, broad frames. Felix had eaten his dinner with his knees up around his ears, and his back ached abominably.

Now, tired from the long days of marching, and a bit drunk from the many toasts that had been drunk to Hamnir and Karak Hirn and the success of the mission, he nodded drowsily in an unscathed high-backed chair, while the others talked and smoked by the fire in chairs edited for dwarf use.

Gorril sighed. 'It was a bad business, and very strange... very strange.' He sucked at his pipe. 'The orcs came up from our mines, but not like any time before: not in a great screaming rush that we could hear coming from the highest gallery, not fighting amongst themselves, and not stopping to eat the fallen and raid the ale cellar. They came silent and organised. They knew every defence we had: all our alarms, all our traps, and all our locks. They knew them all. It's almost as if they had tortured the secrets out of one of us, or there was a traitor in the hold, but that's impossible. No dwarf would give secrets to the grobi, not even under torture. It was... it was...'

'Eerie, is what it was,' said a white-bearded dwarf, an ancient veteran named Ruen, with fading blue tattoos at his wrists and neck. 'In seven hundred years, I've never seen grobi act so. It's not natural.'

Felix noted that, like Ruen, most of the survivors were white-haired longbeards, too crippled or enfeebled to follow King Alrik north to the war. Younger dwarfs had stayed behind as well, for someone had to guard the hold while the king was away, but most of those had died defending it when the orcs came.

'They came when we slept, and destroyed two clanholds outright – slaughtered everyone, dwarf, woman and child,' said Gorril, his jaw tight. 'The Forgefire and Proudhelm clans are no more. There were no survivors.'

Hamnir's hands clenched.

'As I said,' continued Gorril, 'Thane Helmgard was seen to order the Diamondsmith clan to lock themselves in. We don't know if they were successful.'

'Then there is at least a chance,' said Hamnir, more to himself than the others. He sat lost in his thoughts for a moment, and then looked up. 'How does it stand now? What do we face?'

'The orcs defend the hold as well as we did,' Gorril laughed bitterly, 'perhaps better. Our scouts report that the main doors are whole and locked, and they were shot at from the arrow slits. Orc patrols circle the mountain, and there are permanent guards watching all approaches.' He shook his head. 'As Ruen said, they don't behave like orcs. No fighting amongst themselves. No getting bored and wandering from their posts. It's uncanny.'

Gotrek snorted. 'So they have some strong boss or shaman who's scared them into toeing the line, but they're still grobi. They'll crack if we press them hard enough.'

Gorril shook his head. 'It's more than that. You haven't seen.'

'Well, I better see quick,' Gotrek growled. 'I want to be done with this scuffle and heading north before I lose my chance at another daemon.'

'We'll try not to inconvenience you, Slayer,' said Hamnir dryly. He turned to Gorril. 'Have we a map?'

'Aye.'

Gorril took a large roll of vellum and spread it on a shortened table between the dwarfs. They leaned forwards. Felix didn't bother to look. He had seen dwarf maps before. They were incomprehensible patterns of intersecting lines in different colours that looked nothing like any plan Felix had ever seen. The dwarfs pored over it as if it was as clear as a painting.

'So, they guard the main door,' said Hamnir, his fingers moving over the velum, 'and the high pasture gate?'

'Aye. They ate our sheep and rams,' said a hunched old dwarf. 'We'll need to buy new breeding stock.'

'And the midden gate? That lets out into the river?'

'Three miners went up it five days ago, to have a look. They came back down in pieces.'

'What of Duk Grung mine?' asked an old thunderer with an iron-grey beard. 'The Undgrin connects it to our mines. The grobi came up at us from below. We could do the same to them.'

Hamnir shook his head. 'It's three days to the mine, Lodrim, and then two days back underground, *if* the Undgrin is clear. The Diamondsmith clan may starve by then, and the grobi might guard the way from the mines as strongly as they guard the front door.' He tapped the map with a stubby finger. 'Do they patrol the Zhufgrim Scarp side?'

'Why should they?' asked Gorril. 'It's a sheer face from Cauldron Lake to Gam's Spire, and there's no entrance to the hold.'

'Yes there is,' said Hamnir, with a sly smile. 'There's the passage to old Birrisson's gyrocopter landing. You remember? Near the forges.'

'You're out of date, lad,' said old Ruen. 'That hole was closed up when your father took the throne. Doesn't hold no truck with such modern nonsense, your da. He burnt all those noisemakers to the ground.'

'Aye,' said Hamnir, nodding. 'He told Birri to wall it up, but Birri is an engineer, and you know engineers. He wanted to keep one of the gyrocopters, and to have a place to work on all the toys my father frowned upon. So, he walled up the passage at both ends, but set secret doors in them, and made a workshop of it.'

'What's this?' cried Gorril. 'The old fool built an unprotected door into the hold?'

The other dwarfs were muttering angrily under their breath.

'It's protected,' said Hamnir, 'engineer fashion.'

'What does that mean, pray tell,' asked Lodrim dryly.

Hamnir shrugged. 'That secret door has been by the forges for a hundred years, and none of you have found it. The one on the mountain face is as cunningly concealed. If dwarfs can't find it, could grobi? And Birri set every trick and trap an engineer can conceive of inside. If they found the outer door, they'd be chopped meat before they got the inner.'

'It isn't enough,' said Lodrim.

'How do you know of this, young Hamnir,' asked old Ruen, 'and why did you keep such a grave crime from your father's knowledge?'

Hamnir coloured a bit and looked at his hands. 'Well, as you know, I'm not so much my father's son – not the way my older brother is. Perhaps it's because he is crown prince, and I am only a second son, but I am not so hidebound when it comes to tradition. I was only a boy then. I liked the gyrocopters, and all of Birrisson's contraptions. One night I caught him sneaking through the secret door. He begged me not to tell my father. I agreed, as long as he agreed to teach me how to fly the gyrocopter, and to give me use of the secret workshop.'

'But, lad, the danger,' said Lodrim, 'to you, and to the hold.'

Hamnir spread his hands. 'I make no excuses. I know I was wrong in this, as was Birri, but I… well, I liked having a secret from my father. I liked having a place to go that no one else knew of. I took Ferga there a few times.' He smiled wistfully, his eyes far away, and then roused himself. 'The point is, no matter how the grobi learned our hold's secrets, this is one secret that only I and old Birri and a few of his apprentices know, and no one can make an engineer talk. They are the keepers of the secrets of a hold's defence. Grimnir would deny them a place in the halls of our ancestors.' Hamnir tapped the map again. 'The grobi won't be defending this door. If a small force can enter there, and then sneak through the hold and open the front door for the main force, they will not stand against us.'

Gorril nodded. 'Aye. It is our own defences that defeat us, not the grobi. If we can breach our walls, they are finished.'

The dwarfs stared at the map, thinking.

'It'll be certain death for those that open the door,' said Ruen.

'Aye,' said Hamnir. 'Likely.'

Gotrek looked up. Felix thought he had been asleep. 'Certain death? I'm in.'

Felix groaned. Wonderful. Gotrek never seemed to consider how his rememberer was going to live to tell his tale when he made these decisions.

'You are willing to die to aid me?' asked Hamnir.

'Are you insulting me again, oathbreaker?' snarled Gotrek. 'I'm a Slayer. I'd be fulfilling two vows with one deed.' He sighed and lowered his chin to his chest again. 'Not that I'll die, of course, Grimnir curse it. Not at the hands of grobi. But at least I won't have to endure your presence.'

The dwarfs in the room glared and grumbled to hear their prince so abused, but Hamnir just sighed. 'And I won't have to endure yours,' he said, 'so it's all for the best. Good.'

'It'll take more than one dwarf to do the deed,' said Gorril, 'no matter how strong. Two levers in two separate rooms must be pulled simultaneously to open the Horn Gate, and others will need to hold off the orcs while they're pulled.'

Hamnir nodded. 'We'll ask for volunteers at the council tomorrow. That is if we are agreed here?'

The other dwarfs still seemed uncertain.

At last, old Ruen shrugged. 'It's a plan, which is more than we had before. I suppose it'll have to do.'

'I don't care to put the fate of the hold in the hands of a dwarf who seems to care so little for its survival,' said the thunderer, Lodrim, glaring at Gotrek, 'but I haven't a better idea, so I'll second it.'

The others nodded, but with little enthusiasm.

Hamnir sat back, weary. 'It's settled, then. We'll work out the details before council. Now… now I'm to bed.' He rubbed his face with a hand and smoothed his beard. 'I've a dozen grudges to try to sort out tomorrow, Valaya save me.'

CHAPTER FIVE

GOTREK'S JAW CLENCHED and unclenched over and over. His leg bounced restlessly as he tipped back in his sawn-off chair. Felix had his journal open, and was reading through his Araby entries. Rodenheim's dining hall was again full of dwarfs, but not for a meal. The representatives of the dwarf companies sent from the various holds sat before the head table where Hamnir, Gorril and other leaders of Karak Hirn's refugees presided. All were waiting to hear the plan of battle for the retaking of the hold, but before they could proceed to strategy, there were grudges to be resolved that determined who would fight alongside whom, and if some warriors would return home before the battle started.

So far, Hamnir had proved an admirable negotiator, and each of the nine grudges he had heard had been resolved, or at least postponed until after Karak Hirn had been retaken or the battle lost. It was a long process, however. They had been at it since just after breakfast, and lunch was a distant memory. The heat of the hall's enormous fireplace was making Felix drowsy. He was having trouble keeping his eyes open.

'You say the ale delivered was not of the quality you were led to believe?' asked Hamnir. He rested his cheek on his fist, looking bored and frustrated.

'It was undrinkable!' said a sandy-bearded dwarf with a belly that suggested he knew quite a bit about ale. 'The double-dealing Hard-stone clan promised us we would be paid in Bugman's Best. They sent us Bugman's worst, if it was Bugman's at all.'

'If the ale was undrinkable,' said a fierce-looking, black-haired dwarf in a yellow doublet, 'then it was damaged in transit, for it was in prime condition when we sampled a barrel before sending it off. The Widebelt clan should take up this dispute with the traders that we commissioned to transport it.'

'This is fools' work,' growled Gotrek under his breath. 'We should be marching, not talking. If Ranulfsson were the leader his father was, these hair-splitters wouldn't remember their grudges. They'd be rallying around his banner and howling for orc blood.'

It took another ten minutes for Hamnir to resolve the dispute, and required all his cunning and diplomacy to shame the two dwarfs into setting aside the matter of the ruined ale. Gotrek growled under his breath the whole time, shooting dangerous looks at all the participants.

When at last an accord had been reached, Hamnir sighed and looked around the hall. 'Now, are there any other clans who are at issue, or may we proceed with the order of battle?'

'Have you forgotten us, prince?' said a white-haired dwarf with blue eyes, jumping up. His beard was a magnificent snow-white field.

Another dwarf with his hair in long grey braids that hung before his ears was on his feet only a second later, glaring at the first. 'Aye, prince. You have not yet taken up the issue of the Shield of Drutti.'

Hamnir groaned, as did the entire room. Gotrek growled, but although the assembled dwarfs were impatient, they had too much respect for the institution of the grudge, and for the sacred duty of every dwarf to resolve every grudge recorded in his clan's book, to complain, so they did nothing but grumble and fold their arms and settle back in their seats.

'I crave your pardon, Kirgi Narinsson,' said Hamnir to the white-bearded dwarf, 'and yours, Ufgart Haginskarl,' he said to the other. 'Remind me of the grudge. It has been a long day.'

The dwarf with the grey braids bowed. 'Thank you, prince. We of the Stonemonger clan bear grudge against the Ironskin clan for stealing from us the Shield of Drutti, which had been a gift from Gadrid Ironskin, the father of their clan, to Hulgir Stonemonger, the father of ours, two thousand years ago, as a token of thanks when Hulgir rescued Gadrid's daughter from trolls.'

'It was not a gift!' barked Kirgi. 'There were no trolls! It was an affair of business, pure and simple. Our clanfather traded the shield to the treacherous Hulgir for mining rights in the Rufgrung deeps. Rights which were never given.'

Gotrek's leg was bouncing like a steam hammer. Felix could hear the Slayer's teeth grinding.

'Is that the shield in question?' asked Hamnir, pointing behind Kirgi to an Ironskin dwarf who held a massive, rune-carved shield at his side.

'Aye!' cried Ulfgart, angrily. 'They dare to flaunt their stolen goods before us and expect us to–'

'We did not steal it! We merely took back what was rightfully ours. When you pay us what is owed, we will gladly return it to you. It was our clanfather's honest, trusting nature that–'

'Right! That's it!' said Gotrek, standing suddenly and taking up his axe. He crossed to the Ironskin table and snatched the Shield of Drutti from its surprised keeper as if it weighed as much as a pot lid.

'I'll solve this grudge!' he said, and threw the shield on the floor and chopped it in half with his axe, hewing wood and iron with equal ease. He then split the halves, hacking madly as splinters flew.

There was a collective gasp from the assembled dwarfs, but they all seemed too stunned to move.

Gotrek scooped up the mangled fragments of the shield, crossed to the great hearth and threw them in. The fire roared. He turned, grinning savagely at the Ironskin and Stonemonger leaders. 'There. Now you have nothing to fight over. Let's march!'

Ulfgart of the Stonemongers was the first to regain the capacity for speech. He turned solemnly to Hamnir, whose face was buried in his hands. 'Prince Hamnir, the Stonemonger clan formally renounces our grudge against the Ironskin clan, and records instead one against the Slayer Gotrek Gurnisson, and let it be known that this grudge can only be resolved in blood.'

'Aye,' agreed Kirgi Narinsson, his blue eyes blazing. 'The Ironskin clan also declares its grudge against the Stonemonger clan cancelled, and claims a new grudge against Gotrek Gurnisson.' He drew his hammer from his back and stepped towards Gotrek, 'And I ask the prince's permission to resolve this grudge here and now.'

Hamnir raised his head and glared at Gotrek. 'Curse you, Gurnisson! Now we've two grudges where there was only one!'

Gotrek spat on the floor. 'Fah! I thought they were honourable dwarfs, so concerned with the right of things that they would let a karak fall to the grobi over a shield. Will such dwarfs have me break a vow in order to fight them?'

'What vow is this?' sneered Kirgi. 'A vow of cowardice?'

'My vow to Hamnir,' said Gotrek, staring down the old dwarf, 'to aid and protect him until Karak Hirn is recovered. Killing you won't aid him, will it? You'll have to wait to die.'

Kirgi gripped his hammer and glared death at Gotrek, but at last stepped back. 'Let none say that a warrior of the Ironskin clan ever caused a dwarf to break an oath. We will settle this in the feast hall of Karak Hirn, after we have drunk to its liberation.'

'It'll be your last drink,' said Gotrek.

Ulfgart turned to Hamnir. 'Neither will the Stonemongers endanger this enterprise by killing a proven Slayer.' Gotrek barked a laugh at this. Ulfgart scowled and continued. 'We too will wait until Karak Hirn is won.'

Hamnir gave a sigh of relief. 'I thank you both for your forbearance.' He looked around the assembly. 'Are there any other grudges to be brought forward?' When no one spoke, he continued. 'Very well, then listen.' He stood. 'This is the plan we have decided upon. As you know, our own defences protect the grobi, and since they are good dwarf work, they are almost impossible to breach. We are less than fifteen hundred strong. We would lose more than half that before we were inside, were we to attack head on. Fortunately, there is a way into the hold that the greenskins will not have discovered. A small company, led by the Slayer Gurnisson, will enter through this door and make their way through the hold to the main gate. When they have opened it, the throng will enter and split up. The bulk of the force will hold the main concourse, while smaller forces sweep through the rest of the hold, pushing the grobi before them. We will work from top to bottom, and force them out through the mine-head doors.'

'What?' asked a young dwarf. 'Will we leave them the mines?'

'Of course not,' said Hamnir, 'but we must secure the hold before we can retake the mines, or we are in danger of becoming over-extended.' When there were no other complaints, he continued. 'What is yet to be determined, is what companies will do what, and who will volunteer to open the doors. I hope,' he said, his face hardening as a growing murmur rose from the dwarfs, 'that we can reach an agreement on an order of march and a division of duty quickly, without argument or recrimination, for time is of the essence.'

Dwarfs all over the hall began standing and raising their voices, demanding this or that position.

Gotrek grunted and turned to Felix. 'Come, manling, they'll be at it all night.'

'You don't care to learn who you will be leading?' asked Felix.

'Not as much as I care to find a drink.' Gotrek walked out of the room, chuckling darkly as he passed the great hearth, where the Shield of Drutti was burning merrily.

CHAPTER SIX

EARLY THE NEXT morning, while the sounds of the clans forming up in the courtyard came through the open door, Gotrek and Felix looked blearily around the stables of Rodenheim Castle at the dwarfs who sat waiting for them in the dim interior, their packs and weapons, armour and coils of rope at their feet. Hamnir stood in the entrance, dressed in gleaming battle armour, and looking ill at ease. He held an ancient brass horn, filigreed with silver.

'These are your volunteers, Gurnisson,' he said, 'all sworn to follow you unto death, if need be, and to obey your commands.' He gestured to a befuddled looking old whitebeard with rheumy eyes and a wooden leg. 'Old Matrak here helped Birrisson wall up the hangar passage and build his secret doors. He will get you through the locks and traps.'

The engineer broke off chewing his long, white moustache and nodded blankly at Gotrek. Felix noticed that his hands trembled. All that and a wooden leg, he thought. Going to be interesting getting the old fellow up a cliff face.

Hamnir turned to Thorgig and Kagrin, who stood nearest him. 'Thorgig will…' He glared at the young dwarf. 'Thorgig will carry the war-horn of Karak Hirn, and blow it from the Horn Gate watch tower once you are ready to open the doors. We will not advance until we hear it.' He held out the horn to Thorgig, who stepped forwards to take it.

Before he could, Hamnir drew it back, his brow furrowing. 'Thorgig, are you certain of this? There is little hope of survival. There are others who might–'

'Who?' said Thorgig, his lips tight. 'I served as a guard of the Horn Gate for ten years. Who among the survivors knows better than I the mechanism of the gate, the placement of the rooms? It must be me.'

'Gotrek can read a map.'

'Can he blow a horn? Does he know the calls?'

Hamnir growled. Felix had the feeling that he and Thorgig had had this argument many times before.

The prince turned to Kagrin. 'You too, Kagrin? Your skill is in shaping axes, not swinging them. Will you throw your life away and rob us of your art?'

Kagrin shrugged and looked at his feet. 'Where Thorgig goes, I go,' he mumbled.

'I tried to tell him the same,' said Thorgig, angry, 'but he won't listen.'

'Try telling yourself,' snapped Hamnir. 'You have a long life ahead of you.'

'My life is already forfeit,' said Thorgig stiffly. 'I left my clan and my family trapped in a hold full of grobi, and escaped to safety. Only freeing them will expunge my shame.'

'You have no reason for shame. There was an army of orcs in the way,' Hamnir said. 'You would never have gotten through.'

'Then I should have died trying.'

Hamnir's fist tightened around the horn until his knuckles were white. It looked as if he might crush it. Finally, he shoved it at Thorgig, punching him in the chest with it, and turned away.

'You should start at once if you hope to enter the keep before we are in position,' he said as he passed Gotrek. At the stable door, he paused and looked back, his face solemn. 'Luck to you all. You are our success... or our failure.'

He walked out.

A chill settled on Felix's heart. 'Inspiring, isn't he?' he said to Gotrek out of the side of his mouth.

Gotrek shrugged. 'What do you want from an oathbreaker?'

Felix had no idea what that had to do with anything.

'Prince Hamnir is no oathbreaker!' said Thorgig. 'Take it back.'

'What do you know of it, shortbeard?' asked Gotrek. 'You weren't born then.' He turned away from Thorgig and scowled at the others.

'A Stonemonger and an Ironskin,' he said looking from a cold-visaged, black-bearded dwarf wearing the clan rune of the Stonemongers, to a blond-maned, blue-eyed Ironskin who was the spitting image of Kirgi Narinsson, save for being at least a century younger and having a scar that ran down the left side of his face. He had a sliver of charred wood knotted into his huge blond beard like a charm. 'Ranulfsson has a mean streak in him,' said Gotrek, shaking his head. 'He hides it well, but it's there.'

'We are not here at the prince's bidding,' said the blond dwarf, smiling mischievously as he toyed with the blackened wood. 'We volunteered, as he said.'

The black-bearded dwarf nodded. 'The Ironskins and Stonemongers both have an interest in keeping you alive in this venture.' His voice was a soft and cold as snow. 'We do not wish to be cheated of our opportunity to resolve our grudges with you.'

You don't have to worry about me,' said Gotrek, sighing, 'not against grobi.'

'Do we bring the manling into the hold?' asked a grizzled Ironbreaker with a broken nose and braided white hair and beard. He eyed Felix as if he expected him to grow fangs and horns. 'He'll spy out our secrets.'

'He is a Dwarf Friend,' said Gotrek. 'I vouch for him.'

'Dwarf Friend?' snorted the old Ironbreaker. 'The dwarfs have no friends but the dwarfs.'

'No wonder our glory is behind us,' said Gotrek dryly. 'What's your name, doomsayer?'

'Sketti Hammerhand, I am,' said the dwarf, puffing out his chest, 'of the Hammerhand clan. Ironbreaker and Deep Warden of Karak Izor.' And true to his name, the haft of a warhammer stuck up over his right shoulder.

Gotrek turned away from him, unimpressed. 'And you?' he asked, looking at the black-bearded Stonemonger. 'The one who means to protect me so he can fight me later.'

'Druric Brodigsson,' said the dwarf in his mild voice. 'A ranger of the Black Fire Pass, yours to command, for now.' He bowed his head, which was covered in close cropped, bristly black hair. 'Though it may not be me who fights you; he who will have the honour of facing you is still being discussed. I pray I am chosen. I have always wanted to take the measure of a Slayer.'

'Take the measure of your coffin first,' said Gotrek. He turned to the others, his gaze passing over old Matrak, the engineer, who had gone back to chewing his moustache and staring into space, and came to rest upon the blond dwarf with the piercing blue eyes.

'And you're the son of the old blowhard who challenged me last night.'

The dwarf smirked and leaned back, hooking his thumbs in his wide belt. 'Aye, that's me, Narin Blowhardsson. At your service, and your clan's.'

The other dwarfs chuckled.

'What's the kindling in your beard for?'

Narin closed his hand around the sliver of wood, suddenly embarrassed. 'My father's idea, he bid me wear a piece of the Shield of Drutti so that you would always see it and remember our grudge against you.' He scowled down at himself. 'I don't care for it. It's dirtying my beard.'

Gotrek raised an eyebrow. 'You want to fight me too, I suppose?'

'No no,' said Narin. 'My father will not give up the honour. I'm only to make sure you keep your head until he has the pleasure of removing it himself.' He grinned, his blue eyes sparkling. 'You really got the old badger's dander up. Wish I'd been there, but there was a lass from Karak Drazh, and well, it took some time for us to get properly acquainted.' He shrugged. 'About time the old dinner plate was turned to tinder anyway. No use to anybody, save as beard jewellery.'

Druric's head came up. His eyes flashed. 'The shield of Drutti was a great and noble heirloom. The theft of it by the Ironskin clan...'

'Oh come, cousin,' said Narin scowling. 'It has never been taken into battle. It was mounted on the wall of your feast hall for a thousand years before my great-grandfather took it, and then it was mounted on the wall of our feast hall for a thousand years. It was a dinner plate.'

Druric glared at Narin for a long moment, and then sighed. 'Very well, it was a dinner plate, but that is entirely beside the point,' he said, raising his voice as the others laughed. 'Theft is theft. It matters not if it is a bar of gold or a loaf of bread, the dwarf who took it is without honour.'

Narin held up his hands. 'Take it up with my father. It isn't my fight. The dwarfs will have no future if we keep fighting battles two thousand years in the past.'

'And what sort of future will we have if it is achieved at the price of honour?' asked Druric.

'Enough,' said Gotrek, growling. 'Save it for the beer hall!' He passed over Thorgig and Kagrin, who he knew, and looked at the last dwarf, who sat on an overturned bucket with the hood of his cloak pulled so far forwards that his face was entirely in shadow. 'You at the back, what's your name? Let's have a look at you.'

The dwarf didn't speak, only reached up and pulled back his hood. The others swore and laughed. Even Gotrek blinked. Felix didn't blame him, for this dwarf was the strangest of that strange breed he had ever seen.

'What are you?' asked Gotrek, scowling.

The dwarf straightened his shoulders and looked directly at Gotrek, light green eyes glaring out of the eyeholes of the head-covering leather mask he wore. The mask was, in its way, a thing of exquisite craftsmanship, beautifully tooled and sculpted in the square fashion of old dwarf sculptures. Thick strips of orange tinted leather hung in tapering plaits from its cheeks and jaw-line to represent a beard, and a bristling horse-hair crest of flaming orange rose from a flap of leather that went up over the dwarf's scalp and buckled to straps that extended back from the face. 'I am a Slayer,' he said in a low rasp. 'Leatherbeard the Slayer.'

'A Slayer? With no crest?' Gotrek raised a shaggy eyebrow. 'What manner of...'

Leatherbeard put his hand on his axe. He was bare-chested, in Slayer fashion, and wore only the hooded cloak over his shoulders to keep off the morning chill. 'Do I ask of *your* shame, brother?' he growled. 'Do I ask *your* reason for seeking death?'

Gotrek's teeth clicked together. He sobered instantly, and nodded at Leatherbeard. 'Fair enough.' He turned abruptly from the masked dwarf and shouldered his pack. 'Come on, then. Up and out.' He started out of the stable without a backward glance.

Felix gaped at Gotrek as the dwarfs gathered up their gear and followed him out into the wet morning air. That had almost been an apology!

THEY TRAVELLED NORTH and east from Rodenheim Castle all morning, up and down thickly forested hills that rose one after the other like swells in a green sea. There was a road to Karak Hirn – the remains of one of the old dwarf roads – but they didn't take it. The road led to the hold's front door, and would be watched. Hamnir's army was marching up it, bold as brass. With luck, the orcs would keep their eyes fixed on the column, and miss the little company of nine that went the hard way.

They sloshed through rock-choked mountain streams and scrabbled up loose shale slopes, trekked through deep forests and across upland meadows. As they climbed higher, drifts of half-melted snow appeared in the shadows, though the sun was hot on their necks. Felix had thrown back his red cloak and was sweating though his shirt. His calves ached like fire, and they hadn't even reached the real climb yet. Too many months at sea. He'd become a tenderfoot again.

The dwarfs took it all in their stride, maintaining the same dogged pace on flat ground or steep hill. Even old peg-legged Matrak kept up, mumbling, as he limped along, in a monologue that no one else could hear.

Felix wished some of the others were as quiet. Sketti Hammerhand in particular would not shut up for more than two minutes at a time, and it was always the same subject.

'It's the elves behind it all. They want the dwarfs dead because we're what stands in the way of them ruling the world. You can be sure they're behind this grobi trouble.'

'How could they be behind this?' asked Thorgig.

The others groaned as Sketti's eyes lit up. He had only been waiting for someone to give him an opening.

'You don't know elves like I do, young one. I've met them, and a twistier set of shock-headed beanpoles you wouldn't want to find yourself dead in a ditch with. There are no depths to which they wouldn't sink. No plan is too devious.' He licked his lips. 'I'll tell you how it is, lad. You think the greenskins getting too big for their britches is because so many dwarfs and men have gone north, and there isn't anyone to keep them out of the Badlands. That's true as far as it goes, but that's only the surface. A true dwarf doesn't trust the surface of nothing. He looks beneath.'

Gotrek muttered something about true dwarfs knowing when to shut up, but Felix didn't quite catch it.

'What you need to ask yourself, lad,' continued Sketti, 'is why the northmen are invading in the first place. What stirred them up? Put aside the fact that it was the elves messing about with magic they couldn't control that opened the Chaos rift in the first place, making them the fathers of Chaos, you can be sure it was elves put the bee in this Archaon's bonnet as well. Now the "fair ones" like to make out that they have nothing to do with their dark cousins in Naggaroth, but everyone knows that's a trick to blame their evil deeds on someone else. I had it from a dwarf who trades with Bretonnian sailors who deal with Ulthuan that it was the dark elves who whispered in the ear of this "chosen one" and told him his "destiny" lay in the south.' Sketti spread his hands. 'So, he heeds their words and invades the Empire, and the dwarfs, who have pledged since Sigmar's time to protect mankind, no matter how often they steal from us and stab us in the back, go north to defend the ungrateful weaklings, and lo and behold, the grobi "coincidentally" choose that moment to rise and attack! You can't make me believe it isn't all some dark elf scheme.'

'You're saying it was the dark elves who convinced the northmen to attack the Empire just so the grobi could take over Karak Hirn?' said Narin, chuckling.

'And why not?' asked Sketti.

'So the elves give orders to the grobi now?' scoffed Thorgig.

'Not directly. Not directly,' said Sketti. 'But they're in league with the skaven, everyone knows that, and the skaven…'

Everyone groaned again. Felix shivered, recalling all the times that he and Gotrek had encountered the horrid, man-like vermin, and the single-minded grey seer who had dogged their steps so unflaggingly during their travels in the Old World. He couldn't imagine the great Teclis ever conspiring with the likes of them.

'Hammerhand!' said Narin, interrupting Sketti's rant. 'There's a manling among us. Do you truly want to reveal to him all this secret dwarf knowledge? Everyone knows that men are the lackeys of the elves. Do you want the elves to know how much you know?'

Sketti's mouth shut like a trap. He turned and glared at Felix with wild eyes. 'It's true,' he muttered. 'It's true. I have perhaps said too much.' He shot a last suspicious glance at Felix and marched on in silence.

Narin winked at Felix behind Sketti's back as the rest sighed with relief.

Felix nodded his thanks and stifled a grin. A good fellow, Narin. Not as stiff as the others.

JUST BEFORE NOON, the party stepped out of pine woods at the top of a shallow ravine to find the jutting peak of Karag Hirn towering above them, a long feathery scarf of blown snow trailing away from its white craggy peak across the bright blue sky. The rest of the mountain was as black and sober as a judge. Thorgig, Kagrin and old Matrak looked up at it reverently.

'To think the halls of our birth hold run with grobi,' Thorgig spat. 'To think that they defile our sacred places with their presence. We will avenge you, karaz. We will cleanse you of their taint.'

The others murmured answering oaths.

On the west side of the mountain, the gleaming switchback curve of a road could be seen, and above it, almost hidden by rocks and outcroppings, the regular planes of massive dwarf battlements.

'That is the front gate – the Horn Gate,' said old Matrak, pointing. 'Where we…' He choked on the words. 'Where we fled from the silent grobi. Hamnir and the others go there to wait for us. We…' He swung his hand to the right. 'We go there. The Zhufgrim Scarp.'

Felix's eyes followed the engineer's finger to the eastern face of the mountain. The base of it, where it rose from the trees, was notched, as if some dwarf god had hacked out a gigantic foothold with an axe. A vertical wall rose up from the notch, more than half way to the snow-peaked crown, and looked, at least from where Felix stood, as smooth and flat as a sheet of parchment. A thin line of silver glittered down the middle of it.

'At the base is the Cauldron,' said Thorgig, stepping up beside the old engineer. 'A deep lake fed by the falls that pour down the cliff. That is our road.'

Felix swallowed. 'Up the cliff? Do you have wings in your packs?'

Sketti snorted. 'Nothing to it, for dwarfs.'

'Hist,' said Druric. 'Orcs.'

The others went quiet instantly and turned to where he looked. A small company of orcs was pushing through the heavy undergrowth of berry bushes that covered the floor of the ravine below. The dwarfs stepped back from the edge, and squatted down so they could only just see over the lip.

'Twenty of them,' said Thorgig.

'And we are only eight,' said Sketti.

'Nine,' said Druric, 'with the man.'

'As I said, eight,' said Sketti. 'We'll still manage.'

Gotrek snorted at that.

'I'd manage alone!' said Leatherbeard, defensively.

'Forgive me for speaking out of turn,' said Felix, 'but isn't the aim of our mission to reach the secret door without being seen?'

'If they're all dead,' growled Narin, tugging on the charred sliver in his beard, 'how can they tell what they've seen?'

'If others find them chopped to pieces,' said Felix, 'they will know we were here. And if we are to open the Horn Gate in time to let Hamnir in, can we spare the time for a fight?'

The dwarfs hesitated, palpably angry at Felix's attempts at logic. They were tensed like wolves looking down on unsuspecting sheep. Every fibre in their squat, powerful bodies wanted to charge into the ravine and butcher the greenskins.

At last Gotrek sighed. 'The manling is right. This isn't the time for a fight.'

The others grunted their annoyance.

'How much time could it take?' asked Leatherbeard.

'We'll have plenty of fighting in the hold,' said Gotrek, 'enough to kill us. Or the rest of you, at any rate.'

'I have sworn to follow you,' said Thorgig, stiffly, 'but it pains me to let even a single orc live.'

'It isn't the dwarf way,' said Sketti.

'It's *my* way,' said Gotrek. 'Now wait until they pass.'

The dwarfs grumbled, but did as he ordered, watching in hiding as the orcs passed below them.

The greenskins walked in double file, their leader at their head, scanning the landscape. They did not talk or argue amongst themselves as orcs usually did. There was no shoving or fighting, no drinking or eating, or bored hacking at the underbrush with their weapons. They kept at their task with a sad dullness that looked almost comical on their hideous faces. Only occasionally would this listlessness break, when one of them shook its head and twitched, roaring like a bull stung by a wasp, and its eyes would blaze with the accustomed orcish fury. Then, as soon as it had begun, the outburst would end, and the orc would sink back into its stupor.

'What's come over them?' asked Thorgig.

Kagrin shook his head, baffled.

'What kind of orcs don't squabble?' muttered Narin, unnerved.

'It seems almost as if they are asleep,' said Sketti, frowning.

'Then they kill in their sleep,' said old Matrak, trembling, 'for this is how they came when the Karak fell: silent, but bloodthirsty. We didn't hear them until they were on us. We didn't...' He trailed off, his eyes wide and far away.

The other dwarfs looked away from him, uncomfortable.

'Elf work, no doubt,' said Sketti. 'White sorcery.'

Narin considered this. 'Could any sorcerer alive today command the wills of an entire hold full of orcs?'

'One could,' nodded Sketti sagely. 'Teclis of Ulthuan.'

'He could at that,' said Gotrek, stroking his beard thoughtfully.

'You see?' said Sketti. 'The Slayer agrees with me.'

'The Slayer thinks you have elves on the brain,' said Gotrek, sneering, and returned to watching the orcs.

When they had passed out of sight around a twist in the ravine, the dwarfs continued on. Gotrek frowned as they walked, deep in thought. It seemed that he had finally become interested in the task that Hamnir had set him.

CHAPTER SEVEN

AFTER TWO HOURS pushing up Karag Hirn's steep, forested flank, they reached the tree line and came out onto dark, quartz-veined rock, patched with green-grey lichen. The way got harder, the slope steeper and blocked by massive outcroppings, and they had to use their hands as often as their feet to climb. Felix found himself more winded than he expected. The air was thin, and the wind cold, but he was sweating through his clothes.

An hour later, with the flat wall of Zufgrim Scarp getting higher and wider above them all the time, they began to hear a low roaring. It grew louder and louder, until, as they crested a narrow pass between two looming fangs of rock, they came upon a steep-shored mountain lake, surrounded on three sides by low jagged peaks, and on the fourth by the scarp, which rose directly from its frothing waters. The cliff didn't appear to Felix to be any rougher, now that they were closer. It was still as flat as the wall of a fortress. The only break was the waterfall that dropped down its centre in a rushing white torrent and split it in two. The noise of the cataract smashing into the lake was deafening. It churned the water into a roiling boil that made the surface of the whole lake dance, flashing sunlight into their faces from a thousand, thousand ripples. The edges of the lake were crusted with a jagged rime of ice. Flurries drifted down from the snowcap, high above them.

Felix shielded his eyes and looked up. The scarp was even more intimidating from this angle than it had been when old Matrak first pointed it out. He found he had broken out in an icy sweat. 'It's... it's impossible.'

Narin snorted. 'Easy as falling out of bed.'

Felix swallowed. 'Falling is always easy.'

'Eat before we go up,' said Gotrek, 'and get your gear ready.'

The dwarfs fell out, sitting down on the black boulders to eat salted meat and oatcakes, and washing the dry stuff down with beer poured from little wooden kegs they had strapped to their packs. Kagrin as usual got out his dagger and his tools and got to work, ignoring everyone else. Felix found it hard to look away. One mistake, one slip of the tool, and it would be ruined, but Kagrin never slipped. His hands were steady and sure.

Narin munched his hard-tack and sighed as if a great weight had been lifted from him. 'This is the life,' he said. 'Grimnir and Grungni, but I miss it.'

'The life, he says?' said Sketti, cocking an eyebrow. 'Might be the death as well, like as not.'

'Then I'll take the death,' he said with feeling, 'and willingly.'

Leatherbeard looked up at that. 'You don't wear the Slayer's crest. Why would you seek death?'

Narin smirked at him. 'You haven't met my wife.'

Thorgig turned. 'Your wife? Didn't you say earlier you were wooing some maid from Karak Drazh yesterday when the rest of us were at council?'

'As I said,' Narin continued, 'you haven't met my wife.'

Most of the others chuckled at that, but Thorgig and Druric looked offended.

Narin chose to take no notice. He sighed, playing unconsciously with the burnt stick of wood tied into his beard. 'I had the wanderlust when I was a shortbeard. I walked my axe from Kislev to Tilea as a mercenary and adventurer for fifty years, and loved every minute of it. Saw more of the world in that half century than most dwarfs see in five.' He trailed off, his eyes looking far away, and a faint smile on his bearded lips. Then he shook himself reluctantly. 'All that's gone, now that my older brother's dead.'

'Called back to the hold, were you?' asked Druric.

'Aye,' Narin said sadly. 'The second son of a thane has the best of it and no mistake – just ask Prince Hamnir – gold and opportunity, and no more responsibility than a cat. Only now, I'm the first son. The old badger probably has another century in him at least, but still I must come home and learn the running of the hold, and memorise our book of grudges from cover to cover, and make a favourable marriage, and...' He shivered. 'Produce sons with my... wife.'

'Every dwarf must do his duty,' said Leatherbeard, through his mask. 'We are a dwindling race. We must beget sons and daughters.'

'I know, I know,' said Narin, 'but I'd rather have your duty. Killing trolls is a more pleasant task than bedding one, and trolls don't talk as much.'

'Surely she can't be as bad as all that,' said Thorgig.

Narin fixed him with a sharp blue eye. 'Lad, we are all likely to die on this little jaunt, are we not? Prince Hamnir said it was a suicide mission.'

'Aye, I suppose,' said Thorgig.

'Well, let me put it to you this way. I'll be disappointed if it isn't.'

'And I will be disappointed if it is,' said Druric.

'You're afraid to die?' asked Thorgig sharply.

'Not in the least,' said Druric. He turned his cold eyes towards Gotrek, who was wolfing down his food and paying the rest not the slightest attention, 'but if Slayer Gurnisson dies, the grudge the Stonemongers have against him will go unresolved. As long as I know he will live, I don't mind dying.'

Gotrek snorted derisively at that, but didn't bother to respond.

After the meal, there was much rummaging through packs and re-coiling of ropes. Each of the dwarfs hung a bandolier of ringed steel spikes over one shoulder and strapped a pair of cleats to his boots. Fortunately, though dwarfs and men were so dissimilar in size and proportion that they could rarely exchange clothes, dwarfs had big feet, so a pair of cleats had been found for Felix. Old Matrak unbuckled his wooden peg leg and replaced it with one that was a long, black-iron spike.

When all straps were tightened, the dwarfs tapped out their pipes and stood, slinging their packs over their shoulders. Kagrin was last to be ready, tucking his tools and the gold-pommelled dagger away reluctantly.

'Come on, lad,' said Narin. 'There'll be work for the other end of that elf-sticker presently.'

The dwarfs edged around the steep shores of the Cauldron, slip-pery with broken ice and loose shale, until they came to the cliff face, the falls booming to their right, and spraying them with a fine, freezing mist.

Right up against it, the cliff wasn't quite as smooth and feature-less as it had appeared before, but it was still daunting – a long, nearly vertical stratum of grey granite, with few cracks or protrusions. The dwarfs didn't even slow down. They stepped to the wall, reached up to grab handholds that Felix couldn't see, jammed their cleats into the rock and pulled themselves up without ropes or pitons, as easily as if they were ascending a ladder.

By watching closely where Gotrek put his hands and feet, Felix was able to follow him up the face, but it was hard, finger-cramping work, and he was nowhere near as steady as the dwarfs. Even old Matrak was doing better than he was, his iron leg spike biting firmly into the granite.

It struck Felix as odd that dwarfs, with their short, thick bodies, would excel at climbing mountains. One would have thought that a climber with long, spidery limbs and a thin torso – an elf, for instance – would be better suited to the work, but although the dwarfs did have occasional trouble stretching for the next hand or foot hold, they made up for their lack of reach with incredible strength of grip and their uncanny dwarfish affinity for the rock itself. They seemed to find, more by instinct than sight or touch, ridges and cracks to slip their sturdy fingers into that Felix could not have found if he had been staring directly at them.

Unfortunately, this skill, and their vicelike grip, gave the dwarfs the ability to use, as handholds, tiny irregularities in the surface of the cliff that Felix couldn't get a grip on at all. Consequently, by the time the dwarfs were halfway up the cliff, Felix was far below them, his forearms on fire with cramp and sweat running into his eyes. He could no longer hear the others because of the sound of the waterfall roaring past thirty feet to his right.

He paused for a moment to flex his hands and try to shake the ache from his limbs, and made the mistake of looking down between his legs. He froze. He was so high up. One slip – one slip and… Suddenly, he wasn't sure he could hold on any more. A mad urge to just let go and relieve the tension as he fell to his death nearly overcame him.

He fought it off with difficulty, but found he still couldn't move. He groaned as he realised he was going to have to ask for help. Dwarfs hated weakness and incompetence. They had no respect for someone who couldn't fend for himself. Even when they were alone, Felix always felt a fool when he had to ask Gotrek for help. It would be worse here, with a pack of other dwarfs looking on. He would be mocked. On the other hand, better to live and be mocked than literally die of embarrassment, wasn't it?

'Your rememberer is lagging behind, Slayer,' came Narin's voice from above him.

Felix heard a grunt and a dwarf curse, and then, 'Hang on, manling.'

The echoes of dwarf chuckling reached his ears and turned them crimson. Then came a sound of hammering. Felix looked up, but it was difficult to see who was who, let alone what was going on. All he could see were the soles of dwarf boots and broad dwarf rumps.

'Take this,' called Gotrek.

A coil of rope dropped towards him, rushing at Felix's face like a striking snake. He ducked. A small iron hook cracked him on the top of his head. He yelped and nearly lost his grip.

'Mind your head,' laughed Thorgig.

The hook slithered down the cliff face between Felix's legs and stopped with a bounce below his feet at the end of the rope it was attached to.

'Can you get a hand free?' asked Gotrek.

'Aye,' said Felix. He was rubbing his head with it as he spoke.

'Then hook the rope to your belt.'

'Right.' Felix drew the rope up one-handed until he had the hook, then passed it under and around his belt twice and hooked it to the rope again. 'It's done,' he called.

The rope began to slide back up the cliff until it was taut.

'Come ahead,' said Gotrek.

Felix started up again. The rope slackened as he climbed, but then retightened every few feet. Felix looked up and saw Gotrek pulling it through the eyelet of a piton and holding it tight.

The other dwarfs were all watching him as he rose, amused smiles on their bearded faces.

'What's this fish you've caught, Slayer?' asked Sketti.

'Not much meat on it, is there?' said Narin.

'Aye,' said Thorgig. 'Throw it back.'

As he came level with them, Felix saw that Gotrek had tapped two pitons into the cliff, one about five feet above the other.

'Bide a bit, manling,' he said. 'Put your foot on this one, and hold onto this one.'

Felix stepped gratefully onto the lower piton and held onto the other. It wasn't much, but after clinging on with his fingertips for the last hour, it was a blessed relief.

'When you've got some strength back, follow on. We'll leave lines and pegs for you.'

'Lines and pegs,' snorted Sketti. 'Like a baby. No wonder men steal everything from the dwarfs. They can't do a thing for themselves.'

'That's enough, Hammerhand,' growled Gotrek.

'Pardon, Slayer,' Sketti sneered. 'I forgot. He is your "Dwarf Friend". He must be very friendly indeed to be worth the trouble.'

Gotrek fixed the Ironbreaker with his one glittering eye and the mirth died on the old dwarf's lips. His white beard moved as he swallowed.

'Right,' said Gotrek as he turned back to the rock face. 'Upward.'

The dwarfs started up the cliff again while Felix stood on the piton and flexed and stretched each of his arms in turn. When Gotrek had climbed another fifty feet or so, he jabbed another piton into the granite, making it stick with just the force of his hand, then seating it securely with a small hammer. He tied Felix's rope to it, and moved on. From then on, this was how they proceeded. Felix's humiliation at having to use a rope was tempered by the relative safety and ease of the arrangement. He was no longer falling behind, and he didn't freeze when he looked down.

Three-quarters of the way up the scarp, even the dwarfs had to use 'lines and pegs'. The cliff bulged out at the top, like melted wax at the top of a candle, and they had to climb up the underside of the bulge. Gotrek went first, reaching as high as he could to tap in a piton, and then hanging a loop of rope from it in which to sit so that he could tap in the next. Felix shivered at the sight. The Slayer was so heavy, his muscles as dense as oak wood, and the pitons so tiny, that he expected them to pull out of the rock and Gotrek to plummet earthward at any second.

The dwarfs talked, unconcerned, while they waited, as easy clinging to their ropes and resting on their pitons with the wind whistling around them as if they had been bellied up to a bar in a cosy tavern.

'Look there,' said Sketti Hammerhand, pointing and raising his voice to be heard over the falls. 'You can just see Karaz Izor from here: third mountain in, behind the split peak of Karaz Varnrik. You won't have grobi taking *our* hold. My line has been Ironbreakers and deep wardens since my great-grandfather's great-grandfather's time, and no greenskin has ever slipped past us. We've an unbroken record.'

'Do you imply that we lost Karak Hirn out of laxness?' asked Thorgig with a dangerous edge in his voice. 'Do you say we didn't fight hard enough?'

'No no, lad,' said Sketti, holding up his free hand. 'I meant no insult to the bravery of your hold or clan. I'm sure you all fought as true dwarfs should.' He shrugged. 'Of course, if any of your king's line had been there, things might have been different.'

'Now you insult King Alrik,' said Thorgig, his voice rising.

'I do not,' Sketti protested. 'He isn't the only dwarf to fall prey to this elf-birthed Chaos invasion. His heart was in the right place, I'm sure, wanting to help the men of the Empire in their time of need, but a dwarf's first duty is to his own. So–'

'If you dig yourself any deeper, Hammerhand,' said Thorgig, his fists balling, 'You'll strike fire.'

'Quiet!' came Gotrek's voice from above.

The dwarfs ceased their argument and looked up. Gotrek hung above them, craning his neck to see over the curve of the bulge. He had one hand on the haft of his axe.

A sound of movement came to them faintly from the top of the cliff, barely discernible over the roar of the falls. A spill of pebbles rattled past Gotrek to drop towards the lake.

Felix thought he heard a command given in a high, harsh voice, but couldn't make out the word. Whatever it was, the speaker hadn't sounded human or dwarfish.

The dwarfs stayed as motionless as statues, listening. The sounds of movement came again, fainter and to the west, and then were gone. After a moment, Gotrek resumed tapping in the next piton.

'Goblin patrol,' said Druric.

Narin nodded.

'Do they know we're here?' asked Sketti, looking up anxiously.

'We'd be dodging boulders if they knew we were here,' said Thorgig.

Leatherbeard grunted. 'Not a Slayer's death.'

'They know,' said old Matrak in a faraway voice. 'They know everything. They know where the keys are. They know where the doors are.'

The others looked at him. He was staring into the distance, his eyes seeing nothing.

'Poor old fellow,' said Narin under his breath.

Gotrek reached the top shortly thereafter, and threw down a rope. Old Matrak went up first, the line hooked to his belt for safety. As troubled as he was in his mind, he was still sure in his movements. He let go of his piton and swung out on the dangling rope without a qualm. Then he climbed up hand over hand until he reached the bulge and could gain purchase with his foot and iron leg-spike again.

Felix went up fourth, after Druric. He had shinned up many a rope in his travels with Gotrek, and faced many a danger, but swinging out over that drop was one of the hardest things he'd ever done. Only the sceptical scowls of the dwarfs waiting their turn kept him from hemming and hesitating endlessly before letting go. He would be damned if he would let them think him more of a buffoon than they already did.

Of course, this hope was dashed when one of his cleats slipped as he began climbing up the underside of the bulge. He lost his footing and slammed face first into the cliff, bloodying his nose. He caught himself and recovered almost instantly, but he could hear the guffaws of the dwarfs below and above him. His face burned with embarrassment as he topped the bulge and Gotrek held out a hand to haul him up.

'Well done, manling. You're the first to shed blood in the recovery of Karak Hirn,' said the Slayer, grinning.

'The first to shed his own,' said Thorgig, chuckling behind him.

'I'll be happy to shed somebody else's,' said Felix, glaring at Thorgig. The young dwarf was beginning to get on his nerves. He had reason to hate Gotrek, Felix supposed. The Slayer had been more than insulting, to him and to Hamnir, but Felix had given Thorgig no cause to be angry. No cause but his mere presence, he thought. Thorgig was no Sketti, but he had the dwarfish disdain for all things non-dwarf.

Felix looked around. The cliff top was a broad flat ledge, like a landing halfway up the mountain. The rest of the peak still loomed above him, its white snowcap silhouetted against the blinding sun. A deep black pool – a mirror-calm twin to the roiling cauldron below – was cut into the ledge by ages of erosion. To his right, the pool spilled over the edge of cliff to become the narrow silver thread of the falls. There wasn't much room twixt water and cliff edge. It felt as if he and the dwarfs stood on the rim of a giant stone pitcher that forever poured water into a stone cup far below. The top of the falls was thin enough to jump, but the prospect of slipping made Felix's skin crawl.

Druric was studying the ground at the cliff edge. 'It was goblins,' he said.

'So, they're looking for us?' asked Sketti, glancing around warily.

'Not necessarily,' Druric answered. 'There are regular patrols through here.' He pointed. 'New prints over the old.'

Gotrek turned to Matrak as he helped Leatherbeard up. 'Which way to the door?'

Matrak waved to the east, beyond the stream, where the cliff-top ledge rose gradually to a split between the main body of the mountain and a rugged smaller peak – a broad shoulder to the karaz's proud head. 'Up. Through there.'

'The grobi went that way,' Gotrek said. 'Get your armour on.'

The dwarfs took off their cleats and pulled mail shirts, pauldrons and gauntlets from their packs, replacing them with their climbing gear. Felix buckled on a scale-sewn leather jack, and fixed his old red cloak around his shoulders. None of them carried shields, which would have been too heavy and cumbersome while climbing.

Gotrek left the rope over the bulge in place and hopped the roaring falls. The dwarfs followed him across, apparently without a second thought. Felix held his breath as he took a running jump and tried not to imagine falling in the water and being dragged over the edge by the rushing current.

Safely on the other side, the company followed the ledge as it rose to the split between the mountain's head and shoulder. This was a narrow, shadowed cleft that wound crazily between the two peaks, and then opened out onto a sway-backed saddle of hard-packed snow that sloped up to the black flank of Karaz Hirn to their left, and down to a sheer cliff on their right. The last few yards before the cliff were black ice – frozen run-off from the slanting plain of snow, as glossy and smooth as the lip of a wine bottle.

As they were about to step out of the cleft onto the snow, a patch of red and green on the far side drew Felix's eye. A dozen goblins were hacking apart the carcass of a mountain goat, and its blood stained the snow all around them. Like the orcs they had seen before, the goblins were maintaining a very un-greenskin-like silence. They weren't fighting over the choice bits, or devouring their portions immediately, but instead stuffed the bloody legs and flank steaks into their packs for later.

'They're in the way,' quavered Matrak, pointing to a dark gap in the rock face on the far side of the slope of snow. 'The door's beyond that pass.'

'We'll have to take them, then,' said Narin.

'Thank Grimnir for that,' said Sketti. 'The day I hide from goblins is the day I shave my beard.'

Leatherbeard growled in his throat.

'Shut up and attack,' said Gotrek. He started forwards at a run.

The dwarfs charged after him as fast as they could, which, by Felix's standards wasn't very fast. He had to keep to a trot, so as not to get too far ahead.

The goblins saw them coming, but didn't shriek in alarm, or scatter in blind panic as goblins were wont to. Instead, they just dropped the bits of hacked-up goat they held and turned to face the dwarfs, as silent as monks.

Druric loosed a crossbow bolt that took one goblin high in the chest, then threw the crossbow aside and drew a hand axe. He and Felix and the dwarfs crashed into the runty greenskins like a battering ram, mowing them down with their sheer mass. Four goblins died immediately, axes buried deep in their scrawny chests and pointy skulls. Three more were bowled off their feet. Gotrek split one in two. Felix hacked at a second, a tiny, snaggle-toothed horror that rolled away from his blade. Old Matrak stomped on another with his iron leg-spike, impaling it.

The goblin leader chittered an order as he fought Thorgig, and two goblins peeled away from the fight to scamper up the rise. Leatherbeard sent one of his axes spinning after the runners, dropping one, but the other was nearing the opening at the top of the snowy slope.

'After him, manling!' called Gotrek. 'Make those long legs useful!'

Felix sprinted up the incline, his feet smashing holes in the hard crust of snow. The goblin darted through the dark gap and down into a dropping, rocky cleft. Felix charged in after him, gaining with every step. The goblin looked back once, emotionless as a fish, and then ran on.

The floor of the cleft was filled with rocks and loose gravel. Felix slipped and slid as he ran down it, twice nearly twisting his ankle. He came within a yard of the goblin and swiped at it with his sword, but it leapt ahead, ducking around a big boulder and out of sight. Felix swung wide around the boulder, and found himself suddenly on the lip of a wide crevasse that dropped away into blackness. He lurched left, heart thudding, his scrabbling feet kicking pebbles into the abyss, and twisted away from the edge barely in time.

The goblin scampered up a rocky rise before him. Felix surged after it, skin prickling at the closeness of his narrow escape. No one would ever have found him had he fallen into that chasm. No one would know what had become of him: a horrible end for a memoirist.

The goblin slipped on loose scree and fell on its face as it reached the crest of the rise. Felix closed on it rapidly. It picked itself up again and dived over the ridge. Felix leapt after it and tackled it to the ground. They rolled down the far side of the ridge in a tangle of limbs, and jarred to a stop at the base of the slope, the goblin on top. It raised its saw-bladed short sword to stab him, but Felix clubbed it off his chest with his free arm and rolled on top of it, slashing down with his sword. The steel bit through the goblin's skull. The little green monster spasmed and lay still.

Felix collapsed to the side and lay with his cheek on the cold rock, panting and wheezing, glaring at the dead goblin beside him. 'Got you at last, you filthy–'

An enormous fur-booted foot stepped into his circle of vision. He looked up. A huge orc in scrap armour loomed over him, staring down. Twenty more stood at its back.

CHAPTER EIGHT

THE ORC SLASHED down at Felix with a huge double-bladed axe. Felix yelped and rolled. He was deafened as the axe bit deep into the ground, an inch from his shoulder, pinning his cloak. Felix surged up, the cloak nearly strangling him before it ripped free. Another orc swung at him. He jerked aside and ran, stumbling and unsteady, back up the ridge.

The orcs raced after him, unnervingly silent. Felix pounded down the slope towards the black chasm, skidding within inches of the drop as he turned into the narrow confines of the rocky pass. He heard the orcs thundering behind him, and then a fading bellow as one of them missed its footing and tumbled into the depths. The rest came on, not sparing their lost comrade a backwards glance.

A stitch stabbed at Felix's side as he scrabbled up the tight, rising path, and his breath came in ragged gasps. He'd already been winded when he caught the goblin. Now he felt as if he was going to die. He wanted to stop and vomit, but the orcs were so close at his heels that he could hear their breathing and smell their rank animal odour. The ground shook with their footsteps.

The light from the snowfield glowed at the top of the shadowed pass like a beacon of hope. It looked a hundred leagues away. He slipped on a loose rock and this time he did twist his ankle. It flared with sudden agony. He cried out, and nearly fell. Swift steel whistled behind him and an axe rang off the rock wall beside his head.

He scrabbled on, ankle screaming with each step. He didn't have the luxury of favouring it – just jammed his foot down and took the pain as best he could. At last, nearly fainting with agony, he gained the top of the pass, inches ahead of the orcs, and burst out onto the snowfield. A slashing cleaver grazed his scale-covered shoulder and sent him sprawling. He slid face-first down the snowy incline towards the cliff.

The dwarfs were marching up the slope with the dead goblins behind them. They readied their weapons as he sped toward them, looking beyond him with eager anticipation on their faces. Gotrek stepped out and Felix crashed into his knees. The Slayer hauled him up

'Er,' said Felix, probing his throbbing shoulder. The orc had cut through the leather and torn off some of his scales, but he was unbloodied. 'I got the goblin.'

'Good,' grunted Gotrek, and stepped past him, hefting his axe.

The orcs were spreading out in an even semi-circle and marching down in a dressed rank, weapons at the ready. Felix shivered at the sight.

'They aren't orcs,' said Sketti, uneasily, echoing Felix's unspoken thought. 'They can't be. They're something else, dressed up in green skin.'

'Elves, maybe?' said Narin, smirking.

Druric looked over his shoulder, down the slope. 'They mean to keep us in front of them. They want to push us off the cliff.'

'Let them try,' said Leatherbeard.

The orc leader jabbered an order and the orcs charged, uttering not a word. The dwarfs braced and met the attack with an unmoving wall of sharp steel. Gotrek blocked the leader's first strike, shattered its war axe with his return blow, and then cut its legs out from under it. Two more leapt in to take its place.

Narin and Druric fought back to back in a ring of three orcs. Leatherbeard was stepping over one dead orc to get to another, two dripping double-bladed axes in his massive hands. Sketti Hammer-hand and old Matrak fought an orc that wielded an iron mace the size and shape of a butter churn. Thorgig and Kagrin butchered another with their axes and turned to face two more.

Felix fought a short, barrel-gutted brute with a head like a green pumpkin. Strange, he thought, as he slipped an axe stroke and missed with an attack of his own. Though their tactics were vastly improved, and though their fury seemed to be contained, the strange orcs still fought like orcs, slashing with great, clumsy swings that could flatten a building if they connected, but more often than not missed. Why had one aspect changed and not the other? And what had changed them in the first place? Then he stepped awkwardly on his twisted ankle and all thoughts went out of his head in a rush of pain.

The orc saw him stumble. It swung. Felix lurched aside and ran it through the ribs, jolting his ankle again. The orc collapsed. Felix nearly joined it. The world was fading in and out around him. Another orc attacked, this one stringy and tall. Felix groaned. He wasn't ready. He blocked and retreated, limping badly.

Half the orcs were dead, and not a single dwarf had yet fallen, but by sheer weight and numbers, the greenskins had forced the stout warriors back almost to the black ice that glazed the edge of the cliff. Gotrek killed another and it slid past him as it fell, spinning noiselessly into the void.

Felix stepped back again. His bad foot shot back on the ice. His knee hit the slick surface with a smack. His vision went black and red. He was sliding backwards. The tall orc pushed in, eager to finish him off, and instead sat down abruptly as its feet flew out from under it. Felix grabbed at the greenskin's belt, more to stop himself sliding than as an attack, and pulled the orc towards the edge. It scrabbled uselessly with thick yellow fingernails at the hard ice, then it was gone.

Felix shuddered, terrified, then crawled delicately back up onto the snow, hissing and groaning, as the battle raged around him.

To his right, Narin kicked an orc's leg out and it slammed down on its chin before sailing off the cliff. To his left, Thorgig jumped back from a cleaver slash and tripped over the corpse of a dead orc behind him. He fell flat on his back on the ice and started sliding headfirst for the precipice.

'Thorgig!' roared Kagrin, and stepped forwards, only to slip himself. He clutched at a boulder as he watched his friend spin towards the void.

Thorgig recovered at the last second, and slashed down with his long-axe. The hooked heel of the head bit into the ice and held. He swung to a stop, holding one-handed onto the very end of his axe-haft with his feet dangling off the edge.

Thorgig's orc swung at Kagrin, still clinging to the boulder. It swung. The young goldsmith pushed away, and the orc's axe struck sparks off the rock. Kagrin gashed it behind the knee with his hand-axe and its leg buckled. It fell on its side, grunting, and slid, twisting and flailing, across the ice, coming perilously close to dislodging Thorgig as it flew off the edge.

'Hold fast, Thorgig!' called Kagrin, tearing into his pack and pulling out his climbing rope. He began lashing one end around the boulder, but another orc had noticed him and was coming around the fight towards him. Kagrin dropped the rope and stood.

Felix pulled himself to his feet and started for Kagrin, but his ankle gave out and he nearly fell again. He would never reach him in time. He looked around him desperately. Kagrin blocked a brutal blow with his hand-axe and was smashed to the ground, dazed.

A severed orc head lay behind Gotrek. Felix snatched it by its top-knot and turned in a circle. The gruesome thing was amazingly heavy – all skull, no brain, no doubt. His ankle and knee blazed with pain as he spun.

'Hoy!' he shouted, letting go. 'Ugly!'

The orc looked up just in time to take the head of its comrade full in the face. It wasn't a hard blow, but it distracted it long enough for Kagrin to stagger up and bury his axe blade in the thing's gut. The orc stepped back, surprised, and its paunch ripped open, its entrails spilling out of the wound and slapping wetly on the ice. It slipped on them and crashed down into the snow. Kagrin stood and chopped it through the neck. It spasmed and died. Kagrin threw down the axe and turned back to his rope.

Felix limped forwards to defend Kagrin while he uncoiled the rope, but as he looked around he saw there was no need. The battle was over. The other dwarfs stood panting over their kills, the snow all around them stained with blood, both red and black. Gotrek climbed out of a circle of dead orcs and rubbed the blade of his axe with a handful of snow. Leatherbeard had a long gash across his bare chest, but his was the gravest wound. The rest had only nicks and bruises.

Kagrin tossed the end of his rope towards Thorgig.

The other dwarfs turned.

'Careful, lad,' said Narin. 'No sudden moves.'

'That's why a dwarf always carries an axe, not a sword,' said Sketti, looking disapprovingly at Felix's longsword. 'A sword wouldn't have stopped you.'

Thorgig reached out gingerly with his free hand and felt for the rope beside him. He found it at last and gripped it tight.

'Don't try to climb,' said Gotrek. 'Just hold on.'

He took the rope from Kagrin and pulled it in gently, hand over hand. Thorgig slid up the ice in little jerks and starts, his axe dragging behind him, until Gotrek had pulled him to the snowline. Kagrin took his friend's hand and helped him to his feet. Thorgig's face was set and emotionless, but he was white, and his hands shook.

'Thank you Slayer,' he said. 'Thank you, cousin.' He turned to Felix and inclined his head, 'And thank you, human. I saw what you did. You saved my life and the life of my friend. I owe you a great debt.'

Felix shrugged, embarrassed. 'Forget it.'

'You can be sure that I will not.'

'Slayer,' said Druric. 'We should throw the bodies over the edge, and all the bloody snow with them. There may be another patrol, and it would be best if they didn't learn what became of the first.'

'Aye,' said Gotrek, nodding. 'Carry on.'

While the others pushed and rolled the orcs off the edge, and scooped the stained snow after them, Druric, who carried a field kit, dressed and bound Leatherbeard's wound, and wrapped Felix's swollen ankle in bandages.

'Not broken, I think,' he said.

'It may still kill me,' said Felix, thinking of the descent back down the mountain.

Sketti laughed as Felix forced his foot painfully back into his boot. 'Now maybe you'll slow down and walk at a proper dwarfish pace.'

'And maybe if I hung you by the neck you'd grow to a proper human height,' returned Felix.

Sketti blustered and reached for his axe.

Gotrek gave him a look. 'Never get into a war of words with a poet, Ironbreaker. You can't win.'

When all the evidence had been pitched off the cliff and the dwarfs had bandaged their wounds, they set off once again up the saddle-shaped slope of snow and down through the rocky pass.

'There,' said Matrak, after another half hour of winding around the crags and cliffs of Karaz Hirn. 'There is Birrisson's door, that once led to the gyrocopter landing further up.' He pointed to an unremarkable stretch of black granite that looked to Felix no different from the rest of the mountainside.

Druric studied the ground as they paused before it. He shook his head, frustrated. 'The ground is too hard, and there is no snow here. I cannot tell if the grobi have used this door.' He sniffed. 'They have left no spoor nearby.'

'Where else would they have been going?' asked Narin.

'Circling back all the way to the entrance?' suggested Sketti.

'There isn't much of a path that way,' said old Matrak. 'No path at all.'

'If they do use this door,' said Thorgig, 'does it change our course? We must go in even if it is defended. Prince Hamnir depends on us.'

'It is likely not well defended even if it is used,' said Narin. 'They can't expect an attack from this quarter.'

'Open it and we will see,' said Gotrek.

Matrak stepped forwards, but then hesitated, staring blankly at the wall.

'Don't tell me we've come all this way to have you tell us you've forgotten how to get in,' said Narin. He took tinder from his pack and lit his tin lamp. The others followed his example.

'They know we come. They wait for us,' said Matrak. He was shivering. 'We will all die.'

'Enough of that, you old doomsayer,' said Sketti angrily. 'Open the door!'

As the dwarfs lit their lamps, Matrak nodded and did something at the cliff face that Felix couldn't see. He stepped back. The dwarfs went on guard. Felix drew his sword. At first it seemed that nothing happened. Then Felix frowned and shook his head, assaulted by vertigo. His eyes fought to focus. He felt as if he was sliding backwards, though his feet weren't moving. No, it was the cliff-face getting further away! A tall, square section of it was sinking into the surface of the mountain. Felix strained his ears, but could hear no sound of gears or grinding.

After a moment, the square of rock stopped, about fifteen paces into the mountain, revealing the edges of a dark, cut-stone chamber. When a horde of orcs didn't charge out of the door and attack them, the dwarfs started forwards.

'Hold!' said Matrak. 'There is a trap.' He squatted at the groove in the floor, which the sliding door travelled in, and reached down into it. After a moment of fumbling, there was a clunk that Felix felt more than heard, and Matrak stood.

'Now it is safe,' he said.

It didn't feel safe. Though Felix saw nothing particularly alarming, as he and Gotrek and the others stepped warily through the door, he could not shake the feeling that something wasn't right. His back tingled, and he kept looking over his shoulder, thinking he would find evil eyes glowing in the darkness, but there was nothing there.

Matrak closed the door behind them. On this side, a simple lever operated it. The chamber within was only of a moderate size, by the usual standards of dwarf architecture, with a low arched ceiling, crisscrossed with wooden beams that supported iron pulleys and winches hung with heavy chains. Workbenches, forges and writing desks cluttered the space, and old, half-built machines and contraptions were everywhere. Their shadows moved across the walls of the workshop like the skeletons of strange mechanical beasts as the dwarfs passed among them with their lanterns. A gyrocopter lay dismantled in a corner.

Sketti shook his head as he looked around. 'Engineers are mad,' he whispered. 'All of them.'

Matrak led them to a shadowed archway on the far side of the room. Beyond it was a short, narrow corridor that rose, in a series of long, shallow, slightly slanting steps, to a stone door at the far end.

'Be careful,' said Matrak, holding up his hand as he stopped before it. 'Here is where Birri set all his traps and–' He froze suddenly, and then whimpered softly.

'What is it, now?' asked Thorgig, annoyed.

Matrak stepped back, trembling. 'It isn't right. It isn't right,' said Matrak. 'Smells wrong. All wrong.'

The dwarfs lifted their bulbous noses and inhaled. Felix sniffed too, expecting the familiar animal reek of orcs, but could smell nothing. The dwarfs however were frowning.

'Fresh-cut stone,' said Kagrin.

'Aye,' said Druric. 'Not more than a week old.'

'The orcs have taken up masonry now?' asked Thorgig.

Kagrin thrust his lantern through the arch, illuminating the corridor, and examined it with a critical eye. 'Can't be,' he murmured. 'It's all straight and true.'

Felix scowled. 'You can tell how long ago stone has been cut by the smell?'

'Of course,' said Sketti. 'Men can't?'

Felix shook his head. 'None that I know of.'

'Yours is a sad, weak race, man,' said Sketti, pityingly.

'That rules the world,' Felix retorted.

'Only by theft and trickery,' said Sketti, his voice rising.

'Quiet!' barked Gotrek. He turned back to Matrak, who was staring into the corridor with wet, frightened eyes. 'What does it mean, engineer?'

'They've cut stone. Grobi who cut stone? It...' He moaned. 'It can only mean they've changed the traps.' He turned to Gotrek. 'Valaya protect us all. They knew we were coming! They set new traps!'

Gotrek grabbed him by the front of his chain shirt. 'Stop your snivelling, Grimnir curse you!' he rasped. 'If something's wrong, fix it!'

'He's lost his spine,' sneered Sketti, turning away. 'The greenskins stole it from him before he escaped the hold.'

'You didn't see!' wailed Matrak. 'You don't know! We are doomed!'

'Perhaps there's another explanation,' said Narin. 'It doesn't have to be cunning grobi. Perhaps the trapped clans have managed to retake some of the hold. Perhaps they have added new defences against the grobi.'

'Or maybe the greenskins just walled up the far side of the door, and that's what we smell,' said Leatherbeard.

'Whatever the case,' said Druric, 'we'd best go with caution. It would be a grisly joke to be cut to pieces by traps set by those we come to rescue.'

Gotrek released Matrak. 'Right. Get on, engineer.'

Matrak hesitated, staring unhappily into the tunnel. Gotrek glared at him, hefting his axe. The engineer swallowed and at last stepped reluctantly to the arch again, examining every inch of the surrounding floor and wall before finally touching in sequence three square protrusions in the decorative border. Felix heard nothing, but the dwarfs nodded, as if they sensed that the trap had been disarmed. They started forwards.

Matrak held up a hand. 'Just to be sure.' He took off his pack and dropped it heavily on the flagstones just inside the arch. The dwarfs stepped back, but nothing happened.

Matrak let out a long held breath. 'Right.' He took two steps into the corridor and froze, peg leg in the air. He backed away and waved to the others to retreat. 'There *is* a new trap.' He was sweating.

He squatted and examined the floor, running his fingers lightly along the hair-thin seam between two perfectly cut flags, and then looked around at the walls. Something along the moulding on the right side caught his eye and he shook his head.

'Is it dwarf work?' asked Narin.

Matrak chewed his beard. 'It can't be anything else, but it's… No dwarf would admit to work this bad.' He pointed to a section of the moulding. 'Look how poorly it's set.'

Felix could see no difference between it and the next, but the other dwarfs nodded.

'Maybe they were rushed,' said Thorgig. 'Maybe they tried to finish it before the grobi found the passage.'

'Even rushed, a dwarf would take more care,' Matrak said. 'Something's wrong. Something's wrong…' He bent and pressed the new piece of moulding, then let out a breath as he sensed something that Felix couldn't.

'Go on, engineer,' said Gotrek, more gently. 'Test it and move on. We're late as it is.'

Matrak nodded, and tested the new trap with his pack. Nothing happened. He picked it up and inched forwards again, lamp low to the ground. They proceeded in this slow, painstaking way all along the corridor, Matrak disarming traps he knew, finding new ones he didn't, and looking paler and shakier with each. The dwarfs watched his every move, tensing as he searched for the next trap, and relaxing as he disarmed it.

Felix looked around at the walls and ceiling as they progressed, trying to see signs in the stone work of where these traps would spring from, but he could make out nothing. There were no holes or suspicious ornamentation in the shape of axe or hammer. The stone blocks were so well set, and their patterns so regular, that he could not imagine any trap behind them.

While Matrak grew more and more petrified, the other dwarfs grew more at ease, becoming convinced that their brethren inside the hold still lived, and were putting up a spirited defence of reclaimed halls and chambers.

'They're keeping the grobi out,' said Sketti Hammerhand, as they neared the end of the corridor. 'It's as plain as the nose on your face. There'll be dwarfs on the other side of that door, I'll bet my beard on it. We should stop this pussyfooting and call them to let us in.'

'It will be my father,' said Thorgig. 'He wouldn't sit in his hold doing nothing, waiting for rescue. He would be fighting back, attacking the attackers.'

Matrak stopped before the last step. The door was only two strides away. 'The final step is the last of the old traps,' he said. He reached for a torch sconce in the right-hand wall and pushed on the side of the base with his thumb. It turned, and Matrak breathed a sigh of relief. 'There,' he said, turning to the others. 'Only new ones to find–'

Felix felt a deep thud under the floor and a click overhead.

CHAPTER NINE

THE DWARFS FROZE. There was a rolling sound in the ceiling.

Matrak looked up, blinking. 'The cunning villains,' he breathed, with something akin to admiration. 'They've trapped the disarming switch.'

'Run!' roared Gotrek.

The dwarfs turned, but before they had taken two steps, a huge square of the ceiling above the door swung down, its leading edge hitting the floor with a boom. Kagrin screamed, his foot trapped under it, his ankle crushed to paste. A rumbling came from the hole in the ceiling.

'Kagrin!' cried Thorgig, turning back.

'Fool!' Gotrek grabbed him by the collar and dragged him on.

Stone spheres the size of large pumpkins shot down from the hole and bounded down the hallway. The noise was deafening. One landed squarely on Kagrin's head, squashing it flat, and then sped on with the others, leaving red splotches with each bounce.

The dwarfs ran as fast as their short legs could carry them. It wasn't fast enough. Sketti was mowed down by three spheres. They mashed him to a pulp. Another sphere hit his battered body and vaulted up into the air. Gotrek jerked his head aside and the sphere only grazed his temple. He staggered and wove on, bloody. Thorgig recovered his feet and ran past him. A sphere took

Matrak's peg leg out from under him and he landed flat on his back. Another dropped on his belly, bursting it.

Felix sprinted ahead of the dwarfs, ignoring the agony of his ankle, and threw himself left at the end of the corridor. A stone sphere flew past him, missing him by inches. He looked back and saw another sphere knock Druric sideways into the corridor wall. He fell. Leatherbeard scooped him up with brawny arms and dived out of the corridor to the right. Narin was right behind him. Thorgig dodged a careening sphere and landed face first beside Felix. Gotrek came out last, staggering and weaving inches ahead of two spheres, and crashed on top of Narin, clutching his bleeding head.

The spheres barrelled out of the corridor like charging bulls and smashed into Birri's contraptions and workbenches, turning them into scrap and kindling, before finally losing momentum and coming to rest. A tall copper reservoir tank toppled slowly, two of its metal legs bent, and collapsed to the floor with a metallic crash and a billowing eruption of dust.

Felix and the dwarfs lay where they had fallen, catching their breath and collecting their wits. Felix wasn't sure if he was hurt or whole, or how many of his companions were dead. His mind was still a whirl of running and dodging, and the nightmare grinding sound of the rolling spheres.

A groan from the corridor at last brought Thorgig up. 'Kagrin?' He stood.

'Don't get your hopes up, lad,' said Narin, sitting up and rolling his neck. He gingerly tested his left arm.

Thorgig stepped to the mouth of the corridor. Felix and Narin got to their feet and joined them.

Gotrek stood as well, but had to hold the wall. 'Who tilted the floor?' he mumbled.

Leatherbeard pushed himself up and stood behind the others, pulling his mask straight so he could see through the eyeholes. Only Druric stayed where he lay, curled into a tight ball, his eyes clamped shut in pain.

Another moan came from the hall. Felix and the dwarfs stepped forwards. Four yards in, they found old Matrak. He lay, half conscious, in a pool of his own blood, one of the spheres in the place where his stomach had been. He looked up at the dwarfs.

'Knew it wasn't right,' he murmured. 'Didn't I tell you?'

Thorgig took the old dwarf's hand. 'Grimnir welcome you, Matrak Marnisson.'

'Am I dying, then?'

He was dead before any could answer him. The dwarfs bowed their heads, and then Thorgig looked further up the hall. Sketti lay ten feet away, his body shattered, his sightless eyes staring accusingly at the ceiling. Beyond him was another broken lump. Thorgig started into the shadows.

'No lad,' said Narin. 'You don't want to see.'

'I must!' Thorgig cried.

But before he could take another step, the door at the end of the corridor swung slowly open, half hidden behind the granite ramp of the ceiling trap that had released the stone spheres. A crowd of hulking silhouettes filled it. One reached in and touched the decorative border that surrounded the door. There came a sound of gears and counterweights from the walls, and the trapdoor that had released the stone spheres tilted back up into the ceiling. There were clicks and thuds from behind the walls all along the corridor.

'These aren't the survivors,' said Narin, stepping back.

'But it's impossible,' insisted Thorgig. 'Grobi couldn't have set these traps!'

'Perhaps not,' said Leatherbeard, 'but they just disarmed them.'

The orcs pushed into the corridor, looking down at Kagrin's mashed corpse.

'Forget the traps,' slurred Gotrek. 'Get them.' He stepped ahead of the others, weaving drunkenly and slapping his axe haft into his palm.

'Aye,' said Leatherbeard, joining him. 'They've much to answer for.'

The orc leader spotted the dwarfs in the gloom, and barked an order. The orcs stepped over Kagrin and stalked ahead, silent and alert.

'Ah,' said Felix, back-pedalling. 'I hate to be the voice of reason again, but we won't make the front gate. Not with the whole hold roused. We'll leave Prince Hamnir high and dry.'

'The manling's right, Slayer,' said Narin, edging back. 'We must return to Hamnir and warn him off his attack.'

Gotrek spat and growled a vile oath, but stepped back. He plucked up the sphere that had crushed old Matrak as if it was made of wood rather than stone, and bowled it unsteadily, but forcefully, at the orcs. It caught the first two in the shins and knocked them back into the others, toppling them like ninepins and causing a jumbled pile-up. 'Right,' Gotrek said, turning. 'Out.'

As the other dwarfs started after the tottering Slayer, Leatherbeard stopped and squatted by Druric, who was still only semi-conscious.

'Get him on my back,' he called to Narin. 'Hurry.'

Narin turned back and lifted Druric under his arms. The ranger screamed in pain, spraying blood and spit. Narin ignored him. There was no time to be gentle. He draped him across Leatherbeard's broad back. The Slayer caught Druric's legs and stood. Then he went after the others. In the corridor, the orcs were picking themselves up and starting forwards again.

Thorgig pulled the lever and the dwarfs squeezed through the slowly opening door onto the mountainside, turning down the path that led to the Zhufgrim scarp. When they were all out, Thorgig flipped the lever down and ran through as the door began to reverse directions, but it was closing much too slowly.

They ran on.

The sun squatted on the horizon, a bleeding red ball gutted by the jagged peaks of the Black Mountains. All its warmth was gone. The thin mountain air was growing colder by the moment. It froze the sweat on the back of Felix's neck. The hour agreed upon for Hamnir's attack had arrived, if it was not already past, and there was nothing they could do to tell him that the horn blast would not be coming.

'I will repay the orcs ten-fold for the death of Kagrin Deepmountain,' said Thorgig, his face set. 'They have taken a great craftsman and a greater friend.'

Who had no business being there, thought Felix, as he looked over his shoulder. The door was sliding open again, and the orcs were pouring out of it like a green river. There seemed no end to them, and they were already gaining.

'Pointless to carry me,' gasped Druric from Leatherbeard's back. His face was white and slick with sweat. Each of the masked Slayer's jolting strides brought him fresh agony. 'Leg is broken. Hip as well. Won't make it down the mountain.'

'Bah!' said Leatherbeard. 'I'll strap you to my back. We'll get along.'

'We'll fall,' said Druric through his teeth. 'Pegs won't hold two. Leave me with my axe and crossbow. Let me buy you some time.'

'You want a great doom when I am denied one?' snarled Gotrek. 'Not likely.'

Felix observed that Gotrek was having a hard time running in a straight line.

'Aye,' said Leatherbeard. 'If there's anyone stays behind it'll be me. This is Slayer's work.'

'Ha!' Druric laughed. Blood flecked his lips. 'Do you really want to be remembered as a mere orcslayer? Leave me, and save yourself for a better death.'

No one replied, but only ran on in grim silence.

'Valaya curse you for fools!' cried Druric. 'I will not survive these injuries. Let me die as I wish!'

'Leave him,' said Gotrek, at last. 'A dwarf should have the right to choose the manner of his death.'

They carried Druric until the path became a narrow ledge between cliff and mountainside. The dwarfs could hardly walk it with their shoulders squared.

'Here,' said Gotrek.

Leatherbeard stopped and lowered Druric to the ground. Felix looked back. The orcs were hidden around the curve of the mountain, but he could hear them coming – heavy boots stomping, armour clanking.

The ranger slumped across the ledge, cringing in pain. He took off his pack and field kit. 'Pegs,' he said, teeth clenched against his pain. 'I cannot stand. Pin me to the wall.'

The dwarfs didn't question his order. Leatherbeard lifted him and propped him against the wall while Thorgig and Narin deftly tapped pitons through the back of his chain shirt at his neck and flanks.

Druric grinned. His teeth were filmed with blood. 'Good. This way I will block their way even when I am dead.'

Gotrek was still having trouble holding himself upright. He kept shaking his head and blinking his one eye, one hand on the mountain's flank.

'All right, Gotrek?' asked Felix, concerned.

Gotrek grunted, but made no answer.

'It's done,' said Narin, stepping back. He cocked and loaded Druric's crossbow and put it in the ranger's left hand as Thorgig put his axe in his right.

The orcs rounded into view fifty yards back, loping like patient wolves.

'I had hoped that I would be the one to fight you for the honour of my clan, Slayer,' said Druric. 'I regret that will not come to pass.'

Gotrek stood upright and looked Druric in the eye. 'I'm sorry too,' he said. 'Die well, ranger.' He turned and started down the path.

The other dwarfs saluted Druric in dwarfish fashion, fists over their hearts. They followed Gotrek without a word, Thorgig slinging Druric's field kit over his shoulder. Felix wanted to say something in parting, but all he could think of was 'good luck' and that somehow didn't seem appropriate. He turned, vaguely ashamed, and trotted after the others.

Fifty paces on, they heard sharp cries and the clash of steel on steel echoing from behind them. Gotrek and Leatherbeard cursed, almost in unison. Thorgig muttered a dwarf prayer.

Narin growled. 'He was a good dwarf,' he said. 'Stonemonger or no.'

For almost quarter of an hour it seemed that Druric might have stopped the orcs entirely, for the dwarfs heard no sounds of pursuit, but then, as they were climbing the narrow cleft to the treacherous snowfield, the heavy tread of boots found them again. Felix had fallen behind, his throbbing ankle slowing him, and he heard it first. He picked up his pace, hissing with each step, and caught up to the dwarfs.

'They gain again,' he said.

Gotrek nodded. He seemed to have recovered his balance, but the left side of his head was bruised and purple beneath the drying blood.

'We will have trouble at the top of the cliff,' said Narin. 'They will cut the first rope before we can all traverse the bulge to the pegs.'

'I will stay behind and protect the rope,' said Leatherbeard.

'*I* will stay behind,' growled Gotrek. He stopped as they reached the top of the pass. 'I'll hold here. When everyone gets below the bulge, peg the end of the first rope and blow the horn. I'll cut it myself and swing down. Keep them from following us down.'

'Swing down?' said Thorgig, alarmed. 'You'll pull the peg out.'

'Peg it twice then.'

The orcs appeared at the bottom of the pass and Gotrek turned to face them.

'Go,' he said. 'This is all mine.'

But as Felix and the dwarfs turned to step out onto the snowfield, Leatherbeard looked up. 'What's that?'

Felix listened. Boots were running above them. At first he thought it was a weird echo from the orcs in the pass, then he saw long, hulking shadows lurching across the mountainside above the pass. 'They've split up. Found another trail.'

Thorgig cursed. 'They mean to go around the pool and come at us from behind. They'll find the ropes and cut them.'

'Flanked,' Gotrek growled. 'To the cliff!'

He stormed out of the pass and led them down the saddle of snow. The orcs burst out not twenty paces behind them, flowing down the white slope after them like a green stain. The dwarfs ran as hard as they could, but they had been trekking and climbing and fighting all day, and were gasping and flushed. Felix hissed with each step. His ankle felt thick and spongy. By the time the dwarfs reached the mirror pool, the orcs were ten paces behind. As they raced around the shore towards the cliff-edge, they were only five paces distant, and Felix saw the other group coming down from the crags and circling around the opposite side of the pool. They would reach the ropes only seconds after the dwarfs did.

'Ironskin,' rasped Gotrek, as they hopped the rushing falls. 'You're down first.'

Narin grunted. 'Not much on sharing glory, are you?'

Gotrek skidded to a stop next to the rope and turned to face the orcs as they bounded the stream, a silent green avalanche of death. 'I'll hold the left,' he said. 'The rest of you hold the right. Then down on my call.'

With a roar, the Slayer sprang to meet the charging orcs, chopping down three with his first swing, and another two with his backhand. The orcs swarmed him, slashing at his naked torso with savage silence, but they could not penetrate the net of flashing steel he wove around himself. Orc limbs flew and orc axes shattered as Gotrek blocked and bashed, his orange crest bobbing wildly.

Felix shook his head. He had seen it a thousand times, but it never ceased to amaze him. The Slayer in his element was a terrible and awesome sight. He seemed not to have two arms, but six, and three axes, all moving at blurring speed.

The second group of orcs crashed into Felix and the others from the left, nearly driving them off the cliff. They held just at the brink, parrying and hacking furiously. Felix gored an orc and pulled another past him over the edge as it thrust with a crude spear. It bounced down the bulge and into empty air. Narin and Thorgig dispatched one each, and Leatherbeard hacked down two.

'Down, Ironskin!' came Gotrek's voice from the bloody scrum to their right.

Narin cursed as he gutted another orc, but backed from the combat as ordered, while Felix, Thorgig and Leatherbeard closed ranks. Narin snatched up the rope and started backwards down the cliff. 'You dare not die here, Gurnisson!' he shouted over the clash of weapons. 'You owe my father a fight.'

Felix and the others were pressed back to back with Gotrek as the orcs pushed in on them from all sides, a surging green wall, out of which lashed snapping tusks, massive fists and black-iron axes. Every swing and shift of weight made Felix's ankle scream. Gotrek fought the leader, a huge, milky-skinned orc whose beady black eyes glittered silently at the Slayer with cold intensity as they fought. Felix frowned. Didn't orcs have red eyes? Or yellow?

'Thorgig, down!' called Gotrek.

'What?' cried the young dwarf. 'Me before the human? I won't!'

'Down, or I throw you down,' growled Gotrek, swinging his rune axe up through the black-eyed orc's jaw and into his brain. 'The manling's fought by me for more than twenty years. He knows his business.'

The strangeness of the orc's eyes flew out of Felix's head and he felt a burst of pride as Thorgig started, snarling and reluctant, down the rope. He didn't think he'd ever heard Gotrek compliment his prowess as a fighter before. He fought with renewed vigour, inspired by the off-hand praise, protecting the Slayer's flank and rear as he'd always done, while Gotrek dealt brutal death left, right and centre.

On the other hand, he thought sheepishly, he wouldn't have minded entirely if Gotrek had thought less of him and let him go down first.

Dead orcs lay thick on the ground, but there didn't seem to be any less pressing them, and with Thorgig and Narin making their way down the cliff, Gotrek, Leatherbeard and Felix fought harder than ever. Felix wondered if even Gotrek could keep the orcs away from the rope alone. A cleaver grazed Felix's leg, opening up an angry red gash, and a dead orc, falling from Gotrek's axe, nearly knocked him backwards off the cliff. His ankle throbbed, one pain among many. He felt dazed and numb, the green horde blurred before him. He could hardly hold up his sword.

'Down, manling,' Gotrek shouted. 'It's Slayers' work now.'

Felix nodded and backed out of the fight, relieved, and took up the rope. He saw Leatherbeard puff up at Gotrek's words, just as Felix had a moment earlier, and lay into the orcs afresh, pleased to think that Gotrek counted him his equal. Strange how such a taciturn misanthrope could inspire with an unconsidered word.

As he let himself down, hand under hand, feeling gingerly for footholds with his damaged foot, Felix watched the two Slayers fight back to back, axes flashing crimson in the last rays of the sun, their deep-muscled chests and backs streaked with sweat and blood, their thick legs braced wide before the onslaught of the ravening green horde. And the mad thing was, they were laughing. Inches from the cliff-edge – where a single misstep could send them plummeting – battling scores of savage behemoths that lusted for their blood, and they laughed.

Felix understood this to a certain extent. He was not immune to the euphoria of battle, to the mad rush that came with putting one's life on the line, when pain and weariness and any thoughts of the future went away and one was lost entirely in the glorious violence of the moment. But, for him at least, this was a joy that always teetered on the edge of terror, the excitement always well mixed with fear. The Slayers seemed to have no such qualms. They looked entirely content.

As Felix edged below the bulge, he heard Gotrek shatter that contentment with three little words.

'Leatherbeard, go down!'

'Down? No!' shouted the second Slayer through his mask. 'The glory is here!'

'There's no glory in orcs,' said Gotrek. 'You heard what the ranger said. Down!'

'This is not the respect due to one Slayer from another Slayer!' said Leatherbeard angrily, but finally Felix felt the rope jerk above him as the masked dwarf began his descent.

Though Felix could no longer see the fight, the sounds of it rang down from the cliff like the clanging of a foundry, harsh cries and the clash of steel echoing through the thin mountain air. He looked down. Narin and Thorgig waited by the first peg, each hanging from his own pegged rope, looking up. The rope from the cliff top was, as Gotrek had requested, doubled pegged at its nether end.

'Hurry, human,' said Thorgig. 'The Slayer can't hold forever.'

'I begin to wonder,' said Narin thoughtfully. 'He will be a fearsome opponent. If my father dies fighting him, I will become Thane, Grungni save me…'

There was a thunder-crack bang from above. A body with a Slayer's crest hurtled past Felix, plunging down the cliff into the twilight shadows below. Felix gaped. Had it been Gotrek? Leatherbeard? He looked up.

The rope went slack in his hands.

He fell away from the cliff.

CHAPTER TEN

FELIX STARED AT the loose rope as he dropped, stupid with shock. Another body was falling with him, bellowing. He caught a glimpse of Thorgig gaping at him as he plummeted past him, and thought, 'I am going to die.' Then the rope jerked taut, and ripped out of his hands. He spun and slammed upside down into the cliff with teeth-jarring force, stopped short by something that grabbed his left ankle. His leg was nearly pulled out of its socket.

He sucked in a tremulous breath, heart pounding, and body ringing like a bell. His palms were wet with shock sweat. The world was upside down, and dim at the edges.

I'm alive, he thought, though he wasn't sure how. He should have been spinning down the cliff like a straw doll.

Someone groaned below him. He tipped his head back to look down. Leatherbeard held on woozily to the rope twenty feet further down the cliff, the right half of his mask scraped and scarred and his right shoulder bloody.

If Leatherbeard was hanging from the rope, then it was Gotrek who had fallen. Gotrek was...

A searing pain in his ankle drove the thought away. Well, he had twisted it, hadn't he? Then he realised it was the *other* ankle that hurt now. He fought gravity to look up at it. It was caught in a loop of rope – a loop that was being drawn tighter and tighter by the weight of the masked Slayer clinging to it below him. It was agony, a bright fire atop the dull throb of all his other aches and pains.

'Leatherbeard, get off the–'

Felix snapped his mouth closed, terrified by what he had almost done. The Slayer's weight was all that kept Felix from falling. If he let go of the rope and clung to the cliff instead, the loop would loosen and Felix would slip away.

'Hold fast, manling,' came Thorgig's voice, and the young dwarf rappelled down to stop beside him as Narin dropped down to Leatherbeard.

Thorgig held out his hand. 'Take it.'

Felix reached out and clasped it hard. Below him, Narin was help-ing Leatherbeard, swinging his rope towards him. The Slayer caught it and transferred easily. The pressure on Felix's ankle let up and he dropped again, scraping down the rough cliff face to swing free from Thorgig's hand.

'Now, take the rope,' said Thorgig.

Felix grabbed Thorgig's rope with his free hand, wrapped his legs around it, and let go of Thorgig's hand. He and the three dwarfs hung from the ropes and caught their breath. They could hear the orcs marching away above them, as voiceless as ever.

'The Slayer is dead?' Thorgig asked, looking down into the dark-ness below.

'We'll know when we get to the bottom,' said Narin.

'Surely even Gurnisson can't have survived a fall like that,' said Thorgig.

Narin shrugged. 'If anyone could it would be him.'

'But what knocked him off?' asked Thorgig. 'What was that bang?'

'Maybe they had a shaman with them,' said Narin.

'I saw no shaman,' said Leatherbeard wearily.

'Come on,' said Narin. 'Down we go. No point in speculating. We're late for Hamnir.'

Their descent was much quicker than their ascent had been. The dwarfs used lines and pegs the whole way, and rappelled down in grasshopper-like leaps.

Felix took it slower. His ankle would not allow him their long hops, and he went down in silence, his mind struggling to take in the thought that Gotrek, at whose side he had walked for more than two decades, might be dead.

It was too early to grieve – he couldn't yet believe the Slayer was gone. But the idea of a life without him made his head spin. What would he do? Following the Slayer had occupied almost all of Felix's adult life. His duty to record the Slayer's death had gone on for so long that he had a hard time remembering what it had replaced. What had he meant to do with himself before he met Gotrek? Write poetry, plays? Give up his bohemian ways and help his brother with the family business? Marry? Have children? Is that what he wanted now?

How old was he now? Forty? Forty-two? He had lost track of the years during his and Gotrek's travels in the east. Was it too late to pick up where he had left off? Was a forty-year-old student too ridiculous? Of course, even if Gotrek were dead, Felix still owed him some work before he got on with his life. His vow would not be fulfilled until he had written the epic of the Slayer's death.

His heart sank at the thought. Gotrek would be furious to have it recorded that he had died at the hands of 'mere orcs'. It wasn't a fitting death for a Slayer that had, in his time, killed daemons and giants, an anti-climax of the first order. Gotrek would never let Felix hear the end of it. Except... Felix choked back an unexpected sob as it finally hit him. Except Gotrek was...

'There he is,' said Narin, far below him, pointing down.

Felix stared down into the gloom of the cauldron vale, eyes searching, and at last made out a patch of bright red hair on the shore of the churning lake. The Slayer lay motionless on his stomach, half in, half out of the water. Had he fallen there from the cliff, or dragged himself to the shore? Felix almost lost his grip as he hurried to lower himself to the ground.

Narin, Thorgig and Leatherbeard were down before him, but out of some sense of fitness, waited until he had reached the ground before starting around the steep shore of the boiling lake to the broad, prostrate form. At Felix's limping pace, it seemed to take forever, but at last they stood over him. There was just enough light left in the vale to see that Gotrek's back and neck were a flaming, angry red, as if a giant hand had slapped him. His one eye was closed, and his crest was limp and bedraggled. Blood ran from his nose and mouth, and pooled on the black shale under his head. There was more trickling from under his shoulder. His axe lay beside him.

'Gotrek?' said Felix.

There was no answer.

Felix squatted down and reached out towards the Slayer, but then hesitated. If he touched him he would know, and he was afraid to know. 'Gotrek... Are you?'

Gotrek's eye fluttered open. He groaned, and then coughed violently. Water spilled onto the shale.

Felix and the three dwarfs breathed sighs of relief.

Gotrek's coughing subsided. 'Slow-pokes,' he said, barely audible. 'What took you... so long?'

Narin knelt beside him. 'Can you move, Slayer? Anything broken?'

Gotrek thought for a long moment, eyes closed, and then opened them again. 'No,' he mumbled. 'Just... stings a bit.' He tried to turn over and sit up, but his arms trembled and he sank back.

Thorgig and Leatherbeard helped him up and sat him on a rock. He hissed with every movement and touch. Felix saw that he had a deep, bloody wound in his left shoulder.

'What is that?' he asked, pointing.

Gotrek blinked down at the wound. 'That?' He lifted his hand towards it, but seemed too tired. He let it drop in his lap. 'That is the reason I left the orcs.'

'Don't tell me you made that leap on purpose,' snorted Leatherbeard.

'Of course he did,' said Narin. 'A sparrow insulted his great-great-grandfather, and he leapt off to challenge it.'

Thorgig laughed. They all seemed a bit giddy to find Gotrek alive. 'Sparrowslayer, they'll call him.'

'No,' Gotrek said, shaking his head heavily. 'They shot me. Knocked me clean off the cliff.'

'Shot you?' asked Thorgig, confused. 'With what? That's no arrow wound.'

'A long-gun,' said Gotrek.

'Orcs don't have guns,' scoffed Narin. 'They barely have fire.'

'A dwarf long-gun,' finished Gotrek.

The dwarfs fell silent.

'These are very strange orcs indeed,' said Thorgig at last.

Felix's memory flashed back to the orc lieutenant's glittering black eyes. He had to agree.

Thorgig opened Druric's field kit and brought out bandages. He bound Gotrek's shoulder as best he could as the others saw to their own hurts.

When he was all patched, Gotrek tried to stand. He swayed like a wheatstock in the wind and sat back down. 'Curse it. Leatherbeard, your shoulder. We can't wait.'

Leatherbeard helped Gotrek up and slipped his shoulder under his arm.

Gotrek cocked an eyebrow at Felix as they started around the pool. 'All right, manling? You look a little pale.'

Felix coughed. 'I... I'm just glad I didn't have to make "knocked off a cliff by orcs" sound heroic.'

'Didn't think I was dead, did you?'

'It... it crossed my mind.'

Gotrek snorted. 'You should have more faith.' He hissed and stumbled. Leatherbeard caught him and they continued. 'Good thing that pool was deep though.'

THEY HURRIED AS fast as they could around the base of Karaz Hirn. This wasn't very fast at first, but Gotrek recovered himself after about half an hour, and was able to walk on his own. They made better time after that, though it was still hard going, pushing through the rough terrain and dense undergrowth of the pine forests in almost utter darkness. The dwarfs, not wanting to draw the attention of any more grobi patrols, disdained the use of lanterns, and navigated the woods with the keen tunnel-born sight of their race. Felix, however, was constantly cracking his head on low branches, or re-twisting his ankle on protruding roots.

After a further hour of difficult travel, the five companions came to the valley through which ran the old dwarf road that led to Karak Hirn's front door. As they pushed through a thick wood towards the road, Leatherbeard stopped and held up a hand.

'Someone's on the road,' he whispered.

They listened. The clinking and rumbling of an army on the march reached their ears, and here and there torchlight winked through the tangle of branches.

'It can't be Hamnir,' said Thorgig. 'The forward position is a mile north at least. He can't still be getting into position.'

'Who else can it be?' asked Narin tugging on the burnt piece of the Shield of Drutti in his beard. 'Reinforcements from another hold?'

'Orcs coming up from behind?' asked Leatherbeard.

'We won't find out by talking,' said Gotrek. He pushed forwards and the others followed, more cautiously, unlimbering their weapons as they went.

Soon the wood thinned, and they looked out at the road from its shadows to see a dwarf army marching slowly south.

'It *is* Hamnir!' said Thorgig. 'What has happened? 'He's going the wrong way!'

Leatherbeard pointed to the tail of wounded and dead on stretchers and pony carts trailing behind the main column.

'Did the fool attack without our signal?' asked Narin.

'Prince Hamnir is not a fool!' said Thorgig angrily.

'He is if he attacked a buttoned-down hold,' said Gotrek. 'Come on.'

The dwarfs stepped out of the wood and walked up the weary column to its head. Along the way, various dwarfs glared at them, faces hard and angry. Some of them spat at the sight of them.

'Ah, the hero's welcome,' said Narin.

'What are we supposed to have done?' asked Thorgig.

When they reached the front, they found Hamnir marching grimly with Gorril and his other lieutenants. Hamnir had a cut on his forehead, and his chainmail was rent in two places. Gorril and the others were similarly battered. They looked utterly exhausted.

Hamnir gave Gotrek a flat glance as he fell in step with him. 'So, you live. I am sorry to hear it.'

'So am I,' said Gotrek. 'Wasn't through lack of trying.'

Hamnir ignored him. 'Dead, you would have been a hero – the brave Slayer who tried and failed to win his way into the hold to open the door for the army. Alive... alive, you have a lot to answer for.' He looked at Thorgig sadly. 'As do you, Thorgig.'

'The grobi discovered us, prince,' said Thorgig, hurt. 'We would not have reached the front door to open it. We did our best to remain alive in order to return and warn you not to attack.'

'If you attacked without our signal,' said Gotrek, '*you* have a lot to answer for.'

'We did not attack!' cried Hamnir. 'We were attacked! The greenskins raided our position while we waited to hear the horn – archers in the hills that we could not engage, skirmishers who struck and ran, wolf riders. We dared not pursue, for fear of scattering our force, and so we sat, waiting, for a signal that never came, while they picked us off in ones and twos, and we killed one for every five they slew.'

'Prince,' said Thorgig, his young face pale behind his beard. 'Forgive us, we had no–'

'Indeed, I do have a lot to answer for,' continued Hamnir, hotly, interrupting him. 'For when Gorril and the others begged me to withdraw and give the day up for lost, I would not, for I had faith in my old companion, Gotrek Gurnisson. Surely the great Slayer would not fail. Surely it would only be a matter of a few more minutes before we heard the horn.' He hung his head. 'For my foolishness, I lost another fifty noble dwarfs.'

Gotrek sneered. 'You blame me because you're a bad general?'

Gorril and Thorgig bristled at that, but Hamnir waved them down with a tired hand. 'I am no general at all, as you well know. I am a trader, a seller of sharp steel, fine ale and precious gems. It is fate and duty that have brought me to this pass, not inclination. I can only do my best.' He turned hard eyes on Gotrek. 'Just as you vowed to do your best.'

'You think I have not?' Gotrek growled.

'You are alive and the door remains closed. Can you say you gave your all?'

'Our deaths would not have won the door, Prince Hamnir,' said Narin. 'The grobi were alerted to our presence when poor old Matrak tripped a new trap, which killed him and Kagrin, and Sketti Hammerhand. They came through the secret door and attacked us, and even had we defeated them–'

'New traps?' interrupted Gorril, his voice sharp. 'What do you mean, new traps?'

Hamnir moaned. 'Matrak and Kagrin dead?'

'There were traps in the passage that Matrak did not know of, my prince,' Thorgig explained. 'Dwarf work, he said, and built within the last week, by the smell of the new-cut stone. He found and disarmed all but the last.'

'The orcs opened the secret door and touched the secret levers that disarmed all the traps as if they had built them themselves,' said Narin.

'Impossible,' said Hamnir, ashen-faced.

'Aye,' continued Leatherbeard, 'but true nonetheless. We all saw it.'

'Even had we defeated the orcs who came through the secret door,' continued Narin, 'the alarm had already been raised. There would have been an entire hold of angry greenskins to fight through. Perhaps Slayer Gurnisson might have made it, but the rest of us would not have lived to help him open the doors.'

Hamnir's head drooped. He stared at the ground for a long while, and then, at last, looked up at Gotrek. 'If this tale is true, then I suppose I must believe that you have done what could be done.'

Gotrek sneered, unappeased.

'But how can these things be?' Hamnir continued, almost to himself. 'How can there have been traps that Matrak did not know of? How could the grobi know their use? It makes no sense.'

'I fear we may only learn the answers to these questions once we have retaken the hold, my prince,' said Gorril.

'Aye,' said Hamnir, his jaw tight with frustration. 'Aye, but how are we to do it? They seem to have counters for our every move! We thought this the only way possible. Can we find another?'

'Maybe you can convince them to trade the hold for some fine ale or precious gems,' Gotrek growled.

Hamnir's fists clenched. 'If there was a chance that it would work, I would do it,' he said. 'Would you, Slayer? Or would you leave the hold to the grobi because you found the winning of it lacking in glory?' He moved pointedly away from Gotrek, and began talking in low tones with Gorril.

Gotrek glared at Hamnir for a long moment, then grunted and looked away.

The Slayer and the prince remained silent and sullen for the rest of the march. Felix wondered again what it was that had made them hate each other so. Even among dwarfs, the grudge between them seemed particularly malignant. One usually only saw this sort of intense hatred between brothers who had fallen out. Gotrek had said it had been over a broken vow, but what had the vow been? Did it have something to do with Gotrek taking the Slayers' oath? An insult? A woman? As tight-lipped as the Slayer was, Felix might never know.

THE NEXT DAY, after a deep and well-deserved sleep, Felix joined Gotrek as he reconvened with Hamnir, Gorril, old Ruen, and the prince's other counsellors in Hamnir's quarters. It seemed that, however much enmity there was between Gotrek and the prince, Hamnir still wanted his advice.

Before the meeting, Felix was seen to by a dwarf physician, a white-haired long-beard with gold rimmed spectacles, who ignored all Felix's yelps, gasps and curses as he unmercifully prodded and twisted his swollen ankle. It felt as if the old mumbler was breaking what had only been a sprain, but to Felix's surprise, after the dwarf had smeared it with vile-smelling unguents and wrapped it in bandages, the swelling actually went down and he was able to walk on it almost without wincing.

Felix and the other members of the party who had attempted to penetrate Birri's secret passage were invited to attend so that they could relate everything that had occurred: every trap and every trigger they had found, every encounter with the strange orcs. As they finished, the assembled dwarfs shook their heads, bewildered.

'There are only two possibilities,' said Hamnir, 'and neither of them is possible. It can't be the greenskins, they haven't the skill, and it can't be the dwarf survivors, because they would never ally themselves with grobi.'

'Forgive me for speaking out of turn,' said Felix, 'but I can think of a few other possibilities.'

'Go on,' said Hamnir.

'Well,' said Felix, 'perhaps some covetous group of dwarfs has decided to overthrow your family, prince Hamnir, and take the hold for themselves, and are using enslaved orcs as a cover.'

The dwarfs laughed.

Hamnir made a face. 'This is a thing a dwarf would never do. Dwarfs do not war upon each other. We are too few to thin our ranks this way, and even if we did, no dwarf would send our most hated foes against his fellows, no matter what the provocation.'

'Are there not dwarfs that worship the Chaos gods?' asked Felix. 'From what I have seen of them, they would not scruple to use any weapon.'

'Aye,' said Hamnir, 'but their realm is far from here, beyond the Worlds Edge Mountains, and north. It would be extremely strange to find them so far south.'

'They have been known to enslave grobi,' added Gorril, 'but this is done with the whip and the club. Left alone, the greenskins rebel and do what they will. If the grobi we encountered had been slaves, there would have been Dawi Zharr overseers with them, driving them into battle.'

'Then what about sorcerous enslavement?' asked Felix. 'What if some wizard is bending them to his will?'

Hamnir frowned, thinking it over. 'A sorcerer might possibly enslave grobi this way, though so many, and at such great distances? I don't know. Dwarfs are resistant to magical influence, so it would take a very great sorcerer indeed to turn dwarf minds while at the same time maintaining a hold over all those grobi. I don't believe such a one exists in the world today.'

'Sketti Hammerhand suggested the elf mage, Teclis,' said Thorgig.

Gotrek snorted. 'Teclis may be as twisty as the next elf, but even he wouldn't stoop to using grobi.'

Hamnir sighed and looked off into the middle distance for a moment, lost in thought. 'Sorcery, treachery or enslavement, we must retake the hold regardless,' he said at last, 'and immediately! My worst fear was that the dwarfs of the Diamondsmith clan were murdered or starving to death, but Herr Jaeger has made me fear that even worse has befallen them. No dwarf would succumb to torture, but that does not mean the grobi wouldn't try it. If there is indeed sorcery involved, their fate may be more terrible even than that. I can't bear the thought that Ferga–' He broke off, embarrassed. 'I'm sorry, but we cannot allow them to suffer one more day than necessary.'

'Agreed,' said old Ruen. 'Their fate is a shame to us all.'

'The question remains,' said Narin, idly twisting the sliver of wood in his beard, 'how do we reach them? How do we retake the hold with all entrances watched and trapped?'

The dwarfs sat in silence, pondering the question morosely.

After a long interval, Hamnir put his head in his hands and groaned. 'There may be another way,' he said at last.

Gotrek snorted. 'Another "secret" door that the grobi know all about?'

Hamnir shook his head. 'They cannot know about this door, for it does not yet exist.'

The dwarfs looked up, frowning.

'What's this?' asked Lodrim, the thunderer.

Hamnir hesitated for so long that Felix wondered if he had fallen asleep, but then he sighed and spoke. 'I did not mention this way before, for two reasons. One, it requires going over-ground to Duk Grung, and then returning on the deep road to our mines. I had feared our trapped brethren would die during the week this journey would take, but if the alternative is never getting in, then a week it must be. Second...' he paused again, and then continued. 'Second, this is a secret that I have sworn to my father never to reveal, under any circumstances, a secret that only three dwarfs in this world know about – myself, my older brother and my father. Even though I may save the hold by revealing it, I doubt my father will ever forgive me. I may never be allowed to live in Karak Hirn once it is recovered, but I can think of no other way.'

Gorril looked pale. He stroked his beard nervously. 'My prince, perhaps we can discover another way. I would not wish to see you banished from your home. Nor do I want to anger King Alrik.'

'I am open to suggestions,' said Hamnir. 'If there is another way, I would gladly take it. This is not a step I wish to make.'

The dwarfs thought, mumbling one to another.

'Perhaps...' said Gorril, after a while. Everyone looked up, but he trailed off, shaking his head.

'If there were only a way to...' said Thorgig a moment later, but he too left his sentence unfinished.

'We might...' said Narin, and then frowned. 'No, we mightn't either.'

At last Hamnir sighed. 'Very well,' he said. 'Then I must do what must be done.' He sat up and looked around the table, meeting the eyes of all his councillors. 'My father is a true dwarf, and takes a true dwarf's pride in keeping his personal wealth safe from all prying eyes and grasping hands. In pursuit of this goal, he built, with help from only myself and my brother, a vault of which no one else knows the existence.'

'Your father's vault is in the third deep of his clanhold,' said a long beard. 'All know...'

'That is the vault he shows the world,' said Hamnir, 'where he keeps the majority of his gold and his common treasures. But you will not find the Maul of Barrin there, or the Cup of Tears, or the War Standard of old King Ranulf, our clanfather, or the twenty ingots of blood-gold that could buy all the other treasures of the clan vault. They are not to be shown. They are for his eyes alone, as it should be.'

The dwarfs of Karak Hirn stared, amazed.

'Blood-gold,' murmured old Ruen.

'So,' asked Gorril, involuntarily licking his lips. 'So, where is it?'

Hamnir smiled slyly. 'That I will not tell more than those who need to know. Suffice to say that the entrance is hidden near my father's quarters, and from it, a small company might reach the front doors.'

'From it?' said Thorgig, confused, 'But, prince, how do we reach the vault to exit it? Does it have more than one door?'

'No, it does not,' said Hamnir, 'but there is still a way that we might enter. You see, the vault is an old exploratory shaft, from the first King Ranulf's time – sunk, then abandoned, when it struck no ore. My father found it in his youth, and kept the knowledge secret until he had sons to help him make a vault of it. He did everything in his power to erase any record of the shaft, destroying all the old maps and texts he could find.' His hands clasped each other nervously. 'While secret, the vault is not properly secure. We three were not able to reinforce its walls, nor inscribe them with protective runes. The treasures merely sit at the bottom of the shaft, reachable by the steps we cut into its walls, and surrounded by raw rock. The vault's strength was that no one knew its location, or that it existed at all.' He hung his head. 'With this admission, that strength has now vanished.'

'Er, you haven't yet told us how we are to enter it, my prince,' said Gorril gently.

Hamnir nodded. 'I am avoiding it. I apologise. Here it is. The shaft sinks to the level of the mines, near the diggings my great grandfather abandoned when they kruked out unexpectedly fifteen hundred years ago. One of the kruk's tunnels passes within ten feet of the vault shaft.'

The dwarfs looked at him silently.

'So we dig from the tunnel to the vault? Is that it?' asked old Ruen finally.

'Then we climb the shaft and exit the vault within the hold. Aye,' said Hamnir.

'You're right,' said Gorril. 'You father would not approve. Not only do you lead a party to the location of the vault, you open a door to it that cannot quickly be shut. The king's treasures could be stolen from below while we are busy trying to retake the hold.'

'What about the grobi? Won't they hear you?' asked Gotrek. 'They hold the mines too. Or do you expect me to hold them off for you while you mess about with picks and shovels?'

'The kruk is far removed from the active mines,' said Hamnir. 'There are leagues of tunnels and a stone door between them. The grobi haven't dwarf senses. They won't hear us.'

Gotrek snorted, 'Wouldn't surprise me if they're waiting for us inside the vault once we dig through the walls.'

'That is impossible,' said Hamnir, angry. 'Only three dwarfs knew of the vault before tonight, my father, my older brother, and myself, and none of us were in the hold when the grobi took it. They cannot know!'

'A lot of impossible things've been happening lately,' said old Ruen, thoughtfully.

The dwarfs considered Hamnir's plan in silence, puffing on their pipes and glowering. It was clear they didn't like it. A dwarf hold that lost its treasure lost its honour. They would be seen as weak: poor builders who couldn't protect their possessions. If Hamnir won the hold, but lost his father's treasure, many dwarfs would consider his victory a loss.

At last Gorril sighed. 'It seems it is our only option.'

'We could wait for King Alrik to return with his seven hundred warriors,' said the thunderer. 'He would know what to do.'

Felix heard Hamnir's knuckles crack. His face was rigid. 'That... will not do. In the first place, our cousins who are trapped in the hold cannot wait that long. In the second, to allow the grobi to occupy our home for a day longer than is necessary is intolerable. Third, I will not have my father return to find such a tragedy unresolved. It would break his proud heart.'

Not to mention making you look a worthless fool in his eyes, thought Felix. It looked like the rest were thinking the same thing, but no one said anything.

'Right then,' said Gorril. 'Who will go?'

'I will,' said Thorgig immediately.

'As will I,' said Gorril, 'and we'll need some skilled diggers.' He laughed. 'The trouble will be stopping every dwarf in the castle from volunteering.'

'You will not go, Gorril,' said Hamnir.

Gorril looked stricken. 'But, my prince...'

'No,' said Hamnir. 'You proved yesterday that you are a more able general than I. Had you been in command, many dwarfs would be alive today. You will stay and lead the assault on the main door. I will lead the party to the mine. I can burden no one else with the knowledge of the vault's location. Its opening must be on my head alone. No other will suffer my father's wrath.' He turned to Gotrek. 'You, Slayer, may stay here, or go north to fight Chaos if you wish. You have already come perilously close to dying while honouring your vow to me. I free you from further obligation. I have no wish to force my unwelcome company upon you for the duration of our journey.'

Gotrek glared at Hamnir for a long moment. 'You must not think much of my honour, Ranulfsson,' he said finally, 'I swore to help you retake Karak Hirn. Unlike some I could name, I don't break my vows. I'll leave once you're sitting in your father's chair in the feast-hall. Then, we'll talk about another vow we made once. Until then, I'm sticking by your side. If you're going to Duk Grung and back, I'm coming with you.'

CHAPTER ELEVEN

'THIS ISN'T RIGHT,' muttered Thorgig.

Felix, Gotrek, Hamnir and the others lay flat in a ditch, watching as the vague silhouettes of an orc patrol passed by not twenty paces away in a thick predawn fog. The party had left Rodenheim Castle not half an hour before, slipping quietly through the postern gate without lantern or torch, heading down out of the foothills towards the green plains of the Badlands. In addition to Hamnir, four had been added to those who had survived the journey to Birri's door and back – three brothers from Karak Hirn who had mined Duk Grung in their youth, and another dwarf of the Stonemonger clan, who was a skilled mine engineer.

'Woe if any other Slayer ever learns that I twice hid from orcs,' agreed Leatherbeard.

'And ran from them as well,' whispered Narin, helpfully.

'Quiet, curse you!' said Hamnir.

The orcs had been watching Rodenheim Castle ever since Hamnir's army had returned to it. They patrolled around it endlessly, watching every road and goat path. This was more proof of their strangeness. They should have been pouring out of the captured dwarf hold in a frenzied, futile attempt to come to grips with their ancestral enemies. The dwarfs could have wished for nothing more. If the orcs had thrown themselves against the walls of the castle, they could have gunned them down at their leisure, thinning their ranks and making their eventual raid on Karak Hirn all the easier. But the orcs came in skulking squads, observing, not attacking, and staying well away from the walls. It was eerie.

At last, as the dark forms moved off, melting once again into the mist, Hamnir stood. 'Right,' he said. 'On we go, but keep your eyes and ears open. We can't be seen.'

The fog was their friend in this. The party walked down the last ridge and onto the rough plain without hearing or seeing another patrol. Hamnir turned them east and slightly south, and they marched in damp, chilly silence.

After another hour, the fog began to lift, revealing the sparse pines and rocky ground of the barren, hilly land, and then later, the jagged line of the Black Mountains under low, iron-grey clouds. The air remained cold and wet around them, like a clammy embrace. Felix shivered in his old red cloak, and expected at any moment to be drenched with rain, but it never came.

Hamnir walked at the front of the party, Thorgig at his side, eyes moving alertly around the landscape. Gotrek stayed at the back, his brow as clouded as the sky. The Slayer and the prince seemed disinclined to speak, either to each other, or to anyone else.

After a time, the mining engineer, a wide-shouldered, sway-gutted veteran with a red face, a redder nose, and a bushy ginger beard shot with grey, dropped back to Gotrek, sticking his chin out so his beard bristled. 'You know why I volunteered for this company, Slayer?' he asked, loudly.

Gotrek didn't acknowledge him, only stared ahead.

'My name is Galin Olifsson,' said the engineer, slapping his chest with a meaty palm, 'a Stonemonger of the Stonemonger clan, same as Druric Brodigsson. You remember him, Slayer?'

Gotrek spat. A wiser dwarf than Galin might have noticed the balling of his fists.

'Word is, you left him behind to die, Slayer,' snarled Galin, 'while you ran like a coward from mere orcs.'

Felix barely saw Gotrek move, but suddenly Galin was flat on his back with blood streaming from his nose into his moustache and mouth. He blinked up at the sky. Gotrek kept walking, but the rest of the party was turning.

'Curse you, Gurnisson!' cried Hamnir. 'Will every dwarf who marches with me have a broken nose before you're through? We must all be whole and ready if we are to succeed.'

'He asked for it,' said Gotrek, shrugging.

'I wasn't ready, you damned cheat,' said Galin, sitting up woozily and pinching his misshapen nose.

'You call a Slayer a coward and aren't ready to be hit?' asked Leatherbeard, laughing. 'Then you're a fool.'

'Druric asked to stay behind,' said Narin, offering Galin his hand. 'And if you've a fight to pick with the Slayer you'll wait until this business is finished like the rest of us.'

Galin batted aside Narin's hand, sneering, and stood by himself. 'The word of an Ironskin is to be trusted? They who stole the Shield of Drutti from us? You likely told the Slayer to leave my cousin behind.'

'No one tells the Slayer anything,' snorted Narin, then held out the sliver of wood twisted in his beard, his eyes bright with mischief. 'And I have the Shield of Drutti here, what's left out of it, if you care to carry it.'

'You mock me, Ironskin?' said Galin, puffing up his chest. 'You're next after the Slayer if you think–'

'Olifsson!' barked Hamnir. 'If you joined us only to fight us, you can return to the castle. Now stand down!'

Galin glared daggers at Narin and Gotrek, but at last turned away, straightening his armour and dabbing at his still bleeding nose with a voluminous kerchief. 'I can wait,' he grumbled. 'A dwarf is nothing if not patient.'

The other three dwarfs who had joined the party grinned behind Galin's back. They were the Rassmusson brothers, Karl, Ragar and Arn, who looked so alike that Felix had trouble telling them apart – a trio of bald, black-bearded miners whose skin had been permanently begrimed with the dirt and ore they dug. The seams of their faces and their cracked knuckles were grey with it.

'Nice one,' said one – Arn, perhaps, Felix thought.

'Don't see a punch like that every day,' said a second, nodding – Karl, possibly.

'I'll show you one,' snarled Galin, turning and raising his fist.

The third brother, who by process of elimination, Felix decided must be Ragar, raised his hands. 'No disrespect, cousin,' he said. 'We don't say you deserved it.'

'You took it well, too,' said the one that Felix had decided was Arn. 'No weeping or moaning.'

'No calling quits,' agreed the one who therefore had to be Karl. 'On your feet and ready for another right quick.'

Galin eyed them suspiciously for a moment, trying to see if they were laughing at him. 'All right then,' he said finally, and turned back around.

The brothers exchanged sly glances.

'Really was quite a punch, though,' said Ragar.

'Aye,' said Arn. 'Once in a lifetime, that punch.'

'Ha!' said Karl. 'Punch like that could *end* a lifetime.'

Galin's shoulders tensed, but he didn't turn around. The brothers grinned as if they'd won a victory.

FELIX FOUND HIMSELF falling behind the others because of his ankle. The dwarf physician had done a remarkable job, and there was no longer much pain, but it was still stiff, and his stride was stilted. Gotrek, apparently as much to keep at a distance from Hamnir as to keep Felix company, hung back with him.

'What is your grudge against Hamnir, anyway?' Felix asked at last. 'You two were obviously friends at one time. What came between you? A girl? An insult? Gold?'

Gotrek snorted. 'Men can't understand dwarf honour, since they have none of their own. He broke an oath. That's all you have to know.'

'What oath?' pressed Felix. 'What could he have done that was so bad? He seems a decent enough fellow, very even tempered, very reasonable.'

'Ha!' said Gotrek. 'You like him because he acts like a man, with a man's manners and smooth talk, but he's got a man's tricky nature too. He doesn't stick to his word. To a dwarf, an oath's an oath, big or small, but not to that one.' He scowled towards the front of the line. 'A pair of pretty eyes or a better offer and he'll turn his back on a brother. He'll squirm and twist and quote law to get out of his bond.'

'Ah, so it was a girl,' said Felix.

'I'll say no more.'

'Very well,' said Felix.

They walked on in silence for a while, but Felix's curiosity was aroused. 'When did all this happen? Were you already a Slayer?'

Gotrek shot him a sharp glance. 'You trying to pry it out of me, manling?'

'No, no,' said Felix. 'Only, if you die here, I'll need to include Hamnir and the others in the epic of your death: "The brave party the Slayer led", and all that. I'll need to know something about how you met and what you did, to give it some body, some breadth, aye?'

Gotrek thought for a moment, and then nodded. 'I suppose you've a right to some history. Every epic I ever heard told in the feasthall started in the cradle, and it's best you hear it from me and not that silk-tongued oathbreaker.' He shot a sharp look up at Felix again. 'Not that I'll tell you everything, mind. Just enough.'

'Enough will suffice, I'm sure,' said Felix, trying not to sound too eager. It was rare for Gotrek to share anything of his past. 'Go on.'

Gotrek walked on, frowning, as if gathering his thoughts. 'I met Hamnir when he came to the clan of my fathers,' he said at last. 'This was long before I took the crest, when I was still a shortbeard. There was peace in the hold then. Too calm for me. I wanted a fight.' He ran his hand absently through his beard. 'Hamnir was restless too. Wandered all the way from Karak Hirn to the Worlds Edge because of it.' He snorted. 'Read too many books. Wanted to see the world. Wanted to see the wonders he'd read about.' Gotrek shrugged. 'There was fighting in most of the places he talked about – the Sea of Claws, the Empire, Bretonnia – so I said I'd go with him.'

'It was just a travel arrangement?' asked Felix. 'You weren't friends?'

'Me? Friends with that treacherous…' Gotrek paused, and then sighed. 'Eh. Suppose I was. He seemed a good dwarf then. Kept me out of trouble when I was looking to get in it, and got me out of it if I was already in. Talked an elector count out of hanging me once. Whatever army we signed on with, he got us a good deal, and if our commander tried to cheat us, Hamnir always got the money anyway.'

Gotrek smirked and shot another glance towards Hamnir, then grunted and looked away. 'Wasn't much of a mercenary though. Handy enough in a fight, and a good tactician on paper, but he'd get muddled when things went wrong.' Gotrek snorted. 'Didn't have the mercenary spirit either. We'd loot castles and all he took was books. He once punched a captain of ours who smashed a statue. Didn't mind killing man, dwarf or elf, but you couldn't burn a painting around him.'

'How long did you travel with him?' asked Felix.

Gotrek shrugged. 'Ten years? Twenty? Can't remember. Might have been fifty. We fought through the Empire, Bretonnia, down the coast hunting pirates, the border princes, Estalia, Tilea…' He trailed off.

'Tilea?' prodded Felix.

Gotrek came back to himself and scowled at Felix. 'No, manling, I said I'd tell you enough. You'll get no more.'

'But how can you tell a tale and not the finish?'

'He broke his oath,' Gotrek snarled, 'that's the finish. Now leave me be.'

The Slayer strode forwards, catching up with the last of the dwarfs, leaving Felix to limp along behind by himself.

Felix cursed himself for a fool. He'd almost had it. If he hadn't pushed so hard at the end, Gotrek might have told him on his own. Still, he knew now about a stretch of Gotrek's life that even he hadn't known existed before. That was something at least.

ON THE MORNING of the third day, the dwarfs turned north again, winding their way up through narrowing valleys and canyons into the foothills of the Black Mountains until the Badlands disappeared behind a screen of pine-furred hills.

As they pushed on, Hamnir let the Rassmusson brothers lead the way, for in their youth they had worked the Duk Grung and had made the trip many times. The three dwarfs tramped confidently up slopes choked with mountain laurel and clinging nettles, along swift streams and deer tracks, and dirt roads long overgrown with weeds and wildflowers, commenting all the while.

'Isn't this the place where old Enrik dropped an ingot and made us search the bushes for six hours?' asked Arn, as they passed a fallen tree.

'Aye,' said Ragar, 'and he had it in his pack the whole time.'

'I remember,' said Karl, laughing. 'Found it when he bit into his pasty. Chipped his tooth.'

'Always thought Dorn had something to do with that,' said Arn, 'but he never owned up.'

A little further on Karl pointed to a granite ledge overlooking a small, fern-skirted pool. 'The rock of the full moon!' he cried.

His brothers laughed uproariously, but wouldn't explain what he meant.

As the sun reached its zenith, they saw ahead of them the mouth of a canyon that was walled off with thick stone battlements, in the centre of which stood an open gateway guarded by two squat towers.

'There we are,' said Arn, pointing. 'Duk Grung.'

Looking at the old walls peeking through the trees, Felix was struck again by just how long dwarfs lived. For though the walls were sturdy dwarf work and had stood the test of time with barely any weathering, they were thickly overgrown with vines, moss and bushes and the gates had long ago rusted away. The place looked like some ruin of antiquity, and yet Arn, Karl and Ragar had worked here when it was a going concern.

'Grown up a bit, hasn't it?' said Ragar. 'Had a human gardener in our time who did for the pruning.'

'I remember him,' said Arn. 'Wolfenkarg, or something. Luden-holt? Some mannish gibberish. Couldn't hold his liquor.'

'Wonder what's become of him,' said Karl.

'Well, he was a man,' snorted Arn, 'so he's long dead, isn't he?'

'Like may-flies they are,' said Ragar. He shot a guilty glance at Felix. 'No offence, human.'

Felix shrugged. 'None taken.' It was only the truth.

Approaching the rusted remains of the gate, the dwarfs saw a wide, deeply worn track running along the wall and through the gate. They stopped, growing quiet, their hands dropping to their weapons. The two Slayers studied the track intently while the others shot wary glances into the trees around them.

'A troll,' said Leatherbeard, 'and the tracks are fresh.'

'Two trolls,' Gotrek said. 'At least two.'

'One for each of us,' said Leatherbeard jauntily, but his voice was tight.

'Have they made their home in the mine?' asked Hamnir.

'Let's find out,' said Gotrek.

The dwarfs unslung axes and crossbows and followed him through the open gate, on guard. Felix drew his sword. Inside the wall, the canyon rose and narrowed, pinched between two steep, rocky hills. The crumbled remains of old outbuildings peeked out from thickets of young trees on either side of the troll track, which wound up through the centre.

'Cart mule stables,' whispered Karl, waving to the left.

'And Lungmolder's shack,' said Arn, motioning to the right. 'Trouble with wood. Doesn't last.'

'Was it Lungmolder?' asked Ragar. 'Thought it was Bergenhoffer, or Baldenhelder, or–'

'Hush, curse you,' said Galin. His eyes were bulging, and his red face was sweating.

They crept up the troll track to the end of the canyon, a tight funnel between the converging hillsides. In the western slope, there was a black opening, nearly hidden by a thick screen of raspberry bushes. The dwarfs approached it cautiously. As they got closer, Felix saw that the opening was a rough hole, broken through what appeared to be a large, walled-up door, its outlines only barely discernible under the dense cloak of vegetation.

'It's been breached,' said Karl.

'That's bad, that is,' said Ragar.

Arn shrugged. 'Kruked out anyway.'

'Might not have been iron they were after,' said Narin.

'Might have been trying to reach Karak Hirn,' said Thorgig, grimly.

Galin snorted. 'If they tried, lad, it was a hundred years ago, and Karak Hirn survived.' He pointed at the edges of the breach. 'Any dwarf with the eyes Grungni gave him can see that that hole was bashed in long ago. All the breaks are weathered.'

'Call me "lad" again, and I'll feed you the tongue Grungni gave you,' said Thorgig, glaring at the engineer.

'Until you can tuck your beard in your belt, I'll call you what I like,' said Galin.

'I'll tuck your beard up your–'

'Enough!' hissed Hamnir. 'Both of you.'

Leatherbeard pointed to the deep-worn troll track. It wound through the raspberry bushes and right to the hole. 'The hole may be old, but the place is occupied still.'

'Saves us looking for the hidden latch at least,' said Ragar.

'Right,' said Hamnir, taking a deep breath. 'Light your lamps and in we go, Slayers first.'

The dwarfs unhooked sturdy horn lanterns from their packs, lit them from tinder jars, and hung them from their belts so they would have both hands free. Gotrek lit a torch, which he held like a weapon in his off hand. When all were ready, they pushed through the undergrowth to the hole. Though it was small compared with the walled-up door, the break was still twice as tall as Felix, and twice as wide as Gotrek. They peered in. It was utterly black inside.

Gotrek stepped forwards, holding his torch back and to the side, so as not to blind himself. Leatherbeard followed, with the others edging in behind him. A cold wind blew an astounding stench out at them – a rich mix of offal, rotting meat, mildew, and an acrid animal musk even more pungent than that of orcs.

Narin wrinkled his nose. 'Nothing smells worse than a troll.'

'Two trolls?' suggested Arn, or possibly Ragar.

'Quiet!' whispered Hamnir.

On the far side of the door, the hole opened out into a wide chamber. As Felix's eyes became accustomed to the dark, he could make out monumental doorways in each of the walls, and looming pillars holding up a high ceiling. Below this grand dwarf architecture, rubbish lay in swathes: heaped piles of bones, smashed furniture and machinery, rotting carcasses, burnt timber, as well as drifts of brown leaves and tree branches, blown or dragged in from outside.

In one corner, a fire pit had been dug into the stone floor, over which hung a dented iron pot, bigger than a nobleman's bath. Crude log stools and settles surrounded the fire, and two beds of bracken were laid nearby. Limp forms hung from spikes bashed into the walls – two men, an orc, a cow, and a wolf, all skinned and hung to drain. The bones and clothing of earlier feasts were piled within easy flinging distance from the fire pit. Skins were laid out on the floor and held flat with rocks.

'Seems lord and lady troll are not at home,' said Narin.

'Trolls in old Duk,' said Ragar, shaking his head. 'A damned shame.'

'Aye,' said Karl. 'To see the old place mucked up like this, it breaks your heart.'

'Not the tidiest housekeepers, are they?' said Arn, sniffing.

Hamnir looked around uneasily. 'I'd almost rather have found them in their lair,' he said. 'Worse not knowing where they are.'

'Another doom missed,' said Gotrek, morose.

'Which way to the deeps?' asked Hamnir, turning to the Rassmusson brothers.

They looked around, stroking their beards. Then Arn spoke up. 'Barracks that way.' He pointed right. 'Smelters that way.' He pointed straight ahead. 'Workface that way.' He pointed to the left.

'Left then,' said Hamnir.

Gotrek and Leatherbeard led the way across the chamber towards the left-hand arch. Their path took them past the pile of bones, boots and breeches near the cook pot, and as they walked by it, things glinted from it in the lamplight.

Galin stopped, followed by Ragar, and then Hamnir. The others turned to see what they were looking at.

'Is that...?' said Galin.

'Look at that now,' said Ragar.

'It is,' said Hamnir.

'Gold!' said Arn, and stepped to the pile of bones, tossing aside a ribcage and squatting down. The others were right behind him. Even Gotrek was pushing forwards.

Felix looked over their shoulders. The ground amidst the bones and torn clothes was littered with rings, neck chains, unset gems, armbands, gold ingots and the coins of a dozen different nations. The dwarfs snatched them up in handfuls. Narin snapped a finger from a skeleton hand to get at a silver ring. Karl was prying a gold tooth from a grinning skull.

'Stupid trolls,' chuckled Ragar, scooping greedily. 'Throwing away a fortune for stew meat.'

'They're animals,' said Narin. 'The lower orders don't understand the ecstasy of gold.'

'Do we have time for this?' asked Felix, looking anxiously behind him. 'The trolls could come back at any moment.'

The dwarfs ignored him.

Thorgig batted at Galin's hand. 'That was mine, Olifsson,' he snapped. 'I touched it first.'

'And you dropped it,' said Galin. 'It's mine now.'

'Mind your reach!' snarled Leatherbeard to Narin. 'This is my bit.'

'Can I help it if I have longer arms than some,' said Narin, his eyes glowing.

'And stickier fingers.' Leatherbeard shoved Narin, who fell back on his haunches.

'Shove me, will you?' growled Narin, reaching for his dagger.

'Cousins! Cousins!' cried Hamnir. 'Stop this! Stop this! What are we doing?'

Felix breathed a sigh of relief. The prince was going to talk some sense into the others. He at least realised the dangers of their position.

'This is not the dwarf way,' said Hamnir, 'scrabbling like men for scraps of bread. We are a military company on a military mission. This treasure is therefore spoils, and subject to strict division. Now come, take it all out of your pockets and pile it in the centre here. We will see what we have and make our split accordingly. Ten equal shares.'

Gotrek's snort interrupted him. 'Equal shares? That's rich broth coming from you, oathbreaker.' He turned to the others. 'I'd watch him if I were you. He's apt to put a little extra aside for himself.'

Thorgig sprang up, fists bunched. 'Do you call Prince Hamnir dishonest? You go too far at last, Slayer.'

'That's our chief you're speaking of,' said Ragar stepping up beside Thorgig.

'Have a care,' said Arn.

'A red crest don't scare us,' said Karl.

'Come, Slayer,' said Narin. 'Can you truly think that a prince known throughout the holds as a plain dealer would cheat on shares?'

'This from a dwarf who destroyed the property of my clan and won't make recompense,' sneered Galin.

'I don't think,' said Gotrek. 'I know. He's done it before.'

'Gurnisson,' said Hamnir, brow lowered.

'Oh, he'll have a reason,' said Gotrek, 'some excuse why this piece or that piece shouldn't be shared out with the rest. He's good with words. It all sounds reasonable, but whatever it is, in the end, you don't get all that's coming to you with Prince Hamnir the Honest around.'

'You don't get any understanding with Gotrek Gurnisson around, either,' said Hamnir hotly. 'The head and the heart don't matter to him, only the purse. Sometimes I think he's more of a merchant than I am. A dwarf who knows the price of everything and the value of nothing.'

'So, you admit these things he speaks of?' asked Narin, his eyebrows raising.

'Not as he says them,' said Hamnir. 'I cheated no one. In each case, I asked all parties if something could be held out. Put it to a vote. Only Gotrek voted no. The others had some compassion, some belief that the spirit of justice is more important than the letter of the law.'

'Not in every case, oathbreaker,' said Gotrek. 'In one case you just took what you wanted.'

'Because you wouldn't listen to reason!' shouted Hamnir.

His voice echoed through the hall, seeming to come back to them louder than it had left his mouth. The dwarfs looked around warily as the echoes faded to nothing.

'Gotrek, Prince Hamnir,' said Felix, into the silence. 'Perhaps you should return to this debate, and the division of the spoils, at a later date. We are not safe here, and we still have a long way to go.'

'I second that,' said Narin. 'We should move on.'

After a moment, Gotrek shrugged. 'Fair enough. Might be less of us to divide amongst at the end anyway.'

Hamnir nodded. 'Very well,' he said, 'and as my honesty has been questioned, I will not hold it. Nor will any of my hold.'

The dwarfs looked around. Thorgig, Arn, Karl and Ragar, were all of Karak Hirn; that left Galin, Narin, Leatherbeard, Gotrek and Felix.

Gotrek shook his head. 'I'm not carrying all that. It'll get in the way.'

'Aye,' said Leatherbeard. 'No thanks.'

'Nor I,' said Narin. 'I know my weaknesses. I'll not be put in the way of temptation.'

'Er,' said Galin. 'I would be honoured to hold the plunder. The honesty of the Stonemonger clan is known from Worlds Edge Mountains to–'

'And the dwarf who asks for the honour is the dwarf to keep your eye on,' interrupted Thorgig. 'You're not holding my share, Stonemonger.'

'You question my honesty!' said Galin, standing. 'Dwarfs have died for less!'

'Quiet!' snapped Hamnir. He looked at Felix. 'The man will hold it.'

'The man?' Galin gaped. 'But all dwarfs know men are greedy, grasping little–'

Gotrek growled menacingly.

Narin laughed. 'They say the same of us, but you'll note that he was the only one who didn't dive into the pile with both hands grasping. And anyone who's thrown in their lot with a Slayer for twenty years can't be accused of being a man who puts his holdings first.'

'But, prince,' said Thorgig, 'he is the Slayer's companion. He will favour Gurnisson over the rest of us.'

'If he does, I'll kill him,' said Gotrek.

Hamnir nodded. 'Gurnisson may be a stiff, unbending berserker with the disposition of a dyspeptic cave bear, but he is as honourable as an ancestor. It isn't honesty he's wanting, but heart. He will not let Herr Jaeger cozen us.'

Arn shrugged. 'Fair enough.'

'Suits me,' said Karl.

'If the prince says aye, who are we to say nay,' said Ragar.

'If that's the way of it,' said Galin with a stiff shrug, 'that's the way of it.'

The dwarfs quickly emptied their pockets and pouches into Felix's pack and made ready to march again. Felix groaned as he stood and shouldered the pack. The greedy little grubbers had added a stone's weight to his load – they who could lift twice their own weight with ease.

The party took the left-hand arch and started down a corridor lined with long-unused dining halls and common rooms, the outlines of their sturdy furniture softened by centuries of dust. This had not been a true hold, only an outpost, a satellite mine, meant to feed the furnaces and anvils of Karak Hirn. Still, it was built with all the usual dwarf care and quality. There had been no cave-ins in the intervening centuries since the dwarfs had abandoned it. No water stains marred the walls. The flagstones that lined the floor had not cracked. The decorative borders looked as if they had been cut only yesterday.

After a few hundred feet, they came to the rusty rails of a mine cart track, which connected the deeps of the mine with the smelting rooms. The rails branched and turned down crossing corridors, glinting in the darkness. Here and there, they had been pulled up, the wooden ties beneath them too, but most were undisturbed. The dwarfs stuck to the main trunk, which soon led them to the shaft of an ancient dwarf steam lift, meant to raise and lower crowds of dwarfs, carts, mules and tonnes of ore at a time.

Galin, the only engineer among them, had a look at the steam engine that had once powered the thing, built into a room behind it. He came out shaking his head, his beard and eyebrows trailing dust and cobwebs. 'Not a chance,' he said. 'Half the gears have rusted into place, and someone's been at the boiler with a pickaxe. Take a week to make it go. Maybe more.'

'Don't know if the ropes would hold us anyway,' said Narin, holding his lantern out into the shaft. The huge hawser cables were frayed and black with mould.

Felix looked down the shaft. He couldn't see the carriage in the darkness below, but the ropes were tight, so it was down there somewhere.

'Wasn't to be expected anyway,' said Hamnir. 'We'll take the ladder.'

A narrow ledge led out to a square notch in the left side of the shaft, cut just deep enough for a dwarf to climb down into the depths on the ladder that was bolted to its wall without being knocked off by the passing of the lift carriage. Leatherbeard went first. The others lined up behind him.

'Are there any other ways to get down?' asked Felix, waiting his turn. 'I've had my fill of climbing recently.'

'Oh, aye,' said Karl. 'You can walk down through all the deeps by ramp and stair.' He grabbed an iron rung and started down into darkness.

'A lot of walking though,' said Arn, following him.

'This way's faster,' said Ragar.

'I wouldn't mind the walk,' said Felix, sighing, but he stepped onto the ladder behind Ragar and began lowering himself down rung by rusty rung.

Gotrek came last, for the dwarfs were concerned that the trolls might return home and follow them down. He exchanged his torch for a belt-hung lamp, so that he could have both hands free to climb.

For all Felix's grumbling, he found the descent easy. The ladder was dwarf work, and though over two hundred years old, it was still strong and firmly fixed to the wall. At regular intervals, they passed further deeps – wide, rough tunnels, laid with cart rails. Sometimes there would be abandoned mine carts at the lip. In one, something larger than a rat scrabbled away in the darkness. In another, picks and shovels were scattered about.

'Those aren't dwarf tools,' said Ragar.

'No,' said Arn. 'We took everything with us when we closed up shop. Dwarfs don't waste.'

'Someone else looking for scraps,' said Karl, snorting. 'Fool humans, most like. Should know better. Dwarfs don't leave untapped veins.' He looked up the ladder at Felix. 'No offence, human.'

Felix sighed. 'None taken.'

Halfway between the fifth and sixth level down, they found the elevator carriage, an open steel and wood cage hanging straight and true in the shaft as if it had only paused for a moment. Felix looked at it longingly as they passed it. It would have been luxury to step onto it and ride the rest of the way down, but closer inspection suggested that might be a very speedy trip. Near the steel rings that the ropes were fastened to, the hawsers were frayed and thin, as if rats had been chewing on them. It looked as if the merest feather landing upon the carriage would be enough to snap the rope and send the whole thing crashing into the nether depths.

'I am suddenly glad the engine wasn't working,' he said to no one in particular.

Another level down and Leatherbeard held up a hand. 'Something moving below,' he said.

CHAPTER TWELVE

FELIX AND THE dwarfs stopped, listening. At first, Felix heard nothing, but then he caught it – a faint scratching and skittering, echoing up the shaft. It was getting louder.

'What is it?' asked Thorgig. 'Rats?'

'Isn't trolls,' said Arn. 'That's certain.'

'Whatever it might be,' said Hamnir, 'it's coming this way.'

Narin pulled a torch from his pack, lit it from the lamp at his belt, and dropped it down the shaft. The dwarfs watched its ball of illumination fall swiftly away from them. Felix's heart lurched as, two levels down, the torch flashed past a churning mass of hairless, dog-sized monstrosities, briefly glinting off their jagged fangs and bulging black eyes, and the razor claws with which they were climbing the shaft's rough-hewn walls. Then the torch dropped below the things, returning them to darkness. There had been dozens of them.

'What are those?' choked Felix.

'Cave squigs,' spat Karl. 'Grobi rats.'

'Thought we'd killed them all off,' said Ragar.

'We did,' said Arn, 'two hundred years ago.'

'Difficult fighting them here,' said Thorgig, frowning. 'They'll tear us off.'

Felix shuddered. After all his years with Gotrek, he didn't mind a stand-up fight. He would have faced down this pack of horrors

435

undaunted on level ground, but hanging off a ladder over a bot-tomless pit, with only one arm free to defend himself? No, thank you. He could already feel their teeth and claws tearing into him, ripping him savagely from the rungs.

'Wait here,' said Gotrek. He started climbing rapidly back up the ladder.

'Wait here?' asked Felix.

'Where's he off to?' growled Galin.

Felix shrugged. He had no idea.

The squigs were closing swiftly, much quicker than the dwarfs could have climbed back up the ladder. Felix could hear their hungry mewlings, and make out the movement of their limbs in the darkness. Most were in the shaft, but a few climbed the ladder. They reminded Felix of cockroaches scurrying up a storm drain.

The dwarfs drew their weapons and hung, one-handed, from the ladder, grimly awaiting their doom. Felix gripped his sword and prayed to Sigmar that whatever Gotrek was up to, he would hurry up about it. Leatherbeard had undone his belt, and was slipping it through a rung of the ladder to re-buckle it around his waist so he could hang from it and have both hands free.

Scores of glistening eyes reflected their lamplight, and the things' forms were becoming visible – lumpy, misshapen blobs of hairless flesh, all mouth and teeth, with spindly, taloned legs stuck on as if as an afterthought. They were possibly the most hideous things Felix had ever seen, and he had seen his share of horrors.

'Brace yourselves,' said Hamnir, unnecessarily.

'Guess we'll die in the Duk after all,' said Ragar.

'Always thought I would,' said Karl.

'See you in Grimnir's halls, brothers,' said Arn.

'Look out below!' roared Gotrek from above them.

There was a low *tung*, as if someone had plucked the string of a bass viol, and then suddenly the shaft was filled with a deafening, screaming, scraping cacophony.

Felix looked up, and then hugged the ladder as tightly as he could. The dwarfs did the same. With a rush of wind and a screech-ing of steel on stone, the lift carriage plummeted down towards them, then past them, tilting and disintegrating as it went, its tum-bling struts and timbers carving deep white gouges in the walls of the shaft.

Felix looked down, following its passage, and caught just a glimpse of the squigs, eyes wide with fright, bullfrog mouths agape, before it smashed down on them and dropped into darkness, roar-ing as it went.

After what seemed an interminable wait, they heard a thunderous, wall-shaking boom as the carriage at last hit bottom.

'All clear?' came Gotrek's voice from above.

'Nearly,' called Leatherbeard.

Some squigs still scrabbled up the ladder, undaunted by the fate of their fellows, their teeth gnashing for a taste of dwarf flesh. Held in place by his belt, the masked Slayer waited for them, his two axes ready. They leapt up at him, howling with hunger. He chopped down furiously, catching one between the eyes, severing another's foreleg. They tumbled away, knocking others off as they fell, but not all. Leatherbeard slashed into the next wave. Thorgig and Narin fired crossbows over his shoulders. The other dwarfs grunted, frustrated that the narrowness of the ladder wouldn't allow them to get into the fight. Felix was content to watch.

At last, just as Gotrek reappeared above them, the fight was over. The last of the squigs spun squealing down into darkness, trailing a swash of black blood, and Leatherbeard hung, breathing heavily, from his belt.

'Well done, Leatherbeard,' said Hamnir.

'Bravely fought,' agreed Narin.

'Aye,' said Gotrek. 'Good work, squigslayer.'

Leatherbeard growled as he cleaned his axes and freed himself from the ladder. 'Not all of us have been fortunate enough to meet a daemon. I'll get my chance.'

'Not if you travel with Gurnisson,' said Hamnir. 'He may insist on a strict division of spoils, but he takes all the glory for himself.' He looked up. 'Isn't that right, Jaeger?'

Felix opened his mouth, and closed it again. He wanted to deny Hamnir's words, but couldn't quite. Gotrek was certainly always the one out in front when there was trouble, and it wasn't Felix that was called upon to retake holds or venture into uncharted lands. Of course, that was because Gotrek *could* do these things. He wasn't taking any opportunities from Felix. Felix would have died in seconds up against that daemon.

'Leave the manling out of this!' said Gotrek. 'Now let's get on!'

The dwarfs sheathed their weapons and continued down the ladder. They passed another seven levels before they saw the wreckage of the lift carriage glinting below them at the bottom of the shaft – a shattered pile of splintered wood and twisted metal, mixed in with mashed squigs and bleached bones that proved the hideous beasts were not the first living things to fall down the pit.

The party picked their way over the mess and stepped out of the shaft into a low mine tunnel, much rougher hewn than those in the highest levels, but still neatly cut and well braced, if a bit short.

'Is this the deep road?' asked Felix, stooping. He could not stand upright.

The dwarfs laughed.

'No, Herr Jaeger,' said Hamnir. 'This is still the mines. You will know the deep road when you see it.'

'He thinks this is the deep road,' chuckled Karl.

'Still down a few levels,' said Arn.

'Follow us,' said Ragar.

The dwarfs tramped along the dark tunnel, their lanterns making a travelling pool of light around them. Felix limped along behind, bent over like an old man. He hoped the passage would open up before long. He was already getting a crick in his neck. If they had to fight anything in here, he'd have to do it on his knees.

Gotrek walked beside him for a while, muttering under his breath and shooting sharp glances at Hamnir. Then, after the party had descended three more levels in silence, he stepped ahead and fell in with Leatherbeard.

'You did well there, Slayer,' he said. 'You'll find a good doom. I don't doubt it.' He looked forwards and raised his voice, loud enough to carry to the front of the line. 'And it won't matter who you travel with, for glory isn't something you share, it's something you win.'

Felix frowned. This sort of camaraderie wasn't Gotrek's way. What was the matter with him?

'You shouldn't worry about fighting unworthy foes on this journey,' he said, louder still. 'Even a Slayer may put aside his doom to honour his oaths, if, that is, he's an *honourable* dwarf.'

Now it made sense. Gotrek might be talking with Leatherbeard, but he was speaking to Hamnir. Felix was stunned. This level of indirectness was unheard-of for the Slayer. Gotrek was normally as blunt and forthright as, well, as a punch on the nose. Again, he wondered what it was about Hamnir that got under Gotrek's skin.

'Who is the one without honour?' said Hamnir, rising to the bait. He turned his head as they marched. 'You insult me. You strike me, and you know I cannot strike back for I need you in this enterprise. Is that honourable?'

'More honourable than a dwarf calling on an another's oath when he doesn't keep his own,' shot back Gotrek.

The party stepped out into an enormous room – the junction of many rail lines, all coming to a platform in the centre where the mine carts could be dumped into large ore trains. Battered old carts sat where they had been left on the rusty tracks, and neat stacks of rails and wooden ties hugged the near wall. The ceiling soared above the reach of the dwarfs' lamps.

'Only you say I am an oathbreaker,' shouted Hamnir. 'Only you say I am dishonourable. All others know me as a dwarf of my word.' His words rang back from the dark reaches of the room.

'That's because only I know you as you truly are,' growled Gotrek. 'Only I know your tricks. You wear a thicker mask than Leatherbeard.'

'It wasn't a trick,' said Hamnir, stopping and facing Gotrek. The party halted around them, looking warily into the darkness. 'It was a disagreement. You said it should be included in the spoils. I said it shouldn't. It was worthless anyway.'

'Ha!' Gotrek turned to the others. 'You see. He always has an excuse. Worthless, he says.'

'The others agreed with me,' said Hamnir.

'Only because your tongue is trickier than an elf ambassador's!' Gotrek snorted. 'Hah! Maybe that's it. Maybe your mother had a night with some elf lord come to parlay.'

There was an intake of breath from the dwarfs, and Hamnir froze, staring at the Slayer. Finally, he broke, dropped his axe, and began struggling to shuck his pack.

'Right,' he said. 'That's it. We'll have this out here and now, as it seems that's what you want. I will waive your obligation to help me take Karak Hirn and we will fight dwarf to dwarf.'

'I don't want to fight you,' sneered Gotrek. 'I want you to pay me what you owe me. I want you to give me my share of what you held out from the split.'

'I owe you nothing but a thrashing,' said Hamnir. 'Perhaps that will finally penetrate your thick skull.' He threw down his pack and put up his fists. 'Now fight.'

'You're not worth fighting,' said Gotrek. 'Just pay me and you can end this grudge painlessly, as you could have a hundred years ago in Tilea.'

'Coward,' spat Hamnir. 'It's as I have long suspected. You won't fight without your axe in your hands. Without it you are nothing.'

'What do you say?' said Gotrek, bristling.

'I say that it is your axe that deserves your fame,' said Hamnir contemptuously, 'that any dwarf who picked up such an axe would have become great. Without it you are just another dwarf, and perhaps less than most.'

'You think so?' bellowed Gotrek, throwing aside his axe and his pack. He raised his ham-sized fists. 'Come ahead, elf spawn. I'll introduce you to the floor.'

Hamnir started for the Slayer, but Narin and Galin stepped in his way.

'Prince Hamnir,' said Galin. 'This isn't the time for this.'

'Aye,' agreed Narin. 'You must be whole and hale to lead us. Not battered–'

Hamnir pulled himself up, indignant. 'Who says I will be battered?'

Galin and Narin cast sidelong glances at Gotrek, eyeing his massive physique and comparing it sceptically to Hamnir's soft, merchant's body. Felix had to agree with their unspoken assessment. Hamnir didn't stand a chance. Gotrek was wider and more heavily muscled than any dwarf Felix had ever seen, and uncannily resilient, recovering from wounds and blows that would have crippled or killed another dwarf. Not five days ago, he had been shot and fallen the gods knew how many feet, and all he had to show for it was a bandage on his shoulder that seemed to trouble him not at all.

Narin coughed. 'This is all very brave, Prince Hamnir, but there's no need to prove–'

'I do not fight to prove my bravery,' said Hamnir, interrupting, 'but to defend my honour and that of my late mother.' He started forwards.

'But, prince,' said Galin, stepping before him again, 'you can't win. It's obvious. He–'

'Then I will die. At least I will die in the right.' He pushed past them and punched Gotrek as hard as he could in the ribs.

Gotrek didn't even grunt. He buried a fist in Hamnir's belly and the prince collapsed like an empty sack, dropping to his knees and retching.

Gotrek glared down at him. 'There. Had your fill?'

Hamnir shook his head, dazed, and tried to push himself back to his feet. He lost his balance and fell again. There was a harsh chuckle from the darkness. It sounded like someone grinding gravel between millstones.

The dwarfs looked up, grabbing for their weapons. Felix looked towards the edges of the room. Two massive trolls stood in the doorway that the dwarfs had only recently come through, watching the fight with moronic grins on their ugly, mottled faces.

CHAPTER THIRTEEN

THE TROLL ON the left roared something unintelligible and smacked his fists together, as if indicating that Gotrek and Hamnir should continue. The one on the right, a she-troll, even uglier than her mate, clapped her hands and hooted.

'Our hosts have come home,' said Narin.

'Isn't their home,' growled Arn.

'A worthy doom at last,' said Leatherbeard, drawing his two axes.

Hamnir lifted his head, mumbling, but couldn't get up. Thorgig stood over him protectively, glaring savagely at Gotrek. He looked like a hero in a painting.

Gotrek crossed to his axe and snatched it up. The runes upon it were glowing. No one had noticed. 'Start a fire, manling,' he said, and stalked forwards, his thumb stroking the axe's keen edge. It drew blood.

The trolls bawled, disappointed, and motioned again for Gotrek and Hamnir to keep fighting.

'A fire,' said Galin, backing from the trolls uneasily. 'Good idea. The man will need help.'

The others shot sly looks at him as they spread out and readied their weapons and shields.

'Knees shaking a bit, engineer?' sneered Narin.

'It takes more than axes to kill a troll,' Galin said defensively. 'You should thank me for allowing you the glory.' He started across the huge room. 'Come on, man. These ties should do.'

As Felix followed him to the stacked wooden rail ties, memories of the catacombs under Karak Eight Peaks flooded his mind – the hideous mutated troll that guarded the treasure vault, its wounds closing up almost as soon as Gotrek had opened them with his axe, Felix's desperate attempts to light the thing on fire. He was glad that Narin and the others seemed to know what they were about. They were unhooking their lanterns from their belts and holding them in their shield hands, ready to throw.

The trolls roared at the approaching dwarfs and banged clubs the size of tree trunks on the floor. Even twenty strides away, the impacts stung Felix's feet.

'Easy now,' Felix heard Narin say. 'No one get too far ahead.'

'For glory and death!' bellowed Leatherbeard, and sprinted at the male troll, swinging his two axes wildly.

'You mad idiot!' shouted Narin.

He and the others charged after him, Gotrek at the fore.

The troll roared and swung at Leatherbeard's head. The masked Slayer dived right and rolled up in front of the she-troll, gutting her with a swift upswing. She screeched and smashed down at him with her club as her intestines spilled from the bloody gash. Leatherbeard dodged the blow, but was jarred off his feet as the club shattered the flagstones next to him. The she-troll fell back, stuffing the ropes of her viscera back into the cut. It was already healing.

The rest of the dwarfs closed in, swinging axes and hammers, and then leapt back again almost instantly as a backhand from the male nearly decapitated them all.

'Force them this way!' called Galin, kneeling down next to the rail ties and digging in his pack. He pulled out a handful of shiny black coal lumps and placed them around the stacked wood.

Felix looked back at the fight. The dwarfs were dodging back as the troll spewed corrosive vomit at them. Smoking holes appeared in the floor where it had spattered. Arn threw away his shield as it began to disintegrate. The troll's mate was bashing at Leatherbeard again, the rip in her belly now little more than a thin slit. If there was going to be any forcing done, it looked like the trolls would be the ones doing it. It would be a lot easier of if they could take the fire to...

Felix stopped. The cart rails. The dwarfs and the trolls were fighting right on top of them, and they ran past the pile of ties.

Felix hurried to a nearby cart and started pushing at it. 'Olifsson, in here. Put the ties in here!' The rusty wheels complained bitterly, but at last began to move.

Galin looked up, saw the cart, followed the rails to the fight with his eyes, and grinned. 'Good thinking. You must have picked up some dwarf common sense, travelling with Gurnisson all these years.'

Felix nearly choked. Gotrek had many virtues, but he wouldn't have said that common sense was one of them. He stopped the cart at the stack, and he and Galin began hefting the heavy ties into it while keeping an eye on the fight.

The she-troll was taking another swing at Leatherbeard. He ducked and lashed out with a wild backhand, cutting her hand off at the wrist. Hand and club spun away and knocked Ragar and Karl's legs out from under them.

Narin hurled his lit lantern. The he-troll batted it aside with his club, but Arn threw his a second later and it smashed on the brute's shoulder, dousing it.

'That's done it!' cried Karl, getting up.

The flame didn't catch.

Ragar groaned. 'No it hasn't.'

Gotrek charged in under the thing's club and chopped into its left leg at the hip, nearly severing it. It howled in agony and swung at him. The Slayer blocked, and axe and club connected with a crack that hurt Felix's ears. Gotrek tried to pull back for another swing but couldn't. His blade was stuck in the wood of the club.

The troll swung the club up with both hands and lifted Gotrek with it, his hands still clamped tight around his trapped axe. The Slayer lost his grip as he flew over the troll's shoulder and spun through the air to crash to the floor neck-first, ten yards behind it, leaving his axe behind in the club.

The other dwarfs lunged in, smashing and chopping into the troll in half a dozen places, and then darting back as it screamed and fanned them back with the axe-stuck club. The haft of the axe chimed off Arn's pick and knocked him flat.

Leatherbeard continued to slash at the she-troll, trying to cut off her other hand. She vomited at him, but he danced back and the deadly bile missed its mark.

Gotrek staggered up, blinking and shaking his head like a bull, and aimed himself unsteadily at the he-troll's back. 'Give me my axe,' he growled.

'That's enough, Herr Jaeger,' said Narin, as they heaved a last tie into the cart. He lit the lumps of shiny coal from the wick of his lantern and tossed them in, and then smashed the lantern down on the wood. Oil splashed everywhere and the flames spread rapidly.

Felix made to push the cart, but Galin stopped him.

'Wait for it to catch properly.'

'Wait?' Felix looked anxiously back at the fight. Could they afford to wait?

Gotrek shoulder-tackled the troll behind the knees as the others danced and dodged before it. It slammed down on its back, roaring in surprise, and flailed its club at Gotrek, who had ended up half under it. He jerked aside and the troll mashed its own foot. It screeched in agony. Gotrek scrabbled on top of it and ripped the club out of its hand with sheer brute force.

The she-troll clubbed Leatherbeard to the ground with her stump and leapt on top of him, trying to bite his head off. At least her hand hadn't grown back, Felix thought, though there was already new flesh and bone forming at the cut. She didn't renew herself as quickly as the mutated troll had, Sigmar be praised.

The he-troll was up and grabbing for Gotrek. The Slayer dodged back, trying to free his axe from the club. The brute came after him, but without its club, it could no longer keep the dwarfs at bay. They slashed and bashed at it from all sides, cutting gaping wounds in its legs, sides and back, and breaking its bones faster than they could mend. It was giving ground.

'Now, man! Now!' cried Galin, pushing at the cart.

Felix and Galin pushed the flaming cart along the rails towards the fight. The fire and smoke blew directly in Felix's face and he coughed and cursed.

The troll heard the rumble and turned. Its eyes widened at the sight of the flames and it jumped aside. They were going to miss it!

Gotrek freed his axe at last and leapt at the troll, roaring.

'Die, Grimnir curse you!'

He chopped through both of its knees with one mighty blow. It shrieked horribly, and toppled off its severed lower legs to crash into the blaze, knocking the mine cart off the rails and scattering the flaming rail ties.

Gotrek hacked its head off as it tried to crawl from the flames, then tossed its legs on top of it. He grunted with satisfaction. 'Trolls never smell better than when they're burning.'

The others started for Leatherbeard, still thrashing under the she-troll. His right arm was caught in her remaining claw, the other held down with the bony elbow of her handless arm while she tried to bite his head off. He had lost one of his axes.

He glared at the dwarfs through the tangle of her arms and her empty, swinging breasts. 'Leave me be!' he shouted.

The dwarfs reluctantly did as he asked, watching anxiously as he struggled. He had one leg free and was kicking her as hard as he could in the stomach. His neck, below his mask, was crimson and corded with strain. Veins writhed across his trembling muscles.

Gotrek edged forwards.

'You're not going to interfere?' asked Felix.

Gotrek glared at him. 'Of course not, but if she wins...' He hefted his axe.

The she-troll's neck bulged and she made a horrid 'mumphing' sound. She was going to vomit! Leatherbeard would be reduced to a bubbling paste! With a desperate wrench, the masked Slayer ripped his right arm out from under her elbow and swung his remaining axe at her head. She jerked away and took it in the shoulder, spewing her vile puke on the flags beside him. A few spatters burned into his mask and neck.

He swung again. The she-troll let go of his off hand to grab the axe. He thumbed her in the eye. She reeled to her knees, howling and clutching at her face. He surged up and leapt at her, burying his axe in her skull and knocking her back into the flames with his weight. She screeched and lashed him with her claw. There was a ripping sound as he flew back and crashed to the floor on his face.

The she-troll tried to clamber out of the fire, but the split in her head was not healing, and her limbs only twitched weakly before she sank back dead, blackening in the blaze.

'Well done, Slayer,' said Narin, turning to Leatherbeard.

Gotrek nodded in agreement.

Leatherbeard pushed himself up, groggy and groaning. Felix and the dwarfs stared at him, shocked.

He blinked back at them. 'What?'

No one answered.

He reached up and touched his face. It was naked. 'My mask!' he cried, and looked back at the dead she-troll burning in the fire. The leather face hung from her claws, its straps snapped, its edges smouldering.

'No!' Leatherbeard leapt up and grabbed it out of the flames. He hurried to put it back on, but it was too late. They had all seen.

The Slayer had no beard. His chin was cleaner than Felix's. In fact, he was entirely without hair – his scalp was bald, and he was lacking both eyebrows and eyelashes. He looked like a pink, angry baby.

'Now you know,' he choked as he tried vainly to buckle the broken straps. 'Now you know my shame. Now you know why I took the Slayer's oath.'

'Aye, we see, lad,' said Narin, kindly.

'But,' Galin sputtered, aghast, 'what's wrong with you? Are you truly a dwarf? Were you born this way?'

'Grimnir forbid!' The mask wouldn't stay on. Leatherbeard snatched it off again, frustrated. Pain and rage burned in his eyes. 'Last year I fought the skaven in the Undgrin with my clan brothers. They had strange weapons. One exploded in my face when I struck it. The next morning I woke up like this. I ran from my hold before any could see. The priests at the Slayer's hall helped me fashion this mask, and now... now it's ruined. How can I be a Slayer without a crest? How can I continue when all can see my shame?'

'I have needle and thread in my medic kit,' said Hamnir from behind them. 'You are welcome to them.'

Everyone turned. The prince was sitting up unsteadily, rubbing his stomach gingerly. He motioned vaguely towards his pack.

'Thank you, Prince Hamnir,' said Leatherbeard, and stepped to the pack, turning his back as he opened it and dug through it. The others began to tend to their wounds.

Thorgig helped Hamnir to his feet. The prince could barely stand. He glared at Gotrek. 'Just let me gather my strength, Gurnisson, and we will go again.'

'You want some more?' Gotrek shrugged.

'No, prince,' said Narin, looking up from patching a gash on his arm. 'Enough is enough. This cannot continue.'

'Aye,' chorused the brothers Rassmusson.

'Please, my prince,' said Thorgig, 'at least wait until after we win the karak.'

'You will stop a dwarf from fighting for his honour?' asked Hamnir, affronted.

'Never, prince,' said Narin, 'but I will *suggest* that you stop. This is madness.'

'When Gurnisson admits that he was wrong,' said Hamnir, 'I will stop.'

'When Ranulffsson pays me what he stole from me, I'll call it quits,' said Gotrek.

'If it's a matter of gold,' said Felix, 'I'll pay Gotrek what he thinks he's owed. Only let's move on.'

'Don't be a fool, manling,' snarled Gotrek. 'It means nothing for you to pay me. It's him or no one.'

'But what is it all about?' cried Felix, losing patience. 'What's so difficult about a division of spoils? I don't understand.'

'Of course you don't,' said Gotrek. 'You're not a dwarf.'

'The difficulty,' said Hamnir, 'is in the *definition* of spoils.'

'The difficulty,' Gotrek interrupted, 'is that you and I made a blood oath that we would split all spoils evenly! *All* spoils! There would be nothing held back or hidden on either side. We made the oath on the first day we set out, and you broke it.'

Hamnir sighed and sat wearily on the wheel of an old mine cart. 'Here is what happened. Gurnisson and I had hired on with the army of a Tilean nobleman who was in a war with another Tilean nobleman. The usual petty human squabbling.'

Felix snorted at this, but Hamnir didn't see the irony. He continued.

'We fought across the disputed country, retaking villages that our employer's rival had plundered and occupied. In one of them, there was a dwarf tavern keep, with a comely daughter, who showed me her appreciation for our liberation of the town by...' Hamnir coloured. 'Well, she was a very sweet lass, and we developed a fondness for each other in the week I was there, and she gave me a goodbye gift,' he glared at Gotrek. 'A *love* gift – a small book of old dwarf love poems.' He looked at Felix. 'When we came to divide the spoils of the battle, Gurnisson wanted to include it in the tally. I did not. It was not taken in war, it was given in love, and therefore not plunder.'

'It *was* taken in war,' growled Gotrek. 'She gave it to you for winning the battle and freeing the town. I got a gold coin and a new helmet from the blacksmith, because I stopped Intero's men from burning down his forge. I put that in. There is no difference.'

'There is, unless you kissed that blacksmith on the lips and spent the night in his arms,' said Hamnir dryly.

Narin chuckled at that.

'Was it valuable, this book?' asked Felix, flatly.

Hamnir shrugged. 'It was a copy of a copy, worth a few Empire pfennigs at most.' He looked towards his pack. 'If not for the sentimental value, I would have thrown it out long ago.'

'A few pfennigs?' Felix's voice rose of its own volition. 'A few pfennigs! You two lunatics haven't spoken to each other for a hundred years because of a few pfennigs?' He smacked his forehead and turned to Hamnir. 'Why didn't you just pay Gotrek half the cost of the book and have done?' He swung his head to Gotrek. 'And why didn't you tell Hamnir that a few pfennigs don't matter between friends, and forget about it?'

'It's the principle of the thing,' both dwarfs said in unison.

'He puts milk-sop sentiment before law,' said Gotrek.

'He puts law before common decency,' said Hamnir.

'You both put stubbornness before common sense,' said Felix. He turned to the other dwarfs. 'Do none of you find this to be madness?'

The dwarfs shrugged.

'Haven't spoken to my cousin Riggi for nigh on fifty years, because he didn't ask me if I wanted a drink when it was his turn to buy,' said Karl.

'My clan ceased all trade with another clan over a handkerchief,' said Leatherbeard.

Felix groaned. He'd forgotten who he was talking to, but he had to do something. They would be at this stupidity until the end of the world if he didn't. 'Can I see it?' he asked Hamnir. 'I would like to gaze upon the book that kept two friends apart for a hundred years. It must be wondrous to behold.'

Hamnir opened his pack, dug through it, and pulled out a small volume from the very bottom. 'It isn't much to look at,' he said, handing it carefully to Felix. 'Keepsakes rarely are.'

Felix looked at the little book. It was leather-bound parchment, so worn around the edges by its hundred years in the bottom of Hamnir's pack that it was nearly oval. He flipped it open to the centre. The words were in poorly formed Khazalid runes. 'What was her name?' he asked. 'The barkeep's daughter who gave you this?'

'Er...' said Hamnir. 'I... Morga? No... Margi? Drus? It will come to me...'

Felix snorted and ripped the book in two. He held out the halves to Hamnir and Gotrek. 'There,' he said, 'now it is divided equally. Your grudges are at an end.'

The dwarfs gasped. Even Gotrek gaped.

Hamnir started to his feet. 'What have you done, human?'

He grabbed for his axe. Thorgig was beside him, eyes blazing.

'Damned interfering fool!' shouted Gotrek, advancing on him. 'You've just given him an excuse not to pay me at all!'

Felix backed away, gulping and terrified. He hadn't considered what he would do after he destroyed the book. They were going to kill him.

Then Narin started laughing, great roaring belly laughs. After a second, Galin joined him. Gotrek and Hamnir turned on them, glaring.

'You find this humorous?' snapped Hamnir.

'Will you still laugh when I knock your teeth down your throat?' asked Gotrek, raising his fists.

Galin pointed from one half of the book to the other, trying to speak, but he was laughing too hard. Tears rolled down his cheeks and into his beard.

'The Shield of Drutti!' Narin gasped between spasms. He held up the charred wood in his beard and shook it at them. 'The human has smashed your Shield of Drutti!'

He and Galin broke into fresh gales of laughter.

'Not so funny when it happens to you is it, Slayer?' cried Galin.

Hamnir and Gotrek snatched the halves of the book from Felix's hands and turned on each other, eyes blazing with rage. They shook the pages at each other, stuttering and fighting for words. The ancient paper cracked and split. Bits of age-yellowed confetti fluttered to the ground like dirty snow.

Gotrek watched the falling flakes, and then glared at Hamnir. 'When was the last time you read this book?'

Hamnir looked at the pages crumbling in his hand. 'I...' He snorted. 'I...' He exploded in laughter, his whole body shaking.

'What, curse you?' Gotrek shouted, furious. 'What's so funny?'

'I never read it,' yelped Hamnir, his eyes running. 'It was awful!'

Gotrek stood, frozen, for a long moment, staring at Hamnir as if he was going to cut his head off. Then, with a sound like a steam engine exploding, he too began laughing, violent rasping gusts.

Narin and Galin burst into fresh laughter, but Thorgig and the brothers Rassmusson stared, unnerved and confused. Felix was just happy that they seemed to have forgotten about killing him.

'You stubborn, little–' Gotrek wheezed, pointing at Hamnir. 'Never read it. Can't remember her name. Kept it all this time just for...'

'For the principle of the thing!' wailed Hamnir, hysterical.

The Slayer and the prince collapsed upon each other, heads on each other's shoulders, shaking with laughter and slapping each other's backs.

'Maybe...' choked Gotrek, 'maybe you are a dwarf after all.'

'And maybe there's... more to you than an axe,' hiccupped Hamnir.

Their laughter continued for a long time while the others stood around awkwardly, but at last subsided.

Hamnir stepped back, wiping his eyes. 'It has been a quiet hundred years not having you to argue with, Gurnisson.'

'Aye,' said Gotrek, ruffling his crest and snorting noisily. 'And it's been a relief not having you yammering on about everything under the sun night and day. I forgot there was such a thing as silence when I travelled with you.' He shrugged. 'Even the best things have to end.'

They began to collect their packs and pull themselves together.

Thorgig frowned. 'So… so your grudges are cancelled?' he asked. 'You are no longer enemies.' He didn't seem to like this idea at all.

'Aye,' said Hamnir. 'The human ended it, and very neatly too.' He swung around to glare at Felix. 'Though you owe me a book of very bad poetry, man. Or I will have a new grudge.'

'And you owe me some very *good* poetry,' growled Gotrek. 'For this mischief, the epic of my death had better be the greatest poem ever written.'

Felix bowed, hiding a smile. That had gone better than expected. He had thought they would continue to hate each other, but they had put aside their grudge in favour of hating him more. 'I will do my best to oblige both of you.'

Hamnir nodded, and turned to the brothers Rassmusson. 'Come,' he said, 'we've wasted enough time here. Lead us to the Undgrin, miners.'

'Aye, prince,' said Ragar.

'It's just over there,' said Karl, pointing across the room.

'Nearly there,' said Arn.

The dwarfs finished binding their wounds and shouldered their packs, picks and axes, as the trolls continued to turn to black bones in the roaring fire. Leatherbeard pulled on his repaired mask. It was crudely sewn, and didn't fit as snugly as before, but it covered his shame, and he seemed content. When all were ready, they followed the Rassmussons across the vast room, in a more comradely mood than before. Even Galin and Narin seemed to have forgotten their grudges against Gotrek and each other's clans, and talked of this and that. Only Thorgig remained sullen, glaring at Gotrek's back with undisguised contempt.

CHAPTER FOURTEEN

THEY CAME TO the Undgrin at the base of a long descending ramp, down the centre of which two large-gauge sets of cart rails were laid. The system of winches and pulleys that had lifted and lowered the carts up and down the slope still stood, dusty and rusted, but the carts themselves were gone.

When they stepped through the wide curved arch at the bottom of the ramp, Felix stared, gape-mouthed. The scale of the thing was staggering – a gargantuan tunnel at least forty feet wide and sixty high, its granite walls so polished that the dwarfs' lamps reflected in them as if they were mirrors. A double road of rails ran down the middle of the tunnel, glinting like sword blades until they disappeared in the darkness. On either side of these were raised walkways down which ten dwarfs could have walked side by side. The floor was covered in a thick layer of undisturbed dust. No one had travelled the underground road in decades.

The Rassmusson brothers grinned at Felix.

'Told you you'd know it when you saw it,' said Ragar.

'Not bad, eh?' said Arn.

The idea that a tunnel this large had been built, not just between Duk Grung and Karak Hirn, but between almost every dwarf hold from the Worlds Edge Mountains to the Black Mountains was difficult for Felix to comprehend. 'It's… it's astounding,' he said at last.

'This is only a tributary road,' said Galin. 'The real Undgrin is twice as big.'

'Too bad Duk Grung isn't running any more,' said Karl. 'The steam train ran then, taking ore up to the smelting room at Karak Hirn. We could have hopped it and been at the karak in a day.'

Ragar sighed. 'Those were the days. Ten days at the workface, a day up to Karak Hirn for a good bath and two days of slap and tickle with Iylda, a day down again on the Undgrin and back to work.'

'Aye,' said Arn. 'Two days with a lass is about the right amount.'

'With a twelve day break in between,' agreed Karl.

'Mining at the karak, we see them every night,' said Ragar, glum.

'See them every night and they start talking about things,' said Arn.

'Weddings, for instance,' said Karl.

'And babies,' said Ragar, swallowing.

'Hope the chief finds a new mine soon,' said Arn.

The other brothers nodded fervently as the dwarfs started to the right at a brisk pace, lanterns swinging from their belts. The brothers began singing an old dwarf marching song, and the others soon joined in. After the sixteenth verse, Felix started to get a headache.

'Aren't they worried about drawing attention any more?' He asked Gotrek out of the side of his mouth.

'Nothing lives down here,' Gotrek said. 'Too deep, no water, and nothing to eat. Not even insects.'

Felix's wonder at the Undgrin faded quickly as the party marched along its unchanging, unending length for mile upon mile. It was the safest, least difficult leg of their journey by far – a flat, dry, smooth roadway without bends or junctions – and consequently, the most boring, at least for Felix.

Gotrek and Hamnir had no difficulty passing the time. The walls of their century of silence having tumbled down at last, reminiscences and friendly insults poured out of them in a low rumbling flood. They walked side by side, heads together, with only the occasional 'remember...' or 'whatever happened to...' audible to the rest of the company, and now and then erupting in laughter that boomed down the tunnel and back again.

Felix found himself jealous of Hamnir's friendship with Gotrek. Gotrek and Felix had survived adventures a hundred times more desperate than those that Gotrek had shared with Hamnir, but had they ever laughed about them like this? Had they ever truly shared them? It seemed that, as much as they had argued and fought, Gotrek and Hamnir had been true friends. They had fought through the dangers they had faced side by side, not with Hamnir one step behind and to the right, as Felix did. They had caroused together, joked together and devised mad schemes together.

What had Gotrek and Felix done together? Travelled, yes, but had they conversed as they travelled? As little as Gotrek could get away with: 'This way, manling', 'Come on, manling', 'Leave it behind, manling', and more of the same. They had often drunk side by side, but there had hardly been more conversation there – no comradely sharing of troubles, no boisterous joking, no bantering insults. Even at his most inebriated, Gotrek kept himself at one remove from Felix. They were not friends. They were not equals. They were Slayer and rememberer, that was all.

Was it because they were of different races? Gotrek had little respect for men, it was true, but over the years he had come to count on Felix's resilience and prowess with a sword, as well as his opinion. No matter how grudgingly he listened, in the end he did listen – usually. Perhaps it was being Gotrek's rememberer that was the trouble? The Slayer was, in a way, his employer and one was rarely a true friend to one's employee.

But when he thought about it, Felix could think of no one in all their travels that Gotrek had ever treated as a true friend – no one until Hamnir. Not even the other Slayers they had known, Snorri Nosebiter and Bjorni and Ulli. Oh, they had drunk and roared in every tavern and every town they had ever visited, but Felix could not remember Gotrek ever once pouring out his troubles to any of them, or laughing with them over old times, or even hating them as much as he had hated Hamnir before they had buried their grudge.

Then Felix knew what it was. Gotrek had known Hamnir before he was a Slayer. Whatever had driven Gotrek to take the crest had not happened yet during the years he had travelled with Hamnir. Gotrek had been a different dwarf then, a dwarf who had yet to experience the tragedy that would cause him to turn his back on his family, his hold, and whatever plans he might have made for his life, and wander the world seeking a good death.

This was why Gotrek could joke and fight with Hamnir so freely. Hamnir brought him back to a time before his doom, whatever it may have been, and made him feel like the dwarf he had been then, the young adventurer who had fought his way up and down the coast of the Old World. Those were the years when Gotrek's heart had been open enough to allow him friends. Those days were past. Now the Slayer's heart was locked behind walls thicker than those around the vault of a dwarf king.

Felix suddenly felt sad for Gotrek. Perhaps he even understood a little of why the Slayer sought death. To be alone, even when surrounded by your closest companions, for the rest of a dwarf's long life, would be a misery hard to bear. If Hamnir was bringing back to Gotrek some of his lost happiness, why should Felix begrudge him? They were all likely to die at the end of this tunnel as it was. Let the Slayer live first.

The dwarfs made camp for the night around a fire of the same shiny lumps of coal that Galin had used to ignite the rail ties. Only a few of these tossed on the ground burned with the brightness and warmth of a normal wood fire, and for nearly as long. The dwarfs' shadows moved like giants across the soaring walls of the Undgrin in the fire-light, but as Felix looked left and right, down the endless underground road, he felt very small.

When they had all drunk a few cups of strong ale and finished their hard tack and biscuit, the evening turned into a dwarf boasting contest, each trying to top the others with the dangers and outlandish adventures they had experienced. Gotrek was remarkably restrained, considering that, having faced down a daemon, he could top them all. He told only stories from his time adventuring with Hamnir, long before he had found his rune axe or taken the Slayer's crest. Perhaps, thought Felix, that had nothing to do with restraint.

'Well, none of you has ever climbed as high as I have, I'll wager,' said Galin, taking a swig of ale.

'Ha!' said Narin. 'I climbed old Hammertop, just to have a look at the sunset. You climbed higher than that?'

Galin smiled smugly and wiped his lips. 'I was one of the young fools who joined Firriksson when he scaled the Maiden's Tresses.'

Thorgig gaped. 'You climbed the Tresses? With that belly?'

The others laughed.

Galin's eyes flashed, but then he relaxed and chuckled, patting his swelling midsection. 'I hadn't won my ale vault then. In fact, I was younger than you, shortbeard, and I thought Firriksson was the greatest adventurer that ever lived. Of course, we all found out later that he was as mad as a squig in heat, but then, well...' He puffed on his pipe for a moment, his eyes far away. 'You see, he'd heard the old wives' tale that the Maiden's Eye, that winks from the peak of the Maiden at sunrise and sunset, was a diamond as big as a mine cart, and he decided he wanted it. So up we went, a bunch of stripling shortbeards and Firriksson, a lunatic thunderer who used to dance harvest jigs in his tent, by himself, for a half hour every morning before breaking camp. Said it kept him fit. Lost three of us on the way up. They fell down a crevasse in an ice field. Broke every bone they had. Bad business.' He frowned, and then shook off the memory and grinned. 'When we get to the top, after five of the coldest days of my life, Firriksson finds the Maiden's Eye, and it's everything that's promised, big as a mine cart, as clear and clean as spring water... and made entirely of salt.'

The dwarfs guffawed.

Galin shrugged. 'So, we carved our names in it, had a lick for luck, and went back down.'

'You think Kolin Firriksson was mad,' said Hamnir, 'try serving under a human. The sanest human is madder than any dwarf.' He looked over at Felix, suddenly remembering he was there. 'Er, no disrespect meant, Herr Jaeger.'

Felix ground his teeth. 'None taken.'

Gotrek snorted, 'And we once fought for one who was madder than a skaven with a warpstone helmet.'

Hamnir looked at him, laughing. 'You mean Chamnelac!'

'Aye,' said Gotrek. 'Duke Chamnelac of Cres, a pirate hunter out of Bretonnia, fierce as a badger...'

'And almost as intelligent,' said Hamnir, 'but if moustaches had been brains, he'd have been a mage. Had a pair of curling soup strainers you could have hung kettles on.'

Gotrek leaned forwards. 'We'd been chasing old Ice Eye, a Norse raider, who was the scourge of the Bretonnian coast at the time, and finally caught up with him south of Sartosa, on an island well known for being a refuge for pirates.'

'It had been a rough voyage,' said Hamnir, picking up the story. 'A bad storm three days out, a run-in with a Tilean corsair that had killed twenty dwarfs and men and wounded forty more; and Chamnelac had been in such a hurry to get after Ice Eye that he hadn't victualled or supplied himself properly. There was hardly any food or drinking water, and no surgeon. Chamnelac had left him behind by mistake.'

'His crew wasn't too pleased, needless to say,' continued Gotrek. 'We were under strength to be attacking Ice Eye in his hidey hole, and likely to die even if we won, for lack of bandages. There was talk of mutiny, and some of his officers went to him and begged him to turn back.'

'Chamnelac refused,' said Hamnir. 'He called them cowards. He didn't want to let Ice Eye get away. He anchored his ship on the far side of the island from Ice Eye's wooden fort, and ordered the men ashore, supposedly so they could take on fresh water and hunt for food.' He grinned. 'When they did...'

Gotrek laughed. 'When they did, he set fire to his ship! Burnt it to the waterline.'

'What?' said Arn, 'Humans are insane.'

'I see the sense of it,' said Thorgig. 'His men were wavering. He wanted to give them no choice but to attack. The only way to return home was to kill Ice Eye and take his ship. No retreat. No surrender.'

'Very brave, I'm sure,' said Narin, 'but even the boldest commander likes to leave himself an out, if he can.'

'Did it work?' asked Ragar. 'Did he win?'

Gotrek and Hamnir exchanged a sly look.

'Oh aye,' said Gotrek. 'Chamnelac won. Took the island without a fight.'

'Without a fight?' asked Galin. 'How is that possible?'

'Because…' said Hamnir, and then burst out laughing, 'because Ice Eye had seen the smoke from Chamnelac's burning ship and knew he was coming, and…' His laughter overwhelmed him.

Gotrek grinned savagely. 'He sailed away. Ice Eye took off with all his ships and left Chamnelac gaping on the shore!'

'Sailed away?' Thorgig goggled, 'But that means that Chamnelac…'

'Couldn't get off the island!' chuckled Narin, slapping his knee. 'He'd trapped himself! What a fool!'

Thorgig frowned. 'So, er, how did you get off, did you build a raft?'

Hamnir shook his head. 'Too far from shore. We were stuck well and proper. In the end, after three months went by and we were all thinner than human beer, another pirate, an Estalian, dropped anchor to take on water.'

'Did Chamnelac take his ship, then?' asked Ragar.

Gotrek grinned. 'Chamnelac was dead, murdered the first night we were marooned. Half his officers too. No, we signed the articles and joined up, the whole of Chamnelac's crew. Most of them stayed on the account too, as I recall.'

'The poor old duke birthed more pirates than he ever took,' said Hamnir, shaking his head.

Gotrek took a swallow of ale. 'Three months on an island with a bunch of filthy Bretonnians, and only berries and seagulls to eat, ruined my stomach for a year.'

'You had it easy,' said Narin. 'I was trapped in a hunter's shack in the Kislev oblast for two months in the middle of winter, with two ogres for company and nothing to eat but a cellar full of rotten turnips.'

'A dwarf can live on turnips,' said Galin. 'Don't sound such a hardship.'

'A dwarf can, aye,' said Narin. 'Unfortunately, ogres can't. Oh, they'll eat them. They'll eat anything, but it'll only leave them wanting something… meatier. Namely, me.'

The others laughed.

Felix saw Gotrek look over at Leatherbeard as Narin told his story. The young Slayer wasn't participating in the boasting. He sat a little way off from the others, staring into the fire through the eyes of his crudely patched mask. Gotrek glanced at him several more times during Narin's tale. Then, while the Rassmusson brothers were trying to top him by telling a very confused story about tricking a companion of theirs into eating troll dung, he got up and crossed to him.

'All right, Slayer?' Gotrek asked, squatting.

Leatherbeard shrugged.

'Not still troubled about us seeing your face?'

Leatherbeard shook his head. 'That isn't it. Not all of it.'

'Well then, what's the matter? It isn't every day that a dwarf graduates from squigslayer to trollslayer.'

Felix could just see the corners of the young Slayer's mouth turn up sadly through the mouth-slot of his mask.

'I am glad to have won the name, aye,' he said, 'but... but I didn't die. I didn't end my shame. Instead, I lost my mask and made it worse.'

Gotrek chuckled, a black, empty sound. 'Now you know the true pain of the Slayer, lad,' he said. 'Every victory is a defeat, for only if we die do we fulfil our destinies; but if we don't try to win, if we drop our axes and let the troll rip us apart, then Grungni won't accept us into the halls of our ancestors, for he doesn't care for suicides.' He sighed. 'I've been at it eighty years. The pain doesn't go away, but you get used to it.' He stood. 'Beer helps. Have another.'

He returned to the others and the tales continued.

THE NEXT MORNING – if there was such a thing as morning in the stygian underworld of the Undgrin – a few hours after the dwarfs broke camp, they came to a place where it looked as if the tunnel had been crushed by a giant hand. The floor was buckled and broken, and the walls and ceiling had crumbled and fallen in. Boulders as big as houses littered the floor, crushing the twisted cart rails. Other boulders had fallen atop them, some precariously balanced, and the ceiling above the mess was mazed with cracks and missing blocks. It bulged down ominously in places.

'Did you know this was here?' asked Gotrek, his eyes travelling across the wreckage.

'I had heard there was some damage from an earthquake that occurred sixty years after the mine closed,' Hamnir said, 'but that it was passable.'

'I can see beyond it,' said Narin, twisting the sliver of wood in his beard, 'but it doesn't look to be a pleasant stroll.'

'Miner's nightmare,' said Galin, looking uneasily up at the ceiling. 'Those blocks could come down at any minute. Any one of us so much as raises his voice or stamps his feet and… boom.'

'My father meant to repair this,' said Hamnir, swallowing queasily, 'but there were always things closer to home that were more urgent.'

'I heard he left it this way on purpose,' said Karl.

'Aye,' said Ragar, 'so that no army could get through here without it all dropping on their heads.'

'A ready-made trap,' said Arn.

'A trap for us,' said Leatherbeard uneasily. 'A rock fall is no doom for a Slayer.'

'Olifsson,' said Hamnir. 'See if you can find us a way through.'

'Me?' said Galin, eyes bulging. 'Do you mean to get me killed?'

'You are an engineer,' said Hamnir. 'You came for this purpose. I want your advice on this.'

Galin swallowed. 'My advice,' he said, 'is to find another way around.'

Hamnir scowled. 'You know very well there is no other way. It's through, or back the way we came.'

'Are you a coward after all, Olifsson?' asked Thorgig. 'You look a little pale.'

It was true. Galin's normally florid face was mud grey.

'I'm a mine engineer,' he said. 'As the Slayer knows his axe and Prince Hamnir knows his markets, I know walls and ceilings and the weight they will bear. That ceiling is hanging by spider webs. We won't make it through.'

'But we must,' said Hamnir, 'and you're the dwarf to guide us.'

'It's death,' said Galin, his eyes never leaving the crumbling ceiling.

Hamnir stepped to him and looked him in the eye. 'Listen to me, engineer. I have a hold to save. I will not turn back. You are a volunteer. I have not ordered you to follow me. You are free to leave. The rest of us will try to cross through this death trap without you.'

Galin shook his head. 'You'll never make it.'

'Not without you,' said Hamnir, and he turned away to stand next to Gotrek, who was surveying the collapse.

The others turned away too. Galin stood behind them, lips tight, head down. Felix joined the others, as much to spare the engineer his scrutiny as to shun him like the rest.

'All right, curse you,' Galin choked after a long pause. 'All right, I'll have a look. I can't have you fools stomping in and killing yourselves.' He pushed through them, glaring furiously. He stopped at the edge of the mess, removed his pack and laid down his hammer.

Hamnir put a hand on his shoulder. 'Thank you, engineer.'

Galin shrugged him off, snarling, and then swallowed and took a deep breath. It seemed to Felix that he might have lost his courage once more, but at last he started forwards, one cautious inch at a time. Three paces in he looked back. 'Stay quiet.'

The other dwarfs waited as he picked his way cautiously through the boulders, placing every foot with care, testing the floor and the rubble with trembling toes and fingers. He soon disappeared around a fall of boulders, and Felix and the other dwarfs held their breath and craned their necks. After what seemed like forever, he reappeared, his legs trembling and his red face bathed in sweat. He inched back to them as slowly and methodically as he had left them, and at last let out a long breath when he stepped beyond the last bit of jumbled granite.

'Well, there is a way,' he said, mopping his brow, 'but you will all have to step exactly where I step and touch only what I touch. Kicking a pebble or slipping on a bit of scree in that mess will bury us. There're parts of that roof that...' he shivered. 'Well, I don't know what's holding it up.'

'Couldn't we make a big noise now and bring it down before we go on?' asked Felix.

The dwarfs gave him patronising looks.

'That would indeed be safest,' said Narin, smiling, 'but where's the guarantee that the road would still be passable after it fell?'

'I can guarantee it wouldn't be,' said Galin.

'Ah, yes. I see. Of course.' Felix blushed. He felt like a fool.

'Right,' said Hamnir, turning to the others, 'all in one line, close together. Take the exact step the dwarf in front of you took. Galin, you have the lead. Jaeger, you come last.'

Felix's heart thudded. 'Why am I last?'

'Because you have the longest legs to run with, if things begin to fall,' said Hamnir, 'and, forgive me if I'm blunt, you're more likely to put a foot wrong than a dwarf.'

Felix's fists balled. More insults.

'It's true, manling,' said Gotrek. 'We dwarfs were born to tunnels and cave-ins. We know our footing.'

'Aye aye, fine,' said Felix. He wanted to punch all the superior little know-it-alls in the nose, but he restrained himself. It would probably bring the roof down. He took off his red cloak and stuffed it in his pack so it wouldn't catch on anything.

'Follow close,' said Galin, 'and don't say a word.'

The dwarfs started ahead like a caterpillar on the march, walking in lockstep, each with one hand on the shoulder of the dwarf ahead of him. They seemed to have done it many times before. Felix put his hand on Gotrek's shoulder and did his best to follow along, staring intently at the Slayer's feet.

It was slow going. At the front of the line, Galin tested the way with the haft of his warhammer, making certain no rock or slab he put his foot on would shift or slip. Then he would step and test again, step, and test again. The next dwarf would then place his foot where Galin had placed his, and so on. At first, this wasn't difficult, but, as they began to weave through the maze of monolithic boulders and up through places where the floor had buckled and rose at a steep slant, the footing was trickier. The dwarfs braced each other as they went up and down, making sure they didn't slip backwards or tip forwards.

Felix's heart thudded so noisily as he followed Gotrek that he thought the vibrations would surely shake loose the ceiling. He was sweating like a fountain. Every trickle of dust, every clack of boot heel on rock made him cringe and hunch his shoulders. His neck ached with tension.

He watched Gotrek step over a jutting ridge of floor and carefully place his foot on the other side, exactly where the dwarf before him had placed his. Felix lifted his leg over the ridge and stepped down precisely, eyes on where Gotrek was stepping next, and...

Crack! He smacked his head on a low rock overhang. He clamped a hand over his mouth to stifle a yelp. The world was receding and turning yellow and black. His knees buckled. He had been so intent on Gotrek's feet that he hadn't seen the cantilevered slab of granite that Gotrek had simply walked under. He wanted to scream and jump up and down, but both would be suicide. He stood frozen. The tunnel spun around him. He was going to fall.

A grip like iron caught his upper arm. He opened his eyes. Gotrek was holding him steady, a stubby finger on his lips. Felix nodded, and then wished he hadn't. It almost toppled him. He looked past Gotrek. The other dwarfs had stopped, and were looking back at him with expressions that ranged from pity to contempt to amusement. Galin was staring wide-eyed up at the ceiling. His lips were moving as if he was praying.

After a moment, the tunnel steadied and the dizziness passed. Felix's head still ached abominably, and a thread of blood ran down to the tip of his nose, but he had recovered enough to walk. He motioned to Gotrek to go on. The Slayer turned back with the others and took another step. Felix ducked low under the projecting slab and followed.

Felix wasn't the only one who erred. Halfway through the wreckage, Galin's probing axe handle dislodged a skull-sized rock that rolled and bounced down a slanted section of floor as the dwarfs froze and looked up, their shoulders hunched. Dribbles of dust rained down from the ceiling, but it stayed in place. A little further on, Thorgig put his hand out to brace himself on a fallen block of stone and it began to tip. He gasped and stepped back, and the others looked around. The carriage-sized block was precariously balanced on a smaller rock below it, its balance point directly over the bottom rock's edge. The dwarfs froze as they watched it teeter slowly, and then settle back with the softest of thuds. Everyone breathed again.

At last, Galin led them beyond the ruptured floor and out from under the bulging ceiling, and they all let out great sighs of relief.

Felix dabbed at his bloodied forehead with his handkerchief and looked back. His limbs were shaking with reaction. 'I hope we don't have to retreat this way. I don't think I could take it again.'

'Retreat?' said Gotrek, frowning.

He and Hamnir looked at each other, and grinned. As one, they stooped and picked up heavy rocks.

'There is no retreat,' said Hamnir.

'For Chamnelac!' they cried, as they hurled their rocks back at the stretch of broken tunnel. 'Burn the boat!'

Both rocks bounced noisily off the top of the massive teetering block that Thorgig had nearly toppled with a touch.

The other dwarfs stared.

'You madmen!' breathed Felix as the block began to dip.

'Mad dwarfs,' corrected Gotrek.

The block's movement slowed and it looked as if it was going to rock back to its resting position like it had before, but just then the edge of the bottom rock crumbled under its enormous weight, and the top rock slipped forwards a foot, overbalanced and slammed to the floor with a booming crash that shook the whole tunnel.

A long ripping sound echoed from above, like the tearing of some enormous starched canvas, and a whole section of the ceiling tore away, breaking up as it fell towards the floor.

'Run!' shouted Galin.

The first blocks smashed into the rubble like cannonballs. The dwarfs were knocked off their feet. They bounced up again and sprinted away from the collapse in a mad scramble as the tunnel shook and boomed. Felix glanced back as he ran. More and more blocks fell, pulverising those that had fallen before. The walls were folding in and toppling. He was hit in the cheek by a pebble that stung like a bullet. A rock the size of a Marienburg cheese bounced past him, narrowly missing Ragar before rolling to a stop.

Another glance. A rising cloud of dust was obscuring the wreckage and billowing after the dwarfs faster than they could run. Felix choked as it enveloped him, silting his tongue, eyes and nostrils with powdered granite. The dwarfs' lamps were dull orange glows that bobbed around him in the grey murk, while the roar of falling rock continued to batter his ears.

Fifty paces on, they reached the edge of the dust cloud and slowed. The constant thunder was tapering off to individual smashes and booms. The dwarfs stopped.

Gotrek and Hamnir were cackling like naughty schoolboys, choking and laughing in equal measure as tears cut pink channels down their dust-caked cheeks. They and the rest of the dwarfs looked as if they had been dipped in a flour barrel. Felix was the same. They sneezed and hacked and spat, bent double from their sprint.

'Bit close there,' said Hamnir, giggling.

'Aye, a bit,' agreed Gotrek.

'You might have given us some warning!' said Narin.

'Not exactly tactically sound,' huffed Galin. 'It's all very well to say "no retreat", but...'

Gotrek looked up at him, glaring. 'There never was any retreat. This just makes it clear. The only way out is forwards.'

Hamnir sobered too. 'There is no other way into the hold. I will make it in this way or die trying. The same as you swore to do when you volunteered for this mission. If you are having second thoughts, well,' he laughed evilly, 'you're having them seconds too late.' He glared around at them all. 'Now, are you ready to go?'

The dwarfs nodded. They brushed the dust from themselves, squared their weapons and packs, and the party resumed its march. Felix put his red cloak on again. It was cold in the endless tunnel.

Hamnir looked back as they went, though the collapsed section was invisible in the dust and darkness behind them. He smiled grimly. 'Birrisson will be happy – if he still lives. Hasn't had a really big rebuilding project in centuries.'

CHAPTER FIFTEEN

THE PARTY REACHED the under entrance to the mines of Karak Hirn late in the afternoon of what the dwarfs assured Felix was the second day they had spent on the deep road. Felix had entirely lost track. It felt to him as if he had spent a month without seeing the sun. He was beginning to wonder if the overworld was only a dream he had once had. There were dwarfs who lived most of their lives without seeing the sun. It gave him the chills just thinking about it.

His companions hooded their lanterns and crept cautiously towards the entrance. They weren't about to underestimate the orcs again. A train of titanic ore carts, built to the scale of the Undgrin, sat on the tracks near the entrance, and they padded along them, using them as cover. At the end of the train, they squatted down and peered under the last cart. In keeping with the rest of the Undgrin, the opening that led into Karak Hirn was immense – a three storey high archway in the wall of the tunnel, so wide that the eight side-by-side rail lines that emerged from it, bending right and left to connect to the Undgrin lines, fitted in its mouth with room to spare. Giant stone figures of dwarfs stood guard on either side of it, thick stone hands resting on twenty-foot tall battleaxes.

A little ball of light bobbed slowly between the grim granite sentinels as a patrol of six orcs marched back and forth across the door's breadth, carrying torches.

Hamnir was staring beyond them. Inside the door, a broad ramp rose into the interior of the mine, the eight rail lines rising with it. The top of the ramp was illuminated by a flickering orange fire glow, and roaring and rushing came faintly to their ears.

'It appears they occupy the lower foundry,' said the prince. 'We will get past these six easily enough, but if the foundry hall is well lit…'

'No need for that, prince,' said Arn.

'Aye,' said Ragar. 'There's a stair just inside the door on the left, goes up direct to the eighth deep guard room.'

'So the lads at the door don't have to trek all the way around to the main shaft when they go off shift.'

'Excellent,' said Hamnir. 'Then that is how we will go. The old kruk is only five deeps above that.'

The dwarfs waited until the orc patrol was approaching the right side of the vast doorway, and then tip-toed from behind the train and hurried quietly across the tunnel to hide in the shadow of the left-hand statue. They waited again as the patrol marched slowly back towards them, made their turn, and started away again. Again, Felix and the others noted the orcs' strange behaviour – their blank, quiet demeanour, punctuated by short, howling outbursts that stopped almost as soon as they began. They reminded Felix of pit-dogs being bitten by fleas.

As the orcs approached the far side of the door, Hamnir waved the others ahead. They slipped around the statue and through the archway. The Rassmusson brothers pointed to a small, black opening in the left wall. The dwarfs filed through it and up the stairs behind it, then waited once all were in, to hear if an alarm had been raised. All was quiet.

'Well done,' whispered Hamnir. 'On we go. To the east end of the third deep.'

The dwarfs carried on up the pitch-black stair, walking quietly and listening intently. Felix could hear nothing except their own breathing and footsteps, but a few flights up he began to notice a faint red light travelling with them.

'Gotrek,' he said. 'Your axe.'

The Slayer brought the axe up and looked at it. The runes on the head were glowing faintly. He frowned. 'Never shone for grobi before,' he grunted. 'Trolls, daemons, sorcery, aye. Not grobi.'

Hamnir's brow furrowed. 'Could it be the dark powers behind all this? They are strong in the north now.'

Gotrek shrugged. 'Whatever it is, we'll kill it when we come to it.'

But the glow of the rune grew fainter the higher they climbed, and when at last they reached the eighth deep it was entirely dark again.

Orange light shone through the bars of the gate at the top of the stair. Gotrek crept up to investigate while the others waited in the shadows, weapons at the ready. He flattened himself against the wall, peered through the opening, and then tried the gate. It was locked. He cursed under his breath and grabbed the bars, pulling with inexorable strength.

'Gotrek, leave off!' hissed Hamnir, starting up the stairs and pulling a silver key from his belt pouch. 'I am a prince of this hold, if you recall. I have a master key.'

Gotrek grunted and stepped back, letting Hamnir open the door, as Felix and the dwarfs came up behind them. The guardroom was still a guardroom. Orc weapons and bits of crude armour were strewn about, and the rancid remains of an orc meal sat on the table. Dwarf lanterns flickered on the walls.

'Filthy beasts,' said Thorgig, 'defiling our home.'

'Easy, lad,' said Hamnir.

Gotrek crossed the room and looked out into the passage beyond. 'All clear.'

Hamnir led the party into the passage and they crept through the halls and chambers of the vast mine. The sounds of the orc occupation echoed all around them: heavy marching feet, the roar of furnaces, the battering of hammers and picks. The dwarfs were horrified by these sounds, and when they came to a gallery that looked down into a deep excavation ringed with scaffolding, where hundreds of orcs and goblins dug at the walls in dreary silence, they stared, caught between wonder and fury.

'This is madness,' said Narin. 'Orcs don't mine. They don't smelt.'

'Aye,' agreed Galin, 'the shiftless beasts haven't done an honest day's work in their whole history. They steal the iron they have from dwarfs.'

Hamnir nodded. 'I was afraid I was going to find shackled dwarfs under the whip of orc overseers, but this is…'

'Bizarre, is what it is,' said Leatherbeard in wonder.

'It isn't right,' said Thorgig, staring. 'The whole business is unnatural.'

'To think I'd live to see orcs walking around our mine like they owned the place,' said Karl.

'Aye,' said Ragar, 'a black day.'

'We'll chop them to pieces, brothers,' said Arn. 'Don't you worry. Once we open the front door we'll set all to rights.'

They moved on, avoiding lumbering orc patrols as they came to them, and keeping out of sight of the orc work parties that were busy digging and hauling ore and rock on every level. The dwarfs were sunk in a gloomy silence by the strangeness of the orcs and their mere presence in their ancestral mines.

Felix too was infected with gloom. Ever since they had entered the mine, a mood of dread and despair had come over him, and seemed to grow stronger with every step. His heart felt as if it were pumping ice water into his veins. He couldn't pinpoint the source of the anxiety. The party's infiltration had so far gone smoothly. Their mission was no more dangerous than it had always been, and yet he could hardly keep himself from sobbing. He had a sense that they were fated to fail: that some ancient doom had come upon them that there would be no avoiding. They hadn't a hope of succeeding. He should just give up and run straight into the first orc patrol he saw and end it all.

He shook himself. What was he thinking? He had never been prone to death wishes before. That was Gotrek's burden, not his. What was the matter with him? Was the dwarfs' unease about the orcs' un-orcish behaviour rubbing off on him? Was it that Gotrek's axe had glowed? Whatever it was, he shoved the feeling away and forced himself to be calm. The last thing he needed was the dwarfs laughing at him for jumping at shadows. There were plenty of tangible dangers to worry about.

On the fourth level, they had to climb an airshaft to rise above an area crowded with orc work parties. Grated vents along its length glowed red from the rooms beyond, casting the dwarfs' features in grisly crimson. The dwarfs peered through these grates, cursing under their breath. One looked down upon a great forge room, where a hundred bellows roared, and a hundred anvils rang under the hammers of orc smiths.

'They are using our hammers! Our sacred anvils!' said Thorgig, his voice rising. 'We must slay them. They can't be allowed to–'

'Easy,' said Hamnir. But he was trembling too, hardly able to tear his eyes away from the sights beyond the grate.

Galin shook his head as he stared through. 'Axes, spears, armour, and of excusable quality too. Never seen orcs work like that.'

'And what designs are these?' asked Narin. 'Never seen the like. Look like spider parts.'

The red light glittered off Gotrek's one eye as he glared into the forge room. 'What do they make it for? That's the question. Looks like they're getting ready to make war on the whole world.'

The dwarfs looked at him, eyes wide.

'By Grimnir's beard,' said Thorgig. 'What *do* they mean to do? Is Karak Hirn the first hold of many that they mean to take?'

'No,' said Hamnir, grimly, 'it is their last.'

'It is their grave,' said Gotrek.

Felix shivered, the feeling of dread suddenly stronger. He shook it off with difficulty.

The dwarfs moved on, climbing the airshaft to exit into a dark chamber on the third level. Hamnir led them east, through a maze of sorting and smelting halls, forges and supply pantries. The further away from the main shaft they went the fewer orc patrols they passed, and the less populated the corridors and rooms became, until soon they seemed entirely alone. This was an old section of the mine, dug out when the hold was young, and long ago turned into storage rooms and workshops, all of which had been ransacked by the orcs and then abandoned.

Hamnir finally stopped at a large stone door in a dusty and disused corridor. 'The door to the kruk,' he said.

There were orc footprints in the dust before it.

Gotrek peered at the keyhole, holding a torch close. 'Been opened recently,' he said, 'with a key.'

Hamnir groaned. He took a key from his ring and inserted it in the lock. The dwarfs readied their weapons. The lock turned easily and Hamnir pulled it open. The dwarfs looked in. Orc footprints ran off into darkness down a dark old tunnel, smaller and rougher than the rest of the mine.

'Have they found *everything*?' asked Hamnir, angrily.

The dwarfs entered and Hamnir locked the door behind them. They moved quietly through the old mine, glaring into the shadows as they followed the orc trail. It wasn't too long, however, before the footprints stopped and doubled back, and the dwarfs could find no more further on.

Hamnir breathed a sigh of relief. 'It appears that they decided there was nothing to take. Good. Now, this way.'

He led them swiftly, and with a dwarf's unerring knowledge of where he was underground, through the maze of crossing corridors, until he stopped at a section of wall indistinguishable from any other in the kruk.

'Here,' he said. 'My father's vault is ten feet behind this wall.'

Galin stepped up and rapped on the wall with his knuckles. 'May I take a sounding, prince?'

'By all means,' said Hamnir.

Galin turned to Narin, who carried a warhammer. 'Will you strike the wall, Ironskin?'

Narin nodded and readied his weapon. 'At your command.'

Galin took off his helmet and pressed his ear to the wall. 'Strike.'

Narin swung, and the hammer rang off the wall.

Galin listened to the rock intently, and then moved a few yards down the wall and again pressed against it. 'Once more.'

Narin smacked the wall again as Galin concentrated. As the echoes died, the engineer frowned and stepped back, stroking his beard and shaking his head. 'Afraid you've miscalculated, prince. There's a cavity here right enough, but it's closer to twenty feet in.'

Hamnir groaned. 'Twenty feet? Can we dig through that in time?' he asked, chewing his lip.

Galin rubbed a rough palm over the wall. 'Hmmm, sandstone, but there's a fold of gneiss that angles through it and we'll have to get through that first: denser stuff.' He shrugged. 'A seasoned miner should be able to clear a foot deep hole his own height and width through sandstone in an hour and a half, going all out, but he can't do it for more than three hours at the most without slowing considerably.'

He looked around at the dwarfs. 'I've done my share of digging, and I know these lads have,' he said, nodding at the Rassmusson brothers, 'but the thunderers and Slayers and hammerers might not have swung a pick in a century or so. If it's just the four of us, working in shifts…' He paused, doing calculations in his head. 'Thirty hours, probably more, to account for fatigue.'

'I can dig,' said Gotrek.

'As can I,' said Leatherbeard. 'It was as a miner that I fought the skaven.'

'It will still be thirty hours,' said Galin. 'Though, with six digging, we will be less weary when we break through.'

'We must be faster,' said Hamnir, his brow furrowed. 'It is the night of the fifth day, and we told Gorril that we would open the Horn Gate at sunset tomorrow. No more than twenty hours. His force cannot wait for ten hours. The grobi will pick them to pieces as they did before.'

'He will wait, prince,' said Thorgig. 'He would never abandon your cause.'

'I know,' said Hamnir. 'I know.'

'Then stop talking,' said Gotrek, 'and start digging.'

The Rassmusson brothers nodded, doffed their packs and their armour, took up their picks, and without any further preamble, began swinging at the wall with a practiced rhythm. It was deafening. Chunks of sandstone began to litter the floor.

'The first foot or two will go quicker,' said Galin to Hamnir, 'while three can work at once, but when the hole is deeper, only one dwarf will be able to reach the face.'

Hamnir nodded and turned to Thorgig, giving him his ring of keys. 'Cousin, go to the door and see if the digging can be heard from there.' He looked up at Felix. 'Go with him, Herr Jaeger. If we cannot be heard, go into the mine. We will need a barrow and beer or drinkable water, as much as you can carry.'

'And food,' said Galin. 'Digging is hungry work, and we've eaten nearly all we brought.'

'No food,' said Hamnir grimly, 'at least no meat. What grobi eat may be dwarf.'

Felix and the young dwarf set out as the others began setting up camp around the workface, laying out their bedrolls and knocking spikes in the walls from which to hang their lanterns.

When they had reached the door and closed it behind them, they stood still, listening for the clash of pick on rock.

Thorgig cursed under his breath. 'Faint but clear. This is bad.'

'I hear nothing,' said Felix.

Thorgig brightened. 'That is because you are a human. Good. The hearing of orcs is as inferior as that of men, so perhaps we are safe.'

Felix grunted, annoyed once again by the offhand insult.

Thorgig looked up, colouring. 'My apologies, Herr Jaeger. I know you don't like to hear about human shortcomings. You saved Kagrin's life, and mine. I owe you more respect. I will refrain from speaking of them in your presence.'

Felix tensed, choking back the urge to spit a few dwarf shortcomings in Thorgig's face, but what was the use? He wasn't trying to be insulting. In fact, he thought he was being polite. He didn't know any better, and now wasn't the time to educate him.

Felix bowed, hiding a smirk. 'I am humbled and honoured by your sense of tact, Thorgig Helmgard,' he said.

Thorgig nodded, pleased. 'Thank you, Herr Jaeger. The courtesy of the dwarfs seems to be rubbing off on you. This way.'

Felix followed him down the hall, shaking his head in wonder.

They skulked silently towards the more populated area of the mine, and were able to find and take almost all the things on Hamnir's list without arousing the attention of any orcs. The exception was beer. Every cask they found had been broached, smashed or drained. They did however find some stale dwarf flat bread that apparently hadn't appealed to the orc palate. They dumped it into the barrow along with two large skins of water, some shovels, and a jar of lamp oil, and hurried back to the kruk.

Felix was astounded by how much rock the brothers had dug in their absence. The hole in the wall was nearly a foot and a half deep already, and though too short for Felix to stand up in, wider than a dwarf. The three brothers did not appear to have slowed, keeping up their steady, machine-like rhythm without pause. The others had cleared away the rubble of their exertions as best they could, and Felix and Thorgig got to work shovelling it up and dumping it in the barrow. Then Felix wheeled it off down the corridor and dumped it out of the way.

For the next ten hours that was all he did. While the dwarfs chipped at the wall, and the hole got incrementally deeper, Felix shovelled the scrapings into the barrow and carried them away. It was all he could contribute. Asking him to swing a pick would only have slowed them down. He'd have been lucky to dig two inches in an hour.

At the two-hour mark, the brothers had dug as deep as three dwarfs standing side by side could dig, and fell back, exhausted. Galin took over alone, stripped to the waist, swinging at a steady unwavering pace that spoke of long experience. Hamnir and Narin worked behind him, widening the hole and scraping the tailings out to the passage where Felix picked them up.

The other dwarfs rested as best they could, and Hamnir sent Leatherbeard, and then, an hour later, Narin, to the kruk door to listen for orc patrols.

After two hours, Galin stumbled out of the shallow hole, having dug a further foot and a half. He was bathed in sweat and shaking. Leatherbeard took his place, removing his mask so that he might breathe better, but only after he was hidden in the hole. Two hours later and a foot deeper, he was replaced by Gotrek, who set at the rock as if it was a horde of orcs. Stone and dust flew.

'Easy, Slayer,' said Galin, lifting his head from where he lay. 'You won't last at that pace.'

'I know my limits,' said Gotrek, and continued at the same furious rate.

For a time, he was faster than the others had been, cutting through a foot of rock in an hour, but as he entered his second hour, his progress slowed, his bare back running with sweat. Even then, he maintained the pace that Leatherbeard had, and looked as if he could continue at that speed indefinitely. Although the others praised him and encouraged him, he seemed dissatisfied, growling and muttering.

Finally, he stepped out of the hole, wiping his brow and scowling.

'Ready to switch?' asked Ragar, sitting up. He had had six hours' rest and looked reasonably fresh.

Gotrek shook his head, picked up a second pick, and disappeared back into the hole without a word.

The other dwarfs crowded around the opening, watching gape-mouthed as Gotrek attacked the workface with the two picks, swinging them as easily and skilfully as his companions had swung one. Sparks and chunks of sandstone flew everywhere.

His eyes glowed. 'Now we'll make some time,' he growled as he settled down into a rhythm. His massive muscles shone with sweat in the lamplight. The waste rock piled up around Gotrek's feet at an amazing rate.

'He's mad,' said Galin.

'He'll wear himself to a thread,' said Narin.

Hamnir stared hard at Gotrek's back, as if he meant to order the Slayer to pace himself, but instead, he backed into the tunnel and turned away.

Gotrek went three more hours and dug four more feet, an unheard-of feat that had the others, the Rassmusson brothers particularly, stiff with jealousy.

'Isn't proper form,' sniffed Karl, as he approached the workface for his second shift and swung his pick.

'Would never do for real mining,' agreed Arn, holding a lantern behind him.

'Real mining's for the long haul,' nodded Karl.

Felix was becoming unutterably weary, and felt guilty for it. While the dwarfs had laboured heroically, he hadn't done more than stoop and shovel and cart, but after twelve hours of it, he couldn't keep his head up, and shortly after Karl began his second turn, he handed off the barrow to Thorgig and lay down on his bedroll in the darkness beyond the lanterns, pillowing his head with his old cloak.

He fell asleep almost instantly, but it was a troubled slumber. The feelings of malignant dread that he had felt upon entering the mine, and which had never entirely gone away no matter how much he had tried to force them down, bloomed in his dreams like night flowers, pale and putrid. Amorphous fears loomed in his unconscious, pressing in on him from all sides and threatening to smother him. Insectile whispering, like the vibration of glassine wings, buzzed vile urgings in his ears. He felt as if he was being chased down the mine's cramped passages by an intangible evil that was everywhere and nowhere at once, but getting closer with every step. Whatever it was, it was going to kill him. He was going to die here. He would never leave these cursed tunnels. He would never see the sun again. Hands that were not hands were reaching out of the darkness to clutch at his throat. He could feel hard, cold claws slipping around his throat.

Felix snapped awake, panting. Sweat like ice prickled his brow. He sucked in a few deep breaths and looked around, his heart pounding. Flickering lamplight and the monotonous sound of pick striking rock came from the ragged hole in the wall. Around him, the dwarfs were asleep in their bedrolls, snoring like so many bullfrogs croaking.

He looked on them with a sudden loathing. Humans who had never met dwarfs often thought of them as just some breed of short men, but having spent so many years with Gotrek, Felix knew different. They were not men. They weren't even cousins to men. They were another species – a strange race of insular burrowing animals, with the hoarding instincts of pack-rats, and the stubborn intransigence of mules. He stared at Thorgig, snoring next to him. How had he ever thought of these monsters as people? Look at them, with their flat, furred faces, their blunt paws, their coarse, clay-textured hides, their fat, bulbous noses – more like pig snouts, really.

Strange how he had never noticed it before, but all at once he couldn't stand the sight of them – any of them. They repulsed him. Every aspect of them was revolting – and made all the worse by the fact that, unlike skaven or orcs or other monsters, they had somehow tricked men into accepting them as equals, superiors even! No! It was not to be countenanced. They were vile, stunted moles, grubbing in the earth, eating dirt and excreting gold, sacrificing his people to their rock-daemon gods, smashing the cities of his kind when they found them, and forcing him into his long hibernation.

He shuddered. He could no longer stomach their presence. Their stench made him gag. He could not allow them to live. If their wills could not be bent, then they must be destroyed. They stood in the way of his rightful domination of the world. He drew his dagger and stood, looking down at Thorgig. The foolish animal didn't know his doom was upon him. Felix bent and covered the dwarf's mouth as he plunged his blade into the artery under his jaw – hard to find through the beast's cursed fur.

The dwarf struggled briefly, but then sank back. Felix looked around. None of the others had awakened. Good. He stepped to Narin, curled on his side. Felix covered his mouth too, and drove his dagger under the blond dwarf's ear. He twitched and fought, but only for a second.

Beyond Narin was Gotrek. Felix's heart raced. He stood over the sleeping Slayer, glaring at him. He was even more alien than the others – a muscle-bound freak with skin like pink granite, a stiff strip of hair like the coxcomb of a rooster and, as he knew from experience, the strength of ten of his kind. He reached down slowly and quietly. The Slayer was too dangerous. He would have to kill him with the first blow, or he would be ripped to pieces. He cupped his free hand to cover Gotrek's mouth, and angled the tip of his blade towards the hinge of the jaw, as he had with the other two. One quick thrust and...

Gotrek's one eye snapped open and his hand clamped around Felix's wrist with blinding speed. Felix pulled back, trying to break free, but the dwarf's grip was like iron. He fought to get away, punching and kicking, but the dwarf held on, taking the blows as if they were snowflakes falling. Gotrek caught his other wrist.

'Manling,' he said. 'Manling, wake up.'

Felix tried to head butt the dwarf. He couldn't reach him. He thrashed in Gotrek's unshakeable grip. He...

Woke up.

CHAPTER SIXTEEN

FELIX BLINKED, CONFUSED. Gotrek was still in front of him, holding his wrists, but disorientingly, it was Felix who lay on his back and the dwarf who stood over him, scowling. Felix's head spun with vertigo.

'Waving a dagger about in your sleep, manling,' Gotrek said as he let go. 'You'll do yourself an injury.'

Do *himself* an injury? He'd done more than that! He'd... Felix sat up, heart pounding, mind racing. By Sigmar, he'd murdered two of...

Thorgig and Narin were glaring at him from their bedrolls, cross and bleary with sleep. The other dwarfs were glaring at him from the shadows.

'Don't suppose you'd mind keeping your nightmares to yourself?' said Narin sourly.

'We've little enough time for sleep as it is,' said Thorgig, and lay back down.

A dream! Felix's heart flooded with relief. It had only been a dream!

'Sorry,' he muttered. 'I... I was fighting, er... daemons. I'll try to be quieter about it in the future.'

He lay back as Gotrek returned to his bedroll. He didn't want to try to explain to them what he had really been doing in his dream. He couldn't explain it to himself. Where had those thoughts come from?

He had never had a dream so strange, or so real, in all his life. He certainly had plenty of reasons to be annoyed with dwarfs – a surly, unsympathetic lot if ever there was one, so convinced of their superiority over men that they insulted him unthinkingly every time they opened their mouths. But annoyed enough to try to kill them? No.

He tried to remember what it was that had fuelled his murderous anger, but already the dream was fading, becoming unclear. All that remained in focus – vivid focus – as he closed his eyes was the feeling of all-consuming fury, and the image of the tip of his dagger sinking to the hilt under Thorgig's ear.

He shivered and opened his eyes, then sat up and tied off his sword and dagger so it would be difficult to draw them in his sleep. Even with this precaution, he found it difficult to return to slumber, for fear of what he might do.

WHEN NEXT HE woke, his mind clouded and heart heavy from unremembered dreams, Karl was just finishing his second two hours at the rock face, having followed Arn and Ragar before him. Between the three of them, they had dug four feet while Felix had slept, and now there was an argument going on amongst the dwarfs about who should follow him.

'We're not going fast enough,' Hamnir was saying. 'It is now the middle of the afternoon of the seventh day. Gorril's army will have left Rodenheim two hours ago, and if all has gone as planned, they are almost halfway here. In three hours they will be waiting at the advance position to hear the blowing of the war horn, and if Galin reckons right, we still have four feet of rock to dig through. Another six hours of digging.'

'Let me dig again,' said Gotrek. 'I'm fastest.'

'Even you won't be fast enough,' said Galin. He sighed. 'I knew it was impossible when we started it, but…'

'Even if you do cut through in time,' said Hamnir to Gotrek. 'We need you fighting fit on the other side, not worn to a fare-thee-well.'

'Getting into the hold is more important,' said the Slayer. 'I'll do it.'

He took up two picks and stalked into the tunnel. The sharp clash of steel on stone started up immediately, sounding at an unheard-of pace. Gotrek was out-doing even his earlier stint at the workface.

Narin shook his head. 'He won't keep it up. It's impossible.'

Hamnir chuckled. 'He'll keep it up just to spite you for saying so.'

Then there was nothing to do but wait, while the ceaseless rapid-fire hammering of Gotrek's picks battered their ears. And waiting was something that the dwarfs, for all their talk of dwarf patience, didn't do very well. Perhaps the strange oppressive atmosphere, which was clouding Felix's mind, was also having an effect on the dwarfs' tempers. They were snappish and out of sorts, alternately slumping against the walls of the corridor or fidgeting restlessly. Narin and Galin paced moodily up and down the hall, snarling at each other as they bumped shoulders. Leatherbeard tried to sleep, but only tossed and turned. Even the brothers Rassmusson were arguing amongst themselves, fighting over the sharing out of the last of the flat bread.

Then, slightly more than an hour later, Galin jumped up, eyes wide.

'Did you hear?' he cried, pointing to the tunnel.

The others looked up at him listlessly.

'Hear what?' asked Hamnir.

'The boom!' said Galin, excitedly. 'The Slayer's picks are booming as they strike the rock. We are close. Very close. Within two feet.' He stepped into the tunnel.

Hamnir sprang up and followed him in. Felix and the dwarfs crowded around the entrance.

Galin was measuring the distance that Gotrek had cut in the last hour. 'A little more than a foot,' he muttered, scratching his head.

'You said there were six more feet, at least.'

'I, er, it appears I erred on the side of caution,' said Galin.

'Out,' said Gotrek. 'Give me room.'

The dwarfs stepped back. The Slayer was running with sweat. His one eye seemed glazed and unseeing, and the perfect control he usually had was slipping. His swings were wild and he was weaving on his feet, but his pace never slowed. It looked as if, were he to stop, he would fall, so he dared not stop.

'If he keeps up this pace,' said Galin, 'we'll be through in an hour.'

'Excellent news!' said Hamnir. 'We will have half an hour to make our way through the hold and reach the gate. Hardly enough time, but better than four hours late.'

After that, the waiting was even more difficult, for the dwarfs couldn't relax, knowing their goal was so close. They paced and fretted, drawing and then sheathing their weapons over and over again. They cursed each other for being impatient, and cursed Gotrek for being too slow.

Then, slightly less than an hour later, there was a clunk, and a pleased snort, and Gotrek called down the tunnel. 'I've holed it.'

The dwarfs pushed into the tunnel as Gotrek's hacking resumed. There was a fist-sized black hole halfway up the workface, which Gotrek was widening with every strike of his axe. The dwarfs cheered, and nothing Gotrek could say could keep them out of the tunnel, watching over his shoulder.

Fifteen minutes later, the hole was a more than a foot wide and they could see things shining in the darkness through it. Galin stepped forwards. 'Wait. The man will fit through that. Let him go through and work it from the other side.'

Gotrek nodded and stepped back. Galin waved Felix forwards and held up a lantern. Felix leaned through the hole and looked around. A clutter of half-seen golden treasures winked at him in the light of the flickering flame. The vault was a square shaft, about twelve feet to a side, which rose into darkness above as if it was the bottom of a well. With Galin and Hamnir's help, Felix wormed through the hole and lowered himself down until his feet touched. Then he took the lantern and pick that Hamnir passed through the hole and got to work.

With each swing, he had new respect for the strength and endurance of the dwarfs. He was weary after ten minutes, and they had gone for hours. But even Felix's inexpert hacking sped the work, and at last, after another fifteen minutes, the hole was wide enough for a dwarf to pass through. They cheered and then climbed one by one into the vault, Felix helping them to the floor.

Gotrek came through last and sat down wearily on a tapestry-covered casket, mopping his brow and staring blankly in front of him. Felix didn't know if he had ever seen the Slayer look so exhausted. His huge arms were shaking with fatigue.

The other dwarfs held up their lanterns and looked around in wonder at the treasures in the rough-hewn vault. Beautiful suits of gold and gromril armour were displayed on wooden stands, with horned helmets above them, making it appear that ghostly dwarf warriors guarded the vault. Intricately worked caskets of gold and silver were piled on top of each other, nearly as valuable as the treasures they contained. A chalice of gold and polished stone sat on a black marble shrine. A great stone-headed maul, inscribed with runes on its every face, was mounted on the wall. An ancient green battle standard, the horn of Karak Hirn stitched into it in gold thread, was propped against a Cathay vase twice the height of a dwarf. Dwarf books were stacked in the corners, and rolled vellum maps were tucked into gold and silver tubes.

But the thing that drew the dwarfs' attention like a fly to honey was a velvet-lined silver box that sat open on a table, the contents of which shone with a red orange glow in the lantern light.

'Blood-gold,' whispered Narin, licking his lips.

'Look at it shine,' murmured Galin.

'Never seen so much in one place,' said Karl.

It didn't look like a lot to Felix. There were only twenty ingots in the box, and they looked about half-weight, but they had a hypnotic effect on the dwarfs. They couldn't take their eyes off them.

'Beautiful,' said Leatherbeard. 'Worth killing for.'

'Aye,' said Arn. 'Red as blood.'

'Up the stairs!' said Hamnir, slamming the box closed. 'You should not be looking upon any of this. We have less than half an hour. Gorril is already in position.'

The dwarfs blinked and came reluctantly back to themselves. Felix looked up the dark shaft. A rough staircase wound up it inside a dwarf-wide channel carved diagonally into the walls like the threads of a screw. More climbing. Wonderful.

As the others crossed to the stairs, Gotrek levered himself to his feet with the help of his axe and stumped after them. The sweat still boiled from his skin.

Hamnir paused, looking back at the hole in the wall with profound unhappiness. 'Leaving an unguarded door to my father's vault. Perhaps we could block it...' He cursed and forced himself up the stairs after the others. 'There is no time.'

Felix followed the dwarfs up, pressing as close to the wall of the narrow channel as he could. The steps were well cut and true, as was to be expected from any dwarf work, but there was no railing, and as they rose eight, and then ten flights, Felix's knees began to feel weak and his guts watery. There were no ropes and pitons here, and the dwarfs would have ribbed him unmercifully if he had decided to crawl up on his hands and knees, or asked for a rope 'in a stairwell of all places' so he kept his terror to himself.

Seven rotations later, the stair ended at a small landing with no apparent door, only a fat, polished marble pillar set incongruously in one rough wall. A brass lever and something that looked like the lens of a spyglass were placed at dwarf height beside it. Hamnir stepped to the lens and looked into it. He froze, and then stepped back, turning first pale, and then red with rage.

'There are grobi in my father's quarters. They have defiled... everything.'

'Can we get through the door without being seen?' asked Narin.

Hamnir nodded. 'They are not in the sleeping chamber, but I can see them moving in the receiving chamber beyond.' He put his hand on the lever. 'Thorgig, when I open this door, creep to the further door and spy out how many there are. We will have to take them silently.'

Thorgig cocked and loaded his crossbow. 'Ready,' he said.

The others drew daggers and hand-axes.

Hamnir pulled the lever and the fat column screwed down into the floor without a sound, revealing a dark bedchamber that reeked like a garbage heap built over a middens. The dwarfs winced and choked. Piles of rotting food and smashed furniture, broken weapons, squig carcasses, shattered crockery and empty hogsheads of beer were heaped waist deep – shoulder deep for the dwarfs – around the room. King Alrik's grand canopied bed was buried so deeply that only the four posts rose up out of the muck. All the other furnishings had been slashed and smashed.

The dwarfs trembled with rage when they saw the wreckage.

'Green savages!' muttered Galin.

'They will pay for this,' said Thorgig.

'Quiet,' said Hamnir, and motioned him into the room.

Thorgig picked his way through the heaps as silently as he could. Sounds of industry came from the further room, slappings and bangings and sloshings that Felix couldn't identify. And where was the reek of excrement coming from?

Thorgig edged to the side of the receiving chamber door and leaned out. Felix saw his eyes widen as he peered through it. He eased back and returned to Hamnir.

'They've made it into a tannery!' he whispered.

'A... a what?' asked Hamnir.

'A tannery!' Thorgig choked, overcome. 'There's a big vat of... of liquid waste where King Alrik's table was. Goblins are dunking skins and beating them, and stitching them together all over the room.'

'How many goblins?' asked Gotrek.

Thorgig frowned. 'Er, six, and two orcs are squatting over the vat, with one behind, waiting his turn.'

'The door to the corridor is closed?' asked Hamnir.

'Aye, but not locked.'

Hamnir thought. 'We'll wait until the orcs have left, and then kill the goblins, as quietly as possible.' He looked around at the others. 'Make sure we take them in one go, aye?'

They nodded.

Hamnir turned to Gotrek. 'You're not in this,' he said.

'Try and stop me,' said Gotrek. He was still slick with sweat and breathing heavily.

'I'm ordering you,' said Hamnir. 'Save yourself for the Horn Gate.'

Gotrek grumbled, but nodded.

The dwarfs stepped into the bedchamber and began to pick their way warily around the mounds of rubbish. Gotrek and Felix came last. When all were through the door, Hamnir turned to a decorative relief border by the column and pressed a bit of filigree. The fat column rose up again as silently as it had dropped. It looked as if it had never moved.

The dwarfs crossed the room and positioned themselves at the edges of the square of light that shone through the receiving chamber door. The scene was as Thorgig had described it. There was a four-foot high wooden vat in the centre of the room, filled with semi-liquid orc filth. A set of wooden steps led up to a two-holed outhouse bench that was built out over the vat. An orc was just pulling up his breeches and starting back down the steps.

A goblin stood on the rim, stirring the vile soup with a wooden paddle and pushing un-cured hides down into it. To one side of the vat, drying frames had been set up. Treated skins were being stretched in them. Some had dwarf tattoos. Goblins used wooden mauls to beat skins on square blocks of stone. Another cut them with a hooked knife. Two sat cross-legged on regal dwarf furniture, stitching the cut skins into what looked like leather cuirasses. The room was a shambles, littered with half-eaten ham hocks, and black with filth.

Hamnir trembled. 'This is a travesty,' he said under his breath. 'My father would…' He twitched and fell silent.

The orc exited through the door to the corridor. The goblins didn't look up from their tasks. They were as focused and unblinking as clerks at their ledgers.

Hamnir raised his hand. The others gripped their weapons, ready. He dropped his hand. The dwarfs charged through the door. Felix followed them. Only Gotrek waited behind.

Four goblins died on the instant, cut down before they could make a sound. The one with the hooked knife squawked as Leatherbeard ran towards it, and darted into what might once have been a dining chamber. Leatherbeard charged in after it. Felix cut at the goblin with the paddle, but it dived behind the vat. Aside from the first surprised squawk, the last two goblins uttered not a sound. They were as blank and emotionless as all the other grobi they had encountered.

'Get them!' hissed Hamnir.

Narin and Galin swung at the paddle goblin, but it dodged between them and they nearly decapitated each other. Karl, Ragar and Arn scrambled after it as it ducked behind the drying frames. Ragar slipped on a wet skin and fell on his posterior. The frames clattered down. A hollow smash came from the dining chamber.

'Grimnir's mother!' snapped Hamnir. 'Quietly!'

The paddle goblin leapt from the tangle of frames and climbed to the lip of the vat then sprang to the chandelier that hung above it, flailing its absurd weapon around at the dwarfs who tried to reach him.

'I have him,' said Felix, and ran up the wooden steps, swinging his sword. The goblin twisted out of the way and smacked Felix on the shoulder with the paddle. Felix overbalanced, nearly plunging into the vat. He caught himself, heart thumping. That would have been the crown to his regalia of indignities.

A crossbow bolt appeared in the goblin's chest. It squeaked and fell, half in, half out of the vat, drenching Felix's legs in a shower of vile liquid, as the chandelier pendulumed wildly back and forth.

'Little villain!' Felix barked, and slashed down at the thing as it flailed on the lip. He cut its head off and its body toppled down to the floor from the strength of the blow. Its head bobbed for a moment in the vat like a rotten apple, and then sank.

'Shhh!' said Galin. He stood at the corridor door. 'Someone's coming. Sounds like a patrol.'

The dwarfs froze, all but Leatherbeard, who was still chasing his goblin around the dining chamber table. The tramp of marching feet came clearly through the stone walls.

'Thorgig, help him!' whispered Hamnir. 'Karl, Ragar, Arn, hide the bodies, and then yourselves. Galin, Narin, cover the bloodstains. Jaeger…'

The last goblin ran out of the dining chamber as the dwarfs scrambled to obey Hamnir's orders. Leatherbeard dived after the fleeing runt and smashed it to the floor with his axe.

'Get it out!' hissed Hamnir, waving his hand. 'There are more coming.'

The marching feet stopped outside the door. Leatherbeard dragged his goblin back into the dining chamber as the Rassmusson brothers tossed the others to Gotrek, who stacked them up inside the bedroom door. Narin and Galin threw loose skins on top of the various bloodstains that spattered the floor. Felix hopped down the stairs and ran for the bedroom door, but Hamnir poked his head out of an alcove and pointed.

'Jaeger! The chandelier!'

Felix turned. The damned thing was still swinging. He cursed and jumped back up the vat steps. The dwarfs were disappearing through doors and ducking behind furniture. Felix reached up and steadied the chandelier. The handle of the corridor door was turning. He cursed. There was no time to reach any of the doorways. He was trapped in the open.

CHAPTER SEVENTEEN

THE CORRIDOR DOOR began to swing open. Felix jumped off the wooden steps and rolled under them, folding his lanky frame into the tight space. His back was against the vat. A crossbeam pressed painfully across his shins. His breeches clung to him wetly. They stank.

Through the open treads of the steps, Felix watched the knobby green knees of an enormous orc in a studded leather tunic and heavy boots enter the room and approach the vat. A company of orcs at parade rest stood outside the door behind it.

'Oh no,' he murmured.

The heavy boots creaked up the complaining steps and stopped directly over Felix's head. Felix held his breath. If he moved a muscle the orc would hear him.

There was a moment of rustling above him, and then a deep, contented sigh as something plopped wetly into the vat. Felix prayed it would all be over soon, but the orc must have eaten mightily, for the plopping and splashing seemed never-ending. After one particularly violent discharge, a splatter of drops rattled the boards over Felix's head. A bead of stinking brown liquid formed under one plank and hung there, directly over his face.

Felix looked up at it in horror. He daren't move. The slightest motion would alert the orc.

The orc grunted and shifted. The drop fell. Felix shut his eyes. It splashed on his right eyelid, then slid slowly down. Felix tensed, fighting back a scream. The stuff burned like vinegar. He wanted to thrash and kick.

The orc stood, giving Felix a view of parts of its anatomy he could have done without seeing, then pulled up its breeches and started down the steps. Halfway down, it paused and jabbered a question. Its voice had a strange, chittering edge to it, not the usual orc grunt.

Felix groaned. It had finally noticed that the goblins weren't there. This was the end. They were going to have to fight the whole company, and then the whole hold. It was Birrisson's door all over again. Felix rolled his smarting eyes to the side and saw Gotrek and the Rassmusson brothers in the shadows of the sleeping chamber, readying their weapons.

The orc chattered its question again, and then stepped to the door and spoke to its captain. The captain stuck its head in, and the orc indicated the room with a sweep of its hand.

The captain frowned around for a long moment, then shrugged and told the orc to get back in line. Its voice too was sharp and staccato. The orc exited, shutting the door behind it.

A chorus of dwarf sighs came from all over the room. They stepped out from behind doorways and furniture, looking relieved.

Narin grinned as Felix squeezed out from under the steps. 'It's not often a man gets a view like that and lives.'

'It's not often a man gets a view like that and *wants* to live,' said Felix. He wiped his eyelid and looked around for something to dry his breeches with. 'And I got another sort of eyeful as well. Burns like fire.'

'Now that's a hero's brand if ever there was one,' laughed Galin.

'You find it funny?' asked Gotrek, stepping from the bedchamber. 'I wonder if you could have stood it.'

'Is it a hero's part to stand things?' asked Galin. 'I would have jumped up and killed it before the drop fell.'

'And doomed us all,' said Hamnir dryly. 'Very heroic.' He turned to the door. 'Now, hurry, before any more come to fill the vat.' He put his ear to the panels as the others gathered behind him. 'We go left,' he said, 'and then up. The Horn Gate is only three hundred yards due east, but this is the level of the great halls. It will be too populated. Two levels up are grain stores. We will traverse the length of the hold there, and return down a further stairwell nearer the gate. Ready?'

The dwarfs nodded, faces set and grim behind their beards.

Hamnir listened again, then slowly pulled open the door and peered out. The torch-lit corridor echoed with sounds of distant movement, but nothing nearby. Hamnir turned left and slipped quietly down the hall. The dwarfs followed behind him in a single file, Felix looming at the back of the line, feeling clumsy and clammy in his moist breeches. Despite what Gotrek and Hamnir had said, it was hard to feel heroic when you were damp with orc-crap.

The stairwell to the upper levels wasn't more than twenty yards along the hall, but they had to pause and hide three times to let orc patrols and work details march past. Through every door they passed, they saw goblins and orcs busy at their labours, cutting and shaping wood, building torture devices and trebuchets, slaughtering and skinning animals, making food, weaving.

'Weaving?' whispered Galin, nonplussed. 'Grobi don't weave!'

'Place is more like a beehive than an orc nest,' muttered Gotrek.

'And what ails their voices?' said Narin. 'Chittering and gibbering like... like–'

'Monkeys?' suggested Thorgig.

'Mutants, I was going to say,' said Narin.

Hamnir paused at the stairwell and looked in warily, then waved them up. They climbed two levels and stepped out into a broad, unlit corridor. The dwarfs unshielded their lanterns and started down its length. The air was filled with the dusty, musty smell of rotting wheat.

Hamnir sniffed, frowning. 'Have they left a silo open to the damp? We haven't much wheat to spare this year.'

Huge doors lined both sides of the hallway for as far as they could see in the lamplight. They were all open. Hamnir looked into the first one on the right. The room inside was small and stacked along its left wall with barrels and empty canvas sacks. An ironbound door, like a furnace door with a trough beneath it, was set in the back wall. The trough was barely visible, however, because the iron door was open, and pouring from it like a sand dune was a spill of golden grain. The sweet reek of mould grew stronger, and black shadows crawled over the mound – rats, dozens of them.

'Valaya curse them,' sneered Hamnir. 'For all their chittering and weaving, they are still careless savages.'

He looked in the door to the left. That silo was open as well, and the wheat spilled across the floor almost to the door. More rats crawled over the bounty.

Hamnir shivered. 'Two spoiled? It will be a lean winter. It...' He looked up the hall with slowly dawning horror, then hurried ahead.

The others followed quickly. Hamnir looked in the second pair of doors. Both rooms were the same as the first – the iron doors open and mounds of rotting grain alive with rats. Hamnir choked and sped to the next doors. Those silos too had been opened, as had the next set.

Hamnir slumped against the wall, covering his face with his hands. 'Grimnir,' he said, choking. 'They've killed us. Even if we retake the fort and drive them out, they have won. We will starve. No bread. No beer. The hold won't last the winter. Are they mad? Why have they done this? It's suicide for them too.'

'Something's coming,' said Leatherbeard.

The dwarfs covered their lanterns and stepped into the grain room. They peered through the door. A glow of torchlight and looming ugly shadows emerged from around a corner, far ahead. Then a strange procession appeared – two big orcs pushed a mine cart, while ahead of them scurried a dozen goblins, all armed with barbed spears and sacks. The goblins ran into the silo rooms, from which came sounds of struggling and squeaking. Then they reappeared, rats impaled on their spears. They stuffed these in their sacks, and carried on to the next rooms.

When they came out again, one goblin's sack was full. He emptied it in the mine cart, then followed his snaggle-fanged brethren further down the hall.

Hamnir stared open mouthed, but Narin stifled a snort. 'They use the grain to farm rats!' he whispered. 'Brilliant!'

'The fools!' said Hamnir shaking his head. 'The meat-brained idiots.'

'They'll be coming in here, prince,' said Thorgig looking at the rats swarming the grain at their feet.

'Right,' said Hamnir. He glanced around. Barrels were stacked along one wall. 'Behind those. Quick.'

The dwarfs waded through the spill of wheat and edged behind the barrels.

'Hiding from goblins again,' muttered Leatherbeard, disgusted, but he held his breath with the others when three goblins ran into the room, stabbing at the rats with their little spears. The rats squealed and ran for the corners. The goblins didn't bother to chase very far. There were so many vermin that they had each spitted three or four without much effort. They stuffed them in their sacks and ran out again.

The dwarfs remained where they were, listening as the rumble of cart wheels grew louder, and then diminished into the distance. When the rat harvesters were safely past, Hamnir stepped out. 'We must hurry. They may come back. Lamps closed.'

The dwarfs crossed to the door and looked out to the left. The orcs and goblins were fifty yards down the corridor. The dwarfs eased out and continued to the right, Hamnir cursing anew as they passed each new ruined silo.

The corridor turned right at its end, opening into a stairwell that went both up and down.

Hamnir turned to the others. 'We will be very close to the main corridor when we descend. Be careful.'

He led them cautiously down the stairs and they exited two levels down into a shadowy side passage. The glow of lamps from the main corridor, thirty feet to their right, glinted on the blades of their axes, and they heard harsh, gibbering voices. The tramp of heavy feet on the trot echoed to them as well. A large company of orcs armed with dwarf long-guns ran past from right to left.

When they had passed, Hamnir tapped Thorgig on the shoulder and motioned him forwards. The young dwarf padded to the main corridor and leaned out to look both ways. He ducked back suddenly and flattened himself against the wall as more boots echoed from the hall and a second orc company followed the first. They were armed with bows and axes. Thorgig looked after them as they continued down the hall, and then returned to Hamnir and the others.

'The first group went into the guardroom. The second into the passage to the sally port.'

Hamnir nodded. 'Gunners for the turrets and scouts to harass Gorril's line of march: he must be in position. Good.'

'Doesn't sound so good to me,' said Galin scowling. 'If the orcs are positioning gunners in the turrets, your army will be shot to pieces as they come in.'

Hamnir nodded. 'This is why Gorril must be able to run straight in when he arrives, so our brothers won't have to weather more than one salvo while waiting for us to open the gate. The difficulty is, if we are to open the doors, we will have to keep the orcs in the turrets from... Wait.' He frowned and looked around. There was an empty room just behind them. 'Come,' he said. 'I will lay it out for you. There is a lot to tell and not much time.'

He led the others into the bare, dust-thick room, and squatted down. The others hunkered around him.

'Here it is,' he said, sketching in the dust with a thick finger. 'The Horn Gate is approached through a narrow, steep-walled canyon. Our ancestors built eight turrets into those walls, four to a side, so that any force that tries to knock down the stone door can be riddled with crossfire as they come. Twenty feet behind the first door, there is a second, with murder rooms above and on both sides, so that our defenders can pour boiling oil upon, and shoot crossbows at, any attackers that get through the first door, while they are trying to break down the second.' The canyon, turrets and doors took shape with a few deft strokes of Hamnir's finger. Then he began drawing the rooms behind the gates. 'There are two guardrooms to the right and left of the main corridor, just behind the gate. A door in each guardroom leads to the turrets and murder rooms above. Once both of those doors are locked, the orcs in the turrets and murder rooms cannot get back into the guardroom.'

'Unless they bash down the doors,' said Narin.

'Er, yes,' said Hamnir, and continued. 'The two rooms that house the gate levers are also inside the guardrooms. The levers in the rooms must be pulled simultaneously in order for the gates to open. There are two such levers in each room: one for the outer gate, one for the inner. There is a speaking tube between the two rooms so those who pull the levers may act as one, as well as a cunning spyglass that shows the canyon outside the door. Am I clear?'

The dwarfs nodded. Felix would have liked to hear it all again, but didn't care to ask.

'Not as well thought-out as the gates of Karak Varn,' said Galin, sniffing, 'but stout nonetheless. A good system.'

'I'm glad it meets with your approval,' said Hamnir dryly. He turned back to the map. 'Here is what we must do. We must attack both guardrooms at once, subdue what guards we find there and lock the doors to the murder rooms and turrets without alerting the rest of the hold. When this is done, Thorgig...' He paused and looked at the young dwarf with a mixture of sadness and anger. 'Thorgig has volunteered to go up into the first turret and blow the battle horn to let Gorril know we are in position.'

'But... but the turrets are filled with orcs,' said Narin. 'He'll be killed.'

'Aye,' said Hamnir, eyes downcast, 'precisely.' He pounded his leg. 'Curse you, lad. Do you truly wish to throw your life away? Leatherbeard is a Slayer, as is Gotrek. They are looking for a noble death. He–'

'Must we argue this again?' asked Thorgig, interrupting. 'I have been a guard of the Horn Gate for ten years. It was my duty to blow the horn then. It is my duty now.'

'But–'

'Prince, please,' said Thorgig. 'They don't know how to blow the horn.'

'Er,' said Leatherbeard. 'I... I could try.'

Thorgig glared at Hamnir defiantly. 'You see. It must be me. No other can be sure to be heard.'

Hamnir sighed. 'So it seems.'

'So,' said Gotrek. 'Thorgig blows the horn, we open the gates, Gorril runs in with the army, and the day is saved. Is that it?'

'Well, it will be a bit more difficult than that,' said Hamnir.

Felix sighed. Why weren't things ever easier than one expected?

'Go on,' said Gotrek.

'It is fifteen minutes' march from Gorril's advance position,' said Hamnir. 'We cannot open the gates until we see him enter the canyon, otherwise the orcs will form up in front of the gate and block their entrance. We will have to hold the guardrooms for those fifteen minutes to prevent the orcs from retaking them and stopping us from pulling the levers. This will be easy if the rest of the hold is not alerted, but the grobi will most likely hear Thorgig's horn and come running, in which case...'

Gotrek and Leatherbeard grinned.

'In which case we'll have a nice scrap on our hands,' said Gotrek.

'Aye,' said Hamnir. He looked much less eager at the prospect. He dug in his pouch and took out a key ring, which he opened with a twist, and then threaded off four keys. 'We will divide into two groups. One will take the guardroom on the left, the other, the one on the right. Three in each group will kill the occupants while the other two hold closed the doors to the murder room stairs until we can lock them.' He looked around at them. 'Gotrek, Jaeger, Narin, Karl and Ragar, you will take the left room. Who will be in charge of the keys?'

'I will,' said Narin.

'And which two will hold the door while the others fight?'

'I'll fight,' said Gotrek, 'and so will the manling.'

'We want to fight!' said Karl.

'Aye,' said Ragar. 'Let the Slayer be a doorstop! He's still tired from digging!'

'You want to try me?' growled Gotrek.

'Keep your voices down!' hissed Hamnir.

Gotrek gave Ragar and Karl a flat look. 'There'll be enough fighting for all of us when the day is done. You'll get more than you care for, I'll wager.'

The brothers glared back at him, and then shrugged.

Hamnir handed Narin two keys. 'The one with the square loop is for the door to the murder rooms and turrets. The one with the round loop is for the lever room.'

'Square, murder. Round, lever,' said Narin. 'Understood.' He tucked them in his pouch.

Hamnir turned to the remaining dwarfs. 'I will hold the keys for our side. Galin and Thorgig will hold the murder room door. Are we clear?'

The others nodded.

'Good.' Hamnir stood. 'Now, it is past time. Only remember that we must hold the two guardrooms against all comers until Gorril's force arrives, no matter what the cost.' He stepped to the door. 'Let's go.'

Felix followed the dwarfs as they crept down the side passage towards the main corridor. He swallowed, trying to keep his stomach where it belonged. It all sounded very noble and epic, but not particularly survivable.

Even if they managed to hold out until Gorril's force arrived, that was only the beginning of the fighting. They still had the whole fort to subdue after that. Felix had a vision of Gotrek alone in a sea of orcs, with all his companions dead around him, including Felix. It was hard to push it from his mind.

Ten feet from the main corridor, they stopped as they heard footsteps and jabbering voices approaching from the direction of the gate. They shrank back into the shadows, on guard. A massive orc, the biggest Felix had ever seen, strode past, chittering orders to a trailing wake of lieutenants and goblin hangers-on in a sharp, sibilant voice completely at odds with its size, but its voice was the least strange thing about it.

Its eyes were glittering black orbs, and its hide pale and waxy, as if it had been smeared in tallow. Irregular white lumps rose from its skull and forearms, as if tumours were growing under its skin and pushing their way out, and he stank, not like an orc, but sour and cloying, like week-old milk. It wore the strange, spider-shell armour that the dwarfs had seen the orcs forging in the mines, black and glossy and baroque with ridges and spines.

A curiously shaped golden torque twisted snugly around his massive, pale green neck, a faceted black gem glittering from it like a third eye. A hand the size of a prize pumpkin gripped an oddly shaped war axe, bigger than any orc cleaver, but made with almost dwarf skill. Most unsettling of all, though, was the fact that, despite his warlike appearance, his savage tusked face was as slack and dull as a sleepwalker's.

The dwarfs stared as this bizarre apparition continued down the hall, their noses wrinkling at his awful odour.

'What's that when it's at home?' whispered Ragar.

'He's the boss or I'm a halfling,' said Arn.

'But what's happened to it?' asked Karl. 'It looked… it smelled… unhealthy.'

'More proof that there's something amiss,' said Hamnir, hushed. 'The new traps in Birri's hangar, the mining, the weaving, the unorcish jabbering, this strange, ridged armour: it's not right, any of it.'

Gotrek nodded, staring at his axe. The runes upon its head were glowing again. 'Something's amiss all right.' He frowned after the huge orc as it disappeared into the depths of the hold, and then shrugged. 'Come on.'

Hamnir nodded. The corridor was clear to the gate. 'Right,' he said. 'Bolts on the strings and in at a run. Give them no time to react. Go.'

CHAPTER EIGHTEEN

THE DWARFS RAN out, splitting into their two groups, and raced for the guardrooms. The huge stone slab that was the Horn Gate's inner door loomed at the end of the wide hallway like a monolith, solid rock without crack or hinge. Two open doors were set into the corridor walls just inside it. Torchlight shone from them.

The dwarfs had traversed slightly more than half the distance when an orc stepped out of the right-hand guardroom on his way to the left. It turned as it saw motion in the corner of its eye. Thorgig and Narin fired their crossbows. The orc dropped with a thud, one quarrel in its throat, the other in its chest.

Questioning grunts came from the guardrooms. The dwarfs sprinted for them, Gotrek in the lead on the left, Leatherbeard on the right.

Orc heads popped out of the guardroom doors just as the dwarfs reached them. Gotrek buried his axe in the left orc's forehead and drove it backwards into the room with his shoulder. Leatherbeard did the same on the right, and the dwarfs piled in after them.

A single orc jumped up from a table in the centre of the left guardroom as Felix ran in, trying to draw its weapon as Gotrek leapt at it. The Slayer cut its head off before its cleaver cleared its scabbard. Karl and Ragar ran past and closed the door to the murder rooms and turrets. They put their shoulders to it.

Gotrek looked around in disgust. There was a rack of long-guns on one wall, an enormous brass alarm gong on another, and a second door on the same wall as the door the Rassmussons held, but no other orcs in the room. 'Where's my fight?' he asked.

A clash of arms rang from the other room.

'Ha!' Gotrek brightened and hurried for the door. 'Stay here and get the door locked.'

'Aye, Slayer,' said Karl, sneering. 'Go on.'

'We'll just stay here and let you have all the fun,' added Ragar as Narin stepped to them, fishing Hamnir's keys from his pouch.

Felix followed Gotrek across the hall. The right-hand guardroom was a mirror image of the other, complete with gun rack and gong. Four orcs lay dead on the floor, and Hamnir, Leatherbeard and Arn were busy with another six while Thorgig and Galin held the door to the murder rooms and turrets closed. They looked as if they'd rather be fighting.

'Much better,' said Gotrek. He waded in, killing two orcs instantly, as Leatherbeard and Hamnir dropped one each.

The orc facing Arn, seeing its brothers fall, leapt for the alarm gong.

Arn swung after it and missed. 'Watch him! He's–'

Felix dived at the orc and caught it by the ankle, tripping it onto its face, inches from the gong. Gotrek spun and buried his axe in its back.

'Ha!' Gotrek barked.

The last orc stumbled back from Leatherbeard, its guts spilling from its belly. Before any recognised the danger, it tripped over its fallen comrade and pitched, helmet-first, into the gong, dead.

A deafening musical crash rang out, shivering the room with its vibrations. Felix clapped his hands over his ears. Gotrek jumped to the gong and pinched it quiet.

'That's torn it,' said Arn.

Gibbering orcish voices rose in the murder room above, and boots thundered down the stairs. Thorgig and Galin braced their shoulders against the door.

'Quick!' said Hamnir, pointing.

The two dwarfs skidded back as orcs slammed into the door from the other side.

Hamnir pulled out his keys, hurrying towards them. 'Hold fast!'

Gotrek and Leatherbeard added their weight to the door and pushed it closed again. Hamnir stabbed the key with the square loop into the lock and twisted it. It didn't turn.

He paled. 'Have I got it backwards?'

'Hurry, blast you!' said Galin as the door bumped and jumped under his shoulder.

Hamnir stuck the other key in the lock, but just then Narin ran in holding a black iron key ring in one hand and two iron keys in the other.

'They've changed the locks,' he said, and threw the ring to Hamnir. 'Try these. I found mine.'

Hamnir caught the ring, groaning. There were at least a dozen keys on it. He stuck one in the lock. It didn't turn. He tried the next. That didn't turn either. The door bumped and slammed as the dwarfs fought to hold it closed.

'Orcs don't make keys,' muttered Galin.

Ragar stuck his head in from the hall. 'They've heard in the hold!' He shouted. 'They're coming!'

'How many?' called Hamnir.

'The whole damned horde, it looks like!' said Karl over his brother's shoulder.

'Hundred yards away!' called Ragar.

Hamnir turned to Thorgig as he tried another key. His eyes were grim and sad. 'It's now or never, lad. Up the other stairs before they think to try to come down behind us.'

'But they're alerted now,' said Narin. 'He'll be cut down before he has a chance to blow the horn.'

'No he won't,' said Leatherbeard, stepping back from the door. 'Rassmusson, take my place. I'll give him time.'

His eyes glowed through the holes in his mask, with the eager anticipation of battle against impossible odds Felix had seen so often before in the eyes of Gotrek, Snorri Nosebiter, Malakai Makaisson and the other Slayers he had known.

Hamnir clenched his jaw. His beard bristled. 'Right. Go.'

'Yes, my prince,' said Thorgig.

Arn put his shoulder to the door as Thorgig and Leatherbeard saluted Hamnir, fists over their hearts, and then ran across the hall with Narin to the other guardroom. Thorgig unhooked the war horn of Karak Hirn from his belt.

'Damn the world,' said Hamnir. He jabbed the next key into the lock. It too failed to turn.

'Seventy yards!' Ragar chimed from the door.

Felix could hear the orcs now – a rumble like a distant avalanche. He watched across the hall into the other guardroom as Narin unlocked the door to the left-hand murder rooms and turrets, and threw it open. Leatherbeard charged up instantly. Thorgig hesitated the merest fraction of a second, then ran after him, the war horn clenched in one hand. Narin slammed the door and locked it behind them.

There was a muted shout from the orcs in the room above, and then the crisp *tantara* of the horn, blowing a dwarf rally call. Felix heard a roar from Leatherbeard and the clash of axe on cleaver. The horn blew its rally again and again, accompanied by muffled grunts and clangs.

Hamnir found the right key at last and turned it, just as Thorgig's horn squawked abruptly and then cut off.

'Damn the world,' Hamnir said again. He lowered his head until his brow touched the door.

'I only hope they heard,' said Galin, stepping back with Gotrek and Arn.

'Forty yards!' Ragar shouted from the hall. The sound of boots was so loud that it almost drowned him out.

The orcs on the other side of the murder room door started battering it with their weapons. Hamnir continued to kneel before it, unmoving.

'Come on, Ranulfsson,' said Gotrek, gruff. 'Work to be done.'

Hamnir nodded and raised his head, face grim. 'Right.' He crossed to the lever room door. 'Rassmussons, hold the other guard room.' He started trying keys in the lock. 'And one of you, lock Narin into the lever room, in case… in case they get through you.'

'Aye, prince,' said Arn, saluting. He sprinted across to the left-hand guardroom with his brothers, as the thunder of running boots shook the room.

'Thirty!' screamed Ragar, as the brothers formed up in their door.

'Galin,' said Hamnir, not looking up from the lock. 'When I find the key, you will lock me in, and then help the Slayer.'

Galin nodded. 'Right.'

'You know what to do, Gurnisson?' Hamnir called.

Gotrek nodded. 'Keep your sorry hide whole, as usual.' He plodded to the hallway door. 'Manling, fall in.'

'Twenty!'

Felix took up a position to the left of the door and looked at Gotrek. The Slayer swayed slightly as he stood.

'All right, Gotrek?' he asked.

'Never better,' said Gotrek, and looked back at Hamnir. 'Fifteen minutes you said, Ranulfsson?'

'Aye,' said Hamnir.

Gotrek nodded and faced the door, raising his axe. 'I can stand anything for fifteen minutes.'

With a deafening clatter, the orc horde filled the end of the corridor like a green flood. Gotrek roared and swung as they pushed in at the guardroom doors, butchering them as they came. The press of the orcs behind shoved those at the front into Gotrek's axe ready or not. He cut them into flying green pieces.

Felix stabbed into them from the side, hamstringing and blinding them. Through the surging mass of sinewy green arms and armoured green torsos, he caught glimpses of the brothers Rassmusson swinging crimsoned picks in the door to the other guard room, digging into orc flesh with the same tireless swings they had used to cut through the wall to the vault.

At least a hundred orcs choked the end of the hall, and no doubt hundreds more packed the long hall behind them, trying to get to the fight. Fortunately, the doors to the guardrooms were only as wide as a single dwarf, and the orcs could only squeeze in one or two at a time. Gotrek stood a pace back, so he had an unobstructed swing, and split heads and chests, while Felix jabbed at feet, wrists and eyes, before they reached him.

There was a cry of triumph from Hamnir as he found the key to the lever room at last. Felix was too busy to look back, but he heard a door open and clang closed, and then Galin joined them, hewing from the right side of the door as Felix did from the left.

Fifteen minutes? Felix eyed Gotrek uneasily. Could the Slayer do it, weary as he was? Could the brothers Rassmusson? The Slayer's axe never slowed, but he was heavy on his feet, slipping in orc gore, and the savage, bared-teeth grin that usually spread across his face in battle was missing, replaced with a tight-jawed scowl of grim determination.

And would it be only fifteen minutes? What if Gorril encountered unexpected obstacles? What if his force was being ambushed by orcs? What if, Sigmar forbid, Gorril hadn't heard the horn at all? It might be that there was no help coming. Then, no matter how long Gotrek lasted, it wouldn't be long enough. The tide of orcs was never-ending. Eventually, they would force their way into the guardrooms and slaughter them all.

Felix chuckled bitterly. Orcs or no, here was the sort of death that Gotrek had longed for – a heroic fight against overwhelming odds, in pursuit of the noblest of causes. Of course, as always, Felix was as trapped in Gotrek's grand death as the Slayer was, and the chances of surviving in order to write the epic poem of his legendary doom were slim to none. One day, he would have to figure out how to chronicle Gotrek's death from afar – if there were any more days after today.

There was a bellow of pain and then a cry of 'Ragar!' from the corridor.

Felix looked through the crush of orcs to the opposite guardroom. Ragar was falling, his head half severed, blood matting his beard. His brothers butchered the orc who had killed him and fought on.

Felix did the same; there was no time to grieve. He moaned with weariness. It felt like hours had passed, not minutes. His arms ached from stabbing and hacking. The orcs crawled over the bodies of their slain comrades to attack Gotrek with stoic blankness, as if their own lives meant nothing – as if they knew they were the drops of water that wear down a rock. The bodies inside the door were up to Gotrek's shoulders.

Gotrek was weaving with each blow, and Felix and Galin had to do more and more of his blocking for him.

'How long?' the Slayer rasped a while later.

'Ten minutes gone, I think,' wheezed Galin, deflecting a mace, 'maybe more.' He looked over his shoulder to the lever room door, which had a grilled window in it. 'Any sign of them, prince?'

'No sign,' came Hamnir's voice, hollowly.

There was commotion in the hall – an orc voice chittering commands, and orcs shifting around.

Gotrek choked out a laugh. 'Grimnir, that's all we need.'

Felix risked a look around the doorframe and gaped. Ten orcs, armed with dwarf long-guns, were forming up back to back in the centre of the wide corridor, five facing each guardroom door, as other orcs got out of their way.

'Find a way to kill them, manling,' grunted Gotrek. 'If I go out there, the rest will come in here, and if I stay here...'

'I have it,' said Galin. He backed from the door and ran to the gun rack at the far wall. 'Wait there.'

'And where do you think I'd be going?' Gotrek asked through his teeth.

Felix looked back and saw Galin gathering up powder horns.

The orcs primed and loaded their guns like boys on their first day of gunnery drill – clumsy and slow, spilling powder all over the place, but at last they were ready. Their commander growled an order. They raised the long-guns to their shoulders and aimed.

'Olifsson!' shouted Gotrek.

'One moment!'

'Haven't got a damned–'

The orc captain dropped his hand and the orcs fired at Gotrek and the Rassmussons, utterly unconcerned about hitting their fellows who stood in the way.

Two of the guns exploded, their barrels ripping apart at the stock and blowing shrapnel and flame into the faces of the orcs around them. Four collapsed, skulls shattered. Three guns fizzled and failed to fire at all, but five got off shots. Two balls whizzed towards the Rassmussons, three towards Gotrek. One buried itself in the back of an orc. One whistled over his crest. Gotrek swung his axe up and the last spanged off it, and then bonged into the gong.

In the opposite door, Karl staggered back, clutching his arm. An orc cut him down before he could recover. Arn died a second later, alone and overwhelmed.

'The Rassmussons are down!' called Felix. 'The orcs have the other guardroom.'

Hamnir cursed from the lever room.

Having cleared the opposite doorway, all the remaining orc gunners turned to Gotrek's side and began to reload as, behind them, their comrades swarmed into the left hand guardroom and started hacking at the lever room door.

'Hurry, curse you, Olifsson!' called Gotrek.

'Just coming!' said Galin. He ran back to them holding a pair of powder horns with holes in their sides, stuffed with bits of paper wadding. He shook them. They rattled. 'Added some shot.'

He lit the wadding of one with his lamp and heaved it over the heads of the orcs in the door. It hit the floor near the orc gunners, and went off with a concussive crack and an eruption of smoke and flame. Orcs fell, howling and coughing, with holes in their legs and guts, but not as many as Felix could have wished. Five of the gunners were still up, though one of them was on fire and flailing. The captain chopped it down and shoved it aside, roaring at the others to fire.

An orc slashed at Galin as he tried to light the second grenade. He danced back and tried again.

'Throw it!' Gotrek shouted.

The wadding caught. Galin threw the horn just as three of the orcs finished loading, and raised their guns. The powder horn exploded, ripping into them.

It was a second too late. The orcs had got their shots off first.

Gotrek staggered and dropped to one knee, catching himself with his axe. There was a bloody trench along his outer thigh.

CHAPTER NINETEEN

FELIX BLOCKED DESPERATELY as an orc swung for the Slayer's unprotected skull. The cleaver screeched along his sword and missed Gotrek's face by a hair's breadth. Felix hooked Gotrek under his arm with his free hand and tried to haul him up. He was ridiculously heavy. More were coming in. Galin fought two.

Gotrek found his footing again and severed the arm of the orc with the cleaver, but the damage was done. There were five orcs in the room, and more pushing in behind them. The doorway was lost. Felix, Gotrek and Galin backed and fought in a line, trying to keep the orcs from encircling them. Gotrek's left leg was slick with blood.

Felix heard a tinny shout from inside the lever room – Narin yelling through the speaking tube from across the hall. 'They're nearly through to me! The door won't hold long!'

'Courage, Ironskin!' called Hamnir. 'Any minute now.'

There was a smash behind Felix. He glanced back. The blade of a cleaver stuck through the door to the murder rooms and turrets. The orcs from above were breaking through. They would soon be surrounded.

'Where in Grungni's name is Gorril?' grunted Galin, blocking an orc sword.

'Not here,' said Gotrek. He was weaving like a drunk, barely able to stand on his mangled leg. He swung at an orc and missed. Felix nearly dropped his sword in shock. Gotrek never missed. The orc pressed forwards. Felix stabbed it in the neck. Gotrek gutted it, but four more had got past. Gotrek, Felix and Galin had orcs on three sides of them. They were too tired. There were too many.

Then, over the clangour of the fight, very faint, they heard a horn, drowned out almost immediately by muted gunfire.

'A horn!' said Galin.

'They're in the canyon. They're running!' cried Hamnir from the lever room. 'Narin! At the ready!'

'Ready,' came the metallic reply.

'Oh Grimnir, the crossfire!' choked Hamnir. 'So many down. They're... Open the outer door. Pull! Pull!'

An enormous grating and rumbling shook the room as the outer door slowly began to lower, and then came a deafening boom as it sank home. The orcs in the guardroom looked behind them at the sound, and Gotrek, Felix and Galin cut down five of them. The battering stopped behind the door to the murder room, and they heard the orcs running back up the stairs to their stations in the turrets.

A second volley of cannon and small-arms fire resounded through the walls from the canyon.

'Now the inner! Pull, Narin!' came Hamnir's voice. 'Run lads, run!'

Another shuddering rumble and a roaring of wind, and the guardroom filled with cold air and the smell of gunsmoke. As the second door boomed to a stop, the wind rose and steadied to a deafening trumpet pitch that vibrated the whole corridor, as if blown through the throat of an enormous horn. The orcs twitched and cringed at the noise.

Hamnir roared from the lever room. 'The horn of Hirn! Now they will fear us!'

The orcs in the corridor were turning and backing away from the open door, their commanders shouting at them to form up. They were too late.

With horns blowing and banners waving, the dwarfs of Karak Hirn charged through the open doors eight abreast, hammerers at the fore, and punched the disorganised orcs back like a gunner ramming a charge down a cannon's mouth.

Gotrek, Felix and Galin butchered the last five orcs in the guardroom as Gorril's force continued to pour in, rank after rank of sturdy warriors howling for orc blood.

As the last orc toppled, Gotrek staggered back and sank down onto a stool by the guardroom table. His axe head thudded on the stone floor. 'Grungni, I need a drink!' he said. His left leg, below the trench the bullet had cut, was red to his boot.

'Galin!' called Hamnir from the lever room. 'Open the door!'

Galin hurried to the lever room door and let Hamnir out. The prince surveyed the heaps of orc bodies in the room, and shook his head. He looked up at the three of them. 'Your deeds today will be recorded in the Book of Karak Hirn. I swear it.'

Gorril stepped out of the blur of dwarfs rushing past the guard-room, leading a company of his clan brothers. He saluted Hamnir, his fist over his heart. 'My prince,' he said gravely. 'I am glad to see you alive. Your army goes to gain a foothold in the grand concourse, and then awaits your orders.'

'And I am glad to see you, cousin,' said Hamnir, saluting in turn. 'We will need dwarfs here to open the murder room doors and take the orcs within. They must also close the gate when the column is in. There is not the glory to be had here that there will be in the con-course, but our rear must be protected.'

'Of course, prince,' said Gorril. He turned to his clan brothers. 'You heard him, Urlo. Divide up the lads and take the murder rooms.'

'Aye, Gorril.' Urlo saluted and began barking orders to his com-panions.

Hamnir glanced at Galin. 'Stonemonger, take the keys from Arn's body and let Narin out of the other lever room.'

'Aye, prince.' Galin saluted and stepped into the hall.

'And you, Gurnisson,' Hamnir continued, turning to Gotrek. 'I command you to have no more to do with this battle. The physi-cians will dress your wounds and you will take a well-deserved rest. You too, Herr Jaeger.'

'Humph!' said Gotrek.

'Now come, Gorril,' said Hamnir, stepping to the door with the tall dwarf. 'Have you sent thunderers to the second-floor balconies? And are the Ironbreakers on their way through the secondary tun-nels to come at the orc flanks? Have the miners gone to seal the doors to the mines?'

'All as you ordered, Prince Hamnir,' said Gorril. 'They are to secure each passage as they go, so the orcs may not get in behind us.'

Hamnir hailed a mule cart just coming through the front gate. 'Surgeons! Here! See to those within the guardrooms. The Slayer has been shot and is losing blood.'

'Aye, prince.'

The cart stopped and two dwarf surgeons bustled in, field kits in hand. One got busy patching up the minor cuts and scrapes that Felix had collected, while the other cleaned and dressed Gotrek's leg wound. As they worked, Urlo and Gorril's clan brothers unlocked the door to the murder rooms and turrets, and charged up the stairs within. The sounds of battle began to rage above them.

'You're lucky, Slayer,' Gotrek's surgeon said as he began wrapping his leg. 'Missed the bone entirely. Stay off it for a month or two, keep it clean, and it'll heal just fine.'

'A month?' growled Gotrek. 'I'll give you another *minute* before I use your guts to tie it off. Now hurry. There's a battle to fight.'

'Really, Slayer,' said the surgeon. 'I wouldn't advise it.' Nonetheless, he wrapped the wound in record time.

Gotrek surged up almost before he had tightened the last knot, and limped stoically towards the hall. 'Come, manling,' he said, 'I want to find that wax-skinned tusk-mouth in the black armour. An orc like that might almost be a challenge.'

'Not going to listen to Hamnir?' asked Felix, though he knew it would do no good. He followed the Slayer wearily.

'I swore I'd protect him,' said Gotrek, 'not follow his orders.'

Galin and Narin fell in with them as they left the other guardroom, their wounds also bound. All around them, surgeons and victuallers were unloading their carts and setting up cots and trestle tables in preparation for caring for the wounded and weary.

As Gotrek passed a cart piled with barrels and crates, he snatched up a small keg, wrenched the plug out with his fingers and upended it over his mouth, gulping down several pints of the golden brew as it splashed over his beard and crest. At last, he lowered it with a contented sigh and held it out to the others. 'Anyone else?'

Galin and Narin both took and lifted the keg in turn, though with more difficulty, and drank their fill. Felix took it up after them, glad that it was nearly empty, for he would never have been able to raise it full. Gotrek took it from him when he'd finished, had another guzzle, and then slammed it down on the cart and limped on, smacking his lips.

The corridor ended at a high, columned archway, beyond which wide, shallow steps descended into an enormous, marble-floored hall, the grand concourse of Karak Hirn, the central hall from which all the ceremonial and public chambers of the hold stemmed. It was three storeys tall, and pillars as big and round as castle turrets ran down either side of it, holding up an intricately carved, crossvaulted ceiling.

It was swarming with orcs.

The dwarf army held the area around the steps, ranks of doughty warriors, Ironbreakers and miners lined up at their base, while thunderers stood and knelt in two lines on the top step, firing over the heads of their brethren below. The dwarfs were already vastly outnumbered, and more orcs were pouring into the concourse through a dozen archways.

A tattoo of explosions came from beyond the battle. Felix looked up and saw that more thunderers had taken up positions on two balconies, one on the huge room's right wall, one on the left, above and behind the main body of the orcs. Twenty orcs fell at this volley, and there was another right behind it as a second rank of dwarfs stepped up to the rail of the balcony and the first stepped back to reload. A third rank followed the second, and then the first was ready again. Orcs fell like cut wheat. The thunderers' speed and marksmanship was awe-inspiring.

Directly below where Felix stood with Gotrek, Hamnir, and the others, the huge pale orc in the odd armour, and his similarly dressed and milk-skinned retinue, were smashing Karak Hirn's longbeards to pieces. The rancid reek of them was almost blinding. The white-haired dwarfs fought them valiantly, eyes watering from the smell as they struck again and again, but the orcs were incredibly strong, and what was worse, disciplined. For every white orc that toppled, three longbeards had their heads caved in. The longbeards would never break, but neither, it appeared would the orcs. And none could touch the huge warboss. Three longbeards bashed at him, landing blow after blow, but he took their worst and gave back murder. A white-haired dwarf staggered back, clutching his neck, his long beard a bright crimson tabard. It was old Ruen. He fell on his face before the steps.

'Stand aside,' said Gotrek, limping forwards.

'No, Gurnisson,' said Hamnir, stepping ahead of the Slayer. 'He is mine. He took my hold. I will take him. Besides, you're in no shape for a fight.'

'I'm always in shape for a fight,' Gotrek bristled, but then stopped, grunting. 'Bah! It's your hold. I suppose you have the right to challenge him, Valaya curse you.'

Hamnir and Gorril were already charging down the steps to join the longbeards' line. Gotrek glared after them, angry, or perhaps concerned. Felix couldn't tell.

'Come on, manling,' the Slayer said, turning. 'We'll find some other place to get stuck in.'

'Why not take Hamnir's advice and sit this one out,' said Felix. 'You're not exactly at your best.'

'Why do you all say that?' growled Gotrek. 'All I needed was a drink.'

'Listen,' said Narin, trying to see through the gun-smoke that filled the hall like a fog. 'The thunderers on the right balcony have stopped firing.'

'They're being attacked,' said Galin, craning his neck. 'Orcs have got around behind them.'

Gotrek turned to the corridor. 'Then we'll get around behind the orcs.'

'Just the four of us?' asked Felix.

Gotrek looked at the battle. The dwarfs were sorely pressed on every side. 'There's no one else to spare.'

He stumped back into the corridor. Felix, Narin and Galin exchanged a glance, and then shrugged and followed him.

A few strides down the hallway, they reached a rising stair held by a rank of Karak Hirn dwarfs.

'One of you lads, lead us to the right balcony over the concourse,' said Gotrek. 'Your thunderers are in trouble.'

'One of us?' said a dwarf. 'We'll all come!'

'And desert your position?' snarled Gotrek. 'Your prince would like that. Just one.'

The dwarf who had spoken, a gruff veteran named Dolmir, came with them, leading them quickly up the stairs and through the passages of the floor above. Gotrek grunted with each limping step in an effort to keep up with the others.

Soon they entered a high, wide corridor that ringed the grand concourse. On the outer wall of the ring were a series of magnificent doors, each with the insignia of a clan carved above it in stone – the entrances to the holds of the clans who made Karak Hirn their home. Many of their doors hung open, or had been smashed off their hinges, and piles of stone and construction materials littered the corridor, as if the orcs had been attempting repairs. On its inner wall, the ring was pierced by numerous iron-latticed windows, balconies, and galleries that looked down into the grand concourse. The sounds of battle echoed up through them, but a nearer battle was louder. The companions turned.

Halfway down the corridor was the entrance to the balcony that the thunderers had been firing from. A seething scrum of orcs surrounded it. The thunderers had turned and fought them with hand axe and dagger. Both orc and dwarf bodies sprawled at the feet of the combatants, but the dwarfs were getting the worst of it. They were outnumbered two to one. They would be overwhelmed in moments.

'Grimnir take it,' cursed Gotrek as he hobbled forwards. 'I can't run.' He looked around angrily, and then pointed to the construction. 'Manling, that barrow!'

Felix ran to a pile of rubble and pulled out a wooden wheelbarrow. He rolled it to Gotrek. The Slayer climbed in, wounded leg first, and faced forwards, axe at the ready.

'Push!'

Felix tried, but the dwarf was impossibly heavy, much denser than anything made of flesh and blood had any right to be. 'Narin, help me.'

Narin took up one of the barrow's handles and together they ran it down the corridor, Galin and Dolmir pacing them. The orcs and the thunderers were too occupied to notice them coming.

'Valaya's mercy, Gurnisson,' puffed Narin. 'Do you eat stone for breakfast?'

'Shut up. Push faster!'

Fifteen feet from the melee, the barrow's wheel struck a loose brick and bounced wildly. Gotrek catapulted forwards, grunting in surprise, but turned it into a bloodthirsty battle cry and raised his axe in mid-air.

The back rank of orcs turned at the noise and fell to the floor in pieces as Gotrek's axe passed through them, parting armour and bone as easily as it cut flesh. Felix and Narin ploughed the barrow into the orcs, then drew their weapons and charged in with Galin and Dolmir, slashing and chopping.

The thunderers cheered and, heartened by the reinforcements, attacked with renewed fury. The orcs fought with the same blank silence that Felix had come to expect.

Dolmir, however, was unnerved. 'Why don't they cry out? Why don't they break?'

'I don't know, cousin,' said Narin, 'but they won't run. We'll have to kill every last one.'

And they did. Though Gotrek was nearly immobile because of his leg, it didn't matter. The orcs came to him, pushing forwards to swing at him, only to fall before his omnipresent blade. The swarm was quickly obliterated.

'Much obliged, Slayer,' said the captain of the thunderers as his dwarfs recovered and took up their guns again. 'Tougher than we thought they'd be.'

They re-formed on the balcony and started firing down into the mass of orcs once again.

Gotrek, Felix and the others looked over the battle below. The dwarfs and orcs were fighting to a standstill along a curved line in front of the steps. It looked as if every orc in the hold was trying to get at the dwarfs, and in the centre...

'Grimnir curse him!' said Gotrek as he saw. 'Thinks he's a Slayer now?'

In the centre, Hamnir and the orc warboss still fought on, the tattered remains of their squads surrounding them. There were less than ten of the strange pale orcs left, and no more than a handful of longbeards. Hamnir's helmet was dented and his gromril ring-mail torn in a dozen places. His face was red with blood and exertion. The warboss's armour had similarly been smashed and ripped away, but strangely, its pale, green skin didn't have a mark on it.

As Felix and Gotrek watched, Hamnir swung his axe at the giant orc's exposed knee. At first it seemed he had hit it, for Felix could have sworn he saw Hamnir's shoulders jolt with the impact, but it must have been an illusion, for his axe sped on, unbloodied, and the orc took no wound. The orc hardly registered the attack, swinging its own shield-sized axe down at Hamnir so swiftly that the dwarf prince had to fling himself aside to avoid being chopped in two.

'Never was much good in a scrap,' grumbled Gotrek. He pulled himself up onto the balustrade. 'Hang on, scholar!' he roared, and without a second thought, leapt down to the floor, twenty-five feet below.

CHAPTER TWENTY

'GOTREK!' SHOUTED FELIX. He thrust his head over the rail. Narin and Galin did the same, eyes wide with alarm.

'It's all right,' said Narin wryly. 'His fall was broken by a dozen orcs.'

It was true. Gotrek was on his feet in the centre of a cluster of sprawling orcs, slashing around like a red-crested whirlwind as he forced his way towards Hamnir and the warboss. The bandage on his leg was crimson with fresh blood.

Felix's mouth opened and closed. 'Damn him! I... I... I'll break my legs. I...' With a curse he turned and bolted into the hallway towards the stairs. Narin and Galin ran after him, but quickly fell behind.

Felix pounded down the stairs, pushed through the dwarfs at the bottom and sprinted along the corridor to the grand concourse. He skidded to a stop behind the thunderers on the steps and scanned the surging battle for Gotrek.

The Slayer was just reaching the warboss, a wide swath of broken and dismembered orcs behind him. He swung at the warboss's back. The blow ripped the shattered remains of the orc's black breastplate off and sent it spinning. As the brute turned to swing at Gotrek, Felix could see that its back was entirely unmarked. He groaned. Gotrek had missed for a second time today, though it wasn't any wonder: he should have been flat on his back in bed.

With its attention held by Gotrek, Hamnir and the longbeards attacked the warboss from all sides. Their blows did nothing. Felix paled. Were they *all* missing? Or was something more sinister going on? The big orc made no attempt whatsoever to block them. Seven axes struck its back, legs and shoulders, and it shrugged them off as if it didn't feel them. It fought in leather rags and scraps of cloth, and still there was not a single wound on it.

It has some magic, thought Felix, some protective spell. No matter. Gotrek would make short work of that. He and his axe had cut down dragons and daemons. Magic siege engines had disintegrated at the merest touch of that fell blade.

Gotrek knocked the wax-fleshed monster's enormous battle-axe aside and lurched in with a clean unobstructed swing to its belly. The orc roared in pain and staggered back three steps, and Felix raised his fist. That's done it, he thought. But as the warboss straightened, Felix saw only a fading line on its belly, as one might see if one drew one's fingernail across the back of one's hand. The orc had taken a blow that should have come out through its spine, and was unmarked.

'Damned stinking beast!' Gotrek swore. 'What are you made of?'

The orc charged him, raining a storm of blows down on him as the Slayer blocked and swayed on his bad leg, cursing in pain and frustration.

Felix pushed through the thunderers and charged the monstrous orc's back. A stupid thing to do, he knew, even as he did it. If Gotrek's axe could make no impression, what could he do? But he couldn't just stand aside and watch. He swung his long sword at the same time that Hamnir and the longbeards swung their axes. Not one strike broke the skin. They all slid off the orc's pale green hide as if it were oiled marble.

The orc swept a lazy backhand at Felix, Hamnir and the others, splitting open a Longbeard's ribs and knocking him to the floor, dead. Felix leapt back, barely escaping the same fate.

Gotrek lunged in and swung with all his might at the orc's right shin – a blow like that would have severed the leg from an iron statue. The orc grunted and its leg buckled, but it recovered and spun back. Its huge axe shaved a tuft from Gotrek's orange crest.

Felix tossed aside his sword. Perhaps he couldn't wound the thing, but he might blind it. He leapt on its massive back, grabbing it around the neck, struggling to climb it. Its skin was slick with some foul mucus. The smell choked him, and he almost slid off.

The orc grunted, annoyed, and tried to shrug him off. Felix got his legs over its broad shoulders and clapped his hands over its eyes.

'Good, manling!' called Gotrek. 'Stay on him!' He struck the orc's chest with a blow that should have split its sternum.

The orc staggered back, bellowing in pain, but its skin remained whole. It lashed out blind and one-handed with its axe, and groped with its free hand for Felix.

Felix tried to squirm out of the way of the questing fingers, but they caught him by the arm.

Felix scrabbled desperately for purchase and caught at the gold torque wrapped around the orc's neck. The orc threw him crashing into Gotrek, sending them both sprawling.

'Curse you, manling!' grunted the Slayer from under Felix. 'I told you to stay on.'

A shadow of swift movement flashed in the corner of Felix's eye and he rolled instinctively aside. Gotrek rolled the opposite way. The orc's immense axe blade slammed down between them, burying itself deep in the marble floor.

Gotrek staggered up, lurching on his wounded leg, and swung with all his might at the orc's arm as it lifted the axe again. He chopped the massive green limb in half at the elbow.

Gotrek blinked as the orc howled and fell back, its stump spurting black blood. 'What in the name of Grungni?'

Hamnir and the longbeards ran in as the orc staggered, clutching itself. Their axes bit deep, just as Gotrek's had. They chopped it to pieces.

'What happened?' asked Hamnir, as they looked down at its mangled body. 'Why did it suddenly become vulnerable?'

'Haven't a clue,' said Gotrek, ruffling his shortened crest and frowning.

'Er,' said Felix, and held up the thing he clutched in his hand – the orc's golden torque.

FELIX GAVE THE torque to Hamnir as the battle with the orcs continued. He was glad to be rid of it. Perhaps it would have made him invincible too, but it made his skin crawl just holding it. The glittering black jewel in its centre seemed to look at him, and dark whisperings seemed to fill his mind, urging him to put it on. Dwarfs were less susceptible to that sort of thing, he thought as he fought beside Gotrek, better for Hamnir to have it.

Felix's many battles against orcs had taught him that when one kills the warboss, the fight is over. The lieutenants start squabbling, and any cohesion the horde might have had dissipates in an explosion of infighting and panic. Although he and the dwarfs had ample evidence that the orcs they fought now were not like other orcs, it still came as a demoralising shock when they continued fighting just as resolutely after the invulnerable warboss had fallen as they had before.

So, for another weary, blood-soaked hour, the orcs threw themselves at the dwarf line with the dull mechanical ferocity of ants protecting their nest. Gotrek and Hamnir fought back to back in that swirling sea, roaring and joking, and exchanging reminiscences as if they were bellied up to a bar instead of butchering greenskins.

'That wasn't nine, scholar,' Gotrek growled, grinning. 'You only have eight. I finished off the one before last, so he's on my tally not yours. Is this how you count your manifests?'

'I dispatched the one you threw behind you,' retorted Hamnir, grinning. 'Do you think your every stroke is fatal? Someone has to clean up behind you, as it ever was.'

Felix was struck again by unexpected jealousy as he watched them. He had travelled with Gotrek for twenty years and could not recall one instance where Gotrek had been as comfortable and free in his presence as he was with Hamnir now.

Finally, the last orc fell, the echoes of steel on steel faded, and the grand concourse was silent, but for the moaning of the wounded and the dying. Felix could barely lift his sword, and Gotrek was the same, wearier than Felix had ever seen him, but happier too.

The dwarfs looked around in a daze at the piles of the dead and the lakes of blood that spread across the polished marble floor. Some of the survivors mourned over slain brothers and friends. Some clapped each other on the back and drank celebratory toasts from flasks. Some were so tired that they sat down where they were, unheeding of the corpses and the reek.

Hamnir limped unsteadily up the steps and turned to face his troops. He was a mass of cuts and bruises, his armour hanging off him like a gromril rag. 'Sons and friends of Karak Hirn, you have won a great victory here today.'

The dwarfs bellowed a deep-throated cheer.

'This enterprise may have started in my error, but it has ended in your victory. I thank you for your help and sacrifice. Bring our dead and wounded to the shrine of Grungni, but leave the grobi where they lay. We will begin to set the hold to rights tomorrow. Tonight in the feast hall we will dine and drink and toast the valorous dead.'

There was another cheer, and then the dwarfs roused themselves to see to their maimed and murdered. As Hamnir stepped down to the floor again, dwarfs began to jog in from every archway, bearing news.

'Prince,' called the first, 'we have sealed the entrances to the mine. There are many grobi still below, but they will not get in tonight.'

'Prince Hamnir,' said another, 'we have cleared the upper galleries and the grain storage level, but several score of goblins have locked themselves in the third armoury.'

Urlo and the dwarfs of Gorril's clan returned from the guard-rooms, bloody and battered, and missing half their number. Urlo knelt stiffly and held the Battle Horn of Karak Hirn out to Hamnir. The bell was split and crumpled.

Hamnir choked as he took it. 'Thorgig.'

'He died with it to his lips, prince,' said Urlo. 'He never drew his axe.'

'And Leatherbeard? The Slayer?'

'Ten dead orcs surrounded him,' said Urlo, 'and it took as many strikes to bring him down.'

Hamnir lowered his head. 'Their sacrifice won the day. They will be honoured.'

Gotrek nodded gravely. 'It was a good doom.'

More dwarfs approached as reports came from all over the hold. Pockets of grobi resistance here, a decisive victory there, ruined supplies, vandalised rooms, a storage room full of the rotting corpses of dwarfs who had barricaded themselves in and starved to death, looted treasure vaults.

Hamnir took it all, good news and bad, with a weary calm, dis-patching orders and dispensing thanks and congratulations to those who merited it as he walked slowly towards the arch that led to the feast hall, but then came a piece of news that stopped him in his tracks.

'Prince,' called a Karak Hirn warrior, running up at the head of a dozen dwarfs, 'the Diamondsmith clan, their hold is unbreached! It looks as if the grobi tried to break down the door, but it is still whole. They may yet live!'

'Ferga!' whispered Hamnir. He looked around at Gorril and Gotrek, eyes bright. 'Come, we must see!' He strode across the hall, his exhaus-tion a thing of the past. The others hurried after him.

'Don't get your hopes up, prince,' said Gorril. 'It has been twenty days. There can't have been much food in the hall when they closed the doors.'

'Aye, scholar,' said Gotrek, gruff. 'Be prepared for the worst. It may be orcs behind that door.'

'I am prepared,' said Hamnir, but he still sounded eager.

They climbed broad stairs to the balconied corridor that ringed the grand concourse, and travelled past six breached clanholds until they came to a tall iron and stone door with the insignia of a diamond set above its lintel. The door was blackened with smoke, and chipped and dented as if from gunshots and hammer blows, but it was still intact.

Hamnir looked upon it with longing eyes. He stepped forwards, and then turned to the crowd of dwarfs who had followed him there. 'Are there any among you of the Diamondsmith clan? Do any of you have a key or know the clan secret to opening this door?'

None of the dwarfs spoke up.

'No Diamondsmiths save Thorgig and Kagrin escaped the hold, prince,' said Gorril. 'The rest locked themselves in, to the last dwarf.'

Hamnir nodded and turned back to the door, drawing his axe. He reversed it and rapped an odd, syncopated tattoo on the door with the square back of the head. From years in the company of dwarfs, Felix knew what this must be, though he had never heard it used – the mine code of the dwarfs, a system for communicating through miles of tunnels with nothing but a hammer. The code was more jealously guarded than the dwarf language, for with it they could talk though walls and across enemy lines.

Hamnir finished his short pattern and the assembled dwarfs waited for a response. None came. He rapped the door again, and again no response came. Gorril shifted, uncomfortable. Gotrek coughed. Hamnir set his jaw and raised his axe once more, but just as he was about to rap again, an uncertain tapping echoed through the door. It sounded as if the sender was just on the other side.

Hamnir gasped and beat an excited response on the door.

'Easy, scholar,' said Gotrek. 'You're stuttering.'

After a breathless silence, a slow reply came.

'Valaya be praised!' said Hamnir. He turned to the others. 'Stand back. They're opening the door.'

The crowd moved back, murmuring their amazement. Hamnir and Gorril were all smiles, slapping each other on the back and chuckling, but Felix saw that Gotrek kept his hand on the haft of his axe, and his face was wary. Felix understood his caution. If the orcs could learn how to build dwarf traps and shoot long-guns, they might have learned anything.

For a long moment nothing happened, and then there was a deep 'thunk' of stone bolts drawing back and the doors began to swing slowly out.

The dwarfs held their breath, and more than one followed Gotrek's example and lowered their hands to their axes, but when the doors boomed fully open, what faced Hamnir, Gotrek, Felix and the others through the huge arched door, was a handful of dwarfs so ragged and gaunt that it was hard to believe they still lived. Felix heard a horrified intake of breath behind him as the liberators gazed upon the liberated.

Felix had never seen dwarfs so thin. Even in the direst circumstances, dwarfs remained relatively robust, but these poor souls looked at death's door. The dwarf who stood to the fore, an axe hanging from his shaking hand, was practically a skeleton, his cheekbones jutting out above his grizzled and patchy beard like rock ledges. His doublet hung from his bony shoulders like a sack, loose and dirty. His hair and beard were brittle and dull.

Hamnir cried out and stepped forwards, taking the dwarf's bone-thin hand. 'Thane Kirhaz Helmgard! You live!'

'Prince Hamnir,' Kirhaz whispered, his voice as weak as a candle flame at noon, 'you have come.'

'And by Grimnir, Grungni and Valaya, I am thankful beyond all words that we are not too late. Unless,' he choked suddenly. 'Unless we *are* too late, and you few are all that survive!'

Kirhaz shook his head. 'Some have died, but most are spared. We have been allowed to live.'

Felix thought it was a funny way to put it, but Hamnir didn't appear to notice.

'And Ferga?' he asked eagerly. 'Does she live?'

'Aye, Ferga lives,' said Kirhaz.

'The ancestors be praised!' said Hamnir. He turned to the others. 'Summon the physics and surgeons! Bring food and drink! Our cousins are in need.'

More haggard dwarfs were appearing in the hall behind Kirhaz, shuffling forwards like slow-moving ghosts.

'By the ancestors,' said Hamnir, staring. 'What you have endured.'

He started forwards into the Diamondsmith hold. The others followed, calling out to old friends among the survivors and hurrying to them with glad cries and gentle embraces. The survivors met these greetings with wan smiles and blank stares. It seemed as if it hadn't yet sunk in that they had been saved. Their eyes remained haunted and far away.

Felix and Gotrek stepped with Hamnir and Kirhaz and the others into the central chamber of the clanhold. Frail dwarfs came out of arches and doors all around its perimeter, blinking like bears waking from hibernation.

All at once, Hamnir shouted and hurried across the room to a starved looking dwarf maiden, her long hair ratty and unbraided, and her dress like a tent around her bony frame.

'Ferga!' cried Hamnir, taking up her hands and kissing them. 'Ferga, beloved.'

She stared at him uncertainly for a moment, and then reached out and patted his face, frowning uncertainly. 'Hamnir. Prince. Have you come? Or is this yet another dream?'

'I have come, Ferga. You are free. Your ordeal is over.'

'Good. Good.' Her hand fell to her side.

Hamnir swallowed, his face a mixture of confusion and pain. This was obviously not the scene of tearful welcome he had constructed in his head. 'Beloved, you are weak. We must see to your recovery. I...' he paused and looked back at Kirhaz, who was crossing to them. 'I am afraid I must bring sadness to this joyous occasion.' He held up the war horn and looked at them both. He squared his shoulders. 'Your son and brother, Thorgig, is dead, slain by the orcs, but his sacrifice was not in vain. He won the day and freed you. He died summoning our troops.'

'Thorgig.' Ferga's brow furrowed, as if she were trying to remember what the word meant. 'Thorgig is dead?'

'My son,' said Kirhaz hollowly. 'Aye. That's bad. That's bad.'

Felix frowned. Even for dwarfs, Kirhaz and Ferga's response was stoic. They didn't seem to understand.

Hamnir was unnerved, but put the best face on it he could. 'Forgive me. I should not have burdened you with such news before you have had a chance to recover yourselves. I will trouble you no more until you have been fed and tended to.' He turned and addressed the dwarfs of the Diamondsmith hold, masking his pain with an effort. 'There will be a feast tonight in the feast hall. Your courage and steadfastness will be honoured there. If you are well enough, I beg all of you to attend. Let the drinking horns be filled and the trenchers heaped high! Tonight we celebrate a miracle!'

The rescuers cheered. The rescued took the news with dull indifference. The cheers faltered.

Hamnir bowed to Kirhaz and Ferga, and then turned away and whispered to Gotrek. 'It is enough to break my heart. Have you ever seen dwarfs so lost?'

'No,' said Gotrek, 'I haven't.' His hand was still on his axe.

CHAPTER TWENTY-ONE

FOR ALL HAMNIR'S talk of piling the trenchers high, the feast was a lean affair. The dwarfs could not, or would not, trust any food touched by the orcs, nor use the great kitchens until they had been thoroughly scoured, so they had to make do with the provisions that Gorril's army had brought with them from Rodenheim Castle. Fortunately, Hamnir and Gorril had foreseen this situation, and the wagons had been packed to overflowing, though it was still hardly enough.

There was, however, plenty of beer. The dwarfs had been amazed to find two entire storerooms filled with untouched hogsheads – more proof, if any were needed, that the orcs who had held the hold were unusual indeed.

Toast after toast was drunk: to Hamnir, to Thorgig, the survivors, Gotrek, even Felix got a polite cheer. The Diamondsmith survivors – those few strong enough to attend – sat quietly among their roaring, guzzling cousins, sipping at their beer and mouthing their food, and raising feeble smiles at each toast. They seemed glaze-eyed and uncomfortable in the midst of all the uproar.

Hamnir sat between Thane Kirhaz and his old friend, the engineer Birri Birrisson, at the king's table at the head of the hall, trying his best to learn from them what had happened since the orcs had invaded. Whatever Birrisson had looked like before, now he seemed a skeleton with spectacles, his lank grey beard hanging from sunken parchment cheeks.

'But, Birri,' he said as the engineer forked ham mechanically into his mouth with a trembling hand, 'Gotrek reported that the passage from the gyrocopter hangar was laid with new traps, dwarf-built. Those traps killed Matrak, your old colleague, and two others. Are you certain no dwarf helped in their construction? Was perhaps one of your apprentices caught and tortured? Was anyone missing?'

Birri shook his bald head, not looking up. 'No apprentices lost. None that didn't die, at least. Not in our hold.' He frowned. His fork paused. 'Had a dream I set new traps in that hall, but...' He stopped, his eyes far away.

'A dream?' asked Hamnir, eyes wide. 'What sort of dream?'

Birri frowned again for a long moment, then shrugged. 'A dream. Only a dream.' He could not be induced to say more about it.

Hamnir sighed and shook his head as he filled his stein again. He leaned over to Gotrek and whispered in his ear. 'They are still too tired from their privations. I will wait until they have recovered.'

'They aren't just tired,' growled Gotrek, fixing his one eye on Birri, who was staring placidly into space, his food forgotten. 'Something's wrong with them. Dwarfs are made of sterner stuff.'

'Even a dwarf might grow weak after starving for twenty days,' said Hamnir.

Gotrek grumbled suspiciously but said nothing, only drank another stein dry.

Soon the Diamondsmith hold survivors began to nod in their chairs, the unaccustomed amounts of food and beer overwhelming them and making them drowsy. They excused themselves in ones and twos, and returned to their hold while their rescuers toasted each departure. With the last of them gone, the spirits of the remaining dwarfs rose again, and they began to get roaring drunk.

Strange, Felix thought as he watched Gotrek and Hamnir clash their steins together, that the feast's honoured guests had been a drag on the festivities. The listless misery of the survivors had made the victorious army uncomfortable and polite. They had kept their voices low, and courteously tried to keep the survivors engaged in their conversations, but now that they were gone, restraint went with them. Dwarf marching songs rocked the feast hall, and heated arm wrestling and boasting matches were being contested at every table.

Felix knew where it would all lead. He had seen it before. It was a dwarf tradition that they drink themselves into a stupor after a great victory, and it appeared this victory would be no exception. Already, there were dwarfs slumped in their chairs, snoring, steins still clutched in their fists, and those who had travelled with Hamnir were falling faster than the rest – all the marching and digging and fighting of the past days catching up with when they were at last allowed to relax.

Gotrek was slurring his words and leaning heavily on his elbows as he spoke to Hamnir. Narin and Galin, sitting with their respective clans at the long tables below the dais, were both fast asleep, their heads back, snoring heavily. Felix too was drooping, his eyelids getting heavier and heavier until he too sprawled in his chair, unconscious.

FELIX'S HEAD JERKED up from the table. He blinked around blearily, so befuddled with sleep and ale that for a moment he had no idea where he was. The feast hall. Now he remembered. It was dark, the fire in the enormous hearth sunk to red embers, and the lamps and candles guttering. But what had awakened him? He could see no movement in the hall. The dwarfs around him snored softly, heads down on the tables, their beards soaking up puddles of beer and gravy and soup.

A strange feeling of dread came unbidden to his heart, and for a moment, he was afraid that he was having a reoccurrence of the nightmare he had in the mines – that at any moment he would begin stabbing Gotrek and Hamnir and the rest in their sleep. But no, he felt no homicidal urges, only fear.

Then he heard it again, a scream, echoing from the kitchens. That was what had woken him up. Someone had screamed. Around him, dwarfs were snorting and mumbling, their dreams disturbed. He looked towards the kitchen doors. The connecting corridor was bright with lamplight. There was nothing there, and then there was: a weaving shadow. A plump dwarf woman staggered through the door, wailing, and then fell between two long tables. Her back was split open like a melon. Felix could see her spine.

He nudged Gotrek roughly. 'Gotrek!'

The Slayer didn't move.

Around the chamber, dwarfs were waking, muttering and cursing in the darkness.

'What was that?'

'Who's screaming?'

'Ugh, my head.'

'Stop that cursed noise!'

Hamnir lifted his head, murmuring fretfully, and then sank back, his forehead thudding as it hit the table.

More shadows were moving beyond the kitchen doorway, hulking black shapes lurching across the floor, accompanied by harsh scraping sounds.

A dwarf near the door scrambled up out of his seat and backed unsteadily away, pointing. 'The orcsh!' he slurred. 'The orcsh!'

'Wuzzat, lad?' mumbled another, further from the door. 'Don't be daft. The orcs are dead.'

Felix saw Narin amongst his cousins, blinking and rubbing his face. On the opposite side of the hall, Galin was still fast asleep.

'Orcs?' murmured Hamnir. He sat up again, listing in his seat. His eyes blinked open. 'Where…' His chest heaved and he lunged to the side, vomiting over the arm of his chair.

'Gotrek!' Felix shouted, shaking the Slayer.

The shadows pushed into the feast hall, followed by the things that cast them. The dwarfs stared, most still half asleep and entirely drunk, as a dozen orcs shambled through the kitchen door, dragging their cleavers and axes behind them. The first orc was missing an arm. The next had three crossbow bolts sticking from its chest. Another dragged itself along the floor by its hands. It had no legs. The orcs' heads drooped at unnatural angles. Their eyes stared into the middle distance, vacant and dull. Their movements were slow and stiff. A side door crashed open and more jolted through, as ungainly as the first group.

A dwarf staggered up unsteadily from the table closest to the door and stood in the way of the orc procession. 'Grimnir,' he said, pointing. 'They're…'

The lead orc swung his axe around loosely, as if he meant to throw it, and the drunk dwarf went down, the top of his head opened like a hard-boiled egg. All over the room, dwarfs began roaring and fumbling clumsily for their weapons, as ungainly in their drunken stupor as the shambling orcs. More orcs pushed through the feast hall's main archway, a slow, spreading tide of herky-jerk monsters. The doors were choked with them.

Hamnir pushed himself upright, wiping his mouth and looking around. 'What… what is this? Do I still dream?'

'It's no dream, prince,' said Felix. 'Gotrek. Wake up!'

Gotrek's head snapped up, his beard grimy with crumbs. 'Wha?' he slurred. 'Who's that?'

'But the orcs are dead,' mumbled Gorril, blinking around on Hamnir's left. 'How can they…'

'Orcs?' Gotrek looked around, frowning and belching. 'Where? Where are they?'

Hamnir jumped to his feet. His chair crashed to the floor as he sprang unsteadily onto the table. 'Form up, brothers! Form up! Captains rally your men! Hurry!' His voice was lost in the chaos of confused shouting that echoed through the hall.

Gotrek lurched up and nearly fell over. 'What orcs? Light a torch. I can't see.'

A longbeard charged an approaching orc and sunk his axe into its ribcage. The orc swayed under the force of the blow, but showed no pain. It raised its mace, and crushed the old dwarf's skull. The axe was still in its ribs.

The dwarfs bellowed at this horror and charged the orcs all around the room, hacking at them in drunken frenzy. Orc limbs spun away. Orc bones shattered. The orcs kept coming. With hands lopped off and intestines trailing behind them, with torsos pierced by axes and smashed by hammers, they kept coming. They flailed spasmodically with their weapons. Cutting off their legs only slowed them down. Then they clawed forwards, snatching and snapping at the dwarf's legs and feet.

Dwarfs fell with bashed heads and cleaved chests, with severed arms and split bellies. All around the room, they fought in ones and twos as the orcs pushed them towards the centre from all sides. Some were murdered before they woke. Felix saw Narin hack an orc's forearm off at the elbow, and then duck as the orc swung the stump. On the other side of the room, Galin was backing away from an orc with four bullet wounds in its chest and neck.

'Form up! Form up!' shouted Hamnir. 'Form up or we're lost!'

'Light the lights!' roared Gotrek. 'I can't find my axe!'

Felix glanced at the Slayer. 'Gotrek, your patch is over the wrong eye.'

Gotrek snarled and pawed at his face. 'Well, who played that fool trick?' He pulled the leather patch over his ruined socket and blinked around at the chaos in the hall. 'Grimnir's balls,' he breathed. 'What hell is this?'

'The orcs,' said Felix dully. 'They have come back from the dead.'

'It's madness,' said Gorril. 'Nothing stops them. They're unkill-able!'

'We'll see about that,' said Gotrek and drew his axe from under the table.

Hamnir snatched up the battered war horn of Karak Hirn and blew a rally call. Its pure tone was lost. It sounded like a braying donkey, but it was loud. The dwarfs turned at its call.

'Form up!' he cried. 'Captains rally your companies! Thanes call your dwarfs! Form up and face out!'

The horn and the order had an almost magical effect on the dwarfs. As Hamnir and Gotrek, Felix and Gorril leapt down from the high table and hurried across the feast hall to where the orcs were the thickest, clans and companies rallied around their leaders and formed into ranks, facing out from the centre of the hall in a rough square. Companies overturned tables to make barricades, and attacked and defended as one. Hamnir, Gotrek and the others joined Gorril's clanbrothers in the thick of the fighting. Felix found himself beside Galin, still red-faced drunk and cursing like an entire ship of sailors. Narin joined them shortly. He had a cut over one eye, and a ragged gash across the back of his knuckles. The dwarfs slashed unsteadily but unceasingly at the blank-eyed orcs.

It wasn't enough.

Though they had fallen into formation with an organisation so practiced that it was almost instinct, the dwarfs were still too drunk and exhausted to stand against an enemy that felt no pain and was slowed only by the most grievous wound. Hamnir's order had slowed the massacre, but not halted it. Not one of the orcs had fallen, and the dwarfs were dying in droves.

Gotrek cut an orc off at the knees. It crawled forwards on the stumps. The Slayer cursed and jumped back, slashing at its arms.

'We must fall back,' said Hamnir, hacking ineffectually at an eyeless orc. His voice was tight with suppressed panic. 'We cannot hold here!'

'Fall back to where?' asked Gorril. 'We left dead orcs all over the hold. If they're all like this, we've nowhere to run!'

'We could abandon the hold,' said Galin.

'No!' said Hamnir. 'That I will not do. Not after all we went through to win it.'

'What then?' asked Narin.

'The Diamondsmith clanhold!' Hamnir cried at last. 'Their door is still whole. We will retreat there until we can recover and decide what to do.'

'Aye,' said Gorril. 'Good.'

Hamnir stepped back from the front line and blew the war horn again. 'Fall back! Fall back!' he called. 'Pass the word. Retreat to the Diamondsmith hold! Through the kitchens to the stairs and up!'

The dwarf companies began to retire in orderly fashion, forcing a path through the shuffling orcs towards the high table and the door to the kitchens.

The legless orc caught Gotrek's ankle as he tried to follow Hamnir. The Slayer stumbled and nearly fell. He booted it in the face. 'Damned thing! Die!'

The orc shrugged off Gotrek's kick and snapped at his knees with its tusks. Gotrek cursed and decapitated it. It flopped to the ground, its limbs still at last.

'It stopped,' Gotrek said, goggling at it drunkenly.

'Look out!' Felix dragged Gotrek back as an orc axe missed his neck by an inch. Gotrek jerked away from Felix's hand and decapitated that orc too. It collapsed like an empty sack.

Hamnir laughed, still drunk himself. 'You've done it, Gurnisson! You've found the way.'

'Ha!' said Gotrek, indistinctly. 'Knew it all along.'

'The head!' called Hamnir, up and down the line. 'Cut off the head and the body dies! Pass the word!'

'Prince,' said Gorril eagerly. 'Call off the retreat! We can finish them!'

'No,' said Hamnir. 'We are too tired – too drunk. We will die trying. We must recover ourselves first.'

The journey to the intact hold was a nightmare. Even knowing how to stop them, the orcs were hard to kill, and more attacked the dwarfs' flanks at every cross corridor and open chamber, stumbling out of the dark in a grey-green tide. At last, with orcs hemming them in on every side, the dwarfs reached the great doors of the Diamondsmith clanhold.

Once again, Hamnir rapped the mine code with the butt of his axe and, once again, they waited, while the dwarfs held off the press of orcs as best they could.

'Curse them,' said Gorril after five minutes had passed and many brave dwarfs had fallen. 'Where are they?'

'No doubt they sleep soundly,' said Hamnir, 'bellies full and free from fear at last.' He rapped on the door again.

At last there was an answering tap and the doors swung slowly open. Hamnir called the companies back one at a time and they made an orderly retreat into the hold, until only he, Felix, Gotrek and Gorril stood with Gorril's clan brothers, fighting off a wall of unblinking, unrelenting orcs.

'Now! Back as one!' Hamnir cried. Then, 'The doors! Close the doors!'

The dwarfs backstepped quickly, ranks still neatly dressed, as the doors swung in. The orcs pushed forwards, trying to follow them, but the doors closed inexorably, crushing a handful of orcs to paste between them. Gotrek, Felix and Gorril's lads decapitated the few that got in, the doors were locked tight, and all was quiet.

Hamnir leaned against the wall, catching his breath, and then pushed himself wearily upright and turned to the dwarfs ranked up at the ready in the dim corridor – all that remained of the force that had rallied to help Hamnir retake Karak Hirn not three weeks ago. They were much reduced. The battles with the living orcs and the orcs reborn had more than halved their number.

'Well fought, cousins,' Hamnir said, between breaths. 'Now come, let us impose on the hospitality of our recently rescued brothers. We must rest before we can fight again.'

The dwarfs parted and turned about, allowing Hamnir, Gorril, Felix and Gotrek to lead them down the corridor to the hold's central chamber. Galin and Narin came with them, having grown used to travelling with Hamnir.

Felix started as they entered the huge hall. Thane Kirhaz, Birri, Ferga and the other survivors were ranked up like an army in the middle of the hall, staring at them as they entered. All, even the women, were armed, if only with fire tongs and rolling pins.

Hamnir squared his shoulders and saluted them, overcome at this display. 'This is very brave, cousins,' he said, 'coming to our aid when you are in such straits yourselves, but there is no need. We are safe for now, and once we have slept and recovered ourselves, we will deal with the menace in the hold.'

The survivors said nothing. Nor did they move – they only stood and stared, unblinking.

'Kirhaz?' said Hamnir uncertainly. 'Birri? Are you well? Have you room for us to take our rest?'

Kirhaz raised his crossbow. It trembled in his shrivelled hands. He fired – a weak shot. The bolt struck Hamnir in the shin.

'You threaten the Sleeper,' said Birri. 'You must die.'

CHAPTER TWENTY-TWO

HAMNIR CRIED OUT, as much in surprise as in pain, and nearly fell.

'Prince Hamnir!' Gorril caught Hamnir and held him upright.

Everyone gaped at the Diamondsmith dwarfs, stunned. Kirhaz dropped his crossbow with a clatter and drew his axe. He and Birri motioned the other survivors forwards. They shuffled ahead listlessly, raising their weapons.

'Thane Kirhaz, Birri, I don't understand,' said Hamnir, wincing as he put weight on his punctured leg. 'Why do you attack us? Who is the Sleeper?'

Kirhaz and Birri didn't answer. Their gaunt troops came on, staring fixedly at Hamnir and his beleaguered army. Gotrek growled wordlessly.

'Grimnir, what's the matter with them?' cried Hamnir.

'They… they are just like the orcs,' said Gorril. 'How can this be? How did we not notice before?'

Hamnir took a step back. The others did the same. The entire army edged away from the strange, silent dwarfs.

'Is the Sleeper what we sensed in the mine?' asked Felix uncertainly. 'Has it turned their minds with sorcery?'

'Impossible!' said Hamnir, as if trying to convince himself. 'Dwarfs laugh at sorcery. It doesn't affect us.' He called to Kirhaz, who was raising his axe. 'Thane Helmgard, please! Come to your senses. Birri, have you forgotten our friendship? Ferga, make them listen.'

Ferga walked beside her father, as implacable as the rest, a carving knife in her hand. She didn't respond.

Gotrek stared at the approaching dwarfs, his one eye dull and miserable. He put a hand on Hamnir's shoulder. 'They're tainted, scholar,' he said sadly. 'I don't think they can be saved.'

'What? What do you mean?'

'I mean,' Gotrek paused, before going on, his voice rough. 'We will have to kill them.'

'No!' said Hamnir, wild-eyed. 'No! We rescued them! We can't turn around and kill them now! I won't do it!'

'They mean to kill us,' said Gotrek.

'There must be a way!' Hamnir looked around desperately.

A few Diamondsmith dwarfs had reached his lines and were swinging pathetically at their cousins. Their blows were slow and weak. Hamnir's dwarfs parried them easily, some crying out to their attackers by name, begging them to stop. It would have been the work of an instant to cut them all down, but none of the dwarfs had the heart to do it, and instead blocked and held them off.

'The gemcutters' guild hall!' said Hamnir suddenly, pointing to an ornate doorway open on the left wall. 'We will trap them inside, and then descend into the mine and find what has caused this horrible change, this "Sleeper", and kill it! Then they will recover!'

Gotrek shook his head. 'You're fooling yourself, scholar. They're too far gone. Look at them.'

'How can you say that?' Hamnir cried, furious. 'How can you condemn them when there might still be hope?'

'Experience.'

'Damn your experience! I refuse to believe it is too late! Stay your hand. I will not kill my own kin.'

Gotrek growled in his throat, but did not attack.

Hamnir whispered to Gorril. 'Pass the word. Retreat into the guildhall, rearguard first. When they follow us in, we will lock the door behind them, and then exit out the rear door and trap them within.'

Gorril saluted and hurried to each company, murmuring to their commanders, as more and more of the shambling dwarfs closed with Hamnir's army, and the strange, one-sided battle intensified. The dwarfs were relieved not to have to attack their cousins, and obeyed Hamnir's orders eagerly. The companies closest to the guildhall door backed through it while those before them protected their retreat.

Birri, Kirhaz and Ferga angled towards Hamnir and his companions.

Birri raised his hand and pointed. 'Kill the prince. Kill the Slayer. It is the will of the Sleeper.'

The mindless dwarfs obeyed, turning and joining Kirhaz, Birri and Ferga as they slashed at Hamnir and Gotrek, while all along the line the rest attacked Hamnir's troops.

Kirhaz raised his axe at Hamnir. Gotrek knocked it out of his hands. Felix blocked and parried as three dwarfs attacked him. Individually, they were nothing. Together, coming after his drunken slumbers and the mad, breathless retreat from the undead orcs, they were almost more than he could handle. If he could have fought back, the combat would have been over in a second, but he was as reluctant as the dwarfs to slay those he had come to rescue.

Birri aimed a smash at Gotrek with a hammer. Gotrek blocked it easily and kicked at him. The engineer barely seemed to feel it and struck again. Gotrek parried and kicked harder, frustrated. Birri staggered back and tripped over one of his companions, landing hard on his shoulder. He was up again almost instantly. Felix caught a glint of gold around his neck, under his beard.

'Gotrek!' Felix called, pointing at Birri. 'He wears a torque.'

'What?' cried Hamnir, and almost took Ferga's knife in the face as he turned to look.

Gotrek caught Birri's hammer in a bind, and twisted, disarming him. 'Get it, manling. Get it off him.'

Felix started forwards, blocking to both sides, but Birri stumbled back behind the other survivors.

'Stop them!' he murmured. 'Kill them!'

The blank-eyed dwarfs turned to do his bidding, getting in Gotrek and Felix's way as he retreated.

It would have been easy to follow him if they had wished to cut down the dwarfs in the way, but getting through them without harming them was more difficult.

'He's the leader,' rasped Gotrek as he prodded the dwarfs back. 'Not Kirhaz.'

'After him, Gotrek,' said Hamnir. 'Take him, but don't kill him. Perhaps this malaise will lessen if you remove his torque.'

'Aye, scholar,' said Gotrek, pushing forwards another foot. 'Come on, manling.'

They broke through at last, just as Birri was disappearing into a hallway on the far side of the room.

Gotrek stole a glance back at Hamnir as they limped after the engineer. 'Too soft-hearted for his own good. Always has been.'

They entered the corridor. Birri was nowhere in sight. Gotrek cursed. They hurried down it as fast as they could, which wasn't very fast. Their wounds, and all the drinking and fighting they had done had taken their toll. They hissed and grunted with every step.

Felix hobbled down a side corridor and looked in an open door. Birri was not within. He tried a closed door. It was locked.

'Manling,' came Gotrek's voice. 'Back here. I hear him.'

Felix returned to the main corridor. Gotrek was starting down a stairwell. Felix followed. At the bottom was another corridor. They looked left and right.

'There.' Gotrek pointed to the left.

Felix peered down the dim corridor. Far in the distance, he could see a dark form shuffling away from them.

'Got more strength than the others,' he said.

'It's the collar,' said Gotrek.

They started after him. It was a very sad race. Birri might have been fitter than the rest of the Diamondsmith defenders, but not by much. He lurched and staggered like a sleepwalker. Unfortunately, Gotrek and Felix were hardly better. They gained on him steadily, following him through corridors and chambers, and down winding stairs, but it was slow going. Gotrek grunted with each step, his damaged leg as stiff as a board. Felix was so dizzy with drink and weariness that he had to keep one hand on the wall to steady himself.

They had almost caught up with the engineer when he ducked into a side passage and put on a burst of speed. They hurried to the corner in time to see him scuttle through a wide door, through which glowed a steady orange light.

Gotrek and Felix limped through the door after him and stopped dead. They were in an engineer's workshop, its high ceilings lost above a web of girders and gantries, pulleys and heavy chains. The walls were crowded with workbenches, kilns, forges and machines the purpose of which Felix couldn't even begin to fathom. Along the far wall, copper water tanks, steam engines and open cisterns were grouped around a large, grated drain in the floor.

The thing that had taken them aback sat in the centre of the room on a length of steel track. It had once been an Undgrin mine cart. Now, it looked like nothing more than an enormous iron scarab, crouching on six spoked wheels. Curved iron plates covered it like a carapace, and the muzzles of swivel guns stuck out through slotted openings. A huge cannon hung above it on chains, waiting to be lowered into a revolving housing on its roof.

'Sigmar,' breathed Felix, 'it's some kind of steam tank! Like we saw in Nuln!'

'This "Sleeper" means to mount attacks from the Undgrin,' muttered Gotrek. 'With that at the head of an orc army...'

He trailed off as Birri appeared on top of the armoured cart and clambered forwards to an open turret. He grabbed the crank of a strange, multiple-barrelled gun, and swung it towards them.

Gotrek and Felix dived for cover as Birri wound the crank and the gun began spitting a stream of bullets. Felix slid behind a forge as the rain of lead kicked dust off the flagstones where he had stood. Gotrek crouched behind a small smelting furnace. The noise of the gun was deafening.

'You only delay the inevitable,' called Birri over the clatter. 'The Sleeper will not be denied.'

'I'll deny him to my last breath, betrayer,' said Gotrek, looking around at the room's equipment. 'Dwarfs are dead because you set new traps in the hangar corridor.'

'Defended the hold, as I have always done,' said Birri, firing over their heads.

'How did this happen, engineer?' shouted Felix. 'Where did you get the torque?'

'I...' For a moment Birri's calm confidence seemed to falter. 'I wanted to get out. To get help. Too many grobi at the main gate. Used our secret door and made for the hidden hangar door. Caught. Fought. Foolish. None can fight the Sleeper. The others died. I fell and was taken below. Still I fought, but at last... at last I accepted the gift. Brought to my brothers in the hold.' He fired again and his voice strengthened. 'Now I am invincible.'

'We'll see about that,' said Gotrek. He motioned to Felix and pointed to winches bolted into the floor near their hiding places. Felix examined them. The chains that held the cannon above the tank cart wound around them. Gotrek made a hacking gesture.

Felix nodded, but eyed the heavy chains uncertainly. Gotrek would sever his in one blow, but could he?

'Join us,' called Birri. 'Join us and you will be invincible too.'

'Invincible?' said Gotrek, barking a harsh laugh. 'You try to tempt a Slayer with that?'

He held up three fingers, two, and then one. Felix surged up and rolled to his winch, raising his sword. The gatling gun chattered to life. Felix swung down with all his might and the sword bit deep into a steel link, but didn't sever it. He cursed as he heard Gotrek's chain snap behind him. The stream of lead was spewing his way. He hacked again.

The chain parted. Felix dived to the side as bullets smashed into the winch. He rolled behind a massive kiln and looked up.

The huge cannon was swinging down on its two remaining chains like the clapper of some gigantic bell, loose chains flailing, but because Felix's cut had been late, it didn't swing straight. It swerved around Birri like one magnet repulsed by another.

'Ha!' the engineer cried. 'You see? Invincible!'

The cannon swung to the limit of its arc. With a sound like twin pistol shots, the last two chains snapped, and the cannon crashed down behind the tank cart, its butt-end smashing through the iron grate that covered the huge drain. The cannon dropped out of sight like a crossbow bolt dropped down the neck of a bottle. Its chains followed it, rattling violently through their pulleys and lashing like furious snakes.

The end of a chain whipped around Birri's neck and jerked him off the tank cart so quickly that it almost seemed as if he disappeared. Felix stood just in time to see the chain whir into the drain after the cannon, dragging Birri with it.

'Well struck, manling,' said Gotrek.

They limped across the room to the broken grate and looked down the hole. They could see nothing in its pitch-black depths.

'Where does it go?' asked Felix.

'Underground stream, likely,' said Gotrek, spitting into it. 'Hope he rots before he dies.'

'It wasn't his fault, surely,' said Felix. 'The thing took over his mind.'

'Then he was weak. A true dwarf would never have been corrupted.'

Felix raised an eyebrow. 'So all of the Diamondsmith clan were weak?'

Gotrek grunted angrily, and turned towards the door. 'Let's get back.'

WHEN THEY RETURNED to the clanhold's central chamber, nearly all of Hamnir's army had retreated into the gemcutter guildhall. The last few companies backed slowly towards the big door, entirely surrounded by the lost dwarfs.

Gotrek shook his head. 'Pointless,' he said, but started forward nonetheless.

He and Felix pushed through the crowd of frail dwarfs, disarming and knocking down as many as they could as they went, and then joined Hamnir, Gorril and the others on the front line.

'Where is Birri?' asked Hamnir, between parries.

'He fell down a hole,' said Gotrek.

'You killed him, Valaya curse you!' said Hamnir. 'I told you–'

'His inventions killed him,' said Gotrek. 'I never touched him.'

Hamnir gave him a suspicious look, but they had reached the door of the guildhall.

'We hold here,' he said, and then turned to Gorril. 'Have the others fall back to the far door and wait beyond it. You circle back here with some of your clan. When our poor cousins have followed us in, close the doors behind them.'

Gorril saluted and hurried to the other companies, who waited in the middle of the guildhall. Gotrek and Felix joined Hamnir's company in holding the lost dwarfs at the door. It was easy work – in one way, the easiest battle Felix had ever fought – in another, the most unsettling. He fended off the feeble attacks almost without thinking, but looking into the faces of the attacking dwarfs was heartbreaking. Traces of their individuality remained in their clothing and ornament – the way a miner braided his beard, the brooch a dwarf maid wore pinned to her dress, the scars and tattoos of a hard-bitten warrior – but it was gone from their eyes. All had the same blank, dull expression he had seen on the orcs' faces. All fought with the same mindless, passionless ferocity, dampened only by their long starvation.

What made it worse was that, just as had been the case with the orcs, the lost dwarfs would sometimes come to themselves. A brief flash of intelligence would light up their eyes and they would start back in dismay at what they were doing, but then, almost as soon as it had appeared, while Gorril's dwarfs were calling out joyfully at their recovery, the awareness died, the dullness clouded their eyes once more, and they would attack anew. Several dwarfs fell to this phenomenon, as they lowered their weapons and took an axe in the neck from a friend they thought had returned to them.

At last, all of Hamnir's army passed through the far door of the guildhall. Hamnir and the others stepped back from the door and let the flood of lost dwarfs spill in after them. The swarm spread out, trying to encircle the defenders, but they were slow, and Hamnir's company easily outpaced them. Indeed, Hamnir slowed somewhat so as to remain almost within reach and keep their attackers' attention upon them. Felix felt like an Estalian bull-dancer waving a red cape at a herd of somnambulant bulls.

When they reached the far door, much narrower than the main entrance, Gotrek waved the others through. 'The manling and I will hold this.'

Hamnir hesitated, perhaps afraid that Gotrek would change his mind and start butchering the dead-eyed dwarfs. Then he nodded and led the others out the door.

Gotrek refrained from slaughter, though he looked miserable about it. 'Delaying the inevitable,' he muttered. 'Only be worse when the time comes.'

He and Felix held the door until the last of the Diamondsmith dwarfs wandered through the guildhall's main entrance and Gorril's dwarfs closed the big doors behind them.

As they heard the bars fall into place, Gotrek and Felix jumped back from the bizarre melee. Hamnir slammed the small door in the faces of the Diamondsmith dwarfs and locked it. Then he leaned his forehead against it as they beat listlessly at it from the other side.

'We fought so hard to free them,' he said miserably, 'only to lock them in again.' He raised his head and looked at Gotrek. 'My thanks for your mercy.'

'It isn't mercy,' said Gotrek, disgusted. 'It's torture, for them and for you, and it's needless. They won't recover.' He shrugged. 'But they are your kin.'

SAFE, AT LEAST for the moment, with the orcs locked out, and the lost dwarfs locked in, Hamnir's beleaguered army slept. Felix was asleep as soon as he lay down, exhausted by the ceaseless fighting of the past day, but he was again troubled by unsettling dreams. These were the opposite of the last. Instead of murdering the others in their sleep, he was running through Karak Hirn alone, looking for Gotrek. Every dwarf he asked turned blank eyes on him and tried to kill him. Hamnir, Gorril, Narin, Galin, all shambled after him, arms outstretched, as he backed away, his heart pounding.

At last, he found Gotrek, sitting in the guardroom near the Horn Gate, his back to the door. Felix opened his mouth to call out to him, but hesitated, overwhelmed by the fear that if Gotrek turned around he too would stare at him with one vacant eye. He took a step further, reaching out a nervous hand towards Gotrek's shoulder. Gotrek's head lifted as he sensed Felix behind him. He began to turn. Felix shrunk back. He didn't want to see. He didn't want to know. He...

He woke up, his sleep-thick eyes peeling open, and looking around in the dim light of Diamondsmith's central chamber, where he and Gotrek and most of Hamnir's force had laid down the night before. Shouted questions and running feet echoed all over the clan-hold.

Gotrek rolled over and raised his head. 'What now?' he muttered.

Felix sat up, groaning. All his muscles ached. His wounds throbbed. He felt as stiff as a week-old corpse, and half as lively.

Gorril's lieutenant, Urlo, was picking his way through the rows of waking dwarfs looking around. When he spotted Gotrek, he hurried to him, going down on one knee to whisper in his ear.

'Gorril asks that you come see him, Slayer. It is urgent.'

'Gorril asks?' said Gotrek. 'Something wrong with Hamnir?'

'Er,' Urlo looked around uneasily at the other dwarfs. 'Gorril will tell you.'

Gotrek grunted, his jaw clenching. 'All right.' He pushed himself up, hissing as he bent his wounded leg. He collected his axe. 'Come, manling.'

Felix nodded and got painfully to his feet. He and Gotrek followed Urlo out of the room. They could hardly walk.

'HAMNIR'S MISSING,' SAID Gorril.

They were in Kirhaz's private quarters, which Hamnir had taken as his billet. Gorril paced back and forth beside a heavy dining table where an untouched breakfast had been set. Urlo stood by the door.

'Missing?' asked Gotrek. 'Since when?'

Gorril spread his hands. 'He was gone when I went to wake him this morning. I have my company searching the hold top to bottom, but so far, nothing.'

'Any signs of an attack?' asked Gotrek.

'None. I...'

One of Gorril's dwarfs pushed into the room behind them. He had another dwarf with him.

'Gorril. Some news.' Gorril's dwarf urged the other forwards. 'Tell him, miner.'

The miner ducked his head to Gorril. He had a nasty lump over his left ear. 'Aye,' he said. 'Well, last night I was posted to watch the secret door that goes from Diamondhold's third gallery to the main hold grain stores.' He shrugged, embarrassed. 'I must have dozed a bit, because someone got up behind me and gave me a knock over the head that put me on the floor. I opened my eyes just in time to see a dwarf go through the secret door and close it behind him.'

'Did you see who it was?' asked Gorril.

The dwarf shook his head, and then regretted it. 'Just legs and feet,' he said, massaging his brow, 'and all a bit blurred.'

Gorril punched the table. 'When did this happen? Why didn't you tell someone immediately.'

The dwarf flushed. 'I meant to, captain, I did, but somehow in the middle of getting up off the floor I, well, I guess I fell asleep again.' He swayed where he stood. 'Could do with a bit of a nap now, actually.'

Gorril crossed to the dwarf and looked in his eyes. He frowned. 'Take him to the physic. He may have cracked his skull.' He gripped the dwarf on the shoulder. 'Thank you, cousin.'

Gorril turned to Gotrek and Felix as Gorril's dwarf led the other out. 'What does this mean? Was it Hamnir? Why would he go out alone into a hold full of grobi? Could someone have taken him? The guard only saw one dwarf, but there could have been more. Did we miss some of the lost dwarfs?' He stopped, his face pale. 'Grimnir! Have they taken him below? Is he in the mines with their "Sleeper"?'

Gotrek was looking at the floor, his fists clenched. 'Aye. That's my guess.'

Gorril cursed. 'Then there is no time to waste! We must go look for him!'

Gotrek shook his head. 'No, lad.' He tapped himself on the chest. '*I* go after him. You won't be coming.'

'And you'll stop me?' asked Gorril, eyes flaring. 'Hamnir was my cousin, and my best friend. I can't stay here while I know he might be–'

'Do you want to leave Karak Hirn leaderless again?' asked Gotrek, cutting him off. 'You're all that's left.'

'There is you,' said Gorril. 'Why don't you lead them? I no longer…'

'I'm no leader,' Gotrek said. 'I'm a Slayer, and there is something in the mine that needs slaying. You are a leader, so lead. The hold must be cleared of the risen grobi and guarded until King Alrik returns.'

'You mean until Prince Hamnir is found,' corrected Urlo.

Gotrek's face tightened. 'Aye, or that.'

'You don't think you'll find him?' asked Gorril, his eyes troubled.

'I'll find him,' said Gotrek, 'or die trying, but alive? In his own mind?'

'Grimnir!' Gorril swore. 'What turned your heart so black, Slayer? Must you snuff out every spark of hope before it has a chance to kindle?'

'Hope lies,' said Gotrek, stepping to the door. 'Only a fool listens. Now go tell your troops that Hamnir is missing and ready your attack on the grobi. We'll go out when you do.'

Gorril glared at him, and then sighed. 'Very well, we will go in an hour.'

Gotrek nodded, and he and Felix stepped out of the door.

'Slayer,' called Gorril.

Gotrek stopped and looked back.

'If you have no hope, why do you go on?' Gorril asked. 'Why slay monsters at all?'

Gotrek's eye grew hard. 'Because there is one thing anyone may hope for that will eventually be granted them.'

'And what's that?' asked Gorril.

'Death.'

He turned and walked down the hall.

Felix followed. 'Especially if he follows a Slayer,' he muttered.

'What was that, manling?' asked Gotrek.

'Nothing. Nothing.'

CHAPTER TWENTY-THREE

HAMNIR'S ARMY WAS grim and silent as it waited inside the Diamondsmith hold's main door for Gorril to arrive and the sortie to begin. The news of Hamnir's disappearance, on top of the horror and pain of discovering the Diamondsmith clan's empty madness, had hit them hard. They were more determined than ever to take back the hold and rid it of the dread taint that infected it, but it would not be a joyous victory. There would be no repetition of the previous night's drunken celebration.

Gotrek and Felix waited at the front of the column. They were to help with the initial break out, and then split off on their quest to the mines once all the dwarfs had left. Gotrek was as dour as the rest. His eye was on the floor and he muttered angrily to himself. Felix wondered what, besides the obvious, was troubling him, but didn't like to intrude. It wasn't polite, and with Gotrek, it wasn't safe.

Narin and Galin pushed through the troops and stopped beside Gotrek. He didn't acknowledge them.

'I'm coming with you, Slayer,' said Narin at last.

'And I,' said Galin.

'No,' Gotrek grunted, apparently annoyed at being disturbed. 'This is Slayer's work.'

'And if you remember,' said Narin, touching the sliver of the Shield of Drutti in his beard, 'we both have a vested interest in making sure that you are not slain while doing it.'

533

Gotrek raised his head and turned a baleful eye upon him. 'You would rob me of my doom?'

'Will you use your doom to cheat us of our grudge fights?' puffed Galin. 'You cannot die until you face us. The honour of our clans demands it.'

Gotrek snorted. 'I put aside my Slayer's vow until now because of the oath I made to Hamnir long before I took the crest. Now, I might satisfy both oaths at once. A petty squabble over a shield comes a distant third.'

'A petty squabble!' cried Galin. 'He insults us anew!'

'You won't dissuade us, Gurnisson,' said Narin.

Gotrek glared at them, then shrugged and turned away. 'Do what you will. Just don't get in my way.'

The ranks of dwarfs parted and Gorril marched up the column with Urlo and his company to take their place at its head. Gorril turned and faced the dwarfs. 'I've no speech for you, cousins. Remember that they can only be stopped by taking their heads. Fight well. Die well. May Grimnir protect us.'

The companies muttered a short prayer in unison and Gorril signalled the wounded dwarfs who stood at either side of the door. 'Lock it behind us,' he told them, 'and be sure that we are still ourselves before you open it again.'

The dwarfs nodded and pulled the levers that unlocked and opened the doors. They swung slowly in. The undead orcs were still there, waiting, as patient as the grave, and as fragrant. They stumped silently forwards, their weapons raised, the stench of their decay rolling in before them like a fog.

The dwarfs were ready this time. They were rested. They knew what to do. They cut through the orcs outside the door like a hammer through sea foam. Teams of dwarfs worked in tandem, one knocking an undead orc to its knees, the other lopping its head off. The orcs did not bleed.

Gotrek and Felix blocked their ungainly attacks with ease, disarming them – sometimes literally – and separating heads from shoulders left and right. Narin and Galin did the same at their sides.

No matter how many the dwarfs cut down, the mob of walking corpses seemed not to shrink. They filled the broad corridor in both directions. The dwarfs pushed slowly but steadily into them, winning every inch with a decapitation, until all the companies were in the corridor, and the door to the Diamondsmith hold closed behind them.

'Right,' said Gotrek to Gorril. 'You're out. We're off.'

'Good luck to you, Slayer,' said Gorril. 'Bring Prince Hamnir back alive.'

'If I come back, he comes back,' said Gotrek. He looked to Felix. 'Which way, longshanks?'

Felix craned his neck to see over the horde of greenskins. 'Stairs to our left are closest.'

'Right.'

Without another word, Gotrek started hacking a path through the orcs. Felix, Narin and Galin followed in his wake, guarding his back and taking a few heads of their own as they went. After five minutes of the strange, bloodless slaughter, they reached the stairs and the edge of the orc mob. A few orcs followed them down to the grand concourse, but they were so slow that the four quickly left them behind.

Gotrek led them through the hold to King Alrik's chambers. The mineheads were locked tight, and the orcs inside were probably trying to break through them, but with luck, the hole from the vault to the kruk had not yet been discovered, 'with luck'. Felix laughed at that. Their luck had been terrible so far. Relying on it now seemed like madness. Still, it was the best of the bad choices available.

They met no resistance. The hold was deserted. The orcs had all converged on the Diamondsmith hall in order to fight the last of the dwarfs. King Alrik's quarters were as they had left them, minus the goblin bodies, which had apparently risen from the dead and left to fight. They passed through the makeshift tannery into Alrik's bedchamber, covering their noses against the reek of the piles of rotting garbage, and stepped across to the fat pillar on the far side.

'On your guard,' said Gotrek.

Felix, Narin and Galin readied their weapons as Gotrek felt around on the filigreed border beside the pillar. He found the catch at last, pressed it, and the column screwed down into the floor. There were no orcs behind it.

Felix let out a breath.

They descended down the winding, railless stair into King Alrik's vertical vault. At the bottom, Gotrek crossed resolutely to the ragged hole in the wall, but Narin and Galin had a hard time passing all the vault's treasures without slowing. Their eyes lingered longingly on the beautiful axes and suits of armour, and the casket full of blood gold.

'Surely we deserve some reward for our selfless service,' said Galin, licking his lips.

'Aye,' said Narin. 'What's an ounce of gold lost when we've won his hold back for him?'

'You want your reward before you've finished the job?' growled Gotrek.

Galin shrugged sheepishly. 'Only a joke, Slayer.'

'Aye,' said Narin, pulling his eyes reluctantly away. 'Only a joke.'

They followed Gotrek through the hole, and along the rough passage they had cut so laboriously only a day before, and so into the kruk. There was no sign in the abandoned mine that the orcs had yet discovered their diggings, and they hurried through them until they reached the door that led to the mines proper.

Gotrek turned to them. 'Pointless killing grobi until we find what's behind them, so keep quiet.'

'But how will we find it?' asked Galin. 'It could be anywhere.'

Gotrek held up his axe. The runes on its head glowed faintly. 'They burn brighter the deeper we descend. It'll lead us.'

He opened the door and they stepped into the Karak Hirn mines. They saw few greenskins as they trekked through corridors and down shafts, many fewer than they had seen on their way up from the Undgrin, but it surprised Felix that they saw any at all. He had expected that they would all be up battering at the minehead doors, trying to get back into the hold, but in every forge and foundry they passed, at every workface and tailings pit, orcs and goblins still toiled, making weapons, machinery and armour.

It chilled Felix to think of it. How many orcs were employed here that some could still be spared from attacking the doors to continue working? And what supreme confidence must the mind behind this enterprise have to carry on with the day-to-day work as if the retaking of Karak Hirn was a certainty? But then, any mind that could bend the will of a hold full of dwarfs and turn them against their brothers had every reason to be confident. Could such a thing, whatever it was, be defeated? If it could direct the actions of an army of orcs and dwarfs, what could it do if it turned all its power upon a single man or dwarf?

Felix's mind turned more and more often to this hopeless line of reasoning the deeper they went into the mine. Each level down, his mood got blacker and his conviction that there was no way they could win the coming battle got stronger. The knowledge that this gloom was undoubtedly artificial – an invasion of his consciousness by the thing they sought – did not ease his mind. In fact, it reinforced his fears that the thing was unbeatable. Its ability to twist his mind and make him feel hopeless was proof that there was indeed no hope of beating it. He chuckled bleakly to himself. If the rune axe wasn't already showing them the way, they could certainly have used his mood for a guide. The blacker it was, the closer they must be. When he cut his own throat they would know they were at the source.

Though they said nothing aloud, Felix could tell that the dwarfs were affected by the thing's presence as well. They twitched and shook their heads as if beset by mosquitoes, and he could hear them muttering under their breath. Galin occasionally moaned and put his hand over his eyes. Even Gotrek was touched by the malaise, though he showed it by cursing in furious whispers and rolling his shoulders as if trying to shrug off a yoke.

Ten deeps down, three levels below the entrance to the Undgrin, the corridors grew narrower and the side passages fewer. This was the newest area of the mine, many of the tunnels were only tentative feelers pushed through the rock, looking for fresh seams of ore, and had not yet been heavily worked or expanded. The rune on Gotrek's axe glowed so brightly that they no longer needed lamps to see by, and the feeling of dread in Felix's heart pressed down on him like a giant hand, nearly paralysing him. He felt as if his bones had turned to lead. It was a supreme act of will just to put one foot in front of the other.

As they made their way down a cramped corridor, Gotrek paused. There was a light ahead – torch-glow coming from an opening in the left-hand wall. Sounds of movement came from it as well.

'Back and find another way?' whispered Narin.

'Hide until they're gone?' suggested Galin.

Felix blinked at the dwarfs. He had never seen such fear in their kind before. Of course, he felt the same, but he was only human.

Gotrek spat, disgusted. 'Go back if you want,' he said. 'There is no other way.' He held up his axe. 'What we seek is beyond here, and I saw no other branches.'

'Still,' said Galin, chewing his moustache, 'it might be wise to check. Look around a bit.'

Gotrek shrugged. 'It'll only be a few grobi.'

'But, they could kill us,' said Narin. He was shaking.

Gotrek looked around at him, disgusted. 'You're afraid of orcs now?'

'I... No,' said Narin. He shook his head violently. 'No. What's gotten into me? Of course not.'

'I know what's gotten into us,' said Galin, quavering. 'It's the Sleeper. It knows we're coming. It's making us afraid. It can read our minds. It's hopeless. It's–'

Gotrek flattened him with a left hook. 'Pull yourself together, Stonemonger. Whatever it is, if it lives and breathes, it can fall to an axe.'

Galin sat up slowly, rubbing his jaw through his beard. 'I'm sorry, Slayer. It's... it's hard to keep it out.'

'I told you not to come. Now fight it or go back and leave me be.' Gotrek turned and eased towards the torch-lit opening. The others inched along behind him, weapons at the ready. Felix's legs were shaking so much it was hard to walk. He knew it was the Sleeper making him afraid, but that didn't make the fear any easier to dispel, or his heart pound any less.

Gotrek pressed against the wall and leaned forwards to peek into the opening, the light of his rune axe hidden under his arm. He frowned, watching through the door for a long moment, before stepping silently past it and motioning the others to follow.

The other dwarfs were similarly transfixed as they passed the door. Felix came last, and he looked in with a mixture of curiosity and dread, his mind imagining all sorts of horror and filth. Instead, what he saw was a handful of orcs at the far end of a long, low chamber, assembling a wooden crate around a ridged, resinous sack the size of a hogshead of ale. Beneath a sheen of mucus, it had the texture and translucent lustre of insect wings. Through it, Felix could half see something pale and half-formed curled inside. There were at least twenty assembled crates set along the walls of the room, and enough unbuilt to hold twenty more of the glistening sacks.

The dwarfs whispered together a safe distance down the corridor.

'Dozens of them!' Narin was saying. 'Dozens!'

'But... but what are they?' asked Galin. 'And what birthed them?'

Gotrek turned down the dark corridor. 'We'll know in a minute.' He started forwards.

Only a hundred feet further along, they came to a crude side tunnel dug in the right wall. It slanted down at a sharp angle into the earth.

Gotrek's axe blazed like a torch as he stood on the tunnel's threshold. 'This is it,' he said.

He marched into it. Felix tried to follow, but found that he could not. A wave of fear and despair stronger than any that had previously washed over him turned his legs to lead. His little joke about cutting his throat was suddenly no joke. He was so frightened, and so certain that whatever was at the end of the tunnel would not only kill him but turn him into a mindless monster that would turn on his friends and spread the Sleeper's influence far and wide, that he wanted to push his dagger through his neck just to make an end of his misery and save the world. He wanted to tear his eyes out so that he wouldn't have to see it, but his hands were shaking too hard. Narin and Galin were similarly paralysed.

Gotrek looked back at them. 'What now?'

'Don't you feel it, Slayer?' asked Narin, his teeth chattering. 'Are you made of stone?'

'I feel it,' said Gotrek, 'but the worst that can happen is that we die, and that's been true since we left Rodenheim.'

'Death is not the worst,' choked Galin. 'It will take us. It will make us like the Diamondsmith clan. It will turn us against our own kind.'

'It will, if you just stand there and quake,' said Gotrek. 'Stop thinking and start walking. That's the only way.'

He turned and started down the tunnel again, and whether it was Gotrek's words, or the mere fact that listening had freed him momentarily from the bottomless spiral of his imaginings, Felix found that he was able to move again. Narin and Galin too started after the Slayer, following the tunnel deeper into the earth, straight as an arrow.

'This is orc work,' muttered Narin, 'but orcs never dug anything this straight.'

A hundred yards down, the tunnel stopped at a wall of polished basalt blocks, mirror smooth, and so well set that it was almost impossible to see the joins between them. A wide, low door, narrower at the top than the bottom, opened into a pitch-black chamber, a border of strange symbols all around it.

'This is old,' said Galin, caught between wonder and horror, 'older than dwarf-kind. What made this?'

'Not dwarf, nor man, nor elf,' said Narin. 'That's certain.' He pointed at the symbols. 'Are those wards meant to keep something out, or something in? Is this a temple, or a tomb?'

'Whatever it is,' said Gotrek, 'it should have stayed buried.' He stepped through the black door.

CHAPTER TWENTY-FOUR

FELIX, GALIN AND Narin followed Gotrek into the buried basalt structure. Felix had to duck under the low lintel. The red light of the rune axe reflected darkly from the glossy black walls, revealing a large octagonal room with more of the low trapezoidal doorways leading off into darkness. Felix shuddered. There was a feeling of unfathomable age about the place that reminded him of the tunnels of the Old Ones that he and Gotrek had almost lost themselves in during their travels with Teclis. It made him feel very young and small and insignificant.

Something about the scale of the doors made him realise that the place had not been built for anything that walked on two legs. For a moment, he tried to imagine what it might have been, but then he stopped himself. Following that line of speculation would send him screaming up the tunnel again.

It was almost comforting to see signs of orcish occupation in this alien place. Orcs might be horrible viscous monsters, but they were *familiar* horrible, viscous monsters. Long planks had been laid over a wide circular hole in the centre of the room to make a bridge, and a trail of dust, pebbles and orc footprints crossed from the door that Felix and the dwarfs had entered to another in the far wall. The place had the familiar stink of orc to it too – a harsh animal stench, mixed with the reek of death and rotting garbage.

'How did the orcs know this was here?' asked Felix, staring around. 'How did they find it?'

'They didn't,' said Gotrek. 'It called them.'

'Gurnisson,' said Narin. 'Hide your axe a moment. I think I see light.'

Gotrek tucked the head of his axe under his arm, blocking the glow of the rune and plunging the room into darkness. As his eyes got used to the dark, Felix saw a pale green phosphorescence coming from the far door, so dim that it was hard to be sure whether it was really there. Then something blocked it. Huge shadows hunched rapidly towards them along the hall.

'Something's coming!' said Galin.

Gotrek unshielded his axe as Felix, Narin and Galin went on guard. Out of the far door ducked six huge mutated orcs, each the size of the warboss they had faced in the grand concourse, their black faceted eyes glittering red in the rune-glow. A choking rotten egg smell wafted from them like a cloud.

Felix and the dwarfs gagged and covered their mouths as the orcs spread out, moving to encircle them and hefting their weapons.

'Grungni!' said Narin. 'These aren't orcs any more. They've become something else.'

'Mutants,' spat Galin. 'Tainted by Chaos.'

It was true. The mutations that had twisted the warboss were fully realised in the hideous creatures that faced them now. Where the warboss had been pale, these were dead-fish white and glistened with a sticky sheen. Where he had been covered in lumps and tumors, these sported translucent barbs and horns growing from their skulls and shoulders like milky icicles. One had a ring of tiny tentacles sprouting from the centre of its chest around a suppurating stoma. Their arms were long and distorted, reaching almost to the ground, and their forearms were crusted over with spined glassine carapaces, like the shells of albino cave crabs. Gold and onyx glinted at their necks.

Gotrek ran his thumb along the blade of his axe, drawing blood. He grinned. 'Now *this* will be a fight.'

'It'll be a slaughter!' moaned Galin. 'They have torques. All of them have torques. They're all invincible. This is the end.'

'Shut up,' said Gotrek angrily. 'We take them off is all.'

'And cut their heads off,' said Narin, grimly, 'to make sure they don't attack again after they're dead.'

'Manling, with me,' said Gotrek. 'Take the collars and I'll kill them. Galin, do the same for Narin. Go!'

Gotrek and Felix ran at the orcs to their left, while Narin and Galin ran to the right, but it was impossible. The orcs seemed to know instantly what they intended, and when Felix tried to edge around the first, the others attacked him and not Gotrek. He had to skip like a schoolgirl to avoid getting gutted. Gotrek got in the orcs' way and held them off, but they were immensely strong as well as untouchable, and forced him back.

Galin and Narin were having the same trouble. They fell back before the other three orcs, dodging and parrying madly, then ducked aside and ran for the other side of the room. The orcs followed.

'Not working, Gurnisson!' called Narin.

Felix returned to Gotrek's side, slashing around him with all his might, though he knew it was pointless. His sword skimmed off the orcs' slimy white flesh as if it was stone.

'Try again,' grunted Gotrek as he bashed at the orcs.

Felix nodded and made to circle behind the orcs, but they were on him again in an instant. He fell back. On the far side of the covered hole, Galin and Narin were trying to avoid being cornered.

Felix looked at the hole again, and the boards that covered it. 'The hole!' he cried.

'What?' said Gotrek.

Felix broke away and ran to the hole. He dropped his sword and started heaving aside the planks. A wave of death reek rushed up at him like a punch in the nose. Under the planks, the hole dropped straight down for about ten feet. Sigmar only knew what its original purpose had been, but it was a grave now. Heaped at the bottom were a score of orc corpses, so old and rotten that their skeletons were showing through their putrefying flesh.

Felix cursed. He'd hoped it was some sort of well. The orcs would climb out of this in an instant.

'Watch out, manling!'

Felix rolled aside instinctively as an orc cleaver slashed down at him. It splintered the plank he had been about to lift. The orc swung at him again. Felix dived low and rolled past it, snatching up his sword as he came to his feet.

'Good thinking,' said Gotrek, backing away from the other two. 'Narinsson! Olifsson! Clear the boards!'

'No. Won't work,' gasped Felix, ducking another swipe. 'Not deep enough. They'll climb out. Unless...' An idea came to him. He leapt back to Gotrek and snatched the unlit lantern from his belt. Then he dodged around the orcs to the hole again and smashed it on the rim. The glass reservoir inside the tin case shattered and oil leaked out.

Felix shook it along the edge of the hole until the orc lunged after him. He threw the lantern in its face and squirmed past it, barely deflecting an overhand bash.

The orc turned for another attack, slipped on the oil, recovered and came after him. Felix backed away from it, smashing his own lantern as he had Gotrek's, and sprinkled another stretch of the lip with oil. The orc's axe smashed black splinters out of the basalt floor an inch from his foot. He jumped away again.

As the orc lumbered after him, Felix marvelled at how clear his head was. The Slayer had been right. Once the fighting had started, his fear had fallen away. It wasn't gone, coils of dread still slithered in Felix's stomach, but it wasn't all-consuming now. He could think. He could act. He didn't want to give up. He didn't want to die.

On the far side, Narin and Galin were trying to obey Gotrek's order and pull up the planks, but with three orcs chasing them, they weren't having much luck. They were too busy dodging axes to grab the boards.

Gotrek backed towards the hole, luring his two orcs forwards. At the edge, he feinted left, sending one lurching to the side to try to block him, and then veered back and chopped at the other's mid-section.

The orc took the blade of the rune axe on its exposed white flesh with no more than a grunt, and stepped in to swing its ponderous axe at Gotrek's head. The Slayer surged forwards under the slash, ramming his shoulder into the orc's gut and pressing up at it with the haft of his axe, held in both hands like a staff.

Propelled by Gotrek's lift and its own forward motion, the orc went up and over the Slayer's back, and came down with a smash on the remaining boards. They snapped like dry twigs under its enormous weight and it fell into the hole, landing on the mounds of its rotting kin.

Gotrek's second orc charged him, mace raised. Gotrek rolled left, out of the way. The mutated greenskin tried to stop and turn, but he slipped on the spilled oil and skidded into the hole, landing on top of the first.

Galin and Narin ran past Gotrek along the edge of the hole with their three hulking pursuers hot on their heels. The dwarfs deftly avoided the drips of oil, but the lead orc was not so nimble. It crashed down on its back, right arm and leg hanging over the edge of the hole. Felix, backing away from his orc, saw the opportunity. He ran and kicked the orc in the side. It slid into the hole, scrambling with its transparent claws at the slippery edge, before dropping over the side.

Felix spun and ducked a bash from his orc's cleaver and found himself back to back with Gotrek, Galin and Narin. The three remaining orcs surrounded them. Behind them, corpse-white hands were reaching up and pawing at the rim of the hole, trying to gain purchase on the slippery basalt.

'Evened the odds,' said Gotrek, approvingly. 'Now, you three kill one, while I hold the other two.'

'You can hold two?' asked Narin.

'Depends how quick you kill the one,' said Gotrek. 'Go!'

Suddenly the Slayer became a whirlwind of flashing steel, the red glow of the rune axe leaving curving comet trails inscribed on Felix's retina as he pushed two of the orcs back with simple brute ferocity.

Felix, Narin and Galin attacked the third orc, doing their best to emulate Gotrek's ceaseless assault. Felix dodged behind its back and reached for its torque. It jerked away and slashed at him. Felix danced back, a hair ahead of its axe, and Narin made a grab for the torque from the other side. It spun back as Narin ducked. The axe cut a horn off Narin's helmet. The fight reminded Felix suddenly of some children's game, a deadly version of tag or keep-away.

He lunged in again, and this time got his fingers around the gold circlet. He pulled, but it was tight, cutting deeply into the orc's slimy, cable-muscled neck. The brute twisted around and caught Felix on the side of the head with his carapaced forearm. White sparks exploded behind Felix's eyelids and he crashed to the ground, but the torque came with him as he fell.

He dimly saw the orc raise its cleaver over him for the death stroke. Then it grunted and dropped to its knees, thick, clear blood gushing from its mouth as Galin chopped through its spine. Felix flinched and stuck his sword up as the orc pitched forwards on top of him. The point sank into its white gut up to the hilt.

Narin rolled the corpse off Felix, and Galin severed its neck. Felix stood unsteadily and tugged his sword free. The side of his head was running with blood. The world seemed tilted. He tossed the torque aside.

'Well done, manling,' said Narin.

'Only five more to go,' grinned Galin.

'Hurry, you jackdaws!' shouted Gotrek. The two orcs had the Slayer pressed against the wall, and he was blocking and dodging for all he was worth.

Narin, Galin and Felix ran to help. As they passed the hole, one of the fallen orcs hooked its axe over the lip of the hole and another started climbing its back.

'Grimnir!' cursed Galin. 'They're coming out!'

'Go on,' said Felix. 'I have this.'

He grinned. This was not to be missed. As Narin and Galin ran on, he stepped to the edge of the hole and reached out over the climbing orc's head for its torque. The brute snapped at him. Felix jerked his hand back, and tried again.

This time he got it, and ripped it from the orc's filthy neck. 'Ha!' he cried, tossing it aside and drawing back his sword to chop its head off.

The orc threw out its unnaturally long arm and caught Felix's ankle, yanking it. Felix slammed flat on his back, his sword bouncing away with a clang. The orc got its other hand up and tried to lever itself out of the hole, but its palm slipped on the oil and it started sliding slowly back, dragging Felix with it. Felix threw his free leg out and tried to dig in with his heel, but the oil was underfoot. He couldn't get purchase. The orc was pulling him inexorably towards the blade of the axe that the first orc had hooked in the lip of the hole. The blade was going to cut him in two from balls to brains.

Felix flailed for his sword. He couldn't reach it. 'Gotrek!'

The dwarfs were too busy with the other orcs. They didn't hear him.

'Gotrek!'

Gotrek looked around. His eye blazed. 'Curse you, manling! How do you get into…'

He broke away from the fight and ran to the hole. His two opponents charged after him, shouldering Narin and Galin to the floor as if they were children. They seemed to understand that the Slayer was their greatest threat.

The climbing orc was backsliding quickly, its transparent nails scraping across the oily stone like shards of glass. Felix slid with it, his crotch inches away from being bifurcated by the razor-sharp axe.

Gotrek slammed his blade down on the climbing orc's wrist, and then dodged aside, inches ahead of his pursuers. Felix's orc fell back into the hole, stump spurting clear blood, and Felix crabbed back from the axe blade, the severed white hand still gripping his ankle. Near the wall, Narin and Galin were getting to their feet.

Gotrek spun to face his attackers, batting aside one slash and dodging another. They hammered at him unceasingly, pushing him back towards the hole.

As Felix snatched up his sword, he saw the orc who had hooked its axe in the rim of the hole trying to climb its haft. Felix kicked the axe-head on the flat. It screeched across the floor, cutting a white line in the basalt, and dropped off the edge. The orc tumbled back onto its mates.

Felix stood as Narin and Galin ran to help Gotrek. Narin bashed the left orc on the spine. Galin ran straight up the back of the one on the right and grabbed its torque with his thick fingers. The orc spun, hacking at him. Galin flew off and crashed to the floor, his head bouncing off the stone flagstones with a hollow thud. The gold band flew from his limp hand and skittered across the floor.

The orc clapped a hand to his bare neck, grunting. Gotrek swung for its face. It grabbed his arm, but not quickly enough. The axe blade imbedded itself between its eyes. With a gurgling sigh, it toppled backwards into the hole, still clutching Gotrek's arm. The Slayer and the orc crashed down on the mound of rotting bodies as the orcs in the pit leapt aside.

'Gotrek!' Felix cried.

But he had his own problems. The second orc was after him, swiping mightily with its maul. With its elongated arms, its reach was incredible. Narin harried it from the rear, but it still had its torque, and his blows did nothing. Galin lay behind them, blood streaming from the back of his head, struggling to regain control of his limbs. Sounds of furious fighting came from the hole.

'Get behind it, Jaeger,' said Narin. 'I can't reach its neck.'

'Easier said than done.' Felix ducked under a wild swing and tried to slip to the orc's rear, but it turned with him.

Narin joined him in front of the orc. 'I'll hold him. Move.'

Felix slipped left again. The orc turned, but Narin hooked its knee with his axe, slowing it. The orc turned back and swung at Narin to dislodge him, and Felix got behind it. Narin skipped back, laughing, as the maul ruffled his blond beard.

'Come on you unnatural brute!' he jeered. 'Can't you see with those eyes?'

Felix leapt on the orc's back, his sword arm around its throat, and grabbed the torque.

The orc bucked, trying to throw him off. Felix held on, his legs flopping and banging, and pulled again. The torque came free.

'Ha!' Narin ran in, axe high, and chopped into the orc's chest, shattering its ribs.

The orc roared and spasmed, as if it had regained its orcish fury in the moment of death. It swung its maul and hit Narin's chest with a sound like a melon popping. The dwarf and the orc collapsed to the floor as one, their blood mingling.

'Narin!' cried Galin. The engineer was sitting up, a lump like a bleeding plum on the back of his head.

Felix fought back nausea and sadness as he blinked at the red ruin of Narin's chest. There was no time to mourn. Gotrek was still in the hole. He ran to the lip, skidding to a stop just short of the spill of oil, and looked down.

The orc with the severed hand was dead. Gotrek fought the other two on the mound of rotting corpses, which moved and shifted with their every step. The Slayer was bleeding and battered. The orcs didn't have a scratch on them.

Galin joined Felix at the edge. He looked unsteadily back at Narin. 'Poor lad,' he said. 'Died well, for an Ironskin.'

Gotrek dodged behind an orc, putting it in the way of the other. They stumbled around on the uncertain footing, trying to close with him again. It looked as if they had been performing this dance for a while. Gotrek staggered and nearly caught an axe between the eyes. 'Get their torques!' he rasped over the din of steel.

Felix nodded. Yes, get the torques, but how? Jumping into the pit was not an option. There was barely enough room for Gotrek and the orcs, and if he tried to lean in over the oily edge and grab one, he'd fall in. He needed... 'The planks! Galin! A plank! Help me!'

Felix stepped to one of the planks he had heaved aside earlier and took up one end as Galin took the other. They laid it across the hole.

'Hold it steady,' said Felix as he stepped out over the hole.

Galin nodded and sat on one end. Felix carefully lowered himself to his chest on the narrow board, and slid out along it. The orcs fought right below him, but didn't look up. They were too intent on killing Gotrek. Felix reached down a hand towards one. His fingers brushed the torque, but he couldn't grasp it. He strained further. The orc lunged at Gotrek and circled away, taking the torque out of his reach. Felix cursed silently. It was like trying to pluck a brass ring off the horn of a rampaging bull.

The other orc moved under him, angling for Gotrek's flank. Felix strained down again. The orc dodged back and forth as it tried to corner the Slayer. Felix edged his chest off the board for a better reach. The orc backed up – right into Felix's hand. He grabbed the torque. The orc jerked forwards, turning to see who was behind it, and the torque came free.

Gotrek struck too fast to see. One moment the orc was looking blankly up at Felix; the next, its head was flying from its shoulders. It collapsed like a ruined tower.

The other orc also struck quickly, swinging at Gotrek's back in the same instant that the Slayer cut down its comrade. Gotrek dived to the side and the cleaver cut a ragged slice through the meat of his left shoulder. He slammed into the wall and fell among the corpses.

The orc spun to finish him off, raising his axe over his head, right at Felix! Felix yelped and pushed himself up. The axe missed his nose by inches, but smashed through the plank, splitting it in two. The two ends tipped into the hole and Felix went down with them, crashing on top of the orc. He clutched at its arm, as much to save himself from falling as to stop its swing.

The orc hardly wavered. Felix, dangling from the slimy bicep of its axe arm, stared in terror at the greenskin's white, horned face. It was like clinging to a greased statue.

Gotrek lurched up from the mound of corpses. His left arm was red to the wrist. He started unsteadily across the shifting, stinking ground. 'That's it, manling! Hold it.'

Felix laughed mirthlessly. Hold it?

The orc plucked him off like a man picking lint from his sleeve, and held him up by the throat. Felix kicked and fought, choking as the massive fingers tightened around his windpipe. He slashed with his sword at the orc's face. The blow glanced off harmlessly. The orc didn't even flinch. It drew back its axe to cut Felix in half. Gotrek fell as he put his foot through a rotten ribcage and slipped on putrid organs. He wasn't going to make it in time.

'Hoy! Arsebreath!' Galin launched himself from the rim of the hole and caught the orc's axe arm in a bear hug. The orc stumbled, its weapon drooping.

'Come on, Slayer!' roared Galin.

The orc shook its arm, trying to dislodge the dwarf. He held fast.

Gotrek was getting to his feet.

Felix slashed at the orc's head again, the world dimming around him, the torque winking tauntingly at him, only a sword's length away. A sword's length?

As the orc slammed Galin against the wall, Felix stabbed at its neck with his sword. Its point slid across the slick white skin as if it was marble, and wedged under the torque.

The orc bashed Galin into the wall again. Blood flew from the dwarf's mouth. Felix pushed his blade under the torque and twisted. Another bash and Galin dropped, stunned. The torque wasn't coming free. The orc swung its axe at Felix. There was no escape.

'No you don't!'

Sparks flew as a red and silver streak flashed in the way of the orc's strike. The cleaver skimmed an inch over Felix's head. Gotrek!

The orc grunted and raised Felix up as he swung at Gotrek. Through the roaring in his ears, Felix heard a jingle of metal rattling against metal.

Gotrek kicked the orc between the legs. Fool, thought Felix dimly. Axes can't hurt it. Why would a boot? But the orc groaned and let go of Felix's neck. Gotrek hacked its head off with a grunting backhand as Felix fell amongst the corpses. The orc sank to its knees and pitched forwards, its head rolling down its back.

Gotrek sat down heavily on the chest of another orc. The wound in his shoulder gushed red.

'But, how?' whistled Felix through his crushed throat. 'I didn't get the–'

'Didn't you?' Gotrek pointed at Felix's sword. The greenskin's torque dangled from his quillons.

Gotrek shook his head and wiped his brow. 'Grimnir's beard, what a scrap.' He raised his voice. 'Ironskin! Lower a rope.'

'Narin... Narin is dead,' said Galin, sitting up and clutching his head.

'Dead?' said Gotrek. His face hardened.

Felix stood, massaging his throat. He could hardly swallow, and his head throbbed abominably. 'Thank... thank you, Gotrek. I would be...'

Gotrek shrugged. 'Thank yourself. That kick wouldn't have done a thing if you hadn't got its cursed torque off.' He stood and picked up one of the broken planks. He grounded one end in the floor of corpses and leaned the other against the wall. 'Let's get out of this stink-hole.'

One by one they crawled up the narrow board and out of the pit.

When he reached the top, Gotrek looked at Narin, lying in his own blood under the orc he had slain, and shook his head. 'Stubborn fool. Told him not to come.'

'Gotrek...' came a weak voice.

'He's alive!' said Galin.

They crossed to the dying dwarf, their boots splashed in his blood. His ribs rose from his smashed chest like broken white fingers from a red stew.

He looked up at them, grinning glassily. 'Well I... I did it. Escaped being thane. Escaped my... wife. My conjugal bed.' It was an effort for him to get the words out. 'Tell my father I'm sorry I... I didn't give him an heir. But not... very.' He laughed wetly, blood spraying from his mouth.

Gotrek knelt. 'Aye, I'll tell him.'

'And... give him his splinter back.' His hand fumbled in the blood-matted mess of his beard and tugged out the charred sliver of the Shield of Drutti. 'Tell him I... wish him good luck fighting... you.'

'I'll tell him that too.' Gotrek tucked the piece of wood in his belt pouch and took Narin's hand. 'May your ancestors welcome you, Narin Narinsson.'

Narin was already dead. Gotrek and the others lowered their heads.

Felix cursed silently. He had liked the sharp-tongued dwarf. Certainly, he had teased and insulted Felix like all the rest, but it had been different coming from him somehow – the easy familiar ribbing of an old friend, not the sullen distrust of the outsider that he had felt from the others.

There was a footstep. Felix and the others looked up. The surfaces of the room were so hard that it was difficult to tell from what direction the sound had come.

'Who's there?' asked Galin, looking around. 'Show yourself!'

All the dread that fighting the orcs had pushed away closed around Felix's heart again. The hairs raised on the back of his neck. The orcs had only been servants of the thing they were here to destroy. They still had yet to face the master – a thing so powerful it could warp, not only the minds of its minions, but also their bodies.

Another step. A shadowy figure appeared in the far door. They turned to face it, weapons at the ready. It stepped into the red light of Gotrek's axe.

'Hamnir!' cried Galin. 'Hamnir, you live!'

'Welcome, friends,' said Hamnir slowly. 'Welcome to the realisation of our dreams.'

Through the parting of the dwarf prince's beard, Felix could see a glint of gold.

CHAPTER TWENTY-FIVE

GALIN GROANED. GOTREK grunted like he'd been shot. Felix stared.

Hamnir drifted forwards in a somnambulant glide, spreading his hands. 'I am sorry your welcome has been so violent, but you have slain so many of us that the Sleeper was threatened and sought to protect itself.'

'Prince Hamnir,' said Galin, stepping forwards. 'What has it done to you? Take it off.'

Hamnir touched the torque around his neck. 'This is the greatest honour ever bestowed upon me. I wear it with pride.'

'Take it off, damn you!' Galin was red in the face. There were tears in his eyes. 'It's a thing of Chaos! Fight it!'

'Do not threaten me,' said Hamnir, calmly. 'The Sleeper...'

'A plague take the Sleeper! Take it off!' Galin launched himself at Hamnir, reaching for his neck.

Quicker than the eye could follow, Hamnir drew his axe off his back and lashed out at Galin. The blade cut through Galin's armour and his ribs as if they were so much paper and twigs. The engineer fell back, dead before he hit the floor.

'Do not threaten me,' said Hamnir, as calmly as before. Felix and Gotrek stared as he cleaned his axe on Galin's beard. He took another torque from his doublet and looked up. He held it out to Gotrek. 'The Sleeper does not wish to kill you, Gotrek. You are strong. You will be a great asset in the coming struggle. Take this and join us.'

Gotrek closed his eye. His head drooped. Felix had never seen him in such pain. 'Ranulfsson,' he said, his voice rough. 'Hamnir, take it off. Fight it. You are a dwarf: a prince, not a slave.'

'I am still a prince,' said Hamnir, 'a prince that follows a great god. Take the torque, Gotrek, and you will see.'

'No, scholar,' said Gotrek. 'I have no master, dwarf, god or daemon.' He raised his eyes and glared at Hamnir. 'Now take it off, or I'll take it off for you.'

'Listen to me Gotrek,' said Hamnir, his eyes shining with the fire of a zealot. 'For how long have the fortunes of the dwarfs been on the wane? For how long have we lost hold after hold? For how long have we ceded territory and power to elves and men, and even vile skaven? With the torque comes strength, invulnerability. Nothing will stand in our way. With the grobi as our slaves, to dig our ore and work our foundries, we will become mightier even than we were in the golden age!'

'Hamnir...' said Gotrek, but Hamnir wasn't to be interrupted.

'The Sleeper enlisted first the grobi, because their minds are simple and easily reached, but even with its enlightened leadership, an empire of grobi will not stand. They cannot be taught more than the most rudimentary skills.' He stepped closer. 'But the dwarfs, the dwarfs are a great race, a race who will not be slaves, but equal partners in a shared destiny. It will give us its strength and power and the wisdom of ages beyond reckoning, and all it asks in return is to share the torques with our kin and to bring its children to every hold we visit.'

'Its children?' growled Gotrek.

'Did you not see them as you came?' asked Hamnir. 'Even now the grobi ready them for travel. Soon the steam carts will carry them along the Undgrin to every hold in the world.' He held out the torque again. 'Take it, Gotrek. All your doubt, your black moods, your fear, will dissipate like a cloud, to be replaced with blissful peace. You will never be angry again. Take it. Join us.'

Gotrek slapped it out of his hand. It jangled across the floor. 'No.'

Hamnir looked genuinely sad. 'Then, old friend,' he said, sighing, 'I'm afraid you must die.' He licked out with his axe as quickly and casually as a man swats a fly, and nearly caught Gotrek in the throat.

The Slayer jumped back, cursing, wisps of beard fluttering to the floor. Felix dodged back too. Even after Hamnir's words the attack was unexpected. Attacks usually had a preamble – raised voices, threatening gestures, the glint of anger in the attacker's eye. Hamnir's swipe had had none of these.

The prince swung again, as blank as before, and Gotrek blocked the blow with the rune axe, backing up. 'Don't do this, Ranulfsson,' he said, brow furrowed. 'I don't want to hurt you.'

'And I don't want to hurt you,' said Hamnir calmly, slashing again, 'but if you will not take the torque, I have no choice. Those who are not with us are against us.'

Gotrek continued to back away, parrying every blow, but never returning one. Felix had never seen the Slayer so unhappy to be in a fight. It was a battle he couldn't win. Killing Hamnir was a tragedy, not a victory, and being killed by him was no grand doom, and would indeed very likely doom the dwarfs, and perhaps the whole world, to mindless slavery.

But if Gotrek didn't strike soon, he might never be able to. He was weakening with every step. The axe wound in his shoulder had lost him a lot of blood, and it was still bleeding. Felix saw him stagger as he parried a chop to the head. Hamnir wasn't tiring in the least.

Felix edged around Hamnir, angling for the torque.

'No!' snapped Gotrek. 'This is my fight!' He glared at Hamnir. 'And his. Stay back.'

So Felix stood by while Gotrek back-pedalled around the pit with Hamnir in calm, implacable pursuit.

'Fight it, scholar,' hissed Gotrek. 'Fight it! You're the smartest dwarf I know. Can't you see what it's doing? Can't you smell the reek of Chaos on it?'

Hamnir slashed at his belly. Gotrek barely blocked it in time.

'Don't you remember what it made of Ferga?' Gotrek asked. 'Do you want to be like that?'

Hamnir's brow creased momentarily, but then smoothed again. 'Had I known then what I know now, I would have joined her.'

'This god of yours took your hold by force, killing innocent dwarfs and using grobi to do it – the ancient enemies of our people. How can you side with it?'

'We refused to listen,' said Hamnir placidly. 'It did what it had to do. For those who listen there is only joy.'

Gotrek gritted his teeth as he slipped and jarred his leg. 'How long have we been friends, scholar? How many times have we fought side by side, and drunk ourselves blind, and split up a treasure, and argued over everything and nothing?' His voice was hoarse with emotion. Felix had never heard him like this. 'Is that less to you than the joys of being a slave?'

Hamnir was silent, his face troubled. His attacks faltered.

'Good, scholar,' called Gotrek. 'Fight it!'

Hamnir stopped, axe frozen and hands trembling, a war waging within him. 'Fighting it is useless,' he said, his voice strangled. 'We are but two, when it is thousands. We are children, when it is ageless. If I take off the torque a hundred others will pick it up. What I do doesn't matter. We have already lost.'

'We haven't!' roared Gotrek. 'Take off the torque and we'll kill it together.'

Hamnir shook his head sadly. 'Nothing can kill it. It is too strong. Too old.'

Gotrek snarled. 'What kind of dwarf are you? Will you doom your race because you gave up without a fight?'

It was the wrong thing to say.

Hamnir's face became calm again. He raised his axe. 'It is to save my race that I obey it, for if we oppose it we will be destroyed. Only by joining it will we live.'

'With torques around our necks,' Gotrek spat.

'But we will live.' Hamnir swung at Gotrek again.

Gotrek parried and backed away, his face working grief and rage.

'Gotrek,' said Felix, distraught. 'Let me take it off him. Perhaps he'll come to himself.'

'*He* has to do it,' said Gotrek, glaring at Hamnir. 'He has to be strong and take it off himself.'

'Maybe no one is strong enough.'

'A dwarf should be strong enough!'

The pain in Gotrek's voice was almost too much for Felix to bear. 'There's a whole clanhold above that says otherwise,' he said.

Gotrek cursed.

Hamnir hacked again, but this time Gotrek returned the attack, battering at Hamnir's axe and trying to disarm him. Hamnir blocked and countered with blistering speed. He was twice the fighter he had been without the torque. They circled near Galin's corpse.

'You're running out of chances, scholar,' grated Gotrek. 'Take it off or die!'

But it wasn't clear who would die first. Gotrek was fighting one-handed now, his wounded arm useless. He was barely stopping Hamnir's blows from reaching him.

The Slayer backed up, stepping around Galin's body. Hamnir pressed forwards, swinging savagely, and slipped on Galin's blood.

Quicker than blinking, Gotrek caught Hamnir's axe in a bind, and ripped it from his grip with a savage twist of his wrist. It bounced into the hole.

Hamnir stepped back. Gotrek leapt at him like a wrestler, slammed him to the ground, and straddled his chest. He ripped the torque from Hamnir's neck and flung it away, staring into his face, his axe raised.

Hamnir blinked up at him, calmly. 'Will you kill me then, Gotrek? You swore to protect me until one of us should die.'

Gotrek's face collapsed. 'And I failed,' he choked. 'You're already dead.' He buried the axe in Hamnir's chest. Hamnir bucked and contorted, choking, and then lay still, eyes staring at nothing.

Felix gaped, stunned, as Gotrek slumped over his dead friend. Sigmar, he thought, what had the Slayer done?

'Don't look at me, manling,' Gotrek growled, his voice thick. He hid his face in one massive, blood-stained hand, 'or I will kill you where you stand!'

Felix stepped back, shaking, and turned away. He dug his field kit out of his pack, allowing Gotrek his grief while he patched his wounds and tried to make sense of what had happened. Gotrek had killed a dwarf! Hamnir! His friend: without waiting, without giving him time to recover. Felix couldn't stop replaying the scene over in his mind.

How could Gotrek have known if Hamnir had recovered or not? What Hamnir had said hadn't sounded 'wrong'. Had he made a mistake?

After a long interval, Gotrek stood, unsteady. His left arm was red from shoulder to wrist. 'Right,' he said, clearing his throat. 'Let's finish this.'

He pulled a length of bandages from Galin's pack and started winding them around his sliced-open shoulder as he crossed to the doorway from whence Hamnir had come. The edges of the door were carved all over with the same ancient warding symbols that had marked the outer door. Felix was certain now that they had been placed to keep something in, and he was beginning to understand what that something was.

The Slayer's face was as dead and cold as Felix had ever seen it. He wanted to ask him about Hamnir, but he was afraid he would kill him if he did. He held his tongue and followed him.

As they reached the door, the oppressive dread and despair welled up in Felix again, stronger than before. If the Sleeper could turn the mind of a dwarf like Hamnir, what chance did a human like himself have? Worse, what if it turned Gotrek's mind? What if it already had! What if it had decided that Gotrek was a better pawn than Hamnir? Was that why the Slayer had killed his friend? Or perhaps Gotrek had gone entirely mad at last, and couldn't distinguish between friend or foe. Felix felt like running for his life, but he was more afraid of being separated from Gotrek than of being killed by him.

They walked down a short corridor, then ascended a shallow ramp to a wider hallway that curved away to the left and right. The sickly corpse-flesh glow grew brighter with every step, and the thick, sour-milk reek clogged their nostrils. A series of open arches on the inner wall of the curving corridor shone faintly from within. Felix looked in the nearest one, gagged and stepped back. Gotrek scowled into it behind him.

Three-quarters of the large room was filled, floor to ceiling, with what looked, to Felix's unsettled mind, like translucent white custard – custard that had been left out far too long. It was from this bulging, gelatinous substance that the pale phosphorescence emanated, and the smell too. Flickers like green heat lightning flashed deep within its milky depths. Ropy white tentacles protruded from it and lay, long and flaccid, across the floor. They pulsed with sluggish life. Cancerous goiters and weird growths blossomed from it like blackcurrants in a pudding, and thick white cilia stood out like hairs on its surface.

Through the cloudy substance, Felix could just see a doorway on the far side of the chamber. The shattered remains of a stone door lay in front of it, entirely buried under the gelid flesh. It looked like the horrid mass had burst the door and grown to fill the room.

Felix covered his mouth at the smell. 'What is it?' He asked through his fingers, fighting the urge to vomit.

Gotrek stepped up to the bulging white mass. He prodded it with a booted toe. It shivered like jelly. The cilia around the point where Gotrek had touched waved like a field of weeds in a wind.

They moved on. The next room too was overfilled with the translucent stuff, pressed against the walls of the chamber like a mattress full of snot shoved into a too small closet. The white tentacles trailed across the floor like dead snakes, and there was another burst door on the far side of the room.

Gotrek and Felix continued along the curving corridor, passing room after room, each filled with more of the horrible tentacled jelly. Felix began to realise that the corridor was a vast ring. Halfway around its circumference, they came to a second ramp, this one angling down under the centre of the circle.

The corpse glow was stronger here, and Gotrek turned down the ramp immediately. Felix hesitated, the irrational fear filling his veins with ice, then forced himself to go on. If he stopped, he would never be able to start forwards again.

There was another massive trapezoidal arch at the bottom of the ramp, its edges limned with the rancid green light. Gotrek and Felix stepped to it, and then stopped, retching. Felix covered his mouth again and forced his stomach to be still. The smell was overwhelming, but the smell was the least of it.

They looked into a low circular chamber. The floor was littered with black basalt rubble. The ceiling – Felix flinched away from it. It made him want to vomit, to run. The ceiling was of the same gelatinous grub-flesh that had filled the rooms above. The weight of it had caved in the original ceiling, and it bellied down from above like the underside of some filthy bed canopy, making the low room even lower.

And hanging limply from the centre of the mass, like the desiccated shell of some impossibly large praying mantis, was the Sleeper.

There was no question in Felix's mind that this was the thing they had come to kill. It could be nothing else. It was absolutely motionless, head slumped, limbs dangling – asleep. Felix might have thought it already dead, except for the aura of fear and madness that emanated from it like cold from a glacier.

It had once been some sort of insect, but time, imprisonment and some dark pact with the Ruinous Powers had warped it into something infinitely more foul. Its translucent shell was white and waxy, like tallow, and through it Felix could see white, striated muscle and the flow of viscous liquid through glassine veins. Eight long, sharp legs like glass sabres hung below a spined, carapaced head with ten black faceted eyes and a thicket of cruel mandibles. Thick, whip-like antennae curved up from its ridged brow.

Its thin thorax was attached somehow to the gelatinous ceiling, and at first Felix couldn't make out how. Did it cling to it like a bat? Was it somehow trapped in it? Then, with a fresh wave of revulsion, he understood. The jelly was the rest of it! The great fleshy mass, that had grown into every room along the circular corridor, and that had become so heavy that it had broken through the stone ceiling, was the thing's bloated abdomen! Gotrek and Felix had not explored every corner of the crypt. The gods only knew how many other rooms it had filled with its bulk. Felix swallowed convulsively as he realised that he might be looking at the largest living thing in the world.

Other things hung from the bulging ceiling as well – glistening translucent sacs, bulging at the end of twisted umbilical ropes. Felix recognised them as the chrysalises they had earlier seen the orcs putting into crates. There were pale, angular forms inside them, with long forelegs and ten faceted eyes. The Sleeper's children: the end of the world.

The Sleeper did not turn its head, or in any way acknowledge their presence as they stepped into the round room. And yet, Felix was more afraid to approach it than any thing of flesh and blood he had ever faced. Crippling terror paralysed him. He couldn't take another step.

Gotrek hadn't stopped, but he had slowed, leaning forwards and struggling to put one foot in front of the other like a man pushing into the teeth of a gale.

'Fight it, manling,' he said through gritted teeth. 'It's out of servants. It's using the only weapon it's got left.'

Felix couldn't move. If he got any closer, it would eat his brain. He knew this. It was already eating it. If he didn't run, he would end up like the others, a mindless slave, doing the bidding of some Chaos-corrupted insect. It would all be Gotrek's fault – dragging him into certain death time and time again. 'You fight it,' he spat. 'You're the Slayer! Must I always fight your battles?'

Gotrek glared back at him. 'You fight my battles? Ha! That's a joke. Half the battles I fight are to save your worthless hide! Grimnir, what a weakling! Why did I choose a human for a rememberer? A dwarf would have taken care of himself!'

Felix choked, outrage flaring in his heart. 'Weakling? You call me that after all I've been through with you – and all on the strength of a drunken vow I should never have made!'

Gotrek turned on him, the Sleeper forgotten. 'And I should never have held you to it. By my ancestors! Twenty-five years travelling with a snivelling wet blanket too weak to pull his own weight, having to turn back every second step to pull your scrawny arse out of the fire, having to listen to, "That isn't wise, Gotrek", and "Maybe we shouldn't do that, Gotrek", in my ear like a damned mosquito. Why I haven't cut your throat before now, just to shut you up, is beyond me!'

'You think it's been a joy travelling with you?' shouted Felix, his neck pulsing with rage, 'Insulted and ignored every day for a quarter century by a stunted, taciturn bully without a kind word for anybody. I can't think of a single instance when you thanked me or praised me for a job well done. It's always "Shut up, manling", and "Out of the way, manling", and "Get the bags, manling".' He clenched his fists. 'When I think of the life I could have had if I hadn't sworn to follow your ugly posterior around the world until you finally killed yourself! You haven't even had the decency to die quickly like most Slayers.'

'You've seen more of the world than any hundred men of the Empire, thanks to me,' bellowed Gotrek, 'and you complain about it? Grungni's axe! Why didn't I make my peace with Hamnir and ask him to be my rememberer? He at least was a dwarf, not a spindle-shanked weakling!'

'Weakling, again.' Felix put his hand on his hilt. 'You call me weak when I'm still here and your oh-so-sturdy dwarf friend Hamnir is dead? Who's the weakling?'

Gotrek's face went white. His one eye glittered with cold fury. 'You insult the dead? You'll die for that.'

'I insulted him,' Felix sneered. '*You* killed him.'

With an outraged roar, Gotrek lurched unsteadily towards Felix, slashing one-handed with his axe. Felix leapt back, gasping and drawing his sword. He felt the wind of the axe's passing on his cheek.

Terror stabbed through his heart like an icicle. Sigmar, what had he done? Gotrek was attacking him! The axe that had killed daemons and giants was swinging for his neck!

He scrambled backwards, parrying desperately. Gotrek limped after him, the rune axe a blur. Each strike nearly knocked the sword from Felix's hands. He was still alive only because Gotrek fought one-handed, and was weak from his wounds and loss of blood.

Felix cursed himself as the rune axe flashed past, an inch from his chin. What madness had inspired him to goad the Slayer like that? Had he been out of his mind? Then it came to him that the inspiration had indeed been from outside of his mind. It had come from the Sleeper. It was stirring them up like pit dogs. It was defending itself by making them fight each other instead of it.

'Gotrek!' he cried as they circled. 'Stop! It's the Sleeper. It's forcing us to fight! It's in our minds!'

'Trying to trick me into letting down my guard? Ha!' Gotrek hacked unrelentingly at Felix, pushing him further into the room.

Felix could feel the Sleeper's presence behind his left shoulder as he backed closer to it. His skin crawled. 'Gotrek, curse you, fight it!' he shouted. 'What's become of your unbendable dwarf will. Fight it!'

They slashed and hacked directly in front of it, circling slowly, as if they were gladiators, fighting for its amusement. Gods! Why wouldn't Gotrek listen? How dare he accuse Felix of weakness and then fall under the Sleeper's power himself? If he wouldn't listen, Felix would just have to beat it into him. He'd cut the Slayer's head off and shout it down his throat.

'Stubborn fool! I'll teach you!' Felix aimed a lunge at Gotrek's poorly bound shoulder wound.

The Slayer's axe blocked the strike, shivering his sword and stinging his hands.

'It's you who needs teaching, longshanks! Saying you're better than a dwarf!' He aimed a bash at Felix's head that would have sheared it in half if he hadn't leapt back. 'I'll gut you for insolence!'

Felix cursed. Even one-handed and near collapse, Gotrek was stronger and faster than any opponent Felix had ever faced, but the Slayer was reeling, unsteady on his feet. If Felix could make him fall, he could finish him. He continued to circle right, trying to get on Gotrek's weak side.

Gotrek turned with him. 'I'll spit you like a rabbit!' he roared, raising his axe over his head. He tripped on a chunk of rubble. He staggered, off balance.

An opening! Felix darted in, stabbing for Gotrek's bad leg. Gotrek swung down with his axe, blindingly fast, smashing his sword out of his hands, then kicked him in the stomach.

Felix flew back, his sword bouncing away, and crashed into the Sleeper. His arms tangled in its spiny legs. The back of his head smacked it between its rows of eyes. It jerked, waking and hissing, mandibles clattering.

'I'll chop you in two!' Gotrek bellowed, and hurled his axe straight at Felix's head.

Felix yelped and dived to the ground in terror. The axe spun by over his head, ruffling his hair, and severed one of the Sleeper's antennae.

The Sleeper screeched, its legs lashing about, its claws clacking. One clubbed Felix across the shoulder and knocked him halfway across the room. He grunted in pain as he hit the floor, but also in relief. His mind was suddenly clear. All his unreasoning rage was gone. The Sleeper's wound had distracted it.

Felix pushed himself up. Gotrek was diving past the chittering, thrashing thing and snatching up his axe. Felix goggled at him as he turned.

'You... you...'

'Not now, manling,' Gotrek rasped, standing. 'Kill it.'

The Slayer limped towards the Sleeper from behind. The thing twisted and curled itself in every direction, trying to turn to face him, but it was held in place by its gargantuan abdomen. It couldn't move to defend itself.

Gotrek smiled savagely, prepared for the slaughter. Felix stood and recovered his sword. With its vile influence gone from his head, the Sleeper seemed no threat at all. It was pathetic, in fact, made helpless by its own mutations.

Something long and white dropped down beside him. He flinched away from it. It looked like a wrist-thick strand of snot dripping from a giant's nose. Another dropped in front of him. The drips curved towards him like blind snakes, their skins thickening and muddying. They were growing from the Sleeper's bloated abdomen!

The first split at its tip like a seedpod opening, and Felix saw teeth and a purple tongue inside the cavity. The other sprouted hooked barbs and squid-like suckers. They lunged.

He slashed at the one with the mouth, decapitating it. Thick rank liquid exploded from it, making his eyes water. Two more strands dripped down around him. 'Gotrek!'

Gotrek was beset with five of the things. He slashed three in half, and four more dropped down to grapple with him. One looped around his bad leg. Another caught him around the neck. They were trying to hold him away from the Sleeper.

'Chaos-cursed filth!' Gotrek roared.

Felix chopped through two more, but another had his waist and was lifting him off his feet. He swung his sword behind his head and crashed to the floor as he cut through it. He landed in a puddle of grey muck.

The cut tentacles were pouring thick streams of mucus from their wounds onto the floor. It smelled impossibly foul. Felix jumped up, trying to shake it from his hands, and nearly fell again. The basalt floor was slick with the stuff.

The circular chamber was suddenly a swaying forest of slimy white tentacles, all reaching for him and Gotrek. They weren't hard to cut, but there were too many of them. One, with a mouth like a lamprey, bit Felix on the back of the leg. He screamed and chopped it through, but another raked his face with ridges like broken glass.

He hacked at everything that came within reach, slipping and spinning in a mad frenzy. On the other side of the Sleeper, Gotrek did the same, but new tentacles grew out of the bulging ceiling every second, and more than forty truncated tentacles poured viscous goop onto the floor. The stinking mucus was ankle deep. As Felix backed away from three of the mutating pseudopods, he stepped under a shower of muck, and was drenched to the skin. He gagged as it got into his eyes and nose, and plastered his hair to his scalp.

Felix sobbed with frustration as he wiped his eyes. It was hopeless. No matter how many tentacles he cut there would always be more. They would never reach the Sleeper to kill it. The tentacles would tear them apart. He should just throw down his sword and...

He froze. It was back in his head, trying to reassert control. He forced it out savagely, cursing it with each slash of his sword. Then he turned and started slogging, one slippery step at a time, through the lake of snot towards it. He would not let it distract him. It would *not* take his mind from him again.

Gotrek had won free as well, at least momentarily, chopping through the tentacles faster than they could form. The severed heads of three of them hung by their teeth from his arms and legs as he waded towards the thing, and his slime-drenched crest hung in his face like a wet red mop.

The Sleeper chittered in distress and more tentacles writhed the Slayer's way, but he was not to be stopped. He backhanded through six, and then chopped at the thing's face. It lashed out with its glassine legs and the rune axe sheared through two of them at the joints.

The Sleeper shrieked, a deafening insect whine, and swung a pincered foreleg at Gotrek. He made to block, but a tentacle caught his wrist and he couldn't bring his axe in line. A crimson gash opened across his chest. The blood mixed with the slime, and painted his torso red.

Gotrek turned to cut the tentacle, and the Sleeper's other foreleg cracked him on the back of the head. He staggered and almost fell.

'Leave them!' cried Felix, as he finally reached the centre of the room. 'I'll get them!'

Gotrek said nothing, only turned his full attention on the Sleeper as Felix hacked through the tentacle that held his arm, and slashed at all the others that were questing forwards. There seemed to be hundreds of them. All with different mutations, all visions of an unhinged mind.

Gotrek laid into the Sleeper with all his might, but it still had six legs to his one axe, and it blocked every attack, chips and chunks of translucent chitin spinning away with each clash. He cut off another leg, and ducked as the Sleeper lashed out at his head.

Behind him, Felix spun like a dervish as he lopped tentacle after tentacle, but never enough. He laughed bitterly to himself. It was easy to say that he would keep the tentacles off Gotrek, but who would keep them off him? He was fading fast. The mucus was up to his knees – almost to Gotrek's hips – and it felt like he was fighting in quicksand. Worse, the bulging abdominal ceiling was drooping lower, as if it was deflating. Felix kept bumping it with his head. If they weren't torn apart or drowned, there was a good chance the Sleeper would smother them to death. He chopped through two sucker-covered tentacles that were looping around his legs. Then he slashed at three more that were reaching towards Gotrek. His sword arm was as heavy as lead. A tentacle grabbed his left ankle, another bit his right bicep, and more were coming.

Gotrek swung at the Sleeper's right foreleg. It blocked with another leg, and lost it as the axe smashed through it. The Slayer surged forwards, pressing the attack, but suddenly he jerked to a stop, grunting in pain. The Sleeper had him around the waist with its left pincer, lifting him off the ground and squeezing hard. Gotrek grabbed at it with his off hand, trying to keep it from scissoring him in two. He raised his axe to sever the arm, but its right pincer caught it by the haft and tried to pull it out of his hand. The Slayer bellowed in rage and pain.

'Hang on!' Felix cried.

He struggled forwards, hacking through three tentacles. Three more held him tight, and another two were grabbing for him. The Sleeper was lifting Gotrek towards its razor-sharp mandibles as he struggled. The Slayer couldn't let go of the Sleeper's claw to use both hands to free his axe, or it would cut him in two, and he couldn't let go of his axe to use both hands to force open the claw or he would lose the axe.

Felix roared and slashed all around him, chopping through half a dozen tentacles. Still more held him. He freed his arms and dove for the Sleeper, lashing out with the last of his strength as the tentacles around his ankles tried to yank him back.

He connected! The very tip of his blade caught the wrist of the pincer that held Gotrek's axe.

He splashed down face first into the slime and went under. Had he done it? Was it enough? Had the Sleeper let go?

He pushed desperately to the surface, coughing and shaking the muck from his eyes, just in time to see Gotrek, with a guttural howl of triumph, bury the rune axe between the Sleeper's two largest eyes.

The Sleeper shrieked and spasmed, its remaining legs flailing. Every tentacle in the room lashed and writhed like a pinned snake. Gotrek was thrown across the room and crashed into the wall. A dozen frenzied tentacles bludgeoned Felix. His brain was filled with a mad insectile chittering, a thousand crickets sawing violently inside his head, as horrific, shattered-mirror images of blood and dismemberment, and black chambers seething with a million haycart-sized insects crawling over one another, flashed behind his eyes. He thrashed and kicked in the swamp of mucus, screaming, hands clapped over his ears, heart pounding, gorge rising. Gotrek was staggering to his feet, his arms over his head, grimacing and roaring.

The whole world seemed to be shaking. Was it all in his head? A chunk of basalt splashed down beside him, raising a thick fountain of muck. It was not in his head.

'Out, manling!' called Gotrek.

Felix struggled to his feet and sloshed drunkenly through the chaos of waving tentacles after Gotrek, as huge blocks of stone crashed down all around them, and the Sleeper's mental storm continued to batter his mind. Image piled on top of image, each more chaotic and confused than the last: cave-coffered insect cities; towering black basalt pyramids; slave armies – hairy, heavy browed troglodyte humans, digging and building and cleaning up after their chitinous masters; earthquakes; slave rebellions; cave-ins; assassinations; an insect emperor making a pact with entities more ancient even than itself, a pact that gives it new powers, brings it victories, treasure, godhood; then come jealousies; betrayals; invasion by pale overdwellers; battles; defeats; hiding itself in the temple where once the others had come to worship it; the overdwellers locking it in with spells and wards; waiting, growing, waiting.

Gotrek and Felix ran up the ramp and into the circular corridor, which was already half buried in falling rubble. White tentacles flailed from the open doorways as they sprinted and dodged around the ring. Walls crumbled as the vast gelatinous bulk juddered and shook. The Sleeper's psychic scream rose in pitch and volume, losing any semblance of cohesion until it was only a deafening, mind-blasting rush of rage, agony and ancient hate.

A huge slab of black stone crashed down in front of them, missing them by inches. Felix vaulted it. Gotrek dodged around it, and they dived into the ramp, bouncing and rolling down to the hall below as, with a roar like an earthquake, the Sleeper's chambers collapsed altogether.

The Sleeper's presence winked out as the rocks fell, leaving only gibbering echoes. Felix was too scared to care. He lay huddled at the base of the ramp, his head covered with his arms, expecting at any moment that the roof would cave in.

After a while, the rumbling and shaking subsided and all grew still. Felix slowly uncurled, blinking and shaking his head. Gotrek was sitting up too, clutching his temples and groaning.

After a few moments spent leaning against the wall and catching his breath, Felix looked dully over at the Slayer. 'You tried to kill me,' he said.

'What?' said Gotrek. 'Never. You tried to kill me.'

'Only because you wouldn't stop trying to kill me!' said Felix. 'Couldn't you understand? It was the Sleeper. It was forcing you to fight me.'

'Oh, I knew.'

'Then why didn't you stop?'

Gotrek frowned, and looked down, his fists clenching, cha-
grined. 'I couldn't. The thing was damned strong.' He rubbed his
mucus-covered face with his hands and sighed. 'Guess I don't
blame Hamnir so much now. Only broke its hold by giving in.'

'Broke its hold? You didn't break its hold.'

'It got out of our heads when I hit it, didn't it?'

'You hit it by accident.'

Gotrek shook his head and stood up on wobbly legs. 'Couldn't
stop attacking you, much as I tried. Or turn my axe on it, either. It
was too strong for that. But I could put you between me and it.' He
shrugged. 'I knew you'd duck.'

Felix blinked, and surged unsteadily to his feet. His blood
boiled. 'You knew I'd... You... But... but what if I hadn't?'

Gotrek grimaced and cleaned the mucus off his axe as best he
could. 'What choice did I have?'

Felix opened his mouth to argue, but he didn't know what to
say.

Gotrek slid the rune axe through his belt, and turned away.
'Come on.'

They walked down the corridor to the room with the pit in the
centre and stopped at Hamnir's body.

Felix swallowed as he looked at Hamnir's face, calm in death,
and then down at the ruin of his chest. 'How... how did you
know?' he asked. 'How did you know he hadn't recovered? That
he wouldn't recover?'

'I knew,' said Gotrek. 'It was in his eyes. He had spent too long
with it. He wasn't coming back.'

'But...'

'He wasn't coming back!' Gotrek squatted abruptly, slid his
arms under Hamnir's body, and lifted him. He stumped towards
the exit.

Felix stared after him. Perhaps the Sleeper's death would have
ended its dominion over him, he wanted to say. Its corrupting
influence might have died with it. Perhaps Hamnir would have
returned to himself once it was dead. He couldn't force himself to
speak. He followed after Gotrek, his heart at war with itself.

Halfway up the tunnel that led to the mines, Gotrek cleared his
throat. 'You will tell Gorril that Hamnir died well, fighting the
torqued greenskins. It is best.'

'You don't want him to know you killed him?'

'I don't want him to know that he... lost himself.'

'Why don't you tell him?' asked Felix.

'I don't lie.'

'And I do?' Felix was insulted.

'You write plays, don't you?'

A sharp retort rose up in Felix's throat, but he let it die unspoken. He didn't like it, but perhaps it *was* for the best. The last thing the beleaguered dwarfs of Karak Hirn needed to learn was that their prince had betrayed his own race, and it had always been the job of poets and playwrights to put the best face on the deaths of heroes.

'All right, I'll tell him.'

CHAPTER TWENTY-SIX

GOTREK PUT HIS axe through each of the chrysalises in the room where the orcs had been packing them up, and set fire to the crates just to be sure. Once smoke began to fill the room, they turned and continued on up through the mine.

Felix looked with growing despair on the few orcs they passed. He had been afraid their return to the hold would be a nightmare – dodging rampaging orcs newly returned to their ferocity now that the yoke of the Sleeper's evil influence had been lifted from their necks. The reality was worse. The orcs they passed stood blank and lost, staring into space with their weapons and tools hanging limply from their hands. Even when Gotrek and Felix came upon four in a narrow corridor – walked right into them around a corner – the orcs did nothing, only pawed at them lazily, like sleepy bears. Gotrek pushed through them as if they were so much furniture, growling low in his throat. They didn't follow.

Finally, after retracing their steps up the winding stair of King Alrik's vault and through the empty halls of Karak Hirn, they came to the Diamondsmith clanhold. Gorril was just outside its doors, supervising details of dwarfs who were piling the beheaded bodies of the undead orcs onto carts and wheeling them away.

'Gurnisson!' he cried when he saw then. 'We had hope of your success. The last of the walking corpses dropped dead all at once about half an hour–' He stopped when he saw what Gotrek carried. 'Prince Hamnir!' He rushed to Gotrek. 'Is he… Did he…'

'He is dead,' said Gotrek.

'He died well,' said Felix, remembering his part. 'There were more torqued greenskins below, defending the Sleeper. He slew two. Another slew him. He died to stop Chaos and corruption from spreading to other holds.' Which was true enough after all.

'And did you slay the Sleeper?'

'Aye,' said Gotrek. 'It's dead.'

'Then he did not die in vain.' Gorril took Hamnir from Gotrek's arms, his face working, as the other dwarfs gathered around, baring their heads for their fallen prince. As he carried Hamnir into the clanhold, the dwarfs followed him, and more came out into the central chamber to watch in mournful silence as Gorril laid him upon the base of a statue of some ancient dwarf patriarch.

Gorril turned to the assembled dwarfs, tears in his eyes. 'Friends, our prince is dead. We will mourn him as befits a fallen hero, but in this tragedy is triumph, for with his death, he has freed us from the horror that held us in its clutches. The Sleeper is dead. The hold is ours. The worst is behind us.'

'It isn't,' said Gotrek under his breath.

'What?' asked Gorril, turning to him with a frown. 'What do you mean? You killed it. We are free.'

Gotrek sighed and pushed through the crowd of solemn dwarfs to the doors of the gemcutters' guildhall. 'Open it,' he said.

A dwarf brought a key and turned the locks as Gorril and Felix and the other dwarfs filled in behind him. The door swung open.

The dwarfs of the Diamondsmith clan turned towards the door as the light from the hall fell upon them. They stared empty-eyed at the dwarfs who looked in on them, and then slowly started shuffling towards them, their weapons raised, their hands clutching.

Gotrek drew his axe from his belt. 'The worst is still before us.'

Gorril and the other dwarfs moaned in despair, and Felix's last faint hope died.

After a long, stunned moment, Gorril sighed and wiped his eyes. He straightened his shoulders, gripped his axe, and turned to the others.

'Fall in, sons of Karak Hirn,' he said. 'There is sad work to be done.'

EPILOGUE

'PLENTY MEAT ON norther man,' said the ogre. 'Taste funny though.'

The men gagged and edged away from him.

The dwarf grimaced. 'Grungni! Is there anything you ogres won't eat?'

The ogre ruminated for a moment, rubbing his several chins. 'Don't think so,' he said at last.

Felix listened with only half an ear. He and Gotrek were marching with a group of mercenaries who had banded together for safety while traversing the Black Fire Pass. All were heading north to sell their swords and axes to the Empire in its fight against the invasion of the Chaos hordes. Ahead of them was a company of Tilean Pike, outfitted in gaudy red and gold, and behind, thirty Estalian cross-bowmen in brown leather. The dashing son of a border prince trotted past with twenty lances at his back, all on massive chargers, brave pennants fluttering from their lance tips. Ten dwarfs marched slowly beside two pony-drawn cannon, making sure the wheels didn't get stuck in the muddy, snow sprinkled ruts of the rough road.

Gotrek listened not at all. His one eye was turned inwards. He stomped along with his head down, taking no notice of the men, dwarfs or ogres around them. The Slayer had been in the blackest of moods since they had left Karak Hirn ten days before, and Felix

569

didn't blame him. The events of the past weeks had been enough
to depress even the most cheerful, and Gotrek was not known for
his sunny disposition even in the best of times.

In a way, the fact that the Diamondsmith dwarfs had not come
back to themselves had been a blessing, at least for Gotrek's sanity. It meant that he had been right to slay Hamnir – that the
prince would not have returned to his right mind. And yet, what a
bleak comfort that was. Cutting down the lost dwarfs had been the
saddest battle of Felix's life. They had hardly fought back. They
had blinked at the oncoming axes like cattle waiting for the maul.
It had taken moments, and not a dwarf of Gorril's force had got a
scratch, but Felix wondered if they would ever recover.

The thought of losing family made Felix think again about his
own. Were they still alive? He had thought a lot recently about
going home and settling down. Would he still have a home to
return to? Was his brother Otto still running the family business?
What of his old friends and companions? Did Max still live?
Heinz, the innkeeper who had employed them in Nuln? Snorri?
Ulrika?

A pang went through his heart as Felix thought of her. If she
lived, what side did she fight for?

The news that came from the north was a hotchpotch of rumour,
fear and hope. There were some who said the war was over, and the
Chaos-crazed northmen driven back to the Wastes. Others said that
Altdorf was aflame and Karl Franz dead. No two stories were alike.
None could be trusted.

'Yer wasting your time if ye think ye'll get in on the fighting,' said
a swaggering gunner with a Nuln accent and the notched ear of a
convicted thief. 'It'll all be over in a month. Archaon's smashing his
head against the walls of Middenheim as we speak. Pretty soon his
brains will fall out. No one's ever cracked the Fauschlag, no one.'

'So why you march?' asked the ogre.

The gunner shrugged. 'Lot of open positions after a war,' he said.
'Lot of crimes forgotten when the ranks get thin.'

Gotrek raised his head, glowering. 'Better not be over,' he muttered under his breath. 'I must wash the dwarf blood from my axe
in a bath of Kurgan gore.' He held up the axe and gazed mournfully
at its shining steel edge. 'Though it will never be enough.'

He and Felix trudged on in silence as, ahead, the setting sun
painted the northern sky red as blood.

MANSLAYER

'On we pressed, north through the Black Fire Pass, to tread at last on Empire soil for the first time in twenty years. And though my heart sang to be home, it was a grim time in the land of my birth, and it grieved me to see it so wracked with panic and privation.

'Gotrek was eager to reach Middenheim and find his doom in battle against the great hordes of Chaos that had again swept south to threaten the lands of men. In this desire, however, he was to be frustrated, for, passing through Nuln, we stumbled upon a vile and far-reaching conspiracy intended to destroy the beating heart of the Empire from within at the very hour when its greatest enemy attacked it from without.

'While in pursuit of these foul villains, it chanced that Gotrek met an old friend, and I an old love – and never could two reunions have been more different; for Gotrek's was fond and fortuitous, while mine was both sweet, and more painful than I can express.'

– From *My Travels with Gotrek*, Vol VII, by Herr Felix Jaeger (Altdorf Press, 2528)

CHAPTER ONE

'By Sigmar's golden beard, brother!' cried Otto. 'You haven't aged a day!'

'Er...' said Felix, as Otto's butler took his sword and his old red cloak and closed the front door behind him, shutting out the warm rays of a late summer morning.

Felix would have liked to return his brother's compliment, but looking him over top to bottom, the words stuck in his throat. Otto's once blond hair had retreated from his head and turned to silver on his chin – chins, rather. And though he was exquisitely dressed in perfectly tailored velvets and brocades, the best tailor in the world couldn't have hidden the prodigious swelling of his belly.

Otto limped forward, gripping a gold-topped walking stick, and brushed some of the road dust off Felix's shoulders. Gods, he walks with a cane now, Felix thought.

'And you haven't matured a day either, I see.' Otto chuckled. 'Same ragged cloak. Same patched breeches. Same cracked boots. You vagabond, I thought you were going to find your fortune.'

'I have found it,' said Felix. 'Several times.'

Otto wasn't listening. He waved a hand at the butler, who was wrinkling his nose with distaste as he hung Felix's cloak in a closet at one side of the entrance hall.

'Fritz!' Otto called. 'Wine and cold cuts in the study!' He motioned to Felix with a pudgy hand as he stumped down a cherry-panelled corridor towards the back of the townhouse. 'Come, brother. This calls for a celebration. Will you stay to lunch? Annabella – you remember my wife? She will be most interested to see you again.'

Felix followed, stomach growling at the mention of food. 'Lunch? Thank you, brother. You are most generous.'

It had been a lean journey from Karak Hirn, up from the wild lands of the Border Princes through Black Fire Pass then down the Old Dwarf Road into Averland and on. In this time of war even the breadbasket of the Empire had been stripped bare – all its wheat, wool and wine sent north to supply the army fighting to stop Archaon's encroaching hordes. Its men too had gone north, some-times unwillingly. As he and Gotrek had boarded the riverboat *Leopold* at the Loningbruck docks for the long meander down the Upper Reik to Nuln, Felix had seen companies of miserable, pinch-faced farm boys sitting on their packs, all kitted out with spears and bows and cheaply made uniforms in the colours of their lords. Burly sergeants in well-worn breastplates had watched over them like prison guards, making sure none of them slipped off home before the barges came to ship them north. Felix had shaken his head at the sight. How was it possible that these untrained boys, most of whom had never been away from their villages, could turn back the supernatural might of the numberless armies of the Wastes? And yet, for centuries, they had.

'Now then, brother,' said Otto, settling noisily into a high-backed leather chair by the open window of his opulent study. Sunshine and the droning of contented bees filtered in from the garden. 'How long has it been?'

Felix sighed as he sat in the opposite chair. He felt as if he was sinking into a leather cloud. Sigmar! He had forgotten such luxury existed. He smiled wryly to himself. There might be a war on, and privation all around, but one could always trust Otto to do well for himself. In that regard he was just like their father. 'I haven't been keeping track,' he said. 'How long has it been since the ratmen attacked Nuln?'

'Ratmen?' said Otto, looking up as the butler set wine and meat and fancy pastries on a table between them. 'Beastmen, you mean. That was twenty years ago.'

Felix frowned. 'The ones who came up from the sewers and destroyed the College of Engineering and spread plague and ruin? Those were ratmen.'

Otto chuckled. 'Yes, yes. I read your book when it came back from the printers. Very entertaining. But really, there was no need to embellish the truth. The beastmen were bad enough.' He took a sip of wine. 'It sold very well for a time, by the way. As have the others.'

Felix gaped, Otto's absurd insistence that the ratmen were beastmen forgotten. 'You… you published my journals? But…'

Otto smiled, his eyes almost disappearing behind his round cheeks. 'Well, you wouldn't accept my money, and I had some foolish notion that you wouldn't make any yourself.' He gave another amused glance at Felix's threadbare clothes. 'So I took it upon myself to provide for your old age. Annabella read them as you sent them to us, and thought they were quite good. Absolute rubbish of course, daemons and dragons and vampires and whatnot, but just the sort of tall tavern tales that sell these days. Certainly went over better than your poetry ever did.' He helped himself to a pastry. 'I put aside the profits, just in case you ever returned. Of course I had to deduct the printing costs and what not.'

'Of course you did,' muttered Felix.

'But I believe there's still a tidy sum, enough for a man of your, ah, frugal nature to live on for a bit, I should think.'

Felix could feel the blood rising in his cheeks. Part of him wanted to leap out of the chair and strangle Otto for his presumption and condescension. How dare he? Felix had often thought about publishing his journals – about turning them into books – but he had meant it for a time when he was settled, when he would have time to edit them properly, to check his facts, to compare notes with other learned men. He had thought to make them scholarly treatises on the lands and cultures and monsters he and the Slayer had encountered, not a series of penny dreadful melodramas. People would think he was a hack! On the other hand – a tidy sum? There was certainly something to be said for that. He rolled up a slice of ham and stuffed it into his mouth. Sigmar, that was good! He sipped his wine. Heaven!

'How much exactly, is a "tidy sum"?'

Otto waved a hand. 'Oh, I don't know. I haven't looked at those ledgers in years. Come by the office later this week and we'll–'

'Father?' said a voice from the corridor.

Felix looked around. A tall, blond youth with a thin, serious face stood in the study door. He had a stack of books under one arm, and wore the robes and skullcap of a university student.

'Yes, Gustav?' said Otto.

'I am going to the Verenan debating society meeting tonight. It may run late.'

'Very well. I'll send Manni with the coach to wait for you.'

Gustav made a face. He looked about seventeen, perhaps eighteen. 'I don't need the coach. I can make it home very well on my own.'

Otto's face went red. He opened his mouth to speak, then shot a look at Felix and thought better of it. 'Very well, very well. Just don't walk alone until you get to the Kaufman Gate.'

'I know, father,' said Gustav, with infinite disdain.

Otto forced a smile. 'Come and meet your uncle Felix.'

The boy's eyes widened. 'The… the dead one?'

'Only a long away from home,' said Felix, standing and extending a hand. 'A pleasure to meet you, nephew.'

The boy advanced hesitantly and gave Felix a limp hand.

'Gustav studies theology and law at the University of Nuln,' said Otto. 'And he has published poetry.'

'Really?' said Felix. He coughed modestly. 'I once published some poetry. In Altdorf. Perhaps you've…?'

'I don't write old-fashioned stuff like that,' said Gustav airily.

'Old… old fashioned?' stuttered Felix, trying to keep his voice level. 'What do you mean by…'

'I am of the new school, the School of the True Voice,' said Gustav. 'We eschew sentiment, and speak only of what is real.'

'Sounds highly entertaining,' said Felix dryly.

Gustav sniffed. 'Entertainment is for plebeians. We edify. Our philosophy–'

'Gustav,' said Otto. 'You'll be late for your lecture.'

'Ah.' Gustav nodded. 'Of course. Good day, uncle. Father.' He inclined his head solemnly and left.

Otto rolled his eyes at Felix and shrugged.

'I didn't know you had a son,' said Felix, resuming his seat.

'No? He was born… Oh yes, that's right. He was born a year after you left Nuln. Very grave, isn't he?' Otto chuckled. 'Reminds me of you at that age, actually.'

'Me?' said Felix. 'I was never such a…'

'You were worse.'

'I wasn't.'

Otto raised an eyebrow. 'Have you read those poems lately?'

Felix snorted and took another sip of wine.

'So, what brings you back to Nuln?' asked Otto. 'Are you still playing valet to that surly dwarf?'

'I am his Rememberer,' said Felix stiffly. 'And we're on our way to Middenheim, to help turn back the Chaos invasion.'

Otto made a face. 'Bit old for that now, surely. Why don't you stay here and work for me? You can help the soldiers up north and add to your nest egg at the same time.'

Felix sighed, amused. It seemed every time he came to Nuln, his brother offered him a job. Poor Otto. He didn't give a damn about helping Felix 'add to his nest egg.' He just wanted him to get a respectable job and stop being an embarrassment to the family. 'You're helping with the war effort?' he asked, avoiding the question.

'Oh yes,' said Otto. 'Jaeger's of Altdorf won the contract to ship raw iron from the Black Mountains down the Reik to Nuln. We are sole suppliers to the Imperial Gunnery School.' He chuckled to himself. 'Neat bit of negotiating, that. There were three shipping companies with lower bids, but I footed the bill for the Countess's annual Weaver's Guild Ball and buttered her up something shocking and, hey presto, I got the nod.'

Felix scowled. 'So you're not helping the war effort. You're gouging the cannon makers for everything you can get.'

Otto shook his head impatiently. 'Not a bit of it. Our bid may have been higher, but our service is better. Jaeger's is the best in the Empire. Everyone knows that. It just took a little oil to get the Countess to award the contract on merit rather than price. That's the way it is with business.'

'And that's why I'm not in business,' said Felix, a bit more snootily than he had intended. 'I'll pass, thanks. Why don't you ask your son?'

'Him?' Otto snorted. 'He's too much like you. Too high-minded and honourable to get his hands dirty in the real world. Father always did want us to become nobles. Looks like he succeeded, at least with you, and his grandson. Well, I wouldn't want to compromise your ideals, m'lord.'

Felix gripped the arms of the chair. The veins pulsed in his neck. He was no noble. He had nothing but contempt for the nobility. He opened his mouth, then closed it again. If he didn't stop he would say something he regretted, and there was that tidy sum from the sale of his books to consider. He eased back in the chair, forcing himself to relax. Twenty years gone, and he and his brother still couldn't carry on a polite conversation for more than five minutes.

'These books of mine,' he said at last. 'Can I see them?'

'Certainly,' said Otto. 'I think we still have a few copies lying around somewhere.' He lifted a delicate silver bell on the table and shook it.

* * *

LUNCH WAS VAST, and would have been a grim affair, had it been just the brothers at table, for despite his attempts to be civil, Felix had found himself boiling at his brother's every other word. He was such a pompous ass, so ignorant and incurious of the true state of the world, so sure that life was ordered for his pleasure and that he deserved every luxury he had.

Fortunately, they had been joined by Annabella, Otto's Bretonnian wife – as plump and silver as Otto these days, though still a handsome woman – and she had kept up a constant stream of questions about Felix and his adventures, giggling and gasping at all the appropriate moments. This sweet and flattering babble had done a marvellous job of hiding that he and Otto hardly spoke to each other once during the meal.

The only awkward moment had come when, overwhelmed with the spirit of hospitality, Annabella had asked Felix if he wanted to stay with them while he was in Nuln. Otto's head had snapped up at that, and he had glared across the table.

He needn't have worried. Felix felt the same. If this was how he and his brother got along after only a few hours together, a few days under the same roof and they would be at each others' throats. He politely declined Annabella's offer, saying that he and Gotrek were very comfortably lodged in an inn and wouldn't think of imposing.

At the front door after the meal, as Felix collected his sword and cloak from the butler and tried to find room in his pack for the leather-bound books with his name on them, Otto coughed.

'You might want to stop home in Altdorf on your way north,' he said. 'The old man is on his last legs.'

FELIX'S HEAD SWAM as he walked through the Kaufman district towards the High Gate. He had received too much news too fast. Apparently a lot could change in twenty years. Otto had a son who was attending university. Felix's poetry was old-fashioned. His adventures had been made into books. His father was dying.

The tall, gabled townhouses and walled and guarded estates of wealthy merchants passed unnoticed as he wound through the cobbled streets. The sniffs of prosperous burghers and their plump wives as they stared at his shabby clothes went unchallenged. Otto had a son. His father was dying.

His father was dying.

Felix was surprised that news was affecting him so much. He was surprised, actually, that his father was still alive. How old must he be? Seventy? Eighty? Just like the grasping old miser to wring every year he possibly could out of life, just to make sure he got his money's worth.

If there was one person in the world that Felix got on with less well even than his brother, it was his father. The old man had disowned him when he had decided to become a poet instead of joining the family business. He had said Felix was wasting the education he had paid for. Funny really, when it was that education that had opened Felix's eyes to the beauty and variety of life and introduced him to the worlds of literature, philosophy and poetry. Gustav Jaeger had wanted his sons to have all that knowledge, had wanted them to be able to spout it on command, but only because such learning was one of the qualities of refinement that marked a man as noble, and Gustav had desperately wanted his sons to be the first noble Jaegers. As tight-fisted as he was, the old man had poured gold into the coffers of the high and mighty of Altdorf like it was water, trying to buy a title to pass onto his sons – apparently to no avail.

Felix had hated his father for his crassness, his narrow-minded pragmatism that left no room for art or beauty or romance. Gustav Jaeger had sacrificed his childhood to claw his way out of the gutter, becoming one of the richest merchants in the Empire. And, having reached that eminence, he had seemed determined that his sons would sacrifice their childhoods as well. He had made no allowances for youthful follies or indiscretions. Perhaps that was one of the reasons Felix had extended what should have been a passing fancy into a lifelong sidetrack.

Felix sidestepped a rushing carriage and passed under the iron portcullis of the High Gate without looking up. Should he go see him? Should he try to make amends? Should he spit in his face? Should he flaunt the books that had been made of his life? That would show him! Or would it? The thought of seeing the old buzzard, even sick in his deathbed, was daunting. He'd never been able to look him in the eye. Even full of youthful confidence after the publishing of his first book of poems and being the toast of Altdorf University, Gustav had been able to make him feel like he was seven years old and had just wet the bed.

The deep bark of a cannon firing woke Felix out of his reverie. He looked up, wary. Had something happened? Was Nuln under attack? No one else seemed to have noticed. They continued on with their errands as if nothing had happened. Hadn't they heard? Had he imagined it?

Then he remembered. This was Nuln, forge of the Empire. The Imperial Gunnery School test fired new cannons several times a day.

When he had lived here before, he had become so used to it that he too had never looked up from his daily round when they sounded.

He looked around him, seeing for the first time the streets he passed through. Nuln, outside the wall that separated the old city from the new, was a noisy, busy place. The war may have impoverished much of the rest of the Empire, but Nuln made cannons, guns and swords. It thrived in war. Everywhere he looked there was bustle and industry. Wagons hauled heavy loads of coal or saltpetre or finished guns through the maze of streets and tall, soot-blackened brick and timber houses. Grimy workers trudged wearily home from their shifts in the manufactories of the Industrielplatz. Fat merchants trundled by in palanquins, their bodyguards jogging in front and behind.

Sausage and pie sellers shouted their wares from carts fitted with sizzling grills, and the smell of cooking meat mixed with sewer stench and the acrid reek of smoke and black powder to create what was, in Felix's mind, the signature smell of Nuln.

But though Nuln's men of industry were doing well, the same could not be said for the lower classes. Those sizzling pies and sausages were selling for triple what they should have been, and looked to have been made of sweepings from the slaughterhouse floor. The stalls of the fruit sellers and costermongers that fringed the market squares were mostly bare, and the prices for the meagre produce on display were shocking. The press gangs of the state militias were out in force, and there were few able-bodied young men on the street.

On the other hand, there were more beggars than Felix could remember ever seeing in Nuln. They thronged the streets, and lifted their palms in every doorway. He saw whole families camped in alleys and courtyards.

Patrols of the city guard, uniformed in Nuln's colours of charcoal and yellow, sauntered through the shuffling crowd, eyes moving and truncheons swinging. Jugglers and singers jostled elbows with broadsheet sellers, doomsayers and demagogues on the street corners. Sisters of Shallya asked for alms for the upkeep of their hospitals and temples.

'The end times are upon us!' cried a wild-eyed Sigmarite ascetic who carried a hammer fashioned out of wood that was the size of an anvil. 'The wolves of ruin swarm down from the steppes to devour us all! Beg almighty Sigmar for forgiveness before it is too late!'

'We must send the children north!' wailed another, who wore nothing but a loincloth. 'Their purity and innocence is the shield that will turn the sword of Chaos! They are our hope and salvation!'

A group called the Ploughmen called for the shutting down of the foundries. 'We must turn our swords into ploughshares. We must make peace with our neighbours to the north.' They weren't getting much of a crowd.

Another group, The Silver Chalice, was calling for the closing of the Colleges of Magic and the death of all magicians in the Empire. 'The corruption comes from within!'

A young man in a mask that was a bright yellow headscarf with eye holes cut in it held aloft a lit torch while a similarly masked compatriot passed out cheaply printed leaflets. They wore tabards over their jerkins, emblazoned with a crude symbol of a flaming torch. 'The cleansing flame will burn away the corruption that chokes Nuln like the smoke from the foundries!' declaimed the youth. 'No more will the fat priests shear their flocks! No more will the forge owners and factors underpay the brave men who pour the iron that makes them rich! No more will the landlords raise rents on hovels not fit for dogs to live in! Raise the torch, brothers! Join the Brotherhood of the Cleansing Flame and burn them out! Burn the city clean!'

As Felix watched, the masked men caught sight of the watch patrol pushing towards them and they quickly gathered up their leaflets and disappeared into an alley.

Felix continued on. As he got closer to the river and the area known as Shantytown, the buildings became flimsier and taller, and the streets – neatly cobbled within the old city and around the universities – were here unpaved swamps of mud and filth. Felix noticed the symbols of the various agitator groups scrawled more often on the walls of buildings the further he went – the wedge-shaped plough of the Ploughmen, the chalice of the Silver Chalice, the flaming torch of the Cleansing Flame. That last symbol made him shiver, for he remembered the fire that had burned this neighbourhood to the ground during the attack of the ratmen, all those years ago. He found it hard to believe that any organisation advocating flame as a tool of change would gain followers here, but one never knew. People had short memories.

At last, in the very heart of Shantytown, he came to a rundown and ramshackle tavern. The weathered sign over the door was painted with a picture of a pig with a blindfold tied around its head. A few rough mercenaries lounged on benches outside the narrow door, sipping ale and basking in the late summer sun. A pair of towering bouncers nodded to him as he approached.

Felix ducked through the low door and looked around the tavern's dim interior. Gotrek sat at the bar, his squat, massive form perched on a high barstool, his towering crest of red hair aflame in a solitary shaft of sunlight. He hunched forward, massive, muscular arms resting on the bar top, as Old Heinz, the owner of the Blind Pig and an old comrade from Gotrek's mercenary days, filled two tankards from a keg of ale. He handed one to Gotrek and they raised them solemnly.

'To Hamnir,' said Heinz.

'To Hamnir,' agreed Gotrek.

They drank deep, draining the tankards.

Heinz wiped his mouth with the back of a meaty hand. 'But he died well at least?' he asked.

Gotrek frowned and coughed into his mug.

'Aye,' said Felix, stepping forward and taking a seat beside the Slayer. 'He died well.'

'Good,' said Heinz, and turned to draw them all another pint.

Gotrek gave Felix a look that was almost gratitude. The Slayer didn't like to lie, but telling Heinz the truth obviously wasn't appealing either. Hamnir had not died well. He had died betraying his race, and it had been Gotrek that had killed him. This wasn't the first time Felix had saved him from telling this uncomfortable truth. He hoped it was the last.

Gotrek stuck a thick finger under his eyepatch and rubbed his empty socket. 'Heinz says the war will be won or lost at Middenheim. We leave tomorrow at dawn.'

'Right.' Felix sighed. So much for a few days with a roof over their heads. But he wasn't surprised. Gotrek had been like a hunting dog that had scented a fox ever since they had learned at Barak Varr that the hordes of Chaos had once again come down from the wastes to threaten the lands of men. Nothing was going to stop the Slayer from getting north to challenge another daemon.

'Remember the time Hamnir tried to save the entire library of Count Moragio while the orcs were breaking down the doors?' said Heinz as he set tankards in front of Gotrek and Felix. 'Never seen a dwarf so worried about a bunch of books. Mad, he was.'

'Aye,' grunted Gotrek. 'Mad.' He snatched his ale off the bar and stumped angrily off to sit in a dark corner.

Heinz peered quizzically after him with rheumy eyes. The old mercenary was still a big man, but old age had stooped his shoulders, and the bulk that had once been muscle now sagged off his bones. 'What's got into him?'

'Old wounds,' said Felix.

'Aye,' said Heinz, nodding sagely. 'I know the kind.'

'DID YOU SEE the burning today?' asked the harlot.

'What did you say?' shouted Felix.

It was later that same night. The Blind Pig was crowded now, and filled with noise and smoke and the reek of close packed bodies. Boisterous students from the universities and colleges yelled boasts and challenges at each other. Mercenaries and soldiers hunched around tables, telling tall tales at the top of their lungs. Apprentices and smoke-blackened iron workers from the forges across the river bantered with giggling harlots and barmaids eager to strip them of their pay. Slumming nobles' sons kept their backs to the wall and laughed too loudly as they tried to soak up the atmosphere without getting their clothes dirty. Tilean traders talked business with dwarf craftsmen in one corner. A halfling oversaw a dice game in another.

'The burning. Did you see it?' asked the girl, a chubby thing with her hair in red ringlets and rouge caking her round cheeks. 'One of the guards at the Gunnery School. The witch hunters found out he had a mouth under his left arm and burned him on Tower Isle this afternoon.'

'You don't say,' said Felix, disinterestedly.

The girl had squeezed in beside him at the bar hours ago, thinking him an easy mark, and he had fed her wine just to have something to do. Truth to tell, he would much rather have been upstairs in the room Heinz had given him, reading the books his brother had made from his journals, but Gotrek had sunk into one of his blacker moods and Felix had decided that it would be a good idea to stay nearby and keep an eye on him. The Slayer hadn't moved since he had walked away from Heinz, only drunk tankard after tankard of ale and stared all night at nothing with his single angry eye.

He had been this way since he had killed Hamnir deep below the mines of Karak Hirn, grimmer and angrier than Felix had ever known him. Gotrek never spoke of his feelings, so Felix didn't know what was going through his head, but seeing someone who had once been one's best friend succumb to the lure of Chaos and then killing him for it would be enough to make even the most cheerful soul bitter, and Gotrek hadn't exactly been a ray of sunshine to begin with.

'He screamed almost like a human when he burned,' said the girl.

'Who did?' asked Felix.

'The mutant. It made me shiver.'

'Very empathetic of you, I'm sure,' said Felix.

'What does emfetic mean?' asked the harlot. 'Is it something dirty?'

Felix didn't answer. He had heard someone say the word 'Slayer', and turned his head to find the speaker.

A group of drunk students, still in the long sleeveless robes they wore to lectures, were staring openly at Gotrek.

A chinless one with thin blond hair was frowning. 'A Slayer?'

A dark-haired one with a haughty sneer nodded. 'Aye. I've read of them. They are dwarfs who have vowed to expunge some great shame by dying in combat with a terrible monster. There are trollslayers, dragonslayers, what-have-you slayers.'

Chinless guffawed. 'This one looks like a flagonslayer!' he said loudly. 'He's had his nose in that mug since we got here.'

The others burst out laughing at this witticism. Felix cringed and looked at Gotrek. Fortunately, it seemed the Slayer hadn't heard. Now if only the fools would pass on to another target all would be well.

It was not to be. The others liked Chinless's joke so much they felt the need to repeat it, louder.

'Flagonslayer! That's rich!'

'How about aleslayer?'

'Aye! Aleslayer, bane of the taproom!'

'Hoy, Aleshlayer!' called one with jug ears, his words slurring with drink. 'Shlay another flagon for ush! Show ush yer might!'

'Come now, fellows,' said Felix. He pried himself from the harlot and stepped forward, but it was too late. Gotrek had raised his head and fixed the students with a blank, baleful stare.

Most of them paused at that, suddenly aware that the bear they were poking wasn't dead after all. But Jug Ears was apparently dimmer, and drunker, than the rest. He giggled and pointed.

'Well at leash he'll never get crosh-eyed drunk. He only hash one eye!' He raised his glass in mock salute. 'Hail flagonshlayer! Mighty cyclopean drainer of kegsh!'

Gotrek stood, tankard in one hand, knocking the heavy oak table he sat at to the floor. 'What did you call me?'

Felix stepped between them. 'Easy, Gotrek. They're very drunk and very young. We don't want any trouble.'

'Speak for yourself, manling,' said Gotrek, pushing him gently but inexorably out of the way. 'Trouble is exactly what I want.'

The other students backed away uneasily as Gotrek stumped forward, but Jug Ears stood where he was, grinning foolishly. 'I dub thee Flagonshlayer! Aleshlayer! Pintshlayer!' He laughed. 'Thas' it! The pint-shized pintshlay–'

Gotrek's fist connected with Jug Ears's jaw with a crack like a gravestone snapping in two. The boy flew through the air and crashed into a table full of burly Hochland handgunners, knocking their drinks to the floor and soaking them all in ale. Felix's harlot squealed and ran, disappearing into the crowd.

The leader of the handgunners, a black-bearded giant of a man with leather bracers on both wrists, lifted the unconscious Jug Ears off the table by his shirtfront as the other students rabbited for the door. 'Who threw this toff?' he growled. His eyebrows dripped with ale.

'I did,' said Gotrek. He grabbed an entirely blameless smith's apprentice by the front of his leather apron. 'You want another?'

'I want these drinks paid for, is what I want,' said the giant. 'And a cleaning for my best uniform.'

'I'll clean the floor with it,' said Gotrek and, still holding his tankard in his left hand, hurled the apprentice with his right with less effort than Felix would have flung a sack of onions.

The apprentice hit the mercenary high in the chest, knocking him backward through the table and sending his Hochlanders diving in all directions. They leapt to their feet, roaring, and charged at the Slayer, fists and brass knuckles raised high. Gotrek ran to meet them, his drink held protectively behind him, bellowing incoherent insults.

Within seconds the whole tavern was fighting, violence splashing outward from Gotrek and the handgunners like ripples in a pond as elbows were bumped, drinks spilled, then insults and blows exchanged. The dwarfs and Tileans fought a gang of weaver's apprentices. Barmaids and harlots shrieked and dived for cover. A dozen dock workers scrapped with three nobles and their six body-guards. Students of the university brawled with students of the School of Engineering. A company of Bretonnian crossbowmen seemed to be fighting each other. The halfling gambler rode the shoulders of a red-bearded Talabecman, banging on his skull with a pewter dice cup. Everywhere mugs flew, bottles smashed and fur-niture splintered. Old Heinz beat on the bar with an axe handle – roaring ineffectively for order while his bouncers grabbed the col-lars of anyone they could get their hands on and chucked them out of the front door.

Felix fought back to back with Gotrek in a ring of Hochlanders, cursing all the while. Another stupid bar fight over nothing. And Gotrek had started it. He should let him fight his own battles. This was the last thing he wanted to be doing. And yet, in the state Gotrek was in, one of these villains just might get in a lucky shot, and getting trounced in a tavern would do nothing for the Slayer's mood.

He ducked a blackjack and rabbit-punched the mercenary who swung it in the kidneys. The man groaned and doubled up. Felix kneed him in the face. Gotrek back-fisted the captain, sending a spray of yellow teeth flying. The giant's knees buckled and he fell forward. Gotrek jumped back, holding his tankard out of the way. Another mercenary grabbed him around the neck, trying to strangle him. Gotrek reached up and caught him by the top knot and flung him over his shoulder into three others. They went down in a heap.

Four more leapt for the dwarf. Felix tripped one and shoulder blocked another. Gotrek kicked and elbowed the others to the ground.

The captain was up again, a long wooden bench raised over his head for a smashing blow. Gotrek lurched forward and punched up, driving his fist between the man's legs. The captain squeaked like a rat-man and tottered back, eyes wide.

All around the bar the fight was slowing down, the combatants too battered or too drunk to continue.

Heinz's hoarse bellow rose above the moans and groans. 'Who started this? Who smashed up my tap-room?'

The giant mercenary toppled backwards and crashed to the floor like a felled tree, revealing Gotrek, swaying in the centre of a pile of unconscious bodies, still holding his tankard of ale. He hadn't spilled a drop.

Heinz's brow lowered. 'Gurnisson. Did you start this?'

Gotrek drained his drink in one swallow, then smashed the tankard on the floor. 'And what if I did?' he asked.

'And you were bouncers here once.' Heinz shook his head, disgusted. 'Get out.'

Gotrek stumped towards him menacingly. 'And who's going to make me?'

The bouncers started moving in.

Felix stepped beside Gotrek and leaned down to speak in his ear. 'You don't want to fight old Heinz, do you? Your old companion? Your blood brother?'

Gotrek shrugged him off. 'Who says I don't?'

'*You* will, tomorrow morning,' said Felix. 'Come on. If you want to fight, let's go find a tavern where you don't know the owner. There's nobody left here worth fighting anyway.'

The Slayer stopped unsteadily and squinted around the room, taking in the crowd of groaning drunks and battered bouncers. He sneered. 'You're right, manling. Nothing here but a bunch of cowards. Let's find another place.' He turned and aimed himself at the door, then started forward, rolling like a sailor.

As he reached the door, Heinz called after him. 'It was a quiet twenty years, Gurnisson. Don't come back for another twenty.'

AFTER A QUARTER of an hour of meandering through the cramped, overhung streets of Shantytown – deserted at this late hour – with Gotrek muttering and cursing under his breath and changing his mind about which way they were going every few minutes, the Slayer stopped in a small square with a fountain in the centre. The fountain had once been grand – Magnus the Pious holding aloft the hammer of Sigmar with griffins at his feet spouting water into a circular pool. Now the pool was dry, the griffins' beaks cracked, revealing their copper pipes, and Magnus's hammer missing its head and most of its haft. The forms of sleeping beggars and vagrants clung to the walls of the surrounding buildings like dirty shadows.

Gotrek swayed for a long moment in the middle of the square, as if lost in thought, then stepped to the fountain and plopped down on the rim of the pool.

Felix joined him. He was feeling a bit worse for wear and it was a relief to sit. There hadn't been many opportunities for drinking on the road from Karak Hirn, and all the unaccustomed alcohol had gone to his head somewhat.

Gotrek lay back and looked up at the sky, still muttering to himself.

Felix frowned down at him. 'If you want to sleep, we should find an inn.'

'We'll find an inn, manling,' said Gotrek, with every indication of lucidity. 'I'm just thinking.'

'Fine,' said Felix. After a moment he found himself lying back too. The wind was picking up and it was getting too cool for comfort, but lying there was very peaceful. Mannslieb was full and bright, casting a delicate silver glamour over rooftops that by day would have looked shabby and poorly patched. Stars shimmered in the sky like fireflies pinned to black velvet. Felix picked out the constellations. The Hammer, the Wolf, the Dove. His eyes closed, and after a long moment opened again. Then closed again. His breathing grew heavier.

He fought to open his eyes again. 'We really should find some place–' He stopped, blinking up at the sky. A huge black shadow was pushing across his vision, blotting out the stars. Now it was eclipsing Mannslieb! He gaped, frozen with dread and confusion.

What was it? Was he dreaming? Was it some strange swift storm? Was it a daemon come to devour them all? Was it...

Gotrek sat bolt upright beside him, staring straight up. 'It's the *Spirit of Grungni*!'

CHAPTER TWO

GOTREK AND FELIX caromed through the twisting, uncooperative streets of Shantytown like lunatics, trying to keep the receding airship in sight. It was heading due east, and all the streets seemed to head every direction but. They were constantly having to zigzag and double back as the black oblong shape disappeared behind tall, gabled tenements and massive crenellated warehouses, only to appear again as they turned a corner and found it drifting away from them above the moon-washed rooftops.

Harlots and other late-night walkers shied away as Gotrek and Felix staggered drunkenly past, shouting commands and obscenities at the sky. An undermanned watch patrol almost moved to block them, then thought better of it and let them pass. Cats and dogs and rats scurried into the shadows at their approach.

The *Spirit of Grungni* led them out of Shantytown and through the government buildings and trading houses of the Neuestadt towards the Universitat. There the streets became wider and the way easier, and the airship seemed to be slowing. This was good, for Gotrek and Felix were slowing too. Felix was gasping and sucking wind, weakened by too much wine. Gotrek showed no signs of losing his breath, but he was groaning and holding his belly with each step. Felix thought he could actually hear the ale sloshing inside the dwarf, but it was probably his own stomach he heard.

At last, with a roar they could hear from the ground, the airship reversed engines and came to a slow halt over the high grey stone turrets of the massive, castle-like central building of the College of Engineering. Lights on the roof underlit the brass gondola and Felix could just see ropes dropping from it.

Gotrek and Felix fetched up panting and gasping against the College's intricate iron gates a few moments later. Four wary guards stepped out from a guard house just inside, spears at the ready. More watched from the tops of the fortified walls.

'Mak...' said Gotrek. 'Mak...' then vomited a vast quantity of ale all over the wrought iron bars.

'Hoy!' said the guard captain, stepping forward. 'Get away, you filthy drunks! I'm not cleaning that up. Go home and sleep it off!'

Gotrek's hand shot through the bars and caught the captain by the belt, then pulled him down to his level. 'Makaisson,' hissed Gotrek, as the other guards shouted and stepped forward, drawing their weapons. 'Fetch Malakai Makaisson. Tell him Gotrek Gurnisson wants to see him.'

The other guards shouted at Gotrek to let their captain go, but Gotrek wrapped his powerful fingers around the man's neck and he frantically waved them off.

'It's too late,' squeaked the captain. 'College is closed for the night. No visitors. You'll have to come back in the morning.'

Gotrek shook him. 'Fetch him now or I'll come in there and feed you your sword, pommel first.' He shoved him back into his men.

The captain choked and recovered himself as his men started forward again. For a moment it looked like he was going to let them try to chase Gotrek off, then he reconsidered and called them back.

'Leave him, but watch him,' he said, massaging his bruised throat. 'Brugel, go ask Professor Makaisson if he'll see a filthy drunk named Gotrek Gurnisson.'

AFTER WHAT SEEMED like several hours to Felix's foggy brain, he and Gotrek looked up at the sound of approaching footsteps. Out of the shadow of the entry of the college's massive central building came a small squad of guards escorting a short, broad figure in a thick, fleece-lined leather jerkin. He wore a peculiar leather cap with goggles pushed up over his shaggy brows, and a slot at the top to make room for a short crest of bright red hair. It looked like he had just come off the airship.

'Whur's the liar claimin' tae be Gotrek son of Gurni?' spat the dwarf in his strange, thick accent. 'Whur's the eejit dinnae know the Daemonslayer's been deid these seventeen–'

He broke off in mid-sentence as he caught sight of Gotrek stand-ing at the gate. He stopped and stared. 'Weel noo, ye look like him, right enough.' He shot a glance at Felix. 'And this looks like young Felix an' aw.' He crossed his arms over his massive chest. 'But Max-imillian Schrieber said ye went intae some hell-gate in Sylvania and never returned. How am ah tae be sure ye ain't some daemons of the void in disguise?'

Gotrek roared and plucked his axe from his back. He slashed left and right, making a big X in the air with it, then held it at the ready and stumped towards the gate, shoulders lowered. 'Are you calling me a daemon, Malakai son of Makai?'

The guards shouted and advanced, lowering their spears. The cap-tain drew a pistol from his belt and aimed it through the bars, but Malakai just grinned and waved them back. 'Put it awa', boys. Put it awa' and open yon gates. There's but the one who can wield yon axe!'

The guards hesitated, but at last their captain motioned them for-ward and they drew the bolts and pushed on the bars.

Malakai threw his arms wide as the gates swung out and Gotrek and Felix stepped in. 'Gotrek Gurnisson, I'm grieved tae see ye hiv-nae met yer doom, but ah'm glad tae see ye no' the less.'

He clasped Gotrek's hand and slapped him on the shoulder.

'Well met, Malakai Makaisson,' said Gotrek gruffly. 'I hope you have some ale here. I lost some just now and I've got a bit of a thirst.'

'Why am ah here?' Malakai shrugged as he lit an oil lamp and set it on a low desk. 'Ach weel, wae one thing an' another, I'm no' wel-come in the dwarf holds at the minute, so here ah came an' offered ma services. Made me a professor, if ye can believe it.'

Gotrek and Felix sat on an unmade day bed in the middle of a vast, high ceilinged workshop that was apparently Malakai's office, located on the third floor of the college's main building. It was chilly in the room, for it had no roof and the east wall was only half-built. Scaffolding rose before the unfinished wall, and building stones and sacks of mortar were stacked at its foot. Night air and moonlight poured in through it, while high over-head, a canvas tarpaulin snapped in the breeze like the sail of a ship.

In the moonglow beyond the yellow light of the lamp, Felix could make out the looming shapes of partially assembled machines, strange weapons, odd bits of pipe, scrap metal and glass tubing, short-legged tables covered with scribbled-upon sheets of vellum, and what looked like an enormous metal horse. Felix thought he recognised one of the machines as a drill of some sort, and another as a lathe, but the rest were far beyond his understanding.

Malakai pottered about among it all like a gardener seeing to his prize roses, straightening and checking and adjusting things all around the room, and chattering all the while.

'Ah'm sorry for the state o' the place, but ah heard the skaven made a wee mess o' things here at the college some twenty years past and they hiv niver got around to fixing it up again.'

'Er, yes,' said Felix, face flushing. 'We'd heard about that.' *And had a hand in the destruction,* he thought guiltily. He didn't say anything, however. The whole incident was a bit embarrassing.

'That'll change noo ah'm here,' Malakai continued. 'Have this place straight in a jiffy. And better than it was afore.'

'So Max Schrieber survived Sylvania,' said Gotrek, sipping the mug of ale Malakai had found for him. 'And Snorri Nosebiter?'

'Oh aye,' said Malakai. 'They both of them made it back to Praag, ready t'fight the hordes come spring, just as ah wis. But it niver happened. The marauders milled outside the city for a few mair weeks, then just turned aroon an' went back hame. Seemed tae've lost all heart, somehow.' He sounded sad at the memory. 'Max thought it might hae somethin' tae do with the vanishin' of them tae wee sorcerers, but nobody ever really learn't the why of it.'

'Are Max and Snorri still alive?' asked Felix.

'Max is – weel when ah saw him four days ago he wus. He's at Middenheim, wi' the defenders, where ah've just come frae.' His brow creased. 'As tae Snorri, ah dinnae noo for certain. After the spring thaw came tae Kislev that year, he went aff wi' some Empire mercenaries, chasin' a herd o' beastmen south towards the Middle Mountains. No' heard o' him since. Grimnir grant that he met his doom.' He looked pensive for a moment, then shrugged and grinned. 'But enough about aw that. Whur hae ye been these seventeen years? I'll wager that's a tale worth the telling.'

'Well,' said Felix, frowning. 'I'm not sure where to begin.' He looked over at Gotrek and saw that the Slayer was lying back on the day bed, his one eye closed, snoring gently.

Malakai looked over and clicked his tongue. 'Och, the laddie's fallen asleep. Ach weel, no' a bad idea at that. Save yer story, young Felix. It'll keep. Come on. Ah'll find ye a bed.'

FELIX WOKE WITH the familiar feeling of opening his eyes in an unfamiliar place that he had experienced so many times in his travels with Gotrek. He was in a small, clean, cell-like room, lying on a narrow but comfortable bed. His head pounded and, strangely, the pounding seemed to echo through the waking world. For a long, disorienting moment he had no idea where he was. The place was too nice to be a jail. He tried to think back. There had been a tavern, and a fight, and then a drunken walk. He had laid down beneath a fountain. Had he fallen asleep there? No! The *Spirit of Grungni*!

Suddenly it all flooded back. He was in the dormitory of the College of Engineering. The pounding in his head was from last night's drinking. The pounding that shook the room was the morning artillery practice at the Imperial Gunnery School, a few streets away. Felix sat up and rubbed his temples, groaning. Did they have to start so early? It was hardly civilized.

After pulling on his boots and breeches and finding the wash room and water closet, he asked directions of a fresh-faced and much too chipper engineering student, then shuffled at last back into Malakai's enormous workroom. Felix squinted painfully in the blaze of sunlight that streamed through the unfinished wall, and looked around. A work table had been cleared off and Malakai and Gotrek were wolfing down a breakfast of eggs, sausage, bacon, black bread, ham, griddle cakes, pale lager, and that vile Tilean import that some called the black oil of Nuln, coffee.

Gotrek's appetite seemed none the worse for last night's excesses, but Felix's stomach churned at the sight of all the greasy food.

'Welcome, young Felix!' called Malakai, much too loud. 'Sit doon and dig in before Gurnisson eats the lot.'

Felix fought down the urge to heave. He wiped his clammy brow. 'Is… is there some tea, perhaps?'

'Ah'll have one of the lads brew up a pot,' said Malakai, then shouted towards the back of the room. 'Petr! A pot of Cathay fur oor guest!'

Felix clutched his head, certain it was going to shatter.

A moonfaced youth with wild blond hair and a chinstrap beard poked his head up from the innards of a dismantled steam tank. He had wide, watery blue eyes that he blinked rapidly. 'Aye, professor,' he said. 'Right away.' He clambered out of the tank, but caught his foot on a valve and sprawled face-first on the floor. He was up in an instant, blood leaking from his nose. 'No harm done,' he piped. 'No harm done.' He scurried out of the room, bumping into a telescope as he went.

Malakai shook his head. 'Poor wee lad. My best student. Can set the calibrations on a pressure gauge near as weel as a dwarf, but cannae see past his haund, and he could trip o'er a dust mote.' He chuckled as he stuffed a chunk of ham in his mouth. 'He'll be coming to Middenheim to help oot in the engine room. But he's noo allowed on the bridge. He'd wreck us.'

Gotrek looked up, his single eye bright. 'You're flying to Middenheim?'

'Aye. The Imperial Gunnery School has asked me tae tak a shipment of cannon there.'

'You're taking me,' said Gotrek. 'I want to be there before the end.'

'O' course,' said Malakai. 'Always happy tae help a Slayer find his doom.'

'Can we leave today?' asked Gotrek.

Malakai chuckled. 'Much as ah'd like it, laddie, nae. The last cannon won't be test-fired till tomorrow morning. We'll leave jist as soon as it's loaded.'

Gotrek grunted unhappily, but Felix hid a grateful smile. Another night in a proper bed would not go amiss.

'Ye'll still get there mair than a fortnight quicker than if ye marched,' said Malakai, amused.

Petr rushed into the room with a teapot in one hand and a cup and saucer in the other. He wove successfully around a jewellers stove, but his feet got tangled in a block and tackle and he flew forward with a cry. He managed to twist as he fell and landed on his shoulder, saving the teapot and cup from destruction, but slopping scalding tea all over his hands.

He sprang up again and set the teapot and cup before Felix, wincing. 'Sorry! Sorry!' he said. His hands were lobster red.

'Go soak those in cold water, laddie,' said Malakai. 'Ye dinnae want blisters.'

'Aye, professor,' said Petr.

He hurried away. Felix couldn't bear to watch him go.

'Cack-handed pillock,' muttered Malakai. He turned to Gotrek and Felix with a sigh. 'When ye've finished wi' yer breakfast, ah'll take you o'er to the Gunnery School tae meet Lord Groot, who runs the place. As the trip is Imperial business, he has final approval on all ma crew. But dinna worry.' He winked. 'Ah'll put in a good word for ye.'

IF THE COLLEGE of Engineering was big, the Imperial Gunnery School was enormous, a vast complex of workshops, firing ranges, forges, and dormitories surrounding the soaring black granite majesty of the school building itself, which rose above the city like an unimaginably large engine of war, all spires and spikes and sawtoothed crenellations. Fearsome soot-blackened gargoyles jutted from every corner and cornice. Tall, narrow, red-glassed windows gleamed between towering buttresses like the vents in the iron door of some infernal furnace.

Lord Julianus Groot did not look like he should be in charge of such a forbidding place. A thick, cheerful, pot-bellied man with greying mutton chops and a few wisps of hair trailing across his round, bald head, Groot looked more like a village smith than the High Chancellor of the Imperial Gunnery School, which was his official title. He wore a singed leather apron over his black brocade robes of office, and had his trailing sleeves tucked into heavy leather gloves.

'Any friend of Malakai Makaisson's is a friend of mine,' he said, crushing Felix's hand in a powerful grip. 'A better ally the Empire could not have.'

Felix and Gotrek stood with Lord Groot and Malakai in a sweltering forge room where ranks of sweating smiths pounded and shaped steel on regimented rows of anvils as overseers moved among them, observing and criticising. It did nothing for Felix's headache.

Felix was surprised to hear the chancellor speaking with the flat, common accent of the Handelbezirk – the mercantile neighbourhood that was the heart of Nuln's ever-spreading network of trade. He would have expected a man with a title to speak in the more refined and cultured speech of the nobility. Perhaps Groot had bought his way into his title. Rumour had it that the Countess had done stranger things for money.

'It'll be good to have seasoned warriors escorting our guns,' he said, gripping Gotrek's hand. 'When you're up against the Ruinous Powers even a flying ship isn't safe. Some of them beasties have wings. You'll have some sorcerous help too, Makaisson.'

'Oh?' said Malakai, squinting suspiciously. 'And jist who might that be?'

Groot turned and called back into the haze of smoke that veiled the room. 'Magus Lichtmann, come meet your travelling companions!'

Gotrek, Felix and Malakai looked up. Felix wasn't sure what he expected. Some malefic figure striding out of the smoke with glowing eyes? A wizened old man in a pointy hat? What he saw was a tall, beardless man of middle age, bent over an anvil, observing intently as a smith shaped a cannon fitting. He glanced up and firelight winked off his spectacles. 'Hmmm? Oh. Terribly sorry, my dear Groot.'

The magus picked his way through the forges to the chancellor. He was thin to the point of being skeletal, with a prominent throat apple, a weak chin, and a beaked nose beneath a mushroom cap of reddish brown hair. He wore the orange and red robes of the Bright College, and like Groot, he protected his attire with a sooty leather apron. His spectacles were made of delicate steel wire, and his eyes, behind them, were green with flecks of gold.

'Terribly sorry,' he said again in a clear, educated voice as he nodded around at them all. 'Julianus and I have been attempting to develop a new alloy, using magical flame to smelt together metals at temperatures impossible to achieve with mundane fire alone. I was just observing how our latest sample behaved under the hammer.' He smiled at Groot. 'Very malleable, Julianus, but not yet as strong as it could be, I believe.'

'I'll have a look in a moment, Waldemar,' said Groot. He turned to the others. 'Professor Makaisson, Slayer Gurnisson, Herr Jaeger, may I present Magus Waldemar Lichtmann, a Magister of the Bright College, and also an engineer of great renown.'

Magus Lichtmann bowed and extended his left hand, and it was only then that Felix noticed that the magus didn't have a right hand. His right sleeve was pinned up just below the elbow. 'A distinct pleasure, professor,' he said, shaking Malakai's hand. 'Your advances in engineering are well known to me.'

He grinned sheepishly as he turned to shake Gotrek's hand and then Felix's. 'Apologies for the left-handed handshake,' he said. 'People often find it a bit unnerving. I lost the right in a fire. Highly embarrassing for a bright wizard, but I was young then, and hadn't yet learned control.'

Malakai raised an uneasy eyebrow. 'I hope ye have noo. Airships are a wee bit flammable.'

The Bright Wizard laughed, a loud, horsy bray. 'Oh yes, I've gotten a bit better since then, thank you. I can keep my flames to myself.'

'Magus Lichtmann is going to Middenheim to help in the fighting,' said Groot.

'I am very much looking forward to it,' said Lichtmann. 'It has been a long time since I have been in battle, and never anything on this scale. But a man of conscience cannot, at a time like this, continue to hide in the halls of academia. He must act. He must do his part for his homeland and his people. And I am hoping to put some of the new ideas that Groot and I have been developing to the test of war.'

'Weel, yer welcome aboard, magister,' said Malakai. 'Ah'll be happy to hiv someone tae blether wae. This alloy sounds interestin'.'

'It certainly is,' said Lichtmann, his eyes brightening. 'It's a simple idea really, but hard to execute without a Bright Wizard's ability to control the temperature of fire. You see...'

As Lichtmann began to explain – and Felix's eyes began to glaze over – a young man in the colours of the college poked his head through the door of the workshop, saw Groot, and hurried to his side, his face tight with tension. 'My lord,' he murmured in the chancellor's ear. 'Might I speak with you?'

Groot nodded and turned to the others. 'Would you excuse me a moment?'

He stepped away and listened as the student whispered urgently in his ear. Felix and Gotrek waited, sweating in the heat, while Magus Lichtmann continued to babble to Malakai about melting temperatures and tensile strength, whatever that was.

After a moment Groot nodded and said, 'Aye, that's bad,' then rattled off a rapid series of orders and sent the youth running back the way he had come.

The chancellor sighed and returned to his guests. 'Sorry about the interruption. There's been a theft. I'm afraid your flight might be delayed, Malakai.'

'What?' barked Gotrek. His single eye blazed.

'Whit happened?' asked the engineer.

'A barge full of gunpowder was stolen during the night,' said Groot. 'Gunpowder meant for the cannons you will be carrying. The Dwarf Black Powder Guild delivered it yesterday to our landing near Glory Bridge in preparation for loading it onto the *Spirit of Grungni* tomorrow. It was under heavy guard all night, but by morning the guards had vanished along with the barge and the powder.' He shrugged and scratched his bald head violently. 'Wish they'd told me sooner, but they wasted two hours running about seeing if someone from the City Council had ordered the barge moved.'

'You can't leave without the powder?' asked Felix.

'The cannon are useless wi' no powder tae fire them, lad,' growled Malakai. 'Wi'out it they're jus' pretty pieces of iron, an' no reason tae take 'em to Middenheim.'

'Sabotage,' said Magus Lichtmann. 'This is vile. Someone has done this to weaken the defences of the Fauschlag.'

'It's worse than that,' said Groot. 'The fiends could have done that by setting fire to the barge and blowing up the powder. Instead they've stolen it. That means that, whoever they are, they plan to use the powder for their own purposes.'

'And I'm guessin' it won' be tae make fireworks,' said Malakai, grimly.

CHAPTER THREE

A STRONG WIND knocked cold spray off the oily waves of the Reik and blew the pungent stinks of the Industrielplatz across the water. Felix wrinkled his nose and fought down nausea. He smelled burning oil, sulphur, tanning hides, rendering fat, dead fish, and other odours he couldn't name and didn't care to learn the source of. Out in the centre of the river where the current was swift, long, flat barges and high-prowed merchantmen manoeuvred to and from the main docks, further west. Gulls screamed overhead, much too loud for a man in his condition.

Lord Groot had asked Malakai and Magus Lichtmann to accompany him to the river to view the site where the theft had occurred, and Gotrek and Felix had tagged along for want of anything better to do. Now they were waiting while Groot and Malakai and Lichtmann and a few other members of the Gunnery School argued with a gaggle of city officials and a representative of the Dwarf Black Powder Guild on the embankment above the stone landing from which the barge had been stolen the night before.

Felix leaned dully on a piling off to one side, still suffering from his hangover, and watched Gotrek prowl restlessly about on the landing below him, looking down into the water and examining the pilings intently.

'I find it very suspicious,' a trim man in the colours of the city watch was saying. 'The barge was tied up here, in the open, and yet there were no witnesses to its theft, and the crew and the guards have not been found.' He sniffed. 'They were Gunnery School guards, yes?'

Lord Groot drew himself up. 'Surely you can't be suggesting that our guards stole the barge.'

'Not at all,' said the man, in a tone that made it clear that he was indeed suggesting that. 'I just find it peculiar, is all.' His name was apparently Adelbert Wissen, the Ward Captain of the Neuestadt, a position that gave him authority over every watch station north of the river and south of the Altestadt wall. He held himself like he thought he had authority over the winds, the tides and the movement of the sun – a handsome, black-haired dandy in an immaculately tailored uniform and polished steel breastplate, with the haughty, damn-your-eyes look of one noble born. Felix was sorely tempted to splash mud on his perfectly polished boots. 'What need for guards if the powder had been unloaded at once? Then the theft would not have occurred.'

'Didn't I just tell you that we are forbidden by edict of the Countess to store so much in the school?' asked Groot, exasperated. 'Would you have me break the law? And why are you wasting time talking to me? Why aren't you looking for the barge? Surely it can't have vanished.'

'I have men looking for it on both sides of the river,' said Wissen. 'The situation is well in hand.'

'What I want to know is, will I have to pay twice for the same powder,' said a pinch-mouthed older man in chocolate velvet and a mink cloak. 'I only agreed to finance these guns once. If there is more outlay now I will have to charge Middenheim more interest.'

'If you think we're going to give you free powder when you've gone and lost what we've just sold you, you've got another thing coming!' barked a stout red-bearded dwarf in green doublet and brown boots. 'Carelessness, I call it.'

'What patriotism, Lord Pfaltz-Kappel,' said Magus Lichtmann, gesturing with his single hand. 'And such a spirit of cooperation, Guildmaster Firgigsson. It is so heartening to see the peoples of the Empire putting aside their petty grievances and coming together to help fight our common enemy in this time of war.'

Neither the noble or the dwarf seemed to note the sarcasm in his voice.

'I've done my part,' said Lord Pfaltz-Kappel. 'You'd have no cannons at all were it not for me. It would be just like the dwarfs to steal the powder back and make us buy it twice. Gold-hungry little misers.'

'Who are you calling miser, you tightfisted old penny pincher?' retorted Firgigsson. 'I marked down my price almost to half because it was going to the aid of Middenheim. Most like you stole it so you could get two barges for the price of one!'

'Why dinna ye leave the name callin' fur later?' said Malakai, dryly. 'Shouldnae ye be decidin' what yer goin' tae dae about findin' the powder and them what stole it?'

'Agitators stole it,' said Ward Captain Wissen. 'And I do not doubt they mean to use it. I have sent to the Countess and the High Constable to ask that men be placed around the granaries and the palace. And judging by events, perhaps some men should be assigned to the Gunnery School as well, since they don't seem able to mount their own defence.'

Felix saw Gotrek's shoulders tense as the argument got louder and louder. Finally he stomped up the stairs and glared at them. 'Shut up!' he bellowed.

The men all turned to him, looks of surprise and outrage on their faces. Malakai grinned.

Ward Captain Wissen put a hand to his polished breastplate. 'You dare speak to a commander of the watch in such a–'

Gotrek cut him off. 'What colour was this barge?'

The men looked at each other, confused.

Guildmaster Firgigsson raised a shaggy eyebrow. 'It was red and blue, Slayer,' he said. 'With a stripe of gold between. Our guild colours, if it's any business of yours.'

'You interrupted us for that?' sneered Lord Pfaltz-Kappel. 'Groot, is this person a guest of yours?'

Gotrek ignored them as their babbling erupted anew and stumped back down the stairs. Felix followed him, curious. The Slayer began looking at the pilings again, muttering 'red gold blue, red gold blue,' over and over.

Felix stared at him, concerned. Was the Slayer still drunk? Had he gone mad at last?

'Ha!' Gotrek raised his head, grinning. 'Red gold blue!' He turned to Felix. 'Look here, manling. The paint from the barge has scraped off onto the pilings.'

Felix leaned out over the water and looked at the river side of the rough wooden posts. They were covered in faint streaks of paint – layer upon layer of red, green, white, black, blue, yellow, grey and brown. 'Uh, I see red, gold and blue. But I see other colours too. How can you…?'

'Humans are blind,' growled Gotrek. He stabbed his blunt fingers at three points on the post. 'Here, here and here. The red, gold and blue are over the other colours, and much fresher.'

Felix shrugged. 'I'll take your word for it. But what good does it do us?'

'Blind and thick-skulled,' Gotrek snorted. He pointed to the white-capped water. 'Look at that chop. I'll wager its been that way since the wind freshened last night. No matter where the thieves tied up the powder barge, it will have left its mark.' He looked west. 'Now all we have to do is check every dock and tie-up down the river until we find red, gold and blue again.'

Felix laughed. 'Is that all? That could take days.'

'It better not,' Gotrek grunted.

'Why don't we tell Ward Captain Wissen,' said Felix. 'It'll take less time if we have the watch looking.'

Gotrek spat into the water. 'Do you think they see any better than you? I want to be away tonight, not a month from now. Besides...' he shot a glare up at Captain Wissen. 'I don't care for that one's manners.'

The Slayer stomped up the stairs and started off down the embankment without a word or gesture to Malakai or Groot, his head down like a bloodhound's. Felix sighed and started after him. Gotrek was one to talk about manners.

FIVE HOURS LATER they were still looking at pilings. Gotrek had examined every inch of the riverside; every landing and tie-up, every side branch and canal, and the underside of every bridge, and they were only just now reaching the official commercial docks that bordered Shantytown. Felix would not have believed there were so many nooks and crannies and hidden backwaters branching from the Reik's stone banks. His back ached from bending over docksides. His eyes hurt. He was hungry and he needed a drink.

'This is impossible. We'll never find it,' he said.

'That's the trouble with humans,' muttered Gotrek. 'They're not thorough. No patience.'

'That's because we don't live for five hundred years.'

The commercial docks stuck out into the river like cracked grey fingers. The weathered wood boomed hollowly under their heels as they paced each one, out and back, checking both sides. Felix didn't see any red, gold and blue paint, but he saw another crudely drawn torch symbol scrawled on a piling. He had seen scores of them during their search, as well as the symbols of the other agitator groups. They were all over the waterfront.

Longshoremen and carters stepped around Gotrek and Felix as they lugged goods from ship to wagon and from wagon to ship. Cargo guards glared at them as if expecting them to steal something or try to stow away. Felix felt foolish and in the way. This was a bad plan. It wouldn't work. The sun was setting behind the looming ranks of brick warehouses that fronted the river. Soon it would be too dark to see. Felix's aching eyes were already having difficulty distinguishing between the faint streaks of paint. That one, for instance. Was it red or orange? And that one, gold or green? And the one below it, blue or black?

'Red, gold and blue!' rasped Gotrek. He got down on one knee and leaned forward, sniffing like a bloodhound. After a moment he ran a stubby finger down a crack between two warped planks. Grains of black stuck to his fingertip. He sniffed them. 'Black powder,' he said. He lifted his head and looked around, taking in the ships, the warehouses, the sawtooth silhouettes of Shantytown tenements rising behind them.

Felix groaned. If the barrels had been offloaded here they could be anywhere by now. And if Gotrek was going to be 'thorough', it could be a very long night.

'You,' said Gotrek, to a passing longshoreman. 'Did you see someone unloading barrels from a red and blue barge here this morning?'

'This morning?' said the man, without breaking stride. 'I was asleep. I start at sunset.'

Gotrek cursed and strode towards the warehouses, glaring speculatively at the men they passed.

Felix followed. 'Let me try,' he said, afraid Gotrek's brusqueness was going to land them in a fight.

He looked around the dockside. There was a tavern here somewhere. He remembered it from his days carousing with the other sewer jacks, when he and Gotrek had last lived in Nuln. Ah, there it was. A placard painted with a laughing bear standing on a red and yellow ball swung in the breeze just a few hundred yards to the east, and as he had expected, half a dozen shifty looking men lounged around outside it, sipping from leather jacks and watching the comings and goings of the docks with eagle eyes.

Felix felt in his belt pouch until he found a gold crown, one of his last, then sidled up to a likely looking villain with a three day beard and a greasy forelock over one eye.

'Evening, brother,' Felix said, twirling the coin in his fingers. 'Were you here this morning?'

The man turned and stared at the rotating coin. 'Could have been.'

'Did you see some men unloading some barrels from a red and blue barge at the dock over there?' He pointed with the hand that held the coin.

Forelock looked at Felix's face for the first time, and his eyes went as blank as buttons. 'I don't see nothing for no jagger.' He turned away and started into the tavern.

Gotrek grabbed the man before he reached the door. He spun him around and slammed him against the wall, holding his axe an inch from his forelock. 'Do you see this axe?'

The man choked, face pale and eyes wide. The other men stood up from their benches, crying out and reaching for daggers. Felix drew his runesword and faced them. The men paused, considering their chances, then shrugged and slouched with feigned nonchalance into the tavern.

'Please don't kill me,' mewled Forelock.

Gotrek jerked his bearded chin towards Felix. 'Answer his question.'

'But... but they'll kill me.'

'I kill you now. They kill you later. Take your pick.'

Forelock swallowed. Sweat ran down his brow. 'I-I-It was Big Nod's boys! Offloaded this morning 'fore dawn, then set the barge adrift down river.'

'Where are they?'

'I can't...' The man hesitated, then his eyes came back to the axe. 'Cold Hole Lane, by the dog pit. Just follow the docks until...'

Gotrek jerked him away from the wall and shoved him forward. 'Take us there!'

'But they'll see me!' pleaded the man.

'They'll see you dead if you don't move.'

Forelock bit his lip, miserable, but then turned and led the way through the twilight gloom. Felix trailed behind Gotrek, unreasonably annoyed that the villain had marked him as coming from wealth. How had he guessed? It had been ages since Felix had been wealthy. His clothes were as ragged as those of any man in Shantytown – worse in fact. Then he understood. His voice. He still spoke like an educated man. He had been so long out of the Empire that he had forgotten how much accent mattered here.

FORELOCK BROUGHT THEM to a cobbled square that abutted the river. The fish market was closing up for the day. Fishwives and whelk sellers dumped their heads and bones and shells in the river and gossiped as they packed up their carts. All along the north edge of the square wide ramps sank down into the ground, angling back under it. At the bottom of each ramp was a high, wide, arched door, open, but covered with soiled leather curtains. Men rolled carts and barrows up and down the ramps. Though he had never been in one before, Felix knew what they were – commercial cold cellars, built with one wall against the river so that it would transfer its constant chill to them. The cellars were used to store ice, ale, fish and other perishables.

Forelock stopped at the west end of the square and pointed, his hand shaking. 'The third one in. That's Nod's. I don't dare go no farther. They'd see me.'

Gotrek looked at him suspiciously, then sneered and pushed him aside. 'Run away, then.'

He started forward. Felix joined him.

'Hoy,' came Forelock's voice from behind them. 'What about that Karl?'

Felix sighed, then flipped the coin over his shoulder.

Gotrek stopped at the top of the third ramp. A sign over the door said Helder's Ice House. It looked no more criminal than the others. Men were lowering a fully laden ale wagon down the ramp using a block and tackle. Others were sliding still struggling sturgeon down a wet canvas chute to men at the bottom who gaffed them with billhooks and flopped them onto a low cart.

A set of shallow stairs went down one side of the ramp. Gotrek and Felix walked down them and pushed through the leather curtains. It was dim inside, and cold. Haloed torches glowed in the moist air and Felix could see his breath. As his eyes grew accustomed to the gloom, he saw that the cellar was one long, cavernous tunnel that ran under the market square above, all the way to the river wall. The tunnel was about thirty feet wide, with a double row of crumbling stone columns forming an aisle down the centre. Crates and barrels were piled to the left and right of the aisle, pushed up against what Felix at first thought were towering stacks of baled hay. Then he saw that the bales were blocks of ice, wrapped in hay to keep them from melting. The entire room was lined, floor to ceiling, with walls of ice. Below the arched ceiling was a lattice of wooden beams and struts. These supported a crane and winch that could be moved the whole length of the tunnel to facilitate the loading and unloading of carts.

A second ale wagon was being unloaded as they entered – huge man-high kegs winched up and swung across, then set down gently on top of others. To the wagon's left, men in winter coats were laying the twitching sturgeon in beds of crushed ice while, deeper in the tunnel, other men climbed all over the piles of crates, shouting and whistling to each other as they placed inventory or cut ice from the great blocks.

Gotrek marched up to a burly bearded man who stood next to the ale wagon, checking a manifest. 'Where's Big Nod?' he growled.

The man looked down at him, sizing him up, then shrugged and turned back to the wagon. 'Never heard of him.'

Gotrek punched him in the stomach, smashing the air of out him in a rush. The man collapsed to his knees, white and wheezing.

Gotrek grabbed him by the beard and yanked his head up. 'Where's Big Nod?'

'Get... get stuffed,' whispered the man.

Gotrek slapped him to the ground.

Felix winced. Violence was all very well if the man was a thief, but what if he really never had heard of Big Nod? What if the weasel with the greasy forelock had lied to them? All over the underground room men were turning to look at them. Some moved between them and the door.

'Hie!' came a piercing voice. 'What's the trouble?'

Felix looked over his shoulder. A ginger-haired halfling with bushy mutton chops stood in the door of an office, hands on his hips. An enormous man with pig eyes and a slack jaw stood behind him, scratching himself idly.

'Where's Big Nod?' said Gotrek.

'Y've got the wrong place,' said the halfling. 'No one here by that name. Now away with ye before I call the watch.'

The workmen edged closer, hefting billhooks and cudgels.

Gotrek strode forward. 'Where's the black powder? Where are you hiding it?'

'Uh-oh, Nod,' said Pig-Eyes, dully. 'They know about the powder.'

The halfling's cheek twitched, and he kicked Pig-Eyes in the shin. 'Shut yer pie hole, ye cloth-headed orc!'

Pig-Eye cringed away. 'Sorry, Nod. Sorry.'

The halfling shot a nod towards the doors. They began to creak closed. 'Right, lads,' he said, drawing an icepick as long as his arm. 'Now that Hollow Head's let the cat out, looks like we'll have to teach a nosy dwarf to mind his own business. Bleed 'em!'

The warehouse men swarmed in, weapons swinging, as the big doors boomed shut. Gotrek and Felix were surrounded. Felix drew his sword and parried a long pole with a cruel hook at the end. A gutting knife stabbed at his stomach. He twisted away. Gotrek picked up the man he had flattened and heaved him at the crowd. Four men went down, but more surged around them, slashing with barrel hooks, daggers and clubs. Brass knuckles glinted on meaty fists. Big Nod screeched encouragement behind them.

Felix blocked a cudgel, but checked his riposte, even though he had an opening. He felt constrained. He had no compunction about wholesale slaughter when it was orcs or bandits in the mountains, or Kurgan or beastmen in the wilds of Kislev, but this was Nuln. This was the Empire. There were laws here, consequences. Even though these villains were trying to rip his entrails out with their hooks and long knives, he didn't feel right murdering them somehow.

Gotrek too did not kill, fighting only with his fists and whatever sticks and poles he could take from their attackers. He dealt terrible damage regardless. Men lay moaning and writhing all around him, eyes blackening and broken noses gushing blood. He snapped the arm of a man twice his height with a flick from a stolen club. Another's knee bent sideways from a savage kick.

'Practicing mercy?' gritted Felix as they fought back to back.

'Mercy? Bah!' said Gotrek. 'These scum are not worthy of my axe.'

A man in an apron roared and charged Gotrek with a barrow loaded with a huge side of beef. The meat caught the Slayer amidships and drove him back, smashing him into the tubs that held the iced sturgeons. He went down and the barrow went with him, tipping on its side. The half-carcass slid across the stone floor on a smear of blood.

A dozen men leapt on the Slayer, flailing with their hooks and cudgels. One dived from the top of the ale wagon.

'Gotrek!' Felix slashed around with his sword, fanning back his attackers as he attempted to reach his companion. Maybe they should have been killing these hoodlums after all.

Gotrek surged up, kicking and punching, a barrel hook buried in the meat of his left arm. The men dodged back, then darted in again, stabbing and swinging. Gotrek reached behind him, pawing for weapons, and found the tails of two sturgeons. He snatched them up and swung them like clubs. Each was longer than Felix's sword and weighed more than a halfling. The Slayer caught one man on the side of the head with a wet smack that knocked him flat. He took another's legs out from under him.

Gotrek grinned savagely. 'Ha! Now we'll see!'

He strode into the mob, the two massive fish whirling around him in a silvery blur. Warehouse men flew left and right, their heads knocked sideways, spit and teeth flying. Felix caught up a cudgel and followed behind him, cracking the heads and hands of those who had managed to dodge the deadly onslaught.

The tide turned. More than half the workmen were down, and the others were hanging back, wary. Gotrek's left fish slapped a man in the stomach. His right clubbed another in the back of the head. Bits of slimy fish flesh flew everywhere.

Felix slashed with his club and blocked with his sword. His attackers danced back, eyes wide. Was he truly that frightening? Why were they looking over his shoulder?

A hard hand shoved him roughly to the floor and something big whooshed by his ear. He looked up in time to see Gotrek knocked flat by an enormous keg of ale that swung at the end of a rope and pulley. The keg caromed on, mowing down a handful of men, then smashed into one of the stone support pillars in an explosion of ale, smashed staves and tumbling stones.

The ale slopped to the ground in a great spreading tide as men staggered to their feet. The halfling screamed a war cry and ran at the unmoving Slayer, ice pick raised. Felix tried to stand, but slipped in the swamp of ale, blood and filth that covered the floor. His sword flew from his fingers as he tried to steady himself. He wasn't going to make it in time.

'Die, ye nosy dirt eater!' cried the halfling, and jabbed down with the pick.

Gotrek's hand shot up and caught Big Nod's wrist. The halfling screamed in the dwarf's iron grip. Gotrek got to his feet as the little villain scrabbled and kicked at him ineffectually. Still holding him by the wrist, Gotrek raised the halfling over his head, then flung him. He splashed down in the lake of ale.

Gotrek waded in after him and sat on his chest. His fingers closed around the halfling's throat. 'Where is the powder?'

'Please, no…' he sputtered.

A mortar-crusted stone as big as a pumpkin bounced into the ale, drenching them both. The halfling looked up. Felix followed his gaze. The pillar that the keg had struck was falling apart. Men were picking themselves up and running from it. As Felix watched, a huge mass of stone and mortar broke free and sloughed to the ground in an avalanche. The network of rafters groaned. Dribbles of dust rained down from the ceiling above.

Gotrek didn't look up. 'Where is the powder?'

Felix backed towards the wall, staring up warily. 'Gotrek, get away…' He paused, frowning. Was there someone in the rafters? He thought he had seen a white-haired, black-clad figure ducking under a cross-beam, but there was so much dust in the air he couldn't be sure.

The rest of the pillar exploded in a shower of dust and stones as the weight of the roof finally became too much. The rafters warped and splintered with the strain. Men ran for the doors and threw them open, trying to escape.

'The powder,' repeated Gotrek, implacably, as stones crashed down all around him.

A hole was opening in the roof.

'Are ye mad?' squealed Big Nod. 'We'll be killed! Let me up!' A stone impacted inches from his head. He shrieked.

Gotrek didn't even flinch. 'Tell me and I'll let you up.'

'But I don't know where it is!'

Gotrek's hand tightened around the halfling's neck. The hole in the ceiling was getting wider as more stones and mortar peeled away and dropped to the floor. Felix could just see stars in a deep blue sky through the clouds of dust. A rock the size of a fist bounced off Gotrek's back. He didn't seem to notice. Another smashed Big Nod's outflung hand.

'Curse ye!' he wailed. 'I sold it! I sold it to them that ordered it stolen! I don't know where they took it!'

Gotrek surged up and dragged the dripping halfling to the wall. A huge chunk of masonry crashed down right where they had been. Nod gulped, eyes bulging.

Gotrek pressed him against the wall and leaned a forearm across his windpipe. 'Who bought it?'

'I don't know.'

Gotrek pressed harder. Nod's workmen pressed past them, too intent on escaping to be concerned about their boss.

'Come on, Gotrek,' said Felix. 'Bring him outside. It's time to go.'

'Not until he talks.'

'I don't know! Truly!' squealed Big Nod. 'They wore scarves and hooded cloaks. I never saw their faces!'

'It's the truth, dwarf,' said the burly, bearded man Gotrek had first spoken to. 'Came to us at night. Never stepped into the light.'

Another huge chunk of stone slammed down to the floor beside them. Felix felt the impact through the soles of his boots. Big Nod wailed.

Gotrek grunted and dragged the halfling towards the doors. Felix hurried after them, relieved. Halfway there, a flash of white drew his eye upward. There *was* someone up there. A black-clad figure was climbing the rafters. Felix barely registered it before it disappeared through the hole in the roof, its white hair flashing in the starlight. Felix frowned. There had been something disturbingly familiar about the figure, something he was sure he should recognise, but the memory stayed tantalisingly out of reach.

As soon as they were outside the leather curtains, Gotrek pinned Big Nod to the wall again.

'What now?' cried the halfling. 'We already told you. We didn't see their faces. Leave me be!'

'I don't believe you,' Gotrek growled. 'Thieves always make sure of their employers.'

Burly shook his head and made the sign of Taal. 'They was dangerous men. Magickers for certain.' He swallowed. 'Said they could kill us in our dreams if we crossed them.'

'And they paid twice what the job was worth,' said Big Nod. He glared back towards his cellar. 'Won't be enough to fix this though, curse ye. Ye've ruined us!'

'You've ruined yourself,' grated Gotrek.

'Were they Nulners?' asked Felix. 'Could you tell that much?'

'They weren't Shantytowners,' said the halfling. 'I know that. Talked posh, like you. Big words.'

That was something at least. Felix was going to ask another question when he heard shouts and the thud of blows from the top of the ramp. He looked up. Men in the uniforms of the city watch were coming down it, trying to collar scurrying workmen.

'Sergeant!' cried Big Nod, waving frantically in Gotrek's grip. 'Arrest these villains! They attacked my men and smashed up my place! Look at my roof!'

The watchmen started towards them.

'These are the thieves that stole the black powder from the Imperial Gunnery School,' countered Felix. 'They've just confessed to us.'

'We never!' said the halfling. 'They're lunatics, sergeant. Mutants, I shouldn't wonder.'

'Now now,' said the sergeant, a square, stocky fellow with greying hair and enormous moustaches. 'One at a time. And put that halfling down.'

Gotrek glared at him for a moment, then reluctantly lowered Big Nod to the ground and let go of his neck.

The halfling staggered back, gasping and clutching his bruised neck as he glared at Gotrek. 'Y'blackhearted wreckers! Now you'll see! It's the Iron Tower for you, you filthy...!'

'Pipe down if you please, sir,' said the sergeant. 'None of that. You'll have your say.' He turned to Felix. 'Now then, who might you be? And what's your interest in who stole what from the Gunnery School?'

Felix hesitated for a heartbeat, remembering that he and Gotrek were wanted men in the Empire – he for vandalism and incitement, Gotrek for killing Imperial cavalrymen during the window tax riots. Then he chided himself for being foolish. All that was a long time ago, and in Altdorf, not Nuln. Surely no one would remember, would they? It seemed impossible. 'I am Felix Jaeger. My companion is Gotrek Gurnisson. We are guests of the College of Engineering, and...'

The sergeant blinked. 'You're Felix Jaeger?' he interrupted. 'And this is Gotrek the Slayer?'

Felix's heart sank. They *did* remember them. After all these years there was still a price on their heads. Incredible. His hand dropped to his hilt. Gotrek reached for his axe.

But the sergeant laughed and turned to his men. 'Look here, lads! It's the "Saviours of Nuln" come back to protect us from some new menace!'

His men laughed too, dark and nasty, repeating 'the Saviours of Nuln,' derisively.

'You've quite an imagination, Herr Jaeger,' said the sergeant, smirking. 'Ratmen in the sewers of Nuln – skavlings did you call 'em? You and your friend the only ones who could save the day. The watch a lot of incompetent blunderers. Make for a good laugh around the watch station of an evening, your books.'

Felix gaped. This was the last thing he had expected. 'You've... you've read my books?'

'Captain Niederling read 'em to us, as he can read. Never heard taller tales in all my life.'

'What books are these?' growled Gotrek, his single eye turning on Felix.

Felix flushed. He had meant to tell Gotrek the night before, but the dwarf had been in such a foul mood that he had put it off, then forgotten it. 'I... I'll explain later.'

'I don't care who they are,' said the halfling. 'They smashed up my business. Lock 'em up!'

'We were looking for the black powder,' said Felix. 'They stole if from the Gunnery College, then sold it this morning.'

The sergeant cocked an eyebrow. 'Playing out one of your books, Herr Jaeger? Maybe you ought to keep your adventures on paper in the future.' He held up a hand as Felix and the halfling both started talking at once. 'Now now, I think both of you better come down to the watch station and explain it all to the captain.' He grinned. 'Captain will be right pleased to meet you, Herr Jaeger. He loves your books. Highly imaginative, he calls them.'

Gotrek growled in his throat and Felix shot him a warning glance. It would not do for the Slayer to murder an officer of the watch. They had only just returned to the Empire. Felix wasn't keen on going into exile again so soon. On the other hand, an axe through the forehead of this sergeant and his captain might be just the thing. Highly imaginative, indeed! Every word he had put in his journals was the truth. Skaven *had* attacked Nuln. And he and Gotrek had had some part in defeating them. Did they think he was some purveyor of low melodrama? Some Detlef Sierck? How dare they!

'WHAT ARE THESE books, manling?'

Felix swallowed, nervous. He had been waiting for the Slayer to ask that question.

It was many hours later. Gotrek and Felix were walking back to the College of Engineering, trailing behind Malakai Makaisson and Lord Groot, who were talking eagerly about tomorrow. Apparently Lord Pfaltz-Kappel had found more funds, the Dwarf Black Powder Guild had found more powder, and the flight of the *Spirit of Grungni* was back on schedule.

In the end, it had taken the intervention of Groot and Makaisson, and the reluctant confessions of the halfling and his henchmen, before the watch could be convinced to let Gotrek and Felix go. They had been released into Lord Groot's custody like naughty children returned to their father, and told to leave the investigating to the authorities.

Gotrek had been remarkably well behaved throughout the whole ordeal. Not that he was cooperative in any way. He had cursed Nuln and the watch and refused to surrender his weapon or answer any questions, but on the other hand, he hadn't killed anyone, or wrecked the furniture, or punched the captain in the face when he laughed at the sergeant's witticism about them being the 'Saviours of Nuln,' and called Felix's stories of ratmen 'amusing fancies'.

Indeed, every time Felix's books had been mentioned, Gotrek had turned that baleful glittering eye upon Felix, and stared silently at him. Felix quivered each time. It had reminded him of when Gotrek had attacked him in the tomb of the Sleeper, an experience he was not eager to repeat.

Now Gotrek had at last asked the dreaded question.

'Ah...' said Felix. 'Well, as you know, over the years I've kept journals of our journeys – notes for the epic poem of your death, you see. And... and whenever we've found ourselves in a friendly port, I've sent those that I've finished home to my brother for safekeeping. And he... well, he published them without my knowledge.' He swallowed. Gotrek just continued to stare at him. Was he going to attack him here and now? 'I– I meant to tell you last night, but somehow...'

'So you've already begun to tell my saga?' interrupted Gotrek.

'Ah, yes,' said Felix. 'In a way. Although I can't speak for the quality. I haven't begun to read them yet myself, and I have no idea what kind of editing my brother–'

'Good,' said Gotrek, cutting him off again. 'If my fame is great enough, my doom may seek me out and save me hunting for it. I owe your brother a debt.'

He stumped on without another word. Felix gaped after him. He had expected anger, dismemberment even. Never had it occurred to him that the Slayer might approve. On the other hand, he *had* asked him to write the epic. Why should he be surprised that Gotrek was pleased that he had begun?

CHAPTER FOUR

FELIX WOKE AGAIN to thunder. This time it was all outside his head, and much louder than previously. The blast brought him bolt upright in bed. Was it a cannon firing? If so, it must have been much closer. Perhaps one of Makaisson's inventions had exploded. It wouldn't be the first time.

He blinked around sleepily in the pre-dawn light as the reverberations of the explosion faded away and people in nearby rooms raised their voices in alarm. He had not slept well. His mind had been restive. Images of the black-clad, white-haired figure in the rafters of the cold cellar had spun endlessly through his head, trying to resolve themselves into a memory that wouldn't come.

People were running in the halls now. He moaned and climbed wearily out of bed. By the time he had found and pulled on his clothes and stepped into his boots, someone was knocking sharply on his door. He opened it. Gotrek and Malakai stood without, looking grim.

'There's been an explosion on the Gunnery School's testing field on Aver Isle,' said Malakai. 'The last gun of our shipment was tae be tested this morning. We're off tae see what's what.'

GOTREK GRIPPED HIS axe like he meant to butcher someone with it. His face was rigid with rage. 'The gods conspire to keep me from my doom,' he rasped.

Felix nodded. It certainly seemed that some unearthly agency was trying to stop Gotrek from reaching Middenheim in time for the siege. He and the Slayer stood on the neatly clipped green lawn of the Gunnery School's test range, which was situated on Aver Isle, a small island in the centre of the River Aver, and linked by bridges to the Neuestadt district to its north, to the Halbinsel district to the south, and to the west, the forbidding Island of the Iron Tower, the notorious prison of the witch hunters. The testing range was a cool and strangely peaceful place at this time of the morning, silent and wreathed in swirling mists from the river, but evidence that terrible tragedy had recently shattered that peace smouldered before them.

An enormous iron cannon sat broken upon the lawn, its lavishly decorated barrel split into five splayed sections, peeled back so that it resembled some black orchid from the jungles of Lustria. The wooden gun carriage the cannon had been mounted on was shattered and smoking, and the grass all around it was scorched. Patches of red remained on the ground where the bodies of the crew had been flung when the gun had exploded.

Malakai and Lord Groot and other men from the Gunnery School and the College of Engineering circled the cannon, examining it closely and talking amongst themselves. Behind them, a sturdy wagon was being wheeled onto the field in preparation for carrying the gun back to the school. Magus Lichtmann stood to one side, murmuring incantations and making strange gestures with his left hand and the stump of his right arm. By the armoury building, Ward Captain Wissen talked with the administrators of the range. A company of city guard waited near the gate.

Lord Pfaltz-Kappel paced behind Lord Groot, a sour look on his face. 'I suppose I'll have to pay for this too,' he whined.

'Certainly not,' said Groot sharply. 'The school guarantees all its work. You paid for the finest gun the Empire can build. You'll get it. No matter how many times we have to cast it.'

'How long to make anither?' asked Malakai.

'From start to finish, shaping and casting a gun takes fourteen days,' said Groot. 'Twelve if we rush it.'

'Twelve days,' growled Gotrek under his breath. His axe twitched.

'Fortunately,' continued Groot, 'we have a gun just ready to be poured. It is meant for the garrison at Carroburg, but they can wait. Middenheim's need is greater. If we pour it this morning, it can be ready four days from now at dawn.'

Gotrek grunted angrily but said nothing.

'Ah've niver before seen a gun explode wae such force,' said Malakai shaking his head. 'It's almost as though the muzzle wis plugged. Groot, were ye using some experimental ammunition?'

Groot shook his head. 'We would never do that for a test fire. It was loaded with plain iron shot.'

'Perhaps it was loaded wrong,' said Pfaltz-Kappel.

Groot wheeled on him, eyes blazing. 'The crews of the Imperial Gunnery School are the best in the world. The men who died here today were fifteen-year veterans. Great soldiers and personal friends of mine. They did not "load it wrong".'

Magus Lichtmann joined them, frowning. 'I detect no residue of magic,' he said. 'No spell caused this to happen. It seems it may have been an accident after all. Some hidden fault in the iron.'

Lord Groot made a face.

Lichtmann shrugged. 'These things happen, Julianus.'

'Not to my guns,' said Groot. 'I want to look at it more closely when we bring it back to the school.'

'It was saboteurs,' said Captain Wissen, crossing towards them. 'I'll stake my reputation on it. The same villains who stole the powder. Someone from within the school, most likely. Secret cultists among the gun shapers. They want to delay the shipment to aid their masters in the north.'

'There are no cultists in the Gunnery School!' bellowed Groot.

Wissen's lip curled. 'There are cultists everywhere.'

The men stepped aside as workers from the school lowered planks from the back of the wagon and attached chains to the wounded cannon. Four men manned cranks and, with a clattering of gears, began to drag the massive gun inch by inch up the planks. Groot watched in sad silence, like he was at a funeral.

A grey and gold palanquin carried by four men in the livery of Countess Emmanuelle, Elector Countess of Wissenland and ruler of Nuln, came through the high iron gates of the firing range and crossed the lawn. Murmurs rippled through the nobles, and they turned towards it expectantly, waiting to see who it carried. Could it be the Countess herself, Felix wondered? He hadn't seen her since she had thanked him and Gotrek for their help in defeating the rat-men and saving her city twenty years ago. She had been beautiful then. Had she kept her looks?

It was not the Countess.

The bearers set down the palanquin, and one of them opened the door. Out stepped a tall, stooped, delicate old man in severe but exquisitely-tailored black. He had a long, horsy face and thick white hair. The murmurs from the nobles grew louder. Felix frowned when he saw him. He looked familiar, and he knew he had met the man before, but couldn't remember where.

'Greetings, gentlemen,' he said in a soft voice. 'I have come at the request of the Countess. She has heard of the school's troubles and wishes to know what is being done.'

Felix knew him as soon as he spoke. It was Hieronymous Ostwald, the Countess's personal secretary, though he was much changed since he had last seen him. Twenty years ago, when the courtier had called Felix to his offices in the Countess's palace during the skaven crisis, he had been a dark-haired, slightly fleshy man in his fifties. Now he looked like a frail and kindly old grandfather.

But judging by the wary glances Lord Pfaltz-Kappel and Lord Groot and the others gave him, he was more dangerous than he looked.

'I understand that there has been a theft and sabotage,' Ostwald continued. 'I would like to hear the details, and also who the suspects might be. Have the cults been investigated? Have you entertained the possibility that it might be the...' He paused and looked around furtively, then lowered his voice. 'That it might be our "enemies below". I...' His eye fell on Felix and he paused, frowning. 'By Sigmar! Is it... are you related to Felix Jaeger? The bearer of the Templar's Sword? His son perhaps?'

Felix bowed. 'I am Felix Jaeger himself, sir,' he said. 'A pleasure to see you again.' He stifled a smile. It was funny how easily the old courtesies came back.

'Impossible,' said Ostwald, goggling at him. 'You haven't aged a day. You must have drunk from the chalice of youth!'

Felix blushed and didn't know what to say. 'No, sir. I... I feel every one of my years, I'm afraid.'

'My friends,' said Ostwald, turning to the others. 'You know not who you have in your midst! This is Felix Jaeger, who, with the help of his stout – er, stout-hearted – companion, helped turn the tide against the ska... the *beastmen* who invaded our fair city all these many years ago.' He looked at Wissen. 'Captain, I would request that you ask the High Constable to allow Herr Jaeger and Herr Gurnisson to assist you in your investigations, and to share with them all information you have about these crimes.'

Wissen looked appalled, but hid it by bowing and clicking his heels together. 'As you wish, excellency.'

The others looked at Felix and Gotrek with raised eyebrows. He couldn't tell if they were impressed or amused.

Gotrek chuckled almost inaudibly.

Groot stepped forward. 'My lord, if you will come back with me to the school I will tell you what we know.'

'Of course, of course,' said Ostwald. He motioned to Felix as he started back to his palanquin. 'Come, Herr Jaeger. Walk beside my chair so that we may talk. I am no longer able to walk long distances.'

Groot and the others lined up behind the wagon carrying the exploded cannon, and followed it out of the test grounds and onto the stone bridge that connected Aver Isle with the north bank of the Reik. Felix paced next to Lord Ostwald's palanquin with Gotrek beside him. The old man sat at the window and pulled a sable rug around his knees, as if the late summer weather was too cold for him.

A host of memories flooded Felix's mind as they walked, brought on by Ostwald's sudden reappearance in his life, the scenes and emotions coming to him as if they had happened yesterday – killing von Halstadt, the burning of the Blind Pig, Elissa's dark curls, and her betrayal, hideous rat-faces coming out of the dark, the terror of the poison gas, the horror of the diseased skaven in the cemetery, the doctor who had given him the pomander that had protected him from their noxious stew. Felix paused. The doctor was the same man who had introduced him to Lord Ostwald. The two of them had belonged to a secret order of some kind. What had his name been? Oh yes.

He turned to Ostwald. 'Do you still see Doctor Drexler, my lord?' he asked.

'Doctor Drexler?' said Ostwald. 'Oh, but I'm terribly sorry, my dear boy. Doctor Drexler passed away, many years ago.'

'Oh. I'm sorry to hear it,' said Felix. And he was. The old physician had been one of the wisest, most learned men he had ever met, a great healer with a deep understanding of human nature.

'Yes,' said Ostwald. 'He never truly recovered from his fight with that vile skaven warlock. His health remained feeble for a few years, then he succumbed to a cancer of the brain and died.'

'That is sad news indeed,' said Felix, but Ostwald's mention of the skaven sparked another question. 'Tell me, my lord, why no one believes that it was ratmen who attacked the city? Everyone, even men who were there and fought the vermin, seem to remember them as beastmen.'

Ostwald leaned closer to the window and put a finger to his lips. 'Quietly, Herr Jaeger. Quietly.' He looked around, then continued. 'It is strange, I know, but it is for the good of the Empire.'

'The good of the Empire?' Felix looked around too, though he couldn't imagine who would be eavesdropping on their conversation. They were halfway across the bridge now, moving very slowly behind the wagon that carried the huge shattered gun. The only person near them was Gotrek, who was spitting over the balustrade into the water.

'Yes. Don't you see?' continued Ostwald. 'The morale of the people is low enough as it is, and the knowledge that the entire land, from the wilds of Kislev in the north, to the Border Princes in the south, is riddled and undermined by the burrows of an innumerable, implacable foe bent on our utter destruction, would cause widespread despair. So, though we know of their existence, for the good of the people, those of us in possession of this dangerous knowledge must remain silent and fight them in secret. Therefore, the Countess and her advisors tell the people that it was not skaven they fought, but beastmen, and those who say otherwise are arrested – for the good of the community, of course.'

'And this works?' asked Felix, confounded.

'I have found,' said Ostwald, with a sad smile, 'that if you tell a lie long enough and loud enough and from a high enough position of authority, that most people will come to believe it, even with the truth staring them in the face. And those who don't believe it can be disposed of as traitors or madmen.'

'I… I see.' Felix wanted to say that he thought that this was a despicable practice that would only cause the people to come to mistrust the Emperor and his servants, but since Lord Ostwald was one of those servants he decided it was probably in his best interests to hold his tongue.

'I do not approve of this practice,' said Ostwald, pursing his lips. 'For I believe that the skaven thrive in this secrecy. I believe it would be better if we were to speak openly–'

A sound like the gabbling of a thousand geese interrupted him. It came from ahead of them, further down the bridge. Felix looked up, but could see nothing around the great bulk of the cannon. Captain Wissen and his troops were edging around its wagon as Groot and Lord Pfaltz-Kappel craned their necks and asked what was happening.

Gotrek started forward, pulling his axe from his shoulder. 'Trouble,' he said.

'Excuse me, my lord,' said Felix, ducking his head to Ostwald. He drew his sword and followed the Slayer.

The gun wagon was so wide that there was little room between it and the stone balustrades on either side of the bridge. They pushed around it and stopped behind Wissen's men, who had formed a line before the wagon.

Beyond them, an angry mob of Shantytown working men and young men in students' robes was flowing onto the bridge, screaming slogans and waving cudgels, staves and lit torches. Many of them wore yellow strips of cloth around their foreheads or arms. There were hundreds of them. They filled the street beyond the bridge.

'Grain for the people, not the army!' shouted some.

'Iron workers starve while gun makers grow fat and consort with sorcerers!' cried others.

'Smash the guns! Smash the guns!' roared still others.

Standing on his toes, Felix could see men in yellow masks amongst the mob, chanting and shaking their fists with the rest.

As the crowd got closer, the men at the front began to throw bricks, torches and paving cobbles at Wissen's men. The watchmen dodged and ducked. They had no shields, and no bows or guns, so they couldn't retaliate.

'You see?' said Wissen. 'Agitators. Did I not say? Hold your line, men.' He looked back at Groot and Magus Lichtmann and Lord Pfaltz-Kappel, who were peeking around the gun wagon. 'Return to the isle, my lords, and ask Lord Ostwald to do the same. There will be violence.' He glanced at Gotrek and Felix as his men set their spears. 'You too, meinen herren,' he said with a sneer. 'I would hate to be responsible for the deaths of the "Heroes of Nuln".'

'Worry about your own hide, watchman,' said Gotrek, sheathing his axe and smacking his fists together as the crowd swarmed closer. He caught Felix's look and snorted. 'There's no honour in slaughtering untrained fools.'

But that wasn't what Felix had been thinking about. He was wondering if there was any honour in fighting the mob at all. Uncomfortable memories flooded his mind. Hadn't he led the mob during the window tax riots? Hadn't he thrown bricks through the windows of the rich? Hadn't he urged the poor to storm the Lord Mayor's office? Hadn't he fought the watch in the streets? It felt very strange to be on the other side of the spears. He had more sympathy for the mob than he did for the men around him. He agreed with the agitators, at least in principle. The poor should be fed. Working men should be paid a fair wage.

On the other hand, smashing things and fighting the watch never got anyone anywhere, and he doubted these fellows were going to wait for him to explain that he was on their side before they caved his head in. He pulled his sheath from his belt and slid it down over his sword. Gotrek's way seemed best. There was no honour in slaughtering untrained fools, but at the same time, there was no honour in letting them slaughter you either.

In the middle of this reverie, a familiar shape caught the corner of his eye. A figure dressed all in black with a white shock of hair peeking from a voluminous hood, watching from the embankment. He lifted his head up to get a better look, but a flying stone skipped off the top of his head and he flinched down, cursing. By the time he stood again, vigorously rubbing his crown, the figure was gone – if it had ever been there in the first place.

A last volley of cobbles rattled all around them, and then the mob smashed into the watch's line. Wissen's men gored dozens, but they were but one thin line before an unstoppable battering ram of humanity. They were driven back by the sheer mass of the crowd. Some of the agitators squirmed past them, shouting, 'Smash the gun! Smash the gun!'

Gotrek clubbed these to the ground with his heavy fists. Felix laid about him with his sheathed sword, using it as a club. But there were too many. More and more were pushing through and slipping around them. Felix saw a watchman take a brick to the temple and fall. Three workmen dragged down another, even while his spear ripped out the guts of one of their companions. More workers pushed forward, trampling the bodies. They threw glass bottles at the gun wagon. Oily liquid splashed as the bottles shattered. Torches followed, and the wagon burst into flames.

Wissen fired point blank into a protester's face with his pistol and lashed about him with his sword, but he stepped back with every swing. 'Fall back! Fall back!' he cried. 'Use the gun as a barrier!'

'It's the gun they're after,' growled Gotrek.

The watchmen didn't hear him. They backed away, following Wissen as he retreated around the gun. Gotrek and Felix were suddenly alone in a sea of howling workmen. They flattened everyone they could reach, but they were but a small rock in a wide stream. The mob flowed around them on both sides and began clambering onto the gun, some perilously close to the flames, hitting it ineffectually with their clubs and rakes, still shouting 'Smash the gun! Smash the gun!'

'Push it in the river!' shouted someone from further down the bridge. 'Push it in the river!'

The mob took up the cry and began to rock the gun wagon back and forth. 'Into the river! Into the river!'

'No you don't,' said Gotrek, and spun towards the mob around the gun, pulling them off and throwing them aside.

Felix helped, braining the rioters with his sheathed sword and kicking them left and right. He heard glass smash beside him and something spattered his arm and cheek. He turned. Gotrek was drenched in oil. Shards of sticky glass glittered in his crest and slid down his naked back.

Gotrek looked over his shoulder. 'Who…'

A torch sailed over the heads of the mob. Gotrek whipped his axe off his back and blocked it. It spun and glanced off his right shoulder, then bounced into Felix.

Fire bloomed on Gotrek like an orange flower, flowing up the side of his head and wreathing his crest in flame. Felix's cloak and jerkin went up as well. The rioters flailed at them with their cudgels and staves.

'Flame-throwing cowards!' roared Gotrek. 'Come and face me steel to steel!'

He and Felix slapped at the flames as the mob battered at them. They only succeeded in setting their hands on fire. The fire stuck to everything. Felix cursed, his fingers a fiery agony. Heat blasted his face. Gotrek howled with rage. He slashed around with axe, decapitating clubs and severing hands, then surged for the balustrade. Felix followed. The rioters leapt back from their flames.

Gotrek dived off the bridge. Felix was right behind him. The world spun around him – bridge, river, shore, sky, Gotrek on fire – then, with a wet slap, he plunged into the waves. The cold shocked a cry out of him and he sucked in a mouthful of water.

He kicked and flailed in a confusion of bubbles and murk. After a moment of blind terror he broke the surface, choking and retching, eyes tearing.

Gotrek bobbed beside him, throwing his dripping crest out of his eyes. One side of his face was covered in blisters. 'That's what I get for being merciful.' He looked up, then his one eye widened. 'Swim!' he barked.

Felix followed his gaze. The bridge rose up beside them, and looming out over the balustrade, directly above them, was the exploded cannon. It was sliding off the rapidly tipping gun wagon. Felix stared, frozen, as it let go entirely, smashed through the balustrade in an explosion of granite, and began to topple off the bridge.

'Swim, manling!'

Felix snapped out of his paralysis and kicked forward, trying to get under the bridge. Gotrek was ahead of him, swimming strongly. Felix kicked and flailed for all he was worth, but it seemed like he was treading water. He wasn't going to make it.

With a sound like a battering ram hitting an iron door, the cannon smashed into the river. Felix felt himself being drawn back as the big gun opened a vortex in the water, then he was pushed forward again as the water surged back up. His shoulder slammed into a bridge pillar and he spun away on a roiling hill of water.

As they shot out on the other side of the bridge, Gotrek caught him and kept him afloat. 'Can you swim?'

Felix rolled his shoulder and flexed his arm. They were sore, but nothing was broken. 'I... I think so.'

'Then come on.'

Gotrek struck out for the north bank. Felix followed, then paused and looked up. On the bridge, the rioters were dispersing, running for the shore as they whooped and cheered at their victory, Captain Wissen's men chasing after them. Felix cursed them, his earlier sympathy entirely evaporated. The maniacs had set him on fire. He hoped they all roasted alive.

CHAPTER FIVE

'IT WAS A great loss,' Lord Groot said, as he and Magus Lichtmann, Malakai and Gotrek and Felix watched the pouring of the new gun with a group of Gunnery School officials from a metal platform above the casting room floor. 'Not in iron, though that is not cheap these days, with the shippers gouging us with "wartime prices", but in men and honour. Not only did we lose one of the best crews in the Empire, we lost the body and spirit of Johannes Baer, whose ashes were mixed with the iron of the gun.'

'His ashes?' asked Felix.

The heat from the forge was making the burns on Felix's face sting, and his left hand was sweating and itching under his bandages, but the honour of being invited to watch the pouring of a great cannon was not to be refused, so he merely stepped back a pace and hoped it would be over soon.

Felix's left hand had been salved and wrapped, and he was wearing clothes borrowed from a student at the College of Engineering, to replace his cloak and jerkin, which had been badly scorched, and everything else, which was soaking wet. The hand still throbbed, but he didn't dare complain. Gotrek's entire right arm, the right side of his neck, his right ear and part of his back were swathed in bandages, and his Slayer's crest was several inches shorter than usual where the Gunnery School's barber surgeon had cut away the blackened parts, and yet Gotrek bore his pain and indignity with stoic silence.

'Aye,' said Groot. 'It is a long-standing tradition, and a great honour. Artillery men of distinction are cremated when they die, and their ashes added to a new cannon. It is thought to imbue the gun with the fortitude and spirit that the men had in life. Johannes Baer was such a man. A great gunner and a brave soldier who died defending his gun when his position was overrun.' He bowed his head. 'The men who died today will soon be joined with their own guns. Today...' He looked towards the enormous glowing crucible that hung over the casting pit. 'Today, Leopolt Engle will be wed to his gun. He died four months ago in the siege of Wolfenberg, when the city wall collapsed under the bombardment of one of the enemy's hell cannon. He had destroyed two of the foul machines with his marksmanship.'

A bell chimed below. Groot stepped forward. 'They are ready.'

The others joined him. Felix stayed where he was. He could see just fine, and Groot and Gotrek's thick frames protected him somewhat from the waves of brutal heat.

Men in heavy leather aprons and leather hoods that covered their faces and necks stepped back from the casting pit, a square hole in the stone floor that was filled with sand. In the centre of the pit, at the bottom of a slight depression, was set a wide white ring. A shallow groove had been made in the sand, leading to the ring.

'That opening,' said Groot, pointing, 'is the tip of the cannon mould, made of clay, and buried upright in the sand pit. The thick rod that hangs straight down into the centre of it is the bore mould. The molten iron is poured into the mould, then when it cools, the bore mould is removed to make the gun's barrel chamber. We use secrets taught us by dwarf gun makers to make sure that both the gun mould and the bore mould are perfectly vertical and perfectly aligned. This ensures that the cannon shoots straight and is of uniform thickness all around when finished.' His chest puffed up. 'Consequently, our guns are the most accurate in the Old World.'

Above the casting pit was a sturdy wood and metal gantry from which hung the massive crucible that held the molten iron that would be poured into the mould. At the moment the crucible sat over a superheated coal furnace. Foundry workers stood around it in heavy leather, scooping impurities off the top with long steel spoons and dumping them in sand-filled stone buckets. Another bell clanged and the men stepped back. A door opened behind them and onto the gantry stepped a priest of Sigmar and two initiates. These too wore the heavy scarred leather of the forge men, but their gear had the shape of temple vestments, and was stitched upon the breast with the symbols of the hammer and the twin-tailed comet. Their faces were uncovered however, and Felix wondered how they stood it.

The priest held an iron-bound Book of Sigmar folded in his arms. His face, hellishly under-lit by the liquid iron's crimson light, was pocked with circular burn scars. He had obviously performed this duty many times before. One of the acolytes carried a gold-headed hammer, the other carried a stone urn. They too had burns on their faces, but not so many.

The workers on the gantry bowed their heads as the priest took the hammer from the first acolyte, then opened the book and began to read aloud. Lord Groot and the other men from the school who watched the ceremony lowered their heads as well. Felix did not. The ceremony was too fascinating not to watch. Gotrek and Malakai watched too. The priest's words were lost in the roar of the furnace, but whatever the invocation was, it was brief – necessarily so, Felix thought. When he finished, he stepped back and nodded to the second acolyte.

The man stepped forward, his face running with sweat. His lips moved continuously as he opened the stone urn and upended it over the crucible. The dust that poured out glittered as it drifted down into the molten metal, and a swirl of flames and sparks shot up when it touched, splashing the holy men. The acolyte with the urn flinched back and almost dropped it as a spark struck his cheek. With an effort he controlled himself and stood solemnly as the priest finished the ceremony and closed the book.

As they backed away, the forge men stepped forward again, unlocking the crucible from its mooring and then pulling on chains that rolled it forward until it hung over the sand pit. Other chains lowered it until the bottom of the massive container was only inches above the sand. Two heavily gloved men stepped to it and grasped long handles that sprouted from its side. With long-practiced motions they tipped the crucible slowly forward until molten iron began to spill from its spout into the groove in the sand. Sparks leapt in all directions. The men poured carefully, making sure the stream was smooth and constant. It wound down the groove and into the mould like a glowing red snake slipping endlessly into a hole.

Felix blinked to moisten his eyes. The blast of heat from the pouring metal made the room even hotter than before, and they were as dry as eggshells. The entire front of his body felt on fire. He looked over at the others. All were sweating, but none showed any sign of discomfort, curse them.

'Leopolt Engle,' intoned Lord Groot. 'May you, in death, bring victory to the Empire and defeat to her enemies as you did in life.'

'May Sigmar so grant,' said the other men of the school.

For another interminable ten minutes the forge men trickled the metal into the mould while Felix's face felt like it would shrivel up and peel off. At last the mould filled to the brim and the men tipped the crucible back upright.

As the priest stepped forward to say one final blessing, Felix noticed that the initiate who had been burned had fainted. He lay on the gantry, still clutching the urn, while his fellow acolyte knelt over him, shaking him.

Groot and the other men of the school bowed to the cooling gun and made the sign of the hammer, then turned to depart.

Groot smiled at Gotrek and Felix. 'Come,' he said. 'The heroes who defended Johannes Baer's cannon when Wissen and his cowards turned and fled must be honoured. You will feast at my table tonight.'

'Will there be ale?' asked Gotrek.

'Of course!' said Groot. 'As much as you like.'

'Good,' said Gotrek. 'I'm parched.'

As much as *Gotrek* likes, thought Felix. Groot may come to regret those words.

As THEY WALKED through the grounds of the school towards Groot's quarters in the main building, they saw guards in the uniform of the school leading away another guard. The man was raving.

'The guns,' he cried. 'They were looking at me! They want to kill me!'

Groot stopped the strange procession, holding up a hand. 'Sergeant Volker, what is this? What has happened?'

The sergeant looked pained. 'It's Breyermann, sir, who guards the guns before they're shipped. He's come to believe that the guns are alive, and that they mean him harm.'

'They stare at me!' wailed Breyermann from behind him. 'They hate us all!'

Groot shook his head. 'Terrible. First Federeich mutates, and now Breyermann goes mad. What are the odds that such misfortune strikes two of our lads in one week?'

'We thought perhaps that Breyermann caught his madness from Federeich, sir,' said the sergeant. 'Wouldn't be surprised if he shows stigmata soon.'

Groot nodded. 'Aye. You undoubtedly have the right of it. Very sad. Inform his family. And give him to the Sisters of Shallya. Perhaps they can cure him before it becomes a matter for the witch hunters.'

The sergeant saluted and he and his men led the madman away. Groot sighed and continued towards his quarters. Felix looked back at the sad procession, a jumble of half-formed thoughts churning in his head. He noticed that Gotrek was looking back too.

LATE THAT NIGHT, as Gotrek and Felix staggered with Malakai towards the College of Engineering after Groot's lavish feast, Gotrek stopped and turned in the direction of Shantytown.

'I want to go to the Blind Pig,' he said, slurring only a little.

'You want *more* to drink?' asked Felix, amazed. The Slayer had put away an enormous amount of ale at dinner. Felix had seen Groot wince as the third keg had been broached. He supposed Gotrek might be trying to numb the pain of his burns – as Felix had been doing – but then he often drank like that, so who could say?

Gotrek shook his head, then steadied himself. 'I want to talk to Heinz.'

'I'm not sure he wants to talk to you,' said Felix, but Gotrek was already stumping away into the night. Felix sighed and waved goodnight to Malakai, then followed him.

'Watch out for the big 'un, young Felix,' called Malakai. 'He's liable to get intae trouble.'

Felix snorted. There was no other possible response.

'YER NOT TO come in,' said the big bouncer who stood, his arms folded across his broad chest, in front of the Blind Pig's door.

'Try stopping me,' growled Gotrek, aiming himself at the door.

The bouncer braced himself, then wavered before Gotrek's mad, one-eyed glare and stepped aside. He shrugged. 'Ah, go on. There's no one to fight anyway.'

Felix followed Gotrek into the tavern and saw that it was true. It was empty but for one lonely barmaid and old Heinz, half asleep on his elbows behind the bar.

The barman's head came up as he saw Gotrek. 'I told you not to come back, you wrecker!' He didn't seem at all surprised that Gotrek was wrapped in bandages.

'I stayed away last night, didn't I?' said Gotrek. He tossed a gold coin marked with the sigil of Karak Hirn onto the bar. 'Charge me double for my drinks,' he said. 'That'll pay the damages soon enough.'

Heinz looked at the coin for a long moment, then picked it up and pocketed it. 'Suppose I can use all the business I can get.' He turned and drew two pints.

'What happened?' asked Felix. 'Where is everyone?'

Heinz sighed as he set their pints before them. 'It's Ward Captain Wissen and his thugs. Since that ruck on the bridge they've been prowling Shantytown and the Maze, roughing up anyone they find on the streets, trying to find the leaders of the Cleansing Flame. All my regulars are holing up until it blows over.' He snorted. 'I could tell Wissen he's looking in the wrong place. Those troublemakers ain't from around here.'

'Where are they from?' asked Gotrek. He sounded suddenly much less drunk.

'They're toffs,' sneered Heinz. 'Altestadt brats with too much time on their hands. See themselves as do-gooders, standing up for the common man. The Torch, their leader calls himself. Gives fiery speeches about how the poor should rise up and kill the priests and the nobles and the factors. But when the folk start smashing things up and the watch come down on them, where are the Torch and his rich mates? Nowhere. They take off their masks and disappear. Cowards, I calls 'em.'

'I call them worse,' rasped Gotrek.

'So why aren't the watch looking in the Altestadt?' asked Felix.

'They don't know,' said Heinz. 'They think they're all Maze-born rabble rousers.'

'Why don't you tell them different?'

Heinz scowled at Felix. 'No Shantytowner would tell the watch nothing. No matter what it was, they'd find a way to turn it against us.'

'We'd find them in the Altestadt, then?' asked Gotrek.

'If you knew who they were,' said Heinz. 'But nobody knows that. Not even their followers. They have a meeting house in the Maze though. Hidden.'

'Where is it?' pressed Gotrek.

Heinz turned and looked at him, then shook his head. 'No, Gurnisson. I don't want to lose the Pig. They live up to their name, the Cleansing Flame, with them what cross them. Set fire to the houses of many a man they thought betrayed them. Why do you want to know?'

Gotrek raised his bandaged arm. 'They set me on fire.'

Felix touched his face. 'Me too.'

Heinz looked from Gotrek to Felix and back. His lips pulled back in a snarl. 'No one sets my friends on fire and gets away with it!'

Then he paused, uncertain. 'They're dangerous men though. A snake with many heads. You've friends in the palace, if I recall. Maybe they could help you. Save us all some strife.'

Gotrek just grunted and drank his ale.

Heinz rubbed his whiskery chin, visibly melting in the heat of Gotrek's withering silence. 'Of course, there's no connection between us anymore,' he said. 'Been twenty years since you worked for me. And I threw you out two nights ago. Nobody would think it was me who sent you.' He chewed his lip thoughtfully then sighed. 'All right. It might stir up trouble, but I've weathered trouble before, and I hate them muckrakers almost as much as I hate the watch.'

He looked around warily, despite the fact that there was no one in the place, then leaned forward and lowered his voice. 'I overheard one of them telling a new recruit how to get there once. They're in the middle of the Maze, behind a place called the Broken Crown. The fellow said that the building looks like just another old tenement, but it's built atop an old brewery, and the cellars go down and down. The Flame boys keep an eye on it night and day, so watch yourselves when you get close.' He dipped his finger in a puddle of ale and began to draw a map on the bar. 'I'll show you how to get the Broken Crown. After that, you're on your own.'

FELIX WAS LESS than eager to enter the Maze, which was known as the roughest part of the roughest neighbourhood in Nuln, particularly in the dead of night, particularly with Gotrek weaving drunk and him not much better. But he knew nothing could stop a Slayer bent on vengeance, so he followed along warily, one hand on the dragon-figured hilt of his runesword, and his eyes searching every shadow they passed.

The Maze was the haunt of gangsters and cultists and wanted men. There were no street lamps here, and few lights of any kind. Though Mannslieb and Morrslieb were out, the buildings were so crowded together, and so tall – some looming five and six storeys above the alleys – that the moons' light rarely reached the street. Some of them sagged against each other over the street like drunk lovers and blocked the sky altogether.

In most places, the lanterns over the doors of the lawless taverns and gambling halls and low rent brothels that filled the lower floors of the rickety tenements provided the only illumination. Most of the back alleys were pitch black and Felix had to rely on Gotrek's keen tunnel-bred vision to lead them safely through the dark. In some places, new structures, even flimsier than the old, were built upon the rubble of the buildings that had burned down during the skaven invasion, twenty years before. In other places the charred timber bones still stood, patched tents and makeshift lean-tos rising in their midst.

Hard-eyed men watched Gotrek and Felix from doorways and windows. Women in low-cut dresses made kissing noises as they passed. Groups of villains lounged outside open-fronted beer stalls, their legs splayed out into the street, deliberately blocking the way.

Gotrek stumped past them all, ignoring them, his one eye looking for the landmarks Heinz had told them to watch for, and turning where he had told them to turn.

After a quarter of an hour they came to a filthy, rubbish strewn street. On the left was a tavern beneath a crude painting of a broken crown. An alley ran down the side of the tavern. Heinz had said that the Cleansing Flame's meeting house was in a tenement that faced the alley behind the Crown.

'On tiptoes now, eh?' said Felix, thinking of the men Heinz had said watched the area night and day.

Gotrek clomped forward as if he hadn't heard, his boots echoing down the alley. Felix sighed and followed. So much for subtlety. He drew his sword.

Behind the Crown was a crooked alley, so narrow Felix could have reached out and touched both walls at once, if he had cared to soil his hands. To the left and right the alley disappeared into shadow, but across from the rear entrance of the Crown, a slanting slash of moonlight illuminated a dilapidated tenement with a dingy junk shop in its bottom floor, smashed and smoke-blackened furniture and crockery spilling from its unlit but open front. Was this the place? Was it the tenement to the left? The one to the right? Unfortunately Heinz's knowledge had ended at the Broken Crown. They would have to start sticking their noses into doors and looking around. Felix's skin crawled at the prospect.

As Gotrek crossed to the junk shop and looked into it, Felix peered left and right, trying to see into the shadows of the alley, looking for watchers. He gave up. It was too dark, and if there was anything to see, Gotrek would have seen it.

The Slayer jabbed a thumb at the open junk shop door. 'A trap,' he said. 'An open door, but no footprints.' He studied the ground again. The alley floor was hard-packed earth, like all the streets in the Maze. Gotrek followed the prints leading to a closed door, then moved further left, to a spot where it looked like scrap lumber had been used to patch a hole in the wall. 'Here,' he said, and pulled on the boards.

They resisted. As Gotrek stepped forward to pull harder, Felix heard a whistle from somewhere above and behind them. He turned and looked up. Someone was backing away from an unshuttered window. Below it, the back door of the Broken Crown slammed open and seven men swaggered out, swords and daggers dangling casually from their hands. Each of them wore a yellow cotton mask over his face.

'Y'need a key fer that door, stuntie,' said a tall man with the build of a longshoreman, as the others spread out to encircle them.

'I have one,' said Gotrek, drawing his axe and holding it so it glinted in the moons' light.

Some of the men murmured nervously at the sight of it, but the big man sneered, waving them on. 'Come on, lads. They was looking for the Cleansing Flame. Let's not disappoint 'em.'

The masked men lunged forward, swinging their weapons. Gotrek shattered the big man's sword with a slash, then gutted him with a backhand and turned to face three more. Felix backed into an angle of the alley wall so he would only have to face two. He blocked one and kicked at the other as a third tried to find space between them to attack.

These were alley-bashers, not trained swordsmen. Felix countered their attacks with ease and blooded both his opponents on the first pass. But as he recovered to guard, something buzzed past his ear and stuck in the plaster wall beside him. He flinched away. It was a crossbow bolt.

He risked a look up. Someone was reloading in the second floor window. Then, in an eyeblink, they were gone – vanished! Someone or something had yanked them savagely backward out of sight.

Felix was so surprised he almost took the left-hand basher's sword through the belly. He lurched right and the blade grazed his hip. The man on the right was stabbing straight for his eyes. Felix batted his sword aside at the last second and it stuck in the plaster wall next to the crossbow bolt. He kicked the man between the legs, then ducked another thrust from the man on the left and ran him through.

As the dead man fell, Felix slashed at his companion, who was still clutching his groin, and cut halfway through his neck. He turned to face the one who had been trying to push through the other two, but to his surprise, the man was falling forward. A crossbow bolt sticking out of his spine.

He looked up to the window again. There was nobody there.

Gotrek was looking up too. All his opponents were dead as well, one from a bolt behind the ear.

'We have a friend, it seems,' said Felix.

'No one in this place is a friend,' muttered Gotrek. He sidled to the hidden door, keeping his eye on the dark window, then reached back and yanked sharply on the planks. They jerked open with a *ping* of snapped metal, revealing a pitch black opening. Gotrek stole a quick glance inside, then nodded to Felix while returning his gaze to the window. 'In, manling.'

Felix stepped cautiously to the opening. He felt equally reluctant to step into the darkness or stay out in the alley at the mercy of a marksman. With a curse he strode across the threshold and into a narrow corridor. Gotrek backed in after him and closed the door behind him. The darkness was absolute, at least for Felix.

Gotrek shifted around in front of him. 'Put your hand on my shoulder, manling,' he said. 'We'll go without a light.'

Felix reached forward and touched the cloth of Gotrek's bandages. He switched to the opposite shoulder. Gotrek started forward confidently, the wooden floor creaking beneath his feet. Felix followed behind, fighting the urge to put his sword hand in front of his face to shield off any unseen obstacles.

'Stairs down,' said Gotrek, after a few paces. Felix gripped tighter as Gotrek descended, and felt for the edges of each step.

'There would have been a guard behind the door,' he said. 'He must have gone to warn the others.'

'Aye,' said Gotrek. 'They know we're coming.'

At the bottom of the steps, Gotrek froze, holding perfectly still. Felix tried to do the same. After a moment Gotrek started forward again.

Felix let out a breath. 'Do you hear them ahead of us?'

'No,' said Gotrek. 'The front door opened.'

Felix swallowed, and the flesh of his back crawled as he imagined the mysterious sharpshooter from the alley padding down after them in the dark.

Gotrek turned a corner and Felix saw in the distance a faint sliver of flickering orange from under a door. It gave just enough light for Felix to see that the corridor leading up to it had no doors.

'Keep to the walls,' said Gotrek. 'And tread softly.'

The Slayer began edging down the left side of the corridor. Felix went down the right, trying to step on the boards as close to the walls as possible, where they wouldn't creak so much. When they reached the door, Gotrek put his unburned ear to it and listened. Felix held his breath.

'Empty,' breathed Gotrek. He tried the latch. It was locked. He put his palm and shoulder against the door and pushed. The door was much sturdier and better mounted than the hidden door above. Felix could hear the deadbolt groaning with complaint as Gotrek pressed harder and harder. Finally, with a sharp *pang*, the lock gave way and the door flew open. Gotrek jumped forward and caught it before it slammed against the wall. Then he stepped cautiously inside, his axe held at the ready. Felix followed.

The room within was little more than a wide space in the hall. It looked to Felix like a guard station. A low table and two stools sat along one wall. They had not been abandoned long. There was a charcoal brazier on the floor next to them with two sausages cooking on it. A half-eaten loaf of bread sat on the table. A yellow mask was crumpled beside it.

Gotrek glanced around at the walls. 'Hidden panels everywhere,' he muttered.

He stepped forward, peering down the hall beyond the room, then froze and looked back over his shoulder towards the corridor from which they had just come. He motioned Felix to hide to the right of the open door, then took up position to the left. He put a finger to his lips. Felix nodded.

They waited for what seemed to Felix an eternity. From where he stood he could not see through the door, and though he strained his ears, he could hear nothing but the sounds of an old building: creaks and groans, a faint sound of muffled voices, either far above them or far below them, the drip of water from somewhere nearby, the scrabbling of rats inside the walls.

And yet Gotrek remained tensed, axe ready, legs bent to spring, his eye fixed firmly on the frame of the open door. He must be hearing something, but what?

Then, with a movement too swift to see, Gotrek's free hand shot forward through the doorway and pulled a figure into the room, spun it around and slammed it into the side wall. His axe was at its neck. Just as swiftly, a stiletto was at his.

Felix gasped. It was the white-haired figure – the mysterious phantom he had seen in Big Nod's cold cellar and at the riot on the bridge. It raised its shock-haired head, revealing ice-blue eyes and skin like white silk. It smiled, revealing gleaming incisors.

'Hello, Gotrek,' it said, in a voice like honey and sand. 'Hello, Felix. You haven't aged a day.'

It was Ulrika.

CHAPTER SIX

FELIX STARED AT her, a hundred conflicting emotions warring within him: surprise, longing, loathing, anger, regret, nostalgia, bitterness, hope, happiness, grief.

She was beautiful – more beautiful, perhaps, than she had been in life. All her flaws had been polished away. Her skin glowed with the soft lustre of alabaster. Her short-cropped hair, once a sandy blonde, was now snow-white, her eyes were a more piercing blue, her lips a wanton red. A black neckerchief was knotted loosely around her graceful, corded neck. She was as tall as ever, and both slimmer and harder under her tight-fitting black doublet and breeches, and looked the same age as when he had seen her last – twenty-one or twenty-two years old. A bone handled rapier hung low at her trim waist, and black leather cavalry boots encased her long legs to mid-thigh. The hand that held the needle-thin stiletto to Gotrek's throat wore black kidskin gloves of the finest quality.

And yet, for all her beauty, there was something subtly repellent about her as well. Her perfection was that of a statue, lacking entirely in humanity. And as mesmerising as her eyes were, they were equally as unnerving. They looked at him with the unwavering intensity of a hunting cat's – like she saw him only as prey. She smelled wrong as well. The cloying scent of cinnamon could not hide the coppery tang of blood that hovered about her, nor the faint echo of cold, wet earth.

'The bloodsucker.' Gotrek spat on the floor. He did not lower his axe.

'You spared me once,' she said, calmly. 'Will you break your oath and kill me now?'

Felix noted that she still had her slightly slurred Kislevite accent. It was still bewitching.

'Have you broken *your* oath?' countered Gotrek.

'I made no oath,' said Ulrika. 'I was unconscious at the time, if you recall. But if you mean the promise that my mistress made, to teach me to harm no one...' She smiled again, showing long incisors. 'I wager I have killed one for every hundred you have slain in the last eighteen years. And none that didn't deserve it.'

Gotrek snarled and pressed his axe closer to her neck. At the same time, her stiletto pricked the skin of his. A bead of blood ran down and disappeared beneath his beard.

'It would be a shame,' she purred. 'To end so illustrious a career in a spat over the meaning of a word.' She glanced around the room. 'Particularly when our goals appear to be the same.'

'What do you want with the Cleansing Flame?' asked Felix. He could have wished that his first words to Ulrika after eighteen years had been something more personal. He also wished that she and Gotrek would lower their weapons, but he doubted asking would do any good.

'Surely you want what I want,' said Ulrika. 'To discover where these villains have hidden the black powder.'

'The Cleansing Flame have the black powder?' asked Felix.

Ulrika raised an eyebrow. 'You don't know that? Perhaps, then, I can be more useful to you alive than dead?'

'How did you learn this?' asked Felix.

Ulrika shrugged. 'I would find it much easier to talk if your dwarf friend would remove his axe from my neck.'

Gotrek didn't move.

'Gotrek,' said Felix. 'It's Ulrika.'

'Not anymore,' Gotrek rasped.

'Will you break an oath?' pressed Felix.

'She has killed.'

'Then take it up with her mistress,' said Felix.

'I will,' Gotrek growled. 'When I've finished with her.'

He leaned in, looking as if he meant to saw Ulrika's head from her shoulders, but then, from all around them came the sound of running feet. Even the ceiling resounded with footsteps.

Gotrek stepped back from Ulrika, going on guard.

The vampire drew her sword. 'Cockroaches,' she hissed.

Felix turned in a wary circle, scanning the walls and ceiling. Hidden panels, Gotrek had said, but where? The whole place was so patched together and makeshift anything could be a door.

The wall in front of him flew out like the shutters of a cuckoo clock, and four masked men surged out, slashing at him with daggers, axes and cleavers. There were more behind them. At the same instant, panels in the other wall and the ceiling slammed open. Men charged Gotrek and Ulrika. More dropped down in their midst, stabbing in every direction. The tiny guard room was suddenly more crowded than the Blind Pig during Powder Week.

Felix parried and blocked the men in front of him. A dagger from behind gashed his burned shoulder. He hissed in pain and tried to return the attack, but his long sword was cumbersome in this tight space. Still blocking the three men in front of him, Felix twitched away from another backstab and kicked behind him like a mule. The attacker grunted and doubled up, and a back swing from Gotrek's axe took off the top of the man's head.

A man with a short, curved cutlass thrust at Felix and he ran him through. A cutlass! A much better close quarters weapon. Felix left his runesword in the man's guts and stripped the cutlass and dagger from his slack hands. He used them to parry cuts from his other two attackers, then glanced over his shoulder for danger from behind.

A blink took in the rest of the room. All the men who had dropped from the roof were dead, their limbs and heads lopped off – Gotrek's work. The Slayer fought five men who were pushing forward through the far wall. More were dead at his feet. Ulrika stood at the mouth of the inner corridor, teeth bared, her rapier and dagger flickering like humming birds in the brazier-glow. Men fell away from her, blooming red from the chests, necks and groins. A knife was buried to the hilt in her stomach. She appeared not to notice.

Another blink and he was back to his own opponents. He ducked a heavy cleaver swinging for his head, then stabbed the cleaver-man with his dagger and used his cutlass to gash a wrist behind a lunging knife. He had no idea who the wrist belonged to. His vision had narrowed to just the blades coming towards him. A short sword thrust at his groin. He smashed down on the fingers holding it and it clattered to the floor. A hand axe hacked at his head. He ducked and slipped left, shouldering someone in the ribs, and gutting someone else. The hand axe cut his shoulder – the same shoulder the dagger had hit! He hissed and stabbed back angrily, and was gratified to hear a scream. A knife grazed his cheek and he lashed out with his cutlass. The knife-man crumpled, his neck open to the bone.

The last two men backed away from him, squeezing back through the trap and running into the darkness beyond. Felix started forward, snarling.

'Don't be drawn, manling,' said Gotrek's from behind him.

With an effort, Felix restrained himself from chasing the men. It always amazed him how, when his blood was up, he found himself ready to do things you couldn't have paid him to do when he was calm and thinking clearly.

He turned. All the men who had attacked them were dead or fleeing. The room was a charnel house. The bodies were knee deep. Gotrek had a few minor cuts, but was otherwise unwounded. The Slayer was glaring at Ulrika as she drew the dagger from her stomach and tossed it aside with a sniff of annoyance.

'My Tilean doublet,' she said. 'That will take some...' She paused as she met Gotrek's gaze, then rolled her eyes. 'Do you still wish to slay me, Slayer?'

'You are a monster,' growled Gotrek.

'A monster that you allowed to come into existence.'

Gotrek bared his teeth. 'That makes it worse.'

'Perhaps we should settle this later,' said Felix, looking around uneasily as he recovered his runesword from the stomach of the man it had killed.

Ulrika's chin came up. She cocked her head. 'Good idea. More are coming.'

'Where?' said Gotrek eagerly.

She nodded towards the left wall. 'We should elude them.'

'Elude them?' Gotrek sounded as disgusted as if she had suggested he kiss an orc.

Ulrika sighed. 'You were never long on strategy, were you, Slayer?' She continued as if speaking to an unusually slow child. 'If we fight every step of the way, the leaders will have time to sneak away or move the powder.'

Now even Felix could hear footsteps, and they were coming from more than one direction. 'Then let's go.'

But Gotrek was still glaring at Ulrika.

'What?' she snapped, impatient.

At last he snarled and turned towards the inner corridor. 'Follow me.'

Ulrika gave Felix a quizzical glance, as if to say 'did he mean me?' Felix shrugged and they followed the dwarf into the corridor.

Felix could see almost nothing, but he heard men coming ahead of them.

'You call this eluding them?' said Ulrika.

'Shut up, leech,' growled Gotrek. He felt along the walls with his fingers. The composition of the walls changed with almost every pace – brick, wood, plaster, stone. These cellars had obviously been rebuilt countless times. Gotrek turned a corner. The footsteps got louder, and there were more approaching from behind them.

'Ha!' said the Slayer, then felt up and down a section of brick. 'I knew there would be another.'

Felix looked up and down the corridor anxiously. It sounded like both groups of men were almost on them.

With a grunt of satisfaction, Gotrek used a thick fingernail to pry out what looked like a loose chunk of mortar. There was a click and a section of the wall swung back, revealing a stairway going down. 'In. Quick,' said the Slayer.

Felix and Ulrika slipped through the secret door and Gotrek pulled it closed, enveloping them in darkness. Just as it clicked shut again, boots rumbled up from both directions just outside.

'Where are they?' said a harsh voice.

'They were heading towards you,' said another. 'Don't tell me you let them slip by.'

'No one got by us!' said the first voice. 'You must have lost them. Search back the way you came!'

The two groups split up again and the bootsteps faded into the distance.

'A hole even the roaches don't know of,' said Ulrika. 'Interesting.'

Gotrek sniffed. 'I smell smoke and meat. They are below.' He stepped to the stairs. 'Hand on my shoulder, manling.'

They started down the stairs, Gotrek and Ulrika in front, Felix stumbling along behind. He ground his teeth in frustration. Why was he always the one who couldn't see in the dark?

'So, how was it that you learned that these madmen had the black powder?' Felix asked after they had descended a few flights.

'Countess Gabriella hears many things,' said Ulrika. 'Among them was a rumour that the Cleansing Flame would soon make an attack on the Imperial Gunnery School that would be the beginning of the burning of all of Nuln.'

'What!' said Felix. 'They mean to blow up the school?'

'Aye,' said Ulrika. 'When the countess heard that the black powder had been stolen, she wondered if it might be the Cleansing Flame who had purchased it from the thieves. She sent me to investigate. While you were going for your swim in the Reik, I pulled aside one of the yellow-masked agitators who was leading the rioters and questioned him. He told me that the countess's suspicions were correct.'

'He talked?' said Felix, surprised.

'Oh yes.' Ulrika chuckled. 'I bled him for everything he knew.'

Gotrek spat, disgusted. 'And what does your mistress care for the safety of Nuln,' he asked.

'She cares for Nuln precisely the way a shepherdess cares for her sheep,' came Ulrika's prim reply.

Gotrek growled in his throat, but said nothing.

After another flight, the Slayer stopped at a landing. 'Keep back,' he said, and shrugged out from under Felix's hand.

Felix listened, trying to understand from the soft sounds that followed what Gotrek was doing. Then suddenly there was a thin line of torch glow illuminating Gotrek's ugly face, and casting a dim light on the rest of the landing, revealing that the stairs continued further down.

Gotrek peered through the cracked door with his one good eye. Felix stepped behind him and looked over his shoulder.

Though he could only see a narrow sliver of the room beyond, he saw that it was big, with a high ceiling and a far wall more than thirty paces away. There was a large square of yellow cloth on the left wall above what appeared to be a stage of some kind – planks laid over an under structure of old barrels.

'They must have escaped,' echoed a plaintive voice from the room. 'We searched all over the cellars.'

'Escaped?' said an upper class voice. 'I find that hard to believe. Search again. From top to bottom. They cannot be allowed to interrupt us now. Go!'

'Yes, brother. Right away, brother.'

Gotrek closed the door. 'Further down,' he said.

They resumed their descent.

Four flights later, the stairs ended at another hidden door. Gotrek listened at it, then tugged on the catch and pushed it open a crack. He peered through, then opened it wider. There was a hanging of some kind in front of the door. Gotrek drew his axe, hesitating. Felix strained his ears, listening for movement.

'Worry not,' said Ulrika. 'I smell nothing with a pulse in this room.'

Gotrek shot her a look, then eased through the door and looked around the edge of the hanging. He motioned his companions out. Felix and Ulrika stepped through and pushed past the curtain. They were in a small room that looked something like Felix's father's

office in his counting house. A desk with pigeon holes and ledger
shelves stood on the left side of the room, a horn lamp illuminating it. The hanging was a yellow banner with the torch symbol of
the Cleansing Flame stitched onto it. An armoire stood against the
right wall. The far wall had a stout door in it.

Gotrek crossed to the door, listened, then tried it. Felix and Ulrika
stood behind him as he opened it. A short corridor ended at a large,
well-lit warehouse room. Felix could see men rolling barrels past
the door under the direction of masked overseers.

'The black powder,' murmured Ulrika.

'Aye,' said Gotrek. 'But where are they taking it?'

He crept into the corridor with Felix and Ulrika on his heels. They
stopped just out of the square of light that shone from the high,
vault-ceilinged room. It looked like the store room at a garrison
fort. Boxes of steel shot were piled next to pyramids of cannonballs,
racks of spears, swords and bows, a small deck cannon that looked
like it had been stolen off an Estalian galley, and... the stolen barrels of black powder.

On the right-hand side of the room was a wooden loft. Stacked
upon it were sacks of flour, racks of long guns, kegs of ale, barrels of
salted beef and butts of water, as well as small barrels of pitch and
paraffin.

The work crew was rolling the black powder barrels out from under
the loft, and through a ragged hole in the far wall that led into a brick
walled tunnel. The sewers. Felix could smell them from where he
stood. Small boats bobbed in the channel of liquid filth. The men
loaded two barrels on each boat and then other men poled them away.
Only half a dozen barrels remained.

'Destined for the Gunnery School?' asked Felix. 'We should go
back and tell Lord Ostwald,' said Felix.

'Go back?' Gotrek snorted. 'Wait ten minutes and you can tell him
it's over.' He strode forward into the light.

'Fool! Wait!' hissed Ulrika. 'Have you never heard of subtlety!'

It was too late. One of the masked overseers was looking directly
at Gotrek. He pointed, shouting an order. The men pushing the
barrels righted them, then drew weapons and charged. More men
poured out of side rooms, snatching up spears and swords from the
weapon racks. On the loft platform, others began taking the long
guns from the racks and feeding them powder and shot. The
masked overseer started shouting arcane phrases.

Gotrek grinned, his one eye glittering. He ran forward, bellowing
a dwarfish war cry.

Ulrika stared after him. 'He's insane.'

Felix shrugged. 'He's a Slayer.' He raced in after Gotrek, screaming wordlessly.

Ulrika ran right beside him.

The two sides came together with a clash of steel in the centre of the big room. Gotrek killed five men instantly, his fell axe shattering spears, swords and bodies with equal ease. Felix hacked down through the shoulder of a spearman and into his ribcage. Ulrika lunged, recovered and lunged again in a blur, killing two men in the time it took Felix to pull his sword from the spearman's chest.

Then they were surrounded – three whirlwinds fighting back to back in the eye of a hurricane of steel. Spears and swords and hand-axes stabbed in at them from all sides. A sword opened a shallow gash in Felix's chest, tearing and bloodying his borrowed shirt. A spear tore his thigh. This was madness! Why wasn't he wearing his trusty mail? Because he had thought he and Gotrek were going out for a drink, that's why!

More men poured in from the entrances – patrols returning from hunting the passages, Felix guessed – and surged forward to join the press, pushing the melee into the shadow of the loft. Gotrek slew them as they came, wreaking terrible carnage with every stroke. Ulrika floated and flowed like a dancer, her sword everywhere at once. Bodies toppled in her wake, dying from wounds that barely bled. Felix hacked and blocked, more concerned with keeping the spears and swords at bay than with killing anyone. Attacking was too dangerous. Every lunge was an opportunity for five enemies to find an opening and run him through.

The masked overseer finished his incantation and thrust his hands towards the centre of the fight. Nothing happened. Perhaps Gotrek's axe had protected them, thought Felix. It had dissipated spells before. Or perhaps Ulrika could counter magic now that she was a vampire. It gave Felix a good feeling knowing his companions were so powerful – a sense of security. With them at his side he knew he could face the greatest armies and come out on top. Gotrek was unstoppable, and Ulrika appeared to have become an even better swordswoman than she had been when she was alive. In fact, they were so good that Felix didn't really have to do anything. He was tired anyway. Why didn't he just lower his weapons and watch the two of them work? They would protect him. He had nothing to worry about. All was well. Everything would be...

'Wake up, Felix!'

A sharp pain in his cheek snapped his eyes open. Half a dozen spear and sword blades were stabbing towards him. He yelped and leapt back wildly, and smacked into one of the wooden posts that held up the loft, knocking the wind out of him.

To his left Ulrika shouted at him as she impaled one attacker and elbowed another to the ground. 'Beware!' she snapped. 'The mage tries to glamour us.'

Felix growled, furious at the violation. His mind was his own! He renewed his attacks, glaring at the masked sorcerer.

A tattoo of deafening bangs sounded from above. Men screamed. Felix felt hot agony sear his neck. He looked up. The gunners in the loft had got off a volley. They had hit some of their own men, but both Gotrek and Ulrika had been shot as well. Gotrek had a bleeding stripe just above his ear, and Ulrika was clutching her breast.

'Cowards!' roared Gotrek. 'Come down here and fight!'

He lashed out at the support post and chopped it in two with one strike. The platform groaned and sagged in the middle. A flour sack slid off a stack and dropped down into the melee, smacking an agitator on the head. Gotrek pushed for the other post, cutting a swathe through his attackers.

'Gotrek, don't!' cried Felix.

But it was too late. With a fierce backhand, Gotrek smashed through the second post.

'Run!' roared Felix, and bulled into the men in front of him, trying to get clear. They shouted and backed away, tripping over each other as the planks and beams of the loft twisted and snapped above them. Ulrika danced through the mob. Gotrek laughed maniacally, shoving the men aside and grinning back over his shoulder.

With a splintering roar, the loft gave way all at once. The front edge slammed down in a rain of men, guns, kegs, barrels of water and sacks of flour, and crashed right through the ancient warehouse floor, collapsing the supports that held it up, and sending the cannon, the cannonballs, and all the crates of shot smashing into the level below. The sagging planks slanted steeply under Felix's feet as he tried to run, and suddenly he and Gotrek and Ulrika, and all the men that surrounded them, slid backwards down into the hole and fell on top of the heap of debris at the bottom. Felix thudded shoulder first – the *same* shoulder again – into the corner of a wooden gun case, buried under a squirming, moaning, coughing pile of bodies. All around, men called orders and shouted questions. Somewhere nearby, Gotrek chortled madly.

Felix clawed and elbowed his way to the surface. He could see nothing. A cloud of choking dust obscured everything.

Ulrika sat up out of the mound, shoving a body aside. She was covered in dust, making her black clothes match her white skin. She spat. 'Well done, Slayer. Well done.'

'Get them!' the sorcerer's voice rang out from above. 'Kill them!' He began chanting another spell. Felix cursed and tried to stiffen his mind.

All around, men were pushing themselves to their knees and groping for their weapons, their cloaks of dust making them look like some strange snow tribe on the warpath. They turned haltingly towards Gotrek, Felix and Ulrika, groaning as they attacked. The vampire slashed around her, killing all within reach, then helped Felix to his feet. He chopped to his left and right. Every inch of his body felt battered and bruised. His sword weighed as much as a cannon. Sigmar! It *was* heavy! He could barely lift it off the ground, let alone block with it. Beside him, Ulrika was having the same difficulty, losing her balance with every swing of her rapier. Their opponents were not having the same trouble.

'Sorcery!' Ulrika cursed, and tried to scramble back up the slanting floor towards the sorcerer. A thrusting spear tripped her and she slid back.

A man split in two in front of Felix, and Gotrek stepped through the pieces, glaring up at the masked sorcerer.

'Enough of your noise!' he barked, then plucked a cannonball the size of a cantaloupe from the debris at their feet and hurled it at the magician.

The magician squawked and ducked, but not fast enough. The cannonball crushed the side of his head like an eggshell and he fell into the hole, as limp as a sawdust doll.

Immediately Felix's sword was lighter again, and he attacked their foes with renewed energy. Ulrika did the same.

The dust in the air settled as they fought, and the outlines of the chamber they had landed in slowly emerged into clarity. The mound under their feet was a grisly, treacherous jumble. Bloody limbs and crushed heads stuck up out of the mess of shattered timber, spilled long guns, cannonballs and bags of shot. The deck cannon had pinned half a dozen men. They squirmed under it like squashed bugs. The screams were unbearable.

More figures were creeping out of shadowed arches at the edges of the chamber, and at the far end...

Felix froze, and almost took an axe in the knee because of it. He stumbled back as the air cleared and the thing at the far end of the chamber was revealed. 'Sigmar save us,' he choked.

Gotrek and Ulrika glanced up from their fights. Gotrek grunted. Ulrika snarled.

At first it seemed to be a twisted tree, growing from a stone altar and hung with bodies, but then Felix saw that the tree was a sculpture – at least he hoped it was a sculpture – made entirely of bones, of a giant, bird-headed deity, four bodies hanging from its four outstretched hands by hooks that pierced their flesh. The bones of the sculpture were human – leg bones, arm bones, hip bones, skulls and ribcages – all fused together as if they had melted in a furnace. There was no order to the construction. Each of the sculpture's arms and legs was made of hundreds of random bones – skulls and ribs, fibia and tibia – every one of them decorated with swirls of beaten gold. The thing's head was long and narrow and came to a beak-like point. Two gold-sheathed skulls served it for eyes. Dozens of finger bones – still attached to skeletal hands – were its teeth. From the eyeholes of the skull-eyes glowed a sickly greenish light.

The same light shone down into its torso, a lacy, ovoid cage of bones. There was something within the cage, something that writhed and twisted. The bodies that hung from its hands swayed like heavy fruit.

Felix shivered with dread. It appeared that the Brothers of the Cleansing Flame were not mere agitators.

CHAPTER SEVEN

'FOOLS,' GROWLED GOTREK, cutting down two men.

'Dupes of Chaos,' agreed Ulrika, impaling another.

'They must not leave here!' said a new voice from above. 'Slay them, changed ones! Slay the unbelievers!'

Felix looked around. *Changed ones?*

The figures emerging from the temple doors roared and surged forward, clambering up the mountain of debris and clawing at the companions. Felix flinched as he fought them. It was as if he were looking at them through warped glass. Their limbs were stretched and bent, their heads lopsided and bobbing on elongated necks. Hideous goitres and lumps grew from their skin. Some had new limbs – stumpy arms or tentacles or claws growing from their torsos. Some had eyes or mouths where they shouldn't.

But there was worse to be seen beyond them. The bodies hanging from the bone god stirred and pulled themselves free of the hooks to drop, cat-like to the ground. The thing in the bone cage uncoiled and slithered out through a hole near the pelvis. It was pink and blind and foetal, but had stilt-like spider legs that carried it swiftly towards the fight, and the coiled, flexing proboscis of a butterfly.

These new troops swarmed in behind their twisted brethren. Felix's stomach churned as he buried his blade in the spongy head of a man with scaly, seven-jointed fingers. He hated fighting mutants. It was hard to fight something you felt pity for. It was like killing someone with the plague – a necessary, but soul-crushing, task. Not all mutants had dabbled in the black arts. With some, the mutations just came, and there was nothing they could do about it. And once they came, the revulsion of their family and friends, and the persecution of the witch hunters, drove them underground to seek out their own kind. Small wonder that they gravitated to the cults of the Ruinous Powers. They were the only ones who would welcome such creatures with open arms, the only ones who would shelter them and promise them a future.

That was the trouble. It was hard to kill a man when, in the same circumstances, you might have followed the same path. Of course, it became much easier when that man was trying to rip your guts out with a mouth full of shark teeth, but it still didn't make Felix happy to do it.

Neither Gotrek nor Ulrika seemed to have any second thoughts. Gotrek stood on the butt of the fallen cannon, butchering any that came within reach and roaring for the thing from the bone cage to come and taste his axe. He split a mutant with skin like a lobster from head to crotch. The four men who had dangled from the statue leapt to take its place. They appeared to have been skinned. Their exposed muscles were glistening crimson. They bled endlessly.

Ulrika was a blur of black and grey, out of which shot the silver lightning of her blade. Mutants died all around her. A man leapt on her from the warehouse above, stabbing at her chest. She caught his wrist and pulled him off her back, then sank her jutting fangs into his neck, ripping out meat and veins in a spray of blood.

Felix whirled madly, hacking off a clawed hand, ducking a horned fist, then gutting a man with translucent flesh. A tentacle curled around his left ankle. He slashed down at it, but too late. It jerked his legs out from under him, and he fell hard on a bag of shot, hissing with pain. A thing with praying mantis arms and a face of melted wax leapt on his chest. He knocked it off with his arms, then lashed at it with his sword, but the tentacle was still pulling him down the mound, and he missed.

He looked down. The tentacle belonged to a woman dressed like a Shantytown harlot. It came out from under her short skirt. Felix shuddered at the implication. The woman raised dagger-like hands, licking her lips as she dragged him closer.

Suddenly there was a flash of steel and the harlot's head rolled from her shoulders in a spout of blood. It thudded to the floor and her tentacle went slack. Felix looked up. Ulrika was smirking down at him.

'In case you have any compunction about killing a lady,' she said.

The praying mantis thing lashed out at her from behind. She stumbled forward, grunting, and it sprang at her like a flea. Still on his back, Felix thrust up with his sword and gutted it in mid-leap. It landed on him, dead.

Ulrika kicked it off him, then grasped his hand and hauled him to his feet while fending off three others. Her strength was frightening.

'Thank you,' she said.

'The same to you,' said Felix. He returned to the fray. His hand tingled where they had touched. His thoughts flashed unbidden back to other times they had touched. He fought the memories off as desperately as he fought the mutants.

The skinned things were dead, but Gotrek was soaked in their sticky blood. It seemed to be clotting as Felix watched, slowing the Slayer's movements.

The foetal spider clicked forward and lunged at Gotrek. Faster than the eye could see its curled tongue straightened and jabbed. The Slayer blocked with his axe and missed, slowed by the swiftly drying blood, then staggered back, a hole like a gun wound in his right arm. He roared in pain.

Felix beckoned to Ulrika. 'Come on.'

They fought forward to guard Gotrek's flanks, holding off mutants to his right and left as he launched a barrage of attacks at the foetal thing with his axe, crusted blood exploding from his body like brick dust. None struck home. The creature's spider legs seemed to have the ability to jerk its torso out of harm's way in the blink of an eye. Gotrek lashed at a leg, but the thing whipped it away, backing down the mound.

The Slayer cursed, frustrated, then threw his arms wide, cracking off more blood. 'Right then. Have a go.'

The thing lunged in again, snapping out its needle-like snout straight for Gotrek's heart. The Slayer's free hand blurred and he caught the spike at its fleshy root. The spider foetus keened like a newborn and tried to jerk away. Gotrek held it fast, laughing, then brought his axe down in the centre of the creature's unformed body. It disintegrated in an explosion of gelid pink flesh.

Felix heard a ripple of dismay go through the mutants. 'The blessed one is dead,' they whispered, falling back. 'He killed the favoured of the Changer.'

Above them a voice called out. 'Brothers, escape! This place is lost! You will be contacted in the usual ways! The plans proceed!'

Gotrek spun, glaring up towards the voice. 'Get him! He knows what's what!'

Gotrek, Felix and Ulrika tried to run up the broken slanted floor as the mutants scattered for the exits, but just then a black powder barrel toppled into the hole and bounced down the planks, a length of match cord fizzing and sparking from its top. Felix threw himself right. Gotrek and Ulrika went left. Another barrel rolled by. They careened across the floor of the unholy temple and smashed into the statue of the Changer of Ways, toppling it.

'Down!' shouted Gotrek. 'Behind the pile.'

Felix scrabbled over the mound of crates and guns and dived for the ground on the other side.

A thunderclap punched him in both ears, and a wave of blistering air lifted him up and slammed him into the wall behind the mound. A boiling cloud of fire roiled above him as a rain of bricks, boards and body parts battered him. Something struck him on the head, and for an instant all went black. His whole world was noise, heat and pain.

After a moment the noise and blackness receded, though the heat and pain remained. He looked up. Through the hole above him he could see that the warehouse room was on fire. Another explosion rocked it as he watched. Smoke obscured the vaulted brick roof. The temple was ablaze too. Fire licked up the plaster wall beside him, waking new pain in the burns he had taken on the bridge. On the other side of the rubble heap, mutants howled in agony. The hideous statue was gone, blown to pieces, and that end of the chamber was engulfed in flame.

Gotrek staggered to his feet and brushed dust and glowing cinders off his shoulders. He looked like he'd lost a fight with a dragon. 'Time to go, manling.'

'Go where?' asked Felix. They were surrounded by fire.

'The sewers,' said Gotrek.

Ulrika pushed up to her hands and knees, dislodging a long plank. Her beautiful doublet was ruined. The hair on the left side of her head was singed and black. 'A wise plan, Slayer. You surprise me.'

Gotrek grunted, apparently disappointed that she had survived.

'We go through that?' asked Felix, pointing up at the warehouse inferno.

Gotrek shrugged. 'Better than staying here.'

Felix nodded and stood wearily. He didn't feel like he could walk a step, let alone run through a burning cellar, but staying here was death. The sense of where he was and what lay between him and fresh air suddenly pressed down on him like a cart sitting on his chest. His limbs went weak. He was five floors below ground in a burning building, the walls of which were a jumble of old, rotting timber, poorly mortared stone, brick and cheap, dry plaster. He had been far deeper in dwarf mines, but there he had had some confidence that they had been shaped by master masons. This place had been built by a succession of slum lords and criminals. Suddenly he wanted to see the sky more than anything in his life.

He scrambled up the slanted floor behind Gotrek and Ulrika into the burning warehouse, forcing his trembling, exhausted limbs to move. Flames were everywhere. The heat beat on Felix like a hammer. Every breath was like inhaling glass. The sewers were only ten paces away, and the path clear. Only a few steps and they would be safe.

Gotrek started forward, then stopped at a sound from above and looked up. 'Back!' he said, throwing his arms out. 'Back!'

With a rumbling and snapping, the brick ceiling above the hole to the sewers caved in, followed by timbers from the floors above it, all on fire. The debris blocked the hole to the sewers, and the ceiling kept coming down, a rain of bricks, timber and fire, that advanced on Gotrek, Felix and Ulrika like the leading edge of a storm. Dust billowed out towards them in a flaming cloud.

'The hidden stair!' cried Ulrika.

Gotrek made no argument, only turned and ran with Ulrika for the office with the secret door.

In his years with Gotrek, Felix had become used to shortening his stride to match the Slayer's. Not here. Fear lent him wings, and he nearly beat Ulrika to the office, and bested Gotrek by ten paces.

The office was filled with smoke, but was only just beginning to catch fire. Ulrika tore down the banner that hid the door and felt up and down the wall.

'Yebat!' she cursed, scrabbling desperately. 'Where is it?'

'Stand aside, parasite,' said Gotrek. He jabbed a finger at a nail head in a support beam and the door swung open. Ulrika pushed in first, her face rigid with panic. Gotrek and Felix filed in after her and Gotrek closed the door.

The stairs were dark, but at least free of smoke and fire. They hurried up them as the building roared and moaned and creaked all around them.

Felix heard Ulrika mumbling something that sounded like some Kislevite prayer.

'Scared, bloodsucker?' asked Gotrek.

Ulrika laughed, high and tight. 'Swords, daggers, pistol balls; they cannot kill me. But fire, fire means the true death.'

'I'll keep that in mind,' Gotrek growled.

As they raced up, Felix saw firelight glinting through cracks in the walls. Sometimes smoke trickled through and the walls radiated heat like an oven, and more and more smoke was filtering up the stairwell from below. Felix coughed, his eyes watering and his throat raw.

Five flights up, an orange light flickered from above them, and Felix could hear the crackling of flames.

Gotrek stopped. 'Blocked,' he said.

'Back down, then?' asked Felix. They looked over the railing. The smoke below them glowed from within with a hellish red, and the light seemed to be getting closer by the second. The stairs groaned and shifted under their feet, then suddenly dropped several inches and lurched to one side.

'I don't think so,' said Gotrek.

'We're trapped!' whimpered Ulrika.

Gotrek snorted and turned to feel the building's exterior wall, an unplastered mess of thinly mortared brick. Felix copied him. It was cool to the touch.

Gotrek flipped his axe around so that the square end faced out. He smashed it into the wall. Bricks flew. He swung again.

'Ha!' said Ulrika, grinning with relief. She stepped back and kicked at the wall with her boot heel. Mortar crumbled.

Felix joined her, kicking and stabbing at the bricks with his runesword. Sacrilege, no doubt, to use so grand a weapon for so pedestrian a purpose, but if Gotrek was using his sacred rune axe, and if it saved his life...

A hole opened up in seconds, Gotrek smashing through the two layers of brick with ease. Felix and Ulrika's kicks helped him widen it as the flames from below and above crept closer. Felix sucked in great breaths of the cool, clear air that blew in from the hole. He had never tasted sweeter.

At last the opening was wide enough for Gotrek's broad shoulders and they clambered though into another cellar; this one blissfully free of fire.

But as they reached the ground floor it became clear that the building had not escaped the blaze. The narrow corridor that led to the street was filled with weeping, wailing people, all trying to get out at once. Felix could hear crackling and screaming from the upper floors.

The alley, as Felix, Gotrek and Ulrika pushed out into it, was just as crowded. The nearby tenements had emptied and people milled around in panicked circles. Others ran away. Men in the masks of the Cleansing Flame were dotted through the crowd, shouting orders that no one listened to. The cult's meeting house was a roaring hell of flame and blackened beams, half its original height. The buildings to its left and right were burning too, and the wooden shingles of the building that housed the Broken Crown were smouldering.

People in further tenements were spreading wet blankets on their roofs, trying to protect them from the flurries of fiery sparks that whirled up and away over the gables. Others were forming bucket lines that trailed to a small well where two men were hauling up a single bucket and lowering it over and over again. The meagre splashes of water that the men at the front of the line threw on the fire were doing little.

'Sigmar,' breathed Felix. 'All of Shantytown is going to burn!'

Gotrek grunted, his massive fists balled in anger.

Ulrika shook her head in dismay. 'What terrible villainy.'

Gotrek sneered at her. 'What's the matter? You don't like your dinner cooked?'

She drew herself up, offended. 'I'm beginning to think that you are deliberately misunderstanding the Lahmian way.'

'Or maybe you are,' said Gotrek. He started for the well. 'Find a big tub, manling,' he said over his shoulder. 'We need to draw more water.'

Felix nodded, and was about to enter an unburned tenement, when a voice screeched nearby.

'There they are! There are the murderers who started the fire!'

Felix turned with Gotrek and Ulrika to see one of the masked men pointing directly at him.

Another cultist joined the first. 'Get them!' he cried. 'String them up! Throw them in the fire!'

'It wasn't us!' shouted Felix. 'It was them!' But his voice was lost in the roar of the crowd as they turned angry eyes on them.

'Kill the fire starters!' bellowed a man.

'They burned my baby!' shrieked a woman.

All at once the crowd surged in from all sides, snatching up stones and bits of smoking wood.

Gotrek bared his teeth in fury and frustration, and Felix was momentarily afraid that he was going to lash out at the mob, but then, with a dwarfish curse, he turned and made for a narrow alley, shoving the shouting people in front of him roughly aside. Felix and Ulrika followed him, hunching their shoulders against a rain of sticks and stones. Felix didn't want to hurt the poor souls in the crowd, but they were trying to tear him apart. He kicked and elbowed them aside, men and women alike.

They reached the alley mouth. Gotrek let Felix and Ulrika in first and then followed. Here, the mob could only press them from behind. Alone, Felix could have outdistanced them easily, but Gotrek, with his short legs, was too slow, and they railed unmercifully on his back with their makeshift weapons, the cultists urging them on. The Slayer cursed and grunted, but did not strike back. The end of the alley was rapidly approaching. They would be surrounded again.

They dodged around a rickety exterior stairway. Gotrek stopped suddenly. His axe lashed out – once, twice – chopping through the stair's supports, then ran on with Felix and Ulrika.

The crowd flooded after them, but then, with a squeal of tortured nails and twisting wood, the stairway peeled away from the outside of the tenement.

The crowd screamed and backed away, pushing back against their comrades who were continuing to press down the alley as the stairs accordioned down on themselves and crashed to the ground. A dozen or so Maze residents had made it past the crash. They ran out of the alley after Gotrek, Felix and Ulrika.

Gotrek spun on them as they spread out, baring his teeth. Felix and Ulrika drew too. The men and women slowed, uneasy.

'Go back,' said Gotrek. 'Fight the fire.' He raised his axe. It flashed red in the light of the inferno. 'You do not want this death.'

He turned again and the companions ran on. The crowd did not follow.

The Maze was filled with people and noise. Bells rang. People shouted. Men and women ran away from the fire or towards it. Teams of men ran past with ladders. Two women pushed a sloshing hogshead of water on a barrow. Others carried empty buckets, old blankets and brooms.

Felix's heart hung as heavy as a lead brick in his chest as he and Gotrek and Ulrika dodged through them all. He felt useless and miserable. He wanted to do something to help the innocents who were dying and losing their homes because of the Cleansing Flame's callous arson, but he couldn't think of a thing. He and Gotrek were very good at killing and destroying things. Ask them to fight a troll or a dragon, or bring down a corrupt king, or smash some eldritch temple and they would get to work with a will, and more than likely succeed, but ask them to protect someone from hunger or disease, or to save their home from fire or flood, and they were as powerless as the next man. You couldn't slay hunger with an axe. You couldn't kill fire with a sword.

As they came around a corner near the edge of the Maze, they saw Ward Captain Wissen hurrying towards them with a company of the watch. His polished breastplate glinted yellow with reflected fire.

His eyes widened as he saw them. 'You!' he cried, pointing. 'Is it you at the bottom of this?'

Gotrek didn't slow down. 'Out of my way, fool!'

'Arrest them!' shouted Wissen.

The watchmen spread across the road, lowering their spears.

Gotrek stopped, growling and staring them down.

'The culprits are the Cleansing Flame, ward captain,' said Felix quickly. It wouldn't do to have the Slayer slaughter the watch. 'Your agitators are cultists, worshippers of the Changer of Ways. It was they who started the fire. And they plan worse. They mean to blow up the Imperial Gunnery School with the stolen powder.'

Anger flashed across Wissen's face. Jealousy perhaps? 'And how do you know this?' he sneered.

Felix looked around to get confirmation from Ulrika, and realised that she was no longer with them. He looked back over his shoulder. She was nowhere to be seen. Where had she gone? When had she left? 'We heard it from the cultists themselves,' he said, facing Wissen again. 'And we saw them taking the powder into the sewers.'

'But you have no evidence of this?' asked Wissen.

Felix grunted with frustration. 'I don't understand you, ward captain. All along you have suspected agitators of having been behind the thefts, but now that we bring you word that your suspicions are correct, you question it? What is the difficulty?'

'The difficulty is *you*,' said Wissen, stepping forward and jabbing his finger. 'I have had the Cleansing Flame under observation for these past several months. My men have come very close to discovering who their leaders are, and what their ultimate goals are. We were this close!' he held his finger and thumb less than a half inch apart. 'This close to scooping them all up in a bag and jailing the lot of them. We might have uncovered a vast network of agitators and collaborators had we been able to put the screws to them, but then here come the "Saviours of Nuln," waltzing into town like a pair of drunken ogres, and smash up everything they touch. We'll never catch them now! You've scattered them to the four winds!' He cursed and turned to his men. 'Arrest them!' he cried. 'Arrest them for interfering with the work of the constabulary.'

Gotrek went on guard. 'You'll take me when I'm dead.'

Felix groaned. This was bad. Gotrek was going to kill a captain of the watch and they would have to go on the run again before they could warn Groot and Makaisson of the Cleansing Flame's plans. 'Captain,' he said, fighting to keep his voice calm. 'Ward captain, be reasonable. Do I need to remind you that we have been ordered by Lord Hieronymous Ostwald himself to assist you in your investigations? How will you explain to him our arrest? Should you not at least consult with your superiors?'

Wissen paused, grinding his teeth. His men hesitated.

'We were on our way to tell Lord Groot of the danger to the Gunnery School,' Felix continued. 'If you would care to accompany us, I'm sure that the truth of our story will be found below it.'

A nasty smile spread slowly across Wissen's face. 'Ha!' he said. 'I'm sure it will.' He bowed elaborately to Felix. 'Very well, sir. Lead on. Lead on and we will see.'

CHAPTER EIGHT

LORD GROOT UNLOCKED a heavy, iron-bound door and threw it open. 'These are the lowest rooms in the school,' he said in a cross voice. 'And the last that we have not examined – a dungeon we have never found it necessary to put to use.' He stepped aside and let Gotrek, Felix, Malakai, Magus Lichtmann and Captain Wissen step in.

Groot had been roused from his bed more than an hour ago, and was not in the best of moods. He had all of Felix's sympathy. Felix was so tired and sore from all the night's fighting and falling and battering that he could barely put one foot in front of the other. His eyes kept crossing and it was an effort to focus them again.

The dungeon was a very small affair. A guard room with ten cells beyond it, and a 'questioning' room beyond that. It looked indeed like it had never been used. The corners of the few sparse furnishings were sharp and unblunted by use, and everything was furred in a thick coat of dust. None the less, the party made a dutiful tour of the place, poking their heads into each cell and scanning the questioning room. Gotrek and Malakai made a more careful examination, running their hands over every wall, and scrutinising the floors and ceilings closely, while Magus Lichtmann muttered and gestured with his single hand. Groot and Wissen waited for them to finish with exaggerated patience.

At last the two Slayers exchanged an unhappy glance and returned to the door.

'Nithin', said Malakai with a sigh. 'Nae hidden doors, nae hollow walls, nae trapped floors. Same as a' the rest.'

Wissen gave a little snort of triumph.

'And you'll agree that we've seen everything there is to see?' asked Groot.

'Aye, that ah dae,' said Malakai. 'Naught's been left oot. We've seen it a''

'And I detect nothing hidden with magic of any kind,' said Magus Lichtmann.

Groot nodded. 'Then let's return to someplace warmer and wait for the sewer detail's report.'

He led the way back up through the many cellars to the receiving room of the school. Leaders of the sewer detail were waiting for them – a captain and a sergeant of the school guard standing at attention at the entrance with a hunched, haggard man in filthy clothes who carried a lantern, a long-poled hook, and a short sword and dagger on his belt.

Felix recognised the man's accoutrements instantly. He was a sewer jack. A host of memories flooded his mind at the sight – Gotrek and he carrying those very implements, the other men of their patrol – Gant, Rudi, Hef and Spider, the twin brothers who had shared the same girl. He also remembered the vile smell that had taken forever to scrub from his skin and his hair. The memory was so vivid that he thought he could smell the odour even now.

No, no, he thought as he saw Magus Lichtmann wrinkling his nose, it wasn't the memory after all. It was the sewer jack.

'What have you to report, captain?' asked Groot.

The guard captain saluted him and stepped forward. 'Nothing, my lord. Steiger here took us through every tunnel and channel that crosses under the school. There was nothing. No barrels. No loose powder. No fuses. No evidence of digging or recent construction. We even…' He coughed. 'We even had him probe the stew for anything hidden under the surface. There was nothing there either.'

Groot nodded. 'Very good, captain. You are dismissed. Get some rest. And give this man a crown for his pains.'

'Aye, my lord,' said the captain.

The sewer jack touched his forelock to Groot as the captain and the sergeant led him out. The light of early dawn shone into the entry hall as they opened the door.

'You see, Lord Groot?' said Wissen, eagerly, as he and the others followed Groot into the receiving room. 'Nothing! No powder. No sign of the Cleansing Flame.'

Groot only groaned and sank wearily into a deep leather chair.

'Could be it hisnae been placed yet,' said Malakai.

'Or it was never sold to the Cleansing Flame in the first place, perhaps,' suggested Magus Lichtmann.

Captain Wissen scowled at Gotrek and Felix. 'I begin to wonder if any part of their story is true. We only have their word that they found the Cleansing Flame's quarters. Or that the Flame are cultists.'

Gotrek rounded on him, his fists balling. 'Do you think I got these cuts falling down stairs?'

'Falling off a barstool, perhaps,' sneered Wissen.

Gotrek surged forward, lowering his head. 'Right. That's it.'

Malakai stepped in his way and put out a restraining arm. 'Easy laddie, easy. You'll no' catch yer villains like this.'

'You see?' cried Wissen, backing away. 'You see? Whatever acts of heroism these two might have performed in the past, they're mere taproom brawlers now. It may be true that they uncovered sorcery and mutation among the Brotherhood of the Cleansing Flame, but it could be just as true that they were carousing in some Maze ale cellar and kicked over a lantern, then thought to tell this wild tale to cover their villainy.'

Gotrek pushed at Malakai's arm. 'Do you call me a liar?'

'Not at all,' said Wissen. 'I merely say that we can't know, because you burned all the evidence, and we found nothing below the school.'

'We didn't burn it!' snapped Felix, his anger finally winning out over his exhaustion. 'The cultists burned it when they saw that we were in danger of exposing them!'

'And does that make it any less your fault?' asked Wissen. 'If you had not entered their lair they would have had no need to destroy their idols.' He pointed to the line of tall windows that ran along the front wall of the room. 'Look there! Look!'

All heads turned to the windows. Through the diamond panes Felix could see, smudged across the shell-pink dawn like a black smear of dung upon a lady's ball gown, a twisting pillar of smoke that rose from the centre of the Shantytown district. The orange glow of fire still underlit it at its base.

'That is your work,' said Wissen. 'Whether you set it or no. Scores dead. Hundreds without homes. Victims to your bullheadedness.'

Felix couldn't tear his eyes from the rising smoke. He felt as if the words were being stacked on top of his heart like stone slabs, one at a time, crushing it. As much as he hated the man, he couldn't help but think that Wissen was right. It *was* their fault. They had barged in as they always did, and innocents had been hurt. He looked over at Gotrek, expecting him to be trying to push past Malakai for Wissen again, but the Slayer was looking at the floor, his hands clenched. It seemed the words had hit him too. Somehow that made it worse.

Wissen turned to the others, bowing. 'My lords, I will place men in the sewers below the Gunnery School, just in case Herr Jaeger's story is true. It is only prudent. But may I suggest that he and Gurnisson be confined to the College of Engineering at least until the matter of their actions can be put before Lord Ostwald.'

'I think that is wise,' said Magus Lichtmann, his spectacles winking in the dawn light. 'It is a terrible pity. Much as I admire their zeal, I fear that the Slayer and his companion have been perhaps too hasty. If they had reported what they had discovered to Ward Captain Wissen, instead of trying to destroy the cult – if that is indeed what it was – single-handed, much tragedy could have been avoided.'

Lord Groot nodded. 'Aye,' he said. 'Maybe it's best. These sort of tactics no doubt work well enough in the lands of our enemies, but this…' He shook his head sadly. 'This took the lives and livelihoods of honest Nulners. That can't be allowed.'

Malakai banged a side table with his huge fist. His face was as red as his crest. 'Ye empty-headed eejits!' he barked. 'Have ye nae more sense than a bunch o' hens? Yer locking up the wrong lads!' He swept his hand towards Gotrek and Felix. 'Who wis it found the thieves that stole the powder? Who uncovered the vermin who bought it, and learned o' their wicked plans?'

'We have only their word for that,' piped up Wissen, raising a finger.

'Shut it, yoo!' said Malakai. 'I'm talkin'.' He turned to Groot. 'And as to who's tae blame for the fire. Do ye think this wee mannie,' he pointed at Wissen, 'and his lads would hae' fared any better? By Grungni's beard, them Flame boys would have heard 'em coming before they walked down three flights, and set the whole works ablaze. Ye would ha' lost a full company o' the watch as well as all those poor wee beggars in the warrens.' His finger moved to Gotrek and Felix. 'Gurnisson an' young Felix hae come closer than any to catching these lunatics. And it's them yer going tae lock up? Awa 'n boil yer heids!'

Groot raised his hands placatingly. 'Not locked up, Malakai,' he said. 'Not locked up. Only, erm, taking a rest, let's say, until Lord Ostwald can review what's happened. I don't doubt he'll approve of all they've done, and set them on the trail as soon as he's spoken to them.'

'And when can Lord Ostwald see us?' asked Felix.

'Ah,' said Groot, scratching his head violently. 'Well, he's been sent for.'

Lichtmann stepped forward. 'Pardon, Julianus, but I believe Lord Ostwald is closeted with the City Council today and tomorrow, reviewing some sort of fiscal matters.'

Groot looked at Gotrek, Felix and Malakai, embarrassed. 'So, a day or two then? The rest will do you good. You do look a bit the worse for wear.'

Gotrek growled. 'I make no promises.'

Groot and Wissen looked about to protest, but Malakai stepped forward.

'I do,' he said. 'Neither Gurnisson nor young Felix will pass through the gates of the College of Engineering until Lord Ostwald comes tae see 'em.'

Groot frowned and exchanged glances with the others, as Gotrek glared at Malakai.

'You will vouch for their good behaviour?' asked Groot at last.

'Aye,' said Malakai. 'If they step through that gate, ah'll take full responsibility for their actions.'

Groot nodded. 'Very well. Then I release them into your custody. And thank you, Malakai, for your understanding.'

Malakai snorted. 'Oh, I understand fu' weel.'

As they stepped out of the gates of the Imperial Gunnery School and started down the street towards the College of Engineering, Gotrek shot a sidelong glance at Malakai.

'You truly mean to try to keep me locked up?' he asked.

Malakai chuckled. 'Eh? O' course no'! Oh, ye'll no' leave by the gate. A dwarf does no' break a promise. But there's a wee hole down tae the sewers. I said naught about wee holes.'

When they got to the college, Felix went to his room, closed his shutters and his curtains and lay down in bed. But tired as he was, he had difficulty getting to sleep. His mind remained filled with Wissen's damning words. Malakai had made a spirited defence, but Felix still could not convince himself that the fire hadn't been, at least in part, their fault. Should they have gone back and told the authorities instead of wading in? Should they have fought the cultists in a different way? Was there something else they could have done?

When he did fall asleep, his dreams were haunted by the sounds of crackling flames and the screams of the dying.

FELIX WOKE TO a gentle tapping on his door. When he raised his head from the pillows, a man in the robes of a physician was poking his head in. He smiled at Felix.

'Sorry to wake you,' he said. 'But Professor Makaisson asked me to look in on you and change your bandages.'

Felix mumbled for the man to come in and tried to sit up to receive him. He was so stiff and sore he could barely move. The physician came in and helped him up, then went gently but firmly about his work. Felix smiled through his grunts and groans. Makaisson might be mad, but he did well by his guests.

Once all his burns and cuts had been salved and dressed and he had gone about the slow, painful process of pulling his clothes on, he hobbled through the school to Malakai's workshop. Once again he found Gotrek wolfing down an enormous breakfast while Malakai pottered among his inventions. The Slayer too had fresh bandages, but not nearly as many as yesterday. Felix shook his head. Though he had seen evidence of it many times before, he was yet again amazed at how quickly the dwarf's wounds healed. Many of his burns were only shiny pink spots, like punctuation marks among his tattoos.

Felix stepped to the unfinished room's missing wall and looked out over the city. The fires in Shantytown seemed to have died down for the most part, but there was still an ashy pall above the skyline that was not clouds. He sighed and sat down at the table and helped himself to ham, black bread and tea.

'The best cure for yer gloom, young Felix, is to catch yon madmen before they dae worse,' said Malakai. He snorted. 'Ward Captain Wissen willnae catch 'em, that's certain. 'No doubt e's out there now, flogging any poor soul he can catch, but gettin' nae answers, I'll warrant ye.'

Felix nodded, but was not convinced. The best cure would have been to not let the madmen start the fires in the first place.

Petr appeared in the door as Felix took his first sip of tea. He hurried forward, tripping over a coil of rope, then stopped at the table and pushed his wild hair out of his face.

'Good news, professor,' he said, beaming myopically. 'Meyer at the Gunnery School says that the new cannon has cooled and seems to be without fault.'

'Aye. Good news indeed,' said Malakai.

'All that remains,' continued Petr, 'is for the sprue to be cut and the barrel to be smoothed within and cleaned and polished without.'

'And how long will that take?' asked Felix.

'Meyer said that the smiths are aware of the urgency of the situation and will work around the clock to get it done,' said Petr. 'They say it will be done two mornings from now.'

Malakai shook his head sadly. 'Men rush things. Dwarf smiths would take a fortnight tae do it, at the least.' He shrugged. 'But as we have tae be awa' as soon as can be, I suppose quicker may jist be better.'

'Two days.' Gotrek grunted. 'Time enough to find those masked cowards. Eat faster, manling. I want a look in the sewers.'

'Petr,' said Malakai. 'Gae tae the steward and get the key to the sewer door.'

'Aye, professor,' said Petr. He turned and ran out of the room, tripping over the same coil of rope again as he went.

Felix shook his head. How had the boy survived as long as he had?

FELIX SHIVERED AS he and Gotrek stepped through a doorway into the sewers from a cellar under the College of Engineering. It was all as it had been twenty years ago, the crumbling brick walls, the low arched ceiling, the river of filth flowing sluggishly between the two narrow ledges, the rats scurrying away into darkness, the constant echoing plops and drips, the moist reek that flooded his nostrils. Memory once again overwhelmed him – it was here that the fight with the skaven in the College of Engineering had ended all those years ago, with the steam tank crashing through the floor and coming to rest half submerged in the stew. He shivered. No good ever came of entering the sewers.

'Good luck, sirs,' said Petr, as he pushed the heavy door closed behind them.

The boom of it closing was drowned out by a shriek.

Gotrek and Felix spun back, drawing their weapons and holding up their lanterns. There was nothing behind them.

'All right, Petr?' called Felix as the door inched open again.

'It's nothing,' squeaked Petr. 'Nothing. Just pinched my finger a… a little. Good luck.'

The door closed more slowly this time, and they heard locks and bolts clacking shut, and a soft moaning.

Gotrek grunted. 'A dwarf so clumsy would have been smothered at birth.'

Felix frowned. 'How would you know he was clumsy at birth?'

'That one? I've no doubt he tripped coming out of the womb.' He started down the sewer tunnel. 'Come, manling, the Gunnery School is this way.'

They continued down the tunnel, travelling slowly as Gotrek examined the walls on both sides, crossing back and forth over the granite slabs that bridged the stew at regular intervals. The Slayer muttered under his breath from time to time, but said nothing out loud.

A short while later, Gotrek looked up. 'Someone ahead.'

He crept forward, readying his axe. Felix got a better grip on his sword. All manner of possible horrors rose up in his mind as they rounded a curve in the tunnel and the flickering glow of a torch grew stronger before them. Was it ratmen? Cultists of the Cleansing Flame? Mutants?

'Halt!' said a voice. 'Who goes there?'

A trio of Nuln city watch came round the curve, torches held high. They stopped when they saw Gotrek and Felix and thrust their spears nervously before them.

'Who's there?' called the sergeant. 'State your business!'

Gotrek grunted, annoyed. Felix sighed. He had forgotten that Wissen had said he was going to place patrols down here. This was going to be a bit awkward.

'Perhaps we should retire,' he murmured to Gotrek, as the watchmen came closer.

'We need to find the powder,' said Gotrek.

'Aye,' said Felix. 'But we can't kill the watch to do it. We're in enough trouble as it is.'

'Come forward, curse you!' said the sergeant. 'Into the light. What are you doing down here?'

'We can return later,' continued Felix. 'Now we know they're here, we can avoid them next time, once their guard is down.'

Gotrek growled, but finally nodded and began backing away.

'It's the Slayer and the other one,' said one of the watchmen. 'Them that burned Shantytown!'

'Why so it is,' said the other.

'Stop, you!' called the sergeant. 'You're not meant to be outside the College!'

He and his men started forward at a trot.

Gotrek cursed and stopped. Felix groaned and lined up beside him.

The sergeant halted before them and pointed his spear. 'Hand over your weapons and come with me. Watch Captain Wissen will want to hear about this.'

'Tell him about this,' said Gotrek. His hand shot forward and caught the shaft of the sergeant's spear. He twisted it and the sergeant staggered left, then toppled into the stew with a thick splash.

Gotrek advanced on the other watchmen, as the sergeant came to the surface gasping and choking and covered in filth.

'You want to join him?' the Slayer rasped.

The watchmen backed off, wide-eyed, then turned and ran, calling and whistling for reinforcements.

The sergeant slogged after them, waist deep in the flow. 'Come back, cowards! How dare you desert a senior officer!'

Gotrek chuckled nastily and made to continue forward, but there were answering cries and whistles from further down the tunnel. He cursed again and turned away.

'Right, manling,' he said. 'We'll return later. Let's see what we can turn up in the Maze.'

Felix frowned. 'The Maze? Is that wise? We're not well liked down there at the moment.'

'And where are we liked?' asked Gotrek.

FELIX WALKED THROUGH Shantytown with a heavy heart. The men and women of the Maze were wheeling their charred belongings through the streets on barrows and dog carts, their children tailing behind them. Larger wagons were carrying fresh timber, bricks and plaster in the other direction. Priests of Morr carried burned bodies away on carts and stretchers.

Felix wore the hood of his cloak up to hide his face, but Gotrek walked openly, his singed crest and his burn scars showing, and just as Felix had feared, they were getting a lot of looks. People glared. Some whispered behind their hands to each other, but none approached. Perhaps, in the light of day, with the fires of hate somewhat cooled, they didn't relish confronting a dwarf as fearsome looking as Gotrek. Felix was not reassured. It wouldn't take much to spark the Shantytowners to violence again. One voice raised in anger, one pointed finger, and they would be swarmed again.

He held his breath every time they passed another street corner orator. Each was telling the crowds that clustered around them that it was the Countess, or the nobles, or the merchants, that were to blame for the fire – that the rich were burning the poor out to make room for new warehouses and manufactories. The orators urged the Shantytowners to rise up and smash the merchants and the nobles and the fat priests who supported them.

Gotrek stopped at the edge of one such crowd and listened to the speaker, staring intently at him. The man stood on a wooden crate near the mouth of an alley. A handful of other men surrounded him, handing out leaflets and talking in low tones with the listeners. Felix hovered beside him uneasily, anxious to move on before somebody noticed them and started calling for their heads.

'Did we hear that voice last night?' Gotrek asked.

Felix closed his eyes and listened. The voice sounded familiar, but he couldn't be sure. 'I don't know. The message certainly sounds like what the Cleansing Flame were preaching, but these men don't wear masks.'

Gotrek started pushing forward. 'If it squawks like a goblin, and it smells like a goblin...'

'Gotrek, wait,' whispered Felix. 'We'll have the whole neighbourhood after us! We're already getting looks.'

Gotrek paused, considering, then nodded. 'Aye. We need to get one alone.' He rose up on his toes and peered through the crowd. 'This way,' he said, and started down the street, away from the orators.

Felix followed him around the block and then into an alley. Gotrek strode unerringly though the zigzag labyrinth of back streets and mews until they stood in the shadows of an alley just behind the orator and his fellows.

'Right,' said Gotrek. 'Lure one in.'

'Lure...? How?'

Gotrek shrugged. 'You're the subtle one.'

Felix groaned. 'All right. I'll try.'

He edged to the mouth of the alley and looked around. He was standing behind and a bit to the left of the agitators. From this angle he could watch the faces of the crowd as they listened to the speech. The orator was stirring them well. They cheered on cue. They shook their fists. They were angry, and looked to be spoiling for a fight. One of the speaker's fellows was facing the crowd just in front of Felix, holding a fistful of leaflets.

Felix tugged his hood down over his eyes, then stepped out of the shadows and waved at the man. 'Hoy. Let me see one of those.'

'Certainly brother,' said the man. He crossed to Felix, holding one out. 'Did you see the fires last night? Did you lose your home to the villainy of the landlords?'

'Oh yes,' said Felix, taking the leaflet and in the same motion pressing the tip of his dagger against the man's stomach. 'And I saw who started them too.'

The agitator looked down, then up, meeting Felix's eyes under his hood. 'You!' he gasped.

'Shout and you're dead,' said Felix. 'Now, into the alley.'

The man hesitated, and made to back away. Felix caught his arm and twisted it, pressing harder with the dagger.

The man whimpered, eyes wide.

'Shhhh,' said Felix. 'Come on.'

He turned with the man into the alley, bending over the leaflet as if he was discussing it with him, all the while keeping the tip of the dagger pushed firmly against his abdomen.

'What do you want with me?' whispered the agitator, as the shadows swallowed them.

'Me?' said Felix. 'I want nothing. It's him that wants to speak to you.' He nodded further down the alley.

Gotrek stepped forward, the light from the end of the alley glittering in his single angry eye.

The agitator flinched back, almost escaping Felix's grip. 'The dwarf!' he cried. 'Powers of darkness protect me!'

Gotrek's hand shot out and caught him by the neck. He yanked him down to his knees. 'Who are your leaders?' he growled.

'Leaders?' said the agitator. 'I don't know what you...'

Gotrek's thick fingers tightened, and the man's sentence ended in a strangled squawk.

'Who are your leaders?' the Slayer repeated.

'I... I...' squeaked the man. 'I don't know.'

Gotrek slapped him across the ear. It sounded like a branch snapping.

The man wailed in pain. Gotrek clamped a hand over his mouth until he stopped, then let up. 'Who?'

'I swear I don't know!' gasped the man. 'We never see them without their masks!'

'What about the man speaking?' asked Felix.

'He is above me,' said the man. 'But he is only the leader of thirteen men. He only does what he's told, like the rest of us.'

'And who tells him what to do?'

'The leaders,' said the man. 'The masked ones.'

'Maybe he knows who they are,' said Felix.

'No one knows,' said the agitator.

'I'll hear it from him,' said Gotrek. He looked around. There was a flimsy wooden door opening into the back of a tenement beside him. 'Open that,' he said to Felix, then dragged the cultist closer to the mouth of the alley.

Felix tried the door. It wasn't locked. He held it open.

Gotrek shook the agitator. 'Call a name,' he rasped.

'A name?'

'One of your "brothers". Call his name. Ask him to come here.'

'Er, I…'

Gotrek slapped him again. 'Call!'

The man cried out in pain. 'Harald,' he whimpered.

Gotrek raised his fist. 'Louder!'

'Harald, come here!' squealed the man. 'Hurry! I need you!'

'Good,' said Gotrek, and snapped the cultist's neck with a twist of his hands.

The man slumped bonelessly to the ground, dead. Gotrek left him in front of the door, then entered the building and pulled his axe from his back. Felix stepped in after him.

'Close it.'

Felix pulled the door shut and drew his sword. He looked at Gotrek. 'You killed him.'

'Aye.'

Gotrek pressed his ear to the door. Felix frowned, then joined him.

They heard steps and a question, then a cry of alarm.

The steps came closer.

'Dolf!' came a voice, right on the other side of the door. 'Dolf! What happened?'

Felix tensed.

'Not yet,' murmured Gotrek.

The steps ran off again and Felix heard raised voices from beyond the alley. The orator's rant faltered, then continued in the background. The voices got closer. It sounded like four men.

'What happened to him?'

'I don't know. But I think he's dead.'

'Was he attacked?'

'I see no wound.'

'Perhaps his heart just stopped.'

'Come on. Let's get him up.'

'Now,' said Gotrek. 'And stay quiet.'

He pushed the door open. Four men hunched over the body of the dead cultist, lifting him. Gotrek cut down the two nearest before they even had a chance to look up. Felix lunged at a third and ran him through as he let go of the body and reached for his sword. The fourth opened his mouth to scream. Gotrek split his head down to his neck before he made a sound.

'Inside,' said the Slayer. 'Leave the first.' He grabbed two bodies by their collars and dragged them into the tenement.

Felix caught another by the wrists and hauled at it. The body bumped heavily over the lintel and he let it drop next to the others. Gotrek threw the last on top of the others. Felix's stomach felt queasy. He could not remember killing anyone as unprepared as the men who had just died. It did not feel honourable or heroic. He and Gotrek had quite literally caught them stooping.

'That was…'

'Quiet,' said Gotrek. He closed the door and pressed his ear to it again, his axe at the ready.

It took a few minutes, but finally another questioning voice called down the alley, and then another cry of alarm. This time the orator's speech stopped, and Felix heard him calling to the crowd to excuse him for a moment.

His voice rose again in the alley. 'What do you mean, vanished? How could they have vanished? What…?' Footsteps stopped right outside the door. 'Is he drunk? Dolf! Get up! Bah. Get him up. Harald! Feodor! Where are you?'

Gotrek opened the door. Two men were bent over the body, while a third, the orator, stood behind them, hands on his hips. Gotrek slashed left and right, killing the first two cultists, then leapt at the orator and punched him in the stomach. The man folded up with an explosion of breath, and collapsed moaning over the Slayer's shoulder. Gotrek turned back to the door, carrying him.

A chorus of cries came from the mouth of the alley. Felix looked up and saw a clutch of curious crowd members pointing and shouting. They called behind them and started down the alley.

Gotrek stepped through the door. Felix closed it. Gotrek threw the orator to the ground, then began piling the dead cultists against the door. Fists pounded on it from the other side, but could not budge it.

Gotrek picked up the orator and slung him over his shoulder again. 'Come on, manling.'

He carried the orator through the tenement and out onto the street, then immediately entered another tenement on the opposite side and found the stairs to the cellar.

They went down, and Gotrek dropped the man onto the dirt floor amid heaps of trash and broken furniture. He knelt on his chest with one knee and lowered his axe to the man's neck.

'Who are your leaders?' he rasped.

The orator blinked up at him, dazed and frightened. He swallowed. 'I… I have no leaders. I am the leader.'

Gotrek broke his nose with his bony fist. 'Who are your leaders?'

Blood spilled across the orator's cheeks like a red river. 'I... I don't know! They wear masks!'

Gotrek raised his fist.

Felix winced and stepped forward, holding up a hand. 'Who do you *think* they are?'

The man's eyes went wide. 'I dare not! I cannot!'

Gotrek punched him again, further shattering his nose. He screamed.

'Do you dare now?' growled Gotrek.

The orator spat blood and glared up at Gotrek. A mad light had come into his eyes. 'Do your worst, dwarf. Pain ends with death, but if I betray my masters, death is only the beginning of pain.'

Gotrek leaned forward, crushing the man under his enormous weight. He pressed the blade of his axe into the man's neck. 'And what if death is a long time coming?'

'It comes now!' cried the orator, then thrust his head forward and twisted, so that he cut his own throat against the axe blade.

Felix gasped as the man's head slumped back and the clean-edged wound gaped open like a second mouth. Blood pumped from it in a torrent.

Gotrek sat back, annoyed.

Felix let out a breath. He disliked this sort of business. 'A wasted effort,' he said. 'We know nothing more than when we started.'

'Killing seven servants of the Ruinous Powers isn't a waste,' said Gotrek, standing. 'But you are right. These rankers know nothing. We will learn nothing of their masters from them.'

Felix nodded. 'And I don't think we'll find their masters in the Maze.'

Gotrek cleaned his axe on the shirt of the orator, his brow furrowed. 'They have protected themselves well, curse them.' He put his axe on his back and turned to the stairs. 'Come on, manling. A drink will help me think.'

As THEY TURNED the corner onto the street that the Blind Pig occupied, Gotrek grunted as if he'd been shot. Felix looked up, then gaped. The tavern was gone – reduced, along with most of the other buildings around it, to charred beams and mounds of smouldering black rubble. In the street before it, sitting slumped on an overturned water bucket, was Heinz, his face buried in his arms. His clothes were stained with soot. The backs of his hands were burned.

Gotrek stopped in the middle of the street, staring at the sad tableau. Felix stopped behind him. A carriage pulled to an abrupt halt behind them.

'Someone will die for this,' said Gotrek.

Felix nodded, but a nagging voice in his head wondered again if he and Gotrek were responsible for the fire. And if they were, would the Slayer kill *them*?

'Hello, Felix,' said a familiar voice behind them. 'Hello, Slayer.'

Felix turned. Leaning out of the window of the carriage behind them was a heavily hooded and veiled figure. A shock of white hair shone through the black lace of the veil.

'Ulrika,' said Felix. 'What are you doing here?'

'I have been looking for you,' she said. 'My mistress wishes to speak to you. To ask a favour of you.'

Gotrek tore his eyes from the ruins of Heinz's tavern and glared up at her. 'The oath breaker wants a favour?' There was a dangerous note in his voice.

'It pertains to the Cleansing Flame, and may help uncover their leaders and what they have done with the powder.'

CHAPTER NINE

GOTREK STARED LEVELLY at Ulrika for a long moment, then turned back to the Blind Pig. 'You go,' he said to Felix. 'I have things to do.'

'Me?' Felix didn't like the idea of walking into the den of the vampire countess alone. She had dealt honourably with him before, but one never knew with vampires. 'But this might be the information we have been looking for.'

'You're better off without me,' said Gotrek. 'I don't trust my axe in her presence.'

'I don't trust my neck in her presence,' said Felix, but Gotrek was already stumping towards Heinz and didn't look back.

'All right, I… I suppose I'll go, then.'

Felix turned back to the carriage. Ulrika was holding the door open for him. He could see her sharp white teeth smiling through the veil. He swallowed, dread and excitement warring in the pit of his stomach, then shrugged and climbed in.

Ulrika rapped the ceiling with her knuckles and they started forward. She closed the blinds against the twilight, then removed her hood and veil and leaned back, looking at him, her eyes twinkling in the light of a horn lantern. Her hair had been trimmed very close in order to cut out the sections that had been burned the night before, and she looked even more androgynous than usual.

Felix shifted uncomfortably, uncertain what to say or where to look. She was so beautiful, and yet so unnerving. So much like the woman he had once known and loved, and at the same time nothing like her at all.

'I remember you with fondness, Felix,' she said after a moment. 'Is that how you remember me?'

Felix frowned. His memories of their times together rose up before his eyes and he could feel desire stirring within him. At the same time, the smug smirk that had twisted her mouth as she asked the question reminded him unpleasantly of her inborn sense of entitlement, which had always rubbed him the wrong way. There had been so many fights, over so little. She had been so foreign to him, even then. A noblewoman. A Kislevite. A born warrior. She had so little in common with an overly educated merchant's son from Altdorf, who thought himself more poet than soldier. Their ideas of the world had been so dissimilar they might have been different species.

Now they were.

And yet, his most lasting memories of her were not the fights and the sullen silences, nor the jealousies and sadness at the end when things were falling apart, but instead of laughing with her, riding with her, rolling with her, fencing with her, both with sword and word, and most of all, of enjoying the challenge of her.

'Yes,' he said at last. 'For all our troubles, I still think of you... fondly.' He coughed as another thought came to him. 'Ah, have you spoken to... to Max since...'

Her wide grin flashed again. 'Still jealous, Felix?'

'Not at all!' said Felix, hotly. 'I was just wondering what he thought of... of what has occurred.'

'Of course,' she purred. 'Of course. No, I have not spoken to Herr Schreiber since my... "demise". He is in Altdorf, I believe. Teaching. I am not sure he would welcome a visit and, to be honest, I have not thought to seek him out.' She frowned and touched her breast. 'My heart no longer works as it did. Nothing can touch it now.'

For the first time her mask of sly amusement seemed to slip a little and Felix thought he saw a ghost of pain flit across her face.

'Uh,' said Felix, into the silence. 'So, how have you been?'

Ulrika snorted, then chuckled, then doubled over with laughter. At last she flopped back in her seat and looked at him through half-closed eyes. 'Oh, Felix, I *have* missed you.' She sighed, then gazed up at the red damask ceiling, her long white fingers trailing aimlessly across the leather bench. 'It is not an easy thing, becoming one of night's dark masters,' she said. 'One must learn first to master oneself, one's appetites. This is difficult. The hunger is at times... overwhelming. The urge to rend and kill and drink one's victims dry...' She licked her lips and her eyes flicked to Felix's neck, then swiftly away. She coughed. 'Well, it is constantly with one. Fortunately, I have had a very wise, very patient teacher, who has opened the wisdom of her centuries-long life to me without stint. Countess Gabriella, despite what your surly companion believes, has lived up to her vow and taught me how to control my animal hungers, how to sip and savour, rather than guzzle and slaughter. She has taught me how to use my newborn powers, and also, more importantly, how to hide them. And she has tutored me in the twisted family trees of the Nehekharan bloodlines, and in the feuds and internecine jealousies that threaten them.'

Felix frowned. A family tree where no one was related was a strange thing to imagine.

'She has not always been the kindest mistress,' Ulrika continued, and a flicker of some emotion came and went in her eyes that Felix thought might have been pain or anger or fear. 'She is sometimes cruel. It is, I think, part of our nature. And there have been times when I have cringed under the lash of her displeasure. She is wary, as anyone in her precarious position must be – always on guard against betrayal, or incautious words and actions that might expose what she really is. Because of these concerns, she has occasionally scolded me for taking unnecessary risks, or for befriending people not fully under my control.' She shrugged. 'But I owe her my life – or my undeath, rather. For had she not taken me under her wing after that mad idiot Adolphus Krieger turned me, I would have been dead – truly dead – within the day, either by the sun, or Gurnisson's dread axe, or some peasant's bonfire, so I cannot speak too harshly against her.' She chuckled. 'In that, I suppose I feel for her like any daughter feels for her mother, eh?'

All at once, she leaned forward, her face troubled. 'Listen, Felix. You have met her before. Indeed, you knew her before I did. She was cautious then. But you should be aware before you speak to her again that, due to the crazed schemes of Adolphus Krieger and other deluded madmen among our aristocracy, this tendency towards caution has grown. She is, in her way, as suspicious as the Slayer, and extremely unwilling to let live those she feels threaten her existence. So...' She hesitated, then shrugged apologetically. 'So, be polite, eh, Felix?'

Felix swallowed. 'I... I will do my best.'

'Thank you,' she said, then chuckled. 'I must say, I am very glad Gotrek decided not to come.'

AFTER RIDING EAST on Commerce Street through the Reik Platz and on past the squat grey pile of the Nuln town hall, Ulrika's coach turned south into the tidy streets of the Handelbezirk, still alive with wealthy merchants closing up their offices and walking to their clubs or homes, or chatting and drinking in the cafes and taverns that lined the streets.

Another turn to the east, and the coach was rolling down a quiet side street, flanked on both sides by prosperous, well kept townhouses. The warm glow of lamp light shone from diamond-paned windows. The coach made a right down a side alley and pulled at last through a coach yard gate.

Felix stepped out of the carriage behind Ulrika and looked up at the rear of a sturdy, respectable four storey townhouse. He wasn't sure what he had expected, but it wasn't this. It was certainly nothing like Krieger's vast, brooding castle in mist-shrouded Sylvania. There was a distinct lack of towering basalt walls and leering gargoyles and dark foreboding.

Ulrika led the way to the rear door as grooms came out of a coach house and began unhitching the horses. 'It would have been more correct to receive you at the front door,' she said. 'But there are prying eyes everywhere, as the countess says, and she doesn't want any connection to be made between you, for both your sakes.' She paused with her hand on the latch and looked back at Felix. 'One more thing I forgot to mention. Here in Nuln, the countess is not Countess Gabriella of Sylvania, but Madame Celeste du Vilmorin, late of Caronne, a Bretonnian noblewoman.'

'Very well,' said Felix, unsure what he was to make of this information.

Ulrika opened the door and led him into a small room with dark passages leading off into shadows. From further in the house Felix could hear female laughter and quiet music. Ulrika stepped to a narrow winding stair in the left wall and began to ascend. Felix followed.

'The countess...' He caught himself. 'Sorry, Madame du Vilmorin is entertaining?'

'Her ladies are,' said Ulrika.

'Oh,' said Felix. He blushed. 'Oh, I see.'

Ulrika smiled. 'There is no better thief of secrets than a harlot.'

The stairs wound past three more floors, and at each Felix could hear laughter and singing and more intimate sounds.

The fourth floor was much quieter. A thick red Araby carpet ran down the centre of a wide, panelled hallway. Beaded crimson lamps hung from the walls at regular intervals, casting a ruby glow over every surface. Ulrika stepped to a door halfway along the hall and tapped softly at it. After a short wait, the door opened and a young girl in a blue silk dress looked out. Felix almost gasped. She was the most beautiful girl he had ever seen, a little porcelain doll with blonde ringlets, a knowing smile, and enormous blue eyes. She couldn't have been more than fifteen.

'Herr Jaeger,' murmured Ulrika, ducking her head.

The blonde girl curtsied to Felix. 'Welcome, sir. You are expected. Please come in.'

Felix looked uncertainly at Ulrika.

She smirked. 'Perfectly harmless, Felix. I assure you.' She started down the hall. 'I'm going to get out of my hunting clothes. I will join you shortly.'

Felix hesitantly followed the diminutive beauty into a lushly appointed ante-chamber. Tiny, feminine chairs were gathered around low, lacquered tables, all crowded with vases of lush flowers and exquisite statuettes. Crystal chandeliers cast shards of gentle light across the accoutrements of the life of a woman of leisure – a harpsichord, an embroidery frame, a book open to an illustration of a flower. Everything seemed too delicate to be touched.

'Please have a seat, Herr Jaeger,' said the blonde girl. 'I will inform madame that you have arrived.'

She disappeared into a further room and Felix lowered himself warily into one of the filigree chairs, trying to keep his scabbard from bumping into anything. The chair held. He let out a breath, and looked around. There was something wrong with the room. Though it appeared calculated to seem peaceful and exquisite and feminine, it unnerved him somehow, and he didn't know why. What was the discordant element? His eyes roamed from place to place. An enamelled clock ticked quietly on the mantelpiece. Paintings of young lovers walking down sunlit lanes and girls in flower-garlanded swings hung on red brocade walls. A golden ewer and cups sat on a sideboard.

Then it struck him. There were no windows. It wasn't just that the windows had been blocked or curtained. They had been removed entirely.

The inner door opened. Felix turned and made to stand, then stopped, halfway to his feet, paralysed by the sight that met his eyes. Filing out of the inner room was a line of young women, all in simple, elegant white dresses, like novitiates at a Shallyan convent, except that their heads were uncovered, and that they were all astonishingly, painfully, beautiful.

Felix's heart stopped as the first in line looked him in the eye. She was the most gorgeous girl he had ever seen, a dark eyed brunette with lush red lips and a figure to match. Then his gaze was caught by the eyes of the girl that followed her. His heart stopped. She was the most beautiful girl he had ever seen, an ethereal blonde with the regal nose and statuesque bearing of a princess from a fairytale. The girl behind her...

He tore his eyes away and gathered up his jaw. He was making a fool of himself. But what man would not? Each was more bewitching than all the others, and each in an entirely different way. Where had they come from? And why were they here? He couldn't help looking after them as they glided by and sashayed out into the hallway.

'Madame will see you now, Herr Jaeger,' said a voice behind him.

Felix jumped and turned guiltily, nearly knocking over a spindly little table which held a Cathay vase. He grabbed at the vase as it tottered, and nearly succeeded in upsetting it entirely before he managed at last to steady it.

The little blonde girl held the inner door open, a hand over her mouth to hide an amused smile. 'This way, Herr Jaeger,' she said.

Felix followed her through the doorway into a warm, candle-lit boudoir. This was a much darker, more sombre, room, though no less feminine. Books and paintings of beautiful women in ancient dress lined every wall. Rich velvets and brocades in burgundy and cobalt upholstered graceful couches and chairs. A massive canopied bed stood like an altar upon a dais at the far end. Its canopies were closed.

To one side, before a grand fireplace surrounded by a baroquely carved mantelpiece that rose, urn upon corbel upon pillar, all the way to the ceiling, was a luxurious tasselled and fringed chaise longue, upon which reclined the woman Felix knew as Countess Gabriella of Nachthafen, dressed in a robe of crimson silk that spilled off onto the floor like a flow of blood. She had not changed physically in the slightest since the last time he had seen her. She still appeared to be an alabaster-skinned beauty of perhaps thirty, with thick black hair and sparkling black eyes. Her figure was petite but exquisite, and her smallest move full of fluid, feline grace.

'Welcome, Herr Jaeger,' said the countess, her voice silky with soft Bretonnian consonants. 'You have not aged a day.' She raised her hand to him.

'Nor have you, madame.' Felix smiled as he took her hand and bent over it. She had had an Altdorf accent when last they met. It appeared she took her Bretonnian imposture seriously.

The countess motioned behind him. 'Please sit.'

'Thank you, madame.' Felix sank into a velvet covered chair.

'Astrid,' said the countess, as the little blonde girl appeared at Felix's side and placed a glass of wine and a tray of sweets at his elbow, 'Please make sure that Captain Reingelt still slumbers, and then you may retire.'

'Yes, my lady.' The girl curtsied, then stepped to the canopied bed. She drew aside one of the curtains and looked within, then turned back to the countess. 'He does, my lady.'

'Very good,' said the countess.

The girl curtsied again and then drifted silently out into the antechamber. Felix stared uneasily at the hidden bed, alarmed. What had happened to poor Captain Reingelt, whoever he might be?

He turned back to Countess Gabriella and found her gazing upon him. He flinched. She smiled. 'Are you comfortable, Herr Jaeger?'

Felix chuckled. 'I don't know if I have ever been more comfortable and at the same time uncomfortable in all my life.'

The countess laughed, a silvery waterfall of delight.

'You are not the first, Herr Jaeger,' she said, 'upon whom this place has had that effect.'

'Ah,' said Felix, motioning back over his shoulder. 'Those... young women. Were they all...?'

'Not a one,' said the countess. 'We of the sisterhood do not grant the blood gift in so profligate a manner. They are merely girls – children made victims of their own beauty – whom I have rescued and brought here so that they may learn the womanly arts at my... hmm... my atelier.'

It took a moment for Felix to fight his way through the flowery phrasing to the meaning of her words. 'You kidnap pretty little girls and train them to be harlots?'

Countess Gabriella smiled with practiced ease. 'It amuses you to be blunt, Herr Jaeger. But no, the girls are purchased from orphanages or saved from the street, and though it is true that the least of them may indeed find employment within these walls, the best will become the wives and mistresses of the richest, most influential noblemen and merchants in the Old World, and live lives of luxury and leisure of which, in their previous lives, they could never have dreamed.'

'All the while spying for you and your "sisterhood",' said Felix.

The countess nodded. 'But of course. One likes to see a return on one's investment.'

Felix opened his mouth to make a witty reply, but all at once the countess's smile vanished as if it had never been.

'But now to business,' she said.

Felix sat up and waited for her to speak, but despite her words, she paused, her eyes boring into him like a Sigmarite witch hunter trying to see into his soul.

'Before we begin,' she said at last. 'I must ask you a question.' She sat a little forward, her robe falling open to reveal the soft white contours of her breasts. 'I have information to impart to you that will help us both in our fight against these vile cultists, but first I must know that you and your fell companion do not mean me and mine any harm, and will not expose or attack us after our mutual foe is defeated.'

Felix hesitated. For reasons of etiquette and manners, he was glad Gotrek was not present – had he been here there would almost certainly have been bloodshed already – but the Slayer should have been here to answer this question for himself. 'I mean you no harm,' he said at last. 'But I cannot speak for the Slayer. He has said that he feels you forswore the oath you made that you would teach Ulrika to do no harm.'

Countess Gabriella's eyes flashed. 'Does he indeed? And why does he believe such a thing?'

Felix coughed. 'Well, both of us witnessed her kill several men last night.'

The countess waved a dismissive hand. 'She defended herself, and you. It is less than the Slayer does himself. Did he think I would make a sister of Shallya of her?' She raised her chin, defiant. 'Since I accepted her as my get, Ulrika has not killed a single man while slaking her thirst. This was the sum of my promise. More he cannot expect. Ulrika is a warrior. She killed scores of men before entering my service, some of them while fighting at the Slayer's side. In the course of her duties as my bodyguard and my envoy, she has killed to defend me and to protect my interests. Would the Slayer consider these things a breach of my oath?'

Felix pursed his lips, remembering Gotrek's feud with Hamnir, and many others. 'I cannot say, but I know Gotrek has demanded that those who make vows with him honour their most minute points, sometimes beyond all common sense.' He shrugged. 'He is a dwarf.'

The countess slapped the arm of the chaise, annoyed. 'You cannot say? Then why is he not here to speak for himself?' she asked. 'The information I have may be the key to destroying these fiends. But I dare not reveal it to you without protecting myself.' She glared at Felix. 'Can you not give me a guarantee for the dwarf's behaviour?'

Felix laughed, then recovered himself as she saw her anger flare. 'Forgive me, countess, but Gotrek obeys no one but himself. He would not honour any pledge that I or anyone else made in his name.'

The countess's jaw clenched.

'On the other hand,' said Felix. 'The Slayer does not hesitate once he makes up his mind. If he had decided that you had truly broken your vow, he would already have acted. He would be here, and you would be... defending yourself.' He had almost said, 'you would be dead,' but decided at the last second that that would not be very diplomatic.

As the countess mulled this over, the door opened behind Felix and a tall woman in a corseted green satin dress entered and took a seat on a chair near the chaise. She had long wavy auburn hair that hung almost to her waist and a trim, elegant figure. Felix found it hard not to stare at her. Another beauty! Was there no end to them? This one seemed more mature than the rest of the countess's students – a woman, not a girl – but as graceful as a leopardess and as proud as a swan. She met his gaze steadily, then winked an ice blue eye at him. He jerked back in his seat, surprised. It was Ulrika! The auburn hair was a wig. She grinned at his surprise, and put a finger to her lips.

Felix stared anew. He hadn't seen her dressed in so womanly a fashion since their first night together, back on her father's estate. The memory of it made his heart skip a beat.

'So,' said Countess Gabriella, finally. 'You don't think the Slayer means me harm?'

'I cannot say, countess – er, madame,' said Felix, pulling his eyes away from Ulrika and his mind back to the present with difficulty. 'His temper is changeable, to say the least. I do know that at present he wants two things above all others. He wishes vengeance on the Brotherhood of the Cleansing Flame for the burning of the tavern of his friend, and he wishes to reach Middenheim and die facing a daemon in battle. If you can aid him in achieving either or both...'

'Mistress,' said Ulrika, interrupting. 'If I might make an observation.'

'Of course, daughter,' said the countess.

'I think it is perhaps impossible to remove the risk from this venture. I do not think the Slayer will give you the guarantee you wish. But...' she said, raising her voice as the countess opened her mouth to interrupt. 'But, I think that the risk is justified. The Cleansing Flame want no less than the destruction of the Empire and the end of our way of life. They have sided with the Ruinous Powers, and will undoubtedly call upon them for aid. They will bring sorcerers and beasts and daemons against us. They will summon their dark gods to smite us. These are foes that the followers you currently command, loyal though they may be, cannot prevail against.'

'Even yourself, daughter?'

'Even myself,' agreed Ulrika, then continued. 'If we want to ensure the destruction of these evil men, and the defeat of their vile masters. If we want to preserve the life we have now and the future we crave, then we must risk this alliance. Herr Jaeger and Slayer Gurnisson have won battles against the deadliest of foes. I have seen Herr Jaeger kill a dragon. I have witnessed the Slayer destroy daemons. Tides of beastmen have fallen before them. They are our best weapon against these corrupters.'

Felix swallowed. No need to lay it on so thick, he thought. Just because they had fought all those things and won didn't mean they could do it again, or wanted to do it again. Well, he didn't anyway.

Countess Gabriella pressed her fingertips together, her eyes turned inward, thinking. As the silence lengthened, Felix caught Ulrika looking at him. She spread her hands in a pleading gesture.

Felix grunted. He didn't want to convince the countess to dig them deeper into this mess. He didn't like this kind of fight – where one never knew who one's enemies were. He didn't care to guess which of the men around him had worn a mask the night before and tried to blow him up with black powder. He didn't like wondering when a friend or companion might turn on him, dagger raised, the mad light of fanaticism blazing from his eyes. The more he thought about it, the more flying off to Middenheim and fighting enemies out on an open battlefield seemed like the most appealing option.

But he knew it was useless. He had seen the look in Gotrek's eyes when he had found Fritz sitting before the blackened ruins of the Blind Pig. They were going nowhere until the Slayer had found the men responsible for hurting his friend, so if the countess could help them get it over with more quickly, so much the better.

Felix coughed politely. 'Countess, there was a time, some years ago, when you asked *me* to trust *you*. When I was forced to overcome my fear and distrust of your kind so that we could work together to defeat a common foe. I was as hesitant then as you are now, and yet, when, against every instinct, I agreed and we joined together, we triumphed.' He spread his hands. 'As I said, I can make no vow for

Gotrek, but I know he hates these men as much, if not more, than you do. If you give him a way to confront them, he will take it. That, you can trust.'

The countess nodded, still unseeing, then at last sighed and looked up, fixing Felix with a stare as cold and bottomless as the depths of Black Water Lake. 'I suppose I have no choice,' she said. 'Particularly since I can do nothing with the information I have without you, at least not quickly or without weakening my position. But know this; you will not betray me and live. You may be a great hero, and your companion a fell warrior, but the daughters of the deathless queen are everywhere, behind every beautiful smile, and they seldom strike from the front.' She glanced meaningfully towards the canopied bed, then smiled at him. 'You would not die in battle.'

Felix shuddered. 'Threats are not necessary, madame,' he said. 'Your reputation is enough.'

'Good,' said the countess. She looked to Ulrika. 'Tell him.'

Ulrika lowered her head, then turned to Felix. 'As I was ripping out the throat of one of the cultists last night, this came away with his flesh.'

She lifted a golden chain from her bodice, unhooked the clasp and passed it to Felix. He took it reluctantly, but it seemed she had removed all traces of gore. He looked at it. On the chain was a small golden pendant, in the shape of a shield emblazoned with a wolf's head. He vaguely recognised the device, but couldn't remember from where.

'What is it?' he asked.

'A signet chain worn by members of Wulf's, a private gentlemen's club in the Handelbezirk,' said Ulrika.

'Ah, of course.' Once she said it, Felix recognised it instantly. Back in the days when he and Gotrek had been bouncers at the Blind Pig, he had from time to time thrown out members of Wulf's who had come in looking to start trouble. The club had originally been a club for rich merchants, but when the more elegant Golden Hammer had opened, the merchants began to go there instead, and Wulf's was taken over by their sons, idle layabouts with too much money and too much time on their hands. They aped the manners of the nobility and liked to prove their superiority over their poorer brethren with the point of a rapier. Strange that one such would belong to a group that seemed dedicated to overthrowing the established order.

'We want to learn if other members of Wulf's also belong to the Cleansing Flame,' said Ulrika. 'But it is a gentlemen's club. No women are allowed. Even the servants are all male.'

'And you know no men but me?' asked Felix, incredulous. 'Unless I have the purpose of this establishment entirely wrong, you must know half the rich men in this city. None belong to Wulf's?'

'My customers are not my confidants,' said the countess, as if explaining something to a child. 'I extract secrets from them without their knowledge. Asking them openly to spy for me would expose to them my true purpose. Those few men who *are* my confidants and servants...' She nodded towards the bed. 'Some are so besotted that I cannot trust their judgement. Others... well, I will not bore you with internecine intrigues and tales of divided loyalties. Suffice to say that there is no man already within my circle upon whom I can entirely place my trust. So...' She raised her eyes to meet his. 'That leaves you.'

Felix frowned, still confused. 'But I don't understand. I can't help you either. I'm not a member.'

'No,' said the countess. 'But your brother is. Though he no longer dines there, he has never resigned his membership.'

'Wha... How... How do you know that?' gabbled Felix.

The countess smiled. 'As you said, Herr Jaeger, we know half the rich men in this city. And the other half too.'

'Otto comes here...?' Felix was dumbfounded, though he couldn't think why. Why should his brother be any different from any other rich man he had ever known?

'You will ask him to take you to dinner there,' said the countess, placidly. 'Once inside you will hopefully hear a voice you heard in the burning cellar, or recognise someone by their walk. And then...' she smiled prettily. 'Well, you're the hero. I expect you'll know what to do.'

Felix groaned, recalling how he and his brother had left things at the end of their last conversation. How in the world was he going to get Otto to take him anywhere, let alone to a club he no longer frequented?

'You will report to Ulrika all you find, is that clear?' asked the countess. 'I want to know everything before you act.'

'Yes, countess. Certainly,' said Felix, distracted. He rose to go, playing out different ways he might approach his brother, and not liking the outcomes of any of them.

The countess raised a tiny golden bell, but Ulrika stood and held up a hand.

'No need, madame. I'll see him out.'

The anteroom door slammed open. The little blonde girl tumbled in and hit the carpet chin-first as two silhouettes filled the doorway. More figures crowded the anteroom behind them. Felix's hand dropped to his hilt.

'What's this!' Countess Gabriella was on her feet instantly, a dagger in her hand. 'Who dares enter my chambers uninvited?'

Ulrika too gripped a dagger, and was looking like she regretted having changed into womanly garb. She stepped protectively in front of Felix. The little blonde girl was crabbing backwards away from the door, wide-eyed, a smear of blood on her lip.

Two women stepped into the room – well, one of them was a woman. Felix wasn't sure the other was even human – or ever had been.

'Good evening, Madame du Vilmorin,' said the more human of the two, throwing back a rich, velvet cloak. She was beautiful – as beautiful as any of the countess's students – an olive complexion like an Estalian, with pouting lips and heavy lidded eyes as black and cold as a winter sea. Thick waves of glossy black hair spilled down past her bare shoulders to a wide-skirted dress of oxblood satin and black embroidery, so exquisitely made that a queen might envy it.

'What is the meaning of this intrusion, Lady Hermione?' snapped the countess. 'And you, Mistress Wither?' The countess's robe had fallen open entirely and her naked white curves shone in the dark room like alabaster lit from within. 'Give me a reason why I should not set Ulrika upon you,' she said as the little blonde girl clung to her right leg.

'We heard a rumour,' said Lady Hermione coolly, as she tugged off black lace gloves one finger at a time, then tucked them into a beaded drawstring purse that matched the colours of her dress exactly. 'That you thought to bring an outsider into our business.' She ran her eyes up and down Felix with a dismissive sneer. 'It seems we heard correctly.'

The other woman – Mistress Wither – rasped wordlessly at this in a voice that sounded like water splashing on a hot stove. She was tall – taller than Felix by half a head – and appeared skeletally thin under the hooded shroud that hid every inch of her and hissed against the carpet as she glided from place to place. Long sleeves hung down past her hands. Her face was covered with a thick black veil that made it look like there was nothing within her hood but shadows.

'What business is it of yours,' asked the countess, 'what tool I use to achieve my ends?'

Tool, thought Felix. Well, good to know her true opinion of him, he supposed.

Lady Hermione flicked an eye over Felix again. 'He has never been tasted. You have no hold on him. You treat with him as an equal.

We heard you.' She gave the countess a sad look. 'You know better than this, sister. We do not use men that are not fully bound to us. You cannot allow him to leave like this. He will betray us. He will expose us to all of Nuln. Our work will be undone.'

Felix opened his mouth but Ulrika touched his arm with a warning hand.

'Our work will be undone if Nuln falls to the barbarians,' said the countess. 'Our lives will be undone. This man can do what we cannot. Go where we cannot.'

'What?' sniffed Hermione. 'To Wulf's? Yes, we heard that too. Don't be ridiculous.' She motioned behind her. 'Any number of my gentlemen are members of Wulf's. You had but to ask.'

Felix looked through the door. Lounging languidly on the fragile chairs in the anteroom were a handful of dashing, mustachioed heroes, each as handsome as a statue of Sigmar, and certainly just as much a work of art. They did indeed look the sort that would belong to Wulf's.

It was Countess Gabriella's turn to sneer. 'Do you think I would trust any of your creatures? Whose interests would they serve, I wonder?'

'Surely all our interests are one in this calamity,' said Hermione. 'There can be no rivalry when all our lives are at stake.'

'Can there not?' asked the countess. 'If this victory were *yours*, and not *ours* or *mine*, would you not rise in the esteem of our lady, while I sank? Would you not come one step closer to winning my position, as you have been trying to do all these decades?' The countess waved an impatient hand. 'Oh, enough of this. It matters not, for your "gentlemen" cannot win the information that Herr Jaeger can. Only he can do it.'

'Is he so great a hero as all that?' asked Lady Hermione, raising a sceptical eyebrow. 'My gentlemen are some of the finest duellists in all the Empire.'

'No doubt,' said countess as if she didn't believe a word of it. 'But they were not in the burning cellar under the Maze. They did not hear the leaders of the Cleansing Flame order their followers to attack. So how can they hear the voice of a clubman and know that in another part of town he wears a yellow mask and consorts with mutants?'

Lady Hermione sniffed, frustrated. 'Surely there must be another way to learn who these men are!'

'There might be, but there is not time to find one,' said the countess. 'The madmen could burn Nuln at any time – tonight perhaps!'

Lady Hermione exchanged a glance with Mistress Wither, then turned back to the countess. Her face was set and hard. 'Be that as it may, you must still find another way,' she said at last. 'Because this man will not leave here alive having seen us and heard our names.'

CHAPTER TEN

'YOU DARE MAKE demands in my house!' cried Countess Gabriella. 'I still rule here in Nuln, no matter how much it might pain you.'

'You won't after she gets word of this foolishness,' said Lady Hermione. 'Trusting cattle. No good ever comes of it.'

Behind her, her exquisite companions were getting to their feet and resting their hands on their hilts.

'Ladies,' pleaded Felix. 'There is no need for this. I and my companion leave in a few days for Middenheim, where we are very likely to die in the fighting. Your secret will die with us.'

The vampiresses ignored him utterly.

'The foolishness,' said the countess, 'is allowing Nuln to die to preserve your standing in it. Will you be queen of the ashes?'

'There will be no ashes. We will find another way. Now stand aside. Mistress Wither thirsts.'

The tall shadow glided towards Felix, arms raising.

Felix stepped back, drawing his runesword.

Ulrika snarled and advanced, drawing a second blade from her sleeve – a bone handled stiletto that gleamed like captured moonlight in the dark room. 'Come end your misery, mistress,' she said.

Mistress Wither shrank back from the blade, hissing.

'Silver!' gasped Lady Hermione. 'You would use poison against your own?'

Hermione's gentlemen drew their rapiers and pushed in through the door behind her. At the same time, the curtains of the canopied bed were thrown roughly open, and a powerful looking man stumbled out, entirely naked, brushing the hair out of his eyes and groping for a long sword that was propped against a side table. 'Is m'lady threatened?' the man slurred.

'Peace, captain,' said the countess, holding up her hand as he drew his sword.

The man stayed where he was, but remained on guard.

The tableau held for a long moment as the two sides sized each other up.

At last the countess laughed. 'Sisters, you amuse me. To preserve your secrecy you will start a fight that all the gentlemen of the Altestadt who are at their leisure one floor below us will hear. Will you then kill all of them when they come to see what is the matter? Your secrecy is in greater peril if you attack than if you withdraw. Now come, lower your weapons.'

The women stayed where they were.

'The fight may be over quicker than you think,' said Lady Hermione.

'Aye,' said the countess. 'And with at least one of us truly dead. What do you think she will say of that? Has she not said that murder among us is the greatest sin?'

'It is you who drew silver!'

'And you who forced silver to be drawn,' said the countess. She lowered her dagger. 'Now, come, listen to reason. The man will go and learn who these cultists are and what they plan, and he will be watched. Indeed, you may watch him, if that is your wish. If he speaks of our existence before he leaves Nuln, then do what you will.'

'And after he leaves Nuln? How can you guarantee his silence then?' asked Lady Hermione.

Countess Gabriella looked from Felix to Ulrika and smiled. 'Though he is not bound to us by the blood kiss, there are other ties that will stay his hand.'

Lady Hermione curled her lip. 'And all know how great is the constancy of man.'

'Greater than that of sisters, so it seems,' said Ulrika disdainfully.

Lady Hermione remained on guard, glaring at Felix, and though he could not see Mistress Wither's eyes, Felix felt certain that they were fixed upon him too.

'Sisters,' said the countess quietly. 'We fight while our enemies light their fuses. We must act. Now. Let us resume this argument when we know that Nuln is safe.'

Lady Hermione and Mistress Wither exchanged a glance, then at last stepped back. Lady Hermione's men lowered their swords. Ulrika hesitated, then sheathed the silver stiletto.

'It seems it must go as you say,' said Hermione, bitterness dripping from each word. 'But after, we will see. After, we will bring all before the lady, and we will see.'

Countess Gabriella inclined her head. 'So long as the Empire stands, I will be content with her verdict.'

Lady Hermione snorted. 'Oh, the nobility. It moves one to tears.'

Mistress Wither laughed like a steam piston.

The two vampiresses stepped to the right and left of the door. Hermione curtsied to Felix and swept a hand to the door. 'Go then, oh fair and gentle knight. Save us from the machinations of our enemies. But know, champion, that our eyes will ever be upon you.'

Felix's flesh crawled as Ulrika led him forward between them and out through the antechamber under the glowering scrutiny of Lady Hermione's gentlemen. He didn't like this at all. What guarantee did he have that the women wouldn't strike out of spite once he had outlived his usefulness? And would they watch him everywhere? When he slept? When he went to the jakes? He groaned silently. It might have been better to have had the fight then and there and gotten it over with.

'I APOLOGISE,' SAID Ulrika, as the coach swayed smoothly through the streets towards Shantytown. 'Family can be embarrassing.'

'Who are they?' asked Felix.

Ulrika pursed her lips. 'Lady Hermione is the countess's chief rival here in Nuln. She has been longer in the city – almost fifty years. And so was understandably upset when the countess, who though she does not look it, is younger than her by several centuries, was given the ruling of Nuln instead of her. But it is her own fault. Though she has no equals when it comes to seduction, she is quick to anger, and unwilling to compromise. She hasn't the temperament to lead.'

'Yes, I saw that.'

'Mistress Wither…' Ulrika shook her head. 'Mistress Wither is a caution to us all. She was too flagrant in her youth. Too violent. She was caught by hunters, and left naked and shackled to a rock to await the rising sun. She was rescued by her thralls, but not before dawn had come.' Ulrika shivered. 'It might have been better had she died then. Her skin is like burned paper. It never heals. She is in agony every moment of her eternal life. Only feeding gives her some relief, but not much, and not for long. She hates men beyond all reason.'

'Wonderful,' said Felix. 'And do you trust them not to attack us after this is over?'

'I do not know.' Ulrika sighed and looked out of the window into the torchlit night. 'Sad as I will be to see you go, I think it is good that you are leaving soon.'

'Aye,' said Felix. Running towards the daemons to escape the vampires. What a life.

ULRIKA DROPPED FELIX off in Shantytown where she had picked him up. As he walked towards the remains of the Blind Pig, he saw a swarm of activity under the yellow glow of bright lanterns. A wagon had been drawn up beside the ruined tavern, and Heinz and his bouncers were throwing blackened timbers onto it.

''Ware below!' came a familiar voice, and a section of the tavern's roof folded in on itself and crashed to the ground.

Gotrek was revealed on the remains of the upper floor. He was black with soot from head to toe, and had a kerchief tied around his nose and mouth.

'This is why dwarfs hate trees,' he called down to Heinz as he chopped through some ruined beams. 'Trees burn. Stone does not.'

'Aye, well, not all of us can afford to build with stone,' said Heinz.

'You can now,' said Gotrek.

'I won't take your gold, curse you!' said Heinz, standing straight and glaring up at the Slayer. 'I told you once already.'

Gold, thought Felix. Gotrek still has gold?

'You think I'm giving it to you?' asked Gotrek. 'I'm paying for my next thousand drinks.'

'That bracelet is worth a thousand thousand drinks,' said Heinz peevishly.

'I'll bring some friends.'

Heinz snorted and turned away to lift another burned board. 'And what friends have you got, you miserable grouch?' he muttered to himself, but he was smiling in spite of himself.

Gotrek saw Felix coming and swung down a ladder to join him by the wagon. There was an open half keg of ale next to it. Gotrek dipped a mug in it and drank deep, then wiped his mouth, smearing away a thick layer of soot.

'What did the parasite say?' he asked.

Felix hesitated, considering how much to tell him about his visit to the countess's brothel. Did he mention the countess's attempt to force a promise of Gotrek's good behaviour from him? Did he mention Lady Hermione and Mistress Wither and their intention to murder them if they revealed their existence? Perhaps it was better to let sleeping dogs lie. On the other hand, he should know the other players in the game.

'The countess is as wary of you as you are of her.'

'She has reason to be,' growled Gotrek.

'And she has allies – rivals, really – who don't want us involved at all.'

'Allies?'

'Two other vampire women,' said Felix. 'A beautiful seductress and a… a shrouded thing, burned by the sun, apparently, and hiding it under robes. The countess convinced them in the end that we were needed to defeat the cultists, but I think they would sooner kill us.'

'Let them try,' said Gotrek. 'I made no vow with them.'

Felix coughed. 'All the same, the countess may have provided the link to the Cleansing Flame we have been seeking. It might be politic to stay your hand, at least until we find them and the powder.'

'Politic.' Gotrek spat out the word as if it was the vilest profanity. 'What is this link?'

Felix pulled the wolf's head pendant from his pouch. 'Ulrika took this from one of the cultists last night. It's an insignia worn by members of Wulf's, a club for rich burghers. She and the countess think that some of the other cult leaders might be members of the club too. They want me to go there and listen, in hopes I will hear a voice I recognise from the fight.'

'That is a slim hope, manling. Not worth the alliance.'

'I agree,' said Felix. 'But it's the only hope we have at the moment.'

Gotrek grunted, dissatisfied. His gaze travelled back up to the tavern's skeletal upper floor.

'I'll see my brother about going to Wulf's tomorrow night,' said Felix. 'He is a member.'

Gotrek nodded, distracted. He finished his mug of ale in a single swallow and started back towards the ladder. 'Doesn't sound like my sort of work. Come back when you've found me something to kill.'

'Ah, Gotrek,' called Felix after him.

Gotrek stopped and turned. 'Hey?'

'You're… you're giving Heinz gold to fix the Blind Pig?'

'Aye.'

Felix frowned. 'You said we were broke. We didn't eat our last two days before Nuln.'

'We are broke,' growled Gotrek. He held up his thick left wrist, full of gold bracelets, letting them glint in the lamplight. 'Some gold's not for spending.'

'Unless a friend's tavern burns down,' said Felix.

'Aye,' said Gotrek, and started towards the ladder again.

Felix watched as the Slayer climbed it and moved carefully through the ruined upper storey, expertly choosing the next parts to demolish. There was a satisfaction on his ugly face that was almost happiness. Felix suddenly remembered that Gotrek had been an engineer before he shaved his head and took the Slayer's Oath. A strange melancholy passed over him when he thought that, if whatever tragedy had caused Gotrek to become a Slayer hadn't happened, this is what he would have been, a builder of houses and halls. Would he have been happy with just that? Had there really been a time when simple labour could have fulfilled Gotrek's heart?

FELIX VISITED THE Nuln office of Jaeger and Sons the next morning just before noon. The long, dim room was filled with rows of bookkeepers, perched on high stools and bent over their ledgers like an army of hunchbacked storks, quills flying from ink pot to parchment and back. Young boys scurried among them carrying account books nearly as heavy as themselves. The air smelled of candlewick and dust.

'May I help you?' asked a pale man with spectacles and heavy jowls who sat at a high desk near the front door. He had ink stains on his fingers and his lips.

'I'm looking for Otto Jaeger. I'm his brother.'

'Do you have an appointment?'

'No. I'm his brother.'

The bookkeeper sniffed as if this made no difference whatsoever. 'I'll see if he's receiving.' He shouted over his shoulder. 'Rodi! Ask Herr Jaeger if he will see his brother.'

A thin little boy saluted, then scurried back through the rows of tall desks and disappeared around a corner as the bookkeeper went back to his accounts, ignoring Felix. The scritch of quill nibs on paper filled the room as he waited. It sounded to Felix like a hundred rats clawing at the walls of a hundred cages. A shudder went through him. Imagine if he had remained on the path his father had set for him. He would have spent his life in a room like this, adding up accounts, fretting over the delivery of goods, worrying about the price of oats and about how much to bribe the local authorities.

A thought made him smile. Why was it that, when faced with a horde of howling orcs he wished so dearly for this life, and when faced with this life, he wished so dearly for a horde of howling orcs?

A truism could have been found somewhere in that conundrum, if he had had any energy for that sort of thing anymore.

The little boy popped his head around the corner. 'He says he'll see him, sir!' he squealed.

The bookkeeper slapped his desk and stood, roaring. 'Don't shout, you little goblin! You disturb the others! Come up and tell me politely, like a gentleman.' A vein throbbed in his pale forehead.

The little boy cringed and hurried forward, head down, as the clerks stifled amused laughter and shot sly smirks at each other.

'Sorry, Herr Bartlemaas,' said the little boy, his eyes on the ground. 'Herr Jaeger will see, er, Herr Jaeger.'

'Better,' said the head clerk. 'Now show our guest back to Herr Jaeger's office. And no more shouting, or you'll not get your penny today.'

Felix followed the boy's slumped shoulders through the office, fighting the urge to draw his sword and chop the whole place to flinders.

'You'LL HAVE TO be brief, brother,' said Otto without looking up from the papers spread across his massive desk. 'I'm expecting representatives from the bargemen's guild at any moment. I cannot keep them waiting.'

In comparison with the opulence of his home, Otto's office was as plain as a monk's cell – a small room with an iron stove in one corner, a pair of chairs before the big desk, and floor to ceiling bookshelves on every wall, all filled with massive ledgers, each with a month and year printed neatly on the spine. Otto's pens and blotters and ink bottles were all of cheap manufacture. The lantern he used to light his work the same as any farmer would have. Felix wondered if his brother dressed his office down on purpose in order to be able to plead poor mouth to his business associates. He certainly wouldn't put it past him.

'Well, I…' Felix paused, then summoned his courage and continued. 'I've been thinking about your offer.'

Otto raised his eyes in mock surprise. 'What's this? You wish to get your hands dirty, m'lord? You wish to descend from your lofty perch and join us mere mortals in the real world?' He chuckled, then continued in his normal tone. 'What happened? Has the little maniac with the axe fired you at last?'

Felix bit his tongue. A smart reply wouldn't get the job done. 'Fired me? No. But he almost got me burned to a cinder. I'm growing tired of collecting scars.'

'Don't tell me you were behind those fires in Shantytown last night?' said Otto, his eyes widening.

'Not behind them, exactly,' said Felix. 'But certainly in the middle of them.'

Otto shrugged. 'Well, you got out of it at least. And you've done me a good turn. I'll make a tidy profit selling bricks and timber to rebuild it all.'

'At wartime prices,' said Felix dryly.

'Naturally,' said Otto. 'So, what would you like to do?'

The vile little profiteer, thought Felix. Was it any wonder cults like the Cleansing Flame flourished when men like Otto preyed on the poor and the unfortunate? He took a deep breath and relaxed his clenched fists.

'That's what I'd like to discuss with you,' he said at last. 'But I don't want to take up your time here. Perhaps…'

A knock came at the door and the little boy looked in. 'The bargemen are here, sir,' he said.

'Thank you, Rodi,' said Otto. 'Tell them I'll see them in just a moment.' He stood and came around the desk as the boy disappeared again. 'Come have dinner with me tonight at the Golden Hammer,' he said to Felix, then looked him up and down. 'Have you got a good suit of clothes?'

'Ah, no. Mine were singed somewhat. And these are borrowed,' said Felix. 'And I don't suppose we could eat at Wulf's instead?'

Otto made a face. 'Wulf's? Why would you want to go there? It's a dreadful place.'

'I hear it's more, ah, sporting than the Golden Hammer,' said Felix.

Otto sneered. 'Bunch of preening jackdaws who've never done a day's work in their lives. A lot of Gustav's schoolmates go there.'

'Does Gustav go there?' asked Felix, suddenly hopeful. That would make things easier. He could ask the boy about the other members. Perhaps he would have noticed something.

Otto shook his head. 'Not Wulf's. He thinks it represents the antipathy of true speech, or whatever he calls it. Besides, they bully his sort there.'

'I still want to see it,' said Felix. 'If I'm going to live here, I want to know what sort of amusements are on offer.'

Otto smirked knowingly. 'I see how it is. Tired of the privations of the road and want to live a little. Well, I don't blame you. Wulf's is certainly sporting. The evening isn't complete there until some young fool is carried to the surgeons by his friends. But if you want to go…'

'Sounds amusing,' said Felix, with what he hoped was a properly snobbish voice.

'Very well.' Otto fumbled in his pouch. 'Go see my tailor. You remember where he is? Good. Tell him it's on my account. I'll subtract it from your book profits later. And take this and get yourself a shave and a trim. You look like a Kurgan.' He dropped a handful of coins in Felix's hand – gold, silver and copper. 'Rodi!' he shouted.

After a moment the little boy looked in. 'Aye, sir?'

'Show my brother out and ask in the bargemen.'

'Aye, sir.'

'Come by my house at seven, Felix,' said Otto. 'We'll go from there.'

'Right,' said Felix. 'See you tonight.'

He followed Rodi out into the office.

Before they got to the front Felix paused. 'Rodi,' he said.

'Aye, sir,' said the boy, stopping.

'Do you want to be a clerk?'

A terrified expression flashed across his face, and he shot quick looks towards Herr Bartlemass and Otto's office. 'Oh, yes, sir! More than anything, sir.'

Felix scowled. 'I see,' he said. 'And if you didn't want to be a clerk, what would you want to be?'

'A sailor on a ship,' said Rodi instantly. 'My cousin Lani was a mate, sir. He told the most wonderful stories. Been everywhere, my cousin has. Do you know what apes is, sir? My cousin seen one once.'

Felix shuddered, remembering a night under jungle moons, with huge, shaggy shapes lumbering up the steps of a ruined temple towards them. He pushed the scene away and smiled at Rodi. 'A sailor, eh? Well, in case you ever change your mind about clerking, here's something towards your sea chest.' He picked a silver coin from those his brother had given him and handed it to Rodi.

The boy's eyes grew wide as he stared at the coin. 'Thank you, sir!' he said, then darted a wary look at the other boys in the room and slipped the coin quickly into his belt pouch.

Felix shrugged as he wove through the streets towards Otto's tailor. The money would most likely go to Rodi's mother or father and the boy would never leave Otto's office, but at least Felix had tried. He wondered if he would have given him the money if he had said he wanted to be a soldier or an adventurer.

Probably not.

* * *

WULF'S OCCUPIED A grand brick and stone building on Commerce Street in the heart of the Handelbezirk. Golden light spilled from its tall windows, each decorated with a stained glass wolf's head. Wide stone steps led up to its stout oak doors. A huge, uniformed man with the look of an ex-soldier pulled them open for the garishly dressed young men who came and went, chatting boisterously with each other. He seemed to know them all by name, and joked with them as they passed.

The giant sized Otto and Felix up as they stepped out of Otto's enclosed coach and Otto told his coachman and two bodyguards to wait for them down the street. Felix blushed under his scrutiny. He was certain the man had seen in an instant that his doublet and breeches were brand new, and that his gaze could see through the finery to the penniless wanderer beneath. He felt an utter fraud in these clothes, an actor masquerading as a rich man. An uncomfortable actor at that. The stiff lace of the collar chafed his neck. The tight green velvet of the doublet constricted his chest. The glossy, knee-high boots pinched his feet. His face felt dry and hot where the barber had scraped his chin and cheeks clean.

'Your names, meinen herren?' rumbled the giant deferentially as he and Otto mounted the steps.

'Otto Jaeger and a guest,' said Otto.

'Herr Jaeger,' said the giant, bowing. 'Forgive me for not recognising you at once, sir. It has been some time since you visited. Welcome.' He pulled on a huge brass ring that was clamped in the jaws of a brass wolf's head, and the door swung open. 'Please remember that guests are only allowed in the dining room and smoking room, sir.'

Otto nodded and they stepped inside. The entry way was clad in dark wood. The banners of several mercantile guilds hung from the walls. Young men laughed and gossiped on a wide stairway that rose up to upper floors. A deafening torrent of merriment and clinking plates poured from a door to the right.

After depositing their cloaks and swords with a porter, Otto and Felix passed through the door into the dining room. Something flew past Felix's face and he flinched back, wary. The missile hit a young diner in the back of the head and plopped to the floor. It was a hunk of black bread. Laughter erupted to Felix's left.

The diner jumped up, armed with a hunk of bread of his own. 'Who threw that?' he called, eyes flashing. 'Mieritz! Was it you?'

A young man in orange and green velvet spread his hands, grinning. 'Me, Fetteroff? Why would you suspect me?'

Fetteroff flung his bread. Mieritz snatched it deftly from the air and took a bite. 'My thanks, sir,' he mumphed as he chewed. 'My bread seems to have fallen on the floor.'

His friends erupted at this witticism, as did Fetteroff, and everyone returned to their dinners.

'I warned you,' said Otto out of the side of his mouth.

A steward in a high collar bowed and led them to a table for two against the far wall. The dining room was large and high ceilinged, with roaring fires in grand fireplaces at both ends. Rich tapestries – all of them depicting wolves on the hunt – hid the plaster walls, and gold stencilled wooden pillars rose to carved and painted beams. Large circular tables filled the centre of the room, all crowded with preening, posturing young men, each apparently trying to outdo all the rest in the richness and elaborateness of their clothes. Felix had never seen so many colours under one roof. It was as if a rainbow had been violently sick.

'Sigmar's beard, what a cacophony,' said Otto, wincing as loud laughter erupted again from one of the tables. 'Do you really prefer this to the Golden Hammer?'

'I'm not sure I do,' said Felix. 'But I wanted to see for myself.'

A server came. Felix ordered duck in plum sauce while Otto ordered roast beef, and Bretonnian wine for the two of them.

Felix tried to listen to his fellow diners while Otto talked about what job he might do for Jaeger and Sons. He wished he could close his eyes in order to concentrate better on their voices, but Otto would remark on that, so he kept them open. He cursed at the constant din. The room was too loud and echoed too much.

He tried to concentrate on picking one voice out from the hubbub, then another, but found it hard to focus on them without getting caught up in their conversations, and the more he heard, the more his teeth clenched and his hackles rose. It wasn't the noise or the high spirits of the young men at the tables that made him angry – in his travels with Gotrek he had seen more than his fair share of wild taverns and boisterous inns. In fact he liked carousing now and then; singing bawdy songs, arm wrestling, dancing with ladies of less than sterling reputations, having deep philosophical conversations with total strangers that he forgot entirely the next day. He had met Gotrek on such a night.

This was different. There was a cruelty to the laughter, a hatefulness to the jokes and jibes that were bandied between the tables, that was peculiar to the idle rich. These young men were not friends, they were rivals, and deadly rivals at that, for all their blaring bonhomie. Their jokes were not meant to entertain, but to belittle their victims and bolster themselves. They chose their companions not because they liked them, but because knowing them offered some advantage. The symbol of the wolf had been well chosen for this place, Felix thought, for the society of its members seemed based on the pecking order of the wolf pack, where the biggest, meanest, and most cunning predator savaged those below him, and they in turn savaged those below them.

Felix had always despised such behaviour, ever since his days at the University in Altdorf when the nobles had sneered at him for his mercantile upbringing and denied him entry to their clubs and fraternities. It distressed him to see the sons of merchants aping precisely this vile behaviour. One would have thought that, having been snubbed and condescended to by their 'betters', they would have wished to belong to a more egalitarian society. Instead, they were worse snobs than the nobility, exaggerating their viciousness and vainglory until they were little better than beasts in velvet.

The wine came. The server poured glasses for them and retired.

Otto had a sip of his and made a face. 'Gods,' he said. 'Their cellar isn't what it used to be either. Their importer must be cheating them.'

Felix took a sip. It tasted all right to him, but then, after all his years with Gotrek, he was more used to ale.

'Ah well,' said Otto. 'As I was saying…'

Felix turned his attention to the other diners again, trying to blot out their words and concentrate on their timbre and tone while thinking back to voices of the Cleansing Flame. He groaned. Why had Ulrika and the countess invested so much hope in so tenuous a thread? There might be no connection between Wulf's and the Brotherhood of the Cleansing Flame except that they shared one member in common – the man Ulrika had killed when she took his pendant. This whole evening might come to nothing. He might be subjecting himself to dinner with his brother for no reason at all.

He gazed around at his fellow diners, hoping some quirk of gesture might spark a memory. He sighed. They all looked like villains to him, but he tried to measure them objectively. It was difficult. That fop in the purple, with the rouge on his cheeks and the ruff so wide it nearly hung over his shoulders, he certainly looked like the member of some sort of debauched cult. And that fellow in the lemon yellow, with the permanent sneer and the earring. Felix could just imagine him performing blood sacrifices when Morrslieb was full. And the rogue in red and gold who was playing cards with his companions, was he using magic to change the cards? And the handsome, sallow-cheeked dandy who was coughing convulsively into his handkerchief. Was he spreading the pox through every brothel in Nuln? And that fellow...

He almost spat out his mouthful of wine as he saw a man watching him suspiciously from across the room. Was it a cultist? No. Wait a moment. He recognised him. But from where? Where had he see that strong jaw before? That perfectly curled moustache? That proud nose? Then he knew, and almost laughed. It was one of Lady Hermione's beautiful gentlemen, keeping an eye on him. Almost literally. He couldn't have been more obvious if he tried. Perhaps that was the point. Lady Hermione was reminding Felix of her omniscience. Suddenly he didn't feel like laughing anymore.

He gave the man a glare and continued to survey the room. Then stopped again as he saw another almost-familiar face peeking out from behind the nearest pillar. Who was this? He knew the hair, which hung down before the man's sleepy eyes, but the clothing was unfamiliar. Of course! That was because the last time he had seen him, he had been naked. It was the Captain Reingelt, the countess's current swain. It seemed she didn't trust Lady Hermione to share information. And why should she?

Their dinners came, and Otto tucked his linen napkin under his chin and dug in. Felix gave up his search and joined him. Trying to pick out cultists by sight seemed as impossible as trying to recognise them by their speech. He was no witch hunter. He didn't know how to differentiate normal human villainy from the baser horrors of daemon worship. He could recognise a mutant if it looked at him with two heads, but until their corruption showed he was as lost as the next man.

'I know you're not much for sitting at a desk all day,' Otto was saying. 'But we have plenty of jobs that would have you out and doing in the fresh air. Someone needs to go to Marienburg every spring for instance. We buy many of our dyes for our wools there from Bretonnians, Estalians and Arabyans. Araby makes the best indigo. But getting the best prices and making certain the filthy foreign devils aren't cheating us requires being there in person. Does that appeal to you?'

Felix shrugged. 'I've never been much of a one for haggling.'

'Hmmm,' said Otto. 'Well, we also provide guards for our convoys, and we've expanded that service to providing guards for the convoys of other companies. Perhaps you'd like to be involved in the recruitment and training of these fellows. That sounds more in your line.'

Felix was trying to think of an appropriate answer when he overheard an exchange from a group of young men who were passing their table.

'That looks nasty, Gephardt. Get your hand caught in some lady's window when her husband came home?'

'No. Burned it. Stupid, really. Left the poker in the fire by mistake, and when I grabbed it I seared myself.'

Felix looked around at the speaker as the young men laughed. He was a wiry youth with the unlaced doublet and tousled bedroom hair that seemed popular among the more fashionable university students that year. He wore lavender and cream velvet, and had a bandage around his left hand.

'Ha!' said a chinless lad in pink. 'When I leave my poker in the fire too long, it melts! Ha ha!'

Nobody laughed.

'My *poker*, you see,' said the boy in pink, giggling. 'In the *fire*.'

'Do shut up, Kalter,' said the youth with the bandage.

Felix watched him walking away. Burned his hand, had he? And was it Felix's imagination, or was he hiding a limp? He tried to imagine that sly, sneering voice raised in command. It might have sounded something like one of the voices he had heard in the burning cellar, then again it might not, and he needed to be sure. It would be a cruel trick to set the vampires on an innocent man.

He turned to Otto. 'Who is that? The young man in purple and white?'

'Eh?' said Otto, looking up. 'What's this, now? Have you been listening to me at all?'

'Of course I have, brother, but that fellow looks familiar to me. Do you know who he is?'

Otto frowned, annoyed, and squinted across the room. 'Which one?'

'The one in purple and white,' repeated Felix, turning. 'Just now sitting down. He has a bandage on his hand, you see?'

'I see,' said Otto. 'The one next to the fire, yes? I've no idea. Why you would think I would pay attention to the spoiled ne'r-do-wells who frequent Wulf's I don't know. This is why I dine at the Hammer.' He sniffed. 'Looks a bit like old Gephardt, the wine importer, and he's wearing the colours of Gephardt's trading house. Might be one of his sons, I suppose. I couldn't say.'

Felix nodded. Gephardt was the name the youth's companion had called him. Give Otto credit for keen observation. Now the question was, was he a member of the Brotherhood of the Cleansing Flame, or had he only burned himself on a hot poker like he had said? If only Felix could get closer and eavesdrop on his conversation.

Gephardt looked idly around the dining room as one of his companions told a story. His eyes flicked past Felix, then came back. Felix looked away, heart racing. He had forgotten he was staring.

'So, does that appeal to you?' asked Otto, picking up their conversation again. 'Would you like to help us with finding men to guard our wagons? With all your experience fighting – ahem – ratmen and dragons, and so forth, I imagine you know a practiced blade when you meet one.'

Felix stole another look over his shoulder. Gephardt was staring fixedly at him, his eyes wide, whether in fear or anger Felix couldn't be sure. Felix turned back, heart sinking. Well, he had his answer. Gephardt recognised him. He must have seen him during the fighting in the Cleansing Flame's meeting house. Felix could have wished he had learned the information without revealing himself in the process. Now Gephardt knew he knew. Felix would have to catch him before he left Wulf's, or soon all of the Cleansing Flame would know as well. But how was he going to do that with his brother around? He couldn't very well say 'Excuse me, brother, I have to knock out and capture this young man. Do you mind helping me bring him to the College of Engineering so Gotrek can have a word with him?'

Perhaps his so called allies would help him. He looked over at Lady Hermione's man. He was getting up to leave, his gaze fixed on Gephardt. He must have seen the exchange of glances and deduced what they meant. Felix turned towards Captain Reingelt. He too was rising, eyes darting from Gephardt to Hermione's spy to Felix and back again. He knew too. But why were they leaving? Were the two of them going to go wait for Gephardt to exit the club, or were they off to their mistresses to tell them what they had learned? Whatever the case, he couldn't rely on either of them. He would have to take care of Gephardt himself, somehow.

'Felix? Did you hear me?' Otto was looking at him strangely.

'Er,' Felix said, struggling to remember what his brother had been saying. 'Er, yes, that, uh, certainly sounds like the most appealing alternative. I'll most definitely give it some thought. You make a compelling argument.'

Otto's chest puffed up. 'Well, you know, I pride myself on fitting the man to the job and the job to the man. Part of the secret of my success. Shall we order a sweetmeat for after? And a little more wine?'

'Yes, that sounds like a good idea,' said Felix. That would give him more time to come up with a way to kidnap Gephardt. Felix looked across the room again as Otto summoned the server. Gephardt was gone!

Felix's heart thudded violently. He hadn't expected the man to move so quickly! He was already on his way to warn his masters, no doubt. This was bad. He had to get back and tell Gotrek. If they moved immediately, they might be able to catch Gephardt before he talked to the Cleansing Flame.

Felix turned back to Otto. 'On second thought, perhaps we should be getting back,' he said. 'You've given me a lot to think about.'

Otto frowned. 'Are you well, Felix? You look a bit green.'

Felix swallowed. 'The duck, I think. I'm not accustomed to such rich food anymore.' He smiled weakly. 'I suppose I'll have to get used to it.'

A FEW FITFUL raindrops spattered the steps as Felix and Otto stepped out of Wulf's. Thick clouds hid the moons and the wind was cool and wet. Otto summoned his coach and it trotted up. Felix followed Otto into it, glad that it was covered. It looked like a storm was coming.

As they started up Commerce Street towards Kaufman district gate, Otto crossed his hands over his broad belly and burped contentedly. 'You're staying at the College of Engineering?' he asked. 'Shall I drop you there?'

'Thank you,' said Felix. The faster he got back the better. 'Very nice of you. And thank you for the dinner.'

'Not at all. Happy to. I'm just glad you've finally come around to deciding to make something of yourself. Once you start with the company we'll dine out like this all the time. Though I hope you don't want to go to Wulf's next–'

Otto was interrupted by a shout, and the coach slewed to an abrupt stop with a neighing of horses and a skidding of hoofs on wet cobbles. Felix and Otto flew forward out of their seats. Felix heard the bodyguards curse as they were thrown from their perches and tried to land on their feet on the street.

Felix pulled himself up and dropped his hand to his sword.

'Manni! Yan! Olaf! What is it!' called Otto.

'Men, sir,' came the coachman's voice.

'Men with swords,' said one of the bodyguards. 'Near a dozen.'

Fear gripped Felix's heart. Who was it? Hermione's gentlemen? Men from the Cleansing Flame? Had Countess Gabriella decided to kill him after all?

'Easy, gentles, easy,' said a Shantytown voice. 'We only want yer valuables, not yer lives. Hand 'em over peaceable and there'll be no need for violence.'

Felix gaped, amazed. Shallya's Mercy! Was it only a robbery? Could he be so lucky?

'Stand away, you ruffians!' retorted the other bodyguard. 'You'll get steel before you get gold.'

'No no!' cried Otto. 'Don't fight them! It isn't worth your lives. Stand down.' He pulled himself up and peeked out the window. 'Come forward, gentlemen. We'll give you what we have.'

'That's the way, m'lords,' said the Shantytown voice as boots approached the coach from either side. 'Nice and easy.'

'You watch yourselves,' growled a bodyguard. 'No tricks.'

'Sigmar's beard!' said Otto as he wiggled the rings off his fingers and started stuffing them under the cushions of the bench. 'The brass of these fellows. Right in the middle of Commerce Street! Where is the watch when they're wanted?'

Felix sat back on the bench as the bootsteps reached the coach's two doors. His hand went to his dagger. The coach rocked on its springs and two scarred, grinning faces appeared in the windows.

'Evening, gentles,' said the one on Felix's side, a swarthy fellow in a soft hat.

The other, who lacked a right eye, looked from Otto to Felix and back. 'Aye,' he said. 'These are the ones.'

The two robbers drew pistols from their doublets and stuck them through the windows.

Felix struck out in two directions at once, kicking hard against his door with the heel of his boot, while at the same time backhanding his dagger at the man in Otto's window.

There was a splintering of wood and both pistols fired, deafening Felix and filling the coach with smoke. Felix heard a cry, but couldn't tell who it was. He didn't think he'd been hit, so he hoped it wasn't him. He launched himself at his door and was gratified to feel it slam open and to hear a body hit the street.

The words, 'these are the ones,' echoed through Felix's head as he stopped and surged for the opposite door. He came up hard against it. The window was empty. He looked out. The one-eyed man lay on the ground, a messy hole in his throat, shot by his companion it seemed. Beyond him, more thugs were running forward. An ambush then, not a robbery. The only question that remained was, were these cultists from the Cleansing Flame, or hirelings of Lady Hermione or Countess Gabriella?

Felix turned to Otto, just visible now through the clearing smoke. He cowered against the back of the bench, eyes wide and darting, his fat chins trembling.

'Stay in the coach!' Felix barked. 'And defend yourself!'

He leapt out of the smashed door, and almost fell as his new boots slid on the wet street. The taller of Otto's bodyguards – Yan, his name was, Felix remembered – had killed the swarthy shooter and was turning to face the charging thugs. Felix drew his runesword and joined him.

One of the thugs fell before he reached them, a fletched bolt in his leg. Out of the corner of his eye, Felix saw Manni, the coachman, cranking a small crossbow.

Then Felix and Yan were surrounded, swords and clubs swinging at them from every direction. Felix knocked a cudgel from someone's hand and ran through a swordsman. He was relieved to see that Yan was a veteran. He did not flinch or panic. He met the greater numbers calm and alert, and though he made no touches, he took none either. It seemed that Otto had spent wisely when he had hired his guards.

Felix killed another thug, gashing his throat, then unstrung another's knee. The assassins wore no armour, and Karaghul was a heavier, keener sword than their rapiers and short swords. He batted them out of the way with ease. The greatest difficulty was keeping his feet on the slick cobbles.

A shout came from the other side of the coach, and then a shriek from Otto.

'Master Felix!' called the coachman. 'They're getting in!'

Felix cursed. 'Fall back with me,' he shouted to Yan, then flourished wildly with his sword and jumped back out of combat. Yan ran with him as he turned and ran for the back of the coach. Yan gasped and almost fell as a thug slashed him across the back. Felix caught his arm and they surged on, their three remaining opponents close behind them.

Olaf had acquitted himself well. Two corpses lay at his feet, and another was staggering away, trying to hold his guts in. But the bodyguard was slumped, motionless, against the coach door, his chest and face painted with blood. A thug kicked him aside and grabbed at the coach door. There were three more behind him.

Felix bellowed to get their attention, then barrelled into them, slashing left and right. One fell back, torso split from shoulder to hip, and the others dodged away, but one gashed Felix under the left arm and the cold shock of steel burned across his ribs. He grunted and stumbled aside.

Yan hacked the man down, then covered Felix as he turned. Felix's first thought, ridiculously, was that they had ruined his new doublet. Then the pain came in earnest and he forgot about the doublet.

There were seven assassins left between Felix and the coach. Seven against two, and he was wounded, blood running down his side. It would be quite a joke if, after persevering against nearly every horror the Old World had to offer, he was finally killed by common alley bashers on the high street in Nuln.

A thug at the back shoved some of the others forward. 'Hold them off while we kill the fat one!' he said, then screamed as a bolt from the coachman's crossbow punched down through his collarbone.

The others turned their heads at the noise. Felix and Yan charged instinctively. The thugs fell back, caught off guard. Felix and Yan pressed them against the coach, swinging wildly. Felix disarmed one and chopped another's club in half. Yan pinned one to the coach, but took a knife point across the cheek. Felix gutted the one he had disarmed, and clubbed another in the temple with the dragon-headed pommel of his sword.

The assassins had had enough. They broke and ran, scattering to the shadows on both sides of the street. Felix and Yan made no attempt to follow.

Felix put the point of his sword to the neck of the man who had taken Manni's bolt in the collarbone as Yan despatched the rest of the wounded with professional efficiency. 'Who sent you?'

The man spat at him, his eyes wild with fanatical ardour. 'You are dead!' he said. 'The flame will consume you! You and all your kind!' He pushed himself forward deliberately, impaling his neck upon Felix's sword, and laughed wetly as the blood pumped from his throat. 'Change is coming!' he hissed, then slumped back, dead. Felix shivered. Just like the one who had killed himself on Gotrek's axe. Their fanaticism was frightening. At least now he knew who had sent them.

'Is it over?' asked Otto, peeking out from the coach.

Felix nodded. 'It's over.'

He knelt down beside Olaf. The bodyguard was breathing, but only barely. Yan squatted down and the two of them picked him up.

Otto opened the coach door and they laid him on the floor. 'To Doctor Koln's house, Manni,' he said. 'Hurry.'

As Yan pulled himself onto his perch behind, Felix climbed back in the coach. He eased back onto the bench with a weary hiss and closed his eyes. The coach lurched forward, jarring his wound. He grunted, in pain, and opened his eyes.

Otto was glaring at him. 'This was no simple robbery.' he said. 'They were after us. After you!'

'I'm sorry, Otto,' said Felix. 'I...'

Otto wasn't listening. He was too angry. 'This has something to do with Gephardt's son, doesn't it? That's why you wanted to go to Wulf's! You had no interest in talking to me about working for the company. You were having one of your *adventures*, and now you've got me caught up in it! Sigmar! I might have been killed!' His face suddenly paled. 'Gods! I still might! Gephardt must have known me as surely as I knew him. He will come after me. He will come after Annabella and Gustav!' Otto's eyes blazed with fury. His round cheeks flushed red. 'How dare you! How dare you endanger my family with your mad antics!'

Felix hung his head. 'I'm sorry, Otto. I didn't think it...'

'Clearly, you didn't think!' shouted Otto. 'You are insane! Get out! Get out and don't come back!'

'I...' Felix felt like a daemon was twisting his intestines with both hands. It was true. He hadn't thought – not until it was too late. He had been so intent on finding the leaders of the Cleansing Flame that he hadn't considered fully the consequences for those around him. It didn't matter that Otto didn't know anything. The cultists had seen him with Felix, and would assume he was a threat. 'At least let me see you to your house,' he said. 'They might come back.'

'No!' said Otto. 'I don't want you near me or...' He hesitated, his eyes flicking nervously to the coach window, then nodded. 'All right, to my house. But never come again. I will not let you in my door.'

'I understand,' said Felix sadly. He couldn't argue. Otto was in the right. He brought wrack and ruin with him wherever he went. First he burned down whole neighbourhoods, now he had marked his brother's family for death. The hero of Nuln indeed!

THEY DEPOSITED OLAF with the doctor – and Otto waited impatiently as the old man salved and stitched and bound the long gash under Felix's arm as well – then hurried on under clouds that threatened rain, but did little more than spit.

As the coach pulled up to Otto's house, the front door opened, and young Gustav stepped out wearing a rain cloak over his scholar's robes. He had a lantern in one hand and a satchel in the other.

Otto practically leapt out of the coach. 'No!' he said, waving his hands. 'Back in the house! You're not going out!'

'What?' asked Gustav. 'Don't be ridiculous, father. I'm only going to-'

'No! You're not going anywhere!'

'But... but why?'

'Because your *uncle*...' Otto turned to glare at Felix as he stepped out after him, 'Has made us the target of some crazed madmen who he is at feud with!'

Gustav frowned. 'I don't understand.'

'Nor do I,' said Otto. 'Nor do I wish to. One moment he is asking questions about Linus Gephardt's son, the next we are attacked in the street by...'

'Gephardt's son?' asked Gustav, his brow knotted. 'You mean Nikolas? What does Nikolas have to do with–'

'You know him?' asked Felix eagerly.

'Nikolas? He is a classmate at university.' Gustav sneered. 'Fancies himself a pamphleteer. I've read better prose in an account ledger.'

'Do you know where he lives?' continued Felix.

'He lives at his father's house, just–'

'No!' cried Otto. 'I forbid it! He has already wound us too close to his folly. You will not assist him!' He turned on Felix and pointed towards the street with a shaking finger. 'You have hurt us enough. Go. Go and don't come back.'

Felix nodded sadly. 'Very well.' He bowed to his brother. 'I am sorry, Otto. And I will do everything I can to fix this.'

'I don't want to hear any more,' said Otto. 'Just go. Go!'

Felix sighed and started down the street towards the gate to the Neuestadt, his mind boiling with guilt and anger and a determination to honour his promise to Otto and make things right for him and his family. The rain picked up. He pulled up the hood of his fancy new cloak. It, at least, was still in one piece.

CHAPTER ELEVEN

FELIX WALKED OUT onto the roof of the College of Engineering, his brother's words still echoing through his mind. Bright lanterns pushed back the night, making the flat green copper roof and its crenellated edges appear to be a island in a dark and endless sea. Slanting raindrops slashed past the lanterns like little comets.

Students were rolling barrels of black powder out from the stairwell and stacking them in piles beneath the *Spirit of Grungni*, which hovered above them like an iron cloud. A winch was lifting a net full of barrels up through a hatch into the belly of the gondola. Another net was spread out on the rooftop and barrels were being placed in its centre. Beyond all the activity, a gyrocopter sat like the withered husk of some gigantic insect, chains securing it to the roof.

Malakai stood by the net, supervising the loading. Gotrek was with him. Felix limped towards them. There was nothing wrong with his legs, but his wounded side was so stiff he could hardly walk straight. It throbbed with blunt, insistent agony. All he wanted to do was dull his brain with ale and try to sleep, but the Slayer needed to hear of the night's events.

The two dwarfs looked up as he approached.

'Evening, young Felix,' said Malakai.

'You must have found something,' said Gotrek. 'You've been fighting.'

'Aye,' said Felix. 'I found out what a fool I can be.' He cast a distracted eye up at the barrels that were disappearing into the hatch. 'I don't dare to hope that you've recovered the powder in my absence.'

Malakai shook his head. 'This is the new powder, bought with Lord Skinflint-Keppel's money. But what happened tae ye?'

Felix sighed. 'I went to Wulf's. One of the cultists we fought last night wore–'

'Aye, a wolf's head pendant. Ah noo a' aboot it,' said Malakai. 'Gurnisson told me all o' what went on in yon cellar. Nae need tae explain. Go on.'

Felix frowned, uneasy. How much had Gotrek said? Had he mentioned Ulrika? Countess Gabriella wouldn't like that. Well, he couldn't very well ask Gotrek that in Malakai's presence, could he? He coughed and continued. 'Well, I saw a man at the club with a burned hand. Unfortunately he saw me too, and he sent some thugs to waylay me and my brother on our way back to his house. There was a fight. My brother... my brother has told me to never come back to his house.'

'And why, pray tell?' asked Malakai.

'He blames me for getting him involved and bringing trouble to his door.' Felix sighed as the daggers of guilt stabbed at him again, almost as painful as the cut in his side. 'And he is right. I should have found some other way into Wulf's. Now the Cleansing Flame are after him as well. And his family. I fear I have doomed them with a death meant for me.'

Gotrek and Malakai snorted in unison.

'Men,' grunted Gotrek, contemptuously.

'A dwarf would have added his axe tae his brother's and faced his enemy at his side,' said Malakai.

'Did you catch this burned man?' asked Gotrek.

'No,' said Felix. 'But I learned his name, and where he lives.'

'Good,' said Gotrek, turning towards the stairs. 'Let's go.'

'Gurnisson!' snapped Malakai. 'Don't be an ass. Can't ye see the lad needs a wee lie doon?'

Gotrek stopped and looked back, glaring at Felix's blood-soaked shirt. He seemed offended that Felix had got himself wounded. 'There's no time. These fools could use the powder tonight. And the *Spirit of Grungni* leaves in less than two days.'

'I'm fine,' said Felix, though he felt anything but, in body or soul. 'But I don't think we'll be able to reach him tonight anyway.'

'Who says we won't?' Gotrek snarled.

'He's a rich man's son,' said Felix. 'He lives at his father's house in the Kaufman district. The city watch doesn't let commoners through the Altestadt gates at this time of night. Particularly not when they are wanted criminals such as ourselves.'

'Then we'll take the sewers,' said Gotrek. 'Come on.'

The mention of the sewers and of their outlaw status reminded Felix of the encounter they had had with the watch under the Gunnery School earlier that day. He turned to Malakai. 'Did you get a visit from the watch today about us?'

'Oh, aye,' said Malakai. 'I told Gurnisson o' it already. They came asking after ye.'

'And?'

Malakai shrugged. 'I told 'em I didnae know where ye wis, which was the truth. And I told them I'd tell ye, if ye returned, no' tae dae it again.' He grinned. 'So, dinnae dae it again. And dinnae tell me who this rich laddie is, or where his house is, neither. A dwarf niver lies.'

Felix gave a half-hearted chuckle, then groaned and pressed his ribs.

Malakai clucked his tongue. 'Ye shouldnae be goin' anywhere, laddie, except to yer bed.'

'I'll sleep when this is over,' said Felix, and turned after Gotrek. *If I'm still alive*, he thought.

FELIX WALKED BESIDE Gotrek as they travelled again through the stinking brick tunnels towards the Altestadt district, his head down and his mind churning like a stew on the boil. A thought would come to the surface like a mushy onion or a bit of meat or carrot, and then sink back down into the depths as another one roiled up, demanding his attention – his culpability in his brother's danger, his responsibility for the fire in the Maze, the threats of the countess and her even more vicious rivals, the doom that would come upon the Gunnery School if they failed to find the powder, the fact that, not two weeks back in the Empire and they were once again outlaws.

He looked over at Gotrek, striding along with his beard jutting forward, his brow lowered, a picture of unwavering determination. Did he ever have doubts or second thoughts? Did he ever have regrets? Then he recalled the Slayer hunched over the body of his friend Hamnir, whom he had just killed. Of course he did – more than Felix would ever know of, no doubt.

Felix shook himself and tried to clear his mind for the task ahead. 'So,' he said at last. 'When we get there, is your plan to beat this Gephardt until he tells us where the powder is and who his leaders are?'

'Aye,' said Gotrek. 'What else?'

'I don't think it will work.' said Felix. 'The orator we captured in Shantytown yesterday cut his own throat on your axe rather than talk. And the leader of the men who attacked my brother's coach did the same thing when I tried to question him tonight. He threw himself on my sword and died laughing at me.'

Gotrek grunted. 'They're not cowards, at least,' he said.

'No,' said Felix. 'They're mad.' He hissed as the cut over his ribs flared again. 'I think our best bet is to watch Gephardt, and follow him until he brings us to the leaders of the cult.'

Gotrek shrugged. 'All right. But if he doesn't lead us to them before the *Spirit of Grungni* is ready to leave, we'll try it my way.'

'Fair enough,' said Felix.

They walked on, the flow of sludge in the sewer channel was higher and quicker than usual from the rain, and in every direction Felix heard the rush and splash of water pouring down through iron gratings. The brick walls were slick with moisture.

A little further on, Felix slowed and looked around as a familiar fetid smell reached his nostrils. He inhaled deeper, trying to separate it from the pungent background odour of the sewer. Was it? Yes it was. There was no mistaking it – the rancid musky reek of ratman – faint but unmistakable. Was it some old spoor he and Gotrek had stumbled over, or had the skaven returned to Nuln?

Gotrek was turning his head back and forth like a dog sniffing the wind. He caught Felix's eye. 'Aye, manling. I smell it too. But we've no time for diversions.'

He strode on. Felix shook his head as he followed. Only Gotrek could call those horrific abominations a 'diversion'.

A few tunnels on, Felix remembered what Malakai had said on the roof, and his heart thudded in his chest. 'Ah, Gotrek, did you tell Makaisson about our alliance with Ulrika?'

'Of course not,' said Gotrek. 'I might kill her, but I'd not betray her.'

Felix flushed. 'I didn't think so, but when he said you had told him about the pendant...'

'I kept her out of it.'

'Good.' Felix was relieved. That was one lump in his roiling stew of fears that could subside. He could confidently tell the countess and her compatriots that he and Gotrek had kept their existence a secret. Though whether that would matter to Lady Hermione and Mistress Wither he could not say. Their mistrust of men seemed to run too deep.

Gotrek looked up. 'We're under the Altestadt now. This way.'

He led Felix to a side tunnel with an iron ladder as if it had been yesterday that he had used it, not twenty years ago. Felix's wounded side ached as he pulled himself up. The rungs were wet, and a steady stream of drips rattled on their heads as they climbed. At the top of the ladder, Gotrek shouldered up an iron grate and helped Felix out into an alley behind a row of shops. The rain had finally started in earnest. It was pouring. They were wet in seconds.

Felix sighed. 'A perfect night for spying.'

THE GEPHARDT HOUSE stood in the middle of a row of elegant town homes: a four storey granite mansion with tall, narrow windows at each floor and a balcony over the front door. It was nearing midnight when Gotrek and Felix found the place, an hour when most honest Nulners were abed – *and the sane ones were out of the rain*, thought Felix miserably, as a drip ran down his nose – but there was a light behind one of the windows on the ground floor, and when they looked in, they could see young Nikolas pacing before a huge fireplace, and drinking deeply from a wine bottle. There didn't appear to be anyone with him.

The young man was nervous, but what about? Had his thugs reported that Felix and Otto escaped them? Was he frightened that he was going to be exposed? Had he sent his men back out to find Felix? Had they regrouped and gone after Otto? The thought made Felix want to run back to his brother's house and defend it, but Otto had said he didn't want him there and, truth be told, the best way of saving him and his family from the threat of the Cleansing Flame was to find the cultists and wipe them out. Felix just hoped that was possible.

They could not stay too long at the window. Unlike Shantytown and the Neuestadt, the Kaufman district was well patrolled. Gotrek and Felix heard the tap of the watch's spear butts striking the cobbles further down the block before they saw them, and retreated into a service alley, then watched as the men passed, looking wet and out of sorts, their captain carrying a lantern on a long pole before them.

After the watchmen had turned a corner and vanished again into the night, they returned to Gephardt's window. Nikolas was gone, and an old servant was covering the fire and tidying up the wine bottle.

'Around the back,' said Gotrek.

They circled the block. The alley behind the houses was not as neatly cobbled as the street in front and they splashed through puddles and muddy ruts until they came to the right gate. The back of the property was large, and divided into coach yard and garden. As they craned their necks to see over the wall, a light went out in a window on the top floor.

'Gone to sleep,' said Felix.

'Perhaps,' said Gotrek. 'Perhaps not.' He looked around. The coach house of the mansion across the alley from Gephardt's butted up against the alley. Gotrek crossed to it and started climbing the wall to the roof, which was low and partially screened by yew trees. 'I'll watch from here,' he said over his shoulder. 'You go back to where we were. If he leaves from the front, strike your sword against stone. I'll hear it.'

'And if he leaves from the back?' asked Felix. 'I don't have your hearing.'

Gotrek pulled himself up onto the roof and drew his axe. He held it up and grinned. 'You won't need it.'

Felix shrugged. 'All right. Let's hope he leaves quickly, though. I think I'm catching a chill.'

Gotrek snorted. 'Humans are soft.' He settled himself in a valley between the peaks of the carriage house roof.

Felix rolled his eyes, then trudged down the alley and back to the street.

It seemed Nikolas might never leave. Felix stood shivering and sniffing in the service alley across the street from the Gephardt mansion for hours while the rain beat down on his head and his wound ached and itched as if imps were clawing at it from the inside. Nothing happened. Once every hour the watch walked by and Felix stepped further back into the shadows of the alley, but other than that, all was quiet. The rain rained, cats and rats prowled, very occasionally a coach rolled by or deposited someone at one of the grand houses – once even to the house he was hunched against – but none stopped at Gephardt's house.

After a time Felix's legs grew tired and he squatted on his haunches, but then his new boots cut off the circulation in his legs and he stood again, stomping away the pins and needles. At last he sat down on the driest cobbles he could find and tried to keep his eyes open while his seat got wetter and colder. Won't be long now, he thought. Any minute Gephardt's front door will open, or the clash of Gotrek's axe will ring out, and we'll be off and running. Any minute now.

Any minute now.

* * *

'WHAT'S ALL THIS?' said a voice in Felix's ear. 'Are you well, m'lord?'

Felix flinched awake, blinking around in confusion. Booted legs and spear shafts ringed him like a fence. A square face with a broken nose was inches from his, and a loud voice buffeted his eardrums, accompanied by a gust of onions and beer and cheap meat pie. It was still raining.

'Lost yer way home from the club, hey, m'lord?' said the watchman, not unkindly. He offered Felix his arm. Felix took it, and the man hauled him to his feet. 'Upsy daisy, m'lord. That's it.' He dusted Felix down and smiled at him, revealing rotten teeth. 'Best to find your own bed then, hey? You'll catch your death out here in this wet.'

'Thank you,' said Felix, still trying to clear his head. It appeared to be dawn, or almost dawn. How long had he been asleep? Had he missed Nikolas leaving? Had he missed Gotrek's signal? At least with his new clothes they seemed to have mistaken him for a nobleman and weren't suspicious of his being here. 'I... Well, I guess I'll be going.'

But where, he wondered? He pulled his sodden cloak around his shoulders. Would they follow him if he went around the block to find Gotrek? And what if Nikolas slipped out before he could get back in position?

As he started towards the street one of the watchmen stepped to the sergeant and whispered in his ear. Felix saw this and picked up his pace.

It was no good.

'Just a minute, m'lord,' said the sergeant from behind him.

Felix turned at the mouth of the alley. 'Yes?'

'Begging your pardon,' said the sergeant, 'but could you tell me your name? And where you live, exactly?'

'My name?' said Felix, panic rising in his throat. He tried an aristocratic sneer. 'And what business is it of yours what my name is?'

'Well, er, ye see, yer lordship,' said the sergeant, looking uncomfortable. 'Edard here thinks you look like a fellow what's supposed to be under house arrest in the College of Engineering. That one were described as having a sword with a dragon hilt, just like the one you're wearing, and, well...'

'Oh, sergeant,' came a silvery voice from above them.

Everyone looked up. A beautiful woman in green, with long auburn hair trailing out from beneath a shawl, was leaning out of a window of the townhouse beside the alley. She smiled down at them.

Felix stared.

It was Ulrika.

CHAPTER TWELVE

THE SERGEANT TOUCHED his fingers to his cap. 'Morning, m'lady. Terrible sorry if we woke you.'

'Not at all, sergeant,' she said sweetly, and without a trace of Kislev accent. 'But I must ask you to release this man, ruffian though he may be. I threw him out last night after we had a little lover's quarrel. He has pined beneath my window ever since, but I believe he has suffered enough, and I have forgiven him. Let him go and I will open the door for him.'

'Aye, lady,' said the sergeant, uncertainly. 'It's just that we have reason to believe he might be–'

'Nonsense,' said Ulrika, even more sweetly. 'He couldn't possibly be anyone you had any interest in. He is merely my poor, sweet, bedraggled lover, heartsick in the rain.' Her voice was as syrupy and cloying as honey, and her eyes seemed to have gotten very large and very deep. 'My poor, sweet, bedraggled lover,' she repeated. 'Heartsick in the rain.'

'Aye, lady,' the sergeant mumbled. 'Heartsick in the rain. Aye, of course. Thank ye. And we'll be going now.'

'Yes, you will,' agreed Ulrika. 'Goodbye.'

The watchmen turned and shuffled off down the street like sleepwalkers. Felix watched them go, then looked up at Ulrika again.

'How are you here...?'

716

Ulrika put a finger to her lips and motioned to the front of the house, then closed the window.

Felix walked around to the front door, giving the befuddled watchmen a wide berth. After a short wait, the door opened, and a grave looking butler bowed him in. As he was taking Felix's dripping cloak, Ulrika appeared at the top of a curved mahogany staircase and smiled sourly down at him.

'You see how much nicer things could have been if you and Gotrek had honoured your promise?' she said. 'Come up and I will find you some dry clothes.'

'I don't understand,' said Felix crossly, starting up the stairs. It was deliciously warm in here, and dry. The smell of eggs and bacon and spiced tea wafting from the back of the house was making his stomach growl. To think he had spent the whole night getting soaked in the alley, while right behind the wall he had slumped against, Ulrika was sitting in the lap of luxury. 'What promise did I not honour? And how do you come to be in this house?'

'You broke one promise, and Gotrek broke another.' said Ulrika, as she led him along the hall. 'You did not return to the countess and tell her what you had discovered.'

Felix scowled. 'Was there any need? Her besotted knight – what was his name? Captain Reingelt? He was there. He saw it all. As did one of Lady Hermione's dandies. They must have told their mistresses, else you wouldn't be here.'

'Aye, they did, but you forget what I said of the countess's nature of late. She would take even so small a lapse as a deliberate slight.' She opened the door to a bedroom and stood aside to let him enter. It was a comfortable room, with a large canopied bed on one side and a crackling fire on the other. 'But that is by the by. It is Gotrek whose treachery is unforgiveable.'

'Oh come,' said Felix. 'Gotrek has never broken a promise in his life!'

'Indeed he has,' said Ulrika, closing the door behind him and turning, her eyes suddenly as cold and hard as sapphires. 'And you know it.'

'What?'

'Mistress Wither followed you from Wulf's last night, at Lady Hermione's bidding. She was on the roof when you spoke to Gotrek and Malakai. She heard Malakai say, just as you heard him, that Gotrek had revealed my existence to him.'

Felix blinked, confused. 'What? He didn't.'

'Do you lie now too, Felix?' she asked, advancing on him. All her former humour had drained away as if it had never been. 'The Slayer speaks much about honour and keeping vows. Apparently he doesn't hold himself to so high a standard.'

Felix took an involuntary step backwards. She was terrifying. 'Wait! You have it wrong. It must be Mistress Wither that lied.'

'Did she?' she said, still coming forward. 'She reported to us that Makaisson said Gotrek had told him all about the pendant, and the whole truth about the fight with the Cleansing Flame.' She reached out and grasped his collar. 'And the whole truth includes *me*.'

Felix backed into the bed, banging his head against one of the posts. 'Wait! Listen! I can see how she might have construed Malakai's words that way. But she doesn't know Gotrek. He did not give you away. He told Malakai all of it but your part. He left you out.'

Ulrika was inches from him. Her sharp teeth glinted in the firelight. 'And how do you know this?'

'I asked!' Felix swallowed. She was going to kill him! 'It... it troubled me too! Gotrek doesn't do things like that, but knowing how he feels about you and your mistress, I thought perhaps...'

'You thought?'

'I was wrong!' cried Felix. 'He said he might kill you, but he would never betray you.'

Ulrika glared at him, her ice-blue eyes boring into his as if she could dissect his soul with them. Then after a long moment she sighed and backed away, shaking her head and chuckling. 'He might kill me but he wouldn't betray me? Ha! That does sound like the Slayer.'

'You believe me, then?' asked Felix, barely daring to breathe.

'Aye,' said Ulrika. 'I believe you.' Then she frowned. 'But this is unfortunate.'

'What is?'

Ulrika looked up at him apologetically. 'The countess believed Mistress Wither's story, as I did. Therefore she believes that you and Gotrek betrayed me. She is not pleased. In fact, she gave Mistress Wither, Lady Hermione and myself permission to kill you both if we found you.'

'Sigmar!' Felix's heart hammered. Three ancient, powerful, *insane*, vampiresses, all out for his blood! Could it get any worse? 'You have to tell them! You have to call them off!'

'Have no fear, Felix,' said Ulrika. 'I will repair the damage. I will tell the countess what you have said. All will be well.'

Felix swallowed and tried to calm his breathing. 'I hope so.'

'Worry not,' she said smiling reassuringly. 'I am her favourite, and Mistress Wither is a rival. She will believe me.' Her eyes dropped to Felix's clothes. 'But look at you! You're dripping on the carpet. What sort of hostess am I?' She crossed to a wardrobe. 'Let's see what we can find for you.'

Felix blinked at this quick change of subject and mood. Ulrika seemed to have dismissed the countess's death sentence without another thought, but he was having a hard time imagining that all would go as well as she seemed to think.

He looked around the luxurious room as she rummaged in the armoire. Gephardt's father's house was visible through the front window. 'How did you find this place to watch from?' he asked. 'Don't tell me the countess just happens to own a house directly across from Gephardt's?'

Ulrika pulled a dressing gown of blue Cathay silk from the wardrobe and held it out to him. 'Here. This should fit. Put it on.'

Felix took it and set it on the bed, waiting for her to withdraw.

She sat down in an armchair. 'As I mentioned once before, the countess has many clients among the nobility, and she is very good at...' She frowned at Felix. 'What's the matter. Get dressed. You'll catch your death.'

'Ah...' said Felix, colouring.

'Oh, don't be an idiot,' said Ulrika, rolling her eyes. 'It's not as if I haven't seen it all before, when we were...' She stopped as she saw Felix's expression, and snorted. 'All right, all right.' She stood and picked up the chair – a heavy oak and leather behemoth – as if it weighed nothing, then turned it to face the fire. 'Now, go on. I won't look. I promise.' She sat down in it and looked into the flames.

Felix glared at her back, then shrugged and began to peel off his sopping clothes.

'Where was I?' said Ulrika to the fireplace. 'Ah yes. The countess has many rich clients, and she is very good at getting them to do what she wants. Her voice can be very hypnotic when she wishes.'

'As can yours,' said Felix, recalling the befuddlement of the watchmen.

'I am learning,' said Ulrika, then continued. 'This is the house of Lord Jorgen Kirstfauver. When Captain Reingelt reported to the countess – that is, to Madame du Vilmorin – that you had revealed the son of Linus Gephardt to be one of the Cleansing Flame, she knew where he lived – Gephardt senior being of course another client of our house. So it was simplicity itself for her to call upon Lord Kirstfauver and invite him to sample the newest and youngest girls in the house, for as long as he liked, in exchange for the use of his house and servants for a day – with the greatest discretion, of course. Lord Kirstfauver is besotted with Madame du Vilmorin, as are all men, so he readily agreed.'

'And if we must wait longer than a day?' asked Felix, shucking out of his wet linen shirt and taking up the robe.

Ulrika chuckled. 'Time has a way of passing almost unnoticed in Madame du Vilmorin's house. Lord Kirstfauver will find that he was so bewitched by the beauty of his bedmates that the days just slipped away.' She paused, frowning. 'Where is Gotrek, by the way?'

Felix felt a hot flash of shame. He had been here talking all this time while Gotrek was still out in the rain, watching from the back alley. 'Sigmar! He's watching Gephardt's coach yard. As I should be from the front.' He started angrily for the door. 'You've lured me from my post. Gephardt may have gotten away.'

'Fear not, Felix,' said Ulrika. 'I have seven spies watching the house. We will know if he leaves.'

'Seven!' Felix stared at her. Seven spies? And he had seen none of them?

She spread her hands. 'You see? Had you told us as you should have, you might have slept in a warm bed tonight. Your stubborn insistence on going it alone soaked you to the bone, and the fox might have slipped away while you slept.' She smirked. 'Do you want to relieve Gotrek from his misery now?'

Felix flushed again. He did want to bring Gotrek in out of the rain, but the thought of the Slayer finding him in a silk robe in the company of Ulrika made him cringe. 'Yes, I'll... Just a moment.'

He crossed to his sword and unsheathed it. Ulrika looked alarmed until he stepped to the side window, which looked over the alley he had spent the night in. He opened it and rang the flat of the blade against the stone window ledge. Ulrika looked at him curiously.

'Our signal,' Felix explained.

He leaned out of the window until he saw Gotrek's squat form appear at the end of the block and look down the street towards Gephardt's house.

'Hssst!' said Felix.

The Slayer looked up, and Felix waved at him, then pointed to the front door. He saw a look of angry confusion cross Gotrek's face before he started across the street.

Felix and Ulrika reached the entryway just as the butler opened the door.

'What is this foolishness?' said Gotrek as he stepped through the door, water dripping from his beard in rivulets. 'You were only to signal if...' He stopped when he saw Felix's silk robe, then looked past him to Ulrika. He sneered. 'Ah. Not interrupting anything, am I?'

'Let me explain,' said Felix.

'Is it you explaining?' asked Gotrek. He closed the door behind him. 'Or is it her, jerking your strings?'

'I...' said Felix.

'Felix is not beglamoured, Slayer,' said Ulrika. 'I merely invited him in out of the rain, as I invite you now. Had you both come immediately to the countess when you learned about Gephardt, you might have waited out the night in comfort here instead of soaking yourselves out there.'

Gotrek growled. 'And who watches the house while we wait in comfort?'

'I have seven spies watching the house,' said Ulrika. 'Trust me, your quarry will not slip away while you enjoy the countess's hospitality.'

The Slayer grunted, apparently unhappy that all his questions had been answered so reasonably. For a moment he looked ready to turn around and walk back out into the rain, but finally he ran his thick hand through his wilted crest and flicked the water on the floor. 'Then get me a cloth and some food and a pint.'

Ulrika curtsied, her lips twisting into a sly smile. 'At once, sir dwarf. We live only to serve. You will find a fire in the parlour to your left.'

She turned and disappeared through a servant's door.

Gotrek crossed to the parlour door, then looked back at Felix. 'Go and sleep, manling. Alone.'

Felix stiffened. 'All these years, and you don't trust me not to be a fool?'

Gotrek looked as if he was going to snap back with some retort, then he paused and shrugged, looking almost contrite. 'I trust no human when one of those things is around. Now get some sleep.'

He turned and entered the parlour. Felix glared after him for a moment, then started up the stairs for the bedroom where he had left his clothes.

FELIX WOKE SLOWLY. The room was dark but for the low flicker of fire-light. The big four-poster bed was soft and warm and enveloping. The patter of rain on the windows was soothing. The smell of fresh linen and wool was comforting. He yawned and stretched – and yelped like a trodden-on dog as the stitches in his side stabbed at him anew.

He curled up in a ball, hissing and blinking away tears. He saw a face in the blurred dimness. There was someone next to his bed! He jerked back and yelped again as the wound caught him once more.

'Good evening, Felix,' said Ulrika, laughing.

Felix glared at her, panting and sweating. She sat slouched in the arm chair, dressed in her manly garb again, looking as if she had been there for a long while.

'What... what... what do you want?' he finally managed. 'Is it time?'

'No no. Our fox has not yet left his den,' she said. 'But night has come. He may soon. I thought you might want to feed – sorry – to eat, before he moves.'

'Yes.' Felix sat up gingerly. 'Yes. That's a good plan.'

She stood and turned the chair around, as easily as before, then sat down again facing away from him and pointed to the chest at the end of the bed. 'Your clothes have been dried and mended, and there is a wash basin by the fire and a pitcher of water warming before it.'

Felix rubbed the sleep from his eyes, then grunted and hissed his way out of bed. He pulled on his hose and breeches and padded to the fire.

'You will be relieved to hear,' she said from behind him. 'That while you slept, I sent a message to the countess, telling her that you and the Slayer did not betray my existence to Makaisson after all, and asking her to call off Lady Hermione and Mistress Wither.'

'Thank you,' said Felix. 'And has she replied?' He poured the water into the basin. It was the perfect temperature.

'Not yet,' said Ulrika. 'She is unlikely to tonight. Most of her servants are busy, either at the brothel, or looking for the Cleansing Flame.'

Felix shivered as he soaped his hands and face. He was glad to hear that Ulrika had sent the note, but he would be unable to relax entirely until he knew the countess had withdrawn her order of execution.

'You look very young when you sleep, Felix,' said Ulrika. 'Like you did when we first met.'

Felix choked. He looked up, covered in suds. 'You... How long were you watching me?' The thought made him uneasy.

'Our kind do not sleep,' said Ulrika.

Felix frowned and splashed his face. That wasn't really an answer.

'Which is unfortunate,' she continued. 'For it leads to contemplation, and perhaps madness.' Felix heard her sigh. 'I was remembering how it was with us, when last we knew each other, and wondering if things would have been different – if this might not have happened – had you not lost interest in me.'

Felix snorted and water squirted painfully through his nose. He coughed and hacked, convulsing, tears streaming from his eyes and the wound in his side screaming. 'I…!' He wretched and tried again. '*I* lost interest in *you*? You left me for Max!'

She turned in her chair and looked at him, raising an eyebrow. 'Come now, Felix. That was long after things were over between us.'

Felix glared at her. He was surprised at how much the old wounds still stung. 'Is that so? I wish you had thought to tell me.'

'Maybe we didn't speak of it,' said Ulrika, then chuckled. 'We were very good at not speaking of things then, weren't we? But we both knew.'

'I'm not sure I did,' said Felix stiffly. 'I seem to recall your losing interest in me before I lost interest in you. Why else did you start all those pointless arguments? Why else the sullen moods? The sudden anger?'

Ulrika barked a laugh. 'You describe yourself!'

'I was only reacting to you!'

Ulrika's eyes flashed like a cat's, and she sprang from the chair to face him. Felix shrank back, suddenly aware that he was half naked and facing a well-armed and inhumanly strong monster.

Ulrika seemed to come to the same realisation, for all at once she deflated and sat down on the arm of the chair, hanging her head. 'I apologise, Felix. You are entirely right. I started many of those fights, and I did have bouts of sullenness and anger. But you did as well.'

'I… I suppose I did.'

'We were both very young then,' she said. 'Perhaps we still are.' She laughed bitterly. 'I certainly haven't gotten any older.'

Felix crossed to his shirt and drew it on as memories flooded back to him across the years. 'You were very hard to figure out,' he said. 'At times it felt as if you thought me an amusing commoner, not worth more than a summer fling. Other times you seemed to act as if I was your saviour – someone to lead you out of the oblast and show you the world. I didn't know what you wanted.'

'That is because *I* didn't know what I wanted,' said Ulrika. 'I wanted… I wanted…' She paused, her eyes far away, then laughed suddenly, a great guffaw of surprise, and stood, running her hand roughly through her short white hair. 'Shall I tell you when it was over?' She held up a finger. 'And this will prove that you were correct, and that it was me who decided to end it, though I didn't realise that that was so until this very moment.'

'All right,' said Felix, as he tugged on his boots, though he wasn't sure, now that she said it, that he did want to know. Had he said something ridiculous? Had he proved himself a peasant in some obscure manner?

'I set you a test,' she said, leaning against the mantelpiece and crossing her arms. 'Though I didn't know that was what it was at the time. And it was a test that you could not win, no matter your answer.'

'I don't understand,' said Felix. 'What test?'

Ulrika smiled. 'Do you remember, at Karak Kadrin, when I asked you if you would leave the Slayer and come away with me to Kislev?'

Felix's face hardened. 'I do remember. I said yes, I would. It is the only time I have ever betrayed my oath to Gotrek.'

'Yes,' said Ulrika, nodding. 'And because of that, you failed the test. From then on I began to think of you as a man who would go back on a vow, and I no longer had the respect for you that I had previously.'

'So,' Felix said, anger rising in him, 'I would have passed the test if I had said I would not go with you?'

'No! Of course not,' said Ulrika. 'Had you said no, it would have proved that you did not love me enough to go back on a vow.'

Felix blinked. 'But then it was...'

'Impossible. Absolutely!' Ulrika laughed. 'You see? Young and foolish! I thought myself a noblewoman, and a noblewoman must have a lover of unimpeachable honour – a man who would die before he broke an oath. And yet, at the same time, I wanted from my lover such passion and devotion that he would be willing to trample his honour in the mud and forsake his friends and family at my lightest word.'

Felix shook his head in wonder. 'Shallya's mercy, it wasn't Krieger who made you a monster. What madness!'

Ulrika flashed a sharp-toothed grin. 'There is no more dangerous monster than a nineteen-year-old girl with ideals.'

Felix laughed, then winced, and eased gingerly into his doublet. 'I... I must confess to a similar struggle.'

'Oh?'

Felix looked at her sheepishly. 'You were everything I ever wanted – a beautiful girl with spirit and intelligence, who loved life and adventure and...' He paused, '...and love. And yet, you were also everything I ever hated, a noblewoman who'd never done a day's work in her life. A sportswoman who would rather hunt than read, and whose idea of poetry was a Kossar drinking song.'

'Lies!' cried Ulrika, interrupting. 'I worked harder than you ever–'

Felix held up his hands. 'I know. I know. You were not really any of those things. Only a symbol of them. I knew it then too, but I couldn't help it. I spent all my school years being snubbed by the sons and daughters of nobles, and I held it against you. By loving you, I was betraying every ideal I ever held about overturning privilege and ending the tyranny of class, and so I felt guilty. But when I looked at you, and listened to you, and saw you for who you were, rather than what you stood for, I felt guilty for the pigeonhole I had put you in.'

'And so grew sullen,' said Ulrika.

Felix nodded. 'And angry.'

'And started arguments for no reason,' they said in unison, then laughed and caught each other's eyes.

A whole conversation flashed between them in that look. A recognition of regret, of longing, guilt, of understanding come too late – and a pain went through Felix's chest that had nothing to do with his stitches. He turned away, suddenly angry, though whether at Ulrika, or himself, or cruel fate, he didn't know. By the gods, the foolish nothings that drove people apart! It was all so unfair.

'Why couldn't we have had this conversation twenty years ago?' he asked.

'Because we were twenty years younger,' said Ulrika, sighing. 'And twenty years more foolish. And could not name our trouble to ourselves, let alone each other.'

Felix spun back to her. 'But think what those years might have held for us! Think how different our lives might have been if...'

'Aye,' said Ulrika, and the pain in her eyes was like an open wound. 'I do think on it. Often.'

Felix flushed. 'Ulrika.' He stepped towards her. 'Forgive me. It didn't even occur to me.'

He raised a hand to clasp her shoulder, but she flinched back, thrusting out a warding hand and showing her fangs. 'No! You may not touch me!'

Felix stopped, confused.

Ulrika turned away and stared into the fire, hugging herself. 'I could not bear it.'

Felix's hand dropped, his heart breaking. He wanted comfort her, but how? He stared at her back, unable to think of anything to say.

The door opened. Gotrek stood in it. 'He's leaving.'

Ulrika sighed. It sounded to Felix like a sigh of relief.

BUT ALL GEPHARDT did was go to dinner at a nearby restaurant, alone, and then, after an hour, return home, still alone. It was maddening. Felix was certain that somewhere in Nuln the Brotherhood of the Cleansing Flame was preparing to use the black powder for some nefarious purpose, and that something terrible might happen

at any minute. But where? When? And what would it be? He had
thought Gephardt would be part of it, and would bring them to it,
but he appeared to be in for the night.

'Maybe I made a mistake,' he said. 'Maybe I picked the wrong
man.'

Having returned from spying on Gephardt's dinner, he and
Gotrek and Ulrika now watched his father's house from the window
of Lord Kirstfauver's darkened front sitting room. Gephardt's lamps
were on and his figure moved back and forth through the rooms.

'Maybe the look I saw in Gephardt's eye was nothing but indiges-
tion,' said Felix miserably.

'You were attacked,' said Ulrika.

'It could have been some other member of Wulf's who recognised
me and sent those men.'

'It's him,' said Gotrek. 'He is nervous. He paces. He drinks. He is
waiting for something. Something will happen tonight.'

'It had better,' said Felix. 'The *Spirit of Grungni* flies at dawn.'

'And I will let it fly, if need be,' said Gotrek.

Felix looked at him, surprised.

'I will not leave until Heinz is avenged,' Gotrek rumbled. 'No matter how long it takes.'

Another hour passed.

'What if Gephardt's not part of what is going to happen?' said
Felix, from where he slumped in a chair. 'What if he's only waiting to hear of the success of the plan? What if it has already
occurred?'

Gotrek snorted. 'If somebody set off that much powder somewhere in Nuln, we would have heard it.'

Midnight came and went. Gotrek remained at the window, watching intently, apparently untiring. Ulrika prowled from room to
room, restless.

Felix dozed fitfully, dreaming uncomfortable dreams of his times
with her. It had been difficult to think of anything else since their
conversation. Daggers of regret would stab him in the heart when
he would turn his head and see her looking out of the window.
Shards of memory would tumble through his mind, cutting everything in their path with their sharp edges. He would find himself
thinking, there must be some way to fix this. There must be some
way that, now that they knew each other and themselves, they could
return to what they had, older, wiser, and forever. But there was no
way. Ulrika had died seventeen years before, in the arms of Adolphus Krieger, and was given the semblance of life only by darkest
sorcery from the mists of time. There was no way back from what

she had become. There was no way to cure her but the stake or the fire or the sun.

Felix raged silently at the unfairness of it all. How cruel was fate to allow them such an epiphany decades too late? Had they talked then as they talked now, they might have shared their life together, travelling the world side by side, sharing life's wonders and horrors and joys. Instead they had both wandered alone among their companions, divided from each other by unbreachable walls of death, distance and misunderstanding. It was enough to make Felix want to weep, or fight something that would kill him.

It occurred to him that, had Ulrika not been turned by Krieger, Felix might have tried much harder and much sooner, to turn Gotrek back towards the shores of the Old World.

At last, almost three hours after midnight, Gotrek grunted, waking Felix from his fitful slumbers.

'A visitor,' said the Slayer.

Felix and Ulrika stepped to the window. A coach was pulling up before Gephardt's door. A man in a heavy cloak got out. Gephardt's door opened for him, and the coach drove off as he entered the house. It was Gephardt that ushered him in.

'Is he throwing a party?' asked Felix. 'At this time of night?'

'A hunting party, perhaps,' said Ulrika.

For another half hour Gephardt and his guest moved behind the windows, talking and drinking, then another man, this one on foot, approached the house. Again, the door opened before he knocked and Gephardt let him in.

Now, however, Gephardt did not entertain. The lanterns were quickly snuffed and the house went dark. Felix looked back and forth from the front door to the upper floors, expecting them to leave or retire above.

They did neither.

'They are leaving from the coach yard,' said Ulrika. 'I'm sure of it. My spies will tell me in a moment.'

She scanned the roofs of the houses to either side of Gephardt's house. After a second, a dark figure appeared and waved a hand, then pointed left.

'Ah. I was right.' Ulrika turned to the door. 'Come. They are heading south.'

CHAPTER THIRTEEN

IT WOULD HAVE been too conspicuous to follow in Ulrika's coach, so Gotrek, Felix and Ulrika trailed Gephardt's carriage through the Kaufman district on foot. With his short legs, Gotrek was at a disadvantage for this kind of work, but he plodded on tirelessly behind Felix while Ulrika sprinted ahead, disappearing into the shadows and keeping the coach in sight. Felix wasn't much faster than Gotrek. The day's rest had revived him, but it had also stiffened his wounds and tortured muscles. He limped and gritted his teeth with every step.

The night was cold and blustery. Shutters rattled and trees rustled. The rains of the previous night had tapered off to sporadic sprinkles, and the moons appeared and disappeared behind a herd of racing clouds that filled the sky like a stampede of grey bulls.

Ulrika soon vanished entirely ahead of them. Felix carried on in the direction he hoped she had gone, all the while wondering if she was leaving them behind intentionally – revenge perhaps for his not informing her and the countess about Gephardt. But then, after a few minutes, she reappeared in the distance, waving him forward.

'They're going into the Neuestadt,' she said, as he trotted up to her. 'Through the gate. I don't think the watch will let you through.'

'But you they will?' Felix asked, sceptical.

'I don't need the gate.'

'You have wings?'

'Something like that.'

Felix looked down Commercial Way. Gephardt's coach was stopped at the Altestadt Gate while his coachman talked with the guards. How were he and Gotrek going to get through, and do it fast enough to keep the coach in view?

Gephardt was the son of a rich man, with all a rich man's trappings. He had the coach and coachman, faultless clothes, well-bred friends. If he said he was going to some brothel or gambling hall in the Neuestadt, the watch would touch their caps and bow him through. Would they do the same for Felix and the Slayer?

Felix looked down at himself, taking stock. He was dressed well enough at the moment, and was well shaved, and that counted for something – the guard had woken him politely enough when they had found him in the alley this morning, instead of driving him out of the district with kicks and head-knocks – and even though he and Gotrek were being sought by the watch, his face was ordinary enough that he might be able to pass without them giving him a second glance, but Gotrek...

Gotrek could not be called ordinary – not even by Slayer standards. If the guards at the gate had been given a description of him – and Felix had no doubt that they had – he would be recognised in an instant. They would be stopped. There would be questions, and most likely violence. Innocent men would be hurt and Gephardt's coach would get away.

Maybe they should go via the sewers again. But that would take too much time. Gephardt might be anywhere by the time they resurfaced.

Gotrek strode up. 'What's the trouble?'

'They're going into the Neuestadt,' said Ulrika.

'The watch isn't going to let us follow,' said Felix. 'They'll question us. Arrest us.'

The gates were swinging open, and Gephardt's coachman was whipping up the horses.

Gotrek growled. 'If they want to arrest us, let's give them a reason.'

'We can't do that. We...' He paused and gaped at Gotrek. 'Wait! That's good. They want to arrest us. We'll let them.'

'Hey?' said Gotrek.

Ulrika cocked an eyebrow.

'Just long enough to have them take us through the gate.'

'Ah,' said Gotrek. 'Good thinking, manling. Lead on.'

Felix turned to Ulrika. 'Keep them in sight. We'll catch you up on the other side.'

'I'd rather stay and see this,' said Ulrika, grinning. 'But very well. Good luck.'

She turned and ran down a side street, then disappeared into an alley in the direction of the wall. Felix stared after her. Her merry grin had gone through him like a hot poker.

'Well, manling?'

'Right,' said Felix, snapping out of it. 'Sorry.'

He and Gotrek started towards the gate.

'We can't just turn ourselves in,' he said, out of the corner of his mouth. 'They'd know something was up. We need to look like we're trying not to get arrested.'

'And how are we going to do that?' asked Gotrek.

'HALT!' CALLED THE watch sergeant, holding up a hand. He had six stout spearmen behind him, standing in front of the gate, all in breastplates and helmets. 'State your business, sirs.'

Felix and Gotrek halted. Gephardt's coach was still just visible through the bars of the gate, trundling down Commerce Street as it curved east through the Handelbezirk.

'Open the gates, my good man,' said Felix in his snootiest voice. 'I have urgent business at the Gunnery School.'

'At this hour, sir? The school don't receive visitors at this time of night, sir,' said the sergeant as he looked them over in the light of the guard house lantern. 'And no one goes through this gate until sun up.'

'Don't be ridiculous. You let a coach through just now. Let us through.' Felix waved an imperious hand.

'The gentleman was known to us,' said the sergeant. He couldn't seem to keep his eyes off Gotrek. 'And often has business at this hour.'

And slips you a healthy bribe every night, thought Felix.

'I demand you let us through,' said Felix. 'Countess Emmanuelle will hear of this if you don't!'

The sergeant shot a glance back at his men and they began to spread out. 'I'll have your names sir. You and your companion.'

'*My* name?' said Felix. 'Damned if I will. I'll have your commission, you lout. Let me through!'

'Your *names*, sirs,' growled the sergeant.

'My name is… is… Lord Gesundheit, damn your eyes! And this is my servant, ah… Snorri Nosebiter.'

The sergeant blinked for a moment, then shook his head in wonder. 'Gesundheit and Nosebiter. Those are the worst false names I've ever heard.' He turned to his men. 'Take their weapons and put them in irons. I believe these are the "Heroes of Nuln" who are meant to be locked up in the College of Engineering just now. We'll put 'em in Universitat station house until someone can be sent for tomorrow morning. Open the gate!'

'How dare you!' said Felix, as the guards started forward, spears at the ready. He saw Gotrek stiffen. 'Play along!' he muttered out of the corner of his mouth.

'Aye aye,' grumbled Gotrek.

'Your weapons, sirs,' said a watchman.

Felix sighed and unbuckled his sword belt as the gate began to swing open. 'This is a great indignity,' he said, as he gave the dragon-hilted sword to a young watchman.

Gotrek took his rune axe off his back, then paused as if he was reconsidering, his eye blazing. It looked like he might slaughter the watchman instead of handing it over. At last, with a reluctant grunt he held it out. The young watchman took hold of it, then stumbled to his knees, his arms nearly wrenching out of their sockets as Gotrek let go. It clanged off the cobbles.

'Don't dent it,' Gotrek grumbled.

The watchman struggled to lift the axe as he stared wide-eyed at Gotrek. He finally got it up to his chest and cradled it like a man carrying a barrel.

'Your wrists,' said the first watchman.

Gotrek and Felix put their hands behind their backs and a third watchman slipped horseshoe irons around them and locked them.

'Right,' said the sergeant. 'Four of you with Kulich. March!' He bowed slyly to Gotrek and Felix as four watchmen prodded them forward through the gate, followed by the boy who was carrying their weapons. 'Your lordship,' he murmured with mock respect. 'Master Nosebiter.'

Felix could hear the sergeant's men laughing as the others led them into the Handelbezirk. Gotrek rumbled in his throat, but said nothing.

Felix looked ahead. Gephardt's coach was just disappearing around the curve of Commerce Way, far in the distance. They needed to hurry, or they would lose them, but they couldn't act until they were out of sight and earshot of the gate. He hoped Ulrika had made it over the wall as easily as she had said she could. Her scouting was essential.

'Dorfmann, take this axe!' rasped the young watchman, after a few streets. He was staggering under the monstrous weight of the ancient weapon. Even in the dark of the street Felix could see that his face was beetroot red.

'Yer doing fine, Mittleberger' said another watchman, chuckling. 'Be there before you know it.'

The others laughed.

'I mean it,' whined Mittleberger. 'It's slipping.'

The watchmen only laughed harder.

Felix looked over his shoulder. The gate was five blocks behind now, and edging out of sight. 'Now,' he said quietly.

'About time,' said Gotrek. He shrugged his massive shoulders and the chain between his shackles snapped.

The movement was so small and calm that for a second the guards didn't notice. It wasn't until he stepped to the struggling Mittleberger and plucked his axe and Felix's sword from him, that they turned and cried out in surprise.

Gotrek butted Mittleberger in the solar plexus with his forehead. The boy fell back, gasping like a landed fish.

Two guards rushed the Slayer's back. Felix lurched right and shouldered into them. One stumbled into the other and fell. The other continued on. Gotrek spun and chopped through his spear, then shoved him to the cobbles.

The other watchmen hopped back, lowering their spears and shouting at Gotrek to drop his axe. Gotrek slashed down at Felix's back. Felix flinched, but the Slayer's aim was true. The axe blade parted his chains with a *ching*, and he was loose. Gotrek tossed him his sword.

Felix caught it and brained the fallen guard with the scabbard.

The last two guards charged Gotrek. He sidestepped one and knocked aside the other's spear, then upended him over his shoulder.

Felix cracked that one over the head too, then did the same to the one with the halved spear. That left only the one who had charged past Gotrek still on his feet and fully conscious.

Felix and the Slayer turned to face him. He stared at them for a moment, then turned and ran back towards the gate, screaming for the sergeant. Two steps later he staggered sideways, squawking, and fell on his face, unconscious. A bolt with a blunt fowling tip clattered to the cobbles beside him.

'Who...?' said Felix, looking around.

A movement above him caught his eye. He looked up. Ulrika saluted from a nearby rooftop, a mere silhouette against the grey clouds, then waved them on.

'Onward,' said Gotrek, and they hurried down Commerce Street, leaving the dazed watchmen moaning and writhing behind them. Felix rolled his head around on his neck. He felt better. The fight had loosened him up a bit.

* * *

A FEW BLOCKS past the Reik Platz, Gephardt's coach stopped and one of the men got out. His face was now hidden behind a yellow mask, but Felix could tell it wasn't Gephardt. This man was too short and broad.

From the shadow of a trading company office, Gotrek and Felix watched as the man nodded to the coach, then vanished down an alley between two tenements.

'Do we follow him, or the coach?' murmured Felix.

'Gephardt is the leader,' said Gotrek. 'The others came to him. We follow him.'

Felix nodded and they continued down the street as the coach started forward again. Far ahead of them he saw a blur of shadow leap from one rooftop to another, an impossible jump. He shivered. Whatever remnants of her old self remained, leaps like that proved that Ulrika was no longer one of his race. The shiver was followed by a sigh. If only the rest of her were as alien, he might find it easier to accept that what had happened to her was irreversible. But she was still too human – much too human.

A while later the coach turned north into the Weston district. Felix and Gotrek hurried to the corner, then peered around it. The coach was making a left into a side street. They trotted to the next corner. The coach turned again.

From another rooftop, Ulrika waved to get their attention, then motioned for them to hold. Felix saw the wisdom of this. The streets were wider and straighter in this stolid, burgher neighbourhood, and there were fewer places to keep out of sight. If they followed too closely they might be seen.

After a few moments, Ulrika waved them ahead and they moved to the next corner. They travelled for a while in this stop and start fashion until the coach pulled up at a genteel looking tavern, dark and apparently shuttered for the night. Another man got out of the coach and rapped on the tavern door – two short knocks, a pause, then three knocks, another pause, then two short knocks again. It opened and he slipped in.

Felix looked at Gotrek, for the man had been tall and thin, like Gephardt.

The Slayer shook his head. 'Too thin in the shoulders.'

Felix nodded. Gotrek had a better eye for scale and proportion than anyone he knew. If he said it wasn't Gephardt, then it wasn't.

They made to follow the coach again, but it doubled back on them and they had to scramble to find a hiding place in the shadow of a deep door well as it turned onto their street. They held still as statues as it passed them by and continued on the way it had come.

With Ulrika motioning them ahead at every corner, they trailed the coach south again until, after crossing Commerce Street, it entered the Shantytown district and stopped at last at a long wooden warehouse a street away from the wharves.

Gotrek and Felix hid in the shadow of the arched gate of a boat-maker's yard, and watched as Gephardt descended from the coach. And it was Gephardt. Felix recognised him by his strutting walk. The masked youth knocked, using the same rhythm as his companion had at the tavern, then slipped into the warehouse. The coach pulled away and started back in the direction of the Altestadt again. Felix frowned. Whatever Gephardt was up to, he didn't intend to return home tonight.

'This is his final stop,' he whispered.

Gotrek growled. 'More final than he knows.'

Ulrika dropped down beside them, as silent as a falling cloak. 'A big gathering,' she said. 'I smell many scents.'

'Good,' said Gotrek. 'My axe thirsts.'

'We should learn what they're up to first,' said Felix.

Gotrek grunted, impatient, but then nodded. 'Aye.'

Felix turned to Ulrika. 'Can you hear them through the wall?'

'Not well enough, but I have a better idea.'

'Yes?'

She nodded over his shoulder. 'Look.'

Felix turned. Two men in masks and cloaks were walking down the street towards the warehouse. They would soon pass their hiding place.

'Disguises?'

She grinned. 'Aye.'

Felix's skin prickled. He didn't like disguises. So many things could go wrong. 'And how will we disguise Gotrek? A mask and a cloak won't be enough.'

'I need no disguise,' Gotrek said. 'When the fighting starts, I'll come in.'

And what if you come in too late, thought Felix? He and Ulrika could be overwhelmed before the Slayer arrived. But he kept it to himself. It would sound like whining.

'There are skylights on the roof,' said Ulrika, then looked Gotrek up and down. 'If you can get to the roof.'

Gotrek growled. 'I'm a dwarf. There are no better climbers.'

'Shhh!' said Felix. 'They come.'

Gotrek, Felix and Ulrika stepped further back into the arch of the boatyard's gate. The two men walked past, looking nervously over their shoulders, but not into the shadows beside them.

Gotrek reached out and grabbed one by the belt. Ulrika took the other by the collar. They yanked the men into the archway and broke their necks with brutal efficiency. Felix winced in sympathy, then pulled their masks and cloaks off. He recognised neither of them. They looked like shopkeeps.

As Gotrek heaved the bodies over the boatyard gate, Felix handed a mask and cloak to Ulrika and donned the other himself. His mask smelled of sausage and sour sweat. He fought down nausea and looked at Ulrika and Gotrek through the small eyeholes.

'Ready?'

'Ready,' said Ulrika.

'Aye,' said Gotrek.

They stepped out of the archway and started towards the warehouse, Felix and Ulrika making for the front door, Gotrek angling for the alley that ran between it and the next.

When they reached the door, Felix stretched out his hand to knock, then paused. What had it been? Ah yes. He rapped sharply on the door twice, then three times, then twice again.

The door opened, and a short, masked man in workman's clothes looked up at them. 'Welcome, brothers. The password?'

Felix froze, his heart thudding. There was a password? Sigmar, they were sunk before they had begun!

'Er,' he said, for want of anything better to say.

'We have already told you the password,' said Ulrika, speaking in a husky voice and stepping forward.

'You have? said the cultist, his brow crinkling. 'No you haven't. I would have heard.'

Ulrika pressed her mask close to her face so that he could see her piercing blue eyes. 'We have already told you the password.'

She took another step forward. Felix followed her lead and advanced as well. They were in the door now.

'But...' said the man stepping back unhappily. He sounded like he was going to cry. 'But...'

'Don't you see? We must have told you the password,' said Ulrika, soothingly, as she eased past him. 'Or you wouldn't have let us in. You are not to let anyone in who doesn't know the password, correct?'

'That's right,' said the man. 'And...'

'And you are a stalwart man who would not forsake your duty, aren't you?'

'Of course I am! There are none more loyal to the brotherhood than I.'

'Yes. You are dutiful and loyal, and would not have allowed anyone in who hadn't told you the password.'

'Never,' he agreed.

'So since we are in...?' she let it hang.

'I... I suppose you must have told me the password,' said the cultist. 'Yes, of course you did. Why else would I have let you in?'

'Yes,' said Ulrika softly. 'Nothing else makes sense.'

'Yes.' He sighed, glad to have it all resolved. 'Nothing else makes sense.' He pointed to the door at the back of the small office they were in. 'The others are in the back.'

'Thank you, brother,' murmured Ulrika.

Felix shot her a look as they stepped to the inner door. Her eyes behind the mask twinkled with amusement. Felix swallowed. He hadn't seen anything amusing in the exchange. He felt like he had just watched a cat toy with a mouse and then eat its head.

The warehouse beyond the office was dark but for a flicker of lantern light that glowed from somewhere beyond a blocky mountain range of stacked barrels and crates. Low murmurs disturbed the dusty silence. Felix and Ulrika followed the voices around the towering piles of cargo and found a group of men sitting on and standing around a ring of rolled carpets, in the centre of which stood a figure that Felix was nearly certain was Gephardt. There was a lantern at his feet.

'Brothers, welcome,' said the figure. It was indeed Gephardt. 'We will begin shortly. We wait only for two more.'

Felix and Ulrika nodded, but said nothing. They joined the men leaning against a wall of crates at the edge of the circle, staying as far out of the lamplight as they dared. Felix glanced up at the roof. Through the rafters that supported it he could see a line of square skylights. He did not see Gotrek.

After a few minutes, another man came in, and right after him, the guard who had watched the door. Felix counted nineteen in all – twenty-one including Ulrika and himself.

'Good,' said Gephardt, as the door guard took a seat on a rolled rug. 'Now we are complete. And soon our plans will be complete.' He stood straighter and spread his arms. 'Brothers,' he said. 'The time of the rising of the Brotherhood of the Cleansing Flame has come at last. All over the city our fellows meet. Tonight is the last night of Nuln. Tomorrow comes the change!'

The men murmured soft cheers. Felix and Ulrika followed suit.

'I will now tell each of you your target. When we have finished here, go to it and wait in secret until the signal. This will come in a few short hours when the men of the school test the last cannon they shall ever make. When that gun fires, our brave leader will light the powder that will blow the Imperial Gunnery School to the heavens. That explosion is your signal. When you hear it – and have no fear, you *will* hear it – you will set fire to your primary target, then, when it is burning well, light as many nearby buildings as you are able. The houses will burn! The foundries will fall! The manufactories will collapse!' He raised his fists. 'We will raise such a cloud of smoke that Nuln will know no dawn today, and no tomorrow ever after.'

The men cheered.

Gephardt raised his voice to be heard over them. 'The flames of the city will light the way for Tzeentch's glorious armies as they march across the broken empire that will be theirs, and ours!'

The men cheered louder. Felix's heart almost stopped in his chest. By all the gods, they meant nothing less than the destruction of the Empire! For, though they intended to burn only Nuln – only! – Nuln was more than a city. It was the Empire's armoury! Out of it came the cannons and black powder and hand weapons that kept her strong and secure. If Nuln's forges were destroyed and her foundries stilled, no amount of men could defend the Empire's borders, for they would have no arms to do it with. The hordes of Chaos that even now assaulted their northern borders would lumber south unimpeded, and everything that Felix called home would be ground to pulp beneath their iron-shod hooves. The enemy was striking from within, far from Middenheim and the front, and unless he and Gotrek and Ulrika could prevail, no one in power would know it until it was far too late.

Gephardt lowered his arms and motioned for quiet. 'Brother Matchcord!' he called.

'Aye?' said a sturdy fellow at the front.

'Your shift at the granaries starts in an hour, yes?'

'Aye, sir.'

'Go to work as usual, but when the signal comes. Light the silos.'

'Aye, sir! All glory to Tzeentch!'

'Brother Candlewick!'

'Aye,' said a stooped older man.

'Handelhoff's livery stables. Start in the hayloft.'

'Aye, sir.'

'Brother Lampblack!'

'Here, sir!'

And so on through the assembly – Brother Flint, Brother Tinder, Brother Flame, Brother Brand, with each being given a target in the general vicinity of Shantytown. Felix's heart lurched as he all at once realised that they would soon call *his* name, and he didn't know what it was! He looked at Ulrika and she nodded and shrugged.

They both glanced towards the ceiling. There was still no sign of Gotrek. What was keeping him? Had he met with some accident? Was he already here?

'Brother Torch!'

There was no answer. The men looked around.

CHAPTER FOURTEEN

'Brother Torch!' repeated Gephardt, scanning the crowd.

'H-here!' said Felix at last.

Gephardt looked at him, his eyes seeming to burn through Felix's mask. 'You are not Brother Torch.'

'Who says I'm not,' said Felix, remembering belatedly to affect a Shantytown accent.

'Wait a moment,' said the door guard, shaking his head as if waking from a dream. 'Wait a moment. They're the ones who told me they gave me the password when they didn't. I knew something wasn't right about them!'

The masked men all stood, drawing daggers and cutlasses and cudgels from under their cloaks.

'Friends,' said Gephardt. 'You have made your last mistake. Get them!'

His followers surged towards Felix and Ulrika in a mass. Felix threw back his cloak and drew his sword. Beside him, Ulrika did the same. Two versus nineteen, thought Felix grimly. Ulrika might survive it, but he would not. There were too many. If only Gotrek were here.

"Ware below,' grated a familiar voice from above, as the cultists slammed into them.

Felix didn't dare look up. He was too busy blocking and parrying a dozen attackers. But then a groaning of tortured wood followed the words. He stole a glance over his shoulder. The cliff face of crates was leaning precariously out over their heads. Felix yelped and dived left, his stitches tearing as he batted aside the cultists' blades and hit the floor, hissing with pain.

Four big crates toppled down on the masked men just as they realised what was happening. They screamed, and more than half a dozen of them were caught under the crates as they exploded on the floor in an eruption of planks, splinters and brass chamber pots, one of which bounced and clonked Felix on the head.

Gotrek leapt down from the gap he had made, bellowing Khazalid war cries, and cut down three cultists with two swings. Felix surged up unsteadily, the pain from his reopened wound making him dizzy. He slashed around himself, half blinded by his mask, which had turned askew. He tore it off and hacked at a cultist who was engaged with the Slayer. The man screamed in pain and turned, swinging a hand axe at Felix. Gotrek decapitated him without looking around. Beyond the Slayer, Ulrika ran the door guard through the stomach. He squealed as he died.

'Kill them!' cried Gephardt, from behind the pack. 'They know all! They cannot be allowed to escape!'

The cultists pressed forward, calling on their heathen god. Gotrek roared as they came, cleaving one down to his guts, then turning on three more. Felix slashed left and right to keep the ones he faced at bay, then ducked instinctively as something bright flashed overhead. It was Gephardt's lantern, sailing over the heads of the attackers to smash behind Ulrika. It splashed her back with flaming oil. She shrieked and dropped, rolling to put the flames out. A cultist stabbed her through the leg. Another smashed her in the chest with a huge mallet.

'Ulrika!' Felix cried, and tried to scramble through the jumble of crates to reach her. He misstepped, and jammed his foot in a chamber pot. He slipped as the pot skidded on the wood floor. The fire was spreading across the floor. The wreckage and the wall of crates were catching.

Gotrek growled, annoyed, but pushed towards Ulrika, fanning back her attackers with his axe. Felix tried to free his foot, but three cultists were on him. He smashed one's sword out of his hand, but slipped again. A cultist with a cutlass lunged in, trying to take advantage. Felix parried desperately and nearly fell. Beyond the melee he saw Gephardt and another man disappearing around a mound of crates.

'Gephardt's running for it!' he said.

'Well, get him!' said Gotrek, holding off four cultists as Ulrika rolled behind him, still smouldering.

Felix grunted. He could barely stand with this foolish piss bucket on his foot, let alone run. He blocked a smash from an iron-shod club and kicked the cutlass wielder in the face with the pot. The brass split from the impact, and the man dropped like an empty sack. Felix shook his foot as he blocked another bash from the club, but couldn't free it. Curse it! He'd just have to run with it. He bulled past his three attackers, knocking two to the floor, then ran in the direction Gephardt had gone, clanking ridiculously with every step, his attackers in hot pursuit.

As Felix rounded the mound of crates, he saw a door open in the far wall and Gephardt and the other man's silhouettes fill it. He raced towards them as fast as he could go, *clang, thud, clang, thud, clang, thud,* which wasn't very fast. He could feel blood trickling down his side from his torn stitches. He heard his pursuers gaining on him and glanced back. He'd have to fight them before he could fight Gephardt, curse it.

He turned to face them, but as he did, a black shadow dropped down behind them, sillhouetted against the glow of flames from the front of the warehouse. A bright spike of steel sprouted from the last one's ribs. Ulrika! The others turned and cried out as the vampiress laid into them. She was still smoking slightly.

Felix turned and clanked on, his caught foot cramping terribly. Gephardt turned and paused in the door.

'Go!' he called over his shoulder. 'Spread the word! There may be more spies among us! Tell the others to start the fires early!' He tore off his mask and drew his sword, glaring at Felix with wild eyes. 'I'll handle this fool.'

Felix charged at him, swinging, but Gephardt backed out of the door, and Felix's sword bit into the wall beside it. Gephardt lunged through the frame, forcing Felix to twist ungracefully aside to avoid his point. His stitches ripped further. He cursed through clenched teeth. The little snot had him at a disadvantage. Karaghul might be a runesword and a dragon killer, but it was a slashing weapon, not made for quick thrusts, whereas Gephardt's weapon was a slim rapier, a courtier's weapon, made for the lunge. Felix couldn't get a good swing in, with the door frame in the way.

He thrust, but Gephardt parried easily, and returned a riposte that pinked his arm. Felix fell back, his trapped foot slipping sideways and wrenching his groin. Curse this stupid pot, Felix thought. He

Nathan Long

kicked savagely to try to dislodge it. It flew off his foot and through the door, glancing off Gephardt's forehead.

Felix leapt forward before the cultist could recover, and ran him through the belly, tearing it horribly. Gephardt flopped back in the mud of the street, gasping and staring at the ropes of his intestines as they slithered out through the hole in his abdomen.

Felix raised his sword to put the man out of his misery, but a black form blurred past him and shoved him aside.

'No!'

Ulrika straddled Gephardt's chest and thrust her head forward, baring her fangs. 'Burn me, will you?' she snarled, then sank her clawed fingers into his neck as if it was soft butter. Gephardt sputtered and thrashed, but could not throw her off. She ripped his oesophagus out with one hand and showed it to his dying eyes. 'Burn in your master's flames, fool.'

She tossed the mess aside and wiped her hand on Gephardt's beautiful cloak, then caught Felix's horrified look. She shrugged. 'I don't like fire.'

Gotrek appeared in the door. 'Was that the last?'

Felix shook his head and looked up and down the empty street. 'There was one more. And we must catch him. Gephardt sent him to tell the others to start the burning early.'

'Which way did he go?' asked Ulrika.

'I don't know,' said Felix. 'I...'

He paused as he saw something on the ground. He picked it up. It was a mask. He groaned. They were sunk. The man could be blocks away by now, and they didn't know what he looked like. Half the city could be aflame within the hour.

CHAPTER FIFTEEN

'GIVE ME THAT,' said Ulrika. She snatched the mask from Felix's hand and covered her nose with it, inhaling deeply. After a moment she lowered the mask and tucked it away in her doublet, then crouched like a cat on the prowl, sniffing the air and the ground. She took a few steps north, then nodded and stood.

'I'll find him,' she said. Then she sprinted off into the night.

'This is bad,' said Felix, as he helped Gotrek carry Gephardt's body back into the warehouse. The place was filling with smoke from the rapidly spreading fire. 'Did you...' He coughed violently. 'Did you hear their plan?'

'Not all of it,' said Gotrek.

'They are going to blow up the Gunnery School after all, the minute the last Middenheim gun is test fired, and the explosion will be the signal for the rest of the Cleansing Flame to start fires all over Nuln.' He shook his head. 'We'll never stop them all.' He looked despairingly at the inferno that raged at the far side of the room. 'We won't stop even this one.'

'We don't have to stop them all,' said Gotrek, 'just the explosion at the school. Then their signal will never come.'

'But we can't just let this burn!' said Felix. 'We already burned down this neighbourhood once! I won't do it again.'

'Better one neighbourhood than all of them,' said Gotrek. He started for the door. 'Come on, manling. No time to waste. If that gun is ready, they may fire it before dawn.'

Felix followed, reluctant and heartsick. Though he knew in his head that it was the cultists who were responsible for the fires, he also knew that they wouldn't have been set if he and Gotrek hadn't come sticking their noses in. And yet, had they not investigated, they would not have learned that the cultists meant to burn the whole city.

As they stepped into the street they saw Ulrika approaching, wiping her face with the cultist's yellow mask. Her lips and chin were smeared with blood, and her eyes glowed with feverish life.

'I found him,' she said, tossing the mask aside. She licked her lips clean.

Felix shuddered. Gotrek spat, then stumped forward, pushing past her as if she weren't there. Ulrika fell in behind him.

Felix made to follow them, then paused and turned, looking back at the burning warehouse. He couldn't just leave and do nothing. His eyes turned to the surrounding tenements. 'Fire!' he shouted. 'Fire in Pappenheimer's Warehouse! Fire!'

Gotrek and Ulrika stopped and looked back at him.

After a second, Gotrek raised his voice too. 'Fire!' he bellowed. 'Wake up! Fire!' He banged on a stone post with the flat of his axe, making a horrendous racket.

Ulrika joined them, her voice high and clear. 'Help! Help! They're burning Shantytown again!'

Felix heard shutters opening and voices calling questions in the tenements around them. They ran on. It wasn't much. But at least it was something.

'I DON'T UNDERSTAND,' said Felix as they trotted through the Neuestadt towards the Universitat area. 'We searched the school and the watch searched under the school. And they've been patrolling down there ever since. The powder hasn't been found. Where has the Cleansing Flame hidden it?'

'Somewhere we didn't look,' said Gotrek.

Ulrika laughed.

Felix rolled his eyes. He was going to say something snide, but he saw that Gotrek was deep in thought, and so kept quiet.

'The skaven tunnels,' Gotrek said at last. 'The ones that the vermin came out of when they attacked Nuln. These lunatics must have found them.'

Ulrika frowned. 'But would powder placed all the way down there be enough to bring down the Gunnery School?' she asked as the three of them entered the Reik Platz and passed by the Deutz Elm, continuing west.

'Aye,' said Gotrek. 'If it were set correctly. The sewers run under the school. If they found tunnels that run under the sewers, they could cave the sewers into the tunnels. The school would sink like a ship.' He growled deep in his throat. 'They must have an engineer among them.'

Felix groaned. 'But how are we to stop it? If we go down there and try to warn the watch, they'll only try to arrest us again, as they did last time. They won't listen to anything we have to say. Damn Wissen for a thick skulled fool.'

'I'll beat it into their heads,' rasped Gotrek, but then he sighed. 'No, you're right, manling. Arguing with those fools would only slow us down.' He paused and looked around, then started down a side street. 'Come. We will find a rat hole here that will take us under the sewers to the powder.'

Felix and Ulrika followed him half a block to an iron grate set in the street. Gotrek heaved it up and held it open.

'In,' he said.

'Wait,' said a voice behind them.

Gotrek, Felix and Ulrika looked around. Gotrek dropped the grate back into its frame with a clang and pulled his axe off his back.

Ulrika drew her sword and went on guard. 'What do you want?' she asked.

Striding towards them from the main street was a phalanx of dark figures. Some Felix recognised from his visit to the countess's brothel – the tall, impossibly thin shadow of Mistress Wither, hidden entirely within her trailing black robes and impenetrable veil; the beautiful, cold-eyed Lady Hermione, who wore a hooded cloak over her dark blue attire, and who was followed by a handful of her swaggering, immaculately dressed heroes, who were now clad in perfectly polished breastplates and morion helmets.

Beside them were persons Felix had never seen before – a cluster of skulking villains led by a voluptuous, coarse-looking vampiress, fairly bursting from the low-cut red bodice and hitched-up red skirts of a street trull. She might have been ravishing, were it not for the scar that pulled up the left corner of her mouth into a permanent leer. Her followers were just as unnerving – vicious-looking doxies and alley bashers, all scarred and wild-eyed, and armed to the teeth with daggers, cheap swords and iron shod cudgels. A more disreputable collection of human scum Felix had never seen. One of them towered above the rest, a filthy, bearded giant of a man who carried a stone-headed hammer in a huge, hairy fist. Felix could smell him from twenty paces away.

'Good evening, friends,' said Lady Hermione sweetly.

Gotrek growled low in his throat.

Ulrika did not lower her guard. 'Are you here to fight us?' she asked. 'Have you not spoken to the countess?'

Lady Hermione smiled. 'Fear not, sister. The countess informed us of your message, and has sent us to aid you.' She cast a sideways glance at the vampire harlot beside her. 'Madame Mathilda has added her support as well.'

Ulrika frowned, suspicious. 'You're here to help?'

'And why shouldn't we be?' asked Madame Mathilda, in a low accent. 'It's our city as much as it is yers.' She grinned and nodded at Felix. 'This yer lover boy, Kossar? Right sweet little buttercup, ain't he? Worth turnin', of a surety.'

'We do not turn men, Mathilda,' said Lady Hermione with a sniff. 'It only weakens the line. As dearest Gabriella learned to her cost.'

'No!' said Gotrek suddenly. 'I won't do it!' He glared at Ulrika. 'I've stood for you, Ulrika Ivansdaughter. You were a good companion once, and your father a Dwarf Friend and Oathkeeper, but these... these...' He couldn't seem to find a word vile enough to describe the assembled vampires. 'These will die by my axe before they fight by my side.'

'You haven't time to fight us, Slayer,' said Lady Hermione calmly. 'And you waste time arguing.'

'The lady's right, dwarf,' said Mathilda, scratching herself intimately. 'Don't waste yer energy fighting the likes of us when we want the same as you want. It ain't common sense.'

'Damn common sense!' snarled Gotrek. 'You die here, or I do.'

He dropped into a fighting stance. Hermione's handsome swains and Mathilda's ragged bashers did the same. Mistress Wither rattled like dead leaves in a wind. Ulrika looked from one side to the other, as if uncertain who to help.

Felix cursed under his breath. This fight couldn't happen. He was no happier fighting on the same side as Lady Hermione and Mistress Wither than Gotrek was, but there was no time. Win or lose, the fight would slow them and possibly wound them so badly that they would not be able to win the fight that mattered. He hated to play on the Slayer's sense of honour. It seemed a low thing to do, but as regrettable as it was, the vampires were right. 'Gotrek. Did you not vow vengeance on the Brotherhood of the Cleansing Flame for the destruction of Heinz's tavern? Did you not say that you were even willing to give up going to Middenheim to defeat them? Will you then let the Cleansing Flame triumph in order to fight a street brawl with unworthy opponents?'

'Unworthy?' snapped Hermione, but no one paid her any attention.

For a long moment, Gotrek remained glaring at the vampires, his massive chest heaving and his huge fists clenching. Then, at last, he let out a breath and lowered his axe. 'You're right, manling. You're always right.' He turned back to the sewer hole. 'One of these days it will be the death of you.' He wrenched up the grate and tossed it aside as if it weighed nothing. 'Let them follow if they can,' he said, then jumped down into the hole.

UNFORTUNATELY FOR GOTREK, the vampires and their minions followed him with ease. Though he trotted through the foul brick tunnels at a brisk clip, the Slayer was a dwarf, and his short legs were no match for human strides, let alone the vampires' inhuman vitality. And Gotrek wasn't able to travel as fast as he might like, for he stopped to examine the walls and walkways as he went, though what exactly he was looking for Felix wasn't sure. Felix could hardly see his footing in the uncertain light of the lanterns that Lady Hermione's gentlemen carried, never mind signs and traces.

The Slayer spared not a single glance for their companions, only trotted on with his axe in a death grip, all the while cursing bitterly in Khazalid under his breath.

'Ain't no sewers in the Faulestadt,' said Madame Mathilda from behind them. 'More's the pity. Nothing like a sewer for sneaking about, I say.'

'How sad,' said Lady Hermione. 'You'll have to make do with the gutter.'

Madame Mathilda laughed, the echo booming down the tunnel. 'Now now, dearie. No fighting in front of company.'

Ulrika rolled her eyes and gave Felix an apologetic shrug at this exchange.

'Who is Madame Mathilda?' he asked, leaning close to her ear.

'Another of the countess's rivals,' replied Ulrika quietly. 'She rules the slums south of the river as Countess Gabriella rules the Neuestadt. Her web of spies stretches through the mobs and gangs and brothels of the Faulestadt as Countess Gabriella's stretches through the noble houses and the palace. A very dangerous woman.'

'That much I gathered.'

'Whispering sweet nothings, are you?' said Mathilda with a dirty chuckle. 'Ain't they just darling.'

Felix and Ulrika drew apart.

After a few more minutes, Gotrek stopped suddenly and faced the tunnel wall. 'Ha!' he said, then, 'Hmmmf! Even humans could have done a better job.'

'A better job of what?' asked Felix.

He could see no difference between this and any other part of the tunnel, but he had long ago given up trying to see the subtleties of construction and design that were as obvious to the Slayer as the differences in the prose styles of two different authors were to Felix.

Gotrek didn't answer, only stepped up to the wall, reversed his axe, and swung the blunt side at it. It smashed right through, and a fall of crumbling bricks clattered to the floor, leaving a ragged black gap. A cold wind blew from it that reeked of skaven. Felix gagged.

'You say the skaven bricked this up?' he asked.

'Aye,' said Gotrek. 'Hiding their tunnels.' he sneered. 'Or trying to.'

Felix shrugged. He would never have found the tunnel, and it didn't appear that any other human had either.

Gotrek swung again and the hole widened. Felix joined him, kicking at the wall with his boot. Ulrika did the same.

'Here, Pinky,' called Madame Mathilda. 'Give it a go.'

The hairy giant edged forward, pushing his foul stench ahead of him. He swung his stone-headed hammer wildly, nearly taking Felix's head off, and knocked a huge hole in the wall.

Gotrek ignored even this, merely widening the hole with a few more strokes of his axe and stepping through as if the others weren't there. Felix and Ulrika followed him. The others crowded in behind.

The skaven tunnels were round and irregular, like the animal burrows that they were, the walls crosshatched with claw marks of the vermin that had dug them. The air inside was cold and stale. Spider webs hung like drifting lace from the curving ceilings. Felix scanned ahead nervously, looking for signs of recent usage, but did not see any fresh dung or rotting garbage. Perhaps the tunnels had been abandoned since their attack on Nuln had been driven back. But if so, why was the smell of them still so present?

Though the tunnels twisted and turned and rose and fell and branched like the roots of a tree, Gotrek stumped through them as if he had walked through them a thousand times before. He did not pause at intersections. He did not stop to get his bearings. He just turned left, then right, then up, down and back without hesitation. Felix was thoroughly lost in minutes, and it seemed their companions were too.

'Are you certain we go the right way?' asked Lady Hermione imperiously.

'If yer leading us into a trap,' said Madame Mathilda. 'Ye'll get more than ye bargained for, dwarf.'

Gotrek only grunted.

Felix translated for him. 'You are more than welcome to go your own way.'

'Ha!' barked Mathilda. 'No fear! Ye'll not lose us in this stinking warren.'

'You don't feel at home?' sneered Hermione.

A few minutes later Felix found himself walking beside Ulrika, who was apparently deep in thought. Her profile, in the low light, was heartbreakingly beautiful. He looked quickly forward and back. Gotrek was ten paces ahead of them. The vampires and their minions were a ways behind, bickering with each other in low tones.

He leaned in towards her. 'Ulrika.'

She looked up. 'Hmmm?'

He hesitated and licked his lips. 'Ulrika, I just...'

'Don't, Felix,' she said, looking away. 'There is nothing to say.'

'But...'

'Please,' she said. 'Don't you see? There is no way to fix it. There is no way to go back and change our fate, so talking of it – of what might have been – will only make it worse.'

Felix paused, his mouth open, wanted to contradict her, but he couldn't. He hung his head. 'Aye, I suppose you're right.'

'In fact,' said Ulrika, 'it might be better if we never saw one another again.'

'What?' Felix looked up at her. But he had only just found her again! 'That... that seems cruel.'

'Seeing you is crueller, for then the wound stays open, and will not heal.'

Felix hated the cold logic of it, but she was right. Remaining in her presence would only be torture. It would only remind him of what he could never have. And yet separating from her again was just as intolerable. What a choice. What a...

He looked back at her suddenly, struck by a thought. 'This isn't another test, is it? Some impossible conundrum of honour that I cannot hope to win?'

Ulrika smiled, then looked at him wryly, her eyes gleaming sapphires in the torchlight. 'No, Felix. It's not a test. We've outgrown that, remember. It's just the cold, sad truth. We need to find our happiness among our own kind, where...' She paused and took a deep breath. 'Where it is possible to find it.'

Felix sighed and nodded. 'Aye. Though at the moment the possibility seems hard to imagine.'

'When the wound heals, Felix,' she said. 'When the wound heals.'

'Hssst!' said Gotrek suddenly. He held up a hand and cocked his head down a cross tunnel.

The others fell silent.

Felix strained his ears. At first he could hear nothing but his own breathing, but then, at the very edge of his hearing came the faintest chittering and squeaking. It might have been rats, and then again it might not have. As he listened, it faded away.

'They're still here?' asked Lady Hermione, her voice rigid with disgust.

'Oh, aye,' said Mathilda. 'We see 'em now and then, or rather their spoor, but not much, and not often. Think they're still scared of Nuln – thanks to handsome here, and his grumpy little friend.'

Felix heard Gotrek's teeth grinding as he started forward again. It sounded like he was chewing rocks.

ABOUT HALF AN hour later, Gotrek slowed. 'We're close to the school,' he said to Felix. 'Tell them to cover their lanterns.'

Felix turned back to the others. 'Cover your lanterns,' he said.

Hermione motioned to her gentlemen and they closed the slots of their lanterns and hid them under their cloaks. Felix cursed inwardly as the tunnel went black. He didn't want to bump around blindly in the dark, but at the same time, asking Gotrek to guide him in front of Ulrika and the others was embarrassing. But then, just as he was about to give in and ask Gotrek for his shoulder, he realised it was in fact not entirely dark. Far ahead there was a faint red glow on the wall of the curving tunnel.

Gotrek crept forward, his axe at the ready. Felix put a hand on the wall and followed along behind him, Ulrika at his side. The others came after them, moving with uncanny silence.

As they got closer to the red light, Felix began to hear sounds of activity – low voices, thuds, clunks, scrapes, and intermittent hammering. There were more cross tunnels in this area, and even to Felix's untrained eye, it seemed apparent that some of them had been shaped by men, not ratmen. There were wooden support beams holding up the ceilings of some of them, and unlit lanterns hung from the walls that appeared to be of human make.

Just beyond one of the branching corridors, the tunnel slanted steeply down, dropping eight feet in roughly ten paces, then turned sharply to the right and out of sight. Reflected light flooded the base of the slope from around the corner, and the sounds of activity were much louder. A wave of sewer smell made Felix wrinkle his nose.

Gotrek, Felix and Ulrika crept down the ramp, then edged forward and leaned out around the corner. Gotrek grunted as he saw the source of the sounds. Ulrika hissed. Felix choked.

Before them was a large, low-roofed chamber, longer than it was wide, crudely hollowed out of the earth and lit by lanterns hung from hooks pounded into the rock walls. The roof was supported by two rows of rough pillars – no more than thin columns of rock that had not been dug out. Felix was amazed that they could hold up the weight of the earth above them at all. They seemed much too slender. The floor was a muddy soup, dotted with puddles of water that dripped constantly from the roof.

Figures moved among the pillars, roping barrels of black powder to them, drilling holes in the barrel tops, and spooling out long lengths of match cord that they laid on top of planks set on the ground to keep them out of the mud. Most of these figures were human, but others were not – not anymore. The sight of the worst afflicted among them made Felix want to gag.

A flash of green drew his gaze away from a hideous woman with a head like a rotten apple. Between the rows of pillars a pair of mutants – one huge and covered in maroon fur like that of a long-haired cat, the other a translucent blue thing like an upright, man-sized frog – walked from barrel to barrel. The furred beast carried an iron cauldron that glowed from within with a pale green light, and at each barrel, the blue frog dug its webbed hand into the cauldron and pulled out a fistful of glowing green embers. He trickled the embers into the hole that had been drilled in each barrel top, then used a mallet to pound a wooden plug into it and walked to the next, licking glittering green dust from his claws with a tongue like a snake.

Felix's heart thudded as he and Gotrek and Ulrika pulled back into the tunnel and climbed back up the steep slope to where the others waited.

'Well,' said Felix with a shudder. 'We've found the powder.'

'And the cultists,' said Ulrika.

'A crude bit of sapping,' said Gotrek. 'But it'll do the trick. The chamber runs under the sewer that runs under the Gunnery School. When they blow those pillars, everything comes down.'

'But what were they doing with the warpstone?' asked Felix. 'Will it worsen the explosions?'

Gotrek shrugged. 'It might. But worse; it will poison the ground for centuries. Anyone living above will end up twisted and corrupt.'

Felix swallowed, sick and angry and afraid all at once. The Cleansing Flame wasn't just planning to kill Nuln, they meant to mutilate its corpse as well. The city might never be inhabitable again.

'How many are there?' asked Lady Hermione, stepping to them.

Gotrek growled and looked away from her.

'About fifty, lady,' said Ulrika. 'Nearly half of them mutants.'

Madame Mathilda laughed. 'Only that? We're more than enough, then. Let's get to it.'

'Yes,' said Felix. 'But how do we keep them from lighting the powder?'

The vampires paused at that.

'Oh,' said Lady Hermione.

'They won't light the powder,' said Gotrek.

The others turned to him.

'Not if we attack now, before they're set,' Gotrek continued. 'They can't risk a partial explosion. The school might not come down.' He turned back towards the chamber. 'Come on, manling.'

'Slayer, wait!' hissed Ulrika. 'Let us all–'

She paused suddenly and looked into the branching passage. The other vampires did the same. Gotrek and Felix followed their gaze. A glow of lantern light was bobbing towards them, and in it, Felix could see the shadows of walking men.

Quicker than winking, the vampires and their minions vanished silently into the darkness of the tunnel. Gotrek and Felix started after them, but before they got two steps, a voice rang from the passage.

'Who's that?' it said.

Gotrek stopped and turned back. 'Not him,' he groaned.

'Him?' asked Felix. 'Him who?'

Out of the passage came Ward Captain Wissen of the city watch, six watchmen at his back. He gaped when he saw Gotrek and Felix. His men went on guard.

'You!' he said loudly. 'What are you doing here? What have you…?'

'Shhh, captain!' hissed Felix, looking uneasily down the slope towards the big chamber. 'They'll hear you!'

'Eh?' said Wissen, just as loudly. 'Who? What do you…?'

'The cultists,' whispered Felix, pointing. 'Down there, around the corner. They're priming the powder.'

'No wonder he never catches them,' said muttered Gotrek. 'Stomping around like a drunk ogre.'

Captain Wissen blinked, apparently confused, then his eyes narrowed. 'The powder? Here?' He smiled. 'So you were right after all, eh? They're going to blow up the Gunnery School? How many of them are there?'

'Fifty or so,' said Felix.

'Hmmm,' said Wissen. 'Too many for us. Are you alone?'

'Too many?' Gotrek snorted.

Felix looked up the tunnel in the direction Ulrika and the other vampires had gone, searching for some sign of them. They were nowhere to be seen. Had they lost their assistance because of this interruption? Would they not show their faces with Wissen around? Dangerous and uncertain allies they might have been, but given the choice of them or Wissen and his men, there was no question who he would rather have had fighting by his side. He sighed. 'Ah, yes. We're alone. Listen. Maybe you'd better go back and get reinforcements. We'll… we'll keep an eye on them.'

'What?' sneered Wissen. 'And have you burn down the city again with your clumsiness?' He waved a hand. 'Show me where they are. I want to see for myself.'

Gotrek rumbled in his throat. Felix shot him a warning glance. He didn't like it any better than the Slayer did, but starting a fight with Wissen would only alert the cultists. 'This way.'

Felix and Gotrek led the way down the slope, then slipped around the corner and edged towards the opening of the chamber with Wissen and his men shuffling behind them. It looked like the two mutants had finished seeding the barrels with the green embers, and the others were nearly done laying all the match cord. Felix swallowed, anxious. If they didn't attack soon they would have to worry about the cultists lighting the powder after all.

'You see?' whispered Felix, pointing to the pillars. 'They mean to bring down the sewer, which in turn will bring down the Gunnery School. And if we don't attack right away…'

'Brothers!' cried Wissen at the top of his voice. 'Look! Brave heroes have come to stop our villainous plan!'

CHAPTER SIXTEEN

FELIX AND GOTREK spun around. Wissen's six watchmen had levelled their spears at them. Wissen stood with them, grinning and tugging at the buckles of his breastplate.

Felix blinked, uncomprehending. 'What did you say?' He looked over his shoulder into the chamber. The cultists were turning and starting towards them, mutants of every size and description intermingled with their human comrades. He looked back at Wissen. Had the man gone mad?

Gotrek lunged forward, slashing at Wissen. 'Pawn of Chaos!' he spat.

Wissen's men jumped in front of him, stabbing at Gotrek and Felix as the captain stepped back. Gotrek chopped through spear shafts and arms. Two men fell. Felix blocked a spear and ducked another, still off balance by this bizarre turn of events.

'Pawn?' Wissen laughed. 'I'm a knight, at the least.' He let the breastplate fall. For such a trim man, his stomach bulged obscenely. In fact it seemed to be expanding as Felix watched. Then Wissen's shirt split, and angular black shapes ripped through it, unfolding as they thrust forward.

Felix recoiled, his gorge rising. Wissen was a mutant! Black mantis arms grew from his chest where his nipples should have been. They were covered in coarse fur and tipped with cruel pincers. They darted for Gotrek over the shoulders of his men. Gotrek lashed out at one, but it jerked back, faster than the eye could see. The Slayer missed.

The thud of approaching boots was loud in Felix's ears. He and Gotrek whipped around. The cultists from the chamber had reached them, mutants to the fore. Gotrek lurched to one side and gutted a giant humanoid slug as it lumbered past. It squashed Wissen's remaining watchmen as it fell, an evil smelling, custard-like ooze pumping from its belly wound. Felix ducked the claws of a thing like a skinned ape, then chopped through its corded neck with his runesword and ended up back to back with Gotrek in the centre of a frenzied sea of men and mutants. Swords, clubs, pincers and tentacles came at them from every corner.

Wissen laughed maniacally from behind his comrades. 'You see? You should have stayed with Makaisson! I tried to save you.' He lashed out again from behind the others. 'Kill them, brothers!' He seemed to have no interest in leading from the front.

Gotrek roared with something that sounded suspiciously like joy as he lashed out all around him, doing terrible damage to all who came near. Felix, on the other hand, fought down a rising surge of panic. They were surrounded. Two against more than fifty. Gotrek might have faced such odds before and won, but Felix was wounded and weary, and hadn't the Slayer's strength, quickness or stamina to begin with. He was quickly becoming overwhelmed. Where in Sigmar's name was Ulrika? Would she come at all? Would the other vampiresses?

The press of the cultists' attacks pushed Gotrek and Felix into the big chamber. The massive, cat-furred mutant swung at Gotrek with the glowing cauldron. Gotrek dodged back and the mutant kept spinning, the weight of the cauldron pulling it around. It clobbered a handful of its comrades with it, staggering wildly. Felix ducked the huge pot as it came around again and felt his skin crawl and his mind twitter as it breezed past him. The warpstone inside it radiated Chaos like a fire radiated heat.

Gotrek darted in and buried his axe in the furred mutant's spine. It shrieked like a scalded baby and crashed to the ground, its cauldron bouncing noisily away into the chamber, sprinkling warpstone embers as it went.

Felix cut down a thing with legs like a stork, then whipped around to parry attacks from two normal-appearing men. He found that his left hand was bleeding, but he wasn't sure from what. He hacked madly in all directions, though there didn't seem to be any point. The tide of men and mutants was endless.

But then the cultists at the edges of the melee began to cry out and turn. Through clawing limbs, Felix saw Lady Hermione's gentlemen charging from the dark tunnel, swords high. Madame Mathilda's villains were running forward too, led by a huge black wolf bitch with a scar twisting one side of her long snout. She leapt at a massive mutant and ripped out one of its throats. The giant bearded alley basher waded into a pack of cultists, swinging his stone-headed hammer mightily. Mutants and men flew left and right, their heads and ribcages crushed to pulp.

Felix exhaled, relieved, though it was a strange feeling to be glad for the arrival of a host of thralls and a skin-changing vampiress. It was even stranger to realise that his life had become so filled with madness and horror that he could accept the fact that Lady Mathilda had changed into a wolf with little more than a shrug.

Ulrika vaulted a squat cultist, impaling him with her rapier in mid-flight, then dropped beside Felix to guard his back.

'Cut it a bit fine, didn't you?' Felix said over his shoulder.

'I apologise, Felix,' said Ulrika. 'The others paused to discuss, er, "tactics".'

'Ha,' barked Gotrek.

'And where are Lady Hermione and Mistress Wither?' asked Felix dryly. 'Is their tactic to hide?'

'Their skills are not in the art of cut and thrust,' said Ulrika, hacking off the head of a woman with hair like writhing vines.

Felix heard Wissen cursing from somewhere to his left. 'Where did these come from?' he cried. 'This is taking too much time! Leibold, Goetz, Zigmund, break off. Finish setting the charges. We must be ready.'

Three cultists broke away and ran back towards the barrels of black powder. There was no way Felix or Gotrek or Ulrika could go after them. The madmen were four deep around them, fighting with the fearless fervour Felix had noted in them earlier. They seemed to care not at all if they lived or died, so long as the will of their master Tzeentch was done. Some threw themselves on Felix's sword merely to weigh it down so that others might get a strike in.

Gotrek fought an enormous, naked, bloated thing that smelled like rancid cooking oil. It had the head of a kindly old grandmother perched atop a mountainous, wobbling torso. The hands at the end of its fat arms were like mittens, unable to hold a weapon. The fight should have been over before it started, but every time Gotrek swung at the thing, a gaping, shark-toothed mouth opened in its skin wherever Gotrek had aimed, and bit down on his axe, trapping it, while the heavy arms clubbed him unceasingly. It didn't matter where Gotrek swung – at the thing's arms, its stomach, its side – a mouth opened there and snapped at his weapon.

'Little boys shouldn't play with axes, dearie,' it said, in a sweet, quavery voice as it bashed him in the head.

Gotrek swore and slashed at it again, and again a mouth caught his axe.

Beyond this fight, Felix saw the black wolf clamp down on one of Wissen's insect arms. He slashed her horribly with the other, but then she didn't let go. Wissen screamed and flailed at her with his sword. She paid the blows no mind.

'Doctor Raschke!' Wissen called, his voice tinged with panic.

'Aye, aye, coming!' said a harsh voice. 'Turn about, damn ye! Turn about!'

Felix stole a glance towards the voice. A towering woman with the plump, powerful body of a farm girl was tottering slowly towards the melee on thick legs, a look of blank idiocy on her moon face. Surely it couldn't have been her that had spoken. She looked slightly less intelligent than a turnip. Then he noticed she had some sort of basket strapped to her back.

'Turn about, ye great lumbering cow!' the voice said. 'Turn about, or I'll rend your fat for soap!'

Something thin slapped the giantess on the left shoulder and she shuffled in a circle until she was facing away from the battle. There was indeed a basket on her back, and strapped into it, like an infant in a bassinet, was a wizened old man with shrivelled limbs and an enormous bald head that seemed much too heavy for his wrinkled chicken neck. His pale blue eyes flashed with an evil intelligence, and his teeth had been filed to points. He held a horsewhip in one hand, and wore what appeared to be a fortune in gold and lapis lazuli necklaces, pendants, bracelets and rings.

'Now, skin changer!' he cried. 'Feel the wrath of Tzeentch!'

The old man pointed his whip at the black wolf and began to chant in a grating sing-song. A ball of blue and gold light swirled into existence before him. Or perhaps it was a hole in the world that opened into a blue and gold inferno. Felix couldn't tell. He looked deeper into it. It was fascinating.

A hook gashed Felix's arm. He blinked and tore his eyes away, cursing, then hacked at the man with the hook. Gods, he hated magic.

With a shriek, the warlock pushed violently at the swirling ball with his splay-fingered hands, and it flew at the black wolf – and entered her.

The wolf leapt back, rolling and howling like she was being attacked by bees, and suddenly she was Madame Mathilda again, screaming and writhing naked on the floor. She came up snarling to her feet, voluptuous curves swaying, and glared at the sorcerer. 'Ye'll pay for that, witch-man,' she snarled.

'I have the warlock, sister,' called Lady Hermione from the shadows of the tunnel mouth. 'Get the others.' She raised her hands, murmuring under her breath, and squirming shadows began to weave around her fingers.

'Ta, Missy,' said Mathilda. She snatched up a sword and launched herself into the fray again, naked from head to toe. Her guttersnipes and doxies charged after her, howling.

The shadows around Lady Hermione's hands grew solid and stretched out towards the warlock. The old man lifted his voice in a counter spell and the air flexed and stiffened between them. A look of strain appeared on Lady Hermione's face. Her shadow snakes faltered and nosed around as if they had hit a wall. She forced her words out through tightened lips.

'Brother Wissen!' cried a wounded cultist. 'They are too strong! Light the powder now! We cannot risk them defeating us!'

'No!' shouted Wissen. 'Not before the signal! Hold your ground! Only a few more moments!'

Why was it so important to wait for the signal, Felix wondered as he fought on. What was so important about test firing the gun? Were they also going to blow up the testing range? He didn't understand it.

Beside Felix, Gotrek pulled his axe free from another of the blubbery grandmother-thing's mouths. He staggered back, swiping around him to fan back more cultists.

The grandmother-thing bobbled after him. 'Give to mommy,' it said in its kindly old voice. 'Be a good boy.'

'Eat this!' snarled Gotrek, slashing again.

Another mouth opened under the thing's left breast, but this time, just as it bit down, Gotrek twisted the axe so that the blade was facing up. The razor-sharp metal cut through the roof of the closing mouth. Gotrek jerked back hard, and ripped the axe out through its belly flesh in an eruption of meat and gore. The thing squealed like a stuck pig.

Gotrek slashed again, and this time found meat. Felix joined him, hacking off one of its arms. Gotrek split its head, and they turned to face new opponents as the battle swirled around them.

Ulrika killed a mutant with a face like an eel. Mathilda's hairy giant spattered the walls with a cultist's brains, but he was breathing heavily, already exhausted from wielding his too-heavy weapon. Lady Hermione and the shrivelled warlock continued to strain back and forth, neither able to gain any advantage. Dead mutants and cultists lay everywhere, mostly in a ring around Gotrek, but the fight had not been entirely one-sided. Only half of Hermione's gentlemen were still on their feet, and less than half of Mathilda's gutter trash.

Felix found himself fighting a man who looked in every aspect like a counting house clerk, from his spectacles to his buckle shoes, except for the huge, tentacled tumour that grew from his neck. The thing rested on the clerk's shoulder, as big and lumpy as a sack of laundry, pushing his head aside at an awkward angle. He staggered under its weight and apologised meekly as the tentacles lashed out at Felix and everyone else around him.

'Terribly sorry,' the clerk said with each attack. 'Can't control it. Not my doing. Sorry.'

The tentacles sparked with violent black energy wherever they touched. One of Hermione's men fell, twitching, as one slapped him across the face. One of Mathilda's doxies jumped back and dropped her carving knife as another caressed her neck. Cultists killed the stricken before they could recover.

Felix hacked at a tentacle as it snaked towards him. A shock ran up his blade and for an instant his whole body stiffened. He staggered back, arm spasming uncontrollably, numb to the shoulder. Ulrika pushed forward to cover him.

'Apologies,' said the clerk to Felix as the tentacles reached for Ulrika. 'I don't care for it any more than you do.'

'No iron!' cried Felix as he massaged his arm and ducked away from more cultists.

Ulrika nodded and whipped her rapier out of the way, then snatched up a fallen spear instead as Felix took his sword in his clumsy left hand and stepped in to defend her flanks. He flailed awkwardly at a mutant as Ulrika swung the butt end of the spear at the clerk. The tentacles caught it. With difficulty, she wrenched it from their clutches and swept the clerk's legs out from under him. He went down in a heap, tumour first, and she thwacked it with all her strength. It burst, spilling stinking red jelly, and the tentacles slapped at the clerk, shocking him over and over again as he twitched convulsively. Ulrika ran him through. The tentacles flopped, limp, to the floor.

There was no time to take a breath. More cultists attacked them from all sides. Gotrek fought a mutant with axes in each of its four hands. Their fight sounded like a busy foundry. Mathilda's giant staggered as the transparent blue frog-thing clawed out his eyes from behind. The giant roared and dropped his hammer to grab for it. The frog tore his throat out. The giant toppled, blood pouring down his filthy jerkin from under his beard.

All around them the vampiresses' thralls were dying at the hands of the cultists. Felix's heart sank. It seemed they would not be enough to turn the tide after all. He gripped his sword two-handed as the feeling tingled painfully back into his right arm. His blocks and attacks were weak and soft. He wouldn't last long.

Then a chorus of shrieks brought his head up. The cultists and mutants nearest the entrance were screaming and backing away. Felix craned his neck. What could frighten a mutant? And then he saw them – shambling figures with long, shadow-eyed faces, clad in rags and scraps of armour, staggering out of the darkness of the tunnels and reaching for the cultists with cruelly curved claws.

Felix gaped, and had to parry desperately as an axe nearly blindsided him. Skaven! The chisel-toothed heads were unmistakable, but there was something wrong. They were painfully thin. More than thin! He risked another look. They were skeletons! By Sigmar, had the vile ratmen invented some new way to conquer Nuln?

'Skaven skeletons?' he choked, incredulous. 'Were the mutants not enough?'

'Fear not,' said Ulrika, blocking a meat axe. 'They are Mistress Wither's work.'

'She... she raised them?' Felix swallowed. 'Ratmen?'

Ulrika shrugged and ran her opponent through. 'She must use the materials available to her, I suppose.'

Felix heard Gotrek curse viciously in Khazalid. Felix knew how he felt. How had they ended up on the same side of a battle with a necromancer? They had fought against necromancers and their minions whenever they encountered them for as long as he could remember. And yet here he was, almost relieved as the undead servants of one of his allies came to his rescue. How had this happened? What had led him to this mad outcome?

His eyes slid to Ulrika, fighting valiantly beside him. It was she who had brought him here. These were her allies. If he accepted her as a friend, did it mean he must accept her kin as well?

The skeletal skaven swarmed the cultists, clawing and snapping and rattling like dice in a cup. They were not fast. They were not strong. Nor were they difficult to kill. A few bashes and they were reduced to bone shards and powder, but there were hundreds of them. Cultists were dragged down by their sheer numbers, or died at the hands of Mathilda's villains or Hermione's heroes while they were distracted by some meagre scratch or bite from behind.

Felix was aghast at how many of the things Mistress Wither had found to raise. The tunnels must be full of dead skaven. He remembered helping the citizens of Nuln kill hundreds of ratmen in the streets during their invasion, but he couldn't recall anyone taking the fight to the tunnels. What had killed them down here?

The cultists fell back before the skeletal horde, panic rippling through their ranks. Seconds ago they had outnumbered Gotrek and Felix and their allies three to one. Now they were outnumbered ten to one, and more cultists were falling every moment.

Felix crossed swords with a man who had strange, circular burn scars all over his face and hands – a few of them still a fresh, angry red. Felix frowned as he turned the man's thrust and made one of his own. He looked familiar. Where had he seen that face before? In the burning cellars below Shantytown? On the street? During the riot on the bridge?

A dim memory was just coming to the surface of his mind when a man in the uniform of a Gunnery School guard ran into the chamber from the far end.

'Brothers! Master Wissen!' he cried. 'Rejoice! The cannon has sounded! The test was successful! They are loading it on the airship now!'

The cultists cheered. Felix heard Wissen sigh with relief.

'At last!' he said, then raised his voice. 'Liebold! Light the fuses! The rest, hold these meddlers where they are! We will take their souls with us when we go to meet Tzeentch!'

The cultists shouted exultantly and attacked Gotrek, Felix and the vampires with renewed fury as a cultist with a mane of black hair ran for the far end of the room, where the ends of all the match cords came together.

'Push through!' shouted Gotrek. He began surging forward, butchering the cultists in front of him.

Felix cursed as he gutted the man with the half-remembered face and slashed left and right to drive back half a dozen attackers. It seemed the lunatics were willing to die here to make sure their enemies died as well. They were madder than Gotrek – all gleefully looking forward to sacrificing themselves for the greater glory of their daemon god.

Gotrek hacked down four cultists and tried to push past six more. He wasn't fast enough. The black-haired cultist took up a torch and began lighting the ends of match cords, all laid out in a line before him. Sparking flames raced across the floor in all directions as the cords burned towards the barrels.

'Kill the bastard!' shrieked Madame Mathilda.

'Forget him!' roared Gotrek. 'Get the cords!' He battered aside a trio of cultists and tried to run for the nearest barrel, but a broad shouldered mutant with plates of orange, coral-like armour growing from its skin got in his way and swung a fist like a huge, barnacled club at him. Gotrek blocked and slashed back, sending orange gravel flying as he chopped into the crusty armour.

Ulrika hissed a Kislevite curse and leapt over the wall of cultists with a gazelle-like spring. But before her feet touched the ground, a translucent appendage shot out and caught her around the ankle. She fell flat on her face and the blue frog-thing jumped on her back, clawing at her with webbed talons. It had been its tongue that tripped her.

Felix cursed and shoved forward, hacking right and left to reach her. He swung down at the frog-man. It rolled away and shot out its tongue, jerking Felix forward by the wrist while slashing at his face with his claws. Felix blocked with his free arm and the talons tore bloody trenches in his forearm.

Ulrika surged up and aimed a cut at the frog-man's back.

'No!' said Felix, kicking the frog in the stomach and catching one of its arms. 'The fuses! I have him!'

'Right.' Ulrika turned and sprinted for the furthest barrels. Madame Mathilda was right behind her, breaking free of a clutch of mutants. The two vampire women began snatching up match cords and yanking their ends out of the barrels.

'Stop them!' shouted Wissen. 'Put the cords back! They must all go up at once!'

Cultists broke away from the main fight to protect the barrels. Wissen scuttled after Ulrika, using his mantis arms as an extra pair of legs, and launched himself at her back. She spun around and sheared off one of his pincers. He shrieked, but lashed at her with both sword and remaining claw. She parried and returned his attacks.

The frog-thing raked Felix's arms again. Felix hissed in pain and punched it in one of its saucer-sized eyes. It squawked and its tongue let go of his sword arm. Felix slashed at it, but it dodged back, out of range, clutching its eye. Felix raised his sword, then ran for the closest barrel instead. This was no time to fight. He pulled out the cord, then hurried to the next.

The vampires' surviving minions swarmed all over the room, chopping through fizzing match cord or ripping it out of the barrels as they fended off cultists and mutants. Gotrek stepped over the corpse of the coral mutant and ran to do the same. The skeletal skaven lurched forward as well. Only Lady Hermione and the wizened warlock remained where they were, still frozen in their contest of wills.

By Sigmar, we're going to do it, thought Felix as he tugged out another match cord and started for the next. The frog-man's tongue caught him around the neck and slammed him to the ground, knocking the breath from his lungs and his sword from his grip. He clawed at his neck, but the tongue was already gone.

The frog-man sprang, slashing at his face with its talons. Felix rolled over, hunching, and the talons shredded his shoulder and back. He grabbed his sword and swung it in a wild arc. The frog-man hopped away.

Felix scrambled up and faced it. The frog-man was between him and the next barrel. The flame was racing closer along the match cord. The frog-man crouched. Felix went on guard.

'No, Rombaugh!' screamed Wissen. 'Pull out the cord! One blast will only ruin us. We must kill these villains first to keep them from interfering! It's all or none!'

The frog-man backed up, eyes on Felix.

'Stop him, manling!' said Gotrek, pounding towards them. 'Let it blow!'

Felix hesitated, confused by this sudden change in objectives. Let it blow? Why? The explosion would kill him.

The frog-man pulled the cord out and sprang away with it. Felix lunged after him, but too late.

'Now kill them!' shouted Wissen. 'Kill them all so we can reset the charges!' He leapt at Ulrika again, snarling with fury. 'Cursed spoilers!'

'I will set the charges!' rasped a voice from behind them.

Everyone turned. It was the wizened warlock. All Felix could see of the old man behind the fat farm girl's bulk were his outstretched arms, trembling with tension. Glowing blue light stretched towards Lady Hermione from the lapis lazuli on his gold bracelets, and wove a pulsing net around her. Felix could see that the vampire sorceress was fighting to escape the cage with all her might, but it was not enough. Her strands of shadow were dissipating like smoke in a strong wind. She was curling in on herself, her face twisted with agony and impotent rage.

'Lady!' cried Hermione's last remaining gentleman. He rushed towards her. The skaven skeletons ran at the old man. Mutants ran to intercept them.

The warlock clashed his wrists together and the net of blue light tightened around Hermione like a noose. She jerked and dropped, unconscious, flickers of glowing blue fire crawling over her like scuttling rats. Her handsome thrall cried out in anguish as he tried to fight past two mutants.

The warlock cackled, triumphant, then raised his voice in a climbing wail of tortured syllables. Purple clouds began to coalesce over his head. The farm girl just stood there placidly, staring straight ahead.

'No you don't, sorcerer,' Gotrek growled. He ran towards the warlock, knocking aside the skaven skeletons and the mutants as if they weren't there.

Felix ran too. He didn't know what the warlock meant to do, but it had to be bad. He saw Ulrika and Mathilda converging on him too, cultists in hot pursuit. The purple clouds were boiling across the roof of the chamber like smoke.

Something grabbed Felix's ankle and he fell flat. The damned frog! Its tongue dragged him back. He whipped behind him with his sword and chopped the tongue in two. The frog-man fell back on its arse as its tongue snapped back into its mouth. Felix scrambled up and ran on.

Wissen spidered in front of Ulrika, slashing at her with his remaining claw. She fenced with him. Mathilda and Gotrek angled around them, neck and neck, and closed in on the farm girl. Felix didn't want to look. The poor girl hadn't a brain in her head. Killing her would be like killing a puppy.

Gotrek raised his axe. Mathilda raised her sword. But just as they reached her, the girl, as blank as ever, opened her mouth and vomited, spraying Gotrek and Mathilda with vile green liquid that hissed when it touched their skin.

Mathilda fell to the ground, shrieking and writhing as the bile burned her naked flesh. Gotrek stumbled back, cursing and mopping at his bubbling face with his hand, then surged forward again, his left arm shielding his head. The warlock's voice reached a screeching crescendo as Gotrek chopped through the girl's leg, severing it. She toppled sideways, her piteous little-girl cry lost in the foul torrent of the old man's words.

A sound like thunder rumbled overhead as the girl pawed feebly at the ground before Gotrek. Felix ran up in time to see the shrivelled little warlock grinning up at Gotrek from the basket on her back. 'I have done it,' he giggled, his eyes shining. 'The master's will is done.'

'And so are you,' snarled Gotrek. He slammed the rune axe into the warlock's face, splitting his enormous head in two and sinking the blade deep into the girl's back. Her struggles ceased.

The thunder rumbled again and Felix felt something hot on his back. Then on his arm. He looked down. His cloak was on fire. Tiny pink flames dotted it in a dozen places. He beat at them. They didn't go out! Where had they come from?

Beside him, Gotrek cursed as he slapped at his arms and shoulders. There were shouts and squeals behind them. Felix spun around. He gaped.

The warlock's purple clouds hid the roof of the chamber from end to end, and were raining a steady shower of tiny pink candle flames. Wherever they landed, fire spread. The cultists, the mutants, Wissen, Ulrika, Mathilda, her guttersnipes and Lady Hermione's last gentleman were all crying out and running for cover, swatting madly at the flames that burned their clothes and skin. The top of every black powder barrel was burning with little pink blazes, and the wood was starting to blacken. It would be mere moments before the fire burned through the wood to the powder.

'Sigmar save us,' said Felix in a hollow voice as he backed towards the tunnel with Gotrek. 'We'll never put them all out in time. This is the end.'

'Fah!' said Gotrek. 'We need to fight fire with fire, is all.' His face and forearms were a mass of hideous, pus-filled blisters, and he still stank of the farm-girl's viscous vomit. He seemed to feel none of it.

'Fire with fire?' said Felix, confused.

Gotrek put his axe on his back and looked around the floor, then barked a pleased laugh as he saw Mathilda's giant lying dead where the frog-man had ripped out his throat. The Slayer crossed to the giant and picked up his ridiculous stone-headed hammer. He had less trouble lifting it than the giant had. But what did he want it for?

'Into the tunnel, manling,' said Gotrek. He began to spin in a circle.

Ulrika heard and dragged Lady Hermione towards the tunnel mouth. Madame Mathilda's guttersnipes did the same for their barely conscious mistress. Wissen and the cultists had taken cover in an alcove on the far side of the room.

The barrel tops were blazing like torches now. Gotrek turned, faster and faster, holding the huge hammer at the very end of the haft. Was he going to fling it at Wissen, wondered Felix as he backed out of the chamber. What good would that do?

'Back, I said!' Gotrek roared, and let go of the hammer. It flew straight for the closest black powder barrel.

Felix ducked back, gaping with shock as Gotrek dived toward hims, laughing madly.

A huge explosion rocked the tunnel. A fist of hot air punched Felix in the chest and popped his ears painfully. It threw Gotrek into him and sent them rolling backwards into the tunnel. They came to rest in a heap next to Ulrika and Mathilda at the base of the sloping ramp. Pebbles and dust rained down on Felix's head and blistering heat washed over him in a wave. He tensed, waiting for more explosions. They didn't come. A loud roar came from the chamber, but it wasn't an explosion. It was a strange sustained thunder. And what was that horrible smell?

'Ye madman!' screamed Mistress Mathilda, sitting up and glaring at Gotrek. 'What did ye do?' Her face and shoulders where the farm-girl's vomit had splattered them were as blistered as the Slayer's.

'Saved your sorry, undead arse,' rasped Gotrek. 'More's the pity.' He turned to Felix. 'Up, manling. Or you'll be swept away.'

Felix groaned and pushed himself painfully to his feet. 'Swept away?'

A knee-high bow-wave of frothing brown water rushed into the tunnel, nearly knocking him off his feet. Corpses and bits of shattered barrel floated in it, and it reeked of excrement and garbage. Mathilda and Ulrika staggered and braced themselves against the tide, which was rising swiftly. Lady Hermione's last gentleman lifted her unconscious form in his arms and held her above it. He began carrying her up the slope, out of the water. Madame Mathilda and her last few guttersnipes followed wearily.

Felix and Ulrika slogged forward against the current and looked into the chamber, eyes wide with wonder. There was a crumbling hole in the roof directly above the place where the barrel had been, and through it poured a solid, tree-thick column of brown water that was filling the chamber like a teapot filled a tea cup. The tops of the barrels were still burning with pink fire, but the water was already three-quarters of the way up their sides, and climbing fast.

'What a terrifying race,' breathed Ulrika.

Felix nodded, mesmerised. The barrels could still explode at any second. They should all be running for high ground, but he couldn't tear his eyes away.

Then another explosion, far back in the chamber, knocked them back into the tunnel as a ball of fire billowed out across the roof.

Ulrika shook her head as she picked herself up out of the water. She looked at Gotrek. 'It was a good try, Slayer,' she said. 'But not enough, I think.'

'Never doubt a dwarf, bloodsucker,' said Gotrek, grinning as he pushed past her. The water was up to his chest now, and his beard was beginning to float. 'Look.'

Felix and Ulrika followed him back to the door of the chamber. There was another hole in the roof now, above where the second barrel had exploded, and another thick column of water was pouring down. The tide was rising twice as fast. Even as they watched, it began lapping over the tops of the barrels. One by one the pink fires began to wink out.

'Sigmar's hammer,' said Felix, shaking his head in wonder as floating corpses and barrel staves bumped into him. 'We did it! Er, you did it. Ah, it's done.'

Ulrika inclined her head to Gotrek. 'Never again will I question your judgement, Slayer.' She wrinkled her nose. 'Now come. Let us find higher ground. It stinks.'

With a gasping scream, the body floating next to Felix reared out of the water. It was Wissen! He lunged at Felix, his remaining pincer crushing Felix's arm and pulling him close while he clamped his hands around Felix's throat.

'You ruined it!' he screamed, his eyes afire with fanatical hate, his face pock-marked with little circular burns from the rain of pink fire. 'You ruined it all! Our glorious future, drowned in a tide of shit! I'll kill you! In the name of Tzeentch, I'll...'

Felix punched Wissen in the nose. Ulrika ran him through. Gotrek swung his axe underwater and bit into him somewhere below. Felix could feel the brutal impact through the hands that clutched his throat.

Wissen's fingers slackened, and his eyes glazed over as the water around him began to swirl with red. 'At least there is still the master...' he murmured. His skin, around the circular burns, was turning white from lack of blood.

Felix frowned. The burns. The circular burns. Like the man he had killed earlier. Like the... His heart slammed against his chest as realisation dawned. Now he knew where he had seen the man with the circular burns before! He hadn't recognised him at first without his leather robes. He had been one of the Sigmarite priests at the pouring of the last cannon. The initiate who had fainted. The one who had poured the ashes into the molten iron!

Felix grabbed Wissen by the collar. 'Wissen! Don't you die, you fiend! The cannons! What did you do to the cannons?'

Wissen's eyes regained some of their focus and he chuckled weakly. 'Too... late. They have flown.'

Felix shook him. 'What did you do to them?'

'Tainted. All of them,' he said, dreamily. 'Warpstone... in the iron. Once on the walls of... Middenheim, the master will... wake them. Their crews... driven mad... turn them against the gates of the

Fauschlag... shot down from... within. Archaon will enter... Chaos... triumphant at last!'

Felix stared at him, stunned. His arms sagged and Wissen slipped beneath the filthy, bloody water.

Gotrek stepped forward and hauled the captain up again. 'The master!' he growled. 'Who is the master?'

Wissen's head tipped back, a blissful smile on his lips.

Gotrek shook him. 'Grimnir curse you! Talk, vermin!'

Wissen's extremities swayed loosely in the current. His eyes stared at nothing.

Gotrek swore furiously and let Wissen's body submerge. He started up the slope of the tunnel, angling towards the side passage Wissen and the watchmen had entered from. 'Hurry, manling,' he said. 'We have to stop Makaisson before he flies.'

Felix nodded and followed, though he was afraid it was already too late. The *Spirit of Grungni* must certainly have lifted off by now. Still, they had to try.

Ulrika joined them. The three of them pushed forward, rising slowly up out of the water, their clothes soaking and smeared with filth. At the top of the rise, between them and the side tunnel, Lady Hermione, Madame Mathilda and Mistress Wither looked down at them. Lady Hermione propped herself against her gentleman. Mathilda stood naked and blistered and dripping, hands on her hips. Mistress Wither was a tall shadow behind them.

'Get out of the way,' said Gotrek.

The vampire women didn't move.

'Our apologies, Slayer. Herr Jaeger,' said Lady Hermione. 'You have saved Nuln, and we are grateful. But you have also betrayed the countess, making her existence known to Makaisson, the engineer, and perhaps others.'

'I did what?' growled Gotrek.

'For this oathbreaking,' continued Lady Hermione, as if he hadn't spoken, 'she has ordered your death.'

'What!' cried Ulrika.

Behind the three vampiresses, the corridor began to fill with a numberless throng of skeletal skaven.

CHAPTER SEVENTEEN

'COME AND DIE, then!' snapped Gotrek, raising his axe out of the water.

'Wait, Slayer, please!' said Ulrika, sloshing ahead of him.

'There's no time,' Gotrek rumbled, pushing forward. 'Make for the side tunnel, manling.'

Felix joined him. Lady Hermione's gentleman took her up in his arms and backed away with her. Madame Mathilda and her gutter-snipes edged away. Mistress Wither drifted back like a ghost and pointed a bandaged hand at them. Her army of dead skaven advanced, sounding like a thousand marionettes all rattling together at once. They crowded down the slope towards Gotrek and Felix, wading into the water and clawing at them.

Ulrika glared up over the advancing horde at Hermione as Gotrek and Felix chopped into the first wave. 'I don't understand, sister! You said that the countess had sent you to help us! You said the countess understood that I was mistaken – that the Slayer had not mentioned her or myself after all!'

'I said she had received the message,' said Hermione. 'I did not say that she believed you.'

'What? Why?' cried Ulrika backing into the water, as the skeletons advanced.

'She thinks that your loyalties are in conflict.' A sneering smile curled Hermione's lips. 'That you are besotted with cattle.'

Ulrika stiffened with outrage. 'I am a woman of honour, the daughter of a boyar and kin to royalty. I do not lie. I do not break oath.'

Gotrek and Felix advanced another step up the slope, leaving shattered bones and rusted weapons sticking up from the water behind them. The skeletons were pitiful foes, but there were so many. It was maddening. The side passage was only five strides above them, but it seemed they might never reach it.

'Perhaps not,' Hermione continued. 'Perhaps you only believed what you wished to believe. It is a common *human* failing. But...' she said, raising her voice over Ulrika's protests and the sounds of battle. 'Whether you lied or were lied to, the Slayer and the poet must die.'

Felix frowned. Would the countess truly say this? 'Ulrika!' he called, as he shattered a dirt-caked skaven ribcage with a savage cut. 'What if it is Hermione who lies? What if the countess believed you?'

Ulrika looked at him, the light of hope kindling in her eyes, but then, just as quickly, it died. 'But if she didn't, then I would be going against her.' Her eyes narrowed. She turned back to Lady Hermione. 'And I? Am I to die as well?'

Hermione shook her head. 'A mother does not so easily cast aside a daughter. Even an adopted one.' She smiled. 'So that you do nothing to interfere, you are forgiven, and, were you to kill them yourself, why, I believe the countess could never have cause to mistrust you again.'

Ulrika's glance flicked to Felix and then away again. 'I... No! I cannot betray my friends.'

'But you can betray your mother?'

'I did not betray her!' wailed Ulrika. 'Felix and the Slayer did not expose her! They do not deserve her wrath!'

'Whatever they deserve,' said Hermione coolly, 'their death is what the countess wishes. Did you not swear to serve her when she saved you from Krieger? You who claim to never break an oath. Will your vow to her shatter at its first testing?'

If vampires could cry, Ulrika would have been weeping. She stood paralysed, knee deep in sewer water, her face contorted in anguish. Felix cursed Hermione under his breath. There were two battles being fought here, and he could not say which was more savage.

'Ulrika...' he said.

'Don't bother, manling,' said Gotrek. 'She's made her decision. Or she would have killed the bitch already.' He stepped back from the avalanche of skaven and slashed backhanded at Ulrika. 'Defend yourself, bloodsucker.'

'No! she cried, splashing away up the slope through the skeletons. 'No!' She turned at the top and looked into Felix's eyes, her beautiful face twisted with misery. 'I'm sorry, Felix,' she said. 'I will not fight you, but I cannot go against my mistress.'

'But perhaps you don't!' cried Felix, frustrated. 'Perhaps it's all a lie!'

'I... I cannot take that chance,' said Ulrika sadly. 'I am alone in this world without the countess. She saved me. She is my mother.'

And with that she turned and ran down the tunnel, pushing through the army of dead ratmen, and into the darkness. Felix's eyes stung, and he found it hard to swallow around the lump in his throat. No matter. Fighting would fix that.

He ploughed up the slope with Gotrek, wading into the skaven with fevered fury. Suddenly he wanted to see Lady Hermione dead more than anything in the world. The conniving bitch had broken Ulrika's spirit and divided her from Gotrek and Felix as neatly as an executioner lopped off the head of a traitor. She needed to die by his sword. If only these cursed skeletons would get out of the way.

'These puppets won't stop 'em,' snarled Madame Mathilda. 'Come on, me brave ones.'

She dropped into a squat, then launched herself at Gotrek, transforming in mid-air – her body twisting and sprouting black hair, her jaw lengthening, her fingers clumping together into yellow-clawed paws. Her few remaining guttersnipes charged down the slope behind her, howling.

Gotrek hacked off Mathilda's left foreleg as she hit him in the chest. They tumbled backwards together into the water.

Mathilda's half-transformed limb splashed beside Felix, and then her doxies and alley bashers were on him, pushing through the skeletons to stab at him with knives and cutlasses and hooks. He blocked and parried as best he could, but quickly lost all the ground he and Gotrek had won.

Beside him, Gotrek and Mathilda fought under water in a churning froth of limbs. He glimpsed wolf teeth, then Gotrek's axe, then a tail, a foot.

Then he could look no more. He was surrounded. The bashers and doxies and dead ratmen hacking and lunging at him from all sides. He could do nothing but spin in an endless circle, weaving figure eights in the air with Karaghul. It kept them at bay for now, but how long could he keep it up? He felt like he had been fighting for hours. The water dragged at his legs, and the footing was uncertain. Skeleton limbs splintered and spun away as they reached for him and met his blade. A snaggle-toothed harlot gashed his arm with an ice pick.

'Gotrek?' he called.

There was nothing but thrashing behind him.

A basher leapt at him, trying to bring him down like his mistress had Gotrek. Felix sidestepped him and he splashed into the water behind him. Felix stabbed down into the water and found flesh. The skeletons and bashers closed in, hemming him in on all sides. Claws caught his legs and arms.

'Gotrek!'

There was a yelp from behind him, and a great splashing, and the black wolf charged up the slope on three legs, shouldering the skeletons out of her way.

'Cursed wolf bitch!' roared Gotrek, surging up out of the water and charging past Felix, his arms and shoulders running red from a dozen deep wolf bites. The skeletons and bashers turned away from Felix to stop him. The Slayer slashed all around at them. Dead rat-men exploded in showers of bone. The bashers merely died.

Felix breathed a sigh of relief and took up his usual position behind and a little to the left of Gotrek, chopping down any skeletons or guttersnipes that got past him. This was how things worked best – Gotrek taking the brunt and Felix cleaning up behind him. Now they might get somewhere.

Gotrek pressed forward relentlessly against the tide. The last of the alley bashers fell and things went quicker. The Slayer destroyed half a dozen bone skaven with every swing. They were almost out of the water. Felix craned his neck, trying to find Lady Hermione beyond the skeletons.

Just then, what little light there was in the tunnel winked out all at once. They had been seeing by the reflected glow of the lanterns from the black powder chamber. Now everything was black.

'What happened?' he called. Had the water risen high enough to snuff out the lanterns high on the walls? No. That was impossible. It was still only rib deep.

A skeleton ripped at his chest in the dark. He swung blindly at it and heard it shatter. More clawed at him. His skin crawled at their touch and he lashed out. He heard them snap and smash all around him, but still there were more. Gotrek's axe whooshed and whizzed nearby, crushing more of them.

'Sorcery,' grunted Gotrek. 'I can't see.'

Felix gulped. If Gotrek was blind it was indeed sorcery. He had known the Slayer to be able to see in lightless mines.

'What do we do?' said Felix, fighting off panic. He hacked all around him, but kept his strokes tight, afraid of hitting Gotrek.

'Press on, manling,' said the Slayer. 'The passage hasn't moved.'

Felix nodded, then realised that that was foolish in the dark, and opened his mouth to speak. But just as he did, something slithered around his neck and choked him, constricting his windpipe and cutting off his air. He cried out and clawed at his neck, expecting to find some slimy tentacle wrapped around it. There was nothing there!

Teeth and claws continued attacking him in the dark. He flailed about one-handed with his sword, futilely clutching at his throat with his left while panic consumed him. He tried to call to Gotrek, but could only hiss.

'What's that, manling?'

'Chhhikik,' said Felix. 'Chhhht bttthhhh.' Dim stars flared before his eyes. His sword strokes were weakening. He fought to take a breath.

A hard hand gripped his arm and he almost stabbed towards it before he realised it was Gotrek. Something heavy whipped past his ear, and then his other ear. The breeze ruffled his hair. Gotrek's axe! Was he attacking him? Was he mistaking him for an enemy?

Teeth and claws bit his arms and legs. He tried to scream in pain, but only rasped.

Gotrek cursed and, with a swish and a clatter, the teeth and claws fell away.

The Slayer's huge hand moved to his neck and felt around. Then a snarl. 'More sorcery. Fight her, manling. And keep moving.'

The callused hand grabbed his arm again and tugged him forward. Felix stumbled after him, swinging his sword in weak arcs and trying to force down the panic that was consuming him as, all around him, came the sounds of clattering movement and the whoosh and clash of heavy steel chopping bone.

Fight her, Gotrek had said. Fight who? The image of shadowy snakes spilling from Lady Hermione's hands flashed through his mind – stretching out, reaching, strangling. The evil witch. She had snuffed out Ulrika's will with a word. Now she was trying to snuff out his life with black sorcery. He waved his sword in front of his throat, as if doing so could sever the coils. Nothing.

He staggered on behind Gotrek, weak-kneed, the stars in front of his eyes blooming into fireworks, bursting one after another in purples, pinks and yellows. He tried to picture the black coils dissipating into candle smoke. Tried to feel them relaxing their grip on his neck. They remained as tight as ever. The ground beneath his feet became level.

They had reached the top of the slope. Gotrek jerked him left. His shoulder hit the wall. He felt a cross-breeze on his cheek. The clatter of exploding skeletons filled his ears.

'Move!'

Gotrek shoved him towards the breeze, and all at once there were no skeletons around him.

It didn't matter. He was suffocating to death. He couldn't lift his sword anymore. He could barely put one foot in front of the other. His pulse was pounding in his ears like a hammer on an anvil. He could no longer hear anything else. His chest was going to implode for want of air. His tongue was swelling to fill his mouth. His fingers pawed weakly at his throat.

Something hard hit him in the stomach and he was lifted off his feet. His head flopped down towards the ground. His sword dragged on stone. The hard thing bounced him up and down and swayed him from side to side. He could hardly feel it anymore. All he could feel was the pain in his chest and the coils crushing his windpipe, constricting tighter and tighter. If only the bouncing would stop and let him die in peace.

Then, slowly, peace came, black and soft. The bouncing faded. The pain in his chest eased. He had the sensation of drifting down, like a snowflake, through a sweet murmuring darkness. This wasn't so bad. No pain. No loud noises. No horrible smells.

A hard bounce jolted him awake. It knocked the wind out of him. He gasped. Sigmar! He had gasped! There was air in his lungs! He tried again. It was like trying to suck air through a clogged pipe stem, but he was breathing. It hurt like swallowing glass.

Another hard bounce. Another gasp. The world flooded back around him – pain and noise and stink. His head throbbed. His stomach screamed. His chest felt like it was filled with rocks. His ears were battered with thuds and grunts and clanks. His nose was assaulted by the reek of sweat and sewer sludge. He looked around. For a moment he could see nothing. Then came movement and shadow. A dim glow of torches – all upside down. It slowly came to him where he was and what was happening to him. He was draped over Gotrek's shoulder, and the Slayer was running hard. An earthen floor blurred past, inches from his face. They were in a lantern-lit tunnel. Beyond that he didn't know.

'Got… rek,' he mumbled.

'Alive then?' said a harsh voice. 'Good.'

Felix frowned. How was he alive? How could he see? Had he fought off Hermione's sorcery? Had he willed the snakes away? Had Gotrek done it? Had the Slayer's brutal jostling broken the spell somehow? Had the duel with the warlock weakened her so much that she couldn't prolong the spell? Had they simply gotten too far away?

Gotrek stopped and set him down. He groaned in agony. Some-where in the distance came a clicking and clattering. Gotrek did something off to Felix's right. A breeze puffed on Felix's cheek, and more sewer smell filled his nose. He looked towards the breeze. A secret door. Into the sewer tunnels.

Gotrek leaned over him and took his arm.

'I… I can walk.'

'Not fast enough,' said Gotrek, and hoisted him over his shoulder again. Felix's bruised stomach throbbed with agony.

As Gotrek carried him through the door Felix saw movement behind them, a milling throng of wedge-skulled skeletons shuffling towards them. And there were darker figures among them, pushing through them, past them.

Gotrek kicked the door closed, then ran on. The dim grey dawn filtered down into the sewer from above. Felix looked at the sewer channel as they jogged past it. The stew was very low. He had never seen it so low. A gummy brown tide mark was drying high above a sluggish trickle. The holes Gotrek's black powder trick had blasted into the channel must have emptied the sewers. He chuckled. That would take some fixing.

A crash behind them. Felix twisted his head awkwardly to look back. A broken door was toppling into the channel. Two dark fig-ures emerged from the hole in the wall. Or was it three? They surged forward.

'Grimnir take them,' cursed Gotrek. 'No time. No time.' He ran on.

Felix looked back again. The dark figures were closer – much closer. Gotrek turned a corner into a small square space and stopped. He lifted Felix off his shoulder and steadied him against the wall. A set of iron rungs ran up it.

'I hope you can climb,' said Gotrek.

'I hope I can too,' said Felix.

Gotrek started up the rungs. 'Come on. Right behind me.'

Felix nodded and pushed himself away from the wall. The world swirled vertiginously around him. He clutched a rung and held on. The world steadied. He began to climb. One rung. Two rungs. He heard a soft thudding. It got louder. Was it his heart?

Above him, Gotrek reached the top of the ladder and put his shoulder to the grate. A shaft of weak sunlight slanted in and lit up a square of bricks beside the ladder. The Slayer pushed the grate up until it fell aside with a clang.

Felix kept climbing. Halfway there. His vision dimmed. His head pounded. Or was that the thudding sound, growing louder still?

Gotrek climbed out of the hole.

Felix looked back. A black wolf bounded into the room from the tunnel, a petite woman clinging to her back. The wolf had four legs, but one was pale and shiny and had no fur. Behind the wolf and rider was a looming shadow, as thin as a dead tree.

Felix climbed faster, at least he tried to, urging his legs to extend, his arms to pull and grasp. He was sweating like a pump.

'Come on, manling!' called Gotrek from above. He held his hand down into the hole.

The wolf shook off its rider and leapt at him, snapping. Her teeth clashed shut an inch from his ankle. Felix climbed another rung. Only three more! The wolf howled angrily, and transformed. The howl became words as the paws became hands and clambered up the ladder behind him.

'No ye don't, pet!' said Madame Mathilda. 'Haven't had my dinner.' She grabbed his ankle in a grip like a steel talon and yanked down, hard.

Felix's slick fingers slipped off the rungs. But just as he fell, Gotrek's meaty hand grabbed his right wrist and pulled up, hard. Felix barked in agony. He was being stretched like taffy. Another few stitches popped. Every wound on his body screamed.

'Your other arm!' rasped Gotrek.

Felix threw up his left arm. Gotrek caught it and pulled, his legs braced on either side of the hole. Mathilda hauled back the other way. Felix groaned with pain.

Below Mathilda, Lady Hermione was standing wearily and making gestures with her hands and Mistress Wither was floating upwards like a dry leaf, scrawny, bandaged fingers stretching out of her drooping sleeves towards him.

Felix kicked Madame Mathilda in the face with his free foot. She snarled and grabbed his other ankle, pulling with all her weight. Above him, Gotrek heaved mightily. Felix felt his spine pop. His muscles tore and spasmed. But he was rising, slowly – too slowly. Mistress Wither was closing fast.

Gotrek pulled harder. Felix's legs raised up into the slanting shaft of sunlight. The edge of it touched Mathilda's fingers. She screamed and let go, her hands smoking.

Felix came up all at once, scraping his shoulders on the frame of the hole as he shot through it and landed on top of Gotrek. He groaned, in too much agony to move.

Gotrek shoved him off and staggered up, pulling his axe off his back, his eye fixed on the sewer hole.

'Not coming out, maggots?' he called.

There was no answer.

He shrugged, then turned back to Felix and hauled him to his feet.

Felix hissed, nearly passing out from the pain. 'Easy.'

'No time for easy, manling,' he said, starting away. 'Come on.'

Felix looked around as he limped after the Slayer. They were in a side street next to the Imperial Gunnery School. Gotrek's uncanny sense of direction had come through again.

Halfway to the corner, a faint, echoey voice reached his ears. 'It won't always be daylight, heroes.'

GOTREK AND FELIX limped through the gates of the Imperial Gunnery School and headed for the broad flat lawn that stretched along its west side. Men of the College of Engineering and of the Gunnery School were working together to dismantle a tower made of steel beams and guy wires. Other men loaded the pieces onto the backs of a line of wagons and made them secure as the dray horses stamped the grass and snorted steam into the cold morning air.

Off to one side, Lord Groot stood talking with Lord Pfaltz-Kappel and Lord Hieronymous Ostwald. They looked up as the poet and the Slayer approached, then gasped.

'The *Spirit of Grungni*,' barked Gotrek. 'Where is it?'

'You… you have missed it, Slayer,' said Groot. 'Look.'

Gotrek and Felix followed Groot's finger as he pointed west. At first Felix could see nothing but the towers and roof peaks of the city, outlined in pink by the light of the rising sun. But at last he found, just between the sturdy mass of the town hall and the sharp spires of the University of Nuln, a small black oblong shape nosing north and west before a high bank of lavender clouds.

Gotrek's shoulders slumped. He cursed.

Felix groaned. They were too late. The tainted cannon were on their way to Middenheim, to wreak havoc on the Fauschlag's defences from within. But maybe it wasn't too late. Maybe there was some way to warn them, to call the airship back – carrier pigeons or flares or some such.

He turned to Lord Groot. 'My lord…'

Groot, Ostwald and Pfaltz-Kappel were all backing away from them and covering their noses, their eyes wide with dismay and apprehension.

'Did you fall in the sewer, Herr Jaeger?' asked Lord Ostwald, gagging.

'Were you in a fight?' asked Groot.

'Are you diseased?' asked Lord Pfaltz-Kappel.

Felix looked down at himself, then over at Gotrek. He could understand the lords' reactions. He and the Slayer looked a mess. Felix's beautiful new clothes were torn and bloodied and smeared with filth, and he was still bleeding from the gashes the frog thing had torn on his arm. The Slayer was worse. His body was a mass of bleeding wounds. His bandages were soaked and partially peeled away, revealing his healing burn scars, his crest and beard were singed black in places and clotted with sewer muck, and his face, neck and shoulders were covered in angry, pus-filled blisters from the farm girl's vomit. He looked like he had contracted some virulent plague and was in its later stages. Well, perhaps their battered condition would add urgency to their words.

'The sewer fell on us,' said Felix. 'But listen, please, my lords. Something terrible has occurred. The cannon...'

'Another secret plot like the last one you invented?' sneered Pfaltz-Kappel, waving his handkerchief in front of his face. 'The Gunnery School seems to have failed to explode.'

'We only just stopped it from happening, my lord,' said Felix. 'Down in the sewer. Hence our, er, disarray. But please listen...'

'What!' said Lord Groot. 'You say someone was trying to blow up the school after all?'

'Yes, my lord,' said Felix, impatiently. 'Ward Captain Wissen. He was the leader of the Cleansing Flame. He and his followers...'

'Captain Wissen a cultist?' said Pfaltz-Kappel. 'Preposterous. No more zealous defender of the public good exists in Nuln.'

'That was how he covered his actions,' said Felix. 'But who perpetrated the plot isn't important anymore. Wissen has been defeated and his bombs defused. What is important is the fact that the cannons...'

'Wissen has been "defeated"?' asked Lord Ostwald, raising an eyebrow. 'What do you mean by that?'

'We...' Felix paused, suddenly realising how awkward this could become. He shot a look at Gotrek, but the Slayer was staring fixedly at the ground, mumbling to himself. He didn't seem to be listening at all. Well, it would all come out in the end. And it had to be told. 'We... we fought and defeated him and his followers, in order to stop the destruction of the Gunnery School. But unfortunately, part of their plan has succeeded. You see, the cannon...'

'Do you mean you killed him?' pressed Ostwald.

'Er,' said Felix. 'Well, he was killed, yes. But as I say, we discovered part of his plan too late, and...'

'You killed Captain Wissen!' cried all three, stepping back from them.

'And did you also assault the guards of the Altestadt Gate last night?' asked Lord Ostwald.

'And also one of the patrols Captain Wissen placed in the sewers the day before?' asked Lord Pfaltz-Kappel.

'My lords, please,' Felix pleaded. 'I can answer all these charges later. But you must hear me about the cannon. They have been...'

But Lord Groot was waving over a detail of Gunnery School guards as Ostwald and Pfaltz-Kappel continued to back away, hands on the hilts of their swords.

'Herr Jaeger,' said Ostwald. 'I am very disappointed in you. I believed you to be a true and noble knight, a defender of humanity against the horrors that besiege us from all sides, but these actions of yours are very disturbing – assaulting the watch, killing a ward captain of the watch, Sigmar only knows what other villainy. I am afraid I will have to place you under arrest until these matters can be investigated further.'

'Fine!' said Felix angrily. 'Lock us up! Do what you will! Only let me finish what I have been trying to tell...'

Gotrek's head snapped up. 'The gyrocopter!' He barked, then started across the lawn towards the front gates. 'Come on, manling. We've no time to lose.'

'Stop them!' shouted Lord Ostwald. 'Arrest them for the murder of Ward Captain Adelbert Wissen!'

CHAPTER EIGHTEEN

GOTREK GLARED AROUND, pulling his axe off his back. 'What's this?' he growled menacingly as the Gunnery School guards began closing in.

Felix drew his sword. 'I tried to explain about the cannon, but they wouldn't listen. They won't believe that Wissen was a cultist, and...'

'Never mind, manling,' said Gotrek. 'There's no time for explanations.' He lashed about with his axe, making the guards dance back. 'Stay clear if you want to live!' he shouted, then looked around. 'Here, manling,' he said, trotting off. 'Hurry.'

Felix limped after the Slayer and saw that he was heading for the line of wagons from the College of Engineering. Good. As fragile as he felt at the moment, the idea of sprinting to the college with a troop of guards at his heels didn't sound appetising, or possible.

The guards moved with them, maintaining a cautious distance from their weapons, but when they realised Gotrek and Felix were heading for the wagons, they blocked their way, drawing their pistols and resting them across their forearms.

'Shoot, then,' growled Gotrek, without breaking stride. 'But aim well, or it will be the last thing you do.'

'No!' shouted Ostwald. 'Don't shoot!'

'What, my lord?' cried Lord Pfaltz-Kappel. 'They are murderers. Groot! Tell them to fire.'

'No, Groot! Hold!' said Ostwald. 'There is a story here that may have bearing on the security of Nuln, perhaps all the Empire, and I will hear it.' He glared at Pfaltz-Kappel. 'And witch hunters have difficulty wringing confessions from dead men, my lord.'

Gotrek slashed at the guards and they danced back out of the way. He and Felix climbed on the first wagon. Felix took the reins.

Groot stepped in the way of the wagon. 'Be reasonable now, sirs. Turn yourselves in.'

'And face the witch hunters?' said Felix, flicking the reins. 'No fear.' The horses started slowly forward.

Groot backed away, then paced them. 'But you cannot hope to escape the city.'

'Want to bet on it?' said Gotrek.

'Hoy!' said an engineer as he noticed the wagon moving. 'What are you doing? That's the property of the College of Engineering! Get off of there!' He ran at them and tried to climb on board.

Gotrek shoved the man down. Felix slapped the reins again and the horses picked up speed. More engineers started running forward, joining the guards as they ran after them. Gotrek stood wide-legged in the wagon bed, snarling back at them as the wagon bumped and bounced.

'Close the gates!' called Groot, waving towards the front of the school. 'Call for the watch! Call for the army!'

The gate guards frowned and cupped their ears, momentarily uncomprehending, as the horses pounded towards them across the lawn.

'Close... the... gate!' screamed Groot.

The guards understood him at last and scrambled into action, running to the iron gates.

The wagon jolted over a low curb and fish-tailed through the gravel of the drive as Felix pointed the horses at the entrance. The guards pushed on the gates. They groaned, closing slowly, but picking up speed.

'Faster!' shouted Felix, and slapped the reins again.

The horses strained forward, stretching out into a gallop. It was going to be close.

'Hold on!' Felix called over his shoulder.

Gotrek grabbed the back of the driver's bench.

The horses shot the gap easily. Unfortunately, the sides of the wagon stuck out more than a foot to either side of them. The left front corner caught the closing edge of the left gate with a splintering crack, bending the ironwork and ripping away the wagon's left side. The wagon swerved crazily, banged sideways against the right gate, then straightened as the horses plunged into the street, screaming with fright and trying to get away from all the noise and violence behind them.

Felix pulled left on the reins and they careened down Commerce Street as students and labourers and fruit sellers scattered before them in terror. Faint and far behind he heard Groot calling, 'Open the gates! Open the gates!'

At the end of the street Felix turned left again and they thundered down the Wandstrasse, which paralleled the Altestadt wall. The gallop came to an abrupt end just before the Emmanuelleplatz, where it passed through the Great Gate into the Altestadt. The way was blocked by merchants and tradesmen in carts and on foot, all waiting to get through the gate to service their rich clients on the other side. Gotrek and Felix's stolen wagon could go no further.

Gotrek jumped down. 'Come on, manling.'

Felix hissed and climbed down gingerly, looking back down the Wandstrasse. Bobbing helmets glinted at the far end. The Gunnery School guards were still coming. He limped after Gotrek as he turned left onto the Emmanuelleplatz. The towers of the College of Engineering loomed over the street, half way down, casting a long shadow over the tenements on the other side. Gotrek and Felix crossed the street, pushing through the crowds, and hurried to the entrance to the college.

The sergeant at the gate stepped out as they entered. 'Professor Makaisson is gone, sirs. Left with the airship. I'm afraid I can't...'

'It's all right, sergeant,' said Felix, over his shoulder as Gotrek stumped on unheeding. 'We... we're just collecting our belongings. Won't be a minute.'

He pressed after Gotrek before the sergeant could reply.

Inside the main building they wound their way through the maze of corridors and stairwells towards the roof.

As they passed near Makaisson's workshop, a few of the students gave them cheery salutes, then stared after them when they saw the condition they were in.

Gotrek pointed his axe at one. 'Where's the clumsy one? The blind one?'

The student shrank from the axe, and undoubtedly from the smell and Gotrek's blisters as well. 'Who? D'ye mean Petr?'

'Aye. Him. Where is he?'

'He, ah, he went with Professor Makaisson,' said the student, quaking. 'In the airship.'

'You'll do, then,' said Gotrek, advancing on him. 'Is the gyrocopter fuelled? Is it ready to fly?'

'I... I don't know.' The student cowered back against the wall. 'Professor doesn't let us touch it.'

'Where is the black water stored?' Gotrek barked.

'On the roof,' said the student. 'Please don't kill me.'

Gotrek grunted and pushed past him, striding towards the stairs.

'But it's locked up!' the student called after him. 'You have to get the key from the supply steward.'

Gotrek snorted and started up the stairs. As he made to follow, Felix heard a commotion coming from outside – raised voices and angry argument. It sounded like the Gunnery School guards had reached the college and were arguing with their counterparts at the college gate. He hurried on, groaning with each step. There was no place on his body that didn't hurt.

Three weary flights later he stepped panting onto the long, narrow roof. Gotrek was waiting to close the door.

'They're coming,' Felix gasped.

'I heard them, manling,' said Gotrek.

The Slayer looked around the roof. A sturdy cart loaded with heavy brass tanks labelled 'Heberluft' sat at one side. He stepped to it, grasped the handles, and pushed at it, angling it around. Felix pushed too, though he wasn't sure he was helping. Over the sound of the wheels grinding across the copper sheeting he heard a swarm of footsteps pounding up the stairs. Gotrek pushed harder, wrenching on the handles to bring the cart into position.

Just as they eased it side-on to the stairwell door, the door banged open half an inch and slammed against the cart. Fists pounded and knocked on the wooden panels.

'In the name of Countess Emmanuelle, open this door!' said an angry voice.

'You are under arrest!' bawled another.

Gotrek laughed and stumped to a padlocked shed halfway along the roof. He slashed at the lock with his axe and it fell in pieces.

Felix looked back as he heard banging and smashing behind him. The men in the stairwell were attacking the door. It rattled and shook.

Gotrek entered the shed, then returned a moment later carrying two brass tanks and a tin funnel. He lugged them to the gyrocopter, which was tied down with ropes at the far end of the roof. Felix followed, eyeing the flimsy-looking machine warily, as Gotrek chopped through its ropes and threw them aside. The thing only had one seat.

'Are you certain this will carry both of us?' he asked.

'No,' said Gotrek.

He uncapped a brass tank behind the pilot's seat, stuck the funnel in, and began to pour in the black water. The smell made Felix's eyes burn.

'We might not have enough fuel either,' said the Slayer, squinting towards the western horizon. Felix followed his gaze. The *Spirit of Grungni* had disappeared behind the clouds.

Gotrek looked in the cockpit. 'Take out those grenades,' he said, pointing with his bearded chin. 'That'll shed some weight. And find me a spanner. We'll have the cannon off too.'

Felix looked back at the door again. 'Do we have time?'

'The boiler takes ten minutes to build up steam,' said Gotrek, setting down the empty fuel can. 'We can't leave before then.'

'Ten minutes!' Felix cried. He had vague memories of what a boiler was from the lessons Makaisson had given him long ago, but couldn't remember exactly what it did. Whatever it was, he didn't think it was going to do it fast enough. He looked to the door again. An axe blade bit through timbers. It would never last ten minutes. 'We'll be knee deep in Gunnery School guards by then.'

'Just find a spanner.'

Gotrek pulled flint, steel and a curl of tinder paper from his belt pouch as Felix limped back towards the shed. Felix cringed as he heard a *whump* of flame, but when he looked back, Gotrek was closing a door in the side of the machine as if nothing was amiss.

There were no spanners in the fuel shed, but as Felix stepped out again, he noticed a half-dismantled contraption just to his left. It looked like some sort of telescope, or perhaps an experimental catapult. Rusty parts and tools were scattered all around it like fallen leaves. Felix hurried to it and scooped up as many tools as he could carry.

He ran back and spilled them at Gotrek's feet. 'Will these do?'

'Aye, fine. Now remove the grenades.' Gotrek took up a spanner and a pry bar and rolled under the front of the gyrocopter, from which a stubby cannon sprouted. 'And watch the gauge on the side of the tank,' he said as he reached up into the machines innards. 'When the needle points straight up, we're away.'

Felix peered at the gauge. The needle pointed left, parallel to the ground, but was rising slowly, in quivering starts and stops. He looked back to the door. There was a long, narrow hole in it, and axes and swords hacked at it from the other side.

Lord Groot's voice came through it, rising over the clamour. 'Come now, Herr Jaeger! Herr Gurnisson! Give yourselves up! You have no chance of escape!'

Felix swallowed as he leaned into the cockpit and began gingerly taking the heavy black iron spheres from the racks that held them.

He set them carefully on the roof. He remembered too well how deadly and unpredictable the little bombs were. Images of Borek's bespectacled nephew Varek handling them as if they were harmless toys flashed through his mind and made him shiver. And thinking of Varek reminded him of how the young dwarf scholar had died – by crashing a gyrocopter just like this one into the flank of a Chaos-twisted dragon. Felix's shiver turned into full-fledged trembling.

Under the gyrocopter there was a clang, and Gotrek cursed. 'Give me a bigger spanner, manling. And a hammer.'

Felix sorted through the tools and put a huge spanner and a ball-headed hammer into Gotrek's outstretched hand. They disappeared under the gyrocopter and it began to shake as a deafening banging rang across the roof.

Felix checked the gauge again as he resumed unloading the grenades. He moaned. The needle hadn't raised more than a hair's width, and the guards would be through the door at any moment. Of course, they would still have some difficulty after that, having to climb over the cart or under it, but just one man with a pistol would be enough to end Gotrek and Felix's flight before it began.

He looked at the grenade in his hand. That would be one way to solve the problem. One grenade under those lift-gas tanks and everything on that side of the roof would be blown to the four winds. If only it were orcs or mutants or ratmen on the other side of the door instead of Imperial citizens. If he were the black-hearted villain Ostwald and Groot and everybody else in Nuln apparently thought he was, he would have had no qualms about killing them all. Alas, tempting as it was, he was no killer, at least not of innocent men – at least, he thought with a shudder of guilt as he remembered the columns of smoke rising over Shantytown, not on purpose. He was not going to change that now.

He sighed and placed the grenade next to the others, then paused and looked again towards the door. So the men behind it thought him a bloodthirsty killer, capable of anything, did they? Why not use that to his advantage? He grinned and picked up the grenade again.

'I'll be back,' he said, then started to the door.

Gotrek just grunted. The banging from under the gyrocopter continued.

Felix stopped about ten paces from the lift-gas cart. The hole in the door was bigger than a Verenan tome of law now. 'Groot!' he called. 'Lord Groot! Show yourself! I want to talk!'

There was a babble of voices behind the door, and the chopping and banging slowed to a stop. After a second, Groot's face appeared behind the hole, eyes wide and nervous.

'Herr Jaeger?' said Groot. 'You wish to speak to me? Did you wish to give yourself up?'

'No,' said Felix. 'I just wanted to say goodbye.' He raised the grenade so Groot could see it, then mimed jerking the pin out, and rolled the bomb under the cart.

Groot shrieked and disappeared from the hole.

'A bomb! A bomb!' came his scream. 'Down the stairs! Down the stairs! Hurry!'

The sounds of bedlam came through the door – bellows and shouts, the clank and clatter of dropped weapons, the thud of boots and falling bodies.

Felix laughed, then felt ashamed. It was a cruel trick, but when the alternative was murder? He shrugged and limped quickly back to the gyrocopter.

The needle was climbing steadily. It was less than the width of his finger away from straight up. Felix quickly removed the remaining grenades, then looked over the machine again. He frowned. Lightening the load was all very well, but there was still only one seat.

'Where am I to sit?'

'On your arse,' growled Gotrek.

A heavy thud came from under the gyrocopter. Felix looked down. Gotrek was rolling out from under it. The cannon lay on the roof, surrounded by brass lugs.

The Slayer stood and scowled at the gyrocopter, scratching his scalp through his matted crest. 'Hmmm. You'll have to sit behind me, or the balance won't be right.'

Felix looked into the cockpit, frowning. 'But there's no room behind your seat.'

'Aye,' said Gotrek. 'You'll have to sit on the cowling.'

'The cowling?' said Felix. He didn't know the word. 'You mean on top of it? On the outside?'

'Aye,' said Gotrek again. 'It's the only way.' He checked the gauge. 'It's ready. Get on.'

'No no!' said Felix. 'I won't! The airship was bad enough! I'm not going to flit through the sky clinging to the back of a mechanical dragonfly! It's impossible!'

'Use some rope, then.'

'Rope! And what if we crash? Or explode? How will I get away?'

'Stay behind, then,' said Gotrek, starting to climb up the wooden step ladder to the cockpit. 'Do what you want. I'm flying.'

There was a loud crack and something whistled past Felix's ear. He ducked behind the gyrocopter and looked towards the stairwell door. The muzzle of a long gun was withdrawing through the hole.

'Try to blow us up, will you?' came an angry voice. 'Fiends of Chaos!'

Felix groaned. His ruse hadn't bought them as much time as he'd hoped. Another gun poked through the hole, and another ball whizzed past.

Felix swallowed convulsively. 'I'll… I'll get the rope.' He darted out from cover, snatched up one of the ropes that had held down the gyrocopter, then clambered up onto the machine, feeling horribly exposed. He sat down on the skin of it, his back against the column from which rose the spindle that held the three very flimsy looking lift blades. He started lashing himself to it as Gotrek lowered the second canister of black water into the cockpit and climbed in after it.

There was a splintering crash from the far end of the roof. Felix looked up. The door had come down at last. Men with swords and guns were squirming under and over the lift gas wagon.

'Hurry!' he said.

'Easy, manling,' said Gotrek, situating himself and running his hands over the controls. 'I haven't flown one of these in over a century.' He murmured to himself. 'Gear engage. Rudder. Forward down. Backward up. Aye, that's the way of it. Right.' He reached forward, released a lock, and pulled slowly back on a lever. 'Hold on.'

With a hiss of steam and a clunk of pistons, the blades over Felix's head began very slowly to spin. Too slowly.

More guards were pushing out from under the wagon. They stood and fired their guns. Balls whistled past on all sides of Felix. One ricocheted off the fuel tank.

The blades turned faster and faster, making the machine rock and vibrate like a living thing. The first guards knelt and reloaded as more crawled under the cart onto the roof and ran towards them.

Up up up, thought Felix to himself, willing the gyrocopter to fly. *Up up up, damn you!*

As Gotrek pulled the lever all the way back, the rhythmic thump of the blades smoothed out into a steady roar. The gyrocopter shimmied and danced, like a kite straining against its string in a high wind.

The handgunners were standing and aiming again, shoulder to shoulder. A guard ran directly at Felix, sword held high.

'Up!' shouted Felix, terrified.

The long guns cracked. Gotrek pulled backward on the rudder stick. The gyrocopter leaped sideways up into the sky over the bullets. The runners clubbed the sprinting guard to the roof.

Felix flopped over to one side, clutching futilely at the machine's smooth exterior. The ropes cut painfully into his wounded ribs, but at least they held. Gotrek corrected his tilt and the gyrocopter zigged violently back the other way, throwing Felix against the ropes on the other side.

'Controls are a bit sensitive,' shouted Gotrek over the prop wash.

'Really?' moaned Felix.

Vertigo churned his guts as the machine veered over the edge of the roof and his eyes zoomed down the side of the building to the court yard below. With a sickening lurch the gyrocopter dropped and the ground shot up at him. He screamed. He and Gotrek were too heavy. They had overburdened the thing. The blades couldn't keep them airborne. They were going to smash on the flagstones and die!

Gotrek pulled back on the rudder and brought them up short, about twenty feet above the ground. Felix's crotch slammed painfully down onto the fuselage. The world dimmed as he curled forward in agony.

'I think I've got it now,' called Gotrek over his shoulder.

'Oh… good,' said Felix, clutching himself.

He sagged wearily against the ropes as Gotrek manipulated the controls – more gently this time – and the gyrocopter wobbled forward, glancing off a chimney as it rose over the tenements across from the college and started unsteadily across the city.

AFTER A WHILE even terror gives way to boredom.

At first Felix flinched at every dip and swoop that the tiny airship made, his stomach and bowels threatening to void themselves with every midair shimmy. Gotrek might have been the greatest warrior of his age, but he was a middling pilot at best. He flew dangerously close to spires and towers, and seemed to have difficulty staying high enough to clear the rooftops.

Things got better once they passed over the Nuln city walls and started flying above the countryside – there were fewer things to hit – but the machine seemed to be straining to carry them, and Gotrek constantly had to correct their altitude so they wouldn't plough into the tops of trees.

Flying like this was infinitely worse than flying in the *Spirit of Grungni*, Felix decided. He had hated that too, at first – terrified of the unnatural feeling of floating high above the ground – but once he had understood how the cells of lift gas worked, and how resilient the gondola was, he had accepted the fact that it probably wouldn't fall out of the air at a moment's notice, and had come to enjoy it. This horrid contraption was another matter entirely. Here he was exposed to the wind and the cold and the weather, and the only things that held him up were three delicate spinning blades powered by a steam engine that might stutter and die at any moment. That was what had been so reassuring about the *Spirit of Grungni*. Even if its engines stopped, it would remain floating in the air. If the gyrocopter's engines stopped, it would plummet to the ground like a cow dropped from a battlement.

But after the first hour, his terror faded to a dull tension that settled in his shoulders and made them ache. He watched listlessly as the endless green of the Reikwald scrolled past below them and the sun rose higher behind them. His mind, which until they had risen off the roof and out of the clutches of their pursuers, had been entirely occupied with either chasing or escaping their various enemies, began to think back over recent events and link together things that had, at the time, seemed unconnected.

The tainting of the cannons with powdered warpstone explained so much. The Gunnery School guard who had been hanged as a mutant, and the other who had gone insane and said that the cannons were looking at him – the poor fellows must have been warped by the tainted guns they had been guarding. The cannon that had exploded on the testing range – the addition of the warpstone dust must have caused a fatal flaw in the casting. The riot on the bridge that had ended with the cannon being pushed into the river – the Cleansing Flame must have orchestrated it so that the smiths of the Gunnery School couldn't examine the cannon closely and discover the taint. Wissen's insistence that the cultists wait until the new gun had been test fired before blowing up the Gunnery School – he wanted to be sure the last tainted gun didn't blow up like the other had, and so would be able to do its evil work in Middenheim.

It occurred to Felix that the explosion of the cannon on the testing range must have been just as frustrating for Wissen and the Cleansing Flame as it was for Gotrek and Malakai and the others. If the gun had fired successfully, the *Grungni* would have been away that same afternoon, and the shipment of tainted cannon would have reached Middenheim days ago. Had that happened, the mountaintop city might have already fallen to Archaon's hordes!

For a moment Wissen's other actions puzzled Felix. Why had the leader of the Brotherhood of the Cleansing Flame, in his guise as Ward Captain of the Nuln Watch, persecuted the Cleansing Flame so strongly? Why had he gone into Shantytown and beaten and arrested so many people? Was it only to deflect suspicion that he might be a cultist himself? Felix didn't think so. No one had had any reason to suspect Wissen anyway. On the other hand, what better way to make the people rise up against the brutality of the watch than to command the watch to commit worse and worse brutalities? The common people who Wissen, when he wore the yellow mask of the Brotherhood of the Cleansing Flame, stirred up against 'the vicious bullies of the city watch', had no idea that, unmasked, he was the very same Ward Captain Wissen that rousted them out of their beds and beat and arrested their sons for crimes they didn't commit. It was a brilliant scheme. Wissen had driven the common folk towards Chaos with a gauntleted right hand, and then changed masks and lured them to it with a welcoming left hand.

One thing Felix could still not explain. Magus Lichtmann had said that he had sensed no magical energy at the testing range after the cannon had exploded. Why hadn't he sensed the warpstone? Had another sorcerer cloaked its presence somehow? The old man in the basket perhaps? Or was it that Lichtmann wasn't much of a sorcerer? He had seemed more of an engineer to Felix.

'When will we catch up to them?' Felix called to Gotrek.

Gotrek shrugged. 'Not soon. It will take hours even after we see them.'

Felix nodded glumly. And what if they never saw them? It was hard to believe they were travelling fast enough. And what if they were blown off course? What if the *Spirit of Grungni* had been? It had happened before. Twice! He said none of this to Gotrek. He would only get sarcasm in return. He sighed. Hours. His rump and legs were already aching abominably, not to mention the rest of his battered and bruised and sewer-drenched body. He glared enviously at the comfortable cushioned seat Gotrek sat on. It was going to be a long flight.

'MANLING, WAKE UP.'

Felix moaned and opened his eyes, and yelped! He was falling! The ground was a mile away! He... No. No. Now he remembered. He was on the dwarf gyrocopter. He and Gotrek were flying, not falling. He was hanging sideways, leaning against the ropes that held him to the spindle column. He sat up with a groan. Every bone and muscle in his body ached, as if he had been beaten to within an inch of his life. He paused. That was probably because he had been beaten to within an inch of his life. When had he last slept? In a bed? With pillows? Ah, pillows. Pillows were nice. Those clouds looked like pillows.

'Manling!'

Felix jerked. He had drifted off again. 'Aye?' He blinked around. They were still over the Reikwald – or was it the Drakwald now? From the position of the sun, it appeared an hour or so before noon. His cheeks burned from wind and sun. In front of him, Gotrek was wrestling the canister of black water out from between his legs. He lifted it over his head one handed and reached it back towards Felix.

'Take this and fill the reservoir,' he said. 'You'll need the funnel.'

Felix grabbed the canister, and almost dropped it! It was ridiculously heavy.

'Easy!' barked Gotrek. 'We're sunk without that.'

Felix hugged it to his chest like a lover and took the funnel that Gotrek handed back to him. He held onto it with one hand, then leaned forward against his ropes and stretched out his hand. The fuel reservoir's cap was almost out of reach. He unscrewed it with the tips of his fingers, and then fumbled it. It fell, then jerked to a stop and dangled at the end of a chain. Felix breathed a sigh of relief. Dwarfs thought of everything.

He stuck the funnel in the tank, then leaned out to the limit of his ropes and inched the canister forward, resting it on the fuselage. Any sudden moves and he would lose his grip. He tipped it down and black liquid poured from the spout and gurgled into the funnel.

'Ha!' said Gotrek.

Felix jerked and almost dropped the canister. The stream of black water splashed everywhere. 'What!' he said, looking around. 'What's wrong?'

'The *Spirit of Grungni*,' said Gotrek.

Felix raised his head and scanned ahead. Far in front of them and a little to their north, a long black oblong shape hung in the air, just below the clouds.

'At last,' said Felix. He let out a breath he hadn't known he was holding. They had found it after all. He returned to filling the reservoir.

IT TOOK AN agonisingly long time to close with the *Spirit of Grungni*, and the frustration was made worse because it was *right there*, directly ahead of them, and yet never seemed to get any closer. The sun climbed to its noon apex and sank an hour past it and they were still miles away. He kept hoping to see it turn about, or to see some other signal that the crew had spotted them, but it didn't happen.

Felix realized that he had been thinking of the *Spirit of Grungni* as their journey's end, but it wasn't, was it? What did they do then?

Did they return the cannons to Nuln? Did they fly due west and drop them in the sea? How did one safely dispose of a warpstone tainted cannon anyway? Did they go on to Middenheim and try to discover who this 'master' was that Wissen had mentioned?

Felix wondered who the master could be. He would have to be a fairly powerful wizard to bring the guns to life the way Wissen had described. Someone already in Middenheim? A sudden thought made Felix's heart lurch. Max Schreiber! Malakai had said their old companion was there, helping with the defences. Could it be him? Felix had always been slightly suspicious of him. Certainly he had always seemed to fight on the side of the Empire and humanity, but there was also no denying he enjoyed his power, and had seemed at times tempted to use it for personal goals, rather than for the good of all. Had the years and his constant contact with the winds of magic twisted him in some way? Had he succumbed to the lure of Chaos at last? Felix shivered. Max must be a Wizard Lord by now. He did not look forward to facing him in a fight, and if he had turned traitor, Felix had no doubt that he would indeed be fighting him, because Gotrek would not suffer him to live.

At last, with the sun halfway down the sky and glaring in Felix's eyes, the *Spirit of Grungni* loomed ahead and above them like a great black cloud.

Felix gazed up at it in wonder as Gotrek tilted the rudder stick back and they rose slowly towards it. He had never seen it like this before. He had been in it, looking out, and seen it flying from the ground, but there was something beautiful and wonderful about seeing it as a bird would, passing under the riveted brass gondola, rising up beside it, like a salmon pacing a whale, hearing the thrumming of the cables that fixed the gondola to the rigid balloon above it. Who could have imagined that so incredible a thing existed in the world?

Gotrek angled the gyrocopter to cross in front of the *Grungni's* gondola, then held it steady as best he could before it. Felix waved at the large viewing ports that looked into the command deck. He saw young men shouting and pointing at them, and then the broad, squat figure of Malakai stepped to the port and stared out, a look of confusion and concern on his usually cheerful face. Magus Lichtmann joined him at the glass. He gaped, his eyes agog behind his spectacles.

Malakai turned and barked some order to his human crew, then waved at Gotrek and Felix and motioned for them to circle behind the airship. Gotrek saluted, then turned the gyrocopter and angled off to buzz down the airship's side.

In the stern of the *Spirit of Grungni*, a brass door like a draw-bridge was lowered on chains, revealing a narrow hangar constructed of bare metal bulkheads. Another gyrocopter was parked on the metal deck at the far end. Felix didn't understand how it had got in there, for the door looked barely big enough to admit two men walking abreast, let alone a contraption almost as tall as two men, with a wing span considerably wider than that. None the less, Petr, the wild-haired young engineering student, was waving them on as if he had every confidence that they would fit though the gap.

Gotrek tipped the rudder stick forward and they approached it rapidly, too rapidly!

'Slow! Slow down!' cried Felix. 'You'll wreck us!'

'I know what I'm doing,' Gotrek muttered, but he eased back on the stick a little just the same.

The door appeared to get slightly bigger as they approached, but not by much. Felix held his breath as Gotrek nosed the gyrocopter ahead in little fits and starts, raising it and lowering it, then raising it again, as he judged the height of the door and Petr waved his hands this way and that. Finally the Slayer pushed in decisively, and almost precisely.

There was a great clanging racket and the gyrocopter slammed to the deck hard enough to snap Felix's teeth together. He covered his head and looked up. One of the rotor blades was bent, and the whole rotor assembly wobbled in a slow off kilter circle. He looked back at the door. There was a bright gouge in the metal of the frame on the right side.

'Welcome, sirs!' cried Petr, hurrying forward with a wooden step ladder. He tripped over a riveted seam in the deck and the ladder flew out of his hands as he tried to regain his balance. He fetched up face first against the gyrocopter's flank. 'Sorry. Sorry. No harm done.'

He scrabbled under the fuselage, found the ladder and set it up next to the cockpit. 'Welcome to the *Spirit of Grungni*, sirs.' His fore-head was bleeding.

'Ah, thank you, Petr,' said Felix. It was a wonder the airship hadn't gone down with all hands, with this walking disaster on board.

Malakai slid down a ladder into the hangar, then turned, scowling as he crossed towards Gotrek. 'What in Grimnir's name is this? Did ye come all this way just tae wreck yin of my flyin'...?' He choked when he got a close look at the Slayer's face. 'By my ancestor's ancestors, what's happened to ye, Gurnisson? Ye don't look well.'

'Mutants,' said Gotrek, as he climbed stiffly down from the cockpit. 'Now, turn about,' he said. 'The guns are sabotaged.'

'Whit?' said Malakai, raising a shaggy eyebrow. 'Sabotaged? What dae ye mean? They were tested. Passed by the school.'

Magus Lichtmann came carefully down the ladder behind him, his one hand letting go of one rung, then quickly catching hold of the next before he fell.

'Tainted,' said Felix, untying himself from the spindle pillar and sliding down the fuselage to the deck. His stiff muscles screamed as he landed, stabbing pain shooting through them and almost dropping him to his knees. He clutched the side of the gyrocopter for support. 'Warpstone, mixed into the molten iron. We saw it happen, though we didn't know it.' He stood straight, wincing and grimacing. 'The initiate who poured the ashes of the gun captain into the crucible was a secret cultist, a member of the Brotherhood of the Cleansing Flame. There was powdered warpstone mixed into the ashes.'

Petr and the other crewmembers who were lashing Gotrek and Felix's gyrocopter to the deck gaped, horrified.

Malakai looked aghast. 'Can it be true? But why would they dae it? To whit purpose?'

Felix shook his head wearily. 'I don't know many details. Wissen died too quickly to tell us, but...'

'Captain Wissen is dead?' asked Magus Lichtmann, stepping forward alarmed.

Felix nodded. 'Aye. Another cultist. One of the leaders of the cult. We stopped him and his minions from blowing up the Gunnery School.'

'Did you?' said Lichtmann, all agog. 'By the gods!'

'Wissen was a cultist?' said Malakai. He made a face. 'Ah, weel, never did like the wee stuck-up numpty, anyhow.'

'He said that some "master" was to wake the guns once they were in place on the walls of Middenheim,' continued Felix. 'And that the guns would drive their crews mad and cause them to turn them on the defenders.'

'Wake the guns?' Malakai gaped again and turned to Gotrek, as if for assurance. The Slayer nodded.

The engineer opened his mouth and closed it a few times, momentarily unable to put his horror and outrage into words. 'It's no' right!' he said at last. 'Befouling cannon wi' black sorcery! Makin' instruments o' Chaos out o' the purr wee things! The villains! I'll no hae it! It's as bad as the Dawi Zharr and yon daemon gun!' He turned and started for the ladder, his jaw thrust forward. 'Right. We're turnin' about. Make all fast.'

'Professor Makaisson,' called Magus Lichtmann after him.

Malakai stopped and looked back. 'Aye, what is it, magus? Make it quick.'

Magus Lichtmann unpinned his empty right sleeve and pulled it up to his shoulder, revealing a stump tightly bound in linen bandages. 'We will not turn back,' he said calmly. 'We will continue on to Middenheim, and deliver the guns as we have been contracted to do.'

'Whit?' said Malakai. 'Are ye saft in the heid, laddie? Have ye no' heard what's jist been said? Why would ye wannae dae that?'

'Because,' said Lichtmann, tugging at the bandages, 'I am the master.' There was a ripping sound, and the bandages loosened, then uncoiled and dropped to the floor. Beneath them was, not a stump, but something black and dry and crusted. It unfolded with sinewy grace, revealing itself to be a skinny black arm, which crawled with lines of glowing red, like an embered log. Flame yellow claws tipped each of the long, skeletal fingers.

Felix stared at the unnatural appendage, as did Malakai and his crew.

Gotrek cursed, and started forward, head lowered, drawing his axe off his back. 'Warlock,' he spat. 'You die here.' With his face blistered and his body burned and covered in scabbing wounds and filth, the Slayer looked like something escaped from hell.

'I think not.' Magus Lichtmann stepped back through the door that led to the cargo hold and thrust his claw forward. The air before it rippled like waves of heat rising from a tar roof. The fuel reservoirs of the two gyrocopters exploded in billowing balls of flame.

CHAPTER NINETEEN

Felix flew heels over head and slammed into the bulkhead as fire blossomed above him. His head rang like a gong. Burning shrapnel rattled against the metal walls and rained down on him, starting his clothes on fire. He was too stunned to beat out the flames – too stunned to move. He felt like he had been slapped by a giant. His whole body throbbed. Gotrek lay on his back beside him, his one eye blinking up at the roof, his beard and crest smouldering.

The boiling fire dissipated as quickly as it had come, but the ruin it had caused remained. Three of Malakai's crew, who had been standing next to the *Spirit of Grungni's* gyrocopter, were dead, blasted into chunks of meat that were strewn across half the hangar deck. Had Felix and Gotrek not expended almost all of their machine's fuel chasing the airship, they would have been dead too. As it was, the explosion of their gyrocopter was miniscule compared to the fully fuelled one.

Felix raised his head and looked around. Petr lay in a heap beside him, struggling to get up, a deep laceration opening his left forearm to the bone. In the ceiling above, crewmen on the upper deck were gaping down through the ladder hatch at the carnage and calling out to Malakai. The stunned Slayer engineer was in the clutches of Lichtmann, who stood in the cargo hold door, hauling him to his feet with surprising strength. He put a long flame-shaped golden dagger to Makaisson's neck. The edges of it shimmered like heat waves over a hot roof.

'I regret the destruction of such fine machines,' said the magus. 'But no one must be allowed to bring word before we reach our goal. Now, Makaisson, have these two heroes thrown out of the door and maintain course to Middenheim, or I shall be forced to kill you.'

Malakai laughed up at him, eyes wild. 'Ye eejit! I'm a Slayer! D'ye think ah care if ah die?'

He lashed out with a booted foot and kicked Lichtmann between the legs. The magus squeaked and staggered back against the railing of the landing that looked over the cargo hold, gasping and holding himself as more of Malakai's crew slid down the ladder from above, armed with swords, hammers and huge spanners.

Felix saw Malakai stride through the cargo hold door and punch Lichtmann in the jaw with his massive fist. Lichtmann flipped backward over the rail and dropped out of Felix's sight, hitting the floor of the cargo hold with a satisfying clang. Malakai's crewmen pushed through into the hold to stand at their captain's side. Gotrek staggered up and started after them. The runes on the head of his axe glowed cherry red.

Felix groaned and levered himself up to follow. Lichtmann. Why hadn't he thought of Lichtmann? Perhaps because the man had hardly seemed a sorcerer – more a scholarly engineer. The hangar spun sickeningly around Felix, and he had to steady himself against the bulkhead as he limped forward to the cargo hold door. Beside him, Petr picked himself up, moaning, and started after him, clutching his wounded arm.

The cargo hold was as wide as the airship, almost as long, and two decks deep. The door from the hangar opened onto a metal landing with stairs on the right that led down to the deck below. Just below the landing the cannons and mortars were chained to the deck in neat rows, and with their wheels securely blocked. Beyond them were crates of cannonballs, grape shot and other supplies, and beyond those, stacked against the far wall and roped in place, were the barrels of black powder. A pair of crewmen stood among the cargo, looking with wide eyes towards the action at the door.

Magus Lichtmann was just picking himself up behind a row of chained-down cannons as Felix limped into the hold behind Gotrek. The warlock's spectacles were smashed, and his gold-flecked green eyes, behind them, flashed with fury.

'You will come to regret that, engineer,' he said.

Gotrek made to launch himself over the rail, but Malakai threw out a hand.

'No! This yin's mine.' he said, taking a hammer from one of his crew. 'I want this two-faced gowk's head on a platter.' He tsked angrily and started for the stairs. 'Callin' me friend. Takin' an interest in my designs...'

Lichtmann opened his mouth and spat out a stream of harsh foreign syllables, his black hand twisting and thrusting at Malakai and Gotrek. Felix and the students cringed away as a blast of pink fire shot at the Slayers. Felix felt the edges of the spell, flames of fury and madness that boiled up in his head and made him want to kill everyone around him, but Gotrek and Malakai didn't even flinch. The Slayer laughed.

'Ye fool,' sneered Malakai. 'Will a dwarf succumb to magic? Bah!'

Lichtmann backed away, squeezing through the next rank of cannon. 'Then I must try more pedestrian means. Grieg!'

Malakai frowned and looked around. One of the engineering students cracked him between the eyes with a heavy spanner as long as a sword. The engineer staggered and the student caught him again hard over the ear. Malakai hit the floor in a loose flop.

'No!' cried Petr, and leapt at Grieg. The other students followed.

Gotrek roared and launched himself over the rail at Lichtmann, axe held high. The magus fell back, crying out a vile word, and a shimmer of purple snapped into existence between him and the Slayer. Gotrek strode towards him.

On the landing, Petr tripped, knocking the traitorous student into the railing as the murderous spanner swished over his head. The other crewmen swarmed Grieg, and it seemed that the effects of Lichtmann's spell still lingered, for they hacked at him unmercifully with their hatchets and tools.

Gotrek's axe smashed into the warlock's magical barrier and it exploded in pink sparks. Lichtmann flew back a dozen paces at the impact, as if hit by a wave, and crashed to the deck behind another rank of cannon. Gotrek started after him. The crewmen who had been crouching amidst the crates moved towards the sorcerer too, drawing hand axes. Felix crept down the stairs and started edging along the right bulkhead.

Lichtmann lurched up beyond the second line of cannons, glaring at Gotrek, his spectacles gone and his eyes glowing with a hellish inner light. 'That is indeed a mighty axe,' he said. 'It deserves a mighty opponent.'

He spread his arms and raised his voice in an ear-gouging screech of arcane verse. The flame-shaped dagger glinted and rippled in his left hand. His blackened right hand glowed red from within. Flickers of purple and gold light flashed in the air around him.

Gotrek clambered over the line of cannon as the two brave crewmen leapt at Lichtmann's back, hatchets high.

Lichtmann spun like a dancer, dodging their attacks, then lashed out at their throats with two graceful flicks of his golden dagger, all the while screaming his vile incantation. The men staggered past him and, as Felix stared in horror, their heads toppled from their necks and great jets of blood sprayed from the stumps in all directions, showering the nearby cannons and mortars in a red rain before their bodies collapsed to the deck. How could so slight a blade and so thin a man have made such horrible wounds? It seemed impossible.

Gotrek charged, roaring and swinging his axe. Lichtmann dodged nimbly back around a mortar and the Slayer's blow glanced off iron. He continued after the warlock, slow but implacable.

Felix started forward too, but as he moved closer, he heard a strange hissing and bubbling. His eyes followed the sound to the guns, and he stared at what he saw, the hairs rising on the back of his neck. The blood of Lichtmann's victims was sinking into the iron. The cannons and mortars were absorbing it like sponges, and a green glow began to shimmer from them. The chains that held them rattled and shook.

'Gotrek?' Felix called, uneasily.

Gotrek ignored him. He was too busy stalking Lichtmann through the maze of guns.

The warlock's incantation was reaching a crescendo. He gashed his unmutated arm with the gold dagger, then raised both arms over his head as blood welled from the cut. With a final cataclysmic syllable, he pressed his arms together. The blackened flesh touched the bleeding wound. There was a sizzling hiss, and the scent of burned flesh, and Lichtmann cried out, doubling up in pain.

Gotrek rushed him, but the sorcerer threw himself backward over a cannon and crashed down behind it. Felix hurried forward. Lichtmann was down. This could be their chance.

But before he could reach him, he gagged and stumbled, eyes watering. The air was suddenly full of the scent of sulphur and spoiled meat, and there was a noise in the centre of the room like stew on the boil.

Felix looked up through his tears. Gotrek turned.

The blooded guns were glowing brighter now – a pulsating green corona that hurt the eyes. Arcs of arcane energy leapt between them, humming and crackling, and growing stronger by the second. Felix's

skin crawled as the feeling that the guns were looking at him overcame him. Their malevolence was tangible.

Gotrek spat, 'Sorcery.'

There was movement in the midst of the guns. The bodies of the
men Lichtmann had sacrificed were twitching and flopping like
dying fish as blood gushed from their severed necks in arcing
streams. There was too much blood. Gallons of it. Human bodies
did not contain so much blood. It made a spreading pool on the
deck in the centre of the big guns.

Felix stepped back involuntarily as the pool began to bubble and
splash. The smell of sulphur and death got thicker, and Felix's sense
of foreboding became a cloud of oppression that threatened to
crush his soul. Foul whispers tickled his brain. The splashing blood
rose higher and higher, like some grisly ornamental fountain, until
it was the height of a man, and still it rose. At the same time, it
became more viscous, like red honey, and the streams became ropy
and thick. The students on the landing screamed in terror and
scrambled for the door.

'Sigmar save us,' choked Felix. 'What is it?'

'Food for my axe,' said Gotrek. He started towards the thing,
growling deep in his throat.

Felix wanted to scream and run as the students had, but knew that
he could not. His vow to Gotrek wouldn't allow it. He clamped
down on his sanity, willing the mad whispers to be silent. He
looked to where Lichtmann had fallen. The warlock was gone.

Felix turned, on guard, searching for him, and found him circling
on the other side of the Chaos thing, laughing maniacally. The
shapeless horror picked up the two dead crewmen with two dripping pseudopods, then drew them within the frothing, flowing
column of blood that was its body. The gore flowed all around the
corpses, taking on their structure – arms, legs, torsos – and thickening them with layers of red putrescence until the thing looked like
a pair of hulking, headless conjoined twins, fused at the spine,
made entirely of running red candle wax. Faces and mouths formed
on every part of the four-armed, four-legged horror, then melted
away again to appear elsewhere, and Felix heard screams of unimag-
inable anguish join the vile whispers in his brain. The thing had not
just consumed the crewmen's corpses, but their souls as well. He
shuddered.

'Malakai told me that you have been seeking your doom for many
years, Slayer,' Lichtmann called. 'Well, now you've found it.'

'Promises, promises,' growled Gotrek, pushing through the ranks
of cannon.

For once, Felix had reason to share Gotrek's scepticism. As huge and horrible as the thing was, he had seen the Slayer destroy bigger daemons before with little trouble. The daemon-powered siege towers that had threatened the walls of Praag during Arek Daemonclaw's invasion, for instance, had literally exploded at the merest touch of the his axe. This thing looked puny by comparison.

Gotrek charged it, slashing, and opened a great trench in its torso. The horror howled in agony as its gelatinous blood boiled away from the touch of the axe. Felix leapt back, expecting an explosion of gore and pink fire.

It didn't come. The wound melted together again as if it had never existed.

Gotrek blinked, nonplussed. An arm like a sack full of wet sand backhanded him across the face. He flew back, drenched in clotted red mucus, and slammed against a gun carriage. Felix ran to him, aghast. What had happened? The daemon should have vanished in a burst of brimstone.

'All right, Gotrek?'

Gotrek lifted his head. Stinking red slime ran down his face. He growled savagely, glaring at the thing with his single eye. 'Nothing's right with this filth.'

'You will not banish it so easily from this plane, Slayer!' cried Lichtmann from behind the horror. 'Not when the warpstone in the guns strengthens it. Not when the souls of the greatest sorcerers of the age will it to remain!'

Sorcerers? Felix didn't understand. He looked around, almost expecting a phalanx of wizards to step out from behind the cargo crates like the villains in a pantomime. 'What sorcerers are these?'

Gotrek wiped his blistered face with the back of his hand. 'They're in the guns, manling. More foul sorcery.' He pulled himself slowly to his feet.

'In the guns?' Felix said.

Lichtmann laughed. 'Do you think we would sully such fine weapons with the bones of mere soldiers? Some of the most powerful sorcerers of Tzeentch have sacrificed themselves to join with these guns. It was their ashes that were added to them. It is their wills that will turn the gunners of Middenheim against their brothers and bring the Fauschlag down from within.'

As Lichtmann spoke, the bubbling horror reached out its massive, constantly mutating arms to four of the glowing, pulsing cannon, while at the same time a ropy tentacle stretched out from its chest towards a mortar. As the dripping limbs touched the guns, their flowing crimson flesh spilled down over them, covering them, ingesting them. The arms and the tentacle strained and bulged. The chains that held down the cannons snapped, and the horror lifted them out of their carriages as if they were enormous armoured gauntlets. The long tentacle retracted, settling the mortar between the thing's powerful shoulders. Streams of crackling green bale-fire arced between the mortar and the four cannons, forming a glowing cage of eldritch power around the horror. It roared a challenge from a dozen melting mouths as the mortar swivelled towards Gotrek and Felix like the eye of a cyclops. Felix could feel its hate like heat from a furnace.

Gotrek ran at it. Felix gulped and followed, praying to Sigmar for strength. The daemon swung an iron arm. They slashed at it together. Felix's sword clanged off ineffectually and his hands throbbed painfully as it touched the green energy, but the Slayer's axe struck home. The thick slime of sulphurous red matter that covered the gun splashed away from the runed blade like mud after a stone has hit it, showing a bright wound on the cannon's polished surface, then flowed closed again instantly.

Two more iron arms struck down. Felix lurched back, barely in time, but Gotrek ducked them both, slashing for the horror's torso. The axe bit deep, finding white ribs beneath crimson flesh.

The horror howled and fell back. Behind it, Lichtmann thrust out his twisted arm and a ball of fire exploded around Gotrek. The Slayer staggered in the midst of the flames, and a third cannon grazed the top of his head, knocking him flat. He rolled away, smoking, as two more arms slammed down, smashing deep creases in the metal deck. He scrambled back out of range, putting the horror's massive bulk between him and Lichtmann.

'Kill the warlock, manling,' he said out of the side of his mouth. 'The daemon is mine.' A purple bruise was spreading across his scalp to the left of his crest.

'Aye,' said Felix, though he was less than enthusiastic about facing Lichtmann one on one. He looked around, hoping the others might be able to help, that Malakai had perhaps recovered. He had not. Petr and the other students were carrying the engineer's body through the door into the hangar. A thrill of fear went through Felix. Could Makaisson be dead?

Gotrek charged the horror again. Felix summoned his courage and sprinted at Lichtmann, hoping to run him down before he could complete another spell. No such luck. The warlock's charred arm blazed, and a blossom of flame shot at Felix.

Felix yelped and dived aside, crashing down behind a stack of crates and covering his face as the fire billowed above him. The cloud of fire evaporated. He raised his head. All around him the crates were burning. He rose to a crouch, sword at the ready, and looked through the flames. How was he supposed to kill Lichtmann if he couldn't reach him?

On the other side of the crates, Gotrek once again dodged through the horror's slime-covered iron arms and slashed at it, but this time he didn't aim at the limbs or its chest. This time he chopped at the arm just above one of the cannons. The axe hacked through the muck as if it was water, and the cannon dropped to the deck with a clang, flashing and sparking.

The daemon howled in agony, and for the merest instant its crimson flesh became translucent and insubstantial and all the other cannon it carried drooped, as if they had become too heavy for it. The green nimbus around them flickered and hissed. Gotrek pressed his attack, his eye gleaming feverishly.

Lichtmann screeched, horrified, and began carving symbols in the air.

Felix charged him, sword raised. Sigmar's blood! They were going to do it.

Lichtmann saw him coming. He made a circle with his black hand and suddenly a roaring ring of flame sprang up around him. Felix skidded to a stop, throwing up his hands as a wave of heat rushed over him.

Gotrek hacked off one of the horror's legs, then another. Its flesh became nearly transparent. It toppled, cannon dropping. Gotrek tried to spring clear, but one of the falling guns caught him a glancing blow on the shoulder, knocking him sprawling. Another cannon arm smashed through a crate. Cannonballs spilled across the deck. The horror landed on top of the wreckage, all its form lost.

Felix lunged at Lichtmann with his sword, trying to stab him through the wall of fire. He jerked back as the flames seared his arm. Lichtmann ignored him, his eyes on Gotrek. He began another incantation. Felix cursed and looked around for something to throw through the flames. There! One of the dead crewmen's hatchets lay on the deck not ten paces away. He ran towards it.

Gotrek pushed himself up, his shoulder torn and bloody. On the deck in front of him, bathed in the pulsing energy of the possessed guns, the horror was reassembling itself, its legs reconnecting with its torso and its arms once again absorbing the dropped cannon. The cannonballs it had fallen upon were disappearing into its flesh as well.

Gotrek stood and limped forward, hurrying to attack the thing before it completely recovered.

Felix picked up the hatchet as Lichtmann pointed his black claw at Gotrek, the embered cracks glowing.

'Gotrek! 'Ware!'

Gotrek looked up.

Felix hurled the hatchet at Lichtmann through the curtain of fire. It was a clumsy throw. The flat of the axe hit the warlock in the back. He stumbled, but still loosed the fireball.

The Slayer dived aside, rolling behind a mortar. The flames exploded above him.

Lichtmann turned on Felix, flames playing around his right hand. 'It's a pity we do not fight on the same side,' he said, starting forward, his circle of flames moving with him. 'Your bravery and resourcefulness are unquestionable.'

Felix backed away, dodging behind another stack of crates. 'It's a pity you fight on the side of ruin,' he called. He looked towards the Slayer, trying to see if he had survived the blast.

'What choice did I have?' Lichtmann asked, following. 'I would be a loyal son of the Empire yet, had my hand not begun to change. I did nothing to make it occur. I read no proscribed books. I learned no profane rituals. I followed my teachers' instructions to the letter, and *still* I changed.' An edge of anger crept into his voice.

Felix ran behind a pile of barrels.

Across the room, Gotrek staggered to his feet, beard and eyebrows smouldering.

The horror rose before him, once again solid and complete, its pulsing corona of balefire glowing brightly. It lumbered towards him, the cannonballs it had absorbed boiling and subsiding under its skin like black bubbles. It was as if Gotrek's axe had never touched it. The Slayer growled and rushed to meet it, undaunted. Steel rang on steel. Felix groaned as he watched. They were back where they started, only worse for wear.

Lichtmann stepped around the barrels, his ring of flames setting them on fire. 'Could I go to my professors and tell them my plight?' he continued conversationally, as Felix ran and dodged before him. 'Could I ask for mercy at the Temple of Sigmar? No. The only mercy the Empire gives its twisted children is the axe. What could I do? I wanted to live. I did not want my great mind to go to waste merely because one of my limbs had betrayed me.'

Felix squeezed in between two rows of crates as the sound of Gotrek's battle rang in his ears. This was madness. There was nowhere to go. The hold was too small.

Lichtmann circled the rows, looking for him. 'So when Archaon began his march south, I saw that, though I loathed him and his uncultured barbarian followers, his triumph was my only hope for survival.'

A loud clang made both Felix and Lichtmann turn. Gotrek was flying backwards through the air. He crashed down, shoulders first, on the barrel of a cannon, then slid to the floor, dazed.

As the horror slogged after him, the mortar that served it as a head sank into the roiling red protoplasm of its chest, like a bucket disappearing into a swamp.

Felix frowned. He didn't understand what it was doing.

Gotrek struggled to his feet and backed away through the guns while he recovered himself.

The mortar pushed up out of the horror's neck and swivelled towards Gotrek, strands of crimson slime clinging to it.

Felix still didn't understand. Then green fire flickered in the mortar's breach hole, and all became horrifyingly clear.

Gotrek saw the flash too, and dived away just as the mortar fired in a billowing burst of smoke and noise. The cannonball smashed through the right wheel of a cannon and punched a ragged hole in the deck right where the Slayer had been. Sunlight shone up through it.

'No!' shouted Lichtmann.

Felix could barely hear him over the ringing in his ears.

'Do not damage your brothers,' Lichtmann cried to the horror. 'They must be whole or they will not be placed on the walls of Middenheim.' He looked around the hold at all the fires he had started with his magic. 'In fact, we have caused too much damage already.' He stretched out his blackened claw, and the fires snuffed out one after the other.

Of course, thought Felix. Lichtmann has to protect the cannons or his plan won't succeed. And that made them perfect cover. Felix sprinted for the cluster of guns and ducked down behind one. Neither the warlock or the horror would dare to fire at him if he stayed among them.

Gotrek seemed to realise this too. He was back on his feet, beckoning to the daemon with a meaty hand. 'Come on, you overgrown nightmare. Come and face me steel to steel.'

The horror obliged him and waded into the maze of cannon, howling its fury from a multitude of mouths. The dwarf and the daemon clashed together deafeningly.

Felix turned and saw Lichtmann striding towards him, his flame-shaped dagger in his human hand. Felix readied his sword. This might be a fight he could win.

'Die, foul sorcerer!' shouted a voice from behind him.

Felix looked back. Petr and a few other students had returned to the landing, long guns and pistols levelled at Lichtmann. They fired.

Lichtmann threw up a warding hand and the bullets ricochetted off the air in front of him. Felix ducked. One went through his shirt sleeve. Several thwacked into the torso of the horror, to no effect. Others shot off at wild angles, bouncing all over the hold.

'Don't fire, curse you!' shouted Felix. 'You'll kill us all!'

Lichtmann laughed. 'Two can play at that game, fools.'

He sang out a string of profane words and raised his twisted arm. Fire flared from its embered cracks. The horror turned its mortar-head as its arms continued to batter at Gotrek.

'No!' shouted Felix. He ran at the warlock, sword raised.

The students saw what was coming. They made a mad dash for the door, fighting each other to get through it. Petr slipped and fell, then struggled to his feet again.

Almost as one, Lichtmann and the daemon loosed their attacks. A mortar ball punched through Petr's body, bursting him. A mess of limbs and viscera showered down on the guns below the landing, blood splashing everywhere. The students caught in the door were enveloped in Lichtmann's fire. The lucky ones screamed and ran into the hangar, beating at their flaming clothes. The others collapsed where they were, writhing and burning like torches.

Felix slashed down at Lichtmann, enraged at the death of earnest, clumsy Petr. The warlock sideslipped and stabbed backward with his dagger. Felix squirmed aside, barely avoiding its point. A horrible heat radiated from the shimmering blade.

Lichtmann lunged again, lightning quick. Felix swiped with his blade and jumped away, still off balance. He backed into a cannon and put a hand on it to steady himself. The iron tingled to the touch. He glanced back at it. Petr's blood was sinking into it and, just as had happened with the others, it was beginning to glow and crackle with poisonous green energy, as were the rest of the bloodied guns.

Lichtmann smiled. 'Yes, Herr Jaeger. More of my brothers wake. And I will use your blood to wake the rest.'

Felix backed away, flinching as the whispers returned, more strongly than ever, worming their way into his mind. He could feel the rage of the dead warlocks, their lust for his destruction. For the destruction of all his kind. They probed his mind with tendrils of corruption, they ripped at it with thoughts like claws.

Pulsing streams of balefire leapt from cannon to cannon as the spirits within them woke, forming a crackling, criss-crossing lattice of sorcerous energy that made the whole room thrum. The energy arced to the daemon's cannons, and they flared and fizzed with power. The daemon roared and raised its arms. It seemed to grow larger as Felix watched.

Felix's heart sank. The guns were feeding it, making it stronger. They were doomed.

Lichtmann came on, stabbing again. It was all Felix could do to lift his sword to block his attack. He couldn't think. His mind was too full of voices. He wanted to drop his sword and tear at his scalp to make the whispers stop.

To his left Felix saw Gotrek go down hard, a bloody gash across his massive chest. The horror edged through the cannons towards him. Felix knew he should do something, but he couldn't think what. He couldn't think at all.

Lichtmann slashed again with his dagger. Felix's arms wouldn't answer him. He could do nothing but stumble helplessly away through the cannon. He tripped over something and landed beside Gotrek. The sorcerer continued after him. Panic rose in Felix's throat. The whispers told him there was no hope, that he should just give up, that he should offer his throat to Lichtmann's shimmering blade.

Gotrek rose to his hands and knees beside Felix, shaking his head. He glared at Lichtmann and the horror, now only paces away, then grabbed Felix's arm. 'Come on, manling. Get up.'

Felix tried to get his limbs to move. They wouldn't. The whispers were in the way.

'Wake up, manling!'

Gotrek slapped him, hard. The crack was deafening. Pain exploded through Felix's jaw, knocking the voices from his brain.

The daemon loomed above them, raising the hellish cannons. Gotrek yanked Felix aside as they smashed down. They missed Felix's legs by inches and ripped gaping holes in the metal deck. Felix scrambled up, his muscles finally responding, and followed Gotrek, who was charging straight for Lichtmann. The horror crashed after them.

'Thank... thank you,' he said through aching teeth.

Gotrek grunted.

The sorcerer backed away from them, then turned and ran as Gotrek lashed out at him with his axe.

To Felix's surprise, Gotrek didn't pursue him, but continued on towards the stairs to the landing.

'Where... where are we going?' asked Felix.

Gotrek started up the stairs. Felix swallowed. They were leaving the cover of the guns. Lichtmann would be able to blast them!

And he did.

Gotrek shoved Felix forward onto the landing and dived after him as a ball of fire exploded above the stairs. A cannonball whistled overhead, then another. They blasted huge holes in the bulkhead.

Felix looked around. Two shots? The horror was firing with its arms as well as its head! It was bringing the other two cannon to bear.

Gotrek hauled Felix up and pushed him through the hangar door ahead of him. Felix stumbled over the burning bodies of the students that lay across the threshold, and sprawled face first on the hangar deck as Gotrek dived past him. A mortar round smashed a hole in the door frame behind them.

'After them, brothers!' came Lichtmann's voice. The airship shook as the horror stomped towards the landing.

'What are we doing?' asked Felix, getting up. He looked around the hangar. The wreckage of the gyrocopters was still burning. The remaining students were cowering in the far corner. Malakai lay prostrate on the floor at their feet. 'Are we running away?'

Gotrek snarled derisively as he smashed open a locked cabinet and pulled out two canisters of black water. 'We're taking the daemon away from those iron-befouling dead warlocks.' He handed Felix a lantern. 'Outside.'

'Outside?' But they were in the middle of the sky.

Felix glanced back through the door into the cargo hold. The horror was pulling itself onto the landing. The metal groaned under its weight.

'Up the ladder, manling.' Gotrek pushed Felix towards the rungs that were set in the wall beside the door, then picked up a piece of the burning gyrocopter's wooden frame.

As Felix started climbing the rungs, Gotrek split one of the canisters of black water with his axe, then heaved it out into the cargo hold. It bounced off a cannon, splashing black water everywhere. Gotrek pitched the burning wood after it, then clambered up the ladder after Felix.

There was a huge ear-popping *whump* from the cargo hold as the black water caught fire, followed by a blast of heat and orange light. Then a shriek from Lichtmann.

'No!' he cried. 'The guns!'

'That's only the beginning, sorcerer!' shouted Gotrek, climbing. 'A Slayer is not afraid to die. I'm setting fire to the balloon and killing us all!'

Felix stopped, heart pounding. 'You... you're what?'

'Keep moving, manling!'

The horror pushed two cannon arms through the door and started oozing in after them. Felix yelped and scrambled up the ladder, terror in his guts but his mind awhirl. Was Gotrek serious? Was he really going to blow up the airship? It would certainly finish off Lichtmann and foil his plans, but it would kill not just Gotrek and Felix, but Malakai and all his surviving students as well.

Felix clawed up through the circular hatch into the upper deck's central gangway, then took the canister of black water from Gotrek as he heaved himself up through the hole.

The airship shook violently as one of the horror's arms smashed the ladder just inches below Gotrek's boots.

Gotrek lurched up and grabbed the canister. 'Run, manling. The ladder to the roof!'

They ran, though Felix wondered if there was any reason. Could the huge daemon even fit through the hole to chase them?

With a noise like a steam tank crash, one of the cannon arms ripped up through the metal deck, tearing it as if it was paper. The impact knocked Felix off his feet. Gotrek picked him up and shoved him ahead. He looked back. A second smash widened the hole. Two glowing, muck-covered cannons snaked up through it and the horror pulled itself up, deforming like hot wax to fit into the cramped confines of the gangway. Lichtmann appeared behind it.

'Your fire is out, Slayer,' laughed the sorcerer. 'I foiled your little sabotage.'

The horror thundered towards them on four iron legs.

Felix sprinted on, sweating with terror. The ladder to the roof was just ahead to the right. He reached for it and glanced back again.

The mortar burst through the churning skin of the daemon's chest, the wide barrel aiming ahead. Green flame flared in its breach.

'Look out!' Felix threw himself against the right bulkhead. Gotrek did the same.

The mortar fired, battering Felix's ears with its roar. The ball ripped past, inches away, as the gangway disappeared in smoke and flame. Somewhere glass shattered and a man shouted.

Felix groped in the smoke for the ladder. He found it and hauled himself up, blinded and numb, the lantern he held banging off every rung. Gotrek clumped up behind him. The bulkheads vibrated with the thudding steps of the approaching horror.

'Faster, manling!'

Felix's head banged into the heavy hatch above him. He fumbled for the lever as something slammed into the ladder below. He shouldered the hatch back. Sunlight and cold wind slapped him in the face. He scrambled out onto the surface, then turned to take the canister from Gotrek again.

The Slayer squeezed through the hatch and rolled to one side, coming up on his feet with his axe at the ready.

Felix set the canister and the lantern down in a metal box that looked like it was meant to hold grenades, then drew his sword. He faced the hatch with Gotrek. Nothing happened. There was silence from below. Had the horror got stuck in the tight gangway?

Felix glanced around. The surface of the gondola was flat, with a low rail at the edges where the metal curved down on all sides. A score of taut metal cables stretched from sturdy rings in the roof up to the enormous expanse of the balloon, twenty feet above their heads. There was a ladder next to the hatch that rose, encased in a circular safety cage, up to a hatch in the belly of the balloon. All around them was blue sky and sunset clouds. Felix felt almost as exposed and precarious here as he had on the gyro-copter. The last time he had stood on this deck, he had faced the dragon Skjalandir. Memories of that night did not ease his mind. This was not the first place he would have picked for a fight to the death.

'Light the lantern, manling,' said Gotrek. He didn't take his eyes from the hatch.

Felix swallowed. He got out his tinder and flint and knelt, then opened the lantern's door. 'But this is just a ruse, isn't it?' he asked as he sparked a flame.

'If I kill the daemon and the sorcerer, it's a ruse,' said Gotrek. 'If I find my doom first, then it's not. You'll have to finish it.'

Felix lit the lantern, then looked up, following the ladder up to the balloon with his eyes. To be certain of destroying the airship, he would have to enter the envelope, pour the black water from the canister all along the catwalk that ran through the centre of all the lift-gas cells, then light it. He shivered. That would be the last thing he did in this life, for when the gas cells caught, the explosion would vaporise him.

'And if I die before I have the chance?'

'Then Sigmar and Ulric have mercy on their Empire,' said Gotrek. 'For Middenheim will fall.'

A glowing cannon shoved up out of the hatch at the end of a thick red tentacle, swaying like an iron-headed snake.

Gotrek lunged forward instantly and slashed with his axe, decap-itating it with a single blow. Green sparks showered and gore splashed as the cannon dropped to the deck with a deafening clang. It bounced towards the side, hit the low railing and flipped over it, spinning off into space. The slithering voices in Felix's head rose in a keening wail of rage and loss.

'Ha!' said Gotrek. 'You won't get that one back, daemon.'

The beheaded tentacle flailed at the Slayer wildly. He dodged back, continuing to watch the hatch. Felix backed away, a spark of hope flaring in his heart. For once they had the horror at a disadvantage. If it had to push its cannon out through the hatch one by one, Gotrek might be able to cut them off as they came. He could destroy it without a fight.

A second cannon-tipped arm pushed up through the hatch. Gotrek dodged around the first tentacle and hacked at it. It too clanged to the deck, flashing and sputtering. Gotrek stepped back as it bounced past him and crushed a section of the railing before tipping and sliding down the side of the gondola and away. The voices wailed again.

The two headless tentacles shuddered and for a moment grew translucent, their corona of green energy flickering and dimming. But before Gotrek could take advantage, they grew solid again and lashed at him. He hacked at them and circled the hatch.

Felix's heart surged. By Sigmar, it was going to work! Only two more cannon and the mortar to sever and the horror would be so weak that Gotrek would be able to vanquish it with a mere touch of his axe.

A third cannon tentacle shot up through the hatch. Gotrek sprang for it, ducking the attacks of the other two and lashed at it. It reared back and he missed. He lunged forward again, but all at once he was hanging upside down in the air. The first tentacle had him by the ankle.

'Gotrek!' Felix ran forward and slashed the thing with his sword as the Slayer flailed and cursed. The attack did nothing. He drew back for another swing, but the second tentacle clubbed him to the deck.

The first raised Gotrek higher, swinging him about. It meant to throw him off the gondola! Felix struggled to rise. He was going to be too late.

With a violent twist, Gotrek chopped backwards at the tentacle, just below his foot. It parted in a spray of gore and sparks. The Slayer flew across the deck and crashed down on the railing, then rolled over it, sliding towards oblivion.

'Gotrek!'

The Slayer made a one-handed grab and caught the railing. Felix ran to him and offered him a hand. Gotrek took it and pulled himself back onto the roof. They turned.

In the interval, the horror had emerged fully from the hatch. It stood on four tree-trunk legs, its constantly flowing skin glistening in the crimson sunset light as moaning mouths formed and melted away all over it. Its two remaining cannon hung at its sides, the bright ends of their muzzles poking out from the muck that held them and green energy coursing back and forth between them. The other two tentacles rose from behind its back like twin cobras. Its mortar head turned towards Gotrek and Felix menacingly.

The Slayer lowered himself into a fighting stance. He ran his thumb along the blade of his axe, drawing blood. He grinned savagely. 'Now, daemon, you die!'

He charged towards it, roaring a Khazalid battle cry. Felix ran after him, commending his soul to Sigmar.

The red horror came to meet them, clubbing down at them with its iron arms and smashing great dents in the gondola's metal skin as the tentacles snaked forward to grab at them. Gotrek met it blow for blow, bashing at the cannons and hacking through a tentacle. It grew back instantly. Felix hacked at the tentacles too, hoping to keep them away from Gotrek so that he would be able to take off another of its arms. His sword barely scarred them. It was like chopping at a tree limb.

Suddenly he saw green fire flash at the back of the mortar.

'Gotrek! Look out!'

Gotrek looked up, then threw up his axe as the mortar belched flame and smoke. He caught the cannonball on the flat of the axe and it glanced away to skip off the deck and out into thin air. But the force of the blow was too much. It slammed the back of the axe into Gotrek's temple and he stumbled, his legs buckling.

The horror knocked him flat with a tentacle and the Slayer slid across the riveted plates on his back. Felix ran back to him as the horror thundered after them.

The Slayer lurched up instantly, but his balance was shot. He shook his head to clear it and nearly fell again. A bleeding lump was growing over his patched eye. The horror swung in again, raining down crushing blows. Gotrek staggered back, blocking and ducking, but only at half strength. Felix backed with him. The horror pressed forward, pushing them back towards the nose of the gondola.

Beyond the battle, Lichtmann climbed from the hatch, his eyes blazing with fury. 'The cannons you just cast away contained the souls of Magister Valintin Schongauer and Magus Ermut Ziegel – greater men than you will ever be. You will pay for their loss!'

'I'll pay you in steel, warlock!' snarled Gotrek, ducking another cannon blow. He was still unsteady on his feet.

Lichtmann sneered. 'Yes. You will. I will take your axe, and I will melt it down as an offering to Tzeentch.' He raised his charred claw, intoning a spell. His hand flickered with fire.

Felix flinched back, terrified, and almost stepped into a tentacle's grasp. One blast from Lichtmann and the balloon might erupt! Wait! That was it. He looked to the sorcerer, pointing up. 'Do it!' he said. 'Do it and finish us all!'

Lichtmann paused in his incantation. He looked up at the balloon and frowned, then shrugged. 'No matter. There is more than one way to shape a flame.' He started for the fight, drawing his gold dagger with his left hand and murmuring a new incantation. He balled his black claw into a fist, and the flames that wreathed it grew brighter.

Felix eyed him warily. A man armed only with a dagger should not have concerned him, but he had seen Lichtmann sever the heads of two men with that dagger, as easily as he might have clipped a rose from its stem. He had felt the heat that radiated from it. At least with Karaghul he had reach on him.

But just as the thought formed in Felix's head, the flames around Lichtmann's fist extended from it to become a blazing sword. The warlock charged him.

Felix stepped back and parried, almost colliding with Gotrek as the Slayer ducked a whistling swipe from the horror. The sword of flame smashed into Felix's runesword, embers splashing from it like water. He was showered with hissing sparks. Felix staggered, the flames pricking his hands and face. The fire blade had weight! It hit like a great sword, and Lichtmann seemed inhumanly strong. The gold dagger darted for Felix's stomach. Felix twisted away from it, and was knocked sideways by a tentacle. Felix slashed around him blindly, trying to keep Lichtmann at bay until he recovered himself.

The sorcerer laughed and pressed his attack. 'You are running out of roof, Herr Jaeger.' His eyes glowed. In fact his whole aspect was changing. His reddish hair was now flame orange and growing long and wild, and his once hairless face was sprouting curling orange moustaches and a beard.

Beside him, the horror battered at the Slayer with a whirlwind of glowing iron and red tentacles. Arcs of Chaos energy flared all around. Gotrek blocked every attack, his axe seeming to be in six places at once, but he was still not fully recovered, and could not penetrate the thing's defence. He took a step back, and another, his muscle-knotted torso red to the waist from the deep gash across his chest.

Felix beat aside Lichtmann's sword of flame and lunged for his chest. The warlock turned the thrust with the gold dagger then stabbed it for Felix's face. The vile weapon hissed like a snake. Felix jerked back from it and brought his sword up, opening Lichtmann's forearm.

The warlock howled in pain and slashed furiously at him. Felix parried desperately and took another step back. Something pressed against the back of his legs. He glanced back. He was at the rail. Beyond it, the green carpet of the Drakwald spun vertiginously far below him.

Gotrek threw himself back as one of the daemon's iron arms slammed into the deck, tearing a huge trench in the brass plates. He bounced off one of the wrist-thick cables that held the balloon. He too had nowhere to go.

'Ha!' cried Lichtmann. 'Goodbye, brave fools!'

He and the horror attacked as one, Lichtmann lashing out at Felix with both sword and dagger, the horror swinging its iron arms at Gotrek's head. The Slayer dived left. Felix dived right, landing on his face. There was a *spang* like an enormous guitar string snapping, and the roof lurched under him.

Felix rolled over and looked up. Lichtmann was staggering back from the edge, his arms in front of his face, one of the steel cables loose and whipping around behind him.

The horror plunged after Gotrek, who was rolling to his feet beside the rail. Its cannon arms swung again. The Slayer ducked. Two more cables snapped.

Lichtmann fell to his knees as the roof jolted down a foot, broken cables lashing like snakes. The horror staggered sideways, almost tipping off the edge of the slanting gondola, then caught itself with its tentacles and continued after Gotrek. The remaining cables creaked and groaned alarmingly as it moved along the edge.

'No, brothers!' shouted Lichtmann, trying to stand on the metal slope. 'Do not damage the ship! We must make it to Middenheim!'

The horror didn't appear to hear. It swung again. A fourth cable snapped and Gotrek slammed to the deck, blood spraying from his forehead. The nose of the gondola sank further, tilting the roof alarmingly. More cables creaked and stretched.

Felix heard things shifting and thudding below him, deep inside the airship. He pushed himself to his feet and ran to the Slayer. His feet slipped on the slope and he fell again.

The Slayer pushed up, his burned and blistered face a mask of blood, which poured from a gash like a white smile across his forehead. Felix gagged as he realised he was seeing Gotrek's skull.

The horror howled and raised its two iron arms to smash the Slayer to a pulp, but it lost its balance and slid back towards the edge.

With a roar of fury, the Slayer threw himself down the slanting roof at it. It flailed wildly at him with its two cannon. Gotrek ducked them and swung his axe up from below. He chopped through the left arm at the root, severing it in a flash of green fire. The huge cannon dropped, and crashed down right on Gotrek's head and upraised right arm, mashing him flat to the deck, then it rolled off him and bounced down the slanted roof to tumble off into space. Gotrek slid down the slope on his face after it, unmoving.

Lichtmann and Felix stared at Gotrek's body as it bumped to a stop against the rail at the prow end of the gondola and lay there motionless. Felix was frozen in shock. By Sigmar, had he just seen the Slayer's death?

Lichtmann laughed triumphantly and grinned at Felix. 'A good trade, wouldn't you say, Herr Jaeger?' he asked. 'An arm for an enemy's life?' He turned to the horror, who stood beside him. 'Throw him over the side.'

The thing swayed down the incline, tentacles reaching out for the Slayer.

Felix's heart slammed against his ribs. He had to do something. He had to stop it! What could he do?

'At least the Slayer won't have died in vain!' he cried, then turned and scrabbled up the slanting roof towards the ladder. His feet slipped and skidded with every step. 'Prepare to burn, sorcerer!'

'Stop!' shouted Lichtmann, and then, 'Stop him!'

Felix heard the thudding steps of the horror coming after him and looked back, not daring to hope, then groaned with relief. Gotrek still lay at the rail. Lichtmann and the horror had left the Slayer behind to chase him.

Now if only Gotrek would wake up and finish them off, thought Felix, all would be well. He wouldn't have to go through with his threat. He wouldn't have to blow up the airship. He wouldn't have to die. He... he wouldn't have to face the fact that the Slayer was dead.

He looked back again. The horror was gaining, driving its remaining cannon down into the metal of the roof for purchase as if it was a cane, leaving a trail of ring-like dents. Lichtmann was right behind it, lit from below by his sword of flame.

Felix reached the hatch and snatched the fuel canister and the lantern from the grenade box, then ran to the ladder. He started up it one-handed, as fast as he could, which, in his current condition, wasn't terribly fast. The canister clanged off the bars of the safety cage with every step, slowing him.

'Are you certain you want to make this sacrifice, Herr Jaeger?' called Lichtmann. 'You are no Slayer.'

Felix cursed and tried to climb faster, but his battered body didn't respond. The fiends were going to reach the ladder before he reached the top. He was still a dozen rungs away. He felt like weeping. 'I can still die doing the right thing.'

Ten more rungs. Nine.

'Very noble, Herr Jaeger,' called Lichtmann, pacing the horror. 'A sacrifice worthy of Sigmar.'

Eight. Seven.

'A grand gesture to be sung about for all eternity.'

Six. Five.

Lichtmann and the horror reached the base of the ladder. Lichtmann sneered. 'If only you had succeeded.'

The daemon's iron arm swatted the ladder with a horrendous crunch, mangling the safety cage and pinching it shut at the base. Felix lost his grip and slipped several rungs, dropping the fuel and lantern. They rattled through the bars to the deck and clattered away down the slant.

Felix climbed frantically on. Six again. Five again. Oh gods!

The horror smashed the ladder again, and this time ripped it free of the bolts that held it to the belly of the balloon. With a scream of tortured metal, the cage and ladder toppled sideways towards the nose of the gondola, Felix trapped inside. The air exploded from his lungs and pain blasted the wits from his head as his prison slammed to the roof, then rolled towards the side and hit the railing. For a moment it seemed that it might stop there, but then inertia pushed it up and over. Felix clawed up the ladder towards the open end of the cage as he felt the twisted bottom half dip earthward and start scraping down the side of the gondola.

With a last desperate surge Felix pushed his head and shoulders free of the cage and threw out a hand. The gondola's railing smashed against his palm as he slid past it. He clutched at it, caught it, then lost it, and was dragged with the cage down the side of the gondola. He screamed and scrabbled with his hands at the smooth surface. There was nothing to hold on to.

A sharp ridge cracked him under the chin. He grabbed at it – a porthole – brass, and studded with rivets. His fingers clung to it with hysterical strength and he stopped his slide as the ladder and cage fell away, dropping down through wispy, sunset-pink clouds towards the ground far below.

Felix's legs swayed and banged against the side of the gondola as he held on to the porthole. The wind whipped at him, and his fingers were slick with panic sweat. He wouldn't be able keep his grip very long. Already his fingers were cramping. He didn't dare look down again, or the view would paralyse him, so he looked up.

That was no better.

Lichtmann and the horror loomed above him. Lichtmann shook his head admiringly. 'Such tenacity, Herr Jaeger,' he said. 'I do believe if I just left you to die, you would somehow find a way to climb back up and attack me again. I'm afraid I can't leave that to chance.' He looked to the horror. 'Brothers, Herr Jaeger and his uncouth companion have tossed three of our dear colleagues to the winds. I think it only fitting that you do the same for him.'

The horror howled from its melting mouths. The hateful whispers in Felix's head joined the chorus. The mortar and the cannon that were all that were left of the thing's armaments crackled with haloes of scintillating green energy. The mortar sank down into the churning mass that was its chest, and a cannonball floated up to meet it.

Felix swallowed, eyes wide. By Sigmar, it was going to shoot him point blank! He looked down and to either side. There was nowhere to go. The skin of the gondola was smooth until the next porthole, more than a body's length away.

The mortar rose again from between the horror's shoulders, breaking through the pulsing red flesh, then swivelled down towards Felix like a dead black eye. Green fire flared at its breach.

Lichtmann smiled. 'Goodbye, Herr–'

There was a blur of movement behind the daemon, and then a bright flash of steel appeared under the mortar, slashing through its fibrous crimson neck. The mortar toppled from the horror's shoulders, turning as it fell.

It fired.

The deafening report almost shook Felix's fingers from the porthole. He cringed. Was he hit? No. He looked up, and ducked. The mortar clanged off the deck just above his head and bounced down and away.

The smoke from the explosion cleared, revealing the scene on the roof. Lichtmann was staring down at himself, an expression of disbelief on his chinless face. His blackened arm was gone, blasted away by the cannonball. Blood gouted from the stump in a torrent. With a weak whimper the sorcerer tottered and fell to the deck.

Beside him, the headless horror was turning and swinging its sole remaining cannon at something behind it, its multitudinous mouths roaring in fury.

Another bright flash of steel and the last cannon separated from the daemon's arm in a burst of green fire, then sailed out far beyond the edge of the gondola before plummeting out of sight.

The thing shrieked. Its tentacles lashed forward to snatch something up and raise it high. It was Gotrek, axe raised and drenched in blood, roaring with wordless rage. He swung down one handed, and buried the axe deep in the daemon's chest.

It exploded.

Crimson gore spattered everywhere, then evaporated into a sulphurous pink cloud that whipped away on the wind. Out of the dissipating cloud fell the mangled wet bodies of the two crewmen it had ingested. Gotrek fell with them, hitting the deck in a loose jumble of limbs. His axe flew from his fingers and slid a little way down the slanting deck. Felix craned his neck. Was the Slayer dead? Had defeating the daemon taken the last of his strength?

No.

Gotrek was moving. He could just see him over the curve of the gondola, struggling to rise.

'Gotrek?' called Felix weakly. 'Gotrek. Down here.'

The Slayer didn't seem to hear him. He slowly pushed himself to his feet, wincing and pressing his ribs with his left hand. His right arm hung useless at his side. He swayed unsteadily on the angled deck.

'Gotrek!'

Gotrek stepped out of Felix's line of vision, then returned, dragging his axe behind him to stand over Lichtmann, who lay huddled by the low railing at the edge of the roof. Gotrek raised the axe with his left hand.

Felix couldn't see the sorcerer's face, but he saw his remaining hand rise in supplication.

'Mercy,' whispered Lichtmann. 'Mercy, I beg you. I don't want to die.'

'Ask your master for mercy, sorcerer,' rasped Gotrek, spitting blood.

He let the axe fall. Felix heard it chunk into meat, and there was a spray of blood. Lichtmann twitched once and lay still. Gotrek stared down at him, his face blank, blood from his horrible scalp wound dripping from his nose and matting his orange beard.

'Gotrek,' called Felix. 'Gotrek, get a rope.'

The Slayer swayed and took a step, then toppled backwards out of sight, his one eye rolling up in his head.

CHAPTER TWENTY

FELIX GROANED AND his head drooped forward to press against the glass of the porthole. His fingers screamed with agony. They were slipping slowly but inexorably down the curve of the rim. Of all the cruel jokes. Gotrek had killed the sorcerer. The airship, though wounded, was still air-worthy, and had not been blown to flinders, and Felix had miraculously survived it all, but now that it was all over and the day was saved, he was going to die, with no one to see or care.

For all he knew, Gotrek might be dead above him. He might have met his doom at last, and as heroically as he could have wished, saving the city of Middenheim from the most devious, destructive sabotage imaginable. And, wonder of wonders, Felix was alive to record the doom... for perhaps another minute. He giggled hysterically at the ridiculousness of it all, and almost lost his grip. Perhaps he could compose Gotrek's epic on the way down, crafting the final rhyming couplet just before he slammed into the ground. Bizarrely, the verses began to flood into his mind. He knew exactly how it would go. He could see it all transcribed on the page before him. A tear trickled down his cheek. It was all so sad. His greatest work, lost before it was written. No one would know his true genius.

Voices rang out above him.

'Hurry! Hurry! Out! Out!'

'I'm hurrying, curse you! Come on, hand them out.'

'Look! The Slayer!'

'And the sorcerer!'

'Sigmar's hammer! He did it! He killed the dirty traitor!'

'I think he killed himself as well. Tears of the Lady, look at the state of him.'

'And where's the swordsman? Jaeger.'

'Professor! Come up! They're up here! Look!'

'Help,' whispered Felix. And then, 'Help!' as he caught his breath. His fingers slipped another inch. His arms trembled with fatigue.

'Grimnir and Grungni,' came a familiar voice. 'They snapped the cables. That's the cause of it. Here noo, see to the Slayer, and gie him a…'

'Help!' cried Felix again. 'Malakai! Makaisson!'

'Hsst!' said Malakai. 'Dae ye hear something? Wis tha' my name?' The voices stopped.

'Help!' bellowed Felix.

'Over the side,' said someone.

Malakai's round, bewhiskered face appeared over the curve of the gondola. He had a lump on his forehead as big and purple as a plum, and another over his ear. His eyes grew wide. 'Why, Herr Jaeger, what are ye doin' doon there?'

He turned away before Felix could say anything, and was back an instant later with a weird leather bag that looked something like a backpack, but with long, looped straps that would have the thing banging around your calves if you tried to wear it. Makaisson held onto one loop and flipped the other down towards Felix. It slapped against the side of the gondola just above his head.

'Catch ahold of tha', young Felix,' he said. 'And haud on tight.'

Felix was almost too terrified to let go, but there was nothing for it. He threw a desperate arm up and hooked his hand through the loop. He couldn't grasp it as he normally would. His fingers were too cramped to close. He inched his hand forward until the loop was firmly in the crook of his arm.

'Pull,' he gasped.

Malakai pulled, two of his crew holding onto his shoulders to steady him. Felix began to slide slowly up the curve of the gondola, groaning with both relief and pain. His fingers felt like they were on fire. At last strong hands reached out and pulled him over the railing and he collapsed gratefully on the roof, panting like a dog.

He lifted his head and looked around for Gotrek. The Slayer was standing, barely, supported by several of Makaisson's crew. What were they doing to him?

'No time for a kip, young Felix,' said Malakai. 'We hiv tae abandon ship. Now!'

Felix squinted up at him, confused. 'Abandon ship?' He didn't understand. And why were all the young men who stared down at him wearing the strange sagging packs?

Malakai pulled him roughly to his feet and handed him the pack he had pulled him up with. 'Aye. Put this on. Some burning crates slid into the black powder barrels when the gondola tipped. We cannae put it out.'

Felix gaped as he mechanically put on the pack. The powder would blow the ship to pieces and the fire would set the gas cells alight. 'Then we're all dead.'

'Nae, nae. Not at a',' said Makaisson. 'My newest invention will get us all safe tae the ground. But we have to go, *noo*.'

New invention? Felix looked around the roof, expecting to see some weird contraption – a ten-man gyrocopter perhaps. There was nothing. What was Makaisson talking about?

The engineer turned to Gotrek, who leaned wearily against the railing, trying to get his limp right arm through the strap of one of the packs. 'Are ye ready, Gurnisson?'

One of Makaisson's crew took the Slayer's arm, trying to help.

Gotrek winced and shoved him away. 'Leave off,' he growled, then forced the arm through the strap, gritting his teeth. 'Ready,' he said. Something white glinted halfway up his forearm. It was the jagged end of a bone, sticking out from the Slayer's skin.

Felix blanched at the sight. He had never seen Gotrek so hurt. Then again, Gotrek had never fought a daemon with arms of iron before. Could even the Slayer recover from such grievous wounds?

Malakai stepped to the Slayer and shook a brass ring that dangled from the pack's left strap. 'Once ye jump, ye count tae five, then pull the ring. Aye?'

Gotrek nodded. He picked up his axe. 'Aye.'

Malakai looked back at Felix. 'Ye have it, young Felix? Count to five and pull?'

'Count to five and pull,' repeated Felix, not understanding in the slightest. The pack? The pack was the invention? 'But what is it? What does it do? What does it carry?'

Malakai put a foot up on the rail. 'It's a wearable air-catcher. Ah call it a "reliable".' He took a last look around the battered gondola of the *Spirit of Grungni*, and the balloon that rose above it. 'Ach weel,' he said with a shrug. 'Ah always did want tae build a bigger one.' He lowered his flying goggles and waved a hand over his head. 'Awa, lads. Awa!'

And with that, Makaisson jumped off the gondola and dropped out of sight. His few remaining crewmen gave each other wild-eyed looks, then shrugged and leapt after him, screaming 'Awaaaaay!' at the top of their voices.

Felix swallowed as he watched them plummet towards the earth. He turned to Gotrek. The Slayer was lifting a stiff leg over the railing. 'Come on, manling. It's a long walk to Middenheim.'

Felix put a foot up on the rail, then hesitated. A muffled explosion rocked the gondola, jolting him sideways. Another followed right on the heels of the first.

Gotrek leapt into the air, bellowing a dwarfish war cry. Felix jumped after him, a prayer to Sigmar on his lips that, whatever it was supposed to do, the 'reliable' he had strapped to his back was more of a success than Makaisson's 'Unsinkable,' or his 'Unstoppable.'

He dropped towards the ground at an alarming rate. The landscape rushed up at him like something out of a dream – rivers and fields and trees growing larger and more clear with every passing second. It was mesmerising. Sigmar! He had forgotten to count! Had it been five yet? Had he waited too long?

With a loud whump, a huge white shape blossomed beside him, then whipped up out of sight as he shot below it. That was Gotrek! The Slayer would not have forgotten to count. With panicky fingers, Felix fumbled at the ring and pulled.

Another whump, and something grabbed him roughly under the arms and jerked him to a stop in mid-air. It was agony on his wounds, and he nearly blacked out. The pressure lessened quickly and he looked up. A giant white mushroom cap as big as a tent floated over his head. Felix blinked. He was dangling from it by a score of thin silk cords. An aircatcher. Astounding. He looked down. More mushroom caps were floating lazily down towards the trees below him in the golden, late-afternoon light. There was no sound. The beauty of it all took his breath away. How strange to feel so peaceful so high up, with nothing under his feet but air.

An explosion like a hundred thunderclaps punched his eardrums and knocked him down and sideways in the air. Heat like a hammer slammed the left side of his body. He looked up. Beyond the shadowing white circle of the air-catcher, a black cloud of smoke was blotting out the sun. He heard a rushing crackle like coach wheels riding over dry leaves.

As the hot wind buffeted his air-catcher to the side he could see more of the sky above. The gondola of the *Spirit of Grungni* hung nose down from the balloon by a handful of cables, a huge hole blown in its belly. The balloon pointed up towards the sun, its underside on fire.

Why doesn't it explode, thought Felix?

It exploded.

A continent of fire erupted into existence above him, filling the sky, and a tidal wave of sound and heat smashed into him, knocking him up, down and sideways, as if he was a ship caught in a storm. Debris pattered down onto the cloth of the air-catcher above him, then something struck him violently above the temple and his vision dimmed. The last thing he saw was the *Spirit of Grungni's* gondola plummeting nose-first towards the ground, and Gotrek's reliable drifting past below him, covered in smouldering black rubbish.

Then he knew no more.

In his private quarters deep below the city the surface dwellers called Bilbali, the ancient grey seer pored over the correspondence he had just received from Skavenblight, the words inscribed by an elegant paw on the finest man-skin vellum, sealed with the insignia of the Council of Thirteen. He snarled to himself and crumpled the scroll between his claws, then threw it on the fire.

It mattered not how beautiful the vessel, if what it carried was poison. How could they deny him again? How could they refuse him his rightful position in the aristocracy of the greatest of all skaven cities? How could they ask that he continue this exile, this banishment, this insult of a proconsulship in this forgotten backwater, so far from the hub of skaven society? Weren't all his failures – rather, the failures that vile betrayers had falsely called his – almost twenty years gone? Couldn't the council put it all behind them? Couldn't they forgive and forget? Twenty was more years than most skaven lived to see. Had he not lived almost three times that number? Was he not therefore three times – nay, three hundred times – more wise? Was he not the keenest mind of three generations?

Oh, he knew he had little to show for it. All his greatest plans had been stymied, all his certain triumphs brought to crashing, calamitous ruin. But how could they blame him? Was it his fault that he had always been cursed with incompetent underlings? Was it his fault that his colleagues had been jealous backstabbers who had claimed his best ideas for their own, and sabotaged those they could not take advantage of? Was it his fault that he had been stalked by two of the most ruthless, relentless, remorseless enemies ever to cross the path of skaven-kind?

The mere thought of those fiendish beings sent him scrabbling through his papers until he found the stoppered bottle of powdered warpstone. He uncapped it with shaking paws and took a generous snort up both nostrils, then sank back with a sigh as he felt the mellow warmth of it trickle soothingly through his veins. There was nothing like it to calm his nerves. These last years would have been unbearable torture without it.

At least the two monsters were gone, he thought happily. He hadn't heard even a rumour of them for almost twenty years. It had been the one solace of his long exile that they had ceased to plague him. Of course it would have been far more pleasurable to have had them under his power, running them through his maze, testing experimental poisons on them, making their every waking moment a living hell of…

A scratching came at his door.

'Who is it?' he snapped, angry to have been disturbed from such a delicious daydream.

'Only I, oh most ancient of grey seers,' said an obsequious voice. 'Your humble servant, Issfet Loptail.'

'Come come,' said the grey seer. 'Quick quick.'

The door opened and a scrawny skaven with a foolish, simpering look entered, his head bobbing respectfully. He stopped a respectful distance from the grey seer's desk and swayed in place. He was a pitiful thing. He had lost his tail in a raid on a human farm once – to a female no less – and no longer had any balance. But he was smart, and listened well, and – most importantly – obeyed his master's orders without question.

'Speak speak, simpleton,' squeaked the grey seer imperiously. 'Your master is busy. Very busy.'

'Yes, oh pernicious one,' said Issfet, bowing and almost falling over. 'I have news from Nuln.'

'Nuln?' said the seer sharply. 'I wish to hear no news from that ill-favoured place. Have I not told you that I…'

'You have told me always to listen for certain rumours, master, no matter where they spring from.'

'Rumours? What rumours?' the seer asked. 'Speak! Quick quick!'

'Yes, your superfluousness,' said Issfet. 'I discovered a report from our outpost there. Two warriors were seen in our tunnels, travelling with a group of blood drinkers. One of the warriors was a dwarf, with one eye and fur the colour of flame. The other…'

The grey seer reeled back in his chair and nearly fell. He grabbed the stoppered bottle again and upended it on his tongue. 'My nemeses!' he moaned as he swallowed the warpstone snuff. 'My nemeses have returned! Horned Rat protect me!'

'Master!' said Issfet, a look of concern on his snaggle-toothed face. 'Master, wait. Listen further. The news is perhaps not as bad as it seems. There comes a further rumour that these same warriors were killed in an explosion upon a dwarf airship.'

'Killed?' said the seer, rising from his seat, his eyes blazing with weird green light. 'Killed? Those two? Never! I am not so fortunate.' His claws clutched convulsively. 'No. They are not dead. But they soon will be. This time I will be certain of their destruction!'

'Yes, oh most impotent of skaven,' said Issfet. 'How could so wizened, so devoid a grey seer fail to destroy such lowly creatures?'

'How indeed?' said the seer, thinking back with a shudder to his previous encounters with the dangerous pair. 'How indeed.' He turned to the fire, gazing into it. 'Go go,' he said without looking around. 'Disturb me not. I must think.'

'Yes, master.'

'Oh, and Issfet,' the seer said, turning as the crippled skaven backed towards the door.

'Yes, master?'

'Speak of this to no one. There have been times in the past when my rivals have used these two against me. It will not happen again.'

'Of course not, oh most parsimonious of masters,' said Issfet, bowing low. 'None shall hear of it. My snout is sealed.'

'Good good,' said the grey seer and turned back to the fire as his servant backed through the door and closed it behind him. He warmed his cold paws over the flames, then paused and looked over his shoulder, squinting suspiciously. Had there been just the faintest hint of slyness on Issfet's face as he bowed? Had there been the shadow of a cunning smile?

Perhaps the tailless little spy was too smart. Thanquol would have to keep an eye on him.

ABOUT THE AUTHORS

William King was born in Stranraer, Scotland, in 1959. His short stories have appeared in The Year's Best SF, Zenith, White Dwarf and Interzone. He is the author of the much-loved Gotrek & Felix adventures and the Space Wolf novels.

Nathan Long was a struggling screenwriter for fifteen years, during which time he had three movies made and a handful of live-action and animated TV episodes produced. Now he is a novelist, and is enjoying it much more. For Black Library he has written three Warhammer novels featuring the Blackhearts, and has taken over the Gotrek and Felix series, starting with the eighth installment, *Orcslayer*. He lives in Hollywood.

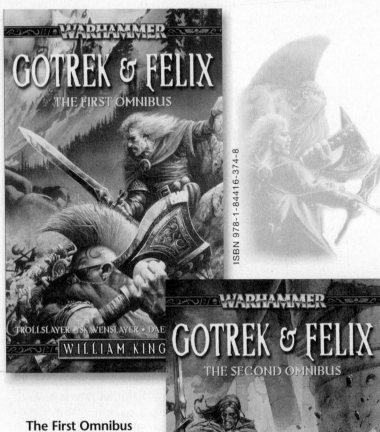

ISBN 978-1-84416-374-8

ISBN 978-1-84416-417-2

The First Omnibus contains the novels *Trollslayer, Skavenslayer* **and** *Daemonslayer*

The Second Omnibus contains the novels *Dragonslayer, Beastslayer* **and** *Vampireslayer*

WARHAMMER

ELFSLAYER

BY NATHAN LONG

A GOTREK & FELIX NOVEL

UK ISBN 978-1-84416-663-3 US ISBN 978-1-84416-575-9

WARHAMMER

Contains the novels Valnir's Bane, Broken Lance and Tainted Blood

Bloodthirsty action from the battlefields of the Old World

BLACKHEARTS
THE OMNIBUS

Nathan Long

UK ISBN 978-1-84416-510-0

WARHAMMER

GREY SEER

BY C·L·WERNER

A THANQUOL & BONERIPPER NOVEL

UK ISBN 978-1-84416-738-8   US ISBN 978-1-84416-739-5

WARHAMMER

HONOURKEEPER

NICK KYME

UK ISBN 978-1-84416-685-6   US ISBN 978-1-84416-684-8

Mischief

In

St. Tropez

Dory Spark Mysteries Book 2

By C.G. Oster

Chapter 1

Covering her eyes with her hand, Dory stared out at the bright, glittering Mediterranean sea. The blue water married with the sky in the distance and a warm sea breeze rustled her skirt. She sighed and turned around to walk back up the vast garden covering the rough terrain at the edge of Lady Pettifer's property.

They had nothing planned for the day, which were Dory's favorite kind of days. Livinia, Lady Pettifer's niece, was at home too, but would most likely dash off to Cannes by the afternoon to seek the company of her friends. Who wanted to be in sleepy, old St. Tropez when the soirees never stopped an hour's drive away?

After initial misgivings, Livinia had grown to love it here on the coast. Granted, she would prefer being closer to the lively towns of Cannes or Nice, but she'd found her set, and they were a wild and varied bunch. Dory liked it here too, although she preferred the more sedate lifestyle of this small fishing village.

Over the last year and a half, her French was perfected and she knew the butcher, the baker and the candlestick maker. In fact, she knew everyone in the village. They weren't, by far, the only Brits here, but it was a certain set that lived out in these smaller villages, and they weren't Livinia's set.

In saying that, the coast in general was now more replete than it had been when Dory had first arrived. The Americans had mostly left, leaving only the more hardy Brits, returning the Cote de Azur to how it used to be in the twenties—exactly how Lady Pettifer loved it. There had always been the British Colony here, but the young, bright and rich Americans had come and ever so gently pushed them out.

That withstanding, it was hard to even recognize that they were officially at war. There had been widespread panic, when in the autumn, both England and France had declared war on Germany. Since then, nothing had happened and life had effectively returned to normal. Even the Duke and Duchess of Windsor were still staying here on the coast. It was the war that never happened.

Obviously, things were more complicated than that, but not here in the endless spring sunshine. People got on with their business and the parties were thrown like they always had been.

Reaching the top of the stairs, Dory put her hat on before crossing the expanse of lawn around Lady Pettifer's villa. She didn't have skin that took the sun well—she burned to a crisp if she wasn't careful. It was a hard lesson she'd learnt to her own misery in her first few weeks here.

Looking comfortable, Lady Pettifer sat in the seating area under a vine leaf covered pergola, a tea service steaming in front of her.

"There you are, dear," Lady Pettifer said. "Any dolphins today?"

"I didn't see any," Dory said as she sat down. She could use a cup. Music started playing upstairs in the house, leeching out of open windows as the breeze shifted. They both looked up at the open window above them. "Livinia is still here, I see."

"I understand Richard is picking her up in an hour." Richard Dormstry was one of Livinia's friends, who essentially did whatever she wished. He drove an hour to pick her up, then an hour back.

Everyone saw that Richard was in love with her—
except Livinia, who refused to see it, or perhaps
refused to acknowledge it.

Lady Pettifer suspected she had her eyes set on
someone else, someone Livinia refused to speak
about, which made Lady Pettifer concerned it was
some married man. As bright and gregarious as
Livinia was, she did keep some things close to her
chest when she wanted to.

Dory had gotten to know her much better in
their time together. These days, Livinia didn't quite
grate on her as much as in the beginning, but she
acknowledged that they were vastly different types of
people. In fact, Dory took to her role as companion
very well, preferring to spend time at Ville Beaulieu
with Lady Pettifer than running around the house
parties in Cannes and Nice. It could also be that
Dory didn't quite belong with any of the groups that
milled around the coast.

In certain settings, Livinia wasn't always able to
be as footloose as she wished and Dory had to serve
as chaperone if any notable doyennes of etiquette
from England would be there. Livinia still had her
mother's scandal to contend with, so couldn't afford

any tarnishing to her own reputation in certain circles.

Accepting her cup of tea, Dory held it to her mouth and drew in the scent. Lady Pettifer was very specific with her tea, and Dory had learned to tell the difference between Chinese, Indian and Ceylon teas just by the smell. It was Ceylon today.

Beauty lay panting under the table and Dory held down the last piece of her biscuit, feeling the dog's wet nose to her fingers before long.

The noisy engine of the mailman's motorcar echoed off the trees as he drove up the long, winding driveway.

"Running a bit late today," Lady Pettifer chided. "No doubt Mr. Merton was giving him trouble." Mr. Merton was their neighbor, a cantankerous elderly man who really enjoyed nothing of life, or even what the lifestyle in the south of France offered. Dory often wondered why he didn't simply be miserable back home. She'd never worked up the nerve to ask, and here on the coast, it was impolite to inquire what brought people here, because there were some who weren't strictly here by choice. Like Livinia, some fled scandal back home—

or worse. For others, the temperate climate agreed with their health.

Livinia came out of the house and sat down in one of the free chairs. The music still played above in her room, almost as if she couldn't stand the silence. She checked her watch. "Where is he? He said he'd be here."

"Something must have held him up," Lady Pettifer said to assuage Livinia's annoyance. It wouldn't do that Richard was less than punctual. "I am sure that all of Cannes will not forget about you simply because you are an hour late."

Accompanying a sour look, Livinia drew a deep breath and crossed her arms. "I do wish we could build a pool. I'm sure even Dory would venture in once in a blue moon."

Lady Pettifer snorted. There is a vast sea right in front of you." Lady Pettifer couldn't abide pools. Her generation didn't build pools. It was a uniquely American import—and hence, avoided. "Besides, there is a war going on. How can we run around building swimming pools at such a time?"

"I think this war is just an excuse for not doing anything. Everyone goes on and on about this war, and nothing ever happens. I feel I have been whacked over the head with this war as far back as I can remember."

"War is simply awful," Lady Pettifer sniffed, her voice drifting off to old memories from the previous war.

Livinia didn't quite roll her eyes, but she had little tolerance for hearing about the war—this or any other.

Almost silently, Mr. Fernley appeared with a silver tray. "The mail, madam," he said in his typical dry tone. There were two letters—none for Dory. She got letters from her mother once a week, and one would likely come in the next day or so, but other than that, she had no one writing to her.

"Oh, an invitation," Livinia said, picking up an envelope of rich, creamy paper. "How exciting."

Now it was Lady Pettifer's turn to grumble as she opened her own letter and read in silence.

"A masquerade," Livinia said with excitement. "Next week. Lady Tonbridge. Well, well, that is a development, isn't it? She must be inviting everyone. That son of hers must be here. What was his name?"

"Marcus," Lady Pettifer stated.

"The invitation is for you as well."

"Not sure I have the constitution for a masquerade," Lady Pettifer said dismissively without looking up. "My knee is still giving me all sorts of trouble. Dory can go."

Automatically, Dory smiled graciously. From having been an observer of such parties back at Wallisford Hall, she was now well past any fascination she'd had for them. Her status here on the coast was not in doubt by anyone. She was never quite a part of Livinia's set, but she wasn't exactly a servant either. The fact that she had been a maid back in England was also known by quite a few. In the beginning, Livinia had pointed it out diligently. Because of this, very few people actually spoke to her at these parties she was sometimes asked to go to. "Of course," Dory said.

"It will be so much fun. It's short notice, though. I think I need a new dress. Where is Richard? I now have to run to the dressmaker as well."

In fact, Livinia's chauffeur was just arriving. They heard the sound of his car, a much deeper rumble than the high-pitched engine of the mailman.

He could be heard even where they sat around the back of the house.

It didn't take him long to find them, walking around the corner of the house. "Aren't you all a picture?" he said with a broad smile. "Smart to escape the midday heat." He took a seat, pulling up the white linen material of his slacks along his long, lean legs. "There's an overturned cart on the road. Took ages to right. Silly bugger."

"I'll just get dressed," Livinia said, bounding into the house.

"I might as well get comfortable, then," Richard said with resignation.

"Tea?" Lady Pettifer offered.

"I would love a cup," he said with a smile.

Chapter 2

Most of the streets in the village of St. Tropez were too small for motor cars to get through. The alleys were tight and dark, most of the buildings three stories, rendered in oranges and yellows. Dory liked walking around here as the streets were typically quite cool, protecting the pedestrians from the heat of the sun.

It was late spring and the sun was getting stronger by the week. The heat and Lady Pettifer's knee kept her mostly at home. Over the last few months, she had increasingly been tired and feeling under the weather. The doctor said it was just a bug and nothing to worry about. Rest and relaxation was all she needed, apparently. Still, Dory couldn't help worrying.

Because of her health, though, Lady Pettifer had not felt up to returning to England for the summer. It meant staying over the hot months, but Lady Pettifer felt she preferred that to spending three weeks on a ship, plus all the trouble with making her way to Wallisford Hall again. Besides, with the war, passage wasn't as readily available as it had been.

Walking into the bakery, Dory was met with the lovely smell of fresh bread, and opened her coin purse to buy a loaf. The French were gifted with bread. Dory hadn't understood how wonderful bread could be before coming here. And the cheese. The French took their cheese as seriously as some did their whiskey.

With a smile, she paid the baker's wife and continued down to the waterfront where the fishermen were selling their morning's catch. It smelled of fish and salt, the entire village seemed to congregate down by the waterfront.

There was no sign of war here. Nothing had changed, and Dory hoped it would stay that way. Still, it felt as though they were living on borrowed time. Everyone hoped that there was sufficient deterrence on both sides to stop either from making an advance. It had kept the war from properly starting so far. God willing it held.

In saying that, anyone new in town, or even in Cannes and Nice, were treated with suspicion. Anyone of German descent had been rounded up and taken into internment—including the ones who would get no welcome in Hitler's Germany.

With carrots, fish and bread in her basket, Dory righted her bicycle and started home. Villa Beaulieu was some ways out of the village, perched on top of a cliff. It had both privacy and spectacular views, which was why Lady Pettifer had bought it with her ailing husband some time ago.

Having spent almost two years here, it was hard to consider going back to Swanley to live with her mother again. Still, Dory had to consider her future at some point, but as long as Lady Pettifer wanted her to stay, she would.

Bicycling up the hills made sweat run down her back and she had to get off and push. This was a route Dory cycled every day, and still, it made her smile every time she looked out at the sea. Small boats sat in the distance, the blue of the sea having turned hazy in the afternoon.

Dory was puffed by the time she made it home and walked into the cool interior of Villa Beaulieu, to find Lady Pettifer sitting in the salon by the large open window. Italian paintings hung on the walls and the sumptuous articles of furniture were all older than Dory was. It was a house where everything had its proper place and little had changed or moved since the time the house had been set up. From what she suspected, the penchant for Italian furniture had been Lady Pettifer's husband, but since his death, she hadn't changed a thing.

The Pettifers hadn't built the house, though. It had been some acquaintance they'd known, an older couple that had passed away quite some while ago.

"The mailman came while you were away. There is a letter from your mother."

"Oh," Dory said and sat down, seeing the letter waiting for her. It had a large sticking along the edge of the envelope that said, 'Opened by the Censor.' Dory opened it. It was strange to think someone had read her correspondence with her mother, but there was nothing for it. it was simply a part of life, these days.

The letter contained nothing but her mother's musings and her ongoing concerns for Dory's siblings. As it was, Dory sent most of her salary back home, so everyone was fed and thriving—but that didn't stop her mother from worrying.

"No news of Margot and her baby?" Lady Pettifer asked, who was by now well-versed in the goings ons amongst the members of the Sparks family. Margot was Dory's cousin and was expecting a baby any day.

"She doesn't say, so I'm guessing she hasn't had it yet. I think it will be a boy, though. I just get that feeling."

"A letter came from Vivian," Lady Pettifer said.

"Oh." Dory felt her shoulders stiffen. She'd heard very little from or about Vivian since they had left England. Her relationship with Vivian, Lady Pettifer's nephew and Livinia's twin, had always been tentative and uncomfortable.

"He says he's in Geneva."

A second rush of discomfort washed over her. His mother, the murderess of Nora Sands, was currently institutionalized in a Swiss sanitorium, and that could be the only reason he would be there.

"I think there is a strong possibility he'll come for a visit, but he doesn't say what his plans are. Only that Honoria is fine and it's a lovely place."

A tight smile twisted Dory's lips. In a sense, Lady Wallisford had gotten away with murder, being subsequently placed in a sanatorium. Technically, she wasn't free to leave, but it was better than she deserved. A young woman was dead for that woman over eagerness to protect her childrens' ambitions. The whole affair turned Dory's stomach.

"It is still a prison," Lady Pettifer said as if reading Dory's thoughts. They remained silent for a while. The tentacles of that dastardly deed still reached far and wide. "Never mind. It's quite exciting about the masquerade."

Dory nodded, appreciative of the change in subject.

"I'm glad you're getting out and about a bit. You shouldn't be stuck here with an old woman all the time."

"I am a companion. This is exactly what I am supposed to do." This was an ongoing discussion between them, and in a sense, Dory was hiding from life a little in this comfortable house. Not that she minded. This had been a place of discovery. She had learned so much during her time here—things she would never have experienced back in Swanley. Lady Pettifer was concerned because she didn't spend copious amounts of time with people her own age, like Livinia did, but Dory's concern was more that her life was a little too easy here. She literally had nothing to worry about other than Lady Pettifer's health.

"I am sure it will be a very diverting party. Livinia seems excited," Dory said brightly.

"Livinia would be excited about a queue at the post office if it had the right dress code."

Dory chuckled. Sadly, it was true. Livinia treasured anyone's company but her own.

But Dory couldn't stop thinking that she should be more like Livinia and seek the company of others. Obviously, Livinia's set wouldn't be welcoming, but surely there would be people in the area who would welcome her as a friend. It just seemed such a hassle to go all the way to Cannes to seek them out.

*

Supper was eaten by candlelight. An officer from the French territorial army had come around a few months back and insisted they stay dark at night. Lady Pettifer had been deeply offended by his tone, but had grudgingly acknowledged the need for it. No one wanted Germans flying around with their bombers at night, did they?

The arrival of German planes had never happened, but that did not provide the excuse for being lax. Granted, many were. Some people along the coast failed to understand the concept of a blackout, and at times, the authorities had to resort to cutting the power.

The cook was an elderly French woman, who created the most divine meals. Lady Pettifer had running battles with the woman who preferred the heavy French palate with thick sauces, scoops of butter and cream. It didn't agree with Lady Pettifer's digestion, but cook had her strict view of what made a decent meal. Gladys, Dory's aunt, would likely be offended by the woman and the meals she served, but Dory could never complain. The French food was marvelous—although, at times, she had to take an extra hour to walk it off.

"Sherry, dear?" Lady Pettifer asked and Mr. Fernley prepared the salon for them.

"A small one would be nice." Dory didn't know how she would live as an elderly lady, but she would never complain with a setup like this. In saying that, though, as time passed and the scandal of Lady Wallisford's activities died down, there would be a time when Dory really should return to England and find a place for herself—unless this war started in earnest and took all choices out of her hands.

The truth was that Dory had no idea what war entailed. Lady Pettifer had once said that the women of England, and broader Britain as well, would have to take over the ongoing operation of the country. It seemed an extraordinary notion, but Dory had to concede that she was probably right. Dory just didn't have a good understanding of how that would work.

DI Ridley entered her mind and she wondered if the Police would need women as well. Could Dory ever consider a profession in the Police? She wasn't sure if she could do what he did. Her eagerness to solve a crime had been a bit of a revelation and she was still deeply offended by someone getting away with an action as awful as taking someone's life.

"Mr. Fernley, would you be so kind to turn the wireless on." Lady Pettifer asked as she settled herself. "Let's hear what they have to say tonight."

The radio started with a rush of static before Mr. Fernley corrected the setting. Music played for a little while and Beauty settled herself down to lie by Lady Pettifer's feet.

It went quiet for a moment, followed by a series of familiar beeps. Everyone in the room was utterly still.

This is the BBC in London calling, the man started with his sharp, deep tone. We start tonight's bulletin with news regarding Germany's advancement into Denmark and Norway, which commenced this morning in the early hours of dawn.

Dory shuddered at what she heard and they all exchanged worried glances.

"It seems they are taking over anywhere they can get a foothold," Lady Pettifer said.

"At least they cannot breach the French Army," Dory said quietly.

"Let's hope that deters them. I do hope Vivian is safe in Switzerland."

Dory noted that she didn't extend the concern to Lady Wallisford, which showed how low a regard she truly had for the woman. At least they agreed on that.

The man broadcasting went on to say the German Army had landed by sea at Gedser and were moving north, and that German troops had sailed up the Oslofjord to the capital of Norway.

Every moment seemed to make it all sound worse. Germans simply invading. It was worse than Dory could imagine. Those horrid Nazis and their relentless ambition. There was no talk of appeasement anymore. They were at war, but opposing sides of equal might deterred any real fighting.

Chapter 3

I have sent Mr. Fernley up in the attic to find my old mask. I bought it in Venice a while ago now, and it will serve you well for the evening," Lady Pettifer said as Dory sat in the salon and read.

"That's wonderful. I had figured I would have to fashion myself something out of the material from an old hat."

"We can do better than that."

Livina's dress had been delivered that afternoon in a large, paper box and Livinia was already upstairs, the dulcet tone of her music playing as it always did.

"If it proves to be too difficult to drive back at night, you can always stay with Lady Dorsey. She wouldn't mind one bit."

Dory had been worried about driving the road back in the dark. It all depended on how bright the moon was. If there was no moon, it was an uncomfortable and perilous journey with steep drops and sharp turns. The coastline undulated violently between St. Tropez and Cannes. "Hopefully, we will make it back."

Another concern was that Livinia would go off with her friends and simply leave Dory to her own devices. Well, perhaps not a concern so much as a real possibility. Livinia was always willing to keep the party going. Dory, on the other hand, was not willing to follow some group around in the wee hours of the night. That would be too much. If Livinia refused to come home, Dory was not prepared to take any responsibility for that—and Lady Pettifer wouldn't expect her to. Livinia was technically old enough to make her own decisions.

In a sense, Dory had some sympathy for Livinia, who was expected to straddle two different social expectations—the old, where she was supposed to be a demure innocent, protected from the world and any real role in it, and also the expectations of a modern girl who made her own way in the world. She needed to be both things at once, and she was managing—perhaps embracing the modern girl a little too gleefully, but that was simply Dory's opinion.

"Have you been successful?" Lady Pettifer asked as Mr. Fernley returned with a box.

"Is this the one you were referring to?" he said, opening the box.

Inside was a white mask with feathers and gold trimming. It looked like a sugar confection, much too fancy, but it was better than any monstrosity that Dory could create, so in that regard, Dory was pleased.

"I think this will go better with your blue dress," Lady Pettifer said.

Dory had two fancy dresses that she used for parties and events. She loved both of them, but she couldn't say she felt entirely comfortable in them. Those dresses were the embodiment of the discomfort she felt about how she fit in here. The truth was that living here and living this lifestyle had changed her in both outlook and in the things she wanted. Or perhaps it was more that she didn't exactly know what she wanted anymore.

"I better go change," Dory said, taking the beautifully embellished mask that Mr. Fernley had found in the treasure trove that was Lady Pettifer's attic. The material was silk, which felt buttery under her fingers. It had a dreamy quality to it and Dory wondered if she'd feel dreamy wearing it. Maybe a masquerade was something a bit special, a place where she could step outside of herself for a little while.

Changing quickly, she pulled the mask over her eyes and considered herself in the mirror. Didn't she look mysterious. Perhaps she would meet a mysterious man and they would dance, the whole while never knowing each other's identities. With a sigh, she pulled it off again and made her way downstairs.

It didn't take long for Livinia to appear, looking wonderful in a sleeveless peach dress. The dressmaker in Cannes was gifted, Dory had to concede. It was a dress far above her own, but Dory wasn't sure she would even feel comfortable in a dress like that. Livinia had no limitations to what she felt comfortable wearing.

"Ready to go?" Livinia asked, pulling up her long, satin gloves. "I'll drive." Which meant it would be an uncomfortable ride for Dory as Livinia's rash behavior was evident in her driving too. The whole family had issues with driving, it seemed. Perhaps it was hereditary.

Dory nodded and Lady Pettifer bid them goodbye, standing at the door to see them off. Lady Pettifer's car was a burgundy-colored Bentley and as it was a dry evening, Mr. Fernley had put the canvas roof down for them.

"Well, I hope the old girl doesn't have too dull a night without us," Livinia stated. "It's so awful with her knee. It must be dreadful getting old."

"Yes," Dory had to agree.

"Andrew should come visit more often. He never comes. Finds it too hot. Such an Englishmen. Positively wilts in the heat. I, on the other hand, adore it. Who wants to molder away in the country all summer?"

More than a few times, Dory had wondered if Livinia told herself so because she was frightened to go home, frightened of the scandal her mother still was. As bright and shiny as Livinia was, she couldn't escape being tarred with that brush. But she had found both excitement and acceptance here on the coast, so Dory expected she would stay here forever if she could—at least until no one cared about the Wallisford Hall murder.

Everyone had their problems, even someone as lofty and flighty as Livinia.

The sky was painted in all shades of orange, red and mauve. It was utterly beautiful and the air was fresh as they drove. Dusk was quickly settling and Dory hoped they would get to their destination before dark. Livinia certainly seemed to be in a hurry to get there.

They drove in silence, because as usually was, they had precious little to talk about, but knew each other enough to sit in silence. Dory had no illusions about what Livinia thought of her—boring and pointless. She was never mean about it. Meanness wasn't actually part of Livinia's personality. Only her brothers brought that out in her.

"You look nice," Livinia finally said.

"Thank you," Dory replied.

"I think your mask is actually better than mine. Who knew Aunt Connie had that up in the attic?"

For a moment, Dory wondered if Livinia wanted it, but she didn't say so. Hopefully not, because Livinia's mask would clash horribly with

Dory's dress. "I wonder if the Duke and Duchess will be there," she said instead, referring to the notorious Windsors.

"They might. I suspect they would love to come to a masquerade and not be noticed. Everyone continually stares at them otherwise." Dory had seen them once at one of the well-known annual parties held by someone with a hyphenated name ending with Rothchild. The ambitious approached them, but mostly, people simply observed them. "I don't think I could stand that."

"You hate being noticed in any capacity," Livinia pointed out. It was hard to argue, but Dory was surprised that Livinia had even noticed that about her.

"That training to never be seen is hard to shake," she said by way of defending herself.

Livinia gave her a chiding glance. "Can't blame your shyness on training."

Dory utterly hated discussing herself and her shortcomings. At least Livinia knew exactly what she wanted in life. She wanted to marry well, with a handsome, rich man who also wanted to be the life of the party. The only ambition Dory had managed to muster was to perhaps go to secretarial school, and even that didn't set her heart alight.

"I'm not planning on coming home tonight," Livinia said after a while. "Duckie is having a party at his house tomorrow, so I thought I'd stay. You don't mind driving back on your own, do you?"

"No, of course not." She didn't relish driving back in the dark, but that had nothing to do with having Livinia's company.

"It's going to be a smashing night. I understand they are having a performance by some American jazz singer."

"You wouldn't know there was a war on, would you?"

"The Germans can keep their war. Miserable buggars. I hope they choke on it."

Dory smiled. There was no holding back with Livinia; she charged ahead with whatever opinion she had.

"Did Lady Pettifer tell you she got a letter from Vivian?"

By Livinia's raised eyebrows, Dory had her answer. "Is that so?"

"He's in Switzerland, it seems."

Livinia's expression clouded over. She wasn't remotely as forgiving of their mother as Vivian seemed to be. It was a hard thing to accept, perhaps.

"Here we are," Livinia said and took an exit off the road. A house was lit up like a firecracker up the side of the hill. It was just about completely dark now and there was no one in doubt there was a party going on. Any German flying over would see a glowing point on an otherwise—mostly—dark coastline.

Chapter 4

The house itself was large, looming over the dark mountainside like a crouching cat. The moon was almost full, so the outline of the hill and the house was seen, as well as the sea beyond. It was a beautiful place, giving Dory the feel of isolation, as though it was an oceangoing ship. Cars were parked along the driveway and Livinia squeezed into a spot with barely enough room to get out.

"Come on," she said excitedly as they walked the rest of the way up to the house. Music was heard even from here, and live music, not the sedate scratchy tunes from a gramophone. Livinia busied herself with her mask and Dory followed. It felt a little suffocating having something on her face, but that was all a part of it.

A neatly dressed servant stood in the doorway with a tray of champagne and Livinia sailed past, picking one up on the way. She really was in her element.

"Thank you," Dory said as she grabbed a glass. Champagne was marvelous and the French really had a way of making the humble grape into something magical.

Meeting her was a room full of exquisitely dressed people, all wearing masks—some elaborate, some plain black. The men all wore black tails with neatly combed hair. This was Livinia's crowd and they was glittering. There was more jewelry in this room than Dory knew how to take in. This wasn't her first event, but this might be the most stylish.

There were some older attendees as well. Their style was slightly different, older in fashion, but there was still a sense of waylaid inhibitions. Obviously, she had heard them exalt what the Cote d'Azur was like in the twenties, with the lavish parties. These days, things were more sedate to reflect the times, and the fact that the country was at war—but not tonight. Tonight was an unapologetic return to opulence.

In a way, Dory was glad she was here. Few of her friends back in Swanley would ever believe there were parties like this. It was too much for the senses to take in.

On a table across the room, a champagne pyramid stood, and a man poured into the very top glass until it overflowed to all the glasses below.

There was also an ice sculpture of a crane with its neck looped around as if it were surveying its own leg.

A girl in a red, tasseled top and small shorts walked around with a silver ice bucket. "For the war effort," she said expectantly as she waited for a man to consult his wallet. In the end, the task proved too difficult so he dropped the whole wallet in. "Good man," she said with a broad smile and moved to the next.

Dory only had five francs in her small purse, but she supposed she would have to part with it when the girl came her way. Everyone needed to do their bit for the war, although she hadn't expected it to be a part of a night like this.

The inside of the main reception room had tall palm trees in pots. The fronds curved across the people milling. Sleek art graced the walls. It really was a lovely house. The floor was black and white checkered, which showed that this house was probably built ten years ago. It was a house built to dazzle and it did its job in that regard. Ville Beaulieu was much older with its cream stucco walls, wood and terracotta floors. As stylish as this house was, Dory preferred the comfort of Beaulieu.

Walking along, Dory smiled to anyone who smiled at her. She was enjoying just seeing this party and the people here. A dance floor was filled with milling couples—some obviously in love. Livinia was one of the dancers, who was laughing at something said by a tall man with glossy black hair. Was this the man she seemed so eager to see, the one she didn't really speak about?

It wasn't Duckie. Dory had met Duckie before, so she knew Livnia was dancing with someone else. It could be that he was the reason she was staying behind tonight—not that Livinia needed a reason. Dory hoped she knew what she was doing.

But then who was she to judge? When it came to love, she wasn't exactly thriving in that department. Back home, she'd never really had time for boys, and it wasn't until she'd met DI Ridley that she'd even managed a proper blush. It was impossible not to face the fact that she had been sweet on him, and to her eternal gratitude, he hadn't noticed. That was all said and done now.

Perhaps part of the reason she stayed on here in the South of France, besides the obvious comfort of her life here, was that she didn't want to go back to England, where she would naturally go to London, to then discover that DI Ridley had absolutely no interest in her now that his case was solved. Part of her obviously feared that was true.

The fact still was that while she had blushed whenever he'd shown a modicum of concern for her wellbeing, he hadn't blushed back. He wasn't the kind of man to blush. With him, he had his objective in mind, and probably didn't notice anything unrelated—like blushing maids.

Changing direction, Dory tried to put all that out of her mind. What she really needed was a seat somewhere, where she could perch for a while like any self-respecting wallflower.

"Hello, Dory," a man said and Dory turned to see Duckie.

"I see my attempts at going incognito have completely failed. What gave me away?" Probably the dress as she only had two to wear. Surely he must have noticed.

Duckie smiled, his eyes looking disturbingly disembodied behind the mask. "Not sure. I think it's the hair. Since you are here, I assume Livinia is milling around."

"Last I saw her, she was on the dance floor." For officially being a chaperone, that sounded awful, but to be fair, she was expected to be the semblance of a chaperone rather than an active one.

A sharp scream echoed across the room, enough to make Dory drop her glass, which smashed into a thousand pieces around her feet. That wasn't the scream of some drunk girl being tickled. There was terror in that scream. Were the Germans invading, was the first thought that stole through Dory's brain.

Duckie's hand was on her arm as if steadying her. The music stopped and confusion spread through the crowd like a malignancy. Then murmurs. Everyone turned and stared in the direction of the scream.

A man cleared his throat. "I think we shall require the service of the Police. There has been an incident."

Livinia pressed unseeingly through the crowd, tears flowing down her face. Dory grabbed her by the arms to stop her. "What happened?"

"I don't know. I went to the bathroom and when I came back… he was dead."

"Who?" Duckie asked avidly.

"Drecsay," Livinia said, distress clearly showing in her eyes. "There was blood." At this moment, she looked like a small child who had been chastised for the first time. "He's dead."

"Bollocks," Duckie said.

People started leaving, finding a place to put their glasses down and headed to the door. Cars were already roaring to life outside, as they made their escape.

"We should go," Duckie said. "Where's Margot?"

"You can't go," Dory said, still holding onto Livinia by the arms as if she'd escape the moment she let go. "You found the body, you need to stay."

Livinia's expression turned to full-on pouting. "I can't."

"You have to. You found the body," Dory repeated.

"I didn't murder him."

"So don't make it look like it by scarpering."

To her credit, Livinia seemed to accept this, but with that acceptance, she now looked faint, as if the shock was catching up with her. Duckie came to her aid and they walked over to a seat.

A few people were still milling about, but from the window, Dory could see a string of car headlights making their way down the mountainside like a sparkling necklace in the darkness.

Couples stood near each other with their arms wrapped around them. A man who had to be the resident butler was trying to take control, and he was flustered, completely unsure what to do.

"Did you call the police?" Dory asked.

The man nodded. "I called them and they said they'd be here in ten minutes."

"Right," Dory said. It was clear where the body was. Down a hallway, a crowd had gathered, all staring down. "We need to clear the area."

The butler still looked confused, too flustered to do anything useful, so Dory walked over to where the crowd was.

"We should probably let the police do their job," she said. "Perhaps we should close the doors until they get here." A couple of people were staring absently at her, as if they didn't understand what she was saying. "Which means you should leave now," she said in a harsher voice. The terseness seemed to motivate the people to move. A voice of authority got through even if it came from her. "Off you go," she continued, eyeing everyone who hadn't gotten the message, until they all left.

A man was crouched next to the body. "You, too," she said and the man eyed her with offense for a moment, before acknowledging that she was right.

The dead man lay on his back, his eyes staring at the ceiling. It was such an unnatural look that goosebumps crawled up Dory's skin. There was clearly blood on the side of his head, and it was the man she had seen Livinia dancing with before, except his mask wasn't on. He was clearly a handsome man, even in death.

Refusing to look more, she grabbed the edges of the double doors and closed what looked like a study. Now, like everyone else, she didn't know what to do with herself. It felt wrong shutting him away to be there alone and discarded. Everything about this felt wrong. It was wrong. A man had lost his life, and by the look of his wound, it hadn't been an accident. He'd been murdered mere yards away from the party.

Chapter 5

The house stood in utter silence while they waited for the police. Another couple decided it was time to go and quietly slipped away. In rushed voices, they spoke to the butler as they left, then their car was clearly heard as they backed up before rushing down the driveway.

Livinia was sitting against the wall, leaning against Duckie's shoulder, while Dory stood in the center of the room, unsure what else to do. One man—clearly drunk—was pouring himself another generous portion of champagne from a discarded bottle.

No one spoke again and from somewhere, Dory heard the ticking of a clock.

How long was it going to take for the police to arrive?

Eventually a car snaked up the side of the mountain and Dory felt relief, as if release from this awkwardness was pending.

Car doors slammed outside and then a man appeared, marching straight into the room in a beige uniform with a pistol holstered at his side, secured with a leather strap crossed his chest. He wore a bored and unhappy expression, showing that he really didn't want to deal with hysterical Brits and their problems.

His gaze traveled across the room, noting the people there. Again, the butler assumed that it was his role to try to deal with this, but the inspector dismissed him with a terse look and the butler visibly deflated.

In the exchange, the inspector had learned where the problem was and walked over to the hallway that led to the study. He opened the doors and stepped inside.

Another policeman stood at the main doors, eyeing them all suspiciously. Everyone else shifted uncomfortably, feeling like naughty school children about to be told off.

Richard appeared, wearing his black tails and holding a small sandwich in his hand. His eyes shifted to Livinia sitting with Duckie and then further, finding Dory. Instead of joining Livinia, he decided to join Dory.

"I hadn't realized you were here," Dory said.

"I came late. Missed the party, but caught the main event."

Dory didn't like how casually he said it.

"Do you think someone snuck in the window and killed him?" he asked.

With a snort, Dory looked away. "The window was closed." In her experience, it was rarely strangers that snuck in and performed some horrid misdeed, even though it was what people liked to assume. No one automatically thought that someone among their friends and acquaintances was a murderer.

"Seems like a dire sort of chap, doesn't he?"

"Drecsay?" Dory asked, recalling the name Livinia had used. Dory had never seen him before tonight, or noticed him if she had.

"No, the policeman."

"Technically, I believe he's a gendarmerie instead of a policeman, but either way, he isn't here to make friends," Dory said dismissively. "He needs to suspect everyone."

"Ohh, I've never been a suspect before. Have you?"

"No," Dory admitted.

"Nothing to put a dampener on a party like a murder," Richard chuckled. "Poor Elsbeth. She had such high hopes for this party. Well, it truly will be the most notorious party of the season. Not quite how she anticipated, no doubt."

"Did you know the man?"

"Drecsay? I suppose. Everyone knows Drecsay. Been around for ages. Handsome bugger. Ladies like him." Richard took a bite of his sandwich and chewed. Well, he was certainly not one to faint with shock. In fact, he seemed completely unperturbed by the events. "I don't suppose we can leave."

"By the look of the man at the door, I don't think any of us are leaving until they've done what they want."

Richard checked his wrist watch.

"Somewhere you need to be?"

"No, not particularly."

"Who was he, this Drecsay?"

"Well," Richard started as if he was about to embark on a rambling story. "Hungarian baron from what I understand—if you believe what he said, because you never know about some of these foreign aristocrats, do you? Poor as a church mouse. You know the type, likes to mingle where the rich ladies are. Flatters them with charm and compliments. They lap it up, of course. The place is filthy with them. He has some rooms at one of the hotels in Nice, I believe."

And that had been who Livinia had been dancing with. Is that what he'd done to Livinia, charmed her? She was, after all, a wealthy heiress. If this man was the type that Richard painted, then he could well have been seeking an improvement in his position through the association. Dory sighed. Surely Livinia wasn't stupid enough to fall for such a man, was she? At times Dory felt like the ugly stepsister to Cinderella, provided Cinderella was resoundingly vacant and a bit of an idiot, chasing after some wildly inappropriate prince. Technically, it was Lady Pettifer's job to keep Livinia out of trouble, but it was Dory's too by extension.

The policeman appeared. "And who is this man?" he said with a flourish of his hand toward the study.

The butler stepped forward. "His name is Baron Dominik Drecsay. I am sure he has a string of middle names, but I do not know them."

The inspector turned to the butler without expression, then nodded to the policeman by the door, who promptly scribbled it down in his notebook.

"And everyone who was here at the time has left," the inspector continued.

"Yes," said the butler with a blush. "Mostly." Now a blushing butler was a rare sight in Dory's book, but then there had been admonishment in the inspector's statement.

"Who discovered the body?"

Everyone turned to Livinia, who still clung to Duckie for support. With raised eyebrows, the inspector walked over. Livinia looked up at him with large, wounded eyes. Dory had to stop herself from rolling hers.

"Who are you, and what were the circumstances in which you found him?"

"Well," Livinia said. "I am Livinia Fellingworth, daughter of Lord Wallisford. I had been in the bathroom and I was walking past."

"But the bathroom is nowhere near the study."

The wounded expression fleeted from Livinia's eyes. She didn't like being challenged, and she certainly didn't like admitting that she had been seeking out the company of Baron Drecsay in the isolation of the study. It wasn't seemly.

"Like I said," she said in a sterner voice. "I was walking past and he was simply laying there. Bloody."

"And the door was open?"

"A little."

The inspector looked down his nose at her. Clearly, the man didn't believe her story, or at least the embellishments.

"And this man was your lover?"

"What? No!" Livinia said with deep offense.

"He is a handsome man. It is understandable if you were sneaking off for a rendezvous in a more private place."

"Absolutely not," Livina said sternly, but she was unable to hide the blush on her cheeks.

"And before you found him in the library? Where did you see him?"

Livinia's mouth drew tight. "On the dance floor."

"You were dancing, yes?"

"Yes," Livinia said through gritted teeth.

The inspector was eyeing her now and Dory knew he was wondering if she had murdered him in some jealous tiff. Absolutely not, Dory thought. For all of Livinia's shortcomings, she didn't feel any emotion deeply enough to drive her to murder.

"I didn't really know him," Livinia filled in as the silence stretched. "The evening has been quite a shock. Can we go now?"

"And where do you live, Mademoiselle Fellingworth?" Her name sounded like an insult in the French accent. Dory wasn't sure if it was intended that way or not.

"Saint Tropez. Ville Beaulieu."

A short grunt escaped the inspector. Seemingly, he wasn't pleased with this. Probably because it was quite some way from this man's office, which Dory guessed was in Cannes.

Then he turned his attention to the rest of the people present, asking who they were, where they had been during the party and the discovery, how they knew the deceased and where they lived. Also if they knew of any enemies the man had. After, they could all go home.

Dory could hear the man request the guest list for the party. He had a big task ahead of him, because it had been large, and someone at the party had murdered this man. The thought made her shudder—someone stalking around the house with such ill intent.

The air was cool as they walked out of the house. Dory had no idea what time it was, but it was late.

"Are you coming home, Livinia?" Dory asked as they stood outside in the darkness. It was too dark to see Livinia's facial expressions. Her whole face had a blue quality from the moonlight.

"I think I will, actually," she said to Dory's surprise. It seemed there was something that could quell her social yearnings.

"Alright, let's go," Dory said and they found their car, which had been standing on its own as everyone else had left. Now there was sufficient space to maneuver as they got in and turned around to leave. The engine whined on the way down the hill and luckily, the moonlight was enough to see the road beyond the short reach of the headlights.

Quiet contemplation seemed to be Livinia's current disposition. It had been quite a shocking night for her, Dory supposed.

"Were you in love with this man?" Dory asked after a while.

"No, of course not," Livinia replied. Her voice sounded thin and distant, so Dory wasn't sure whether she was telling the truth or not.

It hit Dory how incredible this all was. A man had been murdered right there when they were all chatting and drinking champagne. How in the world could something like that happen?

"Do you have any idea who killed him?" Dory asked.

"What I said was true. I didn't really know him that well. I didn't know of any enemies as such. He was just someone around, you know? No one particularly hated him; he was a charming man."

Charming didn't automatically mean no one hated him, but Dory wasn't sure it was the time to point that out.

Chapter 6

Dory was exhausted the next day. Sleep had eluded her and her mind had repeatedly turned over every detail from the night before. And still, she couldn't believe someone had murdered that poor man. He couldn't be more than thirty. His whole life was ahead of him and it had been snuffed out—for apparently no reason at all.

There was a reason, though. No one was bludgeoned at a party for absolutely no reason. Someone hated this man enough to kill him. Then again, murder wasn't always about hate. Lady Wallisford hadn't hated when she'd killed. In her mind, she'd been protecting her family. Murder could be cold and calculating.

Turning herself over, Dory tried fruitlessly to fall off to sleep, but the sun was up and the birds were chirping. Perhaps it was time to give up and embrace a day of sluggish exhaustion. With heavy legs, she dragged herself out of bed and dressed.

Dark shadows were pronounced under her eyes. Brilliant. She looked like a train wreck.

The house was mostly quiet when she went downstairs, although she could hear the tinkling of cutlery. Lady Pettifer was up and breakfasting when Dory walked into the dining room.

"My dear," Lady Pettifer said. "By the look of you, it must have been a long night."

"Not in the way you think. There was an incident at the party which ended it early. A man—someone Livinia knows, and was dancing with, in fact—ended up bludgeoned in the study."

Deep concern marred Lady Pettifer's face. "I hope he's alright."

Dory shook her head, hating that she had to be the one relaying these events.

"Who?" Lady Pettifer demanded.

"Some Baron Drecsay, a Hungarian."

"I don't know him."

"I don't either, but Livinia does—did—and according to Richard, he might not be the type of man she should be spending time with."

"Not if he runs around being murdered. How awful." Lady Pettifer shuddered and Beauty jumped up into her lap. "I suppose the police will let the Hungarian ambassador know."

"That seems logical."

They sat in silence for a moment, and Mr. Fernley placed down a plate of eggs and toast in front of Dory. "Thank you," she mumbled, completely unable to gather her appetite, but she ate to be agreeable. "I am sure the inspector will come around and question Livinia more at some point."

Picking up her coffee cup, Lady Pettifer absently drank and returned it. "What sort of man was he?"

"Well, according to Richard, he was poor and maybe even dependent on the more wealthy ladies of the area."

Lady Pettifer winced. "Still, that doesn't really lend itself to murder, does it? Who would kill a man like that?"

Someone like Lady Wallisford, Dory thought, chewing her toast and looking away. "Maybe he had garnered the attention of some woman and her family objected."

"Hardly cause for murder," Lady Pettifer said. "Then again, people murder for all sorts of reasons, don't they? I don't like that Livinia is caught up in all this."

"No," Dory agreed. With her own eyes, she had already seen that inspector consider whether Livinia was the murderer. There was a good chance he would continue with that line of questioning.

"Bludgeoned, you said?" Lady Pettifer asked after a while. "That most certainly has to be a man. I'm not sure a women could bludgeon a man to death." Dory wasn't sure if that was true, but she wasn't an expert.

"I didn't get a close look, but I don't think he was hit repeatedly. At least not from what I could see. There could have been injuries that I couldn't see. I didn't get a chance to study him. There was a marble clock nearby him on the floor, and I am almost certain that was the weapon."

"Anyone could have walked in, whacked him on the head, and slipped out again. How many people were at this party?"

"It seemed like two hundred."

She winced and a silence prevailed again. It was utterly silent upstairs, too. No music was playing, so Livinia was asleep.

"Had Livinia been carrying on with this man?" Lady Pettifer asked.

Dory could only shrug. "I hope not. They had been dancing together, and—she says otherwise—but she was meeting him in the study, where she found him dead."

"Poor Livinia. She must be distraught. She wasn't built for such knocks. Too high-strung."

As if awakened by people speaking about her, the music started playing upstairs.

"It seems she's awake," Lady Pettifer said. "I hope she isn't too distraught. I haven't heard her mention this man before, so who can say what kind of relationship she had with him."

Livinia eventually appeared down on the patio wearing sunglasses. Her hair had been quickly brushed and she wore a white shirt and shorts. For the terrible night, she looked fresh. "God, I'm parched," she said and sat down. She reached for the jug of orange juice and poured herself a helping.

"I'm sorry to hear about the dreadful events last night."

Livinia shrugged her shoulders. "I can't make heads or tails of it. Who could possibly hate Drecsay enough to do that to him? You don't suppose it was an accident?"

"No," Dory said with certainty. It wasn't that he lay close to the fireplace to suggest he could have accidentally fallen and dragged the clock down upon himself. No, someone had picked up the clock and smashed him over the head with it. In fact, the person had probably been watching Drecsay in the main salon, then watched for an opportunity to strike when Livinia was absent. That had to mean that the person was watching Livinia dance with the man during the evening. The thought made Dory uncomfortable and the hairs rose along her arms. Had the person planned what to do? Had they come to the party with the intention of murdering someone?

"It's such a shame," Livinia sighed wistfully. "He was such a gorgeous man. Do you think someone killed him because they were jealous?"

"No sure people go around murdering others simply because they're pretty," Lady Pettifer said.

"There's a mercy," Livinia responded.

"But people certainly do murder because of jealousy."

"That seems pointless. If there is something you want badly enough, just go out and get it."

"I think often, my dear, there is more a desire for the other person not to have what they have."

"I don't understand it at all," Livinia said dismissively, as though she didn't wish to speak about it further.

"So what do you know about this man?" Lady Pettifer asked.

Livinia sighed audibly. "Well, he's young and handsome. Lives in the Carlone on the Promenade de Anglais as far as I know. I haven't been there if that's what you're thinking," she said defensively. "He was just a nice, charming man. I can't believe someone murdered him." Her mouth was drawn tight for a moment.

"Was there anyone he'd had discord with lately?" Dory asked.

"No. There was a woman he was very close to, a Countess Tirau, but she died recently. Treated him like a son. Obviously, he wasn't a saint. There were more than a few girls vying for his attention, I'm sure. Some of the American girls used to fall over themselves when he came around. It was tiresome, really. Handsome, swarthy baron; they were beside themselves."

Reaching into her pocket, Livinia pulled out a packet of cigarettes and lit one with a gold plated lighter. She blew the smoke across the table and rested her hand to the side until the smoke from the burning tip curled up into the air.

"And where was he from?" Lady Pettifer asked.

"Hungary."

"But where in Hungary?"

"Well, I don't know, do I? Why would I ask that? It wasn't as if I made a detailed study of his family history. His family was old and respected. Ask anyone."

Livinia got up and walked away, having had enough of the questioning. Although she had better get used to it; there were likely more questions to come. The acrid smoke stung Dory's nose as she walked past.

"She is upset," Lady Pettifer stated.

In her jarring and rather dismissive way, Livinia was more upset than she let on. "Everyone on the coast must be talking about her in relation to this murder. She was the one he was meeting in the study."

"The last thing Livinia needs is another scandal."

Well, there might just be one. There would be speculation about who had killed him and why, and Livinia's name would be in the thick of it. Problem was, with a man like Drecsay, who knew what skeletons and misdeeds he had in his closet. From what Richard said, he wasn't an innocent. Even Livinia confirmed it. But Livinia was clearly confused about why he would be murdered, so either she didn't know him well, or he really hadn't done anything that would warrant such a deplorable fate.

Chapter 7

They had a couple of quiet days at the house—days that were constantly accompanied with Livinia's gramophone. Fortunately, she had very good taste in music, so no one minded the dulcet tones of Bing Crosby and Duke Ellington. They even lent a joviality that wouldn't exist otherwise. The death of Baron Drecsay sat like a cloying heaviness, even though neither Dory nor Lady Pettifer knew him. It was the fact that it had happened that was disturbing.

The coast was such a safe community, where everyone was respected and showed a duty of care in return. Normally, the biggest problem around here were motorcar accidents, which happened relatively often late at night after some raucous party.

Dory bicycled down to the village and back, taking Beauty with her. She resupplied them with fresh bread and even bought some lemons to squeeze into drinks during the afternoon heat. Fortunately, they had enough sugar, but she had noticed that the packets of sugar in the shop were fewer than normal. Everything else seemed fine. It was just the sugar that was low. Perhaps it was just an anomaly.

"They had barely any sugar in the village store," Dory said when she returned to the house and found Lady Pettifer sitting in the parlor. She preferred it in there when the midday heat became too strong as the solid walls of the house kept the inside relatively cool.

Lady Pettifer looked up from her book. "I hope they haven't started rationing. We might see less and less of anything coming across the Atlantic."

Dory listened with concern. She hadn't realized that there might be trouble with sugar coming across from South America.

"In 1919, the Germans decided to starve us by sinking any ship coming by water."

"They said on the wireless that the navy was protecting the supply across the Atlantic," Dory said with a deep frown, trying to understand what this all meant.

"France doesn't have the same naval capabilities, so they can't provide the same degree of protection." Lady Pettifer sighed and stroked her fingers across her lips. "Mr. Fernley," she called.

He appeared mere moments later. "Can I be of assistance, Madame?"

"I think we should shore up our stores. Would you go to Cannes and purchase enough of the essentials to last us a good while? Dory has noticed things becoming scarcer down in the village."

Mr. Fernley nodded. He was old enough to remember how things had been in the first war. For all Dory knew, he might have fought in the first war. It had never occurred to her to ask him. "Yes, madame," he said. "If you shall have no use for the motorcar this afternoon, I will go presently."

"We have no plans," Lady Pettifer said and returned to her book.

He didn't wait long and Dory soon heard the car start up and caught glimpse of him drive along the trees in the distance until he was out of sight. It hadn't occurred to Dory that there would be rationing. Of course she had heard of it. Gladys had mentioned it a few times, talked about the things they'd had to do to compensate, but Dory hadn't really paid attention. It seemed vitally important now. What if they didn't have food?

"How bad did the rationing get?" she asked.

"It grew in stages, but it wasn't so bad. Meat, butter and sugar were in short supply over the entire country. I suppose it all depends on how long the war lasts. Technically, the Great War lasted four years, but we really noticed the rationing at the end."

"Four years," Dory said with dismay. Well, maybe it wouldn't be so long this time.

"I spent most of the war at Wallisford Hall, and we didn't really see much of it. In London, though, the Germans came in their great balloons. I never saw them, but we were all terrified one would come, floating to us in complete silence, ready to drop bombs on us."

"It must have been awful."

"The worst was when the letters started coming. Every day there were letters in the village to inform the families of their lost sons. The army took our horses too, as soon as they were ridable. They even took some of our dogs."

"Dogs?"

"I'm not sure why, but they had use of them. My father took to breeding pigeons, too. Everyone had a job, even my father, who bred horses and pigeons. There weren't that many serviceable cars back then—at least not ones that could cover open terrain like horses could, but things are different now."

"I suppose tanks will replace horses."

"I don't know," Lady Pettifer said. "Horses are still extremely versatile. Could be that my brother has been asked to start breeding at Wallisford Hall. If he has, he's probably been asked to keep quiet about it."

Dory listened to everything Lady Pettifer said with both concern and fascination, but they were both distracted by the appearance of a motorcar, and it wasn't Mr. Fernley returning early. It was the same car Dory had seen the night at Lord and Lady Tonbridge, and she knew it belonged to that inspector.

"Who could this be?" Lady Pettifer said, not recognizing the car.

"I believe this might be Inspector Moreau."

They heard Livinia swearing upstairs, and before long, there was a slammed car door and a sharp knock at the door. It was open, along with all windows, to let the air through the building.

"I'll see to him," Dory said as Mr. Fernley wasn't present to perform the duty.

"I suppose you shall have to bring him in here."

Rising, Dory made her way over to the door, where Inspector Moreau stood with his thin frame and straight back. He wore the exact same beige uniform as before, again with his pistol at his side.

"Inspector Moreau," she greeted him.

With a snap, he opened his notebook. "I shall need to speak to yourself," he consulted his notebook, "Miss Sparks, and Miss Fellingworth. Are you both at home?"

"We are. Please come in."

The second policeman he seemed to travel with remained outside as if watching for someone fleeing, ready to give chase at a moment's notice.

Dory led the man into the salon where Lady Pettifer sat. "This is Inspector Moreau," she said, introducing him to the lady. "He is with the gendarmerie. This is Lady Pettifer."

The man gave a sharp bow, but Dory could tell he had no real interest in her. As with DI Ridley, this man only cared about the relevant details of the case.

"Lady Pettifer, you did not attend the soiree at the Lord and Lady Tonbridge house, correct?"

"That is correct," Lady Pettifer said. "Would you like some tea?"

"I will go retrieve Livinia," Dory said and made her way out of the room, to take the wooden staircase up to the second story. Livinia's door was closed and Dory knocked quietly. "That inspector is here. He wishes to speak to you."

The door opened suddenly and Livinia looked sour as if Dory was at fault for bringing her news of their visitor. "I don't know what else I can tell him," she said. "I found him. That's all."

Both returned to the salon, where Inspector Moreau was now sitting uncomfortably in a chair with his legs crossed, the brown leather boots glossy with reflections from the window.

"Miss Fellingworth," he said, rising from his chair. "This is a good time for you tell me everything you know about Baron Drecsay."

Floating down on her seat, Livinia rearranged her skirt, still deeply unimpressed by this interruption. Didn't she realize that her objection to the inconvenience meant nothing to this man. He was hardly going to pack it in because she was annoyed.

"I don't know what else I can tell you," she started.

"When did you meet?"

"Ages ago. I think at a party at Bertie Stringfellow's. We were introduced, but were never really part of the same circle. I've seen him here and there, but we never really knew each other as such," she said with a dismissive wave.

"Yet, you were meeting him in private at the party by Lord and Lady—" He consulted his notes, "Tonbridge."

Livinia's dislike for this interrogation deepened. "He wished to speak in private," was all she said.

"And before that, you were dancing on the dance floor together, no?"

"Yes."

"What was it he wished to say to you in private?"

"How should I know. We never got a chance to speak."

"You must have had some understanding."

"He didn't tell me what was on his mind," Livinia said through gritted teeth.

The inspector looked unimpressed.

"He might have mentioned something about going sailing during the next week," Livinia said, relenting under the inspector's silent pressure. He wrote it down.

"And who was he going sailing with?"

Livinia scratched along her eyebrow for a moment. "That Italian prince… Barenoli, or something some such."

"And you were going with them?"

"No, of course not. I have better things to do than go bob around on some boat."

"Who were his other friends?"

"Like I said, I didn't know him well. Maybe you should talk to Barenoli. He knew him better."

"Have you been to his rooms at Hotel Carlone?"

"No!"

"I think perhaps, Inspector, you are making assumptions where they are not warranted," Lady Pettifer said in a voice with such chill, Dory felt it up her arms. The inspector felt it too. Lady Pettifer stated in no uncertain terms that he was overstepping propriety, and even he, with his investigation, struggled to get past the lady putting her foot down.

Finally, he gave up. "And you, Miss Spark? You knew the man?"

"No, I'm afraid I didn't recognize him in any regard. I'm not sure I've met him before that night."

"He was at the Myrtle party you attended, I believe," Livinia added.

Dory turned her attention back. "If I have met him before, I have no recollection."

"He is a very handsome man."

"Not my kind of handsome," Dory said, refusing to let the blush bloom up her face. But he really wasn't.

Chapter 8

They didn't hear again about the murder for quite a while. Their days returned to normal and Livinia even returned to her social activities—spurred on by Richard coming to pick her up for a tennis match. Livinia left the house in a white sleeveless dress that ended right on the knee, her racquet tucked under her arm.

"I'll be gone for a while. Might be back for dinner, but start without me if I'm not."

The tribulations of the last week had now rolled off her completely and she was swiftly returning to normal. It couldn't be said that she was crushed by Baron Drecsay's death, which showed that she didn't have any deep and lasting feelings for the man.

Maybe what she protested, that she didn't know the man well, was true. Still, Dory felt there was something untoward about the man and his interest in Livinia. It was only his handsome face that would tempt Livinia to stray out of her strict social circle, where status, family and connections mattered. At this point, Dory was learning to see the benefit of it in terms of protecting someone like Livinia from people with less than honorable ambitions.

It was more than Richard's words on the issue now. Lady Pettifer had returned from an afternoon tea with one of the older ladies who lived on the coast with her son, where it had been mentioned that the man did have a reputation for seeking to assure his fortunes. Wealthy heiresses were definitely the kind of women who he kept company with.

With a sigh, Dory tried to dismiss all this from her thoughts. She'd been down this road before and knew how absorbing it could be, gathering and analyzing all information and trying to reach an understanding of what had happened. It wasn't a lie to say that Dory had lost her job, her standing and her friends the last time she had gotten herself caught up in the investigation of a murder. This one she should leave to Inspector Moreau. There was no doubt in her mind that he would absolutely not want her help.

"Why don't you go for a walk, my dear?" Lady Pettifer said. Dory could tell she was tired. "I'll have a little sojourn while you do."

"Alright," Dory said and grabbed her hat. It was early afternoon and the sun was harsh. It didn't have the full heat of August, when it was nearly unbearable with scorching heat built up in the masonry of the house, day after day. The days were still pleasant and Dory walked over the vast lawns to the gardens.

She sought the bench in the garden, where she could sit and stare out at the blue sea. Fishing boats floated in the distance. They weren't so active this time of day, their crew likely sleeping. Dory had never gotten the hang of the siesta, unable to settle down to sleep in the middle of the day. Some days she wished she could sleep away the hottest hours, but her body refused.

So, it was easier to come down here and languish in the garden, or sometimes down by the sea. Below her was a croppy sea shore. It wasn't a bad spot for swimming on the hottest days. A small jetty and a ladder had been built to access the sea, but it wasn't a good place to moor a boat. The rocks were too big and too close, and anything moored there risked being smashed to pieces if the wind picked up.

A lovely breeze came off the sea and she smelled fresh saltiness. The perfume of the flowers around her scented the air as well. In truth, this was a wild garden, left to tend itself most of the time. Dory much preferred it to the neatly trimmed and planned garden at Wallisford Hall, but it was an entirely different thing.

The coast also had citrus. Oranges and lemons that sat like heavy jewels on trees. They were marvelous. Apparently, their lemons were later blooming than most varieties, but they had a more subtle taste. Right now, they weren't ripe.

Dory enjoyed the garden, but she was a little more like Livinia in that she couldn't bring herself to care about the details of gardening and learning the different varieties of plants. Lady Pettifer had a long memory with her garden, remembering the plants and when they were planted, even whom they were planted in honor of.

Dory's mother had only ever invested in one struggling rose bush that against all diversity managed a bloom every other year. It was a tribute to a fallacy of having both the time and inclination to be a gardener, rather than a true passion for her mother, who really was too busy to care for a rose bush as well. Dory smiled at the thought. She did miss home.

For a moment, Dory considered if she should walk to the village, perhaps purchase one of the small bars of chocolate they sold at the village store. It was an indulgence she allowed herself every once in a while. Then she grew worried about the thought of some of these luxury items growing short in supply. Perhaps her love of chocolate would be something she would have to sacrifice to this war.

A renewed discomfort washed over her, like it did every time she thought of the fact that they were at war. Each night, they listened to the BBC and to the relentless German march across Europe. Around here, though, it wasn't the Germans that terrified the population, but the Italians. They were so very close to the border and Mussolini made discomforting noises, and if anyone was to come marching into town, it would be them. The very thought of it was difficult to contemplate. How could life change so quickly? Soldiers coming to disrupt and take control over of a region.

What kind of life would they have if the Italians marched into town? They had no great love for the British. There would be a scramble to flee. But so far, no one had come marching across the Italian Alps. Or would they come by sea like the Germans did? Would she wake up one morning and a battalion full of them would be on their doorstep? Dory shuddered.

*

Livinia did return for supper, still dressed in her tennis whites. A grass stain was prominent on one of her knees, and her nose and cheeks were golden with additional sun. She had skin that could take the sun, turning her skin golden. Dory didn't.

"You won't believe what they are saying in town," Livinia said as she sat down at the table, having changed for supper. Her eyes were lit up with excitement. "That Baron Drecsay had a hidden life and that he was killed for spying for the Italians. I don't believe a word of it, but there are those saying it."

"A spy?" Lady Pettifer said. "That's a little far-fetched, isn't it?"

"Considering he's been here for years. What in the world could he be spying on down here? Although, technically, he's part English, they also said. Tied to the Elmhurst family. I had no idea. Like I keep telling everyone, I didn't actually know him. But a spy, can you imagine?"

Both Dory and Lady Pettifer sat in silence for a moment. Yes, the newspapers were full of talk of spies, but for there to actually be one in their midst, at a party they had attended—that seemed preposterous. Could it be? Dory had to question herself. Could it be that he was a spy and was murdered for being found out? "Surely if he was a spy, they would have dragged him away to be questioned somewhere?"

"He was friends with that Prince Barenoli, who is definitely Italian."

"Few amongst the Italian nobility are friends with that upstart Mussolini," Lady Pettifer said. "One cannot jump to the conclusion that being Italian means one is favorable to either Mussolini or the fascists. The world is more complicated than that."

"Well, not everyone seems that way inclined," Livinia said. "And Hungary has displayed a cozy relationship with the Nazis."

Dory could hear someone else's words coming out of Livinia, because never in a thousand years would she care about such politics if there wasn't a murder involved.

"It's never that simple," Lady Pettifer said. "We can't simply label people sympathetic because of where they're from."

"Still, we've locked up every German in the region," Livinia countered.

Lady Pettifer only sighed. "Unless there is some evidence that he was spying, we cannot treat assertions that he was a spy, and murdered for it, as anything more than rumor."

"And really, would it be appropriate to dispatch a spy at Lady Tonbridge's party?" Dory said.

"Perhaps they took their chance as soon as they could out him?"

"Who?" Lady Pettifer demanded.

"The people looking for spies."

"They're hardly going to be at Lady Tonbridge's party, are they?"

"Who's to say? With the Duke and Duchess of Windsor here, who's to say what kind of hidden military men are lurking around the place? They would definitely act if they came across an embedded spy."

Again Dory heard someone else's words coming out of Livinia's mouth. "We can't assume anything. If there is no proof, there is no fact. Assumptions only mean mistakes." Now she heard DI Ridley's sentiments coming out of her own mouth. "Unless there is something actually proving he's a spy, then it's pure speculation. We have to stick to the facts."

"Which are: someone knocked him over the head at a party."

"So we know it was someone at the party," Lady Pettifer stated.

Chapter 9

Dory had to drive whenever Lady Pettifer came in the car, because Lady Pettifer much preferred it to Lavinia's driving, and Dory couldn't blame her. Lavinia's driving was nerve-wracking for anyone. The road along the coast was winding, with tight corners around the dramatic sheer cliffs. They arrived at the Promenade de Anglaise shortly after noon.

It had taken about an hour and a half to get there, and they were set to meet some friends of Lady Pettifer's in a café along the esplanade, and perhaps wander around some of the shops afterward. Lady Pettifer was in need of new stockings.

It wasn't often that they came to Nice, as it was a bit of a drive, but it was nice to venture away from the house every once in a while. Nice was cosmopolitan compared to the small village of St. Tropez. Even though a good portion of residents had gone back to their respective countries, there was no vast absence of people walking along the promenade, and the cafés were patronised enough.

A parking space was available near the Café de Flore, which was situated on a corner. Cane chairs covered the walkway outside of the Café, encircling small white marble tables. It was quite busy with most tables taken. Multiple languages were heard— Dory identified French, Portuguese and English. With Nice being so busy, it was hard to imagine that so much of the population was now absent. On the streets, it didn't seem so, but perhaps it was less busy than a year ago.

"Finally we're here. You really do drive like an old woman, Dory," Lavinia said as she contorted herself out of the back of the car. With sharp strokes, she straightened her skirt. "I hate sitting in the back. My knees always end up in awkward positions and my skirt crumbles up." There was plenty of space in the back; Lavinia was just annoyed that Dory was asked to drive instead of her.

"I better go call Richard," she continued. "I'll only be a moment, so go ahead without me. I'll catch up." She ran off toward the telephone booth further down the street, while Dory helped Lady Pettifer out of the car.

They walked to the café, where Lady Pettifer spotted her party. "There," she said indicating toward the far side, where in a shaded corner, close to the building itself, sat two elderly women, waving when they spotted the new arrivals.

Lady Pettifer made the introductions. A Lady Summernot and Miss Greer. The women shared a resemblance, so Dory assumed they were sisters.

"Is Lavinia not joining us today?" one of the ladies asked, looking disappointed.

"She's here. Simply making arrangements by telephone. You know the young girls," Lady Pettifer said. "They can't simply do one thing in a day, they have to do several. She's planning the rest of her afternoon as we speak."

The women chuckled lightly and indicated to seats for Dory and Lady Pettifer.

"And how are you, Dory?" Miss Greer asked.

"Well. It was a lovely drive."

The waiter, dressed rather informally without a jacket approached, his hair neatly combed and he smiled beneath his trimmed mustache.

"Tea I think," Lady Pettifer said. "Darjeeling, if you have any."

"I'll have the same," Dory added and the other two agreed.

"The temperature is certainly getting warmer. Not quite intolerable yet." Lady Summernot stated. "We do get the sea breezes, so we are not as badly off as some, but I've had to bring some of my more delicate flowers inside."

Miss Greer shifted in her seat. "We were awfully surprised to hear about that unfortunate incident with the Hungarian man. It's so shocking."

"To think something like that would happen here," Lady Summernot added. "This is such a safe place. It's distressing to hear any such news. Poor man. I understand he has no family here. I don't actually know if he has any family at all."

"I did hear that Lavinia found the body," Miss Greer said. "I hope she's not too distressed by it."

"That has made it around, has it?" Lady Pettifer asked. The two ladies were looking at her expectantly, hoping she would enlighten them further. "Lavinia was returning from the powder room when she saw the poor man lying on the floor in the study, bashed about the head."

Technically it was true, but Lavinia *had* been going to the study to meet the man. The powder room was nowhere near the study, and she couldn't simply have been walking past on her way back. Lavinia had definitely been seeking him out, but it wasn't something that Lady Pettifer wanted these women to talk about. Even Dory had heard that these two were notorious gossips, and anything that came out of their mouths, would be known throughout the entire coast.

"It is very curious, though. I knew the man. Very charming. The kind of handsome that you know would lead a man into trouble," Lady Summernot said knowingly.

"He looked just like Rudolph Valentino," Miss Greer said wistfully. "It's all such a shame."

"From what I understand, they haven't found the culprit yet," added Lady Summernot. "But I gather the police have determined it was a cuckolded husband, an enraged and jealous man being responsible for the act. It seems our Baron Drecsay had been caught in a bedroom or two in his time. So he had more than one enemy amongst the husbands around here. It goes to reason that one of them decided to take their fury out on the man himself."

"That's only conjecture, though," Lady Pettifer added.

"Well this was heard said by the regional head for the gendarmerie himself, so there must be some truth to it. At least that is the direction that the police inquiry had led them to."

Lady Pettifer and Dory exchanged looks. This was news to them. They had heard nothing about an irate husband, but then they were quite far away from the gossip and the tattling tongues of Nice and Cannes.

"Is it a police inquiry or a gendarmerie inquiry? Why do the French have to be difficult and have two police forces? It's so confusing," Lady Summernot added.

"We heard it said by some that he is suspected of being a spy," Dory said and both of the women went silent as their attention turned to her.

"Some are seeing spies around every corner, aren't they?" Miss Greer finally said. "If he were a spy, he was certainly a flamboyant one. I would have thought spies were supposed to blend in and go unnoticed, but Baron Drecsay was anything but."

"It's much more likely that he was caught climbing out of some bedroom or other," Lady Summernot said with amusement in her voice. "He was a lively boy, that one."

"Hello, ladies," Lavinia said brightly as she sat down.

"Has your afternoon been planned out then?" queried Lady Summernot.

"Well, I have just found out what everyone else is up to. Myrtle is having a bit of a pool party at her house later this afternoon. So I wonder if you could drop me off on the way home," Lavinia said, turning her attention to Lady Pettifer and Dory.

"Of course," Lady Pettifer said.

It seemed that Lavinia was being embraced back into her crowd, having survived the ordeal of finding a body in the study at Lady Tonbridge's party.

"It's so awfully hot," Lavinia said, fanning herself with the menu from the table.

It was true that it was heating up significantly in the afternoons, but it wasn't properly summer yet. Likely they were heading for a very hot summer. Or perhaps Lavinia's mind was on the refreshing depths of Myrtle's pool.

"It's such a beautiful day," said Miss Greer, looking around as if just noticing the weather. "We are packing, of course."

"Oh, you're returning to England?" Lady Pettifer asked.

"Well, we have a few more weeks," Lady Summernot said, "but with all the trouble we are hearing on the wireless, we thought we'd better head back to England."

"Others were having endless trouble booking passage," Miss Greer added. "The passenger lines aren't running like they used to. We thought we'd head down to the booking office later this afternoon. It can't be as bad as people say."

"The blockades must be stopping some ships from coming through. No doubt the Navy had commandeered some of the passenger traffic."

"Well, people must still travel," Miss Greer said. "Otherwise we understand some are driving all the way to Calais. I'd hate for that to be the only way to return to England."

"There are still ships sailing," Lady Summernot said. "Perhaps we need to look at booking passage from Marseilles instead."

"I wish they would have communicated the difficulty in booking passage more. If we'd known it would be so difficult, we would have left earlier. But there's been nothing. We haven't heard a thing."

"I'm sure they're not willing to broadcast exactly what's happening with the ships in the area," Lady Pettifer said quietly.

"You don't think the ships are at risk, do you? Nothing's happened so far." Grave concern registered in Miss Greer's face.

"At wartime, there's always a risk."

"Surely they wouldn't interfere with civilian ships?"

"I hope not," Lady Summernot said. "Passenger transport was quite safe during the last war. I doubt even the Germans would sink so low as to torpedo a civilian ship. I think interfering even with merchant ships is a crime. Doing so with the passenger ships, civilian ships, would be an atrocity. Not even the Germans could be that unreasonable."

By the look of Lady Pettifer's expression, Dory knew that she wasn't convinced. Lady Pettifer rarely gave the Germans the same benefit of the doubt as others did. Even her brother, Lord Wallisford, was a little bit more blasé about the Germans, while the Lady Pettifer was deeply concerned about this war, and her suspicions about their safety ran to everything. Dory could only hope she was wrong. It was distressing to think that civilian ships would be targeted as part of the military operations, but they couldn't deny it was a risk.

"I hate all this talk about the war and the Germans," Lavinia stated. "They're not breaching the French lines and that's that. I wish we could all stop talking about it."

Lady Pettifer gave her a circumspect look, almost pitying. Although Dory wished dearly that Lavinia was right. The Germans were moving north because they could, but they wouldn't come this far south as Italy and the French were holding them to the east. Hopefully the Germans had been hemmed in enough to have done all the damage they could at this point.

Chapter 10

The house of Lavinia's friend sat at the top of a very steep hill and a small cable car led from the garage down by the coast road, reaching up through the trees covering the side of the hill. Dory pulled over and Lavinia got out, telling them not to wait up. In a way, Lavinia almost looked relieved escaping their company. She didn't always hide how bored she was with them.

In the slowly rising cable car, she looked a small and lonely figure, inching her way up the side of the hill.

With a wave, Dory pulled away and they continued driving down the road toward St. Tropez.

"What do you think of what Lady Summernot said about the police having concluded some wronged husband had killed Baron Drecsay?" Dory asked.

Lady Pettifer sat quietly for a moment as if considering the idea. "It's hard to say as there's no particular husband anyone can point to. I'm sure the man was no saint, but if passions were so inflamed that they led to murder, wouldn't we know more about it?"

"The theory does sound possible, but you're right, there seems to be no evidence to back it up. At least not anything we've come across. Do you think the police could know something and are refusing to tell anyone?"

"I doubt it. Can't hide anything in a place like this," Lady Pettifer said. "If there was something going on, it would certainly not be quiet. And if he were in the thick with some lover, would he really be sniffing around Lavinia the way he was?"

"Maybe that was a distraction from an affair he was having, a means to deflect attention?"

"If a man were to murder his wife's lover, it's more likely because the news was emerging about it."

"Or perhaps there was blackmail involved," Dory said.

"This is all pure speculation. Speculation means nothing without proof."

"It must be that the police have no proof, otherwise they would've arrested someone by now if there was any truth to their suspicions. Provided their suspicions are correct to begin with."

"I'm sure if Lady Summernot is talking about it, there could well be some truth to it. She is very good at garnering what is true and what is not. I'll give her that. The woman has a good fifty years' experience with receiving and conveying tidbits about the people around here," Lady Pettifer said dryly.

Biting her lip, Dory had to wonder if there were some unpleasant turns in the history between Lady Pettifer and Lady Summernot. On first appearance, they seemed very friendly, but when studying closer, Dory could see that there was tension between the ladies, at least from Lady Pettifer's side. It wasn't her place to dwell about things like that. If Lady Pettifer wanted to inform her of any past transgressions, she would.

Picking a piece of lint off her skirt, Lady Pettifer sighed. "My worry, though, is that the French Police will not look into it further. Like Miss Greer said, 'people are seeing spies in every shadow,' and that is probably true for the police as well. They would be much more concerned about the potential of military presence in the area."

"It is a murder," Dory said emphatically.

"Yes, but it sounds as though the police have no real clue as to who the culprit is. Their assertion that it was a wronged husband must come from assumptions they've made based on Baron Drecsay's character—potentially without any real proof. It's been almost two weeks now, and they haven't apprehended anyone. That worries me."

In silence, Dory considered what this meant. The police were taking their time finding the person responsible. For a moment, she had to wonder if DI Ridley would be more vigilant in his investigation than the French Police appeared to be. The French always had a standoffish attitude to the foreigners here on the coast. They often left any issues for the consulates to take care of.

Technically, the consulates weren't mandated, or even equipped, to investigate murders, and it certainly wasn't within their jurisdiction. It seemed the French Police had done their bit and concluded they could not find the culprit.

Perhaps that was a little ungenerous. The inspector was surely following up on any leads he had. But from what Lady Summernot was saying, no particular lover of this baron had come forth. Either they were very discreet or this man wasn't quite the Lothario that people were making him out to be.

There was no doubt he was a handsome man, and people had naturally assumed he had a lascivious character because of it. It might not be true. He might not be crawling around every bedroom on the coast, even if he had the looks to do so. It was imprudent to assume this was part of his character simply by the way he looked.

One never assumed that beauty was something that would be problematic for people, but apparently their looks got in the way as people made assumptions based on them. Beauty was always assumed to be a wondrous asset, but perhaps it could be a detriment at times too. People always assume certain characteristics went along with that beauty— spoilt, vapid and entitled.

With these thoughts, Dory felt ashamed because she had also assumed attributes based on nothing other than how he looked. She was as guilty as others of expecting that a pretty face translated to a simple and easy life. This man, Drecsay, deserved the same level of justice as anyone else who found themselves a victim of an egregious crime. The man had lost his life. No one deserved that, and no one deserved such a crime to go unpunished.

"I do recall someone saying he was quite close to a Countess Tirau," Dory said. "Did you know her?"

"Everyone knew her," Lady Pettifer replied. "She is not the brightest woman, one has to admit. Petty at times. She would likely be swayed by someone like Drecsay if he was charming to her."

"I can't quite recall who said it, I think it was Richard, but he said that Countess Tirau treated him indulgently, almost like a son."

The car was silent for a moment and Lady Pettifer seemed to consider the thought, worrying her lip between her fingers. "I shouldn't think they were lovers. She was an elderly woman. It certainly would be unseemly if it were true. We don't know if he profited at all from her death."

"It would be good to find out," Dory agreed. "Although if he had profited greatly and Countess Tirau's family were aggrieved by it, that could be motive for murder. Still, I would have assumed there'd have been quite a scandal if that were the case."

"A bequeathment like that would've been taken to court, and I can't see a court being favorable to some Lothario charming inheritances out of an elderly lady. I haven't heard of any gossip to that effect. Lady Summernot would absolutely have mentioned it. Still, it is the strongest connection that has been mentioned with regards to this man. The problem is that we don't know him that well. He could have been getting up to anything—but the gossip mongers were apparently not hearing about it."

"Some people are very discreet," Dory stated.

"A man like that, though, is noticed wherever he goes. There is a curious lack of gossip about anything substantial related to this murder. All speculation and no facts."

"You don't think he could be a homosexual?" Dory asked. That community was notoriously discreet about their activities, collectively watching out for each other as they bore risks simply by associating.

"He would clearly have been a part of a certain crowd if that were true. I suppose it could be," Lady Pettifer said after a while. For a while longer she was silent. "It would be a shame if the police stopped investigating at this point. The man does deserve his justice."

*

They arrived home just before dusk, walking into a mercifully still and silent house after the busy day. Lady Pettifer was tired by the day's activities, even if they'd only sat in the car or at a café for most of it. In the end, they had forgone finding stockings, and had instead returned home. It was still a draining day that Lady Pettifer sat down heavily in her favorite chair as soon as she reached it.

Supper wouldn't be far away and they simply sat and enjoyed the silence for a while before shifting to the dining room. There was no doubt that Lady Pettifer would retire early that night to recuperate from the day. As for Dory, there was still an unpleasant heaviness to her thoughts regarding this man and his death.

It felt as if justice was improperly being done. Just because there was a war didn't mean he should be forgotten and swept under the carpet because his death was inconvenient. Or because he was a foreigner in this land. Surely the police hadn't given up. Still, Dory couldn't escape the heavy feeling that had descended on her, because she suspected that his murder was deemed too inconvenient to deal with at this time, and that went against the grain.

Chapter 11

Livinia sighed as she stood by the window in the salon. Apparently, the news that some cuckolded husband was responsible for Baron Drecsay's murder had spread across the entire coast, and it seemed to have been accepted as truth, even without a scrap of evidence.

"It's as if everyone is ready to sweep the whole incident under the carpet," Livinia said. "Either some husband, or they are saying the authorities are essentially ignoring the case because he really was a spy."

"Some people will believe anything," Lady Pettifer said.

Grabbing one of the small cucumber sandwiches, Dory sat back in the chair and took a bite, chewing it carefully while she thought. "To be fair, quite a few of the aristocracy admire the fascists."

"Posh," Lady Pettifer said.

"Come on, Aunt. There are even quite a few who think Hitler is simply marvelous."

"I wouldn't go that far."

Dory frowned, wondering if Lady Pettifer was applying her own views on others. Dory had heard those sympathizers speaking at Wallisford Hall. They couldn't all have changed their minds because Britain had declared war. "In Italy, families have profited from aligning themselves with Mussolini. It must be that many in Hungary are hedging their bets by making themselves agreeable to the Nazis. I suppose it would be understandable. If Hungary manages to convince the Nazis that they are aligned with their principles, maybe they will spare themselves being invaded by them."

"If he were a spy, he would hardly be spending time at parties dancing with me, would he?" Livinia stated. "Besides, people with Nazi sympathies seem incapable of keeping quiet about it."

"He would if he were a spy," Dory said.

If he were, it's hard to see what he would gain by aligning himself with Livinia. It's not as though anyone of particular importance to the war effort is part of her inner circle. Granted, many have important and influential relatives, but being on the other side of Europe, it's hard to see how that could be of any use.

"There's no point sitting here speculating," Lady Pettifer said. "What does this Prince Barenoli say?"

Silence settled on the room.

"I'm sure the police spoke to him," Livinia said after a while.

"And the friends of Countess Tirau," Lady Pettifer continued. "I did not know her well. I'm not even sure where she was from. She wasn't amongst my friends, but she would have had some. I'm sure Baron Drecsay wasn't the only acquaintance she had."

"I suppose we could ask," Livinia said and they all looked from one to another.

"It's not really our place to ask," Dory said.

Lady Pettifer chuckled. "Could you really rein in your curiosity enough not to investigate?"

Biting her lip, Dory silently fumed that her curiosity was so very obvious. It was true. She would find it impossible not to pay attention if someone mentioned anything related to Drecsay.

"Besides, the police seem to have utterly lost interest in the poor man's death," Lady Pettifer continued. "If he is related to the Elmhursts, then I know his grand aunt. It wouldn't feel right not at least trying to urge the authorities to solve this murder."

"Perhaps we could speak to this prince," Livinia said. "I might as well find out where he lives."

*

For the second time in the week, they drove along the winding road to Nice. Lady Pettifer stayed home, her knee giving her trouble. This time, Livinia insisted on driving and Dory clutched the side of the door during the sharpest turns.

"Most of the princes I've met have been old," Livinia said, "but if he's a friend of Drecsay, he must be quite young."

"I suppose so."

"Drecsay never mentioned him much. I really didn't know Drecsay well," Livinia said earnestly, looking over to gauge Dory's expression. "But heavens was he handsome. Those dark eyes. Sent a shiver down my spine. I can't believe someone killed him. It's such a shame."

As they arrived, Livinia pulled in by one of the large Victorian structures along the Promenade de Anglais with massive white columns and impossibly large windows along the front. It was the Palais de la Méditerranée and a velvet liveried man came forward to open the car door for them. He bid them welcome with a smile and prepared to drive the car away somewhere more convenient.

A darkly dressed man approached them as they entered the lovely lobby of the hotel, decorated with arts décoratifs motifs. Everything in the hotel was modern and of the highest taste. This prince had money. Of that, there was no question. Yet he was friends with a man who was basically considered to be in gentile poverty. Wealth didn't always count for everything, and it stood in this prince's favor that he would be friends with a man of much fewer means— unless it was a relationship built on a common mission to uncover information for their governments.

Dory was increasingly curious about this baron and how he was with his friends and the world around him. How did one identify a spy?

They were directed to an elevator built of rich cherry wood and brass. An operator dressed in red asked who they sought and then proceeded to get the elevator moving.

The carpet in the corridor was cream with flowers and the walls had silk coverings with tropical leaves. Every part of this hotel was stunning.

They arrived at a large, white door and knocked.

"Miss Fellingworth," a man said as he opened the door. "I have been expecting you." Like his friend, this man was dark and beautiful, and he moved with the grace of a man who knew his place in the world. There was an assurance, almost a boredom as he led them in into a sumptuous room, walking past a man who proceeded to close the door behind them. Dory guessed he was a manservant.

The prince sat down on a white brocade sofa and crossed his legs. His waistcoat was unbuttoned and he looked a little less than ready to receive visitors, even if he clearly knew they were coming.

"I know who you are, of course," he said, his attention on Livinia. "You are the one who found Domenik." The man had dark eyebrows that flared elegantly across his face. Dark hair neatly combed in a side part, displaying a uniform wave to his hair.

"Yes. I knew him a little."

The prince rubbed his thumb across his lower lip as he considered her and from her seat, Dory could almost feel Livinia's cheeks burning with the attention. The baron and his friend, the prince, had good looks in common. As for Dory, she was wondering if this man in front of her could in any way have been induced to kill his friend.

"We were hoping you could tell us a little about him," Dory stated after a while. "There are so many rumors about him. The police seem to have made some assumptions about his death."

"The police," the prince said with a hint of disgust in his voice, "couldn't find a whore in a whorehouse."

Okay, Dory said to herself. "There are some who suspect he was a spy." On second thought, was that a stupid question to ask? A spy wouldn't confirm it, would they? "Or that he was murdered by some irate husband. As you are his friend, would you know of any such husband that was particularly upset?"

"Husbands of beautiful wives are always upset. That is the cost of beauty."

The man spoke in generalizations. Well, that was helpful. "Any specific ones that you know of?"

The man shrugged. "Not that he told me."

"And Countess Tirau?" Livinia said.

"They were friends. She enjoyed beauty. There was a price." With a sigh, he shifted slightly as if to alleviate his boredom. "Drecsay was a proud man. He was not a man to accept charity. Still, he found the bills a little harder to pay once the countess passed away."

"So there was no one new to take the countess' place?"

"You mean in his affections?"

Dory got the distinct impression that this man was toying with her, and she didn't understand what it meant. Men like him, men with power and wealth did have a tendency to toy with people. She'd seen it before. Vivian Fellingworth was a little like that. They tended to use the truth as a blunt instrument to beat people with. Was he merciless with Drecsay because of his… solution to his problems?

"The countess was an indulgent woman, but only when it pleased her. She liked to yank the chain at times, ensure he knew who held the reins. Some people use wealth as a means to control. If he displeased her, his debts would build up and she would threaten not to pay them." He certainly wasn't sugar-coating his friend's position. "So was he discreetly visiting the bedrooms of some of the more beautiful members of society here? Absolutely. But he was discreet. Couldn't have the countess finding out.

"Financial difficulties aside, the countess' death released some chains. The countess didn't like him showing interest in the younger ladies of the coast." His attention was back on Livinia as if accenting his point. This man knew of Drecsay's interest in Livinia, Dory bet.

"Financially, though, the death of his benefactor would have been devastating," Dory said and slowly, the Prince stole his attention away and settled on her.

He blatantly studied her for a moment. "He wasn't overly distressed. I don't know the details, but he was very positive about his future, stated that he had secured a way to rebuild his family wealth."

This surprised Dory. Surely, he hadn't meant Livinia, but she was an heiress. "Did he elaborate, or was this something he stated quite often?"

"Are you asking if he was some dreamer who constantly thought up schemes to re-establish the family wealth? Or are you asking if he saw young Miss Fellingworth here as the means to securing his future?"

His assertion was too forward for her to answer, and he knew it.

"Nothing about me was secured," Livinia added loftily. "We barely knew each other. I don't know why I have to keep telling people."

The prince returned his gaze to Dory as if this should provide her with an answer. But it didn't. "Was he a dreamer?" Dory pressed.

"No, he was not. I would go so far as to say some of his actions were the result of desperation, but he wasn't a stupid man—a dreamer. He was very… calculated in his actions. And he did enjoy dealing with Countess Tirau. She might have used her wealth with bluntness, but he had finesse. It was a mutually beneficial arrangement."

"No threats?"

"Have you set yourself the task of investigating his murder?"

"Yes," Dory said frankly and a hint of emotion quickly fleeted across the prince's face.

"And what authority do you have to do so?"

"None. We simply feel the police are not giving this case their due attention."

"There are also some duties felt to his family," Livinia added. The prince only glanced at her. He seemed to have lost interest in her to focus more on studying Dory.

The man's eyebrows rose. "I understand part of his background is English. The English do like to stick together, as you say. Is that why you are here? You feel a duty to him because of his family?" He was speaking directly to Dory.

"No," she said.

"Then why?"

"Because no one deserves to have their life stolen."

"So melodramatic." His eyes traveled down her clothes and shoes. "Your accent is English, but not educated."

Dory blushed as he kept studying her. "Yet here you are. What brings you so far away from your country?"

"I am a companion to Lady Pettifer."

"My aunt."

"Ah," the prince said as if everything made sense now. "And here you are, investigating the murder of some foreigner who wouldn't give you the time of day had you asked." With a frown, Dory tried to understand what this man was saying. He spoke in riddles, eluding to things without actually saying them. "You are an idealist."

Dory had never really put labels on what she was, but perhaps she was. "Someone must be, I suppose."

The prince regarded her some more and then looked away. "I must prepare now. It has been charming to meet you both, but my time is valuable."

"Of course," Livinia said and rose. Dory was less impressed. Could he spare so little time to the people trying to find justice for his murdered friend?

Or had he lost interest because he didn't believe they would achieve anything. The comment about Drecsay not giving the time of day to someone like her stuck. Having mentioned it, Prince Barenoli obviously wasn't unaware of the sentiment. Perhaps he felt the same way.

Chapter 12

The drive back was done in silence. Dory was trying to sort through all of the prince's assertions, accusations and euphemisms. At times, Dory wasn't entirely sure he had been trying to be straight with them, having both disparaged and maligned his friend. But they had learned more about the relationship between the baron and the countess that was his patroness. The assertion that she paid his bills was clear, and he had struggled financially after her death. Also, the baron believed he had some means of restoring his wealth. This did not signify that he had inherited anything substantial from the countess.

"What a curious man," Livinia said. "Very handsome."

Dory rolled her eyes. The man had an acerbic personality. Intelligent but supercilious. There was even something a bit jaded about him. For his honeyed smile, he was in character much too dark for someone like Livinia.

"He wasn't married. Did you see? No ring on his finger."

"That doesn't mean he's not married," Dory said with weariness. Livinia had a habit of being persuaded by the superficial. This man's surface sold a prince charming, but the personality underneath was anything but. The fact that he had counted Baron Drecsay as a friend, despite the difference in their means, pointed to there being some commonality to their characters that gave them common ground.

Were they spies, though? There was too much arrogance there to bow to fascists. Or maybe he was enough of a realist to align himself to the direction the wind was blowing. It would be a mistake to think she knew what it would take to turn someone into a spy.

*

A car was parked in front of the house as they arrived home. Dory had never seen it before. Pulling next to it, Livinia got out. "Who can that be?"

An uncomfortable feeling crept up Dory's spine and at that moment, she heard Vivian's voice drifting out of the open window. Dory sighed. Lady

Pettifer laughed at something he said. As dreadful as he was, Lady Pettifer adored him. Dreadful wasn't the exact word; how Dory felt about him was more complex. He could be very charming, but that was simply a mask. Underneath, he actually was quite dreadful—but also observant and insightful when not obtusely disregarding.

The last time she'd seen him, he'd called her a meddling oik and the insult still stung. Biting her lips together, she automatically checked her hair before following Livinia inside the house.

"Vivian!" Livinia said, gleeful in seeing him when Dory knew they had a contentious relationship—but then siblings always did, and these two were twins, which had to constitute some bond she didn't understand. They certainly weren't best friends.

"Hello, chook," he said and Livinia gave him a pointed look. They embraced, which might be the only time Dory had seen that, but then they had been apart for two years. "And Miss Sparks," he said with a quirky tone to his voice. He kissed her on the cheek, leaving a lingering whiff of maleness and whiskey.

Kissing her on the cheek as greeting was something new too. There had been a time when he'd appeared quite eager to explore her form in some hidden closet, but kissing her on the cheek for greeting wasn't something he did. Perhaps it had something to do with her elevated status as a companion rather than a mere maid.

Even so, there had never been a time when Vivian hadn't made her feel uncomfortable, and he'd done so purposefully on more than one occasion.

"Vivian was telling me about his drive from Switzerland," Lady Pettifer.

"How is Mother?" Livinia asked as she sat down.

For a moment, Dory didn't know what to do with herself, if she should leave them to their familial discussion.

"She's fine," he said.

Apparently that was enough for Livinia, who Dory knew had quite mixed feelings about her mother. She wasn't as readily forgiving as Vivian seemed to be. "You'll never guess what happened here," she said with wide, excited eyes. "There was a murder and I found the body."

Gingerly, she sidestepped the issue that she had been meeting this man for a private assignation. It was a fact that Livinia seemed to have wiped from her memory.

"A murder?" Vivian stated with surprise. "You must be right in your element," he said to Dory, who couldn't find anything to respond with and simply sat there opening and closing her mouth.

"We are investigating," Livinia continued. "Today we questioned his best friend, a Prince Barenoli. An utterly fascinating man. So charming and handsome—you wouldn't believe it. He really is keeping up the standard of the fairy tales."

"Did you find him charming?" Vivian asked, turning his attention to Dory. With that, everyone turned their attention to her, effectively forcing her to answer.

"No."

Vivian's eyebrows rose, but he wasn't surprised, and instead had a reassured expression as if he knew her so well. "Won't be swayed by any Prince Charming, will you? Pray tell, why didn't you find the handsome prince charming?"

"Must be the arrogance," she said through gritted teeth. In a way, it sounded petty because he knew that was what she accused him of. "There was something dark about him, something jaded."

"Tosh," Livinia said. "He was lovely, and so happy we were investigating his friend's death."

Vivian didn't take his gaze away from Dory, and she suddenly found the tea service inordinately fascinating, deciding to pour herself a cup of the cooling tea. It had been a long ride and she was parched.

"How was it traveling across the border?" Lady Pettifer asked.

"It was a mess. It took two hours to get them to let me through. Soldiers everywhere. It seems the French are worried the Swiss are going to roll over for Herr Hitler. I saw garrisons camped a bit further inland, endless fields of them. Tanks and rows and rows of sandbags. The French have made themselves ready."

A silence descended on the room.

"And what did you learn about poor Baron Drecsay?" Lady Pettifer said, breaking the uncomfortable silence, as if she'd heard all she could tolerate about the war.

"Well," Livinia said. "He'd been in some financial strife since the death of his benefactor, Countess Tirau, but he believed he'd found some means out of it."

A frown marred Lady Pettifer's face, but Vivian didn't look concerned. But then, he didn't know about this man's interest in Livinia.

"The prince said he was intelligent and that he considered the commitments he made." Livinia was making it all sound too peachy.

"He confirmed that Drecsay had been a visitor to a few bedrooms he shouldn't be in, and that his benefactor frowned deeply if she even found out about it," Dory added, more for Lady Pettifer's benefit.

"Oh, that kind of benefactor," Vivian said as if he now understood. "A kept man."

"Vivian!" Livinia chided. "No need to be crude. The police say that some irate husband dispatched him. Although other people say he was a spy."

"A spy?" Vivian said with amused expression.

"Well, he was Hungarian and their position can only be described as detached."

"What could a spy possibly garner by creeping around bedrooms in Cote d'Azur?" Vivian asked.

"You'd be surprised what people around here know," Lady Pettifer said. "Who here doesn't have a family member in Parliament? I'm sure quite a few even have relatives in the actual War Cabinet."

"That they wish to speak about to a foreign bedroom hustler?"

"He was not a hustler," Livinia stated with offense. "Why do you insist on painting everything in the ugliest light possible?"

"What other light can one put it in? A man patroned by older women. There is only so much light one can use."

"Children," Lady Pettifer said with exasperation. "Now we are very glad you have come to see us. Are you staying a while?"

"I haven't made any specific plans," Vivian said. "Obviously, I need to get back to England, but I hear the passenger ships are getting harder to book passage on."

"Unfortunately, that is true. Speaking to Mrs. Muiring on the phone today, she mentioned that her neighbors were driving to Spain to book passage."

"That would take days," Livinia uttered.

"Don't worry, Vivian," Lady Pettifer said. "We'll find a way home for you, but there is no reason you can't stay a few weeks."

"No, of course not. It's always lovely down here. Spring seems to be late back home, and things are pretty grim there. This malaise seems to have descended everywhere. It's like we're in a war that refuses to be and no one seems to know what's going on. London has turned into a maze of sandbags. I've never seen it so drab."

"Things are gayer here," Livinia said. "Except for this murder. It's shocking. Who could do such a thing? It's as if people are losing their minds everywhere."

"Things are only going to get worse," Vivian said. "And Mother is basically a stone's throw away from Germany. Half of the people who work at the sanatorium are of German descent."

"I doubt the Germans have raiding the sanatoriums of Switzerland utmost on their agenda,"

Lady Pettifer said. "Still, it is a worry. If the Germans were to invade, the suffering would be indiscriminate."

"They wouldn't take mother hostage, would they?" Livinia said, concern finally registering on her face.

"For what purpose?" Vivian asked.

"I don't know. She is a lady. Maybe they assume she could serve as some leverage."

"What does your father say?" Lady Pettifer asked.

"He refuses to speak about it."

With a snort, Lady Pettifer looked away.

"We must do something about Mother. I just don't know what."

"She's not allowed to leave," Livinia pointed out.

"Yes, thanks, Livinia. I'm fairly sure the sanitorium regulations didn't consider the large-scale invasion by the Germans."

"The French line is holding," Livinia countered. "They will arrest her if she returns to England. That was the deal father struck with the commissioner."

With piercing eyes, Vivian glared at her. Dory couldn't exactly tell what he was thinking.

"Perhaps she needs to be transferred somewhere less volatile," Dory added after a moment of silence.

"There's nowhere that isn't volatile," Vivian said, turning his eyes on her as if she were responsible."

"America," Dory added quietly. "They have absolutely insisted on being neutral in this war, and they are much too far away for the Germans.

"They say Belgium is a bit of a canary in the mine, that the Germans would invade them first, get the small problem tackled before the big problem," Lady Pettifer added. "They might bypass Switzerland entirely. They cannot fight on every border, and Switzerland has never indicated it will serve as a problem for them."

"Would you bet your life on it?" Vivian asked. "Everyone is expecting the invasion to start any day."

A silence descended again, as if no one wanted to say anything more, in case their words brought around the eventuality they all feared.

Chapter 13

Vivian spent a bit of time in his guest room the next day. He slept, Dory assumed. For all his blasé attitude, Dory could tell he was worried, and that worried her. When people like Vivian were taking things seriously, it spelled the situation had to be dire.

Could it be that they had stayed on in France too long? There were still so many here; it was hard to believe they were in grave danger. The heavy militarization Vivian mentioned up north wasn't visible here. Other than the lack of sugar and the half-hearted insistence on blackouts, there was nothing really visible of the war here on the coast.

Most said they were simply going to wait this war out, refusing to be chased out of their house and home to return to cities or families they no longer felt welcome with. Lady Pettifer felt she couldn't endure the travel, and Livinia still feared the remnants of her mother's scandal. But now Dory was frightened.

On the wireless, they reported a great deal of bluster. Communications with the French and agreements to stay strong. Nothing particular was being reported, which on the one hand was excellent, but it almost felt as though the Germans were too quiet, as if they were planning to pounce. Hopefully, Dory was completely overreacting.

Walking outside, she let the gentle morning sun warm her skin. This was the lovely part of the day, before the heat really set in. The breeze coming off the sea was pleasant and there was a stillness. Except for the birds that were chirping away. This place was so lovely. How could something so horrid as war be threatening all around them?

The noise of a car echoed across the trees. Someone had arrived and Dory walked around the corner of the house to see. It was Richard, who was stepping out of his car.

"Has she come down yet?" he asked.

"Livinia? No, I'm afraid not."

He growled slightly. "She told me to come early. I should have known better than to listen to her. But you're up. Trusty Dory. Early to bed, early to rise."

This made Dory wonder what kind of opinion Richard had of her. It wasn't as if she was old enough yet to be considered the dour spinster—not that it strictly mattered what he thought. "Not always, but when I've had a trying day, then yes." And also because Vivian and Livinia had stayed up, and Dory had learned to fear Vivian's tongue when he drank. That was when he tended to be his most vicious and Dory had fled to bed rather than stayed with them. Not that she was going to tell Richard any of this.

"I heard you and Livvie were in Nice yesterday."

"Yes, we met with Prince Barenoli."

"That wanker. Excuse my French."

"I take it he's not your favorite person," Dory said.

"Thinks a lot of himself. Can be a right bastard to the girls. They swoon over themselves for a royal title. It's pathetic."

Dory decided not to mention that Livinia had been in danger of swooning a bit herself. It felt disloyal pointing something like that out, but Richard only confirmed her own impression of the handsome prince. 'Beauty came with a price,' he had said more than once. Maybe he was one to test how much people were willing to pay. He hadn't overtly said anything despicable; it was just a feeling Dory had gotten. With a shake of her head, Dory dismissed the man from her thoughts.

Speaking of low opinions. "You seem to have a very low opinion of Baron Drecsay."

"Really the kind we can do without," Richard said with a disgusted look on his face.

"You mean gentile poor?" Dory said without thinking, or rather without care.

"If you can't afford to be here, you shouldn't be. Sniffing around rich old women. It's disgraceful."

"He was also sniffing around Livinia," Dory pointed out and Richard's mouth tightened. Obviously, Richard was in love with Livinia, but she never quite saw him as anything other than a friend she depended on for just about everything. The truth was that he would probably make her quite a good husband, but she was off being impressed by the superficial beauty of foreign nobles. "Anyone else he was sniffing around?"

"Who knows," Richard stated. "He liked anyone with money. I didn't really know him that well—stayed clear of his lot. Someone who did know him better was Terry Wilcott. They were chums, I suppose. He might be the one who knows who Drecsay was dabbling with. But, you know, I wouldn't dismiss the theory that he was a spy. The man would do anything for money."

"Except spies tend to be carted away and interrogated, not whacked on the head and left at society parties."

Richard's eyebrows rose and sank. "I suppose. Perhaps it is more likely that someone was trying to keep some woman out of the man's clutches."

Which actually gave Richard a motive more than anyone, but by the look on his face, the thought that he was a suspect never occurred to him. At the party, he had claimed to arrive late, but who was to say that was true. It was blatantly clear that Richard had a distaste for the man. He wouldn't be the first person to protect one of the Fellingworth offspring, Dory thought with a snort. It appeared Richard took that snort as agreement with what he was saying.

"Actually, Terry is going to be there this afternoon, maybe you should come along if you want to ask him. Whose is the car?"

"Didn't I tell you? Vivian arrived yesterday."

This time, Richard's eyebrows rose even higher in surprise. "Vivian? It's been an age since I've seen him. Livvie didn't say."

"We weren't expecting him."

"Just like Vivian to go where the wind takes him," Richard said with a smile. "It's been a few years since I've seen him. I don't suppose he is up either?"

"No," Dory said.

"Why is it so hard to get these Fellingworths out of bed?" he said brightly and walked back to the house. "The day is young and the party awaits. Terry is likely to be there. Are you going to come?"

Indecision accosted Dory. The urge to talk to this Terry itched inside her, and she didn't entirely understand why. No one seemed to like this Baron Drecsay, except perhaps Livinia. Even his friends appeared very blasé about his murder. The police seemed to have stopped caring entirely, feeling they had better things to do than investigate the death of some bedroom-creeping foreigner. Maybe it was the fact that no one seemed to care that really got on

Dory's wick. You couldn't just wipe someone away and get away with it.

"Lady P," Dory heard from inside the house. "Smashing day."

"Young Richard," Lady Pettifer replied. "Have you come to steal Livinia away for the day. That would be good. She's been a bit blue about that man's unfortunate demise."

Taking a breath, Dory exhaled. Truth be told, she wasn't sure how deeply Livinia cared about Baron Drecsay's murder. At times it felt like only she cared, and she hadn't even met the man.

Fine, she would go speak to this Terry Wilcott, she decided, taking a few more minutes outside. Lady Pettifer didn't need assistance dealing with the charms of men like Richard.

"Well, I'll be damned," Vivian's voice was heard. It was a little gruff with sleep. "Look who the cat dragged in."

"Vivian," Richard said brightly. "How are you?"

Richard seemed to be just as keen on Vivian as he was with his sister. "Good. About to head off to a party at Archie Wilshire's villa."

"Archie? I didn't know he was here. Haven't seen him since Oxford, second year. I thought he went to work for the Colonial Office. I know they call this a colony, but that's a bit of a stretch."

"Things didn't work out so well there, it seems. Too soft to put his foot down."

"That wouldn't surprise me," Vivian replied.

Standing there, Dory felt like she was eavesdropping, but it hadn't been her intention to. With her head up, she made her way to the salon where everyone had gathered.

Vivian looked no worse for wear from the evening before, but little seemed to dampen his overall golden glow.

"I wish Livinia could be a little more like you at times, Dory," Richard stated. "You never linger in bed all day."

"That's because she's used to getting up at the crack of dawn," Vivian said dismissively and walked over to the tea service.

Dory smiled tightly. Oh, it was going to be a lovely day—a full day of bearing the brunt of Vivian's jibes.

"Be nice, Vivian," Lady Pettifer chided.

"I'm always nice, aren't I, Miss Sparks?"

Dory didn't bother answering and Vivian grinned.

Chapter 14

Archie Wilshire had a lovely house built in art décoratif style, entirely white with large, sweeping rooms and enormous windows. It might be the most modern house Dory had ever seen. The furniture was exquisite as well, dainty with beautifully inlaid wood paneling. Dory spent her first moments in the house simply looking at everything. It was a world away from the two up, two down joined house she grew up in, and even miles away from the staid, old elegance of Wallisford Hall. This was a house of jazz and ideas—a complete rejection of all traditions. Dory loved it.

Vivian was immediately greeted by all and sundry. Everyone seemed to know him, but mostly from England rather than any time spent here on the coast. It seemed all the people of his class knew each other—or at least knew Vivian.

A few of the gathered party was dressed in tennis whites, so Dory guessed that part of the afternoon would involve tennis. A large, covered veranda overlooked a pool and the gardens beyond. With a smile, Dory could imagine how much Lady Pettifer would disapprove of this house, with its showy glossiness and blatant self-assurance.

Livinia was alive in this setting, adored by the people and loving being part of her group. She was practically bouncing on her feet as she walked.

"Archie," she said, greeting their host, whom Dory understood was married to an elegant woman who wore silk blouses with long strands of fat pearls. Meredith was her name and she had polished black hair and a small mouth, accentuated by red lipstick.

In this crowd, Dory couldn't help feeling frumpy. As much as she didn't care about being accepted, and the center of attention as Livinia did, she also couldn't muster the self-confidence that this group seemed to thrive on.

"And you remember Dory, of course," Livinia said to the gentleman wearing a cream linen suit. It cut a lovely line on him, but it wrinkled. Still, comfort in this heat was important. "We wanted her to come along. I hope you don't mind."

With gritted teeth, Dory smiled. When she'd agreed to come, she hadn't realized her presence would be hoisted on the host as a favor.

"No, of course not," he said gregariously. No sign of imposition could be seen on his face and Dory liked Archie more for it. "Do you play tennis, Dory?"

"Two left feet," she said. "I will spare everyone the pain of having to watch me chase a ball."

"You and me both," Meredith agreed, taking a sip of an iced drink from a long, slim glass.

With that, the attention was off Dory and they moved onto discuss what they had done over the last few years. Archie was an ardent sailor, and apparently Meredith could watch him out at sea from the cool of the veranda.

If Archie wasn't so very foreign to Dory, she dared to think she would muster a crush on him. He was kind and generous, and smiled a great deal—but he was also so different from her, she wasn't entirely sure she read him right. Could he really be that nice? Everything about him seemed perfect. His dress was perfect, his manners were impeccable and there didn't seem to be a dark thought in him. By the look of him, he was simply happy to be there with all his friends.

Maybe it was the idea of happiness that seemed so foreign. Dory wasn't sure she trusted it. At no point had she ever seen Vivian happy. Livinia was only happy when she wasn't stuck with her own company. Lady Pettifer was content. But Archie looked happy and bright. Dory watched as he leaned over and kissed his wife on the cheek. A rush of envy bubbled up and she pushed it down. Happiness should be encouraged in the world, not begrudged.

The group moved out onto the veranda, where the pool glittered enticingly. Again, Dory was struck with how far away she was from her station in life. Could she even describe this to her mother? Some of the things she'd experienced, she'd actually omitted from her mother's letters, fearing her mother warning her she was getting above herself. There was a hint in her mother's letters saying so. Their lifestyle was not hers, and she couldn't forget that.

Slowly, the group spilled down the sweeping stairs to the pool below, where a few of the girls sat down along the edge and cooled their legs. Dory stayed back. The truth was that she didn't connect with the girls. They tolerated her presence, but were never friendly beyond politeness. In saying that, they were never overtly unkind, which Dory was grateful for. But she suspected they took their cue from Archie's behavior towards her. They were gracious because he was kind. If he was something other, they would be too.

There was a bar set up by the pool. "Champagne, Dory?" Archie called.

"That would be lovely," Dory answered. He brought over a bulbous glass with the bubbling, slight honey-colored liquid. Dory liked champagne. Before coming to the coast, she had only tasted it after her cousin's baptism. Here there was no occasion that didn't justify popping a cork. Maybe she was getting a little used to life above her station.

Two of the men grabbed racquets and headed across the lawn over the next few minutes, the whole group seemed to gravitate toward the courts. The tennis courts were down in elevation from the house, set amongst orange trees dotted with fruit that were still green. They provided lovely shade for anyone watching the game.

As Dory sat down on one of the benches a little away from the others, she watched Terry Wilcott. He had a very open face with slightly slanting eyes, giving him a perpetually bored look. If she had to guess, she would think he was around twenty-seven. Leather shoes were slightly scuffed as if he didn't care for them properly.

"Your inquisition is going gangbusters," Vivian said wryly. "So far you've only managed to hack a stammering hello to Archie. If you're going to play detective, you actually have to speak to people."

The urge to argue was flaring inside her, but she couldn't. "I just haven't got around to it."

"Too distracted watching Archie on the court?"

Pairs of men had taken to the court, the ball in sharp percussions between them. Archie was one of them. What was this incessant focus on Archie? Perhaps she had been watching him a little. Annoyingly, Vivian pounced on anything she did that indicated the remotest degree of interest, as if he were in cahoots with her mother to ensure she got no ideas above her station. Well, if Vivian was going to point it out, she wasn't going to cower. "I like Archie," she said pointedly. "He's a very kind man. I find kindness very compelling—intriguing. It makes you wonder about a person, who can afford to be so kind." For a moment, Dory felt a flare of panic, wondering if Vivian would from now point out how intriguing she found Archie every moment of the day. It would be utterly juvenile. She didn't, after all, have a crush on Archie. She just liked how kind he was, and how comfortable he seemed in his own skin. That was it—his self-assurance didn't seem put on, and that really was intriguing.

Vivian was silent for a moment, running his finger along the top lip of his glass. The liquid inside was brown, so he was obviously starting with liquor fairly early in the day. Whiskey, probably. He seemed to like whiskey.

"Don't confuse kindness for pity."

Dory's breath stopped in her chest. It was a cruel statement, maybe even the cruelest he'd imparted on her. Was it designed to erode any comfort she felt being there? It had to be designed to do something. She turned to him. "I think that's the point, Vivian. It isn't pity I feel from him, it's just a plain welcome without any underlying need to prove something."

"To prove what?"

"You tell me," she said, refusing to look away.

"All I am saying is that you're not going to prove a great detective if you are always cowering in a corner."

That wasn't what he had been saying at all, and they both knew it. Dory had faced him down and she'd won. She felt it in her bones. A lightness washed over her, but she didn't know exactly what or why.

His gaze lingered for a moment, then he looked away. "Terry, come here," he called and Terry looked up from across the other side of the tennis court. Getting up, he walked around until he reached them.

"Vivian," he said in acknowledgement as he reached them. "What's the urgency?"

"Miss Sparks here wishes to speak to you."

Surprise registered on Terry's face. "How can I help you, Miss Sparks?"

Drink in hand, Vivian walked away.

Chapter 15

Uncomfortably, Dory shifted in her seat.

"How can I help you, Miss Sparks?" Terry repeated.

"Uhmm," she started, not quite knowing how to proceed. She wasn't actually assisting a policeman here; she was doing this because you felt she needed to. "I was hoping you could tell me a little about Baron Drecsay," she said and noted his surprise. "Actually, Lady Pettifer has asked me to talk to you. She is well acquainted with his family." Hopefully that would give her some legitimacy in questioning people about this murder.

"He doesn't have any family," Terry stated.

"He has some relations in England."

"Only distantly."

Why did it matter, Dory wondered. "Yes."

With a sigh, he sat down on the bench next to her. "What do you want to know? I don't know who murdered him. Livinia was the one who found him, but I guess you've already spoken to her."

"Did he have any enemies?"

"I already told the police this."

"And from what we hear, they attributed guilt to some cuckolded husband, but no one has been arrested."

"Perhaps they're still gathering evidence."

Dory refused to be deterred, remembering how nothing would sway DI Ridley from his line of questioning. "Do you know who they suspect?"

Terry looked as if he was about to speak for a moment, but then paused. "I don't, actually."

"You were good friends."

With a shrug, Terry crossed his arms. "I suppose you could say so."

"And he didn't tell you about any married woman he was congressing with?"

"Congressing?" Terry said with a smile. "No, he didn't, but it wouldn't surprise me. Drecsay liked women, particularly since the countess' death. I suppose you heard about his relationship with Countess Tirau?"

"I understand she was very generous to him."

"I think the old bat liked to think someone like Drecsay was actually enamored with her. They're all like that, secretly, wanting to know young, handsome men find them fascinating. Granted, Drecsay could charm any girl out of her knickers, particularly rich ones."

"And he was interested in Livinia, wasn't he?"

"Livinia's a smashing girl. Anyone who manages to set a ring on her finger would be set, wouldn't they? Looks and money. Some would say that's a winning combination. Maybe Drecsay was trying his luck. I don't know; he didn't tell me. But I do know he was seeing some floozy on a regular basis—some French girl. Not the kind you build a future with, if you know what I mean."

"Charming," Dory said dryly.

Terry stood up. "Maybe something related to this girl is responsible."

Unlikely, thought Dory, as the murderer had been invited to Lady Tonbridge's party.

Turning back to her, Terry continued. "Just because he looked like a saint didn't mean he was one. In fact, he left a lot of people on the coast out of pocket. Not too careful with paying people back. Guess he didn't have to be. Countess Tirau eventually took care of everything after some pleading and earnest declarations of devotion." Terry snorted, then smiled. "The guy was a piece of work. You have to give him that. He was fun to know, provided you weren't stupid enough to line his pockets. They guy did as he pleased. It's not a surprise that someone offed him; it was bound to happen sooner or later. Maybe all the better for Livinia."

Picking a speck of dirt off his shirt, Terry gave her the slightest nod before walking away. Dory watched him go, and slip back amongst his friends.

What had she learned that was new? The account of Drecsay's character was consistent with what other people were saying, except for Livinia, who was obviously under the assault of this man's charm. Everyone said he had been charming. And again, the countess with their 'mutually beneficial' relationship. What was new, however, was the mention of a girl he was seeing, a French, local girl— a floozy, Terry had called her.

The way Terry had said it, Dory expected that this girl had been a feature in his life. Prince Barenoli hadn't mentioned her, but then Dory suspected there were plenty of things he hadn't mentioned. Perhaps she needed to go see him again, but she wasn't sure he would agree to a second meeting.

And who was this girl? Was she in some way responsible? The circumstances suggested not, but then she could well know more about what was going on in Drecsay's life around and prior to his murder. But how in the world was she supposed to find this girl? If she had his address book, things would be so much easier. No doubt, the police had it. Surely, they wouldn't be careless enough to overlook such a vital piece of evidence. Could she go and ask to see it? She could well imagine the unimpressed look from the inspector if she did.

Address book aside, the police would not have gathered everything, so his effects would still be somewhere—perhaps even at the hotel he was staying at. It wasn't far away.

A tennis ball flew past her, breaking Dory out of her concentration.

"Sorry, Miss Sparks," Richard said as he passed by her bench in search of the ball. A tight smile fleeted across her lips. The purpose of her visit to this party had been completed with her discussion with Terry—interview, it was in reality. Maybe she would even go so far as to call it an interrogation, she thought with a chuckle.

Now, she was stuck here for hours. Livinia and Vivian were not going to want to return home anytime soon and her coming along had been complicit with their schedules—not her own. Hours of this stretched in front of her. But then Nice was only a short drive away, wasn't it? She could simply pop over and be back well before anyone wanted to go home.

The possibility of doing something useful sat brightly in her chest when she rose from her bench. She decided to tell Livinia instead of Vivian. It seemed her relationship with Vivian had reached a new low and she didn't want a second round of his jabs just at the moment.

"Livinia," she said lightly as she approached where Livinia sat with a group of girls around a table. Livinia looked over guardedly. It was obvious that Livinia was wary of being inclusive, no doubt finding Dory that bit 'not right' for her group of friends. "I thought I'd quickly pop over to Nice. Back in a tiff."

The expression on Livinia's face showed relief. Dory hadn't realized she was quite such a burden for

Livinia, which made her want to escape this company more than ever.

"Alright. Have a good time," Livinia said, not even a bit curious as to why Dory would go to Nice.

Dory almost ran back up the stair toward the house. Meredith looked up as she reached the veranda, where she was arranging the table. There was going to be a meal at some point, Dory realized. "Need to pop out for a bit."

With a gracious smile, Meredith continued with her task. Dory wasn't sure she had ever felt quite so foreign here on the coast, and not foreign in the sense that she was from England, but foreign to the people who lived here. In a way, she told herself off for caring. DI Ridley wouldn't care. He had a job to do and she needed to approach things the same way. He certainly didn't have a crisis of identity every time he investigated a crime. Maybe it was time she grew a backbone and got on with the job.

Her sense of purpose renewed, she went to the car and started it. The engine rumbled to life and it whined as she backed up to make her way down to the coast road. The wind in her hair, she felt wonderful—a little like Vivian's judgment and persecution was lifted off her.

This trip to Drecsay's hotel could be a complete waste of time, but it could also provide some vital clues. In addition, she wondered what had happened to Drecsay himself, his body, she meant. Was he still here? According to Prince Barenoli, he had no family, so what had happened to the body? Had he been returned to Hungary? Was it even possible to return a body to Hungary? It could travel along Italy and Yugoslavia, she supposed. But if he had no family, who was to arrange his travel? Were his distant British family stepping in and offering to help? Nothing about that had been mentioned.

Chapter 16

The Hotel Carlone was a nice Victorian building, painted white with a wealthy display of windows. It was a little further along than the more extravagant hotels, such as where his friend, Prince Barenoli, was staying. Still, it was a respectable address.

Dory had parked right in front and made her way to the reception. A man with neat hair and a carefully preserved suit stood behind the wooden desk. "Mademoiselle," he said with a curt nod as she approached. His name was printed on a brass badge pinned to his lapel.

There were some people milling in the lobby. "I wonder, Monsieur Legrand, if we could speak in private about a delicate matter."

The man's eyebrows rose and so did his chin, so he was now looking down his nose at her. The disapproval wafted off him. Dory had no idea what he assumed that to mean, but it was something he was strictly disapproving off.

"Mademoiselle," he said indulgently, "I am a very busy man."

"Well, Baron Drecsay is not so busy these days and that is who I am here to speak about."

Further surprise pushed the man's eyebrows even higher. Then he frowned. "This way," he said, leading her toward a nondescript door, built to blend into the wood paneling behind the desk. It led to an office of good size. The furniture wasn't the latest, but it was well cared for, and he bid her to sit down by his desk. "How can I help you, Mademoiselle… "

"Sparks," she said. "I have been asked by Lady Pettifer, who is acting in the interest of Baron Drecsay's extended family, to see that poor Baron Drecsay is being properly cared for."

"Oh, would this Lady, or possibly his extended family members, wish to settle the poor baron's account with us?"

"That is a question to put to his estate, I think."

"Well, some of his creditors have already been here, by order of the local *magistrat*, may I add."

This was news to Dory and she must have shown it on her face.

"Some of his creditors came, claiming they had the right to his things in recompense for what he owed."

"They took his things?"

"Not everything. They left disappointed, I'm sure. The baron had some trinkets, but nothing of any real value. I am certain no one has had their accounts paid in full."

"So what is left?" Dory asked, disappointment flaring in her.

"Some toiletries. A rather nice silver comb. His clothes. Some books."

"No diaries or letters?"

"No. You can see the things if you wish. They are in a box."

It hadn't occurred to her that the baron's room had been packed away, but of course it had. A hotel couldn't afford to keep a room for a man who wasn't there to pay for it—or for previous nights, it seemed.

"Yes," Dory said, still battling with her disappointment. She'd felt so assured that some important clue would come out of this. The manager disappeared and returned with a cardboard box. It seemed too small to be the remains of a man's life.

The manager had been correct though, in that there was little inside—nothing that told her anything.

"No one has come for his belongings?" she asked after replacing the lid on his belongings. There really was nothing in there that would be of use.

"Only people seeking something to gain. Obviously people looking for more, because some of his things still have value—his clothes for example. Best quality, but his creditors were not interested."

"What did they take?"

"I did not see. Jewelry, perhaps."

"Was the baron a man who wore jewelry?"

"Obviously, he wore a signet ring. He had a gorgeous Cartier watch. A distinguished diamond tie pin as well." Dory got the feeling this man could describe the jewelry in detail. "But they were not here when he died." It seemed the manager had checked, and probably before anyone else had accessed the room. Dory would bet her arm there was other jewelry in his room that this man wasn't mentioning. The pieces he was describing would likely have been on the baron's person at the time he'd died, which meant the police had them. Dory hadn't noticed at the time and she chided herself. DI Ridley would probably have noticed, but she had been too shocked and distracted to observe such details.

"You never observed anyone act aggressively toward the baron?" she asked.

"No," the man said lightly as if it would never occur to him.

"I understand he was familiar with a local girl," Dory finally said.

The man stroked his chin absently. "Yes. Marie, I believe her name is. Chard."

"Did the police ask about her?"

"No, they were interested in the English women he was associated with. There was obviously the Countess Tirau. Their association was well known."

"What other English women did he know?"

"Sometimes he had women here. They came and went. He was a beautiful man. Usually, they didn't introduce themselves. Mostly Marie. Beautiful man, beautiful woman."

"Was she a lady of the night?" Dory asked lightly.

The man shrugged. "Who is to say?"

"Do you know where I can find her?"

"I don't know. Maybe she wishes not to be found."

With that, Dory sensed that the manager's interest and attention had run out, so she thanked him for his time, and wrote down the Beaulieu Villa number on a card and asked him to call if there was anything else he could think of.

Dory left the building and walked into the sunshine again. For some reason, the hotel manager's office had left her feeling a bit cold, which was unusual. She didn't really want to return to Archie Wilshire's house just yet. Kindness aside, she felt uniquely uncomfortable there, exasperated by Vivian's presence. Because of that, she was in no rush to get back, so she walked along the promenade along the edge of the gloriously turquoise blue water. Never had she seen water so bright before. It looked like a jewel.

On her walk, she recounted all the things she'd heard and knew. There were creditors who had come looking for his things. Marie Chard was undoubtedly his lover—the most consistent one, but not the only one. She could or could not be a prostitute according to Monsieur Legrand's reaction to her question. But if he was seeing her on a regular basis, and his friends knew about her, it suggested there was a relationship there.

It was unlikely Livinia knew about this woman. Dory couldn't imagine that she wouldn't care. Some men had mistresses as a given, but Dory couldn't see Livinia being a person who would tolerate that. Thinking back on it now, Dory realized she hadn't asked the manager if Drecsay's relationship with Marie superseded the death of Countess Tirau. Perhaps it didn't matter. If the countess disapproved of him seeing other women, it might be that he associated with one that would be below her regard.

It was a question she could probably put to Terry, but she wasn't sure if it mattered. Terry might know where to find this woman.

Returning to her motorcar, she turned around and headed along the coast again, trying to put order to all the questions she had. The next thing to do was to find this Marie. If she was in a relationship with him, she might know why he was killed, because no one else seemed to have a clue. It could even be that this woman was responsible, but then again, could she have snuck into a party and killed him? If she dressed the part, perhaps she could. Had she discovered that her lover was waiting for a pretty, rich heiress in a secluded spot and become enraged enough to kill him?

The butler would have kept an eye on anyone arriving at the party and he would have told thc police if anyone unusual or uninvited had arrived. That would have informed their investigation into an entirely other direction, so Dory concluded there had been no unusual person attending the party. It meant she had to focus on the people who were at the party, which was almost everyone belonging to the British enclave on the coast.

To her annoyance, when she arrived back at the party, her parking spot had been taken by some new arrival while she had been gone and she had to find another quite far away. She was looking forward to returning here as much as she would a hole in the head, but she had a job to do.

The party had left the tennis court behind to languish along the veranda, elegantly draped over the equally elegant furniture. Terry was leaning against the wall, standing with drink in hand. His eyes were a little slower and more glossy, and he groaned as she approached. With a bit of drink in his belly, he was more honest about his feelings, not that he had particularly been holding back before.

Dory smiled tightly. "You mentioned that woman, Marie Chard. Do you know where I can find her?"

"God, what would you want to find her for?"

"Just to see what she has to say. She knew Baron Drecsay well. Perhaps he confided in her."

Terry performed an uncaring shrug. "I don't. I don't even know if she's around anymore. It was a while ago since I met her. Not the kind of girl who sticks around, if you know what I mean."

Truthfully, Dory didn't know what he meant, but she also didn't want to reveal her ignorance over what seemed a judgemental throwaway comment.

"Do you know where she was last?"

"I assume they spent most of their time together at his hotel. I wasn't privy to what they did in private. As for where she was when they weren't together, I have no idea."

He took a deep sip of his drink.

"Pretty, though," he said after a while. "The coast attracts pretty girls like flies, and they all want something. Attracted by title or money. They're all after something they don't have themselves."

This was hardly relevant. What was he telling her? Just spreading some form of bitterness? "And what was Marie after?"

"Perhaps she was hoping Drecsay would fall in love with her enough to marry her, give her some respectability. Who wouldn't want to be a baroness? If all other things were equal, wouldn't you?"

"All the barons I've met are miserable people," Dory said tartly. With the exception of perhaps Archie, and Lady Pettifer, of course, she hadn't met an upper-class twit she'd like to know better.

Terry found this inordinately amusing and he laughed. "Purport yourself uncorrupted by titles and wealth?" An edge of sarcasm laced his voice.

"I don't pretend to know myself enough to hazard a guess," Dory said dismissively, having no interest in getting into a discussion about her character with this man. Having dealt with Vivian before, she had no interest in entering some kind of discourse for this man to prove his own prejudices.

Chapter 17

Marie Chard proved difficult to find. She wasn't listed in the phone book, which wasn't perhaps surprising, because it was an expensive service and few could afford it. Trying to call the gendarmerie also proved fruitless and an exercise in absurd frustration, resulting in Dory being told that they could not be used as a meeting service.

With a groan, Dory hung up. She now had no idea how to find this woman. Terry had alluded that she could perhaps have left town, but then the hotel managed had clearly suggested she was a local girl, which meant she lived here somewhere.

If she had been a foreigner, she could easily go to the relevant consulate, who kept track of where everyone could be reached. Who knew it would prove so hard to find a person.

With a sigh, Dory rose from the small chair by the telephone table and walked back to the salon. "I'm afraid the gendarmerie were no help at all. I have no clue how to find this woman."

"Normally the right retailer could push you in the right direction, but I don't think this woman visited the retailers who keep records."

"Perhaps Prince Barenoli will know. I will send him a note later." Dory signed again. "We just don't seem to be getting anywhere. I was hoping Marie Chard would shed some light on why this man died. If there was anyone he would confide in, surely it was her."

"I'm afraid I don't know anyone who would be aware of this girl."

Feeling her spirits flag further, Dory sighed. "You figure this would be the most basic skill involved with investigating."

"We never claimed to be skilled," Lady Pettifer said, popping a candied almond in her mouth. "I wish I had bought some sherbets while we were in Nice."

"I will get some if I go there anytime soon, provided they haven't run out." Along with sugar, the supply of some luxury items were dwindling.

"Well, if we want to know what a professional would do in this instance, perhaps we should ask a professional," Lady Pettifer suggested.

"I tried that, but the inspector won't even speak to me."

"There is another one, though, who might be more willing to lend his ear and offer advice."

"Oh," Dory said. It hadn't occurred to her to ask DI Ridley for help. He may not be able to offer any direct assistance, but he could potentially tell her how to go about finding someone. "I will write to him."

A scrape sounded upstairs.

"Someone's risen," Lady Pettifer said.

Both Livinia and Vivian had returned early in the morning, being driven home by Richard. Livinia had put Dory out of her misery and urged her to drive home, saying they would find a way back without her. It had been a mercy and Dory had jumped at the chance. Now it was close to two in the afternoon and one of them was finally rising.

By the sounds of the steps, Dory knew it was Vivian, who appeared with his shirt open, displaying his white undershirt. "I will change," he said. "I'm just in dire need of something liquid."

"Good night, I take it," Lady Pettifer said.

"It did get a bit messy towards the end. Dory, here, didn't last the distance."

"Much too sensible," Lady Pettifer added.

Again Dory felt the weight of Vivian's judgment. Yesterday it had been for being there. Today his complaint was that she hadn't been there. Could he be so kind as to make up his mind? It seemed like he wanted to complain more than anything else.

"I will go write that letter," Dory said and stood.

"What letter?"

None of your concern, Dory wanted to say.

"We thought we'd ask that policeman back in England how we should proceed from here. We appear to need a little guidance."

Vivian was quiet for a moment. "Perhaps you shouldn't proceed. It could be that the police are not making further inquiries because they shouldn't."

"Or they are simply too busy and too uncaring that some foreigner has been dispatched. If he were a spy, it wasn't as if they are going to publicly acknowledge it." It seemed someone had been discussing the case with him, perhaps at the party last night.

"I really don't think that's the case," Lady Pettifer said.

"Someone at the Tonbridge's party killed him," Dory said and a silence descended. "So either one of the members of the illustrious British enclave is a spy hunter, or there is another reason altogether for this murder."

"It does seem unlikely that anyone would choose to take care of a spy in such a setting."

With a nod, Dory left the spot where she stood by the door and retreated to her room, where she could write her letter. In a way, she felt nervous. She'd had no communications with DI Ridley in any form since he had left Wallisford Hall. It could be that he'd ignore her letter completely. At the time, she had been of assistance to him, but she wasn't sure he would give her the time of day otherwise.

Sitting down at her desk, she pulled out a crisp sheet of paper and tried to think of what to write. Perhaps she should explain the situation first. With some false starts, she finally put her pen to the paper and started writing down what had happened and the things she had found out. What she really wanted to understand was what to do next. She paused. Maybe he would just tell her to leave it to the French police to deal with, like Vivian had—like everyone else was. Dory didn't know this man she was investigating—she didn't particularly like this man, but that was beside the point. Anyone deserved justice in such a situation. And there was a murderer here in this English society along the coast.

For a moment, she wondered if Vivian resented her for her part in uncovering his mother's deed. It was unlikely, but potentially possible that the woman would not have been found out if it hadn't been for Dory.

Still uncertain if she had written down the right things, or if she was even right in asking for guidance, she folded the letter and placed it in an envelope. She didn't know the exact address, so she wrote DI Ridley, Metropolitan Police, London. Surely the police would know how to direct it to the correct place.

Getting up from her seat, she returned downstairs to the salon with the letter in hand. To her relief, Vivian was no longer there. If Lady Pettifer noticed the tension between them, she didn't remark on it.

"Ah, have you written?"

Dory held up the letter.

"Excellent. Mr. Fernley," Lady Pettifer called and her butler appeared after a few moments. She did have a bell for calling him, but she usually bypassed it and simply asked for him. He seemed to hear her wherever he was. "Could you run down to the airport near Cannes and see if you can get this on this evening's flight.

"Yes, madame," he said and took the letter. Dory watched it leave the room and then as Mr. Fernley walked out to the car.

"It should be with him in a couple of days," Lady Pettifer said. "I wonder what he will tell us, but hopefully he will have some advice on how to find this woman. It must be a specialty of a policeman, determining how to find someone."

"I hope he writes back."

"Of course he'll write back. Why wouldn't he?"

"I am sure he's busy."

"It is in the nature of a policeman to assist."

Dory smiled. "Perhaps you are right." She couldn't help but wonder where he was and what he was doing. Was he solving some case somewhere? It could be that he wasn't in London at all, in which case the letter could take much longer to reach him.

"He was a lovely man, wasn't he?" Lady Pettifer said and Dory had to pull herself out of her thoughts.

"Yes," she said quietly.

"Completely unattached, as I recall. He would be perfect for you."

Color flared up Dory's cheeks. She wasn't normally one to get embarrassed about something like that—in fact, she wasn't normally one to swoon over any man, but she had liked DI Ridley. There was something very sensible about him. He also seemed to know exactly what to do when the occasion required it. Without a doubt, he was an excellent investigator, relentlessly pursuing the person responsible for the crime he was investigating.

All in all, Dory wasn't sure her interest in solving murders would have been left unexplored if she hadn't met him. In a way, perhaps she was trying to do what he did.

"Until we hear back, I think it's best we put the whole thing behind us," Lady Pettifer said. "Oh and now the tea is cold and we sent Mr. Fernley away."

"I'll refresh the pot," Dory said with a smile, knowing full well Lady Pettifer hoped she would do so the minute she'd said it.

Chapter 18

The next couple of days were spent trying to avoid Vivian. When he was at the house, she found herself in need of a long walk, returning when he had gone again, or she had been absent long enough. Her strategy didn't always work and he would be sitting either in the covered seating area outside or in the salon. Luckily, he seemed to ignore her much of the time as well. Still, Dory knew she could bear the brunt of his moods anytime he felt like it.

The sky was sunny and pure blue. A warm breeze was coming off the sea, but the house was starting to build up heat in the afternoons.

Today, both Vivian and Livinia were staying at home, which meant the house would likely feel crowded. It was by no means a small house. Perhaps Dory would see herself off to a secluded corner and read. It would be an evening of gin and tonics. Lady Pettifer always liked a gin on a hot day.

Walking into the house, the warm atmosphere felt repressive, and she wasn't in the mood to read.

Surely, she couldn't go for another walk. She'd just returned from one and was hot and sweaty as a result. What she wanted was to cool down. The sea, she thought. Maybe a dip was exactly what she needed, so she went upstairs and dressed in the deep navy maillot she had bought in Cannes. It was lovely and it fit her perfectly. It had a rounded neckline and it finished at on her hips.

With towel over her shoulder and her book in hand, just in case, she left the house again, feeling a sense of purpose. The path down to the sea led through the extensive gardens along the rough terrains of the hillside, then down a rocky path to the small wooden jetty.

Spreading the towel on the jetty, she left everything there and climbed down the ladder into the refreshingly cool water. It had a sting of coldness for only a moment, then it mellowed into wonderful.

The water was so clear she could see all the rocks along the bottom and even some of the sea life. Diving under, all noise disappeared for a moment and she felt alone. The unpleasantness of the day was cleared away and she emerged tasting salt on her lips.

Glittering sun reflected all around her and she swam away from the jetty, where she turned around and floated for a moment. Swimming in the River Darent Lake had always been their summer outing as she'd grown up. They would cycle over and picnic by the lake shore. It had been the most marvelous days growing up—they'd been happy. Lower Darent Lake didn't have the spectacular colors of the Cote D'Azur, but it had its own charm, and Dory felt a pang of longing for home.

Gradually, the water started feeling cold and Dory swam back to the jetty and climbed out, laying herself down in the sun.

Baron Drecsay snuck into her mind. It felt wrong that he would never experience another day like this, just because someone had decided to steal his life from him. There had to be some way of moving ahead.

The sun quickly warmed her and she decided to return to the house before she started to burn. Unfortunately, her complexion wouldn't allow her to lie in the sun for very long and now had to seek shade.

The path to the house felt much steeper on the climb up, the breeze cooling her wet swimming costume as she walked through the shaded parts of the garden.

"Miss Dory," she heard Mr. Fernley call.

"I'm here," she called out.

"A phone call for you."

"Oh," she said and ran up the rest of the path and through the garden. Her towel was flung over her shoulder and she wrapped it around her as she approached the house.

The telephone was sitting on a small table in the hallway, the receiver lying on its side. Picking it up, she held it to her ear. "Hello?"

"Miss Sparks."

Dory recognized DI Ridley's voice immediately, even with the relentless crackling along the line. "DI Ridley. I didn't expect your call. I am so pleased to hear from you."

"I received your letter."

"Yes, I am sorry to bother you with this, but we seem to have stalled in our investigation. I know many feel we shouldn't, but the police here do not have the time to look particularly deeply into this."

"Much is being diverted everywhere," he said. It was hard to hear the exact intonation of his voice. "You mentioned the next step was to find this girlfriend, a local girl."

"Yes, but we struggle to find her. She is not of the community Lady Pettifer belongs to." She was going to add herself too, but it felt wrong in more than one way. "The police cannot assist us, so we do not know where to look."

"Census data is always a good place to seek people if you are looking for someone quite static, but it can be difficult to reach the census office if you are in a more rural location. You could call."

"Of course," Dory said, feeling slightly stupid because in hindsight, it was such an obvious avenue. "I should have thought of that."

"But most likely, if this girl is more of a goodtime girl, as you seemed to allude, just asking for her in some of the pubs is usually a quicker way of finding someone."

Dory didn't see any need to explain that the French didn't have pubs as such, but they did have taverns, and there were clubs and bars around where she could ask. Perhaps any of the drinking establishments near the Hotel Carlone. The baron and Marie were likely regular patrons there. It seemed so obvious now. How had she not thought of it? "I will ask in the establishments around the hotel where the baron lived."

"They might not provide you an answer, but if she was a local girl, then you could probably hone down on her district, then repeat until you get a street. From there it should be relatively simple to find her house, or her family's. If she has left town, her family will know where she is, and even how to reach her. Be careful, though. She might be the person responsible. And perpetrators do rash, irresponsible—even illogical—things when they are cornered. You shouldn't go alone."

"I won't. I promise."

"And I don't mean you and an elderly lady. Take someone who can guard you. It always pays to have someone watching your back."

"Yes, I will." Unsolicitous thoughts turned to Vivian, but she couldn't say he would actually agree. The thought of running around Nice with Vivian, looking for a trace of a woman seemed almost absurd.

"Typically with murder, the motives are primarily jealousy or money. Look to those first. Lady Wallisford didn't neatly fit into those, but most murders do."

Dory nodded even though he couldn't see her. "Thank you."

"You can write to me again if you wish, but it appears I will be at the Pirbright Camp in Surrey in the near future. If you write to the Met, there is a good chance it won't reach me."

"Pirbright?" she said.

"My letter to appear just arrived," he said a little more quietly.

"Oh," Dory said with surprise. "You're being conscripted."

"Effectively yes; technically it's not officially conscription. The expectation is clear. I head off in a couple of days."

"I see." She had no idea what to say to that. The pressure on people like him to join the struggle must be rampant. Was she supposed to send her condolences?

"Apparently they need men with certain skills."

"I hadn't realized," she repeated. The news still stunned her. "I hope you will be alright," she said without thinking.

"It's only training. I'm sure I will survive. Perhaps the French police are having the same issue with many of their officers being pressed into service."

That could explain why they seemed so unwilling to investigate the baron's murder. "I'm not sure England could do without its police."

"Not everyone is being called from the essential services. The firemen have all been exempt, but some of us investigators can be released, it seems."

At this point, Dory had no idea what to say. It felt as though she wanted to say so much, but couldn't think of anything appropriate.

"Are you safe where you are?" he finally asked.

"We seem to be. Lady Pettifer intends to stay put provided the Germans do."

It was silence down the line for a moment. "We should probably end this call."

"Yes, it must be costing you a bit. Thank you so much for your assistance. I know exactly what I need to do now."

There was a chuckle down the phone. "Goodbye, Dory."

Dory didn't want him to go. "I'll let you know how we progress."

"I would appreciate that."

With that, he hung up and the line clicked a few more times as the operators disengaged the calls, until Dory's phone was left with only static silence and she replaced the receiver.

Chapter 19

Dory felt a little stunned as she walked back to the salon, where Lady Pettifer, Vivian and Livinia were all sitting. They all turned to her expectantly, having heard her speaking on the phone.

"It was DI Ridley," she said absently. "He had some good advice."

"So you know how to proceed now?"

Dory sat down, eventually remembering that a question had been put to her. "Yes."

"You seem a bit startled."

"It was just… DI Ridley said he'd been asked to join the services and he was leaving his post."

"Everyone and their dog have been conscripted," Vivian said dismissively and all turned to him. "It's not unusual. Anyone with a hint of education is being conscripted into officer training."

"You have education," Livinia said.

"So I have. Knew it would lead to no good."

"You haven't received a letter, have you?"

"Turns out I have. Wasn't there to receive it, though. Had already left."

The room was silent for a moment.

"Like I said, everyone and their dog. Women too, apparently."

"What?!" Livinia said.

"Mostly nurses and eminently sensible girls, so I think you're safe, Livinia."

"Technically, I don't think women can be required to serve," Lady Pettifer said.

"Not if Sir Beveridge has his way. He seeks to conscript every woman in the country."

"I couldn't possibly go to war," Livinia piped shrilly.

"Don't worry, Livinia," Vivian said. "No one would subject the Germans to you. More likely they will send you to a farm to milk cows or something."

The horror on Livinia's face made Dory chuckle. It wasn't really funny, though. This only showed that the people in power didn't expect that the lack of aggression that had kept things peaceful would continue. And it seemed they could all be a part of the war. This thing that had seemed too abstract and removed had shifted closer. People she knew were being sucked into what she saw as a menacing cloud.

Everyone knew the losses that had occurred with the Great War. A whole generation of men had been lost. With men going to war, the chances of them not returning were high.

Absently Dory stroked her fingers along her mouth.

"Andrew," Lady Pettifer said and rose, marching over to the telephone. In a sense, it felt as though hearing of Andrew's conscription would be worse, because Lady Pettifer was a mother. As much as everyone worried about friends and acquaintances, mothers must be devastated.

This conversation and Lady Pettifer's reaction wasn't something Dory wanted to be a part of. Lady Pettifer wouldn't want it either if it turned out Andrew, her son, had been conscripted. She bore blows in solitude.

"I have to go to Nice," Dory said.

"God, yes, let's get out of here," Livinia said. "All this talk of war makes my skin crawl."

With worry, Dory pressed her lips together, wondering if she should ask Vivian to accompany her. Livinia would be more of a hindrance if there was danger around. But she had no idea if Vivian would be of any use either. Use or not, anyone with ill intent would pause at taking on three people, even if they were essentially useless and oblivious.

Not that it mattered yet. Dory hadn't even located Marie Chard. When it came time to question, perhaps she would ask both of them to accompany her.

"He has received a letter, too," Lady Pettifer said at the door with a strained and tired voice. "I think I will rest for a while."

"In that case, we might continue with our inquiries," Dory said and stood. "Follow up on some of DI Ridley's suggestions."

With a nod, Lady Pettifer turned and walked toward the stairs. Sighing at the sight of Lady Pettifer's silent suffering, Dory felt awful. In a sense, it was hard not to think of it as a death sentence. Or at least Lady Pettifer would, who so remembered the telegrams relentlessly coming with dreadful news.

Without a son or a husband, Dory wouldn't receive such news, and her brothers were yet too young. If the war stretched on for four years like the

Great War, then at least one would be pulled into the malaise as well. She couldn't imagine losing either of her brothers.

Maybe the fact that nothing had really happened yet meant there was still hope of a diplomatic solution. It could be that all of this ended without great loss. Surely no one wanted another war like the one before. It had devastated everyone.

"Come on," Vivian said. "I'll drive."

Still feeling deflated, Dory grabbed her hat off the coat stand. Livinia disappeared upstairs to change, leaving Dory and Vivian to stand by the car. An awkward silence hung between them.

"I am sorry to hear you have been conscripted."

"Wouldn't have happened if I'd been stupid enough to start a parliamentary career like Cedric."

"He's exempt?"

"All parliamentarians are."

Livinia finally appeared and they all got into the motorcar. Dory sat in the back, still feeling heavy from the day's developments. She spent most of the trip lost in her own thoughts while Vivian and Livinia chatted between themselves. Notably, since Vivian had arrived, they hadn't engaged in the petty barbs they used to sling at each other when she'd first met them. His jabs seemed to be exclusively reserved for Dory now.

The drive took long, but happened along beautiful vistas. The coastline was stunning the entire drive from St. Tropez, through multiple small villages and through Cannes.

"Why are you going to Nice, anyway?" Vivian asked.

"I'm going to ask around some of the bars if they know this Marie Chard woman." In a way, the murder seemed like a paltry concern against the looming specter of war, but that was exactly why they couldn't lose focus. Justice was still needed for this man.

Arriving in Nice, Dory asked Vivian to pull over by the Hotel Carlone, where she got out. "I'll meet you back here in two hours," she said.

"And what if we want to stay for more than two hours?" Vivian challenged.

For a moment, Dory was stumped. "Then I suppose I will take the bus." The bus was slow, but it did wind its way back along the coast. By no means was it a comfortable ride, but it would give everyone the flexibility to do as they wished.

"Two hours it is, then," he said before suddenly driving off.

With raised eyebrows, Dory simply watched them as they disappeared down the street, then decided she couldn't be bothered with Vivian and his strange behavior. She had a job to do.

Turning around, she spotted a brasserie. The baron and his girl must have visited there on a number of occasions. It was a nice place with beautiful standing lights between neat rows of wooden tables. The place had a warm, welcoming feeling.

A sharp-featured man stood outside in his starched white apron. It was that quiet period between lunch and supper, when many of the French took their siesta. "Monsieur," Dory said as she approached.

"Are you dining with us, mademoiselle?" he asked with a curt bow.

"No, I'm afraid not. I was wondering if you could assist me to find a woman that I believe frequented here with Baron Drecsay."

The man mused for a moment and Dory feared he would be as unhelpful as the manager at the hotel. "Baron Drecsay had many dining companions."

"I meant specifically Marie Chard."

"Oh, Marie. We have not seen her for a while. The baron met with an unfortunate fate, you know."

"I heard. It is just that his family wishes to give a gift to Marie, but they cannot find her." Dory was lying through her teeth, but she had to do something to get past the suspicion in the man's eyes.

"I see. I can tell her if she comes," he said with a shrug. "And you are?"

"Miss Dory Sparks. I am actually trying to track her down. Do you know where I could ask next?"

"I cannot help you. I don't know her address."

"I understand she is a local girl. Do you know the district she is from?"

"I believe Riquier."

That was quite far away. She would have to take the tram. "Perhaps I will try to find her there."

The maitre'd had lost interest and Dory thanked him before leaving. Riquier was a district she didn't know well, it was known for dense houses and the location of many of the tradesmen in the city. It wasn't a tiny place, but Dory knew it was the kind of neighborhood where the people knew each other.

One of the tram lines would take her straight there and she could relax for a moment and simply watch the busy streets of Nice pass her by. They were busy, but there did seem to be fewer people than the last time she had visited, which was only a week or so back. More people had to be leaving. Dory wondered if Lady Summernot and her sister had managed to find passage out.

Maybe it was time to broach the topic with Lady Pettifer as well. The emptying streets were alarming to see. It felt as though the whole world was anticipating something terrible.

Chapter 20

Marie proved not that hard to find. Dory asked a few vendors and eventually she was led to a second story apartment above a pharmacy. Marie lived with her mother in a small apartment and seeing it, Dory wished the baron's family actually had something for her. Although the chances that they would give any consideration to a girl like Marie were low.

Dory smiled as they sat down in the apartment's tiny reception room. The furniture was old and worn, but well serviced.

"I am trying to find out what happened to Baron Drecsay," she explained as Marie and her mother waited expectantly with their hands in their laps. Marie was very pretty with dark hair and lovely eyes. It wasn't a wonder she had caught the baron's eye. "I have not been able to find any enemies. But I think you know him better, and I was hoping you could set me on the right path."

"You wish to find who killed him? It wasn't me."

The police must have given her a hard time, Dory presumed. She would be the logical suspect. Ridley had told her to look for jealousy or greed first. "Did you observe any specific jealousy amongst his friends?"

"Nothing he was worried about. He liked to have friends of higher position than himself." It had to be Prince Barenoli she was referring to.

"There are some that say that Baron Drecsay was a spy."

Marie laughed. "No, he hated the Germans. Probably they say that because he was friends with Barenoli. Barenoli is only here because he cannot go home. Neither of them are spies. Only stupid people think that. Besides, Drecsay… he didn't like to do difficult things. He liked the easy life. He gets that woman to pay for everything."

"You mean Countess Tirau."

"Stupid woman." There was definitely a hint of jealousy there—or was it resentment.

"But with her death, her support ended. Did he inherit anything from her?"

"No, she gave him nothing!" Marie sounded offended. "All the work he did whispering compliments in her ear and she gave him nothing."

"One of his friends said he had some scheme to rebuild his family wealth. Did he say anything to you?"

"He always had ideas. He spoke of ideas, but he never did anything. Too lazy."

Dory had to wonder if Marie had even liked him. Or was she as dependent on him as he was on Countess Tirau? Did none of these people have the wherewithal to stand on their own feet and have true relationships? With a shake of her head, Dory dismissed the thought. Her judgment wasn't serving her at this moment. "I understood the countess was very generous, at times."

"Every once in a while, she would do what Drecsay wanted. Gifts here and there. Jewelry."

"Anything of note?"

"She gave him a car. Some land to build a house."

"She gave him land?"

"Yes, down in Antibes. Not good land. Average land."

"Do you think anyone would kill him for this land?"

"It was nothing more than farm land. I don't know. When I went, it wasn't much. Mr. Henri can tell you more."

"And who is Mr. Henri?"

"He is the countess' *advokat*."

"Her solicitor? Do you know where I can find him?"

Marie shrugged. "I never met him."

They talked some more, but Dory wasn't getting anything else that resembled a motive. Marie, as it turned out, didn't like Prince Barenoli, but he was rich, the woman pointed out. That forgave him a great deal, Dory assumed. Neither did she like Terry. He drank too much and was handsy. There were also other friends. Drecsay had a lot of friends.

When Dory brought up the subject of Livinia, Marie's face darkened and she called her a stupid English girl. Well, there was certainly jealousy there. It just wasn't directed at Drecsay, even though Marie's anger probably should have been. Women did tend to blame the other woman instead of the man who was inflicting the damage—as if they were incapable of taking responsibility for their own actions. But Marie had never met Livinia, or even knew what she looked like.

There seemed to be nothing else Marie could tell her. Drecsay liked to drink, liked to be the life of the party. And he had enjoyed his time after the countess' control had finished, but his finances had dwindled. Still, he hadn't seemed overly worried.

Bidding goodbye, Dory left, her mind mulling over the things that Marie had said. She painted the picture of a young man who cared little for consequences. In saying that, it seemed Drecsay had turned his attention to marriage and was seeking the most profitable return from it. Livinia had obviously been a target, and for someone like him, it would have been a good step.

Dory shuddered trying to imagine the life they would have—living here on the coast, slowly burning through Livinia's inheritance. Sadly, it wasn't a fate that would unduly disturb Livinia. She, too, would be happy to be the life of the party here on the coast— until the money ran out. But for her, perhaps the money would never entirely run out. She had her own Countess Tirau in her father.

It was a fate that Lady Pettifer would deeply disapprove of, but it was questionable how much control she had over Livinia. Livinia was a young woman of age. It wasn't as if anyone could blatantly tell her what to do. Maybe Marie was right and she was a woman bound to make stupid decisions. Drecsay was no longer in the picture, so perhaps there was hope for her to settle into a good marriage with a half-decent man. Some girls seemed allergic to decent men, though.

The tram took her back to where she had started outside the Hotel Carlone. Right on time, Vivian showed up sans Livinia.

"Livinia is staying," he said, waiting for Dory to get in.

"You didn't feel like staying yourself?"

He didn't answer her question. "So what did you discover in your investigations?"

"It seems Drecsay was looking for an heiress and had his sights on Livinia."

Dory could see the muscle in Vivian's cheek working. He did not like hearing that. If he had been around, Dory had to concede he would have had motive for murder. He'd been nowhere near, otherwise, Dory would have to suspect him again, like she had for the other murder investigation she had been a part of.

"Apparently the countess had given him some land down by Antibes. The girl said it wasn't particularly valuable land, but enough for him to build a house on."

"Land isn't hard to get around here."

"No, I suppose not," Dory admitted.

"Hard to think anyone would murder for a bit of land."

"People have killed for less. I suppose it depends on who inherits the land."

"Some distant relative in Hungary, no doubt. Whoever has inherited the title. So if you find some mysterious Hungarian hanging around, then you might have your man. Someone who would come all the way here to dispatch of a penniless baron for a worthless piece of land."

In Vivian's book, the land might be worthless, but he lived on an entirely different scale from most people. To someone like Marie, that land would be a fortune, even if she hadn't been impressed by it when she'd visited with Drecsay. Like Drecsay with his

countess, Marie would inherit nothing from Drecsay.
It could be said that she had lost more than anyone
out of his death.

Vivian drove, his attention on the road. The
sun was setting, painting glorious colors on the
horizon. Again, Dory was struck with how beautiful
it all was. But it was also starting to feel like an
illusion, a distraction. "There were fewer people in
Nice than the last time we visited."

"People are leaving," he said, but didn't
elaborate further.

"What are you going to do about your
conscription?"

For a moment, he looked over at her, then back
at the road. "Well, I can't hang out here forever.
Sooner or later, I will have to go back."

"Some would say that you could stay here and
avoid it."

"Not if I ever want to show my face in society
again," he said. Dory hadn't realized there would be
such pressure. Ridley had alluded to it as well.
"People are scrambling for excuses for their sons not
to go, but deride others for it. It is the very height of
hypocrisy. None of us are true conscientious

objectors—we just object to our family members being called to serve."

They drove in silence for a while. This war seemed to be steamrolling ahead, unable and unwilling to take a moment to pause and reflect. "Is there any going back now?" she asked.

"It would be a miracle."

Chapter 21

It would be hard to see how some farmland in Antibes would be a motive for murder," Lady Pettifer said as they sat in the dark around the dining table, lit only with candles. Livinia had not returned, and was in the bosom of her social circle for the night. Dory still didn't understand why Vivian had returned home. Perhaps he'd had enough. It could be that he didn't particularly enjoy the company of what was effectively Livinia's friends. They were a bit younger, perhaps.

"It would be truly something desperate."

"I will try to call this Mr. Henri," Dory said. "By the name, it is hard to tell whether he is English or French."

"Perhaps the countess' family can shed some light. I don't exactly know how to reach them." Lady Pettifer looked ponderous. "It wouldn't be something that her friends and acquaintances would know."

"Maybe I should try to reach Inspector Moreau," Dory said with a notion of dread. The inspector seemed less than willing to speak to her. "It's worth a try."

"Try it in the morning. We should be quite insistent. If they prove difficult, I could ask Major Dodds to call him."

"Who's Dodds," Vivian asked.

"The British consul in Nice. He can put a bit of pressure on the French authorities if we need him to."

"Useful," Vivan said. He looked bored as he sat and nursed his wine, or it could be the candlelight that displayed him so. Dory had to wonder if something had happened, or if it was the conscription that weighed heavily on him. That would be understandable. Dory couldn't even imagine what it would feel like to receive such a letter, to be forced to go off to war.

Earlier in the day, he had mentioned that they were recruiting educated men to be officers, which meant him. It was hard to imagine him as someone in charge of a platoon of men. Dory wasn't sure that was the right term, but Vivian would be directing men in the war effort. And Ridley. Ridley seemed more of a natural choice. He had directed men before, but what skills did Vivian really have?

Putting the uncomfortable thoughts away, she returned her mind to Drecsay, which seemed less confrontational to think about. There was no hint of a culprit yet, but the land was a lead she felt they needed to follow.

"Shall we listen to the news?" Lady Pettifer said and rose. "I could use a sherry, I think. Dory, would you like one?"

"I could handle a small one," Dory replied. After all this time with Lady Pettifer, Dory had learned to enjoy a sherry. Initially, it hadn't agreed with her, but over time, her appetite had learned to crave some after supper.

"Mr. Fernley, would you be so good as to turn on the wireless."

The man moved to do so and sharp static invaded their ears for a moment. The remnants of some melody played its last cords. They had made it just in time.

This is the BBC from London, the disembodied voice said gravely. These are today's main events. Germany has invaded Luxembourg,

Belgium and the Netherlands. Both houses of Parliament have been summoned at six o'clock this evening, and the cabinet has met from eleven this morning to prepare our response. The French Parliament has also been meeting today. What news there is comes chiefly from broadcasting stations in Luxembourg City, Amsterdam and Brussels.

They all exchanged concerned looks, but no one spoke. They had been driving around Nice today and no one had been the wiser that Germany was marching across Europe toward them.

Allied troops are preparing their response, and so are our forces in Lille, both mobilizing to meet the Germans.

"It is starting," Lady Pettifer said, her voice completely toneless.

"Our troops will beat them back," Vivian stated. Dory could see the concern in his eyes. She'd actually never seen him truly concerned before.

The presenter went onto detail the resistance being put up in each of the countries to the invading army.

"They're invading three countries at once," Dory said, still not believing what she was hearing.

"There wasn't so much as a peep when we were in Nice. It was just a normal day." She knew full well she was babbling, but she didn't know what else to do with the fear that bubbled up inside her. The Germans were invading, taking the small countries before they marched through to France. Would the French really stop them, like Vivian had asserted? Dory hoped so.

"Turn it off, Mr. Fernley," Lady Pettifer said. The silence was jarring and no one spoke.

"We have to leave," Vivian said after a while.

"I thought you said the French would hold them," Dory asserted.

"When have the French ever held anything. We have to leave. Getting rid of the landed gentry was the first thing the Germans did when they invaded Poland."

Lady Pettifer grimaced. "It is very worrying that the Germans seem to be attacking the civilian population. Very worrying indeed. But all this is happening up north. If not the French, then our troops will beat them back. It is all far away from here."

Vivian rose sharply and paced. Everyone seemed to be saying one thing and then the opposite.

"I might get some fresh air," Dory said and rose herself. Tears were forming in her eyes and she needed some time alone to deal with the emotions that were running away with her. So she walked out into the darkness of the garden outside. The moon was out and lit the landscape around her. It was utterly silent as if the coastline itself didn't care what the stupid people milling on its surface was doing. She felt stupid—on behalf of people in general, she felt stupid. This was a stupid thing to do—war, what use could it possibly serve. It would cause wholesale misery to everyone and for that?

Breathing rapidly, Dory had to slow down or she would start to hyperventilate. Her hopes had been that they would sort this—that it was all posturing and they would sort themselves out. Stupid people were leading them into war, and now they would all suffer. Life as Dory had known it was ending and something awful was going to take its place. Their lovely lives here on the coast could not continue. They had to leave.

Everything had seemed so distant before, but now the ugliness that had been brewing was chasing them away. It was even forcing Ridley and Vivian into the very war itself.

Coming across a bench, she sat down and stared out at the calm sea. Why did everything have to end?

She sat for ages, unable to deal with other people right now, or commiserate with their worry and concern. Too many worries circled around her own heart to have room for the concerns of others. In a sense, she was holding herself back from blind panic and couldn't afford to let anyone test her resolve.

After a long while, she saw headlights snake along the coast road in the distance. Did they know what had happened? Had their life effectively been torn apart too? Or were they blissfully unaware? Just a short while ago, Dory had been blissfully unaware.

Eventually the motorcar drew closer and Dory saw it veer in. It was coming this way. It had to be Livinia. She must have heard. Were the glittering party things in Cannes also panicking?

It really was time to head back, and Dory forced herself to rise. Suddenly, she felt exhausted. It was as though she had used up all her emotions at once and was now left completely empty.

The headlights of Livinia's motorcar, probably Richard's, swung around the tree as it pulled up next to the house.

"Have you heard?" Livinia's voice demanded inside the house. "It's unbelievable. I don't understand. This fucking war! They ruin everything."

Livinia's tirade wasn't far off what Dory was feeling.

"Everyone is shocked," Richard's voice came. "No one knows what to do. There's talk of midnight escapades across the country. They say we should pack up this minute and just drive north or west."

"It serves no one to head off like a headless chook," Lady Pettifer said. "In the morning, we will call Major Dodds and see what he says. We must be orderly with this."

Richard cleared his throat and sat down. "They say the Duke and Duchess left their lunch half eaten and fled earlier today. They must have been told before the announcement on the news. They just left everything and fled."

"Not a word," Livinia said. "They could have warned the rest of us."

"Perhaps they wanted clear roads for their escape," Vivian said and lit a cigarette. His panic had clearly subsided, and he was more or less back to his usual caustic self. Dory had to admire his resilience. "I bet they don't half admire Herr Hitler so much now."

"They were trying to avoid a war," Livinia said in anger. "Maybe if they hadn't been thrown out, they would have succeeded."

"Children," Lady Pettifer said. "We need cool minds. Tomorrow we'll call the consulate and plan what we are to do."

Chapter 22

At no point that night did Dory sleep. It was almost as if she didn't trust the wall to stand if she so much as closed her eyes. It was still unbelievable to think the Germans were marching toward them. It was impossible to imagine what this would entail. No doubt they were going back to England, but it would be an England at war, and Dory had no idea what that meant.

It was a given that she would return to England at some point; she just hadn't anticipated that it would be under these circumstances, which seemed unbelievable even as the war hadn't exactly cropped up overnight. She had always had that hope that it would fizzle to nothing.

With groggy eyes, Dory met the next morning. Her head ached and she felt awful. When she reached the salon downstairs, it seemed Lady Pettifer's night had been similar. "Terrible sleep," the woman said.

"Me, too," Dory confessed.

"It seems we must find some way of leaving here. There are still so many people on the coast.

How are we all going to make our way back to the UK?"

"I don't envy the task that has befallen Major Dodds. You don't think he would simply leave us, do you?"

"It would be cowardly if he did," Lady Pettifer said with distaste. "I think he will do his best. He seems a sensible man."

"You know him."

"Well enough. It seems as our options reduced, traveling home seemed too difficult to deal with, and now we are in the lurch."

"I don't think flying is an option."

"There are too many of us here for it to be the strategy he will choose. The government will have to help us."

"And if they don't?" Dory asked.

"Then we will be in trouble indeed. I still think it will be a long time before the Germans make it all the way down here. The Italians are more of a concern, but so far, they have shown little indication that they want to participate. I don't trust that, though. It is well known that Mussolini dreams of restoring some semblance of the old Roman Empire."

"Well, he will have to compete with the Nazis and their empire," Dory said with distaste.

"I think for the time being, we are safe. We have time at the very least."

Lady Pettifer checked her watch, a bejeweled timepiece that Dory knew she had received from her late husband. "Perhaps I should call Major Dodds now." On painful knees, she rose from her seat and walked over to the telephone in the hall, speaking in French to the operator, who apparently couldn't put her through.

Before long, Lady Pettifer returned to her seat. "There is a queue to access his line," she said. "It seems every person on the coast is having the same idea."

A noise in the hall showed that someone else had risen, and Vivian appeared with his washed hair slicked back from his face. He looked like he had slept at least. "I'm starving," he said.

"Then we shall eat," Lady Pettifer said, and called for Mr. Fernley. "I suppose Livinia won't rise for a while. I understand Richard left early this morning."

Dory had heard a car start and drive away some time well before dawn.

It was going to be a hot day. Heat was already starting to build up. They walked into the dining room and sat down. It would take a few minutes before Mr. Fernley appeared with ham and eggs. Dory's body seemed to crave energy today.

"I think we should wait until tomorrow and then go to the consulate in Nice. It will be utter chaos today, so no need to add to it."

Vivian looked distracted with a deep frown marring his features. "I am going back to Switzerland," he said after a while.

"Vivian, you can't."

"I have to go collect Mother before it's too late."

"The Germans could have invaded by the time you get there. It's not worth the risk."

"If they invade, Mother would be exposed. Centuries past a noble could be assured of good treatment, but that is no longer the case. These Germans would as readily kill anyone with a title."

"I'm sure it is not that severe," Lady Pettifer said.

"Well, I am going shortly. I will collect her and… "

"And then what? She cannot come back to the United Kingdom. Technically, there is still a warrant out for her arrest and if she is arrested, she will hang."

"I know that," Vivian said curtly. "I will have to figure out what to do. Maybe Spain."

"To live under the rule of another insane dictator with dreams of an empire? Who knows what his role is going to be in all this? If he joins with the Nazis, which he could at any point, then things will be very dire indeed."

"The French wouldn't have a chance," Vivian said.

Dory simply looked from one to the other, too afraid to speak in case voicing her thoughts made them real.

"You need to get off the continent," Lady Pettifer said.

"Perhaps we'll go to Algeria or Morocco."

Concern shone through Lady Pettifer's eyes, but even Dory knew that Vivian wasn't changing his mind. As awful as Lady Wallisford was, she was still his mother, and Dory could sympathize with him wanting to fetch her. She would likely do the same if the positions were reversed.

Their food arrived and Dory struggled with her appetite, but she forced herself to eat. A few days ago, her main concern had been the lack of sugar, and now they were all being driven in different directions in desperate flight.

Livinia appeared through the door wearing her sunglasses. "I feel awful. I was hoping I would wake up today and it had all been a bad dream. Where's Richard?"

"He left early this morning," Lady Pettifer said.

"I can't believe he just left without a word. What if we needed him?"

"I guess at times like this, you see who people really are," Vivian said.

"That's unfair."

A silence descended as no one really felt like getting into an extended argument.

"What's going to happen to Mother?" Livinia said.

"Vivian has decided to fetch her," Dory said.

"And then you'll bring her here?" Livinia said hopefully.

"I don't know," Vivian replied noncommittally. "I don't know what options will be open to us. It might be better to head down to Italy. The Italian ports are still open. We could potentially get passage south."

"South?"

"Well, I can't bring her back to England, can I?"

"I'm sure they will make an exception considering the circumstances."

"And will you risk her life on that assumption?"

If Dory didn't feel that capital punishment was gruesome and unnecessary, she would be open to Lady Wallisford meeting the justice she deserved, but she couldn't bring herself to wish someone to hang.

"I will work something out," Vivian said after a while. "There are options."

"There has to be panic all over the country," Lady Pettifer said. "Everyone in the north must be heading south. The poor Belgians. They must be running like rabbits."

"Well, if they ever invade us," Vivian said. "There is nowhere to go."

"Except America," Livinia said.

"If things go very badly, maybe the next time we see each other, it will be in New York."

"Or the Bahamas."

"Not sure the Bahamas can take half the population of the United Kingdom descending on it," Lady Pettifer said. "In saying that though, I am sure Lady Ridgemont will be able to put us up in that villa of hers."

"Along with everyone else she knows."

"Why did we never invest in a villa in the Bahamas?" Lady Pettifer said furtively.

"Because you fell in love with the Cote D'Azur," Vivian pointed out.

"Yes," Lady Pettifer said absently. "Could you imagine traveling across the Atlantic every year?"

The conversation drifted to silence, and shortly after eating, Vivian went upstairs to pack.

"Is he going now?" Livinia asked.

"Yes, I think it is better he goes as soon as possible."

It didn't take him long to return, carrying a leather bag. They all gathered in the hallway.

"If the Germans invade Switzerland, you can't go."

It frustrated Lady Pettifer that Vivian didn't answer, instead kissed her on the cheek. He gave Dory an awkward kiss to, which would probably never have happened if it wasn't for the extreme circumstances. "Get them home," he said quietly so only she could hear. He was placing the task on her to ensure they got home. Dory nodded.

Then he walked outside and placed his bag on the backseat of his motorcar. Livinia followed him and they embraced tightly. That was an affection she hadn't really seen between the twins before. When it came down to it, it ran deeper than either of them let on.

Then he got in and drove without looking back. Not one for long-winded goodbyes. Livinia stood and watched for a while.

An anxious groan escaped Lady Pettifer. "He isn't a stupid boy," she said to reassure herself. "He will know how to watch out for danger."

Will he, Dory wanted to say. As far as she knew, Vivian had a strong sense of entitlement and a puffed-up sense of importance in the world. Hopefully those things would not lead him into trouble.

Chapter 23

The difference in Nice was stark. The streets were empty. They weren't really. People were hurrying along, but at first glance, they looked deserted. There was no one wandering leisurely down the promenade and the cafés were largely empty. Overnight, the world had changed.

Dory drove along the promenade until they reached the building where the consulate was. If there was any question as to where the people had gone, it appeared to be here. A crowd of people stood in a group outside the building, milling and chatting. There were grave expressions of worry on people's faces.

Pulling over, Lady Pettifer and Livinia got out. There were no available parking spaces so Dory had to keep driving down the road to find somewhere. It seemed people had driven from all around to reach the now swamped consulate. Dory doubted they would get much assistance today. Perhaps it had been a mistake coming here, but what else could they do? Hopefully the British Government had some plan for the people here on the coast. Surely they couldn't all be left to their own devices. There were a great many people here without the means of leaving on their own account.

A new set of worry descended on Dory. What would they do if they had to find their own way back? Perhaps Vivian was right and Italy was the best route, but heading into an uncomfortably fascist regime sat badly. Their choices were Italy, Spain, or to find their way north to the Atlantic coast, or even closer to the fighting on the channel coast.

A parking space was available and Dory pulled in. It was a hot day and she could feel the heat of the ground through the soles of her shoes as she walked back toward the consulate.

A lone figure sat along the tables of a café she was approaching, all other tables empty. He was smoking and as Dory came closer, she saw that it was Prince Barenoli. A small coffee cup sat next to him.

"Your highness," Dory said and stopped.

"Miss Sparks," he said as he looked her over. It wasn't a lecherous look, more disapproving of what she was wearing. Dory smiled tightly.

"Going about life as normal despite what's happened?" she asked.

He shrugged and took a drag of his cigarette. "What point is there in panicking?"

"You're not scrambling to leave, then?"

"I have nowhere to go," he said, pulling a piece of tobacco off his tongue. "No one wants an Italian aristocrat."

"The Italians are not a part of this war."

"Not yet, but they will be."

"Do you really think so?"

"Mussolini is too greedy to stand back and watch the Germans claim all the spoils."

The Prince apparently believed the Germans weren't going to be stopped at the border. "So what are you going to do?"

With a shift of his head, he regarded her. "I don't know. Maybe I will go to Spain."

"Some have suggested Algiers," Dory said.

"Maybe that is a good place to wait out this madness."

"What do you know of the land down in Antibes that the Countess Tirau had bought for Baron Drecsay?"

"Even with a war, you do not give up?" he said with a chuckle. He took a drag and regarded her. "It is not worth much."

"Would anyone kill him for it?"

"I suppose it would be worth a few francs to the desperate. It was a joke, I think, on behalf of the countess. Drecsay wanted to build a home and she gave him awful land for it. She had a habit of buying him useless things. It amused her. It wasn't the only useless thing she'd bought him. She even bought him a small Scottish Island once, which I believe is probably the most uninhabitable place in the world. There were others, the more useless, the better. But this property was the first one in an accessible place, I suppose. Maybe that made it all the more vexing."

"So he was never going to build in Antibes?"

"I think he was—maybe just to spite her. But in the end, he had no money to. But a plump, little heiress would take care of that, no?"

He had to be referring to Livina's wealth, because she was certainly not plump in any other regard. "Would he really marry someone simply to build a house?"

The Prince chuckled. "No, I don't think so, but he was certainly looking for ways to recover what his family had lost."

"Apparently a Mr. Henri dealt with the conveyance. Do you know him?"

"I don't know such people," he said chidingly.

"Would Marie kill Drecsay?" she asked, but she already knew the answer. She just wanted to see what he said.

"Without Drecsay, his girlfriend loses everything. Maybe he was going to drop her."

"I haven't heard any indication from anyone I've spoken to."

The look he gave her was almost belligerent. "Well, good luck with finding some place to hide." She knew that sounded a little bit like an insult, but she didn't care. There was nothing likable about the man in her book. In saying that, she did recognize the position he was in. At least she could go home. He had no home and had to run as far as he could.

"And to you, Miss Sparks. Best of luck finding your way home. An invading army is never gentle on the women."

The warning was stark and she knew it was intended to be. She gave him a nod and kept walking, wondering if there was any way he had killed Drecsay. There was nothing to indicate a motive. The Prince was much better off financially, and it certainly didn't seem that he had any jealousy. Nothing seemed to stick there—as unpleasant a man as he was.

Lady Pettifer and Livinia hadn't even gotten inside the building by the time Dory got there.

"The Government is organizing transport," Lady Pettifer said. "They just can't give us any details yet. He knows remarkably little. I'm not sure the advent of a war had actually occurred to him."

"So what are we supposed to do? Go home and wait, they say. Unbelievable. Mrs. Grifton said she was going to drive to Calais."

"Stupid woman," Lady Pettifer said. "They are not going to let her anywhere near Calais."

"I hope you told her," Dory said.

"I doubt she listened. Some people cannot help but do the worst thing for themselves."

"Well, what are we going to do?" Livinia asked.

"I think we are better off doing as Major Dodds says. I do believe the Government is organizing something."

"If they're not too busy with other things," Livinia said pointedly, "like fighting a war."

"There are over a thousand people here. They will have to do something," Lady Pettifer said.

"So we drove all the way here for that—'return home and wait for them to do something.'" Livinia said tartly. "If they would have answered their telephone, it would have saved us a trip here."

"Not much else we can do," Lady Pettifer said with a smile. "Where are you parked?"

"Down this way," Dory said indicating, "but I can go get the car if you wish."

"No, a walk will do me good."

They set off at a leisurely pace. "Can we really afford to wait?" she asked.

"It might be better than setting off like scared rabbits, hurtling ourselves all over France. Who is to say there is any passenger transport if we even reach the northern coast, to get stuck there as the fighting begins in earnest. At least this way, the Government will send something specifically to take us home."

"I suppose you are right," Dory conceded.

The café where she had seen Prince Barenoli was now empty, which was probably a good thing, because Livinia, for some reason, seemed blind to the man's glaring faults. Dory suspected she saw the looks and the title and didn't notice the unpleasantness of the man underneath. That was the kind of man who used women like Livinia and afterward deriding them for their own gullibility and greed. Livinia utterly failed to see such things— perhaps it was her own sense of entitlement falling prey to an even larger sense of entitlement.

"I saw Prince Barenoli before," Dory said.

"Oh, he's here?" Livinia said, looking around.

"He mentioned that Drecsay intended to build on the land that the countess had bought him in Antibes, but he said it was useless land and she had bought it, a little to spite his ambition to build his own house. She bought him a few such places."

"Strange people," Lady Pettifer said with distaste.

"There is something about this that needles at me. I don't know what, but I feel it." Dory chewed her lip. There was something that wasn't clicking into place. "I must find this Mr. Henri and get a list of all his assets."

"What use to anyone is a bunch of useless land?" Livinia said. "Besides, it wasn't as though anyone would inherit. I suppose his extended family would inherit. They are the only ones who had anything to gain."

Dory drove them back along the coast, deep in thought.

Chapter 24

The consulate's telephone remained permanently engaged. It was impossible to reach them, but Lady Pettifer used her trusted network of friends to garner what information was available. The Government had committed to sending transport to Nice to pick up anyone needing to be conveyed back to the UK.

Each night, they listened diligently to the BBC, heard how the Grand Duchess Charlotte of Luxembourg and her family had fled across France as the occupation of Luxembourg had started. The resignation of Neville Chamberlain and the appointment of Winston Churchill as the new Prime Minister. Para shooting troops being defeated. Intense fighting between the Dutch and Belgium troops against the Germans. The Kaiser being offered asylum and the Norwegian and Dutch Governments shifting to London.

There was so much happening every day, they had a hard time keeping up. It seemed as though the world was devolving in front of them. They listened to the French news also, which tended to focus more on the battles in its neighboring countries and the movement of troops eastward in the country.

They sat with their sherries and listened in horror. There was nothing they could do but sit and listen, and wait for this ship that was supposed to arrive. How a ship would transport over a thousand people, Dory didn't know. They intently listened for any news about Switzerland to see whatever hell Vivian was heading toward, but Switzerland wasn't mentioned. Whatever agreement they had with the Germans was keeping them out of this war. It couldn't simply be their ferocious army that was keeping the Germans away. Or perhaps they simply didn't want to deal with the Alps.

Dory didn't dare think what would happen if the ship didn't come. Spain was probably the best answer. It seemed Franco was intent on not getting involved. Every day, more and more people chose to flee instead of wait for the ship. Lady Pettifer felt it was safer to wait, trusted the British Government's promises more than the French officials' lack of concern for the British expats.

Sleepless nights continued and Dory woke feeling exhausted and bleary-eyed in the mornings. The waiting was awful, but another day started and there was no news of a ship arriving. In fact, there was little news at all. Apparently, Major Dodds kept reassuring people that the ship was on the way, but it would take some time to get there.

Even Livinia stayed at home, although she couldn't bear to hide in her boredom. With great sighs, she wandered from room to room, wondering when Richard would come to visit. Instead of banding them all together, the occurring events were making them all seek their own solitude.

It felt wrong to do joyous things like swimming or even reading, so Dory turned her attention to Baron Drecsay and the puzzle it still posed. She wanted to write to DI Ridley about what she had learned, but she felt as though she shouldn't. He would be too distracted to worry about what she was doing. When they'd spoken, though, he'd offered to listen.

With this in mind, she grabbed the receiver and rang through to the operator. At this point, she didn't really know who she wanted to call, but she asked for the office of the prosecutor in Nice and to her surprise was put through straight away.

The woman who answered wasn't impressed when Dory asked if anyone knew of a solicitor called Mr. Henri. Grudgingly, Dory was passed to another woman, and then another, who surprisingly had heard of a Mr. Henri, who had offices in Marseille.

"Oh," Dory said. In all honesty, she hadn't expected this to work, but here she was—a step closer. Thanking the woman, Dory hung up and called the operator yet again, this time asking for Marseilles, where asking for Advokat Monsieur Henri got her put forward to his office. It was ludicrously simple once she put her mind to it and imagined who could help.

A receptionist answered, but Monsieur Henri was not available just at the time. The woman took Dory's details and promised that he would call her at the earliest opportunity.

With a nervous sigh, Dory paced. It seemed nothing she did would alleviate the pervasive nervousness in her, but she knew it had nothing to do with waiting for Mr. Henri's call—even though she did highly anticipate this upcoming conversation.

There was no indication how long the man would be in returning her call. It could be he was engaging in blind panic like so many others.

Dory imagined him haphazardly packing up his office and preparing to flee. Probably not. He appeared to be French, so there was nowhere he would go. For a moment, Dory felt the gravity of the situation that was unfolding north of them. She hoped the poor Luxembourgian and the Belgian peoples were alright, able to imagine the blind panic there. Perhaps it was unkind of her to think derisively about people's unthinking need for action.

"Stop that incessant pacing," Lady Pettifer called from the salon and Dory went over to sit with her.

"Sorry," she said. "I just can't seem to relax."

"That's hardly surprising, I suppose."

The telephone rang and Dory flew up to reach it before Mr. Fernley had a chance.

"Yes," she said when the man on the other end asked for Miss Dory Sparks.

"How can I be of assistance?" he continued.

"Well, I am actually calling about Baron Drecsay. I am sure you are aware of what's happened."

"I am," the man confirmed. Dory could hear the suspicion in his voice.

Again Dory struggled for words. "I wished to ask you about the properties that he had been… given by Countess Tirau."

"Yes," the man said yet again, waiting for her to come to the point.

"Uhh, I heard there were a few properties. One in Antibes and also an island in Scotland."

"That is correct."

"And you handled the conveyance for these properties?"

"Yes." A sigh of annoyed resignation sounded through the phone.

"What other properties were there?"

"Why do you wish to know?"

"Oh, I am investigating his death on behalf of his family." The lie had become familiar now and she was essentially the self-appointed private investigator for the family.

"I see. There are also three properties in Hungary, an apartment in Paris, and a parcel of land in Palestine."

Dory's eyebrows rose. The Baron wasn't exactly destitute. "And all of these properties were gifts from the countess?"

"Yes. This does not cover the properties belonging to the title in Hungary, which are extensive."

"And all of the properties go to the next baron? I understand he had no children or family."

"I do not deal with the succession of the title and his properties, as such, but I understand his heir was a cousin. You will have to direct your queries to his solicitor in Hungary."

"So there is nothing untoward about any of these properties?"

"Not that I know of. They are all quite impractical. There were, of course, some liens from creditors, so the heir will not receive all of the properties. The baron did have debts. His finances were disorderly, frankly. I am still dealing with the liens, and more creditors are coming forward."

"It appears some of the baron's jewelry has been unaccounted for."

"Yes, that seems to be true, but that is an issue for the new baron to take up with the police."

"Can you tell me about the creditors?"

"I don't remember off the top of my head, but I will ask my assistant to send you a list of creditors and their claims."

"That would be much appreciated," Dory said with a smile. Mr. Henri had run out of patience with her, so she thanked him and let him go.

"Anything interesting?" Lady Pettifer called and Dory returned to the salon with the piece of paper on which she had scribbled everything Mr. Henri had said.

"There are a number of properties—an apartment in Paris, the property in Antibes, the Scottish Island, a number of properties in Hungary, and lastly a parcel of land in Palestine."

"Palestine? Why in God's name would he have land in Palestine?"

"Well, the countess seemed to like to give him properties he could not use."

"So you think one of these properties is the reason he was killed?"

With a sigh, Dory sat down heavily. "I don't know. I can't find any other reason. His relationships seemed quite stable. He was interested in Livinia, and we didn't kill him. Unless there is someone jealous of that."

"Like Richard?"

They both chuckled.

"Well, Richard really didn't like Drecsay, but I can't imagine him killing for it," Dory said. "But then he was there. He had opportunity."

"Livinia and Drecsay had only gotten to know each other. It is difficult to imagine that Richard was so incensed he would destroy his rival."

"It hadn't even occurred to me to think of Richard as a suspect, but I suppose I must. He had opportunity," Dory said. "And a semblance of a motive."

"It would be an unhinged mind who would murder for such a reason."

Could it be that Richard was hiding such a dark urge behind a good-natured façade? It was something that had to be considered.

Chapter 25

The detailed list of the properties arrived from Mr. Henri a few days later. Included was a list of creditor liens against Baron Drecsay. They arrived in a large manila envelope that Mr. Fernley delivered with the rest of the post. The postal service hadn't ceased. Normalcy was highly appreciated, seen as a sign that the world wasn't entirely falling apart.

Dory and Lady Pettifer sat in the covered area outside, the shade and the breeze keeping them cool. Midday was starting to be a period for staying in the shade. Livinia's music played above their heads. Like this, everything seemed perfectly normal. It was almost a cruel illusion.

"So what have we?" Lady Pettifer asked as Dory unwound the tie of the envelope and pulled out the sheets of paper inside.

"Here are the properties. The property in Antibes. Five acres some seven miles away from the coast. It is currently an overgrown orchard. It has access to Chermin des Combes."

"Not particularly valuable," Lady Pettifer said.

"The apartment in Paris. Place Vendôme."

"Well, that is nothing to scoff at. It must be worth quite a bit."

"Two rooms."

"Just a bolt hole, then."

"In Hungary, a farm. No, two farms. Quite sizeable."

"I don't think the properties in Hungary will be of any interest to anyone here," Lady Pettifer stated.

"The land in Palestine, which is down to the south, one hundred and fifty miles from the Egyptian border."

"That's nothing but desert. It's not even close to any significant town as far as I know. How much land?

"Twenty-two acres," Dory read.

"Twenty-two acres of desert. I'm surprised she didn't buy him half the Sahara. Is that it?"

"There is the island in Scotland. Unnamed Island, it says. And then it gives coordinates."

"I'm assuming no one is fighting over that one if no one can bother naming it. And the liens."

Dory found the other sheet of paper.

"Well, the Hotel Contano has put a claim in to the estate, but not to a specific piece of property. A number of retailers in Nice have done the same. Prince Barenoli has a lien against the Parisian apartment," Dory said with surprise. "He mentioned nothing about that. If fact, didn't he say something about anyone giving Drecsay money being stupid? Didn't mention he was referring to himself."

"The Prince has money, but some people are averse to losing it."

For a moment, Dory considered what Lady Pettifer said, trying to see if she could find a motive there. "The apartment is worth something, but not a great deal."

"An apartment like that is not something he would choose to stay in. His intention would be to sell it and realize the money."

"He hadn't mentioned any of this."

"I'm sure he dismisses it as nothing, but he must be aware that it does give him some degree of motive."

Hardly convincing, Dory thought. Nothing they had found so far was directly suggested a motive for murder. "Then the land in Palestine. Oh," Dory said as she saw the name. "Terry Wilcott has placed a lien against it. Also something he didn't mention when I spoke to him."

"Why specifically that?" Lady Pettifer asked.

With a gust of wind, Livinia arrived from inside the house. "What are you talking about?" she said as she sat down.

"Terry Wilcott had taken a lien out against one of Baron Drecsay's properties," Dory said.

The scones were more interesting to Livinia than any lien Terry had placed. "Seems everyone is circling like vultures now that he's dead."

"Well, the Prince is as well," Dory stated.

"Is he? Drecsay must have owed him money."

"It seems Drecsay owed quite a few people money."

Livinia was conspicuously quiet on this subject. To her, it didn't really matter now, Dory supposed. Money wasn't something she readily thought about. It simply appeared when she needed it.

"I think I would like to speak to Terry again," Dory said, turning her attention to Lady Pettifer to see if she agreed with her assessment of the next step.

"I suppose I can take you to see him. He has a house in Cannes." Livinia said.

In a sense, Dory was glad she didn't have to go all the way to Nice. Cannes was much closer and it wouldn't take them long to go there and back. Nice required more planning.

"Actually, it would be nice to get out of the house for a bit. We've been cooped up here for days on end."

"Why don't you set off now," Lady Pettifer suggested. "I might go upstairs and rest."

"Marvellous," Livinia sang and rose with her half-eaten scone still in her hand. "Come on, Dory. I'll drive." Livinia was already marching through the house to the other side.

With a wince, Dory grabbed her hat and followed. She hated it when Livinia drove, but Terry was Livinia's friend and Dory wasn't entirely sure how he would behave if it was just her alone.

They drove down the coast and it was lovely. The sun shone, the breeze was cooling. The water glittered where the sun reflected.

"I was going spare in the house all day long," Livinia said, clearly joyful about getting out. "No one is doing anything at the moment. Everything feels so suppressed. I hope this war doesn't go on forever."

In fact, there were troops in Cannes. Dory hadn't seen this before. Endless men dressed in olive green uniforms, with trucks the same color. They had helmets and weapons.

"What are they doing down here?" Livinia uttered.

"I think they must be guarding against the Italians," Dory said quietly. It was disconcerting seeing them. The war was encroaching on the coast as well. They had to be quite worried about the Italians to send so many troops. They passed endless rows of parked trucks with green canvas canopies.

With a sharp turn, Livinia drove down a street leading away from the promenade, until she stopped in front of a white house. It was modest in comparison to Archie Wilshire's house. Nice, in quite a modern style with large windows in what had to be the salon.

With light steps, Livinia walked up the marble stairs to the front door and worked the iron knocker. A butler appeared and Livinia stated their business.

They were led through to the salon with the large windows, which was a lovely room with wood paneling and endless carpets. Terry had good taste in furniture. Everything looked modern and clean.

"Livinia," he said as he rose from his sofa where he was reading the local paper. "And you brought the charming Miss Sparks." His tone defied his statement. He didn't think her charming at all. In fact, he didn't quite know why she was there.

"Dory had a few questions she wanted to put to you."

"Oh?" he said with raised eyebrows. "Regarding?"

"The lien you placed against Baron Drecsay's property," Dory said.

"Oh that," Terry said and visibly relaxed back into the sofa. "What can I tell you? He owed me some money."

"Why the land in Palestine?"

"Uhh," he said in a drawn-out manner. "Well, he didn't owe me a great deal. Two hundred pounds and it seemed to be the property that best approximated the sum."

"You didn't see fit to forgive the sum?" Dory wasn't sure why she asked that; she just did. Maybe because she believed Archie Wilshire would forgive such a sum to a friend, but Terry had not.

"Forgive? We never forgive a sum. Practically a family motto."

"What in the world are you going to do with a plot in Palestine?" Livinia asked.

"It's not worth a great deal. About two hundred pounds, I would assume. Unfortunately, with everything going on, I can't sell it. So I'm stuck with it for a while—at least until the war is over. Drinks, anyone?"

"Yes, a martini would be marvelous," Livinia said.

"Maybe just a splash of gin in some tonic," Dory said, knowing she would be driving home, and Livinia would not be wanting to return to the house in the next two hours.

Terry and Livinia started talking about their friends and what everyone was doing. Archie Wilshire had gone, and taken his wife with him. He was a pilot as it turned out and simply flew his own plane north. Dory hoped it was safe to fly planes across the country now. It was a question that had to be asked of even the mundane things. Surely no one would fire at a small aircraft flying north, but you couldn't take these things for granted.

Like them, Terry was going to wait for the ship to come, which in intervening days had turned into two ships that were definitely being diverted to the coast to pick them up. Everyone sounded so sure. The consulate had even called the house to assure them that the ships were coming and they all had to—absolutely had to—leave on the ships, or they would themselves be responsible for any consequences for staying put.

Means of leaving would be limited after the ships sailed, the consulate had said. Lady Pettifer had learned that some of the older residents were staying put anyway. Many had nothing to return to and would be destitute in England without income or shelter. Taking the risk of staying was simply the easiest option. Dory felt inordinately sorry for them, knowing they had to face down whatever storm came this way.

How bad could it be, some asked. Except there had been worrying reports about the Germans actually attacking civilians in some town up north. It was perhaps the most shocking thing Dory had ever heard and Lady Pettifer had grown increasingly dismayed. That was not within the rules of warfare, but the Germans seemed to have little regard for honor in war. Staying put with such a force coming, might be a disastrous decision. Still, they refused to change their minds.

Chapter 26

The story around Baron Drecsay was like an onion, uncovering new layers the deeper she dug, but the layers never seemed to present themselves fully. There were a number of people who were financially better off with the baron dead, but none of the sums involved were big enough to justify murder, and none of the players appeared disturbed enough to kill someone for such a paltry sum.

"Nothing stands out particularly," Lady Pettifer said as Dory wrote out all the things they had learned. "Even Marie Chard, if she was the one who stole the jewelry. It could be that she robbed the baron while he was at the masquerade. But then she couldn't have snuck into the party unseen and killed him. Lady Tonbridge's butler would never let a girl like that in if she simply appeared at the door without an invitation. Let's face it: she's a girl with a certain reputation and Lady Tonbridge would never abide having such a girl at her party."

"All our other suspects were at the party, but none seem to have a credible reason for killing him."

"I have a feeling we will never know who the killer is until we establish proper motive."

"Maybe I need to talk to Marie again," Dory said with a sigh. "She knew him best. I didn't ask her about any of the properties other than the land in Antibes."

"I suppose we could try to see if anyone has sold the baron's jewelry," Lady Pettifer said, reaching for a biscuit from the tea tray.

"I don't mind telling you it's getting quite frightening driving through Cannes now. The place is full of soldiers. There's probably more in Nice."

"No doubt. Perhaps we should think of them as being here to protect us."

Dory wasn't entirely convinced by the assertion.

"I have to admit," Lady Pettifer stated. "It is the perfect time to commit a murder. No one has the time to look into it."

"Except for us. Poor Baron Drecsay ended up with inept investigators," Dory lamented.

"Don't sell yourself short. You are doing more for this man than anyone—probably more than he deserved, to be completely honest."

"You don't mean that," Dory said.

"No, I suppose not. We must persevere. You should go speak to the girl. Take Livinia with you."

With a smile, Dory wondered if Lady Pettifer was so keen for her to speak to Marie simply to get rid of Livinia for a while. Livinia's boredom was trying for all of them.

After finishing her tea, Dory rose and went upstairs in search for Livinia.

*

Again, Livinia drove and Dory sat with her hand clenched over the top of her door. At least Dory ended up driving home whenever they went on one of their outings. Alcohol invariably appeared somewhere and Livinia was quite happy to hand over for the return journey.

Charlotte Ginsborough was the person Livinia was determined to see. Dory vaguely knew the girl, but had never had much to do with her.

This time, there appeared to be more people in Nice—simply walking or standing around in groups.

The crowd in front of the consulate was even larger, and some had their bags with them. Surely the ship wasn't coming right now.

"They're not British," Livinia said as they slowly drove past.

A frown marred Dory's face. Why were they there, she wondered. They were seeking visas to go to Britain. "Do you think they're Belgians?"

"I think they might be Jews," Livinia said. "They're not waiting around to find out what the Germans will do to them. Poor sods. They've had to leave everything and run."

Dory craned her neck to watch as they drove past. "There's so many. Do you think the ships coming will take them all?"

"I guess that depends on how large the ships are."

Now she watched all the people on the street and many of them looked foreign. Their dress wasn't right for the climate, and they tended to wear what looked like their sturdiest clothes, and there were children—lots and lots of children.

"Where shall I drop you?" Livinia asked.

"I can hop out here and take the tram to Riquiers," Dory said and Livinia pulled over. They agreed to meet again in two hours.

The tram was also full of people, strangers who were consulting maps. They had all their suitcases with them. Dory expected they had all come down on the train. The BBC had mentioned bombings in Rotterdam and Dory expected all these people fled from there. It wouldn't just be Jewish people— everyone needed to escape the Germans. Each night the news got worse and worse. Insanity seemed to be progressing relentlessly, and here were the people escaping it. It was the first true sign that everything they heard on the wireless was true. The people running away from the madness were sitting all around her.

Getting off at Riquier, she made her way to Marie's house and knocked. No one answered. They weren't home or weren't answering. She stated it was her, but still no one came to the door. Had they left?

Dory spent an hour sitting in the doorway to see if either Marie or her mother returned, but they didn't come. Eventually Dory had to give up. This trip had been a dud, a waste of time, so she returned to the spot where Livinia was supposed to pick her up and waited yet again. Sitting down, she watched people. Well, all those empty hotel rooms that the visitors to the coast had deserted in the autumn would be filling up again, but these people weren't here for a pleasant time, they were running for their lives. This all sat very heavily. Some would secure visas and leave, others would have to stay. The Germans were still very far away, so people were safer down here than in their homes. Hopefully it would stay that way.

Livinia finally arrived and was perfectly intent on driving back as well. "People are pouring out of every train that arrives," she said. "It must be an uncomfortable journey all crammed in like sardines. What did you learn from Marie?"

"Nothing. She wasn't there."

"Maybe she left. The Belgians are all trying to come here and we're all trying to leave."

"All these people," Dory said. "Where are they all going to go?"

"Maybe they have family in Britain."

"Maybe. Although if your town is being bombed, I think you'd go even if you didn't."

"Charlotte is waiting for the ships, too. She still thinks Drecsay was a spy, but she couldn't really say why." They had clearly been talking about it. "She did mention something funny, though."

"What?"

"When I mentioned Palestine, she recalled some cartographer that Drecsay had made an acquaintance with some while back. Last year, she said. Anyway, this man had just come from Palestine."

"A cartographer?"

"Something such. Charlotte wasn't entirely sure, but she said he was the type of man who thought well of himself and always wore jodhpurs. Adventurer type."

"Did she catch a name?"

"No. She just mentioned she'd seen them speaking in cafes a few times. Drecsay liked to frequent a café that was close to her apartments. Not that they really knew each other. She said Drecsay was always very polite and friendly."

To an heiress like Charlotte? How was that not a surprise.

A cartographer, Dory thought, trying to turn this over in her head. Why would Drecsay make the acquaintance of a cartographer who'd just come from Palestine? The question kept presenting itself over and over again, but no answers appeared.

The sun was still warm as they returned and Lady Pettifer was sitting on the covered patio with her tea.

"All of Nice is full of Jews," Livinia said when they arrived. "They're coming down on the trains."

"Poor things," Lady Pettifer said. "I suppose they will now face the same persecution as those in Germany, stripped of their jobs, wealth and property."

"The stories from Poland say they can fare worse," Dory said with a shudder. Magazine articles she'd read mentioned horrific things that the Germans did in Poland. People were right to flee.

"So what did you learn?" Lady Pettifer asked.

"Well, Marie was not at home, but Livinia's friend mentioned Drecsay befriending some adventurer type who had just returned from Palestine."

"A cartographer," Livinia added.

"A cartographer?" Lady Pettifer said with surprise.

"I'll just get Mr. Henri's notes," Dory said and went to retrieve them from the desk in the study. Returning, she sat down and turned to the sheet mentioning the property in Palestine. "Oh," she said. "It appears the property was bought last year. In the autumn. So a random property in Palestine was bought just as he made the acquaintance of some adventurer type coming from there. That seems too much of a coincidence. They have to be linked."

"Unless Countess Tirau noted the relationship and bought him a property on a whim," Lady Pettifer. "She seemed to be of that unique disposition."

"I'll call Mr. Henri to see if he knows something about how the property came about." Rising again, she walked over to the phone and asked for the operator in Marseille so she could be put through to his office.

"What do you want, Miss Sparks?" he said with annoyance when his secretary put her through. Dory hadn't expected the tone.

"I am sorry if I am bothering you, I just wanted some more information about Baron Drecsay's property in Palestine."

With a sigh, she heard him sit down. "Umm," he said after a while as if trying to recall something from a very long time ago. "Yes, the property. They bought it not so long ago."

"Was it the countess' idea to buy it and how did she find it?"

"I think this one was actually Drecsay's idea. He was very specific about the land he wanted, had coordinates."

"Coordinates? So the countess bought it at his request?"

"I believe so. I cannot be assured. But as opposed to the other properties, Drecsay came to see me personally to make sure everything was in order. Now, I'm sorry, I can't help you more. I have a hundred things to do. It seems the whole country wants to request exit visas."

"Oh, of course. I won't take more of your time." After a quick goodbye, she hung up. All those people who had come off the trains were seeking the help of solicitors to secure exit visas. The man had to be run off his feet. She fully understood how annoying she would be at such a time. If she had the chance, she would send him a bottle of wine for the trouble.

Dory returned to the patio. "Mr. Henri recalls that Baron Drecsay initiated this purchase."

"So it was different from the other properties," Lady Pettifer said. "It is still land in the middle of nowhere. Useless for all intents and purposes. What would a cartographer want with such land?"

"Well, we don't know why he wanted it," Dory said, pointing out the assumption, "but it seemed Drecsay bought this land based on his conversations with the cartographer."

"If we just knew his name," Lady Pettifer said.

"The High Commission in Palestine might know if any cartographers were surveying in the district," Livinia pointed out.

Chapter 27

The Germans were bombing in England. The news was horrific and depressing that night. Dory wasn't sure she had heard something this distressing since the war was declared. The British forces were in retreat, withdrawing to Dunkirk, the Germans hitting them with a constant bombardment. There was also a report stating that the Germans were massacring the inhabitants of a Belgian village called Vinkt. This was stated by the French radio. The BBC was curiously silent on the topic, which made Dory wonder what else they weren't being told if it didn't bear mentioning when innocent villagers were rounded up and massacred.

The next day, Belgium surrendered with King Leopold being taken and interred by the Nazis.

Each newspaper and radio news program were started with even more dread. The news only got worse and worse. The British were evacuating from the continent. There was too much bad news, and at the same time not enough news. They went for hours without hearing a thing, knowing something catastrophic could have happened.

All along, the sunshine and serenity of Villa Bellevieu were as it always was. They had no visitors, nor did they go anywhere. It was almost as if they lived in a perfect, little bubble, interspersed by horridness coming through the wireless or papers.

There was an unusual amount of cars driving along the coast road. They could see it from a specific spot in the garden, and it looked like quite a few military trucks. The whole country was on the move. The French had to be worried about the Italians, who so far seemed to want to stay out of this war, but Navy ships patrolled out at sea.

A man named Bovis called from the consulate to inform them that the evacuation ships were on their way and would be there in about ten days. He stressed how they had to be there and that there would be no help from the Government from then on if they missed the ship. Dory assured him that they would be there.

They could do nothing but wait. The international telephone lines were increasingly hard to book and mail stopped arriving. Dory tried to turn her attention to Drecsay, but there was too much worry. She had no luck trying to get hold of the High Commission in Palestine, and the mailman refused to take the letter she'd written, saying he could only deliver within the Vichy Government territory.

"Perhaps if we cannot send letters, we could still use telegrams," Lady Pettifer said. "We could send one to the High Commission in Palestine to see if they know this man, or if they are aware of anything noteworthy about this property that Baron Drecsay bought."

Dory nodded. "Then again, what could a cartographer tell Drecsay that would make him rush out and purchase the property?"

"Well, Terry Wilcott had a lien on the property, so it's now technically his. Perhaps we need to mention this in the telegram."

"It's going to be expensive," Dory said, trying to think of ways to say all that in as few words as possible."

"Now is not the time for frugality," Lady Pettifer said and rose. "We are running out of time. The ship is here in mere days. Hopefully we will hear back.

"I'll drive into Cannes to the telegraph office and see if they can send it."

There was no point waiting, so Dory got in the car and took the coast road east. As before, there was an increased level of traffic. The French Navy had their port in Toulon, so it could be that many of them were going there. What did that mean? Were they preparing for something? By the look of it, they were. The most awful thing about this was that they knew so little. It was hard to decide what to do. The Germans were now bombing England and they had to wonder if they were safer where they were. The consulate seemed to think not.

Their neighbor, Mr. Merton, had decided to stay put. The idea made Lady Pettifer uneasy, but he was a grown man—an elderly man—so he did have the right to decide for himself.

These were such grave decisions and they could have catastrophic consequences if they proved wrong, especially if the most disturbing accounts of the German Army's behavior were true.

The drive to Cannes wasn't so long. Cannes was not as busy as Nice, but there were still people who didn't normally dwell there. Rooms were sought everywhere, she supposed, and there were plenty of rooms in Cannes. The cafes were also more busy than they had been a few days ago.

The telegram office was in a brick building down one of the side streets. Dory parked along the main promenade and walked. The streets could be troublesome and it wasn't worth trying to get into the township itself sometimes. Especially now that there were motorcars like black beetles parked everywhere, filled with family possessions—even mattresses strapped to roofs.

The houses were not quite as grand on the side streets. But the town looked busy, as if it had to some degree recovered from the shock of what was happening.

A piece of paper plastered on the wall of one of the building caught her attention and she passed it without really absorbing what it said in stark, black print. 'Mort aux Juifs.' Dory froze and stared at it, not believing what it said. Death to Jews. With a gasp, her fingers pressed to her mouth. This couldn't be real? Could there be someone this callous in their midst—down here where things were sane?

This piece of paper showed that there were. Around here was a person, or people, who wished ill on people they had never met, didn't know—or worse, someone they did—a neighbor. How could this be? It was so unfathomable, she had always assumed that everyone else thought it was utter madness too, but the insidious hatred was rearing its ugly head here, too.

Reaching out, she tore the paper down, unsure if she felt embarrassed as well as mortified. All those people who had come here for find sanctuary were meeting with the same hatred they had fled. It was beyond disappointing for find something like this. Instantly, suspicion formed about every person on the street. Had they put it up? Had they seen it and quietly agreed? Why hadn't they torn it down?

Feeling completely stunned, Dory kept walking to the telegraph office. It was just ahead of her and she had to focus. The shock of seeing a visual display of the hatred she couldn't understand still clouded her mind.

The place was full of people waiting, some in line, others apparently to receive something. This was going to take a while.

A number of different languages were spoken—from German, to French, and other languages she couldn't identify. Everyone was calmly waiting, slowly moving toward the desk.

"Can I help you?" A woman said behind the desk when it was Dory's turn. They were all women, Dory noticed. That was a change from the last time she'd been here—which admittedly was some time ago.

"I need to send a telegram?"

"Where to?"

Dory had trouble getting her mind working. "Uhmm, the British High Commission in Palestine."

"That is a more unusual request," the girl said and pulled out a printed form. "Write here and bring it back," she said and dismissed Dory to serve the person behind her.

"Right," Dory said and moved along. For a moment she felt silly. Here she was, trying to gain information about a piece of land when these people were obviously planning their flight to safety. How could she invest so much time in the death of one aristocrat when there was so much need for attention elsewhere? In a way, it felt wrong, but she also knew that the murderer was probably happy about the distraction the war caused. The idea that someone was benefitting from this war felt even more wrong.

Taking a moment, she devised the telegram as concisely as she could, asking if the Commission knew of a cartographer working in the area, and if there was anything of note about the land that Baron Drecsay had purchased.

It could be that they paid little attention to her request. Should she state that the baron had possibly been murdered because of this land? Then it occurred to her that it was unlikely that she and Lady Pettifer would be here by the time they replied—if they replied.

Please respond to DI Ridley at Pirbright Camp. The 'please' would cost extra, but she just couldn't bring herself to not write it. There was no one else to send it to. Vivian was God-knew-where. She, Lady Pettifer and Livinia would be on a ship for the better part of a month. She would have to use Ridley as a gathering point for any information at this point. She asked for a second telegram form and sent one to him too, saying that she was just about to board the ship to England.

Palestinian property purchased by baron after meeting cartographer returning from region, she wrote. High Commission to send details to you while at sea. Regards, Dory.

Hopefully he would figure out what that meant.

Chapter 28

And then the ships came. They could see them from the house. Two massive merchant ships, slowly sailing towards Nice.

"We best be going," Livinia said, sticking her head out the window above them. "Is everything in the car?"

"I might be best not to take so much with you," Lady Pettifer said.

"Who knows when we'll ever get to see it again?" Livinia said as if Lady Pettifer had suggested something ridiculous.

"You might not be able to find someone to carry the trunk, my dear." With a snort, Lady Pettifer turned her attention back to Dory. "And here we are screaming like fishwives."

Dory had already placed her small suitcase in the back of the car. There were some things she was leaving behind. A pair of shoes and some clothes—especially the party clothes. What use would she have of those in London when war was raging all around them? Dory still didn't know if they were heading toward a more dangerous situation than they were leaving, but it felt important to be at home and not stuck on foreign soil.

"Best go see to Mr. Merton," Lady Pettifer suggested. "Try to see if you can convince him to come with us."

With a nod, Dory rose and hurriedly walked over to the path that led to Mr. Merton's property. It would take a few minutes to get there, but eventually she reached the stone two-story house. It was nowhere near as grand as Lady Pettifer's villa, but the old man seemed happy enough here.

A knock on the door was met with silence. "Mr. Merton?" Again there was silence. Had he gone to meet the ship on his own? He had been so adamant he wasn't going to go.

"Mr. Merton?" she called as she walked around the house, finding Mr. Merton standing in his chicken coup with his trousers rolled up and wearing wellingtons. "There you are?"

"Miss Sparks," he grumbled. He had never been remotely pleasant, but Dory had grown to expect that.

"We are about to leave for the ship. Are you sure you won't come with us?"

"Some bunch of Jerrys aren't going to chase me off my land," he stated pompously. "Never."

"Major Dodds recommends that everyone leaves. You can come back when things are settled again."

"What's he going to do? Come down here and drag me away?"

"No, of course not. He's only thinking with your best interest at heart."

The man grumbled again. "Well, you can tell him where he can stick it."

"I take it that's a no, then."

"Damned right."

Dory sighed. Nothing was going to convince the man, but was he the one making the wiser choice? "If you run out of supplies, Lady Pettifer's stores are still well stocked."

"I'm sure I'll be fine. My chickens won't stop laying because the Jerrys are making a hoo hah."

"I hope so," Dory said absently. "If you're sure?"

"Off you go. Run like scared little rabbits."

"Alright, then. If you insist."

He turned his back on her and Dory made her way back to the path. That was a waste of time even before she started, but she supposed they had to try.

Livinia was downstairs by the time Dory got back, dressed in a summery dress with yellow lemons printed on the material. She looked impossibly smart. "You'll help carry my trunk, won't you, Dory? If it comes to it."

"Sure," Dory said.

"See," Livinia said as if turning to Lady Pettifer in victory.

"We had better get going if we are going to beat the ships to Nice," Lady Pettifer said. "Mr. Fernley? Are you ready?"

"Just about, madame," he called from inside. He had spent the morning placing sheets over the furniture along with Babette from the village. Babette would essentially be the caretaker while they were gone. She normally served that role when Lady Pettifer left for England, but it would be longer than just over the summer this time.

Babette appeared carrying Beauty in a cage and placed it in the back.. "The house will be dusted every week," she said with assurance.

"I know I can trust you, Babette. Take all the perishables when you leave. I don't know how much we have. And if you should ever need to, you can take from the stores as required."

"Thank you, Madame," she said with a quick nod. "I will lock up when you go."

They walked through to the hallway, where Lady Pettifer grabbed her handbag and umbrella. It looked out of place in this weather, but you always needed an umbrella where they were going. "Goodbye, house. I shall miss you. Hopefully it won't be too long before we're reunited."

Guiseppe from the village was there, too. He was to drive them and then return the motorcar to the house. "And we go," he said, holding his brown cigarette between his fingers as he drove. A veteran of the Great War, he drove better than Livinia did, even as he didn't have ready access to a car otherwise.

The acrid smoke from the cigarette wafted back to them occasionally, but telling a French man not to smoke was a waste of breath. Mr. Fernley sat in the small folded up seat at the very back of the car with Beauty. It was unusual to have the butler and the dog with them on an outing, but this wasn't just some outing—they were all fleeing France just like everyone else.

"I wonder if we will see Lady Summernot after all, or if she managed to secure passage prior. I hope Clara Winch manages to make it down. She is so old. Mr. Fernley, perhaps we should go past her apartments to see if she needs assistance. Her knees are dreadful."

"Of course," Mr. Fernley said behind them.

There was a nervous tension in the car. No one spoke and Guiseppe threw his cigarette over the side of the door and lit another.

*

The port was on the other side of Nice, and there were abandoned cars as they drove closer. Quite a few people were leaving everything behind without an expectation that they were coming back. Guiseppe was made to detour down a road where Mrs. Winch lived, and Mr. Fernley climbed out and rang her bell. No one answered.

"That puts my mind to rest," Lady Pettifer said. "Perhaps she took a taxi."

"They are having a busy day, I expect," Livinia said.

Driving on, they reached the port and it was inordinately busy. A crowd was waiting and a man stood with a clipboard, searching for names. Dory recognized him from the consulate. As British citizens, they didn't need the exit visas that the French or Belgians sought. Technically, they weren't emigrating.

French policemen were standing nearby, watching the people swarm around the gateway manned by the consulate man. Everyone was trying to get his attention, to speak to him, some with money in their hands. There were people here without visas, Dory realized. Desperate to get away, they tried to plead.

Spotting them, the consulate man waved them forward. Somehow, Mr. Fernley and Dory had ended up carrying Livinia's trunk, while also carrying their own luggage, and Beauty's cage on top. To Livinia's consternation, she ended up carrying Lady Pettifer's luggage.

They had to jostle through the crowd to the front where they presented their passports. The man carefully checked each one and ticked off their names on the clipboard before giving Lady Pettifer a note and telling her to give it to the man at the top of the gangway. "Go through," he said.

They walked through to join an even larger crowd. There had to be at least a thousand people there—more even. A ship was berthed next to the port and a string of people were walking up the gangplank.

It was not a passenger ship. There would be no comfortable cabins for them to retreat to like they had had on the voyage over two years back. This was a standard cargo ship—and they were the cargo.

With a sigh, Dory surveyed the scene. It was going to be an extremely uncomfortable voyage back to the UK. Mr. Fernley went to register Beauty with the ship's crew. Luckily, Lady Pettifer had had the foresight to sort the dog's papers as soon as the war had initially been declared. Taking her would mean a month's quarantine when they arrived in Britain, but who knew how long this war would last, Lady Pettifer had said when they'd talked about what to do with Beauty. If it really would take years, Lady Pettifer didn't want to be without the comfort of her dog.

It took a good hour to reach the gangplank and they had to awkwardly scramble up while carrying Livinia's trunk. Dory's heels were skidding slightly until they found grip. It was an uncomfortable assent, and Lady Pettifer was exhausted by the time they made it onboard.

The ship was entirely functional. As expected, there were no passenger cabins. Most had to find their places crammed together in large storerooms where they had to find space where they could. This was what the Government could spare at the moment—a ship at its barest minimum. Lady Pettifer was led to a small room with two births on top of each other and a small porthole. There was barely enough room to walk and the three of them together filled the whole cabin.

"Your trunk will have to be outside," Lady Pettifer said.

"Everyone will rifle through it," Livinia whined. "I'll be surprised if I have anything left by the time we reach England. This is horrific. There are three of us and two beds."

"I can sleep on the floor, I suppose," Dory said. "With some blankets, I'm sure it will be comfortable."

"Perhaps we can form a mattress with some of your clothes," Lady Pettifer suggested to Livinia. "Then they will be inside the cabin after all."

Livinia wasn't pleased with the suggestion, which wasn't surprising considering how dusty the floor was. The porthole didn't open, so there was no way of clearing the mustiness. They must be occupying the sleeping quarters of some burly and sweaty sailors.

Looking around, Lady Pettifer sighed. There was nowhere for them to sit other than on the lower bunk. "I have never before been subject to the Government's hospitality. Admittedly, it is grim, but we must be grateful that they are evacuating us, and that they have given us one of the cabins. Not everyone is given that consideration."

Chapter 29

They were served soup with rolls the next day after what could only be described as an uncomfortable sleep. Lady Pettifer snored at close quarters, it turned out. The cabin also remained disturbingly warm during the night, made worse as the Mediterranean sun rose in the morning.

As soon as they woke, they opened the cabin door to try to get some air in. It did help even if there were the occasional wafts of marine diesel. The smell of the sea was lovely. The Mediterranean was a deep blue color and the water rushed against the hull of the ship when Dory looked down over the railing.

All of the external walkways were crowded with people seeking respite from the dark and dingy storage rooms. Some even chose to sit down along the walls and spend the whole day there, slowly watching the coastline move past. The second ship wasn't far behind them, looking like a great leviathan swimming along the water. It wasn't a particularly beautiful ship.

Three weeks on board this ship was going to be trying, probably more so because Livinia was distinctly unhappy with the setup. Luckily, she found an acquaintance in another part of the ship, so she spent periods of time away from them.

Because it was hard for Lady Pettifer to stand for longer periods, she stayed in their small cabin more often than not. There were no seating areas. Every available space was now someone's sleeping area, including the galley.

It really was a far cry from the comforts of the trip to Nice, but at least they were on their way home. Dory knew in her heart that she wouldn't be returning to Nice. It was time to go home, and she'd known that for quite a while. What she would do when she got there, she still didn't know. Need had outpaced her planning.

Returning to the cabin, Dory found that Livinia was back. "And I saw Mrs. Vismouth. You must go say hello to her at some point. I can show you where she is."

"Perhaps later," Lady Pettifer replied. "I wish I had brought more books."

"Maybe we can create a library. I am sure hordes of people have brought books that they will finish. We can all swap," Livinia carried on. Dory knew that Livinia was trying to cheer up Lady Pettifer and it was sweet that she was trying. She had the capacity to be sweet and considerate at times.

"I think that is an excellent idea. I would actually suggest that you organize it."

"I suppose I could. Perhaps we can find a bookshelf somewhere that can be used for the purpose. At least that would give me something to do. I am bored out of my mind already."

"It's only the first day," Lady Pettifer said. "I for one am still trying to think what a cartographer could have said to sway Drecsay to purchase property in Palestine. Maybe he knew something that wasn't general knowledge—such as an upcoming change in borders. There had to be a financial gain Baron Drecsay was hoping to realize. He had clearly stated that he had found some way of recuperating some of the family wealth. I just can't see what a cartographer could have imparted."

"Well, Charlotte said it was a cartographer or something such," Livinia pointed out and Lady Pettifer turned to her.

"I thought you said it was a cartographer," Dory said.

"That's what Charlotte said, but she'd really not the brightest. She couldn't exactly remember what he was, but thought it was a cartographer or something like.

Dory's eyes sought Lady Pettifer and they both knew this changed things significantly. "He could have been anything," Dory said.

"Not just anyone would be out surveying in the deserts of Palestine. Maybe even someone acting on behalf of an organization who is interested. Which meant the land would be of interest to someone, and Drecsay decided to get it before they did," Lady Pettifer said. "Or the man was a prospector."

A piece clicked into place and things made sense. The man was a prospector seeking something. Oil, gold, something. Absently, Dory's fingers stroked across her lips as thoughts churned around her head. "And Terry Wilcott placed a lien against the property."

"That could simply be a coincidence," Livinia stated. "Terry wouldn't hurt anyone. He's always had bad luck. Only he would accidentally involve himself in a murder. He's on the ship, by the way."

"He's here?" Lady Pettifer asked and Livinia nodded.

"I think he was a bit miffed that Archie Wilshire didn't give him a lift on his plane, but apparently there were weight restrictions and Terry couldn't go."

"That is unlucky," Dory said without fully meaning it.

"Now, you better go see about that bookcase, Livinia," Lady Pettifer said. "I think I would like a new book to read."

"Alright," Livinia said and left.

"It is sufficient motive for murder," Lady Pettifer said.

"The word of some fly-by-night prospector?"

"People have killed for less."

They sat in silence for a while. "We don't have any proof that Drecsay told Terry about his plans," Dory pointed out.

"I don't believe in coincidences."

"Nor do I," Dory agreed. "How do we proceed?"

"We don't have access to anything here," Lady Pettifer said. "We are entirely cut off from everything while we're at sea."

"Maybe Livinia's friend can tell us more about what she observed and heard. Perhaps Terry was there at the time."

"Terry Wilcott is onboard this ship. We must be aware of that. If he is the murderer, then he might object to us asking questions about it," Lady Pettifer said.

"Then we must be discreet. I think I should go speak to Charlotte."

There wasn't time to speak to her. They were pulling into the port of Marseille, and even from a distance, Dory could see that the entire port was full of people. Thousands. It was the most disturbing sight she had ever seen. Clearly, people were desperate to leave.

Down the walkway along the ship, she saw one of the first officers.

"Excuse me," she called to the harried looking man.

"One moment, Miss," he said as he continued what he was doing. Dory hadn't realized she had disturbed him working, but he was supervising the men throwing massive ropes down to the dock as the ship was being tied up. "How can I help you?" he said when the men below them completed their work.

"I need to send a telegram. It's important."

"You will have to brave the crowd to get the telegram office. It's right over there," he said, pointing. "Like this, it would be a dangerous crossing. Perhaps if you had a few shillings to spare, you could send one of the ship's boys. They are nimble and quick around the docks."

"Yes, I might do that," she said and the man departed with a nod. The boys were easy to spot. They wore uniforms with sailor's hats. "Young man," she called and pulled out two pound notes from her bag and showed them to him. "I need someone to go send a telegram and they can keep the change," which would probably surmount to a whole pound. "Interested?"

"Yes, madame," he said, his eyes on the notes.

"Excellent. Now, the message." Pulling out a small notebook and pencil, she scribbled DI Ridley as recipient at Pirbright Camp, Surrey.

Not cartographer, probably prospector. Terry Wilcott likely suspect.

Dory had no idea if DI Ridley had the time to look at this, or was even in a position to receive the telegram, but she felt it was a good idea that someone knew of what they had learnt. Who knew what could happen? They were, after all, heading into waters where U-boats sunk merchant ships on a regular basis. So far, at least, they were in what should be safe waters, but as they neared the Channel, things could get dicey. It was too scary to think about.

If nothing else, DI Ridley could follow up and then report to the extended Drecsay family what had happened to their relation.

The ship boy ran off and Dory watched as a few moments later, he fought against the flow coming up the gangway to do her bidding. She would watch until he returned, in case he was forgotten and they left without him.

Over the side of the ship, she could see that they were also taking onboard provisions, which were being hoisted on pallets into a cargo hold—one that people were obviously not sleeping in.

Beside them was another ship and people were streaming up the gangway. *The Pearl of the East* the ship was called. It was taking on a great many people carrying whatever they could.

"Going to Shanghai," a man said next to her.

"Shanghai? That's an awfully long way."

"An open port. You don't need a visa to go. Anyone can turn up and take up residence there." He had an Australian accent.

"Really?"

"These poor bastards are having trouble finding anywhere to go. No one wants them. Mexico is giving out visas, but most other countries are being sparing in the visas they hand out. Some will only take the kids and not the parents."

"That's awful." Why couldn't whole families be taken? Who would care for these children? She wished her own country would be more generous, but there was only a small stream of people coming up the gangway compared to the Shanghai ship. Still, some visas were obviously being granted.

Leaning casually on the railing, the man continued. "Everyone here is looking to go somewhere. Many don't care where, I suppose. I'd fuck off to Shanghai too if I had to. Get the fuck out of this shithole."

That was one way of putting it.

Chapter 30

After the madness of Marseille's port, they slipped away from the French coast, down toward the warm air and sparkling waters of the southern Mediterranean. In a way, it felt as though they were leaving the madness behind, even though that wasn't possibly true.

Even Dory worried about Vivian—not that he would appreciate it. He was so close to where the fighting was. Still, no news had come of the Germans invading Switzerland. In saying that, there had technically been enough time for him to return to the Cote d'Azur, but he hadn't. Perhaps taking someone out of a sanitorium wasn't a straightforward affair, even in wartime.

Then again, he couldn't bring his mother to this boat. Lady Wallisford could not return to the UK. She was effectively in exile—a longstanding tradition for aristocratic criminals.

It was a few days after they left Marseille that Dory spotted Terry Wilcott. He was standing by the railing, smoking while talking to some men, his other hand tucked leisurely in his pocket. He looked as if he hadn't a worry in the world.

Looking over, he caught her watching and waved. They hadn't exactly been friends, but he now acknowledged her. Stuck on this boat, difference in position didn't seem to matter so much. They were in this together, suffering from being transported like livestock.

Was Terry, with his round face and soft eyes, really capable of killing someone—his friend? Livinia said absolutely not, and she had known him a long while. If the land in Palestine was valueless, then there was very little tying Terry to Drecsay in terms of motive. It was just this supposed cartographer that served as an indication that there was more to this story—this land in Palestine.

Quickly, Dory waved back, but she didn't approach. It felt disingenuous being overtly friendly to someone when she was investigating them for murder.

Perhaps it was time to talk to Charlotte. Initially, it had seemed like a good idea, but now, Dory wasn't as convinced that it would tell them any more than they already knew, but it was still worth finding out.

Returning to their area of the boat, she found Livinia who had taken to her role as ship's librarian, having set up a reading corner with makeshift bookshelves she had forced the crewmen to find and retrieve for her. Likely, there wasn't anything she couldn't bully them into doing, speaking with such authority that dissension bordered on traitorous.

"Now, where can we find Charlotte?" Dory asked as she approached Livinia, who was stacking returned books on her shelves. She'd even managed to find a carpet for the reading nook. God knew where she'd got that from.

"Oh, I'll show you. Are you going to interrogate her?"

"I don't interrogate."

"You really haven't heard yourself, then."

Dory opened her mouth to argue, but had to concede that she might not have a leg to stand on. All she did was ask questions. Perhaps some saw it as interrogating. It wasn't, after all, a new accusation. "Fine, I am going to grill her until she squeals like a cornered rat."

Livinia laughed. "Charlotte won't know what's hit her."

At no point had Dory realized there were so many corridors on this ship, and for some reason, Livinia had done a thorough survey of the whole ship. Walking endlessly through areas Dory had never been, they came to a strange compartment where a group of people had set up their quarters. Sheets were hung to provide some semblance of privacy.

"Knock, knock," Livinia said and pushed back a sheet. "Charlotte. Are you in?"

"Here," a woman said, appearing with a book in her hand. Was Livinia bullying people into reading as well? Dory wouldn't put it past her. "Oh, Livinia, what a pleasant surprise. I would invite you to sit, but there is nowhere to sit." The woman's gaze traveled over Dory and she looked back expectantly for an introduction. They had met before. Charlotte obviously didn't remember her. Charlotte was about the same age, and there were similarities between the girls in the way they dressed. Similar type of schooling, Dory would guess.

"This is Dory, Auntie's companion. Remember how you mentioned you saw that man coming from Palestine speaking to Baron Drecsay—cartographer, you said."

"Yes," Charlotte answered. "That's right."

"Now what made you think he was a cartographer?" Livinia asked.

"Well, he had maps. Tons of maps. Some he'd obviously drawn himself."

"He didn't actually say?"

"I didn't actually speak to him. He was only there, around, you know."

"Was anyone else there?" Dory asked.

"It was a café so there were loads of people coming and going every minute, I expect." These questions obviously seemed absurd to Charlotte.

"But anyone you know?"

A slight shrug said no. "No one I noticed."

"How about Terry Wilcott?"

"Why would Terry Wilcott be there? I suppose he and Drecsay were friends, but no, I didn't see Terry there."

"What about at Lady Tonbridge's party?"

Charlotte's expression changed and she looked Dory up and down. Maybe Dory did interrogate people. She didn't seem to be able to ask things casually. That was something she should work on.

"Uhmm," Charlotte tried to think. "I can't quite recall. I saw you dancing with Drecsay, though," Charlotte said while slightly nudging Livinia's arm. "You two seemed to be cozy in each other's company."

"Just friends," Livinia said dismissively.

"I'm sure you got interrogated a time or two about it by the police. You did find him. Whacked on the head. It was bloody from what I hear. I didn't see it myself." There was a certain excited glee in Charlotte's eyes. "I would have been beside myself."

"Yes, it was dreadful," Livinia said coldly and an uncomfortable silence descended.

"Shame," Charlotte said after a while. "He was such a handsome man."

"Do you recall what this cartographer looked like? A name even?"

Charlotte blinked a couple of times. "Average height. Brown hair. Nothing remarkable."

"Age?"

"Young. In his twenties."

"Accent."

"Oh, I think more Oxford than Cambridge, if I were to hazard a guess."

"So he was… " She was going to say 'one of your kind,' but stopped herself, "educated."

"Naturally," Charlotte said as if it was obvious. "John Lobb boots, I'm sure of it. His jacket was obviously Saville Row. Could be Italian, but that would be a stretch."

"No name?"

"We weren't introduced." Charlotte's patience had run out. "I can't believe how hot it's getting. We get no air in here whatsoever, packed in like cattle. It's a disgrace. I should have gone with Stu and driven to Spain. It would have been much more comfortable. I can't believe we have to survive weeks of this." Bringing up her hand, she fanned herself with the book. "And we get nothing to eat but bread and soup. We're all going to starve by the time we reach England."

"We hadn't even considered bringing more from the stores at Villa Bellevieu. Didn't even think about it. If I would have known what this would be like, I would have stuffed my trunk full of food."

It would probably have served them all better if she had.

"Thank you so much for answering our questions," Livinia said, taking Charlotte's hand. "It's been immensely helpful."

"Always glad to help. Are you going to come have a spot of tea with us later? We're trying to make it a regular thing."

"Of course I will."

The invitation was not extended to Dory, which suited her just fine.

"I better get back," Livinia said, urging Dory with her. "She could pick up a man in a line up based entirely on the stitching of his clothes. "But interestingly, as they are John Lobb boots, and I would trust her assessment on that, it is likely the manufacturer could provide us with a name. Perhaps I should get a more accurate description of the boots from her later," Livinia finished absently. She stopped and Dory did too. "I told you that there is no way that Terry would have anything to do with this." She was watching Dory intently now.

"Yes, but that being the case, we need to ensure all the 'I's are dotted and 'T's crossed, otherwise the suspicion would naturally fall on him," Dory said, not feeling the certainty she spoke with. There was technically no evidence to any of this. The only mention of this prospector type was, according to Charlotte's assertion, identified entirely on the clothes he was wearing.

Dory could just imagine how impressed DI Ridley would be if she told him of this supposed 'evidence'. Livinia had at one point asserted that Terry was inordinately unlucky, and being the recipient of a useless piece of land attached to a murder would be seen as the height of bad luck.

There was nothing to say that this prospector had told Drecsay anything. All they really knew was that the man had shown maps. They assumed that Drecsay had purchased the property as a result. There was also no evidence linking Terry to any of this. He was friends with Drecsay—Drecsay owed him money, but he owed other people too, including his other supposed friend Prince Barenoli. They both technically gained by his death through their liens. And of the two of them, Barenoli was the darker character. Terry seemed more good-natured and fun-loving, while Barenoli disdained the world. Both had been at Lady Tonbridge's party. Both liens were resolved with the baron's death. And the apartment, on the surface, was worth much more than this distant land in the desert—but why had Drecsay bought it?

Chapter 31

The coast of Spain was beautiful and a lovely distraction from the ship, where lack of facilities was starting to show in frayed nerves, poorer hygiene, and unruly hair. The rooms were all gradually growing smellier and sniping words were increasingly common.

Dory stood by the railing and watched the Spanish coast slowly glide past. They were too far away to see any life, but they saw buildings, fishing harbors and golden beaches. Well, she had never had the opportunity to go to Spain, but now, she had certainly seen it. The war hadn't reached here and Franco seemed determined to stay out of it. Perhaps that meant there would be something left of it at the end of all this, as the rabble of the German Army seemed to destroy whatever they touched.

The war would end one day. It had to. The Great War had lasted four years. Four years seemed like an impossibly long period of time. Back in history, there was both a thirty-year war and a hundred-year war. The outlook was depressing now that a diplomatic solution seemed less and less likely.

News had filtered through from the people embarking at Marseilles that the Italians had entered the fray by declaring war on both England and France. The news had utterly deflated Dory. Their little safe haven at Villa Bellevieu hadn't been safe at all. For all they knew, it could be run over by Italian soldiers as they spoke. Dory feared for all the people in the village, dreading to think the Italians were as callous and harmful as the Germans. Every corner of the world seemed under attack.

Now that they were at sea, they heard nothing. There was no news about what was happening in the world, which seemed to rewrite itself every single day. But they were sailing away from harm's way, in the nick of time, too.

Over the next few days, they sailed closer and closer to the Spanish coast, eventually seeing Gibraltar in the distance. British territory. There had been no communication about whether they would be allowed to get off or not.

How nice it would be to wander around the streets for a while and do normal things like sit in a café, or browse through shops. It seemed so long ago since she had done something like that. The British Government probably didn't want a thousand people wandering around the streets of Gibraltar with the burden of having to deal with them if they didn't make it back to the ship on time.

Dory was right. They weren't let off and some took the news badly, arguing with the crewmen, saying they needed this or that. Some had legitimate reasons, saying they needed medicines from the pharmacy. There was a doctor on the ship—a very busy doctor, charged with the care of seven hundred some people who were on this ship.

More were coming on, a small and orderly queue of Gibaltarese. Or where they Gibraltarians? Dory didn't know. She also didn't know if they were better off here than back in Britain, but then Gibraltar was always in a strategic position at the mouth of the Mediterranean. It could be that at some point, it became a focal point. Like everyone else, she was trying to determine where would be a safe location as this war progressed. Out of two locations, which would be safer?

By the look of the small crowd waiting to come on the boat, they had decided that Gibraltar wasn't the better of the options available to them. Or maybe they had other reasons to come. There was a Navy ship in the harbor as well, and mariners moved around the port, all seemingly having a task and a purpose.

With a sigh, she watched as provisions were hauled onto the ship again. Managing this ship wasn't a pretty affair. Latrines had been set up along the ship and they had to be emptied overboard every day. A commissary had been set up for purchasing cigarettes and lozenges. It was all they had. Perhaps after this stop, the commissary would have more.

There would be at least ten more days of this. All of them too close for comfort, an absolute lack of privacy and barely enough water for anyone to wash. Lady Pettifer hardly ever left her bunk, while Livinia made herself busy as responsible for the pursuits of higher learning or simply distraction through her library.

Some of the children did put on plays, which were lovely, and probably the best thing about the whole voyage. The only privacy available was gazing out at sea or the distant coast and trying to forget where one was.

"Miss Dory Sparks," she heard a boy call as he walked along the passageway. "Miss Dory Sparks."

"Here," Dory said and held up her hand. People stood aside from her and the boy approached.

"Telegram," he said and handed over a triple-folded paper.

"Thank you," she said, but the boy was gone the moment he was relieved of his burden.

It opened to a printed form with ticket tape glued in the message section.

COPPER MINING LICENSE WITH COLONIAL OFFICE STOP PAYED BY CHEQUE STOP DRAWER TERRY WILCOTT STOP

Dory gasped. This was the link. Terry Wilcott had paid for the mining license for the property. It was all registered and he had paid by cheque. There was no doubt that he knew about the baron's plans and the economic potential of this land. Terry had been a part of the planning. He'd even paid with a cheque from his account. Surely, he could not have intended to kill at that point as there was a clear link between him and the motive.

On flying feet, Dory made her way to their little cabin, where Lady Pettifer was leaning back on their scant pillows and drinking tea.

"Telegram from Ridley," she said and held it out to Lady Pettifer.

After reading it, she looked up. "We have him," Lady Pettifer said. "As much as by lying about it, he admits his culpability."

Lady Pettifer sighed and put the note down on her lap.

"Now what?" Dory asked. "Should we tell the Captain?"

"Now things are complicated. We know he did it, but what jurisdiction is there to do something? Away from France and the people officially responsible for the investigation, there is little we can do. I think we must perhaps talk to the Captain and apprise him of the situation. Whether he can act on this information, we will have to see. The question is if Terry Wilcott presents a danger to anyone else. For now, we know exactly where he is. It may be that we have to leave this until we reach the UK."

"Alright, we'll see the Captain. Should we see him now before we leave port?"

"Yes, probably. Help me up."

Dory moved to assist Lady Pettifer rise from the bunk. It was an unnatural position for her to get up from, dodging Livinia's bunk as she did.

They walked toward where the bridge of the ship was, gingerly stepping over people in their little make-do camps along every available surface. The door to the bridge was gray metal with rounded edges. They had to knock and eventually a uniformed man appeared, eyeing them suspiciously.

"We need to see the Captain," Lady Pettifer said.

"The Captain is busy at the moment," the man said, preparing to close the door.

"It is a matter of some urgency."

"The ship steward is tasked with handling passenger queries."

It was a joke making out like this ship was designed to deal with passengers in any regard.

"This regards a crime," Lady Pettifer said in her most grave voice that only a lady of the aristocracy could pull off. As expected, it made the man waiver.

Lady Pettifer had a forcefulness when she needed it, a communication of authority that only persons of equal authority could face down. "As I said, it is a matter of urgency in light of our imminent departure."

The man weakened. "I will speak to the Captain and see if he will see you."

Lady Pettifer didn't waver in her expectation and the man walked away. A few moments later, the Captain appeared. He wore a dark blue jacket with gold stripes around the cuffs. With his neatly trimmed gray beard, he did look the part. He had to be uncomfortable in this heat in that jacket.

"How may I be of assistance, madam?" the man said dryly.

"I am Lady Pettifer, and certain queries have brought to light the fact that we have a murderer onboard."

The Captain's eyebrows rose, but he didn't look entirely convinced. "Was this a crime that occurred on this ship?"

"No, it occurred in France."

The man was silent for a moment. "That makes things rather tricky as we are now in a British port. Do you have some evidence of this?"

Dory handed over the telegram to the Captain, who looked at it. Obviously, he wouldn't get any understanding from that.

"This telegram establishes the motive, and shows clearly that he has been lying to us. It was sent by a DI Ridley from the Met."

The Captain looked at the telegram again. "It doesn't say so."

"Are you suggesting I'm lying?" Lady Pettifer demanded.

"I am suggesting nothing of the sort, but you have to understand that it would be hard to arrest a man for a crime based on this… evidence. If we called in the Gibraltarian Police, they could only hold him for so long, having no body, no investigation, based on supposed evidence of a DI in the UK. I am, of course, not an expert at this, but I don't expect they could pull together sufficient evidence in time involving such a complex case. It may be better to deliver this man to the UK, where the evidence against him is assembled."

It struck Dory that they didn't even have that. DI Ridley didn't have a case against this man—that was the Gendarmerie in France. The baron wasn't even a British citizen. It was even more complicated than the Captain assumed. Their option was to have him arrested here, where he would assuredly be released in a matter of days due to lack of evidence, to then slip across the border to wherever he wished, or to keep him on the ship where he would be delivered to England.

Unfortunately, this case was too complex legally for any of the assembled party to deal with, Dory realized.

"Under the circumstances, it is perhaps best that DI Ridley deal with this. But be aware of the situation and this man's presence onboard the ship," Lady Pettifer ordered.

"Mr. Terry Wilcott, I take it," the Captain said. "It may be best to keep this information under our hats. Panic is never a good thing on a ship."

"Noted," Lady Pettifer said. "I need to send a telegram."

The man eyed her harshly. "We are just about to leave."

"As we have agreed this investigation and arrest is too complicated for us to deal with here. I would like to send a telegram to the Commissioner of Police. He is an associate of my brothers."

"Tom," the Captain said back into the bridge. A boy appeared. "Get this lady a piece of paper and then deliver it to the Harbor Master to send. Quick as you can, boy."

A paper was found and Lady Pettifer dictated as Dory crouched to the floor and wrote. The boy sprinted away.

"I suggest you stay out of this man's way during the rest of this journey," the Captain said.

With a nod, Lady Pettifer took her leave. They walked over to the ship's starboard side and watched the boy run down the gangway, which was just about to be retracted. The waiting crowd must have embarked already and they were ready to leave. The boy handed the note to one of the men working on the dock.

"Not sure that telegram will ever reach the Commissioner," Lady Pettifer said. "Unfortunately, the Captain is right. A body in France during a war, and a culprit fleeing the country makes everything very complicated. As in France, no one has the resources to see to something like this right now. But if that telegram does reach the Commissioner, he would be duty bound to act. What he will achieve remains to be seen."

"He will do what he can, I'm sure," Dory said. The Commissioner would not come up with some civilized solution as he had for Lady Wallisford in sending her to Switzerland, Dory was sure. Extradition was hard under normal circumstances. During a war, it might be impossible.

Chapter 32

D ory felt strangely deflated when they got back to the cabin. The murder had been solved, the culprit identified. The fact that they couldn't do anything about it was out of her hands. She'd done her part. Baron Drecsay didn't perhaps have his revenge, or even justice, but what had happened to him was now known, and would continue to be so. His family would be told why he died, and hopefully that would be some comfort to them.

"I suppose we have done what we can," Lady Pettifer said as she sat down heavily on the bunk again. "The greed is just unfathomable. I think I will have a little lie-down."

Livinia appeared at the door. "It is said they're selling coffee granules in the commissary."

Coffee would make the next week much more tolerable. "I think I will go buy us some before it's all gone."

"I can't believe how excited we are getting about some coffee granules that we would normally think were undrinkable."

"I don't mind the granules." Dory said.

"Well, you wouldn't."

Thank you, Livinia, Dory thought through gritted teeth. It was easy to get offended by the things Livinia said, but living with her for the last two years had taught Dory that Livinia was largely unintentionally rude. She simply stated whatever entered her mind, and to her simply a statement of fact. As granulated coffee was cheaper and easy to make without the assistance of skilled staff, it would go to show that Dory, being from a more modest background, would like the taste as if it was what she was used to. To Livinia, that was pure logic.

Picking up her coin purse, Dory excused herself and walked toward the walkway along the port side of the ship. The commissary was on the other end of the ship and anything they had picked up from Gibraltar would find interested buyers before long. If Dory wanted coffee, she had to get some now.

The sun was very bright on this side of the ship. Heat radiating from the painted steel added to the sun's harsh rays. There were people who shifted their daytime camps from the different sides of the ship depending on the time of day, seeking shade during the warmest hours.

Right now, this side was largely deserted. Walking past a protrusion, which narrowed the walkway considerably. Just past it, she saw Terry standing next to the railing, leaning casually. He looked up as Dory walked around the protrusion.

"Miss Sparks," Terry said with a broad smile. "Going for a walk? One does need to stretch one's legs on this journey. It is cramped, isn't it?"

"It is not the most comfortable, but the times are dire."

"They are, aren't they?" Terry pushed off the railing where he was leaning. There was something uncomfortable about this. Dory took a step back. "I was wondering," he started as he moved closer. He was still smiling and his stance wasn't particularly aggressive. "Must be on your way to the commissary, I'm guessing. I am, too."

"This isn't near where you are staying."

"Oh, you know where I am staying. Keeping tabs on me?"

"I just assumed. I saw you down the other end of the ship, so I assumed you were staying down that way."

"Assumptions can be dangerous."

That was enough for Dory. His actions weren't overtly aggressive, but he'd even used the word 'dangerous'. "I better go check on... Livinia."

"See, I know you've been asking things you shouldn't. Just can't leave things alone, can you?"

Dory went to briskly walk back the way she had come. They were virtually unseen here. Granted, there were a few people on the story above. Dory could see their arms sticking out over the railing, but they weren't watching.

Suddenly, she got yanked back. He had her by the hair. "You should have just left things alone."

"Let go of me, Terry," she stated, trying to pull away, but he was deceptively strong.

"I just can't let you ruin everything. Nothing personal, Miss Sparks, but you have an incessant habit of sticking your nose where it doesn't belong."

"Let go," Dory repeated, feeling panic flare up inside. Terry pulled her back and over. Dory grabbed the railing in a death grip as Terry's arms snaked around her. His intentions were clear now. He was going to lift her over. With all her might, she pushed back against him as he tried to manhandle her closer to the railing.

Images of her falling into the water filled her mind. They were quite far from the shore now, but there was a chance she could swim back. Thank God she knew how to swim.

"You don't really think throwing me overboard will cover up what you did. More than I know what you did."

"You mean the old crone. I'm sure I can find some way to convince her."

"Then you don't know the lady in the least."

"I can be persuasive. You know, I never wanted any of this. You brought this on by simply not letting it go."

"You killed someone. You killed your friend."

A blow to her head made Dory's vision waiver. If she passed out, she would be over the railing in a heartbeat, drowning in mere seconds. The last thing she could afford right now was to lose consciousness.

Wrenching herself away, she tried to run, but it only gave him more leverage to lift her up, and now she had no grip. She had no way to thwart him in his intentions to hoist her over the side.

There was a thud and she was falling. Panic speared through every thought she had, but he was short, she wasn't over the railing, was falling into it. Then a clear gong just before Dory's shoulder hit against the solid steel of the railing wall. Pain flared across her entire back.

"Terry, you blasted miscreant," Livinia shouted. As Dory looked up, she saw Livinia standing with two books in her hands, ready to strike again. Terry lay with his arm and half his body over Dory—the dead weight was hard to shift, but with all her effort, Dory managed to get out and away.

Splayed face down, he lay unconscious. The gong she'd heard must have been Terry's head hitting the railing.

"You killed him, you sorry bastard," Livinia said, kicking him harshly. The force of it moved him, but he was still unconscious. Others had started to arrive, drawn by the commotion and they stood around, watching agape as Livinia moved to strike him with the books again.

"No," Dory said, moving to intercept her. "They'll arrest him. He needs to be arrested," Dory said, turning her attention to the crowd. A group of men moved in and lifted Terry up by the arms. They dragged him away and at that point, Dory didn't care where as long as he was away from her.

Her heart was still pounding powerfully inside her chest. She'd been very close to being thrown in the sea and left behind. There was a good chance that no one would notice, and it would take hours before anyone confirmed that she was missing from the ship. If it hadn't been for Livinia and her ability to strike true, Dory would be in the sea by now.

"Thank you," she said, her voice breathy.

"I can't believe it. Terry. Why would he do such an awful thing?"

"Money," Dory said. "Plain and simple. He killed Drecsay so he could steal the land in Palestine."

"Why?" Livinia demanded.

"There was copper beneath that land, apparently."

Livinia's face crumpled and her eyes grew glassy. "Drecsay died for a cheap robbery."

"Basically." It seemed Livinia was cut to pieces over Drecsay's death. There really wasn't the point in telling her that he'd been using her. Now Livinia's purpose seemed logical. Both Dory and Lady Pettifer had assumed that Livinia had been the means to which Drecsay would restore the family wealth. An heiress is usually sought for that purpose, but that wasn't his main project. So why the interest in Livinia? It could be that he simply liked her, but for some reason that didn't sit right. An alternative reason would be that he needed money to set up the mine. That had been Livinia's purpose. Drecsay was set to capitalize his mine in exchange for marriage and his title.

The man still wasn't good enough for Livinia, who had never seen the pure commercial aspect of the bargain—and for that, Drecsay didn't deserve someone like Livinia.

As for herself, Terry had just tried to murder her. The reality was only hitting Dory now and she felt her knees weaken. She needed to sit down. "Let's return to the cabin," she said in a shaky voice. In all, she had been useless in a fight against an assailant. If it hadn't been for Livinia, things would not have resolved so well.

People parted as they walked past. In a way, Dory didn't want to tell Lady Pettifer what had happened, because she knew the elderly lady would take responsibility for it, for allowing Dory to put herself in danger. This wasn't Lady Pettifer's fault. It wasn't Dory's fault. It was Terry's fault.

Chapter 33

Nearly every person on the ship was standing along the walkways as they neared the coast of Cornwall. It was still a fraught portion of the journey, where there was no guarantee that they wouldn't meet a German submarine confusing them for a military ship. It did happen. Everyone had heard of the merchant ships that had been sunk by German submarines earlier in the year. And this looked like a merchant ship if one ever did.

But they had reached the coast, which made people hope that they were safe. Surely the Germans wouldn't strike this close to the shore, but Dory honestly didn't see a reason why that would put them off. At least they were close enough to swim to land, one person had said. A sinking ship with close to eight hundred people was never going to end well.

The other ship was in sight not far behind them. So far, they were both afloat, and approaching Southampton. Another day and they would be there.

After Terry Wilcott's attempt on her life, he'd been imprisoned in the brig. It was nothing more than a cabin whose residents had grudgingly been evicted, but Terry was locked in there for the rest of the voyage. Dory wasn't sure what would happen to him now, but in a way, she didn't care. To her, it felt as though her part had been completed. It was up to others now to do what they did. Anything beyond this would be out of her hands. No doubt, she would at some point be called to testify in a hearing against him. It may even be in France. As to when, she couldn't even guess.

Even Lady Pettiford came out of the cabin for the celebration for reaching the English coastline. This journey had been hard on her and she had quietly suffered through most of it. It didn't do her body well to stay in such cramped quarters with barely enough room to move, and everywhere else was so full of obstacles, it was simply easier for her to stay put.

Mr. Fernley had done his best to serve, but there wasn't room for him or really the need. Every day, he came with Lady Pettifer's meals on a tray, then disappeared to wherever he'd found space on the ship. Dory had gotten the distinct feeling he hadn't liked this trip much either. Beauty, who was confined to her crate had to despise it, but there wasn't much for it.

The ship was also running out of water, which had been distressing. Now they were slowly floating past the coast of Cornwall. The end was in sight.

"I do hope George is here with the car," Lady Pettifer said. Livinia stood on the other side of her, quiet for a change. George was Lord Wallisford's driver, and a name Dory hadn't heard for over two years. Her months serving as a maid at Wallisford Hall seemed a lifetime ago. "Shall you come back with us?" Lady Pettifer's attention was on Dory.

There had been considerable time on the ship to consider this question. "No, I think I need to go see my mother in Swanley." Lady Pettifer had no need for a companion here in England, and the thought of going back to Wallisford Hall sat uncomfortably. As Lady Pettifer's companion, she would be given one of the guestrooms and then be served as a guest by the people she used to work with—the people who had made things very difficult for her when she had helped DI Ridley uncover what

316

Lady Wallisford had done. All in all, it would be an uncomfortable affair.

It was time to move onto whatever came next in her life. The close friendship with Lady Pettifer was the hardest thing to let go of. It was what she treasured. Everything else… it was time to put it behind her.

"What will you do?" Lady Pettifer asked.

"I don't know yet. Women are needed for all sorts of jobs, I understand. I am sure they will find some use for me."

"It is true that you will be of more service to the country away from Wallisford Hall. I suppose at times like these, we cannot keep hold of our companions, even if we want to." Putting her arm around Lady Pettifer, Dory squeezed her shoulder. "I honestly have no idea what kind of country we are returning to. I wonder if this war is shaping up to be very different from the last. Still, the country will be run by women, I suppose. I am sure you will be needed. Perhaps you will even be a policeman. I think you do have a knack for it. You too, Livinia. You are going to have to find some way of being useful."

"Not sure my skills will be all that valued," Livinia said.

"Considering that you speak both French and German, I think they will find something for you to do."

"Do you think they'll send me as a spy?" she said humorously.

"I don't think you could hide the fact that you are British even if you tried."

"I might stay in London for a while. See what everyone is doing," Livinia said. The Wallisford family had a townhouse, but Dory didn't exactly know where.

"Your father will want to see you. You have been gone two years," Lady Pettifer pointed out and her tone carried her disapproval.

"Yes, I suppose I will have to go see daddy first," Livinia admitted. "He should be at the hall this time of year."

"If George is there, we can drop you off in Swanley," Lady Pettifer continued.

"I am sure it will be out of your way," Dory said.

"Nonsense. We have traveled this far together, a few more miles isn't going to hurt anyone."

It was strange to think she was going home to Swanley. It had been so long since she'd been back. With the difficulty with mail lately, it had even been hard to get letters through.

"To whatever the future holds for us," Dory said and they all looked out at the passing coastline. Sunshine basked the rugged, dark green landscape, interspersed with white beaches. It was a part of the country Dory hadn't see until she had sailed to France two years back. There was so much of the world she hadn't seen—so much of Britain she hadn't seen. She'd never even been to Scotland.

In truth, she had no idea where she would end up. It felt a little like she was leaving it up to fate. In a way, it was quite scary. She had found a really comfortable place with Lady Pettifer, but she was too young to hide away in comfort in someone else's house. There was too much to be done, too much to be explored. From the start, she'd known this time would come and now it was here.

*

They moved away from the coastline and toward the Isle of Wight. They were nearing their destination. Lunch had been yet another meal of the tasteless, ubiquitous soup. Dory's mouth watered for a proper meal. Tonight, she would dine at her mother's house. The thought of her mother's cooking made her smile. She might not be the cook that Gladys was, but she made a lovely supper.

They were outside again, watching as they sailed past the Isle of Wight. This ship had carried them all the way home. Anxiousness and anticipation were growing around them. Everyone had packed their belongings and were ready to disembark. Dory knew that a few of these people had nowhere to go, had lost ties with England, lost family and friends over time. They would have to find a place for themselves until they could return to their adopted country, who didn't want them in this time of war.

Dory's thoughts turned back to Prince Barenoli, wondering that solution he had found for himself. With the Italians pressing on the border, he had to go somewhere. They might even have invaded for all they knew. There was no news on the ship. By the look of the peaceful Isle of Wight, it seemed the world hadn't ended while they had been afloat along the Atlantic Ocean.

A while later, they sailed past the naval base in Portsmouth, but they were not stopping there. Technically a merchant ship, they kept going to Southampton, where cars were waiting patiently beside the dock they seemed intent for. Southampton port had none of the chaotic scenes in France. Cars were waiting for people. There were other ships around, unloading their pallets of cargo. American by the look of them. They were still getting supplies from America, it seemed.

The lack of chaos was encouraging. Things could not be so bad if no one was desperately fleeing. This was where many wished to flee to, including them.

They felt it in the structure of the ship as the engine slowed, and tugs appeared, working to guide them. It was hard to imagine those little boats being powerful enough to maneuver such a large ship.

Foremost at the doc was a police car and a group of men was standing around—one in uniform. Dory knew instantly that it was DI Ridley and she felt her heart beat powerfully in her chest. He had come—here to arrest Terry.

"Seems your DI is here," Lady Pettifer said.

"He's not my DI," Dory said, flaring red.

"Is there some tenderness between you and that policeman?" Livinia asked. "I never knew."

"Of course not," Dory said, but she knew neither of them believed her. Maybe she didn't entirely believe it either, considering her hands were clammy and a nervousness had set itself deep in her belly.

"They will lead Terry off first. Perhaps you should follow and speak to the good DI. I am sure he will wish to see you before he takes Terry away," Lady Pettifer said.

"Yes, perhaps you are right," Dory said, feeling flustered.

"Go on. We'll see you down on the doc after."

"I am going to have to carry my trunk myself, aren't I?" Livinia said as Dory walked away.

The gangway was a story down and Dory had to fight her way past people who were already lined up. The Captain was standing by the opening to the gangway with some of his sailors, firmly keeping Terry Wilcott in custody.

Dory decided to stay back a little, unwilling to provoke an interaction with Terry. The fact that he hated her was beyond doubt, and there was nothing to be gained by speaking to him. So, she waited. The gangway made grinding, mechanical sounds as it was extended into place, and the gate finally opened. The Captain and his men walked Terry down to the waiting policemen. Dory pushed through to follow, but the crowd surged forward in their eagerness for firm land.

It took a few minutes, but Dory finally made it onto the gangway and started descending, holding her small suitcase in her hand.

DI looked up and saw her, a smile gracing his lips. Her throat went dry as she moved closer. "I heard there was a scuffle," he said when she stepped down on the ground.

"Yes," she admitted.

"You will have to press charges. The murder will be hard to deal with at a time like this, but attacking you, he will stand trial for."

DI Ridley wore a green uniform instead of his typical suit. He was in his military gear, she realized. He seemed to notice her observation. "I am only here temporarily. I need to head back to Pirbright almost immediately. I only came for the arrest."

"Of course," Dory said with a smile. "Thank you."

"Don't thank me. I am not happy to hear he attacked you."

"Livinia Fellingworth saved the day, would you believe it?"

DI Ridley didn't see the humor in it and Dory wiped the smile from her face.

"Where are you heading?" he asked.

"To Swanley."

People were streaming down the gangway behind them, and Terry was seated in the back of the police car with men guarding him. He was resolutely staring straight ahead, a tight expression of displeasure on his mouth. His displeasure wasn't going to change any of the things that were about to happen to him, and he deserved whatever punishment was meted out. Dory turned away and refused to think about him more. He didn't deserve it.

"I can drive you as far as Pirbright, but I can't take you all the way. I only have a few hours," Ridley said, checking his watch.

There were so many things Dory wanted to say and ask, but it wasn't the place for it.

"Lady Pettifer," he said, moving his attention away from Dory. Dory almost felt the pressure of his gaze let. "I am glad to see you've found your way back to England."

"It wasn't a comfortable journey, but these are dire times."

"Yes, they are," he said. It was discouraging to hear him say that, but there was no hiding they were at war.

"Lady Pettifer has offered to drive me home," Dory said.

"Good. It can be hard getting passage, particularly down toward Dover way. Have a safe journey. Watch out for the trucks on the road."

"We will," Lady Pettifer said. "I saw George over to the left. It seemed my brother has not forgotten that we are arriving."

The police car started and DI Ridley gave them a nod, before turning his attention back to Dory. "I will write to inform you what happens from here. You will have to testify in court. I will be there if I can, but I might not be able to. My schedule is… uncertain, but you can reach me at Pirbright if you have any questions. They can forward letters if need be. Miss Sparks," he said with a quick nod before he walked over to the police car and got in next to the driver.

They quickly drove away down the dock, which was now crowded with families reunited.

"The uniform certainly becomes him, doesn't it?" Livinia said. "I think you should definitely come up with some questions to ask him."

Dory blushed but refused to look back. She cleared her throat. "Where was it you saw George?"

"Yes," Livinia said, stretching to look around. "I need him to go get my trunk. It was simply too heavy to lift."

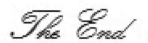

The End

Next book in the Dory Sparks Mysteries series

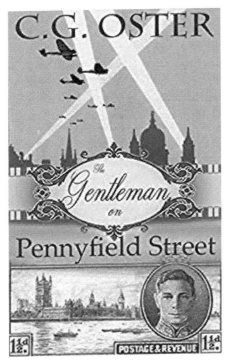

The Gentleman at Pennyfield Street — As the German planes came, London burned. Like everyone else, Dory had a job to do, searching for the threat that came in the night sky. Night after night, she and Vera searched for the enemy, while the bombs fell on street after street. The dark and empty streets of London also concealed the worst of intentions in the rubble and chaos of a blighted city—a perfect place to hide a murder.

Made in the USA
Monee, IL
22 September 2020